ISBN 978-1-334-15449-2
PIBN 10606033

# 1 MONTH OF
# FREE
## READING

### at

## www.ForgottenBooks.com

By purchasing this book you are
eligible for one month membership to
ForgottenBooks.com, giving you
unlimited access to our entire
collection of over 700,000 titles via
our web site and mobile apps.

To claim your free month visit:

www.forgottenbooks.com/free606033

English
Français
Deutsche
Italiano
Español
Português

# www.forgottenbooks.com

**Mythology** Photography **Fiction**
Fishing Christianity **Art** Cooking
Essays Buddhism Freemasonry
Medicine **Biology** Music **Ancient
Egypt** Evolution Carpentry Physics
Dance Geology **Mathematics** Fitness
Shakespeare **Folklore** Yoga Marketing
**Confidence** Immortality Biographies
Poetry **Psychology** Witchcraft
Electronics Chemistry History **Law**
Accounting **Philosophy** Anthropology
Alchemy Drama Quantum Mechanics
Atheism Sexual Health **Ancient History**
**Entrepreneurship** Languages Sport
Paleontology Needlework Islam
**Metaphysics** Investment Archaeology
Parenting Statistics Criminology
**Motivational**

# BARREN HONOUR:

## A NOVEL.

BY THE AUTHOR OF "GUY LIVINGSTON," THE SWORD AND GOWN,"
&c., &c., &c.

---

NEW YORK:

DICK & FITZGERALD, PUBLISHERS.

No. 18 ANN STREET.

# NEW WORKS IN PRESS.

**By the Author of "East Lynne; or, The Earl's Daughter," and "Castle Wafer."**

---

MRS. HALIBURTON'S TROUBLES.
☞ This work will be published from the advance sheets.
GERVASE CASTONEL. OR, THE SIX GREY POWDERS.
THE RED COURT FARM.
MARY GORING; OR, HOW I GREW TO BE AN OLD MAID.
THE DIAMOND BRACELET; OR, GOING INTO EXILE.
RECOLLECTIONS OF CHARLES STRANGE.
MILDRED ARKELL.
PARK WATER; OR, A RACE WITH TIME.
THE EARL'S SECRET; OR, THE SECOND WIFE.
POMEROY ABBEY; OR, THE OLD KEEP.
CLARA LAKE'S DREAM.
BLANCHE LEVEL.
THE SHADOW OF ASHLYDYAT.

☞ The above Works will all be issued at an early date.

---

# BOOKS RECENTLY PUBLISHED.

# BARREN HONOUR:

## A TALE.

BY THE AUTHOR OF "GUY LIVINGSTONE," "SWORD AND GOWN," ETC.

## CHAPTER I.

### NEW AND OLD.

A VERY central place is Newmanham, both by local and commercial position —a big, black, busy town, waxing bigger and blacker and busier day by day. For more than a century that Queen of Trade has worn her iron crown right worthily; her pulse beats, now, sonorously with the clang of a myriad of steam-hammers; her veins swell almost to bursting with the ceaseless currents of molten metals; and her breath goes up to heaven, heavy and vaporous with the blasts of many furnaces.

Whenever I pass that way, as a born Briton, an unit of a great mercantile nation, I feel or suppose myself to feel, a certain amount of pride and satisfaction in witnessing so many evidences of my country's wealth and prosperity; they are very palpable indeed, those evidences, and not one of the senses will be inclined to dispute their existence. If I chance to have an exiled Neapolitan prince, or a deposed grand-duke, or any other potentate in difficulties, staying with me (which, of course, happens constantly), I make a point of beguiling the illustrious foreigner into the dingy labyrinth of Newmanham, from which he escapes not till he has done justice to every one of its marvels. Nevertheless, as an individual whose only relations with commerce consist in always wanting to buy more things than one can possibly afford, and in never, by any chance, having anything to sell, except now and then a horse or two, more or less "screwed," or a parcel of ideas, more or less trivial—as such an one, I say, I am free to confess, that my first and abiding emotion, after being ten minutes in that great emporium, is a desolate sense of having no earthly business there, and of being very much in everybody's way—a sentiment which the natives seem perfectly to fathom and coincide with.

It is not that they make themselves in any wise disagreeable, or cast you forth with contumely from their hive. The operative element does not greet the stranger with the "'eave of a arf-brick," after the genial custom of the mining districts; neither is he put to confusion by a broad stare, breaking up into a broader grin, as sometimes occurs in our polite sea-port towns. A quick careless glance, as if the gazer had no time even for curiosity, is the worst ordeal you will have to encounter in passing a group of the inhabitants, whether at work, or by a rare chance, resting from their labours. There are "roughs" to be found there more dangerous, they say, than in most places; but these do not show much in daylight or frequented thoroughfares. They have their own haunts, and when the sun arises they lie down in their dens. Indeed, the upper Ten Thousand—the great manufacturers and iron-founders or their representatives—will treat you with no small kindness, especially if you have letters of introduction : they will show you over their vast works and endless factories, adapting their conversation always to your limited capacity, becoming affably explanatory or blandly statistical, as the occasion demands, only indulging in a mild and discreet triumph, as they point out some unutterably hideous combination of steel and iron peculiar to their own establishment, which produces results as unexpected as a conjuring trick. Even so have we seen Mr. Ambrose Arcturus, the stout and intrepid voyager, beguile a Sabbath afternoon in exhibiting to a friend's child—to the officer of the day from the contiguous barracks—to a fair country cousin—or some other equally innocent and inquisitive creature—the treasures of the Zoological Society, not a few of which are the captives of his own bow and spear; lingering, perhaps fondly, for a moment, opposite a gigantic bivalve or mollusca which he is reported to have vanquished in single combat.

But, in spite of all this hospitality, the consciousness of being in a false position, of taking up people's time where time is money—in fact, of being rather a nuisance than othewise—cannot easily be shaken off : the eye grows weary with seeking a resting-place where everything illustrates perpetual motion, and the brain dizzy with the everlasting tremor and whir of wheels. It is a positive relief when we find ourselves starting on one of the lines that radiate from Newmanham to every point of the compass, like the feelers of a cuttle-fish, always dragging in "raw material" to the voracious centre : it is an absolute luxury, an hour afterwards, to sweep on through the great grazing grounds again, and to see forty acres of sound, nudulating pasture stretching away up to the black "bulfinch" that cuts the sky-line.

You may easily guess what the political tone of such a borough must be : Liberalism of the most enlightened description flourishes there unchecked and unrivalled ; for no Conservative candidate has yet been found so self-sacrificing as to solicit the suffrages of Newmanham. Were such an one to present himself, it is scarcely probable that the free and independent electors would content themselves with such playful missiles as graveolent eggs or decomposed cabbage-stalks : they would be more likely to revive, for his especial benefit, that almost obsolete *argumentum a lapide* which has silenced, if it did not convince, many obstinate enthusiasts—who, nevertheless, were not far from the truth, after all. In no other town of England are Mr. Bright's harangues received with such favour and sincere sympathy. When the santon-fit is on that meek Man of Peace, and carries him away in a flood of furious diatribe against "those who sit in high places and grind the faces of the poor," it is curious to remark how willingly and completely his audience surrender themselves to the influence of the hour. You may see the ground-swell of passion swaying and surging through the mass of operatives that pack the body of the hall, till every gaunt grimed face becomes picturesque in its savage energy : you have only to look round to be aware that education, and property, and outward respectability, are no safeguards against the contagion : it is spreading fast now through that phalanx of decent broad-clothed burghers on the platform, and—listen—their voices chime in with ominous alacrity in the cheer that rewards a peroration that in old days would have brought the speaker to the pillory.

That same cheer, once heard, is not easily forgotten : there is not the faintest echo of anything joyous, or kindly, or hopeful, in its accent ; one feels that it issues from the depths of hearts that are more than dissatisfied—through lips parched with a fiery longing and thirst for something never yet attained. For what ? God help them ! *they* could not tell you—if they dared. Go to an agricultural dinner (farmers are the most discontented race alive, you know), mark the tumult among the yeomen when the health of the county favorite has been given, or rather intimated, for they knew what the speaker would say, and before he could finish, the storm of great, healthy voices broke in. Those two acclamations differ from each other more strikingly than does the full round shout of a Highland regiment "doubling" to charge, from the hoarse, cracked "hourra" of a squadron of Don Cossacks.

With these dispositions, you may conceive that, albeit Newmanham rather covets land as an investment (they make very fair and not unkindly seigneur, those *Novi homines*), she cherishes little love or respect for the landed interest, its representatives, and traditions. Yet, when a brother magnate from Tarenton or New Byrsa comes to visit one of these mighty burghers, to what object of interest does the host invariably first direct the attention of his honored guest? Deferring to another day the inspection of his own factory, and of all other town wonders, he orders round the gorgeous barouche, with the high-stepping greys, overlaid with as much precious metal as the Beautiful Gate, and takes the stranger fifteen miles away, to view the demesne which, through the vicissitudes of six centuries, has been the abiding-place of the Vavasours of Dene.

The house is not so ancient, nor does it stand on the site of the old Castle. All that would burn of *that* crumbled down in a whirlwind of flame, one black winter's night during the Wars of the Roses. There had long been a feud between the Vavasours and a neighboring family nearly as powerful and overbearing. Sir Hugh Mauleverer was a shrewd, provident man, and cool even in his desperation. When he saw signs of the tide turning against Lancaster, he determined to settle one score, at least, before he went to the wall. So, on New-Year's eve, when the drinking was deep, and they kept careless watch at Dene Castle, the Lancastrians came down in force, and made their way almost into the banqueting hall unopposed. Then there was a struggle—short, but very sharp. The retainers of the Vavasour, though taken by surprise, were all fully armed, and, partly from fidelity, partly because they feared their stern master more than any power of heaven or hell, partly because they had no other chance, fought like mad wild cats. However,

three to one are heavy odds. All his four sons had gone down before him, and not a dozen men were left at his back, when Simon Vavasour struck his last blow. It was a good, honest, bitter blow, well meant and well delivered, for it went through steel and bone so deep into Hugh Mauleverer's brain that his slayer could not draw out the blade; the grey old wolf never stirred a finger after that to help himself, and never uttered a sound, except one low, savage laugh as they hewed him in pieces on his own hearth-stone. When the slaughter was over, the sack, of course, began, but the young Mauleverer, though heated by the fight, and somewhat discomposed by his father's death, could not forget the courtesy and charity on which he rather prided himself. So, when every living thing that had down on its lip was put out of pain, he would not suffer the women and children to be outraged or tortured, magnanimously dismissing them to wander where they would into the wild weather, with the flames of Dene Castle to light them on their way. Most of them perished before daybreak; but one child, a grandson of the baron's, was saved at the price of its mother's life. She stripped herself of nearly her last garment to cover the heir of her house, and kissed him once as she gave him to the strongest of the women to carry, and then lay down wearily in the snow-drift to die.

When Walter Vavasour came to manhood, the House of York was firm on the throne, and another manor or two rewarded his family for what it had suffered in their cause. He commenced building on the site of the present mansion; but it was reserved for his grandson (who married one of the greatest heiresses at the court of Henry VIII.) to complete the stately edifice as it now stands, at the cost of all his wife's fortune, and a good part of his own.

There are more dangerous follies than a building mania; and perhaps it would have been well for Fulke Vavasour if he had ruined himself more utterly in its indulgence. Poverty might have kept him out of worse scrapes. If he resembled his portrait, his personal beauty must have been very remarkable, though of a character more often found in Southern Europe than in England. The Saxon and Norman races rarely produce those long, dark, languid eyes, and smooth, pale cheeks, contrasted with scarlet lips, and black masses of silky hair. Fair form and face were fatal endowments in those hot-blooded days, when lovers set no bounds to their ambition, and *une caprice de grande dame* would have its way in spite of—or by means of—poison, cord, and steel. All sorts of vague rumors were current as to the real cause which brought the last Lord Vavasour to the scaffold. The truth can never be known; for, on the same night that he was arrested, a cavalier (whom no one recognized) came to the Dene; he showed the Baron's signet ring, and required to be left alone in his private chamber. The day was breaking when the stranger rode away; and an hour afterwards a pursuivant was in possession of the house, making, as is the fashion of his kind, minute perquisitions, when there was nothing left to search for. Doubtless all clue to the mystery was destroyed or removed before he came. But it may well be, that, if Fulke Vavasour was innocent of the plot for which he died, he was not guiltless of a darker one, with which statecraft had nothing to do. It is certain that his widow—a most excellent and pious young woman, one of the earliest Protestant converts, and a great friend of The Bishops—made little moan over the husband whom she had long wearied with her fondness; she never indeed mentioned his name, except from necessity, and then with a groan of reprobation. They endure neglect like angels, and cruelty like martyrs; but what *dévote* ever forgot or forgave an infidelity?

Let it be understood, that I quote this fact of the widow's scant regret just for what it is worth—a piece of presumptive evidence bearing upon a particular case, and in no wise illustrating a general principle. I am not prepared to allow, that a fair gauge of any deceased person's moral worth is invariably the depth or duration of the affliction manifested by his nearest and dearest.

The barony of course became extinct with the attainted traitor; but the broad lands remained; for the Tiger, in a fit of ultra-leonine generosity, not only disdained himself to fatten on his victim, but even kept off the jackals. Perhaps, the contracting heart of the unhappy jealous old tyrant was touched by some dim recollection of early chivalrous days, when he took no royal road to win the favor of woman or fortune, but met his rivals frankly and fairly, and either beat them on their merits, or yielded the prize.

The sins of the unlucky reprobate were not visited on his children. The estate gradually shook off the burden he had laid upon it, and during the four succeeding generations the prosperity of the Vavasours rather waxed than waned. Like the rest of the Cavaliers, they had to bear their share of trouble about the time of the Commonwealth; but they were too powerful to be forgotten when the king came to his own again. Indeed, there was a good deal of vitality about the family, though individually its members came curiously often to violent or untimely ends; and the domain had descended in unbroken male succession to its present owner with scarcely diminished acreage. Yet, from a period far beyond the memory of man, there had been no stint or stay in the lavish expense and stately hospitality which had always been maintained at Dene. Twice in the last hundred years the offer had been made of reversing the attainder, and reviving the ancient barony, and each time, from whim or some wiser motive, rejected. No minister had yet been found cool enough to proffer a baronetcy to those princes of the Squirearchy.

It is not worth while describing the house minutely. It was a huge, irregular mass of building, in the Tudor style, with rather an unusual amount of ornamental stonework; well placed near the centre of a very extensive park, and on the verge of an abrupt declivity. The most remarkable features in it were the great hall—fifty feet square, going right up to the vaulted roof, and girdled by two tiers of elaborately-carved galleries in black oak—and the garden-front. The architect had availed himself right well of the advantages of the ground, which (as I have said) sloped steeply down, almost from the windows; so that you looked out upon a succession of terraces —each framed in its setting of curiously-wrought balustrades—connected by broad flights of steps leading down to a quaint stone bridge spanning a clear, shallow stream. Beyond this lay the Plaisance, with its smooth-shaven grass, studded with islets of evergreens, and endless winding walks through shady shrubberies, issuing from which, after crossing a deep sunk-fence, you found yourself again among the great oaks and elms of the deer-park. If there had been no other attraction at Dene, the trees would have been worth going miles to see; indeed, the stanch adherents of the Vavasours always brought the timber forward, as a complete and crushing refutation of any blasphemer who should presume to hint that the family ever had been, or could be, embarrassed. The stables were of comparatively modern date, and quite perfect in their way; they harmonized with the style of the main building, though this was not of much importance, for the belt of firs around them was so dense, that a stranger was only made aware of their existence by a slender spire of delicate stonework shooting over the tree-tops, the pinnacle of a fountain in the centre of the court. The best point of view was from the farther end of the Plaisance. Looking back from thence, you saw a picture hardly to be matched even amongst the "stately homes of England," and to which the Continent could show no parallel, if you traversed it from Madrid to Moscow. The grand old house, rising, grey and solemn, over the long sloping estrade of bright flowers, reminded one of some aged Eastern king reclining on his divan of purple, and silver, and pearl. No wonder that Dene was a favorite resort of the *haute bourgeoisie* of Newmanham on Mondays, when the public was admitted to the gardens, the state apartments, and the picture gallery; indeed, on any other day it was easy to gain admission if the

Squire was at home, for Hubert Vavasour, from his youth upwards, had always been incapable of refusing anybody anything in reason. If "my lady" happened to be mistress of the position, success was not quite such a certainty.

I think we have done our duty by the mansion; it is almost time to say something about its inmates.

---

## CHAPTER II.

### MEA CULPA.

THERE were all sorts of rooms at Dene, ranging through all degrees of luxury, from magnificence down to comfort. To the last class certainly belonged especial apartment, which, from time immemorial, had been called "the Squire's own." For many generations this had represented the withdrawing-room, the council chamber, the study, and the divan of the easy-going potentates who had ruled the destinies of the House of Vavasour; if their authority over the rest of the mansion was sometimes disputed, *here* at least they reigned supreme. There was easy access from without, by a door opening on a narrow winding walk that led through thick shubberies into the stables, so that the Squires were enabled to welcome in their sanctum, unobserved, such modest and retiring comrades as, from the state of their apparel or of their nerves, did not feel equal to the terrors of the grand entrance. Hither also they were wont to resort, as a sure refuge, whenever they chanced to be worsted in any domestic skirmish: though tradition preserves the names of several imperious and powerful Chatelaines, and chronicles their prowess, not one appears to have forced or even assailed these entrenchments. It almost seemed as if provision had been made against a sudden surprise; for, at the extremity of the passage leading to the main part of the building, were two innocent-looking green-baized doors, with great weights, so cunningly adjusted, that one, if not both of them, was sure to escape from weak or unwary hands, and to close with an awful thunderous bang, that went rolling along the vaulted stone roof, till even a Dutch garrison would have been roused from its slumbers. Very, very rarely had the rustle of feminine garments been heard within these sacred precincts; hardly ever, indeed, since the times of wild Philip Vavasour—"The Red Squire"—who, if all tales are true, entertained singularly limited notions as to his own marital duties, and enormously extensive ones as to *les droits de seigneurie.*

It was a large, square, low-browed room, lined on two sides with presses and book-cases of black walnut wood, that, from their appearance, might have been placed there when it was built. The furniture all matched these, though evidently of quite recent date; the chairs, at least, being constructed to meet every requirement of modern laziness or lassitude. An immense mantelpiece of carved white marble, slightly discolored by wood-smoke, rose nearly to the vaulted ceiling, in the centre of which were the crest and arms of the family, wrought in porphyry. There were two windows, large enough to let in ample light, in spite of heavy stone mullions and armorial shields on every other pane—the south one looking to the garden-front, the west into a quiet, old-fashioned bowling-green, enclosed by yew hedges thick and even as an ancient rampart, and trained at the corners into the shape of pillars crowned with vases. Not a feature of the place seems to have been altered since the times when some stout elderly Cavalier may have smoked a digestive pipe in that centre arbour; or later, when some gallant of Queen Anne's court may have doffed delicately his velvet coat, laying it, like an offering, at Sacharissa's feet, ere he proceeded to win her father's favour by losing any number of games.

A pleasant room at all hours, it is unusually picturesque at the moment we speak of, from the effects of many-colored light and shade. A hot August day is fast drawing to its close; the sun is so level that it only just clears the yews sufficiently to throw into strong relief, against a dark back-ground, the *torso* of

a sitting figure which is well worth a second glance.

You look upon a man past middle age, large-limbed, vast-chested, and evidently of commanding stature, with proportions not yet too massive for activity; indeed, his bearing may well have gained in dignity what it has lost in grace. The face is still more remarkable. Searching through the numberless portraits that line the picture-gallery, you will hardly find a dozen where the personal beauty for which the Vavasours have long been proverbial is more strikingly exemplified than in their present representative. There are lines of silver—not unfrequent—in the abundant chesnut hair and bushy whiskers; but fifty-four years have not traced ten wrinkles on the high white forehead, nor filled the outline of the well-cut aquiline features, nor altered the clearness of the healthy, bright complexion, nor dimmed the pleasant light of the large frank blue eyes. There is a fault, certainly—the want of decision, about the mouth and all the lower part of the face; but even this you are not disposed to cavil much at, after hearing once or twice Hubert Vavasour's ready, ringing laugh, and watching his kindly smile. His manner had that rare blending of gentle courtesy with honest cordiality, that the rudest stoic finds irresistibly attractive: you never could trace in it the faintest shade of condescension, or aggravating affability. Presiding at his own table, talking to a tenant at the cover-side, discussing the last opera with the fair Duchess of Darlington, or smoking the peaceful midnight cigar with an old comrade, the Squire of Dene seemed to be, and really was, equally happy, natural, and *at home.*

At this particular moment the expression of his pleasant face was unusually grave, and there was a cloud on his open brow, not of anger or vexation, but decidedly betokening perplexity. He was evidently pondering deeply over words that had just been addressed to him by the only other occupant of the "study."

The latter was a tall man, slightly and gracefully built, apparently about thirty; his pale, quiet face had no remarkable points of beauty, except very brilliant dark eyes, looking larger and brighter from the half-circles under them, and a mouth which was simply perfect. You could not glance at him, however, without being reminded of all those stories of unfortunate patricians, foiled in their endeavours to escape because they *could* not look like the coal-heaver, or rag-merchant, or clerk, whose clothes they wore. If the whim had possessed Sir Alan Wyvern to array himself, for the nonce, in the loudest and worst-assorted colors that ever lent additional vulgarity to the person of a Manchester "tiger," it is probable that the travestie would have been too palpable to be amusing; he would still have looked precisely as he did now and ever—from the crown of his small head to the sole of his slender foot—"thoroughbred all through."

The intelligence which seemed to have involved the Squire in doubt and disquietude was just this. Five minutes ago he had looked upon Wyverne only as his favourite nephew; he had scarcely had time to get accustomed to him in the new light of a possible son-in-law; for the substance of Alan's brief confession was, that in the course of their afternoon's ride he had wooed and (provisionally) won his fair cousin Helen.

Now, when the head of a family has five or six marriageable females to dispose of, forming a beautiful sliding-scale, from 'thirty off' downwards, his feelings, on hearing that one is to be taken off his hands, are generally those of unmixed exhilaration. Under such circumstances, the most prudent of "parents" is apt to look rather hopefully than captiously into the chances of the future *menage*: he is fain to cry out, like the "heavy father," "take her, you rascal, and make her happy!" and indeed acts up to every part of the stage direction, with the trifling exception of omitting the hand over the bulky notecase, or the "property" purse of gold. But it is rather a different affair when the damsel in question is an only daughter, fair to look upon, and just in her nineteenth summer. *Then* it will

be seen, how a man of average intellect can approve himself at need, keenly calculating in foresight, unassailable in arguments, and grandiloquent on the duties of paternity. His stern sagacity tramples on the roses with which our romance would surround Love in a Cottage. It is no use trying to put castles in Spain into settlements, when even Irish estates are narrowly scrutinized. Perhaps we never were very sanguine about our expectancies, but till this instant we never regarded them with such utter depression and humility of spirit. Our cheery host of yesternight—he who was so convivially determined on that " other bottle before we join the ladies"—has vanished suddenly. In his stead there sits one filling his arm-chair as though it were a judgment seat, and freezing our guilty hearts with his awful eye. Our hopes are blighted so rapidly, that before the hour is out not one poor leaf is left of the garland that late bloomed so freshly. We have only one aim and object in life now—to flee from that dread presence as quickly as we may, albeit in worse plight than that of Sceva's sons. How sorry we are that we spoke !

But Hubert Vavasour's voice was not angry nor even cold. If there was the faintest accent of reproach there, it surely was unintentional; but in its gravity was something of sadness.

" Alan, would it not have been better to have spoken first to me ?"

His own conscience, more than that simple question or the tone in which it was uttered, made Wyverne's cheek flush as he answered it.

"Dear Uncle Hubert, I own it was a grave fault. I am so sorry for not having told you the secret first, that I hardly know how to ask even *you* to forgive me. But will you believe that there was no *malice propense?* I swear that when I went out this afternoon, I had no more idea of betraying myself to Helen than I had of proposing to any Princess-Royal. I am sure I have no more right to aspire to one than the other. But we were riding fast and carelessly through Holme Wood; a branch caught Helen's *sombrero*, and held it fast. I went back for it—we could not pull up for a second or two. When I joined her again, she was trying to put in order some rebellious tresses which had escaped from their net; the light shot down through the leaves on the dark ripples of hair; there was the most delicious flush you can fancy on her cheek, and her lips and eyes were laughing—so merrily! I don't believe that the luck of painters ever let them dream of any thing half so lovely. I suppose I've seen as many fair faces as most men of my age, and I ought to be able to keep my head (if not my heart) by this time. Well—*it went*, on the instant. I had no more self-control or forethought than a school-boy in his first love. Before I was aware, I had said words that I ought never to have spoken, but which are very, very hard to unsay. Don't ask me what she answered. I should have been still unworthy of those words if, since my manhood begun, I had never done one ill deed, never thrown one chance away. Uncle Hubert, you can't blame me as much as I despise myself. The idea of a man's having got through a good fortune and the best years of his life, without having learnt—when to hold his tongue."

The clouds had been clearing fast on Vavasour's face while the other was speaking, and the sun broke out, suddenly, in a kind, pleasant smile. Probably more than one feeling was busy within him then, which it would have been hard to separate or analyse. The father's heart swelled with pride and love as he heard of this last crowning triumph of a beauty, that, from childhood upwards, he had held to be peerless. Indeed, he was absurdly fond of Helen, and had spoiled her so consistently, that no one could understand why the *demoiselle* (who certainly *had* a will of her own) was not more imperious and wayward. Besides this, the Squire's strong natural sense of humour was gratified. It amused him unspeakably to see his calm, impassible nephew for once so embarassed as actually to have been betrayed into blushing. More than all, gay memories of his own youth and manhood came trooping up fast, some faint and distant, some so near and brightly-coloured, that they almost seemed tangible—vanishing and reappearing capriciously, as one fair vision chased another from light into shade, like elves holding revel under a midsummer moon.

True, the days of his gipsyhood were past and gone; but the spirit of the Zingaro had tarried with Vavasour longer than with most men, if indeed it was even yet extinct. He could not help owning that, if the same temptation had assailed himself at the same age, he would have yielded quite as easily as Wyverne had done that day, with perhaps rather less of prudent scruple, and with more utter contempt of consequences. Though he had seldom given grounds to Lady Mildred for grave accusation, or even suspicion, gayer gallant never breathed since Sir Gawaine died. A chivalrous delicacy and high sense of honour had borne him (and others) scathless through many fiery trials; yet—not so long ago—hearts had quivered at the sound of his musical voice, like reeds shaken by the wind. Few men had achieved more conquests with less loss to victor and vanquished; for he was satisfied with the surrender of a beleaguered city without giving it up to pillage. Flesh is weak, we know; it would be rash to assert, that in his hot youth, Hubert Vavasour had never regretted a lost opportunity; but perhaps he did not sleep less soundly now, because of all the lost souls who, on either side of the grave, live in torment, not one could lay its ruin at his door. Two or three reputations slightly compromised are surely not an immoderate allowance for a *viveur* of five-and thirty years' standing, and need scarcely entail indulgence in poppies or mandragora. I think it speaks well for the presiding judge if, when a young offender is brought up before the Council of the Elders, those ancient memories stand forth as witnesses for the defence.

So the Squire's tone was cheery and hearty as ever, when he replied to Alan's rather unsatisfactory explanation, and there was a laugh in his eyes.

"It must have been a terrible temptation, for the mere recollection of it makes you poetical. That period about 'the sunlight on the rippled hair' would have done credit to a laureate in love. Seriously, my dear boy, I'm not angry with you; and I don't feel inclined to blame you much. I only meant that if you had spoken first to me, you would have heard one or two things not pleasant to hear, which *must* be told you now, and which had better have been said earlier."

"Uncle Hubert," Wyverne said, gently, " don't worry yourself with going through all the objections which make the affair impracticable. I know them so well. It is easy to give up hopes that one never had any right to cherish. Of course it is clear what you and Aunt Mildred ought to say. See, I accept your decision beforehand. I promise you that I wont murmur at it, even to myself, and I shall not like any one of you a bit the worse. It was written that Ellen should be my first serious love, and my last too, I fancy. *Kismet* —it is my fate; but that is no reason why *hers* should be bound up with it."

The ruffle of brief emotion had passed away from his quiet face, and it had settled into its wonted calmness; though at that instant the happiness of two lives was swaying in the balance, it betrayed no disquietude by the shadow of a sign.

Hubert Vavasour rose and laid his hand upon the speaker's shoulder. There was nothing of mirth left now in the expression of his features; all their grand outline was softened in a solemn tenderness, and his strong voice was low and tremulous as a woman's.

"I have not deserved to be so misunderstood, and—by you. Alan, you are my only sister's son, and I have loved you all your life long like my own. You were too young when your mother died to remember how I mourned her. You never knew either that, when I said good bye to her, after the last Sacrament, I promised her, as plainly as I could speak for tears, that I would always stand fast by you and Gracie. I wish other promises were as easy to keep faithfully. Do you suppose that my interest in you ceased with my guardianship, though my right of interference did? In spite of everything that has happened, there is no man living to whom I would give Helen so readily as to yourself. I am not going to trifle with you. As far as my consent to your marriage can help you, you have it freely; God's blessing go with it. Now—will you listen patiently while I tell you of difficulties in the way?"

If a life dearer than his own had depended on Alan Wyverne's saying anything intelligible at that moment, he could not have saved it by the utterance of one word; but there was eloquence enough in the long white fingers, which closed round his uncle's with the gripe of a giant.

The Squire sate down again, leaning his forehead on his hand that shook ever so little, keeping his face, so, half shaded. He was a bad dissembler, and the effort to speak cheerfully was painfully apparent.

"Alan, have you any idea how the account stands between the world— taking it as a commercial world—and the Vavasours of Dene? I don't see how you should have; for, besides your aunt, your cousin Max, and myself, not half a dozen people, I believe and hope, know the real state of affairs. There is no bankruptcy court for *us*, or I should have been in it years ago. There were very, very heavy incumbrances on the property when I came into it, and— see,— I dare not look you in the face— they are nearly doubled now. I can give no account of my stewardship; but I suppose play is about the only extravagance I have not indulged in; and 'my lady'—mind I don't blame her—is not a much better economist. I wonder our family has lasted so long. It has never produced a clever *financier*, I need hardly say; but, more than that, not one Vavasour for the last seven generations has had the common sense or courage to look his difficulties in the face, and retrench accordingly. Unluckily, rolling debts are not like rolling stones; they *do* increase in volume, diabolically. Well, it's no use beating about the bush or making half confessions. Here is the truth in six words: a quarter of a million would hardly clear us. They said I gave up the hounds because I had got too heavy to ride up to them; perhaps you will guess if *that* was the real reason. It was more as a sop to keep my conscience quiet than anything else though; for £3,000 a year saved only keeps a little interest down, and leaves the principal as big and black as ever. When Max came of age, it was absolutely necessary to make some arrangement. We cut off the entail of all property, sold some outlying farms, and replaced the old mortgages by new ones on rather better terms. But—we raised more money. Max owed seven or eight thousand, and I wanted nearly as much to go on with. He behaved very well about it, only binding me down by one stipulation—that I should cut no timber; for it was suggested then that £30,000 worth might be felled and scarcely missed. He had a fancy, that whether Dene stayed with us or passed away to others, it should keep its green wreath unshorn. It looks as if there were some sympathetic link between our fortunes and our forests—we have cherished them so for centuries: if any White Lady (like her of Avenel) watches over our house, I am very sure she is a Dryad. Alan, the worst is still to tell."

He paused for a minute or so, clearing his throat once or twice nervously, all to no purpose, for when he spoke again his voice was strangely husky and uncertain.

"You don't know much of Newmanham? the greatest iron-founder. There is one Schmidt, a German Jew, whose father was naturalized. They say he is worth half a million. When a man of the people has made money up to that mark, he is always mad to invest in land. Only six months ago, I found out that Schmidt had bought up every shilling of mortgage on this property, and—and—by G——d, I believe he means to foreclose."

The Squire stopped again, and then broke out into a harsh unnatural laugh.

"The patriarch knows where to pitch his tent, doesn't he, Alan? His spies have searched out the length and breadth of the land already, and I dare say he knows as much about the woods now as I do. His lines will fall in pleasant places when he has cast out the Hittite. Dene would be no bad spot to found a family in. Twenty quarterings ought to leave savour enough about the grey walls to drown somewhat of the Newmanham *fumier*. Leah has been prolific, they tell me. The picture gallery will be a nice place for the little Isrealites to disport themselves in in bad weather, and the Crusaders and Cavaliers will look down benevolently on 'the young Caucasians all at play.' Perhaps he will offer something handsome to be allowed to take our name. Faith, he may have it! I don't see why we should keep that to ourselves when all the rest is gone."

The bitter laugh ended in something like a sob, and the lofty head sank down lower still. Looking on Wyverne's colourless face, you would not have guessed that its pallor could deepen so intensely as it did when any strong emotion possessed him. During the last five minutes it had grown whiter by several shades.

"It is punishment enough for all my faults and follies," he said, "to be forced to listen to such words as these, and to feel myself utterly helpless and useless. Uncle Hubert, I remember, when every one thought my ruin was complete, you came the first to offer help, and you never dreamt of taking interest by making me listen to advice or reproaches. Now I hear of *your* troubles for the first time, and I find that I have come in, seasonably to add another grave embarrassment. What a luxury benevolence must be, when it meets with such a prompt return. If you knew how I hate myself!"

The elasticity of Vavasour's gallant spirit had quite shaken off by this time the momentary depression of which he was already heartily ashamed. He threw back his stately head with a gesture full of haughty grace, as if about to confront a palpable enemy or physical danger, and his voice rang out again, bold and musical and clear.

"Don't speak so despondingly, Alan. My weakness has infected you, I suppose? I don't wonder at it. I am not often so cowardly; indeed it is the first time I have broken down so, and I think it will be long before I disgrace myself so again. Yes, you would help me if you could, just as I would help you. I know you, boy, and the race you come of. *Bon sang ne peut mentir.* Whatever happens, I shall never repent having given you Helen. But I want you to see your line clearly; it isn't all open country before you. Listen. I am certain 'my lady' has some projects in her head. She thinks her daughter fair enough to be made the pillar and prop of our family edifice. (Poor child! that slender neck would break under half such a burden.) Now, if either of the young ones is to be turned into an Atlas, surely Max ought to take the part. But he is too proud, or too indolent, or too fond of his comforts, to give himself any trouble in the matter. Faith, I like him the better for it. I think I would rather see the old house go to ruin respectably than propped by Manchester money-bags. *Que diable!* Each one to his taste. I don't imagine that your aunt's visions have assumed shape or substance yet. The coming son-in-law and his millions are still in cloud-land, where I hope for all our sakes they will remain. For my own part, if Crœsus were to woo and win Helen tomorrow, I don't see how it would help us much; besides, it is quite probable that he would have gone away rejected. If you had never spoken, you cannot suppose that I would have seen her sacrificed. Still I warn you that her ladyship has some ideas of the sort floating on her diplomatic brain, so you must not be disappointed if her consent and concurrence are not quite so heartily given as mine."

"I have a great respect for Aunt Mildred's sagacity," Wyverne answered gravely; "whatever policy she might adopt I am sure would be founded on sound principles, and carried out wisely and well. It is very rash to run counter to any plan of hers, even if it be in embryo; I doubt if one ought even to hope for success. My dear uncle, every word you say makes me feel more keenly how wrongly I acted this unlucky afternoon."

The Squire held out his hand again; the strong, honest grasp tingled through every fibre of the other's frame, bringing hope and encouragement with it, like a draught of some rare cordial.

"Alan, I have heard of many rash and wild deeds of yours, never of one that made you unworthy of your blood or mine. It would be rather too good if *I* were to cast mere extravagance in your teeth. I wont hear any more evil auguries or self-reproaches. My word is passed, and I shall not take it back again till you or Helen ask me to do so. We will talk more of your prospects another time. As long as I live you will do well enough; afterwards—we shall see. Thank God, she is the only child I have to provide for. Don't be down-hearted, boy! The Vavasours of Dene are a tough, tenacious race, and die hard, if all tales are true; we are not *aux abois* yet. 'Vast are the resources of futurity,' as some great and good man observed; perhaps we shall pull through, after all. At any rate, we will not be tormented before our time. The thing which is most on my mind at this moment is—who is to tell this afternoon's work to 'my lady?'"

The Squire's bright blue eyes were glittering with suppressed humour as he said the last words, merrily, as if he had never heard of such things as troubles or mortgages. Alan could not help smiling at his uncle's evident eagerness to be spared the responsibility of ambassador.

"I fancy the worst is known to my poor aunt an hour ago. Helen went straight to the *boudoir* when we came in; she wished to tell everything herself, and immediately. It is the best way. Poor child! I hope she has had half the success that I have met with; one cannot count on such good fortune, though."

Vavasour's face was radiant with satisfaction, it was an unspeakable relief to

him to hear that the official communication had been made.

"What a brave girl that is !" he said,
with profound admiration ; " she has ten
times her father's courage. Alan, confess now, you didn't try to be first—
*there ?* Well let us pray for light winds,
for we may have to tack more than once
before we fetch the haven where we
would be. But as the sailors say, 'we
can't tell what the weather will be till
we get outside,' so—*vogue là galère !*
Hark ! there goes the dinner-gong ; go
and dress directly ; of all days in the
year this is the last on which to keep
her ladyship waiting."

---

## CHAPTER III.

### A "MOTHER OF ENGLAND."

If the Squire's study was the most
comfortable room in the Dene, the prettiest, and to a refined taste the most attractive, without contradiction, was "my
lady's chamber." It was of moderate
size, on the first floor, at an angle of the
building ; two deep oriels to the south
and east caught every available gleam
of sunshine in winter, while in summer
time many cunning devices within and
without kept heat and glare at bay.
The walls were hung with dark purple
silk, each panel set in a frame of polished oak ; bright borderings and bouquets of flowers inwoven, prevented the
effect from being sombre ; the damask
of the furniture, as well as the velvet of
the *portieres* and curtains (these last
almost hidden now in clouds of muslin
and lace), matched the hangings exactly.
There was as much of buhl and marqueterie and mosaic in the room as it
could *well* hold—no more ; no appearance of crowding or redundance of ornament. On each of the panels was one
picture, of the smallest cabinet size, and
on three of the tables lay cases of minia-
tures, priceless from their extreme rarity
or intrinsic beauty ; and all sorts of
costly trifles, jewelled, enamelled, and
chased, were scattered about with a studied artistic carelessness. The deli-

cate *mignardise* pervading every object
around you was very agreeable at first,
and finished by producing the oppressive, unhealthy effect of an atmosphere
overladen with rare perfumes. Such an
impression of unreality was left, that
you fancied all the pretty vision would
vanish, like a scene of fairy-land, at the
intrusion of any rude, unauthorized mortal, such as some " mighty hunter," bearing traces of field and flood from cap to
spur. That the hallowed precints had
never been profaned by so incongruous
an apparition since Lady Mildred Vavasour began to reign, it is unnecessary to
say. Her husband came there very seldom ; her son, rather often, when he was
at home. With these two exceptions, the
threshold had remained for years invio-
late by masculine footstep, as that of the
Taurian Artemis. Few even of her own
sex had the *entrée ;* and of these only
three or four ventured to penetrate there
uninvited. It was a privilege more difficult to obtain than the gold key of the
*petits appartemens* at Trianon.

The whole tone and aspect of the
*boudoir* was marvellously in keeping
with the exterior of its mistress. She
occupied it on that August evening,
alone, if we might except a Maltese
lion-dog, sleeping in lazy beatitude, half
buried in a purple velvet cushion, like a
small snow-ball. It may be as well to
say, at once, that this latter personage,
though a very important one in his own
sphere, gifted with remarkable intelligence, and capable of strong attachments, has nothing on earth to do with
the story.

It would be difficult as well as un-
courteous to guess at Lady Mildred Vavasour's precise age ; her dark hair has
lost perhaps somewhat of its luxuriance,
but little of its glossy sheen ; her pale
cheek—tinged with a faint colour (either
by nature or art) exactly in the right
place—and white brow, are still polished
and smooth as Carrara marble ; and her
small, slight, delicate figure, with which
the tiniest of hands and feet harmonize
so perfectly, retains its graceful roundness of outline.

Why is it that, after one brief glance
—giving the lady credit for all these

advantages—we feel sure that she has advanced already far into the maturity of womanhood? Perhaps, when the mind has been restless and the thoughts busy for a certain number of years, those years *will* not be dissembled, and, however carefully the exterior may have been conserved, traces of toil, sensible, if not visible, remain. There is no short cut to Political Science any more than to Pure Mathematics; not without labour and anxiety, which must tell hereafter, can their crowns be won; and Foresight, though certainly the more useful faculty of the two, is sometimes more wearing than Memory.

Now, in her own line, Lady Mildred Vavasour stood unrivalled; she was the very Talleyrand of domestic diplomacy. I do not mean to infer that she was pre-eminent among those Machiavels in miniature, who glide into supremacy over their own families imperceptibly, and maintain their position by apparent non-resistance, commanding always, while they seem to obey. In her own case such cleverness would have been wasted. She no more dreamt of interfering with any of the Squire's tastes or pursuits than he did with hers; and was perfectly content with complete freedom of action, sure of having every whim gratified. Indeed, up to the present time, her talents had been employed in singularly disinterested ways. Very, very seldom had she acted with her own advantage, or that of any one closely connected with her, in view. The position of the Vavasours was such as never to tempt them to look for aggrandizement; the Squire represented his county, as a matter of course, but there was not a particle of ambition in his nature; and her son had always steadily refused to allow his mother's talents or influence to be exercised on his behalf. But she had a vast circle of acquaintance, both male and female, and when any one of these was in a difficulty, he or she constantly resorted to Lady Mildred, sure of her counsel, if not of her co-operation. She gave one or both, not in the least because she was good-natured, but because she liked it. She liked to hold in her little white hand the threads of a dozen at once of those innocent plots and conspiracies, which are carried on so satisfactorily beneath the smooth, smiling surface of this pleasant world of ours. Granting that the means were trivial, and the end unworthy—it was almost grand to see how her cool calculation, fertile invention, and dauntless courage, rose up to battle with difficulty or danger. She loved a complicated affair, and went into it heart and soul; no one could say how many cases that had been given up as hopeless, she had carried through auspiciously, with an exceptional good fortune. With mere politics she meddled very seldom (though she never sought for a place or promotion for one of her own favourites, or an adopted *protégé*, without obtaining it), but in her own circle there scarcely was a marriage made or marred, of which the result might not have been traced to the secret police of Lady Mildred's *boudoir*. If she had a *specialité*, it was the knack of utterly crushing and abolishing—in a pleasant, noiseless way—a dangerous Detrimental. The victim scarcely ever suspected from what quarter the arrow came, but often entertained, in after days, a great respect and regard for the fatal Atalante.

Yes, the work had told even on that calm, well-regulated nature: Lady Mildred's smile was still perilously fascinating; but a certain covert subtlety, when you looked closer, half neutralized its power; and the bright, dark eyes were now and then disagreeably searching and keen. At such times you could only marvel at the manifest contradiction; with all the outward and visible signs of youth about her, she looked unnaturally older than her age.

In all probability, at no one period of her life had she been more attractive than at the present moment. There was extant a miniature taken before she was twenty, and the resemblance of that portrait to the living original was very striking. One charm she certainly never could have possessed—*La beauté du Diable.*

Now we are on the subject, I wish some one would explain this paradox or misnomer. Do we take it in a passive sense, and suppose, that if any emotion of love could fall on "the blasted heart" —like water on molten iron—it would be stirred by that especial type of loveliness—seen now so seldom, but remembered so well? It may well be so. *Væ miseris!* Every other phase of mortal and immortal beauty has ten thousand representatives in Gehenna, save only *this*. Surely few lost spirits carry the stamp of innocence on their brows, even so far as the broad gate with the dreary legend over its door: "Leave hope behind you." Seen very seldom—only when across the great Gulf, the souls in torment catch a glimpse of angelic features melting in intense, unavailing pity; but, perchance, well remembered, for where should freshness and innocence be found, if not in the faces of the Cherubim? And his punishment would be incomplete if it were given to the Prince of Hell to forget sights and sounds familiar to the Son of the Morning.

It is worth while to realize how dwarfed, and trivial, and childish, appears all tales of human ruin and shame and sorrow, by the side of the weird primeval tragedy. Well : the brute creation sympathizes with *us* in our pain; but who are we, that we should presume to pity a fallen archangel? Truly, pious and right-minded men have done so, in all simplicity and sincerity. The story of the Perthshire minister is always quoted among the *Traits of Scotch Humour;* but I am sure the amiable zealot intended nothing irreverent, and saw nothing grotesque in his prayer. He had exhausted, you know, his memory and imagination in interceding not only for his own species and the lower orders of animals, but for "every green thing upon the earth," beside. He paused at last and took breath; then he went on—rather diffidently, as if conscious of treading on perilous ground, but in an accent plaintively persuasive—

"An' noo, ma freends, let us praigh for the De'il; naebody praighs for the puir De'il !"

That is not a bad digression—taking it *as* a digression—from the boudoir of a *petite maîtresse* to the bottomless pit. Whatever connexion may ultimately be established between the two, I am aware that it is neither usual nor justifiable to place them in such close proximity.

But here I make my first and last act of contrition for all such divagations, in season and out of season, past, present, and to come. Reader of mine! you have always the resource (which I would were available in society) of banishing your interlocutor when he bores you, by skipping the paragraph, or throwing the book aside. I may not hope to instruct you ; it is quite enough if your interest and yourself are kept awake. Whether this object would be promoted by writing "to order," is more than doubtful. If one's movements are naturally awkward and slow, they will scarcely gain in grace with the fetters on. Let us not force our talent, such as it is. Few qualities are more useful or estimable than that grave pertinacity of purpose which never loses sight for a moment of the end it has had in view all along. But then, one must *have* a purpose to start with ; and up to the present point, this volume is guiltless of any such element of success. It is in the nature of some to be desultory ; and there are heretics who think that the prizes of Life—let alone those of authorship—would hardly be worth the winning, if one were bound down under heavy penalties to go on straight to the goal, never turning aside for refreshment by the way.

*Peccavimus, et peccabimus.* If this literary ship must be shattered on rocks ahead, we will, at least, make no obeisance to the powers that have ordained the wreck.[1] O younger son of Telamon ! you have spoken well, if not wisely, The wrath of adverse gods is mighty, and hath prevailed ; but let us die as we have lived—impenitent and self-reliant, without benefit of Athéne.

It is nearly time, though, to go back to Lady Mildred. She is still sitting where we left—I am ashamed to say how long ago—in the same attitude of indolent grace ; a very refreshing picture to look upon after such a sultry day, the ideal of repose and comfortable coolness. No mortal eye had ever seen "my lady's" cheek unbecomingly flushed, or her lips blue with cold ; it must be confessed that she seldom threw a chance away in taking care of herself, and had a wholesome dread of the caprices of our English atmosphere. She had been amusing herself for the last two hours with one of the paper-covered *novelettes* which flow in a stream (happily) perennial from that modest fountain head in the Burlington Arcade, mollifying our insular manners, and not permitting us to be brutified. The labour of perusing even this unremittingly, seemed to be too much for the fair student, for ever and anon the volume would sink down on her lap, and she would pause for several minutes, musing on its philosophy—or on graver things—with half-closed eyes.

While she was indulging in one of these reveries or semi-siestas, a quick, elastic step came down the long corridor. Lady Mildred could not have been dozing (nobody ever does allow that they have been sleeping—out of their beds), for she recognised the footfall instantly, though it brushed the deep-piled carpet so lightly as to have been to most ears inaudible : simultaneously with the timid knock that seemed to linger on the panel, her clear quiet voice said—
" Come in, my Helen !"

In these prosaic days of Realism, when Oreads and Undines, and other daughters of the elements, have become somewhat coy and unattainable, it would be hard to conjure up a fairer vision than that which now stood hesitating on the threshold. I will try to give you a faint idea of Helen Vavasour as she appeared then, in the springtide of her marvellous loveliness.

She had inherited the magnificent stature for which her family had for centuries been remarkable, united to the excessive refinement of contour and delicacy of feature which had made "the Dene Beauties" world-renowned. Her figure, though very slight, betrayed no signs of fragility, and you guessed that the development that three more years must bring would make it quite faultless. Her hair was darker than her mother's by many shades—equally fine and silky, but thrice as luxuriant ; its

intense black was relieved by a sheen of deep glossy blue, such as Loxias may have worshipped in the tresses of the violet-haired daughter of Pitané. Her complexion is much fairer than is often found where all the other points are so decidedly a brunette's ; dazzling from its transparent purity, it was never brilliant, except when some passing emotion deepened the subdued shade of delicate, tender pink into the fuller rose-tint that lines a rare Indian shell. So with her eyes—long, large, and velvet-soft, they stole upon you at first with a languid, dreamy fascination ; but you never realized their hidden treasures till amusement, or love, or anger made them glitter like the Southern Cross. It was one of those faces bearing even in childhood the impress of pride and decision, over which half a century may pass without rendering one line in them harsher or harder.

If you have ever taken up a plain photograph, untouched by the miniature-painter, of the form and features (for the moment) deemed fairest of all, you will sympathise with my utter dissatisfaction in reviewing this abortive attempt at portraiture. The stereoscope brings out a certain similitude ; but what a cold, colourless parody on glorious reality ! That very fixedness of expression—in the original so perpetually varied—makes it an insult to our incarnate idol.

Long and attentive study, for her own or her friends' benefit, had taught Lady Mildred to read very fluently the language of the eyes ; the glance of the Expert withdrew their secret from Helen's, during those few seconds while she stood hesitating in the doorway ; and a shy, conscious happiness glowing round her like a soft halo, made surmise certainty.

O laughter-loving daughter of Dioné ! your divinity is trampled in the dust, and none worship now at the shrines of Aphrodité, Astarte, or Ashtaroth ; but one feels tempted at times to turn Pagan again, were it only to believe in your presence and power. Other, and younger, and fairer faces have borne tokens of having met you in the wood, since your breath left a freshness and radiance on the swart features of the false sea-rover, that carried Dido's heart by storm.

Yes, Lady Mildred guessed the truth at once, and all her self control was needed to repress a sign of vexation and impatience, which very nearly escaped her; it bore her through, though, triumphantly. Nothing could be more placable and propitious than her smile ; nothing more playfully than her gesture, as she beckoned Helen to her side :—

"My darling! what has happened in your ride to agitate you so? I can see you are not much hurt. Come and make confession instantly."

This was apparently the young lady's intention, for she had evidently come straight to the boudoir after dismounting; she was still in her riding-dress, and had only taken off her Spanish hat. While her mother was speaking she came near with the swift, springy step which made her inimitable, and knelt down by the low couch, half-concealing her glowing face and sparkling eyes.

If there is any written manual adapted to such rifle-practice, (I mean where a young woman has to fire off at her parent a piece of intelligence particularly important or startling), I fancy, here, it would run thus—"At the word 'three,' sink down at once on the right knee, six inches to the right and twelve inches to the rear of the left heel, and square with the foot, which is to be under the body and upright"—the great difference being, that the fair recruit is "not to fix the eye steadfastly on an object in front."

So far, certainly, Helen acted up to the formula provided for her case; but she had not been much drilled, and was indeed singularly exempt from most of the little weaknesses, conventionalisms, and minauderies which are, justly or unjustly, attributed to modern damosels. Natures like hers affect, as a rule, no more diffidence than they feel, and are seldom unnecessarily demonstrative, however small and select their audience, and however dramatic the piece they are playing. So, after a few minutes'

silence, she looked up and said, quite quietly and simply—

"Mamma, Alan asked me this afternoon to marry him; and—I love him dearly."

The two voices were strangely alike in their accent and inflexions ; but the girl's voice, even when, as now, somewhat tremulous and uncertain, was mellower in its rich cadences, fuller and rounder in its music.

Lady Mildred clasped her daughter's waist, and bent down to kiss her, repeatedly, with passionate tenderness. When the close embrace was ended, she lingered yet for a few seconds with her cheek pillowed on Helen's forehead ; during those seconds her features were set, and her lips tense and rigid; that brief interval of self-indulgence lasted just so long as it would have taken her to utter the words—"It shall never be."

Now, mark ; the daughter was kneeling at her mother's feet, as she might have knelt to say the first prayer of infancy ; she had just told the secret which involved her life's hope of happiness—whether wrongly or rightly founded it matters not ; the mother sate there, with a firm, cool resolve at her heart to crush the hope and frustrate the purpose; and yet she kissed her child without shivering or shrinking. To our rough common sense it would seem, that caress more cruel in its falsehood, more base in its deliberate treachery, never was bestowed since that one over which angels wept and devils shouted for joy—the kiss given in the Garden of Gethsemane.

But who are we, that we should criticize the policy of a Mother of England, cavil at her concessions to expediency, or question the rectitude of her intentions ? They are white-hot Protestants, many of them, but none the less do they cherish and act upon the good old Jesuit maxim—"The end justifies the means." Unluckily, sometimes even their sagacity and foresight are baffled in guessing what the end of all will be. You have read Aspen Court, of course? Do you remember Cyprian Heywood's definition of a parable?—"A falsehood in illustration of truth." "My lady" af fected this convenient figure of speech a good deal; her first words now were decidedly parabolical.

"My dearest child, you have quite taken my breath away. I cannot tell yet whether I am sorry or glad to hear this. It comes so very suddenly!"

"Ah, mamma, say at least that you are not angry—with Alan," the soft voice pleaded.

Lady Mildred did not think it necessary to remain long astounded, being always averse to unnecessary expenditure of time or trouble. So she answered, after drawing one or two deep, agitated breaths (wonderfully well done), with intense gentleness of manner and tone—

"How could I be angry, darling? Next to Max, and yourself, and your father, I think I love Alan better than anything in the world. He has been rash and wild, of course; but I believe he is quite good and steady now. I am sure he will try and make you happy. Every one will exclaim against your imprudence, and mine; but we will not look forward despondently. Only you must not be impatient; you *must* wait and hope. You don't know as well as I do what difficulties are in the way. Perhaps I ought to have foreseen what was likely to happen, when you and Alan were thrown so much together as you have been lately; but I never dreamt—" she stopped, compressing her lips, as if annoyed that a truth, for once, was escaping them. "Well—never mind; confess, Helen, you did not fear that *I* should oppose your wishes? You know my first object in life is to see you happy; and I have not often contradicted you, have I, since you were old enough to have a will of your own?"

I fancy that most damsels, under similar circumstances, would have been of Miss Vavasour's opinion—"That there never was such a darling mother." She did not express it very intelligibly, though; and, indeed, it must be confessed, that the conversation from this point was of a somewhat incoherent and irrational nature. Feminine example is miraculously contagious; if the fountain of tears is once unlocked, the gentle influence of the Naïad will be sure to descend on every womanly bosom within the circle of its spray. I do not mean to imply that upon the present occasion there was any profuse weeping; but they got into a sort of *caressive* and altogether childish frame of mind—a condition very unusual with either mother or daughter. It may be questioned, if the sympathetic weakness displayed by Lady Mildred was altogether assumed. The most accomplished actresses have sometimes so identified themselves with their parts, as to ignore audience and foot-lights, and become natural in real emotion. Five minutes, however, were more than enough to restore one of the parties to her own calm, calculating self. Another yet fonder caress told Helen, as plainly as words could have done, that the audience was ended: as soon as she was alone, Lady Mildred fell back into her old quiet, musing attitude. But the French novel was not taken up again; its late reader had a plot, if not a romance, of her own, to interest her now. Whether the thoughts that chased one another so rapidly through that busy brain were kindly or angry, whether the glimpses of the future were gloomy or hopeful—the smooth, white brow and steady lips betrayed, neither by frown nor smile.

---

## CHAPTER IV.

### A WAIF FROM A WRECK.

"LOOK into a man's Past, if you would understand his Present, or guess at his Future." So spake some sage, name unknown, but probably intermediate in date between the Great King and Mr. M. F. Tupper. The rule is not implicitly to be relied on, but perhaps there is as much of truth in it as in most apophthegms of proverbial philosophy.

So it may save some time and trouble hereafter, if we sketch briefly now some of Alan Wyverne's antecedents; for he is to be the chief character in this story, which has no *hero*, properly so-called, nor heroine either.

The main facts are very soon told: his twenty-first birthday saw him in possession of a perfectly unencumbered estate of £12,000 a year, and all the accumulations that two paragon guardians had toiled to amass during an unusually long minority; his twenty-eighth dawned on a comparative pauper.

The last score of centuries have taught us many things; amongst others, to go down hill with a certain caution and timidity, if not with sobriety. We never hear now of those great disasters to which the very vastness of their proportions lent a false grandeur; where a colossal fortune foundered suddenly, leaving on the world's surface a vortex of turbulence and terror, such as surrounds the spot where a three-decker has gone down. The Regent and his *roués* were wild in their generation, but they never quite attained the antique magnificence of recklessness. The expenses of a contested county election fifty years back, would have shown poorly by the Ædile's balance-sheet, A. C. 65, when Cæsar laughed to see his last *sestertium* vanish in the brilliancy of the Circensian Games. What modern general would carry £20,000 of debt as lightly as he did half-a-million, when he went out to battle with the Lusitanian? If we even hear nowadays of a like liability, it is probably in connexion with a great commercial "smash," involving curious disclosures as to the capabilities of stamped paper, and the extent of public credulity; but the interest of such rarely spreads west of Temple-bar. Truth to say—however moving the tale may be to the unfortunates ruined by the deliquent, there is little romance to be extracted out of mercantile atrocities.

Nevertheless, if you only give him time, and don't hurry him beyond his stride, a dwarf will "go to the dogs" just as easily and surely as a giant. After our *mesquine* fashion, that journey is performed so constantly, that only some peculiarities in Alan's case make it worth noting at all.

Few men have trodden the road to ruin with such a perfectly smooth and even pace; there was no rush or hurry about it from beginning to end; nothing like a crash to attract notice or scandal. He was known to bet high and play deep; but no one spoke of him at the clubs as having lost an extraordinary stake on any one night, nor did the chroniclers of the Turf ever allude to him amongst those "hit hard" on any single event. *One* destructive element never showed itself throughout his career. It must have been gratifying to those much-abused Hetæræ to reflect (do they ever reflect at all?) that none could charge any one of the sisterhood with having aided in Wyverne's downfall. Reckless and extravagant as the son of Clinias, he escaped—at least Timandra. More than one scruple, probably, helped him to maintain a continence which soon became so well-known, that the most persevering of feminine fowlers never thought of laying her snares in his way. Something might be ascribed to principles learnt at his dead mother's knee, which all the contagion of Bohemia failed quite to efface—something to a chivalrous reverence for the sex, which withheld him from deliberately abetting in its open degradation—something to the pride of race, with which he was thoroughly imbued. He loved his ancient name too dearly, to see it dragged through the dust past the statue of Achilles, at the chariot-wheels of the fairest Phryne of them all. For once—hearing a story of human folly and frailty, you asked, "*Dove la donna?*" and waited in vain for a reply.

If the Sirens failed to seduce Wyverne, that was about the only peril or temptation from which he escaped scathless. Profuse hospitality all the year round in London, Leicestershire, and at his home in the north, cost something; a string of ten horses in training (besides yearlings and untried two-year-olds), which only won when their owner had backed something else heavily, cost more: backing other men's bills *currente calamo*, receiving no substantial considerations for so doing, cost most of all. Alan's bold, careless handwriting was as well known in a certain branch of commerce as the official signature on the

Bank of England's notes. There was joy in Israel when they saw his autograph: Ezekiel and Solomon—most cautious of their tribe (those crack bill-discounters are always lineally descended, it would seem, from some prophet or king)—smacked their bulbous lips in satisfaction as they clutched the paper bearing his endorsement: their keen eyes looked three months forward into futurity, and saw the spoil of the Egyptian secure. Alan's own resources, though rapidly diminishing, always sufficed his own wants: but he never tired of paying these disinterested liabilities as long as his friends could furnish him with any decent excuse for his doing so: if the defaulter failed in making out even a shadow of a case, Wyverne still paid, but never consorted with him afterwards. Then the dark side of his character came out. Generous and kind-hearted to a fault, he was at times obstinate to relentlessness: slow to take offence or to suspect intentional injury, he was yet slower in forgiving or forgetting either: he did not trouble himself to detect the falsehood at the bottom of any tale of distress, but against imposture carried with a high hand he set his face as it were a mill-stone.

Hercules St. Levant (of the Chilian Cuirassiers) would tell you—if he could be brought to speak coherently on the subject—that he dates his ruin from the day when he miscalculated the extent of Sir Alan Wyverne's long-suffering or laziness. Surely some of us can remember that wonderful Copper Captain—the round, ringing tones tempting you with a point over the proper odds—the scarfs and waistcoats blinding in their gorgeousness, so "loud" that you *heard* them coming all the way up from the distance post—the supernatural whiskers, whose sable volutes shaded his broad shoulders like the leaves of a talipat-palm? Hercules was very successful at first: he must have started with a nominal capital, but he had plenty of courage, some judgment, and more luck; so, by dint of industry, and now and then picking up crumbs from the table of those by whom the "good things" of the turf are shared, he contrived to ruffle it for awhile with the best of them. Men of mark and high estate would meet and hold communion with him—as they have done with deeper and darker villains—on the neutral ground at "The Corner," without caring to inquire too closely what Cacique had signed his commission, or on what foughten-fields the rainbow of his ribbons was won. With common prudence he might have held his own till now. But St. Levant was a buccaneer to the backbone: he spent his winnings as lavishly as any one of the young patricians whom he delighted to honour and imitate; and took his ease in the sunshine, scorning to make the slightest provision for the season of the rains. It came at last, in an Epsom Summer Meeting. The adverse Fates had it all their own way there: several of the Captain's certainties were overturned, and several promising "plants" were withered in their bud. It was the fourth "day of rebuke and blasphemy," and still the battle went hard against the Peruvian plunger. The Oaks dealt him the *coup de grace:* it was won by an extreme outsider. Hercules saw the number go up, and staggered out of the enclosure like a drunken man, with hardly breath enough left to hiss out a curse between his white lips. "Hecuba" was one of six that Wyverne had taken with him against the field for an even thousand: her name had never been mentioned in the betting at the time, and Alan only selected her because he chanced to know her owner and breeder well.

St. Levant was ruined horse-and-foot, without power or hope of redemption: that one bet would have pulled him through. Some pleasanter engagement had kept Wyverne away from The Corner on the "comparing day," and with his usual carelessness he had even omitted to send his book down by other hands: Hercules saw a last desperate chance, and grasped at it, as drowning men will do. He appeared at the settling with his well-known betting book (gorgeous, like all his other belongings, in green morocco and gold,) but Hecuba's name was replaced by the second favourite's. He chanced to have in his possession a fac-simile. of the original volume, and had copied out, in the interim, every bet it contained, with this one trifling alteration. The matter came before the authorities, of course. The discussion that ensued, though stormy (on one side) was very short and decisive : the swindler's foamy asseverations were shivered, like spray, on the granite of the other's calm, contemptuous firmness. The judges did not hesitate long in pronouncing against St. Levant their sentence of perpetual banishment. All his piteous petitions addressed to Wyverne in after days to induce the latter to obtain a mitigation of his punishment, remained absolutely unanswered. There still survives—a pale, blurred shadow of his former self— as it were, the *wraith* of the Great Captain. We see occasionally a hirsute head rising above the sea of villanous figures and faces that seethe and surge against the rails of the enclosure : we catch glimpses of a meteoric waistcoat flashing through the surrounding seediness ; and we hear a voice, thunderous as that of the elder Ajax, dominating the din of the meaner *mêlée ;* but there is no reversal of his doom. The poor lost spirit must ramp and roar among the "welshers" of the outer darkness, for the paradise of the Ring is closed to him for evermore.

Everybody—including the two or three friends who might hope to ride his horses—was sorry for Wyverne when a heavy fall over timber laid him up, quite early in the season, with a broken arm and collar-bone. The only pity was, that the fortunate accident should not have happened three years earlier. The indoor resources of a country-town, where all one's associates hunt five days a-week at least, are limited. One morning Alan felt so bored, that the whim seized him to look into his affairs, and ascertain how he stood with the world: so he went for his solicitor (as much for the sake of having some one to talk to as anything else), and went in at business with great patience and determination. The men who sat with him on the second evening after the lawyer's arrival, thought

Wyverne looking paler and graver **than** usual, but he listened to their account of the run with apparently undiminished interest, and sympathized with his friends' mishaps or successes as cordially as ever. Only once his lips shook a little as he answered in the negative a question—"If he felt in much pain?" Yet that morning had been a sore trial both of brain and nerve. It is not a pleasant time, when you have to call for the reckoning of ten thousand follies and faults, and to *pay* it too—when the bitter *quart d'heure de Rabelais* is prolonged through days.

Though they arrived then at a tolerably accurate idea of the state of Alan's finances, it took months to complete the final arrangements. When everything in town and country that could well be sold had been disposed of, Wyverne was left with a life-income of just as many hundreds a-year as he had started with thousands. But all his personal debts, and liabilities incurred for others, were paid in full. The only absolute luxuries that he retained (with the exception of all the presents that he had ever received) were the two best hunters in his stud, and his gray Arab, "Maimouna." That residue might have been nearly doubled, if Alan would have consented to dismantle the Abbey. But he could not help looking upon its antique furniture and fittings in the light of heirlooms. He had added little to them when he came into his inheritance : he took nothing away when he lost it. So the great, grave mansion still retained its old-fashioned and somewhat faded magnificence; and few changes, so far, were to be seen there, except that the grass grew long on the lawns, and the flowers wandered over the parterres at their own sweet will, and instead of thick reeks of unctuous smoke, only a thin blue line stole out modestly from two or three chimneys now and then in the shooting season. The game was still kept up, and the farmers watched it as jealously and zealously as if they had been keepers in their landlord's pay.

The sternest Stoic alive could scarcely have fallen into his new position more naturally, or adapted himself to its requirements more gracefully, than did that gay, careless Epicurean. If he had any regrets for the irrevocable Past, he kept them to himself, and never wearied his friends for their sympathy or compassion; he accused no one with reference to his ruin; I doubt if he even blamed himself very severely. There was no more of recklessness in his conduct, than there was of despondency in his demeanour; but he comported himself exactly as you would expect to see a man do, of good birth and breeding, and average steadiness, born to a modest competency. His experience, brief as it was, might have taught him to be somewhat sceptical as to the virtues of our human nature, more especially having regard to such trifles as truth and honesty; but no amount of punishment will beat wisdom or knowledge into a confirmed dunce or idler. His constitutional indolence may have had something to say to it; but to the last hour of his life Alan Wyverne never learnt to be suspicious, or sullen, or cynical.

To be sure, the world in this case broke through an established rule, and behaved better to him when he was at the bottom of the wheel than it had ever done at the culminating point of his fortunes. There seemed to be a general impression that he had been very badly treated by some "person or persons unknown," and it became the fashion to compassionate Wyverne (in his absence) exceedingly. People who in former days met and parted from him quite indifferently, found out suddenly that they had always been very fond of him, and contended as to who should attract him to their house in the hunting or shooting season. The Marquis of Montserrat, for instance, roused himself from where he lay, surrounded by every delight of a Mussulman's paradise, in his summer palace by the Bosphorus, to send a sort of *firmun*, giving Alan powers of life and death over the keepers and coverts of all his territory marching with the lands of Wyverne Abbey; an instance of good-nature which was the more remarkable, inasmuch as the great Absentee not only

carries laziness and selfishness to a pitch of sublimity, but has of late registered a vow against befriending any one under any circumstances whatever. This last and rather superfluous hardening process was brought about in this wise. .

Some years ago there appeared suddenly in the firmament of fashion a little star; no one knew whence it came— though it was supposed to have risen in the East; and when, after twinkling brightly for a brief space, it shot down into utter darkness, no one cared to ask whither it went. Mr. Richardson had advanced just so far in intimacy with the magnates of the land that they began to call him "Tom" (his Christian name was Walter), when the crash came, and he subsided into nothingness. He lived upon that recollection, and little else, for the remainder of his days. Yet one chance was given him. Wandering about the Continent, he met the Marquis of Montserrat. The mighty golden Crater and the poor shattered Amphora had once floated side by side, for a league or two, down the same stream. After a *tête-à-tête* dinner (the *côtelettes à la Pompadour* were a success), old recollections, or his own Clos Vougeot, made the peer's heart warm, and he bethought himself how he might serve the unlucky pauper. At last he said,

"Tom, there is a regular establishment at Grandmanoir, and there always will be in my time, though I never mean to see it again. Go and live there; you'll be more comfortable than in lodgings, and save rent and firing besides. Make yourself quite at home; slay the venison; eat the fruit of the vine, and drink the juice thereof (the cellar ought to be well filled); and grow as fat as Jeshurun, if you like. I only insist on one thing. Whether matters are going on well or ill in the house or out of it—don't bother *me* about them. I don't want to hear a word on the subject. Is it settled so?"

You may fancy Tom Richardson's profuse thanks and his great joy and gladness at finding himself chatelain of Grandmanoir. The *valetaille* treated him at first with no small kindness (he was a meek little man, averse to giving unnecessary trouble), and for some months all went merrily. But before a year had passed there began to dawn on the stranger's mind suspicions, which soon changed into certainties. There existed at Grandmanoir the most comprehensive and consistent system of robbery that could well be conceived. It would have been harder to find one honest menial there than ten saints in a City of the Plain. Everybody was in it, from the agent and house-steward, who plundered *en prince*, down to the scullion (fat, but *not* foolish), who peculated *en paysanne*. There was commercial blood in Tom Richardson's veins, and the sight of these enormous misdeeds vexed his righteous soul exceedingly. One day he could withhold himself no longer, but sat down in a fury and wrote,

"My dear lord,—In spite of your prohibition, I feel it my duty," &c.

And so went through all the disagreeable details regularly. The reply came by return of post, though not exactly in the shape that he expected. The steward came in with scant ceremony, an evil smile on his face (he probably guessed at the truth), charged with his lord's commands that the visitor should quit Grandmanoir before sunset and never return there. Thus rudely was broken the last of poor Tom's golden dreams. The Great Marquis, when the circumstances were alluded to, never could be brought to see any harshness in his own conduct, but spoke of his *protégé's* rather plaintively as "an instance of human ingratitude that he was really not prepared for." He did not give the species many chances of surprising him in *that* way again.

If the chiefs of his tribe were ready to comfort and cherish the disabled "brave," now that he could no longer put on paint and plume, and go forth with them on the "war-trail," be sure that the matrons and maidens were yet more active and demonstrative in sympathy. There must be extraordinarily bad features in the case of distress that fails to secure feminine compassion; except in a matrimonial point of view,

our sisters rarely consider a man deteriorated because he is ruined. Though he was a general favourite in his set, Wyverne possessed many more real friends of the other sex than of his own. If there is anything in reciprocity, it was only fair that it should be so. Alan's reverence and affection for Womanhood in the abstract were so intense and sincere, as to be almost independent of individual attributes. His companion for the moment might be the homeliest, humblest, least attractive female you can conceive; but with the first word his tone and manner would change and soften in a way that she could not but perceive, even if she did not appreciate it. Most of them *did* appreciate it, though, and this was the secret of his invariable and proverbial success. Wyverne could like a woman honestly, and let her know it, without a thought of love, and could always render courtesy where admiration, or even respect, unfortunately, were out of the question. However good the sport might be in other ways, he considered the day comparatively lost in which the feminine element was wanting. While his comrades were resting for an hour before dinner—dead beat with seven hours' hard stalking in the corries of Benmac-Dhui—Alan would be found loitering about the door of the chief keeper's bothy, carrying on, under extreme difficulties of dialect, a flirtation on first principles with his orange-haired daughter. He seemed to derive some refreshment from the process, though the absence of a beard, and the (occasional) presence of a petticoat, were about the only distinctive characteristics of her sex that the robust Oread could boast of. When the season was at the flood, he would spend hours of an afternoon in the quiet twilight of a boudoir in Mayfair, by the side of an invalid's sofa. Sooth to say, that room held no ordinary attractions. Lady Rutherglen had been a famous beauty in the Waterloo year; and though long illness had somewhat sharpened her delicate features, she still retained the low sweet voice and winning manner which had made wild work with the heart of the

Great Czar (the imperial wooing was utterly wasted, for the witty, wayward Countess could guard her honour as well as the stupidest of Pamelas) ; there was hardly a wrinkle on the little white hand, and the lovely silver hair looked softer and silkier now than it had ever done in its golden prime.

Sad and strange shapes of sin and sorrow cross our path sometimes, as we walk home from club or ball through the early morning. Saddest, perhaps, and strangest of all, is the spectacle of one of God's creatures, unsexed and deformed by passion and fiery liquor, struggling in blind undiscriminating rage, and shrieking out defiance alike of friends and foes. The Menad ceased to be romantic when the Great Pan died. Erigone may be magnificent on canvas, but even Béranger failed in making her attractive on paper : in flesh and blood she is simply repellent. Public sympathy would side rather with Pentheus now-a-days than with his cruelly convivial mother ; and we hold the disguise of drink to be the least becoming of all Myrrha's masquerades. Such a sight affected Wyverne with a disgust and pain that few men could have fully appreciated ; but he rarely would pass by without an attempt at mediation. They say that his kind, gentle voice was almost magical in its soothing power. The exasperated guardian of the night would relax the roughness of his grasp ; and the "strayed reveller" would subside from shrill fury into murmurs placable and plaintive, yielding, in spite of the devil that possessed her, to the charm of his cordial compassion and invincible courtesy.

All things considered, woman-kind had rather a better reason for petting Alan than could be given for most of their whims. When his resources were almost unlimited, he was always so perfectly regardless of time and trouble and cost in endeavouring to gratify even their unexpressed wishes, that it was no wonder if, when the positions were reversed, he began to reap his reward, and found out that he had laid up treasure against the time of need.

I have said more than enough to give you some insight into a character in which the elements of hardness and ductility, passionate impulse and consummate coolness, recklessness and self-control, were strangely mingled, like the gold, brass, iron, and clay in the frame of the giant Image that stood beside the prophet in his trance, on the banks of "the great river Hiddekel."

With all his faults and failings, Hubert Vavasour would have chosen him out of broad England for a son-in-law. Lady Mildred thought that such a bridal dress would become her daughter worse than a winding-sheet.

Which of the two was right? Probably neither. There is little wisdom in extremes.

———

## CHAPTER V.

### THE GIFTS OF A GREEK.

When Helen came into the cedar drawing-room (the place of assembly before dinner) she found her father alone. His face was rather thoughtful and grave, but it brightened as she came quickly to his side, and nothing but intense love and tenderness remained, when she rested her clasped hands on his shoulder, and looked up at him with a deepened rose colour on her cheek, and a question in her great, earnest eyes. If she had dreaded the meeting, all fear would have vanished even before the strong, true arm circled her waist, and the kind, honest voice that had never yet lied to man or woman murmured "God bless you, my own darling !" Helen felt happier and safer then than when she rose from receiving her mother's more elaborate caress and benediction.

Nothing, surely, can be more natural or justifiable under such circumstances than a paternal embrace; therefore there was no particular reason for those two starting apart, with rather a guilty and conscience-stricken expression of countenance, when the door opened, and Lady Mildred glided in with the even noiseless step and languid grace that all her friends knew so well, and some admired so much. The appearance of things did not greatly please her, neither did it trouble her much. She had a high opinion of her own resources, and a very poor one of the talents against which she meant to contend; so she regarded the signs of coalition before her with the same contemptuous indifference that a minister (with a safe majority) would display, when the opposition threatens a division, or that a consummate billiard-player would feel, when his antagonist (to whom he gives ten points under the proper odds) makes a grand but unproductive fluke.

As a rule, unless her adversary was extraordinarily skilful or vicious, that accomplished duellist preferred *taking* his fire; so on this occasion Hubert Vavasour had to speak first. He came to time gallantly, though rather nervously.

"You have heard what these foolish children have been doing and saying this afternoon, mamma? I suppose they ought to be scolded or sent to bed supperless, or otherwise chastised; but I cannot play the stern father, and you don't look much like Mother Hubbard. *We* were foolish and childish once, Mildred; surely you remember?"

If his own life or fortunes had been at stake, there would not have been half such pitiful pleading in his eyes and his tone.

Lady Mildred's memory was unusually retentive, but it did not accuse her of any such weakness. Her imagination must have been tasked before she could have pleaded guilty; nevertheless she called up a little conscious look with admirable success, and smiled with infinite sweetness. Perhaps there was the faintest sarcastic inflexion in the first few words of her reply, but it needed a sharper ear to detect it than either her husband or daughter owned.

"Dear Hubert, you are growing romantic yourself again, or you would scarcely call Alan a child. If he is one he is very wise for his years. But on the principle of love levelling every-

thing, I suppose all ages are the same when people forget to be prudent. Of course it was a great surprise to me. I can hardly realize it yet; but—has not Helen told you? I *do* approve more than I ought to do, and I hope and pray that good may come of it to both of them. I love Alan nearly as well as I do my own Helen, and she and you know how dearly that is."

She wound her arm round her daughter's waist as she spoke, and drew her close till 'the two soft cheeks met. It was the prettiest *pose* you can fancy —nothing theatrical or affected about it—enough of tender *abandon* to satisfy the most fastidious critic of attitudes— beautifully maternal without being "gushingly" demonstrative; but not a hair in "my lady's" careful braids was ruffled, nor a fold in her perfect dress disarranged. The embrace was still in progress, when the door opened again and Alan Wyverne joined them, only preceding by a few seconds the announcement of dinner. It is just possible that the caress might have ended more abruptly, if one ear in the cedar drawing-room had not been quick enough to distinguish his footsteps from that of the Chief Butler—a portly man, with a grand and goodly presence, in his gait sedate and solemn—who ever bore himself with the decent dignity befitting one long in authority, conscious of virtue, and weighing seventeen stone.

Nevertheless Lady Mildred's knowledge of her nephew's character made her aware that it would not answer to try with him the line of strategy which might succeed with her husband and daughter. It was very unlikely that he would be taken in by the feint of unconditional surrender. Alan had not devoted himself to the society of womankind for so many years without acquiring a certain insight into their charming wiles. It was very easy to persuade, but wonderfully difficult to delude him. She did not like him the worse for that; indeed she only spoke the truth when she said he was one of her chief favourites. Under any other circumstances she would have grudged neither time nor trouble to serve him, either by gratifying his wishes or advancing his fortunes, and perhaps really regretted the stern political necessity which made it an imperative duty to foil him if possible. Her game now was the temporising one—to treat, but under protest. She looked up once in Alan's face as she leant on his arm on their way to the dining-room. That glance was meant to combine affection with a slight tinge of reproach, but a gleam of covert amusement in her eyes almost spoilt the intended effect. Lady Mildred had a strong sense of humour, and, after the first vexation was over, she could not help laughing at her own carelessness and want of prevision. The fact was, she believed Wyverne capable of any amount of flirtation with any creature wearing a kirtle; but, with regard to serious matrimonial intentions, she had held him safe as if he had been vowed to celibacy ; in default of a better, she would have allowed him on an emergency to play chaperon to Helen. Lo, the sheep-dog not only proved faithless to his trust, but was trying to make off with the flower of the flock, leaving its mistress to sing—with the "lass of the Cowdenknowes"—

> Ere he had taken the lamb he did,
> I had lieve he had taken them a'.

They were rather a quiet quartette at dinner. Helen was by no means sentimental, nor did she think it the least necessary to be nervous, even under the peculiar circumstances; her colour, perhaps, deepened occasionally by a shade or two, without any obvious reason, and the long shadowing lashes swept down over her eyes more frequently than usual, as if desirous of veiling their extraordinary brilliancy ; beyond these, there were no outward and visible signs of perturbation, past or present; her accomplice's face was a study for its perfect innocence and calmness. Nevertheless, neither was quite equal to the effort of discussing utterly uninteresting subjects quite unconcernedly ; both had a good deal to think of, and one had a good deal to prepare for. Hubert Vavasour was

cheerful and happy enough, apparently, but he only talked by fits and starts ; so that it devolved on "my lady" to defray the expenses of the conversation. She performed her part with infinite tact and delicacy ; it was only the fact of her so rarely taking any trouble of the sort in a strictly domestic circle (she thought it quite enough, there, to submit to be amused), that caused the effort to be observable.

It would be just as easy to make a dam-head of sand water-tight, as to prevent the knowledge of an event very interesting to one of its members percolating through a large household within a few hours after it has happened. You may not see the precise spot where the water soaks through, and you may never discover the precise channel by which the intelligence is circulating; but there is the fact, and a very provoking one too, sometimes. It is unnecessary to say that the probable engagement of the cousins formed the prominent subject of discussion that night in the steward's room, though of the circumstances of the *fiançailles* everybody was profoundly ignorant. Of course, Allan could not be closeted with his uncle, and Helen with her mother, immediately after returning from a *téte-à-téte* ride, without the domestics drawing their own conclusions—to say nothing of the traces of emotion which, perhaps, even that haughty demoiselle failed to dissemble from the quick-witted Pauline.

The Chief Butler (before alluded to) during a quarter of a century's servitude in the family had acquired, besides a comfortable competence and considerable corpulence, a certain astrological talent with regard to the signs of the times showing themselves within his limited horizon. He was faithful, too, after his fashion ; but—loving his master much—honoured his mistress more, and was ever especially careful to ascertain how the wind blew from *that* quarter. He was wont to preside over his little parliament like Zeus over the Olympian conclave; hearkening to, encouraging, and, if need were, controlling the opinions of the minor deities; on such occasions his words were few, but full of weight and wisdom. He waited now till, after long discussion, the majority decided that, "it would be a very nice match, and suitable everyways" (a feminine voice remarking "What did it matter about fortune? Sir Alan was good enough for a duchess"); then, slowly and solemnly, said the portly Thunderer:

ὣς ἔφαθ', οἱ δ' ἄρα πάντες ἀκὴν ἐγένοντο σιωπῇ
Μῦθον ἀγασσάμενοι· μάλα γὰρ κρατερῶς ἀγόρευσεν.

According to one proverb, "No man is a hero to his own valet;" another tells us, "Bystanders see most of the game." Combining these two, we may guess how it is that the deepest politicians of private life do not always succeed in blinding the eyes of their own domestics, however great an interest they may have in doing so. Perhaps a rash and quite unfounded contempt for the auricular and mental capacities of a most intelligent class may sometimes help to throw them off their guard; though the proudest *lionne* of our democratic day would hardly care to emulate the cynicism of that exalted dame (she was nearly allied to the Great Monarch) who, when discovered in her bath receiving her chocolate from the hands of a gigantic lacquey, replied to her friend's remonstrancs—"Et tu appelles ça un homme?"

The Squire of Dene was not so clear-sighted as his major-domo: indeed, that pleasant habit of contemplating things in general through roseate medium is apt to lead one into errors with regard to objects distant or near. He thought the aspect of affairs decidedly favourable; so, when they were alone again, he looked across the table at Wyverne with a smile full of hope and intelligence —draining at the same time his first beaker of claret with a gusto not entirely to. be ascribed to the flavour of the rare '34.

"I drink to our castle in Spain," he said; "it seems to me the first stone has been laid auspiciously."

The other filled a bumper very slowly and drained it, deliberately, before he replied. Surely it was more that curious presentiment of some counterbalancing evil in the dim background, which so

"It may be a match, and it mayn't be a match. I've nothing to say against Sir Allan, and I wish him well; but there'll be some curious games up, or I'm mistaken. I doubt my lady ain't altogether pleased about it—she was so uncommon pleasant at dinner!"

often accompanies great and unexpected happiness, than any intuitive knowledge of the real state of things, which prompted the half-sigh—not smothered so soon but that Vavasour's ear caught it 'flying.'

"It is almost too good to be true, Uncle Hubert. I'm modest about my own merits; and I think I know pretty well by this time how much luck I ought to expect. Would it not be wrong to reckon on winning such a prize as that, without some trouble, and toil, and anxiety? I confess I don't like these very 'gay' mornings; the clouds are strangely apt to gather before noon, and one often gets drenched before sunset."

During the short interval that had elapsed since the first confidence was made, the Squire had signed in his own mind a treaty with his nephew, offensive and defensive; he had identified himself so thoroughly with the latter's interests, that it provoked him a good deal now to meet with something like despondency; he had counted on an exhilaration at least equal to his own.

"Your poetical vein fails you, Alan; you are scarcely so happy in your similes as you were three hours ago. That's rather a threadbare one, and certainly not worth of the occasion; it isn't true, either, as you would find if your habits were more matutinal. I don't think you know much about your own merits, or about ' my lady's' intentions; perhaps you do injustice to both. But—simply to gratify you—we will suppose the worst; suppose that she is hostile, and only hiding her game. Well, I believe there is such a thing as paternal authority, though mine has been in abeyance ever since Max was born: I think I should be equal to exercising it if we came to extremities. When all one's other possessions are encumbered, there would be a certain satisfaction in disposing of a daughter. I'm not aware that any one holds a mortgage on Helen."

Now Hubert Vavasour spoke in perfect sincerity and singleness of heart, when he thus purposed to assert a suzerainty quite as unreal as the kingdom of Jerusalem or the bishporic of Westminster. His chances of success in such a reactionary movement would have been about equal to those of a modern French proprietor who, at the marriage of one of his tenants, should attempt to revive those curious seignorial rights, used or abused four centuries ago by Giles de Retz and his compeers. Alan could not but admire the audacity of the resolve; but his sense of the absurd was touched when he reflected on the utter impossibility of its accomplishment. Perhaps this last feeling helped to dispel the gloom which had gathered on his face; at any rate, his smile was gay enough now to satisfy his sanguine confederate.

"I should like to know the man, Uncle Hubert," he said, "who would persist in being suspicious or misanthropical after talking to you for ten minutes. *I* am not such a natural curiosity. 'Sufficient for the day is the evil thereof:' that's the only sound and remunerative philosophy, after all. There has been nothing but good in this day; so I don't know what ungracious or ungrateful devil possessed me: but you have fairly exorcised him. Let us do as our fathers did—burn our galleys, advance our gonfalon, and cry—'*Dex nous aide!*'"

"That's more like the old form," Vavasour replied; "say no more about it now. The claret stands with you; don't linger over it to-night, I fancy we are waited for."

Wyverne's first glance on entering the drawing-room searched for his cousin; he was rather relieved than otherwise at not finding her there; he felt that the difficulties of the next half hour were best encountered alone. Lady Mildred was reclining on her usual sofa; close to it, and just within easy ear-shot of the cushion supporting her head, was placed a very low and luxurious arm-chair. "My lady" was ever considerate as to the personal comfort of her victims, and took especial care that they should not be galled by the ropes that bound them to the stake; acting, I suppose, on the same benevolent principle which prompts the Spaniard to deny nothing to those who must die by the garotte on the morrow.

The proximity was ominous, and far too significant to be unintentional. The instant Alan saw that chair, he guessed for what use it was destined, not without a slight apprehensive thrill. Just so may some forlorn Scottish damsel of the last century, whose flaxen locks snood might never braid again, have shivered in the cold white penance-sheet, recognizing the awful Stool on which she was to "dree her doom." Nevertheless, he accepted the position very gallantly and gracefully, sinking down easily into the *causeuse* and nestling comfortably into its cushions, without any affectation of eagerness or betrayal of reluctance. As he took up Lady Mildred's little soft hand and kissed it, his natural caressing manner was tempered by a shade of old-fashioned courtesy; and even that calm *intrigante* for the moment was not exempt from the influence of a dangerous fascination. Do not, however, do her the injustice to suppose that she once relented in her set purpose, or faltered one whit in its execution.

It would savour somewhat of repetition, and simply bore you, if all the conversation that ensued were given in detail. "My lady's" line was perfect frankness and candour. She alluded pleasantly to the great matrimonial fortunes that she had projected for Helen, and confessed — pleasantly, too — her conviction that the alliance now contemplated was perfectly imprudent, and in a worldly point of view altogether undesirable; she dilated rather more at length on the affection for Alan, indulgence to Helen, &c. &c., which induced the parents to overlook all such objections, and to give their conditional consent; but even on this point she was not oratorical or prosy. Nevertheless her hearer was quite aware that there was some more serious obstacle kept in the background; all these preliminary observations were so many shots to try the distance; the battery did not take him by surprise when it opened in earnest.

"Alan, I know it must bore you, now that Helen has come down stairs, to be obliged to listen to *Madame Mère;* it is very good of you not to show it: be patient a little longer. I must make you look at one side of the question that has escaped you, so far, I think; it is so important to the happiness of both of you that you should see your way clearly. I am not much afraid of your getting into difficulties again, your lesson has been sharp enough to cure you of extravagance; but there are embarrassments worse than any financial ones, which are only tiresome and annoying, after all. My dear nephew— has it occurred to you yet, that in changing your *vie de garçon,* you will have to economize in more ways than one, and wear some chains, though they may be light and silken?"

"I've hardly had time to realize the position, Aunt Mildred," Wyverne answered, "but I am conscious of a perfect flower-show of good resolutions, budding and blossoming already. While I was dressing, I was considering how I could best get rid of my hunters, and I have almost decided where to place them."

"You are too eager in beginning self-denial," Lady Mildred said; "perhaps it will not be necessary to part with your horses *this* season. But you must settle your future establishment with Helen and your uncle. *I* was thinking of some other favourite pursuits of yours —of handsomer and more dangerous creatures than Red Lancer — though I suppose he is a picture of a horse, and it always makes me shiver to see him rear. You may be angry with me, and call me prudish or puritanical if you like; but I *must* say it. Alan—do you know that I consider you the most con-

firmed and incorrigible flirt of my acquaintance?"

To apply to the speaker either of the two epithets she deprecated would have been simply impossible. Her bright eyes sparkled with a malicious amusement and gay triumph, as she marked the effect of her words in the quaint look of contrition mingled with perplexity which overspread Wyverne's face — usually so imperturbable. For once in his life, he felt fairly at a loss for a reply. Those general accusations are remarkably hard to meet, even when one is conscious of innocence; but woe to the respondent, if the faintest shadow of self-conviction hangs over his guilty head! The adverse advocate sees the weak point in a moment, and bears down on his victim with the full flood of indignant eloquence, exulting in a verdict already secured.

On this occasion, however, Lady Mildred did not seem inclined to press her advantage; she interrupted Alan's attempt at a disclaimer, before his embarrassment could become painful.

"Don't look so dreadfully penitent: you make me laugh when I am quite determined to be grave. I did not mean to impute to you any dark criminality. Up to the present time, perhaps, that general devotion has been rather useful in keeping you out of serious scrapes: you certainly have been singularly fortunate in that way—or wonderfully discreet. Besides, I don't mean to lecture you: it is a peculiarity in Helen's character, not in yours, that makes me give you this warning. I suppose you have guessed that she is capable of strong attachments; but you have no idea how exacting she is of undivided love in return. She has only had friendships (and very few of these) to deal with so far: but I remember her fretting for days, because her favourite governess would not give up corresponding with some school friend whom Helen had never seen, but had magnified into a rival. It is no use disguising the truth from you, when I cannot disguise it from myself, much as I love my pet. *You* would not like her to be faultless? Helen is not captious or suspicious;

but she is absurdly jealous, sometimes. I cannot conceive how she learnt to be so: she certainly did not inherit the weakness from her father or me. I believe she would begin to hate a dog or a horse, if you made it too great a favourite; and words or looks of yours— perhaps quite innocent and meaning- less—might make her more miserable than I can bear to think of. Dear Alan, it tires me more to sermonize, than it bores you to be forced to listen; but what would you have? If a mother has any duties at all, it must be one of them to speak when danger threatens her own child and another whom she loves almost as dearly."

A peculiarity of "my lady's" *parables* was, that not only were they always plausible and probable, but they gene- rally contained an element of truth and a slight foundation of fact: it made the deception more dangerous, because more difficult to detect. Really scienti- fic coiners do not grudge a certain ex- pense of pure silver to mix with the base metal: it adds so much sharpness to the outline and clearness to the ring.

So, though Alan had never till this moment heard of that defect in his fair cousin's character, he was by no means inclined to disbelieve entirely in its ex- istence now; simply because he knew his aunt too well to suppose that she would venture upon an utter fiction which would refute itself in a very short time. Most men would be somewhat disquieted by the revelation of a phase in their *fiancée's* disposition which is likely to interfere materially with do- mestic comfort and peace: but it troubled Wyverne wonderfully little. Whatever her mother might say or insinuate, he could not believe that the proud, beautiful eyes would ever con- descend to show signs of unworthy or vulgar passions. He knew that Helen was too frank and impetuous to keep a suspicion concealed for half-an-hour; and he felt that he could rely on himself for not giving her serious cause of un- easiness. It was rather a conviction that he was losing ground every mo- ment, slowly but surely, as his adver- sary's game developed itself, that made

his face very grave as he answered, though he was calm and self-possessed again as ever—

"You don't expect me to be so con- ceited as to allow all you implicate, Aunt Mildred? Still, I fear I cannot deny that I have found many of your sex very charming, and that I have not always refrained from confiding the fact to the parties most interested in hearing it. (I rather pride myself on that circumlocu- tion!) But, you know, I was never bound over to keep the peace till now. I think I can give fair securities, though not very substantial ones. Remember, I pledge all my hopes of happiness—of happiness greater than I ever dreamt would fall in my way. I don't think I should risk them lightly. I cannot tell *when* I began to love Helen; but I know that for months past the temptation has been growing stronger which vanquished me to-day: for months past it has made me proud to compare her with all the women I have ever admired (you say, Aunt Mildred, their name is legion), and to feel that no one could stand the com- parison for an instant. *That* ought to be a safeguard, surely, against other en- chantments? I can hardly fancy Helen playing Zara; yet, if the whim should seize her, I think it would be easy to prove to her that the part did not suit her at all. It is not my way to be prodi- gal of professions; but I am certain of one thing; there is no imaginable friend- ship or acquaintance—past, present, or to come—that I would not give up to spare that child ten minutes' unhappi- ness; and I should not call it a sacrifice. You are right to be distrustful when so much is at stake; but, on my faith and honour, *I* have no fears."

The clear dark eyes were fastened on Lady Mildred's inscrutable face very earnestly, as if beseeching that at least truth might be answered by truth. The trained glance of that great diplomatist did not care to meet the challenge; it must needs have quailed. I would not affirm that a momentary compunc- tion did not assail her just then, while she did justice, in thought, to the kind, generous nature of the man she had de- termined to betray. It behoves the his-

torian to be impartial, and not to attribute an ideal perfection even to his
pet politician. The Prince of Benevento
himself might be pardoned for indulging in a brief self-reproach, after ma-
ligning his own daughter and lying to
her accepted lover, within the same
half-hour. When Lady Mildred spoke
again, her voice, always low and musical, was unusually gentle and subdued.

"I am not so unkind or unjust as you
seem to think, Alan. I do believe thoroughly in your sincerity now, and I am
sure you will try your very utmost at
all times to make Helen happy. I don't
mean to say that it will be necessary to
set a watch on your lips, and measure
out the common attentions of civilized
life by the phrase: the constraint would
be too absurdly evident, if *you* were to
become formal! Nor can I suggest, at
this moment, any one acquaintance that
it would be better you should sacrifice:
your own good sense will tell you when
and where to be careful and guarded.
But I do wish that both you and Helen
should try how far you are suited to
each other, before you take the one step
in life which cannot be recalled. Remember how very young she is. You
cannot call me unreasonable if I ask one
year's delay before we fix the day for
your marriage?"

It came at last—that cunning thrust
under the guard, impossible to evade,
difficult to parry, which the fair gladiator had been meditating from the very
outset of her graceful sword-play: all the
feints of "breaking ground" had no end
or object but this. At those last words
Wyverne set his lips slightly, and drew
himself together with the involuntary
movement which is—*not* shrinking, just
as a fencer might do touched sharply in
mid chest by his opponent's foil. Twelve
months—not a long delay, surely—
scarcely more than would be required
to complete the settlements, *trousseaux*,
and other preliminaries for some matches
that we wot of, especially if a great
house is to be swept and garnished, before the bride is brought home. Alan
might have thought about some such
preparations years ago; now—he only
thought that, whatever forces Lady

Mildred might have in reserve would all
be marshalled in their place before half
the probationary year had passed.

But her position was perfectly safe
and unassailable. When a prospective
mother-in-law consents to ignore a suit-
or's social and financial disadvantages,
he cannot well quarrel with her for endeavouring to make sure that the damsel's affections are not morally misplaced:
of course her domestic prospects ought
to be bright, in proportion as her worldly ones are gloomy. The aspirant ma
have a private surmise, amounting a.-
most to a certainty, that he is being unfairly dealt with. He may murmur to
himself that, if he had been a marquis
or a millionaire, the maternal scruples
would have been mute; but it would
show sad lack of wisdom to express such
feelings aloud. If the case were to come
on for trial, no judge or jury in England
would give the plaintiff a verdict. He
would not only lose his cause, but get
"committed for contempt of court," and
incur all sorts of vague pains and
penalties, besides being held up as a
phenomenon of ingratitude, and a warning to his fellows for the remainder of
his natural life. Most men who come
to grief under such circumstances will
find their position disagreeable enough,
even without the perpetual punishment
of the pillory.

Yes, reason, if not right, was on "my
lady's" side; and she was perfectly aware
of her advantage; for her eyes met Wyverne's steadily enough now as she
waited for his reply.

The latter had reckoned so fully on
meeting with opposition somewhere in
this quarter, that it is doubtful if he was
exactly disappointed at the turn the conversation had lately taken; though perhaps, as a matter of taste, he would
have preferred more overt antagonism
and obstacles more tangible to grapple
with. At any rate, there was not a
trace of sullenness or vexation in his
manner when he spoke.

"I should have thought it unreasonable if you had made my probation as
long as Jacob's, Aunt Mildred; simply
because the span of life is greatly contracted since the patriarchal times, and

everything ought to go by comparison. It would not so much matter to Helen; for, as you say, she *is* very young: she will only be in the prime of her beauty when my hair is grey. But I confess, I should like to reap the reward of patience before I pass middle-age. Men seem to appreciate so few things *then*, that I doubt if one would even enjoy domestic happiness thoroughly. No; I don't think you at all exacting or over-cautious; and I will bide my time with a tranquillity that shall be edifying. I never found a year very long yet, and I shall have so much to do and to think of during the present one that I shall have no time to be discontented."

Lady Mildred smiled on the speaker sweetly and gratefully, but the keen, anxious, *business-like* look still lingered in her eyes.

"Thank you so very much, dear Alan," she whispered, "you have behaved perfectly throughout, just as I expected you would" (she spoke the truth, there). "You will promise me, then, that the day of your marriage shall not be actually fixed till the year has past? You know your uncle is rather impetuous, and not very prudent; I should not wonder if he were to try to precipitate matters, and that would involve discussions. Now I never could bear discussions, even when my nerves were stronger than they are; I think they grow worse every day. If *you* promise, I shall have nothing of this sort to fear. You will not refuse me this, because it looks like a selfish request?"

I have the pleasure of knowing very slightly a Companion of the Order of Valour, who carried the colours of his regiment at the Alma—it was his "baptism of fire." At the most critical moment of the day, when the troops were struggling desperately up "the terrible hill side," somewhat disordered by the vineyards and broken ground; when the Guards were reeling and staggering under the deadly hail that beat right in their faces; the man I speak of turned to the comrade nearest to him and remarked:

"Do you suppose they *always* shoot as fast as this, Charley? I dare say its the correct thing, though."

They say his manner was as listless and unconcerned as usual, with just a shade of diffidence and doubt, as if he had been consulting a diplomatic friend on some point of etiquette at a foreign court. I have the happiness of knowing very well an officer in the sister service who has received a medal scarcely less glorious, for rescuing a sailor from drowning in the Indian Sea. They had had a continuance of bad weather, and worse was coming up all round; great lead-coloured billows weltered and heaved under the lee—foam-wreaths breaking here and there, to show where the strong ship had cloven a path through the sullen surges; there was the chance, too, of encountering one of two sharks which had been haunting them for days; but I have heard that on Cis Hazelwood's face when he went over the bulwarks, there was the same expression of cheery confidence as it might have worn when he was diving for eggs at The Weirs.

Now it is fair to presume, that both these men were endowed with courage and coolness to an exceptional degree; but I very much doubt if, in perfect exemption from moral and physical fear, and in contempt for danger either in this world or the next (if the said peril stood in her path), Lady Mildred might not have matched the pair. When the Vavasours were travelling in Wales, soon after their marriage, something broke as they were descending a long steep hill, and the horses bolted; it was a very close question between life and death, till they were stopped by a couple of quarrymen just at the spot where the road turned sharp to the left over a high narrow archway; no carriage going that pace could have weathered that corner, and the fall was thirty feet clear. The poor Welshmen certainly earned their rich reward, for they both went down, and were much bruised in the struggle, and one got up with a broken collar-bone. When the horses first broke away, "my lady" deigned to lay aside the book she was reading, but showed no other sign of interest in the

**4**

training, before either is brought out for the last grand match against Time. Shall we suggest to Amoret the bride that Fidelio's affections, since they first gushed out from the remote fountain-head, have rippled and murmured—not unmusically—through a dozen *lovelets* at least, caressing on the way several fragrant water-lilies and delicate lady-ferns, before they poured a full undivided volume into the one deep channel, through which (let us hope) they will flow on peacefully for evermore? And then, shall we hint that she ought rather to rejoice thereat than chafe or complain? It were boldly—it were rashly done. However respectable our antecedents—if we could bring testimonials to character signed by ten responsible housewives (which I very much doubt if Sir Galahad himself could have obtained)—the lady would infallibly inscribe our name, foremost, on the Black List of those dangerous and detrimental acquaintances who were the bane of the Beloved's life, before she came—another Pucelle—to the rescue; thenceforward we should certainly "have our tea in a mug," whenever these fair hands had to pour it.

Yet, Madonna, if you would deign to look at the subject dispassionately, you could scarcely help perceiving that the very guilelessness and simplicity which make a First Love so charming and romantic, detract somewhat from its actual value. It is a very pleasant and charitable frame of mind, which "hopeth all things and believeth all things;" but it involves a certain deficiency in discrimination and, I think, in appreciative power. The Object may possibly be superlative in beauty, goodness, or talent; but what is our opinion worth, if we have had no practical experience of the other two degrees? Unless the paired doves take flight at once to some uncolonized island in the Pacific,

And there securely build, and there
  Securely hatch their young—

each must stand comparison, in aftertime, with other birds, tame and wild, whose plumage glistens with every gorgeous variety of colour, whose notes sink and swell through all the scales of harmony. Then it is the old story over and over again. Madame Ste. Colombe does not care so much for modest merit, and considers meekness rather a tame and insipid virtue, since the keen black eyes of haughty, handsome Count Aquila told her a flattering tale; sober drab and fawn no longer seem a becoming apparel since Prince Percinet (the Duchess's favourite lory) dazzled her with his Court suit of crimson and gold. Her innocent consort never dreams, of course, of repining; but he confesses to an intimate friend that cooing *does* sometimes sound rather monotonous: he heard a few days ago, for the first time, Lady Philomelle sing. Surely it were better to endure loneliness a little longer—ay, even till "black turns grey"—than to discover that we are unworthily or unsuitably matched, when to change our mate would be a double sin. There are matrimonial mistakes enough, Heaven knows, made as it is; but, if every one were to marry their first love, a decade of Judges more untiring than Sir Cresswell would be insufficient to settle the differences of aspirants to dis-union.

This is the "wrong side of the stuff," of course; it would be easy to quote thousands of opposite instances—of the Anderson type—where no shadow of discontent has clouded a long life of happiness. Still, the danger remains: you can no more ignore it than you can any other disagreeable fact, or public nuisance; but it will probably be lessened if one or both of the contracting parties have had practical experience enough to enable them to know their own minds once for all. The wise old Stagyrite, after discussing different sorts of courage, places high that of 'Εμπειρία: shall we not, too, honour and value most the Love which has been matured and educated by a course of preliminary and lighter experiments?

If we have wandered far, through many gardens—finding in each flowers fragrant and beautiful, but never a one worthy to be placed in our breast—do we love her less, when we choose her at last—our own Provence Rose? Was it not well that we should review and admire other fair pictures wrought by the Great Artist, before we bought what we hold to be His masterpiece, at the price of all our life's treasure? Had we not acquired some cunning of the lapidary, by studying the properties of less precious gems, could we value your pure perfections aright, O Margarita, pearl of pearls?

(In spite of that last sentimental sentence, which, I swear, was elaborated solely as a peace-offering to Them, I feel a comfortable conviction of having left the prejudices of every feminine reader in precisely the same state as I found them when we broached the subject.)

If you disagree entirely with these premises, you will hardly allow that Miss Vavasour's frame of mind was either correct or justifiable on this same August morning. It would be difficult to conceive any human being more thoroughly and perfectly happy. Yet it ·was not the bliss of ignorance, nor even of unconscious innocence. In some things demoiselle was rather advanced for her years: she could form opinions of her own, for instance, and hold to them, pretty decidedly. Some of our maiden-recruits contrive to acquire a tolerable knowledge of their regiment and its proceedings before they actually join: they have probably several friends who have passed their drill; and these are by no means loth to communicate any intelligence likely to instruct or amuse the aspirant. So, though Helen had not yet been presented, few of the *historiettes* of the last two seasons (fitted for ears polite and virginal) had failed to reach her, directly or circuitously. In more than one of these Alan Wyverne's name had figured prominently. Lady Mildred had not spoken unfairly or untruly when she characterized her daughter's temperament as somewhat jealous and exacting; but the jealousy was not retrospective. Helen decided, very wisely, to bury the past, with its possible peccadilloes, and to accept her present position frankly, without one *arrière pensée*.

It seemed rather a pleasant position, too, as she sate in the deep, cushioned recess of one of the oriel windows of the picture-gallery; the play of light through the painted panes falling fitfully on the grand masses of her glossy hair, and lending a brighter flush to her fair cheek than even happiness could give it; her clasped hands resting on her cousin's shoulder, as he half reclined on the black-bear skin at her feet— (Alan was decidedly Oriental in his choice of postures)—her head bent forward and low, so as to lose not one of many murmured words. Would it have been better if a suspicion had crossed her mind, just then, that the voice she listened to was indebted possibly to long practice in similar scenes for the dangerous melody of its monotone? I think not; there is no falser principle than judging from results.

The line of demarcation between the cousin and the lover is proverbially faint, so much so, indeed, as sometimes to become quite imaginary. There is one advantage about this, certainly; the transition into the affianced state is not so abrupt as to make either of the parties feel awkward or shy; while on the other hand, their transports are probably more moderate and rational. In the present case there was not much danger of extravagance in this way. Wyverne, as a rule, was the personification of tranquillity, and Helen—though impulsive and quick tempered enough herself—held demonstrative damsels in very great scorn. Still it would be difficult, if not impossible, to transcribe their conversation that morning, up to a certain point.

· Fortunately, one is not expected to do anything of the kind. Where the story is meant to be melo-dramatic, it is necessary sometimes to give a good strong scene of passion and temptation, in which either guilt or innocence triumphs tremendously; but the male writers of the present day seem pretty well agreed that it is best to leave *domestic* love passages (where everything is said and done under parental sanction) quite alone. An odd authoress or so does now and then attempt to give us a sort of expurgated edition, which is about as much like the reality as the midnight sun glimmering faintly over the North Cape resembles that which blazes over Sahara. You will observe, that even those dauntless and unscrupulous French *romanciers* of the physiological school rather shirk these scenes.

Perhaps occasionally a curious melancholy feeling mingles with this our masculine reserve. It may be that Mnemosynè (she can be stern enough, at times, you know)stands on the threshold of the half-open door and warns us back with uplifted finger; it may be that of all in the book, we should have to draw hardest on our imagination for this particular chapter. In either case it would not be a very attractive one to have to begin. There is something dreary in sitting down to an elaborate description of luxuries or riches that have passed away from us long ago, or which have hitherto eluded us altogether. I am not inclined to laugh much at Mr. Scrivener's enthusiasm (he writes the "high-life" tales for the *Dustpan* and other penny periodicals) when he dilates on the splendours of Lady Hermegild's boudoir, hung with mauve velvet and silver, or on the glories of the Duke of Devorgoil's banquet, where everything is served on the purest gold profusely embossed with diamonds. He lingers over the details with an extraordinary gusto, and goes into minutiæ which (if they were not grossly incorrect) would imply an intimate personal acquaintance with the scenes he describes. Now, Mr. Scrivener's father is a very meritorious grocer, in the Tottenham Court-road, and the most aristocratic assembly Jack ever attended was a party at Hackney, where (unfortunately for his prudence) he met his pretty little wife. But I know that he composes these gorgeous ᵣchapters in a close stifling room, not much bigger or better furnished than that of Hogarth's poet, with the same wail of sickly children in his ears (the walls are like paper in those suburban lodgings) and with the notice lying on the mantelpiece that the acceptance comes due on Monday, which he must mortgage his brains to meet. I think the incongruity is too sad to be absurd.

Do you see the parallel? Velvet and gold are comfortable and costly, but they are not the most precious trifles that a man may lose or win; bills are very stubborn inconveniences, but there are debts yet harder to meet, on which we pay heavier usury.

Whether that pair in the picture-gallery made themselves in anywise ridiculous, either by word or deed, in the course of the morning, is a question between themselves and their consciences; for the only witnesses were the members of their ancestry on the walls, who looked down on the proceedings with the polite indifference of well-bred people who have seen a good deal of that sort of business in their time, and have found out that "this, too, is vanity." At the moment when we intrude on the *tête-à-tête*, its component parts were in a very decorous and rational condition; in fact they had resolved themselves into a sort of committee of supply, and were discussing the financial affairs of the future. It was delightful to observe the perfect gravity and good faith with which they approached the subject; though it would have been difficult to decide which of the two was most hopelessly and absolutely ignorant of all matters pertaining to domestic economy. Wyverne was especially great on the point of retrenchment, as far as his own personal expenses were concerned.

"You have no idea how much I shall save by giving up hunting," he was saying; "I don't care nearly so much for it as I did, so it is hardly a sacrifice" (he really *thought* he was speaking the truth); "my present stud is too small to be of much use, and I hate being mounted. So that's settled. I shall have no difficulty in getting rid of my horses; Vesey will give me four hundred for Red Lancer any day; and Cuirassier ought to fetch three. Only fancy, Helen, what one will be able to do with seven hundred sovereigns! You must have a brougham to yourself, even if we stay at the great house in town, and it will be useful in the country, for I suppose people will want us to dine with them sometimes. We must have our saddle-horses of course —Maimouna carries you beautifully already—I shall never let you give up riding, if only for the memory of yesterday afternoon; and that will be all, besides the ponies that Uncle Hubert gave you on your last birthday."

"But, dear Alan," his cousin objected, "it seems to me, all those horses will cost more to keep than your hunters do now; for, you know, you always stay somewhere throughout the season, where they get board and lodging."

"Don't entangle yourself in calculations, child," Wyverne answered; "you haven't an idea how expensive hunting from other people's houses is; sending on, costs a fortune. I should like you to see my accounts for last season" (he said this with intense gravity, just as if he had kept them regularly); "I am certain I shall save two hundred a-year at the lowest computation. Yes, we can do it easily. I saw Harry Conway the other day (he married that pretty Kate Carlyon two years ago); he began telling me of his rectory in Herefordshire, what a lovely garden his wife had, and how all the country admired the Welsh ponies she drove. Now, I know their income does not touch six hundred pounds. We can double that, at all events, O cousin, cautious beyond your years!"

The part of Dame Prudence was in reality so entirely foreign to Miss Vavasour's nature and habits, that it amused her very much to play it, so she still tried to look solemn, but the laugh would not be dissembled in her eyes.

"An Abbey is a more expensive residence than a rectory, *M. le Financier*, even if the Lady Abbess should not be enthusiastic about flower-gardens. Have you formed any plans as to our life in the North? I mean to make Mrs. Grant teach me housekeeping; and I shall be *so* severe about the weekly bills! I can fancy the butchers and bakers trembling when they bring up their little red books to be settled."

"Certainly, *il faut vivre;* I quite admit the necessity of that. I have no doubt we shall do wonderfully well. I shall slay a good number of creatures, finned, furred, and feathered, and one does not get tired of game easily. We must not have any one to stay with us, except in the shooting-season; though I believe the chief cost of guests is the claret they drink; fortunately there is a Red Sea of that in the cellars. And now, my Helen, prepare to open your great eyes very extensively; I mean to annihilate your scruples with my last idea in economy. When the present stock is exhausted (it's not large) the supply of champagne at the Abbey will be cut off until I come into another inheritance."

He enunciated the words rather sententiously and solemnly, evidently feeling the confidence and self-satisfaction that might be pardonable in a Chancellor of the Exchequer who has thought of a new and productive tax that cannot possibly hurt or offend anybody, or in a calculator who has elaborated a scheme for materially reducing the national debt. This time Miss Vavasour's musical laugh was not repressed.

"Don't go any further, Alan; Prudence owns herself vanquished by that last tremendous retrenchment. I begin to think we shall manage perfectly; perhaps there is no danger of absolute penury. Whenever I find the larder is empty, and that there are no means of filling it, I shall bring in the Spur in the Dish with my own hands; you were born near enough the Border to know, then, that you and your lances must go out on the foray."

"That's right," Wyverne said; "they say nothing stimulates one to exertion like appreciation, and I've got an exertion before me this morning, in the shape of letter-writing, that I don't much fancy. It's a question of Bernard Haldane. (I can never call him and your father 'uncle' in the same breath, but he did marry my aunt, you know.) He must be absurdly rich by this time; and, when I did not in the least want it, I believe I was to have been his heir. So I might still have been, they tell me, if I had been utterly and irretrievably ruined, and had come to him in the form of the pauper. But he never forgave the poor little salvage out of the wreck which made me independent of his bounty. Very odd old man, that, and intensely disagreeable, I own; but still I wish, now, you two had met. I do believe you would have melted the misanthrope, and a very trifling thaw in that quarter would be of material advantage to us just at this juncture."

Miss Vavasour's haughty lip curled perceptibly; her face did not care to conceal some aversion and disdain.

"I should certainly spare myself the annoyance of writing that letter, if I were you, Alan. I don't think mendicaney would suit you at any time, and it is rather early to begin the trade. *I* should hardly succeed better, even if I had the chance of trying. If I have any fascinations, I think I will keep them for some other subjects than odd, disagreeable, old men."

Wyverne was not in the least inclined to chafe at her tone; in truth, admiration left no place for anger; it would have been hard to quarrel with her, she looked so handsome in her scorn. He knew, too, that her pride was only half selfish, and that she would have dreaded humiliation for his sake, more than for her own. So he smiled quite pleasantly, as he answered,

"O Queen, let your imperial mind be set at rest. Your bond-servant had no intention of making obeisance to any other tyrant. Do I look like one of 'the petitioners who will ever pray?' (He certainly did *not* at that moment.) I only meant to convey a piece of simple intelligence, which perhaps Mr. Haldane is entitled to in courtesy, and leave him to think and act as he would. But I told you I disliked doing even this; and I hesitated till I consulted your mother on the point after breakfast. She decided at once that I ought to do so. I own her look, as she said it, would have puzzled me, if I had not given up long ago trying to decipher 'my lady's' countenance. I imagine she expects not much will result. I'm sure *I* don't. But if Plutus were only to part with a poor thousand, it would help me to furnish two or three rooms prettily at the Abbey for you and your friends. My pet, you will look like Nell

in the Curiosity Shop, in that dismal grey house, with its faded old-fashioned furniture."

Helen was accusing herself already of having been unjust and unkind. Her conscience smote her yet more keenly as her cousin spoke these last words. When she laid her hand on his mouth to stop him, it was half meant as a caress. Wyverne pressed the lithe white fingers against his lips, and made them linger there not unwillingly; but his mood, usually so equable and gay, had become strangely variable since yesterday. The dark hour came on suddenly now. His face seemed to gather anything but light from the bright loveliness on which he gazed. Helen's hand was dropped almost abruptly, and he went on muttering low to himself, as if unconscious of her presence.

"Esau was wiser than I. He *sold* his birthright at all events: I gave mine away. God help us! Instead of these miserable shifts and subterfuges, I ought at this moment to be talking about the fresh setting of my mother's diamonds. I wonder who wore them at the last drawing-room? I took my own ruin too lightly. I suppose that is why it stands out so black and dismal, when I have brought another down to share it. Ah me! If the struggle and the remorse begin so early, what will the end be?"

She broke in quickly, her fingers trembling as she twined them in his, and her cheeks glowing with her passionate earnestness.

"Alan, how can you speak so? Do you want to make me feel more selfish than I do already? I might have known what it would come to when you proposed selling Red Lancer, and I ought to have resisted then. You would sacrifice all your own pursuits and pleasures to me and my fancies, and you take nothing in return except"—(the word-music could scarcely be heard here)— "except—my dear love. See, *I* do not fear or doubt for one instant. Am I to teach you courage—you that I have always heard quoted for daring since I was a little child?"

We have read in the *Magic Ring*

how the draught 'mixed by Gerda, the sorceress, for Arinbiorn, before the great sea-king went forth to fight, doubled the strength of his arm and the sway of his battle-axe. Glamour more potent yet may be drawn from brilliant dark eyes, whose imperial light is softened, not subdued, by tears that are destined never to fall. A tamer spirit than Wyverne's would have leapt up, ready for any contest, under the influence of Helen's glance, when she finished speaking. Very scanty are the relics that abide with us óf the old-time chivalry ; but our dames and demoiselles still play their part as gallantly and gracefully as ever. Even " Sir Guy of the Dolorous Blast," when bound to the battle, will scarcely lack a maiden to brace on his armour.

Alan rose to his feet and leant over his cousin where she sate. He forgot to be ashamed of his own weakness; he felt so proud of his beautiful prize, as-he wound his arm round her delicate waist and drew her close to his side, till the little head nestled on his shoulder and his lips touched her ear as they whispered,

"My own brave darling! you shall never have to revive me again. The dead past may bury its dead; my last moan is made; henceforward will we not hope, even against hope."

In spite of his newly-born confidence, he scarcely repressed a start and a shiver, as, looking up during the happy silence that ensued, he seemed to be answered by the earnest melancholy eyes of the last Baron Vavasour.

There are certain pictures, you know, whose gaze always follows you, however often you may change your position. This portrait was one of such. It ought to have been excepted from the other ancestors, when we spoke of the unconcern with which they regarded the proceedings of their descendants. It was a very remarkable face, as I have said before, and by far the most peculiar feature in it were those same eyes. Notwithstanding their soft beauty, there was something dark and dangerous about them, as if the devil that lurked in their languid depths *would* look out some-

times. They were just the eyes from which an Italian would dread the *jettatura*, seeming to threaten not only evil to others, but misfortune to their owner. In Fulke Vavasour's life certainly both promises were amply fulfilled. If those scornful lips could have spoken now, one might have guessed at the import of the words.

"No change since my time. Those old commonplaces about faith and hope and love are not worn out yet; but it amuses me to hear them again now and then—not too often. I could repeat them glibly enough myself once, and perhaps I believed in them a little. I am wiser now, and so will you be, *beau cousin*, before you have done. I had my romance, of course. You know how that was cut short one cold morning on Tower-hill; but you *don't* know where yours will end."

Some ideas like these shot across Wyverne's mind, but he had no time to give them form or distinctness, even if he had wished to indulge in such absurdity, for one of the doors of the gallery opened just then, and though the drawing aside of the heavy *portière* gave them a moment's grace, the cousins had scarcely time to resume an erect and decorous posture before their *tête-à-tête* was ended.

## CHAPTER VII.

### MATED, NOT MATCHED.

THE new-comer was an elderly man, in a clerical dress. His figure, originally massive and powerful, had thickened and filled out of late years till little of fair proportion or activity remained. In his walk and general bearing there was the same lassitude and want of energy which spoilt his face. The features could never have been regularly handsome; they were too weakly moulded for *any* style of beauty; but their natural expression was evidently meant to be kindly and genial. This, too, had changed. There was a nervous, worried look about him, as of a man exposed to many vexations and annoyances. It was not grave enough to suggest any great sorrow. Geoffry Knowles's story is very soon told. He was three or four years the Squire's senior; but they had been great friends at college. Few of their old set were left when Geoffry went up to keep his "master's term;" so, unluckily, he was a good deal thrown on his own resources. His evil genius lured him one day to a certain water-paty, where he met Laura Harding, the handsome, flashy daughter of an Oxford attorney in large and very sharp practice, who speedily entangled him irretrievably. If Hubert Vavasour had been in the way, it might have been prevented. His thoroughbred instincts would have revolted from the intense vulgarity of the whole family, and the great influence he possessed over his friend's facile mind would all have been exerted to free the latter from a connexion which could only prove disastrous and unhappy. 'Geoffry Knowles himself, the most indolent and unobservant of men, saw from the first that the fair Laura's *entourage* was most objectionable; and certain incongruities (to use a mild term) in the lady's own demeanour and dialect struck him now and then painfully, as they would have done any other man well-bred and well-born. But, though conscious of going down hill, he was too idle to try to struggle back again; and when the moment for the final plunge came, he took it resignedly, if. not contentedly, expecting no countenance from any of his friends, as he had not sought their counsel. Perhaps, after all, retractation would have been worse than vain. The wily lawyer might have said with the Sultan,

Dwells in my court-yard a falcon unhooded,
And what he once clutches he never lets go.

Though Knowles was of an impoverished family and rather an extravagant turn, Mr. Harding knew he had powerful friends, first and foremost of whom was the Squire of Dene; so far he judged rightly. Hubert Vavasour not only disliked "hitting a man when he was down," but never would let him lie there without trying to help him up. So, in spite of the connexion which he thoroughly disapproved, as soon as the rectory of Dene fell vacant, he did not hesitate to offer it to his ancient comrade: it was one of those great family livings that are almost as valuable as a fat priory or abbey might have been; and thenceforth its rector wanted no comforts that affluence could supply. When this event occurred the Squire had been married about three years: he took the step without consulting his wife, or in all probability Lady Mildred would have interfered to some purpose. It was part of her creed never to waste either lamentations or reproaches on what was irrevocable; so she accepted the fact quite composedly, determining to judge for herself as to the feasibility of associating with the new-comer, and to act accordingly.

Neither the Squire's nor the rector's wife ever forgot the first evening they met. Truth to say, "my lady" had prepared herself for a certain amount of vulgarity; but the reality so far transcended her expectations, that the shock was actually too much for her. She could not repress a slight shiver and shrinking sometimes, as Mrs. Knowles's shrill, highly-pitched voice rattled in her ears, and her trained features did not always conceal wonder and aversion at certain words and gestures that grated horribly on her delicate sensibilities. The other's sharp eyes detected every one of these unflattering signs, and she never forgot them: though long years had passed and a reckoning-day had never come, the debt still remained, written out as legibly in her memory as Foscaro's in Loredano's tablets. That evening, when the visitors had taken their departure, the fair hostess leaned back wearily on her sofa and beckoned her husband to her side. When he came she laid her hand on his arm and looked up into his eyes rather plaintively, but not in the least reproachfully.

"Dear Hubert!" she said, "I fancy Mr. Knowles very much, and I hope he will come here whenever he likes. He may bring his wife four times a year (when you have some of those constitnency dinners, you know); but, at any other time or place, I absolutely decline to entertain that fearful woman again!"

There was not a shade of anger, or even disdain, on the placid face, but he must have been a bolder man than Vavasour who would have argued the point with her then. Hubert knew that the fiat just issued by those beautiful lips, ever so little set, was irrevocable.

"She *is* an awful infliction!" he assented, gravely; "I can't call you unjust, dear Mildred. Indeed, I almost regret having brought her so near you. I must manage it with Geoffry as best I can; I should not like to lose his society. Poor fellow! I was very wroth when I first heard of his derogation—but I can do nothing but pity him now. If she affected us so disagreeably this evening, think what it must be to have to live with her all the year round! It is no use saying, 'He's used to it.' There are some nuisances one never gets indifferent to."

Lady Mildred shrugged her round white shoulders slightly, as though to intimate that Mr. Knowles's domestic Nemesis was essentially *his* concern; and so the matter ended.

It was not long before that worried, nervous expression, to which I have alluded, became the habitual one of poor Geoffry's face. He never spoke of his troubles, even to Hubert Vavasour; but they must have been heavy, and almost incessant. His wife had captured him simply as a measure of expediency: she would have married him just as readily if he had been elderly and repulsive when she first saw him; she very soon got tired of keeping up affectionate appearances; indeed, that farce scarcely outlasted the honeymoon. The last phantasm of romance had ceased to haunt the dreary fireside, years and years ago. Laura's sharp tongue and acid face were enough to scare away a legion of such sensitive elves. As soon as she found that their income was far more than sufficient for their wants she took severely to parsimony, and "screwed" to an extent scarcely credible. There never breathed a more liberal and openhanded man than Geoffry Knowles—it must have been a poor satisfaction to him to know that about thirty pounds per annum were saved by economy in beer alone, and that his servants'-hall was a byword throughout the county. The wives of the squirearchy had been very kind and civil to her at first, and were not all inclined to follow the lead of the *grande dame* at Dene; but they couldn't stand her long, and one by one they fell off to a ceremonious distance, doing out their visits and invitations by measure and rule. This did not improve the lady's temper, which was exacting and suspicious to a degree: she never would allow that she ever lost a friend or failed to make one by her own fault; though she had a pleasant habit of abusing people savagely to their nearest neighbours, so that it was about ten to one that every syllable came round to them. They had one child—a son—who might have been some comfort to the Rector if his mother would have let him alone: but she asserted her exclusive right to the child even before he was christened, insisting on calling him by her own family's name—"Harding"—(some one said, "it was to commemorate an incomplete victory over the aspirates"); and maintained her ascendency over his mind by the simple process of abusing her husband to and before the boy, as soon as he was old enough to understand anything; it is needless to say there was always more distrust than sympathy between father and son.

So, you see, Geoffry Knowles had a good deal to fight against, and very little to fall back upon. His one consolation was, his neighbourhood to Dene: he clung fast to this, and would not let it go, in spite of incessant sarcasms levelled at his meanness of spirit for "always hanging about a house where his wife was not thought good enough to be invited:"—(she never missed one of those quarterly dinners, though). It was inexpressibly refreshing to get out of hearing of the shrill dissonant voice—ever querulous when not wrathful, and to share

The delight of happy laughter,
The delight of low replies,

which one could always count on finding at Dene when its mistress or her
daughters were to the fore. Those
visits had the same effect on the unlucky rector, in calming and bracing
his nerves, as change of air will work
on an invalid who moves up from the
close dank valley to the fresh mountain-side, where the breeze sweeps
straight from the sea over crag, and
heather, and tarn. Lady Mildred liked
him—perhaps pitied him a little—in
her own cool way, and the Squire was
always glad to see him; so he came
and went pretty much as he chose, till
it would have been hard to say to
which family he really most belonged.
Helen was very fond of him; it would
have been strange had it been otherwise,
for he had petted her ever since he held
her in his arms at the font, and, indeed,
had lavished on her all the father-love
of a kindly nature, which he was de-
barred from giving to his own child.
As her loveliness ripened from bud to
blossom under their eyes, no one could
have said which was the proudest of
their darling—the Rector or the Squire.

It rather spoils the rómance of the
thing—but, truth to say, there were
other and much more material links in
the chain that bound Geoffry Knowles
so closely to Dene. He had always
been of a convivial turn, and, from
youth upwards, not averse or indifferent to the enjoyment of old wine and
fat venison: of late years he had become ultra-canonical in his devotion to
good cheer. I do not mean to imply
that he drank hard or carried *gour-
mandise* to excess; but certainly not
one of Vavasour's guests, whose name
was legion, savoured more keenly the
precious vintages that never ceased to
flow from his cellars, or the master-
strokes of the great artist who deigned
to superintend the preparation of his
banquets. Was it a despicable weakness? At all events, it was not an uncommon one. The world has not grown
weary of trying that somewhat sensual
anodyne, since Ulysses and his com-

rades revelled on the island-shore till
the going down of the sun—

δαινύμενοι κρέα τ' ἄσπετα καὶ μέθυ ἡδύ

a few hours after he crept out of the
Cyclops' cave, leaving the bones of six
of his best and bravest behind; many
bond-slaves since Sindbad, as the jocund juice rose to their brain, have
forgotten for awhile that they carried a
burden more hideous and heavy than
the horrible Old Man of the Sea.

I have lingered much longer than I
intended over the antecedents of the
Rector; but as one or two members of
his family play rather an important part
in the story afterwards, there is some
excuse for the interruption.

When Mr. Knowles entered the picture-gallery, he was evidently unaware
that it held other occupants; he had
advanced half way up its length, before
Miss Vavasour's gay dress, looking
brighter in the strong sun-light, caught
his eye; even then he had to resort to
his glasses before he could make out
who sat in the deep embrasure.

"This is a new whim, Helen," he
said, as he turned towards them; "I
never found you here in the morning
before. Can you tell me where the
Squire is? I want—"

He stopped abruptly, for he was near
enough now for the fair face to tell its
tale, and, short-sighted as he was, the
rector saw the state of things instantly.
A few steps—very different from his
usual slow, deliberate pace—brought
him into the oriel; he stooped and
kissed Helen on her forehead, and then
griped Wyverne's hand hard, his lips
moved twice before he could say, un-
steadily and huskily, "I am so very,
very glad!"

It was a simple and hearty congratu-
lation enough, but it was the first that
the fair *fiancée* had had to encounter,
and it threw her into considerable confusion, coming thus brusquely. To
speak the truth, she "arose and fled
away swiftly on her feet," covering her
retreat with some indistinct murmur
about going to find the Squire, and left
her ally to bear the brunt of the battle

alone. The Rector was not in the least vexed at her flight; he knew his pet too well to think that she could be ungracious; he only looked after her with a smile of pride and fondness as she glided away and disappeared through the curtained door, and then turned again to Alan.

"I have always dreamt of this," he said; "but so few of my good dreams come true that I scarcely hoped there would be an exception here. I am certain you will take all care of her; and how happy she will make you! And how long has this been going on? You have kept your secret well, I own, but I am so blind that it is very easy to keep me in the dark."

There was a faint accent of melancholy, and a half reproach in the last few words, which did not escape Wyverne's quick ear.

"My dear Rector, don't be unjust. What do you mean by suspecting us of keeping secrets from *you?* You won't give one time to tell you. We were all perfectly sober and sane till yesterday afternoon, when I lost my head riding in the Home Wood; and everybody has been following my lead ever since, for I ought to be crushed on the spot instead of encouraged. You see I'm like other maniacs; they always know their companions are mad, and tell you so—don't they?"

"Imprudent, perhaps, but not insane," the other said, heartily; "and is 'my lady' as bad as the rest of you?"

"Well, not exactly; for, though she refused nothing, she was wise enough to stipulate that the time of our marriage should not be fixed until a year had passed. I believe Aunt Mildred likes me, but I don't think her partiality quite blinds her to my disadvantages."

It would have been hard to decide from Wyverne's face, whether he spoke in earnest or irony; but there was no mistaking the expression of the Rector's; disappointment was written there very legibly.

"You could hardly expect unreserved consent *there*," he said; "but it is a long delay before anything is actually fixed—too long. Alan, trust me. You don't mind my speaking frankly? Helen comes out next season, you know; and even if your engagement is announced, nothing will prevent half the 'eligibles' in London going wild about her. It will be fearfully tantalizing to 'my lady's' ambition, and I doubt if her good faith will last out the year. If that once fails, you will have a hard battle to fight and a dangerous one; none can say what a day may bring forth, and few of Lady Mildred's are wasted when she has determined to carry anything through. Surely you tried to shorten the probation-time?"

Wyverne bit his lip, frowning slightly.

"My triumph is great, I own, but really I don't require to be reminded that I am mortal. Of course there are risks and perils without end, but I have counted them already, Rector; don't trouble yourself to go through the list again. No, I did *not* remonstrate or resist, simply because I think it wiser to husband one's strength than to waste it. I might say to you as Oliver said to Sir Henry Lee—'Wearest thou so white a beard, and knowest thou not that to refuse surrendering an indefensible post, by the martial law deserves hanging?' My position at the moment was not quite so strong, numerically, as the Knight of Ditchley's, for he had *two* 'weak women' in his garrison, and, I fancy, I had only one brave girl. We can count on the Squire's good will to any extent, but he would be the merest reed to lean upon if matters went wrong. It is much the best plan to trust till you are forced to distrust; for it saves trouble, and comes to about the same thing in the end; pondering over your moves don't help you much when your adversary could give you a bishop or a castle. So for the present I believe in Aunt Mildred *coûte qui coûte.* You are right though—there will be a fair crop of rivals next spring; but I am vain enough to think that, with such a long start, I may hold my own past the post."

Alan threw back his head rather haughtily, as he spoke these last words, and once again encountered the eyes of

Fulke Vavasour. He turned quickly to his companion, before the latter could reply.

"An ominous neighbourhood to make love in, is it not? especially considering the resemblance. You have remarked it?"

Geoffry Knowles started visibly, and his countenance fell more than it had yet done.

"I wish you had not asked me. Yes, I have seen it coming out stronger every month for the last year; it was never there before. I have always avoided looking at that picture since I was forced to confess that the family likeness to Helen is far stronger than in her own brother's portrait that hangs there. If the Squire had only some excuse for putting it away! Such coincidences are common enough, of course, but I wish to God the features of the worst of her race had not been reproduced in our darling."

"Not the worst, I think," Wyverne answered, decidedly, "though he was wild and reckless enough in all conscience. It's an odd thing to say, but I've liked him better since I heard how and why he sold himself to Satan. I dare say you don't know that version of the story. Percie Ferrars, who is always hunting out strange family legends, told it me the other day. He found it in some book relating to the black art, written about fifty years after the Baron's death. It seems that he had always been meddling with magic, but he never actually came to terms with the fiend till the night of his arrest. He signed and sealed the contract within an hour after he entered his cell, on the condition that certain papers then at the Dene should be in his hands before the dawn; so he saved a woman's honour from being dragged through the mire of a public trial, and perhaps a delicate neck from the scaffold. This is how the horseman came along at midnight, bearing the Baron's signet-ring, when the arrest was not two hours old; and this is why the pursuivant, who started before the prisoner was in the Tower, and never drew bridle on the way except to change his horses, found no-

thing but empty drawers and rifled caskets, with a mark here and there, they say, as if hot coals had been dropped on them. The author brings the case forward in a very matter-of-fact way, to show for what a miserably small consideration men will sometimes barter their souls, for he observes that Vavasour could not even obtain for himself safety of life or limb. Perhaps he did not try; he came of the wrong sort to stand chaffering over a bargain when he was in no position to make terms. I don't mean to deny that Fulke was very guilty; I don't mean to assert that a man has any right to sell his soul at all; but I am not prepared to admit the absurd smallness of the value received. The Baron himself, it appears, revealed the infernal contract to one man, his cousin and dearest friend. When the confidant, rather horror-stricken, asked 'if he did not repent?' he only answered—'What is done is well done'—and thenceforward would answer no question, declining to the last the consolations of religion or the visits of a priest. But every one knows, that at his trial and on Tower-hill he bore himself as coolly and bravely as if he had been a martyred bishop. Let him rest in peace if he may! If he erred, he suffered. For the sake of that last wild deed, unselfish at least, I will east no stone on his grave."

His quiet features lighted up, and his eyes gleamed, just as they would do if he were reading some grand passage in prose or rhyme that chanced to move him strongly. No enthusiasm answered him from the other's face. The Rector evidently could not sympathize.

"It's a dark story," he said, "whichever way you look at it, and your version does not make me dislike that picture the less. But I'm not a fair judge. If I ever had any romance, it has been knocked out of me years ago. I won't argue the point. I'm only sorry that our talk has got into such a melancholy groove. It is my fault entirely. First I spoil your tête-à-tête by blundering in here, where I had no earthly business, and then I spoil your anticipations with my stupid doubts and forebodings. Just like me, isn't it?"

Wyverne's gay laugh broke in before the Rector's penitence could go further.

"Not at all like you," he answered cheerily; "and don't flatter yourself that either prophecy or warning will have the slightest effect. Ecclesiastes himself would fail if he tried to preach prudence to *us* just now. I told you we had all gone out of our sober minds up here. For my part I don't care how long the Carnival lasts. We must keep the feasts in their order, of course; but, by St. Benedict, we will not anticipate Lent by an hour."

Geoffry Knowles looked wistfully into the speaker's frank, fearless eyes, till his own brow began to clear, and a hearty, genuine admiration shone out in his face.

"I do envy that hopeful geniality of yours, more than I can say, Alan. I have a dim recollection of having been able to 'take things easy,' once upon a time; but the talent slipped away from me, somehow, just when it would have served me best. It was acquired, not natural, with me, I suppose. I doubt if I could translate without blundering, now—*Dum spiro, spero.* I am glad, after all, that I caught you first, and got rid of my 'blue' fit before I saw the Squire. He would not have taken it so well, perhaps, as you have done."

"I don't know about that," Alan said; "Uncle Hubert is pretty confident, and you would most likely have been carried away helplessly by the stream; he put *me* to shame last night, I can tell you. You'll find him in his room by this time; and I can't stay here any longer. I've letters to write, and I mean to have Helen in the saddle directly after luncheon. I must make the best use of my chances now, for, unless the gods would

Annihilate both Time and Space
To make two lovers happy,

(as the man in the play wanted them to do), and cut out the shooting season from the calendar, there would be no chance of keeping Dene clear of guests. They will be coming by troops in less than a fortnight. There is no such

thing as a comfortable *causerie*, with keen eyes and quick ears all around you. *Ay de mi!* one will have to intrigue for interviews as if we were in Seville. I shouldn't wonder if we were driven to act the garden-scene in the *Barbière* some night. Even if I wanted to monopolize Helen, then (which I don't, for it's the worst possible taste), I know 'my lady' would not stand it. Well, thank you for all you have said—yes, *all*. I shall see you at luncheon?"

From the Squire's radiant face, when he came in with the Rector, it might be presumed that the latter comported himself during their interview entirely to his friend's satisfaction.

It was no vain boast of Wyverne's when he said that neither omen nor foreboding would affect his spirits materially that afternoon. Few people ever enjoyed a ride more thoroughly than the cousins did their very protracted one. They would not have made a bad picture, if any one could have sketched them during its slow progress. Alan on the Erl-King, a magnificent brown hunter of Vavasour's; Helen on the grey Arab, Maimouna, whom she mounted that day for the fourth time. The one so erect and knightly in his bearing; the other so admirably lithe and graceful — both so palpably *at home* in the saddle; even as they lounged carelessly along through the broad green glades, apparently lost to everything but their own low, earnest converse, at the first glance one could have recognised the seat and hand of the artist.

If one *must* be locomotive, when alone with the ladye of our love (not a desirable necessity, some will say), I doubt if we can be better than on horseback. A low pony-carriage, with a *very* steady animal in the shafts, has its advantages; but I never yet saw the man who could accommodate himself and his limbs to one of these vehicles without looking absurdly out of his place; his bulk seems to increase by some extraordinary process as soon as he has taken his seat, till ten stone loom as large as fourteen would do under ordinary circumstances. The incongruity cannot always escape one's fair companion, and, if her sense of the ridiculons is once moved, our romance is ruined for the day : perhaps the best plan, on turning into a conveniently secluded road (always supposing that "moving on" is obligatory), would be, to get out and walk by her side, leaving the dame or demoiselle unrestricted scope for the expansion of her feelings and—her drapery. On the whole, I think one is most at ease *en chevauchant.* But then both steeds must be of a pleasant and sociable disposition—not pulling and tearing at the reins, till they work themselves and their riders into a white heat, whenever a level length of greensward tempts one irresistibly to a stretching gallop; nor starting perversely aside at the very moment when, in the earnestness of discourse, your hand rests unconsciously (?) on your companion's pommel ; but doing their five miles an hour steadily, with the long, even, springy gait that so few half-breeds ever attain to,—alive, in fact, to the delicacy of the position and to their own resposibilities as sensible beasts of burden. Maimouna was a model in this respect : she could be fiery enough at times, and dangerous if her temper was roused ; but she comported herself that afternoon with a courtesy and consideration for others worthy of the royal race from which she sprang—

> Who could trace her lineage higher
> Than the Bourbon can aspire,
> Than the Ghibelline or Guelf,
> Or O'Brien's blood itself.

It was pretty to see her, champing the bit and tossing her small proud head playfully, or curving her full, rounded neck to court the caress of Helen's gauntlet; with something more than instinct looking all the while out of her great bright stag's-eyes, as if she understood everything that was going on and approved it thoroughly : indeed, she seemed not indisposed to get up a little mild flirtation on her own account, for ever and anon she would rub her soft cheek against the Erl-King's puissant shoulder, and withdraw it suddenly as he turned his head with a coy, *mutine*

grace, till even tnat stately steed unbent somewhat of his dignity, and condescended, after a superb and sultanesque fashion, to respond to her cajoleries.

Altogether they made, as I have said, a very attractive picture, suggestive of the gay days when knights and paladins rode in the sweet summer-weather through the forest-tracks of Lyonnesse and Brittany, each with his fair *paramour* at his side, ready and willing to do battle for her beauty to the death. Wyverne's proportions were far too slight and slender to have filled the mighty harness of Gareth or Geraint; but Helen might well have sat for Iseult in her girlhood before the breath of sin passed over the smooth brow—before the lovely proud face was trained to dissemble—before King Mark's unwilling bride drank the fatal philtre and subtler poison yet from her convoy's eyes, as they sailed together over the Irish Sea. Yes—no doubt

> It was merry in good greenwood,
> When mavis and merle were singing;

when silvered bridles and silvery laughs rang out with a low, fitful music ; when the dark dells, whenever a sun-beam shot through, grew light with shimmer of gold and jewels, or with sheen of minever and brocade; when ever and anon a bugle sounded—discreetly distant—not to recall the lost or the laggards, but just to remind them that they were supposed to be hunting the deer. Pity that almost all these romances ended so drearily ! We might learn a lesson, if we would ; but we "hear and do not fear.", The modern knight's riding suit is russet or grey; perhaps, at the richest, of sable velvet; a scarlet neck-ribbon or the plumes of a tropical bird are the most gorgeous elements in his companion's amazonian apparel; but I fear the tone of their dress is about the only thing which is really sobered and subdued. People will go on lingering till they lose their party, and looking till they lose their hearts, and whispering till they lose their heads, to the end of time ; though all these years have not abated one iota of the retribution allotted those who "love not wisely but too well;" though many miserable men, since Tristram, have dwined away under a wound that would never heal, tended by a wife that they could never like, thirsting for the caress of "white hands beyond the sea," and for a whisper that they heard—never, or only in the death-pang; though many sinners, since Launcelot, have grovelled in vain remorse on the gravestone of their last love or their first and firmest friend.

Certainly none of these considerations could trouble the cousins' pleasant ride; for every word that passed between them was perfectly innocent and authorized; they had, so to speak, been "blessed by the priest" before they started. When Helen came down (rather late) to dinner, her face was so changed and radiant with happiness that it made "my lady's" for the rest of the evening unusually pensive and grave. Some such ideas shot across her as were in the cruel step-mother's mind, when she stopped those who bore out the seeming corpse to its burial, saying—

> Drap the het lead on her breast,
> And drap it on her chin:
> For mickle will a maiden do,
> To her true love to win.

## CHAPTER VIII.

### CRŒSUS COMETH.

WE have been comfortable in our country-houses for centuries. Even in those rough-and-ready days—when the hall was strewn with rushes, and the blue wood-smoke hung over the heads of the banqueters like a canopy, and the great tawny hounds couched at their master's feet, gnawing the bones as they fell from the bare oak tables, and the maids of Merry England recruited their roses with steaks and ale in the early morning—I believe the Anglo-Saxon squire had a right to be proud of his social privileges, and to contrast them favourably with the short-comings of his Continental neighbours. But it looks as if we had only begun of late years thoroughly to appreciate those advantages; now—there is hardly a tale or a novel written, which does not sound a note or two of triumph on the subject. In truth, it is hardly possible to praise too highly this part of our social system. Nevertheless, in a few of these favoured mansions, there springs up something bitter from the midst of the fountain of delights which, to the minds of many of us, poisons the perfection of hospitality. Sometimes the officer in command is rather too exact and exacting about his morning-parade, insisting upon his company being "all present and correct" within a certain time after the warning gong has sounded. Punctuality is an immense virtue, of course; but our frail and peccant nature will not endure even virtues to be forced upon it against the grain, without grumbling; and there are men—sluggish if you will, but not wholly reprobate—who think that no amount of good shooting or good cookery can compensate for the discomfort of having to battle with a butler for the seisin of their grill, or being forced to keep a footman at fork's length, while they hurry over a succulent "bloater" should they wish to break their fast at a heterodox and unsanctified hour. There is some sense in the objection, after all. If you want to enforce regularity with Spartan sternness, it is better to be consistent, and not tantalize one with contrasts, but recur to the old black-broth and barley-bread form; choose your system and stick to it: it never can answer to mix up Doric simplicity with Ionian luxury.

So few things were done by line and measure at Dene, that it would have been strange if breakfast had formed the solitary exception to the rule of—*Fais ce que voudras*. The general hour was perhaps "a liberal ten;" but if any guest chanced to be seized with a fit of laziness, he could indulge his indolent genius without fear of having to fast in expiation. At whatever hour he might appear, a separate breakfast equipage awaited him, with the letters of that post laid out thereon, decently and in order, and the servants seemed only too glad to anticipate his appetite.

5

The Squire himself was tolerably early in his habits, and kept his times of starting very well in the shooting or hunting season: he would never wait beyond a reasonable time for any one— making no distinction of persons—but would start with those who were ready, leaving the laggards to follow when they would. There was a want of principle, perhaps, about the whole arrangement, but it answered admirably; even those who were left behind on such occasions never dreamt of being discontented, or discomfited; indeed, it was not a very heavy penance to be condemned to spend a home-day at Dene with the feminine part of its garrison. There were few houses that people were so glad to come to, and so sorry to leave.

Wyverne was very capricious and uncertain as to the hours of his appearance, except when any sport by flood or field was in prospect: he was never a second behind time then. If the day chanced to be very tempting, it was even betting that he would be found sauntering about some terrace that caught the fresh morning sun, before the dew was off the flowers; but it would have been dangerous to lay odds about it; taking the average of the year, the balance was decidedly in favour of indolence.

When he came down on the sixth morning from that on which this story began, the Squire and Helen were lingering over their breakfast nearly finished, that Alan might not have to eat his in solitude. Nobody ever thought of apologizing for being late at Dene; so, after the pleasant morning-greetings were over, Wyverne sat down to his repast with his usual air of tranquil, appreciative enjoyment; he did not seem in any particular hurry to grapple with the pile of letters that lay beside his plate.

Have you ever observed the pretty flutter that pervades all the womanhood present when the post-bag is brought in— how eyes, bright enough already, begin to sparkle yet more vividly with impatient anticipation, and how little tremulous hands are stretched out to grasp as much of the contents as their owners can possibly claim? We of the sterner sex·take the thing much more coolly— of course because we are so much graver and better and wiser than *they* are: when a man "plunges" at his letters, you may be quite sure he has a heavy book on an approaching race, or is a partner in some thriving concern, commercial or amatory; in such a contingency the speculator is naturally anxious to know if his venture is likely to prove remunerative. Where no such *irritamenta malorum* (or *bonorum*, in exceptional cases) exist, we are apt to accept what the post brings us with resignation rather than with gratitude, reflecting moodily, that all those documents must not only be read through, but answered—at what expense of time, money, or imagination, it is impossible at present to say.

Some years ago I heard of a female Phœnix—wise and fair, too, beyond her fellows—who actually wrote to a very intimate friend ten consecutive letters, each containing, besides more confidential and interesting matter, all sorts of news and scandal, with the recording angel's comments annexed. They were model epistles, I believe—witty, but not *too* wicked; frank, without being too demonstrative; and to not one of the brilliant decade did the writer *expect an answer*. That was understood from first to last, for circumstances made silence, on one side, imperative. I hope her correspondent appreciated that rare creature, then: I am very sure he did, the other day, when he sat down to his writing-table with a weary sigh and the remark—that "of all fond things vainly imagined, a second post was the most condemnable." If charity covers a multitude of sins, surely such repeated acts of unselfish benevolence ought to cloak most of that poor Rose's little faults and failings. Speaking quite disinterestedly (for I scarcely knew her by sight), I think she deserves a statue—as a marvel of the Post-office—better than Rowland Hill: if I were bound to take a pilgrimage, I would pass by the shrine of Saint Ursula, and go a thousand miles beyond it, to the green Styrian hills where She withered and died—the only woman on record who could persist, for three whole months, in amusing a silent correspondent without proximate hope of recompense.

Wyverne's letters were not very numerous that morning, nor did they appear to interest him much; for he took up one after the other, at intervals, and after just glancing at the contents put them aside, without interrupting a pleasant desultory conversation with his compauions. At last only two remained unread.

The envelope of one was of thick blue-wove paper; the direction was in a large, strong, upright hand; the seal square, and solemnly accurate—such a seal as no man dare use unless he were in a position to set the world at defiance. If you or I, *amigo*, were to risk it, however numerous and unblemished our quarterings, we should lay ourselves open to all the penalties attendant on *lèse-majesté*: the very crest was a menace—a mailed arm, with a mace in its gripe. If any possessor of that truculent coat-of-arms had put it on the outside of a love-letter, all passionate pleading must have been neutralized; the nymph to whom it was addressed would have fled away, swiftly as Arethusa of light-footed memory, or a " homeless hare."

The other letter was of a widely different type; it bore no seal, but a scarlet monogram so elaborately involved as to be nearly illegible; after careful study of its intricacies, with a certain amount of luck, you might have made out the initials N. R. L. There was a *mignardise* about the whole thing quite in keeping with the handwriting—slender, sloping, and essentially feminine; at the same time there was a good deal of *character* about it; without much practice in graphiology, one guessed at once that those lines had been traced by fingers long, lithe, and lissome—fingers that either in love or hate would close round yours—pliant and tenacious as the coils of a Java serpent—fingers apt at weaving webs to entangle men's senses and souls.

Alan took these letters up in the order in which we have named them. The first was evidently very brief; as he read it, an odd smile came on his lip,

not altogether of amusement, but rather bitter and constrained; just such a smile as one might put on to mask a momentary discomfiture, if, in a contest of polite repartee, one had received a home thrust, without seeing exactly how to *riposter*. The other envelope contained two full note-sheets, one of which (of course) was crossed. Wyverne just glanced at the first page and the last few lines, and then, putting it back into its cover, laid it down with the rest; it was quite natural that he should thus defer the perusal, for, however well he might have known the handwriting, ten minutes of undivided attention could scarcely have carried him through it. A very close observer might have detected just then a slight darkening and contraction of his brows; but the change lasted not five seconds, and then his face became pleasant and tranquil as ever.

" Well, that is over, or nearly so," he said, drawing rather a long breath. " Did anybody ever see such a day for riding ? I feel the Tartar humour on me, Helen—do you sympathize ? If so, we'll let our correspondence take thought for the things of itself—*I* don't intend to put pen to paper to-day—and go forth on a real pilgrimage, trusting to fate for luncheon. There's not an atom too much sun, and the breeze might have been made to order."

Perhaps the movement of Alan's arm, which pushed two or three of his letters off the table, was quite involuntary; and perhaps quite unintentionally, when he picked them up, he placed the *last* undermost: but the eyes of Lynceus were not keener-sighted than those dark languid orbs, held by many to be the crowning glory of Helen Vavasour's beauty. Neither the change in her cousin's face, nor one detail of the apparent accident escaped her; and it is possible that she drew from them her own conclusions. Probably they were not very serious ones, and perhaps his careless tone contributed to reassure her; at any rate, nothing could be brighter than her face as she answered—

"I should enjoy it, of all things, Alan. On a day like this I believe Maimouna would tire before I should. I never knew what it was to feel *rested* while riding fast, till I mounted her. Don't be jealous if she begins to know me better than you; you never heard of my visits to the stable, under old Donald's escort, on purpose to pet her. You may order the horses as soon as you please. I must see mamma before we start; but would you like to bet that I am not ready first?"

Alan's reply was on his lips, when the door opened softly, and, gliding in with her usual quiet grace, Lady Mildred joined the party. It was rare indeed that the mistress of Dene favoured the world with her presence before noon. At intervals, upon state occasions, she condescended to preside at breakfast; but, as a rule, took her chocolate and its accessories in her own apartments, and got through the business of her day in solitude. Her letters were always impounded, as soon as the letter bag was opened, by her own maid—a placid, resolute person—a sort of cheap edition of her mistress—who had held her place for many years, and was supposed to know more of the secrets of the boudoir than any creature alive. Women of Lady Mildred's calibre rarely change their confidential servants.

"My lady" was seemingly in a charming humour that morning; she greeted every one most affectionately, and listened to the plan of the long ride with a gentle approval, and even some show of interest. But all the three felt certain that she had good reason for her early appearance. They were not kept long in suspense.

"I had a letter from Max, this morning," Lady Mildred remarked. "Helen, dear, he says all sorts of kind things about you and Alan, but he reserves most of his congratulations, as he hopes to see you so soon. You know he has been shooting with Lord Clydesdale, in Perthshire, Hubert? Before this news came, he had asked him and Bertie Grenvil to come here for the early part of September; but if you don't wish the engagement to stand, you have only to let him know at once."

His astute helpmate could hardly refrain from smiling at the queer embarrassed expression of the Squire's frank face—she read his feelings so well! Indeed poor Hubert was the worst dissembler alive. He looked wistfully at his two confederates, but there was small chance of succour from that quarter. Helen's glance met her mother's for a second, and she bit her scarlet lip once, but remained perfectly silent. Alan was brushing away a stray crumb or two from the velvet sleeve of his riding-coat, with a provoking air of absolute unconcern. Vavasour was so intensely hospitable, that he would just as soon have thought of stabbing a guest in his sleep, as of grudging him entertainment, besides there was no earthly reason why either of the names just mentioned should be distasteful to him, or to any one else present; if he felt any real objection, it was more like a presentiment impossible to put into words. Nevertheless there was an unusual gravity in his voice, as he replied—

"Rather an unnecessary question of Max's, dear Mildred. He ought to know, by this time, that his friends are quite as welcome here as my own. As it happens, we have ample room for those two guns during the *early* (the word was marked) part of September. So many anxious parents will be contending for the possession of Clydesdale, that he will scarcely waste his golden time here beyond a fortnight. Few men are fonder of being persecuted with the attentions of your sex than that very eligible Earl. I believe he thinks it is no use being *the parti* of England if you don't reap its advantages, before as well as after marriage. I dare say Bertie will stay longer; the mothers, at all events, don't hunt him. I hope he will, for there's no pleasanter boy in a house, and his detrimentalism won't hurt us here. Will you write at once and say that we shall be charmed to see them all?"

Those last words were spoken with rather an unnatural distinctness; it seemed as though it cost the Squire an effort to utter them, and he left the room almost immediately, muttering something about "people waiting for him in his study." After a few minutes more of insignificant conversation not worth recording, the cousins, too, went out to get ready for their ride. Lady Mildred stayed her hand for a moment—she was crumbling bread into cream, carefully, for the Maltese dog's luncheon—and looked after them with a pensive expression on her face, in which mingled a shade of pity. Just so much compassion may have softened, long ago, the rigid features of some abbess on her tribunal, when after pronouncing the fatal *Vade in pace*, she saw an unhappy nun led out between the executioners, to expiate her broken vows.

Whatever might be Miss Vavasour's failings, dilatoriness in dressing was certainly not one of them; she would have won her wager that morning; and yet it would have puzzled the severest critic to have found a fault of omission or commission in her costume, as she stood in the recess of one of the windows of the great hall, waiting for the horses and her cousin. He joined her almost immediately, though, and Helen's eyes sparkled more brilliantly, as she remarked a letter in his hand.

"I always quote you and Pauline," Wyverne said, "when people keep their horses at the door for an hour by Shrewsbury clock; but you have outdone yourselves to-day. You deserve a small recompense—*la voilà*. It must be a satisfaction to a minor prophetess to find her prediction perfectly realized. My beautiful Sybil! I don't grudge you your triumph, especially as I did not contradict you on the point. The oldest and ugliest of the sisterhood never made a better guess at truth. Read *that*. I shall give 'my lady' the sense of it; but I don't think I shall show it her."

It was Bernard Haldane's answer, and it ran thus:

My dear Alan,—I thank you for your letter, because I am sure it was courteously meant, and, I believe, disinterestedly too; though, as you are my nearest male relation, it might naturally be expected that I should do or promise something on an occasion like this. I wish you to understand plainly, and once for all, that, in the event of your intended marriage taking place, you need anticipate no assistance whatever from me, present or future, before or after my death. I think it best to enter into no explanations and to give no reasons, but simply to state the fact of my having so determined. I have given up congratulating people about anything; but, were it otherwise, I should reserve such formalities for some more auspicious occasion. Neither am I often astonished; but I had the honour of knowing Lady Mildred Vavasour slightly many years ago, and I own to being somewhat surprised at *her* sanctioning so romantically imprudent an engagement. I will not inflict any sermon upon you; it is only to their heirs that old men have a right to preach. It is unlikely that we shall meet or correspond often again. After what I have written, it seems absurd to say, "I wish you well." Nevertheless —it is so.

Believe me,
Very faithfully yours,
BERNARD HALDANE.

There was disappointment certainly on the beautiful face, but it sprung from a very different cause from that to which Wyverne naturally assigned it. Helen had expected the perusal of a more delicate handwriting. The quaint cynical letter did not interest her much under the circumstances; however she read it through, and as she gave it back, there was a smile on her proud lip partaking as much of amusement as of disdain.

"Let us give credit where credit is due," she said. "I believe it cost Mr. Haldane some pains to compose that answer, short as it is. If you ever speak to him about it, will you say that we considered it very terse and straight-forward, and rather epigrammatic? Don't show it to mamma, though. I wonder when she knew Mr. Haldane? Is it not odd that she never alluded to it when his name has been mentioned?

Ah, there are the horses at last. Alan, do you see Maimouna arching that beautiful neck of hers? I am certain she is thinking of me. I defy the crossest of uncles to spoil *my* ride to-day. Will he yours?"

Every shade of bitterness had passed away, and the sunniest side of Helen's nature—wayward and wilful at times, but always frank and honest and affectionate—showed itself before she finished speaking.

Reader of mine, whether young or old—suppose yourself, I beseech you, to be standing, with none to witness your weakness, by the side of the Oriana of the hour; let the loveliest of dark eyes be gazing into yours, full of provocative promise, till their dangerous magnetism thrills through brain and nerve and vein, and then—tax your imagination or your memory for Alan Wyverne's answer. You will write it out better than I, and it will be a charity to the printer; for, were it correctly set down, it would be so curiously *broken up* as to puzzle the cleverest compositor of them all.

Alan and his cousin enjoyed their ride thoroughly, without one *arrière pensée.* Thus far there was not a shadow of suspicion on one side, not the faintest consciousness of intentional concealment on the other; nevertheless, there was already one subject on which they could not speak quite openly and freely. It was early, too early, to begin even a half reserve. When such a sign appears in the "pure æther" so soon after the dawning of love, however light and small and white the cloudlet may be, the weatherwise foretell a misty noon and a stormy sunset.

----

## CHAPTER IX.

### THE LONG ODDS ARE LAID.

A MAN must be very peculiarly constituted—indeed, there must be something wrong about his organization—if he does not entertain a certain partiality for his female cousins, even to the third and fourth generation. But the same remark by no means applies to the brothers of those attractive kinswomen. Your male cousin either stands first and foremost on the list of your friends, or you are absolutely uninterested in his existence. There *are* instances of family feuds, of course, but these, now-a-days, are comparatively rare. The intercourse between Alan Wyverne and Max Vavasour had never gone deeper than common careless courtesy. It was not to be wondered at. Both were in the best society, but they lived in different sets, meeting often, but seldom coming in actual contact. Just so, they say, the regular passengers by the parallel lines of rail converging at London-bridge recognise familiar faces daily as they speed along side by side, though each may remain to the other "nameless, nameless evermore." Besides this, the tastes of the cousins were as dissimilar as their characters; for the mere fact of two men being extravagant by no means establishes a real sympathy between them.

Alan's favourite pursuits you know already. Max was lady Mildred reproduced, with the exception of her great talents, which he had not fully inherited; but he had the same cool calculating brain, with whose combinations the well-disciplined heart never interfered. This, added to a perfect unscrupulousness of thought and action, many diplomatists besides Vavasour have found to be a very fair substitute for unerring prescience and profound sagacity. Both morally and physically he was wonderfully indolent, and, doing most things well, rarely attempted anything involving the slightest exertion. His shooting was remarkably good; but two or three hours of a battue about the time of the best *bouquets*, or a couple of turnip-fields swarming with birds, round which the stubbles had been driven for miles, were about the extent of his patience or endurance. As for going out for a real wild day after partridges, or walking a quaking bog after snipe, or waiting for ducks at "flight time," he would just as soon have thought of climbing the Schreckhorn: He rode gracefully, and his hand on a horse was perfection; but he had not hunted since he was eighteen, and his hacks, all thoroughbreds with good action, were safe and quiet enough to carry a Premier. He especially affected watching other men start for cover on one of those raw drizzling mornings which sometimes turn out well for hunting, but in every other point of view are absolutely detestable. It was quite a picture to see him return to his breakfast, and dally over it with a leisurely enjoyment, and settle himself afterwards into the easiest of lounging chairs, close to the library fire, with a pile of French novels within reach of his hand. Occasionally, during the course of the morning, he would lay aside his book, to make some such reflective remark as—

"Pours still, doesn't it? About this time Vesey's reins must be thoroughly soaked and slippery. I wonder how he likes riding that pulling mare of his. And I should think Count Casca has more mist on his spectacles that he quite fancies. It's a very strongly enclosed country, I believe, and the ditches are proverbially deep. He must have 'left all to his vife' before this."

And then he would resume his reading, with a shrug of his shoulders, intimating as plainly as words could speak, intense self-congratulation, and contempt for those who were out in the weather. Yet it was not nerve in which Max was deficient. Twice already — he was scarcely twenty-six—his life had been in mortal peril; once at Florence, where he had got into a bad gambling quarrel, and again in a fearful railway accident in England. On both occasions he had shown a cool, careless courage, worthy of the boldest of the valiant men-at-arms whose large-limbed effigies lined the galleries at Dene. In thews and stature and outward seeming he was but a degenerate descendant of that stalwart race, for he was scarcely taller than his sister, and had inherited his mother's smooth dark complexion and delicate proportions. That same indolence, it must be owned, told both ways, and went far to neutralize, for evil as well as for good, the effect of the calculating powers referred to. He had a certain obstinacy of will, and was troubled with a few inconvenient scruples, but wanted initiative energy to entangle himself or others in any of those serious scrapes which are not to be settled by money. So far, Max Vavasour's page in the *Chronique Scandaleuse* was a blank.

The heir of Dene and his friends arrived so late, that they had barely time to dress for dinner. No private conference took place, apparently, between the mother and son that evening; but the latter joined the others very late in the smoking-room. It is scarcely to be presumed that the doffing of *la grande tenue* and the donning of an elaborately embroidered suit of purple velvet, would consume forty-five minutes; so that half an hour remained unaccounted for, during which interval probably the boudoir was witness to a few important confidences.

Max was rather fond of his sister, after his own fashion, and never vexed or crossed her if he could help it; so when they spoke of her engagement on the following morning, he not only forbore to reproach her with its imprudence, but expressed himself hopefully and kindly enough to satisfy Helen's modest expectations. She knew her brother too well to anticipate expansiveness or enthusiasm from *that* quarter. To Alan he was, naturally, much less cordial in his congratulations; indeed, it was only by courtesy that they could be called congratulations at all. Max had a soft, quiet way of saying unpleasant things— truths or the reverse—that some people rather liked, and others utterly abhorred. On the present occasion he did not scruple to confess frankly his opinion as to the undesirability of the match, to which the other listened with at least equal composure.

"I wish I had not gone to Scotland," Vavasour went on, reflectively. "I do believe I could have stopped it, if I had only been on the spot, or forewarned. I needn't say, I have no prejudices against you personally—nobody *has* any such weaknesses nowadays"—(how very old the young face looked as he said it); "but it's a simple question of political expediency. I may be very

the match-makers of Great Britain have been hard on his trail; and his movements, as chronicled in the *Post*, are watched with a keener interest than attaches to the "progress" of any royal personage. He is so *terribly* wealthy that even the great city financiers speak of his resources with a certain awe; for, independently of his vast income, there are vague reports of accumulations, varying from a quarter to half a million. His father died when the present Earl was in his cradle.

There is nothing very remarkable, outwardly, about the other man. Harding Knowles has rather a disappointing face: you feel that it ought to have been handsome, and yet that is about the last epithet you would apply to it. The features individually are good, and there is plenty of intellect about them, though the forehead is narrow; but the general expression is disagreeable—something between the cunning and the captious. There is a want of repose, just now, about his whole demeanour—a sort of fidgetty consciousness of not being in his right place; he is always changing his position restlessly, and his hands are never still for a moment. He had been Clydesdale's "coach" at Oxford for two or three terms, and had acquired a certain hold on the latter's favour, chiefly by the exercise of a brusque, rough flattery, which the Earl chose to mistake for sincerity and plain speaking.

No parasite can be perfect, unless he knows when to talk and when to hold his tongue. Knowles had mastered that part of the science, thoroughly. On the present occasion he saw that the silent humour possessed his patron, and was careful not to interrupt the lordly meditations; only throwing in now and then a casual observation requiring no particular answer. No one dreams of deep drinking nowadays in general society; but the Earl has evidently taken quite as much claret as was good for him— enough to make him obstinate and savage. That pair at the piano seem to fascinate him strangely. He keeps watching every movement of Wyverne's lips, and every change in Helen's colour, as if he would guess the import of their low earnest words. A far deeper feeling than mere curiosity is evidently at work. It is well that the half-closed fingers shade his eyes just now, for they are not good to meet—hot and bloodshot, with a fierce longing and wrathful envy. Not an iota of all this escaped Harding Knowles; but he allowed the bad brutal nature to seethe on sullenly, till he deemed it was time to work the safety-valve.

"A pretty picture," he said at last, with rather a contemptuous glance in the direction of the lovers—Clydesdale gound out a bitter blasphemy between his teeth; but the other went on as if he had heard nothing—"Yes, a very pretty picture; and Sir Alan Wyverne deserves credit for his audacity. But I can't help feeling provoked, at such a rare creature being so perfectly thrown away. If ever there was a woman who was born to live in state, she sits there; and they will have to be pensioners of the Squire's, if they want anything beyond necessaries. It's a thousand pities."

"You mean she might have made a better match?" the other asked: he felt he must say something, but he seemed to speak unwillingly, and his voice, always harsh and guttural, sounded thicker and hoarser than usual.

"Yes, I am sure she might have made a better match: I *think* she might have made—the best in England."

Knowles spoke very slowly and deliberately, almost pausing between each of the last words. His keen steady gaze fastened on Clydesdale, till the Earl's fierce blue eyes sank under the scrutiny, and the flush on his cheek deepened to crimson.

"What the d—l's the use of talking about that now?" he grumbled out, "now that it's all over and settled?"

"Settled, but not all over. I'm not fond of betting as a rule; but I should like to take long odds—*very* long odds, mind, for Wyverne's dangerous when he is in earnest—that the engagement never comes off."

Lord Clydesdale paused quite a minute in reflection. There was a wicked crafty significance in the other's look that he could not misunderstand.

"I don't know what you call long odds," he said at last, "but I'll lay *you* five thousand to fifty that it is not broken off within the year."

There are men, not peculiarly irascible or punctilious, who would have resented those words and the tone in which they were spoken as a direct personal insult; but Knowles was not sensitive when it was a question of his own advantage or advancement, and had sucked in avarice with his mother's milk.

"I'll book that bet," he answered, coolly. "I take all chances in. Sir Alan might die, you know, before the year is out; or Miss Vavasour might come to her senses."

So he wrote it down carefully on his ivory tablets, affixing the date and his initials. They both knew it—he was signing a bond, just as effectually as if it had been engrossed on parchment and regularly witnessed and sealed. But neither cared to look the other in the face now. In the basest natures there lingers often some faint useless remnant of shame. I fancy that Marcus rather shrank from meeting his patron's glance, when he went out from the Decemvir's presence to lay hands on Virginius's daughter.

While this conversation was going on, Max Vavasour had roused himself from his easy chair, and strolled over towards the piano. It is probable that he had got his orders from "my lady's" eloquent eye. As he came near, Wyverne drew back slightly, with a scarcely perceptible movement of impatience, and Helen stopped playing. They both guessed that her brother had not disturbed himself without a purpose.

"It's a great shame to interrupt you, Alan," Max said; "but one has certain duties towards one's guests, I believe; and you might help me very much, if you would be good-natured. You see, all this isn't much fun for Clydesdale; and I want to keep him in good humour, if I can—never mind why. He's mad after *ecarté* just now, and he has heard that you are a celebrity at it. He asked me to-day if I thought you would mind playing with him? I would engage him myself with pleasure; but it would be no sport to either party. He knows, just as well as you do, how infamously I play."

Wyverne very seldom refused a reasonable request, and he was in no mood to be churlish.

"What must be, must be," he replied, with a sigh of resignation. "If the Great Earl is to be amused, and no other martyr is available, thy servant is ready, though not willing. I thought I had lost enough in my time at that game. It is hard to have to lose, now, such a pleasant seat as this. Tell him I'll come directly. I suppose he don't want to gamble? He has two to one the best of it, though, when he has made me stir from here. Helen, perhaps you would not mind singing just one or two songs? I am Spartan in my tastes so far: I like to be marshalled to my death with sweet music."

So the two sat down at the *ecarté* table. Clydesdale betrayed an eagerness quite disproportionate to the occasion when Max Vavasour summoned him to the encounter. He suggested that the stakes should be a "pony" on the best of eleven games: to this Alan demurred.

"I have given up gambling now," he said; "but, even when I played for money, I never did so with women in the room. A pony is a nominal stake with you, of course: with me, it is different. You may have ten on, if you like. I only play one rubber."

The other assented without another word, and the battle began. The Earl was far from a contemptible adversary; but he was palpably over-matched. Wyverne had held his own before this with the best and boldest of half the capitals in Europe. He played carelessly at first, for his thoughts were evidently elsewhere; but got interested as the game went on, and developed all the science he possessed: it carried him through one or two critical points against invariably indifferent cards. At last they were five games all, and were commencing "*la belle.*" Max, Harding Knowles, and Bertie Grenvil (who never could keep away from a card-table, unless some extraordinary potent counter-excitement were present) had been watching the match from the beginning; the last having invested 11 — 10 on Wyverne—taken by Clydesdale eagerly. The cards ran evenly enough. By dint of sheer good play Alan scored three to his opponent's two. As he was taking up his hand in the next deal, Miss Vavasour came up softly behind him, and leant her arm on the high carved back of his chair. She felt sure that her cousin would win, and wanted to share even in that trivial triumph. I wonder how often in this world women have unconsciously baulked the very success they were most anxious to secure? Alan held the king and the odd trick certain; but, if his life had depended on the issue, he could not have helped looking up into the glorious dark eyes to thank them for their sympathy. At that moment his adversary played first, and Wyverne followed suit, without marking. It was one of those fatal *coups* that Fortune never forgives. The next deal Clydesdale turned up the king, and won the *vole* easily.

Even Max Vavasour, who knew him well, and had seen him play for infinitely larger stakes, was astonished at the excitement that the Earl displayed; he dashed down the winning card with an energy which shook the table, and actually glared at his opponent with a savage air of exultation, utterly absurd and incomprehensible under the circumstances.

Alan leant back in his chair, regarding the victor's flushed cheek and quivering lips with an amused smile, not wholly devoid of sarcasm.

"On my honour, I envy you, Clydesdale," he said quietly; "there's an immense amount of pleasure before you. Only conceive the luxury of being able to gratify such a passion for play as yours must be, without danger of ruin! I never was so interested about anything in my life as you were about that last hand; and bad cards for ten years, at heavy stakes, would only get rid of some of your superfluous thousands."

The exultation faded from the Earl's face, and it began to lower sullenly. He felt that he had made himself ridiculous, and hated Wyverne intensely for having made it more apparent.

"You don't seem to understand that we were playing for love," he muttered. "I had heard so much of your play, that I wanted to measure myself against it, and I was anxious to win. It appears that the great guns miss fire sometimes, like the rest of us."

"Of course they do," Wyverne answered, cheerfully. "Not that I am the least better than the average. But we are all impostors from first to last."

The party broke up for the night almost immediately afterwards. Alan laughed to scorn all his fair cousin's penitential fears about "her having interrupted him just at the wrong moment." It is doubtful if he ever felt any self-reproach for his carelessness, till Bertie Grenvil looked up plaintively in his face, as the two were wending their way to the smoking-room.

"Alan, I *did* believe in your *ecarté*," he said.

There was not much in the words, but the Cherub uttered them with the air of a man to whom so wonderfully few things are left to believe in, that the defalcation of one of those objects of faith is a very serious matter indeed.

Yet Wyverne was wrong, and did his adversary in some sort injustice, when he supposed that the spirit of the gambler accounted altogether for the latter's eagerness and excitement. Other and different feelings were working in Lord Clydesdale's heart when he sat down to play. One of those vague superstitious presentiments that men are ashamed to confess to their dearest friends shot across him at the moment. He had said within himself—"It is my luck against his, not only now, but hereafter. If I win at this game, I shall beat him at others—at *all.*" So you see, in the Earl's imagination, much more was at issue than the nominal stakes; and there was a double meaning in his words—"We were playing. *for love.*"

## CHAPTER X.

"A shiny night,
In the season of the year."

It was the third evening after that one recorded in the last chapter; the party at Dene remained the same, though a large reinforcement was expected on the morrow. Only the younger Vavasour was absent; he had gone out to dine and sleep at the house of a country magnate, with whom a Russian friend of Max's was staying. Lady Mildred and her daughter had just left the drawing-room—it was close upon midnight—Wyverne followed them into the hall to provide them with their tapers, and had not yet succeeded in lighting Helen's—there never was such an obstinate piece of wax, or such an awkward πυρφόρος. It is possible he would have lingered yet longer over the operation, and some pleasant last words, but he suddenly caught sight of the chief butler standing in the deep doorway that led towards the offices. The emergency must have been very tremendous to induce that model of discretion to intrude himself on any colloquy whatever; he evidently did not intend to do so now; but an extraordinary intelligence and significance on the grave precise face, usually possessed by a polite vacuity, made Alan conclude his "good-nights" rather abruptly; he guessed that he was wanted.

"What is it, Hales ?" he said, as soon as he came within speaking distance.

The butler's voice was mystériously subdued as he replied—

" My master wishes to see you in his study immediately, if you please, Sir Alan. Mr. Somers is with him."

The said Somers was born and bred in Norfolk, but had been head keeper at Dene for fifteen years — a brave, honest, simple-minded man, rather blunt and unceremonious with his superiors, and apt to be surly with his equals and subordinates; but not ill-conditioned or bad hearted *au fond ;* a really sincere and well-meaning Christian, too, though he would swear awfully at times. He had only one aim and object in life—the rearing and preservation of game ; we should be lucky, some of us, if we carried out our single idea as thoroughly well.

The Squire was looking rather grave and anxious, as his nephew entered.

" Tell Sir Alan at once what you have been telling me, Somers," he said. " There is no time to lose, if we mean to act."

The keeper's hard, dark face, grew more ominous and threatening, as he muttered — " Acting ! I should hope there's no doubt about *that :* there never was such a chance." And then in his own curt, quaint way, he gave Wyverne the sum of his intelligence.

It appeared that the neigbourhood had been infested lately by a formidable poaching gang, chiefly organized and directed by a certain " Lanky Jem ;" their head quarters were at Newmanham, and they had divided their patronage pretty equally, so far, over all the manors in a circle of miles round. They had done a good deal of harm already ; for they first appeared in the egging season, and had netted a large number of partridges and hares, even before the first of September, since which day they had been out somewhere every night. Of course it was most important to arrest their depredations before they could get at the pheasants. The gang had been seen more than once at their work ; but their numbers were too formidable—they mustered quite a score— for a small party to buckle with ; and to track them home was impossible ; they had carts always near, artfully concealed, with really good trotters in the shafts ; so, when they had secured as much as they could carry, they were able to ensure their retreat, and dispose of their booty. In Newmanham they took the precaution of changing their quarters perpetually, which made it more difficult to catch them "red-handed."

That very day, however, one of the lot, partly from revenge, partly on the certainty of a rich reward, had turned traitor. Somers was in possession of exact information as to time and place : about *catching* the poachers that night there was no doubt whatever—*holding* them was another question; for "Lanky Jem" had made no secret of his intention to show fight if driven into a corner; indeed it was supposed that he would not be averse to having a brush, under favourable circumstances, with his natural enemies, the guardians of the game.

"They terms him Lanky Jem," the head-keeper explained; "'cause he comes from Lankyshire. He's a orkard customer in a row, they say, wery wenturesome and wery wenomous; he's taught his gang what they calls the 'rough-and-tumble game;' all's fair in that style they says, and if they gets you down, you may reckon on having their heel in your mouth before you can holler. I don't think that chap would have split, only he had words with Jem; he knocked two of his teeth out, and roughed him dreadful, by the looks on him. You'll see our man with the rest on 'em to-night, Sir Alan, and don't you go to hit him; he'll have a spotted hankercher half over his face, and won't be blacked like the others, that's how you'll know him. I've taken the liberty already of letting Sir Gilbert's folks know; we shall muster a score or thereabouts, and I don't see no fear about matching 'em. The moon won't be down these two hours, and they won't begin much afore that. They'll come back through Haldon-lane, and I thought of lining it, Sir Alan, and nipping down on 'em there, if it's agreeable to you; the banks are nicely steep, and they won't get out of *that* trap in a hurry."

The Squire could not help smiling at the quiet way in which the old keeper took his nephew's presence and personal aid for granted.

"You have not asked Sir Alan if he means to go out with you," he remarked.

"I should think not," Wyverne interposed. "Somers knows me too well to waste words in that way. What a piece of luck, to be sure! Haldon-lane is the very place for an ambush; if we manage well we ought to bag the whole batch of them. You shall be general, Somers—I see your baton's all ready—

I'll do my best as second in command. I think I ought to let the other men know, Uncle Hubert? I shall be ready in ten minutes, and so will they, I'll answer for them. If you've anything to do before we start, you had better see about it at once, Somers. We'll all meet in the servants' hall in a quarter of an hour."

The keeper indulged in a short, grim laugh of satisfaction and approval.

"I like to hear you talk, Sir Alan," he said; "you always comes to the point and means business. Everything's ready when you are; but we needn't start for a good half hour yet. My men are stanch enough, I reckon; but it's no good keeping 'em too long, sitting in the cold."

The Squire laid his hand kindly on his nephew's shoulder, and stood for a second or two looking into his face, with a hearty affection and pride.

"I can't tell you how glad I am you are here, Alan. Even if Max had been at home, I think I would have asked you to go out to-night. I am too old for this sort of thing now; but somebody must be there that I can trust thoroughly. There will be wild work before morning, I fear, and coolness may be needed as much as courage. There has been no bloodshed, for the game, in my time, that the village-doctor could not stanch; and it would grieve me bitterly—*you* can guess why—if any one were dangerously-hurt now. We have had no fray so serious as this promises to be. You will take care, Alan, will you not? I am very anxious about it; I half wish I were going out myself."

"I'll take every care, Uncle Hubert," the other answered, cheerily. "But I don't the least apprehend any grave accident; it isn't likely they will have guns with them, as they are out netting, and don't dream of being waylaid. I must go and tell the others, and g ready. I shall see you before we sta and when we come back, perhaps, wi our prisoners."

It was very characteristic of those two, that Vavasour never hesitated to expose his nephew to peril, nor of exensing himself for not going out to share it; while Wyverne accepted the position perfectly, simply, and naturally. It was evidently a plain question of expediency; the idea that it was possible to shrink from mere personal danger never crossed either of their minds.

Lord Clydesdale and Bertie Grenvil decided at once on joining the expedition; though it must be confessed that the alacrity displayed by the former hardly amounted to enthusiasm: it had rather the appearance of making the best of a disagreeable necessity.

Alan had nearly finished his brief preparations when there came a low knock at his door; when he opened it Lady Mildred's maid was on the threshold. "'My lady' wished to speak to him particularly: she was in her boudoir, and would not detain him a moment."

There Wyverne found her. It struck him that her cheek was a shade paler than usual, but the effect of contrast, produced by her *peignoir* of deep purple and her dark hair braided close round her small head, may have helped to deceive him. There was an accent of annoyance in her voice as she said—

"Alan, what is this I hear about your going out with the keepers? How can you be so rash? What on earth are those people paid for if it is not to take poachers? Surely they know their own business best, and can do it alone."

" Not on an occasion like this, Aunt Mildred: heads as well as hands are useful sometimes. Even as Venice used to send out a pacific civilian to watch the conduct of their generals, so am I deputed to-night to control the ardour of the faithful Somers and his merrymen all. I hope to do myself credit as a moderator."

" I wish you would be serious for once. Even if *you* must go out, which I am certain there is no necessity for, there can be no reason for those other two accompanying you. Of course, I don't suppose there is danger of life; but it is quite dreadful to think of that poor delicate Bertie *aux prises* with some drunken ruffian; and if Lord Clydesdale were to meet even with a slight hurt or disfigurement, I am sure he would detest Dene for ever and ever. Alan, do try what you can do to stop it."

He laughed within himself as he muttered, under his breath, " *Enfin, je te vois arriver ;*" but his manner was quite easy and unsuspicious as he answered her—

" I'm not much afraid for the Cherub; he can take good care of himself anywhere. You all pet him so much that you do injustice to his pluck. You never seem to remember that he is a soldier. He may have to guard his head in sharp earnest one of these days. But you are quite right about Clydesdale. I had much rather he stayed behind; but I fear it would be useless to try to dissuade him now. Aunt Mildred, you don't quite understand these things. He *must* go. But you may sleep in peace. Not a hair of that august head shall be harmed if I can help it. You have read your *Maid of Perth?* Well, your unworthy nephew and other retainers of the house will do duty as a body-guard, like Torquil and his eight sons. The word for the night is, *Bas air son Eachin.* I only hope the parallel won't quite be carried out. All the nine fell, you remember, and then —the young chief ran away. I must not stay another second. Dear Aunt Mildred, give us your good wishes. You may be easy, if you will only trust to me."

He kissed her hand before she was aware, and was gone before she could reply. When Alan came into the servants' hall, he found the whole party mustered, with the exception of the Earl, who joined them almost immediately. The latter had evidently bestowed some pains on his equipment. He wore rather an elaborate cap, with a black cock's feather in the band, white breeches, and boots coming above the knee; but the most remarkable feature was a broad belt of untanned leather, girding the shooting-coat of black velvet. From this was suspended a formidable revolver, balanced by a veritable *couteau-de-chasse.*

Wyverne scanned him from head to foot with a cool critical eye, and then took Clydesdale aside a little from the rest.

"It's a picturesque 'get up,'" he said; "a little too much in the style of the bold smuggler, but that's a matter of taste. May I ask what you intend to do with these?"

He touched the weapons with the point of his finger.

"Do with them? Use them, of course," the earl replied, flushing angrily. "I made my fellow load the revolver afresh, while I was dressing. There's no fear of its missing fire."

The other laughed outright.

"Did you mean to let all those barrels off, and then go in and finish the wounded with that terrible hanger? I give you credit for the idea; but, my dear Clydesdale, we are not in Russia or the Tyrol, unluckily. A man's life is held of some account here, you know, and there's a d—l of a row if you massacre even a poacher. You must be content with the primeval club. See, there's a dozen to choose from. The Squire allows no other weapons. Ask him, if you like. Here he comes."

Vavasour, when appealed to, spoke so decisively on the subject, that the Earl had no option but to yield. He did so, chafing savagely, for he was unused to the faintest contradiction, and registered in his sullen heart another grievance against Alan Wyverne. After a few words of caution and encouragement, addressed by the Squire to the whole party, they started. He griped his nephew's hand hard as the latter went out, and whispered one word —"Remember."

When they had gone a few hundred yards from the house, Wyverne fell back to the rear of the column and took Grenvil by the arm.

"Look here, Bertie," he said, gravely. "I'm rather sorry I didn't go out alone on this business. We shall meet a roughish lot in an hour's time. Now, don't be rash and run your head against danger unnecessarily. I shall not be able to look after you; I've got a bigger baby in charge to-night. I should hate myself for ever if your beauty was spoiled."

The Cherub laughed carelessly and confidently. The burliest Paladin that ever wore a beard was not more utterly fearless than he. He could use those little hands of his (he was in the habit of exchanging gloves with his favourite partners) as neatly and as prettily as he did everything else, and in sooth was, no contemptible antagonist for a light-weight.

"Don't bother yourself about me, Alan," he answered. "I'll look after my face, you may rely on it. I've been very diligent in my practice lately, and if I get hold of an extraordinarily small poacher, perhaps I may astonish him with what the Pet calls—the 'London Particular.'"

They met Sir Gilbert Nevil's men by the way, and when they reached the place of ambush, numbered twenty-two stalwart fighting men. The spot was admirably adapted for the purpose; a narrow deep lane passed just there through the crest of a small hill, and the brushwood on the steep banks was sufficient to hide a larger party. The rest nestled down there as comfortably as they could, while Alan and the head-keeper climbed the ridge to look out over the champaign lying beneath them. They had not long to wait before two lights appeared on the plain below, moving quickly within a foot or so of the ground, and every now and then becoming stationary. They were lanterns fastened round the necks of the steady pointers quartering the stubbles.

The keeper gave vent to a suppressed groan, ending in a growl.

"There they are, d—n 'em," he muttered. "The very beat I meant you to take to-morrow, Sir Alan. They won't be long in filling that ere blasted bag of theirs. I see five coveys on that forty-acre bit this afternoon. We'll take our change out of 'em before we sleep, or my name ain't Ben Somers."

Wyverne shook his head warningly.

"Your blood's hotter than mine, I do believe," he said, "though you are old enough to be my father. But mind, there is to be no unnecessary violence to-night. I've passed my word to the Squire, and you ought to help me to keep it. If they show fight, it's another matter, and they may take the consequences."

"I'll pound it, they fight," the other grumbled; "it comes more nateral to Jem than running, 'specially as he'll find hisself in a middlin' tight trap. We may get back to cover, sir; they'll not be long now; I reckon they'll finish in that stubble close agin' the lane."

So they rejoined their companions. The ambush was thus disposed. Eight men, including Somers, Wyverne, and Lord Clydesdale, took post, four on either bank, at a certain spot; six others, similarly divided, were left about forty yards in the rear—Bertie Grenvil was with this lot—the others concealed themselves at short intervals along the vacant space: the signal was not to be given till the poachers had got well into the space between the two main bodies; that in advance was rather the strongest, as it was expected the maranders would try to force their way into the high road, where carts were sure to be awaiting them. So, without a movement of tongue or finger, they were to bide their time.

Unless one is gifted with exceptional nerves, that time of suspense before action is very trying. To compare great things with small, I heard one of the best and bravest of all who went up to the Redan, confess, the other day, that he never felt so uncomfortable as during those long minutes when the men stood in their ranks waiting for the last orders, and that it was an unspeakable relief when the word was given for the stormers to advance.

Lord Clydesdale evidently liked his position less and less every moment. "Cursedly cold, isn't it?" he muttered, at last, and in truth his teeth were chattering audibly.

"Pocket-pistols are not interdicted, if other fire-arms are," Wyverne whispered, good-humouredly. "Take a pull at mine, and wrap my plaid round you; I really don't want it, I'm better clothed for this work than you are, I fancy; I've been at it before."

The Earl took the plaid, and half drained the flask without a word of thanks; he was still brooding sulkily over the rebuff he fancied he had met with before starting; besides this, the world had spoilt him so long, that self-sacrifice on the part of his fellow-men for the convenience of Lord Clydesdale, seemed to him the most natural condition of things imaginable; he accepted such tributes affably or morosely, according to his humour, but invariably as his proper due.

Alan interpreted his companion's feelings pretty correctly, and smiled contemptuously to himself in the darkness. "You amiable aristocrat!" he muttered between his teeth; "if it were not for vexing Aunt Mildred, and for my promise to her, would I *not* let you look out for yourself this cold morning? I wonder if a thoroughly good thrashing would improve your temper; it were a good deed to allow the experiment to be tried. I do believe the most inveterate ruffian we shall meet, has more natural courtesy than has fallen to your share."

But the momentary bitterness soon passed away. Alan—as is the wont of his kind—never felt so benevolent towards mankind in general as when the moment of danger approached, which was to bring him into conflict with certain units of the species. Surely that perfect physical fearlessness is an enviable, if not a very ennobling qualification; it enables you to charge a big fence or a big adversary, with comparative comfort to yourself; in neither case, unfortunately, will it ensure you against a bad fall; but unless quite disabled, you rise up and go on again, as cheerfully as Antæus, and are at all events spared any pains of anticipation. An interval of silence which seemed very long, ensued. Suddenly Wyverne laid a firm, steady grasp on Lord Clydesdale's arm.

"Take off that plaid," he said, in the lowest and quietest of whispers; "you'll be warm enough in five minutes. They are in the next stubble now."

The ear of the practised deer-stalker, accustomed to listen for the rattle of a

6

hoof far up the corries, had already caught certain faint sounds imperceptible to his companions. Somers heard them, though, nearly as soon; they could just see him through the black darkness, stretching his brawny limbs, and twisting round his wrist the thong of his bludgeon.

The fall of footsteps came nearer and nearer, more and more distinct, as the poachers crossed the low fence one by one, and got on to the harder ground; they were evidently very numerous. They did not come on in detached straggling parties, but appeared to wait till all were in the lane, and then advanced in something like a regular column, in the centre of which four men carried, in two nets made for the purpose, the night's spoil; as this entirely consisted of birds, the weight was overwhelming, though the result had been extraordinarily successful.

"Get on, two of ye, as soon as we top the hill," a deep, hoarse voice said, from the midst of the poachers; "and mind you see all clear."

The slightest touch of Wyverne's arm, and the discreetest chuckle, testified to Somers' intense appreciation of the impending "sell." The gang advanced with their habitually stealthy tread, but evidently quite unsuspiciously, till they were hemmed in by the divisions of the ambush. Then a whistle sounded shrill and ominous as Black Roderick's signal, and a dozen port-fires blazed out at once, casting a weird, lurid glare over the crowd of rugged blackened faces, working with various emotions of wonder, rage, and fear.

In the pause that ensued, while the assailed were still under the influence of the first surprise, and the assailants were waiting for orders, Wyverne's voice was heard, not raised by one inflection above its usual tone, and yet the most distant ear caught every syllable.

"Will you surrender at once? It is the best thing you can do."

The same voice answered which had spoken before—hoarse and thick with passion.

"Surrender be d—d! Here's the chance we've been wanting ever so long. Stick together, lads, and be smart with those bludgeons: there's enow of us to cut the —— keepers to rags."

Alan spoke again; and the curt, stern, incisive accents clove the still night-air like points of steel.

"Stand fast in the front: close up there in the rear. It is our own fault if a man gets through: we'll have all— or none."

He had only time for a hurried whisper—"Somers, whatever happens, look after Lord Clydesdale;" for Bertie and his men came on with a rush and a cheer. The port-fires were cast down and trampled out instantly, and so— darkly and sullenly—the *melée* began. It was likely to be an equal one; the poachers had the disadvantage of the surprise and the attack being against them, but they were slightly superior in numbers, and their bludgeons were of a more murderous character than those carried by the keepers, shod with iron for the most part, and heavily leaded. For a minute or two the struggle went on in silence, only broken by the dull sound of heavy blows, by hard, quick breathings, and by an occasional curse or groan. Lord Clydesdale had drawn slightly aside, and so, avoiding the first rush of the poachers, remained for awhile inactive. Suddenly, as ill-luck would have it, he found himself face to face with the most formidable of all the gang. "Lanky Jem" had forced his way to the front, partly because safety lay in that direction, partly because he fancied that there fought "the foemen worthiest of his steel;" he had his wits perfectly about him, and was viciously determined to do as much damage as possible, whether he escaped or no. He saw the figure standing apart from the rest, taking no part in the conflict, and instantly guessed that he had to do with a personage of some condition and importance: keepers are rarely contemplative or non-combatants at such a moment.

"Here's one of them —— swells!" he growled. "Come on, d—n ye! I'll have *your* blood, if I swing for it."

Clydesdale was not exactly a coward; if any ordinary *social* danger had presented itself, he would scarcely have quailed before it. For instance, I believe he would have faced a pistol at fifteen paces with average composure. But it so happened (he had not been at a public school) that in all his life he had never seen a blow stricken in anger. The aspect of his present adversary fairly appalled him. Independently of the poacher's huge proportions and evidently great strength, there was a cool, concentrated cruelty about the bull-dog face—the white range of grinded teeth showing in relief against the blackness of his sooty disguise—which made him a really terrible foe. The Earl looked helplessly round, as though seeking for succour; but all his party seemed to have already as much as they could do. He saw the grim giant preparing for a spring, and all presence of mind utterly deserted him; he drew hastily back without lifting his hands to defend himself; his heel caught in a projecting root, and he fell supine, with a loud, piteous cry. "Lanky Jem" was actually disconcerted by such absolute non-resistance; but the brutal instinct soon reasserted itself, and he was rushing in to maim and mangle the fallen man, after his own savage fashion, when a fresh adversary stood in his path, bestriding Clydesdale where he lay.

Wyverne had been engaged with a big foundry-man, who chanced to come across him first; but even in the fierce grapple, where pluck and activity could scarcely hold their own against weight and brute strength, he had found time to glance repeatedly over his shoulder. He saw the Earl fall, and extricating himself from his opponent's gripe with an effort that sent the latter reeling back, he sprang lightly aside, just in time to intercept the Lancashire man from his prey. But the odds were fearfully against him now; for his original adversary had recovered himself, and made in quickly to help his comrade. Both struck at Alan savagely at the same instant. He caught one blow on his club, but was obliged to parry the other with his left arm: the head was saved, but the limb dropped to his side powerless. He ground his teeth hard, and threw all the strength that was left him into one bitter blow; it lighted on the temple of the man who had disabled him, and dropped him like a log in his tracks. But, before Wyverne could recover himself, the terrible Lancashire bludgeon came home on his brows, crushing in the low, stiff crown of his hat like paper, and beating him down, sick and dizzy, to his knee. He lifted his club mechanically, but it hardly broke the full sway of another murderous stroke, which stretched him on his face senseless. It looked as if he had remembered his promise to the last; for he fell right over Clydesdale, effectually shielding the latter with his own body.

Alan's life and this story had well nigh ended there and then. Such an abrupt termination might possibly have been to *his* advantage as well as to yours, reader of mine. But it was not so to be. Just as Jem was bracing his great muscles for one cool, finishing stroke on the back of Wyverne's unprotected skull, a lithe active form lighted on his shoulders, and slender, nervous fingers clutched his throat till they seemed to bury themselves in the flesh; and as he fell backward, gasping and half-strangled, a voice, suppressed and vicious as a serpent's hiss, muttered in his ear three words in an unknown tongue—"*Basta, basta, carissimo!*"

The poacher's vast strength, however, soon enabled him to shake off his last assailant, and he was rising to his feet, more dangerous than ever, when a tremendous blow descended right across his face, gashing the forehead and crushing the bones of the nose in one fearful wound. The miserable wretch sank down —all his limbs collapsing—without a groan or a struggle, and lay there half drowned in blood.

The old head keeper stooped for a moment to examine his ghastly handiwork, and then, lifting his head, remarked with a low fierce laugh—

"I gives you credit for that move, Master Bertie, it wur very neatly done."

The poachers had been getting the

worst of it all through; they were so hemmed in in the narrow way that their numbers helped them 'but little; indeed, some in the centre of the crowd never struck a blow. Their leader's fall decided the fray at once; some voice cried out —"Don't hit us any more; we gives in:" and they threw down their bludgeons, as though by preconcerted signal.

So ended the most successful raid that had been heard of in that country for years; they talk of it still. Out of twenty-six men, only three escaped, and one of these was the informer. Neither was any one mortally or even dangerously hurt, though there were some hideous wounds on both sides; but, if you bar gunpowder, it takes a good deal to kill outright a real tough "shires-man." Even "Lanky Jem" recovered after a while from Somers' swashing blow, though they were obliged to carry him back to Dene. The permanent disfigurement which ensued, made his repulsive countenance rather more picturesque in its ugliness, so that it was an improvement after all. He quitted those parts, though, as soon as he got out of gaol, and never returned.

Of all the wounded, perhaps Wyverne was the most seriously hurt; but, though his senses came back slowly, he was able to stagger home, leaning heavily on Bertie Grenvil's shoulder. You must imagine the satisfaction with which the Squire welcomed the conquerors and their captives.

Unwounded from the dreadful close,
But breathless all, the Earl arose.

Even his overweening self-esteem could not prevent Clydesdale's feeling nervous and uncomfortable. He was conscious of having betrayed a very discreditable pusillanimity; and he could not guess how many might be in the secret of his discomfiture. There was nothing in the mere fact of his coming out of the fray scathless, for Grenvil had not a scratch or a bruise; but it struck him as rather odd, that nobody asked "if he were hurt in any way." He was so perturbed in spirit, as hardly to be able to display a decent amount of solicitude about Wyverne's injuries, or to sympathize, with a good grace, in the triumph of the rest of the party. There was one man, at all events, that he could never look in the face again, without an unpleasant feeling of inferiority and obligation. Poor Alan! He meant well; but he did not make a very good night's work of it, after all. He got one or two hard blows, and changed Clydesdale's previous dislike into a permanent and inveterate hate. Virtue is always its own reward, you know.

Perhaps the Earl's *largesse* to every one concerned in the capture would not have been so extravagantly liberal, if he had guessed how thoroughly the old keeper appreciated the real state of affairs. When Somers alluded to the subject—which he did once a month for the rest of his natural life—he generally concluded in these words:

"It wur the prettiest managed thing ever I see; but we wery near got muddled at one time, all along of that there helpless Lord."

----

## CHAPTER XI.

### DIAMONDS THAT CUT DIAMONDS.

HELEN VAVASOUR came of a race whose women, if tradition speaks truth, could always look, at need, on battle or broil without blenching; but it is probable she would hardly have slept so soundly that night, had she guessed at what was going on under the stars. She heard nothing of the preparations; the bustle was confined to those remote regions where a Servile War might have been carried on without the patricians wotting of it; the furlongs of passage and corridor in the vast old manoir swallowed up all ordinary sounds. Pauline would of course have enlightened her mistress, but Wyverne chanced to "head" her before she could "make her point." The quick-witted Parisian saw that he meant what he said, when he begged her not to open her lips on the subject, and kept silence through the night, though it was pain and grief to her. That sentimental *soubrette* kept for Alan the largest share of a simple hero-worship, and she lay awake for hours listening and quaking, and interceding perpetually with her favourite Saint for the safeguard of her favourite Paladin. Judge if she indemnified herself for her reticence, when she woke Miss Vavasour on the following morning! She had got a perfect Romance of the Forest ready, wherein Wyverne's exploits transcended those of Sir Bevis, and the physical proportions of his foes cast those of Colbrand or Ascapart into the shade.

Making all allowances for her handmaiden's vivid imagination, Helen came down to breakfast in a great turmoil of curiosity and anxiety. She had to wait for authentic particulars, till she got fevered with impatience. The Squire, quite determined on doing *his* share of the business thoroughly, had followed the prisoners, already, to the neighbouring town, where they were to answer their misdeeds before himself and other magistrates. Helen had no reason to believe that her mother was better informed than herself, and " my lady's" morning meditations were not likely to be disturbed; no one else had shown any sign of life so far. At last, Bertie Grenvil lounged into the breakfast-room. His appearance was somewhat reassuring; there was not a trace of conflict or even of weariness on the fair face; indeed, the Cherub was so used to turn night into day, that late hours and sleeplessness were rather his normal state. His answers to Helen's string of eager questions were rather unsatisfactory; much in the style of old Caspar's reminiscences about Blenheim:

"Why that I cannot tell," quoth he:
"But 'twas a famous victory."

Perhaps there was no real reserve or affectation about it; one's waking recollections of a midnight fray are apt to be strangely distorted and vague.

"I've seen Alan, this morning," Bertie remarked at length casually. "He's wonderfully well, all things considered, and means to show at luncheon; but I fear they've spoiled his shooting for some time; he won't be able to use that left arm for a fortnight."

Miss Vavasour's cheek lost its colour instantly, and her hand shook so that it could hardly set down the cup it held. "You don't mean that Alan is seriously hurt?" she said. "And they never told me. I have never even sent to ask after him. It is too cruel." She rose quickly, and rang the bell, before Grenvil could anticipate her. "What an idiot I am!" Bertie interjected, actually flushing with a real self-reproach. "I thought you had heard that Alan had met with two or three hard blows, or I would not have mentioned it so abruptly. Don't be frightened; on my honour, they are nothing worse than bruises; he will tell you so himself in an hour's time."

Helen forced a smile, and recovered her composure immediately. But she did not seem comfortable till she had sent Pauline to bring a report of her cousin's state from his own lips. The *soubrette* had been kept in equal ignorance with her mistress as to Wyverne's hurts, and when she came back to repeat his cheerful message, her voice was trembling, and her bright dark eyes were dim with tears.

The whole party—with the exception of the Squire—met at luncheon; for Max Vavasour returned in the course of the morning. The latter congratulated everybody very pleasantly on the success of the night's expedition; and, it is possible, congratulated himself quite as sincerely on having been out of the way; at all events, he affected no regret at having missed his share of peril and glory. Alan Wyverne came in the last. With the aid of a scientific valet, he had contrived to dissemble very successfully the traces of the fray; the dark thick hair swept lower than usual over his brows, and almost concealed the spot where the first blow had fallen; the second had left no visible mark. He seemed in the best possible spirits, and his gay, pleasant laugh came as readily as ever, without an appearance of being forced or constrained; but his face was very pale, and his left arm hung helplessly in its sling.

The worst of Lord Clydesdale's enemies—already he had made not a few—
might have been satisfied at the state of
the Earl's feelings, as he sat there, brooding sullenly over the recollection of
his own discomfiture, and watching the
*empressment* which everybody seemed
determined to manifest towards his
unconscious rival. Miss Vavasour, as
we have before said, was never "gushing" or demonstrative; but she considered it the most natural thing in the
world that her cousin should be petted
and tended under the circumstances.
So she sat by his side, anticipating and
ministering to his wants with the tact
and tenderness that only a woman—
and a loving one—can display, utterly
ignoring the savage blue eyes that kept
glaring at her from beneath their bushy
brows. Clydesdale muttered curse after curse under his breath, and drained
glass after glass of the strong brown
sherry that stood close to his hand; the
rich liquor seemed to be absorbed with
no better effect than a genial rain produces falling on a quicksand.

It was rather remarkable that no one
seemed disposed to question *him* much
about last night's adventure. Possibly,
Lady Mildred knew something of the
truth—though not all—and had taken
Max into confidence; for her maid
might have been seen in close colloquy
with one of the keepers, early in the
morning; and it is probable that model
of austere and dignified propriety would
not so far have derogated without good
cause. However this might be, her
manner towards Alan Wyverne was
kind and affectionate to a degree; when
she spoke to Lord Clydesdale, a very
close observer might have detected a
certain coldness in the perfect courtesy.
"My lady" was only a woman, after
all; and the instincts of her sex, though
tamed and trained, would assert themselves sometimes. She looked at the
Earl as he sat there swelling with
sulky self-importance; ruddy, certainly—perhaps unpleasantly so—but not
"of a cheerful countenance;" then she
looked across at Wyverne, just as a
bright, grateful smile lighted up all his
wan face; and thanked Helen for some

trifling act of kindness. The contrast
was too much for Lady Mildred; for
once, the cold diplomatist yielded
to a real frank impulse and forgot
her cunning. When she rose with the
others, she crossed over to where
Alan sat, and leant over him, on pretence of settling his sling, till her lips
touched his hair. Even Helen, who was
so near, did not catch the whisper—
"Ah, so many thanks! Who can help
loving you—always braver and better
than your word?"

Neither ever alluded to the events of
that night again, but they understood
each other perfectly; and to the end of
his days, Wyverne considered his services over-paid. In truth, it was no
mean triumph to have made "my lady,"
for more than a hundred seconds,
thoroughly honest and sincere.

That day brought a large influx of
fresh guests to Dene; but only four deserve special mention, and perhaps
these might be reduced to three.

Grace Beauclerc was Alan's only sister.
There was a strong likeness between
them, not only in features, but in character. She had the same quiet thorough-bred face, that no one ever called
beautiful, but every one felt was intensely loveable; the same slender,
graceful proportions; the same soft,
winning manner; the same power of
attraction and retaining the affection of
men and women. The resemblance extended still further—to their fortunes.
Grace had not ruined herself, certainly—
with the exception of a few fair specu-
lators of whose daring The Corner and
Capel Court are conscious, they generally leave that luxury to *us*—but she
had gone as near the wind as possible,
by contracting the most imprudent of
alliances. How the Beauclercs lived,
was a mystery to their nearest and
dearest friends. The crash had not
come at Wyverne Abbey when the
marriage took place, and Alan had then
settled £400 a year on his sister; but
this, added to the interest of her own
small fortune, and the pay of a clerk of
nine years' standing in the Foreign Office,
hardly carried their income beyond the
hundreds. A cipher had represented

Algernon Beauclerc's own personal assets long before he married. Yet they lived apparently in great comfort, went out everywhere, gave occasionally the nicest entertainments, at home, on a very tiny scale, that you can conceive; and, it was said, were wonderfully little in debt. It was a great social problem, in its way, and one of those that it is not worth while puzzling oneself to solve. But though Grace's husband had been very extravagant, and was still far from self-denying, he was weak neither in mind nor principle ; he loved his wife and his children, after his fashion, far too well to involve himself in any serious scrape ; and contrived to utilize his amusements to a remarkable degree. He was passionately fond of whist, and had attained an exceptional intelligence in that fascinating game. His plan was to set aside a certain sum each year to risk on its chances : the profits went to the account of *menus plaisirs*, in which Grace had more than her share ; if the card-purse was emptied, nothing would induce him to play again till the time arrived for replenishing it. Algy Beauclerc hardly knew how to be angry, even with an incorrigibly careless or stupid partner, and the world in general found it impossible to quarrel with him. In appearance, he was a curious contrast to his wife—broad and burly, with a bluff, jovial face, half shrouded in a forest of blonde beard, and large, light, laughing eyes. Prince Percinet and Graciosa never got on better together than did that apparently ill-matched couple. The set in which they lived, though neither vicious nor reckless, was decidedly fast; looking at Grace's quiet, rather pensive face, one could not help fancying that she must have felt sometimes uncomfortably out of her element; but she had a singular power of adapting herself to circumstances, without being deteriorated thereby. Presiding over one of those post-operatic *réunions*, where cigars, and even cigarettes, were not interdicted— or playing with her children, as she would do for hours of a morning—she always seemed perfectly and placidly happy.

Of a very different stamp were the other pair that remain to be noticed. Not only her intimate friends, and the men with whom she had flirted more or less seriously—they would have made a fair second-battalion to any regiment— but the whole of London opened wondering eyes when handsome, daring Maud Dacres married Mr. Brabazon, a pillar of the Stock Exchange, five-and-twenty years her senior, after an acquaintance of seven weeks, begun at Boulogne, where—for reasons cogent, though temporary—her father was then residing. It was not that she was more unlikely than another to make a money-match ; but every one was surprised at her selecting that particular millionaire.

Richard Brabazon was not only glaringly under-bred in form, feature, mind, and manner, but he was popularly considered one of the most "aggravating" men alive. He had a knack of hitting upon the topic most disagreeable to his interlocutor or to the company in general, and of introducing the same at the most inappropriate moment, always in a smooth, plausible way, which made it more irritating. Even when he wished to be extraordinary civil, there was an evident affability and condescension about him that very few could stand. His slow, measured, mincing way of speaking — pronouncing *a's* like *e's*— affected one's ear like the hum of a mosquito ; and his plump, smug, smooth-shaven face was intensely provocative, inspiring people, otherwise calm and pacific, with a rabid desire to leap up and smite him on the cheek. This laudable and very general propensity had never yet been gratified; for Richard Brabazon was far too cunning ever to give a chance away. Many men would have given large monies for an opportunity of taking overt offence, but they waited still in vain.

It was a marvel how his wife—high-spirited and quick-tempered to a fault— contrived to live with him, without occasionally betraying annoyance or aversion. It is probable that several bitter duels had in fact taken place; but the antagonists kept their own secret; and it was a perfect neutrality now, though an armed one. The principle of non-interference was thoroughly established, and the contiguous powers did not even take the trouble to watch each other's frontier. Sometimes the spirit of aggravation would tempt Brabazon to launch a taunt or a sarcasm in the direction of his wife or her friends; but it was generally met by an imperial and absolute indifference—at rare intervals, by a retort, not the less biting because it was so very quietly put in. He *would* do it, though he knew he should get the worst of it, just as Thersites could not refrain from his gibe, though his shoulders were shaking already in anticipation of the practical retort of Ajax or Odysseus.

Lady Mildred was goodnatured enough never to cross the plans or pleasures of her friends unless they interfered with hers; indeed, she would further them as far as was consistent with her own credit and convenience; but even in her benevolence some malice was mingled. She was rather glad to give Grenvil an opportunity of following out his love-dream, especially as she felt certain no harm would come of it; but, in mentioning to him the expected guests, she had purposely omitted the Brabazons.

Bertie had been indulging in an anteprandial siesta, and only came down the great staircase as the others were filing past in to dinner; he was in time to see Maud Brabazon sweep by, more insolently beautiful, he thought, than ever. She just deigned to acknowledge his presence with the slightest bend of her delicate neck, and the sauciest of smiles. That wily Cherub could feign innocence right well when it served his wicked ends; but only one visible sign *really* remained to testify that he had once been guileless—perhaps it was a mere accident of complexion—he had not forgotten how to change colour. Lady Mildred watched the meeting. She saw Bertie's cheek flush—brightly as a girl's might do who hears the first love-whisper—and then grow pale almost to the lips. "My lady" laughed under her breath, in calm appreciative approbation, just as some scientific patron of the Arena may have laughed, when the net of the Retiarius glided over the shoulders of the doomed Secutor.

Any one interested in such psychological studies — and, to some people, a really well-managed flirtation is a very interesting and instructive spectacle— would have been much amused that evening watching the "passages" of Bertie's love. It was rather a one-sided affair, after all; for the Cherub was so hard hit as to forget his cunning of fence, and timidity for once was not in the least assumed. The lady was thoroughly at her ease, as women ever are who play that perilous game with their head instead of their heart.

Maud Brabazon was just on the shady side of thirty; but such a pleasant shade it was! The sunniest year in the lives of her many rivals looked dull and tame by comparison. She was rather below the middle height, and rather fuller in her proportions than was consistent with perfection of form; but no one was ever heard to hint that her figure could have been improved upon. Large bright brown eyes were matched by soft abundant hair of a darker shade; a slightly aquiline nose, a delicately chiselled *mutine* mouth, and the ripest of peach-complexions, made up a picture that every one found fascinating, many fatally so.

She was a very queen of coquetry, understanding and practising every one of its refinements. You always saw the most attractive elements of any company converging to the spot where she sat, like straws drawn in by an eddy. Where was the secret of her power? Men who had been led captive at her chariot-wheels asked themselves that question in after days, when freedom was partially regained, and got puzzled over it, as one does over the incidents of a very vivid dream. It was a fair face, certainly, but there were others more brilliant in their beauty, more winning in their loveliness. Her frank boldness of speech dazzled you at first with its natural, careless *verve* — she kept for special occasions the tender confidential tones that lingered in your ears through many sleepless night-watches — but several of her beaten rivals had really thrice her wit and cleverness, and, as conversationalists, could have distanced her easily. Maud Brabazon seemed to diffuse round her an atmosphere of temptation. Cold-blooded men, of austere morals and rigid propriety, felt irresistibly impelled to make love to her on the shortest acquaintance, not wildly or passionately, but in an airy, light-minded fashion, which left no remorse, hardly a regret, behind. It was strange that she had never yet got entangled in any of the toils she wove so deftly : for the bitterest of friends or foes had never dared to impute to her any darker crime than consummate coquetry. One who knew her well when the subject was being discussed, thus expressed himself in the figurative language of the turf, of which he was a stanch supporter :

"Yes, she can win, when she's in front all the way. Wait till you see her collared; *they've never made her gallop yet.*"

Thereby intimating his opinion that the Subduer was still in the future, by whom Maud's peace of mind was to be imperilled.

All things considered, it seemed likely that poetical justice was going to assert itself in the shape of merited retaliation impending over the Cherub's graceless head; a state of things so perfectly satisfactory that we may as well leave them there for the present.

Pressing affairs called Lord Clydesdale away from Dene on the following day. He had probably reasons of his own for cutting his visit short rather abruptly. He thought that whatever interests he might have at stake would be advanced fully as well in his absence, for the present. Somehow or another, before he went, Max Vavasour was made aware of the wager with Harding Knowles. On the occasion of a great robbery—

When the knowing ones, for once, stand in
With some dark flyer meant at last to win—

and the owners of one or two dangerous horses are put on, a "monkey to nothing," I believe they go through the form of registering it as a bet; so we may as well dignify the Earl's compact by that convenient name. It is more than likely that Clydesdale made the confession himself. He had little delicacy in such matters when he knew his man ; and no Oriental despot could be more insolent in his cynicism. If he had thought he could do so safely, he would have offered money to her nearest relation, to serve him in his pursuit of any woman he might fancy, without the faintest scruple or shame.

However the revelation was made, Max Vavasour never betrayed to Knowles his consciousness of the confederacy by word or sign; but he would look at the latter occasionally with a very peculiar expression in his cold dark eyes. There was something of curiosity in that look, more of dislike and contempt. The wily schemer would accept readily the aid of any instrument, however repulsive, that would serve his purpose; but they never were stifled for one moment—the instincts of patrician pride. Harding was no favourite of Lady Mildred's; and her manner towards him could not be said to be cordial now; but there certainly was a shade more of courtesy and attention. She suggested now and then that his name should be added to the dinner-list, which she had never done before; and honoured him at times with a fair share of her evening's conversation. There was nothing strange in this. Knowles was evidently a rising man; and "my lady" made a point of being at least civil to such people, though she would just as soon have thought of asking a real Gorilla to her house, as any living celebrity — soldier, priest, lawyer, or literate—simply because he chanced to be the lion of the day.

----

## CHAPTER XII.

### RUMOURS OF WARS.

HARDING KNOWLES had never been a hard-working man. Very little more reading would have turned a good Second in classics into an easy First, and this was so well known at Oxford that he might have had as many pupils as he liked during the year that he resided there after taking his degree. He would only take two or three—"just to have something to do in the morning," he said; and these were all of the Clydesdale stamp — men whose connexion was worth a good deal, while their preparation cost no sort of head-work or anxiety. He had been called to the bar since then, but had never pretended to follow up the profession. There was not a trace of business about his chambers in the Temple; no face of clerk or client ever looked out at the chrysanthemums through those pleasant windows, the sills of which were framed and buried in flowers. He could write a clever article, or a sharp sarcastic critique, when the fit seized him, and made a hundred or so every year thus in an easy desultory way: the Rector's allowance was liberal, so that Harding had more than enough to satisfy all his tastes, which were by no means extravagant; in fact, he saved money. But he was avaricious to the heart's core, and could be painstaking and patient enough when the stake was really worth his while to win. He did not tarry long at Dene after Clydesdale's departure — long enough, though, to have another incentive to exertion in the latter's cause. Personal pique was added now to the mere greed of gain. The merest trifle brought this about, and you would hardly understand it without appreciating some anomalies in Knowles's character.

There never was a more thorough-going democrat. From his birth his sympathies and instincts had all taken the same direction, and these had been strengthened and embittered by his mother's evil training. He disliked the patrician order intensely; but their society seemed to have a strange fascination for him, judging from the pertinacity he displayed in endeavouring to gain and confirm a footing there. He would intrigue for certain invitations in the season as eagerly as a French deputy seeking the red ribbon of honour. Yet he was always uncomfortable when his point was gained, and he found himself half way up the much-desired stair-case. The mistress of the mansion greeted him probably with the self-same smile that she vouchsafed to nine-tenths of the five hundred guests who crowded her rooms; but Knowles would torment himself with the fancy that there was something compassionate or satirical in the fair dame's look, as if she penetrated a truth, of which he was himself conscious—that he had no business to be there. He felt that, if he got a fair start, he could talk better than the majority of the men around him; but he felt, too, that he had no chance against the most listless or languid of them all. They were on their own ground, and the intruder did not care to match himself against them there; his position was far too constrained, his footing too insecure. How he hated them, for the indolent *nonchalance* and serene indifference that he would have given five years of life to be able to assume! A wolfish ferocity would rise within him as he watched a beardless Coldstreamer dropping his words slowly, as if each were worth money and not lightly to be parted with, into the delicate ear of a haughty beauty from whom Knowles scarcely dared to hope for a recognising bow. The innocent object of his wrath was probably only sacrificing himself to the necessities of the position, while his thoughts reverted with a tender longing to the smoking room of his club, or anticipated the succulent chop that Pratt's was bound to provide for him before the dawning.

In all other respects, Harding was as little sensitive as the most obstinate of pachyderms. He did not know what shame meant, and an implied insult that would have roused another savagely would scarcely attract his notice. You have seen one instance of this already. But he was nervously and morbidly alive to the minutest point affecting his position in society. After assisting at one of those assemblies of the *haute volée*, he would review in his memory every incident of the evening, and would be miserable for weeks afterwards if he thought he had made himself ridiculous by any awkwardness of manner or any incongruity of word or deed. If the choice had been forced upon him, he would have committed a forgery any day, sooner than a *gaucherie*.

I suppose everybody is sensitive somewhere, and it is only a question whether the shaft hits a joint in the harness, and so some go on for years, or for ever, without a scratch or a wound. Sometimes the weak point is found out very oddly and unexpectedly.

There is now living a man whom, till very lately, his friends used to quote as the ideal of impassibility. Even in his youthful days, when he was "galloper" occasionally to General Levin, war-worn veterans used to marvel at and envy the sublime serenity with which he would receive a point-blank volley of objurgation, double-shotted with the hoarse expletives for which that irascible commander is world-renowned. I have seen him myself exposed to the "chaff" of real artists in that line. He only smiled in complacent security, when "the archers bent their bows and made them ready," and sat amidst the banter and the satire, unmoved as is Ailsa Craig by the whistle of the sea-bird's wings. It was popularly supposed that no sorrow or shame which can befall humanity would seriously disturb his equanimity, till in an evil hour he plunged into print. It was a modest little book, relating to a Great War, in which he had borne no ignoble part; so mild in its comment and so meek in its suggestions, that the critics might have spared it from very pity. But unluckily he fell early into the hands of one of the most truculent of the tribe, and all the others followed suit, so that poor Courtenay had rather a rough time of it. They questioned his facts and denied his inferences, accusing him of ignorance and partiality in about equal degrees, and, what was harder still to bear, they anatomized his little jokes gravely, and made a mock at his pathetic passages, stigmatizing the first as "flippancy," the last as "fine writing." Ever since that time, *le Beau Sabreur* has been subject to fits of unutterable gloom and despondency. Only last summer, we were dining with him at the "Bellona." The banquet was faultless, and the guests in the best possible form, so that the prospects of the evening were convivial in the extreme. It chanced that there was One present who had also written a book or two, and had also been evil entreated by the reviewers. A peculiarly savage onslaught had just appeared in a weekly paper, imputing to the author in question every species of literary profligacy, from atheism down to deliberate immorality. The man who sat next to him opened fire on the subject. It so happens that this much maligned individual—as a rule, quite the reverse of good-tempered—is stolidly impervious to critical praise or blame. This indifference is just as much a constitutional accident, of course, like exemption from nausea at sea, but one would think *he* must find it convenient at times. He joined in the laugh now quite naturally, and only tried to turn the subject, because its effect on our host was evident. His kind, handsome face became overcast with a moody melancholy. The allusion to his friend's castigation brought back too vividly the recollection of his own. The cruel stripes were scarcely healed yet, and the flesh *would* quiver at the remote sound of the scourge.

Courtenay's fellow-sufferer would fain have cheered him. The first flask of "Dry" had just been opened (it was *una de multis, face nuptiali digna*—a wine, in truth, worthy to be consumed at the marriage-feasts of great and good men), he took the brimming beaker in his hand, before the bright beads died out of the glorious amber, and spoke thus, sententiously—

"Oh, my friend, let us not despond overmuch; rather let us imitate Socrates, the cheery sage, when he drained his last goblet. Do me right. Lo! I drink to the judge who hath condemned us— Τοῦτο τῷ καλῷ Κριτια.

Courtenay did drink—to do him justice, he will always do *that*—but his smile was the saddest thing I ever saw; and it was three good hours before his spirits recovered their tone, or his great golden moustaches, which were drooping sympathetically their martial curl.

If you realize Harding Knowles's excessive sensitiveness on certain points, you will understand how Alan Wyverne fell under his ban.

The cousins were starting for their afternoon's ride. Knowles had lunched at Dene, but was not to accompany them. He chanced to be standing on the steps when the horses came up, and Miss Vavasour came out alone. Something detained Alan in the hall for a minute, and when he appeared, Harding was in the act of assisting Helen to mount. Now that "mounting" is the simplest of all gymnastics, if you know how to do it, and if there exists between you and the fair Amazon a certain sympathy and good understanding; in default of these elements of concord, it is probable that the whole thing may come to grief. Harding was so nervously anxious to acquit himself creditably, that it was not likely he would succeed. He "lifted" at the wrong moment, and too violently, not calculating on the elasticity of the demoiselle's spring, even though she was taken unawares. Nothing but great activity and presence of mind on Helen's part saved a dangerous fall. She said not one word as she settled herself anew in the saddle; but the culprit caught one glance from the depths of the brilliant eyes which stopped short his stammered apology. It was not exactly angry—worse a thousand times than that; but it stung him like the cut of a whip, and his cheek would flush when he thought of it years afterwards.

While Knowles was still in his confusion, he felt a light touch on his shoulder, and, turning, found Wyverne standing there. Nothing chafed Alan more than an exhibition of awkwardness such as he had just witnessed; besides this, he had never liked Harding, and was not inclined to make excuses for him now. The pleasantness had quite vanished from his face; and when he spoke, almost in a whisper, his lip was curling haughtily and his brows were bent.

"*Fiat experimentum in corpore vili,*" he said. "Your classical reading might have taught you that much, at all events. You want practice in mounting, decidedly; but I beg that you will select for your next lesson a fitter subject than Miss Vavasour."

Knowles was ready enough of retort as a rule; but this time, before he could collect himself sufficiently to find an answer, Wyverne was in the saddle,

And lightly they rode away.

The animosity was not equally allotted, for Alan engrossed far the bitterest share of it; but thenceforward both the cousins might fear the very worst from an enemy capable of much stratagem, recoiling from no baseness, whose hatred, if it were only for the coldness of its malignity, might not safely be defied. For some days after Knowles's departure, everything went on pleasantly at Dene; and nothing occurred worthy of note, unless it were a slight passage-of-arms between Bertie Grenvil and Mr. Brabazon. The latter was so rarely taken at fault, that it deserves to be recorded.

The financier was perfectly aware of the flirtation in progress between his wife and the Cherub; but he never disquieted himself about such trifles; and it was simply his "aggravating" instinct which impelled him one day, after dinner, to select the topic which he guessed would be most disagreeable to both. A certain Guardsman had just come to great grief in money matters, and had been forced to betake himself in haste to some continental Adullam. He was a favourite cousin of Maud's, a great friend of Grenvil's, and in the same battalion. It was supposed that the Cherub was to a certain extent involved in his comrade's embarrassments, having backed the latter almost to the extent of his own small credit. On the present occasion, Mr. Brabazon was good enough to volunteer a detailed account of the unlucky spendthrift's difficulties, which he professed to have received in a letter that morning, adding his own strictures and comments thereon. No one interrupted him, though Lady Mildred had the tact to give the departing signal before he had quite finished. Mr. Brabazon felt that he had the best of the position, and determined to follow up his triumph. When the men were left alone, his plump, smooth face became more superciliously sanctimonious, till he looked like Tartufe intensified.

"There is one subject I would not allude to," he said, "till *they* had left us. I have heard it hinted that Captain Pulteney's ruin was hastened by his disgraceful profligacy. It is said that he lavished thousands on a notorious person living under his name in a villa in St. John's Wood. Mr. Grenvil perhaps knows if my information is correct?"

Brabazon wished his words unsaid as Bertie's bright eyes fastened on his face, glittering with malicious mirth.

"Yes; I know something about it," he replied; "but I don't see that I'm called upon to reveal poor Dick's domestic secrets to uninterested parties. You don't hold any of his paper, I suppose? No—you're too prudent for that. Not quite prudent enough, though. I wouldn't say too much about St. John's Wood, if I were you. You've heard the proverb about 'glass houses?' I believe there's a conservatory attached to that very nice villa in Mastic Road, to which you have the *entrée* at all hours. Have you got the latch-key in your pocket?"

If Richard Brabazon valued himself on one possession more than another, it was his immaculate respectability: in fact, an ostentatious piety was part of his stock-in-trade. For once, he was fairly disconcerted. His face grew white,. and actually convulsed with rage and fear as he stammered out, quite forgetting his careful elocution—

"I don't pretend to understand you; but I see you wish to insult me."

"Wrong again, and twice over," the other answered, coolly. "I never insulted anybody since I was born. And you will understand me perfectly, if you will take the trouble to remember a very warm midnight last spring, when the cabman could not give you change

for a sovereign and you had to send him out his fare. You were in such a hurry to go in, that you never saw the humblest of your servants, about fifteen yards off, lighting his cigar. I don't wonder at your impetuosity. I got a good look at the *soubrette* when she came out with the change; and, if the mistress is as pretty as the maid, your taste is unimpeachable—whatever your morals may be."

The great drops gathered on Brabazon's forehead as he sat glaring speechlessly at his tormentor, who at that moment appeared intent on the selection of some olives, all the while humming audibly to himself, "The Young May Moon."

"It is an atrocious calumny," he gasped out, "or a horrible mistake. I wish to believe it is the last."

"You wish *us* to believe, you mean," the other retorted. "But I won't 'accept the composition,' (that's the correct expression, isn't it?) There was no mistake about it. I saw you that night, just as plainly as I did the morning before, going into Exeter Hall to talk about converting the Pongo Islanders—only you were in your brougham *then*. Quite right too. Never take your own carriage out on the war-trail: it only makes scandal, and costs you a night-horse. I always tried to beat so much economy into poor Dick Pulteney. If he would have listened to me, he might have lasted a month or two longer. I assure you I watched the whole thing with great interest. One doesn't see a *financier en bonne fortune* every day; and the habits of all animals are worth observing at certain seasons. A Frenchman wrote such a pretty treatise the other day about the "Loves of the Moles!"

Many men would have derived much refreshment from the spectacle presented just then by their ancient enemy. You cannot fancy a more pitiable picture of helpless exasperation, nor more complete abasement. Even with his usual crafty reserve, he would scarcely have held his own against the cool insolence of his opponent—thoroughly confident of his facts, and mercilessly determined to use them to the uttermost. If the Squire had been present, the skirmish would not have lasted so long; but he was presiding at a great agricultural dinner miles away. Max Vavasour, who sat in his father's place, was not disposed to interrupt any performance which amused him. Neither he nor any other man present felt the faintest sympathy with, or compassion for, the victim. Brabazon appreciated his position acutely. He was only reaping as he had sown; but some of those same crops are not pleasant to gather or garner. He rose suddenly, and muttering something about "not staying another instant to be insulted," made a precipitate retreat, leaving not a shred of dignity behind. Max Vavasour did rouse himself to say a few pacifying words of deprecation, but they did not arrest the fugitive, nor did the speaker seem to expect they would do so.

When the door closed, Wyverne looked at Bertie with an expression which was meant to be reproachful, but became, involuntarily, admiring.

"What a quiet, cruel little creature it is," he said. "Fancy his keeping that secret so long, and bringing it out so viciously just at the right time. Is it not a crowning mercy, though, that the Squire's 'agricultural' came off to-night? He would have stopped once for once in his life. I wonder whether Brabazon is a 'bull' or a 'bear' on 'Change? Whichever he is, he was baited thoroughly well here; and, I think, deserved all the punishment he got. Cherub, I shall look upon you with more respect henceforth, having seen you appear as the Bold Avenger."

They soon began to talk of other things. A reputation fostered by years of caution, outward self-restraint, and conventional observances, had just been slain before their eyes; but those careless spirits made little moan over the dead, and seemed to think the obsequies not worth a funeral oration. Having once accepted his position, Brabazon, to do him justice, made the best of it. He made no attempt at retaliation, as he might easily have done, by removing himself and his belongings abruptly from Dene; indeed, during the remainder of a protracted visit there, he comported himself in a manner void of offence to man or woman. The Squire, who knew him well, remarked the change, and congratulated himself and others thereupon; but they never told him of the somewhat summary process by which the result had been achieved. It was simple enough, after all. Some horses will never run kindly till you take your whip up to them in earnest.

Though Sir Alan Wyverne had no property left worth speaking of, he still had "affairs" of one sort or another to attend to, from time to time, and of late it had become still more necessary that these be kept in order. Before very long, he too was obliged to go up to town on business He was only to be absent three or four days; but he seemed strangely reluctant to leave Dene. In good truth, there was not the slightest reason for any gloomy presentiment; but Helen remembered in after years, that during the last hours they spent together then, her cousin made none of those gay allusions to their future that he was so fond of indulging in; and that though his words and manner were kind and loving as ever, there was something sad and subdued in their tenderness. So far as Alan knew, it was a simple case of business which called him away; more than once afterwards he thought it would have been better if he had died that night, with the music of Helen's whisper in his ears, the print of her ripe scarlet lips on his check, the pressure of her lithe twining fingers still lingering round his own.

Many men, before and since, have thought the same. It is, perhaps, the most reasonable of all the repinings that are more futile than the vainest of regrets. Two lifetimes would not unravel some tangles of sorrow and sin, that are cut asunder, quite simply, by one sheer sudden stroke of Azräel's sword. Be sure, the purpose of God's awful messenger is often benevolent, though his aspect is seldom benign. The legend of ancient days bears a sad significance still. His arm is "swift to smite and never to spare;" black as night is the plumage of his vast shadowy wings; his lineaments are somewhat stern in their severe serenity; but in all the hierarchy of Heaven—the Rabbins say—is found no more perfect beauty than in the face of the Angel of Death.

---

## CHAPTER XIII.

### THE FIRST SHELL.

So Wyverne went on his way—not rejoicing; and Helen would have been left "sighing her lane," if she had been at all given to that romantic pastime. But they were not a sentimental pair; and did not even think it necessary to bind themselves under an oath to correspond by every possible post—a compact which is far more agreeably feasible in theory than in practice. However, a long letter from Alan made his cousin very happy on the third day after his departure. It was a perfect epistle in its way—at least, it thoroughly satisfied the fair recipient; to be sure, it was her first experience in that line. Two lines evidently written after the rest—said that his return must be deferred four-and-twenty hours. Helen did not hear again from her cousin; but on the morning of the day on which he was expected, the post brought two strange letters to Dene which changed the aspect of things materially. One was addressed to Lady Mildred, the other to her daughter. Both were written in the same delicate feminine hand, and the contents of both were essentially the same, though they varied slightly in phrase. "My lady's" communication may serve as a sample:

"When Alan Wyverne returns, it might be well to ask him three simple questions:—What was the business that detained him in town? Who was his companion for two hours yesterday in the Botanical Gardens (which they had entirely to themselves)? Where he spent the whole of this afternoon? I would give the answers myself, but I know him well, and I am sure he will not refuse to satisfy your natural curiosity. As my name will never oe known, I need not disguise my motive in writing thus. I care not serving you, or saving your daughter; I simply wish to serve my own revenge. I loved him dearly, once, or I should not hate him so heartily now. If Alan Wyverne chooses to betray so soon the girl to whom he has plighted faith, I do not see why *one* of his old loves should engross *all* the treachery."

Helen's letter was to the same purport, but at greater length, and more considerately and gently expressed, as though some compassion was mingled in the writer's bitterness.

I should very much like to know the *fiancée* who would receive such a communication as this with perfect equanimity—supposing, of course, that her heart went with the promise of her hand. Miss Vavasour believed in her cousin to a great extent, and her nature was too frank and generous to foster suspicion; but she was not such a paragon of trustfulness. She was thoroughly miserable during the whole of the day. There was very little comfort to be got out of her mother (it was decided that the subject should not be mentioned, at present, to the Squire); "my lady" said very little, but evidently thought that matters looked dark. When she said— "Don't let us make ourselves unhappy till you have spoken to Alan; I am certain he can explain everything"—it was irritatingly apparent that she really took quite an opposite view of the probabilities, and was only trying to pacify Helen's first excitement, as a nurse might humour the fancies of a fever-patient. Nevertheless, the *demoiselle* bore up bravely; not one of the party at Dene guessed that anything had occured to ruffle her; and there were sharp eyes of all colours amongst them.

Mrs. Fernley was there—the most seductive of "grass-widows"—whose husband had held for years some great post high up in the Himalayas, only giving sign of his existence by the regular transmission of large monies, wherewith to sustain the splendour of his consort's establishment. There, too, was Agatha Drummond—whose name it is treason to introduce thus episodically, for she deserves a story to herself, and has nothing whatever to do with the present one—a beauty of the grand old Frankish type, with rich fair hair, haughty aquiline features, clear, bold blue eyes, and long elastic limbs—such as one's fancy assigns to those who shared the bed of Merovingian kings. She passed the most of her waking hours in riding, waltzing, or flirting; seldom or ever read anything, and talked, notwithstanding, passingly well; but for daring, energy, and power of supporting fatigue in her three favourite pursuits, you might have backed her safely against any woman of her age in England. Both were very fond of Helen, and would have sympathized with her sincerely had they seen cause; but their glances were not the less keenly inquisitive; and, under the circumstances, she deserved some credit for keeping her griefs so entirely to herself.

I have heard grave, reverend men, with consciences probably as clear and correct as their banking books, confess that they never returned home, after a brief absence during which no letters had been forwarded, without a certain vague apprehension, which did not entirely subside till they had met their family and glanced over their correspondence. I will not affirm that some feeling of the sort did not cross Wyverne's mind as he drove up the long dark avenue to Dene. He arrived so late that almost every one had gone up to dress, so he was not surprised at not finding Helen downstairs; it is possible that he was slightly disappointed at not encountering her somewhere—by chance of course—in gallery or corridor. When they met, just before dinner, Alan did fancy that there was something constrained in his cousin's welcome, and unusually grave in his aunt's greeting; but he had no suspicion that anything was seriously amiss, till Helen whispered, as she passed him on leaving the dining-room—"Come to the library as soon as you can. I am going there now." You may guess if he kept her waiting long.

Miss Vavasour was sitting in an arm-chair near the fire; her head was bent low, leaning on her hand; even in the uncertain light you might see the slender fingers working and trembling; there was a listless despondency in her whole bearing, so different from its usual proud eslasticity, that a sharp conviction of something having gone fearfully wrong, shot through Wyverne's heart, like the thrust of a dagger. His lips had not touched even her forehead, yet, but he did not now attempt a caress; he only laid his hand gently on her shoulder—so light a touch need not have made her shiver—and whispered—

"What has vexed you, my own?"

For all answer, she gave him the letter, that she held ready.

He read it through by the light of the shaded lamp that stood near. Helen watched his face all the while with a fearful, feverish anxiety; it betrayed not the faintest shade of confusion or shame, but it grew very grave and sad, and, at last, darkened, almost sternly. When he came to the end he was still silent, and seemed to muse for a few seconds. But she could bear suspense no longer. Yet there was no anger in the sweet voice, it was only plaintive and pleading—

"Ah, Alan, do speak to me. Won't you say it is all untrue?"

Wyverne roused himself from his reverie instantly; he drew nearer to his cousin's side, and took her little trembling hand in his own, looking down into her face—lovelier than ever in its pale, troubled beauty—with an intense love and pity in his eyes.

"The blow was cruelly meant, and craftily dealt," he said, "but they shall not part us yet, if you are brave enough to believe me thoroughly and implicitly, this once. I will never ask you to do so again. Yes, the facts are true—don't draw your hand back—I would not hold it another second if I could not say the inferences are as false as the Father of lies could make them. A dozen words answer all the questions. I was with Nina Lenox, in the Gardens; and yesterday afternoon I staid in town on her business, not on my own. There is the truth. The lie is—the insinuation that I had any other interest at stake than serving a rash unhappy woman in her hard need. That unfortunate is doomed to be fatal, it seems, even to her friends —she has right few left now to ruin. Darling, try to believe that neither she nor the world have ever had the right to call *me* by any other name."

Mrs. Rawson Lenox was one of the celebrities of that time. Her face and figure carried all before them, when she first came out; and even in the first season they set her up as a sort of standard of beauty with which others could only be compared in degrees of inferiority. She married early and very unhappily. Her husband was a coarse, rough-tempered man, and tried from the first to tyrannize over his wayward impetuous wife—who had been spoilt from childhood upwards—just as he was wont to do over the tenants of his broad acres, and his countless dependents. Of course it did not answer. Years had passed since then, each one giving more excuse to Nina Lenox for her wild ways and reckless disregard of the proprieties; but — not excuse enough. Men fell in love with her perpetually; but they did not come scathless out of the fire, like the admirers of Maud Brabazon. The taint and smirch of the furnace-blast remained; well if there were not angry scars, too, rankling and refusing to be healed. Mothers and mothers-in-law shook their heads ominously at the mention of Nina's name; the first, tracing the ruin of their son — moral or financial—the last, the domestic discomfort of her daughter, to those fatal lansquenet-parties and still more perilous morning *tête-à-têtes.*

Was it not hard to believe that a man, still short of his prime, and notoriously epicurean in his philosophy, could be in the secret of the sorceress without having drunk of her cup? That he could serve her as a friend, in sincerity and innocence, without ever having descended to be her accomplice? Yet this amount of faith or credulity—call it which you will—Wyverne did not scruple to ask from Helen, then.

It may not be denied that her heart seemed to contract, for an instant, painfully, when her lover's lips pronounced so familiarly that terrible name. But it

shook off distrust before it could fasten there. She rose up, with her hand in Alan's, and nestled close to his breast, and looked up earnestly and lovingly into his eyes.

"My own—my own still," she murmured, "I do believe you thoroughly, now, even if you tell me not another word. But do be kind and prudent, and don't try me again soon, it is so very hard to bear."

"If I had only guessed—"

That sentence was never finished, for reasons good and sufficient; such delicious impediments to speech are unfortunately rather rare. The kiss of forgiveness was sweeter in its lingering fondness, than that which sealed the affiancement under the oak-trees of the Home Wood.

"Sit here, child," Wyverne said, at last. "You shall hear all now."

He sank down on a cushion at her feet, and so made his confession. Not a disagreeable penance, either, when absolution is secured beforehand, and a delicate hand wanders at times, with caressing encouragement, over the penitent's brow and hair.

It is quite unnecessary to give the explanation at length. Mrs. Lenox had involved herself in all sorts of scrapes, of which money-embarrassments were the least serious. Things had come to a dangerous crisis. She had been foolish enough to borrow money of a man whose character ought to have deterred her, and then to offend him mortally. The creditor was base enough to threaten to use the weapons he possessed, in the shape of letters and other documents, compromising Nina fearfully. She heard that Wyverne was in town, and wrote to him to help her in her great distress. She preferred trusting him, to others on whom she had a real claim, because she knew him thoroughly; and if there was no love-link between them, neither was there any remorse or reproach. She was heart-sick of intrigue, for the moment, and would try what a kind honest friend could do. It was true. Their intimacy had been always innocent. These things are not to be accounted for; perhaps Alan never cared to offer

7

sacrifice at an altar on which incense from all kingdoms of the earth was burned. Mr. Lenox's temper had become of late so brutally savage, that Nina felt actual physical fear at the idea of his hearing of her embarrassments. This was the reason why she had met Wyverne clandestinely in the Botanical Gardens. Her husband was absent the whole of the next day; so that she had received him at home. It was a difficult and delicate business; but Alan carried it through. ✦ He got the money first—not a very large sum—found out the creditor with some trouble, and satisfied him, gaining possession of every dangerous document. It was a stormy interview at first; but Wyverne was not easily withstood when thoroughly in earnest; and his quiet, contemptuous firmness fairly broke the other down. You may fancy Nina's gratitude: indeed, up to a certain point, Alan had congratulated himself on having wrought a work of mercy and charity without damage to any one. You have seen how he was undeceived. He did not dissemble from Helen his self-reproach at having been foolish enough to meddle in the matter at all.

"Some one must be sacrificed at such times," he said; "but, my darling, it were better that all the *intrigantes* in London should go to the wall, than that you should have an hour's disquiet. Trust me, I'll see to this for the future. I am sure Mrs. Lenox would not be a nice friend for you; and it is better to cut off the connexion before you can be brought in contact. One can afford to be frank when one has done a person a real service. I'll write her a few lines— you can correct them, if you like—to say that this affair has been made the subject of anonymous letters; and that I cannot, for *your* sake, risk more misconstruction; so that our acquaintance must be of the slightest henceforward."

So peace was happily restored. We need not go into a minute description of the "rejoicings" that ensued. One thought only puzzled and troubled Alan execedingly.

"I can't conceive who can have written that letter," he said, "or got it writ-

ten. The hand of course proves nothing, nor the motive implied, which is simply not worth noticing. It is just as likely the work of a man's malevolence as of a woman's. Helen, I own frankly I would rather it were the first than the last. But I thought I had not made an enemy persevering enough to watch all my movements, or cruel enough to deal that blow in the dark."

It was evident that the shock to his genial system of belief in the world in general affected him far more more than the foiled intent of personal injury.

When Lady Mildred saw her daughter's face, as the latter re-entered the drawing-room alone, she guessed at once the issue of the conference, and knew that it would be useless now to cavil at an explanation which must have been absolutely satisfactory. She was not in the least disappointed; indeed, the most she had expected from this first shock to Helen's confidence was a slight loosening of the foundations. From the first moment of reading the anonymous letter, she detected fraud and misrepresentation; and argued that the Truth would this time prevail. So, when Alan had audience of her in her boudoir late that evening, he found no difficulty in making his cause good. "My lady" did just refer to something she had said on a former occasion, and quite coincided in Wyverne's idea, that this was one of the dangerous acquaintances that it was imperative for him to give up: indeed, she was very explicit and decided on this point. Otherwise, she was everything that was kind and conciliatory; and really said less about the imprudence in meddling with such an affair at all, than could have been expected from the most indulgent of aunts or mothers. Just before he left the boudoir, Alan read the letter through that "my lady" had given him—he had scarcely glanced at it before. When he gave it back his face had perceptibly lightened, though his lip was curling scornfully.

"I'm so glad you showed me that pleasant letter, Aunt Mildred," he said. "My mind is quite easy now as to the sex of the informer. No woman, I dare

swear, to whom I ever spoke words of
more than common courtesy could have
written such words as those. Perhaps
I may find out his name some day, and
thank him for the trouble he has taken."

Lady Mildred did not feel exactly
comfortable just then. She would have
preferred the whole transaction being
now left in as much obscurity as possible. She knew how determined and
obstinate the speaker could be when he
had real cause to be unforgiving. She
knew that he was capable of exacting
the reckoning to the uttermost farthing,
though the settlement was ever so long
delayed. On the whole, however, she
was satisfied with the aspect of affairs
as they remained. She had good reason to be so. Doubt and distrust may
seem to vanish; but they generally
leave behind them a slow, subtle, poisonous influence, that the purest and
strongest faith may not defy. Of all
diseases, those are the most dangerous,
which linger in the system when the
cure is pronounced to be perfect.

I knew a man well who passed
through the Crimean war untouched by
steel or shot, though he was ever in the
front of the battle. Even the terrible
trench-work did not seem to affect him.
He would come in, wet but not weary,
sleep in his damp tent contentedly, and
rise up in his might rejoicing. When,
quite at the end of the war, he was attacked by the fever, no one felt any serious alarm. We supposed that Kenneth McAlpine could shake off any ordinary sickness as easily as Sampson
did the Philistine's gyves. In truth, he
did appear to recover very speedily;
and, when he returned to England,
seemed in his usual health again. But
soon he began to waste and pine away
without any symptoms of active disease.
None of the doctors could reach the
seat of the evil, or even define its cause.
It took some time to sap that colossal
strength fairly away; but month by
month the doom came out more plainly
on his face, and the end has come at
last. Poor Kenneth's grave will be as
green as the rest of them, next spring,
when the grass begins to grow.

Standing by the sepulchre of Faith,
or Love, or Hope—if we dared look
back—we might find it hard to remember when and where the first seeds of
decay were sown, though we do not forget one pang of the last miserable days
that preceded the sharp death-agony.

———

## CHAPTER XIV.

### THE LETTERS OF BELLEROPHON.

WYVERNE'S valedictory note to Mrs.
Lenox, though kindly and courteous,
was brief and decisive enough to satisfy
Helen perfectly. The answer came in
due course; there was no anger or even
vexation in its tone, but rather a sad
humility—not at all what might have
been expected from the proud, passionate, reckless *lionne*, who kept her
sauciest smile for her bitterest foe, and
scarcely ever indulged the dearest of
her friends with a sigh. A perpetual
warfare was waged between that beautiful Free Companion and all regular
powers; though often worsted and
forced, for the moment, to give ground,
she had never yet lost heart or shown
sign of submission; the poor little Amazonian target was sorely dinted, and its
gay blazonry nearly effaced, but the
dauntless motto was still legible as ever
—*L'Empire c'est la guerre.*

So for awhile there was peace at
Dene, and yet, not perfect peace. Miss
Vavasour's state of mind was by no
means satisfactory; though it seemed,
at the time, to recover perfectly from
the sharp shock, it really never regained
its healthy elastic tone. Miserable misgivings, that could hardly be called
suspicions, would haunt her, though
she tried hard not to listen to their
irritating whispers, and always hated
herself bitterly afterwards for her weakness. She thought how unwise it would
be to show herself jealous or exacting,
yet she could hardly bear Alan to be
out of her sight, and when he was away,
had no rest, even in her dreams. Her
unknown correspondent, in a nice cynical letter, congratulated Helen on her
good-nature and long-suffering, and

hinted that Mrs. Lenox had been heard to express her entire approval of Alan's choice—"it would be very inconvenient, if there were bounds to the future Lady Wyverne's credulity." She did not dare to confess to her cousin that she had read such a letter though, and so only took her mother into the secret. Lady Mildred testified a proper indignation at the spitefulness and baseness of the writer, but showed plainly enough that her own mind was by no means easy on the subject. All that day, and all that week, Miss Vavasour's temper was more than uncertain, and though no actual tempest broke, there was electricity enough in the atmosphere to have furnished a dozen storms. "My Lady" had always indulged her daughter, but she took to humouring and petting her now, almost ostentatiously; the compassionate motive was so very evident, that instead of soothing the high-spirited demoiselle, it chafed her, at times, inexpressibly.

The change did not escape Alan Wyverne. He felt a desolate conviction that things were going wrong every way, but he was perfectly helpless, simply because there was nothing tangible to grapple with; he did not wish to call up evil spirits, merely to have the satisfaction of laying them. Helen's penitence after any display of waywardness or wickedness of temper was so charming, and the amends she contrived to make so very delicious, that her cousin found it the easiest thing imaginable to forgive; indeed, he would not have disliked that occasional petulance, if he had not guessed at the hidden cause. The only one of the party who failed to realise that anything had gone amiss, was the Squire; and perhaps even his gay genial nature would scarcely have enabled him to close his eyes to the altered state of things, if he had watched them narrowly; but, having once given his adhesion frankly and freely, he troubled himself little more about the course of the love-affair, relying upon Alan's falling back on him as a reserve, if there occurred serious difficulty or obstacle. The troubles threatening his house, were quite enough to engross poor Hubert's attention just then.

A few weeks after the events recorded in that last chapter, Wyverne came down late, as was his wont. His letters were in their usual place on the breakfast table; on the top of the pile lay one, face downwards, showing with exasperating distinctness the fatal scarlet monogram.

Seldom in the course of his life had Alan been so intensely puzzled. He felt angry with Flora Lenox for her folly and perfidy—angry with the person unknown, whose stupidity or malice had put the dangerous document so obtrusively forward—angry, just a very little, with Helen, for betraying, by her heightened colour and nervous manner, that she had already detected the ominous letter—angrier than all with "my lady," whose bright quiet eyes seemed to rest on him judicially, not caring to dissemble her suspicion of his guilt. It is always unwise, of course, to act on impulse, and of all impulses anger is supposed to be the most irrational. Such folly was the more inexcusable in Wyverne, because his power of self-command was quite exceptional; it only enabled him, now, to preserve a perfect outward composure; he acted just as stupidly and viciously as if he had given way to a burst of passion. In the first five seconds he had fully determined to burn that letter, unread—a most unwise resolve, certainly—the only pity was, that he could not bring himself to execute his purpose there and then, or at all events confide his intention to the parties most interested therein. But you must understand that Alan—with all his chivalrous devotion to womankind—held orthodox notions (so we should say) as to the limits of their powers, and by no means favoured any undue usurpation of the Old Dominion; he held, for instance, that the contents of the post-bag, unless voluntarily confided, should be kept as sacred from feminine curiosity as the secrets of the Rosicrucians. In the present case, he could hardly blame Helen for betraying consciousness of a fact that had been, so to speak, "flashed" before her eyes;

siastic or unreserved in her trustfulness, and, indeed, hinted her doubts and fears and general disapprobation, much more plainly than she had hitherto done. She believed Alan *now*, of course, but she could not help thinking that the relations between him and Mrs. Lenox must have been far more intimate than she had had any idea of. It would have been much more satisfactory if he could have opened the letter and shown it to Helen. So he had written to say what he had done? That was right, at all events. (What made "my lady" smile so meaningly just then?) But every day made her more fearful about the future.

"I ought to have been firmer at first, darling," she murmured.

The look of self-reproach was a study, and the penitential sigh rightly executed to a breath.

"It is not that I doubt Alan's meaning fairly; indeed, I believe he does his best; but when a man has lived that wild life, old connexions are very difficult to shake off; sometimes it is years before he is quite free. You don't understand these things; but I do, my Helen, and I know how you would suffer. You are not coldblooded enough to be patient or prudent. Even now, see how unhappy you have been at times lately. I was very weak and very wrong."

It is not worth while recording Helen's indignant disclaimer and eager profession of faith, especially as neither in anywise disturbed or affected the person to whom they were addressed. "My lady" kissed the fair enthusiast, with intense fondness, but not in the least sympathetically or impulsively, and went on with her scruples and regrets and future intentions as if no interruption had occurred. There ensued a certain amount of desultory discussion, warm only on one side, it is needless to say. Lady Mildred did not actually bring maternal authority to the front, but she was *very* firm. At last it came to this. "My lady" was understood to have taken up ,a fresh position, and now to disapprove actively; but she consented to take no offensive step, nor even to mention the changed state of her feelings to the Squire or Alan Wyverne, till some fresh infraction of the existing treaty should justify her in doing so. Then, the crisis was to be sharp and decisive. This was all Helen could gain after much pleading, and perhaps it was as much as could be expected. The Absent, who are always in the wrong, don't often come off so well.

The instant her daughter left her, Lady Mildred rang for her own maid, and said a dozen words to the attentive Abigail; though they were alone in the boudoir, she whispered them. All outward-bound letters at Dene were placed in a certain box, which was kept locked till they were transferred to the post-bag. The confidential *cameriste* carried on her watch-chain several keys, one of which fitted the letter-box with curious exactness. It was not often used; but in the dusk of the evening a small slight figure with a footfall soft and light as the velvet tread of a cheetah, might have been seen (if she had not chosen her time so well) flitting through the great hall, and tarrying for a few seconds in that special corner.

That day there were two letters burnt at Dene, both with their seals unbroken.

Though all was not bitter in her recollections of the last twenty-four hours —those few minutes in the picture-gallery told heavily on the right side— Miss Vavasour's state of mind, when she woke on the following morning, was none of the pleasantest or calmest. Her mother's overt opposition did not dismay or discourage her much; for, after the grateful excitement of the first interview had passed away, she had entertained in spite of herself certain misgivings as to the duration, if not the genuineness of "my lady's" favour, or even neutrality. But the demoiselle could not deny to herself—though she had denied it to her mother—that the latter had spoken truly with regard to her own present unhappiness, and wisely as to the perils of the future. Helen's heart, brave as it was, sank within her as she thought of what it would be if she were destined to experience for years the wearing alternations of hope and fear, pleasure and pain, that had been her portion only for a few weeks. She did believe in her cousin's good faith *almost* implicitly (there was a qualification now), but she did not feel sure that he would always resist temptations; and even with her slight knowledge of the world, she guessed that such might beset his path dangerously often. New enemies to her peace might arise any day; and Nina Lenox's pertinacity showed plainly enough how loth Alan's old friends were to let him go free. Could *she* wonder at their wishing to keep him at all risks, so as at least to hear the sound of his voice sometimes—she, who could never listen to it when softened to a whisper, without a shiver and a tingle in her veins?

"Nina!"

As she uttered that word aloud, and fancied how he might have spoken it, and might speak it again, black drops of bitterness welled up in the girl's heart, poisoning all its frank and generous nature; she set her little white teeth hard, and clenched her slender fingers involuntarily, with a wicked vengeful passion. If wishes could kill, I fear Nina Lenox would have been found next morning dead and cold. Helen had seen her fancied rival once—at the great archery-meeting of the Midland shires—and even her inexperience had appreciated the fascinations of that dark dangerous beauty. She remembered, right well, how one man after another drew near the low seat on which Mrs. Lenox leant back, almost reclining, and how the lady never deigned to disturb her queenly languor by an unnecessary look or word, till one of her especial friends came up: she remembered how the pale statuesque face brightened and softened then: how the rosy lips bestirred themselves to murmur quick and low; and how from under the long heavy eyelashes glances stole out, that Helen felt were eloquent, though she could not quite read their meaning. She remembered watching all this, standing close by, and how the thought had crossed her heart, How pleasant it must be to hold such power.

Do you suppose that, because Miss Vavasour did perhaps more than justice to the charms of the woman she had lately learned to hate, she was unconscious of her own, or modestly disposed to undervalue them? It was not so. Helen was perfectly aware that she herself was rarely lovely and unusually fascinating. If she had been cool enough to reason dispassionately, she would probably have acknowledged that the comparison might safely be defied. Both flowers were passing fair; but on the one lingered still the dewy bloom and scented freshness of the morning; the other, though delicate in hue and full of fragrance still, bore tokens on her petals, crisped here and there and slightly faded, of storm-showers and a fiery noon; nor, at her best could she ever have matched her rival in brilliancy of beauty.

But, supposing that Miss Vavasour had over-estimated herself and underestimated her enemy to such a point as to imagine any comparison absurd, do you imagine it would have lightened one whit her trouble, or softened her bitterness of heart? I think not.

Feminine jealousy is not to be judged by the standard of ordinary ethics; you must measure it by the "Lesbian rule," if at all, and will probably, even so, be wrong in your result. Not only is the field more vast, its phases more varied, but it differs surely in many essentials from the same passion in our sex. Don't be alarmed; I have no intention of writing an essay on so tremendous a subject. The pen of Libyan steel, that the old chroniclers talk about, would be worn down before it was exhausted. Take one distinction as an example. I suppose it is because we have more of conceit, pure and simple; but when we once thoroughly establish the fact, that the man preferred before us is really and truly our inferior in every way, it helps materially to soften the disappointment. Comfortable self-complacency disposes us to be charitable, compassionate, and forgiving; we try (not unsuccessfully) to think, that the bad taste displayed by the Object is rather her misfortune than her fault;

nor do we nourish enduring malice even to him who bears away the bride. Remember the story of Sir Gawaine. When the huge black-browed carle would have reft from him his dame by force, he bound himself to do battle to the death; but when the lady had once made her choice, the Knight of the Golden Tongue thought no more of strife, but rode on his way, resigned if not rejoicing. With our sisters it is not so. Let a woman realize ever so completely the inferiority of her rival, —moral, physical, and social—it will not remove one of her suspicious fears, nor dull the sting of discomfiture when it comes, nor teach forgetfulness of the bitter injury in after days.

When wild Kate Goring created universal scandal and some surprise by eloping with that hirsute riding-master, Cecil Hamersley was intensely disgusted at first, but did not nurse his griefs nor his wrath long; when the unlucky couple came to the grief which was inevitable, Kate's jilted lover pitied them from the bottom of his great honest heart, and seemed to think it the most natural thing in the world, that he should help them to the utmost of his power. It was entirely through Cecil, that Mr. Martingale was enabled to start in the horse-dealing business, which he has conducted with average honesty and fair success ever since.

Take a converse example. Ivor Montressor, for the last year or more, has been laying his homage at the feet of Lady Blanche Pendragon, and it has been accepted, not ungraciously; at the end of last season, it was understood that it was nearly a settled thing. But the wooer has not displayed intense eagerness since in pressing on the preliminaries. There is a certain Annie Fern, whose duty it is to braid the somewhat scanty gold of Lady Blanche's tresses—

the most captivating little witch imaginable, with the most provoking of smiles, that contrasts charmingly with her long, pensive, dark-grey Lancashire eyes. She is prettier a thousand-fold, and pleasanter, and really better educated, than the tall, frigid, indolent descendant of King Uther, whom she has the honour to serve; but that is no excuse, of course, for Ivor's infatuation. A dreadful whisper has got abroad, of late, that he admires the maid above the mistress. Lady Blanche is supposed to be not unconscious of all this; but, if she guessed it, she would not deign to notice it in any way, or even to discharge her fatally attractive handmaid. Let us hope that the vagrant knight will be recalled to a sense of his duty, and, remembering that he is a suitor nearly accepted, "act as such." However it may turn out, let us hope, for Annie's sake (she has been absolutely innocent of intriguing throughout), that it will never happen to her "to be brought low even to the ground, and her honour laid in the dust;"—in such a case, I know who will be the first to set the heel of her slender brodequin on the poor child's neck, and keep it there, too.

No; that conscious superiority does not help them at all. As it is now, so it was in the ancient days. Did it much avail Calypso, that in her realm there was wealth of earth's fairest fruits and flowers, while in Ithaca it was barren all—that ages passed over her own divine beauty, leaving no furrow on her brow, no line of silver in her hair, while with every year the colour faded from the cheek, and the fire dried out of the eyes of her mortal rival—if her guest still persisted in repining? Be sure she never felt more wretched and hapless than when, wreathing her swan's neck haughtily, she spoke those words of scorn :

Οὐ μέν θην κείνης γε χερείων εὔχομαι εἶναι,
Οὐ δέμας, οὐδὲ φυήν, ἐπεὶ οὔ πως οὐδὲ ἔοικεν
Θνητὰς ἀθανάτῃσι δέμας καὶ εἶδος ἐρίζειν.

O gentle Goddess! would your kindly heart have been most pained or pleased, if you could have guessed how ample was the final retribution? You

never knew how often—wearied by petty public broils, worried by Penelope's shrill shrewish tongue, overborne by the staid platitudes of the prim, respectable

Telemachus—your ancient lover strode over bleak rocks and gusty sandhills, till his feet were dipped in the seething foam, and he stood straining his eyes seaward, and drinking in the wind that he fancied blew from Ogygia—the island to which no prow of mortal ever found the backward track. You never knew how often his thoughts rushed back, with a desperate longing and vain regret, to the great cave shrouded by the vine heavy with clusters of eternal grapes, deep in the greenwood where the wild birds loved to roost, girdled by the meadows thick with violets—where cedar and frankincense burned brightly on the hearth, making the air heavy with fragrance—where the wine, that whoso drank became immortal, mantled ever in unstinted goblets—where you bent over your golden shuttle, singing a low sweet song—where your dark divine eyes never wearied in their welcome.

I have always thought that, of all men alive or dead, of all characters in fact or fiction, Odysseus, in his declining years, must have been the most intensely bored. But then, you know, though passing wise in his generation, he was wholly a pagan and half a barbarian. Far be it from me to insinuate, that any Christian and civilized Wanderer, when once reinstated in his domestic comforts, ever wastes a regret on a lost love beyond the sea.

------

## CHAPTER XV.

### PAVIA.

It is said, that when a man is struck blind by lightning, he never forgets afterwards the minutest object on which his eyes rested when the searing flash shot across them. Even so, when the crash of the great misfortune is over, and we wake from dull, heavy insensibility to find the light gone out of our life for ever, we remember with unnatural distinctness the most trivial incidents of the last hours of sunshine; we actually seem to see them over again some-

times, as we grope our way, hopelessly and helplessly, through the darkness that will endure till it is changed into night; for it may be, that from our spirit's eyes the blinding veil will never be lifted, till they unclose in the dawn of the Resurrection.

Both the cousins had good cause to treasure in their memories every word and gesture that passed between them on one particular evening; for it was the last—the very last—of pure, unalloyed happiness that either of them ever knew. Years afterwards, Wyverne could have told you to a shade the colour of the ribbons on Helen's dress, the fashion of the bracelets on each of her wrists, the scent of the flowers she wore. She, too, remembered right well his attitude when they parted; she could have set her foot on the very square of marble on which his was planted; she could recall the exact intonation of his gentle voice, as he bade her farewell on the lowest step of the great staircase, for he was to start very early the next morning. She remembered, too, how that night she lingered before a tall pier-glass, passing her hands indolently through her magnificent hair, while the light fell capriciously on the dark shining masses, rejoicing in the contemplation of her surpassing loveliness; she remembered how she smiled at her image in saucy triumph, as the thought rose in her heart—that Nina Lenox's mirror held no picture like this.

Ah, Helen, better it were the glass had been broken then; it may show you, in after years, a face disdainful of its own marvellous beauty, or tranquil in its superb indifference, according to your varying mood; but a happy one—never any more.

The Squire had to go to town for a few days, and Alan, who had also business there, accompanied him. They were to be back for Christmas-day—the last in that week. Wyverne got through his affairs quicker than he had anticipated, so he determined to return a day sooner, without waiting for his uncle. His evil Genius was close to his shoulder even here; for, if Hubert Vavasour had been present, it is just possible, though not probable, that things might have gone differently.

Alan started by an early train, so that he arrived at Dene soon after midday. Perhaps it was fancy, but he thought that the face of the Chief Butler wore rather a curious and troubled expression; if it were possible for that sublimely vacuous countenance to betray any human emotion, something like a compassionate interest seemed to ruffle its serenity. The letters of expected visitors were always placed on a particular table in the great hall. Again—on the top of the pile waiting for Alan, lay one in the well-known handwriting of Nina Lenox. This time it was placed naturally, with the seal downwards.

The first, the very first imprecation that had ever crossed Wyverne's lips in connexion with womankind, passed them audibly, when his eye lighted on the fatal envelope. He knew right well that it held the death-warrant of his love; but even now the curse was not levelled at the authoress of his trouble, but at his own evil fortune. As he took up the letters, he asked, half mechanically, where his aunt and cousin were. The answer was ominous:

"My lady was exceedingly unwell, and confined to her room. Miss Vavasour was somewhere in the Pleasance, but she wished to be sent for as soon as Sir Alan arrived." He had written the night before, to say he was coming.

Wyverne walked on into the library without another word. For the moment he felt stupid and helpless, like a man just waking after an overdose of narcotics. He sat down, and began turning the letter over and over as if he were trying to guess at its contents. From its thickness it was evidently a long one—two or three note-sheets at least. A very few minutes, however, brought back his self-composure entirely, and he knew what he had to do. It was clear the letter could not be burnt unopened, this time. He drew his breath hard once, and set his teeth savagely; then he tore the envelope and began to read deliberately.

Alan once said, when he happened to be discussing feminine ethics—"I can conceive women affecting one with any amount of pain or pleasure; but I don't think anything they could do would ever *surprise* me." Rash words those—perhaps they deserved confutation; at any rate the speaker was thoroughly astounded now. He knew that no look or syllable had ever passed between himself and Nina Lenox that could be tortured into serious love-making; yet this letter of hers was precisely such as might have been written by a passionate, sinful woman, to the man for whom she had sacrificed enough to make her desertion almost a second crime. There was nothing of romance in it—nothing that the most indulgent judge could construe into Platonic affection — it was miserably *practical* from end to end. No woman alive, reading such words addressed to her husband or her lover, could have doubted, for a second, what his relations with the writer had been, even if they were ended now. Griselda herself would have risen in revolt. It is needless to give even the heads of that delectable epistle. Mrs. Lenox acknowledged that she wrote in despite of Alan's repeated prohibition ; but — *c'était plus fort qu'elle*, and all the rest of it. One point she especially insisted on. However *he* might scorn her, surely he would not give *others* the right to do so ? He would burn the letter, she knew he would, without speaking of it, far less showing it to any human being ; she suffered enough, without having her miserable weakness betrayed for the amusement of Miss Vavasour.

Every line that Alan read increased his bewilderment. Was it possible that dissipation, and trouble, and intrigue had told at last on the busy brain, so that it had utterly given way ? Such things had been ; there was certainly something strange and unnatural in the character of the writing, sometimes hurried till the words ran into each other, sometimes laboured and constrained as if penned by a hand that hesitated and faltered. He knew that Nina was rash beyond rashness, and would indulge her sudden caprices at any cost, without reckoning the sin or even the shame, but he could not believe in such a wild *velleité* as this.

" She must be mad."

Wyverne spoke those words aloud; they were answered by a sigh, or rather a quick catching of the breath, close to his shoulder; he started to his feet, and stood face to face with Helen ,Vavasour, who had entered unobserved while he sat in his deep reverie.

Helen was still in her walking-dress; a fall of lace slightly shaded her brow and cheeks, but it could not dissemble the bright feverish flush that made the white pallor of all the lower part of the face more painfully apparent ; the pupils of her great eyes were contracted, and they glittered with the strange *serpentine* light which is one of the evidences of poison by belladonna; but neither cheeks nor eyes bore trace of. a tear. She had schooled herself to speak quite deliberately and calmly ; the effect was apparent, not, only in the careful accentuation of each syllable, but in her voice—neither harsh nor hollow, yet utterly changed.

" Mad, Alan ? Yes, we have all been mad. It is time that this should come to an end. You think, so, too, I am sure."

Wyverne had known, from the first moment that he saw the letter, how it would fare with him; but the bitter irritation which had hardened his heart on a former occasion was not there now; he could not even be angry with those who had brought him to this pass; all other feelings were swallowed up in an intense, half-unselfish sorrow.

" Dear child, it *is* more than time that you should be set free from me and my miserable fortunes. We will drift away, alone, henceforth, as we ought always to have done. It was simply a sin, ever to have risked dragging you down with the wreck; it must founder soon. Ah, remember, I said so once, and you—never mind that —I'll make what amends I can ; but I have done fearful harm already. Three months more of this, would wear you out in mind and body ; even now they will tell in your life like years. We must part now. Darling, try to forget,

and to forgive, too—for you have much to forgive.",

He stopped for a moment, but went on quickly, answering the wild, haggard question of her startled eyes ; she had understood those last words wrongly.

" No—not that ;" he struck the letter he still held, impatiently, with a finger of the other hand. " I told you once, I would never ask you to believe me again as you did then. I don't ask you to act as if you believed, now. But, Helen, you will know one day before we die, whether I have been sinned against or sinning in this thing; I feel sure of it, or—I should doubt the justice of God."

The soft, sad voice quite broke down the calmness it had cost Helen so much to assume ; she could not listen longer, and broke in with all her own impetuosity—

" Ah, Alan! don't ask it; it is not right of you. You know I *must* believe whatever you tell me, and I dare not—do you hear—I dare not, now. It is too late. I have promised—" and she stopped, shivering.

Wyverne's look was keen and searching; but it was not at *her* that his brows were bent. He took the little trembling hand in his own, and tried to quiet the leaping pulses, and his tones were more soothing than ever.

" I know it all, darling ; I know how bravely you have tried to keep your faith with me ; I shall thank you for it to my life's end, not the less because neither you nor I were strong enough to fight against fate, and—Aunt Mildred. I cannot blame her: if I could, *you* should not hear me. She was right to make you promise before you came here. It was unconditionally, of course ?"

The girl's cheek flushed painfully.

" There was a condition," she murmured under her breath; "but I hardly dare. Yes; I dare say anything—to you. Mamma sent for me when that letter came, or I should never have heard of it. She did not say how *she* knew. You cannot think how determined she is. I *was* angry at first;

but when I saw how hard she was, I was frightened; and, Alan, indeed, indeed I did all I could to soften her. At last she said that she would not insist on my giving you up, if—if you would show me that letter. Ah, Alan—what have *I* done?"

He had dropped her hand before she ended, and stood looking at her with an expression that she had never dreamt could dwell in his eyes—repellant to the last degree, too cold and contemptuous for anger. It softened, though, in a second or two at the sight of Helen's distress.

"Did you doubt what my answer would be? I am very sure your mother never doubted: she knew me better."

No answer; but she bowed her beautiful head till it could rest on his arm; a stormy sob or two made her slender frame quiver down to the feet; and then, with a rush like that of Undine's unlocked well, the pent-up tears came. The passion-gust soon passed away; and her cousin kept silence till Helen was calm again; then he spoke very gently and gravely.

"Do forgive me; I did not mean to be harsh. You only gave your message, I know; but it was like a stab to hear your lips utter it. Child, look up at me, and listen. I need not tell you I am speaking God's truth—you feel it. You know what I have done to stop these accursed letters. I believe the writer to be mad; but that will not help us. I think I would stand by and see her burned at the stake, as better women have been before her, if by that sacrifice I could keep your love. But—if I knew, that by this one act I could make you my very own, so that nothing but the grave could part us—I would not show you a line of her letter. It may be, that there are higher duties which justify the betrayal of an unhappy woman, when her very confidence is a sin. I dare say I am wrong in my notions of honour, as well as in other things; but, such as they are, I'll stand by them to the death, and—to what I think must be harder to bear than death. I don't hesitate, because I have no choice. I know that I am casting, this moment, my life's happiness away: Helen—see—my hand does not tremble."

He tossed the letter as he spoke into the wood fire blazing beside them; it dropped between two red logs, and, just flashing up for a second, mingled with the heap of ashes.

Now, Wyverne's conduct will appear to many absurdly Quixotic, and some will think it deserves a harsher name than folly. I decline to argue either point. It seems to me — when one states fairly at the beginning of a story, "that it has no Hero"—the writer is by no means called upon to identify himself with the sentiments of his principal character, much less to defend them. I have not intended to hold up Alan Wyverne either as a model or a warning. He stands there for what he is worth—a man not particularly wise or virtuous or. immaculate, but frank and affectionate by nature, with firmness enough to enable him to act consistently according to the light given him. Whether that light was a false one or no, is a question that each particular reader may settle d son gré. Purely on the grounds of probability, I would suggest that others have sacrificed quite as much for scruples quite as visionary. Putting aside the legions of lives that have been thrown away on doubtful points of social professional honour, have not staid and grave men submitted to the extremes of penury, peril, and persecution, because they would not give up some favourite theory involving no question of moral right or wrong? The *Peine forte et dure* could scarcely have been an agreeable process; yet a Jesuit chose to endure it, and died under the iron press, rather than plead before what he held to be an incompetent tribunal. You constantly say of such cases, "One can't help respecting the man, to a certain extent." Now, I don't ask you to respect Alan Wyverne: it is enough, if you admit that his folly was not without parallels.

Among those who could blame or despise him, Helen Vavasour was not numbered: she never felt more proud of her lover than at that moment when his own act had parted them irrevoeably. She was not of the "weeping willow" order, you know; the tears still hanging on her eyelashes were the first she had shed since childhood in serious sorrow. Quick and impetuous enough in temper, she was so unaccustomed to indulge any violent demonstration of feeling, that she felt somewhat ashamed of having yielded to it now. But the brief outbreak did her good; it lightened her brain and brought back elasticity to her nerves. There is nothing like a storm for clearing the atmosphere. Nevertheless, the haughty, bold spirit was for the moment thoroughly beaten down. There was something in her accent piteous beyond the power of words to describe, as she whispered half to herself,

"Yes, we must part; but it is too, too hard."

"Hardest of all," he said, "to part on a pretext like this. There is either madness or magic, or black treachery against me, I swear. Some day we shall know. But, darling, sooner or later it must have come. I have felt that for weeks past, though I tried hard to delude myself. I must say good bye to Dene in an hour. When shall I see the dear old house again? I am so sorry for Uncle Hubert, too. If he had been here — no, perhaps it is best so— there would have been more wounded, and we could never have won the day."

"Don't go yet: ah, not yet"— the sweet voice pleaded—all its dangerous melody had stolen back to it now, and lithe fingers twined themselves round Alan's, as though they would never set him free.

But Wyverne was aware that the self-control which had carried him through so far, was nearly exhausted. He had to think for *both*, you see; and it was the more trying, because the part of Moderator was so utterly new to him; nevertheless, he played it honestly and bravely.

"I dare not stay. I *must* see Uncle Hubert before I sleep; and it is only barely possible, if I leave Dene in half an hour. Listen, my Helen: I am not saying good-bye to *you*, though I say it to our past. I lose my wife; but I do not intend to lose my cousin. I will see you again as soon as I can do so safely. A great black wall is built up now, between the future, and all that we two have said and done: I will never try to pass it again by thought or word. You will forget all this. Hush, dear. You think it impossible at this moment, but *I* know better. You will play a grand part in the world one of these days, and perhaps you may want a 'friend—a real friend. Then you shall think of me. I will help you with heart and hand as long as life lasts; and I will do so in all truth and honour—as I hope to meet my dead mother, and Gracie, and you, in heaven."

She did not answer in words. The interview lasted about a hundred seconds longer, but I do not feel called upon to chronicle the last details. Writers, as well as narrators, have a right to certain reserves.

Alan Wyverne was away from Dene before the half hour was out; but he left a sealed note behind him for his aunt. "My lady" was waiting the issue somewhat anxiously; it is needless to say, her health was the merest pretext. She read the note through, calmly enough; but, when she opened her escritoire to lock it up safely, her hands shook like aspen-leaves, and she drank off eagerly the strongest dose of "red lavender" that had passed her lips for many a day.

Does not that decisive interview seem absurdly abrupt and brief? It is true that I have purposely omitted many insignificant words and gestures; but if all these had been chronicled, it would still have been disappointingly matter-of-fact and meagre.

Nevertheless — believe it — to build up a life's happiness is a work of time and labour, aided by great good fortune: to ruin and shatter it utterly is a question of a short half hour, even where no ill luck intervenes. It took months of toil to build the good ship Hesperus, though her timbers were seasoned and ready to hand; it took hours of trouble to launch her when thoroughly equipped for sea; but it took only a few minutes of **wave-and-wind-play**, to shiver her into splinters, when her keel crushed down on the reef of Norman's Woe.

———

## CHAPTER XVI.

### MISANTHROPOS.

On the morning after the most disastrous of all his bad nights at hazard, Charles Fox was found by a friend who called, in fear and trembling, to offer assistance or condolence, lying on his sofa in lazy luxury, deep in an eclogue of Virgil. The magnificent indifference was probably not assumed, for there was little tinsel about that large honest nature, and he was not the man to indulge in private theatricals. Since I read that anecdote, I have always wondered that the successes achieved by the great Opposition leader were not more lasting and complete. Among the triumphs of mind over matter, that power of thoroughly abstracting the thoughts from recent grief or trouble, seems to stand first and foremost. Such sublime stoicism implies a strength of character and of will, that separates its possessor at once from his fellows: sooner or later, He must rule, and they must obey.

Alan Wyverne was not so rarely gifted. The bustle of the heavy journey from Dene to the railroad, and the uncertainty about catching the train, helped him at first; but when all that was over, and he was fairly on his way to town, he was forced to *think*, whether he would or no. Anything was better than brooding over the past; he tried desperately to force his thoughts into the immediate future—to imagine what he should say to his uncle, and how the Squire would take the heavy tidings. The effort was worse than vain. The strong stream laughed at the puny attempts to stem it, sweeping all such obstacles away, as it rushed down its appointed channel. All the plans he had talked over with Helen, even to the smallest details of their proposed domestic economy, came back one by one; he remembered every word of their last playful argument, when he tried to persuade her that certain luxuries for her boudoir at Wyverne Abbey were necessities not to be dispensed with; he remembered how they had speculated as to the disposal of the money, if his solitary bet on the next Derby, 1000 to 10 about a rising favourite—should by any chance come off right; how they had weighed gravely the advantages of three months of winter in Italy against the pleasures of an adventurous expedition whose turning-point should be the Lebanon. What did it matter now who won or lost? Was it only yesterday that he had an interest in all these things? Yesterday—between him and that word there seemed already a gulf of years. Yesterday, he had felt so proud in anticipating the triumphs of his beautiful bride; now, he could only think of her certain success with a heavy sinking of the heart, or a hot fierce jealousy; for she was all his own treasure then; one night had made her the world's again. That miserable journey scarcely lasted four hours; but when it ended, Wyverne was as much morally changed as he might have been, physically, by a long wasting sickness.

Does it seem strange that a man, who up to this time had met all reverses with a careless gaiety that was almost provoking, should go down so helplessly now before a blow that would scarcely stagger many of our acquaintance? A great deal, in such cases, depends on the antecedents. Human nature, however elastic and enduring, will only stand a certain amount of "beating." When Captain Lyndon is in good luck and good funds, he accepts the loss of a hundred or two with dignified equanimity, if not with chirping cheerfulness; but supposing the bad night comes at the end of a long evil "vein"—when financial prospects are gloomier than the yellow fog outside—when the face of his banker is set against him, as it were a millstone—when that reckless soldier

Would liever mell with the fiends of hell,
Than with Craig's Court and its band.

O, my friend! I marvel not that a muttered imprecation shot out from under your moustache, last night, when the Queen of Hearts showed her comely face—your adversaries having the deal, at three.

Now Alan Wyverne had been playing for his last stake, so far as he knew: he had put it down with some diffidence and hesitation, and it had followed the rest into the gulf, leaving him without a chance of winning back his losses. Under the circumstances some depression, surely, was not wholly despicable. Remember, he was not so young as he had been: though still on the better side of middle age, he had in many ways anticipated his prime, and had not much left to look forward to.

Qu'on est bien dans un grenier
Quand on a vingt ans!

So sings Béranger, well, if not wisely. But—add another score of years or so—what will the lodger say of his quarters? Those seven flights of stairs are dark and steep; the bread is hard and tasteless; the wine painfully sour and thin; the fuel runs short, and it is bitter cold, for Lisette is no longer there to hang her cloak over the crazy casement, laughing at the whistle of the baffled wind.

Wyverne saw his uncle that night. The Squire was equally provoked and grieved; the intelligence took him completely by surprise, for he had never guessed that anything was going wrong; he would not allow at first that the engagement was irrevocably broken off, and wished to try what he could do to re-cement it; but Alan was so hopelessly firm on the point that Hubert was forced to yield. He believed in his nephew implicitly, and acquitted him of blame from first to last; but he was completely puzzled by Mrs. Lenox's strange conduct; he only dropped the subject when he saw how evidently it pained Alan to pursue it.

"I shall not write, even to reproach her," the latter said. "I am too heartsick of her and her caprices. I suppose she will explain herself if we ever meet, and I have patience to listen."

When they parted, the Squire clasped Wyverne's hand hard, looking wistfully into his face.

"I—I did my best, boy," he said, huskily.

The old genial light came back for an instant, only an instant, into the other's weary eyes, and he returned the gripe right cordially.

"Do you think I don't know that?" he answered; "or that I shall ever forget it? We all did our best; but Aunt Mildred has her way, after all. Take care of Helen; she will need it. And if you would write soon to tell me the truth about her, it would be so very kind."

The next morning Alan started for the North, alone. If the Christmastide was dreary at Wyverne Abbey, it was not a "merry" one at Dene. The Squire did not seek to disguise his discontent, though he said little on the subject of the broken engagement, either to his wife or Helen. There was a gloomy reserve in his manner towards the former, that showed that he more than suspected her of unfair play; to the latter he was unusually gentle and considerate. Miss Vavasour bore up bravely. No one looking at the girl's pale proud face would have dreamt of the dull, heavy pain coiled round her heart, like the serpent round Don Roderic in the tomb. She accepted her father's caresses gratefully, and her mother's with placid indifference. No words of recrimination had passed between these two; but there is an instinct of distrust as well as of love or fear; the last few days had slain sympathy outright, and even the tough sensibility of the cool diplomatist was not always unmoved as she realized the utter estrangement. So even "my lady," though the game was won, did not feel in vein for the festivities of the season. Her conscience had long ceased to trouble her, when it was a question of expediency; she compassionated the sorrows of her misguided daughter about as much as a great surgeon does the sufferings of a patient who has just passed under his knife; but she was not quite philosopher enough, wholly to disbelieve in Retrihution. Her dreams of a brilliant future for Helen were sometimes disturbed by a vision of sad earnest eyes, pleading only that truth might be met by truth— she had answered their appeal so well!

It was an odd sort of life that Wyverne led at the Abbey. He took to shooting over his broad manors, with a dogged determination that rejoiced the hearts of his keepers and tenants and every one interested in the preservation of his game. He went out always early in the morning, and never returned till darkness set in; then he slept for a couple of hours, dined late, and sat smoking and musing far into the night. But it did him good in every way: the strong exercise and the keen north-country air stirred up the iron in his blood, and braced his nerves as well as his sinews. I believe that permanent melancholy implies a morbid condition, not only of the mind but the body. I believe—be it understood this is only a theory, so far—that a man will not *mope* in the Queen's Bench, though he may hate himself occasionally, and find the position irksome, if he sticks to cold water and rackets. The genial hopefulness which had resisted so many rude shocks, was dead in Alan for ever and aye; but it was not in his nature to become sullen and saturnine; he rejoiced simply and sincerely when his uncle's letter brought good news of Helen; he was not selfish enough to quarrel with his lost love because her wreath was not always ostentatiously twined of the willow. Some men are never satisfied unless they leave more than half the misery behind them.

Wyverne had been at the Abbey about a month, when he got a letter which surprised him not a little. Mr. Haldane wrote, to beg his nephew to visit him, for a single night, and pressed it on the ground that his health was failing.

Castle Dacre was situated far up in the hills, thirty miles or so from the Abbey. They had nicknamed it "Castle Dangerous" through the country-side, for the roads all round it were so infamous as to be sometimes impassable. Very few, of late years, had found it worth their while to encounter such perils. It was a huge dreary pile—a tall grey keep in the centre, dating back to the time of the Danes: round this long low ranges of more modern buildings were grouped, all in the same pale gaunt granite. The trees clustering about the castle in clumps, and thickly studded over the bleak park, hardly took away from the bare desolate effect; some of them were vast in the trunk and broad in the top, but it seemed as if the bitter north wind had checked their growth, though it could not waste their strength. You shivered involuntarily when you looked at the house from the outside; the contrast was the more striking when you entered. The whole of the interior was almost oppressively light and warm; great fires blazed in huge grates in the most unexpected corners, and bright lamps burned in the remotest nooks of passage, and hall, and corridor. A Belgravian establishment might have been maintained for a whole season at the cost of the coals and oil consumed in Dacre Castle; but such was the whim of its eccentric and autocratic master.

Alan Wyverne arrived very late, and did not see his uncle till they met at dinner. Mr. Haldane must always have been small and slight of frame; he was thin, now, to emaciation; there was not a particle of colour in the face or the delicate hands; the articulations in the last were so strongly marked as almost to spoil the perfection of their shape. His features might have been handsome once, and not disagreeable in their expression, but evil tempers and physical suffering had left ruinous traces there; the thin lips had forgotten how to smile, though they were meaning enough when they curled sardonically; he had a curious way of perpetually drawing himself together, as if struck with a sudden chill.

He was just the sort of man you would have set down as a great judge of pictures and collector of curiosities. So it was. The whole house was overflowing with the choicest productions of nature and art, gathered from every quarter of the known world. A long gallery was completely filled with the rarest specimens of china that the last three centuries could display. Some of our connoisseurs would have sold their souls for the plundering of that one chamber.

The dinner was simply perfection. You might have feasted for a whole season at half the best houses in London, and have missed the artistic effects which awaited you in that lonely castle of the far North. The wines of every sort were things to dream of. Mr. Haldane drank nothing but Burgundy. Even Alan Wyverne, accustomed as he was to witness deep wassail, felt wonder approaching to fear, as he saw his host drain glass after glass of the strong rich liquor without betraying a sign of its influence, either by the faintest flush on his thin parchment cheek, or a change of inflection in his low monotonous voice. It seemed as if he were trying to infuse some warmth into his veins, in defiance of a curse laid upon him—to remain frozen and statuelike forever.

While dinner lasted, the conversation went languishing on, never coming to a full stop, but never in the least animated. It was evident that the thoughts of both often wandered far away from the subject they were talking of. At last they drew their great arm-chairs up to the fire, one on each side of the horse-shoe table, with a perfect barricade of glass between them in the shape of decanters and claret-jugs. For the first ten minutes after they were left alone the host kept silence, leaning forward and spreading his hands over the fierce fire; they were so thin and white that the light seemed to pass through them as it does through transparent china. He raised his head suddenly and glanced aside at his companion, who was evidently musing, with an expression half inquisitive, half satirical, in his keen grey eyes.

"So everything is at an end between you and Helen Vavasour. I am very glad of it, and not the least surprised."

It is never pleasant to have one's reveries abruptly broken; the nerves are agacés, if nothing worse. Besides this, both words and manner grated on Alan's sensibilities disagreeably. He did not fancy those thin cynical lips pronouncing that name with such scant ceremony; so his tone was anything but conciliatory.

"Thank you. I don't seem to care much about being congratulated, or condoled with, either; and I cannot conceive what interest the subject can have for you. You ignored it pretty decisively some months ago. Perhaps you will be good enough to do so now."

The look on his face, that had been simply listless before, grew hard and defiant while he was speaking. If Bernard Haldane was inclined to take offence, he certainly controlled his temper wonderfully. He filled a great glass to the brim with Chambertin, held it for a minute against the blaze, letting the light filter through the gorgeous purple, and drained it slowly before he replied—

"I am not surprised at your engagement being broken off, because I know right well with whom you had to deal. I am glad, because I have always taken an interest in you, Alan. You don't believe it; but it is true nevertheless; and I do so still. I would sooner see a man I cared for dead, than married to Mildred Vavasour's daughter."

Wyverne's anger ceased, as soon as he saw that the old man had some reason, real or fancied, for his strange conduct; but he spoke coldly still.

"Strong words, sir. I suppose you have strong provocation to justify them?"

Bernard Haldane drew a folded letter from his breast-pocket, and put it into the other's hand, silently. The paper was yellow with age, the ink faint and faded; but Alan knew the handwriting instantly. His astonishment deepened as he read on. Was it possible that his cool, calculating, diplomatic aunt could have penned such words as these—words in which passion seemed to live and vibrate still, untamed by passage through thirty years?

Mr. Haldane drained two glasses in rapid succession while the letter was reading. There was no thickness or hesitation in his voice when he spoke again, but it was hard and hoarse, as if his throat were dust-dry in spite of all the Burgundy.

8

"That is her last letter—the last of forty or more. I have them all still, and I think I know them all by heart. You may laugh out if you like; I shall not be angry. She wrote once more—not a letter, only a note—to break all off, without a word of remorse for herself or pity for me. A fresh fancy or a better match came across her, so she turned me adrift like a dog she was tired of. She would have given me a dog's death, too, if she could, I dare say; for, till she was married, she never felt safe. Do you wonder now, or blame me, for what I have said and done or *not* done?"

Six weeks ago such a story as this would have won hearty sympathy from Alan Wyverne; but he had suffered too lately himself, to be moved by a tale of wrong thirty years old. He could not forget Bernard Haldane's answer to his own letter, and the idea would haunt him that in some way or other it had materially affected his matrimonial prospects.

"I neither wonder nor blame," he said, wearily. "If any one is right in visiting the sins of the mothers on the children, I suppose you were. Certainly, 'my lady' has a good deal to answer for. I understand her look now, when I mentioned your name. Yes, I *do* wonder at one thing. I don't understand why you married my father's sister."

The old man glanced darkly at the speaker from under his strong grey eyebrows.

"I hope my poor wife never knew the lie I uttered at the altar; or, if she did, that she forgave me before she died. But God knew it, and punished it. Alan—you are my nearest heir."

After those significant words there was silence for some minutes, only broken by a faint tinkle and gurgle, as the host filled his glass repeatedly, and his guest followed the example in more moderate fashion. At last Mr. Haldane spoke again.

"Alan, I wonder what would be your line, if you came into this inheritance? Do you know, it is larger than the one you threw away?"

A few weeks ago, when Wyverne's fortunes were bound up with Helen Vavasour's, such a speech as that would have sent a hot thrill of hope through all his being: he heard it now with an indifference which was not in the least assumed.

"It would be a hazardous experiment," he answered, carelessly. "They say there is a great pleasure in hoarding, when you have more money than you know what to do with. I never tried it; perhaps I should take to avarice for a change. But I might take to playing again: it's just as likely as not; and then everything would go, if my present luck lasted—the pictures and the gems, and the china, and the mosaics. It would be a thousand pities, too; I don't believe there's such another collection in England."

Bernard Haldane seemed determined, that night, not to be provoked by anything that his nephew could do or say. He was so accustomed to be surrounded by helpless dependents, bowing themselves without remonstrance or resistance before his tyrannical temper, that he had got weary of obsequiousness. Alan's haughty *nonchalance*, though it evidently proceeded from dislike or displeasure, rather refreshed the old cynic than otherwise.

"You are honest at all events," he muttered; "it's no use trying to bribe you into forgetting injuries; if you *will* bear malice,—there's an end of it. We won't speak of inheritances: they put unpleasant thoughts into a man's head, whose health is breaking faster every day."

Once more a shiver ran through the speaker's emaciated frame, as it cowered and shrunk together; and once more the thin white hands spread themselves eagerly to the blaze. After a pause he rose, evidently to go, and there was something actually approaching to cordiality in his manner.

"It is hardly fair to ask you to stay on in this dreary place; but it would please me very much if you would spare me a few days. They tell me the covers are full of game, and you can have a hundred beaters at half an hour's notice. You will be nearly as much alone here as at the Abbey, for I never appear till dinner-time, and I go to bed very early, as you see. The Burgundy is a good sleeping-draught, but it must be humoured. You will stay over to-morrow, at least? I am glad of that. Perhaps you would like to see the keeper? Give any orders you please, not only about this, but about anything you may fancy: I *can* answer for their being promptly obeyed. Good-night."

His step, as he left the room, was slow and feeble; but not the slightest uncertainty or unsteadiness of gait gave token of the deep incessant draughts of fiery liquor that would long ago have dizzied any ordinary brain. Every family of ancient name, besides its statesmen and soldiers, preserves the moist memory of some bacchanalian Titan, whose exploits are inscribed on bowl, or tankard, or beaker. We may not doubt that there were giants in those days; but the prowess of the mightiest of all those stalwart squires would have been hardly tried, if he had "drunk fair" that night with the little, wan, withered hypochondriac.

---

## CHAPTER XVII.

### A WISE MAN IN THE EAST.

DAY succeeded day, and Alan Wyverne still lingered at Dacre Castle. He could hardly have told you what kept him there. The shooting certainly was a great attraction, for, though the season closed in the first week of his stay, there were snipe and wild-fowl enough to have found work for half a dozen guns; but it was not the only one. The truth was, that a sort of liking had sprung up between the cynical host and his quiet guest. No amount of deep drinking could warm Bernard Haldane into an approach to conviviality; but his morose, moody temper decidedly softened during the few hours that he spent each evening in Alan's society.

There was no sympathy perhaps, strictly speaking, between these two, but there was a certain affinity of suffering. The same soft white hand had stricken them both sorely, though one wound was yet green, and the other had been rankling more than a score of years. After that first night, neither made the faintest allusion to the subject; but ever and anon, when they were talking about pictures or other things in which both took an interest, the conversation would drop suddenly, and a silence would ensue as if by mutual consent; then, each felt conscious that his companion's thoughts were wandering in the same direction as his own, and with equal bitterness. After, a few minutes you might have seen each break from his reverie, with the same half angry impatience, as if despising himself for the weakness of such idle musing, knowing all the while that the return of the dreaming-fit was as much a certainty and a question of hours as the rising of the morrow's sun.

Wyverne's visit would probably nave been still further prolonged, if an invitation had not come one morning, suiting his present humour so exactly, that he accepted it without a moment's hesitation. An old comrade of Alan's was on the point of starting in his yacht for a roving cruise round the shores of Greece and Syria, with an intention of penetrating as far as the hunting-grounds that lie westward of the lower spurs of the Caucasus: indeed, there was a charming indefiniteness about the whole thing; the limits of their wanderings and the time of their return were to depend entirely on circumstances and the fancy of the travellers. Raymond Graham had heard of his friend's late disappointment, though he made no allusion to it in his letter, only enlarging on the sporting prospects of the expedition and the attractions of a very pleasant party. He thought it would be just the proposal to tempt Wyverne, and he guessed right.

None of the new-fashioned remedies beat some of the old ones, after all.

Change of climate and change of scene enable the sufferer to make a stand against sickness of body or mind just, as effectually as they did four thousand years ago.

Hot blinding tears stream down Dido's stricken face as she steals on board her galley in the harbour of Tyre; for nights she will not close her heavy eyes, lest a dead man should stand by her couch pointing to the gash of Pygmalion's dagger; the boldest of her true friends and leal vassals dares not trouble with a word of comfort that great hopeless sorrow. But see—the headlands of Cyprus are yet blue in the leeward distance, and the rich blood has begun to colour the pale cheek again; when the dark lashes lift, men see that the divine light is not quenched in the glorious eyes; nay, the sweet lips do not dissemble a faint, sad smile as she hears Bitias boasting loud of the bride he will win before sundown. Of a truth, I think the fair Queen's dreams will cease to be spectre-haunted, before her prow touches ground in the sands of Bagradas.

They are more definite now as to the seasons of donning and doffing their weeds, and will not set their tresses free a day too soon; but, O Benedict, my friend, are you sanguine enough to believe that so long a voyage would be needed, to replace despairing grief by decorous woe, in the desolate bosom of your widow, or mine?

Remember, we have been speaking of creatures, many of whom must find a certain pleasure in a mild languid melancholy. "They would not, if they could, be gay." Wyverne's temperament, though it contained womanlike elements of gentleness and tenderness, was essentially masculine. He was, indeed, stouter of heart and stronger in will than most of the rough-and-ready Stryver sort, who cannot argue without blustering or advise without bullying; who, neither in love nor war, ever lay aside the speaking-trumpet. The battle of life had gone hard against him of late; but he did not therefore conclude that there was nothing left worth living for. The example just then before his eyes was not without a significant warning. Alan felt that absence from England would suit him best for awhile; but he had no idea of banishing himself indefinitely. The proposed expedition would have tempted him at any period of his life, and he looked forward to it now with a real interest and an honest determination to make the best of everything.

Bernard Haldane did not attempt to alter his nephew's purpose; indeed, he approved of it thoroughly; but he sat much later than usual on the last evening, and seemed loth to say good-bye.

"If I am alive when you return, you will come here, I hope," he said at last. "If I am gone, I am sure you will, for good reasons. Your programme promises well—so well that it would be a pity not to carry it out thoroughly. Don't let money stop you. Where you have to deal with semi-barbarians, it's often a mere question between silver and steel; the first saves an infinity of trouble, and, I think, it's the most moral argument of the two. So take my advice, and bribe Sheikhs and chiefs to any extent. I have written to-day to my bankers, to give you unlimited credit there. Now, don't annoy me by making objections. You know perfectly well that I sacrifice nothing. If I did, my generosity would still begin very late—too late, I fear. It would be the falsest delicacy if you were to refuse; for, though we have been almost strangers hitherto, through my fault, Alan—you are my nephew, after all."

He laid his hand gently, almost timidly, on Wyverne's as he finished speaking, and the thin white fingers quivered with his nervous eagerness, though they remained always deadly cold.

It must be a very mortifying and humiliating time when an old man, who has started in life with exceptional advantages of intellect and fortune, is compelled to admit the probability of the whole thing having been a mistake from first to last; unless there is some grievous sin to be acknowledged and repented of, I think it would be more satisfactory to go blundering on unconsciously to the end. To such a frame of mind Mr. Haldane had been coming gradually for days past. He quite realized the fact that, in default of a son, he would have chosen Wyverne out of all England as the heir to his broad lands and great possessions. He knew enough of Alan's character to feel sure that no more than common kindness in earlier days would have been needed to win his affection and keep it; but he had held him at arm's length with the rest till it was too late to do anything better than change dislike into indifference. For thirty years he had sat alone, "nursing his wrath to keep it warm," fancying that he could make the many suffer for the crime of one. He had succeeded perhaps in discomfiting a few miserable dependents, and in disappointing or disgusting a few relatives and friends; but he had never ruffled a rose-leaf in the couch of the fair "enemy who did him that dishonour." Who had been the real sufferer, after all? The unhappy misanthrope almost gnashed his teeth as he answered the question, and acknowledged the childish impotence of his rancour. If he had only had the courage at first, to look his wrongs and griefs fairly in the face, they might have been easily kept at bay; it was too late to strive for the mastery when they had become a part of his morbid being. He saw all this clearly enough now. The old, old story—theory perfected, when to work it out is physically impossible—the alchemist just grasping the Great Arcanum, without a stiver left to buy powder for the crucible or coal for the furnace.

Nevertheless, that inveterate habit of looking at things *au noir* rather misled Bernard Haldane as to the state of Wyverne's feelings. It would be too much to say that he had begun to conceive a real affection for his uncle; but he was not insensible to the change in the latter's demeanour. He felt that the old man was trying, after his fashion, to make some amends for the past, and rather reproached himself for not having met such advances more cordially. Day by day the wall built up between them

had been crumbling, and this last act of generosity made the breach quite practicable. An orthodox hero would, of course, have taken the "pale and haughty" line, and have rejected the golden olive-branch, preferring sublime independence to late obligation. Alan was much more practical and prosaic in his ideas; he accepted without hesitation, and did not scruple to express his gratitude warmly, though not demonstratively. It is needless to say that he did not intend to work the *carte blanche* unreasonably hard. So those two parted, in all amity. Bernard Haldane knew that he would be alone again on the morrow, and that in all probability he saw his nephew's face for the last time; but he drank less and slept better, that night, than he had done for years.

Wyverne wrote to tell Hubert Vavasour of his plans as soon as they were fixed. He got a very characteristic answer, full of kind wishes and prophecies of great success to the expedition. In truth the Squire rather envied any one who at that juncture could get well clear of England, home, and beauty. He spoke cheerfully about Helen, but his hopes for her seemed about the brightest of his domestic prospects. Evidently he thought that the crash could not be much longer averted, and that the close of the current year would find wrack and ruin at Dene. None the less, from the bottom of his honest heart, he wished his nephew goodspeed.

A fortnight later, strong, healthy excitement tingled in Alan's veins, as he stood on a wet sloping deck, his arm coiled through the weather-rigging, and looked ahead, through spray driving thick and blindly, over a turmoil of black foam-flecked water, betting with himself as to when the next sea would come tumbling in board. The *Goshawk* was a stout schooner, measuring two hundred liberal tons; there was no handier or honester craft in all the Royal squadron; but she had to do all she knew that afternoon, fighting her way foot by foot and tack by tack against a boisterous south-wester, with Cape

Finisterre frowning on her lee. We have not to follow in the track of the outward-bound; our business is, now, with the girls they left behind them.

---

## CHAPTER XVIII.

### A STAR IN THE WEST.

THE season opened early, and promised brilliantly. There was an unusually good entry of "maidens;" but among these one held easily, from the first, an undisputed pre-eminence. They would have made a favourite even of a *protegée* of Lady Mildred Vavasour's; you may guess what *prestige* attached to her only daughter. In truth, the demoiselle could have won upon her merits; before that first drawing-room when, it was said, Royal eyes lighted upon her kindly and admiringly, the triumph was secured. Such a success had not been achieved within the memory of the oldest inhabitant of White's. Hardly any one had heard of her brief engagement, and those who did know, only looked upon it as a childish, *cousinly* folly, entailing no serious consequences. Certainly, there was nothing in Helen's demeanour suggestive of regret or repining. Most people would have laughed incredulously, if they had been told that the superb head, which carried itself so imperially, had ever been bowed down hopelessly and helplessly, or that the lustre of the glorious eyes had ever been drowned in miserably unavailing tears. She seemed generally in good spirits, but they were not equable; her humour was cruelly capricious, and it was impossible to calculate upon her temper; she would be dangerously captivating one evening, and, the next morning, absolutely inaccessible. They very soon found out that she would sometimes be moved to serious anger on absurdly slight pretexts, or—none at all.

To speak the truth, Miss Vavasour was by no means insensible to the admiration she commanded, and appreciated homage thoroughly. It was very pleasant to keep the best men in town *en faction* near the Statue, looking eagerly for her appearance in Rotten-row; and to know, at a ball, that her rivals were waiting with blank tablets, till her own was filled up to the cotillon. She was strictly impartial at first, and the sharpest eyes could not detect the shadow of a preference; she made it a rule not to indulge the best of her partners with more than his one regular turn. There was surprise, if not scandal, throughout Babylon, when Bertie Grenvil engrossed her almost entirely on a certain evening. The Cherub was not disposed to undervalue his advantages of any sort: so he never confided to the world that he had received in the morning a long letter from Alan Wyverne, and had discussed it with Helen, line by line.

Almost all our old acquaintances are in town. Max Vavasour has returned from Northern Italy, where some mysterious attraction had detained him since last November, and signalizes himself by an exemplary attention to his domestic duties; he sacrifices readily all the early part of his evenings whenever "my lady" requires his attendance, and breaks his morning sleep, without a murmur, to chaperon his sister in her rides. Such virtue deserves to be rewarded; and it is possible that Max sees the glitter of a rich compensation not far off in futurity. There is Maud Brabazon, you see—more perilously provocative than ever; her coquetry seems to have blossomed with the spring flowers; she is still disporting herself mischievously with Bertie Grenvil's facile affections, who has not gained a foot of ground since we left them at Dene. The Cherub begins to acknowledge that he is getting very much the worst of it; but finds, apparently, a certain satisfaction in the maltreatment, and submits to cruelty and caprice with an uncomplaining docility worthy of a better fate and a better cause. Harding Knowles, too, has opened the campaign with unusual prodigality and splendour; he rides the neatest of hacks, is profusely hospitable in luncheons at his chambers and suburban dinners, and speaks—always with bated breath and in the strictest *tête-à-tête*—familiarly of "Clydesdale." He is to be seen at all Lady Mildred's parties, who treats him with marked consideration ; but he keeps clear of her daughter, for the recollection of that discomfiture at Dene still rankles bitterly.

Before long, diffidence and despondency showed themselves in the circle of Miss Vavasour's assiduous admirers : the Detrimentals drew back in fear and trembling, and even the best of the Eligibles stood aloof, for a season, watching how things would go. The Great Earl had come to the front, evidently in serious earnest.

Such reserve is, surely, most just and natural. Shall we be ruder than the lower animals, who by their example teach us a proper respect of persons?

See—a company of beautiful brighteyed antelopes are drinking at their favourite pool, deep in the green heart of the jungle ; the leopards have tracked them, and steal nearer and nearer, till a few seconds more will bring the prey within clutch of their spring ; suddenly the ravenous beasts cease to trail themselves forward, crouching lower and lower till their muzzles seem buried in the ground ; there they lie, rigid and motionless, showing no sign of life, even by a quiver of the listening ear ; the sounds close by are significant enough to *them*, though the poor little antelopes hear nothing—a soft, heavy footfall—a deep breath drawn long and savagely—a smothered rustle, as though some huge body were forcing stealthy passage through the tangled junglegrass : the leopards know, right well, that the King of the Forest is at hand, and famished as they are, will not betray their presence even by a growl, till their Seigneur shall have chosen his victim and satiated his appetite. Could the most patient and discreet of courtiers or parasites act more decorously?

The simile is not altogether inapposite, I fancy, nor very new either ; nevertheless, O fairest reader! I *do* pray you to pardon the truculence of that carnivorous comparison.

Clydesdale did not seek to dissemble his admiration ; indeed, he seemed desirous to *afficher* it as much as possible, for he knew that it was the surest way of keeping the ground clear, and that was precisely what he wanted. If it had been possible he would have liked, when he was calling in Guelph-crescent, to have left some visible token of his presence outside, to warn off the vulgar and profane, even as the Scythian chiefs used to plant their spear at the door of the tent wherein dwelt the favourite of the hour. From the moment that he heard, with a fierce throb of exultation, of the breaking off of Helen's engagement, the Earl had made up his resolve, and never doubted as to the event. Alan's departure made him still more confident ; he felt that the last barrier had been taken away : he had nothing to do now but to sit still and win. He was doggedly obstinate in his attentions, yet by no means demonstrative ; he seldom tried to secure more than two of Miss Vavasour's waltzes in an evening, but these were the only ones in which he deigned to exhibit himself ; when she was dancing with any one else, he would stand watching her swift graceful movements, with a critical complacency on his broad sensual face, that was enough to aggravate even an indifferent spectator—the conscious pride of proprietorship was so very evident. With just that same expression, the chief of a great stable watches the Oaks favourite as she sweeps past him, leading the string of two-year-olds—so easily—with her long sweeping stride. Lord Clydesdale was always sparing of his conversational treasures, if he possessed any ; nor did he lavish them even on the woman whom he delighted to honour. His eyes ought to have been more expressive, for they had a good deal of duty to do ; his pertinacious gaze scarcely left Helen's face when he was in her presence, and he seemed to consider this homage quite sufficiently expressive, without translating it verbally. Riding by her rein in Rotten-row, lounging in Lady Mildred's drawing-room for hours of an afternoon—the moody suitor was always the same silent, sulky, self-satisfied statue of Plutus. If the real truth had been known, I believe he would have preferred doing all the wooing by proxy.

No amount of coldness on Miss Vavasour's part would have checked the Earl in his obstinate determination to win her; but it must be confessed that he did not meet with much discouragement.

If a purely conventional marriage had been proposed to Helen, some months ago, she would probably have rejected it with much indignation and scorn; but things were altered now. Women, as well as men, turn readily to ambition — never so readily as when love has just been thwarted— and the demoiselle, though proud as Lucifer, was not too proud to be ambitious. The little she had seen of her admirer had not impressed her very favourably; but no active dislike was working the other way. She knew how eagerly matrons and maidens had striven and schemed to attain the Clydesdale coronet—it was, in truth, better worth wearing than some Grand Ducal crowns —there was a certain triumph in the consciousness that she had only to stretch out her little hand to place it on her brows.

"There's nothing like competition," they say; the maxim holds good in other things beside commerce and Civil Service examinations. I believe that there is hardly any folly, short of sin — let us be generous, and make that possible exception—to which a woman may not be tempted, if she is once thoroughly imbued with the spirit of rivalry. There is no end to the absurdities that they will commit, when this emulous devil possesses them. I have seen a most excellent young person, ordinarily a model of demure propriety, attempt to vault over high timber, and come thereat to grief absolutely unutterable, sooner than be beaten by a companion better versed in gymnastics, who had just performed the feat safely and gracefully, amidst general applause. I have known a fair dame—maturer, it is true, in attractions than in years—utterly ignore her habitual prudence, and compromise herself gravely by waltzing thrice almost consecutively with the same partner, simply because she alone could induce that languid hussar to break an antiterpsichorean pledge which he had entered into for no earthly reason but laziness; yet, on her purity of principle and honesty of intention, I would peril the residue of my life—or, what is more to the purpose—of my patrimony.

The Apple may be crude or withered, and scarcely worth the plucking; but if the fatal legend be once visible on its rind, you will see divine eyes glitter with something more than eagerness; and even chaste, cold Pallas may not repress a jealous pang, when the prize is laid in Aphroditè's rosy palm.

If it had been a question of keeping faith with Alan Wyverne, Miss Vavasour would not have wasted one thought or one regret on the present triumph or the splendid future; but knowing that they were separated for ever and ever, she was inclined to try if "the pomps and vanities of this wicked world" could not make some amends for what she had lost. She would not suppose it possible that a new affection could ever replace the passionate love that had been crushed and thwarted, but which would not die. There was her great mistake. It is in our early years that we ought to be patient; but we never recognize this till we are old: we hope while we are young, but we will not wait. So Helen accepted Clydesdale's saturnine devotion, on the whole rather graciously; her haughty, wayward temper, which would break out at times, rather attracted than repelled him.

It soon began to be noised abroad that the Great Fish was firmly hooked, if not landed. Certain astute chaperons acknowledged, with a sigh, that it was time to desist from a futile pursuit, and to seek humbler and more available victims. Dudley Delamere, the Earl's heir presumptive, who had nourished wild hopes of succession, on the strength of his cousin's notorious habits of self-indulgence, came down to the Foreign Office, two mornings running, with whiskers uncurled, thereby intimating prostration and despair as plainly as if he had rent his perfect garments, or scattered ashes on his comely head.

"I won't fight any longer," he said,

plaintively; "the luck's too dead against me. Throw up the sponge; the Begum has won it fairly."

Those profligates were wont thus irreverently to designate a certain elderly Indian widow — very stout, good humoured, and dark complexioned, with rather more thousands in the funds than she had years on her head—who, for the last two seasons, had manifested an unrequited attachment to the ungrateful but not unconscious Delamere. It must have been the attraction of contraries that made her bow down so helplessly before that slim, golden-haired Irresistible. He rather avoided her than otherwise; made a merit of coming to her artistic dinners, and treated her, when they met, with cruelly cold courtesy; but the impassioned Eurasian still kept hoping and worshipping on; pursuing the reluctant Adonis with pertinacious blandishments, with broad benevolent smiles that terrified him inexpressibly, and with glances out of her great black eyes that sent a shiver through his sensitive organization. Patient fidelity was rewarded at last. When Dudley had once made up his mind to the dire necessity, he accepted the position in a manly and Christian-like spirit, and sacrificed himself for the benefit of his country and his creditors, with a calm, chivalrous bravery worthy of Regulus or —Smith O'Brien. They say it is a very comfortable *ménage*, on the whole; certainly, the Begum's smiles are more oppressively radiant than ever, and I should think she has gained about two stone in weight, since the day that crowned her constancy as it deserved.

Nevertheless, though Lord Clydesdale's attentions were so marked, and his intentions so evident, the season ended without his coming to the point of a formal proposal. It would be rather hard to define his reasons for the delay. Possibly, holding the game in his hand, he chose to dally over his triumph, and play it out to the last card. Possibly, too, when a man's bachelor-life comprises every element of comfort and luxury, he lingers with a fond reluctance over its close. Besides this, the Earl appreciated the advantages of

his position thoroughly; it pleased him to be the centre-point at which the machinations of mothers and the fascinations of marriageable virgins were levelled; he had observed of late — not without regret—a manifest slackening in these assiduities, and, vain as he was, he felt that it would be rather unsafe to rely on his personal attractions for securing such pleasant homage, after his future was once decided irrevocably. Absolutely unalloyed selfishness will make even the dullest of intellects calculating and crafty. But Clydesdale did not vacillate in his set purpose for an instant. His last words, both to Lady Mildred and her daughter, before he left town for Scotland, were perfectly significant and satisfactory.

"My lady" had shown herself throughout worthy of her fame as a consummate tactician. The cunning mediciner was always at hand to give aid if aid was required, but she was far too wise to interfere with Nature when it was working favourably. She guessed aright as to the state of her daughter's feelings; she could understand how bitter memories were perpetually conflicting with ambitious hopes in the poor child's troubled breast; but she knew that a certain order and harmony must inevitably succeed, ere long, the chaos and discord; so she waited for the event in quiet confidence, without irritating Helen by consolation, or advice, or surmises. With Clydesdale, Lady Mildred was equally cautious and reserved; she was always charmed to receive him, of course, and ready to accept his attendance; but her bitterest enemy could not have accused her of betraying any undue eagerness to attract or monopolize it. The accomplished dissembler could afford to despise affectation; when the Earl's marked attentions showed that he was thoroughly in earnest, she did not pretend unconsciousness, but accepted them with a composed courtesy, as if such homage was only her daughter's due. She bore herself somewhat like a monarch of olden days, receiving the fealty of a mighty vassal — evidently gratified by the tribute, yet by no means overpowered by the honour. She did not attempt to conceal her approval, but she would not derogate from her position one step; she was ready to conciliate, not to concede. The suitor soon understood that his position did not entitle him to follow his own fashion of wooing, or to dictate his own terms; he could not claim a single privilege that had not been granted from time immemorial to such as were worthy to aspire to a Vavasour of Dene. Do not suppose that "my lady's" demeanour ever expressed this too plainly; dignified stiffness or majestic condescension were utterly out of her line; her manner never lost the gentle caressing languor which made it so charming. The tacit way in which the understanding was established showed the perfection of the art. The engine would not have been complete, if soft quilted velvet had not masked the steel springs so thoroughly.

Lady Mildred was not in the least vexed or disappointed when Clydesdale left town without bringing matters actually to a crisis. She knew right well it was the simplest question of time. When the Earl spoke, rather eagerly, about meeting the Vavasours again very soon, she only replied "that she hoped they might do so; but that her own summer arrangements were scarcely fixed yet. They would be at Dene in the autumn, certainly, and would be very happy to see him, if he could spare them a week in the shooting season."

Her coolness quite disconcerted Clydesdale; he bit his lip, and looked for a moment as if he were going to be angry; but he checked himself in time, only giving "my lady" a look before he went, that, if she had been at all disquieted, would have set her mind effectually at rest.

It is rather an humiliating confession to make about one's Prima Donna— but, I am afraid, Helen was really more disconcerted than her mother at the abeyance in which affairs just then remained. It is not certain if she had made up her mind to accept Lord Clydesdale at once,; but it is certain that she would have liked to have had the option of refusing him. In truth

there were other disagreeable incidents, besides a passing mortification of vanity. Miss Vavasour's marvellous beauty had not in anywise palled upon public admiration; men gathered round her, wherever she appeared, just as eagerly as at the beginning of the season, and the candidates for inscription on her card were numerous and emulous as ever; but there was a marked reserve and reticence in their homage. When a damsel is once resigned, by general consent, to a high and puissant seignior, even though no contract shall have been signed, a certain wall of observance is built up around her, that few care seriously to transgress, except those incorrigible reprobates who make a mock at all social and conventional obligations, and never see a fence without wanting to "lark" over it. Perhaps it is rather aggravating, to be obliged to conform to all the constraints of affiancement, without having so far reaped its solid advantages.

I am perfectly aware that poor Helen's market-value as a heroine will have gone down about fifty per cent. in this chapter. But what would you have? The ancient answer to the question— "What does Woman most care for?" holds good still. We can solve the riddle, now, without the Fairy's help, affirming boldly that is—Power.

---

## CHAPTER XIX.

### HOW WOLVES AND FOXES DIE.

ONE of our characters need trouble us no more. The summer passed, and autumn came on quickly; but Bernard Haldane never saw the leaves change. Life had been flickering within him, fitfully, for some time past; it went out suddenly at last: the mortal sickness did not endure through forty-eight hours. He betrayed no fear or impatience when he heard that his end was approaching rapidly; only muttering under his breath — "There is time enough for all I have to do." He paid no sort or attention to the remonstrances of the physician, but caused himself to be carried at once into his library where he remained locked in for nearly two hours, with a servant whom he could trust thoroughly. Paper after paper was examined and burned— a packet of yellow faded letters, first of all; and Mr. Haldane retained throughout a perfect intelligence and self-possession. He leant back in his chair when all was done, and closed his eyes with a sigh of satisfaction, but roused himself from the stupor that was creeping over him, to write, with great difficulty, a few lines to Alan Wyverne; the signature was scarcely legible, and as he was trying to direct the envelope, his head fell forward heavily on the table. When they got him back to his room, he was almost too weak to speak, though he rallied somewhat after taking strong restoratives.

The rector of the parish—a meek, single-minded, conscientious man — thought it his duty to offer what comfort and succour he could, though he feared the case was nearly desperate. What doubts, and misgivings, and repinings entered into the system of Bernard Haldane's dark cynical philosophy, God only can tell; he never tried to make a proselyte. As regards any communion with the Church, or outward observance of her ceremonies, he might have been the veriest of infidels; but he had never shown himself her overt antagonist. He listened now to all that the priest had to say, quite patiently and courteously, but with an indifference painfully evident. When asked "if he repented?" he answered, "Yes, of many things." Then came the question, "Are you in peace and charity with all the world?" No word of reply passed the firm white lips, but they curled with a terribly bitter smile; and the skeleton hand that lay on the coverlet was clenched, as though the long filbert-nails would pierce its palm.

The good rector felt utterly disheartened; he had not nerve enough to cope with that intractable penitent; it would have been a sinful mockery to speak of Sacrament, then; so he did the best he could—praying long and fervently, even against hope, for the troubled soul that was so near its rest. The sick man lay quite still, watching the movements of the priest, at first with mere curiosity, soon with a growing interest; at last it seemed as if his eyes would fain have thanked the kindly intercessor; but they waxed dimmer every moment, till the heavy lids closed slowly and wearily, not to be lifted again.

The physician standing by bent down his ear to the lips that still kept moving. He caught one word—"Mildred"—and some other syllables absolutely unintelligible. The frown on the brow and the contraction of the features, just then, surely did not come from pain. So— murmuring a farewell, that savoured, I fear, rather of ban than blessing—died Bernard Haldane—more tranquilly and serenely than saints and martyrs have died, who bore uncomplainingly all the burden and heat, and shrank from no self-sacrifice that could benefit their kind.

The bitter face changed and softened strangely, they say, before the corpse was cold, till it settled into intense sadness, and ten years seemed taken from the dead man's age. That grave, pensive expression perhaps was a natural one, before the keen morbid sensibility was so cruelly warped and withered. It may be that he *did* repent heartily at last, though he could not forgive; thinking of the poverty all round him that he had never stretched a hand to help, of the honest affection that he may have barred out when he shut himself up in his arid misanthropy. If he did once thoroughly realize this, and his utter impotence to make any amends, be sure the latest pang of his life was the sharpest of all. That is the worst of all philosophy—Epicurean or Stoic, seductive or repellant; it *will* often fail just at the critical time of trial. The tough, self-reliant character, that meets misfortune savagely and defiantly like a personal foe, holds its own well for a while; but, if there be not Faith enough to teach humble, hopeful endurance, I think it fares best in the end with the hearts that are only—broken.

Mr. Haldane's will was very brie

though perfectly explicit and formal. Every one who had ever suffered from his temper or caprices found themselves over-paid beyond their wildest expectations. These legacies accepted, he left all that he possessed, without fetter or condition, to his nephew.

There was great exultation among the many who knew and loved Alan Wyverne well, when they heard of his goodly heritage. Bertie Grenvil, on guard at the Palace on the Sunday when the news came to town, called his intimates around him to rejoice over the "pieces of silver" that his friend had found, and presided at a repast such as Brillat-Savarin might have ordered if he had served in the Household Brigade. Algy Beauclerc lost heavily at the club that night, for he was tied, after the Mezentian fashion, to a partner who never played the right card even by accident; but he laughed a great honest laugh, and told the incorrigible sinner, when the penance was over, that "he would make a very fair player in time, if he would only sit still and take pains." The Squire appeared at dinner radiant and triumphant, as if there were no such thing as mortgages or Jews on this side of eternity. Lady Mildred looked delighted and vaguely sympathetic, as if she would like to congratulate *some one* on the spot, but did not quite see her way. Helen Vavasour's cheek flushed for an instant and then grew very pale; her lip trembled painfully, as she whispered to herself, "Too late—ah me! too late!"

The *Goshawk* was lying off Beyrout when "the good news from home" came out. Wyverne received them with a placidity approaching to indifference, which exasperated his companions intensely; but he left the party immediately, and returned alone by the next steamer. When he landed in England, he went straight to Castle Dacre. The first paper that he opened was Bernard Haldane's letter. It ran thus:

"My dear Alan,—I wish I could have seen you once more, though I have little to say besides farewell. Think as kindly of me as you can; but don't try to persuade yourself, or others, that you are sorry I am gone. I leave no chief mourner. If a dog howls here to-night, it will be because the moon is full. It is but common justice that we should reap as we have sown; nevertheless, these last hours are rather dreary. I have left everything undone that I ought to have done for thirty years and more, but I have tried to make amends—at least to you. You are young enough to enjoy this second inheritance thoroughly, and wiser than when you lost your own. I will not attach to my bequest even the shadow of an implied condition; yet I pray you to keep the old house and its contents together as long as you can. You said yourself it would be a pity to part them. I would leave you my blessing if I dared; but it would be a sorry jest, and might turn out badly. I do wish you all the good luck that can be found in this mismanaged world. I wish it—even if you persuade her mother to allow Helen Vavasour to shape your altered fortunes. I am too tired to write more. It has been a long, rough journey, and I ought to sleep soundly. Good night.

Yours, in all kindness,
BERNARD HALDANE."

It would be absurd to say that Wyverne felt deep sorrow for his uncle's death; but an intense pity welled up in his honest heart as he read that strange letter, and fancied the lonely old man tasking the last of his strength to trace the weak wavering lines; in truth, the characters seemed still more hazy and indistinct, when he laid the paper down.

By my faith—it is somewhat early in the day to become funereal. Let us pass over two or three months and change the *venue* entirely.

It is a soft grey December morning, with a good steady breeze, cool but not chilly. The Grace-Dieu hounds are about to draw Rylstone Gorse for the first time this season. It is a favourite fixture, and no wonder—sufficiently central to let the best men in of two neighbouring packs, yet sufficiently remote from town and rail to keep the profane and uninitiate away. There is a brook, too, in the bottom, over which the fox is sure to go; not very wide, but deep enough to hold a regiment, which always weeds the field charmingly. The meet is in a big pasture hard by : while the ten minutes' law allotted by immemorial courtesy to distant comers is expiring, it may be worth while to mark a few of the " notables."

There, leaning over the low carriage-door, and doing the honours of the meet to Lady Mildred, stands the Duke of Camelot. There is nothing of *morgue* or reserve in the character or demeanour of that mighty noble, but his manner is, in spite of himself, somewhat superb and stately. Wherever he appears, there is diffused around an ambrosial atmosphere savouring of the *ancien régime*. Nature never meant him for a warrrior or statesman. His mission through life has been to *poser* before the world, unconsciously, as a perfect type of his order; you see it in every movement of the long taper limbs, in the carriage of the patrician head, in the peculiar sweep and curl of the ample grey whisker, in every line of the clear-cut prominent features, in the smile which—intended to be genial and benevolent—is simply condescending and benign. What his mental capacities may be, it is impossible to say; he has never tried them. But in his own country he hath great honour; the peasantry believe him to be omniscient and omnipotent, if not omnipresent. Were the fancy to seize him to rebel against the powers that be, I fancy the stalwart yeomen would muster strong round the ancient banner, in defiance of the claims of Stuart or Guelph. Nevertheless, the Duke is, on the whole, a very good-natured and convivial potentate; when no state-party is in question, he loves to gather round him pleasant people who suit each other and suit him, without regard to their pride of place or order of precedence. He brings, in one way or another, more than twenty guests to the meet to-day, including, besides the

family from Dene, the Brabazons and Lord Clydesdale.

The Master had just fallen to the rear, after a brief conference with the huntsman. He sits there, you see, with a listless indifference on his dark handsome face, as if henceforth he had no earthly interest in the proceedings; but in reality he is watching everything and everybody with keen, inevitable eyes. Lord Roncesvaux is a cold, stern man, born with tact and talent enough to have made him great in his generation, if he had not devoted both exclusively, together with half his fortune, to the one favourite pursuit. He speaks seldom in society—never in the senate ; but if a thrusting rired gets a step too forward at the gorse, or presses on his hounds to-day, you will hear that well shaped mouth open very much to the purpose.

A little to the left, with a clear space round him, is Clydesdale, looking hot and savage, even this early hour. The horse would be quiet enough if the rider would only let his mouth alone; but the Earl has a knack of bullying his dependents, equine as well as human; so " Santiago's" temper is getting fast exasperated, and his broad brown chest is already flecked with foam.

Do you mark that lithe erect figure, on the wicked-looking bay mare, moving from one group to another in the foreground ? Everybody seems glad to see him, and he has a jest or a smile ready for each successive greeting. That is Major Cosmo Considine, who began life as a Guardsman, and has served since in a more Irregular corps than he now chooses to remember. The habitual expression of the face is gay and pleasant enough, but sometimes the features look strangely haggard and worn, as if the past was trying to tell its tale ; and the thin lips, under cover of the huge blonde moustache, will set, as though in anger or pain. Redoubtable in battle—dangerous, they say, in a boudoir—he is especially hard to beat when hounds are running straight and fast ; no matter how big the fencing may be, if it is a real good thing, Satanella's lean eager head will be seen creeping to

the front; and once there, like her master on certain other occasions, "she is
not to be denied."

Major Considine married a wife,
wealthy and fair, some three years ago,
and has ever since been purposing,
gravely but vaguely, to become steady
and respectable. The pious intentions
have not been carried out with uniform
success. The weak mind of his unhappy spouse is supposed to oscillate almost daily between furious jealousy and
helpless adoration; but the silver tongue
of the incorrigible Bohemian is still seductive as when, in spite of relatives'
advice and warning, it won him his
bride; about twenty minutes' persuasion always reduces' her to the dreamy,
devotional phase, in which she remains
till the next offence awakes her. To do
Cosmo justice, his aberrations are much
more harmless than the world gives
him credit for; nor does he often seek
now to illustrate his theories practically.

There is Nick Gunstone, the great
stock-breeder and steeple-chaser, expa-
tiating to a knot of true believers on the
merits of a long, low, raking five-year-
old, with whom he expects to pull off a
good thing before next April. The
young one looks wild and scared and
fretful, and evidently knows little of his
business yet; but his rider has nerve
enough for both, and a hand as light as
a woman's, though his muscles are like
steel. When the hounds are well away
you will see the pair sailing along in
front, quite at their ease: a "crumpler"
or so is a moral certainty; but Nick
Gunstone is all wire and whalebone, and
seems to rebound harmlessly from the
earth, if he hits it ever so hard; he believes religiously that "nothing steadies
a young one like a heavy fall," on which
principle he generally sends them at the
strongest part of the fence, and the stiffest bit of timber. He is in rather a bad
humour to-day, for objections have just
been made and sustained to his receiving the aristocratic "allowance" in future; and Mr. Gunstone's sensitive soul
chafes indignantly at the injustice—of
course on account of the diminution of
his dignity, not in the least because of
the addition to his weight!

The Amazonian division muster in
great force, displaying every variety of
head-gear, coquettish and business-like.
There is one of the number—far in the
background, with a solitary attendant—
that even a stranger would single out
instantly, but with an instinctive feeling
that his glance ought not to rest there
long. To be sure, her horse is well
worth looking at; for if shape and
"manners" go for anything, Don Juan
must be a very cheap three hundred
guineas' worth. But the rider's appearance is still more remarkable. It would
be rather difficult to define exactly why.
There is nothing particularly eccentric
or "fast" in her demeanour, or so far
as one can judge while she is in repose;
her equipment and appointments, though
faultless in every respect, are perfectly
quiet and unobtrusive; only a very stern
critic would remark that the miraculous
habit fits her superb bust a shade *too*
well. You see a frank fearless face, at
times perhaps a trifle too mutinously
defiant; a broad, brent, white forehead;
clear, bold blue eyes, flashing often in
merriment, seldom in anger; and thick
coils of soft gold-brown hair, braided
tightly under the compact riding-hat.
It is not exactly a pretty picture, though
its piquancy might be attractive to such
as admire that peculiar style.

The solitary horseman who never
leaves her side is Mr. Lacy, the professional artist, who has reduced riding
over fences to a science. In consideration of large monies, perfect mounts,
and unlimited claret and cigars, he consents to act as mentor and pioneer to
the reckless *Reine des Ribaudes:* the
office is no sinecure, and the wages are
conscientiously earned. There is a look
of grave anxiety on his pale intellectual
face to-day, such as may well become a
brave man who estimates aright the importance and perils of a task set before
him, and prepares to encounter them
without reluctance or fear. Of a truth,
in a country like this, where, as a
stranger, she rides "for her own hand,"
and means going, it is no child's-play to
*chaperon* Pelagia.

One other personage remains to be
noticed—I venture to hope you are not

tired of him yet—Alan Wyverne; looking thinner and browner than when we saw him last, but in very fair plight notwithstanding, who had just come down into the Shires, with a larger stud than he ever owned in the old days. He had no idea of the Vavasours being in the neighbourhood, or perhaps even Rylstone Gorse would not have tempted him to ride the score of miles that lay between the fixture and his hunting quarters. He has got over the meeting with his uncle most successfully; how cordial it was, on both sides, you may easily imagine. But he has so many friends to greet, and congratulations to answer, that he has not found time, yet, to approach the carriage in which Lady Mildred is reclining. Alan has nothing in his stable, so far, that he likes so well as his ancient favourite; he rides him first-horse to-day. In truth, Red Lancer is a very model of a fast weight-carrier; you cannot say whether blood or bone predominates in the superb shape and clean powerful limbs, and all his admirers allow "that he is looking fitter than ever." He is apt to indulge in certain violent eccentricities in the first five minutes after he is mounted, but he has settled down now, and bears himself with a quiet, stately dignity; nevertheless, there is a resolute look about his head, implying obstinacy to be ruled only by a stronger will.

The ten-minutes' law has more than expired, and, at an imperceptible signal from the Master, the pack moves on slowly towards the gorse. We will not wait to witness the certain find, but get forward a mile or two, to a point that the fox is almost sure to pass; being invisible we can do no harm, even if we do cross his line.

Did you ever see a more truculent fence than that on your right, which stretches along continuously for twelve hundred yards or more, on the Rylstone side of the road on which we are standing? The double rails, both sloping outwards, are much higher and wider apart than usual, and the charge of a squadron would hardly break the new tough oak timber; to go in and out is impossible, for there is a deep ditch in the middle fringed by meagre, stunted quick-set; and on the landing side there is actually another trench, vast enough to swallow up horse and rider, if by any chance they got so far. The only outlet is through double gates, with a bridge of treacherous planks between them. There was malice prepense in the mind that contrived that fearful barrier. The owner of the farm is a morose, hard-fisted Scotch presbyterian, who regards all sport as a snare and device of the Evil One, and acts according to his narrow light, viciously. When he came into the country a year ago, he was afraid to warn the hounds off his land, but went to a considerable expense to stop them, as he thought, quite as effectually. The pleasant innovation of wiring the fences was unknown in those days (soon, I suppose, they will strew calthrops along the headlands, and conceal spring-guns cunningly, to explode if you hit the binders); but David Macausland did his worst after the fashion of the period; and so sat down behind his entrenchments with the grim satisfaction of a consummate engineer, waiting for the enemy to come on.

You know the occupants of that low phaeton that sweeps round the corner so smoothly and rapidly, pulling up within a hundred yards of us? Miss Vavasour's ponies are too fiery to be trusted in a crowd, so she has listened to Maud Brabazon's suggestion that they should take their chance of seeing something of the run, instead of going to the meet—yielding the more readily because her own fancy, to-day, inclines to comparative solitude. There they are, left entirely to their own devices, with only a staid elderly groom to keep them out of mischief.

The fair adventuresses have not to wait; before they have been posted five minutes, a symphony and crash of hound-music comes cheerily down the wind, and a dark speck, developing itself into shape and colour as it approaches, steals swiftly down the fifty-acre pasture. Fortunately they are not forward enough to do any harm; even the restless ponies stand still, as if by instinct, while a big dog-fox crosses the road, quite unconscious of the bright eyes that are following him; he whisks the white tag of his brush knowingly, just as he clears the fence, evidently thinking it will prove a "stopper," at least to his human foes. Two minutes more, and the pack sweeps compactly over the crest of the rising ground; a little in the rear, on either flank, come the real front-rankers—the ambitious spirits who, wherever they go, will assert their pride of place; the very flower of science and courage; the best and boldest of England's *Hippodamastæ*. Do you think the whole world could show you such another sight as this?

There is Cosmo Considine, sending Satanella along as if he had another spare neck at home, in case of accidents, and as if she had ten companions in the stable (instead of a brace) to replace her if she comes to grief. There is Lord Roncesvaux, riding as jealous as any of them, though he would scorn to confess such a weakness; there is a fierce light now in his broad black eyes, though the listlessness has scarcely left his face. There is Nick Gunstone, holding his own gallantly, discreet enough to give "the swells" a widish berth. And there, in the van of the battle, flutters the bright-blue habit, and gleams the soft golden hair.

"How very fortunate!" Helen Vavasour cried. "We are just in the right place; they must cross the road, and we shall see all the fencing."

Mrs. Brabazon was more experienced than her companion, and, indeed, had been no mean performer over a country in her day. She shook her pretty head negatively, as she answered—

"I am afraid not, dear, unless there is an unusual amount of chivalry out to-day. I have been looking at that place, and I believe it is simply impracticable. They must get round it somehow, and the hounds will leave them here."

The old groom, standing at the ponies' heads, touched his hat, in assent and approval.

"You're quite right, my lady," he said. "There's no man in these parts as would try that fence; no more there

didn't ought to. It's hard on a thirty-foot fly, let alone the drop; and it's a broken neck or back if you falls short, or hits a rail."

The *impasse* is evidently well known, and the leaders of the field appear to be very much of the speaker's opinion; for instead of following the hounds down the middle of the pasture, they began to diverge on either side, the huntsman setting the example. Will Darrell takes fences as they come, very cheerfully, in an ordinary way; but a great general has no business to risk his life like a reckless subaltern; and the idea of being laid up with a broken limb so early in the season is simply intolerable. With Lord Roncesvaux's servants duty stands first of all; they know that no credit won by mere hard riding would excuse a fault of rashness, or soften the implacable Master's anger. Cosmo Considine acknowledges the necessity of a compromise, growling out an imprecation in some strange outlandish tongue; and Pelagia's pilot, after a hurried word exchanged with the Major, for whom he has a great respect and esteem, follows him to the right, utterly disregarding the remonstrances of his impetuous charge. Even Nick Gunstone thinks that this will be rather too strong an illustration of his favourite theory, and reserves the young one's steadying lesson for a more convenient season.

A few sceptics determine to judge for themselves, and ride right down to the fence; but one glance satisfies them, and they gallop along it in both directions, rather losing ground by their obstinacy than otherwise. Amongst these is Lord Clydesdale. Perhaps the Earl is aware of the proximity of the pony-carriage; at any rate, he thinks it necessary to make a demonstration; so he takes a short circuit, and pretends to charge the fence, with much bluster and flurry. Santiago behaves with a charity and courtesy very amiable, considering the provocation he has undergone, and tries to save his master's honour by taking on himself the odium of a decisive refusal. But the sham is too glaring to deceive the veriest novice; Maud Brabazon's smile is marvellously meaning, and Miss Vavasour's curling lip does not dissemble its scorn.

Half a minute later, Maud happened to be looking in an opposite direction; an exclamation from the groom, and a low cry, almost like a moan, from her companion, made her turn quickly. Helen had dropped the reins; her hands were clasped tightly, as they lay on the bearskin-rug, and her great eyes gleamed bright and wild with eagerness and ter-ror; they were riveted on a solitary horseman, who came down at the fence straight and fast.

Alan Wyverne had been baulked at the brook by some one's crossing him, and the pace was so tremendous that even Red Lancer's turn of speed had not yet quite enabled him to make up lost ground. It so happened, that he had ridden along that double on his way to the meet, and though he fully appreciated the peril, he had then decided that it was just within his favour-ite's powers, and consequently ought to be tried.

Truly, at that moment, the pair would have made a superb picture. Alan was sitting quite still, rather far back in the saddle; his hands level and low on the withers, with hold enough on Red Lancer's mouth to stop a swerve, but giving the head free and fair play; his lips slightly compressed, but not a sign of trepidation or doubt on his quiet face. The brave old horse was, in his way, quite as admirable; like his master, he had determined to get as far over the fence as pluck and sinew would send them; so on he came, with his small ears pointing forward dagger-wise, momently increasing his speed, but measuring every stride, and judging his distance, so as to take off at the proper spot to a line.

They were within thirty yards of the rails now, and still Helen Vavasour gazed on—steadfast and statue-like—without a quiver of lip or a droop of eyelash. Maud Brabazon's nerves were better than most women's, but they failed her then. She felt a wild desire to spring up and wave Alan back; but a cold faint shudder came over her, and she could only close her eyes in helpless terror.

9

There came a rush of hoofs sounding on elastic turf—a fierce snort as Red Lancer rose to the spring—and then a dull smothered crash, as of a huge body's falling.

Maud felt her companion sink back by her side, trembling violently: then she heard a hoarse exclamation from the groom of wonderment and applause; then Wyverne's clear voice speaking to his horse encouragingly, and then—she opened her eyes just in time to see the further road-fence taken in the neatest possible style.

There had been no fall after all. Red Lancer's hind hoofs broke away the outer bank of the ditch, and he "knuckled" fearfully on landing; but a strong practised hand recovered him just in time to save his credit and his knees.

Negotiations were entered into soon afterwards with Mr. Macausland, and powerful arguments brought to bear upon his cupidity; the austere Presbyterian compromised with the unrighteous Mammon, so far as to suppress the obnoxious middle ditch and render the fence barely practicable. But they point out the spot still, as a proof of the space that a perfect hunter can cover, with the aid of high courage and strong hind-quarters, if he is ridden straight and fairly. The elderly groom, who is saturnine and sceptical by nature, prone to undervalue and discredit the exploits of others, when one of his fellows speaks of a big leap, always quells and quenches the narrator utterly, by playing his trump-card of the great Rylstone double.

It is almost an invariable rule—if a man by exceptional luck or pluck "sets" the field the hounds are sure to throw up their heads within a couple of furlongs. Fortune, as if tired of perse-euting Alan Wyverne, gives him a rare turn to-day.

There was a scent, such as one meets about twice in a season. The field, spread out like a fan, begins to converge again, and the front rank are riding like men possessed to make up their lost ground. All in vain—nothing without wings would catch the "flying bitches"

now, as they stream over the broad
pastures without check or stay, drinking
in the hot trail through wide up-turned
nostrils, mute as death in their savage
thirst for blood. It was a trivial triumph, no doubt, hardly worthy of a
highly rational being; but the hunting
instinct is one of the strongest in our
imperfect nature, after all; I believe that
it falls to the lot of very few to. enjoy
such intense, simple happiness as Wyverne experienced for about eighteen
minutes, as he swept on, alone, on the
flank of the racing pack, rejoicing in
Red Lancer's unfaltering strength. Such
a tremendous burst must necessarily be
brief. As Alan crashes through the
rail of a great " oxer," an excited agriculturist screams: " He's close afore
you." Close—the hounds know that
better than you can tell them. Look
how the veterans are straining to the
front. Suddenly, as they stream along
a thick bullfinch, old Bonnibelle wheels
short round and glides through the fence
like a ghost; her comrades follow as
best they may; there is a snap—a crash
of tongues—and a savage worry. Alan
Wyverne, too, turns in his tracks; and
driving Red Lancer madly through the
blackthorn, clears himself from the falling horse, just in time to rush in to the
rescue, and—with the aid of a friendly
carter, who uses whip and voice lustily—
to save from sharp wrangling teeth
rather a mutilated trophy.

Now, is not that worth living for?
Wyverne could answer the question
very satisfactorily, as he loosens Red
Lancer's girth and turns his head to the
wind, pulling his small ears, and strok-
ing his lofty crest caressingly. Nearly
five minutes have passed, and the hounds
are beginning to wander about in a desultory, half-satisfied way, as is their
wont after a kill, before Lord Roncesvaux, and the huntsman, and three or
four more celebrities, put in a discomfited
appearance.

It speaks ill for our chivalry that we
should have left the pony-carriage to
itself all this time; but that " cracker"
over the grass was too strong a temptation; we were bound to see the end of
it.

Mrs. Brabazon was the first to speak,
breathing quick and nervously.

" Oh, Helen, was not that magnificent? But were you ever so frightened?"

The wild look had passed out of the
girl's eyes, yet they were still strangely
dreamy and vague.

" It was very fearful," she said; "but
I ought not to have been frightened.
There is no one like him—no one half
so cool and brave. I have known that
for so many years!"

Maud's keen glance rested on the
speaker's face for a second or two.
What she read there did not seem
greatly to please her.

" I think we had better be turning
homewards," she said, gravely; " I feel
tired already, and I am sure we shall see
nothing more to-day."

From Miss Vavasour's flushing cheek,
and the impatient way in which she
gathered up the reins and turned her
ponies, it was easy to guess that she did
not wish her thoughts to be too closely
scanned just then. But before they
had driven three hundred yards, she
was musing again. At last her lips
moved involuntarily. Maud Brabazon's
quick ear caught a low, piteous whisper—" I don't think he even saw me"—
and then a weary, helpless sigh. In
just such a sigh may have been breathed
the dying despair of that unhappy
Scottish maiden, who pined so long for
the coming of her lover from beyond
the sea, and whose worn-out heart
broke when he rode in under the archway without marking the wave of her
kerchief, or looking up at her window.

It was a very silent drive homewards.
One of those two had good right to be
pensive. Last night, Lord Clydesdale,
utterly vanquished and intoxicated by
her beauty, spoke out, right plainly.
The day of grace that Helen claimed
for reflection is half gone already, and
the irrevocable answer must be given to-
morrow.

Shall we say—as they said in olden
times to criminals called upon to plead—
" So God send you good deliverance?"
Truly it was a kindly, courteous formula
enough; but I fancy it carried little

meaning to the minds of the judge or jury, and little comfort to the heavy heart of the attainted traitor.

Throughout the country side that night men seemed unable to talk long about anything, without recurring to the morning's run and the feat which had made it so singularly remarkable. Even Clydesdale did not venture to dissent or show discontent when Wyverne's nerve and judgment were praised up to the skies; he only swelled sulkily, and indulged under his breath in a whole string of his favourite curses, registering another involuntary offence against the name he hated so bitterly. Red Lancer came in for his full share of the glory; they discussed his points and perfections one by one, till you might have drawn his portrait without ever having seen him. He was as famous now, as that mighty war-horse of whom the quaint old ballad sings—

So grete he was, of back so brode,
So wight and warily he trode,
    On earth was not his peer;
Ne horse in land that was so tall;
The knight him cleped "Lancivall,"
But lords at board and grooms in stall
    Cleped him—"Grand Destrere."

In the servants'-hall at Beauprè Lodge, the witness of the feat thus expressed himself, an honest admiration lighting up for once his hard, rough-hewn face—

"It's very lucky I ain't a young 'oman of fortun" (signs of unanimous adhesion from his audience, especially from the feminine division). "Ah, you may laugh. If I was, I'd follow Sir Alan right over the world, without his asking of me, if it was only for the pleasure of blacking his boots."

After this, who will say that "deering-do" is not still held in honour, or that hero-worship has vanished out of the land?

---

## CHAPTER XX.

QUAM DEUS VULT PERDERE.

THE noon of night is past, and Helen Vavasour is alone in her chamber, with-

out a thought of sleep. In truth, the damsel is exceeding fair to look upon—though it is a picture over which we dare not linger—as she leans back, half reclining, on the low couch near the hearth; a loose dressing-robe of blue cachemire faced with quilted white satin, draping her figure gracefully, without concealing its grand outlines: her slender feet, in dainty velvet slippers broidered with seed-pearl, crossed with an unstudied coquetry that displays the arched instep ravishingly; a torrent of shining dark hair falling over neck and shoulder; a thin line of pearly teeth showing through the scarlet lips that are slightly parted; the light of burning embers reflected in her deep eyes, that seem trying to read the secrets of the Future in the red recesses and the fitful flames.

She had been musing thus for many minutes, when a quick step came across the corridor; there was a gentle tap at the door, and it opened to admit Mrs. Brabazon.

"I thought I should find you up," she said. "I'm strangely wakeful to-night, Helen, and very much disposed to talk. Do you mind my staying here till you or I feel more sleepy?"

Miss Vavasour assented eagerly; indeed, she was rather glad of an excuse for breaking off her "maiden meditation;" so there she established her visitor in the most luxurious chair she could find, not without a caress of welcome.

Nevertheless, in spite of their conversational inclinations, neither seemed in a particular hurry to make a start; and, for some minutes, there was rather an embarrassed silence. At length Mrs. Brabazon looked up and spoke suddenly.

"Helen, what answer do you mean to give to the Great Earl to-morrow? Don't open your eyes wonderingly; I drew my own conclusions from what I saw last night. Besides, Lady Mildred is perfectly well informed; though she has not said a word to you, she has spoken to me about it, and asked me to help the good cause with my counsel and advice, if I could find time and occasion. Shall I begin?"

She spoke lightly; but the grave anxiety on her face belied her tone. Miss Vavasour's thoughts had been devoted so exclusively to one subject, that its abrupt introduction now did not startle her at all. Her smile was cold and somewhat disdainful, as she replied—

"Thank you, very much. But it is hardly worth while to go through all the advantages of the alliance; I have had a full and complete catalogue of them already. They chose Max for an ambassador, and I assure you he discharged his duties quite conscientiously, and did not spare me a single detail; he was nearly eloquent sometimes; and I never saw him so near enthusiasm as when he described the Clydesdale diamonds. He made me understand too, very plainly, that the fortunes of our family depended a good deal upon me. Did you know that we are absolutely ruined, and have hardly a right, now, to call Dene ours?"

Ah, woe and dishonour! Is it Helen's voice that is speaking? Have twelve months changed the frank, impulsive girl into a calculating, worldly woman, a pupil that her own mother might be proud of? For all the emotion or interest she betrays, she might be a princess, wooed by proxy, to be the bride of a king whom she has never seen.

Some such thoughts as these rushed across Maud Brabazon's mind, as she listened; great fear and pity rose up in her kind heart, till her eyes could scarcely refrain from tears.

"I had heard something of this," she said, sadly; "though I did not know things were so desperate. There are a hundred arguments that would urge you to say—Yes, and only two or three to make you say—No. It is absolutely the most brilliant match in England. You will have the most perfect establishment that ever was dreamt of, and we shall all envy you intensely; it has been contemplated for you, and you have expected the proposal yourself for months; I know all that. Yesterday—I should not have thought it probable you could hesitate; to-day—I do beg and pray you to pause. I think you will be in great danger if you marry the Earl. Have you deceived yourself into believing that you love him?"

"I don't deceive myself; and I have never deceived him. He is ready and willing to take what I can give, and expects no more, I am certain. I do not love Lord Clydesdale; and I am not even sure that we shall suit each other. But he is anxious to make the trial, and I—am content. I know that I shall try honestly to do my duty as his wife, if he will let me. That is all. Time works wonders, they say; it may do something for us both."

Still the same slow, distinct utterance; the same formal, constrained manner; as if she were repeating a lesson thoroughly learnt by rote. Maud Brabazon was only confirmed in her purpose to persevere to the uttermost in her warning.

"I have no right to advise," she said; "and moral preaching comes with an ill grace, I dare say, from my foolish lips. But indeed—indeed—I only speak because I like you sincerely, and I would save you if I could. One may deceive oneself about the past, as well as the future. Are you sure that you can forget? Are you sure that an old love has not the mastery still? Helen, if I were your mother I would not trust you."

The girl's cheek flushed brightly—less in confusion than in anger.

"You need have no false delicacy, Maud. If you mean that I shall never love any one as I have loved Alan, if you mean that I still care for him more than for any living creature, you are quite right. But it is all over between us, for ever and ever. We shall always be cousins henceforth—no more; he said so himself. If a word could make us all we once were, I don't think I would speak it; I am sure he never would. But, my dear, it does surprise me beyond everything, to hear you arguing on the romantic side. You never could have worshipped Mr. Brabazon, before or after marriage; and yet you amuse yourself better than any one I know."

Miss Vavasour's quick temper—always impatient of contradiction—was in the ascendant just then, or she would scarcely have uttered that last taunt. She bitterly repented it when she saw the other cower under the blow, bowing her head into her clasped hands, humbly and sorrowfully.

When Maud looked up, not one of the many who had admired and loved her radiant face would have recognised it in its pale resolve.

"You only spoke the truth, Helen. Don't be penitent; but listen as patiently as you can. At least, my example shall not encourage you in running into danger. I will tell you a secret that I meant to carry to my grave. You incur a greater risk than ever I did; see, how it has fared with me. It is quite true that I did not love my husband when I accepted him; but I had never known even a serious fancy for any one else. I imagined I was hardened enough to be safe in making a conventional marriage. And so—so it went on well enough for some years; but my falsehood was punished at last. They say, it is sharp pain when frozen blood begins to circulate; ah, Helen—trust me—it is worse still, when one's heart wakes up. I cannot tell you how it came about with me. He never tried to make me flirt, like the rest of them; but when he spoke to me, his voice always changed and softened. He never tried to monopolize me, but wherever I went, he was sure to be; and, some nights, when I was more wild and mischievous than usual, I could see wonder and pity in his great melancholy eyes: they began to haunt me, those eyes; and I began to miss him and feel disappointed and lonely, if an evening passed without our meeting. But I never betrayed myself, till one night Geoffrey told me, suddenly, that he was to sail in four days for the coast of Africa. I could not help trembling all over, and I knew that my face was growing white and cold; I looked up in his—just for one second—and I read his secret, and confessed mine. He had mercy on my weakness—God rewarded him for it!—he only asked for a flower that I wore,

when I would have given him my life or my soul; for I was wicked and mad, that night. It was so like him: I know he would never tempt me: he would save me from going wrong if it cost him his heart's blood. Fevers and horrors of all sorts beset them on that coast: I might read Geoffrey's death in the next *Gazette*, and yet—his lips have not touched my hand. You say I amuse myself. Do you know, that I must have light, and society, and excitement, or I should go mad? I dare not sit at home and think for an hour. I have to feed my miserable vanity, to keep my conscience quiet. I am pure in act and deed, and no one can whisper away my honour; but in thought I am viler than many outcasts—treacherous, and sinning every day, not only against my marriage vow, but against *him*. I often wish I were dead, but I am not fit to die.'"

She had fallen forward as she spoke, and lay prone with her head buried in Helen's lap—a wreck of womanhood in her abasement and self-contempt. The wind, that had been rising gustily for hours past, swelled into fury just then, driving the sleet against the casements like showers of small-shot, and howling savagely through the cedars as though in mockery of the stricken heart's wail. Maud Brabazon shivered and lifted up her wild scared face—

"Do you hear *that?*" said she, "I never sleep when a gale is blowing. The other night Bertie Grenvil was pleading his very best; I answered at random, and I daresay I laughed nervously; he fancied it was because his words had confused me. I was only thinking—what the weather might be on the Western coast, for a gust like that last was sweeping by. Ah, Helen, darling! do listen and be warned in time; if you don't see your danger, pause and reflect, if only for my sake. Have I made my miserable confession in vain."

Miss Vavasour's expression was set and steadfast as ever, though tears swam in her eyes; she leant down and clasped her soft white arms round Maud Brabazon's neck, and pressed a pitiful tender kiss on the poor humbled head.

"Not in vain, dearest!" she whispered; "I shall always love and trust you henceforth, because I know you thoroughly. But I cannot go back. It is too late now, even if I would. I hope I shall be able to do my duty; at least I need not fear the peril of ever loving again. I must accept Lord Clydesdale to-morrow."

Maud drew quickly out of the close embrace, and threw herself back, burying her face in her hands once more; when she uncovered it, it was possessed by nothing but a blank white despair.

"The punishment is coming!" she said; "I can do harm enough, but I can do no good, if I try ever so hard—that is clear. I will help you always to the uttermost of my power; but we will never speak of this again."

She rose directly afterwards, and after the exchange of a long caress—somewhat mechanical on one side—quitted the room with a vague uncertain step. So Helen's very last chance was cast away, and she was left to the enjoyment of her prospects and her dreams.

The decisive interview came off on the following morning. There was not a pretence of romance throughout. Lord Clydesdale manifested a proper amount of eagerness and *empressement;* Helen was perfectly cool and imperial; nevertheless, the suitor seemed more than satisfied. The negotiation was laid in due form before the Squire and Lady Mildred in the course of the day. To do the Earl justice, he had never been niggardly or captious in finance, and his liberality now was almost ostentatiously magnificent. By some means or other he had been made perfectly aware of the state of affairs at Dene. Besides superb proposals of dower and pin-money, he offered to advance, at absurdly moderate interest, enough to clear off all the encumbrances on the Vavasour property; and the whole of the sum was to be settled on younger children—in default of these, to be solely at Helen's disposal.

The poor Squire, though not taken by surprise, was fairly overwhelmed. The temptation of comparatively free-ing the dear old house and domain would have proved nearly irresistible even to a stronger mind and will; still, he felt far from comfortable. He did try to salve his unquiet conscience by requiring an interview with his daughter, and seeking therein to arrive at the real state of her heart. It was an honest offer of self-sacrifice, but really a very safe one. Helen did not betray the faintest regret or constraint; so Hubert Vavasour resigned himself, not unwillingly, to the timely rescue. I have not patience to linger over Lady Mildred's intense undemonstrative triumph.

It was settled that the marriage should take place early in the spring. All the preliminaries went on swiftly and smoothly, as golden wheels will run when thoroughly adjusted and oiled. Miss Vavasour behaved admirably; she accepted numberless congratulations, gratefully and gracefully; in the intercourse with her *fiancé* she evinced no prudery or undue reserve, but nevertheless contrived to repress the Earl's enthusiasm within very endurable limits.

Only one scene occurred, before the wedding, which is worth recording; it is rather a characteristic one. Perhaps you have forgotten that, in the second chapter of this eventful history, there was mentioned the name of one Schmidt, a mighty iron founder of Newmanham, who had bought up all the mortgages on Dene? His intention had been evident from the first; and just about the time of the last affiancement, his lawyers gave notice that he meant to call in the money or foreclose without mercy.

Now the Squire, though he naturally exulted, as a Gentile and a landed proprietor, in the discomfiture of the Hebrew capitalist, would have allowed things to be arranged quietly, in the regular professional way. But this, Lord Clydesdale, when consulted on the subject, would by no means suffer. He begged that the meeting of the lawyers might take place at Dene; and that, if it were possible, Ephraim Schmidt should be induced to attend in person : the paying off of the mortgages was not to be previously biuted at in any way. The whims of great men must be sometimes humoured, even by the law; and this was not such a very unreasonable one after all. " I wouldn't miss seeing the Jew's face if it cost another thousand ?" the Earl said, with a fierce laugh ; so that it was settled that he was to be present at the interview.

Mr. Schmidt and his solicitor arrived punctually at the appointed hour ; there was no fear of the former's absenting himself on so important an occasion. " Nothing like looking after things yourself" was one of his favourite maxims, enforced with a wink of intense sagacity. He was absolutely ignorant of legal formalities, but not the less convinced that such could not be properly carried out without his own superintendence.

The financier's appearance was quite a study. He had for some time past affected rather a rural style of attire, and his costume now was the Newmanham ideal of a flourishing country squire. He chose with ostentatious humility, the most modest of his equipages to take him to Dene ; but he mounted it like a triumphal car. Truly there was great joy in Israel on that eventful morning, for all his family knew the errand on which their sire and lord was bent, and exulted, as is their wont, unctuously.

Ephraim Schmidt was a short bulky man, somewhat under fifty ; his heavy, sensual features betrayed at once his origin and the habits of high-living to which he was notoriously prone. His companion was a striking contrast. There was rather a foreign look about Morris Davidson's keen handsome face, and those intensely brilliant black eyes are scarcely naturalized on this side of the Channel—but the Semitic stamp was barely perceptible. His manner was very quiet and courteous, but never cringing, nor was there anything obsequious about his ready smile. He was choice in his raiment, but it was always subdued in its tone, and he wore no jewels beyond a signet key-ring, and

one pearl of great price at his neck. He was the type of a class that has been developed only within the last half century—the *petit-maître* order of legalists—whose demeanour, like that of the Louis Quinze Abbés, is a perpetual contradiction of their staid profession, but who nevertheless know their business thoroughly, and follow it up with unscrupulous obstinacy. When Mr. Davidson senior died (who had long been Ephraim Schmidt's confidential solicitor), men marvelled that the cautious capitalist could entrust his affairs to such young and inexperienced hands; in truth he had at first many doubts aud misgivings, but these soon vanished as he began to appreciate Morris's cool, pitiless nature, and iron nerves. The wolf-cub's coat was sleek and soft enough, and he never showed his teeth unnecessarily ; but his fangs were sharper, and his gripe more fatally tenacious, than even his gaunt old sire's.

So, through the clear frosty morning, the two Jews drove jocundly along, beguiling the way with pleasant anticipations of the business before them. The lawyer had heard of Lord Clydesdale's engagement to Miss Vavasour, and thought it just possible that under the circumstances some compromise might be attempted. But to this view of the case his patron would in nowise incline, and he discreetly forbore to press it. They passed through the double towers flanking the huge iron-gates ; and the broad undulating park stretched out before them, clumps of lofty timber studding the smooth turf, while grey turrets and pinnacles just showed in the distance through the leafless trees. The Hebrew's heart swelled, almost painfully, with pride and joy. He had been wandering for many a year—not unhappily or unprofitably, it is true—through the commercial Desert, and now, he looked upon the fair Land of Promise, only waiting for him to arise and take possession, when he had once cast out the Amorite. When they drove up to the great portico, he was actually perspiring with satisfaction, in spite of the cold. He grasped his companion's arm, and whispered, hoarsely—

" Mind, Morris, they'll ask for time : but we won't give them a day !—not a day."

The chief butler received the visitors in the hall, and ushered them himself to the library. Ephraim Schmidt, in the midst of his unholy triumph, could not help being impressed by the grave dignity of that august functionary. He began to think if it would not be possible, by proffer of large monies, to tempt him to desert his master's fallen fortunes, and to abide in the house that he became so well. A pleasant, idle dream ! Solomon made the Afreets and Genii his slaves ; but, if the Great King had been revived in the plenitude of his power, he would never have tempted that seneschal to serve him, while a Gentile survived on the land.

The family solicitor of the Vavasours was sitting before a table overspread with bulky papers, with his clerk close by his side. He was thin, and white-haired, with a round withered face, pleasant withal, like a succulent Ribstone pippin ; his manner was very gentle, and almost timid, but no lawyer alive could boast that he had ever got the best of a negotiation in which Mr. Faulkner was concerned. He greeted the capitalist very courteously, and Mr. Davidson very coldly, for,—he had seen *him* b<sub>efore</sub>. There was one other occupant of the library—a tall man, lounging in the embrasure of a distant window, who never turned his head when the new-comers entered : it seemed as though the bleak winter landscape outside had superior attractions. Ephraim Schmidt hardly noticed him ; but Davidson felt a disagreeable thrill of apprehension as he recognised the figure of Lord Clydesdale. It is needless to enumerate the verifications and · comparisons of many voluminous documents that had perforce to be gone through. The mortgagee got very impatient before they were ended.

" Yes, yes," he kept repeating, nervously, " it is all correct ; but come to the point—to the point."

Mr. Faulkner was perfectly imperturbable, neither hurrying himself in the least, nor making any unnecessary delay.

" I believe everything is quite correct," he said, at last. " Now, Mr. Davidson, may I ask you what your client's intentions are ? Is there any possibility of a compromise ?"

" I fear, none whatever," was the quiet answer. " We have given ample notice, and the equity of redemption cannot be extended. My client is anxious to invest in land, and we could hardly find a more eligible opening than foreclosure here would afford us."

" Exactly so," the old lawyer retorted. " I only asked the question, because I was instructed to come to an explicit understanding. It does not much matter ; for—we are prepared to pay off every farthing."

The small thin hand seemed weighty and puissant as an athlete's, as he laid it on a steel-bound coffer beside him, with a significant gesture of security too tranquil to be defiant.

Cool and crafty as he was, Davidson was fairly taken unawares. He recoiled in blank amazement. Ephraim Schmidt started from his chair like a maniac, his eyes protruding wildly, and his face purple-black with rage.

"Pay off everything ?" he shrieked. " I don't believe it : it's a lie—a swindle. Not have Dene ? I'll have it in spite of you all !" The churned foam flew from his bulbous lips, as from the jaws of a baited boar.

The silent spectator in the window turned round, then, and stood contemplating the group, not striving to repress a harsh, scornful laugh. That filled up the measure of the unhappy Israelite's frenzy. He made a sort of blind plunge forward, shaking off the warning fingers with which Davidson sought to detain him.

" D—n you, let me go," he howled out. " Who is that man ? What does he do here ? I *will* know."

The person addressed strode on slowly till he came close to the speaker, and looked him in the face, still with the same cruel laugh on his own.

" I'll answer you," he said. " I was christened Raoul Delamere, but they call me Lord Clydesdale now; and I hope to marry Mr. Vavasour's only daughter. I am here—because I am infidel enough to enjoy seeing a Jew taken on the hip. I wouldn't have missed this—to clear off the biggest of your mortgages. So you fancied you were going to reign at Dene? Not if you had had another hundred thousand at your back. If we only have warning, the old blood can hold its own, and beat the best of you yet. Mr. Faulkner, don't you think you had better pay him, and let him go?"

The change of tone in those last words, from brutal disdain to studied courtesy, was the very climax of insult. It was an unworthy triumph, no doubt, but a very complete one. The Earl remained as much master of the position as ever was Front de Bœuf. The Jew was utterly annihilated. To have come there with the power of life and death in his hand, and now to be treated as an ordinary tradesman presenting a Christmas bill! He staggered back step by step, and sunk into a chair, dropping his head, and groaning heavily. Davidson had recovered himself by this time. The elder lawyer only sat silent, and scandalized, lifting his eyebrows in mute testimony against such unprofessional proceedings.

"We can hardly conclude such important business to-day," Morris said. "My client's excitement is a sufficient excuse. We know your intentions now, Mr. Faulkner, and there is ample time to settle everything. I will call upon you at any time or place you like to name."

So, after a few more words, it was settled.

Ephraim Schmidt went out, like a man in a dream, from the house that he had hoped to call his own; only moaning under his breath, like a vanquished Shylock—"Let us go home, let us go home." The chief butler (who had been aware of the state of affairs throughout) dealt him the last blow in the hall, by inquiring with exquisite courtesy, "If he would take any luncheon before he went?" The miserable Hebrew quivered all over, as a victim

at the stake might shrink under the last ingenuity of torture. Truly, the meanest of the many debtors who had sued him in vain for mercy, need not have envied the usurer then.

O dark-eyed Miriam, and auburn-haired Deborah! lay aside your golden harps, or other instruments of music that your soul delights in: no song of gladness shall be raised in your tents to-night; it is for the daughters of the uncircumcised to triumph.

When the Squire heard an account of the morning's proceedings, he by no means shared in Clydesdale's satisfaction, and rather failed to appreciate the point of the jest. Hubert's thorough-bred instincts revolted against the idea of even a Jew usurer's having been grossly insulted under his roof, when the man only came to ask for his own; besides this, he understood the feeling that had been at work in the Earl's breast, and despised him accordingly. The difference in social position was too overwhelming to make the match a fair one; but in other respects the antagonists were about on a par. It was just this—a phase of purse-pride vanquished by another and a more potential one. Such a victory brings little honour. The transformed rod of the Lawgiver swallowed up the meaner serpents; but it was only a venomous reptile, after all.

Wyverne felt neither wrath nor despair when the news of Helen's engagement came; he had quite made up his mind that she would marry soon; but he was sad and pensive. He did not change his opinions easily, and he had formed a very strong one about Clydesdale's character: he thought the Earl was as little likely as any man alive to rule a high-spirited mate wisely and well. Nevertheless, Alan indited an epistle that even Lady Mildred could not help admiring: it was guarded, but not in the least formal or constrained; kind and sincerely affectionate, without a tinge of reproach, or a single allusion that could give pain. He saw "my lady" twice, Helen once, before the latter's marriage, and was equally successful with his verbal congratulations. Of course the interviews were not tête-

*à-têtes:* all parties concerned took good care of that. Wyverne and his aunt displayed admirable tact and *sangfroid;* but the demoiselle cast both into the shade: her manner was far more natural, and her composure less studied. Truly, the training of the *Grande Dame* progressed rapidly, and the results promised to be fearfully complete.

Alan did intimate an intention of being present at the wedding; but I fear he was scarcely ingenuous there. At all events, urgent private affairs took him abroad two days before the ceremony, no one knew exactly where; and it was three weeks before he appeared on the surface of society again.

*Io, Hymenœe!* Scatter flowers, or other missile oblations, profusely, you nubile virgins. O choir of appointed youths! Roll out, I beseech you, the Epithalamium roundly: let not the fault be imputed to you, if it sounds like a requiem.

So, we bid farewell to Helen Vavasour's maiden history—not without heaviness of heart. Henceforth it befits us to stand aside, with doffed beaver and bated breath, as the Countess of Clydesdale passes by.

———

## CHAPTER XXI.

### MAGNA EST VERITAS.

FIFTEEN or sixteen months are come and gone, and the faces of people and things are but little changed. Yes, one of our dramatic personages is a good deal altered for the worse—Alan Wyverne. He became sadder and wiser in this wise.

I forgot to tell you that the delicate state of Mrs. Rawdon Lenox's health, and of her affairs, had made a lengthened Continental tour very desirable. She remained abroad nearly two years, and did not return to England till the summer immediately following the Clydesdale marriage. It was late in the autumn when she and Alan met. If the latter had been forewarned of the *rencontre*, it is probable he would have avoided it by declining the invitation to Guestholme Priory; but when he found himself actually under the same roof with the "Dark Ladye" (so some friend or enemy had re-christened her), he felt a certain satisfaction in the idea of clearing up a mystery that had never ceased to perplex and torment him. Their first greeting was rather cold and constrained on both sides; but things could not remain on this footing long. Nina had no fancy for an armed neutrality with an ancient ally, and always brought the question of war or peace to an issue with the least possible delay.

When Alan came into the drawing-room after dinner, Mrs. Lenox's look was a sufficient summons, even without the significant movement of the fan, which she managed like a Madrileña. He sat down by her side, his pulse quickening a little with expectation; but curiosity was the sole excitement. For awhile they talked about their travels and other indifferent subjects. The lady got tired of that child's-play first, and broke ground boldly.

"I suppose the interdict is taken off now?" she said. "Will you believe, that I am really sorry that there is no longer a cause for your avoiding me? Will you believe, that no one regretted it, and felt for you more than I did, when I heard your engagement was broken off? Do tell me, that neither I nor my unfortunate affairs had anything to do with it. I have been worrying myself ever since with the fancy that your great kindness to me may have cost you very dear."

Wyverne was gifted with coolness and self-control quite exceptional, but both as nearly as possible broke down at that moment. He certainly deserved infinite credit for answering, after a minute's silence, so calmly,

"Then it would be a satisfaction to you to know this? Have you any doubts on the subject?"

"Well, I suppose I ought not to have any," Nina said, frankly. "The engagement lasted for months after those wretched anonymous things were written, and I am sure I did all I could to set matters straight. My letter was everything that is meek and quiet and proper, was it not? And it was honest truth, too, every word of it."

"Your letter? Yes, of course—the letter you wrote in answer to mine; but the other—the other?"

He spoke absently and almost at random, like a man half awake.

"What on earth are you talking about?" Mrs. Lenox said, with manifest impatience. "What other letter? Did you suppose me capable of writing one other line beside that necessary reply? What have you suspected? I *will* know. Alan, I believed you more generous. You have a right to think lightly of me, and to say hard things, but not—not to insult me so cruelly."

There were tears in the low, tremulous voice, but none in the deep dark eyes that had dilated at first wonderingly, and were now so sad in their passionate reproach that Wyverne did not dare to meet them. He knew that Nina was capable of much that was wild and wicked, but that very recklessness made dissimulation with her simply impossible. If she had been pure and cold as St. Agnes, Alan would not have felt more certain of the truth and sincerity of her meaning and words. The fraud, that he had vaguely suspected at the time, stood out black and distinct enough now. He hated himself so intensely that for the moment all other feelings were swallowed up in self-contempt—even to the craving for vengeance on the conspirators who had juggled him, which ever afterwards haunted him like an evil spirit. Wyverne had always cherished, you know, a simple, generous faith in the dignity of womanhood; if his chivalry had carried him one step further—if, in despite of the evidence of his senses, he had refused to believe in womanhood's utter debasement—it would have been perhaps the very folly of romance; but he might have defied the forger. He took the wisest course now, by telling Nina the whole truth, as briefly and considerately as possible.

"You see, I did you fearful wrong," he said. "Though I have paid for it heavily already, and shall suffer to my life's end, that is no reason why you should forgive me. I don't even ask you to do so."

Mrs. Lenox was, indeed, bitterly incensed. A perfectly immaculate matron might have laughed such a conspiracy against her fair fame to scorn: Nina could not afford to be maligned unjustly. Nevertheless all her indignation was levelled at the unknown framer of the fraud; not a whit rested on Alan. She had been used to see people commit themselves in every conceivable way, and make the wildest sacrifices, for her sake; but she had learned to appreciate these follies at their proper worth. Strong selfish desire and the hope of an evil reward was at the bottom of them all. Truly, when a man ruins himself simply to gratify his ruling passion, the lover deserves little more credit than the gambler. But the present case was widely different. She had not a shadow of a claim on Alan's service or forbearance. Though he seemed to see no merit in a single act of duty, she knew right well what it had cost him to destroy the supposed evidence of her shame; and now, instead of expecting thanks, he was reproaching himself for having misjudged her while believing his own eyes. As she thought on these things, Nina's hard battered heart grew fresh and young again. Not a single unholy element mingled in the tenderness of her gratitude; but, if time and place had not forbidden, she would scarcely have confined her demonstrations to a covert pressure of Wyverne's hand.

"Forgive you?" she said, piteously. "It drives me wild to hear you speak so. I would give up every friend I have in the world to keep *you*. The best of them would not have done half as much for me. And we can never be friends—really. My unhappy name has dragged you down like a millstone; don't attempt to deceive yourself; you must hate the sound of it now and always. Ah, do try to believe me. I would submit to any pain, or penance, or shame, and not think it hard measure, if I could only give you back what you have lost through me."

In despite of his exasperation, the sweet voice fell soothingly on Alan's ear.

A man need not greatly glorify himself for having simply acted up to his notions of right and honour; nevertheless, appreciation in the proper quarter must be gratifying to all except the *very* superior natures. Many are left among us still who "do good by stealth," but the habit of "blushing to find it known" is antiquated to a degree.

So, as he listened, Wyverne's mood softened; and he began quite naturally to play the part of consoler, trying to prove to Nina that she had been an innocent instrument throughout, and that if the conspirators had been foiled in this instance, they would surely have found some other engine to work out the same result.

"But it was such base, cruel treachery," she said, trembling with passion. "Will you not try to trace it, for my sake if not for your own? You must have some suspicions. If I were a man, and could act and move freely, I should never sleep soundly till I was revenged."

Wyverne answered very slowly, and, as he spoke, his face hardened and darkened till it might have been carved in granite.

"You may spare the spur; there is no fear of my sleeping over it. I'm not made of wax or snow, to be moulded like this into a puppet for their profit or pleasure, and I owe you a vengeance besides. Yes, I have suspicions; I'll make them certainties, if I live. Your never having got my note, telling you of my burning the first of the two letters, gives me a clue. They may double as they like, they won't escape, if I once fairly strike the trail. Now, we will never speak of this again till—I give you *the name.*"

The change of Alan's character dated from that night; most of his friends noticed it before long. He was never morose or sullen, but always moody, and absent, and pre-occupied: without exactly avoiding society, he found himself alone, unwontedly often, and solitude did him far more harm than good. To speak the truth, his credit as a pleasant companion began sensibly to decline. A Fixed Idea, even if it be as rosy as

Hope, interferes sadly with a man's social merits; if it chance to be sombre or menacing in hue, the influence is simply fatal to conviviality.

But autumn and winter passed, and it was spring again, before Wyverne could set his foot on more solid ground than vague surmises. He felt certain that Lady Mildred had countenanced, if not directed, the plot—the note having miscarried from Dene was strong evidence—but he was equally sure that her delicate hands were clear of the soil of actual fraud. Who had been the working instrument? For a moment his thoughts turned to Max Vavasour, but he soon rejected this idea, remembering that the latter was not in England that Christmas-tide; besides which, he could not fancy his cousin superintending the practical details of a vulgar forgery; he would far sooner have suspected Clydesdale, but there was not the faintest reason, so far, to connect the Earl with foul play. So he went groping on, for months, in the twilight, without advancing a step, growing more gloomy and discontented every day. It was a curious chance that put him on the right scent at last.

An Inn of Court is not exactly the spot one would select for setting a "trap to catch a sunbeam;" a wholesome amount of light and air is about as much as one can expect to find in such places; heavy, grave decorum pervades them, very fittingly; but it may be doubted if any quarter of a populous city, respectable in its outward seeming, has a right to be so depressingly dull and dingy, as is the Inn of Gray; the spiders of all sorts, who lurk thereabouts, had best not keep the flies long in their webs, or the victims would scarce be worth devouring.

Some such thoughts as these were in Wyverne's mind as he wandered through the grim quadrangle, one cold evening towards the end of March, looking for "Humphrey and Gliddon's" chambers. The firm had an evil name; men said, that if it was difficult to find out their den, it was twice as hard to escape from it without loss of plumage. Alan's temper had certainly changed for the worse, but his good-nature stood by him still; so, when a comrade wrote from the country, to beg him to act as proxy in a delicate money transaction with the aforesaid attorneys, he assented very willingly, and was rather glad to have something to employ his afternoon. He had just come up from his hunting quarters, where the dry, dusty ground rode like asphalte, and scent was a recollection of the far past.

After some trouble he lighted on the right staircase. Raw and murky as the outer atmosphere might be, it was pure æther compared to that of the low-browed office into which the visitor first entered; at any hour or season of the year, you could fancy that room maintaining a good, steady, condensed dusk of its own, in which fog, and smoke, and dust, had about equal shares. Two clerks sat there, writing busily. The one nearest the door—a thick-set, sullen man, past middle age—looked up as Alan came in, and stretching out a grimy hand, said, in a dull, mechanical voice,

"Your card, sir, if you please—Sir Alan Wyverne wishes to see Mr. Humphrey."

It was evidently the formula of reception in that ominous ante-chamber.

The other clerk had not lifted his head when the door opened; but he started violently when he heard the name, so as nearly to upset the inkstand in which he chanced to be dipping his pen, and turned round with a sort of terror on his haggard, ruined face. It might have been a very handsome face once, but the wrinkled, flaccid flesh had fallen away round the hollow temples and from under the heavy eyes; the complexion was unhealthy, pale, and sodden; the features pinched and drawn, to deformity; the lines on the forehead were like trenches, and the abundant dark hair was, not sprinkled, but streaked and patched, irregularly, with grey.

But, at the first glance, Wyverne recognised the face of a very old friend; he recognised it the more easily because, when he saw it last, it wore almost the same wild, scared look—on the memorable Derby day when "Cloanthus" swept past the stand, scarcely extended, the two leading favourites struggling vainly to reach his quarters.

All his self-command was needed to enable him to suppress the exclamation that sprang to his lips; but he rarely made a mistake when it was a question of tact or delicacy. He followed his conductor into the next room, silently; it chanced to be vacant at that moment; then Alan laid his hand on the clerk's shoulder, as he stood with averted eyes, shaking like an aspen, and said, in tones carefully lowered—

"My God! Hugh Crichton — you here?"

"Hush," the other answered, in a lower whisper still; "that's not my name now. You wouldn't spoil my last chance, if you could help it? If you want to see me, wait five minutes after you leave this place, and I'll come to you in the square."

"I'll wait, if it's an hour," Wyverne said, and so passed into the inner room without another word. His business was soon done; even Humphrey and Gliddon could find no pretext for detaining clients who came with money in their hand. Alan did not exchange a glance with either of the occupants of the clerks'-room as he went out; he breathed more freely when he was in chill March air again. As he walked up and down the opposite side of the square, which was nearly deserted, his thoughts were very pitiful and sad.

Hardly a year passes without the appearance of one or more comets in society; none of these have sparkled more briefly and brilliantly than Hugh Crichton. Everybody liked, and many admired him, but the world had hardly begun to appreciate his rare and versatile talents, when he shot down into the outer darkness. He had friends who would have helped him if they could, but all trace of him was lost, and none could say for certain whether he lived or no.

Wyverne had not waited many minutes, when a bent, shrunken figure came creeping slowly, almost stealthily, towards him, keeping well in the shadow of the buildings. In another moment, Alan was grasping both his ancient comrade's hands, with a cordial, honest gripe, that might have put heart and hope into the veriest castaway.

"Dear old Hugh! how glad I am to light on you again, though you are so fearfully changed. Why, they said you had died abroad."

"No such luck," the other answered, with a dreary laugh. "I did go abroad, and stayed there till I was nearly starved; then I came back. London's the best hiding place, after all; and if you have hands and brain, you can always earn enough to buy bread, and spirits, and tobacco. I've been in this place more than a year; I get a pound a week, and I think of 'striking' soon for an advance of five shillings. They won't lose me if they can help it; I save them a clerk, at least; old Gliddon never asked me another question after he saw me write a dozen lines. My work is all indoors, that's one comfort; they haven't asked me to serve a writ yet; my senior—you saw him,—the man with a strong cross of the bull about the head—does all that business, and likes it. But the firm don't trust me much, and they would be more unpleasant still, if they knew 'Henry Carstairs' was a false name. No one has much interest now in hunting me down; it's old friends' faces I've always been afraid of meeting. But I did think that none of our lot would ever have set foot in that den, and I had got to fancy myself safe. You didn't come on your own affairs, Alan, I know. I had an extra grog the night I heard you had fallen in for Castle Dacre. I rather think I am glad to see you, after all."

He jerked out the sentences in a nervous, abrupt way, perpetually glancing round, as if he were afraid of being watched; he was so manifestly ill-at-ease that Wyverne had not the heart to keep him there; besides it was cruelty to expose the emaciated frame, so thinly clad, a minute longer than was necessary, to the keen evening air.

"Why, Hugh, of course you're glad to see me," Alan said, forcing himself to speak cheerily; "the idea of doubting about it! But it's too cold to stand chattering here. I'm staying at the Clarendon: you'll come at seven, sharp,

won't you? We'll dine in my rooms, quite alone, and have a long talk about old days, and new ones, too. I'll have thought of something better for you by that time, than this infernal quill-driving."

Hugh Crichton hesitated visibly for a few seconds, and appeared to make up his mind, with a sudden effort, to something not altogether agreeable.

"Thank you: you're very good, Alan. Yes, I'll come, the more because I've something on my mind that I ought to tell you; but I should never have had the pluck to look you up, if you had not found me. I hope your character at the Clarendon can stand a shock; it will be compromised when they hear such a scare-crow ask for your rooms. I can't stay a moment longer, but I'll be punctual."

He crept away with the same weak, stealthy step, and his head seemed bent down lower than when he came.

Nevertheless, when, at the appointed hour, the guest sat down opposite his host, the contrast was not so very striking. The office-drudge was scarcely recognisable; he seemed to freshen and brighten up wonderfully, in an atmosphere that had once been congenial. Even so, those bundles of dried twigs that Eastern travellers bring home, and enthusiasts call "Roses of Sharon" (such Roses!), expand under the influence of warmth and moisture, so as to put forth the feeble semblance of a flower. The black suit was terribly threadbare, and hung loosely round the shrunken limbs, but it adapted itself to the wearer's form, with the easy, careless grace for which Hugh Crichton's dress had always been remarkable; his neck-tie was still artistic in its simplicity, and the hair swept over his brow with the old classic wave; his demeanour bore no trace of a sojourn in Alsatia, and a subtle refinement of manner and gesture clung naturally to the wreck of a gallant gentleman. Some plants you know—not the meanest nor the least fragrant—flourish more kindly in the crevices of a ruin than in the richest loam.

It was a pleasant dinner, on the whole, though not a very lively one; for

Alan had too much tact to force con-viviality. Crichton ate sparingly, but drank deep; he did not gulp down his liquor, though, greedily, but rather savoured it with a slow enjoyment, suf-fering his palate to appreciate every shade of the flavour; the long, satisfied sigh that he could not repress as he set down empty the first beaker of dry champagne, spoke volumes.

They drew up to the fire when the table was cleared, and they were left alone. Wyverne rose suddenly, and leant over towards his companion with a velvet cigar-case in his hand, that he had just taken from the mantelpiece.

"You must tell me your story for the last few years," he said; "but put that case in your pocket before you begin. There are some regalias in it, of the calibre you used to fancy, and—a couple of hundreds, in notes, to go on with. You dear, silly old Hugh! Don't shake your head and look scrupulous. Why, I won thrice as much of you at *écarté* in the week before that miserable Derby, and you never asked for your revenge. You should have it now if either you or I were in cue for play. Seriously—I want you to feel at ease before you begin to talk; I want you to feel that your troubles are over, and that you never need go near that awful *guet-à-pens* again. I've got a permanent arrangement in my head, that will suit you, I hope, and set you right for ever and a day. Hugh, you know if our positions were reversed, I should ask you for help just as frankly as I expect you will take it from me."

Crichton shivered all over, worse than he had done out in the cold March evening.

"Put the case down," he said hoarsely. "It will be time enough to talk about that and your good intentions half-an-hour hence. I'll tell you what I have been doing, if you care to hear."

Now, though the story interested Wyverne sincerely, it would be simple cruelty to inflict it on you; with very slight variations, it might have applied to half the *viveurs* that have been ruined during the last hundred years. Still, not many men could have listened un-moved to such a tale, issuing from the mouth of an ancient friend. When he had come to a certain point in his story, the speaker paused abruptly.

"Poor Hugh!" Alan said. "How you must have suffered. Take breath now; I'm certain your throat wants moistening, and the claret has been waiting on you this quarter of an hour. It's my turn to speak; I'm impatient to tell you my plan. The agent at Castle Dacre is so wonderfully old and rheu-matic, that it makes one believe in miracles when he climbs on the back of his pony. I would give anything to have a decent excuse for pensioning him off. I shall never live there much, and the property is so large, that it ought to be properly looked after. If you don't mind taking care of a very dreary old house, there's £800 a year, and un-limited lights and coals, (they used to burn about ten tons a week, I believe,) and all the snipe and fowl you like to shoot, waiting for you. I shall be the obliged party if you'll take it; for it will ease my conscience, which at present is greatly troubled. The work is not so hard, and you've head enough for any-thing."

Not pleasure or gratitude, but rather vexation and confusion showed them-selves in Crichton's face.

"Can't you have patience?" he mut-tered, irritably. "Did'nt I ask you to wait till you had heard all? There's more, and worse, to tell; though I don't know, yet, how much harm was done."

He went on to say, that about the time when things were at the worst with him, he had stumbled upon Har-ding Knowles; they had been cotempo-raries at Oxford, and rather intimate. Harding did not appear to rejoice much at the encounter; though he must have guessed at the first glance the strait to which his old acquaintance was reduced, he made no offer of prompt assistance, but asked for Crichton's address, ex-pressing vague hopes of being able to do something for him; Hugh gave it with great reluctance, and only under a solemn promise of secrecy. He did not the least expect that Knowles would remember him, and was greatly surprised when the latter called some five or six weeks afterwards. Harding's tone was much more cordial than it had been at their first meeting; he seemed really sorry at having failed, so far, in finding anything that would suit Crichton, and actually pressed him to borrow £10— or more if it was required—to meet present emergencies. An instinctive suspicion almost made Hugh refuse the loan; he felt as if he would rather be indebted to any man 'alive than to the person who offered it; but he was so fearfully "hard up" that he had not the courage to decline. Knowles came again and again, with no ostensible object except cheering his friend's solitude, and each time was ready to open his purse. "We must get you something before long, and then you can repay me," he would say. Crichton availed himself of these offers more than once, moderately; he began to think that he had done his benefactor great injustice, and looked for his visits eagerly; indeed, few *causeurs*, when he chose to exert himself, could talk more pleasantly than Knowles.

One evening the conversation turned, apparently by chance, to old memories of college days.

"That was the best managed thing we ever brought off," Harding said at last, "when we made Alick Drummond carry on a regular correspondence with a foreign lady of the highest rank, who was madly in love with him. How did we christen the Countess? I forget. But I remember the letters you wrote for her; the delicate feminine character was the most perfect thing I ever saw. Have you lost that talent of imitating handwriting? It must have been a natural gift; I never saw it equalled."

"Write down a sentence or two," Hugh replied; "I'll show you if I have lost the knack."

He copied them out on two similar sheets of paper, and gave the three to Knowles after confusing them under the table: the latter actually started, and the admiration that he displayed was quite sincere: the *fac similes*, indeed, were so miraculously like the original,

that it was next to impossible to distinguish them.

"I can guess what is coming," Alan whispered softly, seeing the speaker pause. "Go on straight and quick to the end, for God's love, and keep nothing back. Don't look at me."

The white working lips had no need to say more: the other saw the whole truth directly. He clenched his hand with a savage curse, but Alan's sad deprecating eyes checked the passionate outbreak of remorse and anger. Suddenly and reluctantly — like a spirit forced to reveal the secrets of his prison-house—Hugh Crichton went through all the miserable details.

Knowles had represented himself as being on such very intimate terms with Wyverne, as fully to justify him in attempting a practical joke.

"Alan's the best fellow in the world," he said, airily, "but he believes that it is impossible to take him in about womankind. There's the finest possible chance just now, and it can be managed so easily, if you will only help me."

Hugh's natural delicacy and sense of honour, dulled and weakened by drink and degradation, had life enough left to revolt suspiciously. But the other brought to bear pretexts and arguments, specious enough to have deluded a stronger intellect and quieted a keener conscience: he particularly insisted on the point that the lady's character could bear being compromised, and that the secret would never go beyond Alan and himself. Hugh had to contend, besides, against a sense of heavy obligation, and the selfish fear of offending the only friend that was left to back him. Of course, eventually he consented. The next morning Harding brought a specimen of the handwriting—a long and perfectly insignificant note, with the signature torn off—(he was a great collector of autographs): he was also provided with paper and envelopes, both marked with a cypher, which he took pains to conceal. Crichton could not be sure of the initials, but he caught a glimpse of their colour — a brilliant scarlet. The tone of the fictitious letter, though the expressions were guardedly vague, seemed strangely earnest for a mere mystification; certainly an intimate acquaintance was implied between the writer and the person to whom it was addressed. The copyist was more than half dissatisfied; he grumbled a good many objections while employed on his task, and was very glad when it was over. The signature was simply "N.," an initial which occurred more than once in the specimen note, so that it was easy to reproduce a very peculiar wavy flourish. The imitation was a masterpiece, and Knowles was profuse of thanks and praises.

He did not allude to the matter more than once during the next few weeks, and then only to remark, in a careless, casual way, that the plot was going on swimmingly. This struck Crichton as rather odd; neither the pleasure of Knowles's society nor the comparative luxuries which liberal advances supplied, could keep him from feeling very uncomfortable at times. One morning, late in December, a note came, begging him to dine with Harding that night in the Temple; the writer "was going into the country almost immediately."

It was a very succulent repast, and poor Hugh, as was his wont, drank largely; nevertheless, when, late in the evening, Knowles asked him to repeat his caligraphic feat, and showed the draft of a letter, it became evident, even to his clouded brain, that something more than "merry mischief" was intended; at first he refused flatly and rudely. Indeed, any rational being, unless very far gone in drink or self-delusion, must have suspected foul play. Not only was the tone of the letter passionate to a degree, but it contained allusions of real grave import; and one name was actually mentioned—Helen Vavasour's. Knowles was playing his grand *coup*, and necessarily had to risk something. He was not at all disconcerted at the resistance he encountered; he had a plausible explanation ready to meet every objection. " He was going down to Dene the next day, on purpose to enjoy the *dénouement ;* it would be such a pity to spoil it now. Miss Vavasour was a cousin who had known Alan from her

10

infancy; she would appreciate the trick as well as any one; but, of course, she was never to know of it. This was the very last time he would ask his friend's help.'' So the tempter went on, alternately ridiculing and cajoling Hugh's scruples, all the while drenching him with strong liquor: at length he prevailed.

Crichton was one of those men whose hand and eye, often to their own detriment, will keep steady when their brain is whirling. He executed his task with a mechanical perfection, though he was scarcely aware of the meaning of each sentence as he wrote it down. Knowles took possession of the letter as soon as it was done, and locked it up carefully.

The revel became an orgie: the last thing that Hugh remembered distinctly was—marking a devilish satisfaction on his companion's crafty face, that made his own blood boil. After that everything was chaos. He had a vague recollection of having tried to get back the letter—of high words and a serious quarrel—even of a blow exchanged; but the impressions were like those left by a painful nightmare. He woke from a long heavy stupor, such as undrugged liquor could scarcely produce, and found himself on a door-step in his own street, without a notion of how he had got there, subject to the attentions of a benevolent policeman, who would not allow him to enjoy, undisturbed, " a lodging upon the cold ground." The next day came a curt contemptuous note from Harding Knowles, to say " that he was glad to have been of some assistance to an old friend, and that he should never expect repayment of his advances; but that nothing would induce him to risk a repetition of the painful scene of last night." They had never met since. Crichton was constantly haunted with the idea of having been an accessory to some base villany; and would have communicated his suspicions, long ago, to Wyverne, if it had not been for the false pride which made him keep aloof from all ancient acquaintance, as if he had been plague-stricken.

Alan sat perfectly quiet and silent,

till the other had finished, only betraying emotion by a convulsive twisting of the fingers that shaded his eyes. All at once he broke out into a harsh bitter laugh.

"You thought it was a practical joke? So it was—a very practical one, and right well played out. Do you know what it cost me? The hope and happiness of my life—that's all. Why, if I were to drain that lying hound's blood, drop by drop, he would be in my debt still!"

Then his head sank on his crossed arms, and he began to murmur to himself—so piteously—

"Ah, my Helen! my lost Helen!"

The beaten-down, degraded look possessed the castaway's face stronger than ever.

"Didn't I ask you to wait till I had told you all?" he muttered. "I knew how it would be; that was why I hesitated to accept your invitation to-day. Let me go now; I cannot comfort you or help you either. You meant kindly though, old friend, and I thank you all the same. Good-bye."

Alan lifted his head quickly. His eyes were not angry—only inexpressibly sad.

"Sit down, Hugh," he said, "and don't be hasty. You might give one a moment's breathing-time after a blow like that. I haven't spirits enough for argument, much less for quarrelling. I know well if you had been in your sober senses, and had thought it would really harm me, no earthly bribe would have tempted you to pen one line. You *can* help me very much; and I will trust you so far from the bottom of my heart; as for comfort—I must trust to God. I hold to every word of my offers. I am so very glad I made them before I heard all this; for I can ask you to serve me now without your suspecting a bribe."

Length of misery tames stoicism as it crushes better feelings: a spirit nearly broken yields easily to weakness that would shame hearts inexperienced in sorrow. The pride of manhood could not check the big drops that wetted Crichton's hollow cheeks before Wyverne had finished speaking.

They talked long and seriously that night. Alan did not trust by halves; he forced himself to go into every detail that it was necessary the other should know, though some words and names seemed to burn his lips in passing. Before they parted their plan was fully arranged. Hugh was to resign his clerkship at once, so as to devote himself exclusively to completing the chain of proofs that would criminate at least the main movers in the plot. Alan clung persistently to the idea that Clydesdale had a good deal to do with it.

It is needless to say that the amateur detective worked with all his heart, and soul, and strength. His temperance was worthy of an anchorite; and, when he kept his senses about him, Crichton could be as patient and keen-scented as the most practised of legal bloodhounds. Before a week was over, he had collected evidence, conclusive and consecutive enough, to have convinced any Court of Honour, though perhaps it would not have secured a verdict from those free and enlightened Britons who will make a point of acquitting any murderer that does not chance to be caught "red-handed." Truly ours is a noble Constitution, and Trial by Jury is one of its fairest pillars; but I have heard a paragon Judge speak blasphemy thereanent. If the Twelve were allowed the French latitude of finding "extenuating circumstances," I believe the coolest on the Bench would go distraught, in helpless wrath and contempt.

Wyverne knew the shop that Mrs. Lenox patronized for *papeterie*. They ascertained there that a man answering exactly to the description of Knowles had called, one day in that autumn, and had asked for a packet of envelopes and note-paper, stating that he was commissioned to take them down in the country, and producing one of the lady's cards as a credential. The stationer particularly remembered it from the fact of the purchase having been paid for on the spot. Trifling as the amount was—only a few shillings—it was a curious infraction of Nina's commercial system, which was, as a rule, consistently Pennsylvanian. Crichton had certainly contracted no new friendships during his office servitude, but he had made a few acquaintances at some of the haunts frequented nightly by revellers of the clerkly guild. He worked one of these engines of information very effectually. Harding had more than once given him a cheque to a small amount, which he had got cashed through one of the subordinates of the bank, whom he had chanced to fraternize with at the "Cat and Compasses," or some such reputable hostel. At the expense of much persuasion, and a timely advance to the official, whose convivial habits were getting him into difficulties, Hugh was in a position to prove that Knowles had paid into his account, early in the January following that eventful Christmas, a cheque for £5000, signed by Lord Clydesdale. The money remained standing to his credit for some time, but had since been drawn out for investment. The dates of the composition of the fictitious letters corresponded exactly with the times at which Alan had received them.

Altogether, the case seemed tolerably clear, and a net of proof was drawn round Harding Knowles that it would puzzle even his craft to escape from.

I do not enter into the question whether the influences of high Civilization are sanctifying, or the reverse; but on some grounds, it surely ought to improve our Christianity, if it were only for the obstacles standing in the path of certain pagan propensities. One would think that even an infidel might see the folly of letting the sun go down on futile wrath. In truth, nowadays, the prosecution of a purely personal and private vengeance is not alone immoral in itself, but exceedingly difficult to carry out. You cannot go forth and smite your enemy under the fifth rib, wheresoever you may meet, after the simple antique fashion. You must lure him across the Channel before you can even proceed after the formula of the polite *duello*—supposing always that the adversary had not infringed the criminal code.

Alan Wyverne's nature was not sublime enough to admit a thought of forgiveness, now. Since he held the instruments of retaliation in his hand, he had never faltered for one moment in his vindictive purpose; but—how best to complete it—was a problem over which he brooded gloomily for hours, without touching the solution.

———

## CHAPTER XXII.

### AN OLD SCORE PAID.

IT is needless to explain, that on Harding Knowles Wyverne's anger was chiefly concentrated. Clydesdale came in for his share; but, so far, it was difficult to establish the extent of the Earl's connection with the plot. When the Divine warning, "Vengeance is Mine," has once been ignored, very few men are so cold-blooded, as to exclude entirely from their plan of retribution, the old simple method of exacting it with their own right hand. As Alan sat thinking, a vision would rise before him, dangerously attractive: he saw a waste of sand-hills stretching for leagues along the coast of France; so remote from road or dwelling, that a shot would never be heard unless it were by a strange fishing-boat out at sea; so seldom traversed, that the body of a murdered man might lie there for days undiscovered, unless the gathering birds told tales; he saw the form of his enemy standing up in relief against the clear morning-light, within a dozen paces of the muzzle of his pistol. I fear it was more the impracticability of the idea than its sinfulness, which made Alan decide that it ought to be relinquished. Sometimes it needs no great casuistry to enable even the best-natured of us to give, in our own minds, a verdict of Justifiable Homicide. But upon calm consideration, it was about a million to one against Harding's being induced to risk himself in a duel, which he might guess would be to the death, where the chances would be heavily against him. As a rule, forgers don't fight.

There were great difficulties, too, about a public exposure—so great that Alan never really entertained the idea for a moment. He would just as soon have thought of publishing a scurrilous libel about those whom he loved best, as of allowing their names to be paraded for the world's amusement and criticism.

While he was still in doubt and perplexity, he chanced to meet one morning, a famous physician, with whom he was rather intimate, though he had never employed him professionally. Dr. Eglinton was a general favourite; many people, besides his patients, liked to hear his full cheery tones, and to see his quaint pleasant face, with the *fin sourire* that pointed his inexhaustible anecdotes; he was the most inveterate gossip that ever steered quite clear of ill-nature.

"You're not looking in such rude health as one would suspect at the end of the hunting season," the Doctor said, "but I suppose there's nothing in my way this morning. I wish I could say as much for an old friend of yours, whom I have just left at the Burlington. It's the Rector of Dene. By the bye, it would be a great charity if you would call on him to-day: he seems lonely and out of spirits—indeed, the nature of his disease is depressing. I know he's very fond of you, and you might do him more good than my physic can. I fear it is a hopeless case—a heart-complaint of some standing—though the symptoms have only become acute and aggravated within the last two years. Do you know if he has had any great domestic troubles or worries of late? He was not communicative, and I did not dare to press him. Nothing can be so bad for him as anything of the sort; and any heavy or sudden shock might be instantly fatal."

It was not only surprise and pain, but sharp self-reproach too, that made Wyverne turn so pale. Revenge is essentially selfish, even when it will reason at all; he had actually forgotten his kind old friend's existence while pondering how to punish his son. He knew right well what had been the great trouble that had weighed on Gilbert Knowles's heart for the last two years. The Rec-

tor was of course unable to intercede or avert the catastrophe; but, when he heard of the final rupture of Helen's engagement, he bowed his head despairingly, and had never raised it since. I told you how he loved her, and how sincerely he loved Alan. On their union rested the last of his hopes; when that was crushed, he felt he should never have strength or spirits enough to nourish another.

No wonder Wyverne's reply was strangely embarrassed and inconsequent: "I don't know—yes—perhaps there may have been some trouble on his mind. The dear old Rector! I wish I had heard of this before. Of course I'll go to him; but not to-day—it's impossible to-day. Good-bye: I shall see you again very soon. I shall want to hear about your patient."

His manner, usually *posé* to a degree, was so abrupt just then, that it set the Doctor musing as he walked away. "There's something wrong there," he muttered, half aloud (it was a way he had); "I wish I knew what it was; he's well worth curing. He's not half the man he was when he was ruined. None of us are, for that matter: I suppose there's something bracing in the air of poverty. I did hear something about a cousinly attachment, but it can't be that: Wyverne is made of too sterling stuff to pine away because an *amourette* goes wrong: besides, he's always with Lady Clydesdale now, they say. What *don't* they say, if one had only time to listen," &c., &c.

The good physician had a little subdued element of cynicism in his nature, which he only indulged when soliloquizing, or over the one cigar that professional decorum winked at, when the long day's toil was done.

"Not to-day." No; Alan felt that it would be impossible to meet the father, till the interview with the son was over. He went back to his rooms, and sat there thinking for a full hour. Then he took some papers from a locked casket, and went straight to the Temple. Knowles's servant chanced to be out, so he came himself to open the door of his chambers. He was prosperous and careful, you know, and could meet the commercial world boldly, abroad or at home; but the most timorous of insolvents never felt so disagreeable a thrill at the apparition of the sternest of creditors, as shot through Harding's nerves when he saw on the threshold, the calm courteous face of the man whom he disliked and feared beyond all living. There was something in that face—though a careless observer would have detected no ruffle in its serenity—that stopped the other in his greeting, and in the act of offering his hand. Not a word passed between the two, till Knowles had followed his visitor into the innermost of the two sitting-rooms, closing the doors carefully behind them. Then Wyverne spoke—

"An old friend of mine has given me a commission to do. I had better get through that before coming to my own business. You advanced several sums to Hugh Crichton at different times, lately; will you be good enough to say, if that list of them is right?"

There could not be a more striking proof of how completely Knowles's nerves were unstrung, than the fact, that he looked at the paper without having a notion as to the correctness of the items, and without the faintest interest in the question. He answered quite at random, speaking quick and confusedly—

"Yes, they are quite right; but it doesn't in the least matter. I never expected—"

"Pardon me," Alan interrupted, "it doesn't matter very much—to us. Perhaps since you have become a capitalist, you can afford to be careless of such trifles. Hugh Crichton does not think it a trifle to owe money to you. Here is the exact sum as far as he can remember it. It is your own fault if you have cheated yourself. I will not trouble you for a receipt. I dare say you did not expect to be paid, still less by my hand. That is settled. Now I will talk about my own affairs."

Though he spoke so quietly, there was a subtle contempt in his tone, that made every word fall like a lash. Again and again, Harding tried to meet the steady look of the cold grave eyes,

and failed each time signally. He tried bluster, thus early in the interview, in sheer despair.

"I can't guess at your object, but your manner is not to be mistaken. It is evident you come here with the deliberate purpose of insulting me. I'm afraid I must disappoint you, Sir Alan. I decline to enter into your own affairs at all, and I consider our conversation ended here."

The other laughed scornfully, and his accent became harder and more *tranchant* than ever.

"Bah!—you lose your head! There are two gross errors in that last speech. I don't come to insult, because, to insult a person, you must presume he has some title to self-respect. I utterly deny your right to such a thing. And you will listen as long as I choose to speak; you may be sure I shall not use an unnecessary word. I come here to make certain accusations and to impose certain conditions—or penalties, if you like. It's not worth while picking expressions."

Harding sat down, actually gnashing his teeth in impotent rage, leaning his elbows on his knees, and resting his chin on his clenched hands.

"Go on, then," he snarled, "and be quick about it."

"I accuse you," Alan answered, steadily, "of having played the part of common spy; of having composed, if you did not write, two anonymous letters to Lady Mildred and her daughter; afterwards, of having maligned a woman whom you never spoke to, by causing her handwriting to be forged; of having made a dear friend of mine, a gentleman of birth and breeding, unwittingly your accomplice, when he was brought so low that the Tempter himself might have spared him; of having done me, and perhaps my cousin, a mortal injury, when neither of us had ever hurt you by word or deed. I accuse you of having done all this for hire, for the specific sum of £5,000, paid you by Lord Clydesdale within a month after your villany was consummated. You need not trouble yourself to contradict one syllable of this, unless you choose to lie for the pleasure of lying. I have the written proofs here."

Knowles's head went down lower and lower while Wyverne was speaking; when he raised his face, it was fantastically convulsed and horribly livid, like one of those that we see in the illustrations to the *Inferno*, besetting the path of the travellers through the penal Circles. He was too anxious to escape from his torture, to protract it by a single vain denial; but he would not throw one chance of palliation away.

" It was not a bribe," he gasped out, " it was a regular bet. Look, I can show it you."

He drew his tablets out and tore them open with a shaking hand; and, after finding the page with great difficulty, pointed it out to Wyverne.

The latter just glanced at the entry, and cast down the book with crushing contempt.

" Five thousand to fifty," he said; " I've been long enough on the turf to construe those odds. The veriest robber in the ring would not have dared to show your 'regular bet.' Now, answer me one question—' How far was Clydesdale cognizant of your plot?'"

" He has never heard one word of it, up to this moment," the other answered, eagerly. " I swear it. You may make any inquiries you like. I *can* defy you there. But some one else did know of it, and approved it too; that was——"

Wyverne's tone changed savagely as he broke in.

" *Will* you confine yourself to answering the questions you are asked ? I don't want any confessions volunteered. I attach no real importance to them, after all; but it grates on one to hear people maligned unnecessarily. Now, I'll tell you what I mean to do about it. I thought at first of inducing you to cross the Channel, and giving you a chance of your life against mine there; but I gave that up, because I knew you would not come. Then I thought—a brutal, last resource—of beating you into a cripple, here. I gave

that up, because I never could thrash a dog that lay down at the first cut, writhing and howling; I know so well that would have been your line. Do you want to say anything ?"

A sudden change in Harding's countenance made Alan pause. You may have seen how utterly deficient he was both in moral and physical courage ; but the last faint embers of manhood smouldered into sullen flame, under the accumulation of insult. He had risen to his feet with a dark devilish malice on his face, and made a step towards a table near him.

Wyverne's keen gaze read his purpose thoroughly, but never wavered in its freezing contempt.

" Ah, that's the drawer where you keep your revolver," he said. " If you drive a rat into a corner, he will turn sometimes. I don't believe you would have nerve to shoot; but I mean to run no risks. I came prepared after I gave up the bastinado. There's something heavier than wood in this malacca. I'll break your wrist if you attempt to touch the lock. That's better; sit down again and listen. Then—I thought of bringing the matter before a committee of every club you belong to, suppressing all the names but my own. I could have done it; my credit's good for so much, if I choose to use it. I only gave up that idea three hours ago. It was when I heard of the Rector's being so seriously ill. The fathers suffer for the sins of the children often enough; but I have not the heart to give *yours* his death-blow. You will appreciate the weakness thoroughly, I don't doubt. On one condition I shall keep your treachery a secret from all, except those immediately concerned; that condition is, that you never show yourself in any company where, by the remotest chance, you could meet either Lady Clydesdale, Mrs. Lenox, any of the Dene family, or myself. I'll do my duty to society so far, at all events. Do you accept or refuse ?"

" I have no choice," the other muttered, hoarsely and sullenly; " you have me in a vice, you know that."

" Then it is so understood," Wyverne went on. "You needn't waste your breath in promising and swearing. You'll keep your quarantine, I feel sure. If not,——" (it was a very significant pause). "After all, my forbearance only hangs on your poor father's life, and I fear that is a slender thread indeed."

The mention of Gilbert Knowles's name seemed to have no effect whatever upon his son; he did not even appear grateful for its mute intercession between him and public shame : but Alan's voice softened insensibly as he uttered it. When he spoke again, after a minute's silence, his tone was rather sad than scornful.

"If you wanted money so much, why, in God's name, did you not come to me?. I would have sold my last chance of a reversion, and have begged or borrowed from every friend I had, sooner than have let Clydesdale outbid me. The plunge was taken, when you could once think of such infamy : you might as well have sold yourself to me. Those miserable thousands must have been your only motive, for you had no reason, that I know of, to dislike me."

For the first time since the interview began, Harding Knowles looked the speaker straight in the eyes : his face was still white as a corpse's, but its expression was scarcely human in its intense malignity.

"You're wrong," he said, between his teeth : "the money wasn't the only motive. Not dislike you! Curse you! —I've hated you from the first moment that we met. Do you fancy, I thank you for your forbearance now? I'd poison you if I could, or murder you where you stand, if I dared. I hated your languid ways, and your quiet manner, and your soft speech, and your cool courtesy—hated them all. You never spoke naturally but once—on the hall-steps of Dene. Do you suppose I have forgotten that, or the look in your cousin's eyes? I tell you I hated you both. I felt you despised and laughed at me all the while, and you had no right to do so—then. It is different— different—now."

His brain, usually so calculating and crafty, for the moment was utterly distraught ; he could not even command his voice, which rose almost into a shriek while he was speaking, and in the last words sank abruptly into a hollow groan. It was a terrible and piteous sight. But you have heard how implacable at certain seasons Alan Wyverne could be : neither the agony of the passion, nor the misery of the humiliation, moved his compassion in the least ; he watched the outbreak and the relapse, with a smile of serene satisfaction that had been strange to his face for some time past.

"So you really disliked my manner?" he said, in his own slow, pensive way. "I remember, years ago, an ancient Duchesse of the Faubourg telling me it had a savour of the *Vieille Cour*. I was intensely flattered then, for I was very young. I am not sure that I ought not to be more gratified now. I think I am. The instincts of hate are truer than those of love. Mde. de Latrêaumont was as kind as a mother to me, and might have been deceived. I have no more to say. You know the conditions : if you transgress them by a hair's breadth, you will hear of it— not from me."

He left the room without another word. It is doubtful if Knowles heard that last taunt, or knew that his visitor was gone. He had buried his face again in his hands ; and so, for minutes sat motionless. All at once he started up, went to the outer "oak," and dropped the bolt which made his servant's pass-key useless, and then returned to his old seat, still apparently half stunned and stupefied.

Do you think the forger and traitor escaped easily? It may be so ; but remember the exaggerated importance that Harding attached to his social position and advancement. I believe that many, whose earthly ruin has just been completed, have felt less miserable, and hopeless, and spirit-broken, than the man who sat there, far into the twilight, staring at the fire with haggard eyes, that never saw the red coals turn grey.

It is true, that when Nina Lenox

heard from Alan a *résumé* of the day's proceedings, she decided at once that the retribution was wholly inadequate and unsatisfactory. But one need not multiply instances to prove the truism, if women are exacting in love, they are thrice as exacting in revenge. I cannot remember where I read the old romaunt of the knight who came just in time to save his lady from the burning, by vanquishing her traducer in the lists. The story is commonplace and trite to a degree. I only remember the one instance that made it remarkable. The conqueror stood with his foot on the neck of the enemy; his chivalrous heart melted towards the vanquished, who, after all, had done his devoir gallantly in an evil cause. He would have suffered him to rise and live, but he chanced to glance inquiringly towards the pale woman at the stake, and, says the chronicler, " by the bending of her brows, and the blink of her ·eyes, he wist that she bade him—'not spare!'" So the good knight sighed heavily, and, turning his sword-point once more to the neck of the fallen man, drove the keen steel through mail and flesh and bone.

Ah, my friend! may it never be your lot or mine, to lie prone at the mercy of a woman whom we have wronged past hope of forgiveness; be sure, that eyes and brows will speak as plainly as they did a thousand years agone, and their murderous message will be much the same.

----

## CHAPTER XXIII.

### DIPLOMACY AT A DISCOUNT.

It would be rather difficult to define Wyverne's feelings after his interview with Knowles. I fear that the utter humiliation of his enemy failed entirely to satisfy him; but, on the whole, I think he scarcely regretted not having pushed reprisals to extremities. At least there was this advantage; he could sit with the Rector now, for hours, and strive to cheer the poor invalid,

with a quiet conscience; he could never have borne to come to his presence with the deliberate purpose at his heart of bringing public shame on Gilbert's son.

At the beginning of the following week, Alan heard that the Squire and Lady Mildred were in town for a couple of days, on their way home from Devonshire. He knew the hour at which he was certain to find " my lady" alone, and timed his visit accordingly. Now, though the family breach had been closed up long ago, and though Wyverne was with Lady Clydesdale perpetually, apparently on the most cousinly terms of intimacy, it somehow happened that he met his aunt very seldom. Still, it was the most natural thing that he should call, under the circumstances, and " my lady" was in no wise disconcerted when his name was announced. The greeting, on both sides, was as affectionate as it had ever been in the old times; it would have been impossible to say why, from the first, Lady Mildred felt a nervous presentiment of impending danger, unless it was—it might have been pure fancy—that Alan's manner did seem unusually grave. So she was not surprised when he said,

" Would you mind putting off your drive for half an hour? I will not keep you longer; but I have one or two things that I wish very much to say to you."

" I'll give you the whole afternoon if you wish it, Alan," she said, in the softest of her silky tones; " it is no great sacrifice; I shall be glad of an excuse for escaping the cold wind. Will you ring, and tell them I' shall not want the carriage, and that I am not at home to anybody?"

So once again—this time without a witness—the trial of fence between those two began; it was strange, but all the prestige of previous victories could not make " my lady" feel confident now.

Alan broke ground boldly, without wasting time in " parades."

" Aunt Mildred, if some things that I have to refer to should be painful to you, try and realize what they must be to *me;* you will see then, that only necessity could make rhe speak. Do you remember when those wretched anonymous letters first came to Dene, I told you I would find out their author and thank him? I did both last week. More than this, I have seen and spoken with the man who wrote those letters which we all supposed came from Mrs. Rawdon Lenox. You never had a doubt on the subject, of course, Aunt Mildred? I thought you would be surprised; you will be still more so when you hear the forger's name—Harding Knowles."

"My lady" really did suffer from headaches sometimes—with that busy, restless brain it was no wonder—and she always had near her the strongest smelling-salts that could be procured; but she did not know what fainting meant, so she was absolutely terrified, when the room seemed to go round, and Wyverne's voice sounded distant and strange, as if it came through a long speaking-tube; the sensation passed off in a few seconds, but while it lasted she could only feel, blindly and helplessly, for the jewelled vinaigrette which lay within a few inches of her elbow. Wyverne's eyes had never left her face for a moment; he caught up the bottle quickly and put it, open, into her hand, without a word.

"It—it is—nothing," Lady Mildred gasped (the salts must have been *very* pungent.) "I have not been well for days; the surprise quite overcame me. But oh, Alan, are you quite—quite sure? I don't like Harding Knowles much; but it would be too cruel to accuse him of such horrors unless you have certain proofs."

"Make yourself easy on that score," Alan said, with his quiet smile; "no injustice has been done. I will give you all the proofs you care to see, directly. While you recover yourself, Aunt Mildred, let me tell you a short story. Years ago, when we were cruising about the Orkneys, they showed us a certain cliff that stood up a thousand feet clear out of the North Sea, and told us what happened there. A father and his son, sea-fowlers, were hanging on the same rope, the father undermost. Suddenly

they found that the strands were parting one by one, frayed on a sharp edge of rock. The rope might possibly carry one to the top—not two. Then quoth the sire, 'Your mother must not starve —cut away, *below*.' As he said, so was it done, and the parricide got up safely. Do you see my meaning? You say you don't like Harding Knowles? I can well believe it; but if you cared for him next to your own children, I should still quote the stout Orkneyman's words —'cut away, *below*.' Now, if you will look at these papers, you will see how clear the evidence is on which I rely."

There was silence for some minutes, while "my lady" pretended to read attentively; in real truth, she could not fix her attention to a line. All her thoughts were concentrated on the one doubt—"How much does he know?" The suspense became unendurable; it was better to hear the worst at once. Suddenly she looked up and spoke.

"Is it possible? Can you believe that Clydesdale was mixed up with such a plot as this?"

"No," Wyverne answered, frankly. "I confess I did suspect him at first; but I don't believe, now, that he was privy to any of the details. I think, after securing his agent's services, he left him *carte blanche* to act as he would. He is quite welcome to that shade of difference in the dishonour. Well, are those proofs satisfactory? If not, I may tell you that I saw Harding Knowles four days ago, and that he confesses everything."

The peculiar intonation of the last two words made Lady Mildred, once more, feel faint with fear. She had never encountered such a danger as this. But her wonderfully trained organ did not fail her, even in her extreme strait; though tiny drops of dew stood on her pale forehead, though her heart throbbed suffocatingly, her accent was still measured and full of subdued music. "Did he implicate any one?"

It was the very desperation of the sword-player, who, finding his science baffled, comes to close quarters, with shortened blade. Alan did indulge vindictiveness so far as to pause for a full minute before answering, regarding his companion all the while intently. But, though he could be pitiless towards his own sex at times, he never could bear to see a woman in pain, even if she had injured him mortally; that minute—a fearfully long one to "my lady"—exhansted his revenge.

"He *would* have done so," he replied, but I stopped him before a name could pass his lips. I am very glad I did. It don't follow that I should have believed him. But it is better as it is. Don't you think so, Aunt Mildred?"

The revulsion of feeling tried her almost more severely than the previous apprehension had done. At that moment "my lady" was thoroughly and naturally grateful. Wyverne saw that she was simply incapable of a reply just then. He was considerate enough to give her breathing space, while he went into several details with which you are already acquainted, and mentioned the conditions he had imposed upon Knowles —which the latter had subscribed to.

Lady Mildred listened and approved, mechanically. Her temperament had been for years so well regulated that unwonted emotion really exhausted her. Her bright dark eyes looked dull and heavy, and languor, for once, was not feigned.

"There is another question," Alan went on;—"it is rather an important one to me, and, I think, my chief reason for coming here to-day was to ask your opinion, and your help, if you choose to give it. What is to be done about Helen? You know, when a man has been in Norfolk Island for several years, and it comes out that some one else has committed the forgery, they always grant him a free pardon. That is the government plan; but it don't suit me. Besides, Helen has forgiven me long ago, I believe, and we are perfectly good friends now. For that very reason I cannot throw the chance away of clearing myself in her eyes. There are limits to self-denial and self-sacrifice. Yet it is delicate ground to approach, especially for me. As far as I am concerned—' let conjugal love continue;' it would scarcely promote a mutual good

understanding, if Helen were told of the part her lord and master played in the drama, and of the liberal odds that he laid so early in their acquaintance. Yet it would be hard to keep his name out of the story altogether: mere personal dislike would never account for Knowle's elaborate frauds. Aunt Mildred, I tell you fairly, I am not equal to the diplomatic difficulty; but I think *you* are. Shall I leave it in your hands entirely? If you will only satisfy Helen that I have satisfied *you*—if you will make her believe implicitly that I have been blameless throughout in thought, and word, and deed, and that black treachery has been used against us both —on my honour and faith, I will never enter on the subject, even if she wished to do so, unless Helen or I were dying. She shall send me one line only to say —'I believe'—and then, we will bury the sorrow and the shame as soon as you will. I think none of us will care to move the gravestone."

For a moment or two "my lady" was hardly sure if she heard aright. She knew that it was impossible to over-estimate the danger to which Wyverne had alluded. Helen's temper had grown more and more wilful and determined since her marriage; it was hard to say to what rash words or deeds resentment and remorse might lead her. She knew Alan, too, well; but she scarcely believed him capable of such a sacrifice as this. And could he be serious in choosing *her* as his delegate? She gazed up in his face, half-expecting to find a covert mockery there; but its expression was grave, almost to sternness.

"Do you really mean it?" she faltered. "It is so good, so generous of you. And will you trust me thoroughly?"

"Yes, Aunt Mildred, I will trust you —*again.*"

A thousand complaints and revilings would not have carried so keen a reproach as that which was breathed in those few sad, quiet words. Lady Mildred shrank as she felt them come home. Involuntarily she looked up once more: it was a fatal error. She encountered the full light of the clear, keen eyes—resistless in the power of their single-hearted chivalrous truth. In another second her head had gone down on Wyverne's shoulder, as he sat close to her couch, and she was sobbing out something incoherent about "forgiveness."

Now, I do not suppose that the annals of intellectual duelling can chronicle a more complete defeat than this. It is with the greatest pain and reluctance that I record it. What avails it to· be a model *diplomate*, to sit for half a lifetime at the feet of Machiavel, to attain impassibility and insensibility—equal to a Faquir's as a rule—if womanhood, pure and simple, is to assert itself in such an absurdly sudden and incongruous way? It is pleasant to reflect, that this human nature of ours is hardly more consistent in evil than in good. There are doubts if even the arch-cynicism of Talleyrand carried him through to the very last. I once before ventured to draw a comparison between him and "my lady"— that was when I *did* believe in her.

Wyverne was intensely surprised, rather puzzled what to do or say, and decidedly gratified. Though he had suspected her from the first, he had never nourished any bitter animosity against Lady Mildred. He had a sort of idea that she was only acting up to her principles—such as they were—which were very much what popular opinion assigns to the ideal Jesuit. Quite naturally and easily, he began to soothe her now.

"Dear Aunt Mildred, I hardly know what I have to forgive" (this was profoundly true); "but here, in my ignorance, I bestow plenary absolution. I fear I have worried you, when you were really not well. I won't tease you with a word more. Mind, I leave everything in your hands, with perfect confidence."

Lady Mildred had fallen back on her sofa again, pressing her handkerchief against her eyes, though no tears were flowing.

"If I had only known you better— and sooner," she murmured.

I dare say she meant every word sincerely when she said it; nevertheless, as a historian, I incline to believe that no insight into Alan's character would have altered "my lady's" line of policy at any previous moment. Perhaps some such idea crossed Wyverne's mind, for there certainly was a slight smile on his lip, as he rose to take an affectionate farewell. The few parting words are not worth recording.

Alan was more than discontented, whenever he thought over these things, calmly and dispassionately, in after days. Twice he had looked his enemies in the face, and on both occasions had doubtless borne off the honours of the day; but it was an unsubstantial victory at best, and a triumph scarcely more profitable than that of the Imperial trifler, who mustered his legions to battle, and brought back as trophies shells from the sea-shore. The recollection was not poisonous enough to destroy the good elements of his character, but it darkened and embittered his nature, permanently.

The fact is, when a man has been thoroughly duped and deluded, and has suffered irreparably from the fraud, it is not easily forgotten, unless retaliation has been fully commensurate with the injury. I am not advocating a principle, but simply stating a general fact. With a great misfortune it is different. We say—"Let us fall into His hand, not into the hand of man." So, at least, is consolation more easily sought for, and found.

Remember Esau—as he was before he sold his birthright—as he is when, in fear and trembling, Jacob looks upon his face again. That score of years has changed the cheery, careless hunter of deer into the stern, resolute leader of robber-tribes—ruling his wild vassals with an iron sceptre—no longer "seeking for his meat from God," but grasping plunder, where he may find it, with the strong hand, by dint of bow and spear—truly, a fitting sire from whose loins twelve Dukes of Edom should spring—not wholly exempt from kind, generous impulses, as that meeting between Penuel and Succoth proves—but as little like his former self, as a devil is like an angel. If the eyes of the blind old patriarch, who loved his reckless first-born so well, had been opened as he lay a-dying, he could scarcely have told if " this were his very' son Esau, or no."

---

## CHAPTER XXIV.

### SEMI-AMBUSTUS EVASIT.

ARE you curious to know how, all this while, it fared with the Great Earl and his beautiful bride? If the truth is to be told, I fear the answer must be unsatisfactory. No one, well acquainted with the contracting parties, believed that the marriage would be a *very* happy one; but they hoped it would turn out as well as the generality of conventional alliances. It was not so. Alan Wyverne was right enough in thinking that Clydesdale was most unfitted to the task of managing a haughty, wilful wife; but even he never supposed that dissension would arise so quickly, and rankle so constantly. There had been few overt or actual disputes, but a spirit of bitter antagonism was ever at work, which sooner or later was certain to have an evil ending.

It would be unfair to infer that the fault was all on the Earl's side. It was his manner and demeanour that told most against him: he had been so accustomed to adulation from both sexes, that he could not understand why his wife should not accept his dictatorial and overbearing ways, as patiently as his other dependents: so even his kindnesses were spoilt by the way in which they were offered, or rather enforced. But—at all events, in the early days of their married life—he was really anxious that not a wish or whim of Helen's should remain ungratified, and spared neither trouble nor money to insure this.

The fair Countess was certainly not free from blame. She had said to Maud Brabazon—" I will try honestly to be a good wife, if he will let me."

Now, her most partial friend could hardly assert, that she had fairly acted up to this good resolve. Perhaps it would have been too much to expect that she should entertain a high respect or a devoted affection for her consort; but she might have masked indifference more considerately, or, at least, have dissembled disdain. Her hasty, impetuous nature seemed utterly changed; she never by any chance lost her temper now, at any provocation, especially when such came from her husband. It would have been much better if she *had* done so, occasionally: nothing chafes a character like Clydesdale's so bitterly, as that imperial *nonchalance*, which seems to waver between contempt and pity. Besides, her notions of conjugal obedience were rather peculiar. The Earl was, at first, perpetually interfering with her arrangements, by suggestions for or against, which sounded unpleasantly like orders; if these chanced to square with Helen's inclination, or if the question was simply indifferent to her, she acted upon them, without claiming any credit for so doing; if otherwise—she disregarded and disobeyed them with a serene determination, and seemed to think, " having changed her mind since she saw him," quite a sufficient apology to her exasperated Seigneur.

An incident very characteristic of this had, somehow, got abroad.

Lady Clydesdale was about to accompany her husband to a tremendous State-dinner, the host being one of the great personages in this realm, next to royalty—no other than the Duke of Camelot. When she came down, ready to start, one would have found, it impossible to have found a fault in her toilette. But the Earl chose to consider himself an authority on feminine attire, and chanced to be in a particularly captious humour that evening: the ground colour of Helen's dress—a dark Mazarine blue—did not please him at all, though really nothing could match better with her *parure* of sapphires and diamonds. She listened to his com ments and strictures without contradicting them, apparently not thinking the subject worth discussion: her silent indifference irritated Clydesdale excessively. At last he said—

"Helen, I positively insist on your taking off that dress; there will be time enough if you go up immediately. Do you hear me?"

For an instant she seemed to hesitate; then she rose, with an odd smile on her proud lip—"Yes, there will be time enough," she said, and so left the room.

But minutes succeed minutes, till it was evident that the conventional "grace" must even now be exceeded, and still no re-appearance of Helen. The Earl could control his feverish impatience no longer, and went up himself, to hurry her. He opened the door hastily, and fairly started back, in wrath and astonishment at the sight he saw.

The Countess was attired very much as Maud Brabazon found her when she paid the midnight visit that you may remember. Perhaps her dressing-robe was a shade more gorgeous, but there was no mistaking its character. There she sat, buried in the depths of a luxurious *causeuse*, her little feet crossed on the fender (it was early spring and the nights were cold); all the massy coils of cunningly wrought plaits and tresses freed from artistic thraldom, a half-cut *novelette* in her hand,—altogether, the prettiest picture of indolent comfort, but not exactly the "form" of a great lady expected at a ducal banquet.

The furious blood flushed Clydesdale's face to dark crimson.

"What—what does this mean?" he stammered. His voice was not a pleasant one at any time, and rage did not mellow its tone. The superb eyes vouchsafed one careless side-glance, a gleam of scornful amusement lighting up their languor.

"The next time you give your orders," she replied, "you had better be more explicit: you commanded me to take off that blue dress, but you said nothing about putting on another. Perhaps my second choice might not have pleased you either. Besides, one is not called upon to dress twice, even for a State dinner. You can easily make a good excuse for me: if the Duke is very angry, I will make my peace with him myself. I'm sure he will not bear malice long."

Now, putting predilection and prejudice aside, which do you think was most in the wrong? The Earl was unreasonable and tyrannical, first; but under the circumstances, I do think he "did well to be angry." He was *so* angry—that he was actually afraid to trust himself longer in the room, and hurried downstairs, growling out some of his choicest anathemas (not *directed*, it must be owned); as has been hinted before, Clydesdale kept at least one Recording angel in full employment. The spectacle of marital wrath did not seem greatly to appal the wilful Countess. She heard the door of the outer chamber close violently, without starting at the crash, and settled herself comfortably to her book again, as if no interruption had occurred.

About this time the Earl began to be haunted by a certain dim suspicion: at first it seemed too monstrously absurd to be entertained seriously for a moment; but soon it grew into form and substance, and became terribly distinct and life-like—the possibility of his wife's despising him. When he had once admitted the probability, the mischief was done: he brooded over the idea with a gloomy pertinacity, till a blind, dull animosity took the place of love and trust. He swore to himself that, at whatever cost, he would regain and keep supremacy: unfortunately he had never had it yet; and it would have been easier for him to twist a bar of cold steel with his bare hands, than to mould the will of Countess Helen. Every day he lost instead of gaining ground, only embittering the spirit of resistance, and widening a breach which could never be repaired. As if all this were not enough, before the year was out, another and darker element of discord rose up in the Earl's moody heart—though he scarcely confessed it even to himself—a fierce, irrational jealousy of Alan Wyverne.

No one who had chanced to witness the parting of the cousins in the library at Dene, would have allowed the possi bility of a free unreserved intimacy, troubled, as it would seem, neither by repining nor misgiving, being established between them within two years. Though Alan spoke hopefully at the time, it may be doubted if he believed in his own words. Yet such contradictions and anomalies happen so often, that we ought to be tired of wondering. They moved in the same set, both in town and country, and were necessarily thrown much together. Wyverne soon managed to persuade himself that there was not the slightest reason why he should purposely avoid his fascinating cousin. As for Helen, I fear she did not discuss the question with her conscience at all. So, gradually and insensibly they fell into the old pleasant confidential ways—such as used to prevail before that fatal afternoon when Wyverne's self-control failed him, and he " spake unadvisedly with his lips" under the oak-boughs of the Holme Wood.

Perhaps there might have been a certain amount of self-delusion; but I fancy that for a long time there was not a thought of harm on either side. As far as Alan was concerned, I do believe that his affection for Helen was as pure and honest and single-hearted as it is possible for a sinful man to entertain.

Nevertheless, the change in the usual demeanour of the cousins, when they chanced to be together, was too marked to escape observation. Her best friends could not deny that marriage had altered Lady Clydesdale very much for the worse: her manner in general society was decidedly cold, and there was often weariness in her great eyes, when they were not disdainful or defiant. The first sound of Alan's voice seemed to act like a spell in bringing the Helen Vavasour of old days, with all the charming impulses and petulance of her maidenhood. Ever since his interview with Nina Lenox, Wyverne had been constantly moody and pre-occupied; but the dark cloud was always lifted before he had been five minutes in his cousin's presence; the frank, careless gaiety which once made him such a fascinating companion returned quite naturally, and he could join in the talk or enter into the project of the hour with as much interest as ever. It was remarkable, certainly—so much so that the Earl might perhaps have been justified in not altogether approving of the state of things, especially as he could not be expected to appreciate Alan's feelings, simply because a chivalrous and unselfish affection was something quite beyond his mental grasp.

Notwithstanding all this, I repeat that his jealousy was irrational. He was sulky and uneasy in Wyverne's presence, and disliked seeing him with Helen, not because he actually mistrusted either, but because he hated the man from the bottom of his heart. He did not believe in the possibility of his haughty wife's ever straying, even in thought or word, from the path of duty; but she was the chief of his possessions, and it exasperated him, that his enemy should derive profit or pleasure from her society. In despite of an inordinate self-esteem, Clydesdale could not shake off the disagreeable idea, that, wherever they had met, so far Alan had got the better of him. He fancied he could detect a calm contemptuous superiority in the latter's tone (it was purely imaginary), which irritated him to the last degree. Added to all this—and it was far the strongest motive of all—was the consciousness of having done Alan a deadly wrong, in intention, if not in fact. It was true that he knew nothing of Harding Knowles's treachery. He had carefully abstained from asking a question, either before or after the result; but he knew that he had bought an unscrupulous agent, on a tacit understanding that a full equivalent should be given for the money; and he could guess how thoroughly the contract had been carried out. In one word, the Earl wished Wyverne dead, simply because he could not comfortably look him in the face. Rely on it, that poison-bag lies at the root of many fangs that bite most sharply.

Nevertheless, Lord Clydesdale abstained from confiding his antipathies even to his wife. Deficient as he was in tact, he felt that a battle would probably ensue, to which all other dissensions would have been child's play. He had no solid grounds to go upon, and he did not see his way clearly to a satisfactory result. So, in spite of his frowns and sulkiness, matters went on smoothly enough up to the time of the disclosures recorded in the last chapter.

It is probable that Lady Mildred discharged her embassage faithfully, albeit discreetly. The subject was never mentioned between them; but Helen's manner towards her cousin perceptibly softened, though she felt a strange constraint occasionally that she could hardly have accounted for. The truth was—if she had indulged in self-examination, at this conjuncture she ought to have begun to mistrust herself. It was dangerous to brood over Alan's wrongs now, when it was too late to make him any substantial amends.

But the world would not long "let well alone." Before the season was far advanced, *cancans* were rife; and Lady Clydesdale's name was more than lightly spoken of: glances, when levelled at her, became curious and significant, instead of simply admiring. Of course, the parties most intimately interested are the last to hear of such things; but Wyverne did begin to suspect the truth, not so much from any hints or inuendoes, as from a certain reticence and reserve among his intimates at the clubs and elsewhere. One evening, Maud Brabazon took heart of grace, and told him all she had heard, after her own frank fashion.

Not even during the hours which followed the miserable parting in the library at Dene, had Alan felt so utterly hopeless and spirit-broken as he did that night, as he sat alone, thinking over the situation, and trying with every energy of his honest heart to determine what he ought to do. Men have grown grey and wrinkled under briefer and lighter pain. It did seem hard: when he was conscious of innocence of intention—when he had so lately, at such costly self-sacrifice, abstained from personally justifying himself in Helen's eyes, sooner than compromise her husband—when he had just found out that

he had been juggled out of his life's hope through no fault or negligence of his own—he was called upon to resign the shadow of happiness that was left him still, merely because the world chose to be scandalous, and not to give him credit for common honesty. But, after his thoughts had wandered for hours in darkness and in doubt, the light broke clear. Half-measures were worse than useless. To remain in England and to maintain a comparative estrangement—to meet Helen only at appointed times and seasons—to set a watch upon his lips whenever he chanced to be in her society—was utterly impracticable. Like other and braver and wiser men, he owned that he had no alternative—he was bound to fly. Weak and fallible as he was in many respects, Wyverne's character contained this one element of greatness — when he had once made up his mind, it was easier to move a mountain than to change his resolve.

He never went near Clydesdale House for three days, and in that space all his arrangements were made, irrevocably. Early in the year Alan had purchased a magnificent schooner; she was fitting out at Ryde, and nearly completed; he had purposed to make a summer cruise in the Mediterranean, it was only turning the *Odalisque* to a more practical purpose, now. Two of his friends had organized a hunting expedition on a large scale, first through the interior of Southern Africa, then to the Himalayas and the best of the " big game" districts of India. Of course they were delighted to have Wyverne as a comrade, especially when he placed his yacht at their service; the *Odalisque*, both in size and strength, was perfectly equal to any ocean voyage. Their absence from England was to last at least three years. Alan felt a certain relief when it was all settled; nevertheless his heart was cold and heavy as lead, as he walked towards Clydesdale House to break the tidings. He found Helen alone; indeed, the Earl was out of town for the whole day, and was not to return till late in the evening. She could not understand what had kept her cousin away for three days—of course she had wanted him particularly for all sorts of things—and she was inclined to be mildly reproachful on the subject. Wyverne listened for a while, though every word brought a fresh throb of pain, simply because he had not courage to begin to undeceive her.

At last he spoke, you may guess how gently and considerately, yet keeping nothing back, and not disguising the reasons for his departure. He had felt sure all along, that Helen would be bitterly grieved at his determination, and would strive to oppose it; but he was not prepared for the passionate outbreak which ensued.

The Countess's 'cheek had changed backwards and forwards, from rose-red to pale, a dozen times while her cousin was speaking, and on the beautiful brow there were signs, that a child might have read, of a coming storm; but she did not interrupt him till he had quite said his say; then she started to her feet; a sudden movement—swift and lithe, and graceful as a Bayadere's spring—brought her close to Alan's chair; she was kneeling at his side, with her slender hands locked round his arm, gazing up in his face, before he could remonstrate by gesture or word.

"You shall not go. I don't care what they say—friends or enemies—you shall not go. Alan, I will do anything, and suffer anything, and go anywhere; but I will not lose you. With all your courage, will you fail me when I am ready to brave them? You cannot mean to be so cruel. Ah, say—say you will stay with me."

Alas! if her speech was rash, her eyes were rasher still; never, in the days when to love was no sin, had they spoken half so plainly.

Wyverne's breath came thick and fast, for his heart contracted painfully, as if an iron hand had grasped it. It was all over with self-delusion now; the flimsy web vanished before the fatal eloquence of that glance, as a gauze veil shrivels before a strong straight jet of flame.

Now—though this pen of mine has done scant justice to Helen's marvellous fascinations—let any man, in the prime of life, endowed with average passions and not exceptional principle, place himself in Alan's position, and try to appreciate its peril. Truly, I think, it would be hard measure, if human nature were called upon twice in a lifetime, to surmount such a temptation, and survive it. Yet he only hesitated while that choking sensation lasted. He raised Helen from where she knelt, and replaced her on the seat she had left, with an exertion of strength, subdued and gentle, but perfectly irresistible; when he spoke, his voice sounded unnaturally stern and cold.

"If I had doubted at all about my absence being right and necessary, I should not doubt now. Child—you are not fit to be trusted. How dare you speak, at your age and in your station, of setting society at defiance, and trampling on conventionalities? You have duties to perform, and a great name to guard; have you forgotten all this, Countess Helen?"

On the last words, there was certainly an inflexion of sarcasm. The bitter pain gnawing at his heart, made him for the moment selfish and cruel. Perhaps it was as well; the hardness of his tone roused her pride, so that she could answer with comparative calmness.

"God help me—I have forgotten nothing—my miserable marriage least of all. Alan, what is the use of keeping up the deception? We need not lie to each other, if we are to part so soon. I never pretended to love Lord Clydesdale; but I think I could have done my duty, if he would have let me.

"How can you guess what I have to endure? I may be in fault too; but it has come to this—it is not indifference or dislike, now, but literally loathing. Do you know how careful he is, not to wound my self-respect? Only yesterday, he left in my dressing-room, where I could not help seeing it, a letter—ah, such a letter—from some *lorette* whom he protects. It was a delicate way of showing that he was displeased with me. And I have dreadful misgivings that I shall become afraid of him—physically afraid, some day—I am not that yet—and then it will be all over with me. I feel safe—I can't tell why—when you are near; and you are going to leave me alone, quite alone."

Now, to prevent mistakes hereafter, let me say explicitly that I do not defend Lady Clydesdale's conduct throughout. I don't know that any woman is justified, on any provocation, in speaking of her husband in such a strain, to her own brother, much less to her cousin, supposing that a warmer sentiment than the ties of kindred is manifestly out of the question. Still, if you like to be lenient, you might remember that a passionate, wilful character like Helen's requires strong and wise guidance while it is being formed; certainly her moral training had not been looked after so carefully as her accomplishments; the mother considered her duty done when she had selected a competent governess; so perhaps, after all, the Countess had as much religion and principle, as could be expected in Lady Mildred Vavasour's daughter.

It was a proof of the danger of such confidence, that Wyverne's blood boiled furiously as he listened, and all his good resolves were swallowed up for the moment in a savage desire to take Clydesdale by the throat; but with a mighty effort he recovered self-control, before Helen could follow up her advantage.

"I did guess something," he said, "though not half the truth. I ought to preach to you about 'submission,' I suppose, and all the rest; but I don't know how to do it, and I'm not in the humour to find excuses for your husband just now. Yet I am more than ever certain that I can do no good by staying here. I should only make your burden heavier; you will be safer when I am gone. Of all things you must avoid giving a chance to the scandal-mongers. Child, only be patient and prudent, and we shall see better days. Remember, I am not going to be absent for ever. Three years or so will soon pass. We shall all be older and steadier when I come back, and the world will have forgotten one of us long before that. Say you will try."

11

Dissimulation is sometimes braver than sincerity. Perhaps Alan got large credit in heaven for the brave effort by which he forced himself to speak half hopefully, and to put on that sad shadow of a smile.

In a book of this length, one can only record the salient points of conversations and situations; your imaginations must fill up the intervals, reader of mine, if you think it worth the trouble to exercise it. It is enough to say, that gentle steadfastness of purpose carried the day, as it generally does, against passionate recklessness, and Helen perforce became reasonable at last. Though the cousins talked long and earnestly after this, the rest of the interview would hardly keep your interest awake. Such farewells, if they are correctly set down, savour drearily of vain repetitions, and are apt to be strangely incoherent towards their close.

"If you are in any great trouble or difficulty, promise me that you will send for Gracie; she will help you, I know, fearlessly and faithfully, to the utmost of her power."

That was almost the very last of Wyverne's injunctions and warnings. If at the moment of parting his lips met Helen's, instead of only touching her forehead, as he intended, I hope it was not imputed to him as a deadly sin; the sharp suffering of those few hours might well plead in extenuation; and, be sure, He who "judges not after man's judgment." weighs *everything* when he poises the scale.

I never felt inclined to make a "hero" of Alan till now. I begin to think that he almost deserves the dignity. You must recollect that he was not an ascetic, nor an eminent Christian, nor even a rigid moralist, but a man essentially "of the world, worldly." If the Tempter had selected as his instrument any other woman of equal or inferior fascinations, I very much doubt if Wyverne's constancy and continence would have emerged scatheless from the ordeal. But here, it was a question of honour rather than of virtue. When his second intimacy with Helen began

to be a confirmed fact, he had signed a
sort of special compact with himself,
and he found that it would be as foul
treachery to break it, as to make away
with money left in his charge, or to
forfeit his plighted word. I do not say
that this made his conduct more admirable; I simply define his motives.

Alan went down to the North the
next day to wind up his home business,
and he never saw Lady Clydesdale
alone before he sailed. But he went
forth on his pilgrimage an unhappy,
haunted man. Wherever he went those
eyes of Helen followed him, telling their
fatal secret over and over again, driving him wild with alternate reproaches and seductions. He saw them while
crouching among the sand-banks of an
African stream watching for the wallowing of the river-horse; at his post
in the jungle ravine, when rattling
stones and crashing bushes gave notice
of the approach of tiger or elk or bear;
oftenest of all, when, after a hard day's
hunting, he lay amongst his comrades
sound asleep, looking up at the brilliant southern stars. His one comfort
was the thought, " Thank God, I *could*
ask Gracie to take care of her."

Alan was expiating the miserable
error of fancying that his love was
dead, because he had chosen formally
to sign its death-warrant. The experiment has been tried for cycles of ages
—sometimes after a more practical
fashion—and it has failed oftener than
it has succeeded.

Think on that old true story of Herod and his favourite wife. Lo! after
a hundred delays and reprieves the final edict has gone forth; the sharp
axe-edge has fallen on the slender neck
of the Lily of Edom; surely the tortured heart of the unhappy jealous tyrant
shall find peace at last. Is it so?
Months and months have passed away;
there is high revel in Hebron, for a
great victory has just been won; the
blood-red wine of Sidon flows lavishly,
flushing the cheeks and lighting up the
eyes of the " men of war;" and the
Great Tetrarch drinks deepest of all,
the cup-bearer can scarcely fill fast
enough, though his hand never stints

nor stays. So far, all is well; the
lights and the turmoil and the crowd
may keep even spectres aloof; but
feasts, like other mortal things, must
end, and Herod staggers off to his
chamber alone. Another hour or so,
and there rings through hall and corridor an awful cry, making the rude Idu-
mean guards start and shiver at their
posts—fierce and savage in its despair,
but tremulous with unutterable agony,
like the howl of some terrible wild
beast writhing in the death-pang—
" Mariamne! Mariamne!"

Does that sound like peace? The
dead beauty asserts her empire once
again; she has her murderer at her
mercy now, more pitiably enslaved than
ever.

Ah, woe is me! We may slay the
body, if we have the power, but we
may never baffle the Ghost.

———

## CHAPTER XXV.

VER UBI LONGUM TEPIDASQUE PRÆBET
JUPITER BRUMAS.

At first it really did appear as if, in
expatriating himself for a season, Wyverne had acted wisely and well.

The purveyors of scandal, wholesale
and retail, were utterly routed and disconcerted. The romance was a promising one, but it had not had time to de-
velop itself into form and substance.
As things stood, it was impossible to
found any fresh supposition on Alan's
prolonged absence, especially as no one
ventured to hint at any quarrel or misunderstanding to account for his abrupt
departure. Some were too angry to
conceal their discomfiture. One veteran
gossip, in particular, went about, saying
in an injured, querulous way, that " he
wondered what Wyverne did next. He
shouldn't be surprised to hear of his
making a pilgrimage to Mecca, having
turned Turk for a change." It was
great sport to hear Bertie Grenvil, at
the club, " drawing" the old *cancanier*,
condoling with him gravely, and encouraging him with hopes " of having
something *really* to talk about before

the season was over." Indeed, it seemed by no means improbable that the Cherub, in person, would furnish the materials; for, having convinced himself by repeated experiments that Maud Brabazon either had no heart at all, or that it was absolutely impregnable, he had taken out lately a sort of roving commission, and was cruising about all sorts of waters, with the red signal of "no quarter" hoisted permanently.

Lord Clydesdale rejoiced intensely, after his saturnine fashion, at Wyverne's departure. It put him into such good humour that for days he forgot to be captious or overbearing, and actually made some clumsy overtures towards a reconciliation with his wife. It must be confessed, he met with scant encouragement in that quarter. Helen was in no mood to "forgive and forget" just then. There are women whom you may tyrannize over one week, and cajole the next, amiable enough to accept both positions with equanimity; but the haughty Countess was not of these Griseldas. Her temper was embittered rather than softened by her great sorrow and loneliness; for the void that Alan had left behind him was wider and darker than ever she had reckoned on. Of course she tried the old counter-irritation plan (nine out of ten do), seeking for excitement wherever it could be found. The result was not particularly satisfactory, but the habits of dissipation and recklessness strengthened their hold hourly. She had a legion of caprices, and indulged them all, without pausing to consider the question of right or wrong, much less of consequences. Before the season closed, Helen was virtually enrolled in the fastest of the thorough-bred sets, and might have disputed her evil pre-eminence with the most famous *lionne* of the day.

Naturally the scandal mongers began to open—first their eyes, and then their mouths again. Every morning brought some fresh story, generally founded, at least, in fact, with Lady Clydesdale for its heroine. They made wild work with her name before long, but so far no one could attach to it the shame of any one definite *liaison*. A circle of courtiers followed her wherever she went, but no' one of these—jealously as they watched for the faintest indication of a decided preference—could have told who stood first in the favour of their wilful, capricious sovereign. Sometimes one would flatter himself, for a moment, that he really had gained ground, and made an abiding impression; but, before he could realize his happiness, the weary, absent look would return to the beautiful eyes, and the unhappy adorer had only to fall back to the dead level of his fellows, in wrath and discomfiture.

No one the least interested in Helen could see how things were going without serious alarm. Lady Mildred, Max Vavasour, and Maud Brabazon, each in their turn, attempted remonstrance. The Countess met her mother's warning apathetically, her brother's contemptuously, her friend's affectionately—with perfect impartiality disregarding them all.

It is more than doubtful if Clydesdale could have done any good by interfering. He certainly did not try the experiment. From first to last he never stretched out a finger to arrest his fair wife on her road to Avernus. He allowed her to go where she would—very often alone—only, indeed, escorting her when it suited his own plans or purposes. Whether he was base enough to be actually careless about her temptations, or whether he resolutely shut his eyes to the possibility of her coming to harm, it would be hard to say. Nevertheless, from time to time, Helen had to endure furious outbreaks of his temper; and with each of these, that strange thrill of physical fear grew stronger and stronger. But jealousy had nothing whatever to do with rousing the storms, which usually burst forth on some absurdly frivolous provocation. The fact was, when the Earl was sulky or wroth, he chose to vent his brutal humour on the victim nearest to his hand that was likely to feel the blows most acutely. He saw that such scenes *hurt* his wife in some way, though he did not guess at her real feelings; and it pleased him to think that there was a vulnerable point in

her armour of pride and indifference.
He would have rejoiced yet more if he
had detected the effort which it cost
her sometimes—not to tremble while
she vanquished his savage eyes with the
cold disdain of her own.

The domestic picture is not pleasant
enough to tempt us to linger over it.
Perhaps, after all, it would have been
better — it could scarcely have been
worse—if Alan had staid on, and braved
it out; but this is only arguing from
consequences.

For a long time there were no certain tidings of the hunting-party : a
vague report got abroad of an encounter
with lions, in which some Englishman
had been terribly hurt, but it was not
even known whether it was Wyverne or
one of his companions. So months became years, and Alan's place in the
world was nearly filled up ; a few of his
old friends, from time to time, " wondered how he was getting on,"—that
was all. Yet he was not entirely forgotten. Every morning and evening,
in her simple orisons, Grace Beauclerc
joined his name to those of her husband
and children ; and another woman—
you know her well—seldom dared to
pray, because she felt it would be a
mockery to kneel with a guilty longing
and repining at her heart.

It was the fourth winter after Wyverne's departure ; the last intelligence
of the party dated from some months
back ; it reported them all alive and
well, in the northern provinces of India ;
there were wonderful accounts of their
sport, but no word as to their intention
of returning.

The Clydesdales were at Naples.
Helen's health, which had begun to fail
rapidly of late, was pretext enough for a
change of climate ; but it is more
than doubtful if her husband would have
taken this into consideration, if other
inducements had not drawn him south-
wards.

The Earl's home was certainly not a
happy one ; but even modern society
does not admit domestic discomfort as
an excuse for outraging the common
proprieties of life ; the most profligate
of his companions agreed, that he

might at least have taken the trouble to
mask his infidelities more carefully ;
they could not understand such utter
disregard of the trite monachal maxim,
*Si non casté, cauté tamen.* Personally,
one would have thought Lord Clydesdale was not attractive ; but a great
Seigneur rarely has far to go when
he seeks " consolations :" there are
always victims ready to be sacrificed, no matter how repulsive the
Idol may be ; for interest and
vanity, and a dozen other *irritamenta
malorum* work still as potently as ever.
It so chanced that the siren of the hour
had chosen South Italy for her winter
quarters, so that the Earl's sudden consideration for his wife was easily accounted for.

Naples was crowded that year ; every
country in Europe was nobly represented there ; so that it really was no mean
triumph when the popular voice, without an audible dissentient, assigned
the royalty of beauty to Lady Clydesdale. Rash and wilful in every other
respect, it was not likely that Helen
would be prudent about her own health;
indeed, if . she would only have taken
common precautions, her state was precarious enough to forbid her mixing in
society as usual.

If you could only have ignored certain dangerous symptoms, you would
have said she was lovelier than when
you saw her last ; her superb eyes
seemed larger than ever; softer, too, in
their languor, more intense in their
brilliancy : the rose-tint on her cheek
was fainter, perhaps, but more exquisitely delicate and transparent now;
and her figure had not lost, so far, one
rounded outline of its magnificent mould.

She had a perfectly fabulous success ;
before she had been in Naples a fortnight they raved about her, not only in
her own circle, but in all others beside.
It was literally a popular *furore ;* the
laziest *lazzarone* would start from his
afternoon sleep to gaze after her with a
muttered oath of admiration when " la
bellissima Contessa" drove by. She had
adorers of all sorts of nations, and was
worshipped in more languages than she
could speak or understand.

At last, one man singled himself out from the crowd—like the favourite "going through his horses"—and, for awhile, seemed to carry on the running alone. That was the Duca di Gravina. Perhaps Europe could not have produced a more formidable enemy, when a woman's honour was to be assailed. The Duke was not thirty yet, and he had won long ago an evil renown, and deserved it thoroughly. Few could look at his face without being attracted by its delicate classical beauty; the dark earnest eyes, trained to counterfeit any emotion—never to betray one—strengthened the spell, and an indescribable fascination of manner generally completed it. There was not a vestige of heart or conscience to interfere with his combinations; to say that he had no principle does not express the truth at all; the Boar of Capreæ himself was no more coolly cynical and cruel. Nevertheless, these last pleasant attributes lay far below the surface; and a very fair seductive surface it was.

The Duke was more thoroughly in earnest now than he had ever been in his life; and people seemed to think there could be but one result—the most natural and reasonable one, according to the facile code of Southern morality. Lord Clydesdale persisted in ignoring the whole affair; and no one cared to take the trouble of enlightening him against his will. It looked as if he had exhausted his jealousy and suspicions on Alan Wyverne, and had none to waste on the rest of the world. One could not help thinking of the old fable, of the stag who always fed with his blind eye towards the sea, suspecting danger only from the land-quarter. It was an ingenious plan enough; but the sea is wide and hunters are wily; they came in a boat, you remember, and shot the poor horned Monops to death with many arrows.

Di Gravina was almost as daring and successful at play as in intrigue; in both he was well served by a half-intuitive sagacity which suggested the right moment for risking a grand *coup*. He began to think that such a crisis was now near at hand. One afternoon Lady Clydesdale and several more of her set went up to Capo di Monte to lounge about in the gardens and drink the fresh sea-breeze. The party then broke up into detatchments very soon, and the Duke found it very easy to bring about a comfortably confidential *tête-à tête*. Helen was in a dangerous frame of mind that day. She had gone through a stormy scene with her husband in the morning, whose temper had broken out as usual without rhyme or reason. The velvet softness of the Italian's tone and manner contrasted strangely with the Earl's harsh voice and violent gestures. At first it simply *rested* her to sit still and listen; but gradually the fascination possessed her till her pulse began to quicken, though her outward languor remained undisturbed. Not a particle of passion, much less of love, so far, was at work in her heart; but in the desperation of weariness she felt tempted to try a more practical experiment in the way of excitement than she had ever yet ventured on. Di Gravina saw his advantage and pressed it mercilessly. For some minutes the Countess had ceased to answer him; she sat, with eyes half closed, just the dawning of a dreamy smile on her beautiful lips, like one who yields not unwillingly to the subjugation of a mesmerizer's riveted glance and waving hands.

At last she looked up suddenly, evidently with her purpose set. How her lips or her eyes would have answered can never be known, for at that instant she became aware of the presence of a third person, who had approached unheard while they were talking so earnestly.

The new-comer leant against the trunk of a palm-tree, contemplating the pair with a quaint expression of mingled curiosity and sadness. His face was sun-burnt to a black bronze, and almost buried in a huge bushy beard; but the disguise was not complete. Helen sprang to her feet impulsively as of old, with a low, happy cry, and in another second she had clasped her hands round Alan Wyverne's arm, with just breath enough left to gasp out a few fond incoherent syllables of welcome.

The Italian did not quite comprehend the situation at first; but he saw instantly that he had lost the game. A smothered blasphemy worthy of the coarsest *facchino* (and they swear hard in those parts, remember) escaped from his delicate, chiselled lips. For a moment his scowling eyes belied their training, and all the soft beauty vanished from his face, malign as a baffled devil's. Nevertheless he was his own silky self again before Helen recovered from her emotion sufficiently to make her excuses, and to present " her cousin." To do the Duke justice, he behaved admirably.

" It is a most happy meeting," he said. " Will the Countess permit the *stranger* to offer his felicitations and— to retire? She must have so much to say to the cousin who has so suddenly returned."

There was not an inflection of sarcasm in his voice; but he turned once as he went, and his glance crossed Wyverne's. These two understood each other thoroughly.

The pen of the readiest writer would fail in recording the long incoherent conversation which ensued. Helen had so much to ask and so much to tell that she never could get through a connected sentence or allow Alan to finish one. She was so simply and naturally happy that he had not the heart to check or reprove her. Even Stoicism has its limits and intervals of weakness, and Alan was a poor philosopher with all his good intentions " given in."

Certain members of her party came to reclaim Lady Clydesdale before half their say was said. (Would they have intervened so soon if the Duca di Gravina had remained master of the position?) So Alan had to content himself with accompanying his cousin to her own door. On the whole he thought it better not to risk meeting the Earl that night; he did not feel quite cool and collected enough for the encounter.

Let me remark casually that there was nothing extraordinary in the opportune apparition. The *Odalisque*

had anchored in the bay late on the previous night. Wyverne met an old acquaintance immediately on landing, who told him at once that the Clydesdales were in Naples. He could not resist the temptation of calling, and the servants directed him naturally to the place where he was sure to find Helen. Nevertheless I own that the situation savours of the *coup de théatre*. I don't see why one should not indulge in a slight touch of melodrama now and then; but there are men alive who can testify that such an intervention, coming exactly at the critical moment, is an actually accomplished fact.

No words can do justice to Lord Clydesdale's intense exasperation, when he heard that his enemy had returned, sound in life and limb. He could not for very shame forbid his wife to receive him just yet, but his whole nature was transformed; the careless, negligent husband became suddenly a suspicious, tyrannical jailor. Besides this, another foe lay in wait for Wyverne. The Duca di Gravina made no secret of his discomfiture or of his lust for revenge. This last enmity came round to Helen's ears, and she confessed her apprehension frankly to her cousin. He only laughed carelessly and confidently.

" I've seen a good deal of the feline tribe in these three years," he said, " and I begin to understand them. That leopard is too handsome to be very vicious. Nevertheless, I think it's as well you've given up *domesticating* him."

There was no bravado in his tone: he had only one honest purpose—to reassure Helen. The event proved the correctness of his judgment. The Duke had been " out" more than once; but it was only when he was compelled to pay with his body for some one of his iniquities. He loved life and its luxuries too well to risk the first without absolute necessity. Exaggerated reports of Wyverne's prowess in the Far East had got abroad; and the crafty voluptuary thoroughly appreciated valour's better part when a formidable foe was to be confronted.

But the ground under their feet was

nothing else than a Solfaterra, and the volcanic elements could not remain quiet long. Early one morning, Wyverne got a hurried message from his cousin, asking him to meet her immediately in the garden of the Villa Reale. As he approached the spot where she was sitting, he was struck painfully by the listless exhaustion of her attitude. When she looked up, as he came to her side, a cold thrill of terror shot through Alan's frame. He saw the truth at last—a truth that Helen had striven so carefully to conceal, that it was no wonder her cousin had failed to realize it. Her cheeks were perfectly colourless, and seemed to have grown all at once strangely thin and hollow; the dark circles under her eyes made them unnaturally bright and large, and a wild haggard look possessed and transformed her face. The signs were terribly plain to read—not of death immediately imminent, but of slow sure decay.

Alan's courage and self-control were well nigh exhausted before he had listened to half of what she had to tell. It appeared that on the previous evening there had been an outbreak of Lord Clydesdale's temper, incomparably more violent than any which had yet occurred. For the first time he had brought Wyverne's name into the quarrel—upbraiding, and accusing, and threatening his wife by turns, till he worked himself to a pitch of brutal frenzy that did not quite confine itself to words. He swore that the intimacy should be broken off at any cost, and signified his determination to start with Helen for England within forty-eight hours. This was the last thing she remembered; for just then she fainted. When she recovered she was alone with her maid, and had not seen her husband since.

"Ah, Alan; will you not save me?" she pleaded piteously. "There is no one else to help me—no one. And I am afraid now—really afraid : I have good reason. Do you see this?"

She drew back her loose sleeve : on the soft white flesh there was the livid print of a brutal grasp—marks such as were left on poor Mary of Scotland's arm by Lindsay's iron glove.

A groan of horror and wrath burst from Wyverne's white lips, and he shook from head to foot like a reed. A few minutes of such intense suffering might atone for more than one venial sin. He knew well enough what Helen meant as her eyes looked over the bay, and rested with a feverish longing and eagerness on the spot where the *Odalisque* lay at anchor, the tall taper masts cutting the sky line. He knew that he had only to speak the word, and that she would follow to the world's end. He knew that her health was failing under tyranny and ill treatment; while gentle nursing—such as he could tend her with—might still arrest the Destroyer. He knew how much excuse even society would find in this special case for the criminals. No wonder that he hesitated, muttering under his breath—

"God help me ! It is trying me *too* hard."

There was silence only for a few seconds. During that brief space Alan's brain was whirling, but the images on his mind were clear. He remembered how he swore to himself to guard Helen from harm or temptation, faithfully and unselfishly ; he thought of the End—possibly very near—and of the dishonour that would cling to his darling even in her grave; last of all rose Hubert Vavasour's face, when he should hear that the man whom he loved as his own son had brought his daughter to shame.' That turned the scale, and it never wavered afterwards. When Wyverne spoke his voice was firm, though intensely sad.

"It is too late to wish that the fever or the lion had not spared me. If I had guessed what my return would cost I would have stayed away till we both grew old. I did hope that we had grown steadier and wiser, and that people would have left us alone, and allowed us to be quietly happy. But I did not go through the pain of parting three years ago, to come back and ruin all. I stood firm then, and so I will—to the last. You will never call me cold or cruel; I feel that. You know how I suffer now while I am speaking; yet I say once more, we are better apart. Dear child, I am powerless to help you, unless it were in a way that I dare not think of. But you shall not be left to Clydesdale's tender mercies defenceless. I'll speak to Randolph to-day. He starts for England immediately, and he shall not lose sight of you till you reach it. He knows enough of your husband not to be surprised at being asked to watch over you. You may trust him as thoroughly as you could trust me. His heart is as soft as a woman's, and his nerves are steel: I have seen them tried often and hardly. Write to Dene, and go there straight from Dover. Clydesdale will have come to his senses before that, and will scarcely object. Remember, I shall follow by the next steamer, and not sleep on the road; so that I shall be in England almost before you. Then we will see what is best to be done. I swear that you shall have rest and peace at any cost. This worry is killing you. Darling, do bear up bravely, just for a little while; and be prudent and take care of yourself. It breaks my heart to see you looking so wan and worn."

His voice shook, and his lip quivered, and his eyes were very dim.

Helen's head had sunk lower and lower while her cousin was speaking; she felt no anger, only utter weariness and despair; she had listened with a mechanical attention, hardly realizing the meaning of all the words, and she answered helplessly and vaguely,—

"Thank you, dear Alan, I dare say you are right. I am sure you mean to be kind; and I know you suffer when I suffer. It is foolish to be frightened when there is no real danger; but I am not strong now, so there is some excuse. Lord Clydesdale is probably ashamed of himself by this time, and I shall have nothing to fear for some days—not even annoyance. Still, if it suits Colonel Randolph to go so soon, I shall be glad to feel there is one friend near me. You are sure you are coming straight to England? And you *will* come to Dene? Even if I am not

there, I hope you will. I must not stay longer than to say good-bye; perhaps I have been watched and followed already. I don't know why I ventured here, or sent for you; I knew it could do no good; but I felt so weak and unhappy. Now—say good-bye, kindly, Alan?"

Though Wyverne knew it was wrong and unwise to detain her, a vague presentiment that it might be long before they met again made him linger before uttering the farewell. While he paused, a heavy foot crunched on the gravel be hind them, and a hoarse, thick voice, close by, muttered something like a curse. The Earl stood there gazing at the cousins, his face flushed with passion, and a savage glare in his pale blue eyes. He essayed to speak with calmness and dignity; but the effort was absurdly apparent and vain.

"Lady Clydesdale, I am excessively surprised and displeased at finding you here, especially after what passed last night. I request that you will return home instantly. You have more than enough to do in making your preparations, and there are some necessary visits that you must pay. We start by tomorrow's steamer, I will follow you in a few minutes."

The assumption of marital authority was a miserable failure. Neither of the supposed delinquents seemed at all awed or discomforted by the Earl's sudden apparition, or by his set speech. Helen rose to depart, silently, without vouchsafing a glance to her exasperated lord; Alan accompanied her a few steps, to whisper a few words of farewell, and to exchange a long pressure of hands; then he came back and waited quietly to be spoken to.

Clydesdale's manner was arrogant and domineering to a degree; but he was evidently ill at ease; he kept lashing gravel, angrily and nervously, with his cane, and his eyes wandered everywhere except where they were likely to encounter Wyverne's.

"I don't mean to have any discussion," he said; "and I choose to give no reasons. You will understand that I decidedly disapprove of your intimacy with Lady Clydesdale; I shall not allow her to meet you, on any pretence, at any future period; and I beg that you will not attempt to visit her. I mean to be master of my own house, and of my own wife. You will take this warning, or—you will take the consequences!"

For once in his life—he reproached himself bitterly, afterwards, for the weakness—Alan fairly lost his temper. When he replied, his tone was, if anything, more galling than the other's, because its insolence was more subtle and refined.

"You might have spared threats," he said; "they would scarcely have answered, even if I had known you less thoroughly than I happen to do. You may frighten women—especially if they are weak and ill—but men, as a rule, don't faint. Consequences! What do you mean? I fancy I have guaged your valour tolerably well; it is superb up to a certain point—when personal risk comes in. If you had staid on here, perhaps you *would* have hired a knife. You might have laid some ruffian five thousand piastres to fifty, for instance, that I should not be found dead within a week—those are your favourite odds, I believe—that's about the extent of what one has to fear from your vengeance. I am not prepared to say how far a husband's dictation ought to extend, who does not take the trouble to conceal his intrigues abroad, and treats his wife brutally at home; and I'm not going to argue the point either. You certainly have a right to close your doors against me, or any one else. I shall not attempt to see my cousin while she remains in your house, or under your authority; her father had better decide how long that ought to last. I am no more inclined for discussion than you are; neither do I threaten. I simply give you fair warning. You had better put some constraint on your temper when your wife has to bear it; she has friends enough left to call you to an account, and make you pay it too. Max Vavasour will do his duty, I believe. If he don't—by G—d—I'll do mine!"

He turned on his heel, with the last word, and walked away very slowly; but he was out of ear-shot before the Earl could collect himself enough to speak intelligibly. If he had received a blow between the eyes, delivered straight from the shoulder by a practised arm, he would hardly have been more staggered. He had been so accustomed, from childhood, to deference and adulation, that a direct, unmistakeable personal insult, literally confounded him; for a brief space he felt thoroughly uncomfortable and humiliated; even his favourite curses came with an effort, and failed to act as anodynes. But he remembered every word that passed, and acted accordingly.

From that day forth, Clydesdale hated both his wife and Wyverne more bitterly than ever; but he entirely changed his tactics, for the present. The idea of a public *esclandre* and separation, did not suit him at all. His manner towards Helen on their journey homewards, was kinder and more considerate than it had ever been; he even condescended to express penitence for his late violence, and went so far as to promise an amendment. He encouraged her wish to go straight to Dene, only stipulating that he should accompany her there. The Countess was neither satisfied nor convinced; but she was weary and wanted rest, and so acquiesced listlessly and passively.

On the very first opportunity after his arrival at Dene, the Earl sought an interview with Lady Mildred. It was easy to make his case good; he lied, of course, literally; he confessed his failings, with certain reserves, and professed great contrition; he only insisted on one point—the necessity of keeping Wyverne at a distance, at least for a time. "My lady" was equally anxious to avoid any public scandal, and she was not disposed to look too closely into the facts. Helen did not choose to make a confidante of her mother, so there was little fear of her contradicting anything. When Alan reached England and wrote to his uncle, he found the ground mined under his feet. The Squire believed in his nephew thoroughly, but he was not strong-minded enough to take any decidedly offensive step, and under the circumstances, inclined to temporize. He talked about "faults on both sides," spoke of a reconciliation being certainly effected, and ended, by begging Alan not in anywise to interfere with it.

Wyverne felt sick and hopeless, he knew how much to believe of all this; but he had only one course open to him now—to avoid meeting the Clydesdales as carefully as possible. He hardly showed at all in town that spring, and encountered Helen very seldom, then only for a few minutes, when there was no opportunity for a confidence, even if either had had the heart to attempt such a thing. He spent all the summer and early autumn in Scotland. ,

Let me say now—for *your* comfort—my patient reader, that the End is very near.

---

CHAPTER· XXVI.

IMPLORA PACE.

THAT same year was drawing to its close, in a damp dreary December—one of those "'green Yules" which greedy sextons are supposed to pray for, and which all the rest of the world utterly abhor. Alan Wyverne was at the Abbey with Crichton for his only companion, who had come over from Castle Dacre to join a large shooting-party which was to assemble on the morrow. He had travelled far that day; and he sat more than half-asleep, before the huge wood-fire, waiting for dinner, and for Hugh, who had not finished dressing yet. He was dozing so soundly, that he never heard the great entrance-bell clang; but he rose to his feet with a start, as Algy Beauclerc came in. From that moment, Wyverne never heard a door open suddenly, without shuddering.

There was no mistaking the bearer of evil tidings; he had evidently ridden far and fast; he was drenched and travel-stained from heel to head; his bushy beard was sodden and matted with the driving ram; and his bluff, honest face looked haggard and weary.

Alan spoke first.

"Where do you come from? Some one is dying or dead, I know. Who is it?"

The other answered, as if it cost him an effort to speak, clearing his throat huskily:

"I have ridden here from Clydesholme. You must come back with me directly: Helen is dying. I don't know if I have done right in fetching you, but I had no heart to refuse her; and Gracie said that I might come. We must have fresh horses, and strong ones, and some one who knows the country: I can never find my way back through such a night as this; the waters were high in two places when I came through, and they are rising every hour. Don't lose a minute in getting ready."

Wyverne turned and walked to the bell without a word; he staggered more than once before he reached it: then he sat down, burying his head in his hands, and never lifted it till the servant entered. His face, when he uncovered it, was ghastly pale, and he was shaking all over; but he gave his orders quite distinctly and calmly.

"Don't talk now, Algy," he said; "you shall tell me all when we are on our way. I shall be ready before the horses are. Eat and drink meanwhile, if you can: you must need it now, and you will need it more before morning."

In less than a quarter of an hour Wyverne returned, fully accoutred for the journey; while he was dressing he had made arrangements with Hugh Crichton about telegraphing to put off the shooting party: his faculties seemed clear as ever; he literally forgot nothing. But Beauclerc was not deceived by the unnatural composure.

"For God's sake, take something to keep your strength up," he said. "It's a long five and twenty miles, and the road and weather are fearful. You'll never stand it if you start fasting."

Alan looked at him vacantly, with a miserable attempt at a smile.

"I don't think I could eat anything

just now," he answered; "and water suits me best to-night."

He filled a huge goblet and drained it thirstily; the horses were announced at that moment. Beauclerc remembered afterwards how carefully his companion looked at girth and bit before they mounted: all his thoughts and energies were concentrated on one point—how to reach Clydesholme as soon as possible—he would not risk the chance of an accident that might delay them for a moment. Two grooms followed them, to ensure a spare horse in case of a break-down; and so they rode out into the wild weather on their dismal errand. It was a terrible journey, and not without danger; the road was so steep and stony in places, that few men even in broad daylight would have cared to ride over it at that furious pace; and twice the horses were off their feet in black rushing water. Strong and tough as he was, Beauclerc was almost too exhausted to keep his saddle before they reached Clydesholme. Nevertheless, he found breath and time to give his companion all the details it was requisite he should know.

It appeared that the Earl had brought his wife to Clydesholme, about a fortnight back, on the pretext of making preparations for a large party, which was to assemble there immediately after Christmas. During the whole of their stay they had been perfectly alone. Her health had been breaking faster every day; while, from some inexplicable cause, his temper had grown more consistently tyrannical and savage in proportion to Helen's increasing weakness and physical inability to make even a show of resistance. On the previous evening had occurred a terrible scene of brutal violence. Early the next morning the Earl had ridden forth, no one knew whither, evidently still in furious wrath. Shortly afterwards the Countess had been seized with a coughing-fit, which had ended in the breaking of a large blood-vessel. As soon as she recovered strength enough to whisper an order, she had sent off an express for Grace Beauclerc, who chanced to be staying within a few miles. She

and her husband came instantly; but it was only to find Helen's state hopeless. You know the rest.

Alan listened to all this, but answered never a word; indeed, he scarcely spoke, except to ask some question about the road, or to give some order about increasing or moderating their speed. Once Algy heard him mutter aloud, "If we are only in time!"—and when they had to halt for some minutes, while a sleepy lodge-keeper was opening the park-gates of Clydesholme, his ear caught the fierce grinding of Wyverne's teeth.

The broad front of the mansion was as dark as the night outside, for the windows of the Countess's apartments looked over the gardens, but several servants came quickly to answer the summons of the bell. There was a scared, puzzled look about them all. Beauclerc whispered to one of them, and then turned to Alan with a gleam of satisfaction on his face.

"We *are* in time," he said; "thank God for that, at least. Stay here one minute, till I have seen Gracie."

Wyverne waited in the huge gloomy hall, with scarcely more consciousness or volition left than a sleep-walker owns. He allowed a servant to remove his drenched overcoat, and thanked the man, mechanically; but he never knew how or when he had taken it off.

Beauclerc soon returned and led the way through several passages into a long corridor; at the further end of this, light gleamed through a half-open door. Algy did not attempt to enter, but motioned Alan silently to go in.

It was a large, dim room, magnificently furnished after an antique fashion, and Grace Beauclerc was sitting there alone. She looked wan and worn with grief, and she trembled all over as she locked her arms round Alan's neck, holding him for a second or two closely embraced, and whispering a warning in his ear.

"You must be very quiet and cautious. She has hardly strength enough left to speak. Call me if you see any great change. I shall be here. The doctors and nurses are close by; but she would not allow any one to remain when she guessed you had come. She caught the sound of hoofs before any of us heard it."

She pointed to where a heavy curtain concealed an open doorway opposite. The gesture was not needed. Wyverne knew very well that in the next chamber Helen lay dying. His brain was clear enough now, and he was self-possessed, as men are wont to be when they have done with hope, and have nothing worse to fear than what the next moment will bring. He walked forward without pausing, and lifted the curtain gently, but with a steady hand.

The entrance nearly fronted the huge old-fashioned couch, shadowed by a canopy and hangings of dark-green velvet, on which the Countess lay. Her cheeks had scarcely more colour than the snowy linen and lace of the pillows which supported her, and, till just now, it seemed as though her heavy eyelids would never be lifted again. But, at the sound of Alan's footfall, the eyes opened, large and bright, and the face lost the impress of Death, as it lighted and flushed, momentarily, with the keen joy of recognition and welcome.

He was kneeling, with his head bowed down on Helen's hand, that he held fast, when the first words were spoken.

"I felt sure you would come," she murmured. "I have been so still, and patient, and obedient — only that I might live long enough for *this*. I heard you, when you rode up, through all the wind and the rain. I am so glad—so glad. I can die easily now. I could never have rested in my grave if we had not said—'Good-bye.'"

Wyverne tried twice to speak steadily, but there came only a miserable, broken moan.

"Ah! forgive—forgive! God knows, I thought I was right in keeping away. I did it for the best."

The thin, transparent fingers of the hand that was free wandered over his brow, and twined themselves in his drenched hair, with a fond, delicate caress.

"I know you did, Alan. *I was* wrong—I, who would have risked all the sin and the shame. But I have suffered so much, that I do hope I shall not be punished any more. See—I can thank you now for standing firm, and holding *me* up too. And, dear, I know how good and faithful you have been from the very beginning. I know about those letters, and all the truth. I am content—more than content. I have had all your love—is it not so? You will look at my picture sometimes, and though she was wilful and wicked, no woman, however good or beautiful, will win you away from your own dead Helen. Ah! it hurts me to hear you sob. I feel your tears on my wrist, and they burn—they burn."

Let us draw the curtain close. Even where sympathy is sure, it is not lightly to be paraded—" the agony of man unmanned." It was not long before Wyverne recovered self-control. They spoke no more aloud; but there were many of those low, broken whispers, half of whose meaning must be guessed when they are uttered, but which are remembered longer than the most elaborate sentences that mortal tongue ever declaimed.

For some minutes Helen's eyes had been closed. Suddenly, though not a feature was distorted, Alan saw a terrible change sweep over her face, and rose to call in assistance. It seemed as if she divined his purpose, and wished to prevent it. The weak clasp tightened, for an instant, round his fingers, the weary eyelids lifted, enough to give passage to one last, loving look, and the slow syllables were just barely audible—

"This once—only once more."

He understood her, and, stooping down, laid gently on the poor pale lips his own—almost as white and cold. Then, for a brief space, there was a great stillness—a stillness as of Death. An awful sound broke the silence—a dull, smothered cry, between groan and wail, that haunted the solitary hearer to her dying day—a cry wrung from the first despair of a broken-hearted man, who, henceforth, was to be alone for evermore.

Grace Beauclerc shivered in every limb, for she knew that all was over. But even then she had presence of mind enough to refrain from summoning any one from without. Helen was past human aid, and Grace knew that she could not serve her better now than by keeping for awhile curious eyes and ears away.

She found Alan standing, with his head resting on his arm that was coiled round one of the pillars of the canopy. He did not seem aware of his sister's entrance, and never spoke or stirred as she cast herself down by the side of the dead, pressing kiss after kiss on the sweet, quiet face, and weeping passionately.

How long they remained thus neither could have told. All at once the door of the outer room opened quickly, and Beauclerc lifted the curtain, and stood in the doorway. The first glance told him the truth. He walked straight up to the foot of the bed, and gazed steadily for a few seconds on the wreck of marvellous beauty that lay there so still; at last he muttered between his teeth,

"It is best—far best—so."

Then he passed round to where his wife was lying, and wound his arm round her waist and raised her gently.

"Darling Gracie, you must rouse yourself. It seems hard, I know, but this cruel night does not even give time for mourning. We must leave this instantly. I have ordered the carriage, and, Alan, I have ordered your horses too. You can find lodging within two miles, but you must not stay here five minutes longer. It is no place for any of us. Clydesdale is in the house at this moment."

For many hours Grace Beauclerc's nerves and strength had been sorely tried but had never given up to this moment. She broke down utterly now, marking the ghastly change in her brother's face, and the murderous meaning of his eyes, as he moved slowly and silently towards the door. She wrenched herself out of her husband's clasp, and threw herself in Alan's way with a wild cry of terror.

"Heaven help us! Have we not suffered enough to-night without this last horror? Alan, you shall never meet while I have sense to prevent it. Algy, won't you stop him? Don't you see that he is mad?"

Beauclerc strode forward and laid his strong grasp on Wyverne's breast.

"Yes, you *are* mad," he said, sternly. "You shall not pass out of this room, if I can prevent it, to work such bitter wrong against that dead woman, who loved you only too well. Cannot you see that if you retaliate on her husband to-night, her name will be dishonoured for ever and ever? She has suffered enough for you to sacrifice your selfish vengeance. Alan, listen now; you will thank God on your knees that you did so hereafter."

Wyverne gazed in the speaker's face, and as he gazed the devilish fire died out of his eyes. He passed his hand over his forehead twice or thrice as if bewildered, and then walked aside to the darkest corner of the room, leaning his face against the wall; when he turned round again, it was settled and calm.

"You are quite right," he said, slowly. "I *was* mad, and forgot everything. You need fear nothing now. I only ask you to trust me. I will see Clydesdale before I go; but I swear I will not speak one angry word. We will go down directly. Leave me here only three minutes, and I will follow you."

They did trust him; they went into the outer room, and never thought of listening or lifting the curtain. It is an example that we may well imitate.

All this while the Earl sat down-stairs alone, in such an agony of remorse and shame that, in spite of his past brutality and tyranny, his worst enemy might have spared reproach. He knew that Helen's state was hopeless, though he had not heard yet that the end had come. He thought of her, as he saw her first, in the radiant bloom of imperial beauty. He thought of her, as he saw her last, pale and exhausted and death-like, after his savage frenzy had vented itself. He *did* repent heartily now, and felt as if he would have given ten years of his life to undo the wrong and make ample amends. And still, the voice that none of us can stifle for ever kept whispering, "Too late—too late!"

He was musing thus in miserable anticipation of the next news, when the door opened slowly, and Wyverne entered, fully equipped for his departure.

What passed between these two will never be known. Beauclerc, who stood outside within ear-shot, ready to interfere in case Alan's self-control should fail, heard absolutely nothing. At first, the Earl's harsh, rough voice, though subdued below its wont, sounded at intervals; but Wyverne's deep, sombre monotone seemed to bear it down, and even this eventually sank so low that not an accent was distinguishable.

At last, the lock turned softly, and Wyverne came out. He just pressed Algy's hand in passing, and went straight to the hall-door, where his horses were waiting. Immediately afterwards the hoofs moved slowly away.

It was five minutes or more before the carriage was ready. Beauclerc had put his wife in, and was standing in the hall, making his last preparations, when Clydesdale came up behind him, and took his arm unawares.

The Earl's face was convulsed with grief; his eyes were heavy, and his cheeks seemed seamed with tears ; and his voice was broken and low.

"I hardly dare to ask you to stay tonight," he said ; "but if you would—— Only consider the fearful weather, and your wife's health. If you knew how bitterly I repent! I only heard the truth ten minutes ago."

Algy Beauclerc could preach patience better than he could practise it. He shook off the detaining hand with a force that made Clydesdale reel, turning upon him the wrathful blaze of his honest eyes.

"I hope you *do* repent," he said, hoarsely. "My wife is not strong, but she should lie out on the open moor sooner than sleep under that accursed roof of yours."

If he had looked back as he went out

he might have seen the Earl recoil helplessly, covering a stricken face with shaking hands.

Wyverne remained at the village inn, not a mile from the park gates, just long enough to rest his horses and men, and then rode back to the Abbey as fast as blood and bone of the best would carry him. His strained nerves and energies were not relaxed till he got fairly home. There was a sharp reaction, and he lay for some time in a state of half stupor ; but he was never seriously ill. It was no wonder that mind and body should be utterly worn out : the dark ride through such wild weather was trying enough, and he had scarcely tasted food or drink for twenty hours. Twice within the week there came a special messenger from Clydesholme ; it was to be presumed that the errand was one of peace ; for, eight days after Helen's death, Alan Wyverne stood in his place among the few friends and relations who travelled so far to see her laid in her grave. But it was noticed that neither at meeting nor parting did any word or salutation pass between him and the Earl. Alan arrived only just in time for the funeral, and left immediately afterwards, without setting his foot over the threshold of Clydesholme.

No one saw anything of Wyverne for some weeks. When he reappeared in society he looked certainly older, but otherwise his manner and bearing and temper remained much the same as they had been for the last four years.

That night left its mark on others besides him. It was long before Beauclerc recovered his genial careless elasticity of spirit ; and for months his wife scarcely slept a night without starting and moaning in her dreams. Judging from outward appearance, Clydesdale was the person most strongly and permanently affected by the events just recorded. He was never the same man again : his temper was still often harsh and violent, but the arrogant superciliousness, and intense appreciation of himself and his position, had quite left him. The lesson, whatever it was, lasted him his life. Very few of the many who were pleased or profited by the alteration in the Earl's character, guessed at what a fearful cost the improvement had been made.

It seemed as if poor Helen had felt for some time before her death that the end was fast approaching. They found not only her will, which had been executed when she was last in London, but divers letters, not to be delivered till after her decease. There was a very large legacy to Grace Beauclerc, and some minor ones to old servants and pensioners. All the residue of the vast sum at her disposal was bequeathed to her father, without condition or reserve. Her jewels—with the exception of Lord Clydesdale's gifts before and after marriage, which reverted to him—were left to to Mrs. Brabazon. There was no letter for Wyverne, and no mention of his name; but Maud sent him a casket, which had been in her hands for some time past. It contained three of Alan's letters, a few trifling relics of their brief engagement, a thick packet in Helen's handwriting, bearing a comparatively recent date, and a small exquisite miniature, taken before her beauty had begun to fade. That casket was the crowning jewel of the testament.

The void that her death made in society was not easily filled up; but after awhile the world rolled on, as if she had never been. The Squire looked broken and grey, and more careworn than when his affairs had been most desperate. He knew scarcely anything of the terrible truth, but a vague remorse haunted and bore him down. Lady Mildred's face was inscrutable as ever, but her smiles grew rarer and more artificial day by day. Max Vavasour, after the first emotion of sorrow, troubled himself little about what was past and gone. If he ever realized his sister's sacrifice, he looked upon it as a great political necessity—to be deplored, but not to be repented of. Maud Brabazon felt as if she could never bring herself to wear the jewels that she inherited; but she got over these scruples in time; and, at the first drawing-room of the following season, her sapphires and diamonds were genearlly envied and admired.

When I said that in Alan Wyverne there was litle outward alteration, I ought to have limited the assertion. Men would have told you so; but maids and matrons are sharper-sighted, and their report would have been very different: *they* knew how utterly he was changed. Their society still had an attraction for him; and he was frank, and kind, and gentle as ever, when a woman was in presence ; but a word never escaped his lips that could be construed into anything warmer than friendship and courtesy. The most intrepid coquette refrained instinctively from wasting her *calineries* and seductions there : she might as well have sought a lover in a deserted statue-gallery of the Vatican.

How Alan fared when he was quite alone it would be hard to say. Such seasons were rare, except at the dead hours of night, when sleep comes naturally to every constitution, unless some powerful momentary excitement is at work; for he mixed more in general society than he had done for years. I doubt if he did not suffer less acutely than when Helen was alive, and in her husband's power. He was at least free from the torments of anxiety and apprehension. If in this world of ours we can defy these two enemies of man's peace, we have gained no mean victory over Fate.

---

## CHAPTER XXVII.

### MORITURI TE SALUTANT.

It is a clear breezy night, out in the midst of the Atlantic, the mighty steam-ship *Panama* ploughs her way through the long, sullen " rollers," steadily, and calmly, strongly, as if conscious of her trust, and of her ability to discharge it—the safe carriage of three hundred lives. A few wakeful passengers still linger on deck ; amongst them is Alan Wyverne; the restless demon, ever at his elbow, has driven him abroad again, to see what sport may be found on the great Western prairies.

Suddenly there is a trampling of hurrying feet between decks, and a sailor rushes up the companion and whispers to the officer of the watch, who descends with a scared face; in five minutes more a terrible cry rings from stem to stern, waking the soundest sleeper aboard—" Fire !—Fire !"

Can you form any idea of the horror and confusion that ensue, when hundreds of human creatures wake from perfect security, to find themselves face to face with death? I think not. No one can realize the scene, except those few who have witnessed it once, and who see it in their dreams till they die. No man alive can say for certain if his nerve will stand such a shock, and the bravest may well be proud, if he emerges from such an ordeal without betraying shameful weakness. I speak of a mixed and undisciplined crowd —not of trained soldiers; we have more than one proof of what *these* can do and endure. I think, that those who died at Thermopylæ were less worthy of the crown of valour, than the troopers who formed upon deck and stood steady in their ranks, till every woman and child was safe in the boats, and till the *Birkenhead* went down under their feet.

Nevertheless, at such emergencies, a few are always found who single themselves out from the rest, as if determined to prove what daring and devotion manhood can display at extremity. First and foremost among these, on this occasion, was Alan Wyverne. He never lost his presence of mind for an instant. Yet he had accidentally become possessed of a secret that few on board had any idea of. English powder was at a high premium in America, just then; and the captain had shipped, at his own private risk, and against his orders, enough to blow all the fore part of the vessel to shivers. Alan reached his cabin before the first upward rush came, and made his preparations deliberately. They were very short and simple. He opened a certain steel casket and took out a packet and a miniature, which he secured in his breast; then passing his arm through the port-hole, he dropped the casket into the sea; a sharp pang of pain flitted across his face as he did so, but he never hesitated; that one fact told plainly enough his opinion of the crisis. Then he buckled round his waist a broad leather belt, from which, among other instruments, hung a long sheathed hunting-knife; he put some biscuits and cakes of portable soup, and a large flask of brandy, into the pockets of a thick boat-cloak, which he threw over his arm; then, after casting round a keen hurried glance, as if to assure himself he had forgotten nothing, he left the cabin, and with some difficulty made his way on deck.

It was a ghastly chaos of tumult and terror—a babel of shouts, and cries, and groans, and orders to which no one gave heed, while over all arose the roar and hiss of escaping steam, for they had stopped the engines at the first alarm, and the *Panama* lay in the trough of the sea—a hugh helpless log; though the weather was by no means rough, the "rollers" never quite subside out there in mid-ocean. The flames beginning to burst out of one of the fore hatchways, threw a weird, fantastic glare on half-dressed, struggling figures, and on white faces convulsed with eagerness or fear; and all the while the clear autumn moon looked down serenely indifferent to human suffering; even so, she looked down on Adam's agony, on the night that followed the Fall.

Personal terror and the consciousness of guilt, had made the captain utterly helpless already; but the chief-officer was a cool-headed Scotchman, a thorough seaman, and as brave as Bayard; he was exerting himself to the utmost, backed by a few sailors and passengers, to keep the gangway clear, so as to lower the boats regularly. In spite of their efforts, the first sank almost as soon as she touched the water, stove in against the side through the slipping or breaking of a " fall." At last they did get the launch fairly afloat, and were equally successful with the two remaining cutters.

There was manhood and generosity enough in the crowd to allow most of the women and children to be lowered without interference; but soon it became terribly evident that fully a third of those on board must be left behind, from absolute want of boat-room. Then the real, selfish struggle began, some of the sailors setting the example, and all order and authority was at an end. As Alan stood in the background, a man came up behind him and touched his arm, without speaking. It was Jock Ellison, whose father and grand-father had been keepers before him at the Abbey; he had accompanied Wyverne through Africa and India; his constitution and strength seemed climate-proof, no peril disturbed his cheerful equanimity, and he would have laid down his life to serve his master any day, as the merest matter of duty.

It did Alan good to see the handsome, honest, northern face, and the bright, bold, blue eyes close to his shoulder. He smiled as he spoke.

"We're in a bad mess, Jock, I fear. Keep near me, whatever happens. You've always done that so far, and we've always pulled through."

The stout henchman was slow of speech as he was ready of hand. Before he could reply, Wyverne's attention was called elsewhere.

A few steps from where they were standing, a pale, sickly-looking woman sat alone, leaning against the bulwarks. She felt she was too weak to force a passage through the crowd, so she had sunk down there, hopeless and helpless. She kept trying to hush the wailing of her frightened child, though the big, heavy tears were rolling fast down her own cheeks, moaning low at intervals, always the same words—"Ah! Willie, Willie!" It was her husband's name, and the poor creature was thinking how hard he had been slaving these three years to make a home for her and "Minnie" out there in the West, and how he had been living on crusts to save their passage money—only to bring them to *this*. Alan had been attracted by the pair soon after he came on board, they seemed so very lonely and defenceless and so wonderfully fond of each other. He had been kind to them on several occasions, and had made

great friends with "Minnie," a pretty timid, fragile child of five or six years.

He went up now, and laid his hand gently on the mother's shoulder.

"Don't lose heart," he said, "but trust to me. You shall meet your husband yet, please God. You will be almost safe when you are once in a boat. The sea is not rough, and you are certain to be picked up by some vessel before many hours are over. The only difficulty is to get to your place. We'll manage that for you. Don't be frightened if you hear an angry word or two. I can carry Minnie on one arm easily; let me put the other round you; and wrap yourself in this boat-cloak—there's enough in the pockets to feed you for days at a strait, and it will keep you both warm."

He hardly noticed her gratitude, but whispered a word or two to Jock Ellison, and moved steadily towards the gangway with both his charges. The gigantic Dalesman kept close to his master's shoulder, rather in his front, cleaving the crowd asunder with his mighty shoulders, utterly regardless of threat or prayer. Some of the better sort, too, when they saw the white, delicate woman, and the little child nestling close to Alan's breast, till her golden hair mingled with his black beard, yielded room, not unwillingly, muttering—"Let *them* pass, at all events: there's time enough yet." So, Wyverne had nearly reached the gangway, when a haggard, wild-looking man thrust himself violently forward, evidently determined to be the next to descend.

"You shall have the next turn," Alan said firmly. "Let these two go first; you see how helpless they are. They are not strong enough to fight their own battles."

The other turned upon him furiously.

"Who the —— are you, that give orders here?" he screamed. "I've as much right to my life as the woman or any of you. I'll have my turn in spite of you all;" and he began to open a clasp-knife.

Alan's face grew very dark and stern.

12

"I haven't time to argue," he said; "stand clear, or take the consequences."

His adversary sprang at him without another word. Wyverne's arms were so encumbered that he was perfectly defenceless; but just then Jock Ellison's hand came out of his breast, grasping a ponderous revolver by the barrel: the steel-bound butt crashed down full on the man's bare head, and he dropped where he stood, without even staggering. The crowd drew back instinctively; before they closed in again the mother was safe in the boat. Even in her agony of terror she found time to kiss Alan's hand, crying "that God would reward him." In truth he *was* rewarded, and that soon.

It was strange—considering their brief acquaintance—to see how the poor child clung to her protector, and how loth she was to leave him, even to follow her mother; it almost needed force to make the thin white arms unloose their clasp of his neck. Young as she was then, "Minnie" will be a woman before she forgets the kind grave face that leant over her, and the soft voice that said, "Good-bye, little one," as Wyverne let her go.

He was turning away, when the man that grovelled at his foot began to stir and moan.

"It's hard on him, too, poor devil!" some one grumbled in the background; "his wife is in the boat; she's five months gone with child, and she'll have to starve if she ever gets to land."

Wyverne stooped down and lifted up his late adversary as tenderly as he had supported the woman.

"Hold up for a minute," he whispered. "You brought the blow on yourself; but I promised you should have the next turn. Your wife has hardly missed you yet. And take care of this: it may help you some day."

He drew a note-case from his pocket as he spoke, and thrust it into the other's breast: no one attempted to interfere as he put the guiding ropes round the half insensible body, and passed it carefully over the ship's side. One determined mind will cow a crowd at most times; and remember, there were two to the fore, just then.

"He has *my* place," Alan said, simply—as if that were the best answer to any objections or murmurs; and then he made his way back again to the clear part of the deck, his trusty henchman following him still.

The dreadful struggle was over at last; the boats, fully freighted, had pushed off, and lay at a safe distance; those who were left on board knew that they had only to trust now to their own resources, or to a miracle, or to the mercy of Providence. There was scarcely any wind, and what there was blew in a favourable direction, so that little of the smoke or flame came aft.

Suddenly Wyverne turned to his companion, who sat near him, apparently quite cheerful and composed—

"You had better look to yourself, Jock. She won't hold together another quarter of an hour. It's no distance to swim, and they may take you into a boat still, if you try it. You've as good a right to a place as any one now the women are gone."

The Dalesman's broad breast heaved indignantly, and there was a sob in his voice as he replied.

"I'll do your bidding to the last, Sir Alan; but you'll never have the heart to make me leave you. I haven't deserved it."

Wyverne knew better than to press the point.

"Shake hands then, old comrade," he said, with a smile on his lip. "You've served me well enough to have your own way for once. I fancy you have few heavy sins to repent of, but you had better make your peace with God quickly; our minutes are numbered."

Just then a boat ranged up close under the ship's quarter, and a smothered voice called on Wyverne by name. It was the chief officer's, who had determined to make this last effort to save him.

"Let yourself down, Sir Alan, there are ropes enough about, or drop over the side. We'll take *you* in; you have well deserved it."

He never hesitated an instant—he

had withstood stronger temptations in his time—but leant over the side and answered, in his own firm, clear tones,

" Thanks, a thousand times: but get back out of danger instantly. It is useless waiting for me; I don't stir. I have given up my place already, and no power on earth would make me take another man's. If a ship comes near, we may all be saved yet; if not, we know the worst, and I hope we know how to meet it."

When the cutter had pushed off, Wyverne sat down again, burying his face in his hands, and remained so for some minutes. Suddenly he looked up, and drew the miniature out of his breast, gazing on it steadfastly and long, with a love and tenderness that no words can express, and a happiness so intense that it savoured of triumph. One of the survivors who chanced to be watching him (unconscious of the catastrophe being so near) said afterwards that a strange light shone out Alan's face during those few seconds—a light that came neither from moon nor fire, but as it were from *within*—a light, perchance, such as saints may, one day, see on the faces of angels.

" Helen—darling Helen," he murmured, " I always thought and hoped and prayed that I had acted rightly; but I never knew it till now."

He pressed the picture to his lips, and kissed it twice or thrice fervently. Let us hope that in that impulse there mingled nothing of sinful passion; for it was the last of Alan Wyverne's life.

In a moment there came an awful smothered roar—a crash of rending timbers and riven metal—all the fore-part of the vessel seemed to melt away, scattered over air and water in a torrent of smoke and flame; the after-part shook convulsively through every joint and seam, and then, with one headlong plunge, went down, like a wounded whale " sounding." Some half-dozen strong swimmers emerged alive from the horrible vortex, and all these were saved. Brave Jock Ellison, after recovering from the first stunning shock, never attempted to make for the boats, but swam hither and thither, till his colossal strength failed him, hoping to find some trace of his master. But Alan Wyverne never rose again, and never will—till the sea shall give up her dead.

And now my tale is told.

I have attempted to sketch, roughly, what befel a man very weak and erring—who was often sorely tried—who acted ever up to the light that was given him, at the cost of bitter self-denial and self-sacrifice—who, nevertheless, in this life, failed to reap the tithe of his reward.

Alan Wyverne was strong, up to a certain point; but he had not faith enough to make him feel always sure that he had done right, in defiance of appearances; nor principle enough to keep him from repining at results. He could neither comfort himself nor others, thoroughly. He was a chivalrous true-hearted man; but a very imperfect Christian. He dared not openly rebel against the laws of God; but he was too human to accept, unhesitatingly, the fulfilment of his decrees. Throughout Alan's life, Honour usurped the place where Religion ought to have reigned paramount; he shrank from shame when he would perhaps have encountered sin.

Just see how complete was the earthly retribution.

To that one principle—sound enough if it had not been the ruling one—he sacrificed love, and friendship, and revenge, and life. Yet the happiest moments that he knew for years, were those when he stood face to face with a terrible death—a dead woman's picture in his hand.

THE END.

Price

THE FOLLOWING BOOKS OF THIS SERIES ARE IN PRESS, AND WILL
BE ISSUED IN RAPID SUCCESSION.

The Housekeeper's Reason Why.  |  The Astronomical Reason Why.
The Botanical Reason Why.  |  The Chemical Reason Why.
The Geological Reason Why.  |  The Grammatical Reason Why.

## The Perfect Gentleman; *or, Etiquette and Eloquence.*

A Book of Information and Instruction for those who desire to become brilliant and conspicuous in General Society ; or at Parties, Dinners, or Popular Gatherings. Containing Model
Speeches for all Occasions, with directions how to deliver them ; 500 Toasts and Sentiments
for everybody, and their proper mode of introduction ; How to Use Wine at Table, with
Rules for judging of the quality of Wine, and Rules for Carving ; Etiquette, or Proper Behavior in Company, with an American Code of Politeness for every occasion ; Etiquette at
Washington, Remarkable Wit and Conversation at Table, &c., &c.  To which is added The
Duties of Chairman of a Public Meeting, with Rules for the Orderly Conduct thereof ; together with Valuable Hints and Examples for drawing up Preambles and Resolutions, and a
great deal of instructive and amusing matter never before published. 12mo, cloth, nearly
400 pages.................................................................... **$1 00**

## Richardson's Monitor of Free-Masonry; A Com-

plete Guide to the Various Ceremonies and Routine in Free Masons' Lodges, Chapters, Encampments, Hierarchies, &c., &c., in all the Degrees, whether Modern, Ancient, Ineffable,
Philosophical, or Historical.  Containing, also, the Signs, Tokens, Grips, Pass-words, Decorations, Drapery, Dress, Regalia, and Jewels in each Degree.  Profusely Illustrated with Explanatory Engravings, Plans of the Interior of Lodges, &c.  By JABEZ RICHARDSON, A. M   A
book of 185 pages.  This is the on'y book ever written which gives a detailed description of
all the doings inside a Masonic Meeting.  In this work nothing whatever is omitted that may
tend to impart a full understanding of the principles of Masonry—the ceremonies as they are
(or should be) performed—the pass-words, grips, signs, tokens. emblems, drapery, dress,
ornaments, jewels, &c., &c.  In short, any Society of Masons, who wish to work in the
higher degrees, or in any degree whatever, will find this book an invaluable aid to them.
Most of the books on Free-Masonry have been written by persons unable to give a clear
description of the ceremonies.  Either they did not understand the subject fully, or else
were careless or incompetent.  We do not hesitate to say that this book gives, in the plainest
possible language, an understandable description of the ceremonies in all the thirty-nine Degrees of Free-Masonry.  No one can be puzzled in reading it  They will know precisely and
exactly the Mysteries (so called) inside a Free-Masons' Lodge, without exaggeration or
detraction.  As this is the only book ever printed that gives these Mysteries complete and
authentic, we expect there will be a great demand for it.  Paper covers................... **30**
Bound and gilt............................................................. **50**

## Lacour on the Manufacture of Liquors, Wines,

and Cordials, *without the aid of Distillation* ; also, the Manufacture of Effervescing Bever-
ages and Syrups, Vinegar and Bitters.  Prepared and arranged expressly for the Trade.  By
PIERRE LACOUR.  This work tells you—How to make all kinds of Liquors, How to convert 10
gallons of Whisky to 100 gallons, How to make Cider without Apples, How to convert the
above Cider into all sorts of Wines, How to make the strongest Vinegar in twenty-four hours,
How to distinguish Imported from Domestic Liquors, How to make the finest Coloring for all
kinds of Liquors, How to make Neutral Spirits and Rectify Whisky, How to make old Barrels
look like new, and new Barrels like old, How to know Poisonous Liquors when you see them,
How to become an Expert Liquor Merchant or a good Bar-Keeper, How to make good, pure,
and healthy Liquors for Auction Sales that the most ruinous prices will pay large profits.
Procure a copy of " LACOUR ON THE MANUFACTURE OF LIQUORS," or, if you do not wish to
purchase, look through the book for a few moments as a matter of curiosity.  Physicians'
and Druggists' pharmaceutical knowledge cannot be complete without a copy of this work
12mo, cloth.................................................................. **1 50**

## The Secret Out; *or, One Thousand Tricks with Cards,* and

Other Recreations.  Illustrated with over Three Hundred Engravings, and containing clear
and comprehensive explanations how to perform, with ease, all the curious card deceptions
and sleight-of-hand tricks extant, with an endless variety of entertaining experiments in
drawing-room or white magic, including the celebrated science of second-sight, together
with a choice collection of intricate and puzzling questions, amusements in chance, natural
magic, &c., &c.  By the author of " The Sociable," " The Magician's Own Book," " Parlor
Theatricals," &c.  Large 12mo, cloth, gilt side and back.  The great merit of " The Secret
Out" consists in the very intelligible manner in which it instructs you how to do, with
ease, what other works on the subject only mystify you about, and make you think impossible to amateurs.................................................................. **1 00**

☞ Copies of the above books sent to any address in the United States, free
of postage.  Send Cash orders to Dick & Fitzgerald, Publishers, N. Y.

# MY UNCLE THE CURATE.

## A Novel.

BY THE AUTHOR OF

## "THE BACHELOR OF THE ALBANY," ETC.

—————

## NEW YORK:
HARPER & BROTHERS, PUBLISHERS,
PEARL STREET, FRANKLIN SQUARE.
1860.

# Ν UNCLE THE CURATE.

## BOOK I.

*Reader.* Pr'ythee, good author, no humdrum commencement now; something dramatic—startli—new, or, at least, not *very* old."

*Author.* I think I shall hit your fancy. 'It was an October morning, and a solitary horseman's seen slowly pacing up a hill—'"

*Reader.* Oh! oh! oh! that dreadful morning—that eternal horseman—that everlasting hill!"

*Author.* Well, what do you say to two horsemen and an inn-door; one of the horsemen masks time night; the moon in the last quarter."

*Reader.* Off, off, off, horsemen and moon both—the moon has been in the last quarter since the eat Cyrus was written."

*Author.* The fire blazed on the hearth; an old couple basked in the kindly light; a kitten sported a terrier on the rug; the table was covered h wine and biscuits."

*Reader.* Mi pardonate, gentle master, do not a to novels at least commence with wine and bisc?"

*Author.* You may have walnuts, if you please, I would undertake to provide nut-cracker Any thing in reason. I have an account the fairies' cutler, and a pair of nut-cracker neither here nor there."

*Reader.* Pray do let us have a new beginning—the request so very unreasonable?"

*Author.* The most unreasonable request in the wc; if your ladyship were a *writer* of fiction, I would know how hard it is to turn up anything new."

*Reader.* Being a *reader* of fiction, that is a truth I don't want the writers of it to tell me."

*Author.* Then ought you to be the more charitable. Time was when readers were gentle in truth—they are only gentle by courtesy—the fault of you are unfair—no allowance for an author's difficulties; no gracious oversight of his little short-comings; and then, like the Athens of old, you keep always calling for something new, as if a writer's brain was like the shop of a Parisian *modiste*."

*Reader.* Very monstrous, indeed!—to expect something new in a novel!"

*Author.* Now, suppose the novel were an Irish, to have nothing novel in it would be quite character."

*Reader.* Well, there has been enough of this parley. It is better to get into the house in any, than to be left in this unceremonious fashion standing at the door."

*Author.* The door is open, madam. I am since distressed it is *not* a new one, to please you.

*Reader.* "A distressed author is nothing new, at all events."

*Author.* "As old, at least, as the scene to which I am going to introduce you—the old hall of an old college; an old table with old books on it."

*Reader.* "Old, old, old, all old indeed."

*Author.* "Not all; there is a young man at the old table, and now that I see the dawn of a smile, madam, on your lips at the mention of the young man, I accept the omen, and respectfully touching your white hand, usher you into my—book."

---

## CHAPTER I.

### CAMBRIDGE.

IT was the beginning of the long vacation of 183–, the universities were growing deserted; students were trooping home to the country houses of their fathers and uncles; the classical antiquary was preparing to sail for Egypt and Asia Minor; the professors of botany and geology were studying the hand-books to Switzerland ; and numbers of grave bachelors and graver doctors in black coats and gray were getting their fishing-tackle in order, and poring over old Isaac and Sir Humphry Davy, preparatory to an indolent tour in Wales, or the Scotch Highlands.

But there are always a few men who linger behind in the long days, as if to keep the lights of science from going quite out, or haply, like culinary vestals, to guard the kitchen fires from extinction. One is too ambitious of academic success to squander a summer roving or fly-fishing ; another loves, but can not afford to travel ; a third would go home if he had only a home to go to ; and a fourth (as there are drones in every hive), is perhaps too sedentary, too lazy, or too corpulent, to think of locomotion with the sun in Leo or Virgo.

The quadrangle of —— Hall, Cambridge, looked particularly desolate and gloomy—all the birds, in fact, had flown but three. One of these—the only one interesting to us—was Frank Vivyan, a young man of good family, handsome person, considerable talents, and very little else to depend upon for advancement and success in life. Vivyan had made up his mind to pass this his first vacation in the monastic repose and almost solitude of his hall. It was not a matter of inexorable necessity, nor yet, on the other hand, absolutely voluntary; at least, not a deliberate choice. His purse, though not full, was not quite empty. His pursuits did not enjoin the sacrifice of health to business. The fact was that he only tarried behind his fellow scholars, because he did not well know where he could enjoy himself more than at Cambridge, having no father's house to harbor him, no invitation elsewhere that he cared to accept, little fancy to wander alone, and no friend to propose to join him in a ramble.

The day was warm, but not sultry, and Vivyan was sitting, or more properly lounging, in a chair too capacious for his size, and too luxurious for his standing, at a small, but very solid, table, close to a tall, narrow window, with an infinity of minute panes. The window stood wide open to admit the genial sunshine and the delicate air. A man is known not better by his companionships than by the arrangements and aspect of his chambers. The disorder of Vivyan's was not inelegant or vulgar, but still it was disorder; there was a negligence that denoted the indolent, or at least the erratic, student; it looked as if there had been a battle of the books, and the papers had the appearance of having been blown about like the leaves in the Sibylline grotto. There were places for books and papers, but nothing was exactly in its place. An open piano was strewed with French mathematics, easily known by their blue and pink *robe de chambre*. The floor adjacent was encumbered with a chaos of loose music. A deep, comfortable sofa seemed to be used as a general repository for articles of all sorts, useful and useless, necessities and luxuries, hats, canes, brushes, pamphlets, boxes, umbrellas, and cigars. All looked careless and desultory, a study in a state of siege. The table was a wilderness of writing materials, pen, ink, paper, envelopes, sealing-wax, seals with antique devices dispersed in all directions, like people in a panic; the books were so multifarious as to afford no grounds for concluding, with any confidence, what branch of study was most in cultivation, or what profession, if any, was the student's aim. There were books of mathematics, history, metaphysics, poetry, politics, a work on geology, and a volume of "Quentin Durward." You could scarcely decide what was the young man's immediate pursuit. A volume of Hobbes was open before him, but other books were open too; Claudian, Shelley, and a treatise of "Conic Sections." He was reading none of the three, but seemingly watching the swallows as they darted across the window.

He was not an idler; only a literary truant. Mental refinement was written on his brow; it spoke in his eye, but the intellect was of an unfixed and airy character. A sheet of paper that lay there among the other straggling leaves let you fully into the story of his mind. It was covered with a maze of characters and hieroglyphics, algebraic symbols, Greek verses, geometrical lines, and lines of English poetry, the exactest possible type of the state of intellectual vagrancy.

A picture stands on the mantel-piece; a green curtain covers it—let us draw it aside—ah!— what a face! what supreme beauty! A face that Raphael might have painted. And how like it is to Vivyan! We have said that he was handsome; he must have been so, indeed, to have resembled that lovely portrait. If his features had a fault, it was owing to their resembling their exquisite original only closely—the style was too delicate and feminine. But then his youth was some excuse; least it was a fair apology for the smoothness of his upper lip, which was only beginning be shadowed by the promise of a mustache His hair was fair, and where its thick clusters were parted with "artless heed" in front, it displayed a forehead of brilliant whiteness and the most intellectual form. His eye was blue, mild, bright, but with something of drainess, or languor, in its very brilliancy. It was, however, not the languor of sensuality; it was that the character of his mouth either, though it was still further, perhaps, from indicating the energetic and heroic qualities. Upon the whole, a physiognomist of no very great keenness might have divined what was indeed truth, that Frank Vivyan was a young man of great attractions and brilliant parts, but deficient in the hardier qualities of perseverance and self-reliance, which so frequently conduce in minor talents to eminence, while great abilities unstrengthened and unsustained by them, are often destined to shame their possessors and appoint the world. If Vivyan escaped these dangers, it was owing to the force of circumstances. Had he been left to be the architect of his own fortune, it is probable the fabric would ne have been raised.

Vivyan was the younger of two others; he had lost his mother early, and his father (an imprudent man) some years previous to the present period. You will easily believe that, in point of fortune, he was no Crœsus; his havings in money, like "his havings in be," were a "younger brother's portion." A small Irish property, yielding something under two hundred a year, had descended to him from maternal side—a revenue sufficient, with strict economy, to maintain him in the position of a gentleman, but totally insufficient to support the expense of the least costly form of university education. For this advantage, therefore, Frank was necessarily a dependent upon friendly aid. It was not from his brother, however, he received it: his brother, Sir Godfrey Vivyan, was a selfish and dissipated man, who, having inherited his father's extravagance along with his estate, found his available income much too mited to supply his own frivolous or licentious pleasures. The benefactor of Vivyan was a distant relative, a wealthy merchant, resident in the south of Spain, whom the young man had never so much as seen. It was, of course, therefore feeling of personal affection or esteem that mulated the munificence of this gentleman. Its origin was of a more tender, indeed of a romantic nature. In his youth he had formed a passionate attachment to Vivyan's mother; inexorable circumstances had not only prevented their union, but united the lady to another; ti passed away, and with it the first bitterness blasted prospects; but what can "raze out written troubles" of the heart—"pluck from memory the rooted sorrow" of frustrated love and hope blighted? The rapturous fascination of Mr. Everard's youth continued to be tranquil charm and innocent solace of his old age. Having heard by report how strong Frank resembled his mother, and that he had been left but poorly provided for, Mr. Everard's irresistibly impelld to promote his advancement in the only way tt seemed open to him; and he proceeded to t/ attainment of his object with a delicacy and fnkness that left the young man no alternative/it to accept the kindness ingenuously, or inft an ungracious wound through a mistaken felng of independence.

Vivyan had cousin, named George Markham, four o five years his senior, generous, brave, cordid and manly, heir to a handsome fortune, and/lready in the enjoyment of so large an alldnce as to place all the pleasures that became gentleman liberally and lawfully within his rch. Virtuously more than intellectually edted, his tastes were happily innocent and hedhy—

"— not of the courtly train,
Or city's rctice, but the country's innocence ;"

he was passnately fond of rural sports, indeed of rural lifin every respect, and spent the greater parif every year at his father's seat, a place calledManor Oakham, in the neighborhood of Sonampton, except when he went to Scotland ithe grouse season, made a pedestrian tour/rough the Alps or Pyrenees, or even rang the world as far as the banks of the Jordand the cataracts of the Nile. He was an ardt lover of natural beauty, as most sportsmen/e, particularly anglers, and Markham was /renowned with the rod as the gun; indeed, thpooks he was most addicted to, if not the q/ ones to which he had ever paid much atttion, were old Izaak and his fly-book.

Vivyarad not seen or known much of this relation /his until some short time after he was estalshed at Cambridge. An accidental circumstce then brought Markham to that part of Egland, and he did not omit paying his fair cou a visit. Nobody was so winsome as Frank Yyan; he was all openness, benevolence, gtleness, courtesy, and good-humor. Markhavas charmed with him: he perceived his men superiority, but the perfect artlessness anmodesty, nay, the very supineness, of Vivyanpharacter, prevented that superiority from bdr disagreeably felt by any body, even by thoshvho were in the position of his intellectual ¡als, which was not the case at all with Mkham. Frank, upon his part, was an easy cquest. He gave his cousin his affections abst in the first hour of their acquaintance; d embraced his invitation to Southampton wiut one thought of Legendre, or Mr. Peters,¡s tutor.

The¡e to which his cousin introduced him was dghtfully idle. All the forms and varieties thpase and idlesse ever took in a countryhouse ¡ere at Vivyan's disposal from cockcrow ¡ sunset. There was not a work on mathdtics in the library to remind him of his deser¡ studies, or a grave academic face at the ta¡ to recall the image of Mr. Peters.

Mdham was not motherless; but his mother, an edntric woman of fashion, lived entirely between¡ondon and Paris; and his father, also an oddit¡and an invalid to boot, was drenching hims¡abroad with all the waters of Germany. The ¡use was thus abandoned to youth, and plea¡e, which is youth's business. Vivyan's mod¡f enjoyment, however, differed in many resp¡s from his cousin's. Markham was ac-

tive and athletic, full of animal spirits, as eager at every thing he engaged in as if his life and fortune were staked on it, habitually an early riser, a man to catch the ¡arks asleep in their nest, and to make chanticleer crow if he neglected his duty. Vivyan, on the contrary, was addicted a little to his couch. He had probably, like most of us, witnessed in his time many more sunsets than sunrises. It is only metaphorically that men in general are much given to worship the rising sun.

At Manor Oakham, Vivyan scarce knew how the time passed, only that it passed agreeably; it was like dreaming—or imagine swimming without an effort down a bright stream that flows over sparkling pebbles, between banks of flowers. Markham adapted himself to his friend's tastes and strength; he shortened his rides and moderated his walks to suit him. For the first time in his life he became something of a saunterer, and it cost him some trouble to become one; he was so used to rapid and energetic movements. But he always took his gun with him. Frank, too, carried a light fowling-piece for a few days, but he found the encumbrance greater than the amusement it afforded; he loved loitering in the woods for the mere love of the woods and the loitering; and he was no great shot either, just enough to frighten a pheasant now and then, or hit a hare couchant. His sportsmanlike essays made Markham and his company smile, but when they smiled, Vivyan himself laughed, and made livelier hits at his own misses than they did. It is only affectation that is ever ridiculous; and Frank, far from affecting to be a shot, did not even assume the garb and externals of a sportsman.

---

## CHAPTER II.

PREPARATIONS FOR A "VOYAGE PITTORESQUE."

"'Tis a rare fortune, but of inestimable solace, to have a worthy man, one of a sound judgment, and of a temper conformable to your own, who takes a delight to bear your company in your travels. I have been at a very great loss for one in mine. But such a companion should be chose, and taken with you from your first setting out. There can be no pleasure to me without communication: there is not so much as a sprightly thought comes into my mind, which it does not grieve me to have produced alone, without one to communicate it to. But yet it is much better to be alone than in foolish and troublesome company."—MONTAIGNE.

THE visit referred to in the previous chapter was made in the vacation preceding that when our story properly commences. Vivyan had given Markham a general promise to return to Manor Oakham whenever his studies and other arrangements should admit of it; but such promises are not considered very binding unless when the memory of them is kept fresh by renewed invitations. Vivyan, however, had never heard from his cousin since his return to Cambridge, and was under the impression that he had gone abroad, when, as he was occupied watching the swallows, in the manner already described, his servant entered, and delivered the following letter:

"Manor Oakham, Southampton.

"MY DEAR FRANK—The Circe. is mine. You remember the boat we saw at Cowes last

September, and which we both admired so much. I have bought her, and have a grand scheme in my head of a 'voyage pittoresque' to Ireland and Scotland—a kind of romantic survey of the coast, islands, sea-ports, &c. What say you? recollect you are an Irish landlord, and ought to look after your property. You have nothing more agreeable on hand, have you? I will bide your convenience, but sail with me you must. You can bring your books, and make a scientific as well as a picturesque tour of it, if you are disposed to combine the *utile* with the *dulce*. Would Mr. Peters join us? as you please, only do not fail.

        "Yours ever truly,
           "George Markham.

"P. S. Don't trouble yourself about a sailor's dress—I can rig you out. I have been at Constantinople and Grand Cairo, and all over the gorgeous East since we met last."

This letter enchanted Vivyan, who really had no such love for his college as to prefer a summer in his chambers, to such a summer as Markham invited him to spend. Yachting, too, was an untasted pleasure; it could not fail to be charming, particularly with his books! He perfectly recollected the Circe—there was sorcery in the very name; but the notion of inviting Mr. Peters upon a party of pleasure of any kind, with his grave, sallow, quadrilateral face, his fluxional eyes, and his blue spectacles—it sounded like asking my Lord Primate to dance a polka.

The Circe, that idle argose, chartered to trade in midsummer amusement, lay at anchor, waiting for sailing orders, within two hundred yards of Manor Oakham, whose fine old woods extended to the very margin of the sea, the outermost trees dropping their branches into it. The yacht was manned by three able seamen, and there was a good cargo of champagne and claret in the lockers, with other stores to correspond; for Markham, though an enthusiastic sailor, and as fond of the sea as Byron, was not the man to neglect victualing his bark, or to be content with pickled pork, biscuit, and grog on a voyage.

It was a lovely, still, gray evening, and the sea lay polished as a mirror, and blue as the sky overhead, save the spaces immediately in the shadow of the impendent trees; and there it was so somber, that at first you were not aware how lucid it was at the same time. The moon was just risen, and promising to repay the world with a flood of silver for the loss it was soon to experience of the sun's golden rays.

The house was a little in disorder. Pieces of sail-cloth, spars, telescopes, compasses, chronometers, fowling-pieces, and even cutlasses, were scattered over the hall and dining-room, in odd association with busts, bronzes, vases, and candelabras. In one corner of the hall lay a small anchor, a swivel-gun, and a marlin-spike, while a billiard-table in the center was covered with flags and streamers of as many kinds, as if the little Circe had been a line-of-battle ship. The young men themselves were about to sit down to their last dinner on *terra firma* ; a small table was placed close to a window commanding a view of the element to which they were soon to commit themselves;

it was no doubt the situation they would have deliberately chosen, but in point of fact the perplexed servant had selected it as the only part of the room unencumbered with nautical implements, naval stores, sailors' jackets, charts, and fishing-tackle, books, cigars, and powder-flasks. A chart of the channel was spread on a sofa, Markham was examining it carefully, while Vivyan, immersed in the most luxurious chair he could find, was turning over Spenser's "View of the State of Ireland," when they were both summoned to dinner, which had been laid on the table without exciting their observation.

"This time to-morrow," said Markham to his friend, as he helped him to sp, "we shall dine in a less spacious apartme, but in point of dinner we shall probably be better off than we are to-day; we shall be unluck if we do not take some good fish, and there is case or two of champagne in the lockers for which I can answer, if there is any faith in wine merchants."

"You think we shall sail to-morrow, George," replied Frank, caring little about the fish or the wine, but bent with all his soul upon the voyage.

"Certainly," said Markham, "the wind is as steady as we are, and some letters arrive which I am expecting. As to the weather, there is no sign of change at present, nor any likelihood of it. The barometer rising; the moon looks well. I have great faith in the moon as an oracle of the weather; you can not see her where you are sitting."

Vivyan changed his position to do homage to the queen of the woods and floods, for both her titles were recalled by the delicate splendor which was just beginning to steal over the tops of the oaks, and beyond them again, a tremulous line of light, athwart the water

"Is she not beautiful?" cried Markham; "to-morrow night she will be nearly full, and a moon-rise by water is a magnificent spectacle. I saw a glorious one on the sea of Glee."

Markham loved nature; not ideal, like Vivyan, but heartily and honestly, nertheless. He was a true sportsman—and all the sportsmen love the moon, though not many see her rise on the sea of Galilee.

"Observe the effect of light upon the Circe's shrouds," said Vivyan, returning to his seat.

"Two blunders," said George, good-humoredly. "Frank, I fear you will always, what we sailors call a land-lubber."

"But how have I blundered now, George?"

"Why, in the first place you insult the Circe by mistaking that clumsy fishing-smac for her; and secondly, you talk of the shrouds when you mean the sails, though I have told you some dozen times that the shrouds are the ropes, not the canvas."

"How precise you are," said Vivyan laughing; "but you will see how I shall improve in nautical lore during our cruise. By the by, are we to make for the Irish or the Scotch coast first?"

"You shall decide," said the good-natured Markham.

"Then I am for Ireland," said Frank; "let us give the more distant expedition precedence ; we can run up the Clyde, or visit the islands later in the season, if there is time for our Irish adventures."

"Content," said Markham; "but we shall incidentally see something, too, on the Scottish coast, as our course will lie between that and the Irish; that is, if you have no objection to proceed northward, and commence our researches after the picturesque along the shores of Donegal."

"What I desire of all things," said Vivyan, "I have heard such accounts of the wild beauties of that part of Ireland; my only wish is that the long vacation were longer by a couple of months."

"We shall make it last as long as we can," said Markham, "and if it should outlast our stock of champagne and our other sea-stores, we must only take in a fresh supply at Belfast, or in Dublin, where we must put in for a day or two, to see the bay which they compare with Naples, and taste the herring for which it is so renowned. But tell me, Frank, how does it happen that you have never visited your Irish estate:—small as it is, it may be worth looking after."

Vivyan smiled, and said that it was the Irish usage to do every thing by proxy, and that he only conformed to the custom of the country.

"What will surprise you more," he added, "my agent has never seen my property any more than myself. He employs a sub-agent, who resides in the neighborhood, and collects the rent, which he transmits to his employer in Dublin, who in turn transmits it to me."

"Probably the sub-agent keeps a deputy also," said Markham.

"Most likely," said his cousin.

"I feel no small curiosity," said Markham, "to see a country that is managed in that sort of fashion."

"Depend upon it," said Frank, "we shall see a great many curious things in Ireland."

"We shall keep a list of Irish anomalies—but in what part of Ireland is your property situate?"

"In Donegal or Enniskillen, I believe," said the young poco-curate absentee.

Markham laughed heartily.

"Enniskillen is not a county, Frank."

"Not a county!—are you certain?"

Markham was not certain, so they called for a gazetteer to settle the question. They then became exceedingly merry at their own expense over a bottle of claret, much merrier than if they had been perfect masters of Irish geography, so that "ignorance was bliss," in this instance, as in many other cases that occur in life.

"At all events," said Vivyan, rising from the table, "I shall be back to my college and my business in the beginning of November. We shall see a great deal of anomaly in three months."

"Of course," said his cousin, "you must not forget your business, but it is no harm, believe me, to lay in a good stock of health and spirits in the long days;—a man returns to his books with such force after a little relaxation."

Markham had much more experience in relaxation than study, and so indeed had his cousin also, though he was not in the habit of unbending himself in the same strenuous way.

The arrival of the expected letters closed the evening. Among them was one which particularly interested them, with a view to their project of invading Ireland. It was from a noble-man, a distant relative of Markham's, who possessed a considerable property in the same county where Vivyan's small estate was situated. Markham had acquainted Lord Bonham (that was the nobleman's name and title) with his intentions for the summer, and his lordship now wrote to place his house in Ireland at his friend's service, and give him one or two introductions, which he might possibly find it useful or agreeable to avail himself of. As not only Lord Bonham himself, but the persons mentioned in his letter, will be found involved (some in no small degree), in the course of the events to be related in the sequel, it may not be amiss to place the letter at the disposal of the reader.

"MY DEAR MARKHAM:—I am both surprised and pleased to hear of your projected cruise. Ireland is worth a visit, and I sincerely wish it were in a state to make it more inviting to visitors than it now is, or probably will be for a longer time than it is agreeable to think of. You are no politician any more than myself, and so much the better for your peace and comfort. As to Ireland, I fear I am no great patriot, but then, as I am not an Irishman (though I have some property there), I neither feel myself bound to wear a green coat or to hold green opinions. Should your voyage lead you to the northwestern coast, you will find much romantic attraction, and you will be in the neighborhood of my more picturesque than profitable patrimony, where my lodge (for it is no more) will be heartily at your service, with the liberty of unlicensed shooting and fishing over some six or seven thousand acres of moor and loch. You will find the fishing good. I am not so sanguine about the shooting, but there will probably be grouse enough for a pie. You will find hospitality whenever you choose to land, but in the part of the country I speak of there are not many people to exercise that good old virtue, which it is the modern fashion to call a barbarous one. I have one excellent friend, whom if you fall in with, you will not fall out with me for introducing you to. His name is Spenser; he is rector of the parish of Redcross, and as great a curiosity as a fly in amber, for he is a liberal parson in the Orange province of Ulster. I hope you will visit him, and I know you will like him if you do. He is not particularly well off in point of wife, as you will probably find out for yourself, but he has two daughters, against whom I would caution both you and your friend Mr. Vivyan to be on your guard, if your object is merely to see the beauties of Ireland, and not to carry any of them off with you. One of the Miss Spensers is a particular friend of Lady Bonham; you have perhaps seen her with us; if so, you will not have forgotten her, even though you have since been in the East, and seen Georgians and Circassians. However, be of good courage and visit Redcross. I send you a letter of mark to my good friend the clergyman, and wish you a fair wind and every other blessing that man or yachtsman can desire.

"I remain, my dear Markham,
"Very sincerely yours,
"BONHAM.

"P.S. I knew the father of your friend Vivyan, and I had also an old acquaintanceship with his amiable and eccentric friend in Spain. By tle-by, my private advices state that poor Mr. Everard is declining in health alarmingly. If Mr. Vivyan has not heard this intelligence, pray do not mention it, as it is possible my information may be exaggerated."

"I can answer for myself," said Markham, as he conducted his friend to his bed-room, after reading all the foregoing letter to him, save the postscript, "I can answer for myself that I have no design on Banham's portable legatee."

"Nor I, unquestionably," said Vivyan, laughing; "but do you recollect the lady his lordship commends so highly?"

"I do not," said Markham, "I fear I have been sadly inattentive to the book of beauty; but as she is a favorite of Lady Banham's, I have no doubt she is very good and very sensible, as well as handsome."

"Quite a dangerous female character," said his cousin, bidding him good-night.

## CHAPTER III.

### THE CIRCE SAILS.

"Fair laughs the morn and soft the zephyr blows,
While proudly riding o'er the azure realm,
In gallant trim the gilded vessel goes;
Youth on the prow and Pleasure at the helm."
GRAY.

The barometer kept rising, the moon was constant to the promise of the previous evening, the morning rose without a cloud on her forehead, and the cousins (almost as early) with minds equally serene and brows alike cloudless. Much of the nautical lumber which we described as so intrusively encumbering apartments never intended for the uses of dock-yards, had been removed on board the night before. What remained was transported at dawn of day, and before the clock in the cupola over the offices struck six, Markham and Vivyan were on their way through the woods and meadows to the cosy little bay where the pinnace was moored, which was to take them to the Circe. They diverted themselves on the way with omens from the ravens, hawks, and pigeons, losing no opportunity, however, afforded by the windings of the path, the undulations of the ground, and the breaks in the forest, of catching a glimpse of their "varmint" vessel, and vying with each other in encomiums upon her. Markham was followed by the two inseparable attendants of his excursions by land or by water; Lawrence, his man, looking prematurely sea-sick, and Pedro his dog, in riotous spirits. Lawrence was a native of Britain; Pedro claimed Newfoundland as the country, not of his birth, but of his parentage. Ashore there is no doubt but that Lawrence was the more serviceable of the two vassals, for he was a faithful, intelligent, attentive domestic as ever served a master. But afloat it was another matter. There Pedro shone to infinitely more advantage; his tastes and delights were so aquatic, his spirits so exuberant, his appetite so keen, his affections so warm, all his doggish virtues so developed, while Lawrence was absolutely good for nothing, not even in "smooth seas," except when their surface was smoother than glass itself. It was indeed a proof of his strong attachment to Markham that Lawrence followed him even in his cruises; nothing was to him so inexplicable as how his master, or any body else, could take pleasure in a treacherous, uncertain element, connected in his mind with every image of terror and danger, with sharks, corsairs, shipwrecks, hurricanes, and the hideous spectre of the Flying Dutchman. He was everlastingly afraid of being boarded, or swamped, stranded, or water-logged, without any distinct idea of the difference between these several disasters. He had heard tales of Spanish privateers, and frightful anecdotes of Kidd and Paul Jones; but in fact such was Lawrence's horror of the high seas that every name he heard mentioned by his master, or Frank Vivyan, with any degree of awe or suspicion, became associated in his mind with piratical ideas. He was not without apprehension of being captured and sold to the Algerines by Daniel O'Connell (whose political exploits were then in the mouth of every body); and fancy dressed up William Cobbett for him in a fierce cocked hat and a blue coat, with a pistol in one hand and a cutlass in the other.

Admirable studies Markham and Vivyan would themselves have made for a painter, who wanted a pair of handsome young corsairs for a wild sea-piece. Markham was tall, athletic, muscular; his figure would have been a model of manly beauty had it not been a little too robust (inclining to the Milo more than the Antinous), but his bearing was graceful and gentlemanlike, which, combined with good, open, manly, though somewhat rigid features, the complexion of vigorous health, a good, cool, daring eye (more that of a sportsman, however, than a poet), made him altogether a very handsome man;—and so he was considered by maid and matron for many miles round Southampton, in which neighborhood the greater part of his stirring life had been spent. His nautical costume became him well, and he wore it with the air and ease of a sailor by craft; for though a young man, George was an ancient mariner, scarcely remembering the time when ropes and cables were not, as "familiar to him as his garter."

A shout of welcome and triumph burst from the little crew, with whom he was highly popular, when Markham, followed by his cousin, and the ghastly Lawrence, jumped with a cheer on the snow-white deck of the Circe. For a few moments, he engrossed all eyes and all admiration, but Frank Vivyan was not long without receiving his full share of attention and applause. He looked an Adonis in his sailor's dress, or a Paris setting out to make a Helen his booty, and perfectly bewitched the rugged tars with the radiance of his countenance, and the singular elegance of his slight person. He was such a contrast to his cousin, of such a different style of beauty; yet his present attire—the loose blue jacket, the cap with its gold band, the checkered shirt, the black ribbon, the white vest and trowsers—had the advantage of taking something from the delicacy of his exterior, and giving him a manlier air than he had yet attained to. In short, you have only to imagine Don Juan following Leander's profession, to form some notion of the picture which Vivyan presented that morning as he came on board, in the direc the mariners were going in quest of.

---

# BOOK II.

## CHAPTER IV.

### THE PARSONAGE.

> "And now they nigh approached to the sted,
> Where these fair mermaids dwelt; it was a still
> And calmy bay, on one side sheltered
> With the broad shadow of a hoary hill."
>
> THE FAERY QUEEN.

A THOUSAND picturesque bays and creeks indent the western and northwestern shores of Ireland, most attractive to the lovers of coast scenery, and most commodious as fishing stations, though shunning, of course, the general marked inattention of the uncivil Irish to the advantages with which nature has blessed them. The scenery at some points of the coast in question is as fine, perhaps, as any of its class in the British islands. The mountain chains of the interior, apparelled in gold and purple by the gorse and heather, terminate in a series of headlands of every variety of shape and altitude, throwing themselves boldly into the Atlantic, which, whirling into the gorges between them, forms a succession of bays, more or less exposed to the fury of the ocean, according to their extent and form, but sometimes exhibiting in their windings all the quiet beauty of the stream-fed mountain lake. Approaching such spots as these by water, the contrast is very striking between the boiling surf through which you make your perilous way into the inlet, and the repose that reigns often at no great distance from its mouth. It is like the calm of settled government after the throes of revolutionary violence, when revolution has the good fortune to be succeeded by peace and order.

There existed some twenty years ago, and probably still exists, a parsonage in the county of Donegal, and parish of Redcross, situated close to the water edge, on the shores of a small but beautiful arm of the sea, which resembled, just at that place, one of the many romantic sheep-pools which abound in the Welsh highlands. The parsonage (a comfortable house, containing accommodation for a large family, but with no great architectural pretensions) stood on the northern side of the creek, or fiord (as such inlets are called in Norway), so that it enjoyed a southern exposure, besides being very well sheltered on the north and northeast by a lofty range of hills, whose steep, rocky sides, strewed with patches of wild vegetation (delicious browsing for sheep), rose like a wall over it. In the westerly direction, where the hills were least precipitous, a copse of oak and birch crept from their base to the very summits; and toward the east, or to the left of the parsonage, a high point of rock, which stood boldly into the water, was crested in a very imposing manner with a group of pines, or trees of that species, whose tops were fired at midsummer with the sun's beams, long before their golden track was visible upon the bosom of the lake. A few acres of greensward—the natural turf improved by not much manual labor—filled up the space between the house and the beach, consisting of a narrow strip of sand, which, not being itself often encroached on by the waves, manifested equal forbearance to the lawn, which it seemed to skirt with silver. From the front of the parsonage the view was exquisite, for it not only commanded the loch itself, with its picturesque banks, distinguished by their air of idle grandeur, but the additional prospect of a not very distant mountain range beyond, one of whose numerous peaks was nearly of a sugar-loaf form, and domineered superbly, with its fine dark blue cone, over the less ambitious parts of the chain. The scenery altogether was the wildest imaginable, but its wildness was chastened by its unity and simplicity. Nature is well compared by a German writer to a great poet, "who produces his greatest effects with the fewest means," a great thought, and a few household words to clothe it.

It was evident that the tenants of the parsonage were in the habit of enjoying the scenery around them from the water as well as from the land; for a' small pier, neatly constructed with square massive blocks of granite, had been thrown some twenty feet out into the loch, forming not only a quay for embarkation, but a kind of diminutive harbor, within which was now moored a small but smart cutter, destined, no doubt, for distant voyages, as well as a boat, like a Thames wherry, designed for cruises not far from. home. At the extremity of the pier was erected a flag-staff, supported by iron stays; there was generally breeze enough in a mountain region so close to the sea to keep the gay ensign floating, but on' the evening 'when our story commences there was scarcely a. breath to stir an aspen-leaf: the flag had ceased to wave, and drooped like' the pendent from a woman's .ear.

The sun was preparing to set in all his pomp, and Mr. Spenser, the rector, with his son· Sydney, two marriageable daughters, Arabella and Elizabeth, and one or two younger children, were assembled after dinner in front of the parsonage, to enjoy the spectacle. Mr. Spenser was sitting, the rest were standing, all more or less intent upon the scene before them; nor were they enjoying it in silence, but, on the contrary, conversing eagerly, noticing the beauties of the prospect, and speculating on the ever-debatable topic in 'these· climes—the· weather of to-morrow.

A cruise of pleasure seemed to be on the *tapis*. At a distance of about half a league from the mouth of the *fiorde* was a very. small but extremely picturesque island, a frequent summer haunt of the Spensers; they held it in joint tenancy with a nation of rabbits, and it was to this little speck in the ocean that they were contemplating a voyage and pic-nic on the following day.

"And a splendid day it will be," cried Sydney, a robust, square-built youth, attired in a kind of sailor's dress, a handsome boy, but with features that indicated both sensuality and willfulness, as if he had either been left untutored and undisciplined, or as if discipline had been thrown away upon him. The tone of his voice, too, was boorish, as if he kept other company occasionally than that in which we now see him.

"I am no weather-seer," said his father, a comely, grave man, between forty-five and fifty, whose attire announced the well-beneficed clergyman, and whose placid countenance, at once benign and intellectual, proclaimed him one of the race of gentle shepherds.

"You have not yet visited your island this summer," he added, addressing the junior branches of his family.

"The island! the island!" shouted the little Spensers, in chorus.

"Listen," said Elizabeth, the rector's second daughter, a radiant brunette of eighteen, with a figure that was perfect, and a face of the sweetest and noblest expression. She spoke with one hand on the bare shoulder of her. little brother, and a finger of the other raised to command attention.

"The island !".replied a voice from ·afar, as of a viewless speaker—it was a voice, and nothing but a voice, for the spot was remarkable for its echo, and. the shrill and joyful cry of the children came back from the rocks and hills with a sharpness and fidelity which the famous echo of Blarney could not have surpassed. . ·

Sydney, however, said, he thought there was a still more wonderful echo on the island, and he hoped his friend Dudley Dawson would bring his French-horn to awaken it. .

. "You surely did not invite Mr. Dawson!" said the brown girl, but in a low but displeased tone, as if unwilling to stir a painful subject. Her elder sister, Arabella, expressed her disapprobation in stronger terms.

"But I did," replied the young man, rudely, and left the circle; perhaps to superintend the preparations for the morrow's amusement. He spoke with a clownishness of phrase and accent, which you were surprised to hear in a member of such a group, and the brother of such sisters.

The placid clergyman made no remark, but sat with one of his courtly legs crossed on the other, gazing on· the· landscape, murmuring to himself lines of Ovid, and verses of Milton, on the phenomena of echo, for his mind was stored with all that is sweet and beautiful in ancient and modern poetry.

The crisis of the sunset was now approaching; the sun descended rapidly upon the brow of the mountain which intercepted the view of the Atlantic. The variegated clouds lay in long, irregular, fleecy masses, parallel to the horizon, their edges burnished by the retiring luminary, whose blazing· disc only appeared in the intervening spaces, sometimes so contracted as only to disclose a slender bar of intense luster, like an ingot of ruddy gold. But directly the sun dropped below the lowest cloud of the strata, there was nothing to obstruct his splendor until he touched the summit of the mountain, when he soon vanished, to illumine and gladden other lands.

Often as the Spensers had witnessed the same imposing spectacle from the same spot, they had never admired it so much. As still they gazed, their contemplation was disturbed by a loud, clear hurrah, proceeding from the heights on the opposite side of the creek.

"Uncle Woodward !" exclaimed several voices instantly. Some· called him "Uncle Hercules."

The quarter from which the shout proceeded was more easily discovered than the personage to whom it was ascribed, for the distance across the inlet was upward of a mile, and the tortuous way in which the road ran upon that side, often altogether hidden by masses of rocks, or clumps of heather and· brushwood, rendered it often· difficult, and sometimes impossible, to detect where the road' ran at all. In fact, it had been carved in days of rough but daring engineering, and when other considerations, besides public convenience influenced road-making in Ireland, in a· continual steep zigzag, from the margin of the creek to the summit of the impending hills, an extent of some four or five miles, without one furlong'which you could travel with tolerable safety, except on foot, or mounted on one· of the sure-footed ponies of the country.

Every eye was strained in the direction of the familiar signal.

"He will shout'again; if it is your uncle," said Mr. Spenser· . . ·

"I think I see him, papa," said one of the children—"see, just at the tall, white rock, where the eagles used to build until last summer, when Sydney shot that grand one."

"It was not Sydney; it was Mr. Dawson," lisped the other little one.

"I see nothing yet," said Mr. Spenser.

Another hurrah was heard as he spoke, and almost at the same instant Mr. Spenser, waving his hat, pointed to a spot where the road came conspicuously into view, directly opposite the parsonage, and about one hundred and fifty feet above the level of the water. The correctness of the discovery was soon acknowledged; the girls waved their handkerchiefs, and their little brother returned his uncle's greeting with a scream, which, though very inferior in sonorous effect, probably reached his ear, for again the same stentorian salute came booming across the estuary, multiplied by a score of echoes.

A few moments brought our new acquaintance to the water's edge, for he had his stout mountain hack under him, a pony in whom discretion and valor were blended in the justest proportions, and who was so familiar with up-hill and down-hill, that he actually never stumbled except upon level ground. There was a snug little deep sandy cove, just where the precipitous road seemingly tumbled down upon the beach; and just above high-water mark was a low rock, to which, by means of an iron ring, was attached a boat, with a couple of oars, designed expressly for the accommodation of those who, having to cross the inlet, like Mr. Woodward, preferred this short cut to a circuitous route, which led you for a couple of miles along the shore, until you gained a point where the estuary was narrow enough to be spanned by a rude wooden bridge.

The Spensers watched their relative's proceedings with the liveliest interest, increased by some little surprise at receiving a visit from him on that particular evening. He loosed the boat from the ring, drew it down along the smooth tawny sand, launched and almost simultaneously stepped into it, leaving the pony to take care of himself, which he was extremely well able to do. A couple of lusty strokes, such as only a very powerful man could have given, pushed the boat into deep water. He then paused, but it was only to throw off his hat and coat, preparatory to resuming the oar with still greater vigor.

"My uncle deserves to be called Hercules," said Sydney, who had just returned, raising a hearty cheer, which his muscular relative as heartily responded to; and the cheering and counter-cheering lasted until the boatman gained the shore, and was surrounded and welcomed by the Spensers. He towered above them all, like a dromedary in a flock of sheep. There was not another such strapping fellow in all the diocese, nay, in all the arch-diocese, in either Protestant establishment, Catholic church, or Presbyterian synod. Hercules Woodward stood six feet three inches in his stocking-feet, and he was broad and brawny in proportion. Though possessing a giant's strength, however, you soon perceived that he was not the man to make giant-like use of it. He had the honestest though roughest set of features imaginable; a face as massive and strongly marked as those which sculptors assign to river-gods, a high bald forehead, bushy, reddish whiskers, and good-humored but powerful eyes, over which a pair of enormous brows beetled, with an endeavor, not always unsuccessful, to give them a ferocious aspect.

Such was his person. His dress was very much in keeping with it. He wore a short frock, or rather jacket, of dark blue cloth, not much finer than frieze; it was something between a sailor's jacket and a shooting coat. His trowsers, very wide and very short, were of strong gray plaid, the coarsest of the kind that is called shepherd's, and his waistcoat was from the same piece; a black silk handkerchief loosely encircled his hirsute throat; his feet were furnished with shoes such as men wear in snipe-shooting, and his head was provided with a low-crowned and broad-brimmed glazed hat. And now that you have him before you, such as nature formed, and the tailor finished him, to what profession would you suppose him to belong? It was difficult enough to believe that he was Mr. Spenser's brother-in-law, but it will be harder still to credit what is equally true—he was also his curate!

There was a marked difference in the greetings and receptions "my uncle, the curate," met with from the two ladies. By Elizabeth he was received with cordiality and tenderness, by her elder sister with cold and fastidious civility. It gave you an insight into the characters of the two girls. Nothing could ever conquer Arabella Spenser's repugnance to her rustic relative, neither her father's regard for him, his own sterling virtues, or the fact that he was the husband of her Aunt Carry, one of the worthiest, as she was one of the largest, specimens of womankind.

To Mr. Spenser, indeed, he was a most striking contrast. Mr. Spenser was so quiet and refined; the intellectual predominated in him so much above the physical; his person was so elegant, his manners so calm and courtly. In fact, it was obvious that they had been born in different spheres of society; the rector was Corinthian, the curate Doric; and moreover, to distinguish them still further asunder, the former was by origin and education an Englishman, while the latter was the genuine indigenous growth of the province of Ulster, descended from a plain, bluff race of ancestors, who had sent many a good rough scholar up to Dublin College, and supplied many a sturdy shepherd to the Irish church.

---

## CHAPTER V.

### THE WEATHER-SEER.

THE curate was a weather-seer, if the rector was not. Not a mountaineer in the country could predict wet or dry, hot or cold, a calm or a hurricane, so unerringly as Hercules Woodward, because in fact, nobody lived so much abroad as he did, and was so conversant with the elements in all their aspects and vicissitudes. With earth, air, and ocean, at least, he lived on terms of daily familiarity. His acquaintance with fire was not quite so intimate, though no man enjoyed a blazing one of turf more of an evening, when he had his wife at his side, and his little Woodwards littered about him.

It was the purest as well as the most active good nature which brought Hercules over to the parsonage that evening, all the long way from the town of Redcross, where he dwelt. "You are not dreaming of sailing to-morrow," he said, with his bluff, stormy voice, and striding at the same time toward the house, with his younger niece, Elizabeth, on his arm, where she looked something like a sprig of geranium hanging from a stalwart mountain ash.

"Yes, indeed we are, uncle," replied several voices, eagerly. Hercules looked unpropitious. "Did you see the sun set, uncle?" cried the little Arthur Spenser.

"Shan't we have a charming day to-morrow?" cried his smaller sister.

"For barnacle and wild ducks, Mysie," replied the curate, looking down at the little girl, as if from the top of a steeple.

"You don't mean to say it will be wet, sir?" growled Sydney, with temper, apprehensive of the effects of his uncle's opinion upon the rest of the party.

"Wet and wind, and plenty of both. The car of day will be a covered car to-morrow, Syd., my boy," replied his uncle, taking no notice of his nephew's ungracious looks and tones, being probably accustomed to such displays of temper.

The prediction, however, caused general surprise; and the little Spensers, as well as their elder brother, looked considerably disconcerted by it.

"I'll tell you more," continued Hercules, not thinking much of the pain he was giving in such a cause, "we are going to have several days of wild weather:—it was nothing else brought me over. I was afraid you might venture out in the morning and get capsized in one of those squalls to which that piece of water there is subject at times, innocent as it looks at the present moment."

Sydney's aspect lowered, but he kept a passionate silence.

"Uncle, you are such a mar-plot," said one of the younger children, half pettishly, half playfully.

"Never mind, Mysie, we shall have our sail," muttered Sydney, in a gruff, refractory tone, which possibly nobody heard, for no notice was taken of it. Elizabeth gently reproved the child for calling her uncle a mar-plot and thanked him over and over again for his kindness, pressing him at the same time to stay that night at the parsonage.

"What would your aunt say to that, Lizzy?" answered her huge relative—"no, Lizzy, my dear, I'll drink tea with you, and then across the water again to the dulce domum. Val., how is Mag this evening?"

Mr. Spenser's name was Valentine, and his wife's was Margaret. The curate had some familiar abbreviation for every body he was related to or intimate with, except his niece Arabella, whose name he uniformly pronounced in full, though her father sometimes called her Bell. The curate was a notable tea-drinker, and as proud of the number of his cups as topers are of the number of their bottles. Al-

though Father Mathew had not yet appeared, there was a Temperance Society in the parish of Redcross, which had Mr. Woodward's cordial support. Mr. Spenser, though any thing but a votary of Bacchus, declined joining the society; he used pleasantly to observe that temperance was "a very proper virtue in a curate."

Uncle Woodward drank six cups upon that occasion. It was not a very lively meal. Sydney was gloomy and morose; Arabella frigid, the rector abstracted; Elizabeth alone exerted herself to make her uncle feel comfortable and at home, nor was it difficult to do so, for nobody was less exacting, though nobody felt more keenly the absence of warmth when he had a right to expect it. But his stay was brief; for the evening was falling rapidly; in fact, it was nearly dark when he rose with even more than his wonted abruptness, and bade them all good-night, shaking hands with every one, and even kissing a few of them. The curate shook hands with a vigor that was sometimes distressing; but friendly, warm-hearted people readily pardoned the momentary pain to their fingers, for the sake of the cordiality that accompanied the squeeze.

Mr. Spenser accompanied his brother-in-law to the little harbor.

"When shall I see you again, Hercules?" he said; "I am anxious to have your advice on a matter of very great importance."

"I'll come over in the morning," said the curate.

"Bring Carry with you," said his brother-in-law.

"The weather won't do for that, Val. There will be a storm, rely upon it. On no account allow Sydney to sail. Good night, Val., good night;" and with that the stout curate seized the oars again, and pushed across the shadowy water.

"I trust," said Mr. Spenser to himself, as he walked back to the house, "that Lord Bonham's friends are not at sea, or that they will get into some port before the gale rises." Lord Bonham had written to advertise him of the probability of his receiving a visit from the Circe about this time.

The rector, on returning to the drawing-room, found his son arranging the details of the next day's expedition, just as if nothing had occurred to render its postponement advisable. It was a great relief to his daughters, no small surprise to them likewise, when their father, with a decision very unusual to him, acted on his brother-in-law's prudent advice, and interdicted the voyage in the most absolute manner.

Before the parsonage was asleep that night the moaning of the wind at intervals, accompanied with the rattling of windows, and the flapping of the branches of rose trees and woodbine against the glass, promised to verify the prophecies of Mr. Woodward only too completely. The rector got very little rest, but it was his wife and not the wind that disturbed his slumbers. Mrs. Spenser was not a very comfortable consort in the calmest weather, but she was particularly disagreeable in a high wind. This, however, is a premature peep behind the bed-room curtains.

## CHAPTER VI.

### THE PARSONAGE ASLEEP.

"Now the cricket's chirp is heard,
Loud as note of any bird;
And the ticking of the clock
Is become a mighty knock;
Enter we the silent house,
With the footsteps of a mouse;
Creep along the corridor,
Mark we every chamber door;
Let the crayon make no sound,
None must know our midnight round."
THE MYSTERIOUS VISITORS.

WHEN people are asleep, it is a very good opportunity for a little gossip on their affairs and antecedents, and not a bad time either to take casts of their faces, and examine the bumps on their heads.

Mr. Spenser had now been incumbent of the parish of Redcross for about ten years. He came to it shortly after his marriage with his present wife (who was the step-mother of Arabella, Elizabeth, and Sydney), and her eldest child was now entering his eighth year. The benefice was a good one, worth from eight hundred to a thousand pounds per annum, and had been bestowed upon him by its patron, Lord Bonham, a nobleman with whom Mr. Spenser had formed a close friendship, originally at Eton, and subsequently at Cambridge. His lordship's estate, which we have already mentioned, lay in the neighborhood of Redcross; but there was no mansion upon it, only a shooting lodge, where he occasionally established himself for grouse shooting or salmon fishing. He offered his agency to his friend along with the parish; but although such a union of offices was a common thing in Ireland at the time, Mr. Spenser's strict notions of clerical duty and propriety revolted at it, and he firmly declined this additional proof of Lord Bonham's friendship, although his increasing family rendered an augmentation of income a point of no small importance. The rector had been more fortunate in his first than in his second marriage. His first wife was a woman of strong sense, sterling worth, and great personal attractions. The beauties of her mind she transmitted to her daughter Elizabeth; those of her person only to Arabella. The present Mrs. Spenser was a discontented, intractable, selfish, and eccentric woman, and had been an invalid, and a most vexatious one, ever since the birth of her youngest child, keeping her bed-room seven or eight months of the year, and talking of returning to it the remaining four or five. Her complaint was one of the nondescript disorders, called nervous, one part real to nine parts fanciful; sources of untold profits to doctors, and untold miseries to husbands. If people were harmless in proportion to their imbecility, it would be all well; but the misfortune is, that those who have the least control over themselves, often possess the most powerful and mischievous ascendency over others. This was remarkably illustrated in the instance of Mr. and Mrs. Spenser. The rector had all the weaknesses of an amiable character, and his wife all the weaknesses of a selfish one. The two sets of weaknesses, united in the bonds of matrimony, made a very uneasy union, and Mr. Spenser would indeed have been very unhappy in his second marriage, only for the extreme placidity of his temper, the society of his daughters, and his passionate love of books. When the living plagued him, he often fled to the dead for refuge, and found in literary pleasures sweet though short respites from his conjugal griefs. And here let us pause, and give a word of advice to men in Mr. Spenser's position of life.

A man in moderate circumstances, particularly a widower with children, who thinks of marrying a lady in delicate health, ought to examine himself, and see that he possesses not only the qualities that befit the master of a house, but those that are indispensable in a mistress likewise. In fact, being destined to discharge the united functions of the father and mother of his family, he ought to be an active, bustling, motherly, managing sort of a gentleman, skilled in nursery affairs, equal to the control of house-maids, and not above "meddling with buck-washing;" he should know as much as possible about chin coughs and teething, to which branches of useful knowledge were he to add some tincture of the science of pickling and preserving, it would not be amiss, under the circumstances. An invalid wife is a very expensive article of luxury even to a gentleman with a thousand a year, and so Mr. Spenser found it. Had he made as good a choice as his curate did, it would have saved him a couple of hundreds annually at the least; he would have had a buxom helpmate to control his servants and govern his children for him, instead of the croaking turtle he had, who gave him more trouble than all the rest of the establishment put together.

Mrs. Spenser had never accommodated herself to life in Ireland particularly to the life of a country parson in the wildest and loneliest part of the island. She quarreled with the people, and she quarreled with the climate; there was always either a storm in the atmosphere, or a tempest in the political world—always something to discompose her; and when there was nothing, nothing answered equally well. You are not to suppose that she would have been happy and contented in a country without a breath of wind, either literal or metaphorical. On the contrary, she was a woman to raise a storm wherever she happened to be; she would get you up a hurricane in an exhausted receiver, and find or make something uncomfortable in Eden itself. The rector was free from avarice, and the only ambition he had was a literary one; but his helpmate was as covetous as Mammon, and as ambitious as Lucifer. She never forgave a tithe defaulter, and was forever instigating her husband to wring the uttermost farthing out of his parishioners; while, at the same time, she thought it extremely hard that he should discharge any pastoral duty at all; continually urging him to settle in Dublin, where a man of his talents and address, enjoying the smiles of a lord lieutenant, and charming with his witty and elegant conversation the vice-regal circle, might fairly aspire to high preferment in the Church—even to change his simple pastoral crook for a crosier. It would have been strange, indeed, if such qualities as these in a wife had not exercised a very decided influence on the life and fortunes of an easy, uxorious husband.

The main defect of Mr. Spenser's character (legible in his countenance) was its deplorable want of energy. With a little firmness he might have been a very happy man; without it, he was the sport of a thousand passions and caprices from which his own mind was perfectly free. He was formed for contemplation, not for action; a man of the study and the bower, not a man of business, or the world. He was vigorous with his pen or at his books; industrious only in his green-leather arm-chair. Control over his children he had none, or extremely little; he spared no expense either on their accomplishments or their amusements, but here his parental interference ended: if Sydney rioted at a sufficient distance from the library, and if he could always have one of his girls to accompany him in a walk, or a ride, and had Arabella to sing little French romances after tea of an evening, he was content.

His eldest son, far from being his comfort or pride, was now beginning to give him much uneasiness, and was destined to give him more. It was the rector's own fault—he had been a careless father, and he could not and did not escape the consequences of neglecting his parental duties. With his daughters Arabella and Elizabeth, however, he had better reason to be pleased; his mild brown eye rested with joy upon them both, but with most delight upon the elder, doubtless because she was her mother's likeness, for in every thing else Elizabeth far excelled.

They differed strikingly in both person and mind. Arabella was tall, fair-haired, with delicate and very handsome features; her figure was also very good, her carriage distinguished, but haughty; and the same expression, mixed with something of petulance and scorn, was visible in her eyes and on her lips, agreeing perfectly with her mode of receiving the homespun curate, although so closely connected with her. At the same time she was not decidedly or strikingly unamiable, only vain, frivolous, cold, and egotistical, not even returning her father's fond preference with one half of her sister's affection and devotedness. In short, she was a woman without passions and without a heart. Elizabeth Spenser was no common girl. In person she was not so tall as her sister, but, though younger, she was even more mature in appearance; somewhat rounder, promising in a short time to be a robust as well as a beauteous woman. Her hair was a dark brown, and nature had been prodigal to her of that loveliest of female ornaments. Her eyes were dark also, only more gray than black. The nose was slightly aquiline; it made her countenance a commanding one; and the expression of her mouth, too, was a further indication of energy and self-reliance. Yet the best part of her loveliness was that with which her mind irradiated her person, as the beauty of a lamp is shown by the pure bright flame within it. Elizabeth's opportunities of improvement had not been greater than her sister's; but as two neighboring vineyards, with the same cultivation to enrich the soil, and the same sun to ripen the grape, will    du e wines of the most different qualities and value, so did the rector's daughters, under the same roof, the same influences, and the same instructions, moving in the same society, keeping the same company, hearing the same conversation, and surrounded by the same

books and other means of improvement, grow up to woman's estate, with minds and characters totally dissimilar in flavor and in worth.

In Elizabeth Spenser the spirits of love and knowledge—the seraphic and cherubic characters, to borrow the old Rabbinical distinction—were beautifully blended. With all the soft attributes of her sex, were combined a solidity of judgment, and a sincerity, depth, and vigor of character, which kept them from degenerating into mere female fondnesses, and enabled her in after life to act a very difficult part incomparably well, in several capacities, and through severe trials. She was the only member of the family by whom Sydney was not systematically spoiled; her influence was, of course, but a feeble substitute for parental authority, but it was sometimes not altogether unavailing. She was more capable, however, of being useful to the little ones, who, between their hypochondriac mother, and a governess—who, though active enough, occupied herself very little with her pupils—were in a very fair way to be ruined. Here Elizabeth had a hard card to play, for Mrs. Spenser was as jealous of interference with her motherly prerogatives as she was deficient in the discharge of her motherly duties. It was not without some address that Elizabeth succeeded in usurping the degree of influence absolutely necessary to prevent Mrs. Spenser from ruining her children by proxy.

For the useful and valuable attributes of her character, Elizabeth Spenser was indebted chiefly to the influence, instruction, and example of Mrs. Woodward, her aunt, the wife of the colossal curate. When Mr. Spenser first went over to Ireland to take possession of his benefice, he was accompanied not only by his present wife, but by his sister Caroline, or Carry, as she was commonly called in the family. We shall presently make this excellent lady's acquaintance. The wonder was how Caroline Spenser had remained single so very long; she had so many of the qualities that marrying men of sense look for in women; her presence was so goodly, her understanding so strong, while for prudence she was a proverb. But she had no fortune, or a very small one, and—she was formidably fat. Besides (so deceitful are appearances and so inscrutable the ways of women), she did not seem to be a marrying woman at all, and least of all did any body dream that she had preserved her heart for upward of thirty years in a polished circle in England, to lose it at the end of that period, and lose it abruptly to a poor curate in the wildest part of Ireland. Mr. Woodward was curate of Redcross when Mr. Spenser was appointed to it. If ever there was love at first sight this was a case of it. There was nothing odd in Hercules falling in love with Caroline Spenser, her attractions were so exuberant; but people did wonder a little at Caroline so promptly returning the fire, the curate was so very rough a diamond, and Carry, though her charms had a tendency to coarseness, was coarse in no other way. But "paucas palabras," as Christopher Sly says. They met, they loved, they married; one of the first duties Mr. Spenser performed in the little church of Redcross was to unite his flourishing sister in the holy bands of matrimony to his gigantic curate.

She was a serious loss to her brother, particalarly as the second Mrs. Spenser soon began to exhibit her physical as well as moral disqualifications for the management of a family.

---

## CHAPTER VII.

### THE CURATE AT HOME.

'From one great source the human nature springs,
And subjects will be indolent as kings;
Hence ev'ry viceroy pays a substitute,
And hence deputed ministers depute;
Kings hireling secretaries keep, and these
Must have their secretaries too; for ease
Bishops place rectors through their holy sees,
And rectors mince them into curacies.
'Mong all the wretches found on Proxy's list,
That crawl 'twixt heaven and earth, and scarce subsist;
'Mong all the lots to which the po..r is heir,
The hardest portion is the curate's share."

THE CURATE. *By the Rev. Evans Lloyd.*

THE curate's house, an old, white, ungainly, three-storied building with a number of long narrow windows, was situated near one end of the town of Redcross, within a courtyard, surrounded by a dilapidated wall, which was decked in summer with red snap-dragons, and gaudy but sweet wall-flowers. A tall gate, with taller pillars, topped with a pair of stone globes, all white-washed, admitted you into the yard; and there, on your way to the door of the house, you probably encountered a couple of young pigs, or a little squadron of ducks and ducklings, bound for a small circular pond in the spacious, luxuriant, well-tilled, kitchen-garden (a wilderness of vegetables and red roses) behind the house. On the ground-floor were three rooms: one was a parlor and drawing-room combined; another was Mr. Woodward's sanctuary; and the third the store-room of his wife, sometimes called "Carry's Miscellany," and sometimes the "Mother's Magazine." The upper apartments were small and numerous (you will find it generally the case in the house of a curate); the highest of all somewhat crazy, and shaky in gales of wind; and none very luxuriously furnished. The whole was oddly surmounted by an hexagonal turret, formed almost entirely of glass, crowned with a weather-cock, and called the Observatory. It was nothing but the distance prevented you from seeing the United States from this belvidere. It contained an old refracting telescope upon a rickety stand, of power enough to exhibit some of Jupiter's moons, but of no great use for the discovery of new planets or nebulæ. A few scattered copy-books, grammars, and catechisms, with a twelve-inch globe, showed that Carry occasionally schooled her children there; but it answered other purposes also: it served as a supernumerary dressing-room when there were visitors; and as a g:ea treat and reward to the little Woodwards after a long career of industry and virtue, tea was now and then taken in the observatory; but this was a secular event, and only took place in very fine weather, about the full of the moon.

Mrs. Woodward did a great deal—perhaps all it was in her power to do—but it was an irregular, harem-soarem house, notwithstanding. The fact was, that with the inveterate propensities of Hercules, more or less inherited or aped by his children, and the careless, untidy, slattern, take-it-easy, and deuce-may-care hab-

its of the Irish maid-servants, it was next to impossible to preserve (with a curate's paltry income) any thing like English order and discipline. Carry soon almost gave it up, contenting herself with keeping her own more especial territories neat, taking care that her children should be scrubbed and curried with all the vigor of some powerful maidenly arm every morning of their lives, and seeing that there was always a scrupulously clean and brilliantly white cloth on her table, no matter how plain the meal was, even an Irish stew, which was turtle and venison to her husband. Often did Carry threaten to enforce general order on some future day, commonly on the next Monday; but *that* Monday was like the Greek calends, or the Feast of Next-Never-come-Tide, and Carry at last gave up even threatening it. Circumstances were too strong for her; nay, so enthusiastically devoted was she to Hercules, that she felt, and owned she felt, herself growing more and more tolerant every day of the domestic disorder and confusion, out of which he was like a fish out of water. Fortunately, she was of such a cheerful, hopeful, elastic temperament—or how else could she have brought up such a troop of Wood-wards half so well and so respectably as she did. Fortunately, too, though the most affectionate creature in the world, she was not a woman to be imposed on, or trifled with; but a little authoritative, and carried matters with a higher hand than she would perhaps have done, had her husband been more at home, or less unfit than he was, by reason of his very size and strength, to deal with the irregularities of children. One day, when her eldest boy was seven or eight years old, he committed some serious infraction of the law, of which Carry made complaint to Hercules, who was forthwith proceeding to punish the malefactor with nothing less than a club. Carry was frightened out of her life, took the culprit into her own hands, settled the matter in a motherly way, and never troubled her husband again with the enforcement of nursery discipline.

She used pleasantly to say that the rod was in her house a branch of economy; it enabled her, for instance, to do without a railing round the pond in the garden, and to dispense with the services of a nursery governess; a title, indeed, by which it was known and respected in the family.

It was dark, and growing late, when the worthy curate returned that night to this queer house and the loving and anxious wife of his bosom. Carry had dispatched her great children to bed, and was sitting up for him, with a little one in its cradle at her side, in the low, spacious, square, unpapered, rudely furnished room, called a study; a very different room from Mr. Spenser's library; but Hercules liked it all the better for the difference, comfort being inextricably associated in his mind with the state of things called "higgledy-piggledy." It certainly was a curiosity. Books, carpenter's-tools, shoes that looked as if they had walked round the world, a very untidy washing-stand, fishing-rods and tackle, old hats and boat-cloaks, a fowling-piece and a duck-gun, with twenty other miscellaneous articles strewed the apartment in "most admired disorder." In one corner was a broken oar, a spade, and a wooden hay-fork; in another, a collection of walking-sticks and cudgels, large and various enough to set up a shop with; a row of shelves intended for books were stuffed with papers, packets of garden-seeds, pruning-knives, a shot-canister, with some horn and tin vessels intended for pic-nics; and all these things were covered with no very thin coating of dust, for the curate was always fidgety when his wife, or her maids, even talked of "settling" his "study," and there was a sort of understanding (sometimes violated certainly) that brush and broom were not to molest him more than once or twice in the year, about certain great festivals of the church.

There was a blazing turf-fire in the grate, the evening having grown coolish, and Carry not being certain whether her husband would take tea at the parsonage or not. Contemplate her by the alternately rosy and golden light from the turf-fire! She is worth looking at, and has comfort enough in her face and her person to make the apartment of the neediest curate in the church comfortable. What age would you give her credit or discredit for? Forty. Not quite so much by four or five years; a year or two younger than her brother, Mr. Spenser. And she is very fair and very fat, too; you can hardly see the chair she sits on, she overspreads it so; but her corpulence has not yet obliterated her shapes, and merged them, as, alas, it will probably do ten years hence, in one huge round mass of maternity. She is a glorious woman, aunt Carry, as she sits there, with her red shawl drawn cosily round her, over her habitual black silk dress, expanded before the hearth, but not very close to the fire, with one plump foot to that of the cradle, making or mending a small pair of sky-blue trowsers, and every now and then listening to catch the sound from the road of the hoofs of her husband's pony. She is a glorious woman within and without; bursting not with comeliness only, but with every ma-tronly virtue, and housewifely accomplishment; her heart is as ample as her person; she is thrice-blessed with good-sense, good-nature, and good-humor inexhaustible; industrious as a working-bee, and for economy (else she would make an indifferent wife for a curate) a very Joseph Hume in petticoats. The features of Carry were good, and massive like her figure. Her complexion was florid; her eyes gray, clear, piercing; her air was that of a woman who was the mistress as well as the mother of a family. If there was a soupçon of severity, or rather combativeness, in her physiognomy, it was the result of her position in life, which had its own difficulties, and required a woman with more than a woman's spirit to meet and con-quer them.

The little pair of sky-blues contained in them-selves the history of a curate's wife. They had been the Sunday dress of each of her three boys in succession, according as each had attained the period when she thought proper to promote him from petticoats. Three times had they been altered, reduced, repaired, and turned with her own hands. When the first out-grew them, they descended to the second; and when the second burst through them, Carry repaired the breach, and they were handed down to the third. The congregation of Redcross church was as familiar with that pair of trowsers as with the cassock of the curate himself, and astonishing it was how well they held out, and how well they looked, after so many transformations.

Twice she was positive she heard the desired step; twice she was disappointed; it was either the wind in the branches of the tall mountain-ash on the right of the hall-door, or the pigs in the yard, or one of the villagers also belated. At length, however, she caught the true unmis-takable, steady, dogged, homeward trot of the pony; and in less than five minutes the bell that communicated between the outer gate (for there was a walled court in front of the house) and the kitchen announced the return of the curate to all his household. His servants adored him. He had three, two maids, and something between a man and boy, called Peter, who was groom, gardener, footman, and butler; at least, if he was not the butler, the curate had no other. Peter had been brought up by his mistress, and stood in great awe of her, but he was always the same giddy illogical fellow, and neither Carry's ratings, or his master's cudgelings, did much to mend him. When the court-yard bell rang at night, Peter always ran to open it with the kitchen candle, although there was a lantern expressly for the purpose. There was no use in lecturing or licking him. It was in his Celtic blood never to make the proper use of any thing. When there was the least wind, the candle of course was blown out, directly the house-door was opened, although the provoking Peter did his best to make a lantern of it with one of his hands. Then he invariably gave the wind a sub-audible malediction for "laving him in the dark," as if the wind was to blame; and registered an oath in the same key that the house was "the windiest house he ever see'd in all his born days."

Yes!—Peter was a very provoking fellow; but then there flowed, united in his veins, two streams of the purest Celtic blood; his father was a Hogg, and his mother a M'Swyne, so that race had probably something to do with it.

Carry never could run very fast, but, as fast as she could run, she ran to meet and embrace her husband as he stumbled into the room, having been, as usual, obliged to grope his way from the court-yard gate to the door of his study. "Dear Hercules!" she exclaimed, flinging her large loving arms about him; and right conjugally did the stout curate return the greet-ing. This done, he hung up his hat on one of the prongs of the hay-fork, and threw himself down, not on a chair, but on a seedy old black leathern trunk, covered all over with torn labels, figures, and directions, and used (when not upon foreign service) for holding all sorts of things, which nobody else would have thought of stow-ing in such a receptacle.

"All well at the rectory?" inquired Carry.

"All well," he replied, unbuttoning his enor-mous outside coat, which was none of your modern paletots, but more of a Boreas than a Zephyr, and throwing it plump down on the cradle.

Carry jumped up with a scream; and it was truly marvelous that the little sleeper was not crushed into a pancake. However, it was not so much as awakened, which made the distressed mother think for a moment that her awkward husband had committed infanticide.

"Who could have thought the baby was there?" he exclaimed, in his own defense.

"The cradle is not a very extraordinary place for a baby," rejoined Carry, a little sharply.

"But in the study, I mean," said Hercules. The notion of any thing being out of place in Mr. Woodward's study was a pleasant one! Probably, however, that subject had been exhausted, for Carry made no remark, but asked her husband would he take tea. Notwithstanding the six cups he had taken at the rectory, Mr. Woodward acquiesced with readiness, and Peter was ordered to make the necessary preparations; which he at length accomplished, after making about ten journeys backward and forward between kitchen and parlor; when one journey would have sufficed, with a grain of forethought, or thought of any kind. Carry was tired of being provoked with him, and sat working at the little blue inexpressibles, raising her eyes now and then to observe Peter's movements, and call her husband's attention to the wonderful amount of unnecessary trouble he was giving himself.

"Upon my word," said the curate, as his man left the room for the last time, "I think the charge of laziness so often brought against Irish servants is a most unwarrantable one."

"At all events," said Carry, "if they do hate trouble, they are the most self-sacrificing people in the world, for they never spare themselves any." And, so saying, she rose to make tea.

"Now I am as happy as a bishop over his Burgundy," cried the good curate, rejoicing in his wife, his home, and his turf-fire, and extending his immense limbs toward the flaming mountain on the hearth.

"Are bishops always drinking Burgundy?" asked Carry, "for I never read a speech or an article about the church but I find bishops and Burgundy always mentioned together."

"Just because they begin with the same letter," said her husband; "bishop and Burgundy, curate and Congo."

"I don't expect ever to see you a bishop, Hercules," said his wife, pouring out the second cup.

"I should not be a jot happier than I am, were I the primate," he replied; "but, Carry, I sometimes think I am a bishop; you are my bonny bishopric, I am bishop of Carolina;" and he rose and kissed her while she was dropping the sugar into his tea.

"You can't say, then, you have not got a fat diocese," she answered, with a smile that seemed the overflowing of a well of warmth and light within her.

"I wouldn't take Canterbury in exchange," said Hercules; "but I honestly confess, Carry, my dear, I should have no objection, for the sake of my wife and my children, to hold a good living *in commendam*."

"If it ever comes," she replied, with a good-humored little sigh—a sigh without a tincture of melancholy in it, "I hope we shall be thankful and enjoy it wisely: we are very happy, poor as we are, and I trust we shall not be less so, if we are ever better off in the world;—I am not impatient for promotion, I assure you, Hercules."

"How much happier we are than your brother, for instance, with one of the best benefices in the north of Ireland; but Val. was not so lucky in *his* bishopric as I was, Carry."

"Oh," said Carry, with feeling, "there is a great deal in my brother's situation that makes me seriously uneasy on his account; not merely his wife, though, Heaven knows, she is quite vexation enough for any poor man."

"I am going over to him in the morning," said the curate, "to consult with him about something he is anxious about—I dare say it is about Sydney."

Carry was vexed to hear that her husband purposed to tramp over the hills again so very soon, but she was too much interested in her brother's concerns to make much work about it.

"Did you see Sydney?" she inquired.

Her husband mentioned how uncivilly he had been received by his nephew, on account of his interference to have the voyage of pleasure postponed.

"Graceless boy," cried his aunt; "but what else is to be expected from the companion of Dudley Dawson? If my brother is thinking of sending Sydney to Cambridge, I trust, Hercules, you won't oppose it."

"Indeed, Carry, I think it would be much wiser in Val. to send him to Trinity College, Dublin."

"As to the relative merits of colleges," said Carry, "I am not qualified to give an opinion; but the further Sydney is removed from his present associates the better—there can not be a doubt of that."

"I don't think as ill of Dudley Dawson as you do, Carry. I think you are all too hard on him; your sister-in-law dislikes him because his father is a tithe-defaulter—why, that's no fault of Dudley's; the girls object to him because he smokes cigars and talks a little too loud, as perhaps I do myself; and you, my dear—"

"As for me," said Carry, warmly, "I dislike him for every reason that could make me dislike a young man—he is designing, vulgar, dissipated—"

"No, Carry, not exactly dissipated—only a little wild. Recollect the life his father led, and how Dudley's education was neglected."

"But that is no reason why he should be suffered to corrupt my nephew."

"Corrupt is too strong a word, Carry."

"Corrupt his morals, and brutalize his manners, for he is doing both," continued his wife, with an earnestness well justified, as we shall soon see, by the real state of the case.

"I shall never forget how he assisted me that night last October, when the two fishing-smacks were capsized in the upper part of Loch Erne," said Hercules; "he behaved like a hero. Between us, we saved the lives of three men and a boy, and only for Dawson, two of them at least would have perished."

"It was very brave, no doubt, and very meritorious," said Carry, folding up the blue trowsers, as it was growing late, "but a brave man may be very bad company; and I have no notion of Mr. Dudley Dawson, on the strength of any exploit of the kind, gaining a footing in my brother's family, and even presuming to inflict his attentions on one of his daughters"

This was the first the curate had heard upon this subject.

B

"Well, Carry, my dear," he rejoined, "you will say I am a great deal too tolerant, but I don't think it's a crime in any man to admire Elizabeth; and if it is a presumption (as I don't say it is not), why, so much the worse for himself, and he is more to be pitied than blamed, in my humble opinion."

"You *are* too tolerant, my dear, very many degrees," said Carry, rising to light her bedroom candle,

"Recollect," said the curate, rising also, "a certain personage is not so black as he is painted."

"But he is quite black enough, notwithstanding," rejoined his wife, retiring, having had the last word in this amicable though warm discussion, so womanly was she in all points. She did not go to bed, however, until she saw that all was still in her son's dormitory, and that Peter in his giddiness had taken no measures for burning down the house.

---

## CHAPTER VIII.

### BAD EDUCATION AND BAD COMPANY.

"Instruct your son well yourself, or others will instruct him ill for you. No child goes altogether untaught. Send him to the school of Wisdom, or he will go of himself to the rival academy, kept by the lady with the cap and bells. There is always teaching going on of some sort, just as in fields Vegetation is never idle."

ESSAY ON MENTAL TILLAGE.

SYDNEY was the principal sufferer by the loss of his mother, his father's weaknesses, and the lax domestic system which grew up out of those causes combined. The mind of the young man had not been left wholly uninstructed, but the formation of his character had been neglected deplorably. The good, easy rector being an elegant scholar, fancied that, with the occasional aid of a resident tutor, he could bring up his son very well at home, where he would also have the benefit of his sisters' governesses for the acquisition of modern languages, and the other things taught, and perhaps taught best, by women. As the boy was quick, if not docile, this plan succeeded well enough for a time, as far as mere learning was concerned; but in other respects it woefully miscarried. Sydney made no intellectual progress which was not more than counterbalanced by the absence of that control which his disposition and temper particularly stood in need of. A too short interregnum of the sensible and energetic Mrs. Woodward's administration (just before his father's second marriage) was the only period of his childhood in which he had been kept in any thing like restraint, or known what discipline was, even in its mildest form. The consequence was, that he grew up, acquiring the meters of Horace, and the names of the Muses, but contracting bad habits in profusion. For one hour spent in his father's library, or his sister's society, he passed six with grooms, game-keepers, boatmen, or with men who kept such refined and improving company. Associations like these rapidly uncivilized him; he grew boorish in his manners, boisterous in conversation, when he was not moodily silent, violent when crossed in any scheme of self-indulgence; and it was only the slight influence, which we have already said, that his sister Elizabeth managed to acquire, that restrained him from continual displays of his overbearing temper, even in the presence of his father, the mildest and most equable of men.

His step-mother had the common fault of step-mothers, which (contrary to the vulgar opinion) is not nearly so much undue severity, as the far worse extreme of neglect and indifference. Even before she fell into her present state of health, she took no pains at all with her husband's children, and never interfered with their management, except in the most absurd and mischievous manner. Indeed, with respect to Sydney, she encouraged his faults in the beginning of her acquaintance with him, and subsequently, when they came to be too offensive and troublesome, she pursued a system equally reprehensible, licensing his absences from home, whenever, upon one pretense or another, he asked permission to join the companions of his riotous pleasures, sometimes for several days together.

It is a great mistake to say that the good points of a character redeem the bad ones, even when the former predominate decidedly. On the contrary, a single uncorrected fault will often make a whole career vicious, notwithstanding a multitude of qualities tending of themselves in the direction of honor and virtue. Sydney Spenser had his good points; he could do a brave and generous thing occasionally. He was popular with the poor in the neighborhood, not merely because he was athletic and enterprising, but because he was really capable of kind actions, and when he had a little money to command, would bestow it on an object of charity, instead of his selfish gratification, if the former chanced to come first in his way. With his companions his propensity was to be lavish, as far as his means went. His guns, dogs, ponies, his boats, and even his clothes, were at the absolute disposal of his favorites, and some of them were by no means backward to profit by his munificence. Sometimes he showed his generosity by being as ready to take as to give; in fact, he had established a sort of communism with several young men of his own age and tastes, the principal and the most objectionable of whom was Mr. Dawson, about whom the curate and his wife differed in opinion so much.

Dawson (whose career, not only as a private but as a public man, is destined to form an important part of our history) was a few years older than Sydney Spenser, but much in advance of him in a vicious acquaintance with the world. He was the son of an embarrassed man, and lived himself from hand to mouth, making the state of his father's affairs the excuse for his own irregularities, while in reality he was running the same dissolute rig which had reduced the once considerable property of the family to almost nothing. He led a kind of oscillating life between Donegal and London, appearing and disappearing suspiciously; but he had always some plausible account to give of himself, and few people knew either how handsomely in debt he was, or to what ingenious resorts he was now and then driven by his financial difficulties. In fact, just at the present period, matters were going so very ill with him, that he was seriously thinking of turning patriot and getting into Parliament; the time being exceedingly propitious for the advancement, in that line, of men of his stamp and character. However, it was not altogether necessity that suggested this high flight, for he was not destitute of vulgar ambition, any more than he was deficient in personal vanity, a quality which, indeed, he possessed in an inordinate degree. His family was respectable (though not as good blood as the Howards and Plantagenets), and he might have moved in good society, had his tastes been different; but he loved low company, and his manners and personal appearance soon became insuperable obstacles to his social reformation. On every return from London (where his conduct was under least restraint), he fell a step lower in the scale; and, as is usually remarked in such cases, he was particularly offensive when he aimed at being particularly polished and well-bred.

Such was the rising young politician, whose rude eye having been captivated by the rector's second daughter, was now daringly, though not avowedly, aspiring to her hand; hoping, by means of his league with her brother, to gain a footing in the family, and confidently relying upon his personal merits, estimated by his enormous self-conceit, to carry all before him afterward.

None of the Spenser family had a notion, at the point of time from which we start in these domestic memoirs, either of the extent of Dawson's presumption with respect to Elizabeth, or that Sydney was involved as much as in truth he was with so dangerous an associate. Dawson was in the habit of advancing him small sums of money, to enable him to purchase articles which he took a boyish fancy for, and had not the means of procuring for himself. For the possession of these things he would account, when any account was required, by stating that they were either loans or presents. Nor was this the worst. Sydney had learned to contract little clandestine debts in other quarters also; and independent of his liabilities to Dawson, he was now in the books of country shopkeepers to the extent of nearly fifty pounds, a serious amount of debt to a youth of eighteen, who had not fifty pence in the world to discharge it.

"Sir," said Doctor Johnson, upon a certain occasion, "small debts are like small shot; they are rattling on every side, and can scarcely be escaped without a wound. Great debts are like cannon-balls, of loud noise, but little danger." The sequel will show how well the truth of this witty remark was illustrated in the case of Sydney Spenser.

----

## CHAPTER IX.

### THE CONSULTATION.

"He keeps his time, as punctual as the sun,
When rising he redeems the pledge he gave
The world at setting, and sent us to our couches
With strong assurance of another morrow.
Oh, Sir, the sun himself is not more faithful
Than strenuous friendship; nor the solar beams
More full of warmth and comfort."

NEW PLAY.

THE following morning verified Mr. Woodward's predictions to the letter. The sun rose red with choler, the sky was surly and foul; the mountains were shrouded with mists, so

that only the outline of their summits was discernible, and that only at intervals, when the wind, which came in sullen fits, dispersed for an instant the accumulated vapors. The gulls and cormorants, retreating from the ocean, like refugees from an impending revolution, flew screaming over the loch to their wonted asylums in the inland valleys. Before the family assembled, it was evidently preparing to blow great guns; the gale moaned and howled in the chimneys, and the waves were dashing over the little strand at the foot of the lawn, and swinging the cutter to and fro so rudely as to extort even from the fool-hardy Sydney himself a surly admission that the weather was unsuitable for aquatic amusements. But the curate had made an appointment with his brother-in-law, and no weather that ever "came out of the sky," as the Irish peasant expresses it, would have prevented him from keeping it. When Hercules set out, "on a raw and gusty day," upon one of his prodigious walks, with his huge dreadnought of dark blue frieze, his oil-skin hat, and a great crooked club in his fist, it was not easy for a stranger to make out who or what he was—whether a farmer, or a pilot, a fisherman, or a mountain shepherd; indeed, he sometimes looked like a man who lived both by hook and by crook, as the saying is. At some distance—particularly when he was encountered on a bleak moor, or upon the crags—he seemed a very desperate character, and made your heart sink within you; but when people were near enough to see him well, distrust vanished, and they felt that it was no small degree of personal security to keep in his company, or within protectorship of his arm. The police of the country had often found him a valuable ally, for being a puissant pedestrian (notwithstanding the possession of so capital a pony), he was intimately acquainted with every recess in the mountains, every cavern on the shore, every house, castle, ruin, almost every rock and tree, within a circle of forty miles round the village of Redcross; and for the capture of a smuggler, or any description of lawless character, not a constable in the north had half the Rev. Mr. Woodward's reputation. His acquaintance with persons, too, was co-extensive with his knowledge of localities; he knew every body all through and round the country, gentle and simple; and there were few to whom he had not done some strenuous kindness. He had saved dozens of lives in shipwreck; and, possessing a certain smattering of physic and surgery, he had cured many a wrinkled crone of her rheumatism or her toothache. Not a blue jacket on the coast but would have died for him; and the old women in red cloaks and blue petticoats, when they could not keep up with him on foot, pursued him with benisons until he was out of sight.

With all Mr. Spenser's knowledge of his curate's hardy habits and character, he was not a little surprised on coming down to breakfast that morning to meet him in the hall, just arrived. He was dripping like a water-dog, and spattered above his knees with the yellow clay of the hills; but he cared little or nothing about it, and was also provokingly thoughtless of the damage he did the floors and carpets by such a needless importation of mud and moisture.

Mr. Spenser induced him to divest himself of

his drenched outer garment, and had less difficulty to make him sit down and eat a breakfast fully proportioned to his size and brawn. All curates are prodigious breakfast-eaters; the reason probably is that they are not always confident of dinner; more shame upon the system that deprives them of what ought to be the well-grounded faith of every honest hard-working man in every path of life. But Hercules had taken a walk that morning, enough to make any man's appetite wolfish.

"I think, Val.," he acknowledged, "I have played the wolf to that cold shoulder of lamb."

"Quite right," said the rector, smiling; "and now play the fox to that cold fowl, I advise you;" and no second invitation was required. Not a fox in the shire could have disposed in much shorter time of two legs and one wing of the fat capon in question. He scarcely spoke a word to his nieces during the meal, except to give Elizabeth a parcel of loves from her aunt, in a kind of parenthesis, between an egg and a cup of tea.

"Now I am your man," he cried, having at length concluded his labors, and rising from the table, with a droll, lingering look at the little that survived the havoc, as if it was scarcely worth while to leave it, and yet impossible to do more than he had done.

"Well, Val., you want to talk to me about Sydney?"

Sydney had not appeared at breakfast, but that was too common an incident to occasion a remark from any body.

"I do. Let us adjourn to the library." They did so. Mr. Spenser seated himself in his own green leather chair; Mr. Woodward preferred striding up and down the room, often visibly agitating his friend for the safety of a bust of Curran and some small groups of statuary—things easily overset by the knock of an awkward elbow or the switch of a coat-tail. The curate was a dangerous person in a drawing-room, or wherever there happened to be any fragile article of *vertu*.

"Hercules," said the rector, "now that the time draws near when Sydney's university education ought to commence, it is time to discuss the question, to what university we ought to send him. Let me at once tell you that Mrs. Spenser—"

The curate made an impatient gesture, as much as to say, "What the — has Mrs. Spenser to do in a matter of the kind?" The rector continued—

"Mrs. Spenser is decidedly for either Oxford or Cambridge."

"Oxford!" muttered Hercules, contemptuously, and, had he not been interrupted, would have proceeded to express the same scorn for the other university.

"I myself," continued Mr. Spenser, "lean to Cambridge—as I was a Cantab, you will understand my feeling—but I wish to do nothing rashly; I desire to combine a due regard to my own circumstances with the best course for Sydney's future interests."

"Why talk, then, of Oxford and Cambridge—of either one or the other—when you have Trinity College, Dublin, where your son would get twice as sound, twice as cheap, and twice as moral an education as it is possible to get any

where else in the world. Since you have asked my opinion, Val., here it is frankly for you. Send the boy up to Dublin—'you may go further and fare worse,' as Father O'Leary said to the Protestant bishop who was abusing Purgatory. Send him, I say, to the college of Swift, Burke, Gold smith, and your favorites, Grattan and John Philpot Curran. There, put him under the tuition of my cousin, Tom Beamish, and I'll answer for it, Val., you'll never repent it."

"So far," said the rector, having listened in the calmest manner to this speech, which was delivered quite in any thing but a calm way "so far I anticipated the opinion you would give; but—"

The curate was on his hobby, and took the word out of his brother-in-law's mouth without scruple.

"I'll show you all the advantages, Val., *seriatim*. First, the economy.—"

"I grant the economy," said Mr. Spenser.

"In the second place, Val.—indeed I should have put this first—comes the moral consideration. Now there Dublin bangs Oxford and Cambridge hollow. It was founded by the maiden queen, remember that, Val. No vice in old Trinity. Not a man there knows a game cock · from an ostrich; no horses, dogs, or curricles. Smash a few lamps, and thrash a sleepy old Dogberry, once a year, that's all—an old usage, only at the feast of the *Sanctæ et individuæ Trinitatis*—no great profligacy in that."

Mr. Spenser smiled at the curate's notions of honoring the Trinity, and, without disputing the positions of the enthusiastic Hercules, said, that he was so far from underrating the moral view of the question, that he considered it far the most important point of all.

"But," he continued, "I can not disguise from myself that Sydney has formed some unfortunate connections in Ireland, which, not exactly prejudicial to his morals, certainly are so to his manners. These connections I am desirous to break off as speedily and as completely as possible, and I see no way so likely to answer the purpose as to send him to an English university, where the company I allude to could not possibly follow him."

"He may get into worse," interrupted the curate. "The worst I know about the Dawsons (for I know you allude particularly to them) is, that they have not paid you the tithes they owe."

"That objection will soon be removed, I am happy to tell you," said Mr. Spenser. "Read this," and he handed the curate the following letter, which we insert, because it may help to throw a light upon the character of the writer.

"Castle Dawson, July —, 183–.

"MY DEAR SIR—I trust I need not assure you what pain it has given me, that owing to the embarrassed state of my unfortunate father's affairs, the tithes due to you from the Castle Daw son property have remained so long unsettled. Had my feelings been regarded, or my urgent solicitations been attended to, your claims would have had the priority to those of any other cred itor; but my father, being a confirmed absentee (not altogether, indeed, a voluntary one), is of course uninfluenced by the profound sentiments of respect and admiration which every resident in this parish must entertain for the most excellent clergyman, and (let me say, without flattery) the most useful country gentleman in Ireland. But my present object in addressing you is merely to say, that I have at length succeeded in making arrangements for the full and immediate discharge of the arrears so long unhappily due from this estate. I have given notice to this effect to Mr. Maguire, your proctor, that he may come over here on some early day and receive the amount.

"Please to present my most respectful compliments to Mrs. Spenser, whose health I trust will improve as the summer advances, and believe me,

"My dear sir, yours,

"With the most sincere admiration and respect,

"DUDLEY DAWSON.

"To the Rev. Valentine Spenser,
"Redcross Rectory, Redcross."

"Now, there!" cried Hercules, with some triumph, "that's what I call the letter of a brave, honest fellow."

"A little too sweet, methinks," said the rector.

"Come, Val., that's a good letter, and an honest letter; if there's a little too much of the *suaviter in modo*, there's the *fortiter in re* along with it. My firm belief is, that you would never have got one farthing of those tithes but for the personal influence and exertions of Dudley. He might as well have left the sweetness *out*, but since he has put the money *in*, I am not disposed to be hard on him."

"But to return to our subject," said Mr. Spenser; "I was going to observe that vicious pleasures are expensive ones, and that my income is not large enough to enable me to make Sydney such an allowance as would give him the means of indulging in pleasures of that description. Moreover, Sydney, though wild and willful, has no actual vices that I have observed, or heard of. He has been brought up, you know, under my own eye."

"Under your *eye*, Val.," said the curate, "but not under your *hand;* and as to the limited allowance which you say is all you can make him, that seems to me to be only an additional source of danger, adding debt and improbity to dissipation, supposing him to fall into bad company, which, as he has done here under your own roof, he is at least as likely to do when some hundred miles away from you."

"There is a great deal, I admit, in what you say," said Mr. Spenser, yieldingly.

Hercules pushed his success with uncouth energy, swinging his arms about, and raising his voice painfully.

"Send him to Dublin—I'll go up myself with him; Tom Beamish is the best fellow and best friend I have in the world. All the vacations will be spent here with you; make him a pensioner; he will get a scholarship if he minds himself—think of that, Val. I'll tell you what a scholarship did for me: I had chambers, Val., books on the buttery, exhibitions, twenty pounds a year, think of that, Val. The college paid me, instead of my paying the college; I had a vote for the member—"

"Yes, and you voted against my friend Plunket, I'll answer for it—ah, Hercules?"

"Yes, that I did," cried the sturdy Woodward,

elate at the memory of the conscientious opposition he had given to the greatest orator of his age, and brightest ornament of his country; "but the best of all is yet to come. I had commons—dinner, you know, dinner, Val.—roast leg of mutton and boiled leg of mutton alternately every day of my life for five years—take your pen and calculate how many legs that was in all—in fact, Val, five years maintenance in the Prytaneum, like Themistocles or Xenophon."

"I was not aware that Themistocles or Xenophon received that honor," said Mr. Spenser, quietly. Mr. Spenser had no great respect for the scholarship of his curate, which, indeed, was not very elegant or exact.

"Can you prove that they did not?" demanded the curate. "And, at all events, Val., if they did not, you can't deny that they deserved it."

"That's another matter," said the rector. "But there is a great deal in all that you have said on the college question, and I will turn it carefully over in my mind, Hercules, you may depend upon it."

"What's the use, Val., of turning it over in your mind? Let me write to Tom Beamish by this post," said the impetuous curate.

"Not quite so fast," said the rector, smiling as he rose.

The curate rose also, and took his leave; not, however, without a sanguine hope that the enumeration of the legs of mutton had carried the day hollow in favor of his own *Alma Mater*.

---

## CHAPTER X.

### STORMS WITHIN AND WITHOUT.

"L'homme propose; Dieu dispose."—FRENCH PROVERB.

THE rector's library was a handsome and spacious semicircular room, fitted up with bookcases of black oak, exquisitely carved, and polished like ebony, containing from two to three thousand volumes, the best editions of the best works in the Greek, Latin, Italian, French, and English languages, the majority superbly bound, for books were the only thing in which Mr. Spenser's personal tastes were luxurious and expensive. He was a bookish man, but not so much a glutton as an epicure in books, and he held that when a work was "glorious within," it was only fit that the "clothing" should be rich in proportion. A taste in bookbinding is essentially a masculine one. No woman has a tincture of it. Women read, and women write books, and often beautiful books, but taste in binding books they have none. It is one of the few elegant things the sex has no gust for. The binding of a robe or a bonnet they comprehend; but the distinctions, proprieties, and niceties of russia, morocco, and vellum—where to gild and not to gild, where to be severe and where to be splendid, what authors and what editions to dress in plain attire, what to clothe in richer garb, what to array imperially in gold and purple—not even your bookish woman has a notion of. Many, are indeed, of opinion that books look best, as ladies often do themselves, *en dishabille*. Bookbinding is twice an art; it is more than the craft of the tradesman, it is part of the study of the scholar, for even in literature it is vain to affect a total indifference to externals. A library is a noble thing, and a taste in books is the politest of tastes. As we love them, we love to embellish and exalt them; the fountains of our purest pleasures, it seems but grateful to deck them with marble and surround them with flowers.

The rector was a thoughtful, exact, careful, and, therefore, a slow writer, no pilferer from Barrow or Massillon, nor one of your mechanical preachers, who take what is called a skeleton discourse, and stuff it with unconnected texts, with the assistance of "Cruden's Concordance." Mr. Spenser, indeed, took remarkable pains with his sermons; his congregation was not a large one, but it consisted chiefly of the lower classes, to whom, as to children, it 's most important that instruction should be conveyed with that perfect clearness and simplicity, which in composition is the summit of art. His curate, however, was of a different opinion. Hercules Woodward thought an *ex tempore* the proper thing for the Protestant shopkeepers and policemen. He roared and bellowed in the pulpit; frightened and bullied his congregation; thumped things into them, and thumped things out of them, and thumped a great deal of dust out of the cushion into the bargain. He was a little addicted to coarseness, too, in his language, particularly when he made a personal attack upon Satan, which he often did, or upon the Pope, which he only ventured to do in Mr. Spenser's absence. But he was an earnest, good man, not more resembling Luther, in the vehemence of his language, than Melancthon, in the mildness and benignity that were under the surface.

"Now," said the rector to himself, when his brother-in-law had taken his leave, to trudge back again to that sweet home, to which the reader has already been introduced, "now," said the rector, "I shall sit down and write my sermon."

Scarce was he seated in his green-leather arm-chair before his library table, preparing his mind for heavenly thoughts, and tuning his tongue to express them in appropriate language, when a rapid running and trampling overhead (my lady's chamber was over the library) and a violent jangling of bells—well-known signals of distress—called him up stairs abruptly. He was used to such disturbances, and bore them only too stoically.

Can you imagine a woman at once handsome and ghastly? Mrs. Spenser's features were good; the complexion actually death-like; her eyes were black, and brighter than was necessary or agreeable. You would not call her face emaciated, but it was so exceedingly pale, or rather pallid, that she looked more like a person escaped from a cemetery than on the way to it. There was, however, no want of vitality about her: just the reverse: she was only too lively, but it was a liveliness the very reverse of pleasant, the animation of selfishness and irritability. A woman more full of whims, whimsies, humors, crotchets, prejudices, envies, jealousies, paltrinesses, pettinesses, peevishnesses, narrownesses, and little miseries, caprices, suspicions, and apprehensions of all sorts, never existed; and she was ruthless in inflicting them on every one about her, particularly, of course, upon her *devoted* husband. Mrs. Spenser was considerate

to only one thing in the world, and that was a black-faced pug, who was lying at this moment at her feet, coiled up in a ball, with a collar of red velvet round his neck, embroidered with the name of "*Bijou.*"

"Calm yourself, Margaret, pray do," said her husband, in a tone of earnest tenderness, approaching the bed-side, where Rebecca, her maid, looking frightened and fluttered, was standing all alert, with opiates, salts, tonics, and many more things than she could well hold in her hands, not knowing what might be first called for. Rebecca's face could almost spare a few roses, and presented a lively contrast to Mrs. Spenser's, which resembled that of a bust in white marble, with two real eyes of unearthly luster glittering in it.

"Calm yourself, Margaret," repeated the rector, "pray do not make yourself uneasy about the chimneys; they have been recently examined by the diocesan architect; believe me they are perfectly secure."

"Secure, indeed!" she cried; those unnatural eyes glancing back and forward between the ceiling and the window, as if she was in instant expectation of seeing the chimney topple down, or Boreas making his appearance in person. "Secure, indeed! as if any thing could be secure in such a terrific storm!"

Then she asked whether there was such another climate on the globe, and said she could stand any thing—any thing but storm;, then she was confident the windows would be blown in the very next gust that came; after which she affirmed that her head was splitting, and applied her long white fingers, not unlike icicles, to her temples, as if to keep the pieces together; and when her hands brought a mass of her hair down from underneath her night-cap, perhaps the luckless Rebecca did not come in for a little hurricane to her own share for her negligent pinning!

"Perhaps, my dear, you would be better up," resumed her husband, to make a diversion in the maid's favor; but instead of noticing what he said, she looked at her watch, and inquired pettishly for Miss M'Cracken. That was the name of the nursery governess, not a very harmonious one, it will be admitted, but she was quite ready to part with it, and what could any girl with an unmusical name do more? Rebecca ran for her, but Miss M'Cracken was not to be found.

"Try the school-room," said the rector, with a *soupçon* of satire in the solemnity of his tone, implying that the room in question was not the most likely place to find the governess in; though it was not to be entirely omitted in a search for her.

It turned out that Lucy M'Cracken was at her toilet. Mrs. Spenser could not bear to have any one about her who was not at all hours nicely, almost elegantly, dressed. Few young women objected to her service on that account; not Miss M'Cracken, certainly.

While the governess was attiring, the rector again suggested to his wife the expediency of rising, at the same time repeating his assurances that the chimneys were as solid as any masonry could possibly be. Mrs. Spenser seemed to be measuring the ceiling with her wild black eyes, and marking the precise spot where the chimney must inevitably smash through it, if the gale continued to rage. It certainly did blow furiously at the moment; close as the wood-work of the windows was, they rattled at every gust, and a tall ash in front of the house, that in general could not be seen from Mrs. Spenser's pillow, was more or less visible every minute, as it bowed under the weight of the blast.

"Perhaps so," she answered, in a tone of peevish acquiescence. "I'll get up and sit in my dressing-room; pray go down, Mr. Spenser, while I dress—no—stay—the exertion would be too much for me—do you not think you and Rebecca could push the bed over to the other side of the room? My poor Bijou—he has been so restless all night—*soyez tranquille, pauvre petit.*"

Master and maid put their shoulders to it, Bijou growling at them the while wickedly. Rebecca was perhaps the robuster of the two, being more in the habit of exercising her arms than her master, who made no great use of his, not even in the pulpit.

Before, however, they commenced moving the bedstead, which was a massive one, they should have thought of putting all impediments out of the way; but they neglected to do so, and the consequence was that they overturned a small table, with all the drops, salts, and tonics, a cup and saucer, a porcelain candlestick, a small silver bell, some French novels, Mrs. Spenser's watch, a china jug, a jar of red currant-jelly, and a wine-glass, the simultaneous fall of which miscellaneous articles made a handsome crash, you may suppose.

Mrs. Spenser concluded it was the chimney at last, in spite of the diocesan architect, and sprang screaming out of bed with an agility that was perfectly marvelous, dragging half the bedclothes after her; and worse, or rather better than all, pitching her ill-conditioned pug into the middle of the room, where he barked and snarled like a little Cerberus.

Mr. Spenser ran round on one side and Rebecca on the other—it was a scene that Wilkie should have painted—the girls ran up stairs, hearing the din, and Miss M'Cracken, dressed *à quartre épingles*, followed by one of the housemaids, with a sweeping-brush in her hand, also rushed to the spot, to see what calamities had happened, and lend their assistance.

A glance would have told any body of the least skill in divining character, who saw Miss M'Cracken enter Mrs. Spenser's bedroom that morning, that she was a person of no little authority and consequence. She was under the middle stature, but made the utmost of her height; her figure was at once neat and stout, and her dress set it off to the best advantage. Handsome she was unquestionably, but disagreeably so; at least many people thought so. Her face was one of those you can't object to, and yet don't quite fancy; it was once attracted and repelled you. In short, it was evident she had a *character* and a mind, while at the same time there was something sinister that bespoke a mind better stored with shrewd projects than good principles. She had reached the mature and stirring age of twenty-seven, and looked as if she had commenced life early in her teens, and seen and done as much as it was possible to see and do in the time.

Every body except Miss Spenser gave way to Miss M'Cracken. She called for explanations, she issued orders, she inquired for the children, she seemed disposed to box Rebecca's ears, although she and Rebecca were generally good friends enough. To the rector alone she was respectful, but there was something condescending in her bearing even to him. Arabella, who did not restrain herself, said in a low but sharp tone, that it would be better for Miss M'Cracken not to talk so much, but to pick up the broken things. Lucy's color mounted, and her eye showed her resentment at this speech; but she commanded her tongue perfectly. Rebecca was instantly on her knees, picking up the shattered glass and china; Elizabeth and the chambermaid assisted: it was too groveling an office for Miss M'Cracken, who occupied herself helping Mrs. Spenser into bed, and appeasing Bijou with Naples biscuits. It is to be presumed she thought these latter employments more dignified.

Mr. Spenser was ridiculously out of his sphere amidst all the petticoats, blankets, and broken china, currant-jelly, and sal-volatile; he felt it, and took the opportunity of the confusion to slip out of the room, picking the feathers from his glossy black coat as he went down stairs, and blaming himself internally for being so weak as to humor his wife's vagaries, a weakness, however, of which he continued to be guilty to the end of the chapter. His grand mistake was, forgetting that he had other duties as well as his conjugal ones; he should have locked himself up in his study, if necessary stood a siege there, and written his pastoral discourse, in defiance of rain and wind, and all the nerves and nonsense in the universe.

Mrs. Spenser continued very excited for some time, unusually fidgety and exacting, always wanting something, and changing her mind before her faithful attendant could get it for her. Lucy took up her position near a window, and applied herself to "Clarissa Harlow," as well as she could, in the intervals of her attendance at the bedside. Never once did she exhibit the least temper, unpleasant as it is to be disturbed reading, particularly such a work as Lucy was engaged with; on the contrary, when the interest became very absorbing, she seemed only to grow more anxious for the comfort and repose of her patient; for she approached her on tip-toe, with a small vial containing a black liquid, and implored her to take a few drops of laudanum on a lump of sugar.

"How many will you take, madam?" she tenderly inquired, her voice as nicely pitched to the tone of a sick room as if she had been educated by Miss Martineau expressly on the point.

"Give me twelve, or thirteen," said Mrs. Spenser.

"Twelve will be quite enough, ma'am," said Lucy; but she administered twenty, and enjoyed Richardson's great work to the content of her heart.

At dinner that day Sydney was missing.

Mr. Spenser asked his daughter Elizabeth whether she knew what had become of him.

"He rode over, I believe, to Castle Dawson," she replied, in a tone that conveyed her displeasure at having no better account to give of her brother.

Mr. Spenser merely remarked that it was an unpleasant day for so long a ride. It was one instance out of a thousand of the parental negligence which caused him so much unhappiness hereafter; and yet Sydney was just now, as we have seen, occupying his mind more than he had ever done before, and more than subjects of direct practical interest usually did.

---

## CHAPTER XI.

### THE NURSERY GOVERNESS.

"A young lady is anxious for an engagement as Nursery Governess, or Companion. She is active, intelligent, amiable, and confidential; teaches English in all its branches, French like a native, and the rudiments of Latin. Has no objection to town or country, or to the education of young gentlemen. Would make herself generally useful. Salary of *some* importance, and the family of a clergyman, or an invalid would be preferred. Address, L. M'C., Post Office, Kensington."
THE TIMES, *Aug.* 3, 1830.

LUCY M'CRACKEN's ostensible employment in the family was not her real one; nominally she was the preceptress of the younger children, she professed the rudiments of Latin, and prepared young gentlemen not only for the studies of Eton, but for its discipline also. But her real and *bonâ-fide* occupation was that of sycophant to Mrs. Spenser. She had a fair salary for the former, but she made a better thing of the latter, not only in the shape of perquisites, but what she valued more, influence and position. Lucy had entered the rector's household a mere nursery-governess, bound by the terms of her engagement to do several things less dignified than teaching grammar and geography; but she had gradually and cleverly shuffled off every function that was in any degree menial, and all that remained was, to shake off her educational duties altogether; an object which, about the present time, she had very nearly succeeded in accomplishing. A more ambitious or more artful young woman never advertised in the "Times" for a post in a nursery. Her grand object was to make herself a lady, and as that was only to be done by captivating and marrying a gentleman, she was always ready for a flirtation with any handsome young man who fell in her way. Beside the face and figure we have described, she had other qualities that made her by no means an undesirable girl to flirt with. She spoke French fluently, sang well, and there was something piquant in the alternate demureness and vivacity of her demeanor. Miss M'Cracken was much too sagacious to rely upon the advantages Nature had bestowed upon her. She perfectly understood the value of accomplishments and manners, and had omitted no opportunity of improving herself in both ways. Her manners, indeed, were already easy and graceful beyond her station; if they were embarrassed at all, it was not by the humble opinion she had of herself, but more by the trouble it gave her to disguise the high one. As to her mind, the pains she took with it would have deserved the highest praise, only that much of the time its cultivation occupied had been purloined from the discharge of her duties; she taught herself Italian when she ought to have been teaching her pupils Latin or English, and the books which she recommended for their use were invariably those which she desired to have for her own mental improvement. In fact, she had little, if any, of the organ of conscientiousness; or, if she originally possessed a conscience, she had contrived to reduce its voice to an almost inaudible tick, which it is quite possible to do, if people will only resolutely and patiently set about it.

When Lucy came first to Redcross, she found Rebecca in the post of honor nearest to Mrs. Spenser's person. But Rebecca was a poor simple country-girl, without a notion above her sphere of life, and the sorry line of her duty. She was pliable and complaisant because she was obliging and good-natured, but she had no turn for flattery, knack at intrigue, or talent for self-advancement. Her prudence began and ended with depositing a few pounds in the Saving Bank of the village; she was born and bred a servant, and a servant was destined to continue all her days, while every thing about Miss M'Cracken announced that if fortune had not a higher sphere in store for her, she was not the woman to sink with alacrity into a lower one. Lucy (who indeed hated children) soon conceived the idea that Rebecca would answer extremely well to superintend the fry of the nursery, while she felt it would be more congenial to her own tastes and talents to pass the greater part of her time in Mrs. Spenser's bed-chamber and boudoir, acquiring lady-like ways of talking and thinking, or doing nothing, and thus fitting herself to move in the walk of life which she had no doubt destiny had chalked out for her, and which, at all events, she had chalked out for herself.

The skill was consummate with which Miss M'Cracken contrived to change places with Rebecca. She began by making herself agreeable; then she made herself useful; and she ended by making herself as indispensable to Mrs. Spenser as her salts and morphine. Nominally, however, she still retained her original appointment; a few hours every day, generally in the morning, were devoted to the young Spensers, during which, by her severe rectitude and her despotic government, she compensated herself in some measure for the lax morality, and the servile behavior of the remainder of the day.

Lucy had contemplated at one time (not long before the commencement of our story) making a little conquest of Sydney Spenser. She would gladly have put him on the list of her pupils, and offered to read "Gil Blas" with him; or be his Italian mistress, if he would prefer Petrarch's Sonnets. But Sydney had the bad taste to scorn Lucy's sentimental schooling; he cared nothing for Petrarch, or for Laura either; the beauty of a bull-dog was that which then had most power over him, and he had more ear for an Irish melody than a Tuscan. In short, he was as repulsive to Miss M'Cracken as St. Kevin was to Kathleen; but his coldness she could have brooked and forgiven, if he had only repelled her advances without ridiculing them, and if he had not gratuitously declared that Rebecca was in his opinion a handsomer girl. Lucy had no notion of being jealous, or quarreling with Rebecca on the subject; but she became all at once a malignant though secret enemy to Sydney. None of his irregularities caped her inquisitorial eye, and she had always a bad word for him whenever she could vent her feelings in safety.

Next to Sydney she disliked Elizabeth. She had no cause for it, only that Elizabeth showed a willingness to discharge the duties which the proper officer neglected, and that her quiet dignity of manner kept the *soi-disant* governess at a lowering and provoking distance. Lucy had not half so much ill-will to Arabella, who openly attacked her and sometimes gave her an opportunity for a "reply churlish," or a "countercheck quarrelsome." The "retort courteous" not often passed between them.

Miss M'Cracken, in short, was one of those people of whom there are many in the world, who are liked by hardly any body, yet of whom nobody can easily find any thing decidedly bad to say. Mrs. Spenser, however, more than liked her, and with very good reason, for Lucy's main business from morning to night was to flatter and humor her; the latter being a much more arduous task than the former, with so capricious and whimsical a woman. Lucy possessed the art of always divining what her mistress wished her to say, or not to say; knew when to congratulate her upon looking charming, or pronounce her looking wretched, which was sometimes the more agreeable compliment; when to coincide with the doctors, when to differ with them; when to be mute as a mouse, when to speak; and what to say when she did speak. To a selfish invalid such an ally was invaluable. Lucy was always ready with the most acceptable suggestions, and of course it was no concern of hers whether the rector could well afford to act upon them or not; she was not his Chancellor of Exchequer; her business was to consult poor Mrs. Spenser's health and gratification, and nobody could accuse that lady of reckless extravagance, or of thinking of herself to the exclusion of every body, and every thing else, when the ideas seemed to originate in the amiable thoughtfulness and inventive good-nature of the governess.

Privations, discomforts and indignities are the lot of hundreds of young woman who devote themselves, or are devoted by their ruthless destiny, to that line of life which the world in its wisdom (or at least a great portion of it) continues to treat as one of the basest of human employments—the education of infancy. But Miss M'Cracken was not the girl to put up with privations or indignities. She knew how to feather her nest, and to butter her bread on both sides, as they say in Swift's "Polite Conversation." Not to speak in proverbs, she possessed the art of making herself snug wherever her lot cast her; and there was scarcely a prettier room in the parsonage than that which she had appropriated to herself. It was handsomely curtained, warmly carpeted, more than comfortably furnished, and, better than all, it was as remote as the extent of the house permitted, not only from the school-room, but from the children's dormitory. In the house the Woodwards lived in, there was no chamber half so well appointed, not even Carry's own, though Hercules did his best to make that comfortable.

Miss M'Cracken's room had the advantage of enjoying the overflow of luxuries and ornaments from Mrs. Spenser's. The rector's wife

was particularly whimsical and extravagant in couches and chairs, and as her chamber could not hold all the varieties her caprice had accumulated, when the inconvenience of a glut was felt, the excess was carried elsewhere, and Lucy was so obliging as to allow a portion of it to be stowed in her own apartment. In the same way she managed to decorate it with a handsome French clock, a buhl cabinet, a mosaic octagon table, and many other like articles, which she wished perhaps to make herself familiar with early in life, lest the possession of them might embarrass or over-excite her at a later period. But many little things in the room and the greater part of the books and prints were her own private chattels. Miss M'Cracken was always acquiring something, and never lost any thing she acquired. She rolled through life like a hedgehog through an orchard, gathering as she went, and probably, as in the case of the prickly and predatory animal, many things stuck to her which were not properly her own. Over the mantel-piece were hung, in little gilt or maple-wood frames, engravings of some of the most eminent Protestant missionaries, preachers, and theologians, interspersed with portraits of several women of celebrated piety, who were, of course, understood to be the female models which Lucy proposed for her study and imitation.

Need it be said that the books were of the same spiritual character. There was a neat little bookcase, well furnished with small editions of the most popular and standard religious works; a few belonged to Mr. Spenser, but the majority had been either bought by Lucy herself, or were presents which she had received from time to time from attached pupils or grateful mothers. Mr. Woodward had given her at Christmas a copy of Wilberforce's "View of Christianity," and the rector had very lately presented her with "Butler's Analogy," a proof of the high opinion he entertained of the powers of her understanding. It often gave him sincere pleasure to find her deeply engaged in its profound pages, while she kept watch and ward at his wife's bedside; for Lucy's novel-reading was generally a clandestine pursuit, which, no doubt, gave an additional piquancy to the scenes of Richardson and Sand.

Very little sleep sufficed Lucy herself, particularly when she had such a book as "Clarissa" to keep her eyes open. It was well for Mrs. Spenser that the stock of novels and romances in the house was limited, for the volumes might have been counted by the phials of morphine administered to her, while Lucy devoured them. That night the dose was doubled, partly because the winds were so mutinous, and partly because Richardson was so absorbing. Long after all the house was under canopies of chintz or dimity, Lucy continued to sit up, with her wax candle, her lively little fire chirping in the grate, her person fused into the swelling cushions of a chair which was all cushions, her feet planted on the fender, her elbow on the table, her eyes riveted on "Clarissa," and taking no notice whatever of either Hannah More, or Mrs. Fry, who were both peering primly at her out of their little frames.

Somebody tapped at the door; she started, though not at all superstitious, listened, threw her handkerchief over the book, and said, "Come in." It was Rebecca, who, kept awake by the tempest, came to pass the night with Lucy, either in her bed, or at her fire-side. Lucy was charitable; drew over another chair, nearly as easy as her own, though made on another principle; planted her shivering deputy in it; and replenished the grate with sods, almost as sable, solid, and full of flame as Newcastle coal. There were soon two pair of feet on the fender, but there was a great difference between them; Lucy's were pretty, and wore silk stockings; Rebecca's were clothed in cotton, or worsted, and deserved no better.

"You hear the storm here mighty little, miss," said Rebecca, "it's mighty loud in the nursery."

"It's because the wind happens to blow from the west," said Lucy.

The fact was, that the wind blew from that point three hundred days out of the three hundred and sixty-five, so that it was very commodious to have a bed-room that was not exposed to the west wind.

"What's a tempest, miss?" asked the deputy-governess, "though I'm sure I ought to know, living in these parts, where it never stops blowing all the year round."

Lucy smiled at the philosophical curiosity of Rebecca, and luminously explained that when the air was agitated, and tumbled things down, blew them about, and turned every thing topsy-turvy, that was a tempest.

"And what's a hurricane?"—was Rebecca's next inquiry.

Lucy again explained, and asked what made her companion so inquisitive that night.

"It was the children that were axing me, as I was putting them to bed," said Rebecca, and then she remarked how curious children were.

"Don't encourage their curiosity too much," said Lucy. "It's a great vice in children to be always asking questions; I have corrected them for it more than once."

"Indeed, it's very troublesome, miss," replied Rebecca, "and I find it so particularly when I don't know what to answer them. But how quiet mistress is to-night!"

"It's the few drops of morphine I gave her in her gruel," said Lucy.

"It's a darling medicine," said Rebecca; "it does the nurse as much good as the sick body."

Lucy sighed tenderly, and said she could sit up forever with such a sweet patient as Mrs. Spenser. Rebecca sighed responsively; and then Miss M'Cracken added that she greatly feared poor Mrs. Spenser would never get a natural night's sleep as long as she remained in the country.

"She never will be asy, anyhow," said Rebecca; "it stands to rayson."

"She never will be well, Rebecca," said Lucy, with sad solemnity.

This was the way the storm within doors was brewed for the easy and unsuspicious rector. Miss M'Cracken's object was to get up a cry in the house that Mrs. Spenser would never get her health in the country. As to herself, she always professed the greatest aversion to town.

"The Dublin doctors would do her a power of good, I suppose, miss?"

"Of course they would."

"But they're very expensive, I'm tould, miss, and won't cure any but rich people."

"And isn't Mr. Spenser as rich as Crœsus?" asked Lucy. "But even if he was not, ought he to think of money when the health of that dear sweet woman is in question?"

"She's his wedded wife, at any rate," said Rebecca, implying some dissent from the flattering epithet Miss M'Cracken had applied to her mistress, but having a clear view of the strength of matrimonial obligations, as all women have.

"She is," said Lucy, with emphasis, "and she deserves better than to be murdered by the sea air, that never agreed with her, and those country doctors, that havn't as much skill as my little finger."

The simile was not very disparaging to the country doctors, for Lucy's fingers had a great deal of skill in them.

"They do well enough for poor bodies," said Rebecca; "but of course, miss, a lady ought to have the best of doctors that's goin'; it stands to rayson."

The clock struck one.

"It's getting very late, Rebecca," said Lucy; "hadn't you better go back to your room?"

"Let me sit here by the fire, miss; do you go to bed, and I'll talk you to sleep, or I'll hold my tongue, just as you please."

"I'm not sleepy myself," said Lucy.

"Read me something," said Rebecca.

"Put some turf on the fire, and I will, then," answered Lucy, complaisantly.

"Shall I read you one of Mrs. Hannah More's 'Sacred Dramas?'"

"Just read me what you were reading for yourself, miss," said Rebecca, perhaps divining that Miss M'Cracken's nocturnal studies were none of the driest, or spying a book that looked more amusing than instructive under the handkerchief.

"I was just looking," said Lucy, taken a little aback, "into a work called 'Clarissa Harlowe;' I suspect it's a novel; but I thought it right to know what it's about, in order to forbid the children to open it, should it contain any thing improper."

"Well, it doesn't sound improper at all," said Rebecca; "Clarissa is such a beautiful name for a lady—"

"—That you think," added Lucy, "her story must be very interesting."

So saying, she resumed her book and took up the story where she had left off herself, without taking much trouble to put her companion in possession of the previous part of it. Nor, indeed, was there the slightest occasion. Rebecca devoured every word with a rapture she had never felt before, and the book was never laid down until the flame of the candle suddenly collapsed into the socket, and left the secret novel-readers in almost total darkness. Lucy drew the curtains to admit the gloomy gray of the morning, and Rebecca, huddling her cloaks and shawls about her, crept back by the same faint light to the children's room.

## CHAPTER XII.

### SUNDRY MATTERS.

" When that I was little tiny boy,
    With hey-ho, the wind and the rain,
A foolish thing was but a toy,
    For the rain it raineth every day."
                          TWELFTH NIGHT.

A STORM always kept the Woodwards, too, in a state of alarm and excitement, though not entirely upon their own account. Mrs. Woodward was not the woman to fall into paroxysms of selfish apprehension, while billows mountain-high, and fierce winds, were threatening, perhaps, hundreds of hapless mariners with destruction within half a mile of her; and as to the curate, he was never so great as when a furious gale was vexing the coast, and threatening to afford fearful occasions for the display of his humanity and prowess.

Redcross was on the shore, and the windows of the curate's house commanded a view of the coast for an extent of many miles. The house was far from being so good as so good a man deserved to inhabit, or as solid as its exposed situation required, in a country so subject to hurricanes. The chimneys were so tall, and at the same time so slender, that their standing was a standing miracle. In that house, indeed, there was rattling of window-frames, and shattering of panes, and creaking of ill-fitted doors, and whistling and howling of wicked blasts through hole and cranny, through ancient crack and modern crevice. Indeed, so continually recurring was the damage done by the wind, that repairing it perfectly was out of the question; it would have taken more than Mr. Woodward's income to have kept the glass in repair, for at that period there was a heavy duty upon that fragile article. The consequence was, that there was scarcely an integral pane in the upper apartments of the house; and many had been shivered over and over again, until it was wonderful how paste and old copy-books kept the fragments together. You might have traced the progress in writing made by the little Woodwards from the first rude pot-hooks, by inspecting the slips of paper with which Hercules had managed to put off, as long as possible, the reference to the man of the diamond, which was inevitable at last. But the wood-work was almost as precarious as the glass, and it was no uncommon incident for a violent gust to burst in a window at one smash, instead of taking the trouble to demolish it by degrees. The curate was then obliged to unite the trade of the carpenter to the glazier's, and fortunately he had a turn for mechanical operations, and could even repair the brick-work a little, or do a matter of slating, to prevent the wind and the rain from becoming absolute masters of the house, while he was constrained to pay the rent of it. Had he required cheering while performing these humble offices, which the poverty of his lot imposed upon him, his wife was there to cheer him, though she was always averse to his labors on the roof, which was very high and slanting, not to mention that the ladder was somewhat rickety by which her brave husband was wont to clamber to his house-top.

In the gazebo, called the *Observatory*,· you may fancy what an uproar there was in such weather as the present. The windows there were boarded up with stout planks, like those of Apsley House in political tempests, but even then it was any thing but a safe place, for it was as obnoxious to the wind as a light-house; without being constructed in the same substantial way.' Still, it commanded so wide a view, that the curate used several times a day to venture up to it to take a more extended survey of the coast than he could obtain from any of the lower parts of the house.

Upon the first day of the gale, a small vessel had been seen in the offing, apparently anxious to run into some of the numerous creeks along the coast; but it was a lee-shore, and Hercules,· who was a pretty good seaman, perfectly apprehended the difficulties she must have to contend with in an attempt of the kind in such ugly weather.

On a minute examination, Hercules had no doubt she was a pleasure-boat; she was certainly not a fishing-smack, and was too small either for merchandise or war. That entire day she was seen beating about, until toward evening, when suddenly she disappeared, apparently behind a group of small islands in the offing, one of which was the romantic rock of which the Spensers considered themselves the suzerains. To send any relief off to the distressed stranger was out of the question; it was possible, however, that the storm might still drive her ashore, and in that case her destruction was almost inevitable, although it was also possible that timely aid might save the lives of her crew. Every exertion that humanity could make to provide against this contingency was made by the brave and worthy clergyman; and Father Magrath, the Catholic priest of Redcross (with whom Mr. Woodward, as well as the rector, lived on the most cordial terms, notwithstanding both political and religious differences), was fully as prompt and energetic in doing all that charity dictated. Parties of the country people were dispatched northward and southward along the cliffs, with poles, ropes, lanterns, and whatever was likely to prove serviceable, should the yacht be driven on the beach. Father Magrath, a bluff, benevolent man, went himself with one of these parties, and Mr. Woodward led another; they heard a gun toward the close of the evening, but saw nothing, and returned to the village in the dead of night, in the midst of the howling tempest, full of the saddest apprehensions as to the fate of the unknown craft. The next day, and the day following, rumors of more than one wreck at various points along the coast reached the inhabitants of Redcross, and it was but too probable that the yacht, if that were her character, was one of the number. There was a bare chance that, by some combination of fortunate circumstances, turned to advantage by very dexterous seamanship, she might have found shelter in a particular cove on the eastern side of the Spensers' island; but it was what the curate called a "potentia remotissima." The odds were enormously against the safety of any vessel situated as she was, much more against one that was obviously a stranger to the coast, and but ill prepared for its peculiar dangers. Familiar as the Woodwards were with storms, and their disastrous effects, they were always thrown into confusion by them. The domestic phenomena, always singular, became at such times doubly curious and striking. The curate sat down to his meals in the dress of the pilot of a life-boat; and Carry, with a double complement of petticoats, cloaks, and shawls, looked vast enough to be the mother of half her species, and almost as anxious as if she had actually so large a family. Ranging from room to room, to patch up the windows as well as she could, according as the wind shattered them, she almost unconsciously huddled on every thing wearable that came in her way, until she grew into an actual mountain; but, with all the disadvantages of this prodigious *dishabille*, and the disorder of her cap and her hair, she was such a mountain as Mohammed would have gladly seen approaching him, or gladly have approached, if it had refused to answer his call. Mrs. Woodward was a very different woman in a hurricane from Mrs. Spenser; there is so wide a difference, even in its influence upon personal appearance, between being uneasy for others, and uneasy for one's self. The lines of the face are affected in quite another manner; the form of the visage is changed differently altogether. It would seem as if benevolence and selfishness acted on two wholly distinct sets of nerves and muscles.

At the parsonage the gale abated considerably, after blowing fiercely for a day and a night; but the rain served equally well to keep Mrs. Spenser in her normal state of unamiable excitement. She was now apprehensive of the glebe-house being washed into the loch by the flood, nor did she know any reason why there should not be land-slips in Ireland as well as in Switzerland; in short, there was no fate so dreadful which might not be naturally expected, in such frightful weather, and such a detestable country. Another year in Ireland, however, would put an end to her sufferings; of that she was quite positive—but no matter, of course, what became of *her*. You might stereotype the speeches of such a woman.

The rector had not ten minutes of tranquillity the livelong day. Hurry-skurry overhead again; running of women to and fro; bells ringing convulsively; doors spasmodically opening and shutting; Miss M'Cracken calling to Rebecca; enormous fuss and humbug, all about nothing in the world but that the wind had cracked the corner of a pane of glass, and that the rain had made its way through the tiny crevice, and trickled down into the room, where it formed what the governess poetically called "a sea"—a sea which you could have drained with a tea-spoon. What a consort this was for a country clergyman! Mrs. Spenser was never quiet and inoffensive except under the influence of morphine, which it was almost to be regretted that her prime minister did not give her in larger doses. She was the wasp in her husband's peach—the nettle in his garland.

It enraged the gentle but ardent Elizabeth to see her father disturbed in so reckless a manner. She was proud of his preaching, and she admired his sermons all the more, because, elaborate as they were, they were not written with the sordid object of establishing a character for pulpit eloquence, and so advancing their author in the church; but simply with the pure and elevated purpose of communicating the most important truths in the manner he believed to be most impressive and intelligible to the "the people of his pasture and the sheep of his fold."

Mrs. Spenser, on the contrary, took particular pleasure in molesting her husband when she knew that he was engaged in writing his sermons; she thought it was a shameful abuse of his talents to exert them, as he did, in a remote rural district, for peasants who had merely souls to be saved, instead of reserving them for the ears of bishops who had livings to bestow, or viceroys with still higher rewards at their disposal. Miss M'Cracken never returned from church, when the rector preached, but she was sure to observe, "What a pity it was, ma'am, to throw away such a beautiful discourse upon a little country church!"

The appetite for Richardson grew with the feeding, and that night again Rebecca took refuge in Lucy M'Cracken's cozy room, from her own comparatively uncomfortable and exposed one. There was of course the usual gossip before the reading. Lucy had noted Sydney's departure for Castle Dawson the day before, and now she did not fail also to remark the fact that this was the second night and yet he was not returned. Upon this subject she made a great many severe, and some very just observations; partly leveled at the young man himself, and partly at his father.

"In such weather as this, Rebecca," she said, "to be galloping through the mountains, and out of his father's house for two nights running, without asking permission, or even informing his family where he was going."

Rebecca said it was very wrong.

"It is very *shocking!*" said Lucy, not thinking Rebecca's word forcible enough; and added, how very differently from Mrs. Spenser would she act, if she were a parent, and if she had a son, and so forth. Lucy, indeed, would probably not have erred on the side of gentleness.

"I'm told Master Sydney went over to Castle Dawson," whispered Rebecca.

"You may speak as loud as you like," said Lucy, implying the strong measures she had taken to quiet her dear mistress for the night. She then said, in answer to her crony's remark, "And he couldn't possibly go to a worse place, if only half what I hear about it is like the truth."

"It bears a bad name, true for you," said the other girl.

"And so do the people that own it," said Lucy. "It's no fit place for the son of a gentleman and a *clergyman* to be seen at."

"Mr. Dudley and Master Sydney are very great, I hear," said Rebecca.

Miss M'Cracken spoke very harshly of Sydney's friend, when her companion interrupted her by asking whether she had ever heard that he was paying attentions to Miss Elizabeth.

This was a surprise to Lucy. It was not often that any one had the start of her in domestic intelligence. She expressed her doubts whether Rebecca was correctly informed, but in truth she was embarrassed between her previous readiness to abuse Mr. Dawson, and a malign pleasure which she instantly felt at the idea of Elizabeth having an unworthy suitor, and perhaps making an unworthy match. In this ill-natured perplexity she abruptly changed the subject by asking Rebecca had she ever been in Dublin.

"No, miss; I was onst in Londonderry," said Rebecca, "to see the gates closed."

The governess smiled with real contempt, but affected good-nature, and again asked her friend if she would not like very much to go to Dublin.

"Why, then, I would, miss," Rebecca answered; "but it's not for the sake of the doctors I'd care to be in it."

"No, I should think not," said Lucy, laughing; "neither you nor I need much doctoring; but I know your tastes, Rebecca, my dear, and I am positive you would be much happier there than here; it was that made me think of it; of course, my dear, we must do our duty wherever it pleases Providence to place us."

Her voice was becomingly low and serious as she delivered the devout part of this little speech, and a well-drawn sigh served for a peroration.

"Dublin is such a big place, I'd be lost in it," said Rebecca, paying much less attention to Lucy's bit of divinity than to the worldly part of her discourse.

"Oh, you would soon find your way," said Lucy, "and you would find more than that, Rebecca—"

"I suppose you mean sweethearts," said Rebecca, giggling.

Lucy admitted that she did, and (protesting her own unchangeable affection for rural scenes) drew a most bewitching picture of the Irish capital, and the life that people lead there, particularly girls in Rebecca's sphere of life, who had no other employment from morn to night (it would appear from Miss M'Cracken's enchanting statement) but tea-drinking, car-driving, play-going, and all manner of fun and diversion.

"Did you ever see Donnybrook Fair, miss?"

Lucy had seen it, or said she had. "But I won't attempt to describe it to you," she said, for I couldn't; and, besides, you wouldn't sleep a wink to-night, if I did, for dreaming of it."

Rebecca was mute with delight and wonder. Lucy left the potion to work which she had so adroitly administered to the girl's love of novelty and pleasure, and resumed the reading of the novel.

---

# BOOK III.

## CHAPTER XIII.

### THE MOUNTAIN RIDE.

"Next him was Feare, all arm'd from top to toe,
Yet thought himselfe not safe enough thereby,
But feard each shadow moving to or fro,
And his owne armes when glittering he did spy,
Or clashing heard, he fast away did fly;
As ashes pale of hew, and winged heeld;
And evermore on Daunger fixt his eye,
'Gainst whom he always bent a brasen shield,
Which his right hand unarmed fearefully did wield."
FAERY QUEEN.

WHILE the rector and curate were holding the dialogue on education, recorded in a previous chapter, the handsome but headstrong youth to whom it referred, in a costume something between a sailor and a groom (not unsuited, however, to the unruly state of the weather), was traversing a bleak mountain road, and caring very little what decision was come to on the academic question, having probably made up his mind to follow the bent of his humor, and enjoy what is called life, whether his lot should be cast on the banks of the Liffey, or those of the more renowned Cam.

Not more than a quarter of a mile from his father's gate he picked up a companion, who was no other than Mr. Randal Maguire, commonly called Randy, his father's proctor, a very odd looking old fellow, and with odd features in his character as well as in his face. Randal was going over to Castle Dawson also, partly in consequence of the intimation he had received from Master Dudley that he was prepared to settle the long pending arrear of tithes, and partly to collect the rent of a small property belonging to an English gentleman who had never seen it, and whose name was all that Randy knew of him. Randy was not himself the agent, but only his deputy. The agent resided in Dublin, lounging about the clubs, being too fine a man to collect rents in person, particularly the rents of a small estate.

Maguire was a short, slender, elderly man, with a feeble frame, but a wiry constitution, always looking as if he had not many years to live, but burying in succession nine tenths of those who had made the remark. In business he was scrupulously exact and honest, in fact, in all respects an admirable tithe proctor, except that his tendency was to apply the screw to the parishioners a little too powerfully; but this was a propensity which in the service of a clergyman of Mr. Spenser's character he was obliged to keep in due restraint. Maguire's physiognomy was extremely queer; a small, withered face, undulating with pock-marks, and ending with scarcely any chin; a pair of prying, decimating little reddish-gray eyes; a miserable crop of scrubby sandy whiskers; and a sharp nose, which had the extraordinary peculiarity of appearing either very long or very short, according to the position in which the spectator viewed it, for it projected horizontally, so as to seem nothing at a front view, while seen in profile it looked like a long spout of a jug, or a tea-pot. This feature gave a peculiarly humorous expression to his face, and, indeed, he was considered a humorous little old fellow in the country; but a little humor goes a great way in a thinly peopled mountain district. Maguire had faults like other men; he was very garrulous, as timid as a hare, and a most inveterate card-player. The passion of the lower orders of the Irish for cards has been noticed by the old chroniclers; Campion gives some amusing instances of the extravagant lengths to which it was indulged in his time by the fellows who were called "carrows;" and though Maguire perhaps did not gamble quite so desperately as those ancient unworthies, he was keen enough, in all conscience, and never traveled without a greasy old dog-eared copy of what the Puritans used to call "the devil's prayer-book" in one of his pockets.

The cowardice of the little proctor made him always glad of a companion in his journeys through a wild and little-frequented country; but it was now particularly satisfactory to him, for though the agitation against tithes which prevailed in other parts of Ireland about this time had not yet reached this remote district, symptoms of a disposition to join it had made their appearance, and the shadow of danger was enough to unnerve Maguire. Accordingly, he was delighted to find that his line of march on the morning in question coincided with that of young Spenser, who, upon his part, was not displeased to have Maguire for a fellow-traveler; not (you may suppose) for the sake of any help in need to be expected from him, but because his eccentricities, especially his open and avowed poltroonery, were amusing, and he had endless tales of the "hair-breadth perilous 'scapes," or more fatal disasters of tithe proctors in the southern counties, where he always cordially congratulated himself that his own lot had not been cast.

"What would become of you, in times like these, Randy. if my father were promoted to a better living in Limerick or Tipperary?" said Sydney, as they jogged along, both indifferent to the rain which pelted them, for the elements were the only thing in nature that Maguire did not fear.

"By the powers, Master Sydney," said the little dastardly old man, "I often thought of that same; I don't think I'd flourish in Tipperary at all, at all. The boys are divils, I hear say, down there; and as to maiming or murthering a chap of my profession, 'faith, they think it no morthall sin to slaughter a minister himself." The proctor was in the habit of finishing his sentences with a noise something between a cough and a laugh; it was partly asthmatic, partly facetious.

"Well, this country, I hope, is quiet enough to please you," said young Spenser. "At the same time, they don't pay my father as cheerfully in some parts of the parish as they do in others; isn't it so, Randy?"

"By my troth, things are not as they used to be, sartinly, Master Spenser," said Randy. "I remember when the minister hadn't to ask for his tithe twice; and when the farmers used to run after me on the high road. Now it's I that have to run after them; and some of thim's not very asy to catch. I don't see the zale that I used to do; of coorse I'm alludin to the Catholics, and some of the Presbyterian boys in particular."

"Some go so far as to say there's a storm brewing against my father," said Sydney.

"It won't signify much, I'm thinking," said the old man, "there's some agitation and harranguin going on, I'm tould, in some parts, but Father Magrath has his eye on the chaps that's doing it, for he tould me as much."

"Where are you bound to, Randy, this beau-'iful summer day?" asked Sydney, the rain and wind almost taking his breath away while he spoke.

The old man's little decimating eyes twinkled with extraordinary satisfaction, as he replied, "I'm going the same coorse as your own self, Master Sydney, for I presume you are going over toward Castle Dawson?"

"What are you going to do at Castle Dawson, Randy?"

"Thin, I'm going to do what nobody has done there for many a long day—I'm going to receive money."

Sydney's countenance expressed his pleasure at this intelligence, for he was aware how the pecuniary claims of his father against the Dawsons had prejudiced Dudley in the eyes of his stepmother, and he was glad to see one obstacle removed to the reception of his friend at the parsonage.

"I didn't know whether I was standin on my head or my heels," continued Randy, "when I was sarved last night with a notice, in Mr. Dudley's own hand-writing, to go over some early day, and he'd settle all demands in cash. By the mass, I could hardly believe my eyes; and I won't be cock-sure of the money until I have it lodged in the ould pocket-book in the buzzom of my coat here." Randy used almost as much action in speaking as a Frenchman, and clapped his little withered hand on the place where he was in the habit of carrying his sacred treasures.

"Is it a large sum?" inquired Sydney.

"Seventy-six pounds seven shillings and sixpence," answered the proctor. "But it's more than the value of the money, Master Spenser; it's the example it will set in the country, where there's any thing going on that's not correct. By my faith, people was beginning to say that Mr. Dawson his own self was disposed to be combinin, as they're doing in other places."

"Combining!" exclaimed Sydney, angrily; "what do you mean by combining?—you don't mean to say that my friend Dudley Dawson, or his father either, are suspected of doing any thing dishonorable, particularly toward our family?"

"I only tell you what I hear said," said Maguire, coolly; "but of coorse, when the arrears is paid up, there'll be an end to all such insinivations."

"Such insinuations," returned Sydney, passionately, "are most impertinent, and I repel them on the part of the Dawsons, and Dudley in particular, with indignation."

"Be that as it may, Master Sydney, it's my duty to your father's son to acquaint you with what I hear and believe, that Master Dudley has some queer people about him just at the present time," said the old man, pertinaciously; using a liberty with Sydney, on account of his youth, which perhaps he would not have ventured to use with a man of more advanced years, in the same station of life.

"We'll drop the subject, if you please," said Sydney, imperiously. Randy submitted, and soon after asked Sydney to sing him "The Boys of Kilkenny"—a song which the old man particularly rejoiced in.

"Here goes, Randy: but it's no easy matter to sing with this wind in one's teeth." However, he managed a stanza or two, to the entire satisfaction of his companion, who had no idea that there was any better vocal music in the world; and, indeed, young Spenser had a good tenor voice, and sung with spirit and humor.

"Oh, the boys of Kilkenny are stout roving blades,
And if ever they meet with the nice little maids,
They kiss them, and coax them, and spend their money free,
Oh, of all the towns in Ireland, Kilkenny for me."

"The wind is too strong for me. Were you ever in Kilkenny, Randy?"

"Then, I never was, Master Sydney, but I often hear talk of it as a mighty quare place, with fire without smoke, and the streets paved with marble."

"Shall we travel together and see the world, Randy?"

The rain was penetrating Randy's short, threadbare, old, brown surtout, and the wind was almost doing the barber's duty on his little wrinkled face. His efforts to laugh were laughable, as he answered—

"At all events, I'm growing too ould to be travelin and roamin such a day as this, Master Sydney."

"If you're old Randy, you're tough," said his companion.

"Yes; I'm purty tough; thank God for it," replied the proctor.

"How do you feel when you ride this road alone?" asked Sydney, who knew the old man's chicken-heartedness perfectly.

"Och, thin, I don't feel at all warlike," said Randy.

"It's a bleak road," said young Spenser.

It was so, indeed; running through a succession of low brown hills, covered with a stunted heath, of which a hundred acres would scarce have afforded a brace of grouse a decent competence.

"It's murtherin bleak," said Randy.

"I'll give you another song, to keep up your spirits," said Sydney, and he struck up the once celebrated Ned Lysaght's popular melody—

"Oh, love is the soul of a neat Irishman,
He loves all that is lovely, loves all that he can,
With his sprig of shillelagh, &c."

Just at this moment a sharp turn brought them to the ruins of what seemed to have been, some centuries back, a castle of considerable strength and size. These ruins stood close to the road, on an abrupt eminence, presenting a very remarkable and picturesque object, known in the country by the name of the "Black Castle."

"A very convenient ambush, that," said Sydney, pointing to the ruins, "for footpads, if there were any in the country."

"Many's the time I've said that to myself," said Randy. "I never pass them ruins without shiverin and shudderin on the hottest day of summer."

"Now, Randy," said Sydney, suppressing a smile, "suppose a highwayman, six feet high, were to jump out of those ruins there upon you, with a blunderbuss or a brace of pistols, to-morrow or next day, when you are returning with all the money in your pocket, what would you do? You'd make a fight for my father's property, wouldn't you?"

"By the holy spider, said Maguire, shrugging his narrow shoulders and scrutinizing the ruins to which his companion pointed with an eye full of comical alarm and suspicion, "I'd make as good a fight for your father's property as I would for my own; but it's a runnin fight, and not a standin one, I'd make for either the one or the other. I'm not come of fightin people, Master Sydney."

"You wouldn't show the white-feather surely!" said Sydney, as if he had now for the first time discovered what a craven the proctor was.

"Then I'm afeard I would so, and a bunch of them into the bargain, as big as the Prince of Wales's plume," said Maguire, with his little tittering cough.

"Now suppose any body were to pull your nose, Randy?"

"I could spare a bit of it, Master Sydney," and he laughed again in his peculiar way.

"Well," replied Sydney, "here's what will protect us both against all the highwaymen in Ireland," and he exhibited a case of very beautiful double-barreled pocket-pistols, his last clandestine acquisition, and the latest addition to the schedule of his small debts.

Randy admired the arms, but seemed very well pleased when Sydney returned them to the pocket expressly made for them in the breast of his coat.

This and other chat of the same kind, with now and then the stave of a comic song, helped a little to beguile the tediousness of a long ride across moor and mountain; so desolate a track that they passed but one human habitation before they arrived at Castle Dawson, itself the bleakest abode that ever disheartened a resident proprietor or justified an absentee. Sydney and the proctor separated at the ruinous gate-house. The latter proceeded to his usual lodging at a small inn hard by; the former trotted up the neglected avenue which led to the house.

It had been in Chancery for fifteen years! Is further description necessary? Do you not see its shattered windows, neglected roof, dilapidated offices, green-white walls, hingeless doors, grass-grown walks, weed-cropped gardens, the stones of the balustrades, dislocated as if by an earthquake, the premature havoc of the ax among such poor timber as there was, and the silent clock in the yard, announcing probably the self-same hour which it announced on the day that the bill was filed in the equity suit? But, in its best days, before it fell into the clutches of the ruthless power so vividly typified by Rabelais in "Gripe-men-all, the Arch-duke of the furred Law-Cats," Castle Dawson was a lonely, savage place (the very abomination of desolation), where the owners resided sometimes of necessity, but where nobody else ever willingly passed two nights in succession. The process-servers demanded double fees for serving a latitat or a subpœna there. It was close to the sea, among hills that were barren without being picturesque; wretched crops of oats composed its harvests, stunted cattle showed the indigence of its pastures; in fact, with the exception of a few acres, the grounds were absolutely good for nothing but snipe-shooting, and the soil only fit for fuel. The word "Castle" was an ostentatious misnomer. The house was so called either because there was nothing at all castellated in its structure, or from the adjacent relics of what had, perhaps, formerly been some kind of fortress, which relics (only a few walls, with an arched gateway) had been incorporated into the offices, and now formed in combination with them a rambling extent of buildings in an advanced stage of architectural decay.

---

## CHAPTER XIV.

### CASTLE DAWSON.

*"Panurge was a very gallant man of his person, only that he was naturally subject to a kind of disease, which at that time they called lack of money ; yet, notwithstanding, he had threescore and three tricks to help himself at his need ; of which the most honorable and most ordinary was by the way of filching ; for he was a quarrelsome fellow, a sharper, drinker, royster, and a very dissolute and debauched fellow ; otherwise, and in all matters else, the best man in the world. And he was still contriving some plot, and devising mischief against the sergeants and the watch."* RABELAIS.

THE remote, dreary, and almost inaccessible situation of Castle Dawson rendered it a most commodious retreat for a man of Dawson's stamp, particularly when he had company with him whom he did not care to acknowledge at the market-cross; for Maguire's information was correct; Dawson had some guests in his house at the present moment, whom (engaging as their manners and conversation may have been) he was far from desiring to introduce abruptly to Sydney Spenser. Indeed he generally affected strict domestic seclusion when he came down to the country; but the fact was, that in such a district, particularly in wild weather, his house might have been filled with the most notorious swindlers and black-legs in the empire—he might have entertained Joseph Ady and Ikey Solomons without much risk of the fact being noticed in the columns of the *Morning Post*, or even in the Dublin newspapers.

On such a day as the one in question, the chance of a visitor was not much greater than if Dawson had lived on the top of the highest peak in the neighboring mountains, or the stormiest island off the coast, and he was consequently not a little, as well as not very agreeably surprised, when Sydney Spenser, after having tried several damp and dismal apartments without success, at length hit on the right one, and found him at dinner, with a distinguished company consisting of two guests, neither of whom carried any very strong testimonials of character in his countenance.

The entrance of young Spenser visibly disconcerted Dawson. He sprang up and vainly attempted to conceal his embarrassment under the mask of a boisterous welcome, horse-laughter, and violent shaking of hands. I do not well know how to describe Dawson. He had not a plebeian and still less a patrician exterior. He looked as if he ought to be a gentleman, and would have called any body out that questioned his title to that appellation, and yet he did not look gentlemanlike, or like the habitual companion of gentlemen. He was vain of his person, and might have once had some grounds for his conceit, but intemperance had bloated and inflamed his face, and injured his figure at the same time. He had naturally good features, but dimmed with passion; the eye alone was originally a bad one —sinister, double, and designing. He dressed flashily, with bright colors, and over-much velvet

and jewelry; strutted when he walked, and talked with a Celto-cockney accent, the tone of the society he kept in England grafted on the brogue of his Irish friends.

Dawson would more gladly have received any other visitor that day than Sydney Spenser. He had no wish to introduce him to either of the gentlemen who were then enjoying the hospitalities of his decayed house. One was a tall, gaunt, muscular man of thirty-five, or forty, in a seedy half-military blue frock, buttoned up to the throat; a black silk stock, or cravat, over which no shirt collar emerged; coarse gray duck, and a very indifferent pair of not very clean boots. When his host presented him as "Major Lamb," he bowed to Sydney in a most ungainly fashion, and smiled in so ghastly a manner that he could hardly have scowled more disagreeably. In fact, Major Lamb looked very like a fellow who you might suppose had been drummed out of the guards, if he had ever been in his majesty's service at all, even with the rank of a sergeant-major. The other guest looked to advantage by his side, and he stood in want of a foil greatly. He was a pale emaciated youth, who had evidently been living on the capital of his health and marrow; he had an aspect at once melancholy and profligate, and was attired in deep black, possibly mourning for some near relation, whose heart he had broken, and end accelerated, by keeping such company as that of Major Lamb and Mr. Dawson.

The first glance at these gentlemen reminded Sydney of Randy Maguire's remark, that "queer people" had been seen of late in Dawson's society; and perhaps Dawson perceived something like surprise and uneasiness in his countenance, for, under pretense of making him change portions of his dress to which the rain had penetrated, he carried him off through a labyrinth of dilapidated corridors up to a bed-chamber, where he accounted in a most satisfactory manner for the presence of the questionable people they had left behind them.

Sydney expressed his regret that he had not found his friend alone, as he had reckoned on.

"I *am* alone," replied Dawson; "you don't take those fellows for friends or guests of mine? one is some sort of a surveyor or valuator, under an order of the coorts, and the other (the poor devil who looks consumptive) is an artist from Dublin, down here sketching the coast—I met him near this, and asked him to dine. I am under the disagreeable necessity of entertaining such people occasionally when I'm at home. You needn't take the slightest notice of them. As soon as dinner's over, they'll probably be off to attend to their business, and then we'll have a cosy evening, my boy."

"All right," said Sydney, whose faults did not include suspicion, "only don't turn the poor devils out such an evening as this on my account."

"Give yourself no trouble about them," said Dawson, "but change your boots—here's a pair of tops of mine that will fit you—and excuse me for a moment, while I give directions to have your sheets aired."

Sydney pulled on the top-boots, and then finding his blue jacket damp, put on a coat of Dawson's, which he found flung on a chair. While he was thus engaged, Dawson flew back to the parlor, very considerately acquainted his guests with the account he had given of them, and prepared them for the part it was necessary for them to act in consequence. He then returned to the bed-room, and reiterated his apologies for having such low fellows at his table under any circumstances.

"Never mind," replied Sydney: "we'll get on very well, depend on it."

Dawson dropped the subject, and commenced admiring his flashy coat on his friend's back.

"That hoonting-coat," he said, "fits you as if it was made for you; it's a little too tight for me, so it's yours, my dear fellow, if you fancy it".

"Thanks," said Sydney, coolly, and surveying himself with great satisfaction in a looking-glass.

The coat thus generously transferred and as liberally accepted was a bright green one, with massive silver buttons—one of the smartest things imaginable—but it required flash manners and green politics to match.

"You are surprised, I suppose," he resumed, as they went down stairs, "to see me on such a day as this?"

"I'm deuced glad to see you; it's a confounded relief to me. You're a darling fellow for coming over in this way."

"The parsonage is so devilish dull in wet weather," said Sydney.

"You'll find it dull enough here, I'm afraid," said Dawson.

"No, I shan't," said Sydney. "We'll smoke, and we'll practice pistol-shooting at the fire-screens in the long drawing-room; we'll get on well enough."

"I hope you have a good appetite," said Dawson, as they reached the parlor, "for you'll have coarse fare, I can tell you; you may suppose I don't treat valuators and strolling artists to French cookery."

"I'm as hungry as a hawk," said young Spenser. And so he was—hungry with the hunger of youth, exercise, and mountain air; and hunger is more concerned about the things *on* the table than critical upon the company *round* it.

It was not the dinner for a man who was at all fastidious; it required the piquant sauce of a keen and a healthy appetite, but with that zest it was excellent. There had been a fish, but it had been disposed of. There remained a corpulent boiled turkey; a dish of mutton-chops, very brown and unctuous; a ham garnished with quartered heads of cabbages, and two great chargers of potatoes—ample provision for a party of four men, though never so pot-valiant. Sydney did ample justice to the viands, and so did the major with the mild surname, so little in harmony with his personal appearance. The young man in black (whose name was Thomson) seemed to have no stomach, except for the fiery port and sherry, the only wines on the table. Dawson kept politely winking at Sydney, as Messieurs Lamb and Thomson evinced every now and then their contempt for many of the little conventionalities of polite society; while at the same time he proved his own superior breeding, by clamorously inviting Sydney to eat, and occasionally blurting out some coarse inquiry about some member or another of the Spenser family. As to the surveyor and painter,

he took little notice of them, and that little in a very lofty and distant way.

The only male attendant was a red-haired slovenly kerne, Terry by name, with a countenance in which savagery and dullness contended for pre-eminence. His dress was a tarnished livery-coat, white turned up with green, with red plush breeches, made for a fellow of twice the height; and he had a villainous trick of wriggling his shoulders as he presented you a plate, or shuffled with the wine round the table. A particularly uncannie and ill-favored old woman, answering to one's idea of the hag of the robber's cave in "Gil Blas,"—and probably the cook—made her appearance at one of the doors more than once during dinner, either to hand in a dish or carry one away; and now and then there seemed to be an interchange of the most virulent abuse between her and the red-headed butler; but it was in Irish, so that its eloquence was lost upon all the company except perhaps Dawson himself, who sometimes swore at the old woman, but took no other step to forbid the colloquy.

Sydney was little of an observer of other men or manners. Even when he had satisfied the desires of nature, he paid less attention to the company than he did to a lank voracious grayhound that was pacing round the table collecting scraps, and to a rifle of Dawson's which stood in a corner of the room.

There was one thing, and one thing only, comfortable in the apartment. It was the fire, which was glorious. The Court of Chancery had exhausted every thing but the bogs on the property, and a capacious grate was filled with a mountain of turf, in a state of triumphant conflagration. The ruddy flame gilded the scanty and damaged furniture (the work of the law-cats), and diffused a glow over the room, which made a young man soon forget the deficiencies of carpets and curtains, though accustomed to Axminsters and chintzes.

The subdued mellow light was exactly the sort of somber yet warm illumination which Dawson would have chosen to set off his professional guests to the best advantage, since he could not well darken the parlor altogether.

The removal of the cloth made an improvement; for it was not spotless, any more than the reputations of some who sat round it. But the next removal was better still: for Messieurs Lamb and Thomson, having finished their dinners, exchanged moody looks, and rising simultaneously, made ungainly obeisances, and left the room, which certainly looked more respectable after their departure.

"Hard work," said Sydney, commiserating the lot of the artist, and the surveyor "under the coorts."

"D—d hard," said Dawson, using the strong word, to which young Spenser had not yet accustomed his lips. But "Rome was not built in a day." Perhaps, in time, Sydney will use strong words as flippantly as his tutor.

Mr. Thomson and the surveyor, however, were not such objects of pity as young Spenser supposed; they only adjourned to a smaller room in a sequestered part of the house, where they soon kindled a good fire with more of the same capital fuel, and made themselves extremely comfortable for the rest of the evening, less by

C

their colloquial resources than by a bountiful provision of that ethereal liquor called mountain-dew, the far-famed vintage of the barony of Innishowen.

As soon as these worthies had retired, said Dawson to his *protégée* and pupil—

"What will you drink, Sydney?"

"No more wine," was Sydney's reply.

"Terry, the black bottle yonder!" Dawson called to his wild butler.

In a few minutes the cold mountain-dew in a black bottle, and the steaming water in a great jug, stood side by side upon the table, flanked with a bowl of sugar and a plate of lemons.

Sydney was just beginning to be familiar with strong liquors as with strong language. However, he had now the excuse of a long wet ride, and probably the contents of the black bottle were purer than those of the decanters. He composed a large glass of punch, and Dawson mingled another, "stiffer" by some degrees, as the phrase goes with punch-drinkers.

"Well, my boy!" cried the host, with hearty emphasis, drawing his chair by one and the same movement nearer both to his friend and the fire, and slapping young Spenser on the knee.

"This is what I call comfort," was Sydney's answer, adjusting his elbows on the arms of his chair, and thrusting out his legs, with the top-boots on, toward the blazing fire.

"Shall we have a cigar, eh?"

"Have you got any of your famous Havannabs?"

Dawson produced a red-leather case from a side-pocket, and extracted a couple of cigars, one of which he presented to his friend, who made an *allumette* of the back of a letter, and lighted first his own cigar, and then Dawson's.

They puffed alternately, and alternately looked at one another in silence, with the mute eloquence of smokers.

Dawson was the first to speak; lowering his cigar, he said—

"I've got good news for you, Sydney; prospects is brightening, my boy."

"I knew that before you told me," said young Spenser.

"How?"

"Randy Maguire rode over with me."

"Oh, indeed, said Dawson; and then added, with a strong expression which need not be repeated, "Sydney, my boy, it was no fault of mine that the tithes due to your father from this property were not settled long ago."

"You need not tell me that," said Sydney.

"There's no man living, Sydney, whom I have the same respect and admiration for, that I have for your father; I swear by his name, so I do. If he only knew what a battle I had with creditors and lawyers, and every body, to have the tithes settled before any other claim against the estate! I was as firm as the Hill of Howth, or I shouldn't have the money to pay Randy Maguire to-morrow morning."

"My father shall know how well you have acted," said Sydney.

"Don't say a word about it," said Dawson, "what's right is right; I only did my duty, and I want no reward, my boy, but the testimony of an approving conscience;—so no more on that head. Sing me something sprightly, now;—have you got any thing new?"

Sydney sang a song that was once popular at the banquets of the Irish volunteers, and which Mr. Crofton Croker has given in his collection

"Love and whisky both
Rejoice an honest fellow," &c., &c.

Dawson either was, or affected to be, in ecstasies at Sydney's performance. It is scarcely possible he could have been sincere, in declaring, as he did, with several oaths, that it far surpassed any singing he had ever heard on the London boards, though he had heard Braham himself. The effrontery is marvelous with which some men can flatter others in the grossest manner to their faces. But then there are people on whom flattery can never be laid too thick to be agreeable; you may lay it on them with trowels; nay, you may shovel it over them; they can bear any weight of it; cartloads of encomium, mountains of compliments, Pelion on Ossa, and Ossa on Olympus. There are gross feeders, or there would not be gross caterers. Dawson knew very well the voracity of Sydney's appetite for praise, but he had other ways of making himself agreeable to his guest beside the fox's trick of commending his voice.

"Now tell me," said he, after some little pause; "tell me something about yourself—have you paid the gunsmith in Letterkenny the ten pounds for the fowling-piece?"

"No," said Sydney, gloomily—Dawson was now coming to the points that he was most concerned about—"but he can wait awhile longer—I'm more uneasy about what I owe *you.*"

"Oh, not a word of that, my boy—light another cigar—no matter if you can never pay me; it can stand over, at any rate, as long as you like; but settle the other matter as soon as you can, for the rogue was saying the other day he'd apply to your father if it wasn't arranged speedily. Small creditors is such harpies."

"I see no way of paying it," said Sydney, with much dejection, "except by applying to my father myself."

"Which I won't hear of your doing; you mustn't be annoying a literary man like him about paltry money matters. I'll see what I can do for you in a few days. It would be pleasanter for you to owe nobody any thing but myself. Between friends it's nothing; but it won't do for a clergyman's son to have tradespeople running after and dunning him for dirty little matters of ten pounds or so. Is there any thing else bothering you?"

"I am sorry to say there is; I owe *your* tailor five guineas for that white bang-up coat, and I owe Amby Hogg, in Redcross, nearly as much more for cigars and gunpowder and sundries. Oh, and there's the brass swivel for the cutter."

"How much did that come to?"

"I don't exactly know; not very much, I suppose."

"Well, altogether it won't break us," said Dawson; "don't make yourself uneasy about the coat—I believe I have worn it as much as you have—but Amby Hogg must get his money, or some of it, for he's a griping rascal, with a dozen hungry brats at his heels, and, if he gets impatient, he'll go badgering your uncle Woodward, who won't think so little of five pounds as you and I do. By-the-by, it's a long time, Syd., since you *did* your uncle for me."

By *doing* his uncle, Dawson did not mean
cheating him, but only taking him off, or mim-
icking him, which Sydney could do capitally.
A very dangerous talent it is, that of mimicry;
it makes enemies and no friends; and, as it is
commonly directed against the gravest and
worthiest characters, those who exercise it
freely, come in time to lose all respect for those
high qualities which they are in the habit of
making sport with for their light companions.
Sydney, however, imitated his uncle's oddities
to the life; and on this occasion he gave an
imitation of Hercules in the pulpit, which threw
Dawson into unaffected raptures.

"Another tumbler, Syd.," he said, after ap-
plauding vehemently.

Sydney declined; he had already taken two—
the first time he had ever made so deep a pota-
tion. "Dudley," he added, warmly, "you are
certainly the best fellow and the best friend in
the world."

"Nonsense, man, nonsense; but what did you
do with Maguire?—take just half a tumbler
more."

"He went to the inn," replied Sydney, yielding
to the sweet temptation, and nearly filling a wine-
glass from the black bottle, while he hummed—

"Love and whisky's joys,
 Let us gayly twist 'em;
 In the thread of life.
 Faith, we can't resist 'em."

"Is Randy as fond of cards as ever?"

"That he is; always carries his soiled old
pack about with him."

"Soiled as they are, I wish we had them; I'd
teach you écarté."

"Send Terry for them," said Sydney; "shall
I pull the bell?"

"Do, if you can," said Dawson, laughing.
The bells of Castle Dawson had ceased to ring
some years back.

He proceeded himself to dispatch the messenger, and found Terry in the room to which
Messieurs Thomson and Lamb absconded so
submissively after dinner. Terry was lying
supine in the middle of the floor, not quite asleep,
yet not exactly wide awake. Thomson was
snoring thunderously upon an old sofa, or settle-
bed; Lamb was sitting doggedly before the
flickering and decaying fire, his arms crossed,
and his red chin reposing on them, looking sur-
prisingly truculent for so tame a profession as
that of a surveyor and valuator. Behind him
was a small deal table, on which stood some
glasses, and what had, a few hours before, been
a bottle of whisky.

"What, now?" demanded Lamb, gruffly.

"It's Terry I want," said Dawson. "Get
up, you lazy good-for-nothing hound," and suiting the act to the word, he gave the recumbent
domestic a kick in the ribs, so violent, that it
made him spring to his legs with an actual howl
of pain and astonishment.

Having thus effectually roused him, he gave
him his commission and returned to Sydney.

"Who's Maguire?" asked Lamb, as Terry
was preparing to obey his orders.

"Randy Maguire, the little ould nosey proc-
thor," said Terry.

"I'll go with you and make his acquaintance,"
said Lamb, seemingly captivated by Terry's
description of Maguire.

"Go without me, Mr. Lamb, honey," said
Terry, "Master Dudley has just kicked the
breath out of me, the d—l's own sweet luck to
him."

Lamb undertook to be Terry's deputy, and
rising from his seat, took down from a peg in
the wall a broad-leaved oil-skin hat, such as
pilots wear, clapped it down over his eyebrows,
wrapped himself in a huge camlet boat-cloak,
and proceeded on his mission, having first, however, further provided himself with an old umbrella, which he found in the hall, and a lantern
which the beldame in the kitchen accommodated
him with. What an envoy to send to the poor
old man, who was as arrant a coward as Acres,
or Sir Andrew Aguecheek, "a coward, a devou
coward, religious in it!"

---

## CHAPTER XV.

MONEY.

" What a god is gold,
 That he is worshipped in a baser temple,
 Than where swine feed?"
 TIMON OF ATHENS.

THE inn where Maguire proceeded to "take
his ease," after parting with young Spenser,
was not much more of an inn than Castle Dawson was of a castle. Randy, however, was in
good luck, both as a collector of rents and of
tithes, for Mr. Branagan, the inn-keeper, paid
him a matter of a few pounds that were due for
a farm he held in the neighborhood, and two or
three other farmers, who chanced to be weather-
bound there that evening, likewise availed themselves of the opportunity to discharge their hold-
ings and their consciences of their debts to their
landlord and the church.

Randy then sat down to his frugal supper.
He was a carnivorous little fellow, when he
was out collecting, and felt himself justified in
exceeding the ordinary bounds within which
poverty confined the ambition of his palate.
Randy was nothing of an epicurean in the primitive and vegetable sense of the term; he had
no objection to a scrag of mutton, or a shin of
beef (the only joints he had much knowledge
of), but his chief delight, as his chief experience, was in the flesh of the unclean beast,
among gammons, and shanks of hams, particularly. He had an extensive acquaintance with
pig's faces, and a pig's foot was one of his dain-
ties. Once in his life he had eaten of a leg of
pork, with the accompaniment of pease pudding. It was in the rector's kitchen, and the
memorable day was registered by the proctor
"among the high-tides in the calendar." This
very evening, he discussed that leg of pork and
pudding over again with Mr. Branagan, and no
doubt the pleasures of memory sweetened the
less delicate meal which was now served up to
him. It was pork, but of what part was a mystery. Randy, however, was hungry, and asked
no questions, but ate of it with as much relish
as if he had been a Turk, or a Jew, with the
sauce of prohibition to make it piquant.

Some of the people in the kitchen, knowing
the old fellow's habits, proposed a game of
cards, while he sipped his grog, but Randy was
wet and weary, and retired that night sooner
than he was wont to do. He was anxious, too,

to be alone with his money. Altogether, when he crept up to his little chamber under the thatch, he had the gratification of counting, smoothing, marking, and otherwise manipulating a sum of between eighty and a hundred pounds in notes of nearly as many different banks, provincial and metropolitan.

The passion for money was illustrated strikingly and curiously in the character of the little tithe-proctor. Randy was remunerated for his services with a fixed salary, and he was scrupulously honest and punctual in making over to his principals all the sums he received; but he delighted inconceivably in the mere act of receiving. The mere sight and touch of the money—the mere flapping of the wings of Plutus passing ever so fleetly over him, gratified his disinterested covetousness inordinately. The uncleanest rag of a bank-note—the filthiest dress that ever filthy lucre wore—a tattered old note, which he was not even to retain possession of, perhaps, for half a day—thrilled with rapture his little yellow palm, made his fingers quiver, and his eyes dance and glitter. So far, his avarice was sensual, almost the only sensual luxury the old man was acquainted with; yet at the same time, was there ever so pure a form of the love of money? For it was not for himself he grasped it; if he was rapacious (and it was only the fear of Mr. Spenser's displeasure that kept him from being a Verres in his line) it was not with the slightest view to his own profit, but simply out of a strong affection for the sight of the paper or the coin itself. Mammon had never a sincerer worshiper. Mammon did little for poor Maguire; housed him poorly, clothed him sparingly, put scarce a pound of flesh on his bones, fed him grudgingly on herrings and potatoes, varied only with eggs and rashers of bacon, supplied his extraordinary length of nose with only a pennyworth of snuff weekly; yet was the devout little old proctor more loyal to his false god, than many a Christian is to the true and bountiful divinity who clothes him in soft raiment, lodges him in a palace, and feeds him daintily thrice a day.

No sooner had he climbed the steep, narrow stair-case, or more properly ladder, which led to his familiar roost than, closing the door, he squatted himself down on a rough-hewn deal chair, over his twinkling farthing candle (a peeled rush dipped in the melted fat of sheep) to reckon out his money, and perform the necessary little operations and tendernesses toward it, previous to vesting it respectfully in the old black-leather case, which (as we have seen) he always carried in a privy pocket wrought into the breast of his coat, on the inner and left side, so as to be as near his heart as possible.

One by one he took up the notes delicately and reverently, as some great scholar and editor in the Vatican might handle a fragment of a lost decade of Livy discovered in a state of extreme decay, dropping to pieces like tinder. Then he very gently smoothed down every piece of bank paper separately; no lady's maid ever handled a berthe of the costliest point more daintily. When every dog-ear was removed, he took from an old pouch, which was also one of his invariable traveling companions, a little short-necked bottle of ink, and the stump of a pen, looking as old as himself, and set about

marking the notes in order, which he did on the upper left corner of each with the initials of his own name in minute cramped characters, placing each as he marked it straight before him, one above another, so as to make a pile which he might afterward sit and contemplate to his soul's content.

He was on the point of completing this labor of love, and was just putting the hieroglyphics to the thirteenth note when there was a step on the creaking ladder, followed almost immediately by a tap at the little door, and Randy said, "Come in;" he had been expecting the maid of the inn, a niece and namesake of his own, to come and arrange his little bed for him, and so certain was he that it was Maggy Maguire who now entered, that he continued his proctorly occupation without looking up from the table.

Dudley Dawson's ill-looking messenger stood glaring at him and his bank-notes, with eyes expressive of a kind of avarice very different from that which constituted Randy's ruling passion. The fellow's imagination probably made the heap of paper look more considerable than in fact it was. He stood glaring fixedly on the little proctor while he marked the fourteenth and fifteenth note, and it was probably the stillness of the room, when he expected to hear Maggy bustling about it, that first made him raise his head. He would have shrieked, had he been less terrified by the apparition that loomed on him. The figure of Lamb was formidable enough of itself, but the dark light of the rush made it still more appalling, and the fellow's head actually nearly touched the ceiling, or the roof, for they were identical. Lamb addressed Randy by name, in what he perhaps considered an amicable tone, but his blandest address was gruff and savage; and it so heightened the proctor's alarm that whatever reply he made, as he huddled up his money, was perfectly inarticulate.

"It's not your bank-notes I'm come for, Mr. Maguire," said Lamb, with a grim smile at the old man's trepidation.

"Who are you?—what do you want?" gibbered the proctor, recovering his speech, and at the same moment crushing up all his paper into a wisp, and thrusting it into the depths of his pocket.

Lamb smiled again in his sinister way.

"I was sent," he said, "by Master Dudley Dawson—"

Directly the name was mentioned, Randy's terror abated, and he saw his visitor in quite another light.

"To settle the arrears," he cried, eagerly; and so excited was he at the prospect of receiving the money, that, without waiting for a reply, he garrulously proclaimed the amount he expected to receive, not leaving the truculent stranger time to mention what his business really was, or to interrupt Randy's revelations, had he been disposed to do so.

When he paused, expecting his grim visitor to rain gold upon him, and learned the trumpery matter about which he came, and that he knew nothing about the arrears until informed by himself, never was a cautious little old man so confounded.

"Why didn't you say that before?" he cried,

with peevish vehemence, and pulling out his pack, he handed it to the demandant with the utmost trepidation, anxious to be relieved as soon as possible from a presence so sinister, and feeling as if the very proximity of a man of Lamb's appearance could not but lessen the number of his bank-notes.

Lamb bid him a surly good-night, as he thrust the cards into his breast, and stumbled under the ladder to return to the castle. Then little Mary Maguire came in for a bit of a scolding. Randy rated his niece roundly for not having given him some notice of the arrival of such an ugly customer, particularly at a moment when he was counting his money.

Mary could tell him nothing about Lamb, and said that nobody in the house could give him much more information; all she knew was that he had very lately made his appearance in the country, and had been observed prowling about the castle and neighborhood. Maguire's thoughts (naturally enough, considering what his vocation was) were all more or less connected with the impost which it was his duty to collect; and every thing about Lamb's appearance suggested and encouraged a suspicion that he was some low itinerant incendiary, who had arrived in this hitherto peaceable district to organize the same system of violent resistance to tithes, which prevailed so extensively in other parts of the island. Then, on the other hand, he appeared to be in the service or employment of Dawson, who was going himself to give, the very next day, so signal a proof of his own determination to support the law and the rights of the clergy. Maguire did not well know what to think, and (after again arranging and fondling his notes) he went to bed in a state of perplexity that made him dream of a great many fearful things, belonging more to the meridian of Thurles than the quiet parish of Redcross. Perhaps his supper of pork had something to do with it.

It was an improving night to Sydney Spenser, for he learned that important branch of useful knowledge and polite education—the game of écarté. After playing for upward of an hour, Dawson ordered the grilled remains of the turkey to be served up. Sydney smoked another cigar, made another libation of the ethereal dew, and then felt nearly as drowsy as if he had taken so much "poppy or mandragora." So soundly did he sleep that night, that he knew nothing of what went on in the house, and had no notion, the next morning, that all its inmates had not been as quiet and well-behaved as himself. It was late when he came down, but Dawson was still later, so that it was just one o'clock when they rose from breakfast, neither having made a meal worth a place in history. Sydney proposed to adjourn with the pistols to the long drawing-room, which was the regular shooting-gallery at Castle Dawson.

"Business before pleasure, my boy," said his exemplary friend; "let us first step down to the inn, pay Mr. Maguire a morning visit, and settle our little account with him. He may, perhaps, be anxious to return home."

"Very well," said Spenser.

They put on their rough coats and water-proof hats, and trudged down the miry grass-grown avenue, Dawson pointing out every mo-

ment some improvement he was on the point of making, a new approach to the house, a belt of wood to be planted, an unsightly wall to be pulled down, or masked with ivy.

They found Maguire on the tenter-hooks of expectation, nervous and fidgety to an extreme. He had been wondering for several hours that he had not been summoned to the castle, and had his receipt ready drawn on the proper stamp, only leaving blanks for the date and his own signature. He thought the happy moment would never come when he should receive the long-pending arrears; and when he descried Dawson and Sydney approaching, he would have jumped for joy, only that he was so old and rheumatic.

"Good-morning to you, Mr. Maguire," said Dawson, in his loud, hearty way, grasping the proctor by the hand.

"Good-morrow, Randy," said Sydney.

"Good-morrow kindly to your honors both," said Maguire, consolidating his acknowledgments.

"Well, Maguire, have you any objection to receive a little money, this morning?" asked Dawson, with a wink at Sydney.

"No, your honor, nor never had," said Randy, with his little laugh.

"Let us to business, then," said Dawson.

Maguire led the way up to the little dormitory, where he had the small deal table (scrupulously washed that morning by his niece) in readiness, with all things needful for the transaction of business. It scarcely occupied five minutes, but there may be enormous bliss as well as enormous suffering in five minutes.

First, down on the table in golden concert chinked six and thirty sovereigns, looking red and almost hot from the mint: had the gold been made into an instrument of music, and had a seraph played on it, the harmony would not have been so sweet to the ear of Maguire. After the chime of the precious metal came the crackling of forty pounds in crisp and maiden paper of the Bank of Ireland, and it would have been hard to determine whether the chink of the bullion, or the sound of the notes were the more melodious. Every passion has its music; love the lute, glory the trumpet, avarice the ringing of coin and the rustle of precious paper. Had Dawson been an Orpheus or a Mozart, he could not have so ravished the ear of old Randy Maguire.

"When do you return, Randy?" asked young Spenser, as he was leaving the room.

"This afternoon, if the weather takes up," replied Randy, "but in the course of to-morrow at all events."

"Perhaps we may travel together again," said Sydney; but Dawson put his veto on that proposition in the most positive manner, not without more than one very unnecessary allusion to the other world, and a certain warm province of it.

Well, if business put pleasure down in the morning, the latter, en revanche, engrossed the rest of the day all to itself. As to Dawson, he seemed almost delirious with excitement. His spirits almost crushed Sydney's. The fire-screens were riddled with pistol-bullets; they played cards and backgammon; they sparred, they leaped, they lunched, and Dawson took a good deal of wine at luncheon. Then, for about half-an-hour, Dawson disappeared, and Sydney occupied himself in the interval with trying on various articles of Dawson's gay and miscellaneous wardrobe. When Dawson re-appeared, they had a bout of fencing, after which they smoked a couple of cigars each; then Sydney shot at a rook on a Scotch fir from one of the parlor windows, with his friend's rifle, and frightened the solitary bird without hurting him, and then—it was near dinner.

A dismal day it was out of doors, and little less bleak within. The rain fell with a melancholy pertinacity, only checked by the sweeping wind. Nothing was visible from the windows of Sydney's room but a wilderness of brown heath and a waste of surly waters. The waves howled sorrowfully along the craggy beach, and thundered in its wave-worn hollows, some of which, from the closeness of the roar, seemed to undermine the house itself. The only question was, whether the sights or the sounds were the most hideous at Castle Dawson. The evening, however, would probably have passed beavily enough, had it been like the preceding one, a tête-à-tête, or a tcat-a-teat, as Mr. Dawson pronounced it. But the dejected artist re-appeared at dinner, and Dawson's agent and man of business, as he called him, a certain Mr. Sharkey, a "special attorney," well known in his profession, arrived unexpectedly from Dublin. This made a pretty quartette ; and after dining, and much smoking and punch-drinking, cards were proposed again, and the game was whist.

At first, Dawson and Mr. Sharkey would only play for amusement, but at Sydney's instance (though he knew almost nothing of the game) they commenced playing sixpenny points. The second rubber the points were shillings. It ended (nobody remembered at whose suggestion) in playing for crowns, and at one o'clock in the morning Sydney rose, having won upward of ten pounds from the pretended artist.

Then there was another fiery supper; more grilled bones, more cigars, more punch; much slang, cock-pit anecdote, and profane swearing. The attorney punned, and repeated his own waggeries at sessions; Dawson vapored about public spirit; Sydney sang bad songs and mimicked good men; and the artist showed a marvelous knowledge of low London life, as if he was the Hogarth of Bethnal-green, or the Wilkie of St. Giles's. Then more cigars, more punch, and to bed without family prayers.

So ended the second day of Sydney's visit. The third was a broken one, for Dawson and Sharkey were called away by sudden business to the county town; Sydney proposed to accompany them; and, as they rode through the village, they found Randy Maguire mounting his little brown hack at the inn-door, to wend his lonely way back to Redcross, full of apprehensions and presentiments of danger; and, in point of fact, although he did his best to argue himself out of his fears, there was only too much ground for entertaining them. At an early hour that morning he had observed two men, whose appearance he disliked, taking the same road he had himself to travel; one of them bore a strong resemblance to his acquaintance of the previous evening, which made him feel exceedingly un-

comfortable, notwithstanding his knowledge that he was a person in Dawson's service. Dawson and Sydney wished the poor little collector a good morning and a safe home, as they passed him, which he returned with such a mournful benediction, and so wistful a look at young Spenser, that the latter could not refrain from lingering a moment behind, to cheer up the old man, and to express his regret that it was not in his power to ride home with him, which he well knew was what Maguire wanted.

"It's only bekase I have so much money about me, Master Sydney," he said, in a very low voice, as if afraid that the very pony should hear the word that had such magic in it.

Sydney had a misgiving that it was wrong to leave the proctor to travel alone under such circumstances, but he had promised to accompany Dawson, so he contented himself with again guaranteeing the perfect safety of the route, and rode forward after his friend. Dawson and Sharkey were both very unsociable; Dawson neither talked himself, nor seemed to wish Sydney to talk to him; he was moody, and seemed to be brooding on some painful and harassing subject. Sydney good-naturedly thought it was, perhaps, the general state of the country that was disturbing him, or that he was pondering deeply on the responsibilities of a member of parliament. At length, however, it occurred to him that it was just possible Dawson might have private business to transact at the place he was going to, and that he would prefer proceeding there unaccompanied by him; so, after about two hours' ride, without the exchange of as many sentences, Sydney pleaded the continuance of a head-ache, with which he had set out, and said he would return to Castle Dawson. Dudley made no opposition, and they separated; but Sydney changed his mind on gaining the village, bethought himself of poor Maguire whom he had before deserted, and not questioning but that he would overtake him in the course of the day, instead of going back to his friend's dreary house, he turned his horse's head toward Redcross, and was soon in the heart of the mountains. He might easily have overtaken the tardy, ill-mounted old proctor, but his horse lost a shoe, so that he was under the necessity of performing the greater part of the journey on foot.

At one moment he was almost on the point of resuming his original intention, for on putting his hand into the pocket where he kept the case of pistols which he had lately been displaying to Maguire he found only one of them in its place. This surprised and vexed him, and he would certainly have returned in search of the missing one had his steed been in traveling order, As it was, he proceeded on his way homeward. soon forgetting his loss, and awakening the echoes of the lonely brown mountains with—

"Bryan O'Linn had no breeches to wear,
So he bought him a sheepskin, and made him a pair,
With the skinny side out, and the woolly side in,
The warmer for that, said Bryan O'Linn."

But now and then he puzzled himself, thinking how the pistol could have been abstracted from the pocket, and repeatedly during that long solitary ride did he recollect, with unpleasant feelings, the faces he had seen under his friend's roof, and even at his table.

## CHAPTER XVI.

### NOCTURNAL DOINGS.

"Light thickens; and the crow
Makes wing to the rooky wood:
Good things of day begin to droop and drowse;
While night's black agents to their prey do rouse."
MACBETH.

It is necessary now that the reader should be informed of the things which were done in Dawson's house on the first night of Sydney Spenser's visit—while he slumbered as deep as a watchman of the old municipal régime, under the combined influence of the mountain air and the mountain dew. We need scarcely say that neither was Mr. Thomson an artist, or the gentleman called Major Lamb a surveyor or valuator. They were profligate acquaintances and instruments of Master Dudley's; and they were now at Castle Dawson for a special purpose, not unconnected with the proceedings in chancery, but one which the chancellor would have by no means approved, had an opportunity been afforded him of giving his judgment upon it.

We must premise that the Dawson property (originally a large one) had been created by Dudley's great-grandfather, in a manner not very uncommon at the period, namely, by a career of successful smuggling, for which the wildness of the coast, and the close proximity of the house to it, afforded every conceivable facility. Such, at least, was the popular belief in the country, and the story was heightened as usual with circumstances of a still more daring and criminal nature; some people going so far as to say that frauds upon the excise were only one source of profit to the founder of the family, who would sometimes evince his hospitality to merchantmen by inviting them on shore, almost under his own windows, with lights put up expressly by himself, and with no expense to the public, at places where the Trinity Board had neglected to erect them. However, all suddenly-raised fortunes are obnoxious to some scandal or another of this kind; certain it was, that in the space of a few years, Mr. Dawson, from a poor became a very rich man; and the glitter of wealth, according to custom, soon blinded people's eyes to the means by which it was amassed, and enabled its possessor to take a place in society commensurate with his fortune. He purchased land, and with the proprietorship of acres, assumed the air of state and importance which acres alone bestow; money, once made, did every thing for him; he married a lady of good family, who added to his estate; he bought a seat in that notorious den of thieves, the Irish House of Commons, which some pleasant politicians are so eager to re-establish; he even discovered that his own family was an ancient and distinguished one, and spent a few thousand pounds in collecting at sales and auctions in both countries a gallery of portraits (some by eminent painters), which served as well to represent his grandfathers and grandmothers, as if they had been painted expressly to commemorate their features.

The story ran that this enterprising gentleman selected his grandfathers by their noses; and whenever he saw or heard of a portrait with what was called "the Dawson nose," which was somewhat cocked up like himself, he purchased, or gave an order to have it secured for him; and

when the picture reached Castle Dawson, it was styled an admiral, a general, an embassador, or a lord mayor, according to the costume in which the figure chanced to be dressed. There were some busts, too, among the family memorials thus oddly collected; and among the number were two which (if you believed your own eyes as well as Mr. Dawson's account of them) established, beyond a doubt, that not only was Mirabeau one of the family, but that it traced its origin and nose to Socrates himself.

The majority of pictures in the Dawson gallery were, as may be imagined, of an order of art not much above sign painting; but there were some portraits of more value than was generally suspected: there were two Vandykes, two Lelys, one by Reynolds, and another supposed to be a Rembrandt. There was also a group of characters by Rubens, including a beauty of enormous development, who might have been passed for Mrs. Woodward's great-grandmother than Mr. Dawson's, only for the decisive circumstance of the *nez retroussé*. The whole collection, however, was soon to be brought to the hammer, under an order of a master in chancery, who, though an old master himself, knew nothing about the old masters of the pencil, and had given no particular directions for the valuation of the pictures by competent judges, nor for their safe custody previous to the sale. Under these circumstances, the idea had occurred to the fertile mind of Sydney Spenser's friend, to turn to his own account the valuable part of the gallery, substituting for it a corresponding quantity of trash, picked up at the old curiosity shops, at the rate of a guinea a portrait. There was also an opportunity for practicing the same little artifice with respect to a few hundred pounds' worth of books, which had been collected by his ancestor, merely on the principle that a great house ought to have something like a library, and that the books ought, at all events, to be superbly bound. Expense had not been spared, so that the books were not only in rich bindings (now indeed damaged by damp and neglect), but some of them rare copies of the works of standard authors; including, for example, a splendid quarto edition of Molière, with finely-executed engravings, which had cost forty guineas, and would now, probably, produce a larger sum. The books to be abstracted were, as well as the pictures, to have their places supplied at a moderate cost; and the business which Dudley Dawson had just now in hand, assisted by Messieurs Lamb and Thomson, was to remove this property clandestinely from the house of his father, and transport it to London, to be there disposed of with the privacy suited to a transaction of so delicate a nature.

No sooner had Dawson assured himself, by applying his ear to the key-hole of Sydney's bed-room door, that his young friend slept profoundly, than he proceeded, with a dim lamp in his hand, to the apartment where his auxiliaries had sequestered themselves, and rousing them from their repose (for it is a mistake to think that rogues don't sleep as well as honest men), summoned them to the work of the night.

"Now, boys," he said, in a low, deep voice, "silence and activity! Follow me!"

The miscreants obeyed, shrugging their shoulders, and knocking against one another, and against the furniture, the room was so gloomy, for there was no light but from the one flickering lamp. Terry had nothing on but his shirt, and his red plush breeches, and was scarcely able to walk, from the effects of the kick he had received from his mild young master in the early part of the evening.

They crept through the passages, not making half the noise which the wind did, whistling through the chinks of the wainscots, and the shattered panes of glass, and slamming distant doors, with that particularly melancholy sound, which writers of ghost stories make such good use of. At the head of a staircase Dawson paused a moment, and held the lamp up to two pictures which hung there. One was the Rembrandt; it was expeditiously unfixed from the wall by the major and Terry, when Dawson took it out of their hands, and carried it down stairs himself, for greater security. In the hall were several of his cock-nosed ancestors, but their descendant treated them with supreme contempt, and passed on to the large dining-parlor, which was not that where Sydney had been entertained. In this room were the marble busts already mentioned, and the rest of the pictures of value; they were taken down with marvelous celerity, and packed, with their frames, in wooden cases which had been provided for them, Dawson looking very sharp to protect the faces of his pretended forefathers from being scratched in the process. The room where the books were was contiguous, and there also stood several strong boxes made expressly to hold those which had previously been selected for embezzlement. The packing of the books occupied more time than the pictures : there were in all four boxes full, and Dawson did this part of the work almost exclusively himself, having probably made himself acquainted with the knack the booksellers have of packing daintily, so as to prevent collision with Russia, or a brush with Morocco. When he came to the splendid edition of Molière, he hesitated for an instant, and then set it aside; his assistants concluded that the book was of little worth, but the fact was, that Dawson reserved it for a judicious present to Mr. Spenser, to whose library he fancied it would be a desirable addition.

The boxes required nailing, but that operation was postponed, out of consideration for Sydney, whose sleep might have been disturbed by it.

Now came the most trying part of the business. Dawson and Lamb being the strongest of the party, undertook the weighty porterage of one of the boxes of books; Thomson and Terry carried a case with the pictures; and then it was that the peculiar subterranean contrivances of Castle Dawson were once more turned to use, and in a manner quite in keeping with their original destination. They were all strong men, except Mr. Thomson, or they could not have done what they did that night. Dawson and Lamb went foremost, with the lamp on the top of the box, and having crossed the hall, they descended a short stair-case which led to the kitchens, and other apartments on the basement story. Few people knew that there was any lower excavation than this, save such as rats or mice might have made to burrow in.

Lamb and Thomson fancied they were going to deposit the booty in some of the ordinary vaults or cellars with which all houses are provided; and in fact it was at the wine-cellar they first halted with their loads.

Hoarse, protracted, and gradually increasing sounds, accompanied with something like the splash of waves, at stated intervals, upon a pebbly beach, were now mournfully audible. Dawson unlocked the door with a thick, short, rusty key. The mournful noise, and the sullen splash, became more distinct.

It was a spacious, desolate vault, with a multitude of compartments; the most of them were quite vacant; the pleasant, profligate fellows, and jovial jobbers of fifty years since had drunk them dry; only a few bins were partially stocked, and but one could be said to be well furnished with wine. The wine, however, was not the present object. The boxes were set down; Dawson scraped away with his feet the thick coating of clay and saw-dust, with which the floor was covered, and presently a trap-door was disclosed to view. It was secured only by a bolt, and when the bolt was drawn, the door opened downward; you saw a ladder descending to unknown depths, and now were fully satisfied that it was the sea itself whose dashing immediately under your feet had for some time been audible. When Thomson, who bore the lamp, lowered it into the opening to examine the rounds of the ladder, the light, faint as it was, probed the obscurity of the cavern, and was visibly reflected in flickering gleams, either by the gushing tide itself, or the bright wet shells and pebbles which the water, retiring with a long-drawn sigh, left behind it.

Not much art, but a good deal of toil, had been required to construct this secret communication with the ocean. A deep fissure in the cliffs, broad enough to admit a small boat at the time of high-water, had been extended by the operation of blasting, so as form something like a subterraneous canal, or the horizontal shaft of a mine, terminating directly beneath the vault where these lawless men were now peering down into it.

Terry was sent down in advance, and scarcely was the splash of his feet heard among the wet shingles, when he raised a howl and an execration, as if Cerberus had bitten him with his three sets of fangs at once. It was not Cerberus, but a huge lobster, which had lost no time in attacking the midnight invader of his retreat. Terry's brogues were none of the slightest, but the angry shell-fish cut one of them clean through, and it was not until after a battle of some minutes that the superior animal, howling and blaspheming all the time like a demon, succeeded in extricating himself from the inferior. Indeed, except that the element was water and not fire, the entire scene was infernal enough; below was the caitiff in red plush struggling with the crustaceous monster; while over-head, straining their eye-balls through the trap to see what was going on, were the faces of Dawson and his knavish companions; Dawson railing and cursing at his unlucky vassal, and menacing him with horse-whips; Lamb witnessing Terry's tortures with the mute and grim delight of an amateur executioner; and Thomson, with his unalterable look of sad and exhausted turpitude, perhaps the most fiendish expression of all.

A boat was secured to a staple in the rock at about an arm's length from the foot of the ladder. It was brought directly under the trap, and the boxes were lowered with ropes into it, Dawson and Lamb placing them so as to let them slide down the latter, and Terry guiding them below, until they were safely lodged in the hull of the boat. Three times did these sons of night go back and forward between the cellar and the great dining-room, until all the boxes and cases were thus mysteriously secreted, preparatory to their being removed to another receptacle known to Dawson, where they were to be shipped off to England at a convenient opportunity. At every return to the cellar, the leader in this piece of midnight villainy knocked off the neck of a bottle of wine with the key of the cellar, to cheer and refresh his comrades, who stood indeed much in want of refreshment, for the job tried the sinews of the party, if it did not sting their consciences. The least guilty was Terry, for he acted merely as a loyal retainer of the Dawson family, and had nothing but kicks for his reward, and the cruel squeeze which the fish gave him. Lamb and Thomson were mercenary accomplices, and had been brought over specially from London to assist in this transaction; not that Dawson could not have found lawless fellows like them nearer home, but that he was already mixed up with them in more than one dark affair, and did not choose to extend unnecessarily the circle of his vicious connections.

It was daylight, but a dim, drizzling morning, when the business was finished, and the four emerged from the basement-story, looking like a low dissolute crew tumbling out of a tavern in Bethnal-green, after a debauch and a boxing-match. Lamb had cut his lip at his last draught from the broken bottle, and his face was not only begrimed with dust, but dabbled with blood, as if he had been at a murder. Thomson and the wretched Terry threw themselves on the naked stone, and the latter was instantly asleep. Dawson crept up to the room where Sydney lay, and assured himself that the seal of repose was still unbroken on his eyelids. Then he descended, and took Lamb aside into a villainous yard, where an old hound was howling in a dilapidated kennel, to give him further directions respecting the embezzled property.

"Very well, Mr. Dawson," said Lamb, after Dawson had concluded, "all that shall be done; and now let me tell you, that both Thomson and myself are of opinion that this job is well worth another hundred pounds."

"A hundred fiddlesticks," said Dawson; "you shall have what we agreed on—not a farthing less, and not a farthing more."

"We must have another hundred," rejoined the major. "We'll not sail for London without the money."

"I wish you may get it," said Dawson, with an irritated laugh. "Come, Lamb, I'll stand no such nonsense; do your duty, and I'll do mine; we ought to know one another well enough by this time." Then he cursed the old hound in the shed, venting on the brute the rancorous feeling excited by his rapacious companion.

"I know you well enough, Mr. Dawson."

"And I know you, Lamb; so no more balderdash. We bargained for fifty pounds and your traveling expenses, and a bargain is a bargain."

The hound continued to whine, and the noise, combined with the whistling of the wind and the bellowing of the waves, made it difficult enough to carry on a conversation. Dawson snatched up a branch of a tree that lay at his feet, and flying at the dog, beat it savagely, in a kind of parenthesis.

"It's a bargain with only one side to it, from this moment," said Lamb, looking diabolical.

So did Dawson after his barbarity to the old dog, but he commanded his temper with the human brute, and said, in a voice comparatively soothing—

"Keep yourself cool, Lamb, and listen to me. I could just as easily pay you ten thousand pounds down at this moment, as the hundred you talk of. The fifty for you is ready; twenty in hard cash, and my note of hand for the remainder. It was no easy matter, under existing circumstances, to raise even the twenty; but it was a point of honor with me to settle partly in cash for this night's job, so I raised the money."

But Lamb was not mollified by this speech.

"And is it also a point of honor with you to pay seventy-six pounds seven shillings and sixpense to Mr. Maguire, the tithe-proctor, to-morrow morning?" he asked, with a fiendish grin.

Dawson's face, red at all times, grew crimson with surprise and rage; then it turned to a livid purple, as he demanded what Lamb meant by his question.

"I mean just what I say," replied the major. "Is it a point of honor with you to pay a rascally proctor, when you can't settle an honest account with a friend?—that's a plain question, Mr. Dawson."

"What the fiend is it to you," cried the other, "what I pay Mr. Maguire or any body else, or whether it is tithe or not?"

"Just this, Mr. Dudley Dawson—that if there's money for the parson, there's money for hard-working men like us;—ours is the prior claim."

"We'll see," retorted Dawson, fiercely and doggedly.

"We will," echoed Lamb, in the same determined way.

"If another guinea would save you and that consumptive varlet snoring in the hall from Tyburn, or a worse place, you should not have it from me," cried Dawson.

Lamb was silent for one moment—it was a moment of rapid, deep, and atrocious meditation.

"Mark what I say," he said, in a hoarse, resolute growl, approaching his companion as he spoke, and thrusting his ill-favored and bleeding face close to his ear, "if we don't get something handsome out of you, we'll manage to get it out of Mr. Maguire."

Dawson regarded him with an eye of fierce scrutiny, and demanded what he meant.

"Coax it out of him," said Lamb, with his atrocious smile; and then added, in a whisper between his teeth, "it wouldn't be a much worse job than we have just been doing, Mr. Dawson."

Dawson's countenance assumed an expression

difficult to understand. It was not approval of Lamb's suggestion, and still less was it horror at it. Perhaps he thought it not worth an observation. However, no more was said. Lamb seemed to abandon his attempt to extort more money from his employer, who seemed, upon his side, glad to have the conference over; and indeed they both wanted some repose after such an extraordinary amount of physical exertion.

# BOOK IV.

## CHAPTER XVII.

### THE FLOOD.

' There is sure another flood toward, and
This couple is coming to the ark."
                                    As You Like It

RETURN we now to the parsonage, which we left with a hurricane blowing, but with very little idea that it was destined to blow one of the rector's daughters a husband. It is pleasant to go back to the haunts of civilization after passing a couple of days at Castle Dawson, and it is agreeable also to mix the proceedings of grim ill-favored men with the doings of women like Arabella and Elizabeth Spenser.

We have mentioned the rudely constructed wooden bridge across the upper and narrow part of the estuary, at a distance of some two or three miles from the residence of the Spensers. For ordinarily rough weather this structure was sufficiently firm; but it proved unequal to withstand the violence of the storm that now raged, with an additional strain of an enormously increased volume of water, partly produced by three days' incessant rain in the mountains, partly by the influx from the ocean under the action of a furious west wind. About five o'clock in the afternoon, on the third day of the storm, the bridge gave way, and in a very few minutes scarce a plank remained to show where it had once stood.

The shooting-lodge of Mr. Spenser's friend, Lord Bonham, was situated about five miles to the north of the parsonage, in the heart of the mountains, an extremely beautiful wild spot, to which the Spensers sometimes made excursions and pic-nic parties with the Woodwards and other neighbors. There was, at the time we speak of, but one practicable and that a very circuitous route, between the lodge and the village of Redcross, and this depended upon the wooden bridge, and was totally interrupted by its destruction. Two gentlemen, one well mounted and attended by a servant, with a good horse under him likewise, the other riding a stout black pony (one of the same breed as Mr. Woodward's), were the first to discover, to their extreme inconvenience and distress, the havoc occasioned by the flood. The party was coming from the lodge, and proceeding southward, intending to dine at a house in the neighborhood of Redcross, and remain there until the weather should clear up. They had had a long, rough ride, and had been comforting themselves for the last half hour by talking of the good table, and the excellent bottle of wine, they expected to bait for the evening. The rider of the black pony was Lord Bonham's agent, a fat, short,

round, red-faced, fidgety little man, with a white hat, a heavy brown coat, and a shawl like a woman's wrapped round his throat, burying half of his amusing physiognomy. He looked, however (as far as the play of his features was visible), excessively agitated and dismayed, on reaching the place where the bridge, to his personal knowledge, had stood only the day before. Surprise seemed to have deprived him of the power of speech, but his companion (a tall man, under thirty, with a showy figure, and gentleman-like appearance, though his air was a little arrogant), exclaimed in a dry, high-pitched voice—

"I say, Trundle, where's the bridge?—I see no bridge, Trundle."

"Nor I, Colonel Dabzac," replied the gentleman addressed, looking comically dismal, and gazing ruefully on the surging and triumphing waters, "all I know is that it was there at six o'clock yesterday, or we should not be on this side now; it's an extremely ugly business, that I can tell you, colonel."

"What's to be done? that's the question. Trundle, you know the country—I don't—are you sure we are at the right point? Is there another road?"

"No road that I am acquainted with but this —no other road to Redcross."

"We must swim for it, I suppose," said the colonel.

"One thing is certain," said the other, "we shall not reach our friends in time for dinner, to-day; I doubt, indeed, if we shall dine at all, without returning to the lodge."

"Which I positively won't do, Mr. Trundle."

"Then, colonel, we have no alternative but to turn to the right and go to Mr. Spenser's."

"That — Whig parson!"—the reader will excuse us for not recording the epithet used by the colonel.

"Then we must either go back all the way to Bonham Lodge, or stay here all night.—The parson has got two handsome daughters, I can tell you that, colonel."

"Has he a good cook?—that's more to the point," replied the other; "however, any port in a storm—en avant, Mr. Trundle; it's getting late; we had better ride hard, or we'll come in for the cold shoulder."

Without waiting for a reply, the colonel set off at a fast trot, and the pony that Trundle rode did its best to go at the same pace, very much to the grievance of his pursy rider, who had not been so long on horseback for several years, and was already uncomfortable enough in his saddle, beside being very embarrassed by a huge roll he was carrying, like a map or survey; and, in point of fact, it was one. Fain would he have remonstrated with his hardier comrade, but the blustering wind, which blew right in his teeth, took away his breath, or prevented the complaints which he tried to gasp forth, from reaching the colonel's ear. It was all in vain to pull in the obstinate pony; poor Trundle, sadly embarrassed by his enormous map, tugged hard at the reins to restrain a speed so adverse to his personal ease, but the beast had the spirit of competition which the man wanted, and seemed perfectly to understand the gestures of Dabzac, who looked back over his shoulder at intervals to see that his friend was not losing ground.

The colonel, however, was obliged to slacken his pace before long, owing to the steepness and roughness of the road, if road it might be called. This enabled Trundle, or rather the pony, to rejoin him; and then it was highly diverting to observe the little round man's physiognomy, as he received the compliments of his companion upon his admirable seat (the sorest subject Dabzac could have hit on), and the merits of an animal, whose only demerit in the eyes of its owner was the stubborn speed at which he insisted on going. The pause was but momentary; the road grew level again, and the colonel, intent on his dinner, pushed forward, the pony again accepting the challenge, and Mr. Trundle in vain endeavoring to call attention to the beauties of the stormy sunset, and its effects upon the ruins of the Black Castle, at which they were now arrived. No man living cared less for sunsets, or ruins, or any thing picturesque and romantic than he did; but he thought to induce his impetuous friend to slacken his pace a little, either not knowing or not reflecting that Dabzac was quite as little sensitive to the charms of scenery as he was himself.

Arabella and Elizabeth Spenser were standing at a window in the library, contemplating the weather-beaten shrubs and down-trod roses, when the two horsemen, such contrasts in all respects, came trotting up to the parsonage, drenched with rain, and bespattered with all the various soils of the country, so that an agricultural chemist could have inferred the rural produce of Donegal from an observation of the state of their boots. Such arrivals create a lively sensation at quiet glebe houses, particularly in such dreary weather. The person of the colonel was not unknown to Arabella, for she remembered having once danced with him at a country ball. Both girls, however, recognized Mr. Trundle instantly, even under the cumbrous disguise of his huge brown coat, and the cotton shawl that enveloped his face. A groan escaped from Elizabeth, which of itself was sufficient to intimate that a more agreeable guest could easily have presented himself. One likes to hear a pretty woman groan, when it is not the expression of actual pain or misery. Elizabeth Spenser groaned charmingly. Why she groaned now will appear very shortly.

Mr. Spenser, who was sitting with his wife, recognized Dabzac directly he saw him, and there were not many men in Ireland whom he would not have more willingly received into his house, for Dabzac belonged to a class for whom, both socially and politically, the rector, having strong Whig prejudices, entertained a decided dislike, the high Tory magnates of Ulster, who, at the period of our story, had not had their crests lowered by the repeated victories of the demagogue, and the triumphs of the popular cause. Such social prejudices, sometimes even amounting to antipathies, were prevalent in Ireland at the time we speak of; they were the growth of laws and systems which, with a few exceptions, have been wisely abandoned, and were themselves irresistible arguments for the abandonment of them.

Mr. Spenser, indeed, had not much reason to be pleased with either of the gentlemen who took refuge under his roof that tempestuous evening. Mr. Trundle, though not formidable in the way the colonel was, was, perhaps, the more formidable of the two. The little round red-faced man was one of the numerous troublesome, self-opinionated, but well-meaning personages, who at the period of our story, had their heads stuffed with projects of all kinds for the improvement of Ireland, and could talk of nothing but the crotchet uppermost at the moment, utterly disregarding fitness of time or place, or the tastes and temper of the company. Now it was the reclaiming of bogs; now the draining of lakes; now mines; now canals; now a scheme of colonization; "every thing in turn and nothing long;" but the plan of the moment was always, of course, the only plan to save the country. As to Mr. Trundle, he had only just abandoned a desperate undertaking against the great bog of Allen, and was now enthusiastically engaged in a terrible design against Loch Foyle and Loch Swilly; mad on the subject himself, and driving every body mad who had the misfortune to encounter him.

The reader will now easily comprehend why Elizabeth Spenser groaned when she saw this gentleman approach the parsonage, with the huge roll in his hand, of which she guessed the nature only too correctly. The groan, indeed, was more on her father's account than her own. The never-failing placidity and benevolence of Mr. Spenser particularly exposed him to bores of every kind, just as a jar of honey attracts wasps, or a sugar bowl on a sunny breakfast-table gathers all the buzzing and droning things in the room about it.

Mr. Trundle introduced his friend the colonel, and Mr. Spenser and his daughters received them with a gracious hospitality which made Dabzac instantly feel that he was the guest of people of refinement, whether of the right sort or not. The colonel's servant had carried a small portmanteau, containing a change of clothes and a dressing-case, but the agent was utterly unprovided, so that Mr. Spenser had to accommodate him with one of his own black suits, in which, when he re-appeared in the drawing-room, he cut a singular figure; the skirts of the coat sweeping the floor, while the tightness of the body gave it almost the stringency of a straight waistcoat, an article of dress (by the way) which many thought that Mr. Trundle should have been provided with long ago. While Colonel Dabzac was indulging a sort of dull, dry facetiousness he had, at the expense of his traveling companion, dinner was announced; and then the struggles and fidgetings of the little agent, in the act of presenting his arm to Elizabeth, were so ludicrous that it was with no small difficulty she concealed from him how much he amused her.

---

## CHAPTER XVIII.

### IMPROVEMENT OF IRELAND.

"*Dogberry.* Truly, for mine own part, if I were as tedious as a king, I could find in my heart to bestow it all on your worship.
"*Leonato.* All thy tediousness on me!—ha!
"*Dogb.* Yea, an 'twere a thousand times more than it is."

                 MUCH ADO ABOUT NOTHING.

It was a momentous occurrence in the lives of both Miss Spenser and Colonel Dabzac, the carrying away of that wooden bridge. The colonel was too busy, however, losing his appetite to lose his heart that day to any lady in the land. But Arabella from the first (although, perhaps, nobody noticed it), regarded him with an eye of favor; and it was not for Mr. Trundle that she came down to dinner, dressed with more than usual care and elegance. She liked his height, his whiskers, his name, his fortune; she had no objection either to his pomposity or his politics; and of all things, she liked his title of colonel.

However, he was a colonel little more than nominally, or figuratively, for he was not an officer in the king's army, but only a lieutenant-colonel in the Londonderry militia, a corps which he had never seen, and which had probably only an existence on paper, just enough to allow some twenty or thirty country gentlemen to give themselves ridiculous martial airs, and swagger in scarlet coats at a Lord-Lieutenant's levees.

As to Arabella, she was just the girl to captivate a man like Dabzac, whose heart, like her own, was a mere animal organ: whose tastes, like hers, were intrinsically vulgar; and whose eye, like hers also, was one of those that are fascinated more by an epaulette, or a livery than by the most glorious prospect in nature.

Miss Spenser, indeed, possessed every charm that could make a woman attractive to an unintellectual, unsentimental man. There was, in fact, only one thing against her—she was the daughter of a Whig parson!

Mr. Spenser was a Whig, and a zealous one; but his politics and his profession were kept totally apart. He never attended political meetings, and scrupulously abstained from the remotest reference to political events, questions, or principles, either in his sermons, or in his pastoral intercourse with his parishioners; but he was not without the natural wish to propagate his opinions, and he did so quietly with his pen, sometimes in a pamphlet, sometimes in the *Edinburgh Review*, or some other liberal periodical. These productions, of course, were anonymous, but known to be his in the literary and political circles. Occasionally, however, he amused himself with essay-writing upon lighter subjects, and his desk contained many pleasant papers, or fragments of papers, which he would now and then read for the entertainment of his daughters, or a few of his friends. As to allowing politics to interfere with the kindly relations of private life, it was utterly foreign to Mr. Spenser's character; and the best proof of this was the fact, that his curate and brother-

in-law, Mr. Woodward, was the most resolute anti-Catholic in all Ireland, the most redoubted champion of Protestant ascendency in church and state, and yet they lived (for it was equally creditable to both) on terms of the most cordial and brotherly affection, having a good-humored battle occasionally about Mr. O'Connell's proceedings, or one of Lord Plunket's speeches, but the same hearty good friends after the engagement as before it. Still, there were certain people who would not or could not differ temperately and politely with a man of the rector's liberal views—people who asserted what they called their Protestant principles in an intolerant, domineering way, that was most offensive to Mr. Spenser; and the Dabzac family, and their connections, were of the number. When he met these people in society, he studiously avoided collision with their prejudices; he knew how useless it is to reason with passion and self-interest, and he never attempted it; but he had no objection to argue a little with a man like Woodward, who, though a bigot on a few points, was a bluff, conscientious, and most good-natured one.

Probably Dabzac expected that the Whig parson would talk nothing but Whiggery all day long; if so, he was agreeably disappointed, for Mr. Spenser never once quoted the *Edinburgh Review*, or mentioned the name of Charles James Fox; nay more, Dabzac might have been under his roof for a month and never have heard a syllable from him upon any of those subjects, or upon politics at all, except in the most general way, or respecting some point upon which politicians of all creeds were pretty nearly of the same opinion; and even in such a case, lightly and almost playfully, without the least approach to vehemence or argumentation. Then, bad as Mr. Spenser's Whiggery may have been, his wine was good, and Colonel Dabzac was enough of a liberal to drink and enjoy a bottle of old claret, although bought from a Catholic wine-merchant, besides being the produce of a Catholic country.

But, indeed, as to that day's conversation, neither Mr. Spenser nor Colonel Dabzac had much share in it, for the ardent Mr. Trundle, albeit not very easy after his ride, and any thing but comfortable in the rector's coat, soon engrossed all the talk to himself; and, of course, his theme was the improvement of Ireland, for he had only the one arrow in his quiver. Mr. Trundle was the most zealous, indefatigable, benevolent busy-body in the world; as in shape he was not unlike a humming top, so the tone of his voice was not unlike the sound of that monotonous toy, when it spins on the nursery-floor. Before he finished his soup, the "hideous hum" commenced; it was all about a meeting, ever so great, that was to be held somewhere the following week, for the purpose of considering his magnificent scheme for a ship-canal between Loch Foyle and Loch Swilly, as the basis of a wonderful system of inland navigation, absolutely essential to the prosperity of Ireland; indeed the only chance she had of escaping "everlasting redemption," as *Dogberry* says.

"I must prevail on you," he said, in a tone of voice amusingly insinuating, with occasionally a forcible-feeble emphasis on his words, "to sign our monster petition, at all events, Mr. Spenser,

and *our address to the Crown*—the most important document that was ever drawn up in Ireland—I drew it up myself—strong but *moderate*
—I am always for moderation, but *I speak out*—
all we want from the government is thirty millions sterling—we don't ask more, and we won't
take *one farthing less.* And I must have the
ladies, too. I can't do without the ladies. The
ladies must join us. A long pull, a strong pull,
and a pull altogether, as I said the other day in
Derry—I did, indeed, Miss Spenser."

Elizabeth endeavored to express, by her looks,
her admiration of Mr. Trundle's eloquence at
Derry; encouraged by the smile, the humming-
top instantly resumed.

"It will bring back our absentees—it will
give employment to *two millions of our poor suf-*
*fering countrymen*—nothing else will ever do it.
I don't want organic changes. I don't want
revolution—I told them so at Derry. I only
want *thirty millions sterling*, for the improvement of our inland navigation. Now, Mr. Spenser, won't you support me ?"

"Thirty millions is a great deal of money,"
said Mr. Spenser, very much at a loss what to
reply.

"A mere trifle. What signifies thirty millions, or sixty, to the British Treasury ?  And
so I took leave to tell the Chancellor of the Exchequer in a letter I addressed to him last year,
to get a little assistance for our General-Lake-
Drainage Company. I want the nobility and
gentry of Ireland to *put their heads together* and
get something for my unhappy country. Is that
unreasonable, Mr. Spenser ?"

"I would rather see them put their *hands* together and *do* something for her," said Mr. Spenser, very quietly.

"We are too poor to do any thing for ourselves; we must get the sinews of war from
John Bull; we must get the thirty millions.
Only give me the thirty millions," persisted Mr.
Trundle, as persuasively as if Mr. Spenser had
the money in his pocket for him at the moment.

"Irish independence would do much more for
the country than English money," said Mr. Spenser, but said it to himself—he was afraid to utter so bold a proposition above his breath, for
fear of exciting Dabzac, who was a fair representative of that class of Irish landlords, who
only "put their heads together" to devise the
means of evading their duties, and only use their
hands to dip them into English pockets.

How charmingly the remainder of the evening
passed, we leave the reader to conceive. Miss
Spenser, indeed, and Colonel Dabzac seemed to
have some agreeable chat; but the rector and
his second daughter had not one moment's respite from Mr. Trundle, and his thousand and
one projects—canals, bogs, fisheries, colonies,
and small-loan funds; quotations from his letters
and pamphlets; abstracts of his speeches, petitions, and correspondence with London and Dublin officials; for he was the plague alike of the
Treasury in London and the Castle in Dublin,
and had made more than one Irish Secretary
think seriously of resigning his office.

Providentially at length the colonel, being
very much fatigued, gave unequivocal symptoms of somnolency, so that Mr. Spenser had
an opportunity of suggesting an early move

bed-wards, which according took place, after
an exchange of the usual drowsy civilities.

"Oh, papa," cried Elizabeth, when her father
returned to the drawing-room, after having conducted his guests to their chambers, "what will
become of us, if the weather does not soon
mend ?  My poor papa !—and you to preach on
Sunday !"

"The bridge ought to have stood just ten
minutes longer," said Mr. Spenser, with Christian resignation.

The girls kissed their father and retired;
Elizabeth meditating how to take the whole
weight of Mr. Trundle on her own shoulders the
next day, or at least diminish the burden to her
father as much as possible. As the girls passed the little round agent's door, they distinctly
heard him humming to himself about Loch
Swilly, for want of somebody else to hum to.
It was (as Mr. Spenser observed the next day) ·
a capital illustration of that bitter curse of *Ther-*
*sites*—"Thyself upon thyself !"

---

## CHAPTER XIX.

### THE ROBBERY.

"Wherein I spoke of most disastrous chances,
Of moving accidents by flood and field."
                                        OTHELLO.

AT eleven o'clock that night the parsonage
was profoundly still, all its inmates (except
Lucy and Rebecca, still reading "Clarissa")
either sleeping or retired to their beds, and
courting repose, if not enjoying it. The gale
was abated, but the rain came down in only
more impetuous torrents. Half an hour later,
Mr. Spenser, who was a light sleeper (probably
having been cured by his wife of the habit of
deep slumber), was awakened by sounds very
unusual at such an hour—the tramping of horses'
feet, human voices, and then the sharp ringing
of a bell. His first idea was, that this untimely
hubbub was occasioned by the return of his son,
and under this impression he made no movement to rise. The domestics had evidently been
roused, for he could distinguish the unlocking
and unbolting of the house-door, and instantly
afterward heard the same voices again, but
louder and more distinct. In a few seconds
there was a quick step on the stairs, and a tap
at the door of his bed-room. He jumped up,
and found a half-dressed servant with a lantern,
who, in a state of excitement, with a countenance pale with alarm, informed him that the
arrivals were Mr. Woodward and Mr. Maguire,
the tithe-proctor, and that the latter had been
robbed and half-murdered.

With an exclamation of astonishment and horror, Mr. Spenser threw on his dressing-gown,
and rushed down stairs, where he found that
part of the story was only too true; the worst
part, however, being happily so much exaggerated, that there was the little old man himself
to tell his tale, only not yet recovered enough
from his fright to relate his adventures very correctly. However, *there* he was, to vouch for the
fact of his having been robbed; and there was
the athletic curate at his side, to verify the statement. Both were in a melancholy pickle, between rain and mire, though only the proctor

had sustained any personal injury, and that was nothing affecting life or limb.

Maguire had been attacked by footpads, and the scene of the outrage had been the Black Castle, the spot which he had so often in his life passed in safety, but never without some apprehension or presentiment of danger. There it was that Randy Maguire, returning from Castle Dawson, and urging his little hack as fast as he could make it trot, past a locality so black and ominous, was set upon, flung from his saddle, rolled upon the road, and robbed of the old black-leather pocket-book, containing all his bank-notes, and also of the little bag in which he had bestowed the thirty new sovereigns in which Mr. Dawson had paid him part of the arrears. This was nearly all Maguire knew about the matter; the state of his clothes bore unquestionable testimony to a liberal rolling in the loose yellow soil of the country, but a scratch on the temple, with one or two not very serious bruises on the ribs, were the extent of his bodily damages. Oddly enough, his nose escaped scot free, though it seemed to project from his face, as it were, expressly to bear the brunt of whatever blows or damages were going. We have now to explain how the curate came to be involved in the events of a night, which in the regular course of events, he ought to have passed in his own house like a peaceable man and a good husband. He had been in the hills during the morning, on an expedition of charity, half pastoral, half medical, to visit the mother of one of his servants, an aged widow, who had been suffering with a rheumatism almost as old as herself. To gain the spot in the mountains where the poor woman lived, he had been obliged to cross the wooden bridge, which he reckoned upon regaining at about five o'clock; and from thence a short hour, with those seven-leagued boots of his, would bring him to the "dulce domum." He arrived at the bridge, or rather the place where the bridge was not, about half an hour later than Colonel Dabzac and Mr. Trundle, and found himself, of course, in exactly the same perplexity. He must either return to the parsonage, abandoning the notion of reaching home that night, or try a shallow place higher up, which Mr. Trundle had not thought of, and which might chance to be still passable without much hazard, as enormous blocks of stone had been placed there for such travelers on foot as were nimble enough to jump over the ugly watery chasms between them. His homeward yearnings, always vigorous, made him choose the latter course, but when he gained the point where he hoped to cross, not a stone was to be seen; the water swelled and roared over the highest and hugest of the blocks, leaving him no alternative but to direct his steps (now not quite so brisk as before) all the weary way to the house of his brother-in-law. It was indeed a severe march in such rain, accoutered so heavily as he was, with a club like that of his namesake, and a coat probably as ponderous as the skin of the Nemean lion. But the greatest weight was the weight on his mind, thinking what Carry would be suffering. The watery moon yielded a dim and uncertain light, but the curate, accustomed to nocturnal walking, could see the objects before and around him distinctly enough to discover any thing unusual, or suspicious, should any thing be stirring which ought not to be stirring at the place and season. The ruins, owing to the winding of the road, were not visible until he came quite close to them. A sharp turn disclosed them suddenly to his view, and two objects immediately arrested Woodward's attention; one was a faint twinkling light through an orifice or loophole in the dilapidated building; the other a figure on horseback, about fifty yards in advance of him on the road, apparently just emerging from the shadow of the ruins. The next instant two fellows sprang out of them, rushed at the man on horseback, who rolled on the road, with one of his assailants over him. Woodward had no doubt about the character of the transaction. He rushed forward, brandishing his cudgel, and had the gratification of saluting one of the miscreants with so hearty a thwack, that the stick was fractured by the blow, and perhaps the bones it encountered were not more fortunate. That was matter for conjecture, for the fellow escaped into the ruins notwithstanding, and Hercules, instead of pursuing him, ran shouting to the aid of the assaulted traveler. Damaged as his club was, it would probably have given a second proof of its strength and toughness upon the person of the other footpad, had he waited the curate's onslaught; which, however, he did not, but effected his retreat to the same asylum with his comrade, only to another corner of it. The first impulse of the brave clergyman was to pursue; but a moment's reflection convinced him of the rashness of doing so, weaponless as he was, while the robbers were probably provided with fire-arms, although, as yet, they had not thought proper to use them. When he first stooped down over the prostrate man, he concluded he was on the point of death, he moaned and gasped in so grievous a manner. Hercules elevated his head, and turning it so as to let such light as there was fall on the face, was equally distressed and astonished to ascertain (which he did at once by the features, particularly the nose, which was unmistakable) that it was the tithe-proctor. Although the poor old fellow was more frightened than hurt, it took the curate a considerable time before he could get him on his legs, and quiet the agitation of his nerves, which shook so, that you could almost hear them vibrate. Woodward often said that he never in his life saw any thing so humorously tragical as the face of Maguire, when, thrusting his hand convulsively into an inside pocket, he discovered that he had saved his life but lost his treasure. He fell back on the road in extremity of mental agony, and would probably have lain there till morning, had not the curate reminded him that the bandits were probably still within a stone's throw, and might possibly renew their attack. This succeeded;—the little proctor suffered his gigantic champion to raise him to his legs; at some short distance they found the horse quietly nibbling the short mountain-grass, as if nothing extraordinary had occurred; Mr. Woodward helped Maguire to mount, and they ultimately gained the parsonage in the manner already described.

Mr. Spenser, after listening in mute astonishment to all these painful details, conducted Hercules to a spare bed-room on the ground floor, and the servants took charge of the maltreated and still quaking proctor. Hercules (fairly exhausted by the incredible toils of the day) slept powerfully, as he did every thing, though still disturbed by thinking of his wife's anxieties, and all the unpleasant events of the night. The loss of so large a sum of money was too grave a matter to Mr. Spenser not to affect his repose very seriously. In strictness, it was true that his proctor (or his security) was liable to make good the sum lost; but the idea of enforcing his strict rights under such circumstances never occurred to the benevolent rector; and it would probably not have been very easy to enforce them, had he been so harshly disposed, the proctor being a very poor man, and his security a still poorer one! But there were other reasons stronger than the pecuniary ones that made Mr. Spenser feel extremely uncomfortable, in consequence of what had occurred.

At an early hour the following morning Hercules rose, literally "a giant refreshed," and made his way to the bed-side of his brother-in-law.

"This is a bad affair, Val.," said the curate.

"Very bad indeed," said the rector, raising himself on his elbow. "It is not altogether the loss, although I shall feel that, too, but to think of a crime like this being committed in our peaceful neighborhood, a quiet pastoral parish like this!"

"I know this country longer than you do, Val.," said Woodward, "and my father knew it before me. The robbery of last night is probably the only outrage of the kind that has been perpetrated for the last hundred years, not only in this parish, but in this barony. Indeed, it is the first case I ever heard of in all Ireland, of a tithe-proctor being robbed. They cut off their ears and noses, and make them eat their applotments, but they never rob them."

"Mrs. Spenser will never consent to live here after this," said the rector, despondingly; now touching the point that agitated him most, and paying little attention to the curate's *resumé* of the attentions usually paid to proctors.

"Fudge!" said the curate. "Fudge!"

"I know her better than you do," said Mr. Spenser.

"Keep it secret, then," said Hercules.

"A very good suggestion," said the rector. "I shall act upon it."

Concealment seemed not very difficult, as it was still early, and only one servant had been roused by the nocturnal disturbance. As to Maguire, he was still in his bed, and not likely very soon to leave it.

"Let us go to him," said Mr. Spenser; "he may stand in need of some of your medical skill. I only cure the soul; you cure both soul and body, Hercules."

"I'm a great hand at a bruise," replied Woodward, "and I've treated a simple fracture before now—but if there's any thing worse, I'll leave it to Wilkins."

Between his robbery and his rheumatism, his bandaged forehead and his bizarre nose, his short cough and his deep groans, there was never such an odd patient as little Randy Maguire; and the oddity of the patient was well matched by the oddity of the doctor. The rector forgot his losses in the diverting contemplation of his curate and his proctor, as the former, with his great hand, manipulated the other from head to foot, in search of breakages, and Randy squeaked, and in vain remonstrated, under the tentative process.

"No fractures," said Hercules, at length, desisting from his painful investigation, "but a good many bruises."

"I should think so," said the rector gravely, and no doubt implying that it could not well be otherwise, after the squeezing poor Randy had undergone in the vice of the curate's fist.

When his pains subsided a little, Maguire gave a prolix account of his adventures; but he concealed almost the only particulars which could have afforded a clew to the discovery of the criminals, being unwilling to mention the pack of cards, as his inveterate gambling propensities had frequently brought down upon him the censure of both the clergymen, particularly the curate, a lecture from whom was a serious affair. Besides, Randy could not have told the whole truth on the subject, without involving Sydney, in some degree, as well as himself, which the proctor thought would neither be discreet nor handsome. He mentioned, however, the fact (of which the rector had not been aware before) that Sydney had been his companion on his journey to Castle Dawson, and bitterly lamented that he had not had the advantage of his protection on his return also. The rector expressed the same regret, and with a wonderful display of parental solicitude, put some questions to Maguire respecting his son, which the old man answered to the best of his knowledge.

Sydney was at that moment in the house, and in his bed, having returned about daybreak, without the cognizance of any of the family, save Lucy and Rebecca, the latter of whom observed him entering his chamber, as she was stealing back to her own, after the night's reading was over.

"Let us now go to breakfast," said Mr. Spenser to his brother-in-law. Hercules obeyed with alacrity; but, before he left the room, he directed the servant who was in attendance to apply some brown paper, steeped in brandy, to the proctor's temples.

"He will probably roar like a bull," said the curate, "but never mind—apply the paper."

---

## CHAPTER XX.

### BREAKFAST.

"The love of woman is a tricksy spirit,
As full of arts and wiles as hate itself,
Deep plots to please, or subtle schemes to save us,
Still practicing some kindly stratagem,
Or setting some fond snare."
NEW PLAY.

RAIN, rain, still rain—we are in for another day of it, beyond all question. It certainly did rain enormously in these Donegal mountains, and at the parsonage particularly, when it set about it. The very trout in the streams got too much of it. Down it came, doggedly, and wickedly, in a forest of small water-spouts, as if the Atlantic were hung up in the air to give the island a douche-bath. Three drops of the Redcross rain was enough to wet a middle-sized man to the skin. The country-people were proud of it, as people always find something to be proud of—even their faults, or their misfortunes, sooner than be proud of nothing.

Think of another day of Mr. Trundle, his ship-canal, Loch Swilly, and the thirty millions! Mr. Spenser, indeed, had now sufficient to distract his mind without Mr. Trundle and the improvement of Ireland. Of this, however, his daughter Elizabeth knew nothing; so she came down to breakfast that morning full, of a notable artifice to deliver her father from the fangs of his tormentor, who was already diligently studying his map to prepare himself to re-commence with effect the assault of the preceding evening.

"Mr. Trundle," she said, motioning him to sit beside her on a sofa at some distance from the table (probably the first time any lady so fair ever gave him such an invitation), "I want you to do me a very great favor;—but first, now, pray tell me candidly, shall you be very busy this morning?"

"Oh, my dear Miss Spenser," cried the little round man, in ecstasies, the more pleased at being thus accosted, as it was so new to him, "I am your humble servant for the whole day—dispose of me as you please—entirely at your service, and only too happy."

"Well, then, my dear sir," she continued, in the same very serious tone, "I'll tell you what you must do for me, if it is not too unreasonable—you must give me a full account of your plan for establishing Small Loan Funds"—[the little black eyes of the agent here actually danced with glee]—"in connection with reading societies and lending libraries"—[here he jumped about]; "and that is not all—I am going to be still more exacting—you must draw out a plan expressly for myself, suited to the peculiar circumstances of this parish and neighbourhood, for it is really full time to have something of the kind here, and with your help—you who are so great an authority—"

"I flatter myself," cried Mr. Trundle, visibly swelling with consequence, and radiant with delight, looking like a triumphant cock-robin, "I do flatter myself I am an authority upon Small Loan Funds. Who was the first man that called public attention to the subject of Loan Funds? Humble me. Who was the first that ever established a Small Loan Fund in Ireland? Humble me. Who—"

He might have gone on forever with this process of self-catechising, had not Elizabeth interrupted him by moving toward the breakfast table, saying, while she winsomely took his arm, "Now remember, Mr. Trundle, you are *all* mine for the *entire* morning;" to which she internally added, "Now papa will be able to write his sermon."

Both the girls were much surprised when Mr. Woodward entered the breakfast-room with their father; but the accident to the bridge, and the vagrant habits of their uncle (the result of his enormous activity in the discharge of his duties), sufficiently accounted for his unexpected re-appearance.

Arabella seized an early opportunity of explaining to Colonel Dabzac that her uncle the curate was only her uncle by marriage. Elizabeth (far from being ashamed of a man who was an honor not only to the church but to human nature) paid him, as usual, every kind attention, supplied him liberally with tea, placed the sugar

bowl within his reach, and privately ordered a couple of turkey-eggs to be boiled for him, which, however, did not discourage that mighty breakfast-eater from also paying his addresses energetically to the pickled salmon and cold meats on the sideboard.

Dabzac was amused at the extent of the curate's devastation, but still more by seeing a tray with coffee, a quantity of toast, an egg, butter, marmalade, and a wing of a fowl, sent up to Mrs. Spenser, who was so great an invalid that she could not make her appearance. Rebecca was scarcely able to support the weight of the tray.

"I need not ask how Mag is this morning," said Mr. Woodward to the rector, who smiled, and said that Mrs. Spenser had got a tolerably good night, and hoped in the course of the day to have the pleasure of receiving Colonel Dabzac and Mr. Trundle.

There was not much conversation, and the little that took place was not on an agreeable subject, for it related to Mr. Dawson. The curate's inquiries for Sydney led to the mention of that gentleman, and Colonel Dabzac, who had heard a report that he was likely to be returned to parliament for the borough of Rottenham, on the ultra-radical interest, spoke of him with a severity against which the curate thought himself bound to protest, though nobody present was more opposed to Dawson's politics than he was.

"He signed my Address to the Crown for the thirty millions," said Mr. Trundle, "so I ought to give him a good word, but I fear he is running through the remains of the property very fast."

"There's not much left to run through," said the colonel.

The curate made a remark to the effect that Dawson's embarrassments were not all of his own creation.

"My uncle," said Arabella, sneeringly, "thinks Mr. Dawson nothing less than an angel, because he once saved a boy from being drowned in Loch Erne."

"No, Miss Arabella, I do *not* think him an angel," rejoined Hercules, somewhat too vehemently, "I have not so high an opinion of any person of my acquaintance, whether a gentleman or a *lady ;* but I do say that the man who saves the life of another at the risk of his own is a fine brave fellow."

"But it does not prove him a loyal man or a good Protestant," said Dabzac, coming to Miss Spenser's aid.

"Nor did I say that either, though I believe the majority of fine brave fellows. are both," said Hercules, with quite too much energy for private life, though it would have done very well at a vestry.

Mr. Spenser smiled, but though he dissented from his curate's last proposition he made no remark upon it.

"When we have drained Loch Erne, as I propose," said Mr. Trundle—

"No more people will be drowned there," said Dabzac, finishing the sentence for him.

"Mr. Trundle has got a new argument for his project," said Mr. Spenser, gravely smiling (every body else laughed) at the little agent's ingenuity in turning the conversation into his favorite channel. However, he was soon cut short by the general rising from the table, when the self-sacrificing Elizabeth instantly pounced on him, as if he was the greatest prize in the world, and carried him off to the hall, there to have him "*all to herself,*" for three or four miserable hours.

Mr. Spenser and Mr. Woodward retired to the library to consult together further upon the steps to be taken in consequence of the events of the night; so that Miss Spenser and Colonel Dabzac had the field all to themselves for amusing or instructive conversation, for flirting, or love-making, at their discretion, or indiscretion, as the case might be.

---

## CHAPTER XXI.

### COURTSHIP AND HORSEMANSHIP.

"Light-winged toys of feathered Cupid."
OTHELLO.

You may say what you will of moonlights, and twilights, and sunset hours, and summer evenings, for the occupation of love-making, but there is no time, or season, half so propitious for the purpose as a desperate wet day in a country house. If, under such circumstances, there is any body to make love to, you must make it out of self-defense ; simply because you have nothing else to do, unless you go to bed, or commit *felo-de-se.* See how Dabzac was situated ! His host was in his library, at his private business ; Elizabeth and her privy counselor were transacting their own affairs ; there was no other resource but chatting, laughing, and flirting with Miss Spenser, and it was by no means a disagreeable alternative, particularly s the colonel could not but see that she had very disposition to chat, laugh, and flirt with him. You may say, why did not the colonel take a book, and sit down and read it in a corner, or on his back on a sofa. Now, would that have been exactly quite polite, unless the lady did the same thing, which in this case the lady did not do ? But the idea of a lieutenant-colonel of the Londonderry Militia reading ! The probability is that Dabzac had never read a book in his life—at least since he left college ; no, not a trumpery three-volume novel from a circulating library. He never thought of reading ; he scarcely knew there was such a mode of passing, or killing time ; he would scarcely have thought of taking a book, had he been sentenced to solitary imprisonment for life in the Vatican or Bodleian. No, he had positively no resource but flirtation. Now flirtation is not love-making, but it is a good introduction to it. It is the skirmishing of the light troops, before the heavy brigades come up, and the action commences. They flirted sitting and standing, and walking up and down the room, sometimes round and round a conservatory, which communicated with the drawing-room. There was not a chair, couch, sofa, stool, chair that could be sat on, or lounged on, which they did not chat and flirt on. They chatted of balls in Derry, and balls in Dublin ; about the Rotunda, and the Castle, about diamonds, trains, feathers, and lappets ; then about horses and carriages, of all kinds and colors, subjects in which Arabella

D

was knowing to a degree that astonished and captivated her gallant companion, who was only eloquent on such a theme as a hunter or a curricle. Then they played backgammon for a fit. Tired of backgammon, they talked again, and by this time the colonel was beginning to think Arabella very pretty, and her hand particularly beautiful; he had seen a great deal of it during the backgammon. The next thing was a discussion on liveries. The Dabzac colors were white and scarlet, which Miss Spenser approved of highly. Then, passing the piano, she ran her white fingers coquettishly up and down the keys, and the colonel insisted on having one of the French chansons, which she sang so agreeably.

It was just the soulless music to charm an empty man, and it had its effect decidedly in heightening flirtation into love-making. But what next ?—there was still half an hour before luncheon. In a corner, on a pile of music-books and newspapers, Dabzac spied a battle-dore, but the shuttle-cock was not to be found—there was a chase and a rummage for it under the newspapers and music-books, and at length the shuttle-cock turned up, and very prettily did Arabella toss the feathered emblem of frivolity to and fro with her admiring playfellow. It had only flown back and forward twice and thrice, when there was a flash of light through the room—was it lightning ? No—it was the sun himself ! Arabella flew to a window, and saw, with a delight only known to those who have been cooped up for a week in a country-house, a clear rent in the clouds, through which the cheery flash had issued, with several still larger chasms near it, revealing the deep blue firmament, and proclaiming that the storm was over.

With still livelier joy, you may well imagine, were the same glad phenomena observed almost at the same moment by Elizabeth in the hall. Figure to yourself a dove escaping from the talons of a kite. Just so did Elizabeth spring from the side of Mr. Trundle to join her sister in the portico, where the warmth and dryness of the air assured them that the breaking up of the clouds was not merely partial or temporary, but a positive guarantee for a charming afternoon A ride was proposed by Miss Spenser, and heartily seconded by Colonel Dabzac. Both were vain of their horsemanship, and each ambitious to shine in the other's eyes. Elizabeth acquiesced, even though it was to separate her from Mr. Trundle, who never rode for pleasure, and as seldom as he could upon business either. The horses were ordered, and the girls went to put on their equestrian dresses. Mr. Trundle had agreed with Dabzac that they were not to protract their stay at the parsonage after the first appearance of fine weather; and he looked annoyed and a little suspicious when the colonel intimated his intention to continue Mr. Spenser's guest until after Sunday.

"The state of the roads, my dear fellow— recollect the state of the roads."

"I fear it is the state of something else," said little Trundle, laughing and giving the colonel a poke in the side.

"Never fear," said Dabzac, turning away. "All safe in that region ; but Miss Spenser is a deuced fine girl, it can't be denied."

"But she is the daughter, you know, of a d——d Whig parson," said Trundle.

"And pray, Mr. Trundle, how have you passed the morning yourself?" asked the colonel. "Perhaps you thought nobody remarked *your* doings?"

"Come, come, colonel, that's too good—that won't do—as if you don't know very well what our *tête-à-tête* was about.".

"If it was not about love," said the colonel, cruelly, as he left the room to put on his spurs, "it must have been about Loch Swilly."

Mr. Woodward, being a living barometer, had foreseen the improvement in the weather an hour before the change actually took place, and (provided with a new cudgel, in the place of that which he had broken on the pate or the ribs of the footpad) had started once more for Redcross. His conjugal affections were as stanch and orthodox as his religious opinions, and were always urging him homeward, while his rather latitudinarian philanthropy and benevolence impelled him to all points of the compass. Anxious, indeed, to appease his wife's solicitude, he had dispatched a bare-footed envoy, at break of day, to assure her of his return that evening, *Deo volente*, without fail; and he was already three good miles from the parsonage, when the horses were brought to the door.

Mr. Spenser, fond of exercise on horseback, jaded with confinement, and uneasy and dispirited by what had occurred, was easily prevailed on to ride with his daughters. However, he paid his wife a visit before he mounted his horse, and had the satisfaction of leaving her heartily dining on a fried sole and a boiled chicken, though she assured him her appetite was entirely a morbid and nervous one—in fact, one of the worst symptoms of her case.

You know nothing of highland glories, if you only see them in calm and sunshine. It is in the coming on and the passing off of showers, and clouds, and tempests, that the magnificence of the mountains is revealed. It still continued a little blustery, but not so much as to prevent the party from enjoying their ride extremely. Their route was superb, one which, gradually climbing the heights over the estuary, commanded the scenery on the opposite side, and ultimately led to the verge of the cliffs over the ocean, whose agitation after so heavy a gale was always a spectacle of singular grandeur. The gradual uprolling of the mists, as the sun exhaled, or the breeze chased them, and the continual coming forth of one object after another, crags, trees, ruins, on the face of the hills, until only the tops remained, turbaned with white vapors, in wavy folds, sometimes transparent like gauze, charmed Mr. Spenser and Elizabeth, but were not much attended to by Arabella and her colonel. Here and there the vapors were obstinate, and clung with lazy tenacity alike to the bottom of the cliffs and the loftiest peaks, while the intermediate region was perfectly free.

"Not unlike what takes place," said the rector, "with respect to prejudice, which is the mist of the understanding; the middle classes are usually emancipated from them first; their hold is much stronger at the base and in the high places of society."

"But, papa," said the bright girl on her prancing pony, "it is only a question of time and patience with mists of both kinds: the sun has only to shine a little longer, and the wind to assist him; then all will be clear from top to bottom. Look—the head of Knocknagoonagh is now quite uncovered."

"Oh, yes," said Mr. Spenser, fond of following out such little analogies, "the triumph of truth and of free discussion—the sun and the wind—is eventually certain, and we must be patient, as you say; but it must not be the patience of inactivity or indifference, but the patience of virtuous perseverance, waging a perpetual, but tolerant and good-humored conflict with bigotry and error."

Arabella and Mr. Dabzac were cantering on before, the road just here admitting of that agreeable pace. She rode well and looked particularly handsome and distinguished on her pretty brown jennet. The broad-brimmed round beaver hat became her extremely; her complexion was freshened by the air and motion, and the disorder into which the puffs of wind threw her luxuriant hair, greatly improved its effect and beauty. Her passionate love of riding, and her fearlessness on horseback, gave her features more than usual animation. In short, Arabella Spenser was never seen to such advantage as in equestrian exercise, and Dabzac, alternately ambling or cantering at her side, never once recollected that after all she was the daughter of a liberal parson, the character which of all others he and his clique most abhorred. But what cares Cupid for political distinctions? he whose glory it is to confound every thing human, the high with the low, the rich with the poor, the brilliant with the dull, the virtuous with the unworthy, nay, even the lovely with the ill-favored; not even respecting beauty itself, licentious leveler that he is, the only thorough-paced apostle of *égalité*. It is little to him to mingle the blood of Whig and Tory, to get up a match between a Spenser and Dabzac.

But to many an eye (though there was no eye that day to regard her with gallantry), Elizabeth, on her humbler steed, in her straw bonnet, coarse in material but graceful in form, would have been far more piquante. She was not so fond of riding as her sister, and preferred a mountain pony to a showy horse like her sister's; still she carried herself well, not with the Amazonian air of Arabella, but with an easy, fearless, lady-like seat, notwithstanding. The breeze brought out her rich color also, and blew the curls of dark-brown hair about her shoulders, and sometimes into her eyes, making her bite her lip in pretty vexation, and often raise the whip-hand, without slackening her smart pace, to keep the rebel locks in subjection.

On they rode gayly, making for the summit that commanded the Atlantic, sometimes all abreast, sometimes in detachments, as when they started, while once or twice, just for a few moments, the girls were side by side, Mr. Spenser and his guest conversing together in advance of them. Mr. Spenser was not as animated and fluent as usual, and Dabzac preserved the same air of grim cold civility, which he never laid aside in his intercourse with men, unless, perhaps, in the tumult of political conviviality, a dinner on the 12th of July, or a revel on the 5th of November. The rector liked him less and less every moment of their acquaintance, little dreaming that his daughter's feelings were of so very opposite a nature. When men of intellect and wit are damped and chilled by dull or uncongenial company, their conversation is apt to sink into a mere common-place, which, from any lips but their own, would excite their contempt and ridicule. Mr. Spenser began soon to be sensible that he was talking not only down to the colonel's mark, but even below it. The consciousness of this was uncomfortable, and it was a great relief to him when Arabella again joined Dabzac in a canter, and he was left once more with his younger daughter.

They soon reached a point that commanded a near and wide view of the ocean, and, having enjoyed for some minutes the magnificent spectacle of its agitation after the late storm, they turned their horses' heads homeward. Nothing occurred of importance during the ride, except that Arabella invited Colonel Dabzac to join them in a pic-nic party to the island already mentioned, proposing the following Monday for the expedition. Elizabeth was pleased at the prospect of resuming the island-scheme in her brother's absence, which promised to secure her against the intrusion of his friend Dawson; and Mr. Spenser never opposed any proposition upon which his daughters were agreed. Chatting of the necessary arrangements for the voyage of pleasure, they reached the parsonage, which they found in a state of confusion nearly as bad as that in which they had left the Atlantic. The secret of the robbery had been ill kept; it had reached Mrs. Spenser's ears with twenty frightful exaggerations; her husband found her in the state that Tabitha Bramble calls "asterisks;" and Rebecca (at her wit's ends) informed him that a groom had been sent for Doctor Wilkins.

---

## CHAPTER XXII.

### HOW THE SECRET WAS KEPT.

**"You would pluck out the heart of my mystery.'**
　　　　　　　　　　　　　HAMLET.

IT was idle to think that a thing of the kind could possibly be kept secret very long, one of the servants being privy to it, and Randy Maguire, the chief actor, or rather sufferer in the transaction, being the most garrulous of men, at the most garrulous stage of life, and actually under Mr. Spenser's roof, confined to his bed with the effects of the outrage. But it was not Randy who broke faith with the rector. In fact, it was Mr. Woodward's careless directions to Cox, the butler, to steep some brown paper in brandy, and clap it on Randy's broken head, it was that made all the mischief. The poor little proctor did roar like a bull, exactly as the curate had anticipated, the moment the smarting application touched him; and it unluckily happened that Rebecca was passing at the instant, on her way to the kitchen to make a toast for her mistress to take with her glass of Madeira. Now, Rebecca had the vice of curiosity (a vice in a lady's-maid, though so admirable a quality in a philosopher), to counterbalance, perhaps, the virtue of patience, which she possessed in so high a degree; so she first tried to

open the door, and failing in that (the cautious Mr. Cox having bolted it inside) she popped down her head to the key-hole, and was very much surprised, you may think, to see an old man in bed, writhing and bellowing in the hands of the butler, who was plastering his temples with something that seemed more piquant than was agreeable. Rebecca, of course, did not wait to be caught peeping, but went down to the kitchen, determined to get a full explanation from Cox, who was her declared lover, at the earliest opportunity. The opportunity was not far off. As she returned up stairs with the toast, Cox was just coming out of the room, having done his best to carry out Mr. Woodward's directions.

"What ails Mr. Maguire?" said Rebecca.

"Why, what should ail him," said Cox, "but that he's sleepy and fatigued after his long jaunt, and has got his old rheumatis that he has had as long as I've known him."

"And has he got the rheumatis in his forehead?" said the maid, looking very sly.

"No, he hasn't," said Cox, "why should he?"

"Because you were putting a blister on it a minute ago," replied Rebecca.

"A blisther on it!" repeated Cox.

"Yes, and you needn't deny it, Mr. Cox, for I seen you with these eyes."

"Then your eyes were where they shouldn't have been," said the detected operator.

"Never mind," said Rebecca, "but tell me all about it this instant."

"I would if I could," said Cox, soothingly, "but it's a secret."

"Don't let mistress's toast get cold," said Rebecca, stamping her foot.

"Go along up with it, then," said the butler.

"Not till you tell me the secret, if the toast was to grow as cold as a lump of ice."

"It's a secret, I tell you."

"Much you know about keeping secrets," said Rebecca, "and at all events, two can keep a secret better than one."

"Well, then, I don't like keeping a secret from you, Rebecca."

"Don't then, Mr. Cox."

A little sentimental bargain was then struck, upon consideration of which, Cox covenanted to betray the confidence reposed in him. The engagement to break faith was better respected than the engagement to keep it, and Rebecca ran up to Mrs. Spenser's room, with the toast somewhat cold, but so full of the story of the Black Castle, that whatever scolding she got made very slight impression on her. A tale of less harrowing import, she might have ventured to communicate herself; but she was an humble girl, and felt that the robbery of her master's proctor was an event that demanded an historian of higher mark. Escaping from her mistress, she flew to Miss M'Cracken. You may suppose the story was colored blood-red by the time it reached Mrs. Spenser's ear. It was, in fact, another tale of the forty thieves, all but the jars and the suet.

Mrs. Spenser recalled all she had been hearing for several months of the insurrectionary state of the southern counties, concluded that the sanguinary warfare against the rights of the church had at length broken out in Donegal, and eventually (being well assisted), worked herself into the hysterical state in which her husband found her on his return from riding. Perhaps there was no ringing of bells, and running to and fro with salts and tonics and aromatic vinegar !

It was in vain the rector tried to quiet her nerves and her apprehensions. She was a woman utterly without self-command at any time, incapable of reasoning or being reasoned with; and besides, her husband's abortive attempt to conceal the occurrence from her, naturally, made her incredulous now, when he tried to undo the effects of Miss McCracken's exaggerations, and reduce the affair to its proper level.

In the midst of all the hubbub, Sydney reappeared. He had arrived indeed, as we have already stated, at an early hour in the morning (having pressed close on the heels of the unfortunate proctor), but being extremely fatigued, had retired instantly to his room, and to bed, where he would probably have lain till dinnertime, had not the confusion in the house prematurely roused him. Perhaps the first warm interest he ever took in the affairs of the family was upon this occasion. He felt exceedingly for poor Maguire, and was now seriously angry with himself for having parted company with the old man on the previous morning, when he stood so particularly in need of a protector.

Randy went over the whole story again, not concealing from young Spenser what he had concealed from his father, namely, how he had been surprised counting the bank notes by the fellow who had been sent for the cards, and how he had also unguardedly disclosed to the same individual that his business at Castle Dawson was to receive the arrears of tithes.

"There's nothing in that," said Sydney; "the fellow you mean was Mr. Dawson's servant."

"He looked as if he never see'd a bank-note in all his born days before," said Randy.

"Possibly he never did," said Sydney; "but are you positive nobody else saw the money, or where you put it ?"

"Nobody else knew nothing about it more han the child unborn," answered Maguire, 'except your own self, Master Sydney, and my bit of a niece, poor Maggy Maguire, at the inn, and she didn't see the beautiful yellow boys, and the illigant new Bank of Ireland notes, only the tattered ould provincials."

"Maggy didn't rob you, at any rate," said Sydney.

"Whoever did it was a cute chap," said Maguire, "howsomdever he got his intelligence, for he never went through the ceremony of axing where I kep the money, but in with his fist into the right place at onst, as if it was his own pocket the thief was ransackin."

"That's an important circumstance," said Sydney; "but now, Randy, I must leave you. Take care of yourself, and to-morrow, or next day, you'll be as well as ever you were."

"Oh, it's all over with me on this side of the grave," grunted the old man; but he had been uttering the same grunt for the last ten years, so Sydney paid it very little attention.

Leaving Maguire's room, the first person he met was his sister Elizabeth, who had not yet taken off her riding-dress. Sydney was dressed in the gay green coat which Dawson had made

him a present of. Elizabeth did not ask him how he came by it, for she knew only too well. In the gentlest possible way, however, she reproved her brother for having so abruptly left home, and so long absented himself from it. She never mentioned Dawson's name, but Sydney knew that she aimed at him, and he eulogized his friend more warmly than ever. He was armed now with the fact that the Dawsons had fully discharged their pecuniary obligations to his father; and to that, of course, Elizabeth had no answer to make, only she thought it strange that a man should be made so much of because he paid a just debt of very old standing; and she intimated this opinion distinctly.

"No," cried her brother, "it was no debt of Dudley's at all—it was his father's debt, not his; his conduct is the most honorable that was ever heard of; but you and Arabella are prejudiced against him, and for no reason in the world but that he smokes a cigar now and then, and wears a green coat."

"For which reason, I suppose," interrupted Elizabeth, archly, "he has transferred his green coat to you."

"What if he has ?" rejoined her unmannered brother, almost fiercely.

"Only this," said Elizabeth, with spirit, "that both Arabella and I like to see you dressed like a gentleman—not like Mr. Dawson."

"Oh, indeed," said Sydney.

"And the companion of gentlemen," added his sister, with energy.

"I am not going to consult you in the choice of my companions," cried the petulant young man, raising his voice; "but Dudley will be a member of Parliament in the course of a week or two, and then, perhaps, you will change your tune."

"The last piece of elegance from Castle Dawson !" cried Elizabeth; and glowing with vexation, she turned contemptuously away from her infatuated and rude brother, murmuring audibly as she went—"A member of Parliament, indeed—will that make him a gentleman ?"

Sydney went chafing to his own room, where, with the passion that youth of his temperament has for fire-arms and ammunition, he first employed himself in cleaning his gun and remaining pistol, polishing the barrels, and seeing that he was well provided with caps and with ball-cartridges. Then he wrote and dispatched a letter to Dawson, to acquaint him with what had occurred, and request him to come over to the parsonage at his earliest convenience, and bring the pistol with him, which would no doubt be found in the room where Sydney had slept, or in the drawing-room, where they had amused themselves riddling the fire-screens. This done, the young man made a more careful toilet than usual (partly in honor of Colonel Dabzac, and partly to avoid Elizabeth's displeasure), and went down to dinner.

A dull, distracted dinner it was; the whole evening, indeed, was a wretched one. Mr Spenser was unable to pay the ordinary attentions to his guests, and Mr. Trundle had no one to listen for five minutes consecutively to his projects. All was at sixes and sevens; nothing but running up stairs and down stairs; ordering and counter-ordering, mixing draughts, preparing baths, and charging stone-bottles with hot water. Every quarter of an hour some new crotchet got possession of Mrs. Spenser's noddle, and at last she sent for her husband, and insisted on his sending to the nearest police-station, and getting an armed party to garrison the parsonage. Mr. Spenser, reminded of "Hamilton's Bawn," suspected shrewdly that either Miss M'Cracken or Rebecca had suggested this idea; a dashing green sergeant would be such an agreeable addition to the company in the servants' hall. But there was no use in remonstrance—the rector was compelled to sit down, and in his wife's presence write to the police officer in command (with whom he was acquainted) requesting the loan of a couple of his men for a night or two. The request was granted (the county being, in fact, so notoriously tranquil, that it mattered little how the police were distributed), and before it was dark, three tall, handsome fellows, in dark green uniforms, with glittering muskets on their shoulders, and short swords by their sides were marched into the rectory; and well-pleased they were to get into such snug quarters, for they had a capital supper with the domestics, good, warm beds to mount guard in, and such fun and flirtation with the house-maids, that the noise of the merriment occasionally reached the library and the tea-table.

Miss M'Cracken, of course, scorned the festivities of the kitchen, above which, indeed, her manners, as well as her education, raised her; but Rebecca, as soon as she had bundled the young Spensers to bed, which she did as fast as the process of untrowsering and unfrocking could be accomplished, hastened to join the rest of the household in entertaining the constabulary, and made herself extremely agreeable to every one but Mr. Cox, who thought she might just as well have remained in the nursery darning stockings, or with Lucy reading "Clarissa."

The police, however, did not satisfy Mrs. Spenser. She must have the lower windows of the house blocked up and barricaded; the carpenter must be sent for without a moment's delay. To this Mr. Spenser good-humoredly demurred, observing that with three armed policemen, and a lieutenant-colonel to head them, all danger was out of the question; but the moment his back was turned, his wife sent for the artificer in wood (who lived hard by the glebe), on her own responsibility, and actually had an interview with him at the side of her bed, and instructed him to put the lower part of the house into as complete a state of defense as possible.

The circle round the tea-table were not a little astonished and diverted when the village Vauban tapped at the door of the library, and asked permission to enter and commence the fortifications. However, it was absolutely necessary to give Mr. Chip something to do, that the noise of his hammer should resound through the house, and accordingly Mr. Spenser took him into the back hall and set him to make a large wooden case for a parcel of books which he was going to send up to Dublin to be bound. When the carpenter sent in his bill some time afterward, one of the items ran thus—"for fortifications, including a box for books, seven shillings and six pence."

## CHAPTER XXIII.

### DAWSON IN SOCIETY.

SYDNEY did not expect to receive an answer from his friend for some days, but he received a reply the following morning by the hands of his own messenger, who found Dawson at home. Dawson's letter was only too cordial and energetic. The robbery astonished him more than any thing that had ever happened in the country, and he pledged himself to strain every nerve, and spare neither fatigue nor expense, to drag the perpetrators of this sacrilegious and abominable crime to light. The sacrilege was what Dawson thought so especially atrocious. He would drive over to the parsonage immediately, for in such a case the loss of a moment might be irreparable. Nor was this all; he proceeded to express a hope that, should the loss of so considerable a sum happen to be the slightest immediate inconvenience to Sydney's father, he would not forget that he had a friend at Castle Dawson, who, while he had a shilling in his pocket, would only be too proud and too happy to accommodate him.

Such was the tenor of the letter, more remarkable for its warmth than its delicacy, particularly the offer of accommodation, but it was written on the spur of the moment, and at all events not likely to find a very severe critic in Sydney Spenser.

Dawson kept his word (as he always did religiously, when it suited his purposes) and arrived the next day at the parsonage in a curricle, drawn by a pair of showy grays, an equipage intended, no doubt, to make a lively impression on Elizabeth Spenser, but which only succeeded in dazzling Miss M'Cracken and Rebecca. Sydney was anxious about his pistol, but Dawson reported that it had not been found.

"Is it possible," said Sydney, "that by mistake that surveyor or the strolling artist—"

Dawson laughed unpleasantly at the suggestion, but thought it unlikely that any such mistake had occurred. Sydney left him to dress for dinner.

Not a word of intimation had either Mr. Spenser or his daughters received of this unwelcome addition to their circle. You may imagine how great was the surprise and displeasure of the girls, when, entering the drawing-room, they found Mr. Dudley Dawson among the guests. There was another increase to their party in the person of Mr. Oliver, the rector of a neighboring parish, a profoundly grave man, who spoke extremely little, and only to draw other people out, particularly Mr. Spenser, whom he enthusiastically admired. When he heard any thing that particularly surprised, or amused him, his eye expressed it by a peculiar twinkle, but he seldom opened his lips when the company exceeded three or four people.

I must try to paint Dawson again, as he appeared on the present occasion, accoutered, it is to be supposed, rather to kill ladies than catch thieves. Take one of those stuffy, pigeon-breasted lay-figures, on whose backs the tailors of Cheapside and the Strand advertise their "fashionable attire;" clothe it in one of their flashiest blue coats with blazing gilt buttons, and let the coat hide as little as possible of a white satin waistcoat, flowered with enormous peonies; let the trowsers be the glossiest black, disclosing at the feet silk stockings of a fiery flesh color, the toes concealed by a square inch of varnished leather, the only visible portion of what is presumed to be a shoe; stud the all-too-beruffled shirt with three massive diamonds, probably not from Golconda; then whisker your figure at the hair-dresser's, next door to the tailor who supplied the coat; perfume it with musk, or essence of lavender; feed it at the oyster-shops and Haymarket restaurants, until the cheeks become red and bloated; carbuncle the fingers with rings and the nose with brandy-and-water; then inflate it with prodigious self-conceit; animate it with a spirit of Brummagem patriotism—any desperate nonsense will do for a political creed, any slang dictionary will furnish a vocabulary—there is Dawson for you, as he approached, with a strut and a wriggle, to pay his homage to the fair Spensers, the elder of whom, certainly, returned his salute with as much contumelious disregard as a clever actress with long study could throw into a glance and a courtesy. The younger, who most disliked him, testified her aversion less, and the coxcomb had the egregious folly to construe in his own favor the mere well-bred suppression of Eliza-beth's repugnance.

The table-talk was not the most interesting : there was talk, but no conversation. Those who can not even talk are too small a minority; and Dawson was not one of them. He talked loud and big; making laborious efforts to ap-pear at his ease, while manifestly out of his element in refined society, and also betraying by the incoherence of his observations and the excitement of his manner, a pre-occupation of mind, not uncommon, indeed, in men living from hand to mouth, and heirs apparent to estates in chancery. As to the robbery, Dawson talked more feelingly than if he had been robbed him-self; he spoke of blowing up the Black Castle with gunpowder, and agreed with Sydney to ransack it the next day armed "from top to toe." He was of great service to Colonel Dab-zac in the eyes of the rector and his second daughter. Dabzac, though only a stiff, grim, vacant, well-dressed nobody, was a gentleman in appearance as well as position; he was no adventurer, or roué; his knowledge and love of horses was that of a squire, not of a black-leg; and, besides, he was disposed to taciturnity, an excellent gift in men who have no bank to draw upon for pleasant discourse. He looked to great advantage beside the presuming, swaggering, restless Dawson, who, if he had only had the tact to sit still in his chair, and hold his tongue, would have been only one half as disagreeable as he actually was. Even Mr. Trundle rose in estimation from the same cause; better loan-funds and Loch Swilly to all eternity than Daw-son's gross politeness, heartless cordiality, and the continual effort to conciliate, which had only the effect of thoroughly disgusting every body. Mr. Spenser was not the man to have such a guest at his table; he neither knew how to silence, or how to talk to him. He would fain have shunned politics, but the conversation be-came political in spite of him. Dawson began by admitting that the Repeal of the Union was all gammon; that good measures were all the Repealers wanted, and when asked why they

raised that exciting and dangerous cry, if their real object was only to carry some minor points, he made a very lame attempt to shuffle out of the difficulty; said that the more people asked the more they got, and compared it to the prac-tice of lawyers who lay the damages in an action at twenty thousand pounds, when they only expect, and would be perfectly content with a verdict for perhaps a fortieth of the sum. Mr. Spenser shook his head, and then Dawson protested that he did not mean to justify the principle; on the contrary, he admitted it to be highly objectionable; he was always himself an advocate for plain-dealing, and would be one to the end of the chapter.

Mr. Oliver's eye twinkled more than once during this speech of Master Dudley's.

The Church having been mentioned, Dawson pronounced a high-flown eulogy upon that in-stitution to captivate Mr. Spenser, who would not have said half so much himself in praise of it. Observing that he had over-done this a little, he declared that the Church had monstrous abuses, not a doubt of it—it was monstrous that any Christian Church should cost the nation two millions *per annum*. Here the eye of Oliver twinkled more than before.

"Two millions, Mr. Dawson!" said Mr Spenser, smiling.

"Scarcely a fourth of the sum," said Colonel Dabzac, with dry asperity, and not so much as looking at the person whose observation he noticed.

Then Dawson drew in his horns, and showed his perfect willingness to estimate the wealth of the Church at any figure the company thought reasonable; after which he added, that if every clergyman in the establishment was only one-tenth part as charitable and exemplary in every relation of life, public and private, as the rector of the parish of Redcross, "far from thinking two millions a year a single farthing too much, he would vote with all his heart to quadruple the sum."

Mr. Spenser could not but say that he was much flattered by this speech, offensively im-pertinent as it was.

"I only say what every body in the world will swear to," proceeded Dawson, still more brazenly, "and what's more Mr. Spenser, if the parish was polled this moment, you'd be the biggest bishop in Ireland to-morrow morning by universal suffrage."

You may fancy how this effusion made the eye of the silent parson quiver with merry meaning.

"Not the biggest," said Mr. Spenser, trying to smile at what revolted him so thoroughly, and devoutly wishing that Dawson had continued a tithe-defaulter, since the settlement had made him (the rector) nothing the richer, while the non-payment had the effect of keeping at a dis-tance a man, whose style of conversation, like his style of living, was so very discordant from that of civilized people.

Dawson rose from his wine only too soon. This was a piece of affectation like the rest of his behavior.

The conversation after he retired naturally turned upon *modesty*, and the rector said "he feared it would be found that the *assumption* of modesty thrives better in the world than the genuine quality itself. Assurance in the mask of humility carries all before it. It is in life," he added, "as in jumping; you must fall back in order to spring forward, but you must be careful not to fall back too far. Backwardness overdone may be as fatal as excessive forwardness. There is an art in this as in every thing else."

"You would seem to give a Machiavellian turn," said Mr. Oliver, "to the divine precept, as if we were directed to take the lower seats, *in order* that the host should desire us to go up higher." This was a long speech for Mr. Oliver, and took up a considerable time, for he spoke with the utmost gravity and deliberation, as if pronouncing judgment in a case of life and death.

"The words *do* in strictness bear that meaning," said Mr. Spenser, "but it is only one of many cases where worldly wisdom coincides with heavenly. The man of the world succeeds best by conforming to the line of Christian conduct. The precept you quote hits the true mean between self-exaltation and undue self-abasement. We are commanded to take the lower seats, but still among the guests, not to go down below the salt."

"There is not much occasion," said Dabzac, "to preach the danger of excessive modesty in this country."

"Perhaps not," said the rector, "yet I know no people who, speaking of them nationally, are so deficient in the virtue or faculty of accurate self-measurement—who are so distrustful of their own strength when they are really strong, and so apt to be over-confident exactly when they ought to be humble. I know no country where there is so much spurious modesty and at the same time so much ill-acted assurance; where the man who is conscious of superiority is so absurdly backward to assert it, and where men of no mark make such ludicrous efforts to seem of consequence."

"How is it to be explained?" said Mr. Oliver.

"I should have to write the history of Ireland to answer you," said the rector.

"No man could do that better," said Mr. Oliver with his great solemnity, "I wish you would undertake the work."

"I have neither industry, nor, I fear, *conscience* enough for such an undertaking," replied the rector, smiling. "'There goes a great deal of conscience to the writing of a history,' as Brown observes truly in the *Religio Medici*."

"There ought to go," said Oliver, couching his remark in the fewest possible words.

"I feel," continued Mr. Spenser, "that, like Hume, I should find it too troublesome to rise from my sofa to hunt for an authority; or, like Vertot, when he wrote his history of the Knights of Malta, and received the valuable information about the siege, after he had composed the account of it with scarce any materials. '*Ma foi, mon siège est fait*,' said the easy Frenchman. The facts came too late!"

Oliver smiled gravely, and repeated his opinion that a history of Ireland by his friend would be a most desirable accession to literature.

"I wrote one history," said Mr. Spenser, "and I do not think I shall ever write another."

"What was that?" said Mr. Oliver.

"A history of Higgledy-Piggledy," said the rector. "You shall have it to read, if you think it worth your while; I'll give it to you in the course of the evening, and you may put it in your pocket, or in the fire."

Oliver's face beamed with delight. They rose and followed Mr. Dawson to the tea-table. Had you seen Dawson enter the drawing-room that evening, you would have perceived how little accustomed he was to such apartments. He threw himself down on the chair nearest to where Elizabeth was sitting, and (mitigating his stable-yard tones as much as he could) commenced by repeating the gross piece of flattery about the bishopric which he had delivered himself of in the dining-room; adding, that her father was the most charming man he had ever known, and what a pity it was such a man should be banished to a country parish in the wildest part of Ireland. Then he spoke of Sydney as the finest, noblest, cleverest, handsomest, most promising fellow in the world, and said magnificent things about friendship, like a Pylades talking of an Orestes. His next move was to ask Elizabeth whether she did not sing; when she replied in the negative, he felt certain that she was at least an instrumental musician, and hoped she would play something, which was, of course, respectfully declined. Then he reconnoitered with his eye-glass the inch of patent leather at the points of his shoes, and talked of dances and balls; making such hash of his wills and shalls, woulds and coulds; such perpetual use of the words elegant, splendid, tremendous, and thrilling; and now and then, also, on the very point of rapping out an adjuration, arresting himself so seasonably at the "by,"—that Elizabeth was a little amused, though much annoyed by his conversation. However, she was happy to escape to Mr. Oliver and the tea-table, and she kept Dawson at an immeasurable distance for the rest of the evening. Though not very thin-skinned, he could not but feel that he was not eminently successful in the drawing-room; but he had vanity enough to support him under still greater discouragements: nay, he formed that very night, for the first time, a deliberate scheme for the conquest of Elizabeth Spenser, far less, however, by gaining her affections (of which, indeed, he could have had but a slender hope) than by the use of influences and instrumentalities much more at his command than the art of captivating the heart of an amiable woman.

Dawson professed himself a passionate admirer and worshiper of beauty. Had he been so in reality, he would not have been the gross sensualist that he was. "There is no more potent antidote," says Schlegel, "to low sensuality, than the adoration of beauty; but there are souls to whom even a vestal is not holy."

He had the shrewdness not to attempt again upon that occasion to break through the rampart of formality and coldness behind which the resolute girl entrenched herself; he had even the skill to assume a distant but profoundly respectful manner toward her, permitting Colonel Dabzac and even Mr. Trundle to perform little acts of attention which he might have performed himself without the imputation of forwardness.

But if he wanted admirers in the drawing-room, he was more successful elsewhere. More than once in the course of the evening, Rebecca crept to the door, and found opportunities for peeping in and feasting her eyes upon the white satin waistcoat, strewed with red peonies, and the dazzling toes of Mr. Dawson's shoes. She gave such a report of his splendor to Lucy, that it was with difficulty the latter controlled her inclination to slip down and enjoy the same spectacle in the same clandestine way; but it was against her system to demean herself without a sufficient motive, so she not only restrained her curiosity, but lectured Rebecca for peeping, and told her sharply that she would have been better employed teaching the children their catechism or putting them to bed. Rebecca took the latter part of the hint without delay, and then hastened to the kitchen, where she enraged Mr. Cox exceedingly, by dancing a jig before supper with one of the policemen.

Mr. Dawson certainly did exhibit amazing vigor in the rector's service the following day; he started with young Spenser and one of the police-constables in quest of the robbers at day-break, provided with arms of various kinds, a hamper of provisions and a powerful and ferocious bull-dog, to whose society Sydney was not a little partial, and of whose exploits he had wonderful things to tell.

Sydney was active and brave. The prospect of a raid through the hills was just the thing to excite to the highest pitch a boy of his turbulent disposition, and who plumed himself so much on his animal strength. However, nothing came of that day's expedition; Sydney wanted to explore the Black Castle, but his comrade thought it would be mere waste of time to do so, so they contented themselves with scouring the country between the parsonage and Castle Dawson, diverging here and there into the wild glens to the right and left of the road, but not getting a shot the live-long day at any thing more important than a hare.

———◆———

CHAPTER XXIV.

MR. SPENSER'S ACCOUNT OF THE ISLAND OF HIGGLEDY-PIGGLEDY.

"In the Commonwealth I would by contraries
Execute all things, for no kind of traffic
Would I admit; no name of magistrate;
Letters should not be known; no use of service;
No use of metal, corn, or wine, or oil,
No occupation; all men idle, all,
And women too."            THE TEMPEST.

THE grave Mr. Oliver, enthusiastic about every thing that Mr. Spenser said or did, thought he would never be permitted to retire soon enough, so anxious was he to peruse the paper which the rector put into his hands on the night recorded in the foregoing chapter. Putting on his spectacles and his robe-de-chambre, and establishing himself in a great chair with his feet on the fender, he read as follows:—

"Higgledy-Piggledy is an island in 96 deg. 0 min. 0 sec. south longitude, and 396 deg. 70 min. 3 sec. west latitude, as laid down in the maps of the Swiss Admiralty, from the accurate surveys of the Great Chartists. Its place on

the globe is almost the antipodes of the Insulæ Fortunatæ. Strabo has not mentioned it, probably because he was ignorant of its existence; and the silence of Malte-Brun in later times may plausibly be accounted for upon the same hypothesis.

"The island is so called from the Higgledies, who constitute the smaller and wealthier part of its population, and the Piggledies, who constitute the greater and poorer portion. The Piggledies again derive their name probably from 'pig,' either because that animal abounds among them, or because in its character and general habits it resembles them very strikingly. In fact, it is a common saying that there is nothing so like a Piggledyman as a pig, and nothing so like a pig as a Piggledyman.

"The country is divided into four provinces, called Bluster, Funstir, Spunster, and Donaught. Funstir is the finest and most remarkable; what a pleasant land it is, you may conclude from its appellation; the Piggledies have it nearly all to themselves, and it includes the celebrated and eccentric district or shire of Topsiturvia, where, in peaceable times, the people are always in insurrection, but, when rebellion is afoot, they are actual models of good behavior. Spunster, the northern part of the island, is the province where the Higgledies are found chiefly. Many of them are as gay fellows as the Topsiturvians themselves; but others are as orderly and shabby as any population can be—low industrious creatures, who work for their bread, generally at weaving or spinning, whence comes probably the name of the province.

"The metropolis of Higgledy-Piggledy is the great city of Hubbub, in the neighborhood of which is held annually, about the time of the summer solstice, the elegant festival of Brokenhead, corresponding to the Olympic games among the barbarous Greeks.

"The Piggledies lodge for economy in the sties erected for their swine, and they live upon a certain root, which they are so passionately fond of, that they prefer the risk of starvation to propagating any other. Although a certain mixture of blue and yellow is the color of the nation, they can not abide it in crops, and a Piggledyman will cultivate even nettles and ragweed rather than turnips or mangold-wurzel. There is corn grown in many places—wheat, because the climate is singularly unfit for it; and oats and barley; not to make the vulgar article of bread, but for the wiser and nobler purpose of extracting from these grains a certain liquor, which has a marvelous effect on the eyes, making the drinker see objects twice over, so that all the blessings of Providence seem doubled, and man is, of course, doubly grateful and twice happy.

"The ancient constitution of Higgledy-Piggledy was a mixed anarchy, a form of government on which De Lolme is strangely silent, and of which Locke says nothing. But it was a glorious constitution notwithstanding, and, if not 'the envy of surrounding nations,' it might certainly have been said to be 'one of the wonders of the world.' At all events, the Higgledy-Piggledidians enjoyed under it for many a century a degree of happy confusion, such as no other country in the world has ever been blessed with; and as it promoted all the great objects of misrule and merriment, their devotion to it is not very difficult to understand.

"Up to the beginning of the present century the island had a sort of a legislature of its own, not extremely unlike the British Parliament in form, called the National Harem-Scarem. Marvelous things are recorded of the Harem-Scarem of Higgledy-Piggledy, which the Higgledies kept all to themselves, with all its profits and honors, in order that the Piggledies, by their efforts to get into it also, might never want a motive to keep the country in its normal state of uproar and disorder. At length a more powerful neighboring state, the Whitelanders, envious of the prosperity of the people of Higgledy-Piggledy in the possession of this inestimable domestic treasure, determined to rob them of it, and actually committed the robbery about the beginning of the present century. To the Higgledies this was perhaps a serious blow, but the Piggledies might have been expected to have rather rejoiced than grieved at it. The contrary, however, took place. The Piggledies have been howling like maniacs from that day to this for the restoration of their native Harem-Scarem, an assembly into which they were never suffered to put their snouts; and although they can not justly complain that the stronger state has inflicted many good laws, or afflicted them with much good government, yet nothing will content them but to have the mismanagement of their own affairs in their own hands, the indofeasible right of *self-misrule*, or (as their demagogues sometimes express it) ' *Higgledy-Piggledy for the Higgledy-Piggledymen !* '

"There are two codes of laws in the island, one the dullest system imaginable, diametrically opposed to public opinion, at least, to the public opinion of the Piggledies, the other called the code of Topsiturvia, the work of an illustrious native of that part of the island, who may be considered as the Numa, the Zoroaster, or the Moses of Higgledy-Piggledy.

"The courts by which this admirable code is administered are held, like the Areopagus of old, by night, or in the dark; nothing can be simpler, cheaper, or more expeditious than their processes : they bring justice to every Higgledy gentleman's hall door; in fact, every thing is done by the plaintiff himself; he is prosecutor, witness, judge, jury, and executioner, by which it is inconceivable what a saving is effected both of time and money; and so uninfluenced by personal feelings are those august tribunals, that even after judgment in capital cases, the traverser is allowed to appear by his attorney or agent, and is shot, or otherwise executed by *proxy.*

"Whenever the Piggledies have the power, they proceed against the Higgledies (who are generally the nominal lords of the soil), according to Topsiturvian law. On the other hand, the Higgledies, when they have the advantage, take care to cite the Piggledies before their own judges, and try them by their own formal, tedious, and ruinously expensive system. However, when the object is to regain possession of the soil, the processes of Higgledy justice are rapid enough in all conscience, nearly as *swift* and *mortal* as those of the other code.

"One of the strangest things connected with the state of the law in the island is a system

they have by which the bulk of the soil is vested in a high legal functionary, corresponding with our chancellor. In fact, the entire island may be said to be 'in chancery,' and the general state of tillage is exactly what might be anticipated from such a droll arrangement; for, except the process of *draining*, what branch of agriculture can any court, either of law or equity, have a *practical* acquaintance with ?

"There are two religions in the island, the Piggledy religion established in fact, and the Higgledy religion established in law; the opposition of law to fact being an admirable provision for keeping the country in that highly comic and convulsive state, without which it would not be worth living in. Indeed they draw largely upon their religious institutions for what they consider the prime comfort of existence; and in this they are highly to be commended, inasmuch as religion, no doubt, ought to constitute the happiness of every people. The great temple, or state pagoda of the island, only frequented by the Higgledies, though supported at the cost and charges of the Piggledy-men, is a gorgeous and astonishing pile; it stands on the edge of an awful precipice, and is in the singular form of a cone, or sugar-loaf, turned upside down, the broad summit representing its ample possessions, the small point in contact with the earth being perhaps emblematic of the small fraction of the community which enjoys its benefits. Nothing can be more terrific, seen at a distance, than this strangest of edifices that the hand of man ever raised. Foreigners who visit the island shudder to think of such a dangerous pile overhanging them and threatening to topple on their heads every moment. But this state of unstable and perilous equilibrium is what charms the people themselves; and particularly the Piggledies, who might long since have reversed the fabric and placed it on its base, had such been their will and pleasure. As to the Higgledies, their zeal in defense of the sacred structure is perfectly natural, for they must take it as it is, or forego its advantages altogether. They are always fidgety about its safety, and keep a vast army on foot, ready at a moment's warning to surround the building and prop it up with their lances and spears.

"The vernacular language of the country is a sort of dialect between high Bluster and common Rigmarole. It is so highly figurative that it is found to be almost impossible to state facts, or convey simple truth in it. The accent is also a mixed one, something between a roar and a whine, which makes it excellent to bully or beg in. You may fancy what a Babel the isle is, particularly in the chief cities, where the most notorious whiners and bawlers congregate.

"Besides Hubbub, the metropolis, there are other important towns, for instance Riotville on the mighty river Trash, and Hocus-Pocus on the banks of the Drivel. In every town there is a great chamber, or senate-house, called Balderdash Hall, and the loudest and the longest speaker is the Demosthenes of the place. The principal subject of discussion is always the restoration of the Harem-Scarem; but when strangers demand of the Piggledies, what the Harem-Scarem did for them when they had it, or what they expect it would do for them, if they had it again, not an orator of them all has a word to answer; but so much the worse for the interrogator, for he is sure to be bespattered with mire from head to heel, and runs a serious risk of being flung bodily into the Trash or the Drivel.

"Being a proud and haughty people—most of them descended from kings, and not a man of them who is not a gentleman born—they generally despise trade. In their cities you will see but few cheesemongers, or fishmongers; but some branches of industry find more favor with them; there are enough of news-mongers and grievance-mongers, these occupations not being deemed disparaging to their gentility, on which no people plume themselves so much. You are not to suppose, however, that there are no degenerate, low-minded creatures among them, who use their heads for thinking, and their hands for working, more than their tongues for talking. There are several such perverse, poor-spirited people, sprinkled over the island, but they are in a wretched minority, and are despised, as they deserve to be, pretending to be better than their neighbors, and not having the patriotism to conform to the genius and character of the country.

"So thoroughly averse to commerce is Higgledy-Piggledy in general, that the most popular cry in the island is for the total destruction of the only branch of commerce open to them, the exportation of their own superfluous food, for they raise food in enormous quantities, the soil being as fertile as any in the world. Nothing enrages the orators at Balderdash Hall more than the spectacle of a drove of pigs going to market, or a sack of corn sold to a foreign merchant. They insist upon cramming their farmers with their own bacon, and would throw the corn into the Drivel sooner than see it exported abroad. Nor is this school of political economy confined to the Piggledy provinces. Many of the Higgledies take the same wise views of the interests of the public. Indeed, this is one of the few points upon which the orators of both races concur in opinion, but as their agreement in this respect tends to promote the general happy confusion, it must be regarded as a fortunate circumstance; and the great pity is, that both parties have not their old Harem-Scarem back again, that they might have to say, that, for once, they acted cordially together, and *ruined* their country *in concert*.

"It ought to be mentioned that the Higgledies of Hubbub have a hall of their own, like their poor fellow-citizens. It is a vast round building, which perhaps accounts for the frequency with which Higgledy debaters argue in a circle. The prevailing mendicant turn of all classes, Higgledies as well as Piggledies, will sufficiently explain another of their logical characteristics, namely the habit of begging the question. In short, the round building we speak of is named with justice the Temple of Twaddle. Faction, Fanaticism, and Fashion preside there in turns, and there the general congresses of all the States in Noodledom are holden annually, about the time of the vernal equinox.

"At Balderdash Hall is to be seen one of the greatest curiosities in the whole country, an enormous engine (said to be of forty-ass power) for keeping the island constantly in *hot water*.

The hot water, however, is not for the purpose of bathing or ablution, for there are no public baths, and cleanliness is not one of the besetting virtues of the people. It is a political and social institution altogether, and has hitherto worked admirably, to the great credit and content of the engineers.

"There is a famous Castle in Hubbub, for the possession of which the Higgledies and Piggledies are forever squabbling, and in truth it seems of no great use except as a bone of contention between them. The Castle itself is in the possession of the Whitelanders, the same people who formerly plundered the island of that wise and virtuous legislature which was once its glory. The Whitelanders commit the fortress from time to time to the custody of some great giant, who is occasionally, but *not often*, a wizard also. The giants of Hubbub Castle had such indifferent characters in former days, that one of the wits of Higgledy-Piggledy is reported to have said that their deeds ought to be found recorded in the history of Rapin (e). However, the more giant-like the giant, he pleases the people the better, for he keeps the fun stirring which they love so dearly. When he is more wizard than giant, wise as well as strong, he is not so popular by half. Either the Higgledies, the Piggledies, or both combined, are sure to assail and besiege him, while he has no support from any quarter, but from the good-for-nothing and shabby minority already mentioned, who, being capable of industry (the greatest vice in a citizen), are equally prone, of course, to be loyal, which in Higgledy-Piggledy is considered the greatest vice in a subject.

"The state of education in the island is one of transition, and measures are now in progress, which threaten the best interest of Ignorance with ruin, if the mind of the country is not awakened in time to so awful a danger. How great the danger is may be judged from the unquestionable truth that Higgledy-Piggledy educated would be Higgledy-Piggledy no longer. However, the sprightly feuds of the two races will probably prevent the poison from spreading with extravagant rapidity, so as to save the island from any thing like a deluge of enlightenment, or at least afford time for the construction of an ark.

"Nothing, indeed, can be more presumptuous than the attempt to instruct the Higgledy-Piggledians, as if they did not, or could not, instruct themselves; the fact being that they have one of the completest systems of public instruction in the world.

"Of all things, no traveler should omit to visit their Polytechnic School. I found (when I inspected it) a professor of mathematics teaching a great many curious things, which had bearings on other subjects as well as on algebra and geometry. He taught, for instance, that a crooked line is the shortest between two points; that enormous social virtue resides in *sixes* and *sevens;* that researches after *impossible* quantities is one of the noblest pursuits that a Piggledy or a Higgledy can engage in; that the most interesting spiral is the common cork-screw; but of all things, he took the greatest pains to explain and apply the principle of the inverted cone, which he contended was the very type of stability, naturally dwelling on it the most, as, in fact, it is the fundamental *idea* of the Higgledy-Piggledy constitution.

"Passing into the hall of Ethics, the chair of morality was filled by a learned doctor, who was just then developing some curious views on the subject of *meum* and *tuum*, to which he stated that he had been led by analytical reasoning from the religious institutions of the island. 'Assuming,' he said, 'our great conical temple (with the renown of which the whole earth is filled) to be in reality, as it is professedly, a moral and religious fabric, it follows that the endowments it possesses can not have had any origin but a strictly moral one; now that those endowments were forcibly taken by the Higgledies from the Piggledies, merely because the former were stronger at the time, and had a fancy for the pious property of their neighbors, is beyond controversy. It, therefore, can not be immoral (he argued), in any case, to deprive people forcibly (nor, of course, fraudulently) of any thing they possess that you happen to covet, for if such an action were criminal at all, it could not but be criminal in the highest degree in a case where religious uses are in question. for there it would not be a simple robbery, but one aggravated by the profane dedication of the spoil to heaven.' It was impossible not to be forcibly struck by a train of reasoning, which sent away a large ethical class thoroughly convinced that the immorality of rifling a pocket was nothing more heinous than the process by which the great inverted cone came by its property.

"The school of oratory is held at the fish-market. Indeed, whatever little encouragement the exhaustless fisheries of the island receive is to be attributed to the immemorial connection between dealing in fish and dealing in foul language. The very professors of rhetoric at Hubbub and other places are fish-wives. One of them has reduced the art of scolding to a system, and given it to the world in a treatise called 'The New De Oratore.' I was formally introduced to this lady, and picked up some curious information from her. Among other things, she told me that the word *harangue* was derived from the French *hareng*, a herring; and that it was not for the purpose of shouting with pebbles in his mouth, that Demosthenes was accustomed to frequent the beach, but to invigorate and enrich his style by listening to the invectives of the *poissardes* of Athens. For the same reason, she added, eloquence had always flourished most in maritime states, and most of all in islands; witness Rhodes in ancient times (where the Romans sent their sons for those advantages of marine instruction which the inland position of the imperial city did not afford); and in the present day, Higgledy-Piggledy itself, where orators so abound, that the only difficulty is to find a man who is not one.

"Passing through an obscure quarter of the city, after leaving the fish-market, I was surprised to observe a modest building dedicated (as an inscription announced) to Industry and Independence. It proved to be a sort of academical institution. Curious to hear how far a lecturer would presume to go upon subjects so distasteful to the bulk of the community, I entered, and opening the door of a chamber where I was told the business of the school was going on, saw a professor delivering from his chair a most elaborate and interesting—*soliloquy*. Pleased at having at length an auditor, if not an auditory, he was proceeding with considerable increase of animation, when the shouts of an infuriated multitude were heard distinctly, and in a few moments the institute was beleaguered by a rabble of Piggledies, hot from Balderdash Hall, who, with furious noises and gestures, expressed their resolution to pull the edifice down, and tear the unfortunate professor of industry piece-meal. How I escaped I never distinctly understood, but the lecturer was not so lucky, for he fell into the hands of the mob. In vain he protested that he was only a *professor*—that he had never *practiced* what he taught —that in his heart he despised both industry and independence as much any man could do, and that as to his lectures, it was impossible they could do much mischief, inasmuch as he had uniformly delivered them to empty benches. The crowd was not to be appeased; a variety of frightful deaths was proposed, and I learned afterward that he only escaped ending his days in some appalling way by the humane suggestion of one of the bystanders, who cried out that the fellow was a madman, and that a whip and a straight-waistcoat were the proper treatment for him.

"Going some while afterward to visit one of the hospitals for lunatics in Topsiturvia, I saw my poor professor there, among the other maniacs and idiots. This lunatic institution is one of the greatest curiosities in the country, for all those things which elsewhere in the world are looked upon as characteristics of a sound mind, are regarded in Higgledy-Piggledy as evidences of an incurably disordered one. In the next cell to the frantic professor of industrial philosophy, was an insane political economist, who had protested against a project for the exclusive use of Higgledy-Piggledy manufactures. 'When Higgledy-Piggledy cloth is as good and as cheap as the cloth of other countries'—this was his argument—'it will be time enough to buy a coat of it.' The doctrine procured the poor wretch a Higgledy-Piggledy waistcoat, which, however, was not so tight but that he managed to amuse himself, in the usual manner of Tom-o'-Bedlams, by scribbling the walls of his cell with a bit of coal, an employment at which I found him busily engaged; and being curious to see what the scrawl was, I examined it, and found it consisted of scraps from authors as mad as himself, named Smith, Malthus, and Ricardo. In the next cell was a crazy agriculturist, who had announced the doctrine of rotation of crops, and driveled upon draining, until at length a commission of lunacy was issued against him. The keepers would allow him nothing but potatoes, but I threw him a few Swedish turnips, which seemed for the time to make him very happy, and he 'babbled of green' *crops* as long as I remained near him. The next wretched being that I met with seemed so profoundly melancholy that I could not refrain from asking him what folly he had committed to bring him into such dismal company.

"'I denied,' replied the idiot, 'that the Piggledies were the finest peasantry in the world— I said they had their faults, like other people.'

"'But you do not say so still?' I asked him, in a tone of profound commiseration.

"He mumbled a reply in the affirmative, and turned mopingly away to confer with the mad agriculturist, who charitably shared his turnips with him. 'Them's a pair of the incurables,' growled the keeper, a tall, savage Topsitturvian, who then took me into a ward where I saw a variety of singular cases, including one of a grocer, who insisted on placing his sugar-loaves on the broad end, to keep them from falling, and an astronomer, who adhered to the Copernican system, in opposition to the received opinion of the island, that the sun goes round the earth, and the earth round the moon, a celestial arrangement which would certainly be in perfect accordance with the institutions of Higgledy-Piggledy.

"Shocked and distressed at those sad spectacles of mental imbecility, I left the asylum with much more satisfaction than I entered it. It was such a comfort to be with the sane people once more.

"Among them I observed a wagoner yoking his cart before his horse—several farmers were shearing their pigs, and great was the cry and little the wool, as usual—a Piggledy ostler was carefully looking a stable-door, while a Piggledy thief was riding off with the horse—some industrious old women were making silk purses out of sows' ears—a wife was burning her candle at both ends—Old Piggledy was throwing the house out of the windows, and Young Piggledy was flinging his loaf into the kennel, and scampering after a rainbow. Failing to catch the airy glory, the boy commenced bawling lustily, and fell into a fury of childish passion, whereupon his mother, instead of correcting, appeased him, by setting him to blow bubbles, the only use made of soap and water by the great majority of these fantastic islanders.

"The natural history of this country is well worth attention. Its zoology is rich and curious. The sloth there attains a gigantic size, and, notwithstanding its habits of torpor, commits greater ravages than wolves and tigers in other countries. The common jackass abounds, chiefly in the precincts of the cities, and the neighborhood of Balderdash Hall, where it is not easy to distinguish its braying from that of the politicians and economists. There are wolves in sheep's clothing to be met with in many parts, and it is odd that bears are not more numerous, for the island has the strongest possible resemblance to a bear-garden.

"Among birds, the wild goose is prominent. The chase of it constitutes one of the favorite amusements of all classes. There are numerous owls, too; and the Higgledy grandees provide ruins liberally for them, by expelling the poor Higgledies, and demolishing their habitations. But the bird that is most plentiful is the gull, and though the kites and cormorants devour them in great quantities, they seem never reduced in number.[*] The insect and reptile tribes swarm; the working bee is, indeed, rare, and one species of flea is also deficient—namely, the industrious variety.

"Fish is extremely plentiful, and not more plentiful than excellent; so much so, that it is universally abjured by the people as an article

of food. They will perish of hunger sooner than eat fish, and, to strengthen this aversion, their priesthood enjoins the eating of fish as a religious penance. You may conceive how light the yoke of a religion is where the mortifications are to dine on turbot and John Dorys; but there is no end to the eccentricities and comicalities of this strange people.

"Higgledy-Piggledy is the country for meteors. The chief employment of its natives is running through their bogs after Will o' the Wisp, Jack o' the Lantern, and other *ignes fatui*.

"Vegetation flourishes. The country would be a garden, only that the taste of the people is for wildernesses. A richer field to go *simpling* in does not exist in the world. In Topsiturvia, and most parts of Funstir and Donaught, the herbs that flourish most are wormwood, ragweed, monk's-hood, and the wild variety of Justice, generally found in the crops of hemp. But the same districts are also fertile in numerous other plants, such as docks, nettles, tares, brambles, considered weeds in most countries, but by the Piggledies cultivated with almost as much attention as is elsewhere bestowed upon the gifts of Céres. There are but few bays and laurels in the island, and those few are but little cultivated. The soil seems totally unfit for the olive; attempts have been made to domesticate it, but hitherto without success.

"Higgledy-Piggledy has produced some great men, but it is not the delight of that singular island to erect statues to Genius, or monuments to Public Virtue. In revenge, however, they honor *Little Men* exceedingly. In some parts are to be seen colossal statues of Mediocrity, and the Temple of Faction *there* corresponds with the temples raised in other nations to Fame and Public Spirit. Literature is of no account whatever. Men of letters are as much despised at Hubbub, as they are honored and courted in other capitals.

"The national music is the Hurdy-Gurdy. That instrument is sculptured on their coins, and its melody is supposed to inspire the population with that national *Higgledy-Piggledy spirit* to which they are, no doubt, as much indebted for their wild institutions, as England is to the spirit of liberty for her tame ones.

"Sore puzzled is the chronicler of this bizarre commonwealth to determine what is most curious in such a profusion of natural and artificial curiosities. Upon the whole, I am disposed to admire nothing more than the little eating that satisfies the bulk of the inhabitants. They are as indifferent to the loaves as they are to the fishes, and content themselves (as we have seen) with a few roots, requiring little culture, and constituting a not more wretched than precarious subsistence for the people. The art of cooking is not much more known and practiced than the art of embroidering or sculpture. Yet, to crown all, there is a state kitchen, kept up at prodigious cost, with cooks and arch-cooks, not only to the unspeakable comfort of the Higgledies, who are amazing gourmands, as well as passionately fond of ruling the roast, but (what would be incredible if related of any other nation in the world) apparently to the no less contentment of the Piggledies, who have not so much as a bone to pick, or even the crumbs that fall from the State table."

---

[*] In Latin, the *larus communis*. It is observable that Larry (evidently from *larus*) is one of the commonest names among the Piggledies.

# BOOK V

## CHAPTER XXV.

### THE BLACK CASTLE.

'The danger hid, the place unknowne and wilde,
Breedes dreadfull doubts: oft fire is without smoke,
And perill without show: therefore your stroke,
Sir Knight, withhold, till further triall made.'
'Ah, ladie,' sayd he, 'shame were to revoke
The forward footing for an hidden shade,
Virtue gives herself light through darknesse for to wade."
FAERY QUEEN.

IT is a question often asked, what it is that makes the lives of some people so full of incident, that they seem never to make so much as the tour of their chamber, without meeting with some entertaining or remarkable adventure, while those of others are so dull and monotonous that place them in Faeryland itself, in the midst of giants, Saracens, dragons, and enchanters, nothing would ever occur to them out of the ordinary routine of the vulgarest animal life. The answer is, a radical difference of character; and the particular traits of character which, perhaps, more than any other, often make one man's career almost a novel, while the want of them renders that of his neighbor as unromantic as a treatise on logarithms, are certainly enthusiasm and courage. Both qualities were possessed by Hercules Woodward in an eminent degree, and accordingly it was not often that he took one of his prodigious walks, or made a journey on his pony, or, indeed, in any other way, without seeing, or doing, or at the very least hearing, something notable or extraordinary, of either a serious or a ludicrous description. When we saw him last, he was starting from the parsonage, on the day that the weather cleared up. His homeward route (as the reader must be aware, if she has ever so little of the organ of locality) led him to the Black Castle, the scene of his exploits the night before; and from thence his course (in fact, the only course left him now that the bridge was gone) was to proceed to the stepping-stones, far up the estuary, which his experience in the tides and floods assured him he would find, at a certain hour in the evening, high and dry above water. On arriving at the ruins, it suddenly occurred to him to make a short halt and search them, not with the idea of catching the villains themselves who had perpetrated the robbery, but because he thought it just possible that they might have inadvertently left a weapon, an article of dress, or something of the kind behind them, which might prove hereafter an important link in a chain of circumstantial evidence.

These ruins (whatever their story was) afforded not only a picturesque object to the landscape-painter, but a most convenient ambush to highwaymen; they stood within a few yards of the road, and their extent and intricacy were such, that miscreants familiar with them might use them with the greatest confidence, either for personal concealment, or a receptacle for booty. Three circular towers (one of an imposing height) remained: the loftiest provided with stairs, which, though disjointed and in decay,

were not impracticable to a supple climber; the parapets connecting these towers were broad, and in some places mantled with ivy, or overgrown with long grass, thistles, fox-glove, and even brushwood, and it was commonly said, and probably not untrue (like some tales of a ghostly nature, which were also rife), that there were subterraneous passages likewise, to add to the mystery and perils of the place.

In fact, there was not a little risk in the examination which Mr. Woodward proposed to make; but he was not the man to think of danger when he had what he considered a duty to perform, and as to fear, he did not very well know what it was. The spaces between the walls on the level of the ground were mostly stuffed with heaps of fallen rubbish, or choked with brambles, docks, nettles, and other plants that exult and expatiate in stony places. They grew there with the utmost luxuriance, affording most enviable cover for foxes and other wild animals, but the most uninviting harbor imaginable for any human creature, even for an outlaw, or a thief. Still it was possible, in two or three places (with the help of a stick for beating down the insurgent briars), to penetrate this thorny and tangled labyrinth; and Hercules laid about him vigorously, being determined to leave nothing unexplored. Once or twice he thought he had made a discovery;—some shining object caught his eye; it might be a pistol; it might be a knife, or a dagger;—but it turned out, after he had stung his fingers, and prickled his legs, over and over again, to be nothing but a fragment of mortar, or a piece of wet slate glittering in the sun. With but a single exception, he detected nothing in this part of his investigation from which he could so much as divine that any thing living had lately resorted to the place. In one spot, opposite to a breach in the outer wall, on the side toward the road, the brambles and weeds appeared to have been recently crushed, as if somebody, or something had couched there. Struck by this little circumstance, Mr. Woodward made the minutest search for several yards round among the bushes and fallen materials (literally leaving no stone unturned), but to no purpose; he found absolutely nothing, and accordingly proceeded to prosecute his inquiries in the upper part of the ruins, availing himself of the dilapidated stairs already mentioned. He commenced with the lowest of the turrets; the ascent and descent occupied but a few minutes; he startled a small white owl, and saw either a mouse, or a lizard (he was uncertain which) run out of one crevice into another; but not a trace of a robber or a robbery. The second tower gave him a little more trouble, for the stair was in such decay that, to reach the first step that was trustworthy, he had to swing himself up by the branches of a vigorous young mountain-ash, which sprang out of the rubbish underneath, as it were expressly to supply the place of the broken-down masonry. It was a feat of strength thrown away; he pulled some bunches of the red berries, to amuse his little Woodwards with on his return, and swung himself down again, debating in his mind whether it was worth while to climb the third turret, which was twice as high as the higher of the other two. A school-boyish feeling decided him; he recollected that he had never been at the top of it, and no doubt it commanded an extensive and bold view. The ascent for about thirty feet was almost quite dark; the loop-holes being choked with ivy, or loose mortar. For the next ten or a dozen the winding stair was lightsome enough, but proportionally dangerous, for the outer wall was gone entirely, and he had to mount the small, triangular, slippery steps, with no protection upon one side whatsoever. It required caution as well as courage to achieve this in safety. The next and last stage was easier, though longer than the first, and quite as dark. Hercules, however, soon surmounted all difficulties, and emerging into the light, stood instantly face to face, and within less than a yard, of one of the fiercest and wildest-looking men he ever remembered to have encountered in his life, even when he used to go out on amateur revenue duty, still-hunting through the Innishowen moors, or to protect the police.

If the fellow who confronted him so startlingly was not one of a gang of robbers, he certainly looked sufficiently like one to warrant the strongest doubts of his respectability and good intentions. He had the countenance of one who had seen the inside of prisons, and the pale ferocity of a man who was abroad more by night than by day. He was at least as tall as Hercules himself; his shoulders were broader, and his figure more erect and compact, suggesting (along with something in the style of his dress, shabby as it was) the idea that, if he had received any education, it must have been that of the drill-serjeant. However, he did not appear to be armed, which was something. It was a fearful spot, however to encounter such a fellow in—a small circular platform, not more than five or six feet in diameter, surrounded with a parapet indeed, but one that was broken down in several places and not more than two feet high when it was perfect; in fact, no protection at all, considering that if you fell, or were flung over it, there was a sheer descent of full thirty or forty yards into the road, or the court-yard beneath. The plain honest man and the palpable villain scrutinized and measured one another instinctively—the curate with a deliberate, dauntless eye, the other with a keen, but unsteady glance, which, with all its atrocity, betrayed apprehension, and even some degree of dismay and confusion. Woodward saw in an instant that the ill-looking stranger was there upon no lawful business; it alarmed him, but he showed no sign of it—his color underwent no change, his eye never wavered. The stranger was equally swift in making the discovery, to him still more alarming, that the formidable figure before him was that of a true man, although externally nearly as rough and formidable as himself. For a moment neither spoke a word. The stranger broke silence first, muttering some common-place allusion to the state of the weather. Hercules observed him, while he spoke, eyeing the cudgel in his hand with intense interest, not unmixed with suspicion and fear.

"You have chosen a commanding place for making your observations," he replied, with a fixed look and a firm voice.

"Ay," said the ruffianly stranger, shrugging his brawny shoulders, and forcing a haggard smile, "it would be an ugly fall from this into the court below."

"I shouldn't like to try it, my man," said Woodward, with the utmost coolness possible, but taking a swift comprehensive view of all the perilous circumstances of his situation, in such a place, with such an antagonist, should a contest ensue between them. In fact, it was utterly impossible that any two men (much less such men as these) could have a personal struggle where they stood without both going headlong over the parapet. Perhaps it was the conviction of this inevitable result that kept both parties from resorting to or provoking violence. At all events the peace was kept. Hercules took as leisurely a survey of all that was to be seen from the tower as if he had only his wife by his side, and was about to descend, when the stranger made a motion to do so likewise. Instantly, Hercules recollected the part of the stair where the wall was broken down for so many feet, and, resolving not to put himself in the ruffian's power by going foremost, made a step back—one was all there was room to make—and civilly, but standing firm as a rock, and, with another of his most determined looks, desired or rather commanded his unpleasant companion to take precedence. Whether it was the power of the strong man's honest eye, or the tone in which he spoke, or that the other had really no violent purpose, certain it was that he obeyed; and Hercules followed him at an interval, of a few steps. When they came to the dangerous part, how easily could he have dashed the fellow to pieces! The slightest push would have sufficed; there was nothing to grasp, nothing but the weeds or the ivy; the fall would have been inevitable and mortal; how pleased he was that he had so courteously waived his precedence. The last stage was perfectly safe as we have already seen; the curate now lost sight of the stranger in the dark, and began to turn over in his mind how to act when he rejoined him at the bottom; but he was spared all trouble upon that head, for when he issued from the lower arched doorway of the tower, among weeds and briars, the robber (for such it was now impossible to doubt that he was) was nowhere to be seen.

All quest was fruitless. Hercules recalled the traditions of subterraneous passages connected with the ruins, and at length, but very reluctantly, continued his journey. He found the stepping-stones barely passable, so that he had lost no time, and, having crossed the water (n without some hazardous jumps), was not displeased also to find that his wife had sent a gossoon with Sligo (his eccentric pony), to meet him, for it was growing late, and between climbing, walking, and other modes of motion, he was beginning to feel that he had exercised his muscles enough for the day. As fast as the pony could carry him he rode into Redcross, but before he went home, he called at the police-station in the village, and gave the *renseignements* of the mysterious miscreant he had encountered; height, size, hair, beard, complexion, expression, dress, just as they do in the "Hue and Cry," or in a French passport; and not even satisfied with this degree of accuracy, the zealous curate drew a clever sketch of the fellow in pen and ink, and left it with the constabulary for Hercules possessed in a degree the double talent of Titmarsh, whose pen, however, does not want the aid of his pencil to insure his works a permanent popularity.

Perhaps there was not a stack of turf flaming on his hearth, when he regained his dear crazy old home; and perhaps the copper kettle was not singing its ancient song, nor the preparations for tea shining in the light of the fire, nor a wife, as good as she was great, waiting to receive him in her loving arms.

Carry was deeply grieved at the robbery, alternately delighted and terrified at her husband's share in the dangers, and amazed beyond measure at the simplicity of the rector and curate, in thinking it practicable to keep such an event a secret for twenty-four hours.

Hercules then took his tea, and protracted his potations so long, that it was past midnight when his temperate carouse was over. He then poked out the fire with the nose of the bellows, although the poker was just as near him, and followed his blooming Omphale to her bower; where the last thing he said before sleep o'er-mastered him, was to deplore for the hundredth time, that he had not been successful in tracking the desperado to his den.

"Indeed, Hercules, I am heartily glad you were not," was the last speech of his spouse.

CHAPTER XXVI.

THE BOROUGH OF REDCROSS.

"Whether the bulk of our Irish natives are not kept from thriving by that cynical content in dirt and beggary, which they possess to a degree beyond any other people in Christendom?"
"Whether it be not true that the poor in Holland have no resource but their own labor, and yet there are no beggars in the streets?"
"What should hinder us from exerting ourselves, using our hands and brains, doing something or other, man, woman, and child, like the other inhabitants of God's earth?"
BERKLEY'S QUERIST.

IT was the custom of Mr. Spenser and his children to breakfast on Sunday morning at Redcross, with the Woodwards, and upon the Sunday that now came they were accompanied by Colonel Dabzac, and by Mr. Trundle, who was always quiet enough upon horseback. It was a balmy bright morning in July; just air enough on the water to curl the surface, and upon the hills beyond to make every plant that had a sweet breath yield it abundantly.

As Redcross was a corporate town, it is only respectful to give some account of it before we enter its jurisdiction. It was a small and a poor place, but might have been a respectable one, both in size and wealth, had the inhabitants devoted half as much time to honest industry as they spent in complaining about any thing, or nothing, shrugging their shoulders, whining about the times, lounging about with their dirty hands in their empty pockets, and wondering what the Lord-Lieutenant, and this Board, and that Board, meant to do for them, or whether they meant to do any thing at all. The Prot-

estant population belonging to the Established Church consisted of a grocer, a publican, two tailors, three policemen, and four revenue-officers, with their respective complements of wives and children. The Presbyterians numbered one shoemaker, two blacksmiths, a baker, a carpenter, and a wheelwright. There was one Quaker, who met in his own house; and the rest of the burghers of all trades and vocations, a vast majority of the entire population, were Roman Catholics, principally McSwynes, with a few O'Gogarties, races of old renown in the country, but generally at feud with one another, for no assigned reason except a tradition that, fourteen hundred years ago, an O'Gogarty had pulled a McSwyne by the nose; which most legitimate cause of quarrel had been honestly transmitted from generation to generation, and was indeed at present the only inheritance that remained to either of those illustrious tribes. The scenery of Redcross was remarkably fine in its way; I mean, of course, the dunghill scenery. There was a charming picturesque mount, not so sweet as Hybla, fronting almost every house, the loftiest towering before the piggeries of the McSwynes, who were as vain of them as the Swiss are of their Alps. The streets of Redcross (for it possessed three or four) were never swept except by the wind, or watered but with aqua celestis; they were consequently as dusty in dry weather, as African plains, and in wet weather perfectly Parisian—in point of mud. The Protestants, who were mostly Hoggs, threw all the dirt of the place upon their fellow-townsmen, the McSwynes, and even went so far as to say that dirt and Popery always went together. Unfortunately, however, for this theory, Amby Hogg, the sexton, and Ralph Hogg, the Presbyterian shoemaker, were the slovenliest fellows in the borough, save the Quaker, who was perhaps the slovenliest fellow in the world, and had probably for that reason taken up his abode at Redcross. Then there was Mary Jane Hogg, wife of Luke Hogg, the grocer, who was a match for any slattern in Europe; but, to be sure, she made up by her finery on Sunday for the neglect of her person on the week-days. Besides, in these days of Protestant ascendency the Hoggs had an authority and power which the McSwynes and O'Gogarties had not. The town had a corporation, and the members of it were all Hoggs, or of the Hogg faction. They might have paved, and swept, and washed, and whitewashed the municipality if they pleased. There were two aldermen of the name, three burgesses, two water-bailiffs, an officer called a bang-beggar, and another styled a butter-taster. The buttertastership was a very snug thing (two hundred a year with perquisites), and the holder of it lived at Carrickfergus. The bang-beggar was resident, and terrified the Celtic lazzarone by a furious display of authority annually, every Michaelmas. The rest of the year (three hundred and sixty-four days), mendicancy flourished better than any other profession, calling, or trade, in the borough of Redcross. There were beggars of all sorts, young and old, male and female, lame and blind, feeble and able-bodied—ay, even rich and poor. The majority were strapping women and powerful men, women who should have had the alternative of the spinning-wheel or the stocks, and men who should have been put in a dilemma between the tail of the plough ai d the tail of the cart.

As to the theaters, museums, academies, halls, and institutes of the town, there are good reasons for being silent about them. But it had one or two establishments deserving of notice— a savings' bank, a dispensary, a circulating library, and two schools. The circulating library had been established by the joint exertions of Elizabeth Spenser and Carry Woodward. They had greater difficulties to encounter than you will easily believe; their funds were so limited, and there was so much fanaticism to be encountered in some quarters, and so much selfishness in others. The wives and daughters of many of the neighboring squirearchy wanted to stock the library exclusively with the usual trash of sentimental novels, and romances of "thrilling interest," (to use a favorite phrase of Mr. Dawson's), ghosts and mysteries, love and murder. The ladies of the evangelical party would hear of nothing but sermons and tracts, lives of godly children, biographies of Calvin, and all manner of keys and antidotes to Popery. But what Elizabeth and Mr. Woodward wanted was a useful little library for the poor people of all persuasions, not excluding religious books (except such as were controversial and probably offensive), but including every thing moral, amusing, and instructive, suited to the young, and to people in humble life. However, nothing is to be done in this world, even the foundation of a village circulating library, without mutual concession and compromise; and fortunately the Spenser party were not as obstinate as others, or the library would never have been formed. As it was, it contained intellectual diet for every sort, condition, and taste; and the books (most of them in a very hoggish and swinish condition) were jumbled together on the shelves, or paraded at the little unclean window, mixed with nuts and gingerbread, tops, balls, sealing-wax, and pop-guns, for Betty Hogg, the librarian, was allowed to improve her situation by dealing a little in other toys and sweets besides those of learning.

One of the schools, too, was entirely aunt Carry's. It was a school for boys and girls under ten, and the school-mistress was an Ellen Hogg, who understood her craft, every art and branch of her profession, as well as Shenstone's school-mistress herself. She was a tall, stern-looking, middle-aged, powerful woman, kindly to the industrious and docile, but the terror of truants and evil-doers. There grew no birchen-tree in her garden, but there were birches on the neighboring hills, which provided her with abundant discouragements to sloth, and stimulants to virtue. Mrs. Woodward was a disciplinarian herself, and discipline reigned wherever her influence reached. Then Ellen Hogg was as neat in her person (though people did not expect it from her name), as any woman could well be. Before her door there were no beauties of dunghill scenery to be seen. Brushes and brooms were known to her. She used, and she enforced the use of them.

Encouraged by Aunt Carry, she aspired to reform the personal habits of the rising generation radically, and the urchin who was not washed by his mother at home was sure to be washed by Ellen at school, and whipped at the pump into the bargain. The blooming Carry visited the school frequently, always after church on Sunday, with her swarm of children about her, like little satellites about a great primary; and then and there was a muster of all the pupils, and much catechising, and a report made of the doings and misdoings of previous week.

The party from the parsonage reached the village and the curate's house in the highest spirits; the cheeks of the girls glowing with healthy color, after their brisk mountain ride, Mr. Spenser sedately cheerful, Mr. Trundle perfectly inoffensive, and the colonel looking not quite so grim as he generally did. Hercules and his wife received their company in their several styles, but both with the utmost cordiality. The cordiality of the curate was blunt and rustic, with his Lizzy, his Vals, and Mags, cutting every name down but the repulsive Arabella's, in his homely, affectionate way.

Carry's reception was as lady-like as it was hearty. She was habited in her dark blue Sunday silk, with a plain straw hat, or open bonnet, with cherry-colored ribbons, which streamed upon such a bust and pair of shoulders as you may see in Rubens's picture of the abduction of the Sabine women, or in his works passim. Her bulk gave a momentum to her embraces that was almost alarming when she pressed a child to her breast, or even grown girls like her nieces. Elizabeth, whom she clasped twice as fondly as she did Arabella, seemed for a moment lost in the arms of her portly aunt, whose bracelet, indeed, might almost have served either of the Spenser girls for a girdle.

"Carry, let me introduce Colonel Dabzac," said Mr. Spenser, when the first rush of the embracing and ardor of kissing was over.

Carry courtsied with buxom dignity, and said she was very happy to see Colonel Dabzac in her house. Trundle was presented next, and received the same courteous notice. The curate made some excuses, as awkward as they were needless, for the apartment was neat and clean; the repast substantial and excellent, the table-cloth the most beautiful fabric of Downshire, and white as the driven snow; in short, every thing was quite good enough for Dabzac, had he been a field-marshal. The only thing that happened untoward during breakfast was the sudden incursion of a couple of very pretty pigs (a particular breed which Carry was rearing) into the parlor. This was certainly a little amiss; but the pigs were the cleanliest little animals of the kind you ever saw, and the excuse for their escapade was, that the door of their sty was off its hinges, and Hercules had neglected to repair it, no doubt with a little of the procrastination of his country.

"I hope I don't intrude," said aunt Carry, pleasantly, being the first to perceive the invaders.

The little Woodwards jumped from their seats with the greatest glee to pursue the little pigs back to the yard. Every body laughed, even the dry Dabzac.

"Do you remember, Val," said Hercules, "the morning the gander paid you a visit while you were dressing in my study?"

"It was in the Observatory," said Mr. Spenser, with the gravity of a man correcting a serious historical mistake.

"Come, Val., it was not quite so good as that."

"It *was* the Observatory, papa," said the eldest boy, from the side table, "for that was the morning the refractory telescope was broken—the gander broke it.

Another laugh, of course, at the boy's blunder, which, after all, was no very great one, for the telescope *was* a refractory one, sometimes showing none of Jupiter's moons, sometimes double the actual number.

The curate repeated the nursery rhyme, certainly very appropriate—

"Goosy, goosy gander,
Whither do you wander?
Up stairs,
Down stairs,
And in my lady's chamber."

The Woodwards had five children, two fine, flourishing, large-limbed boys, and three rosy, bright-eyed girls. They had their breakfast apart, and were not very silent at it, but, at the same time, not very boisterous either. Carry, and her nursery-governess, had them in too good order for that. Her children were striking proofs that affectionate and judicious discipline has no tendency whatever to break the spirit— at least, that it breaks no spirit which ought not to be broken.

There was never, perhaps, a more animated breakfast—plenty to talk about as well as plenty to eat. The curate had his last adventure at the Black Castle to tell, and the rector related the explosion of the secret, and the garrisoning and fortifying of the parsonage, with a quiet humor that diverted every body extremely. When Carry heard of Dawson having dined and slept at her brother's house, her features assumed their severe and displeased expression instantly, though perhaps only Elizabeth observed it; but when she learned that her nephew was actually at that moment ranging the country with his scampish friend, she roundly expressed her opinion that it would have been much seemlier in him to have accompanied his father and sisters to church. Mr. Spenser made no reply.

Children are sharp observers! Before breakfast was half over, the little Woodwards had settled that Dabzac was courting their cousin Arabella, and we need scarcely say that their mother was not less quick in arriving at the same conclusion.

The two families and their visitors went to church in a long procession, taking the middle of the street, the better to avoid the odoriferous mountain chains which adorned the fronts of the wigwams to the right and to the left—almost every where, except opposite to the academy and residence of Mrs. Ellen Hogg, whom they found at her door, flaming in pink calico, marshaling a troop of her Protestant pupils, all scrupulously washed, though by no means all as well clothed and fed as philanthropy could have wished. Boys and girls made the most respectful obeisances to the majesty of aunt Carry, as she paused for a moment in her stately progress to review the line and drop a word of gracious civility to the "crassa Minerva" of the village. Two of the children, who had stuck orange lilies in their breasts, got alarmed as Mrs. Woodward approached them, and dropped them on the ground by stealth. Elizabeth, also, received not a few rustic salutations, of a less

E

ceremonious character. As to the rector and curate, they were so engrossed by the interesting subjects they had to talk and consult about, that they had no eyes for Mrs. Hogg and her herd, who very properly, therefore, economized their genuflections for another occasion.

The police station was hard by the church; Hercules looked in to see whether any steps had been taken in consequence of the information he had given the night before, and was pleased to find that a search had been made that very morning, at break of day, through the ruins, and for several miles round about them. The police had made no capture, but they reported that they had discovered a pit, or chasm, in the ground floor of the castle, nearly concealed by weeds and rubbish, and communicating with a vault underneath, into which it was not improbable that the villain seen by the curate might have disappeared. Two of the party had ventured down, and it was an enterprise that required no little courage. The smell of tobacco established the fact that something human had recently harbored there, for (as one of the men observed) it couldn't have been a rabbit or a fox that was smoking. They struck a light, and minutely examined the vault, but found nothing but the back of a letter, which the chief constable produced. The direction was in a gentlemanlike hand, but such a hand as the acutest clerk in the post-office could scarcely have deciphered. Mr. Spenser said it looked like the name of Dawson, but Hercules thought it was Lawlor; one of the constables suggested Roberts, and another was positive it was Moran. There was an initial before it, which might have been almost any letter of the alphabet, but it certainly bore a strong likeness to the first letter of the surname. On the other side was a scrawl in another hand, but in pencil, and so much defaced as to be nearly as illegible as the writing in ink. It looked like an inventory of some kind, and the word "pictures" was tolerably plain, at all events. Hercules took the paper from the officer, saying that his wife was very skillful in deciphering bad writing, and now the bell ceasing to toll announced that it was time for divine service to commence.

It was a small, modest, whitewashed church, a little ruinous, and not like the picturesque old village churches in England screened and adorned with those ancient yews that furnished the British infantry with their good bows, before the bow was superseded by the firelock. But the ivy for which Ireland is justly renowned had taken a great fancy to one side of the rude edifice, and had crept up to the very summit of the belfry, so as to impede the swinging of the bell a little. This relieved the otherwise naked aspect of the building, and harbored flocks of sparrows, which made no scruple of chattering often in the very midst of the Litany. The church-yard was small, and so populous with the fathers and forefathers of Redcross, that the green graves rose in hillocks, up to the level of the windows, and sometimes still higher, obstructing disagreeably both the light and the air. It was an ancient burial-place. One or two of Mr. Spenser's predecessors had inhumanly endeavored to monopolize it for Protestant interment, but there had been no such detestable bigotry and foul injustice in his time: it was the common resting-place for the dead of the parish;·the Hoggs, McSwynes, and O'Gogarties slumbered side by side, their differences at an end; their feuds forgotten; setting an example of peace and tranquillity, which few of them set when they were above ground.

Nothing happened very remarkable during the service of this Sunday. Hercules read the prayers with stentorian voice and energy. Mr. Spenser read·his quiet, rational, and impressive sermon, upon brotherly love and Christian charity, not without reference to an approaching anniversary, on which it was too much the custom of his Protestant parishioners to indulge in demonstrations which gave umbrage to their Catholic fellow-townsmen, and led to counter exhibitions of the opposite color, not always terminating without infractions of the peace. In the midst of the discourse, the sparrows happening to be particularly loquacious in the ivy, the curate (who, orange as he was in principle, made it a point himself to be as soothing and pacificatory as possible at this exciting time of the year) gave a nod to Amby Hogg, the sexton, to go out and chase away the disturbers, but Amby either performed this (an ordinary duty of his office) very imperfectly, or not at all, for the chattering continued all through the sermon. The truth, indeed, was, that the sexton was very far from approving of Mr. Spenser's dissuasives from strife and faction, for he kept a small public-house which did twice the usual business when the orange lilies were in blow, and the sparrows, in his opinion, were doing no great harm in drowning a discourse so prejudicial to his trade. The shrewd aunt Carry, too, whose roving and piercing eye let nothing pass that passed around her (even when the little Hoggs in the aisle whispered one another on a matter of gingerbread), could easily perceive, by the slightest·possible scornful curl of Colonel Dabzac's insolent lip, that he was saying to himself " we wouldn't stand that sort of talk at Tanderagee."

But Dabzac was doomed to undergo something still more revolting to his feelings before the day was over, for Mr. Spenser met the benevolent and burly Father Magrath·in the street after church, and invited him home to dinner. Magrath (who had ·been ·as zealous that day at the altar as the rector had·been, in the pulpit to inculcate the doctrines of peace and charity) accepted the invitation cheerfully, and promised to overtake the party· on the mountain. It was a chapter of Irish history to mark how the colonel looked at the priest, just as if he was a dog, or the priest of a religion in which a dog was the divinity. Father Magrath, on the other hand, eyed the colonel with the defiant air of a man who felt that he represented the people, and that the cause of the people was "conquering and to conquer." The intense enmity with which they regarded one another was, indeed, ·the means of keeping the peace between them ;·for, feeling that any converse must inevitably lead to a warmth of altercation incompatible with good manners, particularly in ladies' company, they·refrained, by mutual consent, from holding any intercourse whatsoever.

But what had become of Mr. Trundle ? · He certainly·came out of church with the·rest, yet,

when Mr. Spenser began to collect his little flock of relatives and guests, whom he was that day to provide with carnal as 'well as with spiritual food, "the little, fat, round, oily man" of projects was not to be seen. There was a game of "hide and seek" about the precincts of the church to find him ; and where' should he turn up at last but in Mrs. Hogg's school-room, getting the strapping Ellen herself and all her scholars, male and female, down to the smallest thing that could make a scratch with a pen, to sign his petition and address to the Crown for the ship-canal between Loch Foyle and Loch Swilly.

---

## CHAPTER XXVII.
### THE RETURN.

"Here we go up, up, up,
And here we go down, down, downy."
NURSERY RHYMES.

THE return to the parsonage resembled the march of a caravan.· In front rode the Spenser girls and Colonel Dabzac. Then came the curate's inside car, a curious, square, spacious vehicle, of very rude construction, painted dark-green, and drawn by a mule ; it contained Carry herself (no bad proof of its capacity), one of her little girls on her knee, another by her side, rather pinched for room, and the two boys, poor Billy· Pitt and little Hercules, both still petticoated, on the opposite seat, their red and white legs now and then appearing amid the ample folds of their mother's.dress. The car was followed by the· rector on his brown mare, Mr. Trundle triumphing in his accession of signatures, the curate bestriding Sligo, and Dr. Wilkins, the. doctor of the neighborhood, who always paid Mrs. Spenser a Sunday visit, and generally dined at the parsonage on that day. Sometimes $E_{l_i-a}b_{e_{th}}$ ·fell back to chat with her aunt, and point out some beauty in the prospect; sometimes Hercules bolted forward to join his nieces, take his little namesake up before him on the pony, or ask the elder boy the Latin for a goat or a sea-gull, just to see how he was improving under his mother's tuition. He had a prodigious stock ´of nursery hymns, too, for the entertainment of children, and tales of Æsop's immortal fox, to whose deeds he sometimes gave a political complexion, so much so that the rector used to· say, " Hercules, your fox is always a Whig."

· Doctor Wilkins· was a remarkable man ; he had the most lugubrious· countenance you ever saw, yet he seldom spoke but he made you die laughing. He was well worth a college of your grave, formal physicians. ·It was hard to say how it was Doctor Wilkins made you laugh, but he did it, never once smiling himself; on the contrary, seemingly quite unconscious, that he was at ·all amusing, and looking the picture of the· profoundest melancholy, while every body within hearing was holding his sides. · He knew every body, and had a dry, solemn, historical way of reproducing the preposterous things he heard or witnessed, which (enhanced by a smooth, rich brogue)· was absolutely. irresistible. He embellished very little, but he brought out the ridiculous points to admiration, and in the most artless way.in the world, more as if he was talking to himself than trying or wishing to entertain the company. It was in reality comic talent of a high order, but he was an able physician likewise, and justly popular with both rich and poor all round the country.

It was a sultry day in the valleys, but on the heights and on the water there was a delicious breeze. Mrs. Woodward, not being partial to boating, lamented the destruction of the bridge, and began to stir up the gentlemen to have the mischief repaired promptly.

"I was over at Major Armstrong's yesterday," drawled the doctor, "and they were talking on that subject. O'Madden was dining there, and one or two more."

"The bridge is, or I should say was, on the major's property, I believe," said the rector.

"One side of the water is the major's ground," replied Wilkins, "and the other, it appears, is the O'Madden's."

"The expense will be trivial—I should say under twenty pounds," said Mr. Spenser.

"So they were saying," said the doctor, "but, from all I could collect, I doubt if the work will ever be done, necessary as it is, unless the county takes it in hand, or his excellency the lord lieutenant."

"The lord lieutenant!" exclaimed Mr. Spenser—"why, it's not a bridge in the Phœnix Park!"

"The major says it's the business of the grand jury; O'Madden is for throwing it on the government. I'll tell you more," added the doctor; "there was a bit of a memorial drawn up in my presence, and I left them seriously talking of sending up a deputation to the castle, tomorrow or next day."

"You astonish me," said Mr. Spenser, "though I have been long enough in Ireland, too. Why, in England—"

"But we are not in England," said the doctor.

"I sometimes think we are in Higgledy-Piggledy," said Carry Woodward.

"And the O'Madden, too! a man who never opens his lips but to bluster on patriotism and independence," cried Mr. Spenser with unusual warmth.

"And isn't it the height of patriotism to keep our own money in our pockets, and get as much as we can out of Johnny across the water?" drawled the doctor.

"I've a good mind," said the curate, "to go up with the deputation to Dublin, and put in my private claims at the same time. I want a hinge to the door of my pig-sty, as you know, Val."

"A capital satire it would be," said Mr. Spenser.

After some time the rector and curate recommenced their argument on college education, and Hercules, as before, had the best of it decidedly, clearly proving that it was far more difficult for a young man to go through the Dublin university without some improvement, than through either Oxford or Cambridge, and again enumerating with enthusiasm all the legs of mutton he had eaten, and all his ambrosial nights with Tom Beamish.

While this dialogue was going on, Elizabeth was riding close alongside of the car, conversing on the same topic with Mrs. Woodward. They talked also of Mr. Dawson, whose connection with Sydney was growing every day a source of greater uneasiness to the ladies of the Spenser family.

"Has your father no control?" asked Mrs. Woodward, earnestly.

"He is so occupied with Mrs. Spenser and his books," said Elizabeth.

"I have no patience with my brother," cried Carry, in great vexation; "the worst of this unfortunate robbery is, that it seems likely to entangle Sydney still more with that dangerous man. What an evening you must have had with him! Was he as coarse as usual?"

"Indeed, aunt," said Elizabeth, smiling, "his coarseness is not half so disagreeable as his refinement; but I would freely forgive both if he would only not be so excessively attentive to me as he always is; he was particularly odious the other evening."

"My poor girl," said Carry, with compassionate vehemence, "if I were your father, or your brother, I would not allow such a person as Mr. Dawson to come within twenty miles of you, if there was a pistol, or a horsewhip to be had in the world."

It was curious to observe the looks of admiration and awe with which Mrs. Woodward's children regarded her when she delivered herself in this impassioned sort of way. Their eyes were riveted on her face, and the play of her animated though massive features was indeed very imposing.

"I am sometimes surprised at papa," said her niece, after a moment's pause, "he is so observant, and so naturally fastidious; but I never saw him so annoyed by Mr. Dawson's manners and conversation as he was on Friday."

"Very well," said Mrs. Woodward, "but will he forbid Sydney to keep his company?—that's the question."

"But my uncle, you know," rejoined Elizabeth, "sometimes takes Mr. Dawson's part, so we must not be so hard upon papa."

"Oh, many a battle I have with your uncle on that subject," said Carry; "indeed, I think it's the only thing we ever fight about, except the state of his study."

Before dinner there was a grand levee held in Mrs. Spenser's boudoir; Miss M'Cracken and Rebecca officiating as maids of honor; and the salts and tonics, with a bouquet of magnificent green-house flowers, duly arranged on a little oval table, covered with a fair napkin. Doctor Wilkins, the state physician, had recommended her to receive visitors, knowing the efficacy of a little gossip and excitement in female disorders of the nervous class. The bed-room was the prettiest room in the house, overlooking a flower-garden, with the water and hills beyond, and furnished both with taste and luxury, the taste being the husband's and the luxury the wife's. The lady sat near the window, with pillows behind, pillows under, and pillows on each side of her, richly attired in black satin, and looking so very pale that you expected to hear some news from the other world every time she opened her lips. Mrs. Spenser was one of those women who know something about every body in a certain sphere, and who are expert at discovering some sort of relationship or connection more or less remote between themselves and every body else in the same privileged circle. She graced Dabzac at once with her special favor, knew some near relatives of his intimately, and presumed he was related to Sir Thomas Dabzac, of Shropshire. Her reception of aunt Carry (whom she stood slightly in awe of), was civil enough, more because she was a Spenser than because she was the best of women; but she returned the friendly greetings of the curate with a coldness which, however, hurt the rector more than it did Hercules himself, who despised the lady too much to care for the temperature of her courtesy, had it been down to zero. Mrs. Spenser, indeed, looked on curates in the light of tutors and such low people. As to the doctor, he was too useful to be snubbed; but, indeed, he would not have brooked it from her; he was one of the few people who kept her in any subjection, contradicting her with a courage that astonished Mr. Spenser, and returning slight for slight, the true way to deal with impertinent women, whether in their boudoirs or their drawing-rooms.

"Who preached to-day, my dear?" she said to Elizabeth, who sat close to her. She knew very well that her husband had preached, but she had her own small reasons for asking.

"Papa," replied her step-daughter.

"Papa!—again!" exclaimed the white lady in black satin, in a weak but perfectly audible tone.

The point of this short speech was in the "again," or rather in the tone and look with which the word was pronounced. It conveyed most distinctly, and was intended to convey "what is the use, Mr. Spenser, of keeping a curate, if you preach yourself so often?"

Carry fired up, and bit her lip—only for the strangers present she would never have put up with it. She sometimes gave Mrs. Spenser a bit of her mind, as well as Doctor Wilkins. The fact, however, was, that Mr. Spenser did preach much more frequently than most rectors do who have curates to preach for them. People sometimes said that he was the curate and Mr. Woodward the rector. It arose from Mr. Spenser's considerate regard for his brother-in-law, who, having so large a family, and so poor a stipend, was compelled to have other irons in the fire to make out a respectable livelihood.

The rector now expressed his hope that Mrs. Spenser would join the family at dinner: "What do you say, Doctor Wilkins?"

"I say yes, by all means; it will do her all the good in the world," answered the doctor, bluntly and decidedly.

"Ah, I am not equal to it—I am not indeed, Doctor Wilkins;—the very idea of dinner makes me ill—doesn't it, Miss M'Cracken?"

Miss M'Cracken assented, of course;—it was in the routine of her office.

Mrs. Spenser continued, speaking as if it was an effort far beyond her strength, "She hoped Colonel Dabzae would excuse her, she was always such a wretched invalid; the climate of Ireland was killing her; and you may imagine," she added, "that the late awful event has almost finished me; I can bear any thing—any thing in the world—but this dreadful state of things, when we can't call our lives our own, without having one's house fortified like a castle, and the police at one's very door."

"Oh, be asy, my darling," audibly muttered Doctor Wilkins, in his long-drawn, comical way.

Mrs. Woodward had been watching his countenance, which had been growing longer and longer during Mrs. Spenser's speech, until at last it grew as lugubrious as possible, and then he came out with his amusing "Oh, be asy."

"Indeed, Valentine," the lady went on, affecting not to hear the doctor, "I would greatly prefer having a military force; soldiers are so much better disciplined; I'm positive, if you would write to your friend Mr. —, at the castle, he would order a regiment to be quartered here."

"A regiment, my dear!" exclaimed Mr. Spenser, smiling.

"Well, a company," said the silly invalid.

"Fudge, nonsense, humbug," interrupted Wilkins, unable to stand this any longer; "the best company for you is our company at dinner; that's the company you want, ma'am. Come, we must strengthen your nerves; rout you about, and put some flesh on your bones, ma'am. 'Faith, I'm not so sure that if Captain Rock was to pay you a visit in earnest, it wouldn't do you more good than the doctors. I'll order you an insurrection if you don't behave yourself."

Every body laughed but Miss M'Cracken. Mrs. Spenser was struck dumb by the doctor's audacity, and enraged at the effect it produced on the circle.

"The doctor's a regular $trump$," said Hercules to his wife, as they went down stairs to have a little conjugal stroll on the sands and examine together the paper found by the police.

"I trust they will not persuade her to come down to dinner," said Carry, highly incensed at Mrs. Spenser's impertinences.

"So do I, devoutly," said her husband; "I sometimes think that poor woman is possessed with a fiend."

"God help the fiend," answered Carry, "that were possessed with her; I should say poor fiend, not poor woman."

"What a person for your brother to place at the head of his family!" said Hercules.

Something between a sigh and a groan that came from the abysses of Carry's voluminous person, heaving up her stomacher like a great billow, testified her cordial concurrence in the sentiment.

Directly Mrs. Woodward glanced at the paper, she said the name was Dawson, but the curate still insisted that it was Lawlor, and said he had no doubt about it. His wife was just as positive on her side.

"But, my dear," said Hercules, "how is it possible a paper belonging to Mr. Dawson could have found its way into a vault under the Black Castle?"

"Easily enough," replied Carry, looking very mysterious, and speaking very deliberately, "if Mr. Dawson had a hand—"

The curate was too indignant to allow her to finish the sentence. He gave her an awful lecture on what he called the female vices of suspicion and detraction. Carry bit her lip, but made no answer.

# BOOK VI.

## CHAPTER XXVIII.

### THE ISLAND.

" Oh, had we some bright little isle of our own
In the blue summer ocean far off and alone !"
MOORE.

" Blanda pericla maris." CLAUDIAN.

MR. SPENSER proposed to put off the pic-nic voyage to the island until the return of his son; —a cruise without Sydney seemed, indeed, like a fleet going to sea without an admiral;—but his daughters and their aunt were unanimous against the postponement; not that they were pleased to be without Sydney (rough as he was), but his presence would probably involve that of his friend Dawson, the feeling against whom was so strong, that the party would have been broken up had the postponement been insisted on. Mr. Spenser intended to have made one of the voyagers, but he was compelled to do service on that day upon terra firma. At an early hour in the morning he was waited on by the commandant of the police force, whose object was to intimate that he was under the necessity of withdrawing the garrison from the parsonage, as the services of the men were required in a neighboring parish, where some slight disturbances had actually broken out connected with the collection of tithes. This intelligence was doubly unpleasant; the agitation was approaching alarmingly near, and protection was about to be withdrawn at the very moment it seemed to be really desirable to have it. How to communicate the news to Mrs. Spenser was, however, the practical difficulty that first occurred. There was, of course, another hubbub, quite as great as what took place when she discovered Maguire's robbery. There was no resource but to write to the Under-Secretary for the aid of the military. Mr. Spenser doubted the absolute necessity of the application, but he was compelled to sit down by his wife's bedside, and an urgent letter, dictated by that lady's own lips, was sent by the next post up to Dublin Castle.

The Woodwards (having pressed Doctor Wilkins into their service) sailed from their own place of embarkation close to the village. The curate had a good stout well-built smack of his own, called the Caroline, after his wife. The arrangements were rough, but not very uncomfortable, and, when a pic-nic on the island was in view, the smack was always provisioned for a week, to guard against casualties, such as an unlucky shifting of the wind, or a sea-fog. Hercules was never so glorious as on a day like this. It developed his animal strength, and excited his animal spirits. It made him a boy again, and no boy could have more fully, or almost more boisterously, enjoyed it. Carry promoted such expeditions on his account chiefly; it was his only relaxation after weeks of such pastoral labors as no pastor in the church but himself could have gone through. Indeed, his very relaxation would have broken down most other men.

The Spensers had their trim cutter, the Gipsy, and a pretty boat she was, though not to be mentioned on the same day with George Markham's Circe. Dabzac understood something of navigation, but there were better seamen on board the Gipsy, or Mr. Spenser would not have committed his children to the Atlantic in her. The girls went on board immediately after an early breakfast, accompanied by the colonel, and Miss M'Cracken, with the second brood of the Spensers.

There was so little air on the water near the parsonage, that the cutter had to be towed for a couple of miles down the creek, where she caught a breath of wind from the hills to the northward, just sufficient, with the help of an ebbing tide, to waft her gently toward the sea. The scenery was beautifully bold, and grew wilder and loftier every moment, while the inlet narrowing at the same time toward its mouth brought the heights on each side closer and closer, until at length the voyagers found themselves in a marine gorge, through which for some minutes there seemed to be no passage. The height of the mountains just here was so great as to exclude the direct rays of the sun at that early hour, so that a certain air of somber magnificence distinguished the scenery at this spot, which had therefore acquired the romantic name of the Dark Glen of the Ocean. A few knots further changed the view remarkably. As you emerged from these gloomy waters, you passed as it were through the jaws of the gulf, and the prospect of the Atlantic burst upon you in all its splendor. There was always a little agitation here on the stillest day in summer. The Spensers were always distracted between their admiration for the view at this point and the disagreeable motion that universally accompanied it. Here, too, when there was any breeze, you were sure to get either all the benefit or all the disadvantage of it. The breeze was now as propitious as possible. The cutter showed all her canvas, and flew through the waves merrily.

" Why, that is a castle before us !" cried Dabzac, struck by the singular appearance of a pile about half a league distant, in the direct line of their course.

It was not a castle, but only a huge castellated cliff, forming the eastern face of the islet toward which the Gipsy was bound. The resemblance to an extensive castle, like that at St. Goar on the Rhine, was very remarkable; geologists accounted for it by the basaltic character of the rock of which the islet was composed. It seemed a group of ruinous turrets, of various heights, some very commanding, and connected by parapets and battlements, in which the eye, aided a little by fancy, discovered embrasures and portholes, and every thing that a regular fortress ought to be provided with. The mouth of a cavern near the center of the mass had all the appearance of a low-browed arched gate with a portcullis. The deception, on the whole, was very complete and singular. It was sometimes called The Isle of the Tower, either from this remarkable peculiarity, or from a real tower or fort, the ruins of which still existed in the interior. But the name it commonly went by was T ry Island, probably a corruption of the other appellation; or it may have been a Tory fastness in by-gone days, when Tories were synonymous in the north of Ireland with robbers and rapparees. Mr. Woodward, who was a passionate antiquary, had a long and learned story from that extremely barren chronicle, "the Annals of the Four Masters," about the original occupation of this island by the Fomorians, a race of gigantic corsairs, or sea-kings, sons of Ham, and consequently grandsons of Noah. Mr. Spenser used to say that Hercules looked extremely like a Sea-King himself.

The Gipsy was joined, amid mutual cheers, by the Caroline, immediately under the gigantic crags we have described. The water there was deep enough for a frigate to ride in, almost up to the very edge of the rock, so that (the sea being smooth as crystal) the smack and cutter cast their anchors within a yard of the shore, and the party actually jumped on land, all but aunt Carry for whom a stout plank was provided.

At first sight you thought there was no issue from the short and narrow strip of beach on which you stood, after landing at this spot; it seemed as if you were completely hemmed in by the water on one side and the tall towered cliffs on the other. But a steep stair, as winding as a cork-screw, had been roughly, but ingeniously, hewn out among the fissures and crevices of the rock, enabling you to climb with considerable labor, but without much risk, not exactly to the summit, but to a cleft, as it were, between two bastions, from which a hollow slope of beautifully smooth and verdant turf introduced you at once into the ferny interior of the island, right among the panic-stricken conies. The whole extent was not more than some dozen of acres; a little hollow or basin, with the richest wild vegetation, presenting a rocky front to the ocean on every side.

You may fancy how the young Spensers and their cousins, the still bolder little Woodwards, reveled in a place like this. The latter were the first to gain the top of the ascent, and they were a little scared and surprised to find the island apparently in possession, not of the rabbits, as usual, but of an enormous Newfoundland dog, whom they saw careering through the brake, lost in its deep masses, now appearing again, rushing up to them with apparent hostility, and as swiftly scampering off once more, in exuberance of canine spirits. It puzzled them extremely to find such an animal on the island, and it puzzled the wiser heads of the party, too, as they toiled up the craggy parapet in succession. Carry Woodward always felt this part of the expedition sensibly, and often and often had declared that she never would undergo it again; but still there had never been a party to Tory Island without her.

The proper way to go down the green slope was running; the curate, Doctor Wilkins, and the boys, were already up to their hips in the fern; the great Hercules, quite as wild as the little, who was as wild as one of Cadwallader's goats. The curate had already shot a brace of rabbits. Carry stood puffing and panting to rest herself, looking quite overcome and exhausted. Dabzac offered her his arm to make the descent, but she said she always managed it best by herself, with just the help of her parasol. The girls made the race with their usual activity and suc-

cess. Miss M'Cracken got down with the help of Doctor Wilkins, and poor Mrs. Woodward got down too, only that just at the last the bank was too slippery, or her parasol too frail, or her momentum too considerable, for she fell in the most amusing manner with the utmost possible safety, and came sliding down to where the turf was level, and further slipping was against the laws of nature. Elizabeth was at her side in an instant, and there was merry laughing, of course, Carry laughing herself as pleasantly as the rest, as soon as she got on her legs again. Meanwhile the dog continued to make his evolutions through the fern, occasioning a dozen speculations as to how he came there and who could own him. Once or twice he disappeared on the opposite side over a brow which led to the ruin already mentioned, under which, upon a spacious flat rock, about thirty feet long by twenty broad, the Spensers had long ago fixed a rustic table of great massiveness, and surrounded (except on the side next the sea) with a bench formed of huge stones, cushioned with green sods. This was the point to which parties of pleasure (always more or less sensual) generally made in the first instance. The boatmen carried the panniers with the provisions, and Mrs. Woodward herself superintended the dispositions for what many people consider the most indispensable part of a *fête-champêtre*.

"There must be other people, papa, on the island besides ourselves, to-day," said Billy Pitt to his father.

"I can't think it possible, Billy," said the curate, "my fear is that there has been a wreck; it is only too probable that the yacht we saw in danger during the gale has been lost here; I can not account in any other way for a dog like that being on the island, and see, he has a collar round his neck."

The dog rushed past them at the moment up the slope that commanded the ruins and the rustic table beneath them; Billy Pitt ran forward with nearly equal speed, and in a few moments made a signal to his father to hasten after him, which, of course, he did with his giant strides, expecting to see something surprising, and he was not disappointed.

At the rustic table, about fifty yards beneath the place where he stood, sat two young men, attired in seemingly naval uniform, actively engaged in discussing an excellent dinner, and seemingly as much at their ease, and at home, as if the island belonged to them in fee-simple. The dinner was not entirely a cold one, for a wreath of smoke was perceptible ascending from one of the dishes, which seemed to consist of broiled fish; a supposition which was confirmed by the circumstance that a fire had been kindled, and was still burning within the adjacent ruins, which had an arched gate-way communicating with the flat rock.

"They have turned the hall of Conaing's Tower into a kitchen," said Billy Pitt, highly excited and irritated at what, to his ingenuous and enthusiastic mind, appeared a most sacrilegious proceeding.

"Yes, and I am mistaken," said Mr. Woodward, "if that is not the cook lying on his back in the shadow there under the wall, resting from his labors."

"See, papa, they are drinking cider."

"More probably champagne, Billy," replied his father; "upon my word, they seem to be a pair of luxurious young pirates." The curate knew what champagne was, probably not so well by the report of the cork, as the report of the world. Even Mr. Spenser did not drink expensive wines, and as to episcopal dinners, the curate had only read of them, and scarce believed half that he read.

"They do look piratical," said Doctor Wilkins, "the taller of the two wears a cutlass, and I see something behind the other like a blunderbuss— it is either a blunderbuss or a telescope."

At this moment, one of the banqueters on the rock gave a shrill whistle, and cried Pedro in a sonorous voice, which made the cliffs and caves ring again. Pedro was chasing the rabbits and other innocent little wild beasts many a yard away, too far to be within hearing of the signal, and the young man who had made it stood up to look after his dog, and in so doing discovered Mr. Woodward, his son, and Doctor Wilkins peering down upon him from the edge of the precipice. If the curate had been surprised at the sight of the strangers in naval dress, they, upon their part, were far more startled at the sight of him. He was indeed a figure that might well have been taken for a pirate, and a formidable one. His gigantic size, his features, which looked at a distance so truculent, his round, broad-brimmed, low-crowned glazed hat, his blue jacket, and the fowling-piece on his shoulder, formed an *ensemble* which led irresistibly to the conclusion that he was some bold smuggler, or sea-attorney, who had made this almost inaccessible islet his stronghold. Doctor Wilkins wore a blue jacket also, and might be very well taken for a mate or a coxswain.

The curate was soon made sensible of the impression he produced, for the young man who was on his legs seized a rifle which had been lying beside him, and made a sign to his comrade to arm himself, too, which he immediately did, grasping the gun which Billy had taken for a telescope. At this critical moment arrived aunt Carry, escorted by the colonel, and followed by her beautiful nieces and the rest of the party. The young men looked at one another, and conversed in a low tone.

"The pirate or smuggler, or whatever he is has got a jolly fat wife," said George Markham.

"And a fine family," said Vivyan.

"I fear it will turn out that we are the intruders," said Markham.

"I fear so," said his friend; "these people may possibly be the proprietors of this island, they look wild enough for it;—*we* certainly are not;—in my opinion we ought to parley with them."

"And invite them to join us," added George, "the women look civilized, at all events, and so do two of the men—that tall fellow in the pea-jacket with the gun is certainly a very ill-looking desperado."

"Probably a kind of amphibious game-keeper; —remember we are in Connaught."

"Well, here goes," cried Markham, "I'll face the party, strong as it is; do you make that lubberly Lawrence stir himself; threaten to mast-head him, and set a few flasks of champagne to cool in the water; there's a great lobster left in the square basket—make him

dress it;—I'll give a whistle should I want you to come to me,"—and so speaking, the active young sportsman sprang up the rocks in an oblique direction by a track he had before discovered, and which conducted him in less than five minutes to the group on the top of the cliffs, who were eagerly discussing who the invaders of their island might be, and where they should spread their dinner, now that the flat rock had been usurped so unceremoniously.

The curate, feeling himself the leading personage of his sex present, advanced to meet Markham, who did not at once renounce the opinion he had formed of him at a distance; but the misapprehension was removed directly Woodward spoke, which he was the first to do, apologizing most civilly for having interrupted the young men so unseasonably.

"It is our part to apologize," said Markham, with a gesture of courtesy intended for the ladies who stood close by, as much as for the strange personage with whom he talked—"but our story is simply this: we are mariners in distress—all but shipwrecked—we have been cast upon this island, where we are doing our best to make ourselves comfortable; among other things, we have been trying to-day to make out a dinner; and if you and your party will only honor my friend and myself with your company down on the table-rock yonder, we shall esteem it the greatest kindness you can possibly confer upon a pair of weather-beaten tars."

The curate looked at his helpmate, and she in her turn looked at the curate, and the looks of both were so decidedly affirmative that very few words were necessary to conclude the treaty of peace and hospitality between the parties. Markham stated his own name and his friend's, and Mr. Woodward (at his wife's prompting) observed the same formality, following it up by presenting the young Englishman to Carry, his nieces, and the rest of his faction in order. This done, he directed the crew of the Caroline to proceed to the usual place with the baskets (for he insisted on contributing to the entertainment), and in less than a quarter of an hour the whole human population of the island was assembled on the flat rock, as happy and animated a circle as ever met together on a convivial occasion. If Markham made a favorable impression on the women, you may conceive how much they were struck with Vivyan, whose appearance had been much improved by the exposure to the sun and air, which had slightly bronzed his complexion, and given him a manlier look than he wore when he sailed from Southampton.

His address was grace itself, his smile the blandest and brightest; there was a quiet joyousness about him, a love of pleasing, and a disposition to be pleased, which, joined with his elegant person, cultivated taste, and a natural facility of expressing his thoughts in lively and agreeable language, made him one of the most fascinating young men of his time.

## CHAPTER XXIX.

### THE PIC-NIC.

"Medio in fonte leporum,
Surgit amari aliquid, quod ipsis in floribus angit."
LUCRETIUS.

THAT probably was the most remarkable and

romantic pic-nic that ever took place. What a spot it was! In the front of the party lay the glorious expanse of the Atlantic, with not an inch of dry land, no, not so much as a rock for a sea-mew to perch on, between the place where you stood and the mouth of the Mississippi. Behind, a gray ruin, with a legend, of course, and many a controversy, which we shall not molest the reader with, about its date and its architecture, among the Oldbucks of the Irish Academy. The curate (a little of a bore on Irish antiquities) is already warm on the subject with Markham, quoting Doctor Petrie, and warning him not to let himself be led astray by the heresies of Sir William Betham. Markham is looking at the ladies, and uncertain which of the girls to admire most, or whether the matron is not better worth looking at than either. Vivyan is speaking to Arabella, just because she happens to be nearest to him; he has scarcely seen Elizabeth's face yet. All is tumult, surprise, and gayety, on that strange wild place for a dinner-party. Miss M'Cracken is opening the hampers from the parsonage, and repaying herself for her pains by taking a foretaste of their contents. Mr. Lawrence (heartily weary of his "voyage pittoresque") is dressing the great lobster (a superb one it is, calling for lettuce, as big as cabbages) and, Peter, the curate's butler, is committing all manner of gaucheries in the discharge of his office, and somewhat undecided whether the blunderbuss is a flask of champagne, or the flask of champagne a blunderbuss.

"We have heard a great deal," said Markham, at length escaping from the curate and the archæology, and addressing Mrs. Woodward, "we have heard a great deal of the 'wild sports of the west,' but we never dreamed of enjoying any thing at once so wild and so charming as this." The "charming" was meant for the lady he was accosting, and she replied with her goodliest smile that "she feared the wildness was all upon the side of her party, for, often as she had visited the island, this was the first time she had found it in the possession of such a civilized and agreeable population."

It was a compliment to the Englishmen at the expense of the rabbits.

"We are only adventurers," said Vivyan, "something like Stephano and Trinculo, only we don't think of usurping Prospero's island."

"Our Prospero is not with us," said aunt Carry. "I mean my brother, the Rev. Mr. Spenser, (father to those ladies," she added, in a parenthetic tone), "who will regret not meeting you here; but I hope before your cruise is over he will have that pleasure upon an island of more respectable dimensions than this."

"Spenser!—the name struck Markham, and added to his surprises. He was on the point of inquiring whether the Mr. Spenser mentioned was Lord Bonham's friend, when one of the sailors came up to receive some directions from Mr. Woodward, and, addressing him, called him "your reverence."

If they had called him "your holiness," or "your majesty," they could not have more electrified the young Englishmen. Wild sports of the west, indeed!—they both exclaimed internally, for the idea that Mr. Woodward was a clergyman had never occurred to them, nor was there any thing about his appearance at all suggestive of it, but entirely the reverse. It heightened their spirits to find so much to divert mixed with so much to attract and delight them. Men so odd and uncouth, and at the same time so replenished with good nature as the curate and Doctor Wilkins neither Vivyan nor Markham (who had been in the East, and seen Arabs and dancing dervishes) had ever encountered; and to find them in the society of three women, not merely with fine persons, but well-bred and accomplished, was one of those surprising things which people like to meet on their travels, and it was agreeably surprising, too, which made it so much the better. They saw some surprising things in Ireland, that long vacation, which were quite of another character.

Elizabeth that day looked supremely bright and joyous; she was passionately fond of nature, a girl who loved the gayety of the open air, in the fern and heather among the rocks, the wild flowers, and the wild birds, better than the gayety of any ball-room. Though her father was absent, she had people with her who were very dear to her, and to whom she knew that she was dear; she idolized Carry Woodward, and was greatly attached to uncle Hercules, without being blind to his oddities and mannerisms; then she had Arabella, and her little step-brother and step-sister, toward all of whom she felt exactly as a pure, healthy-minded girl ought to feel, solicitous for their happiness, and happy herself when she saw them happy. What an inestimable quality it is, that of deriving pleasure from the mere prospect of it in others;—that basking in the light reflected from other faces;—how it multiplies the enjoyments of those who are fortunate enough to possess it; how it exceeds in intensity as well as dignity, and in durability still more than either, all satisfaction of a selfish nature; how wise and independent, as well as how good is it, to be capable of being thus made happy! Elizabeth Spenser abounded with this beautiful attribute; it was this, and nothing else, that gave that sweet, soft, glad luster to her eye, that, serene, sunny, musical expression to all her features, which, before his cruise in the Circe was over, flung its dazzling spell over one of the young Englishmen, and made that day on the Atlantic islet the most important and critical of his life.

Markham (who was not long in establishing the identity of Mrs. Woodward's brother with the gentleman to whom he had introductory letters) took the lead on the part of the English invaders, as the curate did on the part of the Irish residents, during the protracted festivities of the rock. Vivyan, in the beginning of acquaintanceships naturally shy, conversed a little with Mrs. Woodward. who sat upon his right during the banquet, seldom addressing the whole party, and never except when Markham stimulated him to the effort. Elizabeth was his neighbor to the left; he often marveled, afterward how little impression she made on him in the first moments of their acquaintance.

The expertest reporter of a London journal would probably have failed to give a tolerably correct report of the mirthful, hearty, enthusiastic, and motley conversation of that day. The curate's spirits were naturally somewhat too exuberant, but they were just sufficiently controlled by the less turbulent hilarity of the rest of the party. In a company of Irishmen Hercu.es was Irish, but when you diluted the Hibernian alcohol with English milder spirits, you produced a very agreeable and indeed civilized mixture.

Mr. Lawrence's lobster was applauded by all who tasted it, and the champagne did not diminish the vivacity of the circle. The very opening of it caused considerable merriment, for Peter, being the Ganymede of a man with an income of seventy-five pounds a year, and having consequently never witnessed the phenomenon before, was very near tumbling over the cliff into unfathomed water, when the first cork bounced into the air. Mrs. Woodward is reported to have drank three glasses on that ever-memorable day, one with Markham, one with Vivyan, and one with Colonel Dabzac, who, on the whole, behaved himself very socially, for a lieutenant-colonel and a grand-master. Then uprose the curate, and "in his rising seemed," not "a pillar of state," but rather a church-steeple; he rose to propose a general health to a reunion as agreeable as it was unexpected and picturesque, accompanied with a jovial prayer that the same society might assemble again at some future time on the same rock with hearts as light and faces as cheerful. The glasses were filled, the sunbeams danced on the sparkling foam of the Epergnay grape, when a shrill shout from the younger members of the party, who were disporting themselves in the heath above the cliffs, attracted attention and interrupted the libation. The cry was "Sydney, Sydney." Mrs. Woodward and her nieces were disturbed and vexed by it; Elizabeth, indeed, reproached herself with feeling as she did when the approach of her brother was announced, but it was not her brother whose approach she dreaded—it was that of Dawson, and almost the next moment he stood at her side.

He and Sydney had returned to the parsonage that morning, soon after the expedition set out, and on receiving information of the pic-nic, they instantly took a boat and rowed to the island, Dawson not hesitating to join the party on his friend's invitation.

You could not, without the eyes of Argus—eyes to see every body at the same moment—have had an idea of the effect produced upon this occasion by the sudden apparition of Sydney and his companion. The Irish party fell at once several degrees in the estimation of the Englishmen. Sydney of himself would not have produced such a result, for his face was not yet fevered by dissipation, or deformed by passion; his eye had not lost its ingenuous light; he looked a wild, ungóvered, but still a handsome and well-born, if not well-bred, boy. With Dawson, however, in conjunction with him, it was different. Markham instantly thought that he had seen Dawson somewhere in London, whether smoking in the Quadrant, betting at Tattersalls, or lounging and whispering in the gallery of the House of Commons, he was not certain. Both he and Vivyan soon learned that Sydney was brother to the fair girls whose acquaintance they had just made, and that Dawson was Sydney's friend, relative, or both, required no sagacity to discover. Let the reader imagine what must naturally pass through the mind under such circumstances; the disappoint-

ment of the Englishmen on the one nand, the uncomfortable feelings of the Spensers and Woodwards on the other, the feeling of being ashamed of an acquaintance and a relative, and that relative such a very near one.

There was an end of all hilarity and easy conversation. The efforts of the new comers to restore both only made the effect more remarkable. The curate alone received Dawson with any thing like cordiality; he rose to make a place for him at the table, but Frank Vivyan rose at the instant with the same object, and little dreaming of the pain he was causing both to Mrs. Woodward and Elizabeth, was instrumental in planting Dawson between them. In the act of performing this civility, he encountered Dawson's sinister and ambiguous eye, with one so freezingly disregardful, that the look was never forgiven or forgotten.

Both aunt and niece had dined as well as Vivyan, so they saw no reason why they should linger at the table, while Sydney and Dawson satisfied the cravings of nature, particularly as another gorgeous sunset was on the point of taking place. They rose simultaneously, and a proposition was soon made and accepted to ramble over the island. The broad-brimmed white hat which Dawson wore, concealed the scowl with which he regarded the graceful Vivyan, as now conversing with Elizabeth he mounted the steep path that led to the top of the cliffs. However, he applied himself to his dinner notwithstanding, devoured the remnant of the lobster, and divided with Sydney a flask of champagne, neither inquiring from what cellar the wine came. Miss M'Cracken paid him little attention, knowing that he was no favorite with Mrs. Spenser; but the honest curate, who never deserted a friend in need, took the best care he could of him, and conversed with him for some time. Among other things he asked Dawson whether the report was true that he was on the point of going into parliament for Rottenham.

The question excited Dawson's vulgar vanity,' and made him swagger a good deal, and talk and eat simultaneously. He replied, that there was something in the wind, he believed, on the subject; but he would look before he leaped; no constituency should make a cat's-paw of him, and he was equally resolved to be no man's warming-pan; he didn't deny he was a liberal, and he didn't, assert that the country had no wrongs and grievances, but he wouldn't pin himself to the tail of any agitator; he would blush, so he would—he pronounced it bloosh—to be a mere shillelagh in the' hand of Daniel O'Connell himself.

Dawson often talked of blushing, but he never did.

The curate, however, felt that his principal obligation for the time being was to entertain the young Englishmen, and accordingly he now strode after Markham, who was following the women, having been intensely disgusted with Dawson's display.

Miss M'Cracken, however, had overheard the conversation between Dudley and the curate, and taking a very different view of the former gentleman when she learned that he was of sufficient mark for a seat in parliament, she now did all she could to make him comfortable helped him plentifully to tongue and chicken, and not only smiled and courtesied graciously, when he proposed a glass of champagne to her, but drank off the glass with the same amiable complaisance.

"Your country is remarkable for the magnificence of its sunsets," said Markham to the curate, as they walked together, immediately behind Mrs. Woodward, her nieces, and Frank Vivyan.

"Men of your profession, sir," replied Woodward, "have constant opportunities of observing and enjoying such phenomena."

Markham smiled, and undeceived the curate as to his profession, acquainting him that both himself and his comrade were only amateur sailors, though they wore a costume something resembling the naval.

"But where is your yacht?" asked the other. "You did not lose her, I trust, in the late gale."

"No," said Markham, "but how we preserved her, or indeed saved ourselves, I can hardly inform you; I fear it was less by our seamanship than our good-fortune. However, we sustained so much damage that this morning we ordered our men to carry her into the port of Derry, to undergo the necessary repairs. We lost our bowsprit and our rudder."

"We could have managed all that for you at Redcross," said the curate; "but what do you propose to do while your boat is repairing?".

"We propose, with your permission, to bivouac here, on this pretty isle of yours," answered Markham, coolly. "We are tolerably well armed and provisioned; we have a tent, plenty of cloaks and blankets, lots of books; oh, we shall do very well, I assure you."

"But we must try to provide you with somewhat better quarters, sir," said Woodward. "I hope you will kindly prefer our hospitality, rude as you will find it, to that of the rabbits and the sea-gulls. Besides, I don't think your friend looks as if his frame was quite equal yet to the hardships of a Robinson Crusoe life."

"Oh, is it Vivyan?" said Markham. "I assure you he is a hardier fellow than you take him for. He was squeamish enough for the first week, but, faith, now he is the best hand in the Circe. However, your proposal is a very kind and agreeable one, and I have no doubt my friend will concur with me in accepting it very thankfully."

Markham then gave the curate a full account of the plan and the course of their voyage; told him a good deal about Vivyan, a little about himself; assured him that pleasure was their sole object; and that they were visiting Ireland, neither as politicians to meddle with state affairs, artists to paint her scenery, or commissioners of the *Times* newspaper, to investigate the relations of landlord and tenant. He could not help thinking, as he said this, that finer subjects for sketches, either with pen or pencil, than the singular personage he was talking to, and his fair, vast wife, it would not be easy to find between the tropics, or beyond them.

That fair wife was now sitting on a cushion of turf, soft as Lyons velvet, and green as oriental emerald, save where a tuft of purple heath broidered it, contemplating the glories of the evening, the sun, the ocean, and the mountains, with an eye to enjoy, and a mind to feel them. She had partly conquered Vivyan's reserve, and was now holding with him the sort of conversation that cultivated women are so fond of, fanciful, poetical, lively, sentimental without melancholy, a grain of philosophy in it to make it serious, a strain of wit to make it brilliant, and a little touch of gallantry to throw a rosy hue over all. Perhaps no woman loves this sort of parley so well as a clever and handsome one of ripe years, with such a companion as Vivyan, young enough to be her son, but capable, as he was, of holding such discourse with her. Carry, too, enjoyed it the more, because it was rarely now that she met with a man of elegant mind and soft acquirements, with the exception of her brother, Mr. Spenser. Elizabeth sat in her shadow, on the same natural couch of green and purple, eagerly listening, but taking no part in the dialogue, except with her eyes, which incessantly chatted with those of her aunt, though they seldom encountered Vivyan's, who indeed was not seated so as to have the same full view of her that he had of Mrs. Woodward.

The curate had one fault on a pic-nic—he was as eager to get home as he was to set out.

"Your uncle is getting fidgety," said Carry, to her niece, as Hercules approached with Markham.

"It is still early, aunt," said Elizabeth, reluctant to leave the sunset, and finding the conversation pleasing, though participating little in it.

Much, indeed, as Carry herself loved her husband, and dutiful wife as she was, she would very gladly have lingered another half hour on the green couch with her fascinating new acquaintance. But Mr. Woodward was commodore of the squadron, and when he gave sailing orders, his wife was not the person to mutiny, so she gave her hand to Markham, who helped her to rise, while Frank gave his arm to Elizabeth just in time to save her from the offer of Dawson's, who came up at the moment with the rest of the party, all now in motion for the beach. Dawson next addressed himself to aunt Carry, who repelled him in a certain dry way she had, and which she well knew how to employ on proper occasion. She was a porcupine to men of his stamp, or rather a rhinoceros, for she was content with defensive operations, and made herself as impenetrable to the people she disliked, as she was affable and buxom to her favorites.

It ended in Dawson being obliged to put up with the governess, who, indeed, wanted the assistance of his arm to descend the rude winding stair among the rocks, and it was the least return he could make for the tongue and chicken she had helped him to. Lucy, being an accomplished coquette, managed to make herself extremely agreeable; and perhaps Dawson foresaw that so clever a girl might possibly hereafter be useful to him, for, though he was a little morose at first, he grew even more than polite after some moments, and formed on that occasion a sort of flirting friendship with Miss M'Cracken, which continued to the end of his career, and was not without important results.

Hitherto the day had passed without any incident more provoking than the intrusion of a disagreeable guest; but a painful occurrence took place just as the party was all mustered on the little narrow quay already described, and on the point of embarking in their respective vessels. Billy Pitt Woodward was playing somewhat riotously with his little cousins and the dog Pedro, and though several times warned that the space was too limited for such gambols, persevered, in the intoxication of his boyish spirits. Elizabeth Spenser happened to be standing within a foot of the edge, just between the yacht and the smack, and the boy in passing was pushed against her by the dog. She stumbled, lost her equilibrium, and before any body could grasp her dress, or give any assistance, she fell into the water. A general shriek accompanied the horrid splash. Instantly it was followed by another. A young man had thrown off his coat and plunged after her—it was Mr. Dawson!

It was gallantly and admirably done. Not two minutes elapsed between the fall and the rescue; but nothing, of course, was thought of but attention to the almost lifeless girl. She soon, however, came to herself, and was carried by her afflicted uncle (who was almost as skillful in cases of drowning as Doctor Wilkins himself) on board the Gipsy, which was fortunately provided with blankets in sufficient quantity, and several other appliances useful on such occasions. It was a disastrous termination of a day of pleasure, and not the least annoying part of it was the circumstance that the girl's deliverer was the last man in the world whom she would have chosen to owe her life to. But the curate, as soon as he returned upon deck, embraced Dawson (dripping as he was) in the transports of his gratitude, and Markham and Vivyan agreed that he was a fine bold fellow, after all, and only another Irish anomaly. Sydney pressed his friend to return with him to the parsonage; but Dawson accepted Mr. Woodward's invitation to go to Redcross in the Caroline. Neither Mrs. Woodward nor Doctor Wilkins thought it prudent to leave Elizabeth. As to Vivyan and Markham, they decided, under the circumstances, to revoke their acceptance of the curate's hospitality for the present, and they passed the night adventurously on the island—the hares and rabbits their bedfellows, the heather their pillow, the blue concave their canopy, and the moon their night-lamp.

---

## CHAPTER XXX.

BIVOUAC ON SPENSER ISLAND.

"For now I stand as one upon a rock,
Environed by a wilderness of sea."
TITUS ANDRONICUS.

"I DON'T apprehend any serious consequences," said Markham, as he and his cousin walked leisurely back to the place where they had dined; "she seems a hardy as well as a handsome girl, and I never saw or heard of a rescue so prompt —almost so instantaneous; in fact, I scarcely knew which of the party had met with the accident, until I saw her in the arms of that reverend Goliath, who, it appears, is her uncle."

"I feared she was drowned," said Vivyan.

"I knew that was impossible," said Markham; "I have seen cases of the kind more than once."

"Well, George," said Frank, after some pause, "if our Irish expedition goes on this way, it will be romantic enough, at all events."

"But either you or I should have saved the lady," said Markham, "by all the laws of romance."

"Ah, if things would only happen in life as they do in a novel," said Vivyan.

"However," said his cousin, "we have no great reason to murmur, wrecked upon such a picturesque islet as this is, and after a day so full of startling events."

"Such strange men, and such lovely women," added Vivyan; "only think what a charming little realm this was only an hour ago—in the whole female population not a woman who was not a beauty. Even the lady who seemed a governess was decidedly good looking."

"Handsome, but decidedly not *good* looking," said Markham. "You mean that, fair, fierce girl?—she made me think of arsenic."

"A little fierce, certainly," said Vivyan; "but only think, George, what a world this would be if there was nothing physical but beauty, and nothing moral but love."

"The word moral has a very convenient vagueness in it," said Markham.

"The pleasure in beauty is moral, surely, essentially moral," said Vivyan, who was at the age when the night and the ocean make young men desperately sentimental.

"Then, if a man admired a plain woman, you would say he was immoral," said Markham.

"Not exactly," said the other; "but, as a general proposition, I maintain that the love of beauty is virtue, and the love of deformity, vice."

"Well, it is a vice we need scarcely preach a crusade against," said Markham; "but while we have been talking metaphysics and sentiment, how splendidly the night has advanced upon us!"

"How brilliant the stars are," cried Vivyan; "let us sit down on this smooth rock and gaze on them."

"Like Jessica and Lorenzo," said Markham, who was tolerably well acquainted with Shakspeare; and he that is so has an encyclopedia of poetry in his memory.

"I think I never saw the heavens so glorious as they are to-night," said Vivyan.

"Do you know the names of the constellations, Frank?"

"Only a few," said Vivyan. "I am of Biron's opinion on that subject. Is it not Biron who says—

"Those earthly godfathers of heaven's lights,
Who gave a name to every fixed star,
Have no more pleasure in their starry nights
Than those who gaze, and know not what they are."

They were both mute again for a few moments, their eyes riveted upon the blazing firmament.

"How solemn, how beautiful, how grand all this is!" exclaimed Vivyan, breaking the silence. "Never shall we forget our first night on the coast of Ireland."

"Never," said Markham, deeply feeling the splendor of the scene.

"Had I ten thousand prejudices against the country, George, upon this memorable rock I should abjure them all—if this island were my property I should have a cottage on it assuredly—but look, the moon rises yonder, let us move toward the beach, and watch the effect upon the water."

The moon rose that night of a pale gold color, a flickering causeway of the same delicate tint seemed to traverse the face of the waters from the base of the cliffs to the lower limb of the planet. They made their way out to the extreme point of a lofty ledge of rocks, and seating themselves on the uttermost gray splinter, fancied that they could almost step on the radiant road that terminated trembling at their feet.

"One can't help believing in the planetary influences," said Vivyan. "I try in vain of moon-light nights to recollect my astronomy, and think of nothing but the moon's nodes and librations; but to no purpose—the poetry still returns, Diana won't allow me to think of Newton."

While Frank was thus rhapsodizing, his relation was watching, with his keen nautical eye, an object upon the water, apparently at about a quarter of a mile from them. He called Vivyan's attention to it, and in a few moments it was evident that it was a small brig, and that it was standing in right for the island.

"Our adventures, perhaps, are not yet over," said Vivyan.

"Probably smugglers," said Markham—"the wise course is to arm ourselves, and be prepared for an attack, at the same time avoiding observation as much as possible."

They rose, and proceeding to the spot where they had left Lawrence with their arms and other accouterments, both pacific and warlike, each provided himself with a gun and cutlass, and thus equipped, they moved forward among the rocks, keeping out of view of the brig, until they found a convenient station for watching the behavior of her crew.

Almost immediately a boat left her, rowed by two men, who pulled lustily for the beach, and in a few minutes disappeared in the shadows of the cliffs. Markham and Frank, like Crusoe and Friday, crept as close as they safely could to the spot where the boat seemed disposed to land; but when they saw her again, she was pushing back rapidly to the brig.

Vivyan was for clambering down the rocks and searching for the cave where it seemed likely the free-traders had been depositing some articles of their irregular traffic.

"Not yet," said Markham, "the boat may return."

It did return; and now they distinctly saw the men run her into what appeared to be the mouth of a cavern, almost directly under the crags from which the y ung Englishmen were watching their proceedings. The boat was invisible for about twenty minutes. When she reappeared, Vivyan could perceive nothing but the sailors who rowed her (the moonbeams glancing on their broad brimmed glazed hats), but Markham, who had the vision of a falcon, saw that she contained several large wooden cases, to carry off which it was now evident she had been sent ashore.

The young men remained still until the boat returned to the brig. What took place then, the shadows prevented them from observing, but the boat did not come back; on the contrary, the brig weighed anchor, and stood out to sea on a southerly course, as if she intended to make for the port of Galway.

Never did a chamois-hunter in the Bernese Oberland spring from rock to rock with the speed of George Markham, in his eager curiosity to discover the haunts of the pirates, or smugglers, whatever they were, and detect the nature of their operations. He called to Vivyan not to follow him, and indeed, there was not much occasion for the remonstrance, the descent was so rugged and perilous (particularly by the faint light of the moon), and Frank was so unused to exploits which his cousin, from his habits of deer-stalking, thought as little of as if he had been bred a smuggler himself.

Markham was soon lost to Vivyan's view, and after some time the latter became uneasy, and followed his footsteps as far as he could with any consideration for his personal safety, shouting at intervals, but receiving no answer. Just as he was beginning to be seriously alarmed, he heard a slight noise close to him, and he was rejoined by his cousin, who had found a shorter and easier way back than that by which he had descended the cliffs.

"Well," said Vivyan, "and did you find the cave?"

"I did," said Markham, looking as if he had discovered something a great deal more surprising.

"And what did you find there, George?"

"A hall of statues, or a sculptor's studio," answered Markham, "the light was so bad, I could not decide the question, but I found two marble busts unquestionably."

"You are jesting," said Vivyan.

"I am not," said Markham, "and I can tell you more, I strongly suspect that the cave contains a picture-gallery also. It seems incredible, but it is true, I assure you."

Frank was disposed to be incredulous—not very unreasonably—and Markham, instead of repeating his story, conducted his cousin down the comparatively easy path he had struck upon, and in a few seconds they stood at the mouth of the marvelous cave, the floor of which seemed to be just above the ordinary high-water·mark. Had the moon been commodiously situated with respect to the cavern, or the cavern with respect to the moon, the interior might probably have been more accurately surveyed, but the light fell obliquely, and was half interrupted by the rocks upon one side, so that the illumination was very dim and imperfect.

Markham led his cousin by the hand, and stopped at what seemed at first to be a mere lump of white, or grayish stone.

"That's not a bust," said Vivyan.

"Pass your hand over this part of it," said George.

Vivyan did so, and at once confessed that his cousin was in the right.

"Now come on a little further," said Markham. Frank followed him, and could hardly discern the next object of vertu to which his attention was called; but on again applying his hand, there was not a doubt on his mind but that he stood in the midst of the fine arts, strange as it was to find such an institution in such a place.

"Now come this way," said George, "you see I am a capital cicerone; but tread cautiously" Immediately Frank's foot struck against some thing that returned a hollow sound.

"I thought at first it was a coffin," said Markham, "but I ascertained the shape; it is a square box, such as pictures are packed in; and as the cave contains the works of the chisel, it is only natural to expect a few works of the pencil also."

"Nothing would surprise me after this," cried Vivyan. "What a high notion it gives one of the refinement of this part of Ireland to find a contraband trade in statues and pictures carried on so actively."

"Unfortunately for that view of the matter," said Markham, "the trade seems to be an export one. I own there is something in this that surprises me extremely. One can not help suspecting that it is not the rightful owner of these articles who has concealed them here, and who seems to be shipping them off by degrees in this clandestine manner."

The young men having further searched the cavern, groping with hands and feet, but without succeeding in finding any thing more of consequence, were very glad to find themselves under their lady the moon again, for the air of the cave was extremely cold, and the floor was damp, although not with the influx of the ocean. Fortunately there was no dew upon the heath, which was their couch that night; and luckily, too, they had abundance of blankets and cloaks above and beneath them, or a cold and a fever might have discouraged their somewhat rash enterprise of sleeping *al fresco* even at midsummer, in the humid and fickle climate of Ireland.

At break of day, while Lawrence was making their coffee, they hastened back to the cave, and found sufficient light to confirm fully all the conjectures they had already made. It occurred to them to try if they could move the busts and carry them close to the entrance, so as to see what they were. It required all their strength to effect this object, but they ultimately achieved it, and found that one was a bust of Socrates; the other they were not so clear about, but both were apparently well executed, and in the finest Carrara marble. When they returned to examine the wooden box, it was not to be found. The smugglers had carried it off during the night.

After a wild but substantial and various breakfast, the y ung men decided upon availing themselves of one of the boats of the Circe, which they had retained, and pulling over to Redcross to pay their respects to the Woodwards, and inquire for Miss Spenser, for they were not sufficiently acquainted with the coast to have found their way to the parsonage, if they had proposed to make their first visit there.

They found the great and good curate in that extraordinary study of his, and the apartment amused and astonished them as much as its occupier had done the day before. The ruins of a morning meal were scattered over several tables, the chief one not much more than half covered by the cloth, and the curate was sitting among them, like Marius in the wreck of Carthage, only that Marius was not employed darning his toga, as Hercules was repairing a rent in his huge pea-jacket, not having his wife to perform that delicate little office for him. The manly simplicity of the rustic clergyman, so cheerful and independent in the midst of his sacred poverty, struck his visitors forcibly. He chased a glossy and corpulent black cat from an oaken chair to present it to Markham, and dusted a stool with a sleeve of the jacket to make it fit for Vivyan to sit on. Then he flung the jacket aside, and, forgetting that he wanted it on his shoulders, entered lustily into conversation, suffering the cat to jump on his knee, to compensate her for ejectment from the chair. Hercules had a partiality for cats, in common with many other remarkable men (including Tasso and Newton); and had surprising stories to tell of their affection as well as their sagacity, contrary to the prevailing opinion with respect to that most domestic of all animals.

The first inquiry of the yachtsmen was, of course, for the lady whom so alarming an accident had befallen. Hercules had been actually preparing to walk over to the rectory, to satisfy himself on the same point, and he was in raptures at the proposition which Markham made to bear him company.

"But will your friend be equal to it?" he asked, compassionately contemplating Vivyan's slender frame, much as Pantagruel may be supposed to have contemplated the pilgrim whom he found in the salad.

"Any thing under ten miles, sir," said Vivyan, smiling.

"Not five, by the rout I shall take you," said the curate; "so I'll put on my coat and my shoes, and we'll start immediately."

"I foresee I shall fall in love with this cu rate," said Markham when he left the room. "How odd that Bonham said nothing of him!"

They were not half done admiring the detail of the study, when Mr. Woodward reappeared, wonderfully metamorphosed, for, out of respect to the travelers, he had put on his full black suit. The coat, indeed, was an iron-gray, but he called it his black one, and it answered the purpose. His wife was the only person living who thought the clerical dress improved him; and indeed his frame and his features were more in keeping with the garb which he commonly wore on week-days.

"Now," said he, taking down the hat that was intended to match the suit (a low-crowned and broad-leaved one, but nothing of the shovel), "now, gentlemen, let us take the road—but come, I must provide you with sticks."

"We have been admiring your formidable store of them in the corner," said Markham, smiling.

"Ay," said Hercules, "I'm a stick-fancier. There's a cudgel *there*, I believe, of every wood that a cudgel was ever made of, oak, ash, hazel, holly, blackthorn, and bamboo, and some there have seen service. Take your choice, but I recommend you, Mr. Vivyan, to choose the bamboo; you will find it stout enough, and light into the bargain."

Vivyan took the curate's advice; Markham selected a powerful oak sapling, and Hercules himself sallied forth with the blackthorn.

"And so you actually bivouacked!" said Woodward, as they crossed the courtyard, "that's a thing I never did myself, and I thought I had done most things of that kind."

Markham gave a full account of the night they had passed, and the story of the cave excited the curate's curiosity greatly. It was utterly incomprehensible, and for some time he could talk of nothing else, minutely inquiring into all the circumstances, and framing theory after theory to explain them, then demolishing them himself without mercy. At length the charms of the scenery diverted the conversation into another channel.

The walk was enjoyed prodigiously by all three. The curate was never so vigorous, either in mind or body, as when he was on the hills; he seemed to grow greater and greater as he got higher and higher; his mind became elastic as the turf he strode on; and his heart as expansive as the concave over his head. Markham resembled him in his passion for the heath and his insatiable love of muscular exertion.

"You would make a capital mountain curate," said Hercules, as George kept pace with him manfully, Vivyan lagging a little behind, and thinking that men might be very good pedestrians without walking quite so fast.

"I fear," said George, "I should have no other qualification but a love for the mountains."

"You would soon begin to love the mountaineers," said Hercules; "the only fault I find with my brother-in-law is that he can't walk—or won't walk; it comes to the same thing;—but now we are on the brow, and there is Redcross Rectory, that white house in the wood beyond the water."

"How quiet, how very beautiful!" exclaimed Vivyan.

"The descent is nothing," said Woodward, resuming his speed, and giving Frank very little time to admire the prospect, so anxious was he to get news of his niece.

### CHAPTER XXXI.

THE PARSONAGE VISITED.

"In recreations be both wise and free;
Live still at home, home to thyself, howe'er
Enriched with noble company."
                    THE LADY'S TRIAL.

GEORGE MARKHAM was right. Elizabeth Spenser was not the girl to succumb under a couple of minutes' immersion in cold water; her strong and elegant mind was cased in a frame, which also united elegance with strength. It was as much, indeed, as Carry Woodward could do to keep her in bed the next morning until after breakfast.

"Really," she said, "my dear aunt, I was not much longer under the water than if I had been bathing; and the water was so beautifully bright!"

"But it's not pleasant to be ducked with one's clothes on in the brightest water," said Carry.

Elizabeth was sitting up in her little dimity-curtained bed at her breakfast; aunt Carry sat expanded by her side; the casement was open, the sun was brilliant, the air fresh and balmy, and the long shoots of the monthly roses and woodbine, that covered the front of the house, were flapping every now and then into the room, encumbered with flowers. It was a picture better worth seeing than many a modern cartoon.

A tap at the door. Enter Lucy, curt and ceremonious, with Mrs. Spenser's compliments (that was her style with her step-daughters) to know how Miss Elizabeth felt herself, and would she try just five drops of the "Royal Soothing Restorative," recommended for all cases of sudden fright or over-excitement; indispensable for fires, hurricanes, inundations, and earthquakes, in fact, every disorder in nature, as Carry said, except moving bogs.

Then came the rector himself, kissed his pale daughter affectionately, and received an account from his sister of the agreeable young men whose acquaintance they had made the day before. Mr. Spenser was happy to hear of the safe arrival of the Circe, for he had been anxious about her fate during the gale. He then mentioned all he knew about Markham and Vivyan, which was not much; but Elizabeth was pleased to learn that the former was the friend of the Bonhams, a circumstance which had not transpired on the previous day. In making new acquaintances it is always agreeable to discover some link or another to connect them with old ones.

Tap the third. Now it was the head girl of Elizabeth's little school, with an address of condolence from the scholars, in the misfortune of their young mistress, and also to know whether they were to tarry or to disperse to their several homes. Carry sent them a cheering account of her niece, and took upon herself to proclaim a truce with popular ignorance for a day or two. It was not often she was so pacific in that way.

Shortly after noon, the fair girl rose, the first time for many a day that the meridian sun had seen her head on the pillow; and, still a little weak, leaning on her portly relative, descended to the library, where she found her father on the point of setting out with Doctor Wilkins for Redcross, to thank Mr. Dawson, both in his daughter's name and his own, for his heroic conduct.

"We are all very thankful to him, I am sure," said Mrs. Woodward. What would she not have given, notwithstanding, that her niece's life had been saved by almost any one else in the world?

"You have very good reason," said the doctor, "promptitude is every thing in such cases; minutes count for hours when young ladies are at the bottom of the Atlantic. I am grateful to Mr. Dawson, myself," he added, "for I haven't so many patients in the neighborhood that I can afford to lose them in so summary a way."

Smiling at the physician's speech, the rector kissed his rescued child, who repaid his smile in the same bright coin, and proceeded to the door, where he had not been standing a minute, before he heard a well-known shout from the water, and saw a boat within a bow-shot of the land, containing the redoubted curate, and two other gentlemen, whom he had never seen before.

Grateful as niece and aunt were to Mr Dawson, neither regretted that he had not come to receive their acknowledgments in person. It was much more agreeable to see the Englishmen enter. As to Dawson, Mr. Woodward only knew that he had slept the night before at the hotel at Redcross and had started by an early mail for Dublin. A note, however, which Sydney received from him, gave the important additional information, that his friend had been suddenly summoned to town, in consequence of a vacancy having unexpectedly occurred in the borough which he had for some time past aspired to represent.

Carry welcomed Markham and Vivyan in her

radiant, overflowing manner, and Elizabeth as became a maiden receiving agreeable strangers in her father's house; her cheek at the same time almost recovering its wonted color, that lovely brown with a delicate under-current of carmine in it.

The yachtsmen called to pay a morning visit, and remained the guests of the polished parson many days. Charmingly wild as Tory Island was, and enthusiastic as Markham and Vivyan were about its scenery, and the luxury of the life they had led there, not much persuasion was necessary to induce them to shift their quarters to the cosy and rosy parsonage. Mr. Spenser prevailed on them to promise him a week's sojourn in his pastoral cot; and the Woodwards consented to remain also, Carry having a very discreet nurse, to whom she did not hesitate now and then to confide her brood for a few days; all but Billy Pitt, who still required her own immediate supervision, and whom she had not yet promoted to the paternal oak, or blackthorn, though strongly tempted to do it by his late pranks on the island.

The parsonage, however, lost a guest that evening in the person of Colonel Dabzac, and nobody but the rector himself was in the least surprised at the circumstances under which his departure took place. He completed the conquest of Miss Spenser on Tory Island, and just before he mounted his horse, he drily asked, and reluctantly received, her father's consent to the match. In fact, there was no valid objection to it. Dabzac was a young man of good fortune, without a stain upon his insipid character, and though very far from being the person whom Mr. Spenser would have chosen for a son-in-law, he was not to allow his own tastes, and still less his own politics, to interfere in a matter of the kind. Besides, Mrs. Spenser highly approved of it, which was enough to settle the question. In short, there never was a matrimonial affair arranged with much less fuss. A not distant wedding-day was provisionally fixed, and Mr. Spenser gave his brother-in-law notice, that he might not be on his rambles when wanting to tie the knot.

Beauty and gayety, wit, wine, and worth, made that day's dinner the most charming of domestic convivialities, and it was succeeded by many equally delightful. The custom was (when the elements were propitious), after the removal of the cloth, to enjoy the dessert and wine al fresco, in the portico. One of the pastimes on such occasions was the remarkable echo, mentioned early in our story, and which the rector called his oracle, the mode of consulting it being to frame the question so that the last word, or syllable, would be a plausible answer, on the plan of the well-known dialogue of Erasmus.

"Now you shall hear, Mr. Vivyan, how well our Echo understands the state of Ireland."

Then he proceeded to catechise the nymph as follows, taking care to pronounce the final word of each sentence in a sufficiently loud tone.

What is the chief source of the evils of Ireland? Echo—Land.

What is the state of Munster?—Stir.

What are they doing in Connaught?—Naught.

Why don't they reclaim their morasses?—Asses.

Should we not excite them to industry?—Try.

Inform us what the derivation of Erin is?—Erinnys.

Then the curate, with his stentorian lungs, proposed the following interrogatories, shaped with a view to show that the echo was of his way of thinking.

What would you give the Catholics?—Licks.

Who best deserves a fat rectory?—Tory.

But the Echo answered questions of another kind, equally to the satisfaction of the company; for, on being asked—

"In what wine shall we drink the health of Colonel Dabzac?" the airy tongue replied, with the same promptitude and sharp distinctness—"Sack."

It made an amusing variety in an Irish night's entertainments; and, what with a lively tea, a little music, and another hour's miscellaneous conversation, the rector had every reason to think that the first day was a tolerably successful one.

At breakfast the ensuing morning a singular discovery was made, which connected Vivyan in a way none of the most agreeable with the fortunes of the Spensers. This was nothing less than the fact that the principal part of the money of which Maguire had been robbed consisted of the rents of Vivyan's small Irish estate, to which it turned out that the little proctor was bailiff, or collector. These were the rents which Maguire had received at Mr. Branagan's inn, near Castle Dawson, when he was surprised counting his money, as has been related in a former chapter.

"A provoking discovery for a landlord to make on his first visit to his property," said the rector.

"Perhaps only a fit punishment for his not having visited it before," said Vivyan, although the loss of so much money was no laughing matter to a young man with his limited income.

"You deserve extremely little credit for visiting it now," said Markham; "only for this unfortunate affair, you would probably never have known that your estate lay in this part of the country."

"It must be submitted to, I suppose," said the easy Frank, "as a sort of local absentee-tax."

"You take the loss of a gale of rent very coolly," said his friend; "but since we are on the spot, we must use our best exertions, in conjunction with Mr. Spenser, to probe this business to the bottom."

The curate was delighted with Markham's energy; it was a quality which he possessed himself in almost a superabundant degree; so he declared his readiness to co-operate in any plan that might be agreed on (and the more prompt and strenuous the better) to discover the offenders, and bring them to justice. The parties who seemed apathetic and remiss were the rector and Vivyan, the principal losers in the transaction. The former thought that every thing that was right to be done would be done by the police and the authorities, while the latter seemed infinitely to prefer the pleasures of boating, sauntering, and chatting with Mrs. Woodward and the Spenser girls, to the fatiguing amusement of hunting bandits through the mountains. The weather, however, was now exceedingly warm, so that for several days nothing was attempted, even by the energetic part of the company, which could give the most sensitive malefactor in the country the slightest uneasiness for his personal safety.

One of those sultry days was agreeably spent in a second party to the island, to which the discoveries of the strangers had attached a new interest almost as great as if they had found an Herculaneum there. No accident threw a shade over that day's pastime; not even Carry slipped on the verdant slope, the muscular Markham sustained her so ably. The breeze palliated the heat; there were no guns to scare and slaughter the *feræ naturæ;* all disagreeable thoughts and disagreeable people were left behind. As to Sydney Spenser, nobody knew where he was that day, but this was no uncommon occurrence; and displeased only Elizabeth and Mrs. Woodward, who were always anxious to keep him in the safe circle of his friends, however little the pleasure they derived from his company. The truth was, that Sydney's spirits had just received a serious shock, which unfitted him for partaking in any social enjoyment; he had seen the clever sketch drawn by his uncle for the guidance of the police, and had recognized with horror the tall ruffian with whom he had dined at Castle Dawson. He had also inspected the paper found at the Black Castle; and though he could make nothing of the writing in ink, the pencilling, faint as it was, bore a striking resemblance to his friend's hand.

The party scarcely expected to find the busts still in the cavern, it seemed so likely that the brig would have completed her business, but, whatever the cause was, Socrates and Mirabeau were found just where the yachtsmen had left them, gazing with their lack-luster eyes on the Atlantic, which had evidently risen to do them homage, for a wreath of sea-wrack was twisted round the brawny neck of the French orator, and the claw of a crab was sticking in the forehead of the philosopher. The latter incident caused great merriment, for the rector insisted it was one of the fingers of Xantippe, and ought not to be removed upon any account.

In order to show the ladies the wonders of art which their favorite island contained, the curate performed one of his great feats of bodily strength. Markham suggested that as the women could not come down to the grotto, the contents of the grotto should be carried up to them.

"By all means," said the curate, "do you carry the Frenchman, and I'll carry the Athenian."

Markham and Vivyan together had with difficulty moved the busts from the interior of the cave to its mouth, but, nevertheless, the former had no doubt but that he could do what Hercules proposed. Now, however, he had not only to bear the load a greater distance, but he had to carry it up a steep and broken path. He carried Mirabeau about a third of the way, and was then very glad to deposit him on a shelf of the rock. The curate then cried "Come, old fellow!" addressing the marble Socrates, and heaving him up in his brawny arms, he strode up the precipitous ascent, and never paused until he deposited the bust at the feet of his wife, who was sitting with her nieces in the heather. Markham was loud in his applause, and acknowledged that Mr. Woodward was the most powerful man he had ever met with. But the curate was not satisfied with this; he went down the rocks again

and completed the task that Markham had left unfinished, after which, indeed, he was glad to stretch his giantship on the turf, and refresh himself with beef and mustard.

They puzzled themselves in vain, during their repast (for a visit to the island always implied dining there), to frame some plausible theory to account for the mysterious apparition of Art in the wildest domains of Nature; but it is no disparagement to their sagacity to relate that the shrewdest guesses were wide of the mark.

What to do with the spoil was the next question. Mr. Spenser decided it sensibly and promptly; the presumption was, he said, that the marbles had not been brought from the main land for honest purposes, or by honest people, and consequently it was his duty (especially as he was a magistrate) to take possession of them in the name of the law, until the rightful owners should appear to claim them. This opinion having been received with general approbation, the crew of the Gipsy were sent for, and it was as much as four lusty seamen could do to transport the busts on board the cutter. The rector was excessively amusing all the way back on the subject of Socrates and Xantippe, and said, among other things, that "it was very hard on the philosopher to have had two demons," implying, of course, that Mrs. Socrates was *one.*

"*One* is quite enough for any man, even for a philosopher," said Markham.

"As my poor brother knows to his cost," said Mrs. Woodward, *sotto voce,* to her husband.

"Well," replied Hercules in the same tone, "she has allowed Val. one pleasant day at all events."

"And how he has enjoyed it!" said Carry.

That same evening the busts were enrolled with those of Burke, Grattan, Fox, and Curran, in the rector's elegant library. He happened to possess two vacant scagliola pillars, to one of which he elevated Socrates, and promoted Mirabeau to the other, placing the latter by the side of Mr. Fox, whom he resembled in the fervor of his character and the impetuosity and abundance of his eloquence.

The rector had, indeed, spent a happy day, and he continued comparatively tranquil, as long as his application to the government for troops remained unanswered. The longer the reply was delayed, his wife, though fidgety, continued to cherish stronger and stronger hopes that her wishes would be liberally complied with. At length arrived the official letter with its huge seal, and if Mrs. Spenser was the most disappointed, her husband was certainly the most astonished at its contents. It ran as follows:

"Dublin Castle, July 17, —31.

"Sir,—In reply to your letter of the 5th instant, applying to the Government for military aid to protect your house and property from attacks which you seem to apprehend (without, perhaps sufficient grounds, considering the general tranquillity of the county in which you reside), I am commanded by the Lord Lieutenant to state that His Excellency considers the safety of the district in question amply provided for by the police-force stationed there, supported as it is by the troops quartered at Letterkenny and other towns at no great distance; but *under no circumstances whatsoever could His Excellency consent to allow artillery to be employed for the defense of a private house*, even that of a clergyman of the Established Church.

"I have the honor to be, Sir,
"Your obedient humble servant,

\*    \*    \*

'To Rev.Valentine Spenser, Redcross Rectory, Redcross.'

Conceive the rector's amazement on reading this!—He had never said one word of artillery in his letter. It was an after-thought of his wife's, which she had added in a postscript, without acquainting him with what she had done.

---

# BOOK VII.

## CHAPTER XXXII.

### PRELIMINARY CONQUESTS.

"Folk that love idlenesse,
And not delite in no kind besinesse,
But for to hunt and hawke and pley in medes,
And many other such like ydle dedes."
THE FLOURE AND THE LEAFE.

THE curate and Markham soon fraternized; not in the shallow sentimental way of French or Irish clubbists, but honestly, heartily, as one brave man should cleave and cotton to another. They both loved sport and exercise, and both abhorred a sedentary life. Woodward excelled Markham in physical strength; but the latter had the advantage in every thing that required skill and address. The curate was the better pedestrian, Markham was the better horseman. Markham was a better shot with a rifle; but the curate killed more hares and rabbits in a given time. The curate was as poorly armed for the field, the moor, or the loch, as any sportsman could possibly be—a rusty single-barreled gun, a powder-horn and shot-bag which had been worn at the fight of the Boyne, a wicker-basket instead of a game-bag, and dogs that set at grouse and partridge when they met with them, but took the same polite notice of larks, corn-crakes, and water-wagtails. Now Markham piqued himself upon the completeness and accuracy of his accouterments. He could afford to spend the double of Mr. Woodward's income upon his sporting apparatus; his gun never missed fire, his rifle was infallible, his fishing-tackle was perfect, and his dogs knew what was game, and what was not, as well as if they read the *Sporting Magazine*, or had assisted in passing the game-laws. It was wonderful what execution Hercules did with his deficient machinery, and how close he trod on the heels of Markham, who had every sportsmanlike equipment, and made the expertest and ablest use of them. Had it not been for Mr. Woodward, it is possible that Markham might have felt his time hanging somewhat heavily on his hands at the parsonage; his tastes were so widely different from his cousin's, who seemed to have found in the rector and his family the exact kind of society and kind of life which by its freedom from restraint, and its intellectual cultivation, was best adapted to his temperament and his talents. The life, indeed, which Vivyan now led was almost as happy a form of existence as he had ever imagined in his castle-buildings. The rector's conversation, combining classic taste with polished pleasantry, various, discursive, fanciful, suggestive, with a strain of seriousness in its gayety, and most sparkling when it was most solid, exercised a powerful fascination over all who had the faculty to appreciate it. His beau-

F

tiful and luxurious library was just the place for an indolent lover of books like Frank to revel or repose in. Out of doors were the Oreads and the Naiads, if his fancy led him to wander on the hills, or loiter along the warbling brooks or sonorous torrents; and within doors, when the sun or the showers interdicted roaming, in the company of his new female acquaintances, he had only a too charming and accessible resource if ever he was threatened with *ennui*. Thus was every thing propitious to the intensest enjoyment that the eye, the ear, the mind, or the fancy was capable of; and intensely did Vivyan enjoy every thing, as oblivious of Cambridge as if he had been born to a dukedom, and as thoughtless of the pecuniary loss he had sustained (amounting to half of his slender income), as if he had been as rich as Mr. D'Israeli's marvelous Jew.

But it was not in the nature of Vivyan to be happy himself, without being the cause of happiness to those who made him so. He was never so captivating as to those by whom he was captivated. His first Irish success was with the no less benign than intellectual Carry Woodward. His second victory was over the rector himself. He resembled Mr. Spenser remarkably in the delicate qualities of his mind, and not a little also in the ease and softness of his character. Mr. Spenser, when at college, must have been just such an engaging young man. How painfully he was struck with the contrast between Vivyan and his own son! Yet he had the gratification, not unmingled with considerable surprise, of observing that Sydney, though so rustic and unlettered, so inferior to Frank in all respects, and particularly in manners and conversation, seemed not unsmitten by his attractions any more than other people. In fact, singular though it may seem, Vivyan made a most decided conquest of Sydney Spenser; and his sister Elizabeth and his aunt Woodward observed it with the liveliest satisfaction. Just about this time a certain thoughtfulness, and even gloom, was becoming visible in Sydney's looks and demeanor, and his relatives were glad to perceive the change, attributing it to the revolution of sentiment produced by the contrast between his new acquaintance and his old associates. It was not an unnatural explanation, but unhappily it was not the right one.

It was certain, however, that Sydney was smitten deeply by the daily contemplation, in a young man not much his senior, of those accomplishments and graces in which he was himself so sadly deficient. Probably it was partly owing to the depression of spirits under which he manifestly now labored that Markham did not attract him more than his cousin; Markham, who was so athletic, so renowned with the rifle, so skilled in all manly sports and exercises, while Vivyan had so little in common with young Spenser; in fact, nothing but the love of pleasure—and in their ideas of what constituted pleasure they differed as widely as in any thing else. But Markham, though not so fastidious as his friend, was less careful to conceal any dislike that he conceived; and having been from the first disgusted with Sydney, he continued to manifest his feeling by a reserve and dryness of manner which kept young Spenser at a severe distance, and disposed him doubly in Vivyan's favor. On the other hand, the extreme placidity and benevolence of the latter, indeed his better breeding, made him totally incapable of repelling the advances made by the son of his host, and the brother and nephew of the charming women, with whom he laughed and chatted the livelong day. Then the management of women, the most artless women, is so clever! Bent upon availing herself of the present occasion to produce a beneficial impression upon her brother, Elizabeth, carefully concealing her design, not only encouraged his attempts to converse with Vivyan, but created opportunities for him, brought him forward at favorable moments, and threw a timely shield over his coarseness or ignorance, when she feared he was on the point of committing himself in some alarming way. She had no very great difficulty now to make him appear at dinner in the costume of society; his attire in the morning was of less moment, particularly as the prevailing taste was for the sailor's jacket or the shooting coat. Indeed, Markham retained his naval dress, though Vivyan laid his aside, and resumed the ordinary garb of a man who was neither soldier, sailor, or sportsman, but a plain citizen of the world. Markham was astonished to observe how tolerant Vivyan seemed to be of a degree of uncouthness and rusticity which he himself found so offensive.

"He seems brave and good-natured," said Frank; "we must put him down among our anomalies."

"In the same class with Mr. Dawson; they may be very brave fellows, both of them, but they are very bad company, nevertheless."

"Young Spenser has the advantage," said Frank; "he seems to have run wild, and to have lived in a society quite different from that in which his family moves, but his father talks of sending him to Cambridge; we'll civilize and polish him there, depend upon it."

"My dear Frank," said his friend, in the tone of remonstrance, "don't engage yourself for a bear-herd. Very well to see every thing on one's travels; very well to peep at bears in a pit, but to undertake to lead and teach them to dance is neither a very creditable employment nor a very safe one." Vivyan laughed.

"What I mean is, Frank," continued his friend, "that I would not have you involve yourself with loutish fellows in Ireland, whom you may find it difficult to shake off, when you return to England."

"But what a fascinating family this is!" said Vivyan.

"Fascinating people," replied Markham, "with relatives and friends who are just the reverse. Just be a little guarded—I ask no more."

Vivyan promised.

But circumstances threw young Spenser more into companionship with Frank than with the other stranger. Mr. Spenser was sometimes entirely engrossed by his demon-wife, torn from his books, his children, and the society of his guests. Hercules and Markham frequently paired off together upon some prodigious undertaking, far transcending Vivyan's or even Sydney's pedestrian powers. At such times Aunt Carry, her nieces, or one or other of them, with Vivyan and her nephew, would set out, assisted, perhaps, by a jaunting-car, on a quieter expedition, with generally some little object in view, a lake, a water-fall, or some interesting remnant of other days. Carry, you may suppose from her tonnage, was no great pedestrian, and got particularly soon knocked up when there was much up-hill work, as there commonly is (topographers agree) in a highland region. Then she and Arabella would sometimes return and leave Elizabeth and the two young men to pursue their ramble; or, when the object was too distant, or the day too sultry, all the ladies would give it up in despair, and creep back to the parsonage, escorted perhaps by Billy Pitt, while Vivyan and Sydney would proceed to accomplish the purpose of the day.

Vivyan, indeed, would almost always have preferred returning with Mrs. Woodward and her nieces, for he much preferred young women to old castles, and Carry's conversation infinitely to her nephew's; but Carry would not allow it, and Sydney, sometimes recovering his buoyant and too riotous spirits, was eager to show his visitor what was to be seen in the country, and was perhaps, moreover, not disinclined to try the young Cantab's mettle over the mountains of Tyrconnell.

---

## CHAPTER XXXIII.

### PIG-DRIVING.

"Believe me sir,
That government is no holiday employment,
No velvet couch, or journey over flowers,
But a laborious, rugged, uphill task,
Demanding god-like force and faculties,
A righteous hand to wield the sword of justice,
A vigorous arm to hold her balance even,
Deep knowledge, old experience, high courage,
The hands of Briareus, and the eyes of Argus."
NEW PLAY.

IT blew a stiff gale for a couple of days about this time, and the party had a most agreeable excursion on horseback to view the ocean; it was the same ride which the Spensers had before taken with Colonel Dabzac, after the memorable storm with which these chronicles commenced. Carry did not often ride, and, when she did, it was a great event, and caused a sensation in the stables, and much pleasant remark everywhere. The rector had a fine old glossy black mare—a formal, sleek, monastic animal, with a long tail and a broad back, strong and steady as an elephant, and this was the mare that aunt Carry rode. The rector and Markham helped her to the saddle, where, when she was seated, she looked like some Amazon queen, save that she was slightly nervous, and, if fierce at all, only fierce with timidity. Mr. Spenser guarded her on the right flank, George Markham on the left, and Arabella, Elizabeth, and Vivyan brought up the rear. The pace of the black mare regulated the pace of the whole party. She was just the sort of discreet and solemn creature that you read of in Spanish novels, ambling under comely priests, mitered abbots, or other such sacred burdens.

"You have immense water-power," said Markham, "in·this country." The hills were pouring down·torrents all round their line of march, making wild, loud music to the ear, and sometimes taking dashing-leaps over the rocks, forming picturesque.water-falls.

"And wind-power,· too," said Elizabeth, smiling. . The zephyrs were playing with her hair and riding-dress somewhat rudely.

"Yet I see no mills," continued Markham. "You do not seem to turn your advantages to account."

It pained the rector to be forever censuring and complaining of the country, and it was with a very serious and almost melancholy tone he said, in reply to Markham's observation—

"Our very winds and waters are idle; not a wheel is turning within twenty miles of this spot. In other countries man revenges himself on the elements by making them do work enough to compensate for all their ravages; but here the flood and the storm are our absolute masters. We are deluged one day, and blown off our legs the next, without the satisfaction of punishing a single ruffian blast, or lawless torrent, by setting them to turn a mill."

They had now gained a point that commanded the view of the ocean, and its imposing splendor abruptly terminated the conversation.

"A more agreeable way, this, to enjoy the commotion of the waves than from the deck of the Circe," said the rector, breaking the silence, and addressing Markham.

"I have no wish whatever to be afloat in that swell," said George, "I feel quite content upon terra firma."

"And I'll answer for my aunt," said Sydney; "she prefers riding the black mare to riding the billows, any day."

It was the first observation Sydney made during the ride.

Carry assented, and said she feared America would never have been discovered if Columbus had left the adventure to her; but she had no objection to a·short cruise in very smooth water; and to witness the agitation of the deep from a safe position on shore, she thought a pleasure of a very high order.

The Atlantic was indeed a glorious spectacle that day. The waves thundered in the caverns, and hurled the spray in clouds over the. tops of the cliffs, tossing the shells and sea-weed among the heather, and impregnating with saline particles the whole atmosphere. The shattered crests of the billows, as the sun glanced upon them, looked like mountains of crystal smashed into dazzling fragments by invisible. sledges; and innumerable rainbows (combining the loveliest with the most formidable objects in nature) beautified the terror of the scene. They approached as near as was consistent with safety to the edges of the crags, to peep into the anarchy of the·waters, where it was most triumphant; how they boiled and tumbled, as if

seething in the crater of a volcano, and as if rocks of adamant could oppose but poor resist·ance to their fury. Here and there were enormous insulated masses of the fallen cliff, which the retiring breakers for a moment left totally uncovered, and then, recollecting their wrath, returned with fearful energy, and left not a stone unsubmerged large enough for a cormorant to perch on. In one or two instances it happened that the points of rock were sufficiently lofty to escape all but the mere spray.of the insurgent flood, and these points had been seized upon by the most daring of the sea-fowl, who screamed defiance of the threatening surf, well knowing, perhaps (feathered soothsayers ,that they are), by their unerring instincts, that its threats were impotent, as the exhausted winds were retiring from the fray. It looked as if the ocean would never be at peace again, as if Halcyon would never brood on its bosom more. Nothing that ever carried oar or sail could live an instant in a sea like that, to whose prodigious violence the destruction of the noblest ship that ever carried the flag of a Nelson or a Napier would have been no greater feat upon such a coast, than the cracking of an egg-shell or a vase.

They returned through Redcross, and the Englishmen had an opportunity of observing the municipal curiosities of that distinguished and important place.

"You see,·Mr. Markham," said the rector, as they rode through the streets, "if.we don't manure our fields in this country, we manure our streets liberally."

Markham smiled, and said that undoubtedly a commerce in manure might be established with great advantage between town and country. The rector then was pleasant on pigs. He compared the government of Ireland to pig-driving, and said that the Lord-Lieutenant was the Schwein-General.

"You will find," he observed, "parallels in the Irish population to every variety of the pig species, as they are enumerated so humorously by Sir Francis Head in his 'Bubbles.' The pigs, 'with a jaded, care-worn appearance, evidently leaving behind them a numerous litter,' how only too easy it is $_{to}$ find their exact human likenesses ! ·Then, there.is 'the great, tall, monastic, melancholy-looking creature, which seems to have no other object left in this wretched world than to become bacon,'—there Mr. Markham, yonder is just such an animal upon two legs. And look·at that group of my young parishioners disporting themselves on their patrimonial dunghill !—in them you see the 'thin,·tiny, brisk, petulant piglings, with the world and all its loves and sorrows before them.'"

.Had¯there been a Young Ireland at the period of this conversation, how forcibly Mr.· Spenser would have been struck hy.the resemblance of the "tiny, brisk, petulent pigling" to the members of that party !

"Noscitur à sociis, would appear .to be extremely applicable in the present instance," said Vivyan. ;

"Well," said the curate's bouncing wife, who loved the people, with all their faults, and, indeed, devoted much of her time and thoughts to improve them. "Well,·but we must not be too hard upon the swinish multitude; I assure you, Mr. Vivyan, there is a reformation going on, and we are growing less and less piggish every day."

"The pig is excellent, when *cured*," said the rector, "but it is a perverse, grunting, bristling animal; and to drive it requires great tact and patience inexhaustible, a quick eye, and a strong hand; you must be willing to encourage, and you must be prepared to goad. The worst, too, of the office of Schwein-General of Ireland is that he is not the *only* drover; there are other drovers, unfortunately, who are quite as disorderly and swinish as the herd itself; the agitator drives one way with his shillelagh, the bishop another with his crozier, the agrarian captain with his pike, the Orange ringleader with his bayonet. The Schwein-General has to drive the drovers as well as the drove, and that is an arduous duty for the swine-herd of a people."

It was an unlucky day for the poor citizens of Redcross, for, as the party rode through that part of the town, which the McSwynes principally occupied, and where the houses were generally thatched, a most diverting and surprising scene presented itself. The inhabitants were observed, some perched like birds, others lying on their faces, upon the roofs of their humble dwellings; for what purpose the Englishmen tried in vain to conjecture.

"It is an oriental custom," said Markham, "and perhaps confirms what I have heard stated, that the Irish are of Eastern and Hebrew origin."

The Spensers smiled at this learned solution, but Vivyan naturally wondered how they could enjoy this house-top recreation in such a high wind.

"Why don't they come down," he asked, "until the gale abates a little."

"On the contrary," said Mr. Spenser, "they will never come down while the gale lasts; if they did, their roofs would be blown into the air."

He then explained to his amazed guests this singular usage of the McSwynes, who prefer keeping their thatch steady in stormy weather with the *vis inertiae* of their own bodies, to taking the trouble of putting it in a state of permanent security by any mechanical means.

"It shows a degree of passive industry, and also fortitude," said Markham, "which can not be too much admired."

"You hit the truth exactly," said the rector, "if the virtues of these poor fellows were only *active* instead of *passive*, they would be one of the finest races in the world."

"But what is it," said Vivyan, "after all, but an old school of philosophy revived, the sect of the Cynics."

"Very true," said Mr. Spenser; "I have no doubt but Diogenes was an Irishman."

"Or a native of Higgledy-Piggledy," said Mrs. Woodward. "By-the-bye, Valentine, you must show our English friends your history of that country."

Carry herself read it that evening after dinner for the entertainment of the company. Mr. Spenser made amusing strictures upon his own performance, and was never once interrupted during the reading of it by a summons from his wife.

It was never well understood what kept Mrs.

Spenser so quiet, and made her so inoffensive, as she was during this last fit of tempestuous weather, and indeed during the greater part of the time passed by Markham and Vivyan at the parsonage. The rector, certainly, had not enjoyed so much tranquillity for some years. What made his wife's good behavior at this period the more singular was that Doctor Wilkins now, for the first time, pronounced her case to be one requiring regular medical treatment. Her irritable and discontented disposition had, at length, in his opinion, produced a morbid state of the nervous system, which might contain the seeds of more than one serious disorder, and which therefore, required to be watched with care. He recommended as much amusement and as little medicine as possible; made her a present himself of a macaw, and gave Miss M'Cracken a number of private directions for her management, one of which was to be as sparing as possible of artificial means to produce sleep. Indeed, his orders were, that no opiate of any kind should be administered without express directions from himself; but upon this point it would seem that Lucy differed in opinion from Doctor Wilkins, for she continued in secret the same liberal use of morphine which she had hitherto found so convenient, taking care, however, not to supply herself with it at the shop of Mr. Spenser's apothecary. No doubt the firmness of the governess in persevering in her own system, though contrary to the doctor's prescription, contributed not a little to keep Mrs. Spenser in order; but other circumstances were favorable likewise. If she was denied a military force for her protection, she soon had the satisfaction, as we shall see presently, of having the little garrison of police restored, and she not only took a great fancy to George Markham, but discovered that she was related to him on the maternal side, and opened a correspondence with Mrs. Markham at Paris, on millinery and mesmerism, gloves, poodles, bon-bons, and Angora cats, which filled up many a vacant hour, and promised a little harvest of Christmas presents and New-year's gifts, which no child in the nursery was fonder of receiving.

---

## CHAPTER XXXIV.

### THE 'MODEL' FARM.

"Intereunt segetes; subit aspera sylva, Lappæque, tribulique; interque nitentia culta Infelix lolium, et steriles dominantur avenæ."
 THE GEORGICS.

THE curate could never be prevailed on to write a sermon, or even to set about the mental composition of one, until toward the close of the week, seldom, indeed, until Saturday morning. His plan then was to take one of his bludgeons in his hand, and wander out alone, either along the cliffs, near Redcross, or over the adjacent mountains, when the cattle might sometimes be seen scudding before him, terrified by his vociferous preparations to preach the gospel of peace on the following day.

Hercules disappeared one Saturday morning after breakfast, and Carry made no secret of the cause of his absence. The day was then spent by the remaining gentlemen in a little agricultural survey of the neighborhood, so that the present chapter, being Georgical and bucolical, will probably be skipped by those readers who want nothing in a novel but love and mischief, comedy or tragedy, forgetting that human life has something corresponding to every form of the drama, and, among the rest, to those enumerated by Polonius as " pastoral-comical and historical-pastoral," under either of which heads you are free to class this chapter, or under both if you please.

As Markham was something of a farmer as well as a sportsman, you may fancy how he was amused and interested by what he saw in Donegal. Indeed, he saw a great deal that was instructive as well as entertaining, for bad examples have their uses as well as good ones, and in this way some of the Donegal farmers were as good preceptors as Coke of Norfolk, or Smith of Deanston.

Mr. Spenser, too, was a husbandman after a fashion. The history, literature, and poetry of agriculture seized on his imagination, and led him to take a kind of scholarlike concern even in its practical details. He had some original English principles on the subject, but he had lived so long in Ireland that he was growing rather loose in his practice, partly in consequence of the general law, which makes popular systems and habits triumph over conflicting individual efforts, partly through his innate and invincible indolence, a quality in which he was much more of a Celt, than a Saxon or Norman.

Compared, however, with the majority of farms through the neighborhood, the glebe lands exhibited a very superior tillage; the principle of rotation was evidently recognized and acted on; the farm-buildings were in tolerable order; draining was attended to; manure was economized; and there was none of that wretched confederacy of sloth, nastiness, and poverty, which, wherever it prevails, strips the name of husbandman of every agreeable and picturesque association.

"I need not ask, Mr. Spenser, if you are a farmer," said Markham to the rector, as they rode about one day together, accompanied, as it happened, by Vivyan—"your lands show it plainly enough."

"Ah, they do not deserve so much praise," replied the clergyman. "I take some interest in agriculture without being an agriculturist; I sometimes think that if Virgil had not written the Georgics, I should never have known a plow from a spade, or a heifer from a kid."

"How poetry has exalted and beautified the subject!" said Vivyan.

"Yes," said the rector, "Virgil has wreathed the handle of the plow with flowers—but, in truth, the subject has an intrinsic dignity and charm which naturally recommended it to so great and so wise a poet. The merest utilitarian, the most prosaic Benthamite, must admit the practical value of the Georgics."

"They were the work of a great poet," remarked Vivyan, "writing at the suggestion of a great statesman."

"And the state of Italy when they were written, wasted with civil wars and commotions, bore considerable resemblance," said the rector, "to that of Ireland at present. It were idle to expect a second Virgil in the same field, but it is not too much to hope that a minister may yet

arise, who, with the spirit and sagacity of Mæcenas, may give the impulse, so much wanting, to the rural industry of this fine island."

"It were devoutly to be wished," said Markham. "What strikes me as so curious is, that having always heard Ireland described as a country essentially agricultural, I find, on coming here, that if there is one pursuit more despised and neglected than another, it is the cultivation of the soil."

"Shamefully true," said the clergyman; "I am Irishman enough to be ashamed of it. Had we your inexhaustible coal-fields, we should, doubtless, be equally neglectful of manufactures. Then, perhaps, we should take to the plow and the harrow. *Optat ephippia bos piger.*"

"The Irish, of all classes, it seems to me," said Markham, "attach over much importance to legislative reforms, instead of applying their minds to improvements within their own reach and power."

"Yes," said Mr. Spenser; "but it is also true that the legislature, by deferring measures of obvious justice, divert the public mind from the species of improvements you allude to, and delay the hour of self-amelioration. The people are foolish, and their rulers are too often no wiser."

"That doctrine seems to lead to the repeal of the union," said Vivyan.

"No," said Mr. Spenser, smiling; "I do not see that it does. When an English government is merely foolish, an Irish one would be stark mad; mal-administration is much better than anarchy; the frying-pan is uncomfortable, but the fire is much more so. Let ill alone may be sound policy, when ill can only be changed for worse."

"Besides," said Markham, "a more liberal spirit is growing up daily in the governing classes in England."

"Unquestionably," said the rector; "but at the same time I see such an abundant crop of evils on all sides (like that crop of weeds yonder), so much ignorance, so much prejudice, so much passion, so many sinister interests, so little truth or patriotism in popular leaders, so little courage in statesmen, such enormous abuses to be reformed, and such a dearth of moral power to grapple with them, that I confess myself one of those who think the regeneration of Ireland will be a very slow process; and I think it is important to keep this steadily in view, for there is nothing leads to despondency so much as indulging in over-sanguine expectations. I do not despair; but the deliverance I see is afar off."

"I perceive no green crops any where but on your own ground," said Markham, bringing the conversation back to Georgical matters.

"No," said the rector, "neither my precept nor my example has ever produced a single turnip beyond the precincts of my own farm. I do not predict that any one will ever induce the Irish peasantry to grow turnips, or cease to scourge the earth for grain-crops, but whoever does will be a Mæcenas indeed."

"Then you think, sir," said Vivyan, "that the glory is reserved for a minister?"

"I am positive, Mr. Vivyan, that enormous good would be effected by a statesman who would but conceive the idea of making himself Farmer-General as well as Governor-General of Ireland—who would aim at making his rule illustrious, neither by the glitter of the bayonet, nor even by the flashing of the sword of justice, but by the splendor of the plow-share burnished by the clod."

"I have somewhere read," said Vivyan, "that the Emperor of China is annually informed of the husbandman who has distinguished himself most in the culture of the so⸺and he makes him a mandarin of a certain order."

"The idea might be adopted," said the rector, "with great advantage; and I am reminded of an observation of Montesquieu, that lazy nations are generally proud, and that the effect might be turned against the cause, and laziness be extirpated by bringing the feeling of pride into play. But no!—it is not on the improvers of society and the benefactors of mankind that our governments bestow their rewards."

"Perhaps," said Vivyan, "when your Mæcenas appears, to raise with his potent hand the drooping agriculture of Ireland, this idea may occur to him, and we may see the fountain of honor in the crown playing on worthier objects than those who are now usually sprinkled with it. We shall have an order of the plow, perhaps, or something of the kind."

"There's a farmer, yonder," said Markham, laughing, "who is well entitled to be decorated with the order of the thistle. I think I never saw so fine a crop of thistles in my life as he has raised in that field to the left of his cottage."

"Magnificent," said the rector; "but you must know that is what we call our model farm. You will see exhibited there the entire system of our Celtic husbandry in perfection, with the solitary exception of plowing by the tail, which it is surprising farmer M'Swyne has not returned to."

"The land is not bad," said Markham.

"By no means; some of the best in this parish; that is the beauty of it," replied Mr. Spenser—"but I see the model husbandman himself digging yonder; let us dismount, and walk over to him."

They left their horses with the grooms, and entered the fields. Vivyan plucked a superb thistle, as he moved along, and remarked, that as a cultivator of wild flowers, the farmer was entitled to much praise.

Roger M'Swyne was a model farmer, indeed. He would have been a saint in the Indian theology, which places human perfection in a state of the utmost inactivity. He was at work, but his work was as like relaxation as one egg is to another; he dug passively; his sinews were unbraced, and so were his nether garments. Like Canning's knife-grinder,

"his hat had got a hole in't,
So had his breeches."

But he was very civil and g⸺d-humored, gratified at being visited and talked to, with a great deal of natural politeness and plenty of " God bless you's." Markham observed with intense curiosity Roger's manner of digging. At what a very acute angle the spade entered the ground, just scratching the old face of mother Terra, as if to elude as far as possible the original blessed curse of labor. Not more than six inches of the spade were bright with the friction; the rest was as rusty as you could wish the soldier's bayonet or the rebel's pike to be.

"Why, Mr. M'Swyne," said Markham, "you don't call that digging, do you?—why don't you go down deeper ?"

"Och, then," replied the pattern agriculturist, "is it deeper your honor says ?—sure there isn't a man in the townland giving his bit of ground such a diggin."

Markham gently took the spade out of his hands, put it almost perpendicularly into the earth, stood up straight to it, pressing it down with a strenuous exertion of the muscles of his right foot, and turned up thirteen or fourteen inches of new virgin soil.

"Now, there is a spade-full of earth," said Mr. Spenser, "that never saw the sun before since the creation of the world."

Roger gazed with a comic expression of indolent wonder at the phenomenon of Markham's exploit, and the result of it.

"That's what we call digging in England," said Markham, returning the spade.

"Och, then it is diggin," said Roger, shrugging his broad shoulders, the chief use he made of them.

"Why, man," continued the young Englishman, "there's gold under those acres of yours, if you would only dig for it."

"There's gold's worth, at any rate," replied the farmer, who perfectly understood the metaphor, not being at all defective in intelligence.

"Your thistles, Roger," said Vivyan, too pleasantly to be at all offensive, even if the farmer had been touchy, which he was not at all, "are so luxuriant, that I have plucked one to stick in your button-hole; and I must have the pleasure, at the same time, to dub you a knight of that ancient and distinguished order."

Frank then, amid great laughter, in which Farmer M'Swyne heartily joined, invested him with the appropriate reward of his agricultural success, and Roger was known for many a year afterward, all round the country, as the Knight of the Thistle.

They had their choice of egresses from the model farm, for though there were twenty superfluous fences, there was not one through which elephants, or even mammoths, might not have ranged with the utmost comfort and facility. Roger's cows were grazing at large on the road-side, where there was better vegetation than in their proper pastures, which were usurped by his neighbor's cattle, as indifferent to meum and tuum as their owners. There was a pound in the parish, but as straying seemed to be the established usage, it is to be presumed that only perverse beasts, which staid at home, were ever committed to it.

---

## CHAPTER XXXV.

### A LOVE CHASE.

"If such you seek,
It were a journey like the path to heaven
To help you find them."
COMUS.

WHEN Vivyan returned from that ride, he went in quest of the ladies, or at least of Mrs. Woodward, for it was only for her that he inquired.

He was pretty well acquainted by this time with all the little out-door haunts and resorts of the women of the family, and he went rapidly from one to another, his heart fluttering for no reason but that he had not heard a female voice, or seen a female form, since breakfast. A room, close to the laundry, had been fitted up in a rude, temporary way for the rector's daughter to hold her little school in, for the children of the laborers on the glebe and the cottiers in the immediate neighborhood. Frank raised the latch. The place was silent and sunny. A robin, which had got in through the open casement, was hopping over the books and slates, picking up crumbs of bread more probably than crumbs of knowledge. The bird hopped out when Vivyan entered. The school had been over for some time; he looked into some of the books that were nearest his hand.. Elizabeth's handwriting was in most of them; her name with a few kind words conferring the little rewards of infant merits, or incitements to it. There was her chair, too, and a little scarf of hers on the back of it: trifling circumstances, but they did not escape the attention of Frank Vivyan, though the name on his tongue was still aunt Carry.

The laundress had a little daughter, a round four-year-old, bright-eyed, rosy, merry creature, that nobody in female form, except Miss M'Cracken, ever passed without saying something, or giving something to, were it only a cowslip or a kiss. It was always clean, too, for the mother had been a pupil of Ellen Hogg. The wonder was that the little laughing lump had not long ago been kissed away, it got so much kissing; but it seemed to thrive upon the diet, and there it rolled and tumbled about with its short clothes, among the daisies, the livelong day when it was not raining, still laughing, playing with the laughing flowers, or munching laughing potatoes, which possibly helped the kisses to keep the laundress's daughter so florid and fat.

"Miss Lizabeth not dere," cried the little joyous she-urchin to Frank Vivyan, as he came out of the vacant school-room. The impertinence of the infant provoked him. Vivyan was no kisser of infant beauty, but he tapped the thing playfully on the cheek. It fell back crowing with its habitual glee; Venus at four could not have been a more laughing child.

The bare-armed mother, unseen by Frank, stood at the door of the laundry, hot from the tub, exulting in the precocious sharpness of her rosy rogue of an infant, and probably admiring at the same time the handsome Vivyan, a pleasing respite from the labor of washing on a summer day. Her eyes met Frank's, as he was passing on, and the sly twinkle in them almost brought the color to his cheek, for it made him feel that every body divined the soft current of his thoughts, from three years old to thirty.

He hastened on, not without a gracious notice of the glowing laundress; and between two lofty hedges, or rather walls, of laurel and yew interwoven, he next encountered the demure nursery-governess, wrapped in a little scarlet mantle, pacing the natural cloister alone. Vivyan still thought her handsome, but he now distinctly perceived the sinister expression which had struck Markham the first time he saw her. Lucy, indeed, looked more like a conspirator, with a white powder in her pocket, or a dagger under her cloak, than a nun telling her beads.

She had for some time admired Vivyan more than she had confessed to any body, and had frequently thrown herself in his way, and tried to inveigle him into little flirtations. The present meeting, however, was purely accidental, but Miss M'Cracken thought she might as well turn it to advantage; so she began by falling in love with a sprig of the broad-leaved myrtle in full flower, which Frank chanced to wear in his button-hole. He presented it to her, and she instantly stuck it tenderly in her bosom.

"Myrtle is my favorite tree," said Lucy, sentimentally.

Frank was compelled to remark the curious coincidence of Lucy's taste in trees with that of the Paphian queen. Lucy simpered, and wished Mr. Vivyan would tell her why Venus had made the myrtle her own. He scarcely heard the question, so impatient was he to escape from the querist, pretty as she was. She then inquired if he was a botanist. A monosyllable answered that interrogatory.

"Would you like to learn?" she pursued gliding by his side.

"Why, to be instructed by you," said Vivyan; of course—what else could he have said?

"I should be very happy to teach you, sir," she rejoined, with the grave air of a person solely intent upon the duty of communicating knowledge. Frank knew not how to extricate himself, for she plucked one of the flowers of the myrtle and actually began her lecture.

"These are called petals, one, two three, four; this in the middle has a very hard name, the pistil, and all those little things round it with the dust on them, are called anthers; the dust itself is named the farina—oh, Mr. Vivyan," she then exclaimed, with a sudden burst of enthusiasm, "there is absolutely no end to the wonders and beauties of nature; are you fond of natural theology?"

So abrupt a digression surprised Frank much more than even the voluble anatomy of the flower had done; scarcely knowing what reply to make, he said he hoped Miss M'Cracken would give him credit for not being uninterested in the sacred subject she had alluded to. She then asked him his opinion of Paley, Butler, and a host of moralists and divines.

What a heavenly-minded young woman, thought Frank, to meet between two laurel hedges! But, whether he gave her implicit credit for sincerity or not, he decidedly thought her conversation a bore, and, with all his politeness, he was unable much longer to conceal the fact, that the pains of his fair lecturer were utterly thrown away upon him. Directly Lucy perceived this, her looks and manner underwent a sudden and marked change; she bit her lip, with ill-concealed resentment, dropped a ceremonious courtesy, and bade him his inattentive scholar good evening; adding, as she turned on her heel—

"You will find Miss Elizabeth, sir, in the flower-garden."

This annoyed Vivyan, and indeed he was vexed too, at having unintentionally wounded the girl's *amour propre*, by having been so absent in her presence—a crime that women, more angelic than Lucy M'Cracken, are slow to pardon. Besides, what crime is more heinous in the eyes of a governess, than neglect or scorn of her lessons; so that Frank had offended in every way.

He was half inclined to follow her, and make the *amende* for his abstraction, and seeming incivility, when he saw a young man emerge from a side-alley and join her. He distinguished his features but imperfectly; they were strange to him, and as disagreeable as strange. There was something, too, in the furtive way in which he glanced about him, which struck Vivyan as singular, but it was not his humor, or his business, to be suspicious, so he went his way in the direction of the garden, and soon thought no more either of Miss M'Cracken or her companion.

Against the garden wall, close to the door, grew an ancient fig-tree. Barren enough it was in point of figs, for the climate was not like that of the plains of Lombardy, but its foliage was luxuriant, so that Mr. Spenser would not hear of its being cut down; but, on the contrary, had a bench placed under it for his old gardener, Pierce Byrne, to sit and smoke on, when it was either too hot, or too cold, too early, or too late to work; or when there was nothing to be done that could not be done by proxy, which was the commonest case of all.

The gardener was now sunning himself there with his pipe; his right leg was crossed on his left knee; his blue Connemara hose ungartered; his red waistcoat open, as much for want of buttons as because of the heat; and a pair of shears at his side, with a comfortable coat of rust on them, showing how charitable they were to the excesses of vegetation. He was an aged man, who had mismanaged the horticultural department under three rectors; but he was hale and hearty, having been always temperate and a singularly early riser, probably to have more time for dawdling and doing nothing. If his plants grew, well and good; he was too easy to force them. Perched now on the same bench, smoking likewise, and coughing and groaning at intervals, was another old man, very diminutive, with the oddest features Vivyan had ever seen, his nose projecting from his shriveled face like the bill of a fowl; no chin, or the same as none, and a patch on his forehead, just under his little gray wig, as if he belonged to the nation of the pigmies, and had recently had a brush with the cranes. The reader will instantly recognize Mr. Maguire, the proctor. Vivyan ought to have known him, too, as Randy was in his employment, but Randy had gone up to Dublin before Vivyan's arrival, and had only that morning returned to the country. The reason of his journey to the capital will be collected from the dialogue with the gardener which Frank overheard, and which, indeed, made him acquainted with the fact that the queer disconsolate little old fellow smoking and croaking under the fig-tree was the acting agent of his Irish estate. The hedge was still between Vivyan and the old man, so that he heard the following conversation unseen by them.

"Ugh, then, it's a hard, hard world, Pierce, so it is, and there are hard people in it; but they won't be hard on myself much longer, ugh, ugh, ugh," coughed the withered little proctor.

"Och, then, it *is* a hard world," echoed the gardener, who had no right at all to say so, for not a man living in his sphere of life had found it such an easy one.

"It will be all aqual to Randy before Christmas comes round, ugh, ugh;—well, I never wronged any one living, Pierce, of the value of that ould withered leaf on the ground there, and to be put out of my bread in my ould age—ugh, ugh, ugh," coughing (much increased by the smoking) prevented Maguire from finishing the sentence, and his companion finished it for him.

"And for no crime, Randy, but the robbery," said the gardener.

Vivyan's first impression was, that the two old men thought very lightly of the crime of robbery, which seemed good ground enough for turning a person out of his employment; but Maguire soon relieved his mind upon that point by his next observation.

"Sure I didn't rob myself," said Randy, "but it's the innocent that suffer in this world, and the wicked that prosper—it's a quare world, Pierce, and I don't care how soon I lave it for a better."

"I'll take my davy," said the gardener, in a similar strain of piety, "the villains that got the money arn't much the better for it. Though I'm nothing but a poor hard-working man, up early and late, and out at all saisons, I wouldn't change with the richest rogue in Ireland, and take his conscience along with his plundher."

"And there's no country where there's such rich rogues as in ould Ireland," said Randy.

"What else is them blood-sucking absentees?" asked the gardener.

"It's no lie to say that," said Randy. "When I tould the agent up in Dublin that I'd petition the head-landlord (a chap of the name of Vivyan, rowling in luxury over in England), and see if there was no justice or mercy for a poor man, who had done no harm to nobody, he up and he tould me that I might petition the pope, or the d—l, if I plazed, for all the good petitioning would do me."

"And so you might, Randy;—my sister's son held a bit of land onst up at Carrickmacross, under that same Mr. Vivyan, and I know all about him. I'm tould, and I believe, there's not such a desolate young man any where; doesn't know where his wealth comes from, only thinks of squanderin' it on horses and curricles, drinking, gaming, smoking, and divarting himself."

"Drinking, gaming, and smoking—ugh, ugh, ugh," repeated Randy after him. You may fancy how astonished and amused Frank was to hear this account of his riches followed by such a catalogue of his vices. It was time to join the conversation, and an opportune opening in the tall hedge enabled him to do so instantly.

"That's an indifferent character to have," he said, as if he had only caught the gardener's last words.

"It's a too true picthur," said Randy, "as your honor would own, if you only knew the gintleman who's the subject of discoorse."

"His acquaintance would appear to be a very undesirable one," said Frank, "but I think," he added, glancing at the pipes which the old cocks had in their hands, "you might both have some little mercy on the gentleman, whoever he is, for the crime of smoking."

"Och, thin, we ought to be merciful, as we hope for mercy," said the gardener, rising to open the door for Frank, and growing very charitable all of a sudden.

◄ "It's a vanial sin, partiality to baccy," said the proctor, "in either a rich man or a poor man."

Vivyan entered the garden, explored it rapidly, found nobody there, and returned to the same door in about five minutes. The two hoary sinners were now playing cards. Oh, if Mr. Woodward had caught them!—but they knew very well that the curate was many miles away. Randy had produced his pack, and he and Pierce Byrne were deep in the old popular game of five-and-forty, for halfpenny stakes, with the bees humming about them under the fig-tree.

"What!" cried Frank, who now despaired of meeting the ladies before dinner—"gambling, too, as well as smoking!—come, old fellows, one little vice more, and you will have all the qualities of the gentleman you were abusing just now so heartily; to smoking and gaming you must add a little drinking for my sake—only be more temperate in your liquor than you have been in your language."

He put a sovereign down on the ace of clubs, and went toward the house, resolved that poor Randy Maguire should not be deprived of his employment because he had the misfortune of having been robbed.

---

### CHAPTER XXXVI.

#### HUE AND CRY AFTER HERCULES.

"*Dogberry.* You shall comprehend all vagrom men. You are to bid any man stand in the Prince's name.
"*Watchman.* How, if he will not stand?
"*Dogb.* Why then, take no note of him, but let him go."

THE curate had a whimsical adventure to amuse the party with when they were assembled at dinner. He had taken a discursive ramble over the hills, preparing his sermon in his usual odd way that alarmed the mountain cattle so exceedingly. At length (little thinking that any thing in human form was observing his proceedings) he found himself in a lonely glen, rarely visited by tourists, but of a strikingly beautiful and bold character. Only a footpath, known to shepherds or goatherds, traversed this wild gorge, whose steep sides, here and there terminated in sharp white cliffs, which at twilight looked like sheeted apparitions, showed no sign of a human habitation, or even of animal life itself, except a few small mountain sheep, and the "feeble folk that make their houses in the rocks." Roaming this deserted valley, he came to a small lake, and observed at one side, at a considerable elevation, the gleaming and flashing of a stream through some patches of birch and hazel, the noblest trees that grew there. It was evidently a cascade, and he had the curiosity to clamber up through the copse to reconnoiter it. A path wound along the side of the fall, which, as you approached it, was very beautiful in its small way, tumbling over a ragged precipice of some thirty feet into a rocky basin, where it bubbled and sparkled a moment in any stray gleam of sunshine that pierced the shade, and thence pursued its course more modestly until it identified its waters with the lake.

Hercules was a little fagged when he reached the rocky basin, and was glad to seat himself upon a stone while he contemplated the cataract. He had not been many moments thus reposing, when he was suddenly pounced on by two armed constables, and apprehended on a charge of no less a crime than highway robbery. Greatly astonished, and still more amused at such an incident, he made somewhat curt and rough replies to his captors, eying them very fiercely, and both by his voice and his looks strongly confirming them in the opinion that they had captured an atrocious criminal.

At length he desired to know where they intended to take him.

"Before the nearest magistrate, and that's the Rev. Mr. Spenser," said one of the officers.

"That's convenient," said Hercules, "for I'm going there myself to dinner."

Not wishing to be troubled with such companions, he then informed them who he was, and verified his account of himself by letters which he had in his pocket.

The constables looked extremely foolish, particularly when they admitted that they had been dogging him all the morning, and Woodward was curious, of course, to know how they came to make such an absurd mistake. Upon this, one of them, who seemed the most annoyed, and most anxious to vindicate his conduct, produced a paper from his pocket, and exhibited to Hercules the identical pen-and-ink sketch he had drawn himself of the fellow with whom he had the rencounter at the Black Castle.

Hearty was the laugh with which the curate's adventure was received by the company; only Carry affected to be very angry with the police for taking her husband for a bandit under any circumstances.

"Was it a very striking likeness, Hercules?" inquired the rector.

"Well, Val.," said the curate, "I believe it was sufficiently like to excuse the peelers."

In fact the sketch did resemble Hercules, as much as if it had been done for him, and his wife hoped it would be a lesson to him not to stroll the country in future in the same outlandish attire.

"What would you have done, my dear," she added, "if the men had been going in an opposite direction, and insisted upon taking you with them?"

"Why, in that case," said the powerful curate, "I should perhaps have taken *them* with *me*."

"I have no doubt you could have done it," said George Markham.

While they were thus conversing over their wine and fruit, three men were coming toward them up the principal avenue.

"Hey day, what have we here?" cried the rector, directing the attention of the company to the new comers, who were advancing with a rapid but measured tread. "The police again, I protest—Hercules, I fear there is some fresh charge against you."

It was, indeed, a party of three constables, and the curate soon recognized in two of them the identical fellows by whom he had been dogged in the morning. They halted within a few yards of the table, and one of them, who seemed to command, and who was personally known both to Mr. Spenser and the curate, advanced respectfully, touching his hat with a movement of his arm, as rigid as if it had been made of metal, and turned on a pivot.

"Good evening to you, Mr. Crumpe," said the rector.

"Good evening to you humbly, sir," answered the officer, with a second salute, the stiffest and most formal possible.

"Your business, I presume," continued the rector, with well-feigned gravity, "is with that gentleman there, my unfortunate brother-in-law." Mr. Crumpe now turned to the curate, made another of his cast-iron obeisances, and commenced an awkward and prolix apology for the mistake his men had made in the morning, excusing them on the ground of their being young men in the force, and only lately under his orders.

"Oh, then," said Mr. Spenser, "your business is not with Mr. Woodward *this* time."

"No, sir," said Mr. Crumpe, "my business is with you."

"The tables are turned, Val," cried the curate, with the loud laugh he had brought from college with him, and which Carry had never succeeded in moderating.

The rector affected to be uneasy for his personal safety, and rose to talk with the officer apart, leaving the rest of the party in a high state of enjoyment.

He returned in less than ten minutes, his face considerably lengthened, and evidently not too well pleased by the result of the private conference with the chief constable.

"Well, Valentine," said Carry, "the police have not come to apprehend you, at all events."

"Apprehend me!" replied her brother—"they have come to do worse a great deal, they have come to *protect* me. I am to be garrisoned again, it appears, in spite of myself. Some obliging friend has been exerting his influence on my behalf with the government, and Mr. Crumpe and his men have received orders to quarter themselves on my premises, and consider themselves at my disposal."

"How absurd," said Carry.

"The best way of disposing your troops," said Hercules, "is to send them trooping."

The serious looks of the rector and his relatives showed Markham and Vivyan that there were grave domestic considerations involved in what seemed, at first sight, a mere ludicrous incident. They rose, accordingly, from the table, and joined the girls in the many charming little promenades with which the glebe and its neighborhood abounded.

"Who is your obliging friend at court, Val.?" asked the curate, as soon as the party was reduced to a council of three.

"Mr. Crumpe tells me," said the rector, "that he supposes some members of parliament of my acquaintance have been using their influence at the Castle, but I know no member likely to be so officious; I am positive that I never directly, or indirectly, sanctioned such interference on the part of any body."

"This is Mr. Dawson's doing, I have no doubt," said Mrs. Woodward, with vivacity and decision.

"I can't think it, Carry," said the curate.

"Nor I," said the rector; "besides, Dawson is scarcely an M.P. of ten days' standing."

"Mind what I say, Valentine," said Carry; "your friend at court is Mr. Dawson, and nobody else. Who else would take such an impertinent liberty? Is there another man living

who would have the assurance to make an application to the government in your name, without your request, or your permission?"

"It's a most extraordinary occurrence," said the rector; "but I must now go up and sit awhile with Margaret, and leave you and Hercules to your conjugal stroll."

"But you will send the police packing, at all events," said the curate, as his brother-in-law left the room.

Mr. Spenser made no reply: perhaps he did not hear what the curate said.

"He will do no such thing," said Carry, with severity, biting her lips, and swelling with vexation at her brother's weakness. She then rose from her chair and paced up and down the portico, like a corpulent queen in high displeasure with a minister; she abused her brother in feminine but sharp language, and she did not let her husband escape either, but told him he was a great deal too simple even for a clergyman; that he had too much of the dove, and too little of the serpent, and more in the same strain of ladylike invective; all because Hercules had not divined what she had divined at the first glance, that not only was Dawson at the bottom of this police affair, but that his interference was a scheme of that gentleman to ingratiate himself with Mrs. Spenser.

"There are wheels within wheels, my dear," she said, at length reaching the peroration, but speaking with great earnestness, but you and my brother are as blind as those bats that are flying past the windows."

"But you women," said her husband, a little subdued by her energy, giant as he was, "are like watchmakers—you have a microscopic eye for wheels."

"And you men," rejoined Carry, "or some of you, at least, have no eyes for wheels, until they are as big as mill-wheels."

So ended that week at the parsonage. There was one member of the household to whom the return of the police was no mystery, nor the influence to which that event was owing. The acquaintance which Mr. Dawson made with Miss M'Cracken upon the island had not been left unimproved. It was from her he had learned the fact that the police force had been withdrawn from the parsonage, and to her he privately communicated, not only the steps which he designed to take in order to secure its restoration, but the object which he had in view, namely, to gain the good-will of Mrs. Spenser. Lucy engaged in this privy correspondence, with little motive, in the first instance, but the pure love of clandestine doings. Her views of mischief, however, widened as she advanced; and she soon began to feel an especial gratification in secretly supporting a man whose addresses she knew were intolerable to Elizabeth Spenser, toward whom she bore an intense dislike, and of whom she had of late been growing absurdly jealous. How Vivyan's indifference to her (of which she had so decided a proof in the laurel walk) tended to exasperate this state of feeling may easily be imagined. The young man who secretly joined Miss M'Cracken upon that occasion was an envoy of Dawson's, and the junior of the two suspicious personages whom Sydney had met with at Dawson's house. He was the bearer of a letter to her, containing a present of a pair of bracelets, and was under the impression that Lucy was Dawson's cousin, not that he would have objected to undertake the same mission had its legitimacy been ever so open to question. His instructions from his employer were to take Miss M'Cracken's orders, and execute promptly any little commission she might intrust him with; but Lucy did not task him heavily—she merely sent him of an errand to Redcross for a surreptitious supply of laudanum for her black bottle.

---

## CHAPTER XXXVII.

### ◄ 'THE CURATE'S SERMON. ►

"His preaching much, but more his practice wrought,
A living sermon of the truths he taught."
THE GOOD PARSON.

THE exordium of the curate's discourse alarmed Mr. Spenser exceedingly, for it proclaimed roaring war with a power which the preacher reprobated as the grand enemy of mankind, and of Irish mankind especially, the foe to all improvement and civilization, a spirit in open rebellion to the divine word, and against which he wished he had ten thousand tongues to testify, and as many thousand hands to lift.

The rector trembled for the Pope—he folded his arms resignedly in his surplice, and awaited the assault on the Vatican, which seemed inevitable. Before the end of the exordium Hercules had actually made himself invisible in the dust which, with his tremendous action, he knocked out of the old red cushions; and the deep thundering voice issued as it were out of a cloud. Markham and Vivyan, accustomed to the repose of the English pulpit, were amazed at such a display of muscular energy and vocal power in a quiet little country church. But it was not against Rome the curate took up his parable on the present occasion; it was neither against the Pope, or Antichrist, that he bolted his invectives, but against the sloth and indolence of his countrymen. It was a capital, trenchant discourse, full of broad sense and sound morality, but as termagant as any harangue could be. He felt that he was entitled to inveigh against sloth, being himself the most laborious and energetic of mortal men; and inveigh against the vice he did, as if he had it before him incarnate; he bespattered it with the foulest language, branded it with every crime, imputed every human misery to it, stuck it up in a pillory, and scolded and pelted it for half an hour, with such a copiousness and variety of epithets and reproaches, as would have better become the red or the blue petticoat than the black gown. But the abuse was mixed with so much undeniable truth, and came so naturally from the curate's lips, and so palpably from his heart, that it seemed at length perfectly germane to the subject. He made his audience feel that sloth deserved all he said of it, and sent some of the Hogg family home with uncomfortable forbodings as to their fate both here and hereafter.

He went back to the beginning of things, and pointed out the deep moral in the simple tale of the Creation; how there were six working days to one sabbath; then he demanded whether earth was to dictate to heaven, or heaven to earth; what right had man to seven days of rest, when

God, by precept and example, had declared there should be one only, and that at the close of a week of toil? As for you, he cried, ye Hoggs and M'Swynes, a perpetual sabbath is what you would fain keep, if Providence would only send ravens to feed you, and shower manna down upon you; but I say unto you that the sluggard's sabbaths are Satan's sabbaths, and that it is wrath heaven will rain on you and not manna; his ministers of vengeance, not of mercy, Providence will send to visit you, if you do not repent and mend your lives; and the only repentance that will be worth a button to you is to cease to be the drowsy knaves you are, and work for your bread like honest men. There never was an honest man who was not a laborious one, and there never was a sluggard but he was a rogue into the bargain. Now I'll let you into one of the secrets of the next world, and you may publish it from the tops of your neat cabins and at the corners of your dainty streets;—if there is one thing under the sun that heaven detests and abhors more than another, it is the very thing you love most—the abominable and rascally vice of idleness. It is the will of heaven that man shall eat his bread in the sweat of his own brow, and you want to eat yours in that of your neighbor's. See what a country Providence has given to a crew of lazy lubberly varlets, who would be only too well off in Zahara or Stony Arabia! Dare you say that God is not goodness and bounty itself to you? Ay, that he is, a thousand times too bountiful: I could almost quarrel with Heaven for not having given this charming and fertile island to the honest hard-working independent Dutch, and settled you in the swamps of Holland, to pump for your lives. No thanks to you if your fields are as green as they are; though they are not half so green as they ought to be, and would be, if Providence had given them to industrious people. Beware, I say unto you, ye Hoggs and M'Swynes; Heaven withdraws the blessings that man abuses; "a fertile land," it is written, "maketh he barren for the wickedness of them that dwell therein." And do we not see the scripture already fulfilled in the meager produce of your neglected or exhausted fields? No sirocco withers your lands; no army of locusts desolates your crops; the only blight is human sloth; the only locusts are your own selves.

Then he discharged a volley of texts at them, principally from that magazine of practical every-day wisdom, the Book of the Proverbs. "As the door turneth on its hinges, so doth the slothful on his bed." "The slothful hideth his hand in his bosom; it grieveth him to bring it again to his mouth." "He that tilleth his land shall be satisfied with bread, but he that followeth vain persons is void of understanding." "The slothful man saith, there is a lion in the way; a lion is in the streets." Here the curate paused, and sternly demanded of his congregation, which of them did not see a lion every day of his life? "Why," he exclaimed, "Afric is not so infested with lions as Ireland is."

The junior part of the audience looked a little startled at this asseveration, and Billy Pitt felt abashed at his father's ignorance of the natural history of his country. But the curate vehemently protested that he affirmed the truth, and that he would proclaim from the house-tops that all the miseries of Ireland were owing to the lions. Why were the bogs unreclaimed? For fear of the lions: Why were the fields untilled? Fear of the lions. Why were the very streets of Redcross unpaved and unbesomed? Because there was a lion in every one of them. Then he told them that the lion seen by the slothful is a phantom sent to scare them from their duties by him who is represented as a lion himself, and a roaring lion, seeking to devour, and who would eat up the sluggards first of all.

Having thus sufficiently terrified his audience, he proceeded to inform them how the lions were to be combated. "Face them," he cried, "and they will scamper away like hares. I have made lions run in my time—so I speak from experience, my friends. Resist the devil, and the best way to resist him is to work. Christianity is the religion of work. Its divine Author was himself a workman; its apostles were fishermen and mechanics, expressly to teach us that there is nothing so good, nothing so holy, nothing so godlike as industry, as there is nothing so shabby and diabolical as sloth. The God of Christianity is a God of industry; he took his kings from the sheep-fold, and his prophets from the plow." This idea led the enthusiastic preacher into a rhapsody which delighted Markham. The curate broke forth into a glowing panegyric upon rural life, with its pastoral and agricultural occupations; their calm pleasures, their salubrious nature, their transcendent usefulness, their true dignity; how the plow exceeded the sword in glory—how no foughten field, not the memorable fight of the Boyne itself (which in Mr. Woodward's estimation exceeded all the battles of history in glory), is half so illustrious as the field that industry finds a waste and leaves a garden; how the cultivator of the earth is the victor for man to honor; how the Pagans understood this when they adored the givers of the corn, the olive, and the vine; and how he panted for the day when some greater conqueror than had ever yet appeared—greater than Strafford, or Cromwell, or glorious and immortal William himself—would visit their shores, not with the sword to ravage, but with wisdom to reclaim and cultivate; not to subdue the people, but to vanquish their follies and their crimes; not to win gory honors by the slaughter of men or the sack of towns, but to bind his brows with unbloody and unfading laurels, gathered with the sickle, not the sword, with all "the pomp and circumstance of glorious Peace."

"You laid it hard on them," said the rector to Hercules, after service, as they all walked back together to the curate's house to lunch there. The fact was, that Mr. Spenser winced a little himself under his curate's invectives; and so, indeed, did Vivyan too, as he confessed to his friend in the course of the evening.

"I give them a blast like that once a year," said Mr. Woodward; "it does them no harm, at all events."

"No harm!" cried Markham. "I should think it ought to do them all the good in the world."

"Ah, the Syren, sloth, is a sweeter singer than I am," said the curate. "That was not a bad hit about the Dutch, eh, Val.?"

"It was capital," said the rector; "but it was all excellent, only perhaps a little too—what shall I say—too termagant."

"I have no patience," said Hercules, "with the lazy varlets, starving in rags, and wallowing in the mire, when, with a little common industry, they might be as well housed, clothed, and fed, as any peasantry in Christendom."

"You don't think them the finest peasantry in the world, Mr. Woodward?" said George Markham.

"The flatterers that tell them so are not their friends," replied the curate—"it's not often the rogues hear so much plain truth as they heard from me to-day. Truth is a scarce commodity in this country, Mr. Markham."

"It ought to be abundant," said the rector, "for we are exceedingly economical of it."

"You think there ought to be a great accumulation somewhere?" said the curate, laughing. "Well, I wonder where it is?"

"But, Mr. Woodward," said Vivyan, who had not yet spoken, "were you not a little too hard on the Piggledies, pa　u a y as you let the Higgledies go scot free?"

"I gave it to the Higgledies at Easter," replied Hercules, "and there is no part of Ireland where they deserve a rating better than in this very county. Formerly I used to have them both up together, landlords and tenants, but the result was, that each thought himself abused merely to humor the other; and besides, it was only encouraging the notion, already far too prevalent, that the faults of the rich excuse those of the poor, and *vice versâ*."

---

## CHAPTER XXXVIII.

### YOUNG LOVE.

"Beauties, have ye seen this toy
Called Love, a little boy,
Almost naked, wanton, blind,
Cruel now, and then as kind?
If he be amongst ye, say,
He is Venus' runaway."
HUE AND CRY AFTER CUPID.

THE fonder Vivyan grew of the society of Mr. Spenser and the ladies of his family, the more gently and good-naturedly did he bear with the comparative clownishness of Sydney, the more incapable he was of repelling his advances with the coldness and hauteur of his less complaisant and less facile cousin. Greatly to Markham's chagrin, it was soon settled that young Spenser was to be sent to Cambridge at the end of autumn; and Vivyan, in fact, undertook to introduce him to his own college, his own tutor, and his own circle of acquaintance. There was another party as well as Markham, who disapproved as strongly as possible of the arrangement; we need hardly say it was the curate, who never for a moment swerved from his opinion that Dublin University was the best in the world, and his friend, Tom Beamish, the best scholar in that academy, and therefore the best scholar in the world, by a plausible, if not very sound or original process of reasoning. Carry, however, kept her husband quiet; she "hoped it was all for the best," and in truth she was secretly pleased that the point was carried against Hercules, for (independently of her English notions) she wished her nephew to be removed as far as possible from his Irish assoɛiates, and she thought it extremely fortunate that at so critical a moment he should have formed a friendship with a young man of Frank Vivyan's stamp.

Simple George Markham! While he was tormenting himself about his cousin's entanglement with Sydney, he was utterly blind to a much more serious complicity with another member of the rector's family.

Ah, it was a dangerous atmosphere for fiery and waxen youth to breathe, that which two such women as Mrs. Woodward and her niece made round about them; an atmosphere of light and love, warmer and brighter than the very air of those summer days. When Vivyan sailed in the Circe—nay, when he landed on the emerald isle —he was heart-free and heart-whole; scarcely, indeed, knew he had a heart at all, except as a scientific fact, learned from a cabinet cyclopedia. Woman had entered his eye, but her image had never penetrated beyond the retina; he had only seen or read of beauty, and of passion knew no more than that it was something that inspires sonnets, and goes to the composition of a romance. It boots not to inquire how it happened that the revelation was now made to him —the old mystery that is revealed to every son of Adam, individually—that "man is not made to be alone." At what particular moment the rich golden shaft smote him, or whether it was in the boudoir or the library, or the gardens, or on the glassy water, or on the pine-clad height to the left of the parsonage, a favorite resort in the sweet summer evenings, was known perhaps only to himself. It is idle to pretend acquaintance with facts of this nature, as many writers of domestic history are wont to do. He was young, ardent, imaginative, soft, susceptible, and it is enough to say of Elizabeth Spenser, that it would have been almost a reproach to Vivyan had he been proof against her charms; her companion, as he was, from morning to night in some amusing occupation or busy amusement; sitting with her, or sauntering, or sailing, conversing or reading; no "strict age or sour severity," to check the flow of youthful spirits, or the play of fancy; the serenity of Mr. Spenser, on the contrary, and his admiration of Vivyan, sanctioning and promoting freedom, and Carry Woodward licensing with the broad seal of her comely presence and goodly countenance the growing familiarities in which she did not perceive the sweet mischief that was latent.

It was not by her accomplishments that Elizabeth Spenser fascinated Frank Vivyan, for no girl of her rank had so few of what are commonly so called. She understood and loved music without being a performer; she neither drew nor painted; in fact, her accomplishments were of a higher kind; her mind was accomplished by the habit of elegant and solid reading; her character with tenderness, modesty, truth and courage. There was every thing feminine about her, and nothing frivolous. She was the only woman Vivyan had ever met who was, not perpetually inquiring for new books. Her father had taught her to see in old books a variety, a freshness, a fullness and vigor to be sought in vain in the annual teemings of the literature of the day. But Elizabeth did not use to talk of her reading. You might find out that

she was familiar with Shakspeare, with Milton and Pope, with Massillon, or Jeremy Taylor, for she was as far from the affectation of concealment as from that of display. It was by the tone of her conversation, and the good taste and sound judgment of her remarks that you discovered the superiority of her intellectual training. Then she had a keen appreciation of wit in conversation; the pleasures she loved were the calm, pure, healthy enjoyment of books, flowers, friendships, and beneficent occupations. Vivyan saw her not merely by her own light, but by the light reflected from the faces of those that loved her, and from the numerous objects of her care. Her spirit of usefulness was visible through a wide circle round her father's house; she supplied, in a great measure, his deficiency in point of vigor; there was no want of benevolence in Mr. Spenser's nature, and his daughter supplied the place of that active usefulness without which benevolence resembles the tree that gives no shade, or the flower that yields no fruit:

A relative of Vivyan's had once shown him a character of his mother, written by Mr. Everard long after his retirement to the continent. It had many features in common with that of Elizabeth Spenser, and (as he afterward owned) it was the perception of this resemblance that first led him to indulge in the dangerous pursuit of studying the mind of a captivating woman, with her person at the same time before his eyes, inevitably blending the admiration of form and feature with the moral or metaphysical pleasure of contemplating inward beauty.

It was a strange but a natural thought that occurred to him one evening, as he sat alone in a little bocage close to the house, the creation of Elizabeth's hands, and one of her favorite resorts, either to crop her carnations, or provide for a little colony of robins and blackbirds, which had settled there under her protection. It was a singular thought, but a natural one— "My mother, at her marriage, was probably just such a girl." How long did he sit dreaming there in that bocage? No matter.

The clock struck seven; he started up to perform the duties of the toilet, and on his hurried way to his chamber, he met Elizabeth descending to the drawing-room. She seemed to his view a miracle of loveliness; lovely she was indeed, but what beauty is it that imagination does not heighten; imagination, that paints the lily and perfumes the violet? Its magic beams falling full at that moment on Elizabeth made her a blaze of beauty; it deprived him of the power of expression, and he never saw her afterward but in that enchanted light of love. 'For it is not by the light of the sun that young love sees its idols, but by the fairy light of its own dreams. Love's vision is not subject to the laws of optics; it has optics of its own, to which every line is a line of beauty, and in which every ray is couleur de rose.

But of all passions love is the most unsociable. Your lover is the worst company in the world. Vivyan was unconvivial that day as a specter at a banquet. Mr. Spenser's wine and Mr. Spenser's wit sparkled in vain for him. Even Mrs. Woodward's cordial affability, that seldom failed to warm and animate all within the sphere of her fascinations, was entirely thrown away. His abstraction, however, was ascribed to a cause different from the true one, for it was known that he had received a letter acquainting him with the serious illness of his friend and benefactor in Spain, and that seemed sufficient reason for the depression of spirits under which he manifestly labored

Indeed, nobody but Carry herself seemed up to the conversational mark at dinner. The curate and Markham were manifestly done up after what they called a *saunter* of fifteen or twenty miles, and had little more force left than they wanted for the exercise of the knife and fork. As to Sydney, he had not been seen since breakfast.

With coffee, however, a light breeze of conversation sprang up; but it threatened to fall again in a few minutes, so that Mrs. Woodward, alarmed at the prospect of being becalmed for the rest of the evening, dropped a hint to the effect that if Mr. Spenser would amuse them either with his "Directions to Governesses," or his "Advice to Curates," the company would take it as a great favor.

"Do, Val., and keep Mr. Markham and me awake," said the curate, rousing himself, and conquering a disposition to yawn with a muscular effort not much more polite.

"I shall more probably put you asleep," said the rector.

"No, no, no," said Markham, not very distinctly knowing what he was negativing, but conscious that he ought to negative something.

"Which will you have, Carry?" asked the rector, rising.

"The Governesses, Val.," answered Hercules for her, "for I'm not equal to controversy tonight, and the other paper would provoke one, as sure as a gun."

"Be it so," said the rector, and, producing a small manuscript, handed it to Carry, who, with a good discretion, read it to the circle.

----

## CHAPTER XXXIX.

### ADVICE TO GOVERNESSES.

"But pardon me, I am too sudden bold:
To teach a teacher ill beseemeth me."
LOVE'S LABOR LOST.

"While the most celebrated wits have not thought it beneath them to advise all other classes of domestics, it has been your misfortune, ladies, and not the least of the wrongs of which you are entitled to complain, that no pains have been taken by any competent authority to instruct *you* in the principles of your profession and duty. Without going the length of affirming that your vocation is equal in importance and respectability to that of the cook, or the butler, I may assert, without flattering you too much, that it is not inferior to that of either the house-maid or the kitchen-maid, from which it follows that you have at least an equal right to a place in any complete system of *directions to servants.*

"Regarding you in the light in which you are considered by the greater part of the world, I do not know how I can better commence the advice, which in the most friendly spirit I desire to offer, than by earnestly warning you against the fatal error of thinking more highly of yourselves than you are thought of by your masters and mistresses. Connected with this is another mistake, no less serious, into which I have observed many of you prone to fall—that of taking a deeper and livelier interest in your pupils than is felt by their parents themselves, whose value for their children may fairly be measured by the respect and consideration they pay those into whose hands they confide them at the tenderest and most critical season of life. Divest yourselves, at once and forever, of all romance and sentiment upon the subject of education. Your sole business is, like other menials, to make the best of your place ; and as the wages are commonly trifling (if, indeed, salary is 'an object' to you at all), you must only endeavor to eke them out as well as you can, with every little incidental emolument and advantage which your situation throws in your way. Always recollect that nobody can have a *right* to greater services than they choose to *pay for,* and that you are only bound in conscience to give your scholars an equivalent for the pittance you receive; and not even that little, if you are expected to combine the office of instruction with the collateral duties of the laundress or the mantua-maker. You stand (as learned writers agree) *in loco parentis ;* you represent the mistress of the family you enter, and you have, consequently, as clear a right to neglect or mismanage your subjects as if you stood literally in the maternal relation toward them. Ponder this principle well, and it will save you from a great deal of anxiety and vexation. What can be more preposterous than to see a lady exhausting her patience, overworking her brain, and sometimes even wearying her hand, for the benefit of a set of turbulent young people who are not related to her ever so remotely, while the woman who bore them sees them perhaps only once a day, scarcely ever thinks of them at all, and probably never corrected one of them in her life ?

"Begin by keeping your pupils at an awful distance. The further you keep them from you, the less you expose your temper to be ruffled by their disobedience or their inattention, and a serene temper is, in your situation, a quality of the first importance. Besides, the communication of knowledge implies the previous acquisition of it, and how can a young lady improve her own mind as she ought to do, if she squanders the greater part of the day in the nursery or the school-room, in the worst possible company, that of ignorant, ill-behaved children. You will at least be always justified in bestowing as much time upon the cultivation of your own mind as the mother of your pupils devotes to fashionable frivolities and amusements.

"If you are forbidden to correct your pupils upon any occasion, or for any transgression whatsoever, strictly comply with the injunction. A mother is free to ruin her children, if she pleases, and it is extremely presumptuous in a hired governess to try to hinder her. It is another question, when you find it impossible to retain your situation in consequence of the turbulence of your subjects, which you are not permitted to repress. You will in such a case consult your own generous impulses only, and not resign your place and your salary without leaving a character for energy behind you, which may probably be of use to the lady who succeeds to your enviable post.

"Be very particular in the choice of books for your pupils. The best rule is to select them exactly as if you were selecting them for your own use. You will, of course, take care that they relate to those branches of knowledge with which you are *least* familiar, should you happen not to be one of those omniscient young women who teach *all* things teachable, and 'make themselves useful' into the bargain. Suppose the mother to remark that the works you have ordered from the family bookseller are too abstract or advanced for the school-room, nothing is easier than to tell her that she greatly underrates the abilities of her children; and, as this is always an agreeable remark to the maternal ear, you may order another batch of similar publications very soon after, upon the strength of it.

"It is very convenient for you when the mother has a reasonable share of ignorance for a woman, and knows little or nothing of modern languages. You may then purchase the novels of George Sand, and pass them off as the works of a French Mrs. Ellis or Mrs. Trimmer. Besides, should you happen to be a daughter of a Welsh parson, nothing would be easier than to make the language of the ancient Britons answer for German, and increase your reputation, if not your income, by the device."

Just at this point, Carry suddenly dropped the paper she was reading on her lap, and glanced over her shoulder at the door, near which she happened to sit, as if she heard some noise in that direction or expected somebody to enter. It was but a momentary interruption. She resumed as follows.

"Another excellent and approved mode of improving yourself is by securing the assistance of eminent masters. Many a young governess has entered a family illiterate and unaccomplished, and left it a well-informed and highly polished woman. You can not afford yourself to incur the expense of the best professors of music and dancing, or Italian and German, but your employers *can;* impress the advantage of masters upon them strongly, and if you have any relatives or friends of your own in the line, you will have an opportunity of serving them at the same time that you serve yourself. Should you be in love with any handsome young pianist, or drawing-master, a charming arrangement will easily occur to you, by which you can at one and the same time improve your scholars, and secure happiness as well as improvement for yourself. If you are extremely frank and confiding, you will let your flirtation with the gay artist be known to the family; if you take my advice, you will keep it as quiet as you can.

"Do not encourage the mother to be always popping into your school-room, and prying into your proceedings. Some ladies have the meanness to be always watching their governesses, and controlling their hours and their movements. Keep your mistress at as great a distance as her children. If she has confidence in you, she should mind her own business, and leave you to manage yours; if she has not, she ought to declare it frankly, and then you would know how to act. Establish yourself either at the top of the house, or in some remote wing of it, so as to make it, at all events, a long journey for madam, or my lady, to visit your apartment, either to call you to account for chastising her favorite son, or, perhaps, to pry after your Angelo, or your Tamburini."

Here Mrs. Woodward again glanced over her shoulder, but without discontinuing her reading.

"Some mothers think their children can never get governessing and schooling enough. They desire to make prodigies of them, and for that object would sacrifice not only the health of the poor things themselves, but what is of much more consequence (at least to you), the health of their preceptress. Combat this system resolutely. Be prepared with the fable of the bow kept always bent, and ready with cases of fine boys, who, to your knowledge, became absolute idiots in consequence of too close attention to their books. You ruined a charming little fellow yourself (did you not) by over-teaching him, and what would you not give now that you had acted upon the opposite system. How you reproach yourself with all the severities you employed to please a mother and to produce a dunce! Not for worlds would you commit again the same fatal folly."

Now Mrs. Woodward not only dropped the manuscript again, but bounced up, and sharply opening the door, received Miss M'Cracken in her arms. In fact, that young lady would probably have tumbled into the room, head foremost, had she not been supported by Carry's voluminous person.

"Miss M'Cracken!" exclaimed the matron, in her most formidable manner, drawing herself up to her full height, and sternly regarding the detected eavesdropper.

Lucy, however, encountered her looks undauntedly, and with the utmost composure simperingly addressed the rector, and said that Mrs. Spenser desired to see him. He obeyed, of course, and the governess withdrew along with him.

"You don't think she was listening at the door, aunt?" said one of the girls.

"I am positive of it," said Carry, "I have a quick ear, my dear."

"You may be mistaken, after all," said the charitable curate, drily, "but go on with your reading."

"At all events," said his wife, preparing to obey, "she has given Valentine a hint to improve his essay." She then continued without further interruption to the end.

"If this sound reasoning should fail to answer its purpose, there are various methods to which you may resort, to relieve both yourself and your scholars from the irksomeness of too close application. Their health. as well as their instruction, is in your province. See that they take abundant out-door exercise. Accompany them when you please, but a head-ache, a cold, or a sprained ankle, will always enable you to remain quietly at your fire-side, and the children's maid is, or ought to be, a perfectly safe person to trust them to. You, at least, may always have as much confidence in her as you think proper; and should any accident ever befall a child in her custody, it will always be easy to demonstrate that the same would have happened had the mother herself been on the spot at the moment. When you can not escape walking with your pupils, carry out their mother's wishes effectually, and give them enough of it. Should a trifling illness result from over-walking them, it is no fault of yours, and you will gain a few days' repose for your feet, and also save your shoes, which is no trifling consideration. Never be without Buchan at your elbow, have a medicine-chest of your own, and be on a good understanding with the family apothecary. Many an hour of relaxation is to be procured by proper attention to the little illnesses of young people. It is much wiser to anticipate a disorder than to wait for it to make its appearance formally. Such of you as teach 'the rudiments of Latin' will understand the meaning of '*principiis obsta.*'

"As I have alluded to Latin, let me drop a hint upon the subject while I think of it. Do not suffer the elder brothers of your pupils to entrap you into classical discussions. You only profess the rudiments, and though, of course, you know much more, you ought not to parade it in society, but rather keep it in the background, and reserve it all for your scholars in private. Apply the same rule to other things as well as Latin. Many of *our* sex preserve a reputation for learning by shunning every opportunity of displaying it; how much more becoming, then, is the same modesty in people of *yours*.

"With French it is otherwise. You can not be too lavish or ostentatious of whatever French you know, be it much or little. Lard every thing you write, and interlard every thing you say, with it; nothing makes such an impression on people who don't understand the language, and the less they comprehend what you mean, the higher opinion they will have of you. At breakfast ask for the *pang* and the *boor*. At dinner, say you will take some *dingdong*, and afterward have some of the *buff bully*. You have no conception what an effect these little feminine displays (for French is essentially feminine), produce in Bloomsbury and about Hackney. I have known wine taken with a governess in an irresistible burst of admiration, occasioned by a quotation of two words from the '*Echo de Paris.*' It will always, however, be well to be on your guard against disagreeable surprises. Beware of the exiled Poles, and the young wine-merchants from Bordeaux. When you hear that M. Latour, or M. St. Etienne, has been asked to dinner, you can have one of those convenient aches and indispositions, of which a governess ought always to have a large stock on hand. If you have exhausted those excuses in other ways, do any thing sooner than let the extent of your French acquisitions be discovered. You may say that *you don't understand the patois of Gascony!*

"So universal is the notion that the British governess possesses every qualification under the sun, and so common is it to pledge them to be 'generally useful,' that in many houses you would be required to act as *garde-malade* to the children in the measles, nor do I well know how you are to escape the duty, except through the friendly interposition of the apothecary, who (at your suggestion) may insist upon calling in a professional nurse-tender. You would then have a few weeks at your disposal to visit your father at his curacy in Ireland, or your uncle Williams, at his vicarage in Wales. The danger of a deduction from your salary need not much alarm you, for few people understand fractions well enough to calculate what it ought to be.

"Do not expect civility and good-nature, and you will never be disappointed at not meeting with it. Truly wise and good people will always treat you with urbanity and kindness, but to shape your conduct with reference to the wise and good would argue a degree of ignorance of human nature inconceivable in a woman who is bound to be ignorant of nothing. Never remain an instant in any place after you find another more advantageous and at your disposal. Be just as considerate and grateful to your employers as they are to you—no more. If you confine yourself, as many ladies do, to the education of young gentlemen, take care that they are not much above your shoulder, or over the age of twelve, unless you happen to be a Thalestris, or a lineal descendent from Boadicea. In that case I do not see why you should not prepare them for college, as well as for Eton and Harrow. If you belong to the class of finishing governesses, as you are paid much better than the rest of your profession, be as slow in finishing your young ladies as you can; you may be certain they will be finished soon enough, if you give them the last exquisite touch just when you have amassed a hundred pounds, and are resolved to keep your attachment to Angelo no longer a secret.

"If you could command your personal appearance, I would advise you to be good-looking rather than handsome. If you are beautiful, the mother will dislike you; if you are plain, you will be equally unfortunate on the other side of the house. The most comfortable post for you is the family of a widower. There you may be as absolute with your subjects as you please, and it is your own fault if you do not speedily turn the maiden aunt out of doors, and raise yourself from the low condition of a governess into the haughty station of a step-mother.

"But the natural close of a governess's career is the opening of that of a school-mistress. You are a fish in a frying-pan, and the only transition for you is into the fire. Tyrannize now over the young as you have been tyrannized over by the old. As education, in a narrow sphere, has been made painful and degrading to yourself, so let it be to others in the wider circle where you are now supreme. Be a Czarina to boys at Brompton, or an Ogress to girls at Blackheath. The great world has been harsh to you, revenge its harshness upon the little one. Return neglect with neglect, and cruelty with cruelty, or continue (if you are very simple, and very good) to be an amiable, conscientious, and Christian woman, filling the sacred post that mothers abdicate, earning ill-usage hardly, and receiving no wages worth mentioning but those of scorn and ingratitude.',

The curate and Markham had been sound asleep for some time, before Mrs. Woodward had done reading.

"Very flattering to Valentine," she said, rising to shake Hercules, and affecting to be hurt at this practical criticism on her brother's production.

As she crossed the hall a few minutes afterward on her way to her chamber, she encountered her nephew, and would fain have inquired where he had dined and spent the day; but he looked more than usually morose and gloomy, and scarcely vouchsafed her a civil return to the affectionate good night she wished him.

---

## CHAPTER XL.

### A DISCOVERY.

"I understand you very well (quoth Pantagruel): But preach it up; prattle on it, and defend it as much as you will, even from hence to the next Whitsuntide, if you please so to do; yet in the end will you be astonished to find how you shall have gained no ground at all upon me, nor persuaded me by your fair speeches and smooth talk, to enter ever so little into *the thraldom of debt*. And I am fully confirmed in the opinion, that the Persians erred not when they said that *the second vice was to lie, the first being that of owing money*." RABELAIS.

THE brow of Sydney Spenser was growing daily darker and darker, and an expression of care was visible in his features, not only foreign to his age, but to his former character. His disappearances were growing at the same time more frequent and abrupt; he made appointments and broke them on slight pretenses; he walked or rode out with the rest of the party, and suddenly quitted them, sometimes giving an account of his conduct, but often vouchsafing no explanation.

Mrs. Woodward, and his sister Elizabeth, had been far enough indeed from conjecturing the true cause of his depression of spirits, when first they remarked it. Now they did not observe him as closely as before; the mind of the best of sisters can not be always occupied with solicitude for a brother, and Carry surely had enough to engage her thoughts and affections, active and warm as they were, without anxieties for a graceless nephew.

But Sydney was now, indeed, an object of compassion, and he would not have wanted pity and sympathy, had his distresses been but known; had he only possessed the courage, or the prudence to reveal them to the relatives who were so tenderly interested in his welfare.

The days of his unbounded confidence in false friends were nearly over. Though far from being convinced of the profligacy of Dawson, he had begun to be painfully sensible of the influence which, even in his absence, he exerted over him. Those small debts, from which his false friend had obligingly promised to relieve him (having first encouraged him to contract them), remained still undischarged, or at least the greater part of them; they considerably exceeded Sydney's rough estimate, and though Dawson had made some small advances, they only sufficed to keep the creditors quiet for a few weeks. The residue still hung over him—a millstone round his neck by day, an incubus on his breast by night. Let young men beware of contracting small debts, for small debts may be great calamities. There are few sadder, and at the same time more unnatural, spectacles in the world, than a young man under twenty with the cares of the Fleet prison written on his forehead, with the anxieties of debt clouding his eye and hollowing his cheek. Had Sydney candidly disclosed his embarrassments to his father, there was nothing in them so serious that he could not have been extricated from them with facility. But Mr. Spenser had never been in his son's confidence. He was too negligent to seek it, and Sydney, left to himself, and depending for the means of

enjoyment upon the acquaintanceships of his own making, had never felt the want of his father's friendship, or even conceived the idea that such a relationship could exist between them. Then, to have had recourse to his father would have involved the necessity of numerous confessions, which false pride deterred him from making; he had contracted those small debts disingenuously, and he now concealed them, with the folly which uniformly accompanies indirectness, and aggravates its evil consequences.

Moreover, he could not but feel that the recent loss of a considerable sum of money made it a particularly unfavorable moment for adding to the rector's burdens. No, it was no longer the pursuit of coarse and boisterous pleasures elsewhere that led Sydney to absent himself from the society of the parsonage, or the festive expeditions from it. How little dreamed the virtuous and affectionate Elizabeth that the copses on the heights over the house, and the heathery nooks on the edge of the water, where she and her brother had a thousand times played hide and seek in their childhood, were often used now for a like game in real life, the undiverting and degrading one of debtor and creditor, which, though it supplies the stage with so much farce, and though the riotous wit of a Rabelais may torture mirth out of it, will never, to the end of the chapter, be fun and frolic to the actual players at it. Respect for Mr. Spenser kept his son's creditors from coming up boldly under his library windows and asking a settlement of their little accounts. Some of them were now beginning to menace Sydney with that extreme course, but he had hitherto, by excuses, promises, even threats, and a variety of tricks and stratagems, kept them from the house, though the more impatient of the number sometimes penetrated the glebe, and drove him to skulk, not always with success, about the grounds, or in the farm-offices.

Cheerfully, without a murmur or a moment's hesitation, would Elizabeth have given all she possessed in the world, to the very rings on her fingers, to have extricated her brother from such disgraceful difficulties. Cheerfully would Carry have sold her diamonds, if she had had diamonds to sell, for the same purpose; but the truth was utterly unknown to them, and indeed to every member of the household but Miss M'Cracken, to whom nothing was unknown that was said or done in the parsonage, or round about it, particularly by Sydney, over all whose doings she had long exercised a malignant and unsuspected surveillance.

But, as we have already seen, he had another cause of uneasiness. He had little doubt, from the description his uncle had given, and still less from the portrait he had drawn of the person he had seen at the Black Castle, that he was one of the two suspicious characters, whom he himself had not only met, but sat at table with at Dawson's ill-omened house. To be sure, Dawson had stated the man's profession, and explained what brought him to the country; but then, on the other hand, it seemed impossible not to connect him, in some way or another, with the robbery. Fearful ideas flashed for a moment across his mind; he laughed at them, but still they returned. Was his confidence in Dawson diminished?—he *said* to himself that it

G

was not, yet he *acted* as if it was, for he could not bring himself to disclose to his uncle his suspicions respecting Messieurs Lamb and Thomson, although it might have furnished a clew to the detection of the thieves, and could not possibly compromise Dawson, assuming the statements to be true which he had made to Sydney.

Thus, not only haunted by the faces of creditors (aspects which would be repulsive, were we in debt to an Adonis, or in the books of Apollo himself), but dogged as it were by the still more terrifying apparition of the soi-disant Major Lamb, the misguided Sydney was visibly and greatly altered. The ruddy health and the noisy spirits were gone; he no longer lounged about the house or the grounds, whistling, like Cymon, "for want of thought," or singing the "Boys of Kilkenny, or the Fortunes of Brian O'Linn," at the top of his good sonorous tenor; he was grown wonderfully quiet and gentlemanlike, civilized by debt, and subdued and polished by mental anxiety. ."

The curate one day proposed at breakfast a walk to the Black Castle. Markham agreed cheerfully, but Sydney declined to accompany them, pretending a slight indisposition, but really apprehensive of encountering his, formidable Castle Dawson acquaintance.

Hercules and Markham then armed themselves, more, however, to shoot hares than robbers, and proceeded on their expedition without him. The rector and Vivyan sauntered about together, quoting Milton and the Georgics, and conversing about Cambridge. Sydney passed the morning differently. One of the most troublesome of his creditors was Amby Hogg, the sexton of the parish. Amby had walked over from Redcross that morning to press once more his little demand, being probably pressed himself to procure food and clothes for his dear though dirty children. One of Sydney's scouts (of whom he retained several in his service) informed him of this arrival, and he retired to a favorite fastness of his in the Haggard.

The bull-dog already mentioned was eminently useful on such occasions. It was a savage animal, called Brutus, that barked wickedly, and would have flown at a lion. Amby knew he was running a risk, but he suspected that Sydney was in the yard, and creditors are proverbially daring. Directly the poor shop-keeper raised the latch and put his nose into the haggard, Brutus sprang at him with a terrific growl. If he had not stepped back and banged the door to with the utmost celerity, his leg or his throat would have been in the bull-dog's fangs. One of the farmservants ran up and Sydney called to him to lock the door. The boy executed the order promptly, being used to adopt such defensive measures; and then there was the following short parley between him and the creditor outside.

"What does your masther mane by keeping a dog to ate the people?" growled the terrified sexton.

"My masther's dog ates nobody that oughtn't to be aten," replied the gossoon through the key-hole. .

Then: they reviled one another like fishwives in Redcross, and the stable-boy, prompted by Sydney who was close to him, but so placed as not to be discoverable through the key-hole, told lies enough to bring down lightning, if falsehood

were a conductor of the electric fluid, which for tunately it is not, in a part of the world so "given to lying" as Ireland.

However, Sydney eluded once more his creditor's grasp, and after lurking some time longer in the straw, caressing his amiable and useful friend Brutus, he crept into the house to luncheon.

Some hours were then spent delightfully upon the water. Vivyan suggested it to Sydney, and Mrs. Woodward and Elizabeth were easily prevailed on to accompany them. Never was the surface of a summer sea smoother; the water was alternately gray, purple, gold, and azure, as it reflected the rocks the heath, the gorse, or the blue concave.

It was through Mrs. Woodward's medium that Frank had become acquainted with Elizabeth, that is to say with her mind, its cultivation, solidity, and loveliness. Carry possessed in an eminent degree the talent of developing the talents and characters of every body round her who had talents and character to be developed; and Elizabeth never revealed herself so freely as in her society, or expressed her thoughts and emotions with the same confidence. Hers was not the enthusiasm that shows itself in exaggeration and emphasis, or in looks, sighs, and gestures, but the enthusiasm whose very strength conceals it from observation; it was not the perfume of the flower, perceived and enjoyed by all the world, but the essence of its incense, yielded to few, perhaps entirely only to one. That was a glorious ripening day, not to the mountain crops alone, but in love's harvest Vivyan fully experienced the rapturous feeling of the oft translated and oftener imitated fragment of Greek song—

"Blest as the immortal gods is he,
The youth who fondly sits by thee,
And sees and hears thee all the while
Softly speak, and sweetly smile."

Never did he take so little part in conversation himself; the little he did say was either to Mrs. Woodward, or to Sydney, and chiefly on the subject of Cambridge; but this was to Elizabeth a most agreeable topic, so happy was she in the thought that her brother was on the point of being delivered, as it were, by the accomplished and amiable Vivyan, from the hateful influence of Mr. Dawson. However, silent or eloquent, Vivyan pleased her, and Mrs. Woodward perceived it that day for the first time, and inwardly resolved to make all the inquiries suggested by a motherly prudence respecting Vivyan's position and prospects, and to make them without delay.

The hour of dinner and of sunset was approaching when they ran their skiff ashore alongside of the small pier, under the flag which was now gayly streaming in a delicious evening breeze. Sydney remained behind a moment to secure the boat by its chain and padlock. The ladies and Vivyan went up to the house, and found in the porch the curate and Markham, just returned from their excursion, and conversing with unusual eagerness with Mr. Spenser and his eldest daughter. The visit to the Black Castle had not been a fruitless one. The new comers shared the excitement directly they joined the group; and Sydney hearing the exclamations and the earnest speaking, hastened

to the spot. As he came up he perceived that George Markham held something in his hand, and he heard him say— •
"The robbery was committed by the owner of this pistol."

Sydney advanced another step.

The pistol was his own—the pistol he had lost during his visit to Castle Dawson. It was natural that the incident should astonish and disconcert him; but his confusion was remarked by nobody. Indeed, his position at the moment, and the shadows of the portico and its pillars, were sufficient to protect him from observation, even had attention been directed toward him, which of course it was not in any degree.

Candor at that moment would have saved Sydney and his family untold troubles. Had his father or his sisters ever seen the pistol in his possession, concealment would of course have been useless; but he knew they had not, and to have acknowledged it would have made it indispensable to relate a multitude of incidents, which might possibly and undeservedly throw suspicion on Dawson. In such cases, too, the truth must be told at once, or it is too late. Sydney suffered the moment to pass, through his moral cowardice, and thus deprived himself of a testimony in his own favor, that would have rebutted all the circumstantial evidence which was only too soon accumulated against him.

Markham retained possession of the pistol, fully determined to trace its owner by every means in his power, and he heartily congratulated his fair cousin, as they went to dress for dinner, upon such a practical result of their voyage to the Irish shores. But different thoughts from pistols and robberies were occupying the mind of Frank Vivyan. He returned from that day's boating over head and ears in love.

Sydney Spenser would that evening have given a thousand pounds for that small weapon, which had not cost him five. He shuddered to think that he had its fellow in his bed-room, and rising in the dead waste of night, he stole out of the house, unmoored the boat again, pushed out a hundred yards from shore, and flung it into the loch.

---

CHAPTER XLI.

CLOUD AND SUNSHINE.

"Love! yield thy quiver and thine arrows up
To this triumphant stranger. Before him, Fortune!
Pour out thy mint of treasures; crown him sovereign
Of all his thoughts can glory to command."
THE SUN'S DARLING.

THE next day Mrs. Woodward begged a private interview with Vivyan's friend and cousin. There was a directness about George Markham that inspired you with confidence almost on the first acquaintance : you saw that he was a man of worth and honor, of moral as well as physical courage, on whose word you might rely with profound assurance, and who would infallibly take the right-minded view of any practical question you proposed to him. Mrs. Woodward resolved to open her mind to him freely upon a subject to her niece of paramount importance, and to young Vivyan of no small consequence also. Markham fully justified the reliance placed on him : he stated, with the utmost candor, his

cousin's circumstances and prospects; completely satisfied Carry as to h'is family and connections, but entirely concurr ed in opinion, that nothing could be more unfortunate than that Miss Spenser's affections sh ould be engaged by a young man with no fortun e but his talents, his attractions, and his hopes.

"Fortune on neither side, Mr. Markham," said Carry; "it may seem a strange objection," she added, smiling, "for a curate's wife to make, but poverty and happiness combined is the lot of few indeed in this world.; it has been mine, but I would not willingly see the risk run again by any girl I love, or, indeed, by any young man in whom I take the interest nobody can help taking in your charming friend."

"It is very well to despise money, Mrs. Woodward, when we have it to despise," said Markham, with his blunt good sense, and inwardly resolving to hurry Vivyan away from this enchanted ground with relentless celerity. The resolution was taken too late. While Markham and Mrs. Woodward were conversing calmly on the necessity of loving with discretion, Vivyan was declaring his passion to Elizabeth in another place, without a thought of any thing but the sentiments with which she inspired him.

Markham left Carry to go, in quest of his cousin, vexed with himself for not having kept a sharper eye upon his conduct, but not dreaming that matters had gone as far as in fact they had. Vivyan resembled Telemachus more than his cousin did Mentor.

"But you have made no declaration, Frank, I hope."

"I have," said Vivyan.

"Then I trust the girl has not been as rash as you."

"Her heart is mine," Vivyan answered "but her hand will depend upon the approbation of her friends."

"Ah, that is always the phrase," said Markham; "all imprudent marriages begin that way. With your little Irish property, Frank, you seem to have inherited the proverbial improvidence of the country. I fear you have not considered how remote is even the prospect of professional success for you who are still so young, and not yet of two years' standing at college !"

Vivyan, of course, had considered nothing but that Elizabeth was fair, and that, like Shenstone's shepherdess, "she was every way pleasing" to him. Consideration was left, as usual, to fathers, aunts, and friends. The usual conferences and debates took place. They ended in Elizabeth and Vivyan being both brought to acknowledge (she far more easily than he) the prudence of immediate separation. Under such circumstances it is the best thing that can be done, and the pity is that the prudence does not much diminish the pain of it to the parties principally concerned. Various are the results with which such separations take place : they are, in fact, appeals to time and fortune, either to confirm rash engagements, by preserving their spirit and removing the obstacles to them, or to quash the original proceedings altogether, by giving the eye leisure to review its decree, or the fancy to revise its judgment.

But Vivyan seemed to be fortune's darling, and the appea: to time in the present instance was not kept long pending. The cloud was scarce gathered over the heads of the rash lovers, before a propitious gale dispersed it, and the sun shone forth with unexpected luster. Markham had sent orders for the Circe to be in readiness to sail. While she was wearing round the coast from the port of Derry, where she had been sent to undergo the repairs necessary after the storm, Markham, all impatience for her arrival, Vivyan miserable, though his understanding was convinced that his speedy departure for England was most advisable, a letter addressed to the latter, but in a hand which he did not recognize, arrived from Grenada. Vivyan was comparatively a rich man.

The previous letters acquainting him with the rapidly-declining health of his friend, Mr. Everard, prepared him in some measure for the account of his death, which he now received; but he had never reckoned upon being enriched by that event, and it was with no little astonishment he now learned that his romantic benefactor, whom he had never seen, had bequeathed to him a large portion of his property, so considerable a sum as probably to yield an income of nearly two thousand a year.

Vivyan mourned sincerely, if not poignantly, the loss of the friend, who living had been so kind, and who dying was thus munificent. A mind more indifferent to pelf never informed a human frame. He only valued it now as it removed the barrier between himself and Elizabeth Spenser, and blotted out the word separation almost as soon as it was written. It is wretched to record a farewell in the first leaf of a love story, but how seldom does a reprieve follow so close on the heel of a sentence !

There was, however, one little drawback; there always is. It was necessary that Vivyan should go to Spain to take some legal steps, in order to obtain the dominion over the property bequeathed to him. To Spain! He could scarcely have thought more of a voyage to China. A

few weeks before, how the prospect of visiting one of the most picturesque and romantic of European kingdoms would have enchanted him ! Now he infinitely preferred to linger on the shores of the little bay of Redcross ; an humble parsonage had more charms for him than the Alhambra ; and the barren hills of Tyrconnell, with scarce a ballad in their praise, pleased him more than the Sierra Morena, immortalized by the genius of Cervantes.

Vivyan was greatly discouraged by the thought of having to take this journey to the peninsula. Markham laughed at him, and indeed it did seem to be excessively unreasonable in Vivyan to be depressed by the prospect of an absence of two or three months, he who had only a few hours before been sentenced to a separation of perhaps as many years. But it did dispirit him exceedingly, and he tried in vain to reason himself out of his melancholy, and to conceal what he considered his weakness from Elizabeth's observation. But she perceived his dejection, and it infected her. The voyage to Spain was an indispensable preliminary to their union, yet both one and the other contemplated it with alarm, and would willingly have long delayed it. Neither spoke of a presentiment, yet both felt something like a boding that the first obstacle to their happiness had only been surmounted to make room for another which might not be overcome so easily.

Had a foreshadowing of misfortune been visible to her mind's eye alone, events would soon have proved it only too clear a peep into futurity. A serious calamity was even now impending over the rector's family, and it was Vivyan's lot to leave the parsonage in extreme confusion and distress, though utterly unconnected with his engagement to Elizabeth Spenser.

To give the history of this, it is necessary to see what Mr. Dawson has been doing since we saw him last, or rather what fortune has been doing for him.

---

# BOOK VIII.

## CHAPTER XLII.

### DUBLIN CASTLE.

"My good Mr. Dean, there are few that come here,
But have something to hope or something to fear."
                                        SWIFT'S WORKS.

WE have not seen Mr. Dawson since his gallant service to our heroine, nor heard, indeed, any news of him, except that he advanced a certain sum of money to Sydney, and was pitchforked into Parliament by a little knot of priests and attorneys, who jobbed at that time the representation of the borough of Rottenham.

Another man would have presumed upon his brilliant exploit, and his now distinguished position, and prosecuted his love-suit vigorously on the strength of both; but Dawson seemed above taking advantage of adventitious circumstances; he seemed to think nothing either of personal hazards, or personal advancement. It was little to him to save a lady's life at the risk of his own, and as to the House of Commons, that was only his proper sphere.

Such were the appearances, and they were certainly in his favor ; but the truth was that for some time after his return for Rottenham he had too much business on his hands of a financial nature to leave him much time to think of his affairs at Redcross. Among other things, he had to make a clandestine sale in London of the books and pictures, and it was no easy matter to squeeze out of the Nathans and Mordecais money enough to cover the honestest of his electioneering expenses, although he had called the powers of earth and heaven to witness, at a public banquet, that his election had not cost him a single shilling.

There were several constituencies at that period (it is to be hoped there is more public virtue extant at present), which had a positive antipathy to respectable men. They exacted two qualifications, and only two, from their representatives ; a certain sum of money, and a readiness to take any pledge required of them on the hustings. The necessary money Dawson managed to raise by the well-known fiscal operation called hook and crook (chiefly by selling the portraits of his fictitious ancestors); and as for the pledges, there was not the slightest difficulty on that head, Dawson's swallow being prodigious, only comparable to that of the giant in the French romance, whose ordinary diet was windmills. He pledged himself to dismember the British empire without a scruple, and would have entered into an equally solemn engagement to repeal the law of gravity and dissolve the universe, with just as little remorse of conscience. That great political bubble, the cry for the Irish Harem-Soarem, was then newly blown, and beginning to soar and glitter in the public eye; fascinating with its rainbow colors all who were ignorant of its flimsy materials and utterly hollow nature. Some, no doubt, were honest in espousing the question, sincerely believing in its vitality, and flattering themselves that they had reasons to give for "the faith that was in them;" but to many it was only an hurrah, which they stupidly echoed, or a game which they profligately played. A frenzy against the union actuated some of the most popular constituencies, and a little phalanx of repealers was sent into the House of Commons, where (whether they retarded the prosperity of the country or not) they certainly did not advance their cause an iota. With this phalanx Dawson aspired to connect himself, and he was qualified to act with it in several important respects. He had studied eloquence in that great national school of oratory, whose fundamental principles are to divorce logic from argument, truth from statement, and decency from language; a system of rhetoric which considers violence strength, and rigmarole reasoning, and where abuse and personality constitute the graces and delicacies of elocution. Such was Dawson's intellectual education for the senate. As to his patriotism and public spirit, they were hereditary; he prized his country too highly to sell her for a trifle, and he thought it the indefeasible right of an Irish gentleman to have a parliament of his own, wherein to carry his jobs. The last generation had driven their parliamentary trade in College Green, and he saw no reason why the present should be forced to do their dirty work at Westminster; so far was Dudley a thoroughly sincere repealer.

With his parliamentary career, however, we have little to do, indeed nothing, except as far as it was curiously mixed up with the affairs of the Spensers.

The influence of Dawson as a public man was felt at the parsonage, and felt agreeably, at least by one member of the family, almost immediately after his return to parliament. Dawson's behavior in the affair of the police was so very handsome, that it is a pleasure to record it. In the first place he addressed an elaborate letter to the Chief Secretary, and represented to him that, though the peace of the country about Redcross was not disturbed, or in immediate danger, yet that circumstances had happened well calculated to alarm the family of a clergyman living in a wild and remote place in the mountains. This effect, he added, had unfortunately been produced in the present instance; the wife of the clergyman, "a most amiable and highly-accomplished lady" (so Mr. Dawson painted her), was an invalid, and a state of apprehension was not merely dangerous to her health, but to her life;

in short, what he feared and predicted was that, unless the protection he asked was granted, the result would be that Mr. Spenser would be forced to leave the country, than which a greater calamity could not happen, inasmuch as, in losing him, they would lose not only a pious, learned, and exemplary clergyman, but a man whose services as a magistrate and a country-gentleman it was impossible to over-rate. Dawson, however, not merely wrote the letter, of which this was the substance, but he proceeded to the castle and demanded an interview with the minister. There were circumstances connected with this first act of Mr. Dudley Dawson in his parliamentary character which incline us to describe it in some little detail.

He excited not a little attention as he swaggered one day about five o'clock into the waiting-room of the castle, generally thronged about that hour with officials having appointments on business, deputations, suitors, claimants, expectants, political quacks hawking their sovereign remedies for all manner of public disorders and social evils, news-mongers, outrage-mongers, vote-mongers, pamphleteers (dirty fellows, some of them in more ways than one), reporters, messengers, loungers, tattlers, idlers, and spectators. It was capital to overhear the different little groups into which the assemblage was divided whispering together, and mutually despising and abusing one another as hirelings, place-hunters, and castle-hacks. Mr. Trundle was there, with his address to the crown, and enormous chart of Loch Swilly, determined to see the Chief Secretary, who, upon his part, was equally determined not to see Mr. Trundle. Mr. Fosberry was there also, as great a bore in his way as Trundle, with his pockets full of samples of all kinds of guano, liquid and solid. He perfumed the ante-room in not the most agreeable way.

Mr. Trundle was acquainted with Dawson, and running up to him, congratulated him on his entrance into parliament, begged his signature to the address (forgetting that Dawson had signed it before), and desired at the same time to know whether the world had ever produced such another booby as Mr. Fosberry? At the very same moment Mr. Fosberry was regaling with one of his phials of guano the nostrils of a group of barristers of six years' standing (in chase probably of a vacant chairmanship), and expressing himself most contemptuously of Mr. Trundle and Loch Swilly. A well-known, clever, and popular attorney, Tom Conolly by name, was there among the rest, having some little business of his own to transact, and beguiling the time before his interview with poignant jests and humorous anecdotes, keeping a large circle in fits of laughter. Conolly was the shrewdest, cleverest, pleasantest, jolliest limb of the law that ever the sweet south, whence he came (and which alone could have produced him), contributed to the hall of the Four-Courts. He had fun enough to make a dozen funny fellows, and he knew more law than all the place-hunting barristers put together. His electioneering talents were matchless; craft, daring, good-humor, with a strong voluble court-house elocution; a Machiavelli in the committee-room, a Wilkes on the hustings. His broad round face was as full of sensible drollery as the part of one of Shakspeare's clowns. It was intensely Irish; its music, if faces are musical, played "Patrick's day," or "the Boys of Kilkenny," audibly. He looked comedy and he spoke farce, the comedy Goldsmith's, the farce O'Keefe's. His lips quivered with mirth, and he had an eye for the hole in every man's coat, or co uld pick one at his pleasure.

And comedy there was strewn thickly about him; nobodies affecting to l . se somebodies; people whom nobody knew pret( )nding to know every body; fellows taking airs of independence, who were ready the next mor nent to clean the secretary's shoes, if ordered t( ) do so; men pretending to the most conscientiou s and exalted patriotism, yet having no other bu siness there, but to solicit remuneration for their votes at an election. Some came to ask any thing ; some to ask every thing; some to ask nothing, but only to make it known that something woul .d be extremely acceptable. One declared that h .e cared not a fig for reward himself, but his frie nds would never let him rest until he preferred his claims; another thought it his duty to offer his services where he felt he might be of use t o the public; a third abhorred the idea of office ), but he had a sincere regard for the Whigs, ? .nd would accept any little post with a thousand . a year, just to oblige them.

Then to hear : some men talk of what they had done, and what .they were doing, you would have concluded tha .t they bore the whole weight of affairs on thei r own shoulders, and that viceroys and secretar ies did nothing but give dinners. There was one man there who had been the prime move( ) in every event of importance which had taken l lace for a quarter of a century. He had actual( ) y done nine things out of ten, and what he ha d not actually done he had suggested, or advised . No matter who thundered, every clap was l \_( )is; he had documents in his pocket to prove it. Then the degree of intimacy that subsisted be tween some of the shabbiest people present and the heads of the gov .rnment was astonish ing. One of the hack writers was evidently t he bosom-friend of the Lord-Lieutenant, for he r lever called him any thing but Anglesea, just as if he had been a marquis himself, instead o f being little above the rank of a printer's devil.

The re was incessant ringing of bells, the Chief Secretary's bell, the Under Secretary's bell, and other bells, which kept such a jangling as was never before heard, except in a Flemish town, or in Mr. Spe use house, when his wife was hysterical. Tom Co. nolly pretended that he knew by the bells what t he result of each interview was. If a bell rang sharply and waspishly, the last person introduce d was no favorite; the Secretary was provoked by his application, and impatient to get rid of h im. If it rang steadily, and not immediately af ter the bowing out, an impression had been p. roduced, and the claim was worth consideration . All this time the messengers and junior cler! ss were bustling to and ro, some with red boxe: s, some with black, some with bundles of papers, some taking cards and etters from those in w aiting, and promising to and them in at the very first opportunity. Daw on arrest:d one of the messengers, and said, in a authoritative tone, that he wanted to see ord ——.

"Impossible, sir, to-d iy," said the ready fellow. Dawson blazed up, and presenting his card,

ordered the messenger to hand it instantly to the Chief Secretary; adding, so that the whole ante-room heard him—"I'm a member of parliament."

Every body looked at the self-advertised legislator, and Conolly, who was acquainted with every thing and every body, soon made it known who Dawson was, telling stories of his father and grandfather, and the Dawson nose, which forced his audience to hold their sides.

Dawson's card was handed in; the messenger re-appeared, but, to the astonishment of every body, the person summoned to have his audience was Mr. Fosberry. Triumphant at being so promptly admitted, he snatched one of his phials of guano from the hand of one of the barristers, and in doing so spilled half the contents upon the floor of the apartment, the smell of which was now vile enough to stifle a sanatory commissioner.

Every one held his nose but Mr. Trundle, who thought of nothing but the iniquity of the great man in receiving Fosberry before himself.

"This is enough," he muttered audibly, "to make a man a repealer. Here am I having most important business—no less than the improvement of Ireland—kept waiting for two hours, and that booby, Fosberry, gets an audience before me."

"Lord —— doesn't know who you are, Trundle; or he wouldn't keep you waiting a moment," said Tom Conolly, winking at his friends.

"I must say," said an elderly gentleman, with a sour face and a querulous voice, in another group, "there is great inconvenience in this system of sending us over young English lords, who know no more about people in this country than they do of the Cherokee Indians; only think of Lord —— having been more than a year in Ireland, and yet it was only the other day he was aware of the fact that I have a son in the Church."

"His lordship ought to be impeached," said Conolly, sotto voce.

Now a bell rung petulantly.

"That's Stanley's ," said the dirty pamphleteer, to show his intimacy with the noble lord who then held the agreeable office of Chief Secretary of Ireland.

"A short interview that," said one of the barristers.

"Short but not sweet," said the waggish solicitor.

At the same moment the messenger came up and said—

"Now, Mr. Dawson, this way."

Dawson swaggered out of the ante-room, as he had swaggered into it; with difficulty avoided collision with Mr. Fosberry, who appeared to have been almost kicked out; and in a moment was ushered into the presence of Lord ——. Scarcely rising from his chair, the Secretary made a supercilious inclination of his head, as he motioned Dudley to a seat which was placed on the opposite side of the table, and between it and the door.

The Secretary had seen some bad specimens of popular representatives, but he thought the gentleman now before him was the sorriest he had yet seen. Dawson wriggled on his chair as usual, endeavoring to assume a parliamentary look and tone, for it is one of the characteristics of such men to think there is a particular way of looking and speaking for every rank and situation of life. They are always acting, and never act well.

Dawson's business surprised the Secretary not a little. He expected to be solicited for a place in the Excise for an independent elector, or a colonial appointment for a brother, or a cousin, and he was agreeably disappointed when the application proved to be one on behalf of a clergyman, for his lordship had taken the clergy under his special protection, and indeed was accused of showing an undue partiality to the Church.

"The case you have stated, Mr. Dawson," he said, "is a strong one certainly; and if such is the state of the clergymen of the Established Church and their families in those parts of the country which are comparatively tranquil, what must be their condition in the actually disturbed districts? I trust you and your friends will seriously reflect upon it."

Here a messenger entered, and said that the Lord-Lieutenant desired to see Lord —— for a moment. His lordship rose, excused himself to Dawson, and saying he would return in a few minutes, left the room.

Dawson was not idle during the Secretary's absence. He looked over several of his lordship's papers, with the feeling that an honest government can have no wish to conceal any part of its conduct; then he examined the traces left upon some blotting-paper with that sort of appetite for truth which despises or neglects no source of information; and he was beginning to amuse himself with the scraps of a torn letter, just trying if he could arrange them in their original order and position (like a Chinese puzzle), when the minister reappeared. Dawson's gentlemanlike occupation would have been discovered, if he had dropped the fragments, so he crumpled them up and put them in his pocket.

"Mr. Dawson," said the Secretary, without sitting down, "I was sorry to be under the necessity of refusing Mr. Spenser's application for a military force—indeed, he wanted some pieces of cannon, which was quite out of the question—but, to the extent of a small detachment of police, I have no objection to comply with his wishes and yours. As long as I hold office, the clergy shall be protected, and whenever you have any favor to ask on their behalf I shall be always happy to see you either here or in London."

As he made this speech, he bowed the member out of the room as adroitly as if he had studied the rules Mr. Taylor gives in his "Statesman" for putting an abrupt end to official conferences.

When Dawson passed through the waiting-room again, it was less crowded than before. The droll solicitor had departed, and so had the least hopeful of the briefless barristers; but the sour old man with the son in the Church was standing his ground still, and so was poor Mr. Trundle, who might as well have been seeking a personal interview with the Ottoman Porte.

Leaving the Castle, Dawson proceeded instantly to the office of a newspaper, with the editor of which he was intimate, and procured the insertion of a short paragraph to the effect that "Dudley Dawson, Esq., M.P. for Rottenham, transacted business to-day with the Chief Secretary." He then paraded the principal streets for half an hour, with a cigar in his mouth, in company with two more legislators of the same stamp; after which he dined with Bob Sharkey, who called him his "honorable friend" at least a hundred times in the course of the evening. ' .

---

## CHAPTER XLIII.

CUPID AMONG THE CONSTABLES.

"Even as one heat another heat expels,
Or as one nail by strength drives out another,
So the remembrance of my former love
Is by a newer object quite forgotten."
THE TWO GENTLEMEN OF VERONA.

THE police party which, in consequence of Mr. Dawson's exertions at head-quarters, were sent to garrison it against dangers which were purely imaginary, consisted (as we have seen) of a chief constable and three sub-constables, all respectable men, and one of them a particularly good-looking young fellow, whose language, as well as whose features, intimated that his birth and education were above his position in life. The name of this young man was Edward Peacock; he was tall, his figure was good, he wore a private's dress in an officer-like manner, and in short the coarse cloth in his coat did not altogether conceal the gentleman. The fact was that he was a younger son of a younger brother of a good family in the south of Ireland. His father, without land, capital, or profession, had committed matrimony without an extenuating circumstance; his wife was prolific, his income small; the rest may be imagined; he was only too happy to procure for his eldest son a subordinate appointment at the Castle, and his second was the handsome young sub-constable now doing holiday duty at Mr. Spenser's. This Edward Peacock had one fault—at least in a policeman it was one—he had a very susceptible heart, and was very apt to take tender impressions wherever he happened to be stationed. In truth, he would have been long ago dismissed from the force, only that he was exceedingly brave and active when not under the sway of Venus. Already he had been removed three times from quarters where his amorous temperament had involved either himself or some equally tender-hearted damsel in embarrassments. His last scrape had been a serious one (the object of his transitory admiration having been the daughter of a gentleman of good fortune), and it had occasioned his abrupt transfer from the county of Longford to his present station, where directions had been given to his superior officer to keep a sharp eye upon him, and instantly report his first relapse into "la belle passion." Peacock himself had been made sensible of the indiscretion of his conduct, and it was clear that he would never offend again—until the next time.

One of Mrs. Spenser's cravings—almost the only one she had that was innocent—was her craving for flowers. It was part of Miss M'Cracken's regular daily duty to ravage the gardens and conservatories to gratify this passion; and she was a Tamerlane in her devastations, thinking of nothing else but how to ingratiate herself with her mistress by the enormous size of her bouquets. It happened on a certain morning, that Edward Peacock was on guard at the door of the green-house—guarding the geraniums and balsams, I presume, for there was nothing else to be sentineled—when Miss M'Cracken arrived as usual with her flower-basket on her left arm, her scissors and the key of the green-house in her right hand, meditating havoc to every plant that was in bloom or blossom. Now Miss M'Cracken, though so crafty and servile, made decidedly a pretty flower-girl; she looked particularly smart and grisettish of a morning; and when she had no great distance to go, only about the grounds or the garden, her out-door dress in general was a coquettish little French cap, with gay ribbons, and a short scarlet cloak, which, over a white frock, looked very smart and distinguished. Very little attention her governess-ship paid the policeman as she glided demurely along, and he, upon his part, tried to be equally inattentive to her, but scarlet is a very attractive color; it seizes the eye whether we will or not, and so it happened quite unavoidably that the eye of the young sub-constable did rest for a moment upon the pretty and piquant Lucy. A plague upon keys! They certainly hold a high place among the minor ills of human life. Twenty, ay, a hundred times over, had Miss M'Cracken opened that glass door without the slightest difficulty; yet now the key stuck in the lock, and refused to turn one way or the other. Miss M'Cracken was never very patient, and she soon grew provoked with the key, just as she would have done with one of her pupils, but still the key would not open the lock. She set down her basket and tried it with both her hands, uttering little peevish exclamations, scolding the key for stupidity and obstinacy; not loud enough, however, to be very distinctly heard by Peacock. Then she looked into the lock (and she had an eye sharp enough to pick one), lest there might be something obstructive in it—a leaf, or a snail, perhaps· but she could see nothing, and she tried the key again, but to no purpose, though she used all her strength, and uttered more of her little angry sub-audible objurgations. It was full time for the policeman, therefore, to step forward to help her; it was no part of his positive duty, but it was civil, and policemen are expected to be civil to every body.

"Allow me to try, ma'am," he said, advancing deferentially, and bowing to Red-Riding-Hood.

"I suppose it is not the right key," she said, scarcely looking at the person who accosted her, but presenting the key to him at the same time. The sub-constable took it respectfully, not without an eye to the governess's rosy fingers, which peered out of her half-handed gloves. He put the key into the lock—

"Open sesame," said he, and at the first trial the glass-door flew open.

Miss M'Cracken was surprised to meet a policeman who had read the Arabian Nights, and she could not help smiling as she slightly courtesied and thanked him. It would have been civil to have asked him to step in and look at the plants, but she was in too great a hurry to fill her basket, and commenced her ravages, nipping, snipping, clipping, and whipping into her basket every thing odoriferous or gay that was not beyond or above her reach. Peacock was fond of flowers, and knew more about them

than was necessary for his profession, so he could not resist the temptation of entering this palace of Flora, though not invited by the governess. However, he entered modestly, and was very careful not to follow the scarlet mantle. The scarlet mantle, however, came round to him in the course of its ravages, and surprised him gazing admiringly on a group of balsams. He retired a little, making awkward excuses, and Miss M'Cracken began to fell the delicate green stalks; but there was one which she could not come at even standing on tip-toe, and she was glad to avail herself of the aid of the tall sub-constable, who, having the scissors in his hand, not only cut her down the particular plant she longed for, but a great many other beauties also, which were far beyond the range of her arm. In fact, she never carried off such a booty before, and she could not but look thankful and ask her assistant whether he liked flowers.

"I love them," he answered, heightening the expression used by Miss M'Cracken. She could not but remark the improvement, nor help observing, as she took the scissors from his hand, that it was nearly as white as her own.

"You never were in a green-house before, I dare say," she continued, condescendingly. He smiled, and said, "Pardon me, we had a larger one than this at my father's."

"Miss M'Cracken concluded that the civilized and communicative policeman was the son of a seedsman, or florist, and there was no more conversation between them, for the children came running into the garden, calling their governess with their shrill voices, and Peacock saw a man approaching at some distance, who, he suspected, was the chief constable watching his movements, so that he was glad to make his retreat in time.

It so happened, however, that several mornings successively, the green coat and the red mantle met either in the garden, or the conservatory. Peacock, perhaps, thought it his duty to prevent a civil war breaking out afresh among the roses, or to keep the factious lilies in order; and Miss M'Cracken was not sorry to have a tall young man to help her to crop those flowers which had hitherto been safe from her depredations. But the upshot was that they knew each other better and better every day; before the end of a week the susceptible Peacock was once more over head and ears in love, and Lucy, on her part, made up her mind to receive his addresses, having at length found an admirer who was not only a handsome man, but a gentleman, with a name she fancied, and the other qualities which she considered indispensable in a husband. As to the swain's present position, it only served to throw an air of romance over his fortunes, and besides, there were precedents enough of young men, of even higher birth, compelled, by adverse circumstances, to begin their career in the lowest ranks both of civil and military service.

Meanwhile, the chief constable had not been inattentive to what was going on. As Peacock had little to do but to fall in love, so his chief had little to do but to watch his proceedings, which he did so warily, that Peacock flattered himself that for once in his life he had managed to keep his love affairs secret. One morning, after a longer colloquy than usual with his fair, he was suddenly confronted by his superior, in a retired part of the garden, whither he had ro paired, either to compose a sonnet, or to indulge in a reverie. They had a short, sharp, decisive conversation.

" You seem partial to the garden," said the chief constable.

" The moss-rosés are so beautiful," said Peacock, coloring like one of them.

" Humph," said the chief, " I know the sort of rose you come here every morning to look at."

" Hear me," said the young man, abashed and imploringly.

" Hear me, sir," said the other; " this is your third offense, and it is not only a breach of duty, but a violation of your word of honor. I shall not only report it to head-quarters, but I shall take it upon myself to act in a summary way, so far as to send you up this night to Dublin."

" Hear me, sir," said poor Peacock, earnestly.

" I will not, sir," rejoined the chief with warmth, " you shall go up to town by this night's mail, so be ready to start from Redcross in half an hour from the present moment." So saying, the officer turned on his heel, and the desperate Peacock went in quest of Miss M'Cracken, resolved to disobey his orders and brave all the consequences. But he had a prudent young woman to deal with, who, though she was astonished and distressed at a blow so unexpected, was far from being thrown off her center by it. She would not hear of her lover not only flinging away his bread for the present, but ruining all his chances of promotion, and she not only advised, but enjoined him to obey his commanding officer.

" I shall be dismissed," he said, ruefully.

" Better be dismissed for love, Edward, than for insubordination," said the shrewd Lucy.

" You are right, dear Lucy," said Peacock. —" Oh, if I had only a little parliamentary influence,"—he added, " all would be right soon."

A thought seemed to flash across her mind, but she said nothing, and parted with her lover on the spot, much firmer than he was, and crying very sparingly, if at all, for there never was a girl so little tearful as Lucy M'Cracken, though she was the cause of tears to others occasionally, but that, to be sure, was in the way of her profession.

Going straight up to her own little room, she sat down and wrote a letter to the only member of parliament she knew, namely the member for Rottenham; told him the whole tale, how she had lost her heart to a friendless gentleman in disguise, and earnestly besought his interposition in the gentleman's behalf, renewing at the same time her protestations of steadfast devotion to his interests at the parsonage, and assuring him that she was resolved to remain in her present situation for another year, notwithstanding her engagement to Peacock.

Dawson was only too happy to have so fair an opportunity of confirming his hold upon Lucy. He not only exerted his own influence for Edward Peacock, but induced another member of parliament, a friend and crony of his, to work for him too. Day after day they besieged the castle, until their faces were as familiar as that of the state porter. The job was not an enormous one, but a job it was, and of course it was prosecuted with zeal and assiduity. Had Peacock done some signal public service, and

not had two members of parliament to back him, the secretary would probably never have heard his name; as it was, he not merely escaped the unpleasant consequences which would have followed in the case of another man, but he was actually promoted for his misbehavior in the police to a place in the excise. As this appointment, though worth a hundred a year, and one that a gentleman might becomingly hold, involved residence in Dublin, the amorous simpleton grumbled exceedingly at the arrangement which removed him to it, and wrote a romantic epistle to his Lucy, full of quotations from Moore and Petrarch, about the insupportable horrors of absence, and offering, of course, to fling office and salary to the winds, and live with her in a cottage, a grotto, or a tent. Not a girl in Chirstendom had less of such nonsense about her than the woman to whom all this sentimental stuff was addressed. Lucy had no notion of living in tents or grottos, nor indeed had her lover any very serious thoughts of it either. In fact, he had already made similar Arcadian propositions to several fair maidens, one or two of whom were silly enough to have embraced them, had things been suffered to go to such a length. Miss M'Cracken thought him very simple, and would have told him so, had she thought it prudent. She was overjoyed at the success of Mr. Dawson's kind offices, congratulated her lover in the tenderest manner on his good fortune, convincing him that he was a lucky fellow, while at the same time she studiously kept the flame burning, which made him feel that his lot could never be completely blessed until she was at his side to share his prosperity and continue to promote it. In fact, though Lucy was not much alive to the horrors of absence, she was fully conscious of its dangers. She had got some little inklings of her Edward's past career in love, and she soon became fully as anxious to join him in Dublin as he was to join her in the country. The difference was, that she was a girl of business, and he was a youth of sentiment. The policy of following her lover as soon as possible no sooner impressed itself upon her, than she cast about in her ingenious mind for the practical means of accomplishing it. To resign her situation would have been the simplest course of all, but that would have been imprudent in two ways, involving both the loss of another year's salary, which she was bent on securing, and the abandonment of a position in which she might fairly hope to turn Dawson's interest to still better advantage. In this difficulty it occurred to her to make more effectual use of her mistress's nerves than she had yet done, and by a bold stroke accomplish the long-desired object of the migration of the family

---

## CHAPTER XLIV.

DAWSON'S SECRET JOURNEY TO REDCROSS.

" There is no secresy comparable to celerity, like the motion of a bullet in the air, which flieth so swift as it outruns the eye." BACON.

WHEN Dawson had established his claims on the friendship of Miss M'Cracken, in the politic manner related in the foregoing chapter, he began to turn his mind in what way he could make her gratitude serviceable to his own objects. Indeed, he did not rely on her gratitude altogether, and took care therefore to represent what he had already done for Peacock as but a trifle compared with what he might hereafter be able to do for him. For it is the well-known way of the world to be more influenced by favors expected than favors received; at least, it was the way of Miss M'Cracken.

Upon the whole, Dawson thought it would be wise to have a personal interview with Lucy as soon as possible; matters of delicacy are sometimes managed so much better, and with so much less hazard, by conversation than in writing. Another matter, too, required immediate looking after in the country. The busts were missing among the property transported to London, and he was not so anxious on account of their intrinsic value, as of the risk of detection to which they might expose him, were they to fall into the hands of suspicious or inquisitive people. Actuated by these two motives, he made a rapid and secret journey to Redcross; arrived at the village, while all the Hoggs and M'Swynes were immersed in slumber; and by the light of the stars and the waning moon, being well acquainted with the country, walked alone across the shadowy hills in the direction of the rectory.

Had he been an innocent man, how the freshness, the intense quiet, the balm and the cool of that romantic walk at that spiritual hour would have charmed him! Nature does not reveal herself to men like Dawson. The first heraldic streaks of day were just visible in the orient as he gained the summit of the ridge, commanding the earliest glimpse of the loch and the country on its further side.

" Jocund day
Stood tip-toe on the misty mountain-top."

An upper sea of fleecy vapor hung over the waters of the fiorde; and the hills above the still and sequestered parsonage had the aspect of an island emerging from this silvery ocean, the mansion itself being as yet only dimly visible. As he descended toward the loch, the haze grew thinner and thinner; and the eastern tints brighter, until at length, suddenly as a bright arrow darts from the string, an horizontal ray of the most glorious crimson smote the summits of the clump of pines on the rocky headland to the right, and proclaimed the day.

Gorgeous miracle it is! In the union of repose with splendor, what sign and wonder in all the range of nature can compare with the sun's rising? How sweet, yet how stupendous; its beauty how majestic, its magnificence how calm! The commonest, yet royalest and solemnest of all spectacles, a prodigy wrought in the heavens every morning, oldest and newest of celestial glories, the Advent and Apocalypse of Light. The powers of darkness are defeated, the spirits of life and health resume their empire, a general song—the carol of birds, the strains of poets, the hymns of early pilgrims—greet the renewed dispensation. Earth hails it with a thousand voices, and ocean welcomes it with unnumbered smiles. Cheering, vivifying, purifying, strengthening hour; dear alike to genius and devotion, precious to virtue and to beauty.

But what cared the profligate young man, who had now all those purple mountains to himself, and seemed the only waking witness of the enchanting change that was in progress—what cared he for the loveliness that was beneath and above and round about him? As he stood, ankle-deep in the rich heather, which decked his unworthy feet with pearls, a flood of rosy light bathed him, but there was no light in his breast, save the lurid one of passion and low designs. To him, beauty was but an object of appetite, and virtue only a difficulty to be evaded; an obstacle to be overthrown. Now he could distinctly see the picturesque abode of the Spensers, the residence of the fair, wise girl, on whom, with folly equal to his presumption, he had fixed such affections as he had. The exhalation still lingered, but it was now transparent, and gave an airy beauty to the substantial objects discerned through it. The mountain behind looked fanciful, and the irregular house, with its raiment of roses, and its pale gray wings, one of which was the library, looked speculative and dreamy, like its master's mind. A parsonage in the air it seemed, such as Mab constructs with her no materials in the visions of young divines.

The descent of the mountain-side was rapid; the boat was in its wonted receptacle; Dawson was in his lusty prime, and Mr. Woodward could scarcely have pushed across the water with greater expedition. He did not land, however, at the usual point, but higher up, in a little cove, surrounded with a wilderness of heath and wild shrubs, immediately under the pine-clad promontory, and only accessible from the land by one approach, and that so steep and so tangled that it was rarely visited by any one, and known, indeed, only to very few; but Dawson had a sort of instinctive knowledge of crypts and caverns and all manner of solitary places. The clock of the parsonage struck four as he stepped out of the boat upon the narrow strand. He sat down on a lichened stone, and taking out his watch held it in his hand, evidently expecting the arrival of some person, or some event. A quarter of an hour elapsed and he grew impatient and began to look round about him, but he had a small horizon for circumspection, being inclosed on all sides by a wall either of rock or of wild vegetation. Presently there was a slight rustling in the heather and bushes not far from him. He looked to the right and left, but observed no motion; it might have been only a linnet or a hare; still, however, the rustling continued, and grew more audible. "She is coming," he said to himself; and at the same instant he was struck on his hat with a few small cones of the pines, and, raising his head, saw a girl, wrapped in a shawl of gray plaid, cautiously descending by the precipitous path already mentioned. She had plucked the cones, and on discovering Dawson, and thrown them down upon him to advertise him of her coming.

Lucy M'Cracken was strong, agile, and daring, equal to any thing that any girl of her age and size, perhaps indeed that any young woman was equal to. Dawson thought her very pretty that morning, and she certainly did look attractive enough, particularly as the consciousness that she was not where she ought to be at that hour, and in such company, made her a little fearful, and her fears gave her a touch of maidenly bashfulness, which was just the charm she lacked most. She had exchanged her red mantle for the gray shawl, probably because she was less anxious to look an Aurora in Dawson's eyes, than to pass through the rocks and woods as unnoticed as possible.

Time was precious; both seemed equally aware of it, and but few moments were wasted n civilities and compliments. Dawson's object was to gain over Lucy to his interests; Lucy's was simply to gratify and flatter Dawson. He was inordinately vain, and she was shrewd, dexterous, and insinuating. She could not, or would not, see any serious obstacle to the accomplishment of his designs upon Elizabeth Spenser. He spoke of the prejudices that existed against him.

"They are nothing but prejudices, sir, and of course they will wear out in time," said Miss M'Cracken.

"You think, then, my prospects are fair?" said Dawson.

Lucy smiled ironically.

"Fair," she said; "as if any gentleman ever stood in a better position than you do, to win any lady in the land. I grant Miss Elizabeth is handsome—if she was not, Mr. Dawson, you would not be the man to admire her—but I think even you will not say she is positively a beauty; so that why a gentleman like you should not succeed with her, or with a much greater match, is more than I can understand; to say nothing of the fact that you are her brother's bosom friend, and that only a week ago you saved her life so gallantly, at the imminent hazard of your own."

"Well, really," said Dawson, tickled by this speech; but Lucy had not finished.

"I am sure I don't know what fair prospects are; if yours are not fair," she continued, earnestly; "you have the three grand recommendations of family, fortune, rank—and—and—I could mention another thing that can't be much in your favor, Mr. Dawson, if I dared." She looked at him in a very peculiar way, and then she looked down, and played with the strings of her little black apron.

"Say all that you think—every thing that comes into your mind, my dear Lucy," said Dawson, seizing her hand.

"It was only this, sir," she answered, with admirably counterfeited modesty and reluctance, "I do think you such a very handsome man."

Dawson was exactly of the same opinion himself, so that he was not electrified, though greatly pleased, by the last link of Miss M'Cracken's argument. The personal hit told so well, that she tried another moment's interval.

"The first time I ever saw you, sir, was riding with Mr. Sydney; did any one ever tell you, sir, that you look particularly well on horseback?"

We have seen that Dawson plumed himself on his horsemanship, and indeed he rode extremely well; only that his seat was a little theatrical, in keeping with the general ostentation of his character. It was now time for him to take his part in the conference.

"I must see her," he said, "I have never seen her since that night upon the island."

"So much the better, perhaps," said Lucy; "your sudden disappearance had a good effect, and besides, you were much better employed getting into parliament; but now that you have got such a fine feather in your cap, I do not see why you should keep in the back ground a mo-

ment longer—though I would not advise you, sir, to do any thing too hastily."

"Mrs. Spenser is my enemy, Lucy, and the consequence is, that I am not invited here;— Sydney has told me so repeatedly."

"Can you do nothing to make her your friend, Mr. Dawson?' You have no notion how fond she is of getting presents—a parrot, a French watch, or any trifle of the kind would make a wonderful change—some ladies are so shocking mercenary—even such a pretty ring as that on your little finger."

"This ring is for you, Lucy," said Dawson, taking her hand again.

"Oh, Mr. Dawson!"—but she did not decline the ring, which was a small emerald, handsomely set, which he had purchased in Dublin, expressly for the corrupt purpose to which he now applied it.

"I am in hopes," he went on to say, while Lucy was admiring and even kissing the brilliant transferred to her hand; "I am in hopes that my exertions in the police affair will be of some little use to me."

Lucy assured him that the exertions alluded to had already been of the greatest service to him in the quarter alluded to, and "I am sure," she added, with all the outward signs of grateful emotion, "I ought to be thankful to you, too, Mr. Dawson, as only for you I should never have seen or known my dear Edward."

"It was not an easy job to manage, I assure you," said Dawson.

He then told her of his letter to the Chief Secretary, and lamented that he had not kept a copy, as it would not fail to impress Mrs. Spenser most favorably toward him, she was spoken of there in terms of such glowing compliment.

Lucy instantly recollected that her lover's brother held a subordinate place at the Castle, and that she had no doubt but that she could manage, through him, to procure a copy of the letter, or, indeed, even the letter itself, if it were required.

"A copy would do," said Dawson, "you could let Mrs. Spenser see it, as if it came to your hand by mere accident."

This little matter was easily settled; but he subsequently hit upon a better modd of turning the letter in question to good account.

Dawson was most grateful to his fair friend for her zeal and ingenuity in his service.

"Rely upon it, Lucy," he said, "I will do all in my power for your Edward; I never met a young man who so captivated me on a short acquaintance; I am greatly mistaken if he is not destined to make a splendid figure in the world."

The eyes of the worldly-minded Lucy glittered. Her love was one of those adulterated varieties of the passion, in which other passions, particularly avarice and ambition, are very largely mixed. She was on the point of bringing her honorable friend to promise something specific for the advancement of Peacock, when a loud barking at no great distance threw both parties into the greatest consternation.

"Oh, dear!" exclaimed Lucy, pale as ashes, "that's Pedro's bark."

"Who is Pedro?" whispered Dawson, scarcely less agitated.

"Mr. Markham's dog; oh, what will become of me?" She paid no attention to the effect which the name of Markham had upon her companion, to whom it conveyed the fact that the young Englishmen, whom he had seen on the island, had ever since been the guests of Mr. Spenser. He moved a step aside to conceal the passion which suddenly seized him, and made him for the instant thoughtless of danger. When he turned again, the nimble Lucy was springing up the steep bank, to hide herself in the darkest thicket she could find. He naturally thought that she feared to be detected in his society under circumstances so suspicious, but the false girl had another and still stronger motive (which will be disclosed in time) for shunning all observation at that hour, and she succeeded in regaining the house and her own bed-room without any eye but that of Heaven upon her doings.

It was altogether a busy and exciting morning with her; a whim took her to school the children before breakfast, and in the course of the proceedings she detected, or fancied she detected, little Arthur Spenser in an offense which, to her pure eyes, was unpardonable—an aberration from the paths of truth. She corrected the child severely, and immediately after sat down to her desk, and with the rod actually before her with which she had punished deceit, wrote a letter to her lover in town, directing him to procure a surreptitious copy of Dawson's letter to the Chief Secretary. This done, she carefully arranged her hair and her dress, and went down to breakfast, for she now breakfasted with the family, though she still dined with the children at two o'clock. Several times during the meal she thought of poor Mr. Dawson, in the little alcove under the hill, probably still besieged by Pedro. She would have carried the honorable gentleman his breakfast, if she could have done it clandestinely, but that was impossible; so she ate her own heartily, for both her mind and her body had been exercised that morning.

---

### CHAPTER XLV.
#### THE THREATENING NOTICE.

"It is the nature of extreme self-lovers, that they will set a house on fire, an it were but to roast their eggs."
BACON'S ESSAYS.

ON the heathery verge of the picturesque point overhanging the senator's hiding-place the rector had long ago placed a semicircular bench of rough-hewn timber, affording seats for about half-a-dozen persons, and as the view from it was fine, and the ascent, by a winding path, not quite as hazardous as that of Mont Blanc or Chimborazo, it was a common thing to loiter an hour there, chatting or reading, musing or speculating. Some elegant sermons had there been imagined and partly written; much solid sense had been talked there, and much airy nothing too; there the rector and Father Magrath had often bewailed the discords which raged between two branches of the same great Christian family; there the rector and curate had often wrangled about Demosthenes and Plunket; and there had Carry and Elizabeth held many a little council of charity for the benefit and improvement of the poor of the neighborhood, and raised many an orison for the peace and happiness of every body round about them.

On the day in question they resorted with their books and work to this favorite haunt soon after breakfast. It was still a somber but sweet morning; the lingering haziness of the atmosphere mitigated the solstitial heat, and beautifully softened every object by land and water. The surface of the latter was motion at rest; the wing of a sea-bird agitated it visibly. The silence was profound, save where a grasshopper or two chirped in the fern, a gull screamed as he lazily flitted over the loch, or the faintest distinguishable murmur reached the ear from the ripple of the water upon the beach beneath. Indeed, Carry had to raise her cap, and a cloud of her bright-brown hair also, before she was able to catch this almost noiseless sound. Elizabeth neglected her book, but her aunt's needle was industrious, and the musical tongues were busy also. Carry's voice was remarkably decided, clear, distinct, and fluent; Elizabeth's was a liquid, loving, warbling one. They were discoursing of many things and many persons, when Mr. Spenser joined them, in extreme agitation. He held a piece of soiled paper in his hand, with some writing scrawled upon it. "Carry, my dear," he said, sitting down beside her; but he could say no more, he was so moved and out of breath, and he placed the paper in her hands, with a gesture that showed how much he was affected by it.

It was a threatening notice, which he had found himself, only a few minutes before, posted on the old fig-tree close to the door of the garden. The document ran as follows:—

"TITHES—TITHES—TITHES!

"I hereby caution the Rev. Mr. Spenser to have no more to say or to do with the tithes of the parish of Redcross, and to refund what he has received for the six months last past. Any person who pays tithes to him, or to any other parson whatsoever, will meet a villain's fate, which is sharp and sudden death; so let them mark and digest the consequence. If Mr. Spenser (or any others) violates my rules and regulations, I will pay him an early visit, and all the police and troops in the county will not save him. Here is the coffin prepared for extortioners and robbers of the poor.

"Given under my hand,
"Captain KILL-PROCTOR or KILL-PARSON
(as the case may be)."

Carry could not help smiling while she read this proclamation of the blood-thirsty unknown, to which a representation of a coffin was annexed, in the established form of such instruments.

"For myself," said Mr. Spenser, recovering his speech, "I do not attach as much weight as some people do to notices like this, which are so easily forged, and are often, I believe, nothing but malicious hoaxes; at the same time, it is most unfortunate that such tricks should be played just now."

"If you take my advice, Valentine," said Carry, regarding the paper contemptuously, "you will tear it in pieces this moment, throw it into the loch, and not say a word about it to a human being."

"Do, papa," cried Elizabeth, "it has all the look of a foolish forgery; destroy it, and do not give the author the satisfaction of knowing that he has even succeeded in alarming you. Of all things, do not let mamma hear of it."

"Ah," said the rector, "the mischief I fear is done—she has heard of it already."

"Oh, Valentine," exclaimed Carry, about to reproach him with having communicated such a thing to his wife, of all people in the world, but he had his defense ready; it appeared that Rebecca was just coming out of the garden at the moment, and had been present when he and George Markham discovered and took down the notice.

"It can't be helped, then," said Mrs. Woodward, "we must only do the best we can under the circumstances, and try to trace the writer, who I dare say has as little notion of shooting either a proctor or a parson as I have myself."

Mr. Spenser wished Carry to accompany him back to the house. She did so, and left Elizabeth with no other society but her book and her maidenly meditations. She had not enjoyed these excellent companions many minutes when she heard a step close to her, and concluded it was either her father or her aunt returned; imagine her astonishment and dismay when she beheld Dawson!

He was equally unprepared to meet Elizabeth, and far more embarrassed than she was, as he had no good excuse to give for so abrupt an appearance in her presence. He had merely clambered up the height to gain a path by which he knew he could in all probability effect his retreat in safety. It was necessary to speak, but not so easy to say any thing apropos under the circumstances. His dress disordered by travel, and his extreme confusion of manner, impressed her with the notion that he was intoxicated. He began by stammering out something to the effect that he was delighted to find she had not seriously suffered by the late accident, and made a number of inconsistent and needless apologies for being so late in waiting upon her after it.

"Oh, no, Mr. Dawson," said Elizabeth, tremulously, "you have no apologies to make; it is I that have cause to regret not having had an earlier opportunity of thanking you, as indeed I do, most sincerely."

"Don't thank me, Miss Spenser," he replied, "what I did is not worth your thinking of; all I hope is, that you don't consider me utterly unworthy of the honor I had on that occasion."

"Indeed, sir," replied Elizabeth, still more nervously, "I hope I feel every thing that I ought toward a gentleman who so nobly hazarded his life for mine."

"Who would willingly have sacrificed it," interrupted Dawson, vehemently, and sitting down close to her.

"I am indeed very grateful," she said, her voice husky with agitation, and with difficulty preventing herself from withdrawing herself to a distance from him.

"Don't say grateful, charming Miss Spenser," said Dawson, in a low deep voice, passionate more than tender.

Elizabeth affected not to hear, and tremblingly inquired whether he had seen her father or her brother.

"No," he replied, "I have only this moment arrived in the country: I am on my way to Castle Dawson; I came here to see you, and nobody but you."

"Me, sir!" said Elizabeth, recovering a little self-possession, as the occasion for it increased.

"You," said Dawson, gazing at her—"to tell you that I admire you—that I adore you."

"Oh, Mr. Dawson," said Elizabeth, starting up amazed and indignant—"I can not listen to this—excuse me, I must return to the house."

"Not until I tell you how I love you," cried Dawson, attempting to seize her hand, which she nimbly withdrew, her face glowing with resentment, while her frame quivered with alarm.

"Not until I tell you that I love you, that I have long loved you, that I will never cease to love and adore you," he pursued violently, now succeeding in holding her, which he did, however, but for an instant, for she was robust as well as fair, and she liberated herself with a single strong effort, and fled down the hill, not even keeping the path, but rushing like a fawn through the copse and heather. She never ceased to run until she gained the skirts of the lawn, where she met Carry Woodward, and almost fainted in her arms. Carry and Elizabeth agreed, after a long consultation, to communicate what had taken place to the rector himself only; they feared to let Sydney know that his dangerous friend was again in the country; but it was indispensable that Mr. Spenser should write to Dawson without delay, to complain of his unwarrantable intrusion (particularly in so clandestine a manner), on the privacy of his glebe and his family, and acquaint him, unambiguously, with the utter hopelessness of his design to gain the affections of his daughter.

The rector was, indeed, as much incensed at Dawson's conduct, when it was related to him by his sister, as it was in his placid nature to be incensed at any thing; but the letter he wrote at Carry's suggestion (unfortunately not her dictation) was far below the mark, both in vigor and precision. It was not much to be wondered at. The device of the threatening notice had succeeded only too completely. Mrs. Spenser had already extorted a promise from him that he would remove to Dublin with the least possible delay. There was an end of his pastoral life—an end of his rural happiness; all the many ties of duty, affection, taste, benevolence, love of ease, love of retirement, love of nature, which bound him to his picturesque parish, and simple, loyal, attached parishioners, were to be torn asunder, and the gentle-natured man poignantly felt it.

Several hours elapsed before he could muster up the courage to confess to his sister and daughters the decision to which he had come. The grief of Elizabeth was extreme. That of aunt Carry was mingled with just indignation at her brother's deplorable weakness, and her sister-in-law's enormous selfishness. But no one in the family seemed to feel so much on the occasion as Lucy M'Cracken, for whom it is hoped the reader will feel the due degree of pity, if he does not harbor suspicion that she had a hand in the threatening notice. She was confident she never could live in Dublin; the happiest days of her life had been spent in the Irish highlands. Mrs. Spenser began by trying to console her, and ended by scolding and telling her sharply that, if she wanted to continue in the country, she must look out for another nursery to govern. Then Lucy commanded her feelings, and went resignedly to pack her trunk.

# BOOK IX

## CHAPTER XLVI.

### THE PARSONAGE DESERTED.

"The place is now forsaken;
The house is dark and silent; on the threshold
Professors soon shall botanize, and within
Arachne weave unharmed her subtle web."
NEW PLAY.

THE curate was at Redcross on some business of his sacred calling, when the vexatious incident took place which has just been recorded. On the previous evening he had taken his leave of Markham and Vivyan, who were only waiting for a favorable wind to weigh anchor. Markham returned his cordial squeeze with one of nearly equal power. But Vivyan's more delicate hand long retained the sense of the lusty clergyman's too strenuous-adieu.

Carry was not sorry that her husband was absent when the threatening notice, like the fall of a bomb-shell, threw the whole household into confusion. Had he been at the parsonage at the time, he would probably have made confusion worse confounded, he was so much in the habit, not only of speaking the truth upon all occasions, but laying it on in the most energetic and unsparing manner.

The Circe sailed. The parting of lovers has been described so often, both in prose and rhyme, that we may safely leave the reader to imagine the parting-scene between Elizabeth Spenser and Frank Vivyan. But mingled with the grief of separation were tender solicitudes for others, and concern for objects beyond themselves. Vivyan had become strongly attached to Mr. Spenser, and felt acutely for the distress in which he saw that he was involved by seemingly uncontrollable circumstances. Elizabeth not only felt for her father, but for her brother still more deeply. Her anxiety for Sydney, indeed, had been extreme, ever since the change in Vivyan's fortunes (by preventing his return to Cambridge) had deprived her brother of the anticipated advantages of such a friend to introduce him to the University, and protect him from corrupting associations within its dangerous precincts. In all the ardor of her love for Vivyan, this tender care for Sydney never ceased to occupy her mind; and gladly would she have seen the plan of sending him to England overruled, and the advice of her uncle followed. But it was too late. Sydney was now bent upon going to Cambridge, and with a degree of eagerness which astonished, while it could not but please his family, to whom his principal reasons for wishing himself far removed were totally unknown. At the same time, it was not without regret he parted with Frank Vivyan, whose ascendency over him had been steadily increasing from the beginning of their acquaintance. Sydney embraced him affectionately before he sailed, and Elizabeth felt (as she witnessed their farewell) how completely it was in Vivyan's power to reform him completely, and how unfortunate it was that their intercourse was broken off thus prematurely. Carry Woodward had precisely the same feelings, and the last thing she said, as maternally she took leave of Frank, suffering him to kiss her mellow

cheek, was that Elizabeth would feel his departure most, but that Sydney would be the greatest loser by it.

All that the amiable Vivyan could do for the brother of his betrothed he did with more than the zeal of friendship; he left a warm letter of introduction behind him to Mr. Peters, his own tutor, and a few other letters of judicious recommendation to such of his college acquaintances as he knew would make safe companions, and who he thought would, out of friendship for himself, tolerate Sydney's deficiencies in manners and refinement.

The Circe sailed. The rector was called away to his wife's chamber, while in the act of shaking hands with Markham; but Elizabeth, Mrs. Woodward, and Sydney, never left the little quay until the last inch of canvas disappeared, where the bend of the fiorde abruptly terminated the prospect seaward.

Elizabeth shed a few tears, and Carry wiped them away, as she led her back to the house, speaking as comfortably as she could; and it was a hard task to speak so, for she was heavy at heart herself, and felt as if a long course of life's sunshine was about to be succeeded by a period of gloom and difficulty.

Elizabeth went to her room. It was still day-light. Carry called Billy Pitt, and directed him to go to the stables and order the black mare to be saddled, as well as his cousin Elizabeth's pony; to have both put on board the boat, and to equip himself also without delay, as he intended to ride home that evening. Billy Pitt was enchanted at the novelty of being his mother's escort and champion upon an equestrian expedition; and it never once occurred to him, when they were both mounted, after crossing the water, how much he resembled Tom Thumb squiring the princess Glumdalca. At a marvelous pace, for both the mare and her burthen, the journey was accomplished before the end of twilight.

The curate was engaged in supplying his pigs with clean straw, when his wife and his son trotted up to the gate, and he was not slow to divine that something extraordinary must have happened at the rectory. When he learned what it was, no words can express either the agitation of his mind, or the commotion of his frame. Carry never saw him so moved before, not even when the Duke of Wellington struck to Mr. O'Connell. He was somewhat calmer when he and she were together once more in his untidy study, but it was the mighty swell of the sea on the day after a hurricane, and quite alarming enough to witness.

"A worthy shepherd," he cried, "to abandon his flock in this fashion, on the very first cry of wolf. But Val. was always a coward; a cowardly father, a cowardly husband, and now he is going to show himself a cowardly shepherd, and run away from his sheep. Cowed by a slip of paper pinned to a fig-tree! I would as soon be cowed by that spider there on the ceiling. I should like to see Val. with a grove of pikes at his throat, as I saw my own father in the '98 (I was not half as big as Billy at the time), since a scratch of a pen makes a woman of him. A man might as well be a woman at once as be the slave of a woman's *fears and vagaries. Down, puss, down, down." The great black cat was preparing to spring on his knee, as if it desired to mollify him. "Carry, Carry, much as I scorn a dastard in a red coat, I hold a dastard in a black one to be twice as contemptible." "Ten times," responded his wife, bitterly, and pacing up and down the study as rapidly as she could with the encumbrance of her riding-dress. She was almost as excited as her husband, though thinking more of the domestic unhappiness involved in her brother's determination than of its effects upon the parish.

"It all comes of uxoriousness," continued the curate, as if summing up his invective, and still repelling the advances of the corpulent black cat. "It comes of having married a silly, selfish woman," said Mrs. Woodward, "and it comes of cherishing a viper in the bosom of his family."

Carry then related Mr. Dawson's strange apparition and behavior at the parsonage that morning; she could not but suspect that there was some mysterious alliance between Miss M'Cracken and that gentleman, particularly as Elizabeth was decidedly of opinion, from the negligence of his dress, that his scene with her was not a premeditated one.

For the first time in his life Hercules made no apology for Dawson; his tenderness for his niece was extreme, and never did any man abhor more intensely than he did duplicity and dark practices of all kinds.

"I don't understand," he said, after some moments of grim silence, "how Dawson could possibly have passed through Redcross without my knowledge; I'll send Peter down to the inn to inquire whether he arrived by the night-coach."

Peter brought word that Mr. Dawson had not been seen in the country for several weeks, and that, to the best of the innkeeper's belief, the honorable member for Rottenham was then in Dublin. The curate was Mr. Dawson's friend no longer.

Now there commenced a ferment not commonly witnessed in a rural parish, and one of the singular features of it was the triple alliance of a Catholic priest, a Presbyterian minister, and a clergyman of the Established Church. Rare, in Ireland at least, was such a confederacy; but people of all persuasions were afflicted at the thought of losing Mr. Spenser, and Hercules had no difficulty whatsoever in rousing a spirit of determined opposition to his brother-in-law's cowardly resolve. He, who had all his life been railing at agitators, and denouncing aggregate meetings, was now a flaming agitator himself; and convened so vast an assemblage of the inhabitants of the parish that the meeting was held in the church-yard, no building in the town being large enough for the purpose. The chair (placed on the summit of a heap of tombs), was taken by Father Magrath; resolutions, prefaced by enthusiastic speeches, were unanimously passed, expressive of the most devoted attachment to Mr. Spenser, and declaring the determination of men of all sects and parties to support and protect him; a subscription was entered into and a reward offered for the discovery of the writer of the notice, which was ascribed with one accord either to private malice or wanton mischief; and, finally, an address to the rector was voted, which Father Magrath and the Presbyterian divine undertook to prepare between them.

Mr. Spenser would have prevented all these proceedings, particularly the address, if it had been in his power; but the parochial feeling was too strong, and the expression of it placed the rector in a difficult position; so much so that Hercules was not without hope at one moment that his brother-in-law would return to his senses, take the true view of his duty, and retract the rash vow he had made to his wife.

"I am miserable, Hercules," said the rector, looking very unhappy indeed, and walking up and down his library, with his clasped hands sometimes behind and sometimes before him. A draft of the address lay on the table, having been sent to him before presentation, to enable him to prepare his answer.

"To be weak is to be miserable," said the vigorous curate, quoting the speech of one of Milton's angels.

"I have *promised* her, Hercules," said Mr. Spenser, with melancholy emphasis on the word "promised."

"You are not the first man who has made a hasty promise," said Hercules, "but you know Val., as well as I do, that in case of a foolish or a wrong engagement the moral obligation is to break and not to keep it."

"I'll go up to her," said the distracted rector, passing his hand over his pale and throbbing temples.

He went, and Hercules remained in the library, striding and straggling about, to the imminent danger of the busts, as usual. In about ten minutes the rector came down again, and entering the room with an excitement and vehemence such as he rarely exhibited, slapped the table with his hand, and exclaimed—

"It's her health, Hercules—it's her health—her health makes it indispensable."

Hercules saw that all was over, and rushed out of the library without uttering a word. Never did he walk at such a pace as he did back to Redcross that evening; never did he look so truculent and unlike a minister of the gospel of peace.

Within a fortnight from that date the parsonage was deserted. The rector's library was consigned to the spiders, and there was nobody left to feed Elizabeth's robins, or talk playful politics with the echo from the hills.

---

## CHAPTER XLVII.
### THE SPENSERS IN TOWN.

"Matto in testa, Savio in bocca."—ITALIAN PROVERB.

THE Spensers passed the autumn at a favorite watering-place in the neighborhood of Dublin. The beginning of winter found them in the capital, tenants of a handsome house in one of the principal squares, looking at straight dull rows of brick houses, instead of picturesque mountain chains; the lazy Liffey and shriveled Dodder in place of the foaming streams of Tyrconnell; miry streets for the clean, fresh, elastic heather, and the smoked sparrows of the city, for the white-winged sea-birds of the coast, or the broad-pinioned eagles of the hills.

Sydney had gone to Cambridge almost immediately after the removal of his family from Redcross. His father, with his characteristic negligence of every thing that did not immediately press, or pinch him, after one admirable letter, in which he laid down a course of study such as an Aristotle might have prescribed to an Alexander, soon dismissed him almost entirely from his thoughts. Elizabeth, however, wrote to him frequently, and when her letters either remained unanswered, or were hurriedly and curtly replied to, she amiably ascribed it to the intensity of her brother's application to mathematics.

However, she had a correspondent in Spain, who was not chargeable with neglecting her letters, or answering them too briefly.

Vivyan was forced to protract his absence far beyond the period within which he had hoped to conclude his business. The affairs of his deceased friend were involved in no small degree of complication between the law and the lawyers of two nations, and Frank had occasion to remark that all he had heard of the romance of Spain was certainly borne out by his personal experience of the jurisprudence of that country. A voluminous correspondence passed between him and Elizabeth, and perhaps some of the letters were as prolix as the pleadings of any court of justice in the world.

The frivolous and selfish Mrs. Spenser was really reduced in strength when she arrived in town. The laudanum system was rapidly turning imaginary disorders into actual ones, and she suffered, besides, considerably by the fatigues of the journey. The novelty, however, of a town-house, and the excitement of new faces and acquaintances, produced a salutary re-action, and for some short time she was a marvelously amiable patient, her bed-room crowded with doctors, and her boudoir with fashionable gossips, alternately a college of physicians and a school for scandal. Some of the doctors, indeed, were first-rate gossips themselves, and probably did her as much good by their talk as by their tonics. They gave her old complaints new names, they favored her with several new disorders, consulted her palate as much as her pulse, and operated occasionally on her risible muscles.

Too much of the rector's money, more than he could afford, went in doctors' fees; but he never complained, and often, indeed, declared that he found the leading members of the faculty any thing but grasping. Some, when they learned that he was a beneficed clergyman, driven from the country by the league against tithes, had too much good feeling to conspire with Captain Rock to fleece him. Others found in Mr. Spenser a most agreeable accession to Dublin society; they enjoyed his acute and pleasant conversation, and declined to have their friendly visits counted and enumerated as medical calls. Those who were convivial were delighted to have a new man at their dinners, with such a fund as the rector possessed of the cleverest table-talk, for in that Mr. Spenser had few equals. He missed his library chiefly, and used to say that, like Prospero, he was "a sot without his books." Though his social success in Dublin was complete, there was not much society that he greatly relished; and he could not but observe that he was much more prized and courted as a clergyman of rank, than for his wit or his literary eminence. There was also a certain narrowness and timidity about the Dublin circles which struck him as distinguishing society there remarkably from society in London. He thought he never saw people so absurdly afraid of ridicule, and so apt to suspect literary men of dealing in small satire and anonymous personalities, meannesses from which such men are particularly free. As Mr. Spenser (when he did indulge his humor) never intended to wound individuals, he was hurt at having the design imputed to him; but, indeed, he was accused of lampooning people of whose very existence he was ignorant until their preposterous charges reached his ear. Of course he never condescended to notice either such accusations or such accusers; he merely remarked in general that it was discreet to be dull in provincial capitals.

In one of his letters to Carry Woodward he observed, speaking on this subject, that "small satire is like small cutlery, and those who use such weapons are more likely to wound themselves than seriously hurt others. Satire ought to be a sword and not a penknife."

Very soon after his arrival at the seat of government, he was appointed, through his wife's little ambitious intrigues, one of the Lord-Lieutenant's chaplains, an honor he was not solicitous of; it gave him some trouble and no emolument; he had to preach for the mimic court, and dine at trumpet-dinners, and unfortunately the dinners were not as concise as his sermons.

"I am not fond of a diffuse dinner any more than of a diffuse discourse; I like to dine *laconically*, as Marshal Turenne used to say," he remarked one day, talking in the street to his friend Sir Florus Bloomfield, an eminent surgeon and accomplished member not only of his profession, but of society.

"Dine with me in that fashion to-morrow at seven," said the courtly baronet, and cantered away to perform one of his brilliant operations. Sir Florus did every thing brilliantly, lectured, operated, talked, dressed, and rode. Nay, he sometimes hunted, and even rode a steeple-chase, but that was perhaps to encourage and give éclat to amusements, of which the members of the surgical profession are the natural and proper patrons. At least Mr. Spenser used to say so.

The dinner at Sir Florus's proved far more Attic than Laconic. Several distinguished guests had been invited to meet the rector, who made on that day some valuable additions to his list of friends. Two men particularly pleased him. The first was a lawyer by profession, a demagogue by necessity, and a poet and orator by nature; the warmest of friends, the most attractive of companions; a mind all fancy and fire; a heart all frankness and good-nature; Catholic in genius as in creed. The fortunes of his country had determined his career. He started at a time when it was patriotic to be turbulent. But his was a turbulence embellished by wit and illumined by eloquence; born of just discontent, and extinguished by the achievement of its high objects. He generously coveted, and fairly won, the first privileges and honors of the constitution, forced his way into parliament to adorn, not to snake the empire; serving Ireland best by making Irish talents useful, and Irish worth conspicuous in his person.

The other was Sir Charles Freeman, a physician profoundly versed in the science and learning of his humane profession, though he did not prosecute it as a source of income. His wit resembled Mr. Spenser's, at once playful and scholarlike, drawn from every sparkling fount in ancient or modern letters. Probably no man in his time had hived up so much elegant and curious knowledge, or had his infinite reading so much at command. With French literature he was as familiar as the best educated Frenchman, and in Greek learning he was altogether unrivaled. He was an equally acute and good-natured observer of manners; a brilliant essayist, and a politician whose liberality was not adhesion to party, but a deduction from his studies, and a confidence in moral truth. Yet his enlightenment and his wit were but a small part of his value; he was the humanest, simplest, and worthiest of men, though his virtues, no more than his talents, won for him in Ireland the consideration they deserved. The jealousies and bigotries were too strong for him. He required another sphere, a higher and wider stage, and a more judicious and magnanimous society. It was his fortune, some years after the period when Mr. Spenser made his acquaintance, to live admired and loved, and to die honored and lamented, by the statesmen, the wits, poets, and philosophers, of the metropolis of England and the world.

The company of such men, and a few others of kindred character and genius, was delightful to the rector, and had his wife allowed him to enjoy more of it, he might easily have been reconciled to life in Dublin. But Mrs. Spenser was not less perverse in town than country, and Elizabeth could not help thinking that she made it a point to be taken ill, when her husband was invited to some particularly agreeable dinner.

In the mornings he walked or rode about a good deal with his daughters, when the weather was not too atrocious. They visited all that was sight-worthy in the city, and it took no very long time to complete the survey. There were lions enough, in the curate's sense of the word, but very few in its more popular meaning. A court without nobility, an exchange without merchants, a theater without the drama, and a zoological garden without a wild beast. So Mr. Spenser described the Irish capital in a letter to his curate, but his wife had been troublesome in the morning, and perhaps there was more gall in his ink than usual. When she was quiet and well-behaved, he took a different view of things, and sometimes gave a very agreeable picture of life in Dublin.

### CHAPTER XLVIII.

#### PERSECUTIONS.

"Had I been seized by a hungry lion,
I would have been a breakfast to the beast;
Rather than have false Proteus rescue me.
O heaven be judge, how I love Valentine,
Whose life's as tender to me as my soul;
And full as much (for more there can not be),
I do detest false, perjur'd Proteus:
Therefore be gone, solicit me no more."
THE TWO GENTLEMEN OF VERONA.

ELIZABETH hoped, as parliament was now sitting, that Mr. Dawson would forget a subject so insignificant as herself in the cares of statesmanship and the toils of legislation, but whether it was that the talents of that gentleman were not decidedly parliamentary, or that his feelings toward Miss Spenser overpowered his sense of public duty, or that there was room enough in his great capacity for the affairs of the heart as well as those of the nation, certain it was that he spent more of his time in Dublin than was consistent with the duties he had to discharge at Westminster.

The rector had written him a sharp letter immediately after the incident of the Signal Rock, but it was not sharp enough, and it wanted that tone of decision which Mrs. Woodward would have given it, and which might have shown Dawson once for all the utter folly of his attentions to Miss Spenser. The consequence was, that an opening was left for a letter of explanation and apology, which Mr. Spenser had the weakness to reply to in such gentle and forgiving terms that Dawson's position was rather improved than injured by the result of the whole transaction. But his success with Mrs. Spenser was still more complete. He had written, the reader will recollect, a letter to the government, in which, with the utmost indelicacy, he had introduced Mrs. Spenser's name, extolling her in the most fulsome language as another Eleanora, or Mrs. Killigrew. Miss M'Cracken had undertaken to procure a copy of this state-paper through a brother of Peacock's, who had some appointment at the castle, but she over-rated her corrupt influence, and this drove Dawson to devise a still cleverer way of gaining his object. He prevailed on one of his parliamentary associates to move for copies of papers and correspondence connected with the anti-tithe agitation, shaping the motion so that his own letter must necessarily be produced among the other documents. It succeeded to admiration. The returns were made, printed in a blue book, published in the newspapers, and Mrs. Spenser's graces and virtues became part of the public records of the kingdom.

The rector himself, uxorious as he was, had no notion what a divine helpmate he had, until, to his amazement, he read her character in the newspapers, extracted from the blue book; and as to the lady herself, not even in the mirror of Miss M'Cracken's most abject and daring flattery, had she ever seen herself arrayed in such a panoply of charms. You may conceive how high Dawson stood in her opinion after this. Lucy assured her mistress that she had read Lord Chesterfield's letters, and thought Mr. Dawson's worth them all put together, "it was not only so very beautiful, but so very true."

Still nothing but the most enormous personal conceit could have urged him to persevere in addresses which Elizabeth had upon all occasions repelled with the utmost coldness. Dawson's vanity was more than mere satisfaction with himself; it amounted to admiration and rapture. When he had accomplished himself from top to toe in what he considered, or what tailors, hatters, and hair-dressers assured him was the acme of fashion—when he was mounted on a showy horse, or seated in a dashing cab —he thought himself the most redoubtable lady-

H

killer; and when, to crown all, he recollected that he was a public character and a member of parliament, he believed that nothing in female form, however beautiful, wealthy, or exalted, could possibly resist him.

One day Elizabeth had spent the morning with her friends, the Ramsdens, who lived in a neighboring street. A servant attended her home. Pacing up and down before the door was a groom in a handsome livery, mounted on a superb horse, and leading another nearly as fine. Not having paid much attention to such matters, she concluded that Sir Florus Bloomfield was visiting Mrs. Spenser, and, as his company was always agreeable, instead of going to her own room, she proceeded to her step-mother's. Just as she reached the door, Rebecca was coming out; a glimpse into the interior was thus afforded, and that glimpse revealed Mr. Dudley Dawson. Miss Spenser recoiled, as if she had inadvertently approached the mouth of a dragon's den, and flew on tip-toe to her own apartment. She had not been there many moments, when Miss M'Cracken came tapping, and said that Mrs. Spenser desired to see her. Elizabeth excused herself, saying (which was indeed the truth) that she was changing her dress, and Lucy went away disappointed, to give a still greater disappointment to Mr. Dawson.

Mrs. Spenser had given Dawson the most cordial reception imaginable. In return for his adulation of herself, she loaded him with compliments, congratulations, expressions of gratitude, and civil speeches of all kinds. She would never forget his kindness; she lamented that her health had prevented her from seeing more of him in the country, she thought his waistcoat the handsomest of the season, asked him for franks, and hoped to see him frequently, as long as he remained in town.

While the excited invalid was making this long oration, Miss M'Cracken was sitting at a window with a devout book in her hand, looking meek as a nun, but now and then directing furtive glances at the senator, expressive of her triumph in the success of their schemes. What followed almost threw her into ecstasies. The rector entered as Dawson was taking leave. A sudden thought struck Mrs. Spenser.

"Would Mr. Dawson, if he happened not to be engaged—would he kindly return to dinner?"

Mr. Spenser had, of course, no alternative but to concur in the request, but Dawson was to dine that day with the Lord Lieutenant. "Happy condition of vice-regal state," thought the rector.

"To-morrow?" Mr. Dawson was only too proud and too happy to consent.

Mr. Spenser pitied the viceroy for having to entertain such a man as Dudley, but he ought to have rather compassionated his daughter, who had not the formalities and ceremony of the Castle to protect her against a repulsive guest. The state that accompanies great employments is not necessary merely to make them imposing in the eyes of the vulgar; it is absolutely essential to defend those that fill them from the importunities, familiarities, and thousand indecorums of scores of persons, who, unless kept back by troops of aids-de-camps and ushers, would make the service of the public in high offices an intolerable burthen. As to Dawson, he was a man to be received with a file of battle-axes and the whole college of heralds, Ulster, Cork, and Athlone pursuivant.

The dreaded day came and went, with less pain to Elizabeth, however, than she could have anticipated, but unluckily with more satisfaction also to Dawson than he had hoped for. Elizabeth received him with cold civility, but being under the impression that he was aware of her engagement to Vivyan (with which, however, Miss M'Cracken had not acquainted him), her manner was less freezing than it would otherwise have been, and his vanity, of course, interpreted this negative symptom as a favorable one.

The next day Dawson paid a visit; it was expected and endured.

On the following evening Elizabeth went to the theater with her relations, the Ramsdens. The greatest actor of the age was playing Macbeth. In the interval between the first and second acts, she happened just to turn her head round for a moment to make a remark to one of her friends in whose party she was, when the door of the box opened, and Dawson appeared, blazing in gold chains, gilt buttons, and pink velvet. He bowed, and she could not but return the salute. There was a vacant place in the box; he closed the door and took possession of it in such a flourishing way as to attract general attention. The great drama went on, but Macbeth and Macready no longer engrossed Elizabeth's mind. She never could cease thinking of the offensive personage behind her.

"Hence, horrible shadow!"

The words seemed strangely applicable to her situation, but unfortunately Dawson was no "unreal mockery." Before the play was over, a gentleman in the row immediately behind her, but not of her party, quitted the box. Dawson instantly seized the vacant post, and then she thought the green curtain would never fall. His criticisms, however, amused her friends, if they disgusted her. Every second word was either gorgeous, or splendid, or magnificent, or tremendous. "Thrilling," too, was a favorite phrase of his. Something was always thrilling Dawson, he was of such an extremely sensitive constitution. Scotland was not more relieved than Miss Spenser was, when the sword of Macduff concluded the tragedy. But she was not quite delivered from Dawson yet; he assisted her in shawling, and intrusively offered her his arm to conduct her to the carriage. She took the arm of one of her cousins, but Dawson followed her, making odious attempts to be agreeable, hoping she would not catch cold, and wondering how, after witnessing such stupendous acting, any one could remain to see a paltry after-piece. Directly, however, the Ramsdens' carriage drove off, our man of such delicate taste and refinement returned to the house; sought out a knot of his friends, and after laughing vociferously at a low farce, passed the residue of the night in the pleasures of loo and lobsters.

Now, indeed, scarcely a day passed without Elizabeth experiencing more or less annoyance from the same gentleman. She underwent nearly the same persecution that another lady, more known to the world, was doomed to undergo some years afterward from another Lothario of the emerald isle. If Elizabeth walked in the squares, with the Ramsdens, or any of her female friends, Dawson seldom failed to inflict

himself upon them. If she went shopping, she
was pounced on in the same manner. At con-
certs and other public places, there was no protection from him, and his visits to Mrs. Spenser
were now events of almost daily occurrence.
Dawson gave her all his franks, and was so
obliging as to offer to receive all the letters of
the family, which, if sent under cover to him,
would thus come to them free of postage. Of
this privilege, however, Elizabeth did not avail
herself, but her step-mother made use of it
liberally, and made the rector do so too.

Mr. Spenser, however, had the misfortune
accidentally to involve himself at this time much
deeper with Dawson than by the mere acceptance of a few franks. He had taken a first-class
house, furnished in the handsomest manner, and
this, with the increased expenses of a town residence, the outlay at his daughter's wedding, and
the necessary advances to Sydney, was now beginning to press so heavily on his means, that
he was under the necessity of negotiating a
loan of five hundred pounds. With three hundred of this sum his bookseller, more generously than prudently, accommodated him, and he
found it no easy matter (having but few friends
in Dublin) to raise the remainder. At length
he heard of an obscure solicitor, by whom matters of this kind were adroitly and confidentially
managed, and to this gentleman he repaired for
assistance. It turned out that this person was
Dawson's attorney, and Dawson was actually
in his office when a clerk entered and informed
the man of the law that the Reverend Mr. Spenser desired to see him. Sharkey and Dawson
whispered, and Dawson stepped into a very
small closet behind the attorney's chair, where
he was almost stifled with old coats, boots, and
musty parchments, but could hear what went
on in the office as well as if he had stood his
ground like an honest man. When Dawson
heard the rector state his little embarrassments,
how deeply it affected him in his hole must be
to the reader to imagine. Mr. Sharkey
and what low money-jobbers always say upon
such occasions: talked of the times, the scarcity
of money, (with which the market then chanced
to be actually glutted), but concluded by promising to see what could be done, and requesting
the rector to call again in a few days. The
clergyman departed, and the senator emerged,
the former feeling deeply the indignity to which
his necessities reduced him, the latter actually
vain of having wantonly played the part of a
knave.

"Will you lend the money, Dud.?" asked
the attorney, who was Dawson's boon companion and bosom friend. He was a small man.
with a red face and sharp features, but not as
sharp as his practice. In the hall of the Four
Courts he was considered a dandy, and when he
was engaged in any particularly dirty business,
he invariably wore canary gloves and a white
waistcoat.

"You best know whether I can or not," replied Dawson; "but there's not a man living,
Bob, to whom I'd rather lend a couple of hundred pounds, if I had it. You know who he is,
don't you?"

"To be sure I do; the father of the girl you're
after," said Sharkey.

"The same," said Dawson.

"I don't think you'll ever get her, Dud."

"By —— I will, as sure as I'm member for
Rottenham. But I tell you what it is, Bob, I
think it would do me no harm to be in her papa's
books for the two hundred."

"Upon my sowl, Dud., it's the very thing would
do the business for you. And didn't you save
her life?"

"But about the money," said Dawson.

"Why, you haven't it, and that's all about
it," said the attorney, and, lowering his voice,
added with a facetious grim, "are there any
more pictures by the ould masters at the castle,
Dud.?"

"By ——, Bob," whispered Dawson, elate at
the thought of his management of the affair, alluded to, "that was the cleverest job I ever
did."

"But, tell me, Dud.;" the attorney lowered
his voice again, and still more than before—
"what's become of the major and Thomson?"

"The major's gone abroad," said Dawson.

"For seven years?" said Sharkey.

"Not so bad," said the other; "but he got
wild about the repeal of the union, and he
thought he could serve the question in New
York as well as in ould Ireland."

"And you didn't discourage him," said the
attorney.

"No," answered the M.P., "but, touching
the money—is there no way?"

Mr. Sharkey now looked very deliberative,
and his eyes corresponded with Dawson's for
several moments, with that sort of silent but
most intelligible language which it is a mistake
to think confined to the interviews of swains and
shepherdesses. It can take place just as well
on two stools in an attorney's dingy office, over-
hung with cobwebbed papers, as upon banks of
violets, under canopies of roses and eglantine.

"It just occurs to me," said the attorney,
breaking this eloquent silence first, "that there's
a client of mine who is anxious to get a poor
boy of his something or other in the public service—any thing that's going worth a hundred a
year, or even less, but you see the poor fellow
has nobody to ask for him, though I think he'd
come down with two or three hundred pounds,
if the thing could be managed in an honorable
way."

Dawson looked as roguish as he well could
look, but did not answer for a moment or two.

"Confidential, Bob," he said at length.

"Honor bright, Dud."

Dawson took his hat, reminded his legal ad-
viser of an appointment for the night, and went
his way. He was seen a good deal for a few
days about the castle, swaggering in the ante-
room, or wriggling in the corridors. What
success he had is unknown, or what place he
got for the son of Sharkey's client; but the attorney managed in the course of the week to
accommodate the rector with the sum he required, securing a pretty per centage for himself, and concealing the name of the real lender,
Dawson being too delicate to appear in the
transaction, though he put the rector's accept-
ances into his pocket.

Dawson would have been a happy man had
all the sex been as devoted to him as Miss
M'Cracken, but tenderly as she watched over
his interests, she was more on the *qui vive* about

her own, and as just about this time she thought it prudent to bring matters with Peacock (the amorous exciseman) to a matrimonial crisis, she judged it also to be only discreet to get him another shove forward in life.

Mr. Spenser continued to take a Donegal newspaper, called the *Tyrconnell Mercury*, and it happened one morning that Lucy, glancing over the columns of this rural journal, saw recorded among other news the promotion of the postmaster of Redcross to the like office in the city of Cork. The announcement at first made no impression on her mind, but in the course of the day the thought flashed across it, that the office of postmaster would suit her lover, and that through Dawson's exertions it might not be an unattainable object. At first she found the M.P. a little impracticable. He had been using his influence freely of late, and had a hundred more applicants for places on his list than he had the least chance of providing for, though not a few of them were ready to accept any office, however mean, at any salary, however moderate, in any part of the world, no matter how distant or pestilential.

Dawson, one Sunday afternoon, did a very unusual thing—a thing he had never done before on the same day, and at the same hour—he went to church. In the morning he had received the following short note from Miss M'Cracken:—

"DEAR MR. DAWSON—Miss S—— will be at the —— chapel, this evening.
"Your obliged and devoted,
"L. M'C."

Dawson attended punctually; but, though Elizabeth was there, as the female spy had correctly informed him, he might as well have been losing his time under the walls of the most jealous harem in the East, trying to get a glimpse at the Fatimas and Zobeides. Miss Spenser was with her father and the Ramsdens, in a private pew, well pavilioned about with curtains, and inaccessible to strangers, even with the silver key, which Dawson would gladly have applied to the lock. Never was a mind less in unison with the spirit of prayer and thanksgiving than his was, as he dodged about the aisles and galleries, in the dim religious lamp-light, seeking a position, whence seen or unseen, he might command at least a view of the pure girl, with whom he fancied himself in love, in his absolute ignorance of what love is.

After he had stood some time, like Satan among "the sons of God," his frivolous design completely baffled by the crimson hangings of the pew where Elizabeth was ensconced, he bethought himself that he was wasting his evening with unprofitable hypocrisy, and was stealing out of the church to resort to the tavern, just as a sacred song was given out to be sung by the congregation. The voices were almost all female, and one drew general attention, not merely by its real sweetness, but by the impassioned energy with which it lifted the note of praise far higher than any other voice that was raised upon the occasion. In the midst of the hymn that divine voice ceased abruptly, and the people looked about them, wondering what could have struck it dumb. But the surprise did not extend to Dawson, who recognized the tones of an instrument of his own, and perfectly well understood

that Miss M'Cracken was about to sacrifice the sermon for a chat with him in the vestibule. It was exactly so. She came out immediately after him, wriggling through the crowd on tiptoe, every body thinking that the girl with the enchanting voice was overpowered by the heat, and in want of fresh air. The sermon, that night, was delivered by one of the most celebrated preachers of the time, and even the pew-openers and beadles pressed into the aisles to hear him, leaving the vestibule deserted, so that our worthy pair had it all to themselves. They sat down together on a wooden form that was there, and were not much disturbed, on the whole, by the distant thunders of the pulpit.

Their remarks on the service were not edifying, and shall, therefore, be omitted. Lucy was sorely grieved at Dawson's disappointment, and said many harsh things of the pew system, and on the exclusiveness of crimson velvet curtains. No such things were allowed in Scotland; they would not be tolerated, she said, in the Church that she belonged to; and Dawson paid her a just compliment upon her liberality in attending the services of the English Church, though born and bred a Presbyterian. He was then about to leave her (not wishing her, perhaps, to lose the sermon), when, after sundry little hesitations, and beatings about the bush, she brought the subject of her own little fortunes and her Edward's promotion on the tapis.

"The post-office at Redcross is a very snug thing, Lucy," said the senator, musingly and dubiously.

"It would suit Edward and me so very nicely," said the amiable girl in her most persuasive tones.

"Well, Lucy," said Dawson, "suppose you were post-mistress, would you take great care of the Castle-Dawson bag? would you take particular care of my letters and newspapers?"

Lucy thought she might make herself useful in the situation, if she was appointed to it. The member of parliament thought so too, though neither he nor she stated precisely in what way the usefulness was to be shown. There are some things which it is not either pleasant or politic to speak of with precision even in the most confidential communications.

"Well," said Dawson, rising, "you are a jewel of a girl, Lucy, and to-morrow. I'll see what can be done; but do not be too sanguine. I am by no means confident of carrying the point."

It was raining when they looked out of the porch of the edifice, which they had thus been desecrating, into the gloomy street, but Dawson had an umbrella and proposed to conduct Lucy home. This, however, she declined, having some curiosity, she said, to hear a little of the sermon; and besides, she just made the discovery that she had left her hymn-book behind her. They parted, however, affectionately, he braving the elements out of doors; she, with still greater hardihood, venturing back into the house where the worship of God was still going on.

The rector walked home from church that evening, having resigned his seat in the carriage to a lady. As he moved along, keeping the most sheltered side of the street, and musing on the arrangements for his daughter's wedding, which was to take·place in a few days, a tall ·young man, who was walking rapidly, ·passed ª him, and it ·struck 'Mr.· Spenser immediately ʳ that he bore a striking resemblance to George Markham.

·· He instantly turned, and overtook him; it was Lindeed Markham, but the pleasure of the meeting seemed to be all on the rector's side, for when Mr. Spenser informed him where he was quartered, and hoped to see him at his house, George declined with obvious embarrassment, and pleaded the urgency· of the affairs which had brought him over, and the very limited time he· had at his disposal while he remained in Ireland. They spoke of Vivyan,· but Markham had no news of a recent date to give of his ·friend, and upon this, as upon other subjects, he ·was strangely uncommunicative, though the few ·words he did exchange with Mr. Spenser were not unfriendly, and at parting he shook his hand, and thanked him with warmth for his past and his proffered hospitality.

· Mr. Spenser thought there was something ¹ strange in all this, but ascribed it to the pre-occupation of the young man's mind with the urgent affairs he had spoken of, and continued his walk home, in doubt whether to blame himself or not for having omitted to invite Markham to assist at Arabella's marriage.

Elizabeth, however, was extremely pained and perplexed when she heard from her father what had occurred; she remembered what a frank, joyous fellow George had been at Redcross; and found it difficult to avoid the thought that Vivyan must be connected in some way or another with the circumstances, whatever they were, which had brought his friend back to Ireland.

"Did he ask for the Woodwards ?" she inquired, with anxiety.

" No," replied her father.

This she thought very unaccountable, Markham having taken such a prodigious fancy to her uncle : it looked like either profound absorption in business, or as if, after all, there was no great solidity in the attachments which George formed yachting.

.A letter from Vivyan, however, arrived the next morning, all tenderness and eloquence, as usual, and Elizabeth, having the cares of a .wedding on her shoulders, thought little more of Markham, his business, or his abstraction.

The first event of any consequence that took place in Dublin was Arabella Spenser's marriage, and it was as heavy an affair of the kind as was ever transacted at St. George's, Hanover Square, or St. Peter's, in Dublin. Indeed, it only deserves to be chronicled as an illustration of Arabella's littleness and her uncle's magnanimity. It had been considered a settled point ·that the curate was to perform the ceremony, and we may remember that the rector had advertised him to keep himself in readiness to discharge that interesting duty, when called upon. In fact, Hercules had ordered a new coat (not .an iron-gray, but an actual black), and had been very urgent and impatient with his tailor about it. " Do be patient, my dear," Carry said more than once, " recollect what a time it must take to make a coat for *you*." The tailor, however, kept his engagement better than other people did. About a week before the wedding, it was decided that no ecclesiastic under the rank of a bishop would answer to unite so important a personage as Lieutenant-Colonel Dabzac in the bonds of matrimony with Miss Spenser, and as the bishop of one of the. northern sees was a connection of the bridegroom, the bride had a shabby pretext for cashiering ·her uncle ·the curate. The rector was excessively ' mortified and distressed, and indeed he was secretly more grieved than he owned to any body at the whole of his daughter's conduct in relation to her marriage ; she showed such little concern at leaving her father's roof, and such a precipitate eagerness to identify herself with her husband's family and ·connections. As to Mrs. Woodward, though very indignant, she knew her niece's character too well to be much surprised at her paltry conduct, so she was not · an excuse for not being present at the wedding. Hercules, however, made it a point to go up to town, and he could not have more effectually revenged himself on Arabella, had such been his wish, for the curate's exterior was unquestionably ill-calculated. to adorn a "marriage à la mode." The provincial tailor had done him more justice in the quantity of cloth than in the elegance of his cut. His shoes were very new, but made for the bogs, rather than the carpet; and as for the delicate white gloves with which he was duly presented, after a single glance of curiosity and contempt, he thrust them into his pocket for Carry, with grave doubts whether they were not much too small for her plump hand as well as' his own. Indeed, it was no easy matter to adapt the curate to a drawing-room at any time ; and now that he was left to his own devices, with no good wife to look after his toilet, the more he studied to be a *beau*, the more extraordinary was the figure he cut. Even Elizabeth herself could not help wishing that he had not got his hair curled so egregiously, and that he had seen the impropriety of putting cambric enough into his cravat to make a surplice. There were no fewer than five lieutenant-colonels (either relatives or friends of Dabzac's) present at the wedding. There were also old Mrs. Dabzac and her sister, old Mrs. Loquax, Lord and Lady Brabble, Mr. and Mrs. Pepper, several young Peppers, and a certain angelical Miss Vallancey, all of the Dabzac faction. The Spensers were inferior in number, but in number only. There was the rector himself and his daughter, the good curate (well worth an army of the colonels) the Ramsdens (excellent people, related to the Spensers), Sir Florus Bloomfield, and last and least of all, little Mr. Trundle, in full feather, and chattering at the very steps of the altar about Loch Swilly and the thirty millions. Mr. Trundle had been invited by both parties, being not only agent to Dabzac, but also to Lord Bonham, Mr. Spenser's friend and patron.

If Hercules was snubbed at breakfast by some of the company, he was compensated in some measure by the honor of an introduction to the bishop, who kindly shook· his hand, and graciously said that he had heard of ·Mr.· Woodward, and was happy to have the opportunity of making his acquaintance. Hercules was pleased to be thus noticed by one of the heads of the Church, and indeed the prelate was ª man by whom it was almost promotion to be praised, for his life was as spotless as his lawn, and the luster of his virtues outshone his miter.

On the evening of the wedding-day the curate returned to his parish, having been absent from his pastoral duties only three days. He had not been in Dublin for ten years before, and it was a sore grief to him not to have had a single jolly night with his friend Tom Beamish. He breakfasted, however, with Tom one morning, and was accompanied by Elizabeth, whose beauty and affability made such a sensation in the university that to this day her visit to it is matter of table-talk at college commons. Hercules showed her the chambers which he had occupied himself when a scholar; conducted her to the hall, and pointed out the precise spot where the illustrious Doctor Prior had examined him in Thucydides; led her to the academic kitchen, and explained the machinery by which one fire roasted innumerable legs of mutton; from thence to the buttery, where he and Beamish joked all their jokes, and punned all their puns over again, enormously exaggerating their old potations of October, while Miss Spenser unaffectedly laughed with them, although far from understanding one-half of their quips and quiddities. She was greatly pleased, on the whole, with her reception in the college of her royal namesake; the only fault she found with it was that it was not sufficiently national, but her uncle luminously explained to her, as they walked home, that to admit a single Catholic on the foundation would be tantamount to placing a barrel of gunpowder under it, and blowing the establishment into the air.

---

### CHAPTER XLIX.

MARKHAM REVISITS THE PARSONAGE.

"Revisit, say you?
Who ever visited the same mansion twice?
The walls remain, the roof, the gables, chimneys;
The mason's work will stand a century,
But 'tis not stone and mortar makes the house,
The bricks, or timber, but the hearts and faces,
And these change every day and every hour."
NEW PLAY.

ALMOST immediately after the curate's return home, he went to reside at the parsonage, which was a central point in the parish, whereas the town of Redcross was situated on the edge of it, bordering on Mr. Oliver's benefice. Hercules did not feel half so comfortable as if he had been in his own dear disorderly old house, for he was obliged to forego a number of his little innocent freedoms and enjoyments; he was no longer in a position to repel the invasions of housemaids; the sweeping-brush now swept all before it, and the Pope's head was too strong for him, sturdy Protestant as he was. Carry now kept him in reasonable order; only she could not prevent him from sometimes clapping his oil-skin head-piece on the bust of Curran in the library, the worst of which was that Billy Pitt followed the paternal example, and took the same liberty with the bust of Fox, who, in Billy's straw hat and green ribbons, looked like a superannuated Colin, or an Alexis of sixty.

Carry had just been talking one morning of writing to her friends in Dublin, when the cu-

rate was called out to speak to a shopkeeper of Redcross, who had come over the water to inform him that he thought he had discovered a clew which might possibly lead to the detection of the robbery of the tithe-proctor. The clew consisted in a bank-note for five pounds, on one corner of which the shopkeeper recognized a mark, which he thought exceedingly like Mr Randy Maguire's signature. There was also a date immediately under, and apparently in the same cramped hand. The curate was not familiar enough with the proctor's writing to give an opinion; but Randy was sent for, and not only identified the initials and the date, but was enabled by the latter to pronounce the note to be one of those which he had received at Branagan's house from a tenant of Mr. Vivyan. Hercules hurried back to Carry with the joyful news of the probable discovery of the criminals in consequence of this occurrence; and then, taking the shopkeeper and Maguire with him, proceeded to Redcross to prosecute the inquiry. The shopkeeper had a dispute with his wife as to the quarter from which they had received the note. He maintained it was from a grazier in the neighborhood; the wife was positive it had been received from Amby Hogg, the sexton, who has been already honorably mentioned in the course of our story...

"Well," said Hercules, "let us go to Amby first."

Amby was a vain little tradesman, who wished to be thought more familiar with considerable sums of money than in fact he was, so he talked of ascertaining the hand from which any particular note came to his as a thing not to be done.

"I'm happy to find you receive so many of them, Amby," said the curate.

"It would be a bad business, your reverence," said the sexton, "if five-pound notes were as scarce as green peas at Christmas."

"They're not quite as plenty, howsomdever, as blackberries at Michaelmas," muttered the other shopkeeper, not pleased at his fellow-townsman's ostentation of wealth.

While these observations were passing backward and forward, Amby Hogg's daughter, a quiet but smart little girl of about fourteen, who kept his shop, and indeed made the m's of his money for him, gave her father sundry winks and plucks by the coat, which the curate perceived sooner than the sexton himself did.

"Your daughter has got something to say to you," said Hercules. "Perhaps she may be able to jog your memory, Amby."

Amby followed the girl into a little parlor behind the shop, where much of the profits of the trade were drank in toddy by himself, and in tea and toddy by his wife. In a moment he returned, and, with a mysterious face, said to the clergyman—

"Will your reverence step this way?"

Amby took the curate into the inner room, and there informed him that his daughter said the note in question had been received from Mr. Sydney Spenser.

"Why make a mystery of that?" said Hercules; "we must only try to find out how it came into my nephew's possession."

The curate was returning to the shop, when Amby held him back; and, in a low voice, vised him not to mention his nephew's name in connection with the business.

This still more surprised Hercules, and he desired to know why Amby recommended such reserve.

"When I'm alone with your reverence, I'll tell you my maning," said Amby.

The curate was at a loss what to say to the other shopkeeper, who stood outside, but Amby's invention was quicker.

"Tell him," said he, "just nothing at all about it; only keep the bank-note in your own possession."

"It's a serious thing," said the considerate Hercules, "to detain so large a sum of money from a poor fellow like him."

"Then your reverence must only give him another note in place of it," said the sexton, flippantly.

Never was the ascendency of moral dignity over mere pecuniary consequence more conspicuous than it was in the aspect of Mr. Woodward, as calmly and silently it intimated the fact, that it was entirely out of his power to adopt Mr. Hogg's last suggestion.

"I'll see if I've got as much in the till, myself," replied Amby, but not as conceitedly as he would have said it, if his little pride of purse had not been rebuked by the high-minded simplicity with which the man of education, and the minister of the Gospel, had confessed how little he possessed of the world's wealth.

However, Amby went to his treasury, and produced the required sum of money, without seeming to have much trouble in making it up. The sexton of Redcross was a richer man than the curate!

As soon as they were alone together, Amby made a statement which wounded Mr. Woodward to the soul. Sydney, on leaving Redcross, had left several unsettled accounts behind him. Some of his debts (among others, that to Amby himself) he had discharged; but by so doing he only exasperated those creditors whose demands he left entirely unsatisfied, and nothing, in fact, but a feeling of delicacy toward the rector (particularly as he was parting from them under painful circumstances) kept them from making a noise about their accounts, and calling on Mr. Spenser to settle them. Imagine the feelings of the honest and humane uncle, when he heard that in some instances his nephew had actually borrowed small sums of money, on sundry pretenses, from the poor shopkeepers, and that these sums had not been repaid. He was not in the least surprised when the sexton proceeded to inform him that some people in Redcross had begun to speak hardly of Sydney.

"Of course they have," cried Hercules, impetuously—"to be sure they have."

"But," continued Amby, with hesitation, "there's some of them says what they have no call to say at all, but perhaps I'm wrong in telling your riverence any thing about it, as it's sure to aggravate you and make you unasy."

"That's the very reason I ought to hear it," said the curate, with stern composure.

"Why, then," replied the sexton, "I needn't acquaint you, sir, that there are people in Redcross, as elsewhere, with malice in their hearts, and bad tongues in their heads; and thim that

have no character to lose themselves are the first to take it away from thim that has."

"Come to the point, Amby."

"I didn't like to tell your reverence before (but there's no help for it) that Master Sydney owes a trifle to the widdy Grogan, who keeps the little shop for ship's stores down at the harbor."

The curate's eye expressed his indignation; but he was too impatient for the upshot of Amby's narrative to interrupt him by a word.

"Well, she is a poor creature," said Amby, still beating about the bush, "and that's why people say it's so hard upon her in times like these."

"What do they say of my nephew?" demanded Hercules, almost savagely.

"They say," said Amby, at length driven to extremity, "that a young man who would rob a poor widdy, wouldn't think much of robbing his own father."

"What do they mean by that?" cried Hercules.

"Then," said Amby, "they have no ground to stand upon the size of a sixpenny bit, for their wicked surmises; only that Ned Grogan, the widdy Grogan's husband's brother (they're black Presbyterians, your reverence), swears he met Master Sydney within a stone's throw of the Black Castle on the night of the robbery."

The curate's wrath, when he heard how his unfortunate nephew was slandered by the ruthless tongues of his little creditors, knew no bounds.

"It's well for him, you're a minishter," said Amby.

"My ministry shan't protect him," cried the enraged clergyman; but, of course, upon reflection, he abandoned his first violent intentions, and also perceived the prudence of the sexton's advice, that nothing ought to be said or done to give an appearance of countenance to what at present was a mere slanderous imputation, without a scintilla of evidence to support it; for as to Sydney having been seen near the Black Castle on that memorable night, what was there in that to support such a charge against the son of a clergyman; and moreover, as the curate remarked, there was just the same evidence against himself.

Leaving the suspicious five-pound note in the custody of Amby Hogg, who was indeed now its rightful owner, Mr. Woodward trudged back to the parsonage. What he had heard about Sydney grieved him sorely, and Ellen Hogg, the schoolmistress, whom he visited for a few moments, perceived that something was wrong with him, but she thought he had been visiting some death-bed, or performing some other melancholy office of charity, and after the performance of such duties, Hercules did not speedily get up his spirits, for though his exterior was so rough and hard, his heart was of another texture. He was a nut with a rugged shell and a sweet and oily kernel.

The first occupation of his thoughts was how immediately to pay off those small debts which his nephew had so shamefully contracted, and still more shamefully left undischarged. He then employed himself speculating upon the nature and singularities of circumstantial evidence; he put the case that his nephew should be unable to state how the note which he had given to the sexton had come into his possession; that some other circumstances with a sinister aspect should come to light; and he then figured to himself how difficult it might become for his nephew to meet a case of the kind, notwithstanding the apparent improbability that such a robbery had been committed by a gentleman, the son of a clergyman, and the identical clergyman who was the chief sufferer by the crime. That such a charge should ever be actually made, seemed, of course, altogether out of the question; but it was painful to contemplate the bare possibility of the event happening; and shocking to think that Sydney should have left a character behind him at Redcross, such as to suggest and countenance, instead of being itself an overwhelming answer to the daring insinuations of calumnious people.

There was another distressing view of the matter which did not occur to Mr. Woodward at first. The sums of which Maguire had been rifled, included money of Frank Vivyan's as well as Mr. Spenser's; so that the imputation hanging over Sydney was not merely that he was concerned in defrauding his father, but that he had also robbed the man to whom his sister was then actually contracted in marriage.

This view of the case struck Mrs. Woodward at once, and she trembled to think of what Elizabeth would feel and suffer, were the lightest rumor to reach her of what slander was whispering in the miry streets of Redcross.

"These small sums must be paid instantly," said the curate.

"You had better write to Valentine at once," said Carry.

"Val. has had a load of trouble lately," said her husband, "and a heavy increase to his expenses, what with removing to town, and sending that unfortunate boy to Cambridge—it was against my judgment—but there's no use in talking of that now. What I think of doing is to dispose of Sligo. Wilkins offered me twenty pounds for him not long ago."

"My dear, good, good Hercules!" cried Carry, jumping up and running to him; "to think of selling the pony!"

"Carry, my dear, I would do more than that to save Val. trouble, and, after all, it's not doing much, for I'm not a bad walker, you know; and, at a pinch, I can always take one of the plough-horses."

Hercules sent the pony to Doctor Wilkins that very evening, with a letter stating that he had reconsidered his offer and felt disposed to accept it. The next morning the doctor called at the parsonage and paid him the twenty pounds; upon receiving which the curate set off instantly to Redcross, and went all through the town, accompanied by the sexton, settling the demands against his scampish nephew, carefully, however, concealing the fact that the money came from his own pocket. It gave him no great trouble to hide his good deeds, he was so accustomed to that kind of under-hand proceeding.

Hercules, however, grossly misreckoned in expecting that the arrangement of these little matters would silence the tongue of defamation. Already had an ill construction been put upon the detention of the five-pound note, virtually by Sydney's relative; the sexton had repeated to his wife (the slattern sextoness) all the conversation he had held with the curate about Sydney, and what people were saying of him, so that when the payment of the debts followed so speedily, the slattern sextoness shrugged her broad shoulders, only one of which was as much covered by her gown as it should have been, and said, "she knew very well the matter would be hushed up, and that, for her part, she thought it better it should be."

The curate's next step was to write to Sydney. Carry and he concocted the letter between them, sitting at the fire-side in a small parlor, connected with the library. It was wearing toward dusk on a dry but gusty evening in March. The letter was finished and dispatched to Redcross for the next post by one of the farm-servants, who took the bull-dog with him for company and protection.

Carry and Hercules sat down to their plain but neat and excellent dinner. Neatness was Mrs. Woodward's luxury; she was satisfied when she had a snowy cloth on her table, and a substantial dish or two for the masculine stomach of her spouse. On this occasion there was part of a turbot, which had been caught opposite to the house, with a piece of boiled pork and peas-pudding (a union which the curate was nearly as much attached to as he was to that of England and Ireland). It was abundance in all conscience for two people, particularly as Carry's appetite was not, like the curate's, in direct proportion to the scale of her person.

They had not long been seated, when Carry's maid entered and announced a visitor. She thought she had seen the gentleman last summer, but was not very certain, he was so wrapped up. Hercules went out; and his boisterous greetings reaching his wife's ear, assured her that it was no stranger who had arrived, but some old and very welcome friend. It was George Markham, whom the curate found in the hall, disencumbering himself of his coats and shawls. He had not dined, and after a few minutes' attention to the toilet (during which the fish and the joint were sent back to the kitchen to be kept hot), he made a third at the curate's table, but did scanty justice to his substantial fare. He appeared to be much fatigued and way-worn, so that neither host nor hostess pressed him with many questions, though one was nearly as curious as the other to learn what it could be that brought him back so unexpectedly to Donegal. When dinner was over, Markham preferred a glass of the rector's old Innishowen to wine, and dispelled the reserve which a very unlooked for visit occasions as long as the motive of it is unknown, by saying, in his usual frank way that he had come down to the country on a matter of business, which he would mention to the curate in the morning. "I must be your debtor," he added, with something of his natural vivacity, "for this night's lodging, as I find you have not yet repaired your bridge."

The evening was a short one. Carry fancied that it was not altogether fatigue that made Markham unsociable; unpleasant thoughts occurred to her; her niece was uppermost in her mind, and she naturally apprehended that something or other had occurred to verify the old adage about the course of love. It was a relief to her when their visitor requested permission to retire, for she wished to be alone again in council with Hercules, to discuss what it possibly could be that brought Markham to the parsonage, and was evidently weighing on his spirits more than sleep on his eyelids.

"Sufficient to the day, my dear," said Hercules, half quoting the text; "but Mr. Markham's business is obvious enough; he is come over about his friend's affairs, of course."

"Oh, Hercules, I am certain of it," she answered; "something is going wrong."

The curate laughed, and said he only alluded to the affairs of Vivyan's little estate, which it was but natural he should have begged Markham to attend to in his absence. Carry was not to be persuaded of this, though her husband said he had no doubt on the subject, and in this divided state of opinion the curate and his wife retired to rest.

Terrible was the disclosure of the following morning. Through the gun-smiths of London and Dublin, Markham had traced the ownership of the pistol found at the Black Castle to Sydney Spenser.

---

## CHAPTER L.

### LETTERS FROM TOWN.

"Let us hear from thee by letters,
And I likewise will visit thee with mine."
TWO GENTLEMEN OF VERONA.

MARKHAM went as abruptly as he came. With the utmost delicacy and tenderness he discharged what he considered his duty, and no man could have felt more poignantly for the distress he caused. His principal object was to enable Sydney's friends to send him out of the way in time, before the discovery of his assumed criminality through some other channel.

It was some time before Hercules saw all the painful bearings of the case, as it now stood. The marriage of Elizabeth Spenser was involved in the result; it was evidently impossible it could take place until everything connected with this unfortunate business was cleared up, and cleared up honorably to the reputation of her brother.

Markham grasped the hand of the tender-hearted curate, in whose eye a great drop of manly sorrow glittered, as he thought of the grief that was in store for Carry and the niece, whom both he and she loved like a daughter. Hercules brushed away the tear with his sleeve. Markham stooped and plucked a primrose which grew opportunely at his feet, the firstling of the Irish spring. They walked side by side for some moments without speaking; then Markham again wrung his friend's hand, and hastened to the boat which waited for him.

Mrs. Woodward was as quick as her husband had been slow to see the connection between Elizabeth's union with Vivyan, and even the shadow of guilt upon Sydney's character. The idea stirred all the woman, the friend, the sister, and the mother within her; she entered with only too lively an imagination into all the miseries with which even a doubt was pregnant; the anguish to her sensitive brother, the ruin of Elizabeth's happiness, perhaps for life; the disgrace of the family, the cruel wrong to her, nephew himself, who was redeeming his youthful follies at Cambridge (at least she thought so), little dreaming of the cloud that was gathering over his head at home. Some time, indeed, elapsed before her husband could make her understand that there was any thing in the aspect of affairs by which Sydney could be seriously compromised. Carry was not as familiar with the nature of circumstantial evidence as if she had been the wife of a lawyer, and probably few lawyers' wives know much more about it than what they read in slip-shod novels while their husbands go their circuits. Even when the curate did make her see what the cumulative effect of the various circumstances would be in a court of justice, Carry still took a woman's view of the matter, and said—

"But it is all nonsense, Hercules. Surely you can't think for a moment that Sydney is really guilty."

"On the contrary, I firmly believe him innocent," said her husband, "but it is not a question of fact at present—God forbid it were—it is a question of opinion; not of your opinion, or mine, Carry, but what the opinion of strangers will be—of a man like Mr. Markham, for example, or a man like Vivyan."

"As to Vivyan," she replied, "he would just as easily be brought to believe that Elizabeth herself committed the crime."

"Sit down, Carry," said Hercules, and, leading her to a sofa, he seated himself beside her, and then resumed, speaking slowly and collectedly—"Elizabeth was not out of her bed on the night of the robbery; she was not seen that night close to the scene of it; she did not settle an account with money that bears Maguire's private marks; she was not the possessor of a brace of pistols, one of which was found by George Markham and myself among the weeds, not many yards from the spot where the outrage was perpetrated."

"Oh," cried his wife, with strong emotion, "are all these facts in evidence against Sydney?"

"There is, unhappily, not a shadow of a doubt upon one of them; but support yourself, my dear Carry, for this is a severe trial, and may possibly require all our strength to sustain, not only ourselves, but others."

"Oh, Hercules, if it should be true, when the very imputation is so shocking to think of!"

She threw herself back on the sofa, and spoke with her hands clasped over her forehead.

"Let us face it boldly," said the curate, "and shut our eyes to nothing; it is the wise course, were it only for the sake of the unfortunate boy himself, whom I firmly believe guiltless, despite of all the appearances against him."

"Guiltless!—impossible!" cried Carry, almost distracted, and now thinking it hopeless to reconcile the facts which had been just recapitulated with her unfortunate nephew's innocence.

"Not so; far from impossible," said her husband, "and yet I have not enumerated all the adverse circumstances—two just occur to me; I now recollect that Sydney declined to visit the Black Castle with Markham and me on the day we found the pistol—I thought it odd at the time—and when we exhibited it on our return in his presence, he did not claim, or seem to recognize it."

"It was growing dark, Hercules; I remember the evening perfectly."

. "Well," said the curate, rising, "I shall write to the unfortunate boy again; I trust and hope he will be able to explain every thing."

As he was leaving the room, Peter brought letters which had just arrived, and among them was one from Elizabeth and one from the rector. They were both for Carry. Miss Spenser did not write from home, but from a villa in the neighborhood of town, which the Bonhams had lately taken for a short period. The health of Lady Bonham, whom, next to her aunt, Elizabeth loved most tenderly, had recently been declining; and as it was always her greatest happiness and comfort to have Elizabeth with her, it was so particularly now, when her illness unfitted her for general society, and made that of one beloved friend more than ever valuable. This part of the letter was written in great depression of spirits, for Lady Bonham was a woman who was loved enthusiastically by the few who knew her sufficiently to love her at all. She was indeed a woman of the Eleonora race, though when she died, as, not many months after she did, she had no Dryden to honor her memory in verse that will never die.

She was a woman of lofty figure, and singularly fascinating and gracious aspect; her mind was highly cultivated and richly stored, not with common-place acquirements, but with the knowledge that is at once elegant and profitable. Her taste in books and conversation was, perhaps, somewhat masculine, like that of Elizabeth herself, but not to the extent that displeases men, though it disqualified her to live with the frivolous of her own sex. Distinguished and remarkable in many ways, her most striking attributes were the earnestness and fervor of her character. This showed itself most in her religion, which was not so much a principle as a divine and sweet enthusiasm, which made her a very apostle in her sphere. She did more than many divines to diffuse the spirit of Christianity wherever her influence extended, and she enjoyed, if ever woman did, that "heaven upon earth" described by Bacon, when "the mind moves in charity, rests in providence, and turns upon the poles of truth."

Such was Lady Bonham. She deserves this passing notice, were it only for the sake of the rector's daughter, who was so devotedly attached to her.

Mr. Spenser's letter was, full of interesting matter. Exclamation after exclamation escaped from Mrs. Woodward, as she ran her eye rapidly over it. "Miss M'Cracken gone—such a scene—such a fracas—my poor Valentine—and Elizabeth absent—a monster of ingratitude—married to that policeman—post-mistress—impossible! Oh! Hercules, only think of that abominable woman being at this moment postmistress of Redcross!"

. "Of Redcross!" cried the curate, in amazement.

' "Mr. Dawson's interest, of course," said his wife.

' The rector gave the following detailed account of the circumstances connected with the departure of Lucy.

He was sitting one morning after breakfast reading the *Edinburgh Review.* Miss M'Cracken entered in a particularly smart walking-dress, and approached him smiling.

"Well, Lucy," said the bland clergyman, laying down on his knee the book in blue and yellow.

"I have news to tell you, sir," she said, with a sly simper.

"Something good of yourself, I hope, Lucy."

"Yes, sir." Then she cast her eyes on the ground, like a marble modesty, and added, "I was married this morning."

"The clandestine marriage," said Mr. Spenser, with good-humored surprise; "but I congratulate you with all my heart upon the happy event, though I suppose its ultimate effect will be to deprive us of you."

"Yes, indeed, sir, I fear it will," she replied, with well feigned regret; and then, in a falter ing tone, also assumed for the occasion, she announced her second piece of intelligence—the appointment to the provincial post-office.

"Have you communicated all this good news to Mrs. Spenser?" asked the astonished rector.

"Not yet, sir; I was so afraid of agitating her, sir."

"Indeed, Mrs. Peacock, I fear it will," he replied, anxiously.

"Mrs. Edward Peacock, please, sir; my husband is only a younger son."

The rector found it difficult to suppress a smile at the girl's ridiculous airs; but the sequel was no laughing matter. It was absolutely necessary to break the news to Mrs. Spenser, and as neither the rector nor Lucy would undertake the task alone, they agreed to go about it together.

The first question the hysterical lady put was —"By whose interest the appointment had been obtained?"

"My husband's parliamentary connections," replied Lucy, with ludicrous importance. Dawson had charged her to keep his share in the business a secret.

Mrs. Spenser scoffed like a maniac at the parliamentary connections of a police-constable. Lucy was about to reply in the same tone, but the rector laid his hand on her arm, and in a low, earnest voice, besought her to be quiet. She bit her lip, and commanded her busy member.

Then came the critical question—"When did Mrs. Peacock propose to resign her present employment?"

Lucy knew the effect her answer would produce, and had armed herself in triple brass to make it.

"To-morrow, madam, if you please," she said, with the most impudent composure.

"I do not please," shrieked the irritated invalid, not irritated, indeed, without cause in the present instance.

Lucy contented herself with replying, that Mr. Edward Peacock had already taken places in the Donegal mail.

The excitement and rage of Mrs. Spenser were indescribable. The distracted rector, while he sought to calm her, could not but join in severely censuring Mrs. Peacock, who at length waxed hot, too, stoutly defended herself against her master, and repaid the invectives of her mistress with usury.

The rector was eventually compelled to push the termagant young lady out of the room; and when he returned to the bedside of his wife he found her in a truly alarming state, and a serious apprehension was entertained for some time that she had ruptured a blood-vessel in the paroxysm of her passion. When Mr. Spenser wrote, she was not entirely out of danger.

"Well," said Carry, "I am heartily glad they are rid of that odious woman, at all events; although I wish she had been provided for any where else in the world but in our neighborhood."

"She can do no great harm as post-mistress," said the curate.

When he walked into the town that same evening, and went to the post-office, among other places, he actually found the Peacocks installed, and Lucy transacting in person the business of that confidential department. She had only arrived the preceding day, and almost the first letter committed to her charge was that which Mr. Woodward had just written to Sydney, at college. After congratulating his old acquaintance upon her marriage and advancement—being extremely anxious about the subject of his correspondence, he was particular in his inquiries as to the hour of forwarding the mail, and strict in his injunctions to Lucy to take care to dispatch his letter by the earliest post. Perhaps this piqued the new post-mistress's curiosity, or perhaps she was impelled by her more general thirst for information;—be this as it might, the curate was no sooner gone than Lucy Peacock, putting the letter into her bosom, retired into a neat little bed-chamber, adjoining the office, bolted the door, lighted a taper, and very cleverly slipping the heated blade of a small pen-knife under the wax of the seal, raised it daintily from the paper, and made herself rapidly acquainted with every syllable of the dispatch to Cambridge. This done, she heated the knife again, nicely melted the under surface of the seal, and brought the edges of the paper again into contact with an adroitness that would have been wonderful if this had been her first attempt of the kind; which it probably was not. This delicate little proceeding having been taken, the new post-mistress deposited the letter in the bag with the strictest probity, and went about her household arrangements. She had a small, but neat and cheerful suite of apartments, which she tastefully decorated with all the little nicknacks, gimcracks, and articles of cheap *vertu* which she had accumulated in the days of her governess-ship. Over the mantle-piece of her "drawing-room" she hung up, in seemly order, her gallery of exemplary men and pattern women, to which she had made some nice additions in Dublin; and, on the shelves of a very gay glass-case, she displayed all the pretty books of her own property, with several to which her right might have been fairly disputed, particularly by members of the Spenser family.

---

/ CHAPTER LI.

⅂ :⸝ DAWSON IN PARLIAMENT.

"Master Robert Shallow, choose what office thou wilt in the land, 'tis thine. Pistol, I will double-charge thee with dignities."

SECOND PART OF KING HENRY IV.

IF the curate's first letter to his nephew did

not much alarm him, the second had more success. It found Sydney occupied with neither

" Wit, eloquence, or poetry,
Or search of deep philosophy,"

but carousing in a circle of young debauchees of his own age, whom he was treating to wine, fruits, and ices, and enchanting with his Irish melodies and mimicries, comic songs and stories, some of which he sang and told as cleverly as Mr. Lover. Never had greater folly been committed than to launch a youth like Sydney Spenser, without studious habits or tastes, without the ballast of principle or judgment, upon the dangerous sea of an English university. He scarcely made a week's stand against the multitudinous seductions of the place. Accustomed not merely to the gratification of his senses, but to the practice of many little clandestine and unworthy arts to procure the means of self-indulgence, he arrived at Cambridge in a high state of preparation for a course of extravagance and sensuality; and if Science and Literature found him a slow scholar, Vice and Folly, on the contrary, had no cause to be dissatisfied with his progress. The progress from dissipation to debt, and from debt to dishonor, has too often been related to need reiteration here. It is enough to say, that Sydney Spenser found the road to ruin as free from obstructions, as broad, smooth, flowery, and inviting as any young man who ever traveled it. It was easier to raise a hundred pounds at Cambridge than it had been to raise ten in the county of Donegal. At Redcross, the position and means of his father were known to every body, and besides, the shop-keepers were too poor themselves to give long or considerable credits; but on the banks of the Cam it was quite different. Instead of soliciting credit from the tradesmen, the tradesmen solicited him to become their debtor; and such was the current impression as to the wealth of the Irish Church, that directly it was known that Sydney was the son of a beneficed clergyman, there was scarcely an amount to which the tailors, hatters, confectioners, and fruiterers would not have accommodated him; and, what was more, there was no so monstrous price for their goods, or no usury on the sums of money they supplied him with, which they did not think it perfectly fair to impose. It was only to be wondered at, considering all this, that his involvements at the present period were not greater than they actually were; what they did amount to, he himself had no notion, but had all the demands of his Cambridge creditors been totted up, and his various debts of honor added to them, five hundred pounds would not have cleared off the score, even after a smart taxation, and he had not yet been six full months a pupil of the excellent Mr. Peters.

Sydney had not seen Dawson for some time, but on receiving the letters from his uncle, he determined to go up to London, seeing by the newspapers that there was a call of the house, which would probably bring together the scattered elements of the council of the nation. But it was necessary to write to his uncle before he left Cambridge, and again he might have redeemed himself by frankly stating the truth upon both the points that so urgently required elucidation—the hand from which he had got the bank-note, and the way in which he had lost the pistol. He persisted, however, in the same course of infatuated insincerity; declared that it was utterly out of his power to say, after so long an interval, from whom he had received a particular sum of money; and with respect to the pistol, he made a careless statement, partly true and partly false, namely, that he had lost a brace of pocket-pistols about the time in question, that it was possible they might have fallen into bad hands, but he suspected there must be some mistake about the identity of the pistol found last summer by Markham and his uncle, as he had not recognized it at the time. So much of Sydney's letter was lamentably defective in truth and good sense; but the scorn and indignation with which he repelled the monstrous charge which his base slanderers at Redcross seemed disposed to fix upon him, were perfectly sincere, and exactly in the tone to be expected from the son of a gentleman accused of a crime so inexpressibly heinous. He concluded by saying, that, though he thought it right to reply to questions put to him by his relatives, yet he would not stoop to vindicate himself in any other quarter; the enormity of the imputation was an answer to itself, and he would take no further notice of it except with one of his uncle's clubs, or with another pair of pistols which he fortunately had still in his possession.

Dawson was at the Burlington, confounding night and day as usual, legislating, drinking, jobbing, gaming, leading a life of miscellaneous profligacy between clubs, committees, taverns, and billiard-tables. There is always a little knot of lawgivers who live in this sort of way during the session, call it parliamentary life, and make a great merit of sacrificing in the public service the health and strength which they really squander in disgracing the legislature, not in performing its duties.

Sydney called at the Burlington at twelve o'clock on the day of his arrival in town. Mr. Dawson had not been long in bed; he generally breakfasted at three in the afternoon. Sydney called again at four. Mr. Dawson had gone down to the house, leaving a line for Sydney on a card, requesting him to follow and send his name by the door-keepers.

Who ever forgot his first impressions of the lobby of the House of Commons? It seemed at first sight to Sydney merely a dim, dirty, noisy room, crowded with people, either passing to and fro in several directions, or standing chatting in groups. The first intimation he had that there was any regularity in its seeming confusion, was a civil but peremptory order to stand back, given him by a stout, short, elderly man in a plain black suit. Sydney perceived a baton in his hand, and thence inferred that the elderly man was a constable, and not the Speaker. His next discovery was, that there was one leading thoroughfare in the apartment, between two rows of wooden pillars. There was a double door at the far end, continually opening and shutting, and revealing, when it opened, momentary glimpses of a hall, lighted with gilt chandeliers, and not very unlike a parish church. Now and then Sydney thought he saw a personage at the upper extremity in a big wig, who might have stood for the rector, while a couple of lesser wigs beneath him represented the curate's assistant. Incomprehensible things were going on at the door. In the first place there were posted there, one upon each side, two men in complete black suits, with white heads, very red faces, and an alternate gentleness and fierceness of aspect and demeanor which seemed as difficult to understand as the British constitution itself. Sometimes these mysterious red-faced men bowed to the ground, and seemed all blandness and servility. Then, again, they seemed to wax suddenly ferocious, and sometimes even flew like bull-dogs at gentlemen who approached them, though in many instances of much less questionable exterior than those upon whom they fawned. Repeatedly people stepped up to them, and with the utmost humility presented them with cards or papers, which sometimes they superciliously received, and then anon contemptuously spurned. This looked almost as if they were two of his Majesty's principal Secretaries of State; but then the deference they were seen to pay the next moment to shabby fellows, not half so well dressed as themselves, negatived that supposition, and left their functions still a conundrum. While he was trying to solve, and on the point of asking some of the bystanders to solve it for him, he spied Mr. Trundle not far off, still carrying his roll, now nearly as thick as himself, so easy is it to get millions of signatures to any document, no matter how preposterous its contents. Trundle, however, was probably the honestest man in the lobby, for he was seeking nothing for himself, only a modest thirty millions of money for the drainage of Loch Swilly. Sydney watched his movements with interest. He was pressing forward with vigor, as fast as he could with his burden, and had just gained a position within about a yard of the door, when the two red-faced men sprang at him simultaneously, which was the first circumstance that seemed clearly to establish their janitorial functions. Poor Mr. Trundle was good-humor itself, and being also supported by his patriotic enthusiasm, he was returning to the charge, when the valves of the door were opened from the inside; a gentleman walked rapidly out—"Lord ——"—"one of the ministers"—ran through the crowd; the red-faced men did homage as he passed, and Mr. Trundle rushed, or rather rolled, after him. This was highly amusing to Sydney; but there was more diversion in store for him, for Mr. Connolly, the droll attorney, whom the reader has already seen in the waiting-room of Dublin Castle, was one of the throng, and was keeping, as usual, every body near him in roars of laughter, by the never-ceasing flow of his fun, anecdote, and shrewd remarks upon men and things. Connolly, however, had his eyes bent upon the door like others, and at length approached it. He was put back. After some interval, he tried it again, but again was repulsed. A third time, and one of the fierce men with red faces ran at him as he had done before at Mr. Trundle, and Sydney heard him say—

"You must stand back, sir; you are not a member of the house."

"Thank ye for the information," retorted Connolly, with humorous composure, and undauntedly regarding the gruff official; "but if I'm not a member of the house at this present moment, may-be it won't be so some of those days, and the first motion I'll make, my fine fellow, after taking my sate, will be that you and your colleague opposite shall wear red plush inexpressibles."

A burst of laughter followed this sally, particularly from Connolly's countrymen, who were present in great force, and most of whom had, doubtless, received what they considered affronts from the fiery officials at the door, which were now handsomely avenged by the disparaging speech of the humorous attorney. But the wrath of the red-faced man in black was not to be described; dreadful deeds would have been done, as Homer says, and Connolly might have been committed to the coal-hole for his audacity, had not the scene instantly changed.

The door of the house was suddenly flung open, and poured forth an impetuous tide of senators, flying from a speech of Sir Andrew Agnew, or some other dinner-bell, and the Urquharts and Ansteys of the period. Foremost in the rout was Dawson; he spied and seized Sydney by the arm, and carried him away to Bellamy's.

Sydney spoke during dinner of what was uppermost in his mind, the annoying news he had received from Ireland. Dawson treated the matter with the utmost levity and contempt, and advised his friend to do so too.

"I have always through life, my dear fellow," said Dudley, "made it a rule to stand on my character; it's the best way, rely upon it; never defend yourself against the charges of a rascal; thrash him, or kick him, if you like, but give him no other answer."

"But one can't thrash cobblers and tinkers," said Sydney. "I only wish a *gentleman* would impeach my honor."

"You are very well off, I think," said Dawson, "to have your honor only impeached by cobblers and tinkers."

"I shall never be at ease," said Spenser talking in the lowest possible tone of voice that could be heard by his friend, "until the fellows are found out who committed the robbery. For my part, I can not but strongly suspect the men who were at Castle Dawson that day at dinner."

He then informed Dawson that he had positively received from Thomson, in settlement of the account of the whist-table, the five-pound note which he had paid over to his father's sexton. Dawson said it was very strange, and quite possible that Sydney might be right.

"Did you ever see him since?" Sydney inquired.

Dawson said he had not, and thought he would scarcely recognize, were he to meet him.

The conversation then changed. Dawson was dull and abstracted, as usual, until the wine operated; he drank port freely, and grew more parliamentary and patronizing at every glass. He began by talking in a strain of indignation of the scandalous exclusion of Irishmen from high offices in the government.

"I don't care for salary," he said, "but I care for place, and place I'm resolved to have. I want to be able to advance my friends, and first of all yourself, my dear fellow; I pledge you my word of honor as a gentleman you shall be my first object."

They drank more wine, and Dawson next requested Sydney to say what he would like to have; from what branch of the public service

he would like to have a thousand a year or so dropping into his mouth.

Sydney's eyes glistened, as he answered that he would count himself a lucky fellow to have such a salary in any department of the state. He thought of his debts at Cambridge, and how pleasant it would be to pay them off out of the public purse. Then he inquired what office his liberal friend proposed to fill himself.

"Men generally begin with the Treasury," said Dawson; but after another pint of port, he was disposed to think that he might possibly, in certain contingencies, and with particular stipulations, be prevailed on to accept a situation abroad, but nothing under the government of a colony, or an island.

"In such an event," he added, now overflowing with generosity and friendship, "what would you think, my dear fellow, of going out with me as my secretary?"

Sydney had no time to answer this serious question, for immediately a bell rang loud and sharply; Dawson jumped up; the house was going to divide, and every one flew to his place.

"Breakfast at one to-morrow," said Dawson, shaking the astonished Sydney by the hand, and flying with the rest.

Between the unusual noise and bustle, the port wine, and the visions of place and power which his parliamentary friend had filled his mind with, Sydney's brain was now seething like a kettle; his eyes were beginning to swim; he felt feverish, and the cool air of the streets was an agreeable relief. He wandered about for some time, and then feeling drowsy, returned to his hotel, threw himself on a sofa in the coffee-room, and slept for more than two hours. He then rose, and seeing that it was only eleven o'clock, he went out again, intending to drop into one of the minor theaters, to see John Reeve or Liston. Liston was then killing the public with laughter at the Olympic, and Sydney, having ascertained this from the bills, proceeded there to lay in a fresh stock of fun for his boon-companions at Cambridge. Several people of both sexes were loitering about the piazzas, as usual. Two men stood so close to the door that he had to brush close by them in order to enter the house; a stream of light from a lamp fell directly on the face of one of them. Sydney's memory for faces was good; he thought he recognized the ghastly features of Mr. Thomson, and a second glance assured him that his conjecture was right. Instead of entering the theater, he now withdrew to some little distance under the vestibule, undecided whether to accost his suspicious acquaintance, or only watch his movements. He had not been debating this point with himself for three minutes, when a cab drove up within a couple of yards from where he stood. A gentleman jumped out; it was Dawson, and Sydney was just running up to him, when he was anticipated by the man he had been observing. Sydney was amazed. Only two or three hours ago his friend Dudley had stated that he had never seen Mr. Thomson since last summer, that he scarcely recalled his features, and now he saw him shake him by the hand, and they walked away together immediately in close conference toward the Strand.

Sydney neither kept his appointment with Dawson the following morning, nor sent him any message or communication. When Dawson inquired about him at the Union Hotel, he was informed that he had left town by a morning coach for Cambridge.

Dawson wrote to him at the University, but received no answer. Sydney had started for Ireland.

## CHAPTER LII.

### THE CURATE IN TOWN.

"A poor man, sir, in point of gold and silver; he has not land enough to serve him for a grave, but he has a treasury of worth in his heart, and will travel round the globe barefoot, to be at the side of a friend in need."

NEW PLAY.

THE vindictive Mrs. Peacock was not long in turning to account the information she had picked out of the curate's letter. Lucy had an old flirtation with the sub-editor of the *Tyrconnell Mercury*, a certain sentimental Mr. O'Dowd, whom she had once even thought of marrying, but was deterred by the name, which she did not think a pretty or imposing one. Through her influence with this literary gentleman she procured the insertion of the following piquant little paragraph in the journal with which he was connected :—

"Strange reports are current on the subject of the robbery committed last summer on the proctor of a well-known clergyman in this county. A small pistol, of exquisite workmanship, is said to have been found on the spot where the crime was perpetrated, which will probably lead to the detection of the guilty parties. In the mean time we deliberately suspend our opinion; but it would seem highly improbable that such a pistol could have been in the possession of any person under the rank of a gentleman."

The pain which these few lines gave the Woodwards was intense. They tried in vain to conjecture how the fact alluded to could have become known to the conductors of the *Mercury*, and were apprehensive that Markham had not been sufficiently reserved upon the subject. Mr. Spenser, when he saw the paragraph, wrote instantly to his brother-in-law, being naturally curious to learn what the reports were to which allusion was made. Hercules and Carry consulted together, and the result of their deliberations was, that Hercules resolved on a journey to Dublin. The old portmanteau was again compelled to yield up the extraordinary miscellany of odds and ends of which it was the depository when off regular duty, and Carry packed it herself with the curate's Sunday suit, and put in his gown and cassock, in case he should be invited to preach some charity sermon.

The rector, indeed, never was more in want of the presence and support of his strenuous friend. His wife's illness had assumed a dangerous aspect; and on the very day of the curate's arrival in town, Mr. Spenser received his first intimation, in a letter from Mr. Peters, of the career of extravagance which his son had been running at college.

The letter coolly stated that the debts, on the whole, did not probably exceed six hundred pounds, and the writer excused himself for not having made a very minute inquiry, on the ground that he was then deeply absorbed in some abstruse mathematical researches. Six hundred pounds was more than one-half of Mr. Spenser's income, and he had already, as we have seen, contracted a debt of five hundred, to meet the expenses consequent upon his removal to town. Dearly was he now beginning to pay the inevitable penalty of his conjugal facility and his parental *insouciance*.

The critical situation of Mrs. Spenser had already recalled Elizabeth to town. How lovingly she flew to welcome her uncle, when, totally unexpected, he entered the drawing-room; how tenderly the huge good man returned her affectionate embraces. Mr. Spenser was in his wife's room. Elizabeth saw anxiety on Mr. Woodward's forehead, and concluded that he, too, had heard the untoward news of Sydney, and had good-naturedly come up to cheer and advise her father. Mr. Spenser appeared in a few moments. Each saw dejection in the visage of the other, and each ascribed it to the cause of uneasiness with which he was acquainted. It was not until Elizabeth retired that they mutually discovered that there were two sources of trouble instead of one, and that Sydney was concerned equally in both.

But Mr. Woodward was more deeply affected by the information his brother-in-law communicated, than the latter was by the business which brought the curate to Dublin. Mr. Spenser thought that the curate was frightening himself with a bugbear in attaching so much weight to the gossip of idle and malicious tongues of Redcross.

"This is one of those accusations, Hercules," said the rector, "which would require the most positive and direct evidence to support it. What the boy states in his letter you is no doubt the simple truth. Besides, no human being in his senses would ever suppose that the paragraph in the *Mercury* could possibly refer to Sydney. I heartily wish his follies were as visionary as his crimes. His debts are unfortunately only too real."

"How will you meet them, Val. ?"

The rector looked profoundly melancholy, but made no answer, and Hercules did not allude to the subject again. On the other point, too, he said as little as possible, trying to persuade himself that his brother-in-law took the right view of it, and unwilling to add to the cares of a man who had care enough on his mind already. In conversation with Elizabeth he never alluded to either subject; she had not as yet a notion of the suspicions afloat to her brother's prejudice, and as to the newspaper paragraph, she fancied that it was aimed at Dawson.

It was fine weather, and as Mrs. Spenser repelled the attentions of her niece, and preferred to be waited on by a hired nurse-tender, Elizabeth was her uncle's constant companion during his stay in Dublin; they perambulated the town a good deal together, and much speculation they caused in the fashionable thoroughfares. The tall, uncouth, formidable man in clerical attire, with that refined and handsome girl hanging on his arm, looking so ill-assorted, and yet perfectly well-pleased with her rough companion, like the fair maiden in romance under the escort and patronage of the lion. Every body saw that Hercules was a country clergyman, at most a rural dean; and it was a question whether Elizabeth was his daughter or his wife, though it was difficult to conceive how she could be connected with him in either or in any way.

The Dabzacs were now in town, having taken a house for the season, not far from where the Spensers resided. Mrs. Dabzac called almost every day to inquire for her step-mother, and sometimes dropped in for a moment to see her father or Elizabeth : but it was only a moment, for she was always on her way to some gay scene, a *déjeuner*, a concert, or a flower-show; or Lady Brabble was in her carriage, or she expected Lord and Lady Western to lunch. Then the curate saw her name daily in the news-papers, in the accounts of drawing-rooms, balls, dinners, in short, all the festive doings of the Dublin world, and he thought it strange that a daughter should lead such a life, while her father was in so much trouble. But Elizabeth made twenty excuses for her sister, and often reminded her uncle that Arabella was not long married, and that her husband was not the sort of man to forego his social enjoyments because his wife's step-mother was indisposed. Hercules met Mrs. Dabzac only once. Elizabeth took him with her to pay a visit of civility, which he was the more particular to do, as he had been so ill-used at the wedding. A chariot, with a lady in it, was standing at the door, which opened almost directly Mr. Woodward knocked, and Mrs. Dabzac appeared at the same moment, tripping down stairs, superbly dressed, and thinking of any thing but her rural relations. She uttered an exclamation of unaffected surprise, but feigned and ill-feigned pleasure, and received her uncle the curate with her habitual cold simper, only giving him two of her fingers, to save her gloves from being violated, and pouring out a torrent of frigid nothings, partly addressed to him and partly to her sister, while at the same time she kept beckoning to her friend in the carriage, as much as to say, "what a bore!—what a *contre-tems!*" She kindly offered, however, to return to the drawing-room, and have "a long chat about old times" with her unwelcome visitors ; which they, of course, would not hear of; and they also declined to go into the parlor, where there was luncheon, as they had lunched before. So far Hercules acted perfectly to the satisfaction of his heartless niece, but he spoiled all by insisting on handing her into the chariot. It certainly made an amusing scene. A group of Mrs. Dabzac's gayest acquaintance were passing, and two superfine men of a hussar regiment also rode up at the moment, so that poor Hercules found himself suddenly surrounded by a set of people who looked at him as if he was an orang-outang ; and as to Mrs. Dabzac, she could not have felt or looked more ashamed of her uncle, had he actually been an animal of that species.

The next day the cards of Colonel and Mrs. Dabzac were left for Mr. Woodward, and also an affectionate note, in which his niece proved to a demonstration, by a list of her engagements, that it was out of her power to have her uncle to dinner any day for the next week, but trusted she would see a great deal of him on his next visit to Dublin, or perhaps at Dabzac House in the course of the summer. The only remark Hercules made upon this (whatever he may have

thought of it) was that "it was no time for dining out." Nor indeed was it, at least for people like himself and Elizabeth, for not only was Mrs. Spenser sinking apace (having, in addition to her regular train of maladies, been attacked by an epidemic then raging in Dublin), but Lady Bonham was declining also. Elizabeth knew that her friend would gladly receive a visit from such a man as her uncle, and Hercules was always ready to go to the house of mourning. He held a long private conversation with the declining lady, and when he rejoined his niece in another apartment, he found her alone and in tears. She had seen Lord Bonham, and had heard from his own lips that the physicians had abandoned all hopes of their patient. Elizabeth wept again upon her uncle's shoulder as she told him the cause of her sorrow. "She deserves those tears," he said, as he comforted her and shed one or two himself ; "she is a noble crea-u e, Lizzy ; she is fit to live and she is fit to die."

The next day was Sunday. It was Mr. Spenser's turn to preach at the Castle Chapel, but at nine o'clock in the morning, his wife was pronounced in imminent danger, and the rector had no one to do the duty for him but his brother-in-law. It was a trying situation for the modest country parson to preach at a moment's notice in the presence of the court; Carry never dreamed of such an event, when she packed up his gown and cassock; but Hercules acquitted himself well, and his robust style and fervent manner attracted the gracious attention of the excellent viceroy himself. When he retired to lay aside his sacred garments, an aid-de-camp was announced, and was in the act of inviting the astonished curate to dine with the lord-lieutenant, when a hurried note from his niece was put into his hand—Mrs. Spenser was no more.

At the same hour, and perhaps the same moment, Mrs. Woodward, having just returned from church, was in her dressing-room at the parsonage, when she was startled by the abrupt appearance of Sydney Spenser. His agitated looks, his disordered dress his excited manner, frightened her. She sharply scrutinized his features, holding him at a little distance ere she embraced him, but the scrutiny was satisfactory; she found alarm there and indignation, but no guilt. He understood the meaning of her eye, and said, with a scornful smile—

"No, aunt Carry, I am not an highwayman."

"You did well to come over," she answered, sitting down on a sofa to recover herself, and motioning Sydney to sit beside her.

"Where is my uncle?" he asked.

"In Dublin."

"Then I shall not stay here an hour; I must see and consult with uncle Hercules without loss of time."

Carry approved of his resolution, but was naturally anxious to have from his own lips an account of the circumstances which had awakened suspicion, not doubting but that, when related by him, they would make the groundlessness of the charge as plain as the light of the day. But he had not gone far in his story before she clearly perceived that he was not making a clean breast; that he was concealing some things and varying in his statement of others. In truth he was driven to and fro between his

suspicions of Dawson, and his reluctance to implicate a man whose spell was still upon him,
and of whose power to injure or to serve him he
entertained an habitually exaggerated notion.
i Those doublings and falterings alarmed Mrs.
Woodward more than she had been alarmed yet.

"Sydney," she exclaimed, with passionate
emotion, "you are not adhering to the truth, even
with me, whom you can have no earthly object
in deceiving. Beware, I implore you—I warn
you—how you make your innocence look like
guilt by unavailing concealments, dictated, I am
convinced, either by false shame, or by your
desire to screen somebody, I know not whom.
Nobody will believe your guilty, if you do not
condemn yourself by acting the part of guilt."

Her feminine vehemence produced a sensible
effect. It was as if a Siddons had thus accosted
him. Carry pressed her success.

"I fear nothing," she said, "but your own want
of candor and directness. Sydney, I implore you,
as your near relative, as your true friend, as you
value your father's character, your sister's happiness, the respectability of your family, and
your own personal safety, do not tamper with
the truth. Frankly disclose every circumstance
connected with your visit to Castle Dawson
previous to the robbery; disclose them fully,
without considering what construction they may
bear, or what inference may be drawn from
them, and my life upon it, Sydney, you will come
out of this cloud without a shade of suspicion on
your character."

It was the advice of a wise woman, given
with a force of which only women of a certain
mettle are capable; Sydney walked about the
room and promised to act upon it.

"There may be circumstances," added Mrs.
Woodward more calmly—indeed she had fatigued herself with the foregoing appeal, and was
now reclining upon the couch were she had just
been sitting so erect and commanding—"there
may be circumstances which to me you may not
think it necessary or proper to reveal; but in
the name of heaven, my dear boy, conceal nothing from your uncle; put him in possession
of the whole truth, from the first to the last, and
remember, spare no false friends at the expense
of your true ones—you well know my meaning."

So saying, she rose, hastily adjusted her hair,
which had fallen into disorder in the agitation
of the scene, and took her nephew down to the
dining-room, where she prevailed upon him to
take some refreshment before he returned to
Redcross.

She embraced him and kissed him at parting
with the affectionate fervor of a mother, and now
for the first time remarked the improvement in
his personal appearance. If Cambridge had not
moralized and intellectualized, it had mannered
and dressed him. He looked like a gentleman,
though a foppish one, not like Dudley Dawson
any longer. The flash coat, the gaudy cravat,
and the check shirt had disappeared. His coat
was the work of a Bond street artist, his boots
the handy-work of Hoby. They were not paid
for, but they looked none the less handsome and
well made on that account.

Very little now passed at Redcross that escaped the piercing eyes of the new postmaster's
wife, or lady, as he called her. She was up
early and late, people that are so see twice as

much as sluggards and snoozers do; at least
Lucy did. However, it was not very suprising
that Sydney's arrival and departure were not
unknown to her, for at least twenty pair of eyes
saw him as well as Mrs. Peacock's.

"There's something mysterious in it," said
the sexton's slut of a wife, shrugging her broad
shoulders at her shop-door, and alternately disclosing them to view, her draperies were so
loose and classical.

"It's above my comprehension," said the tobacconist's spouse next-door, taking a curl-paper
from her head, to wrap up a penny-worth of
snuff for old Randy Maguire.

"Randy knows more anent it than he likes to
let on," said Farmer M'Swyne, the knight of
the thistle, who had come into town to sell a slip
of a pig, and discourse about the weather with
the idlers in the market-place.

"Then I just know as much as your own self,
Sir Roger," said old Randy.

There was a laugh at the farmer's expense,
so he went up the street with his slip of a pig,
which was making as great an uproar, and with
as little meaning in it, as if he had been the
leading politician of the place.

The sexton's wife and the tobacconist's lady
prolonged their gossip at the shop-door, until it
was time for tea, when the former invited the
latter to share that repast with her; and the
sexton coming home soon after, accompanied
by the proctor, the four of them sat down to a
game of cards, which they enjoyed exceedingly,
while on the kettle on the hearth performed a
sprightly overture to a supper of punch and
oysters.

----

## CHAPTER LIII.

### THE REWARD.

" *Plutus.*  What!—I!—can I do such mighty matters ?
" *Chremes.* Can you ?  Ay, by Jupiter, and many more,
too, for no man ever had his fill of thee.  Of all other,
things we may be surfeited, even of love ; of you never."
ARISTOPHANES.

SYDNEY arrived in Dublin at an early hour on
the day but one after his sudden appearance at
Redcross. On reaching the street where his
aunt had informed him that his father lived, he
found the thoroughfare obstructed by the mournful preparations for a funeral. If there was
'sorrow, it was not a silent one. There seemed
to be no mutes assisting at the ceremony.
There was a crowd assembled, and a great
bustle among coachmen, footmen, and the regular standing army of the horseboys, beggars,
and idlers of the quarter. The undertakers',
men were distributing, and the servants were
wrangling for those trappings of mock distress,
called scarfs and hat-bands, a custom introduced into Ireland by way of encouraging the
linen manufacture. Sydney had never before
had an opportunity of observing the details of a
funeral as it is managed in the Irish capital,
and he stopped to observe what went on. The
black hearse, waved over by black plumes, and
drawn by large black horses, led by grooms in
sable livery, stood at an open door, thronged
with faces of which few were even grave.
Behind the bier was a train of some half-dozen
carriages, two evidently belonging to the funeral
state, for like the hearse they were black, and

drawn by horses of the same color. The other carriages were private ones; two looked like those of the physicians who had either accelerated or failed to defeat the triumph of disease and death. The windows of the upper apartments of the opposite and adjoining houses were thrown up, and curious cooks and excited housemaids were eagerly gazing down upon the obstreporous scene, as if they had never seen black plumes and white scarfs before. Sydney, with his fondness for coarse humor, could not but enjoy, as he could not but hear, the singular mixture of drollery and pathos which characterizes the dialogue of the lower classes in Ireland. While he stood listening, a stir took place in the throng; the people gave way upon each side as the coffin was borne out. For a moment the crowd was still. The chief mourners followed. Sydney marked them as they issued from the door, and notwithstanding their downcast heads, and the sable mantles that enveloped their persons, he recognized his father and his uncle.

The truth immediately suggested itself, for he had heard from Mrs. Woodward of the dangerous illness of his step-mother.

But one servant remained in his father's house after the funeral had slowly moved away. Sydney asked for his sister; she had been removed the day before to the house of her friends, the Ramsdens. He obtained the direction, and hurried to find her. It was now about ten o'clock, and the streets were beginning to look lively, if not business-like. Those strange, uncouth, wild, convenient and inconvenient vehicles, the jaunting-cars, drawn by wild horses and driven by wild men, were beginning to career about the town, obeying no law, human or divine, reckless of the lives and limbs of the passengers, the most of whom, indeed, seemed reckless of their own carcases, for they preferred the middle of the street to the trottoirs, and when any of the Celtic charioteers, having a drop of the milk of human kindness left, raised a shout of warning to his probable victims, as he drove a muck among them, the fellow warned either doggedly despised the caution, or profited by it with a savage execration.

As Sydney was walking rapidly along, rather closer than was prudent to the edge of the pavé one of those unsightly conveniences came sweeping down, the driver on one side yelling to the populace, a passenger on the other swearing at the driver, and the intermediate space crowded and piled with portmanteaus and traveling-bags. Sydney recoiled to save his knees from collision with the iron steps of the vehicle, and at the same moment meeting the eye of the passenger, discovered that it was his honorable friend, the member for Rottenham.

Dawson instantly jumped off, and Sydney's hand was in his grasp before he could agree or disagree to be so embraced. They stood before the hotel where Dawson was in the habit of staying when in Dublin.

"You are cold to me," said Dudley: "how have I offended you?"

The question was not hypocritical. Dawson was really ignorant what offense he had given to young Spenser, who returned some gruff reply, but with an agitation which the other did not fail to notice and take advantage of. He spoke in his most soothing tones, merely inviting Sydney to step into the hotel, and candidly state what he complained of. To so much Dawson was fairly entitled, and Sydney accompanied him into the house, where the senator, being well known, was speedily accommodated with a private room.

"Breakfast for two," he said to the waiter, as coolly as if nothing had happened to vary his relations with young Spenser.

Sydney's bolt was soon shot. He charged his friend Dudley with playing him false respecting his acquaintanceship with Mr. Thomson. Dawson winced under the charge visibly, if Sydney had been collected enough to mark it, but he was over-excited, and at no time very observant. Dawson, however, recovered himself instantly, burst into an affected laugh, and exclaimed—

"Well, they are strikingly like one another; I am not in the least astonished at your mistake, ludicrous as it is. Why, man, the fellow you took for Thomson was a reporter of the Morning Chronicle; I had an assignation with him, certainly, and I'll tell you for what, to correct his report of my speech that night on the state of the country."

Sydney remarked that the piazza of the Olympic was an odd place for an appointment with a reporter.

"Quite the contrary," said Dawson, "the office of the Morning Chronicle is in the Strand, you know, hard by."

"And did you speak that night?" continued Sydney, fancying that he was cross-examining his friend very acutely.

Dawson rang the bell.

"Did I, indeed?" he replied, triumphantly; "the Tories know whether I spoke or not. I made a speech, and, what's more, it was a hit, my boy; why, I spoke for one hour and twenty minutes. Sheil only spoke for half an hour, and O'Connell was not on his legs much longer. Waiter, bring me the file of the Morning Chronicle. You shall read my speech, corrected by myself from the report of the very fellow you took for Thomson."

"I see I was mistaken," said Sydney completely hood-winked, "but he was extremely like Thomson, Dudley."

The waiter re-appeared with the file, followed by another with breakfast. Sydney then had to listen to two mortal columns of that species of declamation of which the imperial House of Commons has such a lively horror, but which, it is to be presumed, would rank in an Irish one with the speeches of Cicero, or above them. It was a proper punishment for young Spenser's simplicity. Had he even examined the dates, he would have detected the imposition.

Thus was the misplaced confidence once more re-established, and the fatal ascendency once more restored. Sydney breakfasted with Dawson, who seemed profoundly affected by the account of Mrs. Spenser's death (much more, indeed than Sydney himself), and made several touching remarks about the precariousness of earthly things. Then they separated for the morning, after an appointment to meet again at a later hour in the day.

Sydney and Elizabeth met. Elizabeth was in the deepest grief, not for the loss of a step-moth-

I

er, in whom she had never had so much as a friend, but for the sorrow in which the event had plunged her father. But she little knew the extent of his distress that melancholy morning. The rector confessed to Hercules, as they returned together in one of the gloomy carriages, after the performance of the funeral rites, that he had no means of paying off his son's debts and his own (the latter now amounting to a large sum) but by a sequestration of his living and the sale of of his furniture, and even his books.

"Not the books—not the books, Val.," said the good curate, his eye moist and his voice tremulous with sympathy; "we won't let the books go, come what will."

"Hercules, I ought to have taken your advice respecting that boy," said the rector.

"You acted for the best," said Woodward. Such was the short sad conversation of the mourning coach.

They reached the silent house and entered it unnoticed. The rector buried himself in the inmost chamber, and Hercules went to make arrangements for the immediate return of the family to the country. Elizabeth hastened to her father's side, and informed him of Sydney's arrival. Mr. Spenser declined to see his son, and sent him a message by his uncle, conveying his desire that he should go to his sister, Mrs. Dabzac (who had gone down a few days before to her country seat in the north), and remain under her roof for the present. Uncle and nephew met. Dawson had regained his dangerous influence upon Sydney since the latter had conversed with his aunt at the parsonage, and all Carry's wise and eloquent advice might as well have been given to the winds. To such an extent, indeed, did the misguided young man now waver in his statements, and equivocate in his replies to the questions put to him, that he actually forced upon his uncle the terrifying conclusion that to some extent or another he was not unimplicated in the crime. All unhappiness about his nephew's debts disappeared from the mind of Hercules directly the idea of his guilt entered it. It was not without some difficulty that he brought himself to suggest a course which he had been turning in his mind for some time, namely, the expediency of offering a large reward for the discovery of the person or persons who robbed Maguire.

But Sydney seized on the idea with alacrity. "Let my father offer five or six hundred pounds," he exclaimed, flippantly, as if the sum he named was a mere trifle.

He never forgot the tremendous look which his uncle gave him, as he passionately answered, "Five or six hundred pounds, ill-conditioned boy—that is about the amount you have squandered in six months in wine and gluttony, on horses and dogs, and your idle and unprincipled associates, reckless whence the money was to come to pay for your profligacy, never thinking what burdens you were heaping on the back of your father, what privations you were bringing on your good sister, what disgrace and misery on all your relations and connections! Five hundred pounds—you talk glibly of hundreds of pounds!"

Fiercely and impetuously delivered, this speech of Hercules amazed and overwhelmed his nephew: he quailed and cowered under every word

as if it had been a blow, twirling a foppish little cane round his finger, and looking extremely foolish.

Sydney was at a loss to divine how the news of his excesses had reached the ears of his family. He exclaimed, doggedly and at random, that his enemies exaggerated his wildnesses, as usual.

"No, sir," resumed his uncle. "I believe the exact contrary is the fact. Your enemies, indeed! Your enemy, sir, is yourself; and, let me tell you, you have a great fool and a great coxcomb for your enemy. Your tutor has inquired, and admits that your debts exceed six hundred pounds—some of them, no doubt, gambling debts—debts of honor, I understand you call them; and pray, sir, what do you call your debts to the poor shopkeepers at Redcross, to the widow Grogan, for example?"

"All this, sir, is beside the present question," said Sydney, with provoking hauteur, though almost livid at the same time with shame and vexation.

The curate was out of breath, and admitted that, to some extent, it was so.

"To return, then, sir, to the question of the reward," continued the nephew, with the supercilious air of one who has gained an advantage in argument, and slapping his refulgent boots impatiently.

"My opinion is," said the curate, despising his nephew too much to continue a dispute with him, "that the reward ought to be offered by the government."

"Of course, that would answer equally well," said Sydney.

There was no difficulty about it. Mr. Spenser, that same evening, addressed a note to a leading member of the Irish government, which Hercules the next day presented at the castle. It procured him an immediate interview, much to the surprise and envy of the throng in the anti-room, who had been making merry at the curate's expense, and marveling what he could be, or what he could be looking for, unless it was the office of chaplain to Newgate.

The following evening the *Dublin Gazette* announced that the lord-lieutenant would give a reward of three hundred pounds to any person who would prosecute, to conviction, the robbers of Mr. Spenser's proctor, and one hundred pounds to any body who would give such information as would lead to the discovery of the offenders. On the same evening a traveling-carriage drove up to Mr. Spenser's door, and the rector, his daughter, the curate, with the two children, stepped into it, and accomplished the usual first stage of the journey to Redcross.

Dawson heard of the reward first from Sydney. Sydney was dining with him, intending on the following day to go to Mrs. Dabzac's, should she be able to receive him, which he internally hoped she would not. Mr. Spenser had written to her before he left town, requesting her to send her answer to her brother directly. Dawson said the reward was a very proper step; he wondered it had not been thought of before; and then he asked Sydney to take wine.

"Bring some champagne," he cried to the waiter.

"Let it be well iced," added the luxurious young spendthrift, whose father's heart was at that moment breaking in a country inn, bitterly thinking of his benefice about to be mortgaged, and his library going to the hammer. But the iced champagne was drank—to be sure the senator was to pay for it—and after the champagne they drank a bottle of claret each, and then they went to the play. After the play they resorted, accompanied by two of Dawson's Dublin friends (Bob Sharkey was one of them), to a notorious house, where they smoked cigars, ate lobsters, and drank mulled port, Sydney objecting to punch, and paying for his supper with his celebrated mimicry of his uncle Hercules. With this amiable effort of genius that virtuous night closed, and the next morning Sydney found on his table the following tender epistle from his married sister:—

"Dabzac House, Tanderagee.

"MY DEAR SYDNEY—My feelings so completely overpower me, that I hardly know what I am writing, or whether I am writing or not. Oh, my poor, poor father! what he has gone through—what he has endured; but what a blessing it was to have Elizabeth with him, and my dear good uncle, and you, Sydney, who came over so providentially, just when he required every support. Oh, what would I not have given to have been with you all : but Colonel Dabzac would not hear of it, and two of the carriage-horses are laid up, so it was not to be; and I hope it is all for the better; I fear I should have broken down under such a trial. Oh, Sydney, let this be a warning to all of us. No one can tell whose turn it may be next to appear at the dread tribunal. Oh, that we may be all prepared. I am sure, my dear, dear Sydney, if your coming to us just now would be any relief or amusement to you, it would only make me too happy to have you with us, and it would gratify my husband, too, more than I can tell. The way we are situated is this :—Lord and Lady Western are here for the summer, I fear, and the odious Dalrymples ; then the assizes are coming on, and we are to have those stupid old judges, and the high sheriff, and half a dozen Dabzacs, as a matter of course ; I don't expect to survive it, I assure you ; but, my dear Sydney, if all this does not frighten you as it does me, do come down, I entreat ; indeed, I do so want somebody to support me ; I hardly dare promise you a bed, but you would put up with a sofa, I am sure, for the sake of being near me; and recollect, Sydney, you have not been my guest since I was married. Colonel Dabzac begs to join me in all I have said, and in condolences upon the late melancholy, but, I hope, instructive event.

"Your ever dear sister,
"ARABELLA DABZAC.

"To Sydney Spenser, Esq.
&c., &c., &c."

The truth was, that Mrs. Dabzac figured Sydney to herself as she had last seen him at her father's house, dressing, talking, laughing, blustering, and swaggering like Dudley Dawson; she had no idea how effectually the tailors of Cambridge had brushed up his exterior, and its society rubbed down his manners ; how the consciousness of owing large instead of paltry sums had quieted and dignified his bearing ; how familiar he had grown with expensive luxuries and fashionable occupations ; with the systems,

nomenclatures, and usages of the great world, or she would not have been ashamed to present her brother to Lord and Lady Western and the odious Dalrymples.

Sydney forwarded his sister's letter to his father, as his excuse for not going to Dabzac House ; but the rector had surely distress enough without the additional pang of a daughter's heartlessness.

---

## CHAPTER LIV.

### THE EXPLOSION.

"Oh, what was love made for, if 'tis not the same
Through joy and through sorrow, through glory, through
shame."                                           MOORE.

THE gold offered by the Castle operated quickly—only too quickly. Vivyan, returning from the Peninsula, found his Elizabeth the sister of a denounced criminal, and a fugitive from the hands of justice.

The curate, whose strong, keen eye was always on the watch under his beetling brows for opportunities of doing his fellow-creatures some service, or saving them from some harm (a faithful shepherd, if ever a flock had one), observed prowling about the neighborhood of Redcross, soon after his return home, a stranger whose features, at once profoundly melancholy and expressive of hardened guilt, exercised a painful fascination upon him. Once or twice he met him hanging about the post-office, and he asked Mrs. Peacock if she knew who he was, and what was his business in the town. She answered promptly that she believed he was a poor young artist, who had come down to sketch the scenery on the coast. This was plausible, but still Hercules kept his eye upon him, probably thinking that it was not the pencil which had drawn those deep lines in the stranger's cheeks, nor the fine arts which had given him that air of pensive profligacy. Upon one occasion it happened that the curate was walking with Mr. Spenser (the first day the poor rector had been prevailed on to take the air), when this remarkable yet mean personage crossed their path.

"Of what age would you take him to be ?" said Hercules.

"Young," said the rector ; "but age is not altogether measured by years."

"A young man and an old scoundrel, I should say," added the curate.

They re-entered the curate's house (for the Spensers had not returned to the parsonage, nor was it their intention to do so for some time), and sat down to a homely dinner. Time was when the homeliest dinner in that house was a happy one ; but now the faces were sad, and the voices spoke with effort. Mr. Spenser was mourning both as a husband and a father; Elizabeth had also her complicated grief; Carry's big heart was bursting with solicitude for them both ; and Hercules was all tenderness to every body in his own rugged, colossal way. Their sorrow at that moment resembled one of those somber masses of vapor that so often brooded in calm wet weather over the mountains of the region, mists which poured down steady rain, and involved every object in the landscape in dense but serene obscurity. How different was it after the blow which followed! In the course of that same evening, a gentleman with whom both Mr. Spenser and Mr. Woodward were slightly acquainted, a magistrate of the county, rode up to the gate of the court-yard. He solicited a private interview with the rector, who received him in the curate's study.

Thomson had that morning tendered informations on oath against Sydney Spenser.

It is almost unnecessary to state that the outrage had been actually committed by the two fellows who had been employed at Castle Dawson, in aiding and abetting its proprietor in a lawless proceeding of another character. We have seen that one of those fellows, Lamb, had already been sent out of the country; and Dawson would have gladly disposed of Thomson in the same way, but he was not successful in inducing him to expatriate himself. His last attempt had been on the late occasion, when Sydney had accidentally witnessed their meeting by night in London. Whether Thomson had followed Dawson over to Ireland, or had returned to that country in search of another job, is uncertain, but he was in Dublin when the reward was offered, and its first effect was to agitate and alarm him exceedingly, for he did not know what had become of his accomplice, and the lively faith he had in Lamb's villainy assured him that no time would be lost on his part in turning approver to clutch the money. Haunted by this well-founded apprehension, he accidentally met with Mr. Sharkey, his old employer, and from him he learned the fact that Lamb was gone to improve his fortunes and morality among the Yankees. How devoutly Thomson then wished that they had been a party of three at the Black Castle, that he might have somebody to transport and make three hundred pounds by. Brooding still on the money, he recollected that he had met a man on the night of the robbery, and near the scene of it, whose features he thought he would recall if he was to meet him again. Acting on this hint from the author of all roguery, he crept by tortuous ways to Redcross. He had personated an artist at Castle Dawson to blind Sydney Spenser, and he now resumed the same easily-supported character; it only required a portfolio, a scrap of chalk, and a few terms of art gleaned from a penny cyclopædia. Ned Grogan (the man who saw Sydney that night in the neighborhood of the old castle) had a narrow escape, for it was he who had been seen by Thomson, and whom the miscreant would infallibly have sacrificed, had he not been diverted from that scheme by accidentally falling in with his old acquaintance, Mrs. Peacock. Thomson had not been many days in the society of the unprincipled and revengeful Lucy, before he abandoned his designs against Grogan, and (having the benefit of all the information which the post-mistress had collected, not only from the gossip of the town, but from official sources) determined to fly at higher game. It was equal to him, of course, whether he earned the reward of the government, or extorted the money from Mr. Spenser; and it was probably in the latter way that he reckoned upon securing his object.

To Elizabeth there was nothing to break the shock occasioned by the explosion of this "infernal machine;" the other members of the family had been in some slight degree prepared, at least, as far as knowing that malicious people had for some time been making free with Sydney's character, and that there was a singular concurrence of circumstances to support a charge against him; but to his sister the first disclosure came in its last and most appalling shape; she fell with a harrowing shriek into Carry's arms, and Hercules carried her, almost lifeless, to her room.

That same night, at a late hour, a traveling-carriage arrived at the principal inn of the town. The handsome young man, browned by southern suns, who alighted from it, was Frank Vivyan. What fearful changes had taken place since he had been last in Redcross! But the saddest change of all was, that his return gave his Elizabeth no joy, but, on the contrary, made her sorrows more hard to bear.

He returned not to be a comforter, for dishonor admits of no solace; and alike incapable of performing the active offices of a friend, for the case seemed equally beyond the reach of friendship. He came back, too, in what a harrowing relation to herself! Elizabeth's share in the misfortune was the largest and bitterest of all.

Mrs. Woodward, knowing the force of her niece's character perfectly, was fully prepared for the determination to which she came in the first moment of recovered self-possession—to cancel her engagement to Vivyan. Mrs. Woodward communicated this inevitable result to the miserable young man before Elizabeth had directly alluded to the subject. In fact, so clearly did the noble-minded girl see the path which duty and high-minded love pointed out to her—so plain did the road to be taken lie before her, shining in the bright sun of honor—that her resolution to tread it was rather implied that expressed in her conversation, and Carry was not slower to divine, than her niece was to form a right and high-souled purpose.

Vivyan, on his side, would have thought himself the blackest and most heartless traitor, had any guilt of Sydney's, whatever its amount, or how clear soever its demonstration, led him for one moment to waver in his devotion to Elizabeth. Some days elapsed before she was strong enough to support the severe trial of an interview with him. These days were passed by Vivyan in no company but that of Mrs. Woodward, for the rector and his brother-in-law had gone up to Dublin to be directed by professional advice as to the conduct to be pursued with respect to their son and nephew. Vivyan never doubted Sydney's innocence for a moment. Every circumstance attending the charge seemed a complete answer to it—the nature of the accusation—the position of the accused—he might well have added the character of the accuser, as well as his personal appearance, had he been acquainted with either. All these topics were urged by Vivyan over and over again in long interviews with Mrs. Woodward.

"But, as to myself and Elizabeth," he repeatedly added, "let the issue of this unfortunate business be what it may, it does not alter our affections, and it can not and must not prevent our union."

"Cherish no such hope, I implore you, Mr. Vivyan," replied Mrs. Woodward, who was already beginning to show in her cheek, and her diminished figure, the outward signs of sorrow and anxiety—"Elizabeth's love is too pure, too elevated, to suffer you, in the violence of your attachment, to connect yourself with a dishonored family. Oh, no, nothing now but the most complete vindication of her brother in the face of the world, and in the eyes of the law—in fact, nothing but the discovery and conviction of the actual offenders—if, indeed, my unfortunate nephew is innocent—" Her voice and her tears fell at the torturing thought that it might be otherwise.

"Innocent! of course he is," cried Vivyan, taking her hand with affectionate warmth; "none of us, at least, have a doubt of it."

"Alas, my husband has," said Carry, and, no onger controlling her grief, wept abundantly.

Before Elizabeth was able to receive Vivyan, the rector and curate returned from Dublin. Sydney had been sent to Canada. It was the result of a consultation with an eminent lawyer and an old friend of the family, who, having had all the circumstances of the case before him, and viewed it in all its bearings, formed the adverse opinion upon which Mr. Spenser immediately acted.

Strong suspicion also fell at the same time upon Dawson. Indeed, the impression upon the mind of the lawyer was that Sydney had committed the crime at the instigation of his dangerous associate; in fact, that Sydney had been what is commonly called a cat's-paw in the transaction. Dawson had been invited to be present at the secret inquiry, but had excused himself on the plea of urgent parliamentary business, whereas in truth he was apprehensive of being cross-examined inconveniently as to the character and real employment of Thomson and Lamb. Besides, he had no direct evidence to give which could have been of use to young Spenser. The only way in which he could possibly have served him would have been by destroying Thomson's credit, which no man could have done more effectually, but he would have destroyed himself at the same time.

But Sydney had damaged his own case from first to last by his fatal deviations from truth. He reserved to the eleventh hour the statement that he had received the bank-note, which he had paid to Mr. Hogg, the sexton, from the hands of Thomson himself. There was no corroboration of this assertion, and he had previously assured his uncle that he had no recollection whatever of the way in which the note came into his possession. Again, he prevaricated with respect to the arms in the same suicidal manner. He had disowned the pistol found by Markham, a suspicious circumstance in itself; but when a solemn address from the lawyer extorted from him the other fact, that he had thrown its fellow into the loch, his unhappy relatives hung their heads down; the inquiry was considered at an end, and the unfortunate young man was sensible himself that he had no longer any support but the unavailing consciousness of his own innocence. "It is possible," said the lawyer, privately to Mr. Woodward, "it is possible that your nephew may not be guilty; the crime may, in fact, have been committed by the fellow who now appears to accuse him; but your nephew has done so much to give his case

the aspect of criminality, and deprive himself of the benefit of character, that I can not recommend you to trust to the verdict of the jury. My advice is, to send him out of the country before informations are sworn, after which it may be too late."

Elizabeth and Vivyan met. Her resolution, taken in the depths of her sorrow, and conceived in the spirit of the purest and most disinterested love (the love that prizes not its own gratification, but the happiness, and above all, the honor of the loved object), never wavered for a moment. Its strength consisted in the very excess of its delicacy and tenderness; never did woman need the support of a lover and a husband more than in the circumstances under which this generous girl steadfastly declined it; never was more fervent attachment, more passionate remonstrance, brought to bear upon a woman's purpose, to warp her from it. It was the contest of two spirits of the truest love, the struggle of two rival principles of the finest honor;—Elizabeth prevailed.

"No, dearest Frank," she said, with the sweetest sadness; "I shall always love you, only not in the character to which I formerly aspired."

He urged, and urged in vain, that love's trial was in the storms and vicissitudes of life, and that she was robbing love of its best privilege by repelling its sympathy and protection at a moment when both were most needful.

"Oh! Frank," she answered, "if this were a misfortune which I ought to share with you, if it were only poverty, if it were any thing but disgrace, do you think I would have come to this decision?"

"Dearest Elizabeth," he replied, "I will not hear you talk of disgrace. There is a mystery unexplained, that is all that can be said; I still believe firmly that your brother is innocent as I am; the criminal is his accuser, or Dawson himself; but at all events, does dishonor touch you?—oh, you talk of dishonoring me, and yet you would deprive me of the only honor I seek, all I am ambitious of—that of calling you my wife."

"Ah," she answered, "with what delight I once listened to that language, and from you did not call it flattery; but how can I now deceive myself? I am no longer an object of ambition, but only, only—of pity."

"Only of love, nothing but devoted and eternal love," cried Vivyan, clasping her in his arms. "How can you talk of separation, dearest girl, when I know your love is unchanged?"

"Unchanged it is, indeed," she answered; "unchanged and unchangeable. Alas! I love you too well to marry you."

From that determination neither tears nor eloquence, persuasion nor argument could make her swerve. Vivyan's last appeal was founded upon the unfavorable inference which the world would draw from the breaking-off of their marriage; but Elizabeth had taken her stand upon a clear broad principle of conduct, and all considerations of a secondary nature were pressed upon her to no purpose.

They met once more, and Vivyan went abroad soon after, miserable himself, and leaving those he loved best in the world in misery behind him.

# BOOK X.

## CHAPTER LV.

### UNCLE AND NIECE.

> " Oh, Goneril,
> You are not worth the dust which the rude wind
> Blows in your face; I fear your disposition."
> LEAR.

THE world talked with its usual flippancy, impertinence, ignorance, and often malice, of the reverses of the Spensers. The great world in London and Dublin gossiped pretty much in the same style as the little world in Redcross. People judged every thing without knowing much about any thing; and arranged what every body was to do, and the relative duties and obligations of every member of the family precisely as if they constituted a tribunal fully informed upon the whole of the case, and authorized to pronounce a decree settling the rights and responsibilities of all the parties. Most coteries agreed that the Spensers must quarter themselves upon somebody, or at least distribute themselves among their rich friends and relations; Elizabeth was to go to the Ramsdens, the children were to be taken by the Woodwards, and Mr. Spenser himself would naturally devolve upon his married, wealthy, and favorite daughter, Mrs. Dabzac. This was all very nice and comfortable; but you may be certain many things were said by the world, in the course of these arrangements, which were not altogether so good-natured.

"I am not quite so sure," observed Lady Brabble, for instance, "that the Ramsdens will like to have Elizabeth Spenser again, after this very awkward affair about her brother; Mrs. Ramsden is very particular, and I really can not blame her, as she has daughters."

"I know, for my own part," said old Mrs. Loquax, "I always judge girls by their brothers; it's a principle I have always acted on, and I advise every body to do the same."

"Then, you know, that was all extremely unpleasant about that terrible Mr. Dawson; and I'm told it's going on still," said Miss Vallancey, a wickedly virtuous old maid.

"Mr. Spenser, I'm told, is going abroad," said Lady Brabble.

"I can't tell you how I pity him," said Lady Towser; "at the same time, he has brought it all on himself, poor man; there's no denying it."

"Oh, I should think nothing about it, Lady Towser, if it had happened in any other family but that of a clergyman," said the godly Miss Vallancey. "Things like this give the enemies of religion such a handle."

"By-the-by," said Lady Brabble, "talking of the Spensers, reminds me of the Dabzacs;—we are going down to them next week—what a dear good creature she is, and how much she is to be pitied."

This is just a specimen of the way in which the Dublin world discussed the affairs of the Spensers, shooting their poisoned little shafts at random, in morning visits, and the talkative corners of ball-rooms.

The Spensers did not quarter themselves any where, at least in the free and easy sense in which the Dublin ladies used the word. They certainly quartered themselves in no sense at all upon the Ramsdens, or even upon the Dabzacs. If they lived at free quarters any where at all for a short time, it was under the humble roof of the plain curate of Redcross, the roof which he was wont to repair with his own hands, when the storms stripped it.

As to Mrs. Dabzac, she wrote, indeed, several rigmarole letters, in the style of her epistle to Sydney, full of anxieties and tendernesses, commiserations and remembrances, but she never invited either her father or sister to her house, angelical as Lady Brabble pronounced her. Arabella, however, had excuses as plenty as blackberries for not doing what a daughter of any feeling would have done under the circumstances. Perhaps they did not altogether impose upon the rector; but if he questioned their validity he was silent upon the subject.

He had a child, however, who did not fail him in his troubles, who stuck the closer to him the more the tempest raged and the storms of life buffeted him.

"You have a daughter left, Val.," said Hercules, when Mr. Spenser was speaking of his reduced circumstances, "who has worth enough to make any man who possesses her a Crœsus."

"Yes," said the rector, "Elizabeth has always done her duty."

"Nobody has lost so much as she has," said the curate.

So in truth it was; but minds that are strong and good are supported by trial under trial; the very variety of their afflictions sustains them. They are like the strong-rooted tree of the forest, which many winds conspire to overthrow, but which remains upright, though shaken, by the very conflict of the opposing blasts.

Those who saw the parsonage in a few months after the calamities recorded in the previous book, witnessed a melancholy revolution there. The house was shut up; its furniture had been sold; the rector's pictures, bronzes, busts, and, what he valued and regretted most of all, his select and beautiful library, with its curiously carved oaken bookcases, had been removed to Dublin, and were destined to the hammer, to satisfy the demands of his son's Cambridge creditors, and discharge his other pecuniary obligations. The horses and carriages had been disposed of; even the old black mare on which Carry Woodward used to sit so portly; and the Gipsy was no more to be seen moored alongside the little pier.

The curate did not let the books go without a vigorous effort to save them.

"All nonsense, Carry," he said, "the books can't be sold; it is impossible; I have turned it all over in my mind; his daughter will never allow it."

Carry looked surprised, thinking that he meant Elizabeth.

"Not allow it, my dear Hercules!—she is perfectly resigned on that as upon every other subject."

"I'm not talking of Lizzy, Carry—I'm talking of Arabella, Mrs. Dabzac."

"Well, my love," said Carry, regarding him with curiosity, not knowing what he was driving at, "what of Mrs. Dabzac?"

"Why," said Hercules, "only that she is his daughter, and was always his favorite; I can not but think, if she knew the actual state of his affairs, she would at least redeem his library—if Val had only his books he would weather the storm."

"My dear, good Hercules," cried his wife, smiling affectionately on him, in a way that clearly intimated her opinion that he was much too simple for a man of his years. He perfectly understood her looks, and vociferated, slapping his thigh—

"Why, Carry, she is not a Goneril, or a Regan."

"Very far from a Cordelia," said Carry. "Why, my dear, not to speak of her recent behavior to her father himself, her very conduct to you—I mean the way she acted at her marriage—might show you how little is to be expected from her."

"Come, Carry, love, let by-gones be by-gones; I have forgiven her long ago. She probably thought that a bishop would tie the knot faster than a curate, and perhaps she was right. That is no reason for denying her the common feelings of a daughter for a father."

At day-break the next morning, Hercules rose, saddled Sligo with his own hand, and set out on a long journey across the country, taking the line of road that led to the county of Armagh. The reader may think it strange to see him bestriding Sligo again, as he had sold that redoubted steed to Doctor Wilkins for twenty pounds; but Sligo was a pony who had a will of his own, and whether it was that he preferred divinity to physic, or had grown so attached to his old shed in the curate's yard, that he could not make himself comfortable any where else, certain it was that the doctor could get no good of him; for, whenever he found the stable door open, or had any opportunity of making his escape, he invariably trotted back to his former abode, and was found with his nose against the latch, as if trying to raise it and let himself in. After this had happened several times, Doctor Wilkins thought he might as well reconvey him formally to his ancient master, but he steadfastly refused to take back the twenty pounds, insisting that he bought the pony, subject to all his faults and eccentricities.

Dabzac House was a spacious, gray, formal building, with a story more than a country-house ought to have; it looked cold and ceremonious; there was a dull, square piece of water in front of it, with two stiff swans lazily navigating it; the trees and shrubs seemed to have been trimmed by a carpenter, and the only flowers to be seen were holly-hooks and orange lilies. The house was just now full of company. A great many frigid and fashionable people were gathered together, the personages enumerated in Mrs. Dabzac's letter to Sydney, and several more whom she had not referred to, including two or three lieutenant-colonels and grandmasters.

Arabella, habited in graceful and almost gay mourning, was standing, shortly before dinner,

at a window, chatting with the Honorable John Dalrymple and the Honorable Tom Flinch; they were talking of Cambridge, and Arabella had been actually boasting of her brother's extravagant career there (that having been the cause publicly assigned for Sydney's abrupt expatriation), when with horror indescribable she espied her uncle riding up the rigid avenue, between the regular rows of beeches.

"Whom have we got here?" said the Honorable Tom, the first to call attention to the approaching curiosity.

"I think," said the Honorable John, "it must be Dominie Sampson."

"Or Doctor Johnson redivivus," said the other.

Arabella was a little short-sighted, though in the present instance she had been the first to descry her relative, and she now reconnoitered him through her eye-glass, just to gain time to arrange her ideas. While she was doing so, Colonel Dabzac came to the window, and instantly recognized his wife's uncle.

"Can it be possible?—really I believe Dabzac is right—my uncle, my dear good odd uncle," exclaimed his amiable niece, with her little affected simper.

The colonel went out instantly to receive Mr. Woodward with his habitual starched civility, but still as became a gentleman in his own house. Arabella received him, too, with a great deal more warmth in her manner than she really felt, and yet she looked any thing but cordial.

The honorables John and Tom were too well bred to jest any more on the curate's personal appearance, now that he proved to be a relation of the family, but they saw in a twinkling that their hostess was disconcerted by the new arrival, and despised her vulgarity of mind much more than they did the curate's coat.

Hercules had all the great points that constitute the true gentleman. He was independent and unselfish, respected others, and respected himself; he knew his position, and though no man had a higher sense than he had of the dignity of a minister of the Gospel, no man knew better the practical difference in society between the opulent drones and the indigent working-bees of the hive. As a clergyman, and a relative of Mrs. Dabzac, he was received respectfully by the company, who were accustomed to the homely manners of the northern clergy, and did not want to be assured that Hercules was a plain blunt man and an eccentricity, points that were repeatedly pressed by his niece.

As the people began to assemble before dinner, the Honorable John said to the Honorable Tom—

"Do you know, Tom, this is the first time, to my knowledge, that I was ever in the same room with a curate."

"Well," replied the Honorable Tom, "I have no recollection whether I ever met a curate before, but I was once in the same room with an attorney."

"That must have been very unpleasant," drawled his brother coxcomb.

Lady Brabble observed to Lady Western that she was positive Mrs. Dabzac wished her uncle in Jericho.

"Dear me," exclaimed Lady Western, and being a little deaf, she began to examine Mr.

Woodward very attentively, under the impression that he was a missionary, just returned from the city named by Lady Brabble.

When dinner was announced, Hercules was amazed. He had dined on the road, at two o'clock, and had purposely delayed his arrival at Dabzac House to an hour when he thought that dinner would be over, having no notion of spunging on his niece for more than a tea and a night's lodging. An eight o'clock dinner had never entered into his calculations, and he had hardly made up his mind whether the announcement was serious, ere he found himself seated at a pompous banquet, with the deaf Lady Western on one side of him, and the Honorable Tom Flinch on the other. Hercules was called on to say grace, and his performance of that office drew all eyes upon him, it was at once so brief and so devout, so energetic and sonorous. Lady Western began immediately to attack him about his travels in Palestine. She was particularly inquisitive about Jericho, and it was to no purpose the curate explained over and over again, that though he took the greatest interest in the part of the globe she was talking of, his only knowledge of it was from the Bible and books of travels. At length he gave up the contest, and suffered her ladyship to take him for an oriental missionary during the rest of the evening.

With the Honorable Tom he got on capitally. Tom took good care of him, though he puzzled him a little with dry champagne; but the best of it was, that Tom turned out to be an aid-de-camp to the lord-lieutenant, and the identical officer who, after the curate's sermon at the Castle Chapel had been commissioned to invite him to the viceroyal table.

Mrs. Dabzac was in hopes of concealing her uncle's humble position in the church under the general denomination of a country clergyman, but she was not successful in this little manoeuvre. Mr. Pepper and Lord Brabble began to talk of the state of the country; and the distress of the clergy being alluded to, Lord Brabble said he believed very few clergymen were receiving the half of their incomes, "as, I dare say, you know very well, sir," he added, addressing himself to Hercules.

"Not by my own personal experience, my lord," replied Mr. Woodward.

"Then your income is paid; you are a lucky man," said Mr. Pepper.

"I never received my seventy-five more regularly," said the curate, in a tone that reached the four corners of the table; and if he had taken up a decanter, and flung it at his niece's head, he could hardly have shocked her more than by his blunt mention of the sum which, being the exact arithmetical symbol of curacy, at once dispersed all the obscurity that belonged to the phrase "country clergyman."

Several people present (Lord Brabble and Tom Flinch, for instance) liked Hercules all the more for his honest speech, but some looked scornful, and Arabella herself devoutly wished him at the place from which Lady Western insisted on believing him just returned.

It seemed, however, as if the presence of a poor working clergyman had the effect of a wet blanket on the company in general, for there was no more conversation until the ladies were gone,

and then it took an acrimonious political turn, which brought forth the curate again, and afforded him an opportunity of reading the grandmasters and grand-secretaries a lecture which they did not soon forget. He told them, that if they could not reconcile peace and charity with their orange principles, the sooner they plucked the orange ribbons from their coats the better; that bad as the pope was, there was another spiritual personage against whom Christians ought to be still more on their guard; that they were to purify politics with religion, not defile religion with politics; that he detested popery as much, he hoped, as any man could, but that he utterly despaired of smothering it with orange lilies, or bawling and drumming it out of the country. This speech caused a general set to be made upon the curate, who had need of all his prowess to sustain his numerous assailants. Colonel Dabzac said, dryly, that he had heard Mr. Woodward was one of themselves.

"My principles are orange, sir," replied Hercules; "but I am very far from approving of the doings of a great many of our party."

"Pray which of our doings do you disapprove of?" asked Mr. Pepper, sneeringly.

"As I was riding here, this day," said the curate, "I passed a church ten miles from this, and I saw an orange flag floating from the steeple. I disapprove of that, sir; I disapprove of it mightily;—that, sir, is what I call defiling religion with politics."

"Is that all you have to find fault with?" asked Lord Brabble.

"No, nor t e half, my lord," answered Hercules, roundly. "I don't like your orange lodges, what you call your organization; I don't see the sense, and still less do I see the grandeur of it. Grand men ought to be above meeting in holes and corners. I don't like secrecy, my lord. What legitimate object is there which may not be achieved by proceedings in the face of the world? The presumption is, and will always be, that when men enter secret associations, whether in Tanderagee, or in Tipperary, their objects are of a nature that look better in a weak light than a strong one. And another point, my lord, is this, that if we have our John Knox lodge, and our Beresford lodge, depend upon it the time will come when others will have their Emmet clubs and Wolfe Tone clubs. I disapprove of all such bodies, whether the ribbon is green or orange; they are all capable of doing mischief, and the best of them can possibly do no good."

"My uncle's a fine fellow," said the Honorable Tom to the Honorable John, as they both moved together from the dining-room.

"Devilish fine," said the Honorable John, heartily weary of the political squabble, during which the wine had been kept standing half an hour before Lord Brabble.

Hercules thought the rest of the evening dreadfully tedious, so anxious was he to have a private conference with his niece, who, upon her part, was equally fidgety to learn what could possibly have brought him to her house, and no undisturbed by shabby suspicions that his visi was connected with the distressed affairs of he family.

At length the drawing-room was left to themselves, and Arabella, throwing herself on a sofa, afflicted exhaustion, attered a kind of thanks-giving for being at length delivered from the odious Dalrymples and that insupportable Lady Western.

"How I did pity you, my dear uncle," she said, with her counterfeit earnestness; "a clever man like you seated between that prosy old woman, and an absolute idiot like Tom Flinch."

"He seems a very good-natured young man," said Hercules; "he was very obliging and attentive to me at dinner."

"Oh, but, sir, I should have so liked to have had you all to myself; we have so many things to talk about."

"So many things, Arabella, and such sad things," said Hercules, with deep solemnity, seating himself at her side.

"Sad, sad indeed," said his niece; "I can't tell you, sir, how distressing it is to be obliged to receive all this company at such a time." And, as she spoke, she raised the corner of her little handkerchief of snowy gauze, to receive any pearly tribute which her eyes might be disposed to pay to the claims of sympathy and kindred.

Arabella looked, spoke, and dressed sorrow very respectably. Black lace, white cambric, and downcast eyelids do a great deal; besides we all know what an advantage a handsome Mrs. Haller or Mrs. Beverley has over a plain one. Arabella imposed upon her uncle, and yet he found it no easy matter to bring the conversation to the desired point. At length he found what he thought a tolerably fair opening—

"I suppose you have heard," he said, "that it has been found necessary to dispose of the furniture and other property at the parsonage."

Arabella answered in the affirmative, with a most touching expression of regret.

"The furniture—plate—pictures—horses—carriages"—repeated Hercules, detailing the items of poor Mr. Spenser's sacrifices.

"Not the books!" exclaimed Mrs. Dabzac, interrupting him; "my poor father always set such a very high value on his library."

Hercules was overjoyed; his niece was actually anticipating the object of his mission. He hastened to tell her that the books were not yet disposed of, and, for the first time in his life, fondled down her stately name from Arabella to Bell.

"It was only this very morning," she added, "the colonel and I were talking on this very subject."

Hercules seized both her small white hands with his huge brown ones, and could almost have knelt to her.

"We were saying," she added, "that the book-cases alone would produce several hundred pounds at a London auction."

Hercules dropped her hands as if her fingers were adders. He was expecting her pretty mouth to drop pearls and diamonds, and it opened to let out reptiles. He gave a very loose and unsatisfactory account of the remainder of his interview with Mrs. Dabzac. Carry concluded that he had given too loose a rein to his indignant emotions. Certain it was that he left Dabzac House the following morning long before breakfast, and arrived at Redcross the same night, a ride almost as remarkable as Turpin's.

"She's a Regan, Carry; she's a Goneril," he exclaimed, rushing into his study, where his wife was sitting up for him alone. For a full half hour he continued repeating, "A Regan, a Goneril;" as he tugged off his boots and his coats, and flung them to all corners of the room.

---

## CHAPTER LVI.

### THE MICROSCOPE.

"Oh, coward conscience, how dost thou afflict me!"
RICHARD III.

THE Spensers continued for a considerable time the guests of the Woodwards, and fortunately the crazy old white house was elastic, or it would not have answered the demands now made upon it by the consolidation of the two families. Though Dabzac House was not open to the rector in his adversity, many more agreeable mansions were, both in Ireland and England; but it did not suit his depressed spirits to make tours of visits; and Elizabeth, in the spirit of retrenchment, had taken upon herself the education of her little brothers and sisters, which was an additional reason for remaining stationary and retired. A happy domestic revolution it was to the little Spensers, after the negligent tyranny of Mrs. Peacock. The boudoir of an affectionate and accomplished sister was now their school-room; they were instructed by the lips of beauty, and governed by the hand of love. Carry called it the golden age of Queen Bess, and Hercules said it was a little 1688, the greatest era in his chronology.

The death of Lady Bonham, while it added to Miss Spenser's sorrows, produced an unexpected change in the arrangements of the family. Lord Bonham went abroad immediately after his loss; but, before he went, prevailed upon Mr. Spenser to settle himself for some time at his shooting lodge, in the mountains to the north of the parsonage. It was painful to leave the Woodwards, but the rector felt that he had been long enough a burden to his curate; and another consideration, of a totally different kind, disposed Elizabeth also to accept the offer of Bonham Lodge. Her deceased friend had left three children of a tender age, who were now at the lodge, under the care of a person in whom Miss Spenser knew that Lord Bonham placed but little confidence. The idea of being useful to these little ones immediately occurred to her, for her mind was something like her good uncle's house, it was always so ready to expand itself for any number of new virtues or new duties.

As to Carry Woodward, she was more satisfied upon the whole than displeased at this new turn of events, for she knew that her niece required all the support of constant and engrossing occupations through her complicated trials; Mrs. Woodward's own experience told her how little time maternal offices leave for brooding on recollections, or indulging fancies; and she encouraged and applauded Elizabeth's benevolent resolution, as the wisest she could possibly take in her present circumstances.

The idle and talkative women of Dublin (for there were a few such women in that capital at the period of these events) took a different view of the matter.

"It's easy to talk," said Lady Brabble to Mrs. Pepper, "of Lord Bonham being Mr.

Spenser's old college acquaintance; there's no disguising the fact, that Miss Spenser is going to Bonham Lodge in the capacity of a governess; the world will look upon it in no other light, at all events."

"I'm told Lord Bonham is to allow her fifty pounds a year," said Miss-Vallancey.

"Don't you pity poor pretty Mrs. Dabzac, with such relations—such a brother and such a sister?" said Lady Towser.

"It's positively beginning to affect her spirits and her looks, poor thing," said another member of the group.

"I foresaw what it would end in, when I heard of the scrapes the brother got into," said old Mrs. Loquax; "my rule is always to judge of girls by their brothers."

But, undeterred by the slanderous gossip of her sex, Elizabeth Spenser entered upon her enlarged sphere of usefulness, and in the employment of the present labored to forget the griefs and the impressions of the past. It was a lovely September morning when the Spensers parted in tears from their affectionate relatives, and at a late hour in the evening of the same day they reached their new abode.

Bonham Lodge was situated in an angle of the coast, about a mile from the beach. The mountains were piled about it in fantastic masses, possessing every variety of picturesque attraction that wood, rock, heath, and water, with their infinite combinations, could give them. The house was a cottage in form, but had some excellent rooms, and was built in the massive style that the stormy character of the coast rendered indispensable for stability and safety. Being comfortably furnished, and so charmingly situated, it was a most desirable place to pass a few weeks at, particularly at the season when the Spensers went there; and Mrs. Woodward was wont to say, that the only thing against it was the circumstance that the only road by which it was accessible from Redcross was also the road to Castle Dawson.

But it was now a good while since the proprietor of that dismal mansion had presumed to molest Elizabeth; she had almost ceased to think of him, and little dreamed of the fresh persecution that even now, in her grief and solitude, was impending over her. Little did the rector dream that he was actually connected himself with Dawson in the most unpleasant way; namely, as his debtor for a considerable sum of money. The reader will recollect the loan which Sharkey, the attorney, had negotiated for Mr. Spenser; the money had been found by Dawson, and the rector had accepted bills, which Dawson held not only as securities for the repayment, but (as he sordidly and vaguely calculated) as a means of influencing the daughter through the father's difficulties. In this scheme, however, he was baffled by the curious train of circumstances which we have now to relate.

When the bills were about to fall due (which was soon after the removal to Bonham Lodge), Mr. Spenser was but ill-prepared to meet them, and wrote to Mr. Sharkey with a view to procure renewals, or, in other words, to postpone the period of payment. Dawson was pinched for money at the time quite as much as the rector was; indeed it was nothing but the desperate state of his affairs which, engrossing all his thoughts, had so long protected Miss Spenser from his attentions, but he could not resist the temptation now thrown in his way, of at once revealing himself as Mr. Spenser's benefactor, and confirming his hold by preserving that generous character still longer. The rector's surprise and Elizabeth's horror were extreme, when Sharkey's reply disclosed who the owner of the bills really was. The affair was managed adroitly enough by both worthy solicitor and worthy client. The former communicated Mr. Spenser's request to the latter; the latter wrote to the former, cordially agreeing to the proposal, and graciously offering any accommodation the rector desired; then Mr. Sharkey forwarded the substance of this interesting correspondence to Bonham Lodge, not without the expression of a fear that Mr. Dawson would be displeased at having his name made known in the transaction. It was no easy matter to unriddle Mr. Sharkey's writing, he wrote such an execrable hand; and to this circumstance the rector owed his escape from the trap laid for him, for he was obliged to call in the aid of his daughter to read the letter, and she fell at her father's knees almost swooning, when at last she deciphered the name of Dawson.

"Oh, papa!" she exclaimed, recovering herself, "do not put yourself under any further obligation to that man; surely you are not driven to have recourse to such assistance."

In the most earnest and touching manner was this petition made, and the amiable rector loved her too tenderly to refuse it, although his constitutional weakness, and the facility of renewing an old negotiation, would probably have led him to continue Dawson's debtor, had not this fortunate accident happened to prevent it. He wrote that day, nay that very hour (for Elizabeth anxiously pressed him), to thank Mr. Dawson for his kindness in grateful terms, declining, however, to avail himself of it, on the ground that altered circumstances made it desirable to him to close the transaction. How to raise the money to pay the bills was then the next question, and while both father and daughter were deliberating on that point, and taking such steps as seemed most advisable, a man rode up to the lodge, mounted on a strong white horse;—it was Dawson himself.

A great alteration had taken place not only in his position, but in his personal appearance, since the last time the rector saw him. The portrait we drew of him in a previous chapter must now be retouched. He was no longer the picture of robust vice, and immorality with a good digestion. Anxiety was plowing his forehead, and delving hollows in his cheeks; even his carbuncles were beginning to pale, though intemperance supplied their fires with even more than their former fuel. His eyes, however, had grown red, as if at the expense of his cheeks; they looked languid, as if sleep rarely visited their lids, yet watchful as if they momentarily expected the approach of an enemy, or the explosion of a mine. How his position was altered will be related afterward; it is sufficient to mention here that he was no longer a member of parliament.

Elizabeth fled, terrified, to her chamber, and immured herself there on the pretext of indisposition, firmly resolved not to appear as long as a visitor so detested haunted the house. He inflicted his bad company on the rector for three days, pressing his services upon him, and still hoping that Miss Spenser would come forth and receive his homage. It would be injustice, however, to Dawson, not to add that he was far from being unconcerned at the misfortunes that had befallen Sydney, and that he would have done any thing in his power, short of personal risk and exposure, to repair the evils of which he himself was so much the cause. It was even possible that he might have involved himself, by his feelings on this point, in admissions of a dangerous nature, had not the rector, on the first mention of his son's name, begged to be spared the fruitless discussion of a painful topic.

The seclusion of Elizabeth, and her firmness in maintaining it, embarrassed and mortified Dawson beyond measure. He scarcely refrained from making it a subject of complaint to the rector, but with all his assurance did not venture to hazard the rebuff to which such extreme presumption would have exposed him, even from Mr. Spenser. If ever Dawson felt distinctly and painfully the utter hopelessness of his pretensions, it was in the presence of the object of them, or in the society of her family. Still he was always courting the position in which he felt most humiliated. His pursuit of Elizabeth had all along been a sort of monomania more or less active at particular times, according as circumstances chanced to excite it, or other passions more or less engaged him; but its roots were deep, for it had its origin in his inordinate self-conceit, and for the same reason it was utterly incurable even by the strongest possible demonstrations of repugnance on the part of the lady. Otherwise the delusion would long ago have been dispelled. Such men feel as if they were actually under recognizances to their own vanity never to take a repulse, or own that any woman has been found to resist their captivations. They have committed themselves to a hopeless adventure; possibly made their object notorious by boasting and swaggering among their associates; and they prefer the ostentation of vainly persisting, to the ridicule of pocketing all their affronts and going about their business. No consideration for the person, the peace of whose life is sacrificed in this barbarous and selfish game, ever enters the minds of the daring yet despicable coxcombs who play it.

Mr. Spenser had also been peremptory at first on the subject of the accommodation which his guest desired to force upon him; but on the morning of the third day, the answers he received from the parties to whom he had applied for assistance to discharge his obligations, proving extremely unfavorable, he began to waver in his resolution, and was on the point of violating the promise he had made to his daughter, and again involving himself with Dawson, when the opportune arrival of the Woodwards (to pay their first visit to the lodge) changed the posture of affairs.

Great was the vexation of both the curate and his wife, but of Carry especially, when they found the rector entertaining a man whose presence was intolerable to his fair and virtuous daughter. Dawson was not in the house at the moment of their arrival, so they expressed their sentiments freely.

Carry went immediately to visit her niece in her captivity, and Mr. Spenser took his brother-in-law apart to put him in possession of the state of his affairs, and particularly the difficulty which immediately pressed him. Hercules no sooner cast his eye upon Mr. Sharkey's letter, than he cried out immediately that the hand-writing was the same as that on the paper which the police had found in the subterraneous chamber under the Black Castle.

"Carry has it in her pocket," he added; "she has kept it there ever since; it will be curious to make the comparison."

"Hercules strode away to his wife, who came back with him; the two papers were placed side by side, and the ascertained characters on the one serving to determine the doubtful ones on the other, not only the identity of the hands was placed beyond dispute, but it was also most satisfactorily established that the paper discovered in the vault was the envelope of some letter which Dawson had received from his attorney.

"Now," said Mrs. Woodward, "if we could only decipher the writing in pencil on the other side!"

She had scarcely uttered the words, when the curate's eye was attracted by a solar microscope which stood on a table near a window, where the rector had, that very morning, been exhibiting the seed of the fern and the blazonry of a butterfly's wing to his little son. Hercules took the paper, placed it under the glasses, arranged the instrument properly, and the experiment was so successful, that he actually read aloud the list, or inventory, of which it had already been suspected that the writing consisted. Among other things he came to the following item:—"Two marble busts"—upon which Mrs. Woodward instantly suggested that these might possibly be the busts found in the island, and at that moment in the rector's library at the parsonage.

"Whose hand is the inventory written in?" asked Mr. Spenser.

Carry applied her eye to the glass; and did not recognize it; Hercules failed also; then the rector looked himself, and pronounced it Dawson's, without a question.

Carry went off to communicate all this to her niece.

Almost at the same moment Dawson entered. Hercules had not met him since he had first changed his opinion of his character, in consequence of his stolen visit to Redcross, now two summers since. In the interval many things had occurred to corroborate the impression which that occurrence left upon the curate's mind. Dawson quickly and keenly felt that Hercules was his friend no longer. There was no mistake about Woodward's manner; he never smiled when he was frowning inwardly; and when he took the hand of a man he despised or disliked, he never squeezed his fingers. He made Dawson extremely uncomfortable, by the way in which he now received him, so clearly did it show that, for some cause or another, he had utterly forgotten the night on Loch Erne, and even the gallant saving of his niece's life. But worse was in store for the unwelcome guest. Wandering about the room he approached the microscope.

"We have just been trying its powers upon the faint writing on that scrap of paper," said Hercules, in tones as deep and hoarse as the murmur of the waves upon the neighboring shore.

Dawson stooped and looked in. There he saw and recognized with the dismay that may be imagined a rough catalogue made with his own hand of the property of which he had rifled the creditors of his father's estate. His posture prevented the rector and curate from remarking how the wonders of the microscope affected the muscles of his face, but no doubt they expressed a stronger feeling than that of a gratified philosophical observer.

"Extremely curious," said Hercules, intently gazing in Dawson's face, the instant he raised it from the glass.

"Extremely," said the other, neither liking nor understanding the curate's keen, steady scrutiny.

Woodward then withdrew the paper, turned it up, as if without intention, and again fixing his alarming eye on the disconcerted profligate, addressed him, and said—

"By-the-by, Mr. Dawson, this is a scrap of paper which the police found at the Black Castle—it seems to be the back of a letter—perhaps you can help us to read the writing."

Now Dawson's face turned all colors in less than a second; and, divided between the fear of being frank and the danger of excessive caution, he pretended inability to decipher the address, but said, with an awkward laugh and a husky voice, that the hand was not unlike his attorney's.

"So we were just saying," said the rector, in his quietest manner, but it cut Dawson as if with a stiletto; for it made him apprehensive that some secret investigation or discussion was going on about his dark practices at Castle Dawson, and that the Spenser family knew much more than he wished of his secret history.

It was a relief to him when Mrs. Woodward entered. Her notice of him was studiously supercilious and unpleasant, for, in truth, she came down with a deliberately-formed resolution to drive him from the lodge before dinner; but it did not deter him from hoping that she had found her niece better. Carry's reply was contemptuously inarticulate. Dawson, whom it was the hardest thing in the world to abash, persevered, and said he hoped Miss Spenser would soon be able to leave her room.

"She has no present intention of it," returned Mrs. Woodward; not inaudibly, as before, but with the utmost possible distinctness, and in a tone that left no doubt whatsoever as to the meaning of her words.

Dawson mounted his white horse and went almost as abruptly as he came. The house looked brighter and the air felt purer when he was gone. Elizabeth came forth from her hiding-place, and instantly placed a letter in her father's hands, which relieved him from the embarrassment of his obligation to her persecutor. She had been more successful in her financial operations than the rector. No sooner did he consent upon her account to repudiate Dawson's offer of accommodation, than she felt herself called upon to make every exertion in her power to procure from some other quarter the aid he wanted. After much anxious consideration of the subject, she could think of nobody so likely to stand her friend as Mr. Trundle, though she felt that to apply to him (after the little fraud she had formerly committed, during his visit to the parsonage) was something like an attempt to impose upon him a second time. However, she made up her mind to write to him, not only as her father's friend, but as Lord Bonham's agent and representative; and his prompt and cordial answer, actually inclosing a draft for the sum required, proved beyond a doubt that a man may have his mind stuffed with idle crotchets, and his heart at the same time replenished with solid worth.

While the Spensers and Woodwards were spending the evening in something like the old way, before misfortune overtook them, Dawson was galloping across the dreary brown mountains, not to his own house, but in the direction of Redcross. He looked, when the shades of night began to gather round him, not unlike the dreary horseman of a Rhenish legend; he looked defeated, yet dangerous; even since morning his visage seemed to have grown darker, and his eye more expressive of evil, as if his mind was beginning to harbor some purpose deeper and blacker than had hitherto entered into his most licentious calculations. And if then you could have turned that corrupted and tumultuous mind inside out (as naturalists do with certain zoophytes to examine their internal structure), you would have seen that it was so.

His route, on leaving Bonham Lodge, lay by the Black Castle and the parsonage, across the water; he passed the perilous ruins at full speed, eying them apprehensively over his shoulder, as they glimmered in the twilight, and reared their gaunt towers against the faded sky. The whistling of the evening wind in the ivy seemed to interrogate him as to his past life, and the few rays of light that straggled through the chasms or loop-holes in the walls glared upon him like the stern, pale eyes of justice. He would have shunned the parsonage, had it been possible, for it was only associated in his mind with mortification and repulse; but to reach the water it was necessary to pass beneath its very windows. Those of the library stood partially open: the servants had been airing the apartment and had lighted a fire there, which faintly illuminated the walls, no longer hidden by literary treasures. Dawson peered in, but there was nothing left of all that had once made that room so refined and beautiful, save two busts, which stood seemingly staring at one another, like Calpe gazing at Alyla. Dawson trembled and raised the window-sash. There was nobody at hand to mark or hear what he did. He stepped into the library, and instantly recognized the pieces of statuary which had formerly done duty in the gallery of his mock ancestors. There was nothing very wrong in an acquaintance of the Spenser family, as he was, raising a window and stepping into an unfurnished apartment; he had seldom been guilty of a less shabby action, yet he felt like a housebreaker at that moment; and the sound of a door opening and shutting at a distance scared him as if in the middle of a burglary. He rushed back to his horse, and hurried to the little quay, but there was no boat there to transport him across the loch. His only resource was a desperate one; but he was in the mood to dare any thing. He sprang upon his steed, with whip and spur impelled him into the water, and with the utmost possible difficulty gained the further side of the creek in safety. Thence, dripping and jaded, he pursued his way to Redcross, where he passed the night in a low carouse with the Peacocks and the caitiff Thomson. The following morning, at a late hour, he had a private conference with Lucy and Thomson at the inn where he stopped, and almost immediately afterward started in a chaise for Dublin, *en route* for London.

The conference with the perfidious post-mistress was an important one. Dawson obtained from her an account of proceedings and movements in which he was deeply concerned; he learned that Vivyan had for some time maintained a correspondence not only with Mr. and Mrs. Woodward, but with Mr. Hogg, the sexton, and Maguire, the proctor; that letters had also passed between the curate and Markham, and that several had also been dispatched to Sydney, directed to Quebec. Lucy had actually taken down in writing the substance of some of these letters, and the dates of all; and it was evident to Dawson that in one quarter, at least, there was no intention of letting the investigation drop. It enraged him to think that, of all men in the world, it was Elizabeth's accepted lover who was thus secretly hunting him. He had never seen Vivyan but once, at the pic-nic upon the island, and upon that occasion, (although Vivyan and Spenser were then total strangers), Dawson had conceived a violent dislike to him, which was subsequently strengthened and inflamed by jealousy, when he discovered that Frank occupied the proud place which he vainly coveted for himself. Dawson paid sharp attention to the dates of the correspondence betrayed to him, and observed that for nearly three weeks there had been no letter received at the Redcross post-office. This looked as if the inquiry had been given up, or intermitted; but there was another conclusion to be drawn from the circumstance, and one which was strongly confirmed by a letter of Markham's, namely, that the course of investigation might have led Vivyan to America. Lucy herself was of that opinion. It seemed natural that he should have followed Sydney, to consult with him upon the proceeeings to be taken; but another and more disagreeable view of the case occurred to Dawson himself, whose conscience poignantly hinted that, if Vivyan had indeed crossed the Atlantic, his motive might be to discover and produce Lamb. It was in Lamb's power completely to·establish Sydney's innocence, but unluckily he held the fate of the guilty in his hands as well as of the innocent, so that the very idea of his being found and induced to return to Ireland, made Dawson perspire with alarm. Without confiding to his fair friend·the extent of his fears, or the true nature of them, he adjured her at parting to watch the correspondence of the Spenser family with redoubled vigilance, and to be particular in apprizing him of the import of all American letters. Between fear, jealousy, rancor, and despair, he carried a little private pandemonium with him on his journey to England.

## CHAPTER LVII.

DOWNWARD CAREER OF DAWSON.

"Who plays the knave, without a knave's advantage,
Plays the fool also; 'tis the sharper's fortune,
Who played with loaded dice and lost the game."
						THE TABLES TURNED.

NOTHING had thriven, for some time back, publicly or privately, with Dawson. It is necessary to trace briefly his recent parliamentary career, in order to explain the precise position in which he stood at the present moment. He had, of late, been growing heartily sick of the life of a legislator, or, to speak more correctly, he was become thoroughly disgusted at having turned his influence hitherto to no good personal account. He procured an appointment for Sharkey; it was the last Dawson job; and Sharkey, in return, urged his generous patron to press his own claims, "make his hay while the sun shone," and demand something from the government commensurate in emolument and dignity to the rank of a member of Parliament. Dawson then worried the ministry for himself, as a hundred times before he had worried it for others; he became as formidable as Mr. Fosberry with his liquid guano, or Mr Trundle with his petition for the thirty millions; he badgered the Home Office, he beleaguered the Treasury, he infested·Downing-street, and he laid siege to Dublin Castle.. Gladly would the government have promoted and extinguished him; but it was not an easy matter to manage; he was too vain, as well as too grasping, to accept of small offices, and it was impossible to confer any considerable post upon him without damaging the public service to a degree not to be hazarded, either by a conscientious or a prudent administration. At length his necessities became too pressing, and since he could make nothing by his seat in any other way, in a tempest of rage and disappointment, he made up his mind to sell it. Dawson sold the good-will of Rottenham for a thousand pounds, and accepted the Chiltern Hundreds, the only situation in life he ever filled without a blemish upon his character. He parted with his constituents with more hilarity than honesty. They gave him a farewell dinner, and he made them an oration, crammed with honor and virtue, as full as the speech of the expiring fox in the fable. He put his retirement on the grounds of his utter despair of ever achieving any thing for Ireland·in the Imperial Parliament—he, whose name had never been attached as sponsor to a single bill, who·had never even suggested to others a measure of the slightest public utility, who had never done a day's work on any committee of useful inquiry, and who had never requested an interview with a minister, except to propose or promote a job. Nobody at the farewell dinner taunted him with this, for every guest at the table was either his dupe or his accomplice; the worthy elector who proposed his health was as arrant a p        a swindler as the retiring senator himself, aind expected to make a nice thing of the new election for the borough. The feast ended with an extraordinary melange of brutality and sentiment, a scene not to be witnessed except in the political conviviality of a place like Rottenham. The banqueters grew tender as they grew tipsy. Their eyes filled as the bottles emptied, and at length it came to falling on each other's necks, and embracing each other frantically. Every body tried to embrace Dawson, who wept like Niobe, and at three o'clock in the morning by the town clock, overpowered by punch and pathos, he rolled on the floor in the arms of his friend Sharkey, while another disconsolate attorney tumbled and rolled over both, vainly endeavoring, in the frenzy of fondness, to clasp Dudley to his breast.

In a few days after this affecting incident Dawson received the sum for which he had bartered his parliamentary position. In a few days more, not a shilling of that sum remained in his pocket; yet it was at that very moment he sought to force his aid upon Mr. Spenser, who had only declined the benefactions of a bankrupt.

No sooner did the rector find a friend in need in Mr. Trundle, than he hastened to acquit himself of his previous obligations. In fact, Dawson received the amount of the bills before they were strictly due; but it was no longer in the power of money to save him. Between his debts and his passions, there was a gulf that would have swallowed up a large fortune; his creditors snatched what they could; the rest was hazarded and lost at the gaming-table, or on the turf, and the characterless roué was cut in the morning by the men who had fleeced him the night before.

The day on which he received the amount of the bills from Mr. Spenser was almost the last of his London life. Flushed by the fullness of his purse, and being always social in a dissolute way, he invited Sharkey and some more worthies to a dinner at Blackwall. Dawson had ceased to be an eater; but he drank the deeper in proportion, and on this occasion outdid all his former Bacchanalian exploits. Before dinner was half over, he had commenced vaporing about conscience and duty, as he always did when the wine began to tell upon his brain. With the claret he began to swagger about his plans as a country gentleman; vowed he would put Castle Dawson in thorough repair; blustered about planting and draining; threw himself back ostentatiously in his seat, flung open his tawdry waistcoat, and deplored the time and talents he had squandered in the House of Commons, which might have been spent so much more profitably living on his estate and improving the country.

"In the buzzom of a happy and continted tin' antry," stammered Sharkey, dropping his head on the table, and instantly dreaming of ejectments.

By what road, or by what conveyance, that jovial party got back to town, after that night's entertainment, was utterly unknown to all of them except Dawson, whom wine unfortunately inflamed without stupefying; for it left him in that state of excitement which usually drove him to Crockford's. Thither he repaired, after seeing his company safe in the hands of the watchmen, and dice ended the night, as debauchery counts the hours.

CHAPTER LVIII.

THE BURLINGTON.

"Mischief, thou art swift<br>
To enter in the thoughts of desperate men."<br>
ROMEO AND JULIET.

IMAGINE yourself now in a bed-room in the Burlington. A bed has just been deserted. The late occupier is flung in a great chair near a table at some distance from the couch. It is Dawson, just risen at two o'clock in the day. His posture and attire is that of the ruined gamester in the "Rake's Progress." The table is covered with all the appliances of vulgar foppery, in addition to letters, newspapers, pistols, and soda-water and brandy. The room is filled with parliamentary and rakish rubbish of all sorts. In one corner is a chaos of blue books; in another a heap of clothes unpaid for, and bills never to be settled; in a third, a collection of brass-knockers torn by the senator from hall-doors. Scarce an article in the chamber but tells a tale of profligacy. Wonderful it is how some men live as they do, surrounded night and day with the monuments of their follies and their crimes.

Dawson is a ruined man. He lost last night the entire of the sum repaid him by Mr. Spenser. Even his bill at Lovegrove's will never be discharged. He is utterly ruined, and sits there in the savage gloom of desperation, nobody yet knowing how utterly and hopelessly lost he is, not even the friend of his youth and the attorney of his bosom.

He has just dispatched a note to Sharkey, in order to acquaint him with the results of last night's amusement.

"Bob," said Dawson, when his friend arrived, wonderfully fresh after the night's excess, "Bob, I'm done at last."

"I don't feel quite comfortable myself," said Sharkey, supposing that Dawson alluded to the effects of last night's dissipation.

"It's not that, Bob; I'm done brown." Sharkey laughed.

"It's not brown you are," he said, "but blue, Dud.;—you are always blue before breakfast."

Dawson acquainted him with the mishaps of the night.

"I'm cleaned out, Bob, and that's the long and the short of it; I must run."

"What's come over you this morning?" asked Sharkey, growing a little serious.

Dawson then made the fullest financial statement he had ever made to his man of business in his life, and in ten minutes fully convinced him he was worth several thousand pounds less than nothing.

"It's a bad business, Dud."

"You may say that, Bob."

"And where do you think of running to?"

"I have a brother in Van Dieman's land, and I'm thinking of joining him, scraping together all I can, and speculating desperately in sheep."

"It's a bad business, Dud."

"Bob, I haven't told you half my business with you this morning," said Dawson.

"I hope you have told me the worst half," said the other.

"I'm thinking of going to Castle Dawson for a few days, to wind up affairs there."

"I wouldn't advise you to do any such thing," said the attorney; "people might be looking for you whom you wouldn't like to have at your heels; and besides, what affairs have you to wind up there or any where else?"

"Yes, but I have," said Dawson; "and, at all events, wouldn't I like to see the old place once more before I leave it forever; many a rollicking day we had there, Bob."

"Many a queer thing was done there, Dud."

"Many a queer thing," said Dawson, repeating the attorney's words, whether abstractedly, or with a new meaning, it was hard to say. His looks puzzled Sharkey, and made him ask Dawson what he was thinking of.

"I was just thinking," he replied, "that almost the only queer thing that was never done at Castle Dawson, to my knowledge, was—but no matter; that's neither here nor there," he added, suddenly checking himself.

"No," said Sharkey; "but take my advice, and don't set your foot in Ireland again, whatever you do; it would be a risk, Dud."

"What care I for risk," roared Dawson, starting up and striding melodramatically up and down the disordered room, with his gorgeous dressing-gown hanging about him, unshaven, ghastly, and hideous with sudden passion, to a degree that frightened Sharkey, who concluded him delirious between the wine and the losses of the previous night. At length he stopped abruptly opposite to the attorney, and broke out with furious earnestness, although still in the "Cambyses' vein," which was second nature with him—"What care I for risk? I never succeeded in any thing in my life, and I tried every thing; I played every game—I played for money, I played for office, I played for beauty—I played boldly, too; I was no dastard—was I, Bob? I ask you, Bob—was I?"

"No one can say that, Dud., at all events," said Sharkey, too much alarmed by the frenzied manner of his companion to dispute any point with him.

"No, by heavens they can't; I was no coward and I was no churl; I was liberal of my life and my money—I risked all and I won nothing. Nothing did me any good. I set my heart on a girl; you know who I mean, Bob—was there any thing I didn't do to deserve her? I need not tell you, Bob, all I did for her and her ungrateful family. My money, my talents, my parliamentary influence, my life; I put all at their service."

"You did, and I always said so," said Sharkey, heartily wishing himself out of the house.

"Is she a great fortune—is she a Miss Coutts? Is there any thing against me?—I mean, that any one can prove." The voice altered and fell with this very proper salvo. The point would have told well on the stage.

"What's between you and me," said Sharkey, "is neither here nor there."

"Am I a Caliban, Bob?" was Dawson's next interrogation.

"You are not that, at all events," replied his friend, probably thinking that Dawson meant a cannibal.

"Well, Bob," continued Dawson, "the upshot of it all is, that by"—(it is unnecessary to quote Dawson's phrases *verbatim*)—"I'm not going to put up with it any longer. I'll right myself, if the world won't right me. Either it's fate or it's witchcraft that's fighting against me, and by ——, I'll try one fall more with the one or the other, before I shoot myself. My plan, Bob, is what I have just told you."

"You told me no plan."

"I told you I was going to Castle Dawson."

"I see no plan in that," said Sharkey.

"It's a resolution, then," said Dawson.

"It's a foolish one," said Sharkey; "and I don't see what good it will do you with the lady."

"I'll take leave of her at all events," said Dawson.

"You are too sentimental, Dud.," said Sharkey, "but if you must go back to Ireland, go by long say, I recommend you."

"You don't suppose I'm such a blockhead as to go any other way, in existing circumstances," said Dawson. "Captain Dowse is in the river with the brig that did the job for me before."

"Well, there's some sense in that," said Sharkey.

"You must come with me, Bob," said Dawson.

Sharkey at first positively declined the invitation, which seemed indeed no very tempting one, falsely alleging that he had a case to attend to in the House of Lords, but Dawson overcame his reluctance, partly by holding out the prospect of a glorious farewell debauch with a few choice fellows like themselves, and the remnant of the wine in the Castle Dawson cellar, partly by tender reminiscences of their old rascally friendship. Sharkey, in truth, was not much better off in point of fortune or prospects than the ex-senator himself; and when a man lives from hand to mouth, the ties are never very strong that attach him to any particular spot on the earth's surface. The attorney further undertook to go down that very day to Blackwall, and order Captain Dowse to be in readiness to sail within twenty-four hours.

Sharkey was not long gone upon this mission, leaving Dawson ruminating upon some dodge to effect his escape from the Burlington without settling his bill, when a servant entered and brought him letters. One was from Mrs. Peacock. He tore it open. Its effect was like the pouring of oil upon a furnace, or vinegar into a wound. He started on his feet, tore his hair, tugged at his neckcloth, and ranged the room grinding his teeth and stamping like a maniac. The intelligence more than confirmed his apprehensions as to Vivyan's movements and the object of them. Two letters, in Vivyan's handwriting, bearing American post-marks, had reached Redcross. The first was addressed to Mrs. Woodward, but it had been sealed in a manner that baffled Lucy's ingenuity, and with all her expertness she was forced to content herself with as much as she could read through the folds of the paper, without violating the wax. This was enough, however, to prove that Vivyan had found Sydney, and that they were both in quest of the fellow whose evidence was of such vital consequence. The second, which arrived with the first, although dated nearly a fortnight later, was more manageable, as the post-mistress expressed it; it was a letter to Elizabeth herself, and, as if Mrs. Peacock desired to drive Dawson frantic, she had copied almost the whole of it for his information. The name of Lamb was not mentioned, perhaps advisedly; but the letter (which seemed to have been written in a delirium of joy) announced in general terms that the means had been discovered not only of triumphantly acquitting Sydney, but of establishing charges of almost incredible enormity against parties who little dreamed of the exposure, that awaited them. The rest of Vivyan's letter was all made up of language, which, though perfectly innocent in its nature, the writer would never have committed to paper, had he dreamed of its meeting any eye but Miss Spenser's. Perhaps this was the part that most infuriated Dawson. Accustomed to indulge in violent bursts of passion, he dashed the furniture about the room, uttered a thousand horrid imprecations, snatched up a pistol and seemed on the point of blowing out his brains, then swallowed brandy, and looked as if about to tumble into a fit of apoplexy. The brandy, however, had a composing effect, and Mrs. Peacock's dispatch only confirmed Dawson's previous intentions. He shaved himself, and looked a degree less rakish and desperate when Sharkey rejoined him close to dinner time. They dined together, and when the attorney learned, among the confidences of the evening, that the return of Lamb to Europe was a probable event, he heartily concurred in the prudence of his friend's resolution to follow his brother to Van Dieman's Land.

The following evening, Captain Dowse's ill-looking brig, with an ill-looking crew, and several ill-looking passengers, in addition to Dawson and his agent, sailed for the west of Ireland. It was on the deck at midnight, while they were both smoking cigars, and the captain was blaspheming to his men, that Sharkey first learned the real object of the voyage.

---

# BOOK XI.

## CHAPTER LIX.

### CAROUSALS.

*"At one time he assembled three or four especial good hacksters and roaring boys, and made them drink like Templars."* RABELAIS.

CAROUSAL at Castle-Dawson. Old times come back again; wine flowing like water; awful drinking in the ruinous parlor; furious gaming in the decayed drawing-room; a select party of insolvents, black-legs, and desperadoes. It was always a stormy place. The wind never slept there; nothing reposed within five miles of it; its atmosphere was the type of modern Irish patriotism, never a calm, or even a steady gale; nothing but squall and bluster. Now, as if expressly to suit both the riotous mirth of the guests assembled, and the gloomy habit of the proprietor's mind, the weather was dark as well as gusty; it was cold, too, for it was the fall of the year—a damp insinuating cold which penetrated your bones, and either cramped you with rheumatism, or wrung you with tooth-ache.

It was a house that demanded huge fires, mountains of blankets, and perpetual motion, to keep its inmates warm; and even then it called for, and almost justified, deep drinking to make them forget, as soon as possible, what a dreary place it was at best. Some ruinous houses tell, even in their decay, that they had once been virtuous buildings, that the feet of worthy men had once trodden their halls, and that honest faces had once gathered round their hearths; but Castle Dawson told no such story. There was something more than bleak about its dilapidation. Its decline was not the decline of respectability; its antiquity was ill-looking; it reminded you of the old age of vice, which no lip blesses, and to which no knee bends.

Perhaps it was that the blankets were not mountainous enough, but certainly the party did not waste much of their night in bed. Dawson was of course master of the revels; he was dissolute and uproarious certainly, but he was too haggard and abstracted for a Comus. Still he drank himself, and he cheered the topers; many a time, too, did he descend into that mysterious wine-vault of his, which corresponded with the ocean, and bring forth remnants of bins, which had been stocked in the gay but wicked days chronicled by old Sir Jonah.

The dinners were solid and coarse, but the company was not fastidious. They drank generously, and generously overlooked the deficiencies of a bachelor's establishment. The "Repeal of the Union" was drunk vociferously every day; Dawson proposing it in a mad speech, and Sharkey always roaring for "one cheer more."

There was an anachronism in these festivities. They savored of the jovial times before the union, more than of the saturnine age which Pitt and Castlereagh had the honor of introducing. Not only day and night were reversed at Castle Dawson, but even centuries were turned topsy-turvy.

But Dawson had not revisited his paternal mansion on this occasion with mere designs of hospitality and mirth, however coarse and licentious.

Within a pistol-shot of the house, which Dawson used swaggeringly to call his ancestral mansion, a brig was swinging at anchor, which Markham's eye would have recognized at a glance as the same respectable craft which he had seen trading so mysteriously in books and pictures on the memorable night of his bivouac on Spenser Island. If you had gone on board the Dolphin (for so the brig was named), you would have seen that active proceedings were in progress to furnish and decorate her small cabin with something more than comfort; there was an obvious, if not a very successful, effort to fit it up with some degree of luxury and refinement. Nay, more, you would have been struck by observing that the arrangements were of a feminine character; and, in fact, there was a tight, active, bustling, and good-looking young woman on board, not merely superintending, but, with her own smart hands, briskly and cleverly assisting in putting every thing into the neatest possible order.

The bed-rooms of Castle Dawson had been ransacked for the principal part of the furniture of the cabin, for you may suppose that dressing-tables, sofas, looking-glasses, and such articles, were somewhat scarce on board a ship like the Dolphin, when in the best sailing trim. To transfer these things from the house to the brig, the secret communications between the cellars and the clefts or caves along the beach had been found extremely convenient; and the small black skiff employed in the transportation had not yet completed its work, but was still to be seen darting in and out of the mouth of the cavern, like a boat plying on a subterraneous canal.

It was night-fall, and the red lights thrown by the brig's lanterns upon the two rough faces in the skiff, as well as those which their flambeau, in return, cast upon the people, on the deck of the brig, made the scene as picturesque as the transaction was irregular.

The features of the young woman were very imperfectly seen, and she seemed not anxious to display them: Her bonnet was close, and her hair, disordered by the breeze, and occasionally by the spray, streamed about her face and assisted to conceal it. There was nobody, perhaps, whom she cared to favor with a peep at any part of her person, for she was most comfortably and impenetrably wrapt in a scarlet mantle, with a gray plaid shawl or scarf folded over it, and both were not more than the evening required, for it was damp, raw, and blustry, as indeed it generally was at this dismal part of the coast.

Occasionally a gust came from off the shore and brought with it sounds like those of gross merry-making. Dawson's friends, if not Dawson himself, were evidently carousing deeply.

There seemed to be three seamen in the brig at the time; two of them were minding their business, the third, who seemed to have some command, was overlooking the operations going forward, and occasionally trying to engage the young woman in conversation. But she seemed disinclined to converse with him, and intent upon nothing but the business for which she had come on board. Though the wind evidently annoyed her, blew her bonnet half off her head, and made her grapple her shawl about her, she scarcely spoke at all, but only bit her lip, or uttered some little peevish but inarticulate exclamation.

The boat issued once more from the cavern: the effect then was particularly striking. A ruddy glow strongly illuminated for a moment the low-browed arch under the cliffs, and the next instant was diffused over the agitated water. The boat came along-side, and this time its cargo was a fractured looking-glass in a tarnished gilt frame of carved wood, a fragile table of some fanciful shape and material, and a couple of old tapestry screens, one of which was much torn, probably by Sydney Spenser's pistol-shooting. The articles were not heavy, and were easily hauled up into the brig.

"Is that the last?" demanded the young female.

"; One of the boatmen replied in the affirmative.

"Then I'll just see those things put in their places," she said, "and I'll return with you."

In about ten minutes she was ready to leave the brig; the seaman who had been desirous to flirt with her now handed her civilly into the boat; she thanked him curtly, and ordered the men to pull back into the cave. She was evidently a bold girl; for the place she was going to, the fellows she was trusting herself with, and the time of the day were sufficient to make most young women a little nervous.

The skiff plunged into the hole in the crags, whose jagged points and splinters sometimes
K

caught the jackets of the boatmen and the dress of the young female, while the wreaths of sea-wrack pendent from the roof of the chasm bobbed against their foreheads, and now and then filled their eyes with brine. The air was cruelly cold, and the light only just enough to show the extremities of objects, the points of the rocks, the tips of the noses, the illuminated edges of the oiled-skin hats.

The young woman was well pleased when she reached the foot of the ladder. Directly the trap-door was opened, down came in gusts the noise of the coarse conviviality in the dining-room; and the kitchens, with the entire basement story, rang with it, to the exclusion of all other sounds.

In ordinary times you heard nothing in this part of the house but the squall and the surge, and they made sufficient hubbub. But now the roar of the gayety drowned the thunder of the waves against the beach, and their dismal groaning under ground. The girl untied, partly raised her bonnet, and listened with attention, as if she wished to distinguish some particular voice among the rest; she then called to one of the wild attendants who were lounging about the passages, and ordered him to conduct and light her to her room. The fellow snatched a blazing brand of bog-pine from the kitchen-hearth, and preceded her through the moldering corridors.

"Your master is still with his company," she said, interrogatorily to her torch-bearer, who, uncouth as he was, wore a tarnished suit of the Dawson livery.

The clownish footman, ill at ease in a garb that had not been made for him, shrugged his shoulders, and replied in the affirmative.

The room she repaired to was the same remote and small one to which we may remember that Dawson, upon one occasion, dismissed two guests of his who were not presentable in decent society. There was no furniture there now, save a few creaking chairs and a crazy table; a sofa which it formerly contained had been sent on board the brig. There was, however, a good turf fire on the hearth, and the lady was not sorry to see it, after her long exposure to the night air. She flung her bonnet on the table, and sat her down before the blaze, her feet close to the embers, her arms folded on her bosom, and her eyes fixed on the flickering flame, with an expression that did not imply the most virtuous train of inward meditation.

She probably slept, for on the door being abruptly flung open, she started up with a slight scream, and then laughed at herself for being frightened. It was only Dawson, just escaped from the dinner-table, at which he had left his friends—perhaps a few of them under it. The room was very dark, but there was light enough for present purposes. Dawson's voice announced the depth of his potations, if not of his designs.

It was thick and stammering, as he said—
"Is all ready, Lucy?"

She replied in the affirmative. He then asked her whether she had had supper and wine; but she was doggedly temperate, and only requested an immediate escort back to Redcross.

"Not to night, woman," said Dawson.

But she was peremptory; her work was done, and she must return to her husband. Dawson pressed her, and cracked some thrice-cracked jokes at the expense of conjugal fidelity, as if Lucy had been renowned for fidelity in any relation of life. However, she was constant to her resolution now; and the same kerne who had lighted her with the blazing faggot was now directed to convey her on a swift horse across the hills. Dawson himself helped her on horseback. She mounted behind her wild conductor, and soon disappeared in the mountain mists. Until that night Lucy Peacock had always been a brave girl. If cowardice is a feminine quality, she was now feminine enough. She quivered with every bull-rush which the wind stirred in the fens; the wings of the moor-fowl, fluttered from their nests by the horse's hoofs, dismayed her. She clung with convulsive tenacity to the waist of her escort, and the little light that was in the pitchy sky, instead of being a source of comfort and hardihood, only ministered to her terrors, and, metamorphosed every gray stone and wandering sheep into an object of alarm.

Dawson spent the residue of the night more soberly than his company. He tore himself from the social circle to hold clandestine conferences with Sharkey and the commander of the respectable craft at anchor under his windows. Captain Dowse was the name of that distinguished officer. He was a short, square, cadaverous, one-eyed villain, who looked as if nature had cut him out for the diabolical trade in men, and as if the horrors of the middle passage would be cakes and ale to him.

---

## CHAPTER LX.

### THE ABDUCTION.

"Beauty, like the fair Hesperian tree
Laden with blooming gold, had need the guard
Of dragon watch, with unenchanted eye,
To save her blossoms and defend her fruit
From the rash hand of bold incontinence,
Of night, or loneliness, it recks me not:
I fear the dread events that dog them both,
Lest some ill-greeting touch attempt the person
Of our unowned sister."        COMUS.

It was a Friday evening. In September the days are generally bright in Ireland, but their span is of course much contracted; the sun departs precipitately for the other hemisphere, and, when there is no moon to "take up the wondrous tale," the sovereignty of darkness is soon established. Mr. Spenser had gone over to Redcross after breakfast to transact some parochial business, intending to bring the Woodwards back with him to the lodge; and Elizabeth (radiant with joy at the happy news from America, which had reached her only the day before), having occupied herself within doors the entire morning, toward the close of the day went out alone, to take a short stroll, not purposing to go very far from the house. Lord Bonham had interspersed the heath that clipped in his wild retreat with little patches of shrubs and flowers, such as the sea air and the mountain soil suffered to thrive; Miss Spenser, having old gardening habits, was wont to pay occasional attentions to these tiny oases in the desert, and she commonly carried a garden-knife in the pocket of her apron, to assist her in her little horticultural operations. Thus occupied on the day in question, she strayed unconsciously to the edge of the inclosure, and lingered there awhile, smitten by the beauty of the evening, and of the scenery that surrounded her; the view bounded at some points by glorious glimpses of the sea, at others by the rocky summits of the hills, which were now attired in the richest autumnal colors. The laborers' bell rang six as she reached the spot we have mentioned, and, as she did not expect her father to return until near seven, she passed the inclosure by an opening in the fence, and planned a short tour, calculated to lead her back to the lodge in about twenty minutes. She had not proceeded far before she encountered a young man, whose countenance impressed her painfully. It was a face familiar to the reader, but to Miss Spenser entirely unknown. The fellow, however, was not physically formidable, even to a woman; his shoulders were contracted, and his cheeks pale and hollow, so that Elizabeth could not help pitying, while she gladly withdrew her eyes from him. A few moments brought her to the road side, and there she was greatly surprised to observe a chaise, with four horses, drawn up in the shadow of some trees which grew there. A charming thought instantly suggested itself, that it might be Vivyan returned. She advanced to speak to the postillion, who was standing near; he uttered something unintelligible, and she turned, disappointed, to resume her walk. In an instant two ruffians, masked and otherwise disguised, sprang on her from behind the fence; there was nobody to hear her shrieks, as they dragged her to the chaise. Terror now almost bereaved her of reason. When she first came to herself, she was alone in the carriage, and the postillion was urging the horses, at the top of their speed, across brown hills unknown to her. Her first thought was to open the door and cast herself upon the heath, which the wheels of the chaise grazed as it swept along. But she heard the clattering of hoofs behind her; she was guarded by outriders; and she opportunely recollected that if she was hurt by the fall, which was so likely to happen, she would only be the more at the mercy of the villains in whose hands she was. Who could they be?—what could this undreamed-of violence mean? whither were they whirling her across the mountains? The fearful thought quickly flashed upon her that this could be the atrocity of only one man in the world. As far, too, as she could form a notion of the direction in which she was moving, it was toward Castle Dawson. The agony of her mind under that conviction (for it soon became one) is beyond painting. The dangers before her seemed as great as ever woman was exposed to: she stood in need, at that trying moment, of all the strength of mind, steadfastness of purpose, and energy of will, of which nature had implanted the seeds in her character; and fortunate now it was that her recent experience in life had educated and corroborated those hardy qualities. Yet what was any former trial to that which now awaited her? Now, it was brute force she was the victim of; no passive courage would carry her through the struggle that impended. She was in Dawson's fangs! She was going to the house, at the very name of ᴠ uch she was wont to shudder, as children do a. the castles of ogres. The very name was a guarantee for every thing lawless and licentious, and her heart sank within her when she reflected that the violence which she was now experiencing, was designed but as a mere preliminary to further deeds, which her blood ran cold to think of. Frantically she clasped her hands to her eyes, as if she could thus exclude the images of horror that presented themselves—images of danger to what was dearer than life. One hand fell down upon her lap; it touched the garden-knife. She was not without a weapon to face a Tarquin! She opened it; the blade was short, thick, but keen enough to deal a mortal wound. While she was gazing upon this heaven-sent protector, one of the masked horsemen rode up close to the carriage window. Instead of returning the knife to the pocket in her apron, she thrust it open into her bosom.

It was now darkening apace. The horseman who rode up seemed to have done so only to quicken the postillions, for the carriage now flew like the wind, the course being down a long declivity, at the base of which the unhappy girl thought she could just discern the waste of the ocean, with a dim gray object on its margin, which, with unutterable horror, she concluded was the reprobate mansion of her persecutor.

It was black night when the chaise halted before the dilapidated porch. The movements were all so rapid, and the house was so dark, that Elizabeth could scarcely distinguish the objects she passed, while with force, but not with violence, she was hurried through gloomy passages and up dreary staircases, to a chamber on the first floor. Repeatedly and sternly she demanded whither they were bearing her; by what right or pretense of right her liberty was thus violated; and who was it that dared to commit this intolerable outrage? Her questions received no answers, her taunts no notice.

She now found herself a prisoner in a spacious room. It was hung with old and tarnished draperies; it contained a bed, some presses, and other bed-room furniture; there were two windows looking over the wide, dismal yard, where the old hound was still howling, and there was a large, ruinous fireplace, with some burning peat in it, which afforded all the light in the apartment, save the glimmering of a thin candle on a three-legged table in the midst of the floor.

About a quarter of an hour elapsed before any thing occurred to prove that the house contained any inhabitant but herself; not a sound reached her ear but the whining of the hound, the melancholy dash of the waves, and the intermitted moaning of the blast. It was a dreadful interval. The appearance of her ruffian foes would have been a relief to its mysterious horror. She felt a desperate anxiety to know and to brave the worst—to see her assailants and to cope with them. Could she have unlocked the door, she would have ranged the house, seeking the villains who had dragged her there; she would have gone in quest of the ruffianism that seemed now to be skulking with some infamous design, perhaps biding its own time to pounce upon her when exhausted with fatigue, and less able to combat force. But the

door was securely fastened on the outside; and the windows seemed equally to forbid egress. There are men, it is to be feared, who, in the situation of this fair young woman of two-and-twenty, would have lost some of the composure so important in great dangers. It is high praise of a girl to say that from the beginning to the end of the struggle to which she was now committed, she scarcely neglected any precaution, or failed to try any resource, which there was the slightest use in resorting to under the circumstances. She felt more and more every moment that upon her own resolution, and probably upon her own hand, her deliverance must depend. Inspired by a sacred enthusiasm, she fell upon her knees before the table, and with clasped hands besought the support of the God of purity and innocence to deliver her out of the power of wicked men, whatever shape their guilty purposes might assume. Rising already reinforced by that brief and fervent act of devotion, she recollected her secret weapon, drew it forth again, sheathed it in the folds of her soft raiment, and felt the spirit and resolution of a Lucretia to use it at her need.

Just as she returned the knife to her bosom, a step was audible—it approached—a hand was upon the key of the door—it grated in the wards—the door opened.—When it closed again she was shut up in the same lone room with the man whose approach to her person, even in her father's house and presence, had often made her shudder. His villainy faltered under the eye of the outraged maiden; she faced him with an energetic composure that unnerved and petrified him. He forgot the love-speech he had framed to give the color of romance to his nefarious conduct, and stammered forth a foolish apology for the unworthiness of the apartment and the badness of the fire.

"Confine yourself to an explanation of your behavior, Mr. Dawson," she replied, with indignant scorn. "Why am I here?—why have I been torn from my friends by brutal force? Why am I thus barbarously insulted and abused?"

"Calm yourself, adorable Miss Spenser," he replied; "calm yourself, and I will explain all—do not tremble so—sit down."

"I do not tremble, sir—though I am in your house, Mr. Dawson, I do not tremble."

"Hear me, charming girl—but you are fatigued—be seated."

"I shall not sit down while I am at Castle Dawson," she answered bravely. "I demand my freedom; I neither ask nor shall I receive courtesy from you—let me go, and instantly."

She moved toward the door—he placed himself so as to obstruct her approach to it.

"No, Miss Spenser—you do not leave this tonight; you are in my power; it is my turn now to conquer; we shall see whether my passion is not as resistless as your charms."

"Oh, you shall dearly rue this atrocious outrage; you shall answer it dearly both to my family and to the laws of the country."

"Do not talk of your family—I do not wish to speak of them except with respect and affection. The old friend of your brother—"

"His corrupter—his betrayer."

"I did not betray him, Miss Spenser. This is more of your injustice—your cruel injustice to one whose only crime is to love you"

"I am not going to argue with you, sir—it is getting late—again I demand my freedom—release me—release me at your peril. Why do you thus cruelly detain me?"

"Do you talk of cruelty," he replied, now beginning to recollect some of his prepared address, "you, whose cruel insensibility to the truest, noblest, and sublimest passion that ever thrilled a human bosom, has driven me to this last resource of desperate affection. No, not esperate, I will not call it desperate; you see oefore you a frantic, but not despairing lover. You are one of those women—the grandest of their sex—who are not to be won by the ordinary tokens of sincerity. When I saved your dear life, adorable girl, did I not well know that it was not by such common-place gallantry a heart like yours was to be gained? No; you were only to be convinced by enormous sacrifices, such as my ambition and my country. I have already sacrificed one by retiring from parliament, and I am on the point of sacrificing the other by leaving Ireland forever."

"What is all this to me, sir; what are your intentions to me?" Elizabeth naturally demanded, seeing no drift in this oration, and beginning to apprehend that she was in the power of a lunatic as well as a ruffian.

"That shall be explained to-morrow, or sooner, if the wind changes," said Dawson.

"No, no—I leave this to-night—this instant," she cried vehemently.

"Resistance is vain; but need I assure you that in this house you shall be safe from harm?"

"Depend upon it I shall, sir," she said, with quivering energy.

While he promised her security he looked dangerous in the extreme; he still stood between her and the door; his eye was sometimes rudely fastened upon her; sometimes it wandered strangely about the room. Again he alluded to her fatigue, and offered to take her hand to conduct her to a seat. With tremulous vigor she repelled the hateful attention, and repeated her declaration, that she would never sit while she remained his prisoner. He uttered some scarce-articulate words, half reproachful, half passionate, and moved to the door. She thought he was about to relieve her from his presence, but he went to the door only to lock or bolt it. The terrified girl raised a scream that pierced through every corner of the dreary house. He advanced toward her with a savage declaration that her cries would call no one to her aid. She repelled him with her extended arms, with the fierce action of beauty and virtue in the face of danger. He approached another step and attempted to catch her waist.

The garden-knife flashed in his face.

He recoiled before the instrument of death and safety.

"Do you depend on that?" he asked between his clenched teeth, with affected contempt for the weapon, and the resistance of a girl.

"Yes, Mr. Dawson," she cried, "upon this, and upon the support of heaven, is my resolution to defend my honor with it."

He laughed fearfully, and looked at once dubious and dreadful. The thought now occurred to her, that if she could but drive him from the room and fortify herself there, it would afford time for her father and friends to come to her rescue, as they would not fail to suspect Dawson to be the author of the outrage. Possessed of this thought, she did not content herself with standing on the defensive, but menacingly commanded him to leave her presence.

"Retire instantly, Mr. Dawson," she cried, almost unsexed by the exigency of her situation, and assuming the post and attitude of active hostility; "leave me this moment, or I will compel you with this weapon. If I am a prisoner here to-night, I shall pass it not only in safety, but in solitude. Begone, or I will chase you from me."

So speaking, she advanced upon him with no feigned determination, but with the actual fierceness of a noble, high-passioned woman. As a beaten hound slinks from his chastisement, so did the baffled and degraded Dawson, white with rage and fear, retire from a garden-knife in the lifted hand of a girl.

Directly he was gone, she secured the door, not only with the key and the bolt, but with as much of the furniture as she could accumulate against it with the remains of her exhausted strength. There was no other door to the chamber. She examined the windows. The fall to the ground from one of them was some twenty or thirty feet. Immediately under the other was the roof of a stable; or some out-office slanting toward the yard. Her defense on this side was therefore but slight—only the shutters of the windows, which she made as fast as the arrangements permitted. There was then nothing to be done but to rely upon the providence which had so far protected her, and abide the course of events; but it was a harrowing situation; she thought of her very securities with terror; a few chairs and boxes her only barricade against the extremity of outrage. How weak she felt, too, now that the excitement of instant peril had ceased to give a hysterical vigor to her limbs! It was impossible to keep the resolution she had announced not to sit during her captivity. She sat for upward of an hour almost motionless, listening intensely to catch any noise that might intimate either the approach of friends, or the return of the enemy; sometimes she thought she could distinguish voices, but in general the only sounds were those of the winds and the waves, to which she would gladly have committed herself to escape from Castle Dawson. The fire was lowering, and the candle was growing short and dim. The room grew more gloomy and ghastly every minute. She shuddered with cold; there were blankets and a counterpane on the bed, but she would have thought their touch contamination. It was now, she calculated, about eleven o'clock. She paced the room for a while, then returned to her chair, still listening and marveling, either at the dismal noises, or the more dismal silence in the intervals between them; alternately shrinking with dread, and composing herself with calm reflections; struggling to keep down fearful bodings with cheerful courage; trying to fathom the mystery of Dawson's designs, to divine what shape his violence would take, should he storm her in her present fortress before the arrival of assistance; often thinking of her father's despair and misery, on his return from his ride, and trusting that the Woodwards would not hear of her danger until after her deliverance—all the reflections and feelings of a brave and virtuous girl beset with perils, but not discomposed and unnerved by them.

Another hour elapsed, as well as she could mark the passing of time by the agonizing train of controlled but not vanquished fears. Though unmolested, she was not unvisited during that interval. A hobbling step in the corridor, followed by a hoarse croaking voice at the door, varied the monotony of her dismal situation. It was the withered crone of the kitchen with the offer of refreshment, and the tender of her delicate services to her master's fair visitor. Had Miss Spenser recognized female accents, she might have appealed for assistance to those female sympathies which are rarely quite extinct in the foulest form of womanhood; but the characteristics of sex were wanting in the voice at least of Mr. Dawson's housekeeper. Elizabeth declined her hospitable attentions, and the same hobbling step retraced the passage until its noise was lost, as well as that of the growl that accompanied it, in the other discords of the place.

Anxious to form a notion of the progress of the night, the thought now occurred to her to unbar the shutters of one of the windows and observe the heavens. She knew some of the leading constellations, and she thought if she could only see the Great Bear, she might divine the hour with some degree of accuracy. With extreme caution she removed the fastenings and peered out into the dark. It was a wonderfully calm night for the locality, and as bright as was possible without a moon. The concave blazed with stars, and the aspect of the room being fortunately northward, the remarkable group she wanted was easily distinguished, and its inverted position assured her that it was probably an hour or two past midnight. As still she gazed forth upon the firmament, which had nothing purer beneath it than herself, her eye glanced upon the slanting roof under the window, which seemed to slope downward to the very pavement of the yard, and the idea of escape suggested itself. The difficulties seemed enormous, but the idea possessed her strongly. To flee from such detestable confinement, to get beyond the reach of such ruthless villainy, were it to the most savage heath or the wildest cavern along the shore, was so desirable, that the more she thought of the dangers, the less formidable they seemed. Her resolution to venture it was taken in a few minutes. The advantage of disguise was obvious, and the completest and most commodious would be the attire of the other sex. One of the wardrobes was unlocked and open. She looked into it, and discovered with surprise and joy, a kind of sailor's dress, a blue jacket, loose trowsers of gray plaid, and a round oil-skin hat, which she instantly recognized as belonging to her brother; in fact it was the suit Sydney had worn on the memorable day on which he rode to Castle Dawson with the proctor, and which he had changed there for a hunting-dress of Dudley's. Elizabeth remembered how sharply she had reproved him for appearing in the flashy green coat, and now the jacket he had left behind him in its place was about to save her from worse than death.

She speedily metamorphosed herself into a sailor's boy, retaining as much of her female gear as she could; gathered up her beautiful hair under the hat, took her gray tartan shawl on her arm, to protect herself from cold, and thus, not forgetting her faithful knife, she proceeded to attempt the descent into the yard. Noiselessly she raised the window, and crept out upon the shed beneath it. Fortunately, the inclination was gentle, so that she crept on to the edge without difficulty, but she was then at a height above the ground which far exceeded her estimate, and for a few moments her progress was balked. The yard was very obscure, but at some short distance she fancied she could discover what seemed to be a heap of litter. At all events it did not appear to be stones or any hard substance, and she thought she could gain it by a leap. She raised herself to her feet, and with a vigorous effort sprang upon the heap, which proved to be straw, and received her with a soft and rustling welcome. The egresses from the yard commanded her attention in the first instance. There were two, a gateway, which was secured, and a door at one side, which was also locked; but the key was in the hole, so that her escape so far was unimpeded. Her heart now, however, sank within her, when she thought of the wide waste of unknown heaths and hills that stretched between her and her friends. How could she hope to traverse them in safety; nay, to traverse them at all? A horse—had she but a horse—"a kingdom for a horse!" Familiar with the ponies of those mountains, it occurred to her that she might find one of them in the stables, and she returned and searched the sheds in the yard with that view. She found two animals of that small, hardy, sagacious species; and what was more, she found a side-saddle, the identical one that had been provided for Mrs. Peacock's use on a former night. The beast was more courteous to her than man had been, and she succeeded, to her own astonishment, in preparing him for the road. She found a whip, too, which she seized to her use, and leading the pony out of the yard, she mounted him eagerly, and having no choice of roads to distract her, simply turned her back upon Castle Dawson, and fled into the hills.

On rode the dauntless girl over moor and mountain, in the visible darkness, only bent upon leaving the abhorred house, and its more abhorred master, as far as possible in the rear. The pony was a brave sure-footed animal, and seemed to feel that he was bearing distressed beauty from the reach of ruffian aggression. On she rode, not fearless, but with no fear that misbecame or overwhelmed her. The sounds of the heath and of the distant sea occasionally startled but never bewildered her. Hers was

"The virtuous mind that ever goes attended
By a strong-siding champion, conscience,"

and hers was the unwavering assurance

"That he, the Supreme Good, to whom all things ill
Are but as slavish officers of vengeance,
Would send a glistering guardian, if need were,
To keep her life and honor unassailed."

On she rode, with unflagging spirit, with unabated speed, with undismayed heart, agitated yet constant, like the fair tree in the storm—how different from the girl who rode over the same moors a night or two before, after having atrociously aided Dawson to accomplish his nefarious purpose. Pursuit was what Elizabeth chiefly dreaded; into worse hands she could not possibly fall than those from which she was a fugitive; but to be pursued and overtaken was a mischance so likely to befall her, that she resolved never to slacken her pace while the horse that carried her did his duty. Often she wondered how it came to pass that her friends had not already tracked her out; sometimes she feared that she had taken a wrong course; sometimes she conjectured, what proved to be the truth, that their pursuit had been diverted into a false scent by one of the stratagems of the gang.

It was not until just before sunrise, that exciting morning, that the distracted rector and curate discovered the artifice that had been practiced upon them, and, tortured by the fear that its success had been fatal to Elizabeth, at length, after hours of vain search, and upon jaded horses, took the rout they should have taken at first.

The curate was clothed in terror from head to heel. His passion was so towering that it seemed to add a good cubit to his stature. He looked like the incarnation of a whirlwind; his teeth were clenched, and he was dumb with the intensity of his indignation. The staff which he brandished was out of the category of all ordinary cudgels, for it was literally a young forest-tree, such as painters and poets arm a satyr with, or a Cyclops.

The two clergymen, with Lord Bonham's gamekeeper and two officers of police, were now riding hard toward Castle Dawson, when, on gaining the crown of an eminence, from which miles of road could be seen winding through the moors, like an immense serpent, they discerned a rider approaching them at the top of his speed. The dress of a sailor was noticed before the features could be distinguished. As the speed on neither side was checked for an instant, the distance diminished rapidly, and Mr. Spenser exclaimed, with amazement—

"Good God, it is Sydney!"—his daughter looked so like her brother, in the garb which the latter had been accustomed to wear. But the next moment Hercules was supporting his lovely niece in his arms, to save her from falling exhausted from her horse.

---

## CHAPTER LXI.

### THE SHIPWRECK.

"Truth will come to light; murder can not be hid long;
a man's son may, but in the end truth will out."
MERCHANT OF VENICE.

IT was not the great curate's fault that Dawson effected his escape. The minister of the gospel that day performed the work of a dozen officers of justice. His assault on Castle Dawson bore no faint resemblance to the actual storming of a fortress, except that, to his sore disappointment, no enemy appeared to defend its approaches. No nook or corner of that iniquitous mansion did the besiegers leave unransacked. When they reached the vault which communicated so craftily with the sea, Hercules, in the tempest of his fury, shivered into atoms the few bottles of wine which remained after

the late debauchery; his tremendous weapon made the glass fly and the liquor spout in cataracts round about him, until some of his auxiliaries were literally drenched with claret. But the trap-door eluded observation in the din, fortunately for those who escaped by that way on board the brig. For some time it was feared that the whole gang had got off, but at length a dapper little fellow in a white waistcoat, with a physiognomy of the same hue, through the excess of his terror, was detected on an upper shelf of a huge wardrobe, where he had endeavored to conceal himself behind some bundles of old linen. Hercules, who alone was tall enough to make the discovery, dragged him down by the collar of the coat, and had he recognized him as Dawson's man of the law, he would infallibly have given him as good grounds for an action of assault and battery as ever a plaintiff had. Not knowing Mr. Sharkey, he only delivered him over to the constables, by whom he was securely handcuffed; but though repeatedly questioned as to his name and calling, he was far too shrewd to confess either. Sharkey was the only prisoner made in the house, notwithstanding several hours' search, during which no probable or improbable place in which a man could conceal himself, and which a bludgeon could demolish or break open, escaped the curate's secular arm. Indeed, like the jealous Ford, he searched even impossible places. They were slow to relinquish the chase while a chance remained of discovering the principal malefactor; but the sun was going rapidly down, and the lurid coloring of the sky, with the surly tone of the blast, and other indications which the curate well understood, admonished him to think of withdrawing his forces, in order to have a reasonable chance of regaining Bonham Lodge that night. As it was, the shattered windows of Castle Dawson were reflecting the last dismal gleams of day, when, thoroughly exhausted with their exertions, they retraced their steps to Branagan's inn, carrying the captive solicitor with them, who preserved the determined silence of Iago, after the consummation and detection of his crimes.

While they tarried at Branagan's to refresh themselves, the wind, which had been turbulent by fits all day, increased to a gale, and the night set in so frightfully, that anxious as Hercules was to travel, it was not to be thought of until there was some abatement of the storm. He passed several hours dismally enough in the same little loft which Mr. Maguire had occupied when he was surprised counting his money; and the curate's supper was very little better than what had been served to the proctor upon the same occasion. However, he was more accustomed to the rough than the smooth of life, and never complained of his hard fare, but after he had supped, stretched himself on the little settle-bed to enjoy a nap, while the wind was doing its best to batter the house down. There he slept until past midnight, but without outsleeping the hurricane, and he would probably have slept longer, had he not been startled from his slumbers by a cry which had startled many a sleeper in that little inn before, the cry that there was a ship upon the rocks. Hercules was already out of bed, huddling on his clothes in the dark, when Mr. Branagan rushed

MY UNCLE THE CURATE.

into his room with a lantern to announce the intelligence, well knowing the curate's reputation for skill and bravery in such emergencies. His renown, indeed, was known to all about him, so that they instinctively ranged themselves under his command, and obeyed his directions. Having marshaled his force, and provided himself and them with every thing the inn contained likely to be of use in saving lives, he led them forth into the dark and howling tempest, and hastened to the point where the halloos of the peasantry who were already on foot intimated that the disaster had occurred. It was no easy matter so much as to walk in the wind that blew, for it was furious enough to have plucked up the trees by their spurs, had there been any trees on that bleak shore to be plucked up. The waves roared, too, so that a thousand bulls could not have out-bellowed them. The ship had struck upon a reef of rocks at a point of the shore, about a mile from the inn, and close to Castle Dawson. Hercules had never witnessed a scene so fearful as the shipwreck of that night, inured as he was to scenes of this kind, and with all his familiarity with that terrible coast. A party of the country-people, however, had assembled, and, having now experienced and able directors, they succeeded in saving numerous lives, though many a corpse was flung upon the beach, and the vessel itself, an American brig from Quebec, went, before the spectators' eyes, to a thousand pieces. The naked and the wounded (for few escaped without more or less injury), received all the attention and relief that could be afforded them under the circumstances. Some were carried to the inn, indeed as many as it was possible to accommodate there; the rest were distributed through the huts of the poor fishermen about the spot, whose dwellings were not more open to the storms than were their hearts to all charitable sympathies with their fellow-creatures in distress.

It was sunrise when Hercules again threw himself down on a long bench before the kitchen fire, to recruit his strength after his prodigious exertions during the night. But scarcely had he closed his eyes before he was roused by the game-keeper, and requested to get up and visit one of the sufferers, who was reported to be on the point of death. The report was brought by a miserable old woman, in whose hut the dying man lay. The curate sprang upon his legs instantly, and huddled on his still dripping garments.

"I can't confess the poor fellow," he said, "but I may be of use to him, nevertheless."

It was no easy matter in the storm to reach the dreary place to which the crone conducted the curate, accompanied by the game-keeper and Mr. Branagan of the inn. The old woman literally crept along the ground, grasping the tufts of sea-pinks to prevent the wind from whirling her aloft like a truss of straw. She led the way, however, to a small, deep hollow, close to the shore, surrounded, except toward the west, with an irregular wall of cliffs, and destitute of all vegetation, except a few amphibious plants, and patches of stunted fern. The winds collected and howled there like twelve legions of demons. At high tides, with a western gale, the sea usurped it completely, and left the blasted fern strewed with wreaths

of sea-weed and shattered shells. It was an awful place either to die, or live in. but Mr. Woodward was accustomed to such scenes, and to find in them the haunts of men.

They entered the hut. The den of a fox could scarcely have been more unfurnished. A hole in the roof was the chimney, and a hole in the wall was the window. The ocean's spray bounded through both apertures. There was an iron pot, and a straw pallet, no other visible household stuff. Mr. Woodward approached the straw, which rustled with the writhings of the poor wretch who lay upon it; otherwise no one could have known that any thing living lay there, so dark was the wretched place. Mr. Branagan, by the curate's directions, held a lantern which he carried, so that its slender thread of light fell upon the face of the wounded man. It instantly struck Hercules that he had seen that gaunt and truculent face before. The idea agitated him, but he made no remark, not being certain that recognition would be prudent, supposing his impression to be correct. The man was as tall and muscular as himself; his countenance singularly fierce and forbidding. He had evidently received a dangerous, if not mortal hurt, and answered the questions put to him with an effort that seemed to cause him acute anguish, and in a voice scarcely audible in the hurly-burly of the waves and winds. The humane curate stooped over him; administered some drops of a cordial he had provided himself with at the inn; and, examining the wounds, came instantly to the conclusion that the case was past the resources of the ablest surgery. The cordial, however, restored strength, if it did not mitigate pain; the wounded man raised himself on his elbow, and expressed an eager desire to see a clergyman, naturally concluding the curate to be a surgeon, or a doctor.

"I am a clergyman, not a doctor," said Hercules, "but I am not a priest," he added, meaning that he was not a Catholic priest, and could not therefore administer the rites of the Church of Rome to the dying man.

He tried to reply, but failing in the attempt, made a gesture with his hand, intimating that he wished to be alone with Mr. Woodward.

The game-keeper and Mr. Branagan were very reluctant to leave the shelter, but Hercules (anxious himself for a private conference) insisted on their retiring; directing the former to remain within call, and Branagan to return to the inn and dispatch a messenger for the nearest medical assistance. The old woman had crept into a corner of the hut, where she lay rolled up like a bundle of rags, and nobody saw or knew she was there.

"If I am not mistaken," said the curate seating himself on the stool, and holding the lantern in one hand, while with the other he again administered some drops of the cordial; "if I am not mistaken, I have seen you before, my poor fellow."

The man looked as if he desired to ask where.

"At a place in this county called the Black Castle," said Hercules.

The man again raised himself for a moment, gazed with intensity on the face of his interrogator, muttered assent to his recognition, and fell back on the rustling straw. Hercules gave him time to rally, and then said, with deep solemnity—

"You have crime upon your conscience." ...

Crime, indeed a life of crime, was suggested by the pale ferocity of that countenance upon which Mr. Woodward gazed with the same strong eye with which he had once before encountered it, only that now there was pity in the curate's look, for to the expression of violence and guilt, in the face before him, was now added the awful physiognomy of rapidly approaching death.

"Ay, crime enough," was the answer.

"I will hear any statement you choose to make," said Hercules, "but I must reserve to myself the right to make what use of it I please; on that condition I am prepared to receive any thing you have to say."

The voice was faint, hoarse, interrupted with the moans of pain, and often almost inaudible, in which the confession was made. It commanded the attention of Mr. Woodward so profoundly that he scarcely breathed while he listened. Portions of it agitated him extremely and suggested various eager inquiries. At length he said—

"This must be stated in the presence of a third person, and taken down in writing, otherwise it can not advance the ends of justice."

To this the dying man mutely but willingly assented, and Hercules stepped out and dispatched the game-keeper for the policemen, not untortured by fear lest the vital functions should be exhausted before their arrival. It was a dreadful interval, and more than once it seemed as if death purposed to destroy the evidence, on the preservation and record of which so much depended. But it was not so ordered by Providence; the police came in time to be of the service required, and by one of them the examination was put in writing, as slowly and intermittingly the story was repeated, or the answers returned to the questions which Mr. Woodward proposed. Life meanwhile was ebbing fast. Few moments remained for the exercise of the curate's good offices as a minister of religious consolation, but he made the most devout and zealous use of them, pouring all the balm he could into the hurt spirit, and devoutly hoping it was not, like his wounded body, past healing. The final struggle soon came and was soon over. When Hercules left the hut, the Atlantic foam was washing the pale grim features of the dead.

---

## CHAPTER LXII.

### THE HOUSE-TOP.

For 'tis the mind that makes the body rich,
And as the sun breaks through the darkest clouds,
So honor peereth in the meanest habit."
           TAMING OF THE SHREW.

THUS providentially was the curate the means of preserving from destruction the evidence on which the vindication of his nephew and the happiness of his family depended, for it has already been divined that the man who perished that night in the fisherman's hut was the accomplice of Thompson in the robbery of Mr. Spenser's proctor. It was owing to accident that Vivyan and Sydney had not made the voyage home in the same fated vessel. They had, in fact, secured their berths in it, when the captain of a British sloop of war, a friend of Vivyan, who was about to sail for England a day or two later, offered a passage to him and his friend, which was too agreeable a proposition not to be gladly accepted, and by accepting it they probably saved their lives When Hercules first discovered who the dying man was, his alarm had been extreme, lest the two young men should prove to have been also among the passengers, and numbered with those who perished. Lamb, however satisfied him on that point before he became speechless; but his strength failed before he could relate the circumstances under which he had been discovered, and the motives which had induced him to return to Ireland.

The curate's curiosity, however, was not destined to remain long unsatisfied, for the sloop of war had outsailed the merchantman, and was actually at that moment in the harbor of Plymouth.

Hercules hastened back from the scene of death to Mr. Branagan's inn, the storm still pelting him furiously. In defiance of all obstacles, he then mounted his pony, and, followed by the game-keeper, rode back to Bonham Lodge at the swiftest pace to which, without inhumanity, he could urge Sligo. Never was an arrival more anxiously looked for. Carry had passed the night in a fever of apprehension for his safety, and now he rushed into her arms, not merely to assure her that he was alive and well, but to give her the happiest tidings of which he could possibly have been the bearer. Doctor Wilkins was in attendance upon Elizabeth, who did not recover the horrors of the night at Castle Dawson as speedily as she had done the plunge in the ocean on a former occasion. Her physical exertions, as well as her mental tortures, had been inconceivable. She continued so ill for some days that it was not thought prudent to add to her excitement even by the communication of the most joyful news. Her aunt attended her day and night with the solicitude of a dozen mothers; indeed, Carry suffered by sympathy quite as much as if she had been the victim of the abduction herself; an exploit which in her case would have been one of the hardest. As to the curate, there seemed no rest for him. He had scarcely drawn his breath at the lodge before he thought of his old tumble-down house; the damage it was likely to have sustained in the tempest, and the hazard to which his children had been exposed, made him excessively uneasy and he ordered one of the plough-horses to be saddled to convey him to Redcross, for the pony was quite done up. So great was his anxiety, particularly about a stack of chimneys immediately over the room where Billy Pitt slept, that he totally forgot he had made no breakfast, and his wife and the rector were too much engrossed to think of matters of that kind; but Lord Bonham's housekeeper had a great reverence and affection for Hercules, who had once brought her son through a fever, and she now proved her gratitude by bringing him a great bowl of tea and some proportionate huge slices of brown bread and butter, which he took sitting on the back of the plough-horse, who was by no means impatient for the road. The reader is aware that to reach the town he had to pass close by the parsonage for it was the same route which

Dawson had taken not very long before. When Hercules arrived at that point of his journey, he found certain things going on for which he was utterly at a loss to account. A small trading vessel lay at anchor, just where the smart Gipsy used to be moored in the prosperous days past, and she seemed to have just discharged herself of her cargo, for several boxes and bales of goods, covered with mats and tarpaulins, stood on the strand, while the crew and some of the rector's people were busy transporting other bales, seemingly of the same description, and depositing them in the house. Very little inspection showed that the goods consisted principally of household furniture; but Hercules got very little satisfaction from the people at work, when he inquired by whose orders they were thus employed, for he very well knew that the rector had no idea of what was going forward. Entering the house the first person he met was the little proctor, who threw quite as small light on the matter as any body else, although the curate could not but suspect, from the mysterious twinkle of his shrewd little pair of eyes, that he knew something more than he chose to admit.

Randy almost wept for joy, when he learned what had taken place at Castle Dawson, and how Providence had brought the guilt home at last to the real criminals. He said he knew all along that the truth would come out sooner or later, though he never expected to be spared to see the day, closing the speech with his queer little twittering cough.

"But," said Randy, "there's a bit of a question I wishet your reverince had axed the poor sinner, before his sowl passed, for it's too late to talk of it now."

Hercules desired to know to what he alluded.

"How he knowed," said Randy, "that I kept the money in the pocket in the left buzzom of my coat."

"Why, man, he saw you thrust your pocketbook into it the night he paid you the visit at Branagan's."

"The Lord be praised!" ejaculated the proctor, "I always said that was the villain that done it. And did he tell your reverince all about it, and how he terrified the seven sinses out of my poor ould self? Och—ony—oh, it's myself that will never forget the looks of him when he seed the bank notes."

"He did, Randy," said Hercules, fixing his eye severely on the little officer of the Church, "he did, and he told me also what it was that took him down to the inn that night, and afforded him the opportunity of making acquaintance with you and your bank-notes. Randy, Randy, you incorrigible old gambler, it was that old pack of cards of yours brought this pack of troubles upon us all."

"Thin in some sense it was, sartainly, and I won't gainsay it," said the little proctor, greatly abashed, and coughing very pitifully.

"You never said a word about the cards; not a word about the cards, Randy, did you ever mention."

"I thought it would only aggravate your reverince to hear talk of them," said Maguire, "and I never liked displasing you, Mr. Woodward, honey, for you were always kind to me and mine, and always gave good advice."

"Some of it very unprofitably bestowed, Ma-guire," said the curate, moving away; "but enough of the subject, for the present. I see there is some good-natured scheme on foot to give your old master an agreeable surprise; however, I won't ask you to let me into the secret."

"I'm mighty thankful to your reverince," said Randy, almost touching the ground with the tip of his nose, "and may providence pour his blessings on you and your good lady and all your beautiful darlings, and may you live to have many more of them."

The curate shook his head very doubtfully at the latter part of this benediction, and pursued his way across the water, after which a short time brought him to Redcross. He found his little Woodwards all safe and sound, but his mansion had suffered woeful detriment. The hurricane had smashed numerous panes of glass, which Peter was trying to repair with wisps of hay and as many old hats of his master as he could find; but the roof had been still more unfortunate; the court-yard was literally strewed with slates and fragments of tiles, and Billy Pitt and his brother were swimming their paper boats in the pools of water which had found its way into the upper story. Meditating how to remedy all this ravage of the elements with his own honest hands, Hercules walked down to the post-office for letters. Mrs. Peacock did not appear; her husband was on duty in person, and after considerable shuffling and going backward and forward between the office and an inner room, he handed the curate a letter, the seal of which he instantly perceived had been tampered with. It was a short note from Vivyan, announcing his arrival in England, and there was an allusion in it to a letter which Sydney had written to his father by the same post.

"Any letters for Mr. Spenser?" said the curate.

"None, to-day, sir."

"Be so good as to try, Mr. Peacock."

The post-master was very confident, but turned over his packets, and persisted in his answer. The curate then stated the good reason he had to believe that there was a letter for the rector, and peremptorily commanded a further search. Peacock was visibly fluttered, and again repaired to the inner room. The curate's eye followed him, and directly the door opened he spied two persons in the background; one was Lanty and the other was Thomson. Hercules said not a word. Peacock returned in a few moments with a letter in his hand. The seal, however, showed no sign of having been outraged like the other. Hercules paid the postage, put the letter in his pocket, and then, coolly walking into the office, accosted Peacock, in a deep stern voice, and ordered him to go back into his privy chamber and inform Mr. Thomson that the Reverend Mr. Woodward desired to talk with him. Peacock turned white as a shroud, and trembled from head to foot as he obeyed the mandate. The moment the curate's message was delivered, the fellow who was the object of it rushed at the door, and made a desperate effort to escape into the street. But Hercules sprang after him, seized him by the nape of the neck, and actually lifted him for an instant off his legs, as if he had been a hare or a rabbit. Peacock shrank cowering into a dark corner, not daring to interpose between the curate and his prey. Lucy remained paralyzed with terror in the inner room, expecting to see her hollow-checked accomplice torn to pieces, or cudgeled to death before her eyes. But Hercules had too strong a sense of dignity to use any more violence than was absolutely necessary. Without addressing a word either to the post-master or his wife, he strode out of the office, holding a terrible gripe of his captive, and trailing him along the principal street, just as Ellen Hogg, the schoolmistress, might have done with one of her scholars, who had vainly attempted to escape from her hand. A bare-headed and bare-legged mob was soon collected, and upon this occasion assuredly the sympathies of an Irish rabble were enlisted on the side of justice, for they cheered Hercules vociferously and lustily hooted his prisoner, probably judging from his aspect that he was more likely to be guilty of some petty larceny than any crime of dignity, such as an abduction or a homicide. Arrived at the police barrack, the curate found the Castle Dawson party just returned with Mr. Sharkey in custody, and Thomson and the attorney were locked up together for the night. It was not a very discreet arrangement, as the result soon proved.

By the time this adventure had ended, it was drawing toward dusk, and Hercules went home to his children, followed all the way with the applauses and benisons of his parishioners of all persuasions, every second blessing including a prayer for the fertility of Mrs. Woodward, and a rapid multiplication of the poor man's offspring. He found his progeny (numerous enough in all conscience), hungrily expecting his return; and a glorious Irish stew (a savory compound of mutton, potatoes, onions, pepper, and gravy) soon smoked on the table in the study, round which they all pressed; the father looking like an affectionate giant entertaining a party of delighted dwarfs, and the corpulent cat going round and round the company, fawning on great and small, and purring parasitically, as loud as he could, to earn his share of the national dish. But the table-talk that day was far the best part of the entertainment. The curate had scarcely time to appease his appetite, whetted as it was by an unusually long fast, so eager were the little folks to hear all about their fair cousin's escape, and so proud were they of their father's prowess. He had only told his tale some three or four times over, when an uproar reached their ears from the main street of the town, and Hercules sprang up and rushed out to ascertain the cause of the hubbub. Thomson and Sharkey had made their escape out of the window of the room they had been confined in. It was owing to the gross negligence of the police, and Hercules was justly incensed at their conduct. He consoled himself, however, by reflecting that the attorney might have proved a troublesome customer, and that the conviction of the other miscreant was comparatively immaterial, after the dying confession of Lamb. Neither Thomson, nor Sharkey, was ever retaken, or any tidings heard of one or the other from that day to this.

The curate retired to rest not very early that night, for the town continued long in a ferment, yet he was up with the first lark to resume the duties of his hard but happy life. Billy Pitt was an early bird also, and the morning being as

bright a one as ever cheered the world, the curate and his son held a consultation whether they should set about repairing the roof, or mount their hacks and visit mamma and cousin Elizabeth at the lodge. Billy was for the latter plan, and Hercules was very well inclined to it also; but the former was more prudent, and the curate was careful never to set his children an example of postponing duty and business to pleasure in any shape. So Peter was dispatched to the lodge to bring an account of Miss Spenser's health, and immediately after breakfast, and as soon as the curate had paid one or two pastoral visits to sick people in town, the slating commenced with vigor. Upon this occasion it was not by a ladder that Hercules got on his roof, but out of the windows of the observatory, which was a much safer way, and one that Carry always urged strenuously. The curate exchanged his coat for a flannel jacket, which he kept for his mechanical operations, and borrowed a coarse linen apron of Peter, for his worst clerical suit was too good to have spoiled with lime and mortar. The mortar was made in the garden, and Billy Pitt carried it up the stairs in a coal-scuttle, having previously collected the slates in the yard and conveyed them to the observatory also. Then the work went on actively; Billy remarking every five minutes that no regular slater could do it much better, and Hercules himself very well pleased with his performance, and now and then, in the midst of his stories of Scipio and Epaminondas (for he and Billy were very classical at such times), stopping and surveying it not without considerable vain-glory. The sun grew very strong, but still they labored until noon, when the curate said he would set only half-a-dozen slates more, and then they would take an hour's repose and have luncheon. Scarcely had he spoken the words, when the bell attached to the outer gate rang, and the other children, who were diverting themselves about the court, ran to open it. Hercules paid no attention until he heard his name pronounced, and the sound of horses' feet in the yard below. Then he peered over the parapet and saw that a gentleman on horseback, accompanied by a servant, had arrived at the house-door. The gentleman's figure was too much fore-shortened to be distinguishable; all Hercules could see was that he was attired in black, so he concluded it was Mr. Oliver, or some other clergyman of the neighborhood, and sent down Billy Pitt to ascertain. But before Billy got half way to the hall he was met by his little brother Hercules, running up in violent excitement, screaming—

"Father, father! A bishop, a bishop! Put on you, put on you!"

The curate heard the scream of the juvenile from the roof, and, not believing his ears, put his head in at the window to catch the sounds again, when the door burst open and little Hercules rushed in, vociferating—"A bishop, a bishop!" It was as true as holy writ. A bishop was below—an actual live bishop—and had asked to see the Rev. Mr. Woodward.

"What did you say?" said the curate, extremely dismayed for a moment or two, and thinking ruefully that he had left his coat in the study.

"I said you were slating in the observatory,

father," said the little Hercules, who had been brought up by both his parents in the ways of truth and simplicity.

While the child spoke, the solemn tread of clerical boots was heard outside, and the grave voice of the eminent visitor in conversation with Billy Pitt; the door opened, and instantly the curate in his working costume, with his narrow trowel in his hand, stood in the presence of the same excellent bishop, to whom he had been introduced at the marriage of Mrs. Dabzac. His lordship, both amused and puzzled at the reply of little Hercules, had desired Billy Pitt to conduct him up stairs, determined, (at the risk of intruding too far behind the domestic scenes), to witness with his own eyes what promised to be a striking picture of poverty dignified by worth. Such a picture indeed was now presented to his view, and there was nothing in the bearing of Hercules to detract from its full effect. It was profoundly respectful without an approach to cringing; as Shakspeare says of the elephant, "his legs were for necessity, not for flexure;" and he was too much of a practical philosopher, and far too much of a true Christian clergyman, to be ashamed of his narrow circumstances or of the quaint occupation at which he was surprised. He stood in presence, indeed, of a man who would have despised him had it been otherwise; a prelate, whom riches had not corrupted, nor temporal elevation lowered; who represented in his person the glory of well-used wealth, as the curate did the dignity of nobly-supported poverty. But these considerations were perhaps too abstract for a boy of Billy Pitt's age, for while his father was entering into conversation with the bishop, Billy kept hovering round him, trying to untie and remove the white apron, probably being the more shocked at its impropriety by contrasting it with his lordship's black one. The two good churchmen noticed the boy's proceeding almost simultaneously, and were equally diverted by it. Still Hercules could not conjecture to what he owed the honor of a visit so unexpected, and his right-reverend visitor seemed equally at a loss to state the business which he really had in hand. His lordship looked out of the windows, and remarked the immense extent of view from them, the magnificence of the ocean, and the fine coloring of a small group of rocky islets in the offing. Then he made some observations on slate and slate quarries, and gave the curate a word of advice on the dangers of his employment and the perfidious nature of ladders; but still it was evident from his manner that it was not to speak of ladders, or quarries, or coast scenery, that he had pushed himself to the top of the house.

He was a shy, reserved, though well-bred man, and it was not always those acts which he performed with most pleasure which he performed with the greatest ease. At length, after briefly alluding to his first meeting with Mr. Woodward in Dublin, and expressing his regret that he did not see more of a clergyman of whom he heard so much, he came bluntly to the point, and said, there was a preferment vacant in his diocese, more valuable for its rank than its income, and "I am come, Mr. Woodward," added his lordship, "to request your

acceptance of it, because I know no worthier man to offer it to, and I am anxious to have you in my diocese."

The bishop, hurried away so fast that he actually mounted his horse before he thought of informing Hercules what the preferment was, or gave him time to express his surprise and gratitude in a connected sentence. The curate, by that unexpected visit, was made an archdeacon; there was a small living attached to the dignity worth about three hundred a year, but there was a good house on the glebe; and the best of all was that it was at no very great distance from Redcross parsonage, which would have been a serious drawback.

The news reached Bonham Lodge in a few hours. The post-boy happened to be just starting, and Hercules wrote a line to Carry. Then he went to his luncheon with Billy, after which he returned to the roof and finished his repairs in silence, thanking God in his heart for having increased his means of educating his children, but otherwise not expecting to be a happier man for his preferment.

Had the prime minister written to Mr. Spenser and offered him Canterbury, he could not have made him happier than he was made by the promotion of his curate. Indeed, that promotion made a great many good people happy; and if it be true, as most true it is, though a poet said it, that there is "care in heaven," and "love in heavenly natures to us creatures base," it is scarcely a fiction to say that the advancement of Hercules made the angels themselves glad. As to Carry Woodward, she rejoiced serenely in the turn of her husband's fortunes, and longed to have the whole history of it from his own lips.

But the first members of the family who hailed him by the title of archdeacon were Sydney and Vivyan, who arrived late that evening at Redcross. The arrival, though not expected, was no very great surprise. The meeting of the nephew and uncle was at once affectionate and solemn. The curate was reluctant to acquaint Vivyan with the sufferings and outrage to which his Elizabeth had been exposed, but it was necessary to do so, and it was no easy matter to restrain him, or Sydney either, from pushing on to Bonham Lodge at midnight. Peter, however returned with capital news of Miss Spenser, and a note from Carry, in which she said that Doctor Wilkins had pronounced her niece able now to bear any amount of good news, and hoped that, to-morrow or next day, she would be equal to any amount of agreeable company. There was no allusion to the promotion in the note, for the post had not arrived at the lodge when Peter left to return to Redcross. Vivyan and Sydney slept that night at the inn, and ere the following morning was past its prime, the whole party, on good mount ain hacks all of them, were trotting over the hills to the hunting-lodge, Vivyan and Sydney beguiling the road with the narrative of their meeting at Quebec, and the adventures they both had met with in pursuit of the wretched Lamb. Hercules was astonished at the energy displayed by Vivyan, until he thought of the motives and passions under the sway of which he acted, and remembered that love, which makes hard natures soft as wax, has the opposite effect of rendering soft ones hard as iron. From the day that Vivyan parted in tears and misery from Miss Spenser, in her uncle's house at Redcross, he became an altered man, altered in character and constitution! the extreme gentleness of the former and the almost fragility of the latter disappeared; the necessity for great efforts seemed to produce not only the mental vigor but the physical hardihood to make them; he renounced all that bordered on the woman in his delicate and refined nature, and started on his almost quixotic enterprise as manly and brave a fellow as George Markham, or even Hercules himself. Markham would have accompanied his relative upon an expedition so germane to his taste for travel and exploit, but he was prevented from leaving England at the time by the death of his father, and the domestic affairs in which that event involved him. He beheld the revolution in his cousin with agreeable surprise, hardly recognizing the same young man who a short time before had almost fainted under the load of a fowling-piece, and who was quite broken down by a walk of five miles in the Tyrconnell mountains.

---

## CHAPTER LXIII.

### THE RESTORATION.

" On to the temple! There all solemn rites
Performed, a general feast shall be proclaimed.
Sorrows are changed to bride-songs. So they thrive
Whom fate, in spite of storms, has kept alive."
THE LOVER'S MELANCHOLY.

No disparagement to physic and physicians, one can not help thinking that there is great healing virtue in a happy turn of fortune, and something extremely tonic and cordial in the spirit of love and friendship. Doctor Wilkins was a very skillful as well as a very amusing man, and no doubt he acted discreetly in keeping Miss Spenser very quiet for a few days after the terrible trial to which she had been exposed; but she certainly recovered with marvelous rapidity from the moment she saw her brother returned, reformed, and saved, and her lover again at her side, in the character of Sydney's reformer and deliverer. Then she had also her uncle's prosperity to exult in, and it was almost enough in itself to restore elasticity to her ankle and bring the carmine of health back to her cheek.

There was no end of rejoicing in the curate's promotion, no end of practicing to call him archdeacon, discussing whether he ought to assume the shovel or not, and making him repeat the story of the bishop's visit. Carry almost died laughing at the part borne by her little son in the transaction, and did nothing for whole evenings but repeat—

"A bishop, a bishop—put on you, put on you:—my poor little Hercules—a bishop, a bishop."

The story is told to this day round the firesides of the family in all its branches, Spensers, Vivyans, and Woodwards, and causes almost as much mirth as it did when the event was fresh. The newspapers in a few days announced Mr. Woodward's advancement, in the article of ecclesiastical intelligence, and letter came upon letter to congratulate him from his old college cronies Tom Beamish and others, from many

of his wife's friends and relatives, and a few short but warm lines from the Hon. Tom Flinch, who never forgot him. But the warmest of all, at least in terms, though a little prolix, as usual, was the letter that arrived from Mrs. Dabzac. However, it had the rare merit of being perfectly sincere. No member of his family saw the poor, homely curate exalted into a titled dignitary of the Church with greater content, and (as Carry remarked) it would have made Arabella still happier to have seen her uncle a bishop. It was not the least of the curious circumstances connected with the curate's fortune that he was partly indebted for it to his niece's vulgar vanity on the occasion of her wedding, and partly to his own magnanimity in overlooking her pettiness.

" Well," said the rector, "Elizabeth will have an archdeacon at least to marry her : that won't be so very bad, after all."

But the rector had to provide himself with a new curate, and that was a grief and trouble to him, for such another man as Hercules was not to be found on every coast, or met on every mountain. The choice of his successor was wisely left to the archdeacon himself, who wrote on the subject to Tom Beamish, upon whose fervent recommendation a fresh-colored, simple-minded, and able-bodied young man was appointed to the curacy of Redcross, and inducted by the rector himself into the humble abode where his brother-in-law had dwelt so long in happy and honored indigence. Upon that occasion Mr. Spenser made a happy application of Evander's speech to the Trojan hero, in the 8th book of the Æneid; for, laying his hand gently and impressively on the arm of the young clergyman, as they stood at the door of the old white house, in his solemn, melodious voice, he pronounced the lines—

" Hæc limina victor
Alcides subiit; hæc illum regia cepit.
Aude hospes contemnere opes, et te quoque dignum
Finge Deo."

The last clerical duty Mr. Woodward performed in the parish of Redcross was the marriage of his niece; but this did not take place during the sojourn at Bonham Lodge. One serene and sunny morning, when Miss Spenser's recovery was complete, an excursion to the parsonage was proposed by somebody, and though the rector would more willingly have gone any where else, he made no opposition, when he saw that the plan was popular. There was a phaeton, a jaunting-car, and ponies for the equestrians. The party set out, and some members of it certainly were astonished beyond measure to find the old house in complete order, furnished from bottom to top with its pristine taste and luxury. Mr. Woodward, we have seen, had some inkling of the matter, but to his brother-in-law it seemed the work of magic. The glee of the old proctor, as he beheld Mr. Spenser's amazement at the unexpected preparation to receive him was the best comedy ; but Randy had kept the secret so long that there was no keeping it any longer, so it was soon known that Vivyan was the sorcerer at whose command the upholsterer and cabinet-maker had made all comfortable again. But it was not until the rector entered the room which had contained his library, sadly thinking how it had once been peopled, and never expecting to see so much as the backs of his troops of silent old friends again, that his astonishment was complete. Here, indeed, a necromancer seemed really to have been at work, for his books were all there, marshaled by their nations and languages to receive him, in their ancient cases of curiously carved oak, folios, quartos, octavos, and duodecimos, according to their several dignities, and critically in their own arrangement, looking in fact as if they had never been molested or sent roving about the world. It was natural that this also should be attributed to Vivyan, and it was in vain he protested that he was as much surprised as the rector himself; but such was the fact; and only for Carry Woodward, who was in this part of the secret beyond all doubt, the restorer of the library might have remained a good while unknown. The truth was that almost every body connected by relationship or friendship with Mr. Spenser, had been anxious to replace him in his former ease and comfort, with the shabby and unnatural exception of Mrs. Dabzac. Mr. Oliver, among others, had never enjoyed a day's happiness, since misfortune fell on the man whom he loved and admired. Being a literary man himself, he entered more keenly than any one else into the rector's sorrow when his very books were reft from him; but being unable himself to redeem them, he could only indulge his feelings in complaints and lamentations to his friends and correspondents, which he did so bitterly and incessantly, that at length Lord Bonham heard of the circumstances at Rome, where he was, and instantly wrote home to Mr. Trundle to purchase the library at a liberal valuation and thus secure it from irretrievable dispersion. Mr. Trundle, friendly himself to the rector, and zealously devoted to his daughter ever since the day that she gave up a whole morning to his loan-fund schemes, performed his part of the business with the utmost zeal and efficiency. The library was bought, the cases as well as the books, and by Lord Bonham's directions consigned to the care of the enraptured Mr. Oliver, who valued it beyond the Bodleian for his friend's sake, and would willingly have taken ten times as much trouble as it actually gave him to put it up and arrange it in its original order. The only member of the family he communicated with, while thus employed, was Mrs. Woodward, for it was necessary to have some confidant in order to gain access to the parsonage, and be secure from interruption and discovery while engaged in this clandestine labor of love.

Well, if friends did all that friends could do to make the return of the Spensers to their picturesque home as happy as possible, they, upon their part, made a great many people happy also. The reoccupation of the parsonage made many an eye bright and gladdened many a heart. There were fêtes given, addresses presented, and bonfires kindled on many a hill to celebrate the event. The first person to visit the rector was Father Magrath, the second was the Presbyterian minister, the third was the excellent Doctor Wilkins, with his face that disposed you to weep and his conversation that made you expire of laughing. Last came Mr. Oliver, more than ever shy and monosyllabic;

nay, looking as if he had actually given some particularly heinous offense to the family, and was greatly ashamed to present himself before them.

But no one was welcomed back so cordially and enthusiastically as the fair and good Elizabeth. No prince would have been thought too good a husband for her. She had always been not only so humane to the poor, but still actively useful to them, so beneficent as well as so benevolent, so considerate for the old, so tender to the young, so kind and so patient with every body. So popular, indeed, was Miss Spenser, that had she been possessed with a proselytizing spirit, she would have been an actual little wolf in the Catholic and Presbyterian folds. In the midst of all the preparations for the wedding, and all the tumult of her new but still incomplete happiness, she resumed her attention to the children of the neighborhood, and reopened her school, which was, indeed, a model one. Again the robins hopped on the slates at play-hours, and again the fat rosy child of the laundress came in for the cowslips and kisses, as it rolled and rollicked on the little green paddock. Again the yard echoed the multitudinous lisp and murmur of infant education, and the lusty matron at her tub hard by used to rest a moment from her sultry labors, with her bare stout arms in the suds, and try to distinguish the hum of her own brats in the Babel of tiny sounds.

One personage and one only regarded with an evil eye the happy revolution in the fortunes of the Spensers, and particularly the triumphs of Elizabeth's love and of Sydney's reputation. The rage of the malignant post-mistress knew no bounds; but her career in that capacity was cut short abruptly, for Hercules, who never gave a malefactor a moment's rest in his own parish, or indeed any where within the reach of his influence, had no sooner leisure to attend to the matter than he forwarded to head-quarters a charge against the Peacocks of tampering with the letters of his family, called for an official inquiry, fully established his case, and succeeded in chasing the wicked Lucy and her husband with ignominy out of Redcross. Nothing was heard of them for a long time, until one day that Mr. Spenser observed in the Times newspaper the advertisement of a Mrs. Edward Peacock, who announced her desire to receive a certain number of young gentlemen into her house, promising to instruct them in the rudiments of Latin, to pay them more than motherly attention, and above all things to train them rigidly in the ways of truth and virtue. The bold hand of Lucy was not to be mistaken, although she neither referred to the Spensers or Woodwards for testimonials of her qualifications.

There was no reason for deferring the marriage, and it was not deferred longer than was necessary to give time for the arrival of George Markham, and worthy little Mr. Trundle. It was a fine spectacle to see how Markham and the archdeacon embraced, and how the former triumphed in the honor and reward of the man whom he venerated more than all the men he had ever met with, for his heroic combination of physical energy with plain sterling moral worth. The Dabzacs were present, of course; but despite of their frost and formality, the nuptial ceremony was performed with the devout hilarity that becomes it, and all the festivities before and after were as gay and hearty as ever ushered a bride and bridegroom into the holy and hazardous state of marriage.

"And so that extraordinary Miss Spenser is married at last," said Lady Brabble to old Mrs. Loquax, at a ball which Mrs. Pepper gave in Dublin some short time after the wedding.

"To Mr. Trundle, of course," said old Mrs. Loquax.

"To Lord Bonham, I suppose," said Mrs. Pepper.

"Oh, no; not quite so good a match as that; to a Mr. Vivyan," said Lady Brabble.

"I am sure I am very glad she is married to somebody," said the sour and sanctified Miss Vallancey; "it was exceedingly unpleasant to hear a girl so very much talked about."

"She had beaux enough to her string, at all events," said Mrs. Pepper. "In my opinion, she treated poor Lord Bonham excessively ill."

"I'm told," said Mrs. Loquax, "that the dress she wore at her wedding was actually a present from his lordship."

"That's nothing," said another, "Lord Bonham gave her a superb suit of diamonds, which she never returned. I know it from Carcanet, the jeweler."

"Does any body know any thing about that Mr. Vivyan?" asked one of the clique.

"Oh, nobody," said Lady Brabble, laying down the law.

Tom Flinch came up at the moment, and as he was a know-every-body-that's-knowable sort of man, Mrs. Loquax pounced on him and inquired if he knew any thing about the Mr. Vivyan who had married Miss Spenser.

"Dab.'s sister," drawled the honorable Tom. "Oh, he is Sir Thomas Vivyan's brother; he got a large property some time since by the death of a rich relation in Spain."

"That explains Miss Spenser's conduct most satisfactorily," said the heavenly Miss Vallancey; "how shocking worldly?"

But the Vivyans cared extremely little for the chit-chat of any coterie; they were too happy even to recollect that there were such talkative and malicious people in the world as the Brabbles, Peppers, and Vallanceys. Soon after his marriage Vivyan succeeded to his brother's fortune and baronetcy, and when Elizabeth became Lady Vivyan, and the mistress of a handsome fortune, she was deluged with civilities and flatteries by the same people who before were so busy pulling her beautiful character to pieces. Even old Mrs. Loquax was graciously pleased to forget that our heroine's father had once been a scamp; and if Lady Brabble remembered the revolting fact that Elizabeth had acted as governess to the young Bonhams, she was good enough never to talk of it, nor did it in the least diminish her anxiety to push herself and her daughters into Lady Vivyan's circle.

The fate of Dawson continued a mystery for several years. It was Mr. Woodward's opinion that he had effected his escape in the brig commanded by the respectable Captain Dowse; but the brig was traced to an English sea-port, and, though several persons of suspicious appearance, and some who were known to have been

Dawson's associates, were found on board of her, not a vestige of himself was discovered, nor any thing to serve as a clew to his detection. Various other efforts were made with the same object and the same ill success. It seemed unaccountable; but after some time it ceased to be discussed, at least at the parsonage, except at long intervals on winter evenings, when in every family old topics are sure to turn up again, often for want of new ones of greater interest. Castle Dawson passed into other hands, and was ultimately taken by a mad doctor for a private lunatic asylum, a purpose for which it was ill-suited, if the recovery of the patients was contemplated, but eminently fit, if the doctor's design was merely to make money, and to have his establishment as free from inspection and control as possible. It happened one day that Doctor Wilkins was dining with Mr. Spenser, when he received a summons from the coroner of the county to attend an inquest at Castle Dawson. He rode over there at the time appointed, not doubting but that some inmate of the asylum had come to a violent end, requiring legal inquiry into the circumstances attending it. But on his arrival he found that the case was one of a very different kind. The subject of investigation was a body, or rather a skeleton, which had been discovered in the subterraneous passage under the wine-cellar. It had been found at the foot of the ladder, which was all in a state of decay, the upper rounds fallen to pieces, so as to suggest the idea that they had given way under the weight of some one attempting to descend, and occasioned his death by precipitating him into the chasm beneath. But the first object was to identify the remains. They were produced before the jury, a hideous spectacle, without form or feature, the limbs scarcely continuous, the clothes in shreds, and tangled with sea-wrack. Tattered, however, as the clothes were, they led not only Doctor Wilkins, but several persons present, to conjecture instantly that the corpse before them was that of the wretched Dawson. A minute investigation confirmed this impression irresistibly. Among other things, a signet ring was found, bearing his crest and initials, which, joined to the fact that the remains were those of a middle sized square-built man, like Dawson, settled the question beyond a reasonable doubt. The evidence which Doctor Wilkins gave as to the cause of death, also confirmed the conclusion come to in the first instance. In fact the neck of the skeleton was broken exactly as in cases of falls from considerable heights. The verdict of the jury recorded their perfect satisfaction upon both points.

Little remains to be added; yet, little as it is, our domestic chronicles would be imperfect without it.

Vivyan was faithful to the romantic country where he found his incomparable wife; he loved it for her sake, and entered with zeal into all her benevolent schemes (now enlarged by her increased means of usefulness) for the improvement and happiness of her father's parishioners. Sir Francis purchased the wild islet where he first became acquainted with the Spensers, and built a cottage of solid blocks of granite nearly on the spot where he and his cousin were startled by the apparition of the formidable curate peering down upon them from the cliffs. He also rebuilt the wooden bridge at his own cost and charges, instead of waiting any longer for the county, the government, or a miracle to reconstruct it. The Hoggs and M'Swynes improved visibly under the indefatigable tuition and encouragement which they received from their resident benefactors. No doubt a chapter of the Knights of the Thistle might still be convoked in the neighborhood of Redcross; an ancient father or mother of the borough may still be seen perched on the house-top, to steady the thatch in a gale of wind; there are still dirty faces in the streets, and still a few lions roaring at the Celtic sluggards and terrifying them from honest exertion; but, upon the whole, advice and example have not been thrown away. Between the rector's good-natured ridicule, the patient perseverance of his daughter and her husband in well doing, and the occasional thunders of the archdeacon, who frequently visited Redcross and preached in his old pulpit—there are not so many anomalies as when the Circe sailed on her *voyage pittoresque ;* or, as Carry Woodward said only the other day, "Things are not quite so Higgledy-Piggledyish as formerly."

The archdeacon himself did not reform his ways entirely. He continued to wear very odd hats and coats, and brandish extraordinary cudgels, for a dignitary of the Church, though he no longer glazed his windows and repaired his roof with his own hands. He attained no higher rank in his profession, but he got a better living a few years later, having a second time attracted the notice of the lord-lieutenant, before whom he preached. A few days after his promotion he was commanded to dine with the viceroy, and he obeyed very reluctantly, not being accustomed, he said, to the "ways of courts, or how to talk to a lord-lieutenant."

"Just talk to him as you would to Carry," said the rector.

"Ho, ho," said Hercules, laughing as loud as when he was a stipendiary curate, "I say a great many things to Carry which it wouldn't do to say to a chief governor."

**THE END.**

# JOHN MARCHMONT'S LEGACY

## A Novel.

BY M. E. BRADDON,

AUTHOR OF

"AURORA FLOYD," "ELEANOR'S VICTORY,"

&c., &c., &c.

NEW YORK:

HARPER & BROTHERS, PUBLISHERS,

FRANKLIN SQUARE.

1864.

# By M. E. Braddon.

AURORA FLOYD. 8vo, Paper, 50 cents.

ELEANOR'S VICTORY. 8vo, Paper, 50 cents.

JOHN MARCHMONT'S LEGACY. 8vo, Paper, 50 cents.

Published by **HARPER & BROTHERS**, Franklin Square, New York.

☞ Sent by mail, postage free, to any part of the United States on receipt of price.

# JOHN MARCHMONT'S LEGACY.

## CHAPTER I.

### THE MAN WITH THE BANNER.

THE history of Edward Arundel, second son of Christopher Arundel Dangerfield Arundel, of Dangerfield Park, Devonshire, began on a certain dark winter's night upon which the lad, still a school-boy, went with his cousin, Martin Mostyn, to witness a blank-verse tragedy at one of the London theatres.

There are few men who, looking back at the long story of their lives, can not point to one page in the record of the past at which the actual history of life began. The page may come in the very middle of the book perhaps; perhaps almost at the end. But let it come where it will, it is, after all, only the actual commencement. At an appointed hour in man's existence the overture which has been going on ever since he was born is brought to a sudden close by the sharp vibration of the prompter's signal-bell, the curtain rises, and the drama of life begins. Very insignificant sometimes are the first scenes of the play—commonplace, trite, wearisome; but watch them closely, and interwoven with every word, dimly recognizable in every action, may be seen the awful hand of Destiny. The story has begun: already we, the spectators, can make vague guesses at the plot, and predicate the solemn climax; it is only the actors who are ignorant of the meaning of their several parts, and who are stupidly reckless of the obvious catastrophe.

The story of young Arundel's life began when he was a light-hearted, heedless lad of seventeen, newly escaped for a brief interval from the care of his pastors and masters.

The lad had come to London on a Christmas visit to his father's sister, a good-natured widow, with a great many sons and daughters, and an income only large enough to enable her to keep the appearances of wealth essential to the family pride of one of the Arundels of Dangerfield.

Laura Arundel had married a Colonel Mostyn, of the East India Company's service, and had returned from India after a wandering life of some years, leaving her dead husband behind her, and bringing away with her five daughters and three sons, most of whom had been born under canvas.

Mrs. Mostyn bore her troubles bravely, and contrived to do more with her pension, and an additional income of three hundred a year from a small fortune of her own, than the most consummate womanly management can often achieve. Her house in Montague Square was elegantly furnished, her daughters were exquisitely dressed, her sons sensibly educated, her dinners well cooked. She was not an agreeable woman; she was, perhaps, if any thing, too sensible—so very sensible as to be obviously intolerant of any thing

like folly in others. She was a good mother, but by no means an indulgent one. She expected her sons to succeed in life, and her daughters \ to marry rich men; and would have had little patience with any disappointment in either of these reasonable expectations. She was attached to her brother, Christopher Arundel, and she was very well pleased to spend the autumn months at Dangerfield, where the hunting breakfasts gave her daughters an excellent platform for the exhibition of charming demi-toilets and social and domestic graces, perhaps more dangerous to the susceptible hearts of rich young squires than the fascinations of a *valse à deux temps* or an Italian scena.

But the same Mrs. Mostyn, who never forgot to keep up her correspondence with the owner of Dangerfield Park, utterly ignored the existence of another brother, a certain Hubert Arundel, who had, perhaps, much more need of her sisterly friendship than the wealthy Devonshire squire. Heaven knows, the world seemed a lonely place to this younger son, who had been educated for the Church, and was fain to content himself with a scanty living in one of the dullest and dampest towns in fenny Lincolnshire. His sister might have very easily made life much more pleasant to the Rector of Swampington and his only daughter; but Hubert Arundel was a great deal too proud to remind her of this. If Mrs. Mostyn chose to forget him—the brother and sister had been loving friends and \ dear companions long ago under the beeches at Dangerfield—she was welcome to do so. She was better off than him; and it is to be remarked that if A's income is three hundred a year, and B's a thousand, the chances are as seven to three that B will forget any old intimacy that may have existed between himself and A. Hubert Arundel had been wild at college, and had put his autograph across so many oblong slips of blue paper, acknowledging value received that had been only half received, that by the time the claims of all the holders of these portentous morsels of stamped paper had been satisfied, the younger son's fortune had melted away, leaving its sometime possessor the happy owner of a pair of pointers, a couple of guns by crack makers, a good many foils, single-sticks, boxing-gloves, wire masks, basket-helmets, leathern leg-guards, and other paraphernalia, a complete set of the old *Sporting Magazine* from 1792 to the current year, bound in scarlet morocco, several boxes of very bad cigars, a Scotch terrier, and a pipe of undrinkable port.

Of all these possessions only the undrinkable port now remained to show that Hubert Arundel had once had a decent younger son's fortune, and had succeeded most admirably in making ducks and drakes of it. The poor about Swampington believed in the sweet red wine, which had been specially concocted for Israelitish dealers in jewelry, cigars, pictures, wines, and specie. They smacked their lips over the mysterious liquid, and confidently affirmed that it did them more good than all the doctor's stuff the parish apothecary could send them. Poor Hubert Arundel was well content to find that at least this scanty crop of corn had grown up from the wild oats he had sown at Cambridge. The wine pleased the poor creatures who drank it, and was scarcely likely to do them any harm; and there was a reasonable prospect that the last bottle would by-and-by pass out of the rectory cellars, and with it the last token of that bitterly regretted past.

I have no doubt that Hubert Arundel felt the sting of his only sister's neglect, as only a poor and proud man can feel such an insult; but he never let any confession of this sentiment escape his lips; and when Mrs. Mostyn, being seized with a fancy for doing this forgotten brother a service, wrote him a letter of insolent advice, winding up with an offer to procure his only child a situation as nursery-governess, the Rector of Swampington only crushed the missive in his strong hand, and flung it into his study-fire, with a muttered exclamation that sounded terribly like an oath.

"A *nursery*-governess!" he repeated, savagely; "yes; an under-paid drudge, to teach children their A B C, and mend their frocks and make their pinafores. I should like Mrs. Mostyn to talk to my little Livy for half an hour. I think my girl would have put the lady down so completely by the end of that time, that we should never hear any more about nursery-governesses."

He laughed bitterly as he repeated the obnoxious phrase; but his laugh changed to a sigh.

Was it strange that the father should sigh as he remembered how he had seen the awful hand of Death fall suddenly upon younger and stronger men than himself? What if he were to die, and leave his child unmarried? What would become of her, with her dangerous gifts, with her fatal dowry of beauty, and intellect, and pride?

"But she would never do any thing wrong," the father thought. "Her religious principles are strong enough to keep her right under any circumstances, in spite of any temptation. Her sense of duty is more powerful than any other sentiment. She would never be false to that; she would never be false to that."

In return for the hospitality of Dangerfield Park, Mrs. Mostyn was in the habit of opening her doors to either Christopher Arundel or his sons whenever any one of the three came to London. Of course she infinitely preferred seeing Arthur Arundel, the elder son and heir, seated at her well-spread table, and flirting with one of his pretty cousins, than to be bored with his rackety younger brother, a noisy lad of seventeen, with no better prospects than a commission in her Majesty's service, and a hundred and fifty pounds a year to eke out his pay; but she was, notwithstanding, graciously pleased to invite Edward to spend his Christmas holidays in her comfortable household; and it was thus it came to pass that on the 29th of December, in the year 1838, the story of Edward Arun-

del's life began in a stage-box at Drury Lane Theatre.

The box had been sent to Mrs. Mostyn by the fashionable editor of a fashionable newspaper but that lady and her daughters being previously engaged had permitted the two boys to avail themselves of the editorial privilege.

The tragedy was the dull production of a distinguished literary amateur, and even the great actor who played the principal character could not make the performance particularly enlivening. He certainly failed in impressing Mr. Edward Arundel, who flung himself back in his chair and yawned dolefully during the earlier part of the entertainment.

"It ain't particularly jolly, is it, Martin?" he said, naïvely. "Let's go out and have some oysters, and come in again just before the pantomime begins."

"Mamma made me promise that we wouldn' leave the theatre till we left for good, Ned," his cousin answered; "and then we're to go straight home in a cab."

Edward Arundel sighed.

"I wish we hadn't come till half-price, old fellow," he said, drearily. "If I'd known it was to be a tragedy, I wouldn't have come away from the Square in such a hurry. I wonder why people write tragedies, when nobody like them?"

He turned his back to the stage, and folded his arms upon the velvet cushion of the box preparatory to indulging himself in a deliberate inspection of the audience. Perhaps no brighter face looked upward that night toward the glare and glitter of the great chandelier than that of the fair-haired lad in the stage-box. His candid blue eyes beamed with a more radiant sparkle than any of the myriad lights in the theatre; nimbus of golden hair shone about his broad white forehead; glowing health, careless happiness, truth, good-nature, honesty, boyish vivacity, and the courage of a young lion—all were expressed in the fearless smile, the frank, yet half-defiant gaze. Above all, this lad of seventeen looked especially what he was—a thoroughly gentleman. Martin Mostyn was prim and effeminate, precociously tired of life, precociously indifferent to every thing but his own advantage but the Devonshire boy's talk was still fragrant with the fresh perfume of youth and innocence still gay with the joyous recklessness of early boyhood. He was as impatient for the noisy pantomime overture, and the bright troops of fairies in petticoats of spangled muslin, as the most inveterate cockney cooling his snub nose against the iron railing of the gallery. He was as ready to fall in love with the painted beauty of the ill-paid ballet girls, as the veriest child in the wide circle of humanity about him. Fresh untainted, unsuspicious, he looked out at the world, ready to believe in every thing and every body.

"How you do fidget, Edward!" whispered Martin Mostyn, peevishly; "why don't you look at the stage? It's capital fun."

"Fun!"

"Yes; I don't mean the tragedy, you know but the supernumeraries. Did you ever see such an awkward set of fellows in all your life There's a man there with weak legs and a heavy banner that I've been watching all the evening

He's more fun than all the rest of it put together."

Mr. Mostyn being of course much too polite to point out the man in question, indicated him with a twitch of his light eyebrows; and Edward Arundel, following that indication, singled out the banner-holder from a group of soldiers in medieval dress, who had been standing wearily enough upon one side of the stage during a long strictly private and confidential dialogue between the princely hero of the tragedy and one of his accommodating satellites. The lad uttered a cry of surprise as he looked at the weak-legged banner-holder.

Mr. Mostyn turned upon his cousin with some vexation.

"I can't help it, Martin," exclaimed young Arundel; "I can't be mistaken—yes—poor fellow, to think that he should come to this! you haven't forgotten him, Martin, surely."

"Forgotten what—forgotten whom? My dear Edward, what *do* you mean?"

"John Marchmont, the poor fellow who used to teach us mathematics at Vernon's; the fellow the governor sacked because—"

"Well, what of him?"

"The poor chap with the banner," exclaimed the boy, in a breathless whisper; "don't you see, Martin? didn't you recognize him? It's Marchmont, poor old Marchmont, that we used to chaff, and that the governor sacked because he had a constitutional cough, and wasn't strong enough for his work."

"Oh yes, I remember him well enough," Mr. Mostyn answered, indifferently. "Nobody could stand his cough, you know; and he was a vulgar fellow, into the bargain."

"He wasn't a vulgar fellow," said Edward, indignantly; "there, there's the curtain down again; he belonged to a good family in Lincolnshire, and was heir-presumptive to a stunning fortune. I've heard him say so twenty times."

Martin Mostyn did not attempt to repress an involuntary sneer, which curled his lips as his cousin spoke.

"Oh, I dare say you've heard *him* say so, my dear boy," he murmured, superciliously.

"Ah, and it was true," cried Edward; "he wasn't a fellow to tell lies; perhaps he'd have suited Mr. Vernon better if he had been. He had bad health, and was weak, and all that sort of thing; but he wasn't a snob. He showed me a signet-ring once that he used to wear on his watch-chain—"

"A *silver* watch-chain," simpered Mr. Mostyn, "just like a carpenter's."

"Don't be such a supercilious cad, Martin. He was very kind to me, poor Marchmont; and I know I was always a nuisance to him, poor old fellow; for you know I never could get on with Euclid. I'm sorry to see him here. Think, Martin, what an occupation for him! I don't suppose he gets more than nine or ten shillings a week for it."

"A shilling a night is, I believe, the ordinary remuneration of a stage-soldier. They pay as much for the real thing as for the sham, you see; the defenders of our country risk their lives for about the same consideration. Where are you going, Ned?"

Edward Arundel had left his place, and was trying to undo the door of the box.

"To see if I can get at this poor fellow."

"You persist in declaring, then, that the man with the weak legs is our old mathematical drudge? Well, I shouldn't wonder. The fellow was coughing all through the five acts, and that's uncommonly like Marchmont. You're surely not going to renew your acquaintance with him?"

But young Arundel had just succeeded in opening the door, and he left the box without waiting to answer his cousin's question. He made his way very rapidly out of the theatre, and fought manfully through the crowds who were waiting about the pit and gallery doors, until he found himself at the stage-entrance. He had often looked with reverent wonder at the dark portal; but he had never before essayed to cross the sacred threshold. But the guardian of the gate to this theatrical paradise, inhabited by fairies at a guinea a week, and baronial retainers at a shilling a night, is ordinarily a very inflexible individual, not to be corrupted by any mortal persuasion, and scarcely corruptible by the more potent influence of gold or silver. Poor Edward's half a crown had no effect whatever upon the stern door-keeper, who thanked him for his donation, but told him that it was agen his orders to let any body go up stairs.

"But I want to see some one so particularly," the boy said, eagerly. "Don't you think you could manage it for me, you know? He's an old friend of mine—one of the supernu—what's-its-names?" added Edward, stumbling over the word. "He carried a banner in the tragedy, you know; and he's got such an awful cough, poor chap."

"The man as carried the banner with a awful cough," said the door-keeper, reflectively; "why, I'm blest if it ain't Barking Jeremiah."

"Barking Jeremiah!"

"Yes, Sir. They calls him Barking because he's allers coughin' his poor weak head off; and they calls him Jeremiah because he's allers doleful. And I never did see such a doleful chap, certainly."

"Oh, do let me see him," cried Mr. Edward Arundel. "I know you can manage it; so do, that's a good fellow. I tell you he's a friend of mine, and quite a gentleman too. Bless you, there isn't a move in mathematics he isn't up to; and he'll come into a fortune some of these days—"

"Yes," interrupted the door-keeper, sarcastically, "I've heerd that. They chaffs him about that up stairs. He's allers talking about bein' a gentleman and belongin' to gentlemen, and all that; but you're the first gentleman as have ever as't after him."

"And can I see him?"

"I'll do my best, Sir. Here, you Jim," said the door-keeper, addressing a dirty youth, who had just nailed an official announcement of next morning's rehearsal upon the back of a stony-hearted swing-door, which was apt to jam the fingers of the uninitiated, "what's the name of that super with the jolly bad cough, the one they call Barking?"

"Oh, that's Morti-more."

"Do you know if he's on in the first scene?"

"Yes. He's one of the demons; but the scene's just over. Do you want him?"

"You can take up this young gentleman's card to him, and tell him to slip down here if he's got a wait," said the door-keeper.

Mr. Arundel handed his card to the dirty boy.

"He'll come to me fast enough, poor fellow!" he muttered. "I usen't to chaff him as the others did, and I'm glad I didn't, now."

Edward Arundel could not easily forget that one brief scrutiny in which he had recognized the wasted face of the schoolmaster's hack, who had taught him mathematics only two years before. Could there be any thing more piteous than that degrading spectacle? The feeble frame scarcely able to sustain that paltry one-sided banner of calico and tinsel; the two rude daubs of coarse vermilion upon the hollow cheeks; the black smudges that were meant for eyebrows; the wretched scrap of horse-hair glued upon the pinched chin in dismal mockery of a beard; and through all this the pathetic pleading of large hazel eyes, bright with the unnatural lustre of disease, and saying perpetually, more plainly than words can speak, "Do not look at me; do not despise me; do not even pity me. It won't last long."

The fresh-hearted school-boy was still thinking of this when a wasted hand was laid lightly and tremulously on his arm, and looking up he saw a man in a hideous mask and a tight-fitting suit of scarlet and gold standing by his side.

"I'll take off my mask in a minute, Arundel," said a faint voice, that sounded hollow and muffled within a cavern of pasteboard and wickerwork. "It was very good of you to come round; very, very good!"

"I was so sorry to see you here, Marchmont; I knew you in a moment, in spite of the disguise."

The supernumerary had struggled out of his huge head-gear by this time, and laid the fabric of papier-mâché and tinsel carefully aside upon a shelf. He had washed his face before putting on the mask, for he was not called upon to appear before a British public in martial semblance any more upon that evening. The pale wasted face was interesting and gentlemanly, not by any means handsome, but almost womanly in its softness of expression. It was the face of a man who had not yet seen his thirtieth birthday; who might never live to see it, Edward Arundel thought, mournfully.

"Why do you do this, Marchmont?" the boy asked, bluntly.

"Because there was nothing else left for me to do," the stage-demon answered, with a sad smile. "I can't get a situation in a school, for my health won't suffer me to take one; or it won't suffer any employer to take me, for fear of my falling ill upon his hands, which comes to the same thing; so I do a little copying for the law-stationers, and this helps out that, and I get on as well as I can. I wouldn't so much mind if it wasn't for—"

He stopped suddenly, interrupted by a paroxysm of coughing.

"If it wasn't for whom, old fellow?"

"My poor little girl; my poor little motherless Mary."

Edward Arundel looked grave, and perhaps a little ashamed of himself. He had forgotten until this moment that his old tutor had been left a widower at four-and-twenty, with a little daughter to support out of his scanty stipend.

"Don't be down-hearted, old fellow," the lad whispered, tenderly; "perhaps I shall be able to help you, you know. And the little girl can go down to Dangerfield; I know my mother would take care of her, and will keep her there till you get strong and well. And then you might start a fencing-room, or a shooting-gallery, or something of that sort, at the West End; and I'd come to you, and bring lots of fellows to you, and you'd get on capitally, you know."

Poor John Marchmont, the asthmatic supernumerary, looked perhaps the very last person in the world whom it could be possible to associate with a pair of foils or a pistol and a target; be smiled faintly at his old pupil's enthusiastic talk.

"You were always a good fellow, Arundel," he said, gravely. "I don't suppose I shall ever ask you to do me a service; but if, by-and-by, this cough makes me knock under, and my little Polly should be left—I—I think you'd get your mother to be kind to her, wouldn't you, Arundel?"

A picture rose before the supernumerary's weary eyes as he said this; the picture of a pleasant lady whose description he had often heard from the lips of a loving son, a rambling old mansion, wide-spreading lawns, and long arcades of oak and beeches leading away to the blue distance. If this Mrs. Arundel, who was so tender and compassionate and gentle to every red-cheeked cottage girl who crossed her pathway—Edward had told him this very often—would take compassion also upon this little one! If she would only condescend to see the child, the poor pale neglected flower, the frail exotic blossom, that was so cruelly out of place upon the bleak pathways of life!

"If that's all that troubles you," young Arundel cried, eagerly, "you may make your mind easy, and come and have some oysters. We'll take care of the child. I'll adopt her, and my mother shall educate her, and she shall marry a duke. Run away now, old fellow, and change your clothes, and come and have oysters, and stout out of the pewter."

Mr. Marchmont shook his head.

"My time's just up," he said; "I'm on in the next scene. It was very kind of you to come round, Arundel; but this isn't exactly the best place for you. Go back to your friends, my dear boy, and don't think any more of me. I'll write to you some day about little Mary."

"You'll do nothing of the kind," exclaimed the boy. "You'll give me your address instanter, and I'll come to see you the first thing to-morrow morning, and you'll introduce me to little Mary; and if she and I are not the best friends in the world, I shall never again boast of my successes with lovely woman. What's the number, old fellow?"

Mr. Arundel had pulled out a smart morocco pocket-book and a gold pencil-case.

"Twenty-seven Oakley Street, Lambeth. But I'd rather you wouldn't come, Arundel; your friends wouldn't like it."

"My friends may go hang themselves. I shall do as I like, and I'll be with you to breakfast, sharp ten."

The supernumerary had no time to remonstrate. The progress of the music, faintly audible from the lobby in which this conversation had taken place told him that his scene was nearly on.

"I can't stop another moment. Go back to your friends, Arundel. Good-night. God bless you!"

"Stay; one word. The Lincolnshire property—"

"Will never come to me, my boy," the demon answered sadly, through his mask; for he had been busy reinvesting himself in that demoniac guise. "I tried to sell my reversion, but the Jews almost laughed in my face when they heard me cough. Good-night."

He was gone, and the swing-door slammed in Edward Arundel's face. The boy hurried back to his cousin, who was cross and dissatisfied at his absence. Martin Mostyn had discovered that the ballet-girls were all either old or ugly, the music badly chosen, the pantomime stupid, the scenery a failure. He asked a few supercilious questions about his old tutor, but scarcely listened to Edward's answers; and was intensely aggravated with his companion's pertinacity in sitting out the comic business—in which poor John Marchmont appeared and reappeared; now as a well-dressed passenger carrying a parcel, which he deliberately sacrificed to the felonious propensities of the clown, now as a policeman, now as a barber, now as a chemist, now as a ghost; but always buffeted, or cajoled, or bonneted, or imposed upon; always piteous, miserable, and long-suffering; with arms that ached from carrying a banner through five acts of blank-verse weariness, with a head that had throbbed under the weight of a ponderous edifice of pasteboard and wicker, with eyes that were sore with the evil influence of blue-fire and gunpowder smoke, with a throat that had been poisoned by sulphurous vapors, with bones that were stiff with the playful pommeling of clown and pantaloon: and all for—a shilling a night!

---

## CHAPTER II.

### LITTLE MARY.

POOR John Marchmont had given his address unwillingly enough to his old pupil. The lodging in Oakley Street was a wretched back-room upon the second-floor of a house whose lower regions were devoted to that species of establishment commonly called a "ladies' wardrobe." The poor gentleman, the teacher of mathematics, the law-writer, the Drury-Lane supernumerary, had shrunk from any exposure of his poverty; but his pupil's imperious good-nature had overridden every objection, and John Marchmont awoke upon the morning after the meeting at Drury Lane to the rather embarrassing recollection that he was to expect a visitor to breakfast with him.

How was he to entertain this dashing, high-spirited young school-boy, whose lot was cast in the pleasant pathways of life, and who was no doubt accustomed to see at his matutinal meal such luxuries as John Marchmont had only beheld in the fairy-like realms of comestible beauty exhibited to hungry foot-passengers behind the plate-glass windows of Italian warehouses?

"He has hams stewed in Madeira, and Perigord pies, I dare say, at his Aunt Mostyn's," John thought, despairingly. "What can I give him to eat?"

But John Marchmont, after the manner of the poor, was apt to overestimate the extravagance of the rich. If he could have seen the Mostyn breakfast then preparing in the lower regions of Montague Square, he might have been considerably relieved; for he would have only beheld mild infusions of tea and coffee, in silver vessels, certainly, four French rolls hidden under a glistening damask napkin, six triangular fragments of dry toast, cut from a stale half-quartern, four new-laid eggs, and about half a pound of bacon cut into rashers of transcendental delicacy. Widow ladies who have daughters to marry do not plunge very deep into the books of Messrs. Fortnum and Mason.

"He used to like hot rolls when I was at Vernon's," John thought, rather more hopefully; "I wonder whether he likes hot rolls still?"

Pondering thus, Mr. Marchmont dressed himself—very neatly, very carefully; for he was one of those men whom even poverty can not rob of man's proudest attribute, his individuality. He made no noisy protest against the humiliations to which he was compelled to submit; he uttered no boisterous assertions of his own merit; he urged no clamorous demand to be treated as a gentleman in his day of misfortune; but in his own mild, undemonstrative way he did assert himself, quite as effectually as if he had raved all day upon the hardship of his lot, and drunk himself mad and blind under the pressure of his calamities. He never abandoned the habits which had been peculiar to him from his childhood. He was as neat and orderly in his second-floor back as he had been seven or eight years before in his simple apartments at Cambridge. He did not recognize that association which most men perceive between poverty and shirt-sleeves, or poverty and beer. He was content to wear threadbare cloth, but adhered most obstinately to a prejudice in favor of clean linen. He never acquired those lounging vagabond habits peculiar to some men in the day of trouble. Even among the supernumeraries of Drury Lane he contrived to preserve his self-respect; if they nicknamed him Barking Jeremiah, they took care only to pronounce that playful sobriquet when the gentleman-super was safely out of hearing. He was so polite in the midst of his reserve that the person who could willfully have offended him must have been more unkindly than any of her Majesty's servants. It is true that the great tragedian on more than one occasion apostrophized the weak-kneed bannerholder as "BEAST," when the super's cough had peculiarly disturbed his composure; but the same great man gave poor John Marchmont a letter to a distinguished physician, compassionately desiring the relief of the same pulmonary affection. If John Marchmont had not been prompted by his own instincts to struggle against the evil influences of poverty, he would have done battle sturdily for the sake of one who was ten times dearer to him than himself.

If he *could* have become a swindler or a reprobate—it would have been about as easy for him to become either as to have burst at once, and without an hour's practice, into a full-blown

Léotard or Olmar — his daughter's influence would have held him back as securely as if the slender arms twined tenderly about him had been chains of adamant forged by an enchanter's power.

How could he be false to his little one, this helpless child, who had been confided to him in the darkest hour of his existence; the hour in which his consumptive wife had yielded to the many forces arrayed against her in life's battle, and had left him alone in the world to fight for his little girl?

"If I were to die I think Arundel's mother would be kind to her," John Marchmont thought, as he finished his careful toilet. "Heaven knows I have no right to ask or expect such a thing; but she will be rich by-and-by, perhaps, and will be able to repay them."

A little hand knocked lightly at the door of his room while he was thinking this, and a childish voice said:

"May I come in, papa?"

The little girl slept with one of the landlady's children in a room above her father's. John opened the door, and let her in. The pale wintry sunshine, creeping in at the curtainless window, near which Mr. Marchmont sat, shone full upon the child's face as she came toward him. It was a small, pale face, with singularly delicate features, a tiny straight nose, a pensive mouth, and large thoughtful hazel eyes. The child's hair fell loosely upon her shoulders; not in those cork-screw curls so much affected by mothers in the humbler walks of life, nor yet in those crisp undulations lately adopted in Belgravian nurseries, but in soft silken masses, only curling at the extreme end of each tress. Miss Marchmont—she was always called Miss Marchmont in that Oakley Street household—wore her brown-stuff frock and scanty diaper pinafore as neatly as her father wore his threadbare coat and darned linen. She was very pretty, very lady-like, very interesting; but it was impossible to look at her without a vague feeling of pain that was difficult to understand. You knew by-and-by why you were sorry for this little girl. She had never been a child. That divine period of perfect innocence—innocence of all sorrow and trouble, falsehood and wrong—that bright holiday-time of the soul had never been hers. The ruthless hand of poverty had snatched away from her the gift which God had given her in her cradle; and at eight years old she was a woman—a woman invested with all that is most beautiful among womanly attributes—love, tenderness, compassion, carefulness for others, unselfish devotion, uncomplaining patience, heroic endurance. She was a woman by reason of all these virtues; but she was no longer a child. At three years old she had bidden farewell forever to the ignorant selfishness, the animal enjoyment of childhood, and had learned what it was to be sorry for poor papa and mamma; and from that first time of awakening to the sense of pity and love she had never ceased to be the comforter of the helpless young husband who was so soon to be left wifeless.

John had been compelled to leave his child, in order to get a living for her and for himself in the hard service of Mr. Laurence Vernon, the principal of the highly select and expensive academy at which Edward Arundel and Martin Mostyn had been educated. But he had left her in good hands; and when the bitter day of his dismissal came, he was scarcely as sorry as he ought to have been for the calamity which brought him back to his little Mary. It is impossible for any words of mine to tell how much he loved the child; but take into consideration his hopeless poverty, his sensitive and reserved nature, his utter loneliness, the bereavement that had cast a shadow upon his youth, and you will perhaps understand an affection that was almost morbid in its intensity, and which was reciprocated most fully by its object. The little girl loved her father too much. When he was with her, she was content to sit by his side, watching him as he wrote; proud to help him, if even by so much as wiping his pens, or handing him his blotting-paper; happy to wait upon him, to go out marketing for him, to prepare his scanty meals, to make his tea, and arrange and rearrange every object in the slenderly furnished second-floor back-room. They talked sometimes of the Lincolnshire fortune—the fortune which might come to Mr. Marchmont, if three people, whose lives were each worth three times John's feeble existence, would be so obliging as to clear the way for the heir-at-law, by taking an early departure to the church-yard. A more practical man than John Marchmont would have kept a sharp eye upon these three lives, and by some means or other contrived to find out whether number one was consumptive, or number two dropsical, or number three apoplectic; but John was utterly incapable of any such Machiavellian proceeding. I think he sometimes beguiled his weary walks between Oakley Street and Drury Lane by the dreaming of such childish day-dreams as I should be almost ashamed to set down upon this sober page. The three lives might all happen to be riding in the same express upon the occasion of a terrible collision; but the poor fellow's gentle nature shrank appalled before the vision he had invoked. He could not sacrifice a whole trainful of victims even for little Mary. He contented himself with borrowing a *Times* newspaper now and then, and looking at the top of the second column, with the faint hope that he should see his own name in large capitals, coupled with the announcement that by applying somewhere he might hear of something to his advantage. He contented himself with this, and with talking about the future to little Mary in the dim firelight. They spent long hours in the shadowy room, only lighted by the faint flicker of a pitiful handful of coals; for the commonest dip-candles are sevenpence half-penny a pound, and were dearer, I dare say, in the year '38. Heaven knows what splendid castles in the air these two simple-hearted creatures built for each other's pleasure by that comfortless hearth. I believe that, though the father made a pretense of talking of these things only for the amusement of his child, he was actually the more childish of the two. It was only when he left that fire-lit room, and went back into the hard, reasonable, commonplace world, that he remembered how foolish the talk was, and how it was impossible—yes, impossible—that he, the law-writer and supernumerary, could ever come to be master of Marchmont Towers.

Poor little Mary was in this less practical than

her father. She carried her day-dreams into the street, until all Lambeth was made glorious by their supernal radiance. Her imagination ran riot in a vision of a happy future, in which her father would be rich and powerful. I am sorry to say that she derived most of her ideas of grandeur from the New Cut. She furnished the drawing-room at Marchmont Towers from the splendid stores of an upholsterer in that thoroughfare. She laid flaming Brussels carpets upon the polished oaken floors which her father had described to her, and hung cheap satin damask of gorgeous colors before the great oriel windows. She put gilded vases of gaudy artificial flowers on the high carved mantle-pieces in the old rooms, and hung a disreputable gray parrot —for sale at a green-grocer's, and given to the use of bad language—under the stone colonnade at the end of the western wing. She appointed the tradespeople who should serve the far-away Lincolnshire household; the small matter of distance would, of course, never stand in the way of her gratitude and benevolence. Her papa would employ the civil green-grocer who gave such excellent half-pennyworths of water-cresses; the kind butter-man who took such pains to wrap up a quarter of a pound of the best eighteen-penny fresh butter for the customer whom he always called "little lady;" the considerate butcher who never cut more than the three-quarters of a pound of rump-steak, which made an excellent dinner for Mr. Marchmont and his little girl. Yes, all these people should be rewarded when the Lincolnshire property came to Mary's papa. Miss Marchmont had some thoughts of building a shop close to Marchmont Towers for the accommodating butcher, and of adopting the green-grocer's eldest daughter for her confidante and companion. Heaven knows how many times the little girl narrowly escaped being run over while walking the material streets in some ecstatic reverie such as this! but Providence was very careful of the motherless girl; and she always returned to Oakley Street with her pitiful little purchases of tea and sugar, butter and meat. You will say, perhaps, that at least these foolish day-dreams were childish; but I maintain still that Mary's soul had long ago bade adieu to infancy, and that even in these visions she was womanly; for she was always thoughtful of others rather than of herself, and there was a great deal more of the practical business of life mingled with the silvery web of fancies than there should have been so soon after her eighth birthday. At times, too, an awful horror would quicken the pulses of her loving heart as she heard the hacking sound of her father's cough; and a terrible dread would seize her—the fear that John Marchmont might never live to inherit the Lincolnshire fortune. The child never said her prayers without adding a little extempore supplication, that she might die when her father died. It was a wicked prayer, perhaps; and a clergyman might have taught her that her life was in the hands of Providence; and that it might please Him who had created her to doom her to many desolate years of loneliness; and that it was not for her, in her wretched and helpless ignorance, to rebel against His divine will. I think if the Archbishop of Canterbury had driven from Lambeth Palace to Oakley Street to tell little Mary this he would

have taught her in vain; and that she would have fallen asleep that night with the old prayer upon her lips, the fond foolish prayer that the bonds which love had woven so firmly might never be roughly broken by death.

Miss Marchmont heard the story of last night's meeting with great pleasure, though it must be owned she looked a little grave when she was told that the generous-hearted school-boy was coming to breakfast; but her gravity was only that of a thoughtful housekeeper, who ponders ways and means, and, even while you are telling her the number and quality of your guests, sketches out a rough ground-plan of her dishes, ponders the fish in season, and the soups most fitting to precede them, and balances the contending advantages of Palestine and Julienne, or Hare and Italian.

"A 'nice' breakfast, you say, papa," she said, when her father had finished speaking; "then we must have water-cresses, of course."

"And hot rolls, Polly dear. Arundel was always fond of hot rolls."

"And hot rolls, four for threepence half-penny in the Cut."—(I am ashamed to say that this benighted child talked as deliberately of the "Cut" as she might have done of the "Row.")—"There'll be one left for tea, papa; for we could never eat four rolls. They'll take such a lot of butter, though."

The little housekeeper took out an antediluvian bead-purse and began to examine her treasury. Her father handed all his money to her, as he would have done to his wife; and Mary doled him out the little sums he wanted—money for half an ounce of tobacco, money for a pint of beer. There were no penny papers in those days, or what a treat an occasional *Telegraph* would have been to poor John Marchmont!

Mary had only one personal extravagance. She read novels—dirty, bloated, ungainly volumes—which she borrowed from a snuffy old woman in a little back street, who charged her the smallest hire ever known in the circulating-library business, and who admired her as a wonder of precocious erudition. The only pleasure the child knew in her father's absence was the perusal of these dingy pages; she neglected no duty, she forgot no tender office of ministering care for the loved one who was absent; but when all the little duties had been finished, how delicious it was to sit down to "Madeleine the Deserted," and "Cosmos the Pirate," and to lose herself far away in illimitable regions, peopled by wandering princesses in white satin, and gentlemanly bandits, who had been stolen from their royal fathers' halls by vengeful hordes of gipsies. In these early years of poverty and loneliness John Marchmont's daughter stored up, in a mind that was morbidly sensitive rather than strong, a terrible amount of dim poetic sentiment; the possession of which is scarcely, perhaps, the best or safest dower for a young lady who has life's journey all before her.

At half past nine o'clock all the simple preparations necessary for the reception of a visitor had been completed by Mr. Marchmont and his daughter. All vestiges of John's bed had disappeared; leaving, it is true, rather a suspicious-looking mahogany chest of drawers to mark the spot where once a bed had been. The window had been opened, the room aired and dusted, a

bright little fire burned in the shining grate, and
the most brilliant of tin tea-kettles hissed upon
the hob.  The white table-cloth was darned in
several places; but it was a remnant of the
small stock of linen with which John had begun
married life; and the Irish damask asserted its
superior quality, in spite of many darns, as positively as Mr. Marchmont's good blood asserted
itself in spite of his shabby coat.  A brown tea-
pot full of strong tea, a plate of French rolls, a
pat of fresh butter, and a broiled haddock, do
not compose a very epicurean repast; but Mary
Marchmont looked at the humble breakfast as a
prospective success.

"We could have haddocks every day at
Marchmont Towers, couldn't we, papa?" she
said, naïvely.

But the little girl was more than delighted
when Edward Arundel dashed up the narrow
staircase and burst into the room, fresh, radiant,
noisy, splendid, better dressed even than the
waxen preparations of elegant young gentlemen
exhibited at the portal of a great outfitter in the
New Cut, and yet not at all like either of those
red-lipped types of fashion.  How delighted the
boy declared himself with every thing!  He had
driven over in a cabriolet, and he was awfully
hungry, he informed his host.  The rolls and
water-cresses disappeared before him as if by
magic; little Mary shivered at the slashing cuts
he made at the butter; the haddock had scarcely left the gridiron before it was no more.

"This is ten times better than Aunt Mostyn's
skinny breakfasts," the young gentleman observed candidly.  "You never get enough with
her.  Why does she say, 'You won't take another egg, will you, Edward?' if she wants me
to have one?  You should see our hunting-
breakfasts at Dangerfield.  Four
sorts of claret, and no end of Moselle and Champagne.  You shall go to Dangerfield some day
to see my mother, Miss Mary."

He called her "Miss Mary," and seemed
rather shy of speaking to her.  Her womanli-
ness impressed him in spite of himself.  He had
a fancy that she was old enough to feel the humiliation of her father's position, and to be sensitive upon the matter of the two-pair back; and
he was sorry the moment after he had spoken
of Dangerfield.

"What a snob I am!" he thought; "always
bragging of home."

But Mr. Arundel was not able to stop very
long in Oakley Street, for the supernumerary
had to attend a rehearsal at twelve o'clock; so
at half past eleven John Marchmont and his
pupil went out together, and little Mary was
left alone to clear away the breakfast, and perform the rest of her household duties.

She had plenty of time before her, so she did
not begin at once, but sat upon a stool near the
fender gazing dreamily at the low fire.

"How good and kind he is!" she thought;
"just like Cosmos—only Cosmos was dark; or
like Reginald Ravenscroft—but then he was
dark too.  I wonder why the people in novels
are always dark?  How kind he is to papa!
Shall we ever go to Dangerfield, I wonder, papa
and me?  Of course I wouldn't go without papa."

----

### CHAPTER III.

WHILE Mary sat absorbed in such idle visio
as these Mr. Marchmont and his old pupil walk
toward Waterloo Bridge together.

"I'll go as far as the theatre with you, Marc
mont," the boy said; "it's my holidays' no
you know, and I can do as I like.  I'm going
a private tutor in another month, and he's
prepare me for the army.  I want you to t
me all about that Lincolnshire property, old bo
Is it any where near Swampington?"

"Yes; within nine miles."

"Goodness gracious me!  Lord bless my sou
what an extraordinary coincidence!  My unc
Hubert's Rector of Swampington—such a hol
I go there sometimes to see him and my cous
Olivia.  Isn't she a stunner, though!  Kno
more Greek and Latin than me, and more mat
ematics than you.  Could eat our heads off
any thing."

John Marchmont did not seem very mu
impressed by the coincidence that appeared
extraordinary to Edward Arundel; but, in ord
to oblige his friend, he explained very patient
and lucidly how it was that only three lives stoc
between him and the possession of Marchmo
Towers, and all lands and tenements appertai
ing thereto.

"The estate's a very large one," he said, fin
ly; "but the idea of my ever getting it is,
course, too preposterous."

"Good gracious me!  I don't see that at all
exclaimed Edward, with extraordinary vivacit
"Let me see, old fellow; if I understand yo
story right, this is how the case stands: yo
first cousin is the present possessor of Marchmo
Towers; he has a son, fifteen years of age, w
may or may not marry; only one son, reme
ber.  But he has also an uncle—a bachelor u
cle—who, by the terms of your grandfathe
will, must get the property before you can su
ceed to it.  Now, this uncle of the present po
sessor is an old man; of course he'll die soo
The present possessor himself is a middle-ag
man; so I shouldn't think he can be likely
last long.  I dare say he drinks too much po
or hunts, or something of that sort; goes to sle
after dinner, and does all manner of apoplect
things, I'll be bound.  Then there's the son, on
fifteen, and not yet marriageable; consumptiv
I dare say.  Now, will you tell me that chance
are not six to six he dies unmarried?  So, y
see, my dear old boy, you're sure to get the fo
tune; for there's nothing to keep you out of i
except—"

"Except three lives, the worst of which is be
ter than mine.  It's kind of you to look at it
this sanguine way, Arundel; but I wasn't bo
to be a rich man.  Perhaps, after all, Providen
has used me better than I think.  I might
have been happy at Marchmont Towers.  I'm
shy, awkward, humdrum fellow.  If it wasn't f
Mary's sake—"

"Ah, to be sure!" cried Edward Arund
"You're not going to forget all about—M
Marchmont!" he was going to say "little Mary
but had checked himself abruptly at the sudd
recollection of the earnest hazel eyes that h
kept wondering watch upon his ravages at t
breakfast-table.  "I'm sure Miss Marchmon

born to be an heiress; I never saw such a little princess."

"What!" demanded John Marchmont, sadly, "in a darned pinafore and a threadbare frock?"

The boy's face flushed, almost indignantly, as his old master said this.

"You don't think me such a snob as to think I'd admire a lady"—he spoke thus of Miss Mary Marchmont, yet midway between her eighth and ninth birthday—"the less because she wasn't rich? But of course your daughter will have the fortune by-and-by, even if—"

He stopped, ashamed of his want of tact; for he knew John would divine the meaning of that sudden pause.

"Even if I should die before Philip Marchmont," the teacher of mathematics answered, quietly. "As far as that goes, Mary's chance is as remote as my own. The fortune can only come to her upon the event of Arthur's dying without issue, or, having issue, failing to cut off the entail, I believe they call it."

"Arthur! that's the son of the present possessor?"

"Yes. If I and my poor little girl, who is delicate like her mother, should die before either of these three men, there is another who will stand in my shoes, and who will look out perhaps more eagerly than I have done for his chances of getting the property."

"Another!" exclaimed Mr. Arundel. "By Jove, Marchmont, it's the most complicated affair I ever heard of! It's worse than those sums you used to set me in barter: 'If A sells B 999 Stilton cheeses at 9½d. a pound,' and all that sort of thing, you know. Do make me understand it, old fellow, if you can."

John Marchmont sighed.

"It's a wearisome story, Arundel," he said.

"I don't know why I should bore you with it."

"But you don't bore me with it," cried the boy, energetically. "I'm awfully interested in it, you know; and I could walk up and down here all day talking about it."

The two gentlemen had passed the Surrey toll-gate of Waterloo Bridge by this time. The Southwestern Terminus had not been built in the year '38, and the bridge was about the quietest thoroughfare any two companions confidentially inclined could have chosen. The shareholders knew this, to their cost.

Perhaps Mr. Marchmont might have been beguiled into repeating the old story, which he had told so often in the dim fire-light to his little girl; but the great clock of St. Paul's boomed forth the twelve ponderous strokes that told the hour of noon; and a hundred other steeples, upon either side of the water, made themselves clamorous with the same announcement.

"I must leave you, Arundel," the supernumerary said, hurriedly; he had just remembered that it was time for him to go and be browbeaten by a truculent stage-manager. "God bless you, my dear boy! It was very good of you to want to see me; and the sight of your fresh face has made me very happy. I should like you to understand all about the Lincolnshire property. God knows there's small chance of its ever coming to me or to my child; but when I am dead and gone Mary will be left alone in the world, and it would be some comfort to me to know that she was not without *one* friend

—generous and disinterested like you, Arundel —who, if the chance *did* come, would see her righted."

"And so I would," cried the boy, eagerly. His face flushed and his eyes fired. He was a preux chevalier already, in thought, going forth to do battle for a hazel-eyed mistress.

"I'll *write* the story, Arundel," John Marchmont said; "I've no time to tell it, and you mightn't remember it either. Once more, good-by! once more, God bless you!"

"Stop!" exclaimed Edward Arundel, flushing a deeper red than before—he had a very boyish habit of blushing—"stop, dear old boy. You must borrow this of me, please. I've lots of them. I should only spend it on all sorts of bilious things; or stop out late and get tipsy. You shall pay me with interest when you get Marchmont Towers. I shall come and see you again soon. Good-by."

The lad forced some crumpled scrap of paper into his old tutor's hand, bolted through the toll-bar, and jumped into a cabriolet, whose high-stepping charger was dawdling along Lancaster Place.

The supernumerary hurried on to Drury Lane as fast as his weak legs could carry him. He was obliged to wait for a pause in the rehearsal before he could find an opportunity of looking at the parting gift which his old pupil had forced upon him. It was a crumpled and rather dirty five-pound note, wrapped round two half crowns, a shilling, and half a sovereign.

The boy had given his friend the last remnant of his slender stock of pocket-money. John Marchmont turned his face to the dark wing that sheltered him and wept silently. He was of a gentle and rather womanly disposition, be it remembered; and he was in that weak state of health in which a man's eyes are apt to moisten, in spite of himself, under the influence of any unwonted emotion.

He employed a part of that afternoon in writing the letter which he had promised to send to his boyish friend.

"MY DEAR ARUNDEL,—My purpose in writing to you to-day is so entirely connected with the future welfare of my beloved and only child that I shall carefully abstain from any subject not connected with her interests. I say nothing, therefore, respecting your conduct of this morning, which, together with my previous knowledge of your character, has decided me upon confiding to you the doubts and fears which have long tormented me upon the subject of my darling's future.

"I am a doomed man, Arundel. The doctors have told me this; but they have told me also that, though I can never escape the sentence of death which was passed upon me long ago, I may live for some years if I live the careful life which only a rich man can lead. If I go on carrying banners and breathing sulphur, I can not last long. My little girl will be left penniless, but not quite friendless; for there are humble people, relatives of her poor mother, who would help her, kindly I am sure, in their own humble way. The trials which I fear for my orphan girl are not so much the trials of poverty as the dangers of wealth. If the three men who, on my death, would alone stand between Mary and the Lincolnshire property, die childless, my poor darling will become the only obstacle in the pathway of a man whom, I will freely own to you, I distrust.

"My father, John Marchmont, was the third of four brothers. The eldest, Philip, died, leaving one son, also called Philip, and the present possessor of Marchmont Towers. The second, Marmaduke, is still alive, a bachelor. The third, John, left four children, of whom I alone survive. The fourth, Paul, left a son and two daughters. The son is an artist, exercising his profession now in London; one of the daughters is married to a parish surgeon, who practices at Stanfield, in Lincolnshire; the other is an old maid, and entirely dependent upon her brother.

"It is this man, Paul Marchmont, the artist, whom I fear.

"Do not think me weak, or foolishly suspicious, Arundel, when I tell you that the very thought of this man brings the cold sweat upon my forehead, and seems to stop the beating of my heart. I know that this is a prejudice, and an unworthy one. I do not believe Paul Marchmont is a good man; but I can assign no sufficient reason for my hatred and terror of him. It is impossible for you, a frank and careless boy, to realize the feelings of a man who looks at his only child, and remembers that she may soon·be left helpless and defenseless to fight the battle of life with a bad man. Sometimes I pray to God that the Marchmont property may never come to my child after my death; for I can not rid myself of the thought—may Heaven forgive me for its unworthiness!—that Paul Marchmont would leave no means untried, however foul, to wrest the fortune from her. I dare say worldly people would laugh at me for writing this letter to you, my dear Arundel; I address myself to the best friend I have—the only creature I know whom the influence of a bad man is never likely to corrupt. *Noblesse oblige!* I am not afraid that Edward Dangerfield Arundel will betray any trust, however foolish, that may have been confided to him.

"Perhaps, in writing to you thus, I may feel something of that blind hopefulness—amidst the shipwreck of all that commonly gives birth to hope—which the mariner, cast away upon some desert island, feels when he seals his simple story in a bottle, and·launches it upon the waste of waters that close him in on every side. Before my little girl is four years older you will be a man, Arundel; with a man's intellect, a man's courage, and, above all, a man's keen sense of honor. So long as my darling remains poor her humble friends will be strong enough to protect her; but if ever Providence should think fit to place her in a position of antagonism to Paul Marchmont—for he would look upon any one as an enemy who stood between him and fortune —she would need a far more powerful protector than any she could find among her poor mother's relatives. Will *you* be that protector, Edward Arundel? I am a drowning man, you see, and catch at the frailest straw that floats past me. I believe in you, Edward, as much as I distrust Paul Marchmont. If the day ever comes in which my little girl should have to struggle with this man, will you help her to fight the battle? It will not be an easy one.    . . .

"Subjoined to this letter I send you an extract from the copy of my grandfather's will, which will explain to you how he left his property. Do not lose either the letter or the extract. If you are willing to undertake the trust which I confide to you to-day, you may have need to refer to them after my death. The legacy of a child's helplessness is the only bequest which I can leave to the only friend I have.                JOHN MARCHMONT.

"27 OAKLEY STREET, LAMBETH, *Dec.* 30, 1838.

"EXTRACT.

"'I give and devise all that my estate known as·Marchmont Towers and appurtenances thereto belonging to the use of my eldest son Philip Marchmont during his natural life without impeachment of waste and from and after his decease then to the use of my grandson Philip the first son of my said son Philip during the term of his natural life without impeachment of waste and after the decease of my said grandson Philip to the use of the first and every other son of my said grandson severally and successively according to their respective seniority in tail and for default of such issue to the use of all and every the daughters and daughter of my said grandson Philip as tenants in common in tail with cross remainders between or amongst them in tail and if all the daughters of my said grandson Philip except one shall die without issue or if there shall be but one such daughter then to the use of such one or only daughter in tail and in default of such issue then to the use of the second and every other son of my said eldest son and successively according to his respective seniority in tail and in default of such issue to the use of all and every the daughters and daughter of my said eldest son Philip as tenants in common in tail with cross remainders between or amongst them in tail in default of such issue to the use of my second son Marmaduke and his assigns during the term of his natural life without impeachment of waste and after his decease to the use of the first and every son of my said son Marmaduke severally and successively according to their respective seniorities in tail and for default of such issue to the use of all and every the daughters and daughter of my said son Marmaduke as tenants in common in tail with cross remainders between or amongst them in tail and if all the daughters of my said son Marmaduke except one shall die without issue or if there shall be but one such daughter then to the use of such one or only daughter in tail and in default of such issue then to the use of my third son John during the term of his natural life without impeachment of waste and from and after his decease then to the use of my grandson John the first son of my said son John during the term of his natural life without impeachment of waste and after the decease of my said grandson John to the use of the first and every other son of my said grandson John severally and successively according to their respective seniority in tail and for default of such issue to the use of all and every the daughters and daughter of my said grandson John as tenants in common in tail with cross remainders between or among them in tail and if all the daughters of my said grandson John except one shall die without issue then to the use of such one or only daughter in tail and in default of such issue then to the use of the second and every other son of my said third son John severally and successively according to his respective seniority in tail and in default of such issue to the use of all and every the daughters and daughter of my said third son John as tenants in common in tail with cross remainders between or amongst them in tail and in default of such issue to the use of my fourth son Paul during the term of his natural life without impeachment of waste and from and after his decease then to the use of my grandson Paul the son of my said son Paul during his natural life without impeachment of waste and after the decease of my said grandson Paul to the use of the first and every other son of my said grandson severally and successively according to their respective seniority in tail and for default of such issue to the use of all and every the daughters and daughter of my said grandson Paul as tenants in common in tail with cross remainders between or amongst them in tail and if all the daughters of my said grandson Paul except one shall die without issue or if there shall be but one such daughter then to the use of such one or only daughter in tail and in default of such issue then to the use of the second and every other son of my said fourth son Paul severally and successively accord-. ing to his respective seniority in tail and in default of such issue to the use of all and every the daughters and daugh-·

ter of my said fourth son Paul as tenants in common in tail with cross remainders between or amongst them in tail,' etc., etc.

"P.S. Then comes what the lawyers call a general devise—to trustees to preserve the contingent remainders before devised from being destroyed; but what that means perhaps you can get somebody to tell me. I hope it may be some legal jargon to preserve my *very* contingent remainder, as it appears to me."

The tone of Edward Arundel's answer to this letter was more characteristic of the writer than in harmony with poor John's solemn appeal.

"You dear, foolish old Marchmont," the lad wrote, "of course I shall take care of Miss Mary; and my mother shall adopt her, and she shall live at Dangerfield, and be educated with my sister Letitia, who has the jolliest French governess, and a German maid for conversation; and don't let Paul Marchmont try on any of his games with me, that's all! But what do you mean, you ridiculous old boy, by talking about dying, and drowning, and shipwrecked mariners, and catching at straws, and all that sort of humbug, when you know very well that you'll live to inherit the Lincolnshire property, and that I'm coming to you every year to shoot, and that you're going to build a tennis-court—of course there *is* a billiard-room—and that you're going to have a stud of hunters, and be master of the hounds, and no end of bricks to your ever devoted friend, countryman, and brother,

"EDGARDO.

"42 MONTAGUE SQUARE, *Dec.* 31, 1838.

"P.S. By-the-by, don't you think a situation in a lawyer's office would suit your better than the T. R. D. L.? If you do, I think I could manage it. A happy new year to Miss Mary!"

It was thus that Mr. Edward Arundel accepted the solemn trust which his friend confided to him in all simplicity and good faith. Mary Marchmont herself was not more innocent in the ways of the world outside Oakley Street, the Waterloo Road, and the New Cut, than was the little girl's father; nothing seemed more natural to him than to intrust the doubtful future of his only child to the bright-faced, handsome boy, whose early boyhood had been unblemished by a mean sentiment or a dishonorable action. John Marchmont had spent three years in the Berkshire Academy, at which Edward and his cousin, Martin Mostyn, had been educated; and young Arundel, who was far behind his kinsman in the comprehension of a problem in algebra, had been wise enough to recognize that which Martin Mostyn could not understand—a gentleman in a shabby coat. ' It was thus that a friendship had arisen between the teacher of mathematics and his handsome pupil; and it was thus that an unreasoning belief in Edward Arundel had sprung up in John's simple mind.

"If my little girl were certain of inheriting the fortune," Mr. Marchmont thought, "I might find many who would be glad to accept my trust, and to serve her well and faithfully. But the chance is such a remote one. I can not forget how the Jews laughed at me two years ago, when I tried to borrow money upon my reversionary interest. No, I must trust this brave-

hearted boy, for I have no one else to confide in; and who else is there who would not ridicule my fear of my cousin Paul?"

Indeed Mr. Marchmont had some reason to be considerably ashamed of his antipathy to the young artist, working for his bread, and for the bread of his invalid mother and unmarried sister, in that bitter winter of '38; working patiently and hopefully, in despite of all discouragement, and content to live a joyless and monotonous life in a dingy lodging near Fitzroy Square. I can find no excuse for John Marchmont's prejudice against an industrious and indefatigable young man, who was the. sole support of two helpless women. Heaven knows, if to be adored by two women is any evidence of a man's virtue, Paul must have been the best of men; for Stephanie Marchmont and her daughter Clarisse regarded the artist with a reverential idolatry that was not without a tinge of romance. I can assign no reason, then, for John's dislike of his cousin. They had been school-fellows at a wretched suburban school, where the children of poor people were boarded, lodged, and educated all the year round for a pitiful stipend of something under twenty pounds. One of the special points of the prospectus was the announcement that there were no holidays; for the jovial Christmas gatherings of merry faces, which are so delightful to the wealthy citizens of Bloomsbury or Tyburnia, take another complexion in poverty-stricken households, whose scantily-stocked larders can ill support the raids of raw-boned lads clamorous for provender. The two boys had met at a school of this calibre, and had never met since. They may not have been the best friends, perhaps, at the classical academy; but their quarrels were by no means desperate. They may have rather freely discussed their several chances of the Lincolnshire property; but I have no romantic story to tell of a stirring scene in the humble school-room, no exciting record of deadly insult and deep vows of vengeance. No inkstand was ever flung by one boy into the face of the other; no savage blow from a horse-whip ever cut a fatal scar across the brow of either of the cousins. John Marchmont would have been almost as puzzled to account for his objection to his kinsman as was the nameless gentleman who so naïvely confessed his dislike of Dr. Fell. I fear that a great many of our likings and dislikings are too apt to be upon the Dr. Fell principle. Mr. Wilkie Collins's Basil could not tell *why* he fell madly in love with the lady whom it was his evil fortune to meet in an omnibus; nor why he entertained an uncomfortable feeling about the gentleman who was to be her destroyer. David Copperfield disliked Uriah Heep even before he had any substantial reason for objecting to the evil genius of Agnes Wickfield's father. The boy disliked the snake-like schemer of Canterbury because his eyes were round and red, and his hands clammy and unpleasant to the touch. Perhaps John Marchmont's reasons for his aversion to his cousin were about as substantial as these of Master Copperfield's. It may be that the school-boy disliked his comrade because Paul Marchmont's handsome gray eyes were a little too near together; because his thin and delicately-chiseled lips were a thought too tightly compressed; because his cheeks would fade to an awful corpse-like whiteness under circumstances which would have brought the rushing life-blood, hot and red, into another boy's face; because he was silent and suppressed when it would have been more natural to be loud and clamorous; because he could smile under provocations that would have made another frown; because, in short, there was that about him which, let it be found where it will, always gives birth to suspicion—MYSTERY.

So the cousins had parted, neither friends nor foes, to tread their separate roads in the unknown country, which is apt to seem barren and desolate enough to travelers who foot it in hobnailed boots considerably the worse for wear; and as the iron hand of poverty held John Marchmont even further back than Paul upon the hard road which each had to tread, the quiet pride of the teacher of mathematics most effectually kept him out of his kinsman's way. He had only heard enough of Paul to know that he was living in London, and working hard for a living; working as hard as John himself, perhaps, but at least able to keep afloat in a higher social position than the law-stationer's hack and the banner-holder of Drury Lane.

But Edward Arundel did not forget his friends in Oakley Street. The boy made a morning call upon his father's solicitors, Messrs. Paulette, Paulette, and Mathewson, of Lincoln's Inn Fields, and was so extremely eloquent in his needy friend's cause as to provoke the good-natured laughter of one of the junior partners, who declared that Mr. Edward Arundel ought to wear a silk gown before he was thirty. The result of this interview was, that before the first month of the new year was out John Marchmont had abandoned the classic banner and the demoniac mask to a fortunate successor, and had taken possession of a hard-seated, slim-legged stool in one of the offices of Messrs. Paulette, Paulette, and Mathewson, as copying and outdoor clerk, at a salary of thirty shillings a week.

So little Mary entered now upon a golden age, in which her evenings were no longer desolate and lonely, but spent pleasantly with her father in the study of such learning as was suited to her years, or perhaps rather to her capacity, which was far beyond her years; and on certain delicious nights, to be remembered ever afterward, John Marchmont took his little girl to the gallery of one or other of the transpontine theatres: and I am sorry to say that my heroine—for she is to be my heroine by-and-by—sucked oranges, ate Abernethy biscuits, and cooled her delicate nose against the iron railing of the gallery, after the manner of the masses when they enjoy the British Drama.

But all this time John Marchmont was utterly ignorant of one rather important fact in the history of those three lives which he was apt to speak of as standing between him and Marchmont Towers. Young Arthur Marchmont, the immediate heir of the estate, had been shot to death upon the 1st of September, 1838, without blame to any one or any thing but his own boyish carelessness, which had induced him to scramble through a hedge with a superb fowling-piece, the costly present of a doting father, loaded and on full-cock. This melancholy event, which had been briefly recorded in all the newspapers, had never reached the knowledge of poor John Marchmont, who had no friends to busy them-

selves about his interests, or to rush eagerly to carry him any intelligence affecting his prosperity. Nor had he read the obituary notice respecting Marmaduke Marchmont, the bachelor, who had breathed his last stertorous breath in a fit of apoplexy exactly one twelvemonth before the day upon which Edward Arundel had breakfasted in Oakley Street.

<hr />

## CHAPTER IV.
### GOING AWAY.

EDWARD ARUNDEL went from Montague Square straight into the household of the private tutor of whom he had spoken, there to complete his education, and to be prepared for the onerous duties of a military life. From the household of his private tutor he went at once into a cavalry regiment, after sundry examinations, which were not nearly so stringent in the year one thousand eight hundred and forty as they have since become. Indeed, I think the unfortunate young cadets who are educated upon the high-pressure system, and who are expected to give a synopsis of Portuguese political intrigue during the eighteenth century, a scientific account of the currents of the Red Sea, and a critical disquisition upon the comedies of Aristophanes as compared with those of Pedro Calderon de la Barca—not forgetting to glance at the effect of different ages and nationalities upon the respective minds of the two playwrights, within a given period of, say half an hour—would have envied Mr. Arundel for the easy manner in which he obtained his commission in a distinguished cavalry regiment. Mr. Edward Arundel therefore inaugurated the commencement of the year 1840 by plunging very deeply into the books of a crack military-tailor in New Burlington Street, and by a visit to Dangerfield Park, where he went to make his adieus before sailing for India, whither his regiment had just been ordered.

I do not doubt that Mrs. Arundel was very sorrowful at this sudden parting with her yellow-haired younger son. The boy and his mother walked together in the wintry sunset under the leafless beeches at Dangerfield, and talked of the dreary voyage that lay before the lad; the arid plains and cruel jungles far away; perils by sea and perils by land; but across them all, Fame waving her white arms, beckoning to the young soldier, and crying, "Come, conqueror that shall be! come, through trial and danger, through fever and famine—come to your rest upon my blood-stained lap!" Surely this boy, being only just eighteen years of age, may be forgiven if he is a little romantic, a little over-eager and impressionable, a little too confident that the next thing to going out to India as a sea-sick subaltern in a great transport-ship is coming home with the reputation of a Clive. Perhaps he may be forgiven, too, if, in his fresh enthusiasm, he sometimes forgot the shabby friend whom he had helped little better than a twelvemonth before, and the earnest hazel eyes that had shone upon him in the pitiful Oakley Street chamber. I do not say that he was utterly unmindful of his old teacher of mathematics. It was not in his nature to forget any one who had need of his services; for this boy, so eager to be a soldier, was of the chivalrous temperament, and would have gone out to die for his mistress, or his friend, if need had been. He had received two or three grateful letters from John Marchmont, in each of which the lawyer's clerk spoke pleasantly of his new life, and hopefully of his health, which had improved considerably, he said, since his resignation of the tragic banner and the pantomimic mask. Neither had Edward quite forgotten his promise of enlisting Mrs. Arundel's sympathies in aid of the motherless little girl. In one of these wintry walks beneath the black branches at Dangerfield the lad had told the sorrowful story of his well-born tutor's poverty and humiliation.

"Only think, mother!" he cried, at the end of the little history. "I saw the poor fellow carrying a great calico flag, and marching about at the heel of a procession, to be laughed at by the costermongers in the gallery; and I know that he is descended from a capital Lincolnshire family, and will come in for no end of money if he only lives long enough. But if he should die, mother, and leave his little girl destitute, you'll look after her, won't you?"

I don't know whether Mrs. Arundel quite entered into her son's ideas upon the subject of adopting Mary Marchmont, or whether she had any definite notion of bringing the little girl home to Dangerfield for the natural term of her life, in the event of the child being left an orphan. But she was a kind and charitable lady, and she scarcely cared to damp her boy's spirits by holding forth upon the doubtful wisdom of his adopting, or promising to adopt, any stray orphans who might cross his pathway.

"I hope the little girl may not lose her father, Edward," she said, gently. "Besides, dear, you say that Mr. Marchmont tells you he has humble friends, who would take the child if anything happened to him. He does not wish us to adopt the little girl; he only asks us to interest ourselves in her fate."

"And you will do that, mother darling?" cried the boy. "You will take an interest in her, won't you? You couldn't help doing so if you were to see her. She's not like a child, you know—not a bit like Letitia. She is as grave and quiet as you are, mother—or graver, I think; and she looks quite a lady, in spite of her poor, shabby pinafore and frock."

"Does she wear shabby frocks?" said the mother. "I could help her in that matter, at all events, Ned. I might send her a great trunk full of Letitia's things. She outgrows them long before they are shabby."

The boy colored and shook his head.

"It's very kind of you to think of it, mother dear; but I don't think that would quite answer," he said.

"Why not?"

"Because, you see, John Marchmont is a gentleman; and, you know, though he's 'so dreadfully poor now, he is heir to Marchmont Towers. And though he didn't mind doing anything in the world to earn a few shillings a week, he mightn't like to take cast-off clothes."

So nothing more was to be said or done upon the subject.

Edward Arundel wrote his humble friend a pleasant letter, in which he told John that he

had enlisted his mother's sympathy in Mary's cause, and in which he spoke in very glowing terms of the Indian expedition that lay before him.

"I wish I could come to say good-by to you and Miss Mary before I go," he wrote; "but that's impossible. I go straight from here to Southampton by coach at the end of this month, and the *Auckland* sails on the 2d of February. Tell Miss Mary I shall bring her home all kinds of pretty presents from Afghanistan—ivory fans, and Cashmere shawls, and Chinese puzzles, and embroidered slippers with turned-up toes, and diamonds, and attar of roses, and such like; and remember that I expect you to write to me, and to give me the earliest news of your coming into the Lincolnshire property."

John Marchmont received this letter in the middle of January. He gave a despondent sigh as he refolded the boyish epistle after reading it to his little girl.

"We haven't so many friends, Polly," he said, "that we should be indifferent to the loss of this one."

Mary Marchmont's cheek grew paler at her father's sorrowful speech. That imaginative temperament, which was, as I have said, almost morbid in its intensity, presented every object to the little girl in a light in which things are looked at by very few children. Only these few words, and her fancy roamed far away to that cruel land whose perils her father had described to her. Only these few words, and she was away in the rocky Bolan Pass, under hurricanes of drifting snow; she saw the hungry soldiers fighting with savage dogs for the possession of foul carrion. She had heard all the perils and difficulties which had befallen the Army of the Indus in the year '39, and the womanly heart sank under those cruel memories.

"He will go to India and be killed, papa dear," she said. "Oh, why, why do they let him go? His mother can't love him, can she? She would never let him go if she did."

John Marchmont was obliged to explain to his daughter that motherly love must not go so far as to deprive a nation of its defenders; and that the richest jewels which Cornelia can give to her country are those ruby life-drops which flow from the hearts of her bravest and brightest sons. Mary was a poor political economist; she could not reason upon the necessity of chastising Persian insolence, or checking Russian encroachments upon the far-away shores of the Indus. Was Edward Arundel's bright head, with its aureola of yellow hair, to be cloven asunder by an Afghan renegade's sabre, because the young Shah of Persia had been contumacious?

Mary Marchmont wept silently that day over a three-volume novel, while her father was away serving writs upon wretched insolvents, in his capacity of outdoor clerk to Messrs. Paulette, Paulette, and Mathewson.

The young lady no longer spent her quiet days in the two-pair back. Mr. Marchmont and his daughter had remained faithful to Oakley Street, and the proprietress of the ladies' wardrobe, who was a good, motherly creature; but they had descended to the grandeur of the first floor, whose gorgeous decorations Mary had glanced at furtively in the days gone by, when the splendid chambers were occupied by an elderly and reprobate commission-agent, who seemed utterly indifferent to the delights of a convex mirror supported by a gilded but crippled eagle, whose dignity was somewhat impaired by the loss of a wing; but which bijou appeared to Mary to be a fitting adornment for the young Queen's palace in St. James's Park.

But neither the eagle nor the third volume of a thrilling romance could comfort Mary upon this bleak January day. She shut her book, and stood by the window, looking out into the dreary street, that seemed so blotted and dim under the falling snow.

"It snowed in the Pass of Bolan," she thought; "and the treacherous Indians harassed the brave soldiers, and killed their camels. What will become of him in that dreadful country? Shall we ever see him again?"

Yes, Mary, to your sorrow. Indian cimeters will let him go scathless; famine and fever will pass him by; but the hand which points to that far-away day on which you and he are to meet will never fail or falter in its purpose until that day comes.

We have no need to dwell upon the preparations which were made for the young soldier's departure from home, nor on the tender farewells between the mother and her son.

Mr. Arundel was a country gentleman *pur et simple*; a hearty, broad-shouldered squire, who had no thought above his farm and his dog-kennel, or the hunting of the red deer, with which his neighborhood abounded. He sent his younger son to India as coolly as he had sent the elder to Oxford. The boy had little to inherit, and must be provided for in a gentlemanly manner. Other younger sons of the house of Arundel had fought and conquered in the Honorable East India Company's service; and was Edward any better than them, that there should be sentimental whining because the lad was going away to fight his way to fortune, if he could? He even went further than this, and declared that Master Edward was a lucky dog to be going out at such a time, when there was plenty of fighting, and a very fair chance of speedy promotion for a good soldier.

He gave the young cadet his blessing, reminded him of the limit of such supplies as he was to expect from home, bade him keep clear of the brandy-bottle and the dice-box; and, having done this, believed that he had performed his duty as an Englishman and a father.

If Mrs. Arundel wept she wept in secret, loth to discourage her son by the sight of those natural, womanly tears. If Miss Letitia Arundel was sorry to lose her brother she mourned with most praiseworthy discretion, and did not forget to remind the young traveler that she expected to receive a muslin frock embroidered with beetle-wings by an early mail. And as Algernon Fairfax Dangerfield Arundel, the heir, was away at college, there was no one else to mourn. So Edward left the house of his forefathers by a branch coach, which started from the "Arundel Arms" in time to meet the "Telegraph" at Exeter; and no noisy lamentations shook the sky above Dangerfield Park, no mourning voices echoed through the spacious rooms. The old servants were sorry to lose the younger-born, whose easy, genial temperament had made him

an especial favorite; but there was a certain admixture of joviality with their sorrow, as there generally is with all mourning in the basement; and the strong ale, the famous Dangerfield October, went faster upon that 31st of January than on any day since Christmas.

I doubt if any one at Dangerfield Park sorrowed as bitterly for the departure of the boyish soldier as a romantic young lady of nine years old, in Oakley Street, Lambeth, whose one sentimental day-dream, half childish, half womanly, owned Edward Arundel as its centre figure.

So the curtain falls on the picture of a brave ship sailing eastward, her white canvas strained against the cold gray February sky, and a little girl weeping over the tattered pages of a stupid novel in a shabby London lodging.

------

## CHAPTER V.

### MARCHMONT TOWERS.

THERE is a lapse of three years and a half between the acts; and the curtain rises to reveal a widely-different picture: the picture of a noble mansion in the flat Lincolnshire country; a stately pile of building, standing proudly forth against a back-ground of black woodland; a noble building, supported upon either side by an octagon tower, whose solid masonry is half hidden by the ivy which clings about the stonework, trailing here and there, and flapping restlessly with every breath of wind against the narrow casements.

A broad stone terrace stretches the entire length of the grim façade, from tower to tower; and three flights of steps lead from the terrace to the broad lawn, which loses itself in a vast grassy flat, only broken by a few clumps of trees and a dismal pool of black water, but called by courtesy a park. Grim stone griffins surmount the terrace steps, and griffins' heads and other architectural monstrosities, worn and moss-grown, keep watch and ward over every door and window, every archway and abutment, frowning threat and defiance upon the daring visitor who approaches the great house by this, the formidable chief entrance.

The mansion looks westward; but there is another approach, a low archway on the southern side, which leads into a quadrangle, where there is a quaint little door under a stone portico, ivy-covered like the rest—a comfortable little door of massive oak, studded with knobs of rusty iron—a door generally affected by visitors familiar with the house.

This is Marchmont Towers—a grand and stately mansion, which had been a monastery in the days when England and the Pope were friends and allies; and which had been bestowed upon Hugh Marchmont, gentleman, by his Sovereign Lord and most Christian Majesty the King, Henry VIII., of blessed memory, and by that gentleman commoner extended and improved at considerable outlay. This is Marchmont Towers—a splendid and a princely habitation, truly; but perhaps scarcely the kind of dwelling one would choose, out of every other resting-place upon earth, for the holy resting-place we call home. The great mansion is a little too dismal in its lonely grandeur; it lacks shelter when the dreary winds come sweeping across the grassy flats in the bleak winter weather; it lacks shade when the western sun blazes on every window-pane in the stifling summer evening. It is at all times rather too stony in its aspect, and is apt to remind one, almost painfully, of every weird and sorrowful story treasured in the storehouse of memory. Ancient tales of enchantment, dark German legends, wild Scottish fancies, grim fragments of half-forgotten demonology, strange stories of murder, violence, mystery, and wrong, vaguely intermingle in the stranger's mind as he looks, for the first time, at Marchmont Towers.

· But of course these feelings wear off in time. So invincible is the power of custom, that we might make ourselves comfortable in the Castle of Otranto after a reasonable sojourn within its mysterious walls. Familiarity would breed contempt for the giant helmet, and all the other grim apparitions of the haunted dwelling. The commonplace and ignoble wants of everyday life must surely bring disenchantment with them. The ghost and the butcher's boy can not well exist contemporaneously; and the avenging shade can scarcely continue to lurk beneath the portal which is visited by the matutinal milkman. Indeed, this is doubtless the reason that the most restless and impatient spirit, bent on early vengeance and immediate retribution, will yet wait until the shades of night have fallen before he reveals himself, rather than run the risk of an ignominious encounter with the postman or the parlor-maid. Be it how it might, the phantoms of Marchmont Towers were not intrusive. They may have perambulated the long tapestried corridors, the tenantless chambers, the broad black staircase of shining oak; all the dead and gone beauties, soldiers, and lawyers, and parsons, and simple country squires of the Marchmont race, may have descended from their picture-frames to hold a witches' sabbath in the old house; but as the Lincolnshire servants were hearty eaters and heavy sleepers, the ghosts had it all to themselves. I believe there was one dismal story attached to the house—the story of a Marchmont of the time of Charles I., who had murdered his coachman in a fit of insensate rage; and it was even asserted, upon the authority of an old housekeeper, that John Marchmont's grandmother, when a young woman and lately come as a bride to the Towers, had beheld the murdered coachman stalk into her chamber, ghastly and blood-bedabbled, in the dim summer twilight. But as this story was not particularly romantic, and possessed none of the elements likely to insure popularity, such as love, jealousy, revenge, mystery, youth, and beauty, it had never been very widely disseminated.

I should think that the new owner of Marchmont Towers—new within the last six months—was about the last person in Christendom to be hypercritical, or to raise fanciful objections to his dwelling; for inasmuch as he had come straight from a wretched transpontine lodging to this splendid Lincolnshire mansion, and had at the same time exchanged a stipend of thirty shillings a week for an income of eleven thousand a year, derivable from lands that spread, far away over fenny flats and low-lying farms, to the solitary sea-shore, he had ample reason

to be grateful to Providence, and well pleased with his new abode.

Yes; Philip Marchmont, the childless widower, had died six months before, at the close of the year '43, of a broken heart, his old servants said—broken by the loss of his only and idolized son; after which loss he had never been known to smile. He was one of those undemonstrative men, who can take a great sorrow quietly, and only—die of it. Philip Marchmont lay in a velvet-covered coffin, above his son's, in the stone recess set apart for them in the Marchmont vault beneath Kemberling Church, three miles from the Towers; and John reigned in his stead. John Marchmont, the supernumerary, the banner-holder of Drury Lane, the patient, conscientious copying and outdoor clerk of Lincoln's Inn, was now sole owner of the Lincolnshire estate, sole master of a household of well-trained old servants, sole proprietor of a very decent country gentleman's stud, and of chariots, barouches, chaises, phaetons, and other vehicles—a little old-fashioned and out of date, it may be, but very comfortable to a man for whom an omnibus ride had long been a treat and a rarity. Nothing had been touched or disturbed since Philip Marchmont's death. The rooms he had used were still the occupied apartments; the chambers he had chosen to shut up were still kept with locked doors; the servants who had served him waited upon his successor, whom they declared to be a quiet, easy gentleman, far too wise to interfere with old servants, every one of whom knew the ways of the house a great deal better than he did, though he was the master of it.

There was therefore no shadow of change in the stately mansion. The dinner-bell still rang at the same hour; the same tradespeople left the same species of wares at the low oaken door; the old housekeeper, arranging her simple menu, planned her narrow round of soups and roasts, sweets and made-dishes, exactly as she had been wont to do, and had no new tastes to consult. A gray-haired bachelor, who had been own man to Philip, was now own man to John. The carriage which had conveyed the late lord every Sunday morning and afternoon service at Kemberling conveyed the new lord, who sat in the same seat that his predecessor had occupied in the great family-pew, and read his prayers out of the same book—a noble, crimson morocco-covered volume, in which George, our most gracious King and Governor, and all manner of dead and gone princes and princesses were prayed for.

The presence of Mary Marchmont made the only change in the old house; and even that change was a very trifling one. Mary and her father were as closely united at Marchmont Towers as they had been in Oakley Street. The little girl clung to her father as tenderly as ever —more tenderly than ever, perhaps; for she knew something of that which the physicians had said, and she knew that John Marchmont's lease of life was not a long one. Perhaps it would be better to say that he had no lease at all. His soul was a tenant on sufferance in its frail earthly habitation, receiving a respite now and again, when the flicker of the lamp was very low, every chance breath of wind threatening to extinguish it forever. It was only those

· B

who knew John Marchmont very intimately who were fully acquainted with the extent of his danger. He no longer bore any of those fatal outward signs of consumption, which fatigue and deprivation had once made painfully conspicuous. The hectic flush and the unnatural brightness of the eyes had subsided; indeed, John seemed much stronger and heartier than of old; and it is only great medical practitioners who can tell to a nicety what is going on *inside* a man, when he presents a very fair exterior to the unprofessional eye. But John was decidedly better than he had been. He might live three years, five, seven, possibly even ten years; but he must live the life of a man who holds himself perpetually upon his defense against death; and he must recognize in every bleak current of wind, in every chilling damp, or perilous heat, or overexertion, or ill-chosen morsel of food, or hasty emotion, or sudden passion, an insidious attack upon the part of his dismal enemy Mary Marchmont knew all this—or divined it, perhaps, rather than knew it, with the child-woman's subtle power of divination, which is even stronger than the actual woman's; for her father had done his best to keep all sorrowful knowledge from her. She knew that he was in danger; and she loved him all the more dearly, as the one precious thing which was in constant peril of being snatched away. The child's love for her father has not grown any less morbid in its intensity since Edward Arundel's departure for India; nor has Mary become more childlike since her coming to Marchmont Towers, and her abandonment of all those sordid cares, those pitiful everyday duties, which had made her womanly.

It may be that the last lingering glamour of childhood had forever faded away with the realization of the day-dream which she had carried about with her so often in the dingy transpontine thoroughfares around Oakley Street. Marchmont Towers, that fairy palace, whose lighted windows had shone upon her far away across a cruel forest of poverty and trouble, like the enchanted castle which appears to the lost wanderer of the child's story, was now the home of the father she loved. The grim enchanter, Death, the only magician of our modern histories, had waved his skeleton hand, more powerful than the star-gemmed wand of any fairy godmother, and the obstacles which had stood between John Marchmont and his inheritance had one by one been swept away.

But was Marchmont Towers quite as beautiful as that fairy palace of Mary's day-dream? No, not quite; not quite. The rooms were handsome—handsomer and larger, even, than the rooms she had dreamed of; but perhaps none the better for that. They were grand and gloomy and magnificent; but they were not the sunlit chambers which her fancy had built up, and decorated with such shreds and patches of splendor as her narrow experience enabled her to devise. Perhaps it was rather a disappointment to Miss Marchmont to discover that the mansion was completely furnished, and that there was no room for any of those splendors which she had so often contemplated in the New Cut. The parrot at the green-grocer's was a vulgar bird, and not by any means admirable in Lincolnshire. The carrying away and providing for her favorite tradespeople was not practicable; and John Marchmont had demurred to her proposal of adopting the butcher's daughter.

There is always something to be given up even when our brightest visions are realized; there is always some one figure, a low one, perhaps, missing in the fullest sum of earthly happiness. I dare say, if Alnaschar had married the Vizier's daughter, he would have found her a shrew, and would have looked back yearningly to the humble days in which he had been an itinerant vendor of crockery-ware.

If, therefore, Mary Marchmont found her sunlit fancies not quite realized by the great stony mansion that frowned upon the fenny country-side, the wide grassy flat, the black pool, with its dismal shelter of weird pollard-willows, whose ugly shadows, distorted on the bosom of the quiet water, looked like the shadows of hump-backed men—if these things did not compose as beautiful a picture as that which the little girl had carried so long in her mind, she had no more reason to be sorry than the rest of us, and had been no more foolish than other dreamers. I think she had built her airy castle too much after the model of a last scene in a pantomime, and that she expected to find spangled waters twinkling in perpetual sunshine, revolving fountains, ever-expanding sunflowers, and gilded clouds of rose-colored gauze—every thing except the fairies, in short—at Marchmont Towers. Well, the dream was over, and she was quite a woman now; a woman, very grateful to Providence when she remembered that her father had no longer need to toil for his daily bread, and that he was luxuriously lodged, and could have the first physicians in the land at his beck and call.

"Oh, papa, it is so nice to be rich!" the young lady would exclaim now and then, in a fleeting transport of enthusiasm. "How good we ought to be to the poor people, when we remember how poor we once were!"

And the little girl did not forget to be good to the poor about Kemberling and Marchmont Towers. There were plenty of poor, of course; free and easy pensioners, who came to the Towers for brandy, and wine, and milk, and woolen stuffs, and grocery, precisely as they would have gone to a shop, and expected that there was to be no bill. The housekeeper doled out her bounties with many short homilies upon the depravity and ingratitude of the recipients, and gave tracts of an awful and denunciatory nature to the pitiful petitioners. Tracts interrogatory, and tracts fiercely imperative; tracts that asked, *Where are you going? Why are you wicked? Will you repent? What will become of you?* and other tracts, which cried, *Stop, and think! Pause, while there is time! Sinner, consider! Evil-doer, beware!* Perhaps it may not be the wisest possible plan to begin the work of reformation by frightening, threatening, and otherwise disheartening the wretched sinner to be reformed. There is a certain sermon in the New Testament containing sacred and comforting words, which were spoken upon a mountain near at hand to Jerusalem, and spoken to an auditory among which there must have been many sinful creatures; but there is more of blessing than cursing in that sublime discourse, and it might be rather a tender father pleading gently with his wayward children than an offended Deity dealing out denunciation upon a stubborn and refractory race. But the authors of the tracts may have never read this sermon, perhaps; and they may take their ideas of composition from that comforting service which we read on Ash Wednesday, cowering in fear, and trembling in our pews, and calling down curses upon ourselves and our neighbors. Be it as it might, the tracts were not popular among the pensioners of Marchmont Towers. They infinitely preferred to hear Mary read a chapter in the New Testament, or some pretty patriarchal story of primitive obedience and faith. The little girl would discourse upon the Scripture histories in her simple, old-fashioned manner; and many a stout Lincolnshire farm-laborer was content to sit over his hearth, with a pipe of shag-tobacco and a mug of fettled beer, while Miss Marchmont read and expounded the history of Abraham and Isaac, or Joseph and his brethren.

"It's joost loike a story-book to hear her," the man would say to his wife; "and yet she brings it all hoame, too, loike. If she reads about Abraham, she'll say, maybe, 'That's joost how you gave your only son to be a soldier, you know, Muster Mooggins'—she allus says Muster Mooggins—'you gave un into God's hands, and you troosted God would take care of un; and whatever cam' to un would be the best, even if it was death.' That's what she'll say, bless her little heart! so gentle and tender loike. The worst o' chaps couldn't but listen to her."

Mary Marchmont's morbidly sensitive nature adapted her to all charitable offices. No chance word in her simple talk ever inflicted a wound upon the listener. She had a subtle and intuitive comprehension of other people's feelings, derived from the extreme susceptibility of her own. She had never been vulgarized by the associations of poverty; for her self-contained nature took no color from the things that surrounded her, and she was only at Marchmont Towers that which she had been from the age of six—a little lady, grave and gentle, dignified, discreet, and wise.

There was one bright figure missing out of the picture which she had been wont of late years to make of the Lincolnshire mansion, and that was the figure of the yellow-haired boy who had breakfasted upon haddocks and hot rolls in Oakley Street. She had imagined Edward Arundel an inhabitant of that fair Utopia. He would live with them; or, if he could not live with them, he would be with them as a visitor—often —almost always. He would leave off being a soldier, for, of course, her papa could give him more money than he could get by being a soldier —(you see that Mary's experience of poverty had taught her to take a mercantile and sordid view of military life)—and he would come to Marchmont Towers, and ride, and drive, and play tennis—what was tennis? she wondered—and read three-volume novels all day long. But that part of the dream was at least broken. Marchmont Towers was Mary's home, but the young soldier was far away; in the Pass of Bolan, perhaps— Mary had a picture of that cruel rocky pass almost always in her mind—or cutting his way through a black jungle, with the yellow eyes of hungry tigers glaring out at him through the loathsome tropical foliage; or dying of thirst and fever under a scorching sun, with no better pillow than the neck of a dead camel, with no more tender watcher than the impatient vulture flapping her wings above his head, and waiting till he too should be carrion. What was the good of wealth, if it could not bring this young soldier home to a safe shelter in his native land? John Marchmont smiled when his daughter asked this question, and implored her father to write to Edward Arundel, recalling him to England.

"God knows how glad I should be to have the boy here, Polly," John said, as he drew his little girl closer to his breast—she sat on his knee still, though she was thirteen years of age —"but Edward has a career before him, my dear, and could not give it up for an inglorious life in this rambling old house. It isn't as if I could hold out any inducement to him, you know, Polly. I can't; for I mustn't leave any money away from my little girl."

"But he might have half my money, papa, or all of it," Mary added, piteously. "What could I do with money if—"

She didn't finish the sentence; she never could complete any such sentence as this; but her father knew what she meant.

So six months had passed since a dreary January day upon which John Marchmont had read in the second column of the Times that he could hear of something greatly to his advantage by applying to a certain solicitor, whose offices were next door but one to those of Messrs. Paulette, Paulette, and Mathewson's. His heart began to beat very violently when he read that advertisement in the supplement which it was one of his duties to air before the fire in the clerks' office; but he showed no other sign of emotion. He waited until he took the papers to his employer; and as he laid them at Mr. Mathewson's elbow murmured a respectful request to be allowed to go out for half an hour upon his own business.

"Good gracious me, Marchmont!" cried the lawyer; "what can you want to go out for at this time in the morning? You've only just come; and there's that agreement between Higgs and Sandyman must be copied before—"

"Yes, I know, Sir; I'll be back in time to attend to it; but I—I think I've come into a fortune, Sir; and I should like to go and see about it."

The solicitor turned in his revolving library-chair and looked aghast at his clerk. Had this Marchmont—always rather unnaturally reserved and eccentric—gone suddenly mad? No; the copying-clerk stood by his side, grave, self-possessed as ever, with his forefinger upon the advertisement.

"Marchmont—John—call—Messrs. Tindal and Trollam—" gasped Mr. Mathewson. "Do you mean to tell me it's you?"

"Yes, Sir."

"Egad, I'll go with you!" cried the solicitor, hooking his arm through that of his clerk, snatching his hat from an adjacent stand, and dashing through the outer office, down the great staircase, and into the next door but one, before John Marchmont knew where he was.

John had not deceived his employer. Marchmont Towers was his, with all its appurtenances. Messrs. Paulette, Paulette, and Mathewson took him in hand, much to the chagrin of Messrs. Tindal and Trollam, and proved his identity in less than a week. On a shelf above the high wooden desk at which John had sat, copying law-papers, with a weary hand and an aching spine, appeared two bran-new deed-boxes, inscribed, in white letters, with the name and address of JOHN MARCHMONT, ESQ., MARCHMONT TOWERS. The copying-clerk's sudden accession to fortune was the talk of all the *employés* in "the Fields." Marchmont Towers was exaggerated into all Lincolnshire and a tidy slice of Yorkshire. Eleven thousand a year was expanded into an annual million. Every body expected *largesse* from the legatee. How fond people had been of the quiet clerk, and how magnanimously they had concealed their sentiments during his poverty, lest they should wound him, as they urged, "which" they knew he was sensitive; and how expansively they now dilated on their long-suppressed emotions! Of course, under these circumstances, it is hardly likely that every body could be satisfied; so it is a small thing to say that the dinner which John gave—by his late employers' suggestion (he was about the last man to think of giving a dinner)—at the "Albion Tavern," to the legal staff of Messrs. Paulette, Paulette, and Mathewson, and such acquaintance of the legal profession as they should choose to invite, was a failure; and that gentlemen who were pretty well used to dine upon liver and bacon, or beef-steak and onions, or the joint, vegetables, bread, cheese, and celery for a shilling, turned up their noses at the turbot, murmured at the paucity of green fat in the soup, made light of red mullet and ortolans, objected to the flavor of the truffles, and were contemptuous about the wines.

John knew nothing of this. He had lived a separate and secluded existence; and his only thought now was of getting away to Marchmont Towers, which had been familiar to him in his boyhood, when he had been wont to go there on occasional visits to his grandfather. He wanted to get away from the turmoil and confusion of the big, heartless city, in which he had endured so much; he wanted to carry away his little girl to a quiet country home, and live and die there in peace. He liberally rewarded all the good people about Oakley Street who had been kind to little Mary; and there was weeping and regret in the regions of the Ladies' Wardrobe when Mr. Marchmont and his daughter went away one bitter winter's morning, in a cab which was to carry them to the hostelry whence the coach started for Lincoln.

It is strange to think how far those Oakley Street days of privation and endurance seem to have receded in the memories of both father and daughter. The impalpable past fades away, and it is difficult for John and his little girl to believe that they were once so poor and desolate. It is Oakley Street now that is visionary and unreal. The stately county families bear down upon Marchmont Towers in great lumbering chariots, with brazen crests upon the hammer-cloths, and sulky coachmen in Crown-George wigs. The county mammas patronize and caress Miss Marchmont—what a match she will be for one of the county sons by-and-by!—the county daughters discourse with Mary about her poor, and her fancy-work, and her piano. She

is getting on slowly enough with her piano, poor little girl, under the tuition of the organist of Swampington, who gives lessons to that part of the county. And there are solemn dinners now and then at Marchmont Towers; dinners at which Miss Mary appears when the cloth has been removed, and reflects in silent wonder upon the change that has come to her father and herself. Can it be true that she has ever lived in Oakley Street? whither came no more aristocratic visitors than her Aunt Sophia, who was the wife of a Berkshire farmer, and always brought hogs-puddings, and butter, and home-made bread, and other rustic delicacies to her brother-in-law; or Mrs. Brigsome, the washer-woman, who made a morning call every Monday with John Marchmont's shabby shirts. The shirts were not shabby now; and it was no longer Miss Mary's duty to watch them day by day, and manipulate them tenderly when the linen grew frayed at the sharp edges of the folds, or the button-holes gave signs of weakness. Corson, Mr. Marchmont's own man, had care of the shirts now; and John wore diamond studs and a black satin waistcoat when he gave a dinner-party. They were not very lively, those Lincolnshire dinner-parties; though the dessert was a sight to look upon, in Mary's eyes. The long, shining table, the red and gold and purple and green Indian china, the fluffy woolen d'oyleys, the sparkling cut-glass, the sticky preserved ginger and guava-jelly, and dried orange rings and chips, and all the stereotyped sweetmeats, were very grand and beautiful, no doubt; but Mary had seen livelier desserts in Oakley Street, though there had been nothing better than a brown-paper bag of oranges from the Westminster Road, and a bottle of two-and-twopenny Marsala from a licensed victualer's in the Borough, to promote conviviality.

---

## CHAPTER VI.

### THE YOUNG SOLDIER'S RETURN.

THE rain beats down upon the battlemented roof of Marchmont Towers this July day as if it had a mind to flood the old mansion. The flat waste of grass, and the lonely clumps of trees, are almost blotted out by the falling rain. The low gray sky shuts out the distance. This part of Lincolnshire—fenny, misty, and flat always—seems flatter and mistier than usual to-day. The rain beats hopelessly upon the leaves in the wood behind Marchmont Towers, and splashes into great pools beneath the trees, until the ground is almost hidden by the fallen water, and the trees seem to be growing out of a black lake. The land is lower behind Marchmont Towers, and slopes down gradually to the bank of a dismal river, which straggles through the Marchmont property at a snail's pace, to gain an impetus farther on, until it hurries into the sea somewhere northward of Grimsby. The wood is not held in any great favor by the household at the Towers; and it has been a pet project of several Marchmonts to level and drain it, but a project not very easily to be carried out. Marchmont Towers is said to be unhealthy, as a dwelling-house, by reason of this wood, from which miasmas rise in certain states of the weather; and it is on this account that the back of the house—the eastern front, at least, as it is called, looking to the wood—is very little used.

Mary Marchmont sits at a window in the western drawing-room, watching the ceaseless falling of the rain upon this dreary summer afternoon. She is little changed since the day upon which Edward Arundel saw her in Oakley Street. She is taller, of course; but her figure is as slender and childish as ever; it is only her face in which the earnestness of premature womanhood reveals itself, in a grave and sweet serenity very beautiful to contemplate. Her soft brown eyes have a pensive shadow in their gentle light; her mouth is even more pensive. It has been said of Jane Grey, of Mary Stuart, of Marie Antoinette, Charlotte Corday, and other fated women, that in the gayest hours of their youth they bore upon some feature, the shadow of the End; an impalpable, indescribable presage of an awful future, vaguely felt by those who looked upon them. Is it thus with Mary Marchmont? Has the solemn hand of Destiny set that shadowy brand upon the face of this child, that even in her prosperity, as in her adversity, she should be so utterly different from all other children? Is she already marked out for some womanly martyrdom; already set apart for more than common suffering?

She sits alone this afternoon, for her father is busy with his agent. Wealth does not mean immunity from all care and trouble; and Mr. Marchmont has plenty of work to get through, in conjunction with his land-steward, a hardheaded Yorkshireman, who lives at Kemberling, and insists on doing his duty with pertinacious honesty.

The large brown eyes looked wistfully out at the dismal waste and the falling rain. There was a wretched equestrian making his way along the carriage-drive.

"Who can come to see us on such a day?" Mary thought. "It must be Mr. Gormby, I suppose"—the agent's name was Gormby—"Mr. Gormby never cares about the wet; but then I thought he was with papa. Oh, I hope it isn't any body coming to call."

But Mary forgot all about the struggling equestrian the next moment. She had some morsel of fancy-work upon her lap, and picked it up and went on with it, setting slow stitches, and letting her thoughts wander far away from Marchmont Towers. To India, I am afraid; or to that imaginary India which she had created for herself out of such images as were to be picked up in the "Arabian Nights." She was roused suddenly by the opening of a door at the farther end of the room, and by the voice of a servant, who mumbled a name which sounded something like Mr. Armenger.

She rose, blushing a little, to do honor to one of her father's county acquaintance, as she thought; when a fair-haired gentleman dashed in, very much excited and very wet, and made his way toward her.

"I would come, Miss Marchmont," he said—"I would come, though the day was so wet; every body vowed I was mad to think of it, and it was as much as my poor brute of a horse could do to get over the ten miles of swamp between this and my uncle's house; but I would come. Where's John? I want to see John.

Didn't I always tell him he'd come into the Lincolnshire property? Didn't I always say so, now? You should have seen Martin Mostyn's face—he's got a capital berth in the War Office, and he's such a snob!—when I told him the news! It was as long as my arm. But I must see John, dear old fellow; I long to congratulate him."

Mary stood with her hands clasped, and her breath coming quickly. The blush had quite faded out, and left her unusually pale. But Edward Arundel did not see this. Young gentlemen of four-and-twenty are not very attentive to every change of expression in little girls of thirteen.

"Oh, is it you, Mr. Arundel? Is it really you?"

She spoke in a low voice, and it was almost difficult to keep the rushing tears back while she did so. She had pictured him so often in peril, in famine, in sickness, in death, that to see him here, well, happy, light-hearted, cordial, handsome, and brave, as she had seen him four and a half years before in the two-pair back in Oakley Street, was almost too much for her to bear without the relief of tears. But she controlled her emotion as bravely as if she had been a woman of twenty.

"I am so glad to see you," she said, quietly; "and papa will be so glad too. It is the only thing we want, now we are rich, to have you with us. We have talked of you so often; and I—we—have been so unhappy sometimes, thinking that—"

"That I should be killed, I suppose?"

"Yes; or wounded very, very badly. The battles in India have been dreadful, have they not?"

Mr. Arundel smiled at her earnestness.

"They have not been exactly child's play," he said, shaking back his auburn hair and smoothing his thick mustache. He was a man now, and a very handsome one; something of that type which is known in this year of grace as "swell;" but brave and chivalrous withal, and not afflicted with any impediment in his speech. "The men who talk of the Afghans as a chicken-hearted set of fellows are rather out of their reckoning. The Indians can fight, Miss Mary, and fight like the devil; but we can lick 'em."

He walked over to the fire-place, where there was a fire burning upon this chilly wet day; and began to shake himself dry. Mary, following him with her eyes, wondered if there was such another soldier in all her Majesty's dominions, and how soon he would be made Generalin-chief of the Army of the Indus.

"Then you've not been wounded at all, Mr. Arundel?" she said, after a pause.

"Oh yes, I've been wounded; and I got a bullet in my shoulder from an Afghan musket, and I'm home on sick-leave."

This time he saw the expression of her face, and interpreted her look of alarm.

"But I'm not ill, you know, Miss Marchmont," he said, laughing. "Our fellows are very glad of a wound when they feel home-sick. The 8th come home before long, all of 'em; and I've a twelvemonth's leave of absence; and we're pretty sure to be ordered out again by the end of that time, as I don't believe there's much chance of quiet over there."

"You will go out again!"

Edward Arundel smiled at her mournful tone.

"To be sure, Miss Mary; I have my captaincy to win, you know. I'm only a lieutenant as yet."

"It was only a twelvemonth's reprieve, after all, then," Mary thought. He would go again to suffer, and to be wounded, and to die, perhaps. But then, on the other hand, there was a twelvemonth's respite, and her father might in that time prevail upon the young soldier to stay at Marchmont Towers. It was such inexpressible happiness to see him once more, to know that he was safe and well, that she could scarcely do otherwise than see all things in a sunny light just now.

She ran to John Marchmont's study to tell him of the coming of this welcome visitor; but she wept upon her father's shoulder before she could explain who it was whose coming had made her so glad. Very few friendships had broken the monotony of her solitary existence; and Edward Arundel was the only chivalrous image she had ever known out of her books.

John Marchmont was scarcely less pleased than his child to see the man who had befriended him in his poverty. Never has more heartfelt welcome been given than that which greeted Edward Arundel at Marchmont Towers.

"You will stay with us, of course, my dear Arundel," John said; "you will stop for September and the shooting. You know you promised you'd make this your shooting-box; and we'll build the tennis-court. Heaven knows there's room enough for it in the great quadrangle, and there's a billiard-room over this, though I'm afraid the table is out of order. But we can soon set that right, can't we, Polly?"

"Yes, yes, papa; out of my pocket-money, if you like."

Mary Marchmont said this in all good faith. It was sometimes difficult for her to remember that her father was really rich, and had no need of help out of her pocket-money. The slender savings in the little purse had often given him some luxury that he would not otherwise have had in the time gone by.

"You got my letter, then?" John said; "the letter in which I told you—"

"That Marchmont Towers was yours. Yes, my dear old boy. That letter was among a packet my agent brought me half an hour before I left Calcutta. God bless you, dear old fellow; how glad I was to hear of it! I've only been in England a fortnight. I went straight from Southampton to Dangerfield to see my father and mother, staid there little over ten days, and then offended them all by running away. I reached Swampington yesterday, slept in my uncle Hubert's, paid my respects to my cousin Olivia, who is—well, I've told you what she is—and rode over here this morning, much to the annoyance of the inhabitants of the Rectory. So, you see, I've been doing nothing but offending people for your sake, John; and for yours, Miss Mary. By-the-by, I've brought you such a doll!"

A doll! Mary's pale face flushed a faint crimson. Did he think her such a child, then, this soldier; did he think her only a silly child, with no thought above a doll, when she would have gone out to India, and braved every peril

of that cruel country, to be his nurse and comfort in fever and sickness, like the brave Sisters of Mercy she had read of in some of her novels?

Edward Arundel saw that faint crimson glow lighting up in her face.

"I beg your pardon, Miss Marchmont," he said. "I was only joking; of course you are a young lady now, almost grown up, you know. Can you play chess?"

"No, Mr. Arundel."

"I am sorry for that; for I have brought you a set of chessmen that once belonged to Dost Mohammed Khan. But I'll teach you the game if you like?"

"Oh yes, Mr. Arundel; I should like it very, very much." ·

The young soldier could not help being amused by the little girl's earnestness. She was about the same age as his sister Letitia; but oh how widely different to that bouncing and rather wayward young lady, who tore the pillow-lace upon her muslin frocks, rumpled her long ringlets, rasped the skin off the sharp points of her elbows by repeated falls upon the gravel-paths at Dangerfield, and tormented a long-suffering Swiss attendant, half-lady's-maid, half-governess, from morning till night! No fold was awry in Mary Marchmont's simple black-silk frock; no plait disarranged in the neat cambric tucker that encircled the slender white throat. Intellect here reigned supreme. Instead of the animal spirits of a thoughtless child there was a woman's loving carefulness for others, a woman's unselfishness and devotion.

Edward Arundel did not understand all this, but perhaps the greater part of it.               ·

"She is a dear little thing," he thought, as he watched her clinging to her father's arm; and then he ran off about Marchmont Towers, and insisted upon being shown over the house; and, perhaps for the first time since the young heir had shot himself to death upon a bright September morning in a stubble-field within ear-shot of the park, the sound of merry laughter echoed through the long corridors, and resounded in the unoccupied rooms.

Edward Arundel was in raptures with everything. There never was such a dear old place, he said. "Gloomy," "dreary," "draughty," pshaw! Cut a few logs out of that wood at the back there, pile 'em up in the wide chimneys, and set a light to 'em, and Marchmont Towers would be like a baronial mansion at Christmastime. He declared that every dingy portrait he looked at was a Rubens or a Velasquez or a Vandyke, a Holbein or a Lely.

"Look at that fur border to the old woman's black velvet gown, John; look at the coloring of the hands! Do you think anybody but Peter Paul could have painted that? Do you see that girl with the blue satin stomacher and the flaxen ringlets?—one of your ancestresses, Miss Mary, and very like you. If that isn't in Sir Peter Lely's best style—his earlier style, you know, before he was spoiled by royal patronage and got lazy—I know nothing of painting."

The young soldier ran on in this manner, as he hurried his host from room to room; now throwing open windows to look out at the wet prospect; now rapping against the wainscot to find secret hiding-places behind sliding panels; now stamping on the oak flooring in the hope of discovering a trap-door. He pointed out at least ten eligible sites for the building of the tennis-court; he suggested more alterations and improvements than a builder could have completed in a lifetime. The place brightened under the influence of his presence, as a landscape lights up under a burst of sudden sunshine breaking through a dull gray sky.

Mary Marchmont did not wait for the removal of the table-cloth that evening, but dined with her father and his friend in a snug oak-paneled chamber, half breakfast-room, half library, which opened out of the western drawing-room. How different Edward Arundel was to all the rest of the world, Miss Marchmont thought; how gay, how bright, how genial, how happy! The county families, mustered in their fullest force, couldn't make such mirth among them as this young soldier in his single person.

The evening was an evening in fairy-land. Life was sometimes like the last scene in a pantomime, after all, with rose-colored cloud and golden sunlight.

One of the Marchmont servants went over to Swampington early the next day to fetch Mr. Arundel's portmanteaus from the Rectory; and after dinner upon that second evening Mary Marchmont took her seat opposite Edward, and listened reverently while he explained to her the moves upon the chess-board.

"So you don't know my cousin Olivia?" the young soldier said, by-and-by. "That's odd! I should have thought she would have called upon you long before this."

Mary Marchmont shook her head.

"No," she said; "Miss Arundel has never been to see us; and I should so like to have seen her, because she would have told me about you. Mr. Arundel has called once or twice upon papa; but I have never seen him. He is not our clergyman, you know; Marchmont Towers belongs to Kemberling Parish."

"To be sure; and Swampington is ten miles off. But, for all that, I should have thought Olivia would have called upon you. I'll drive you over to-morrow, if John thinks we whip enough to trust you with me, and you shall see Livy. The Rectory's such a queer old place!"

Perhaps Mr. Marchmont was rather doubtful as to the propriety of committing his little girl to Edward Arundel's charioteership for a ten-mile drive upon a wretched road. Be it as it might, a lumbering barouche, with a pair of overfed horses, was ordered next morning, instead of the high, old-fashioned gig which the soldier had proposed driving; and the safety of the two young people was confided to a sober old coachman, rather sulky at the prospect of a drive to Swampington so soon after the rainy weather.

It does not rain always even in this part of Lincolnshire; and the July morning was bright and pleasant, the low hedges fragrant with starry, opal-tinted wild roses and waxen honeysuckle, the yellowing corn waving in the light summer breeze. Mary assured her companion that she had no objection whatever to the odor of cigar smoke; so Mr. Arundel lolled upon the comfortable cushions of the barouche, with his back to the horses, smoking cheroots and talking gayly, while Miss Marchmont sat in the place of state opposite to him. A happy drive: a drive in a fairy chariot through regions of fairy-land, forever and forever to be remembered by Mary Marchmont.

They left the straggling hedges and the yellowing corn behind them by-and-by, as they drew near the outskirts of Swampington. The town lies lower even than the surrounding country, flat and low as that country is. A narrow and dismal river crawls at the base of a half-ruined wall, which once formed part of the defenses of the place. Black barges lie at anchor here, and a stone bridge, guarded by a tollhouse, spans the river. Mr. Marchmont's carriage lumbered across this bridge, and under an arch-way, low, dark, stony, and grim, into a narrow street of solid, well-built houses, low, dark, stony, and grim, like the arch-way, but bearing the stamp of reputable occupation. I believe the grass grew, and still grows, in this street, as it does in all the other streets and in the market-place of Swampington. They are all pretty much in the same style, these streets—all stony, narrow, dark, and grim; and they wind and twist hither and thither, and in and out, in a manner utterly bewildering to the luckless stranger, who, seeing that they are all alike, has no landmarks for his guidance.

There are two handsome churches, both bearing an early date in the history of Norman supremacy: one crowded into an inconvenient corner of a back street, and choked by the houses built up round about it; the other lying a little out of the town, upon a swampy waste looking toward the sea, which flows within a mile of Swampington. Indeed, there is no lack of water in that Lincolnshire borough. The river winds about the outskirts of the town; unexpected creeks and inlets meet you at every angle; shallow pools lie here and there about the marshy suburbs; and in the dim distance the low line of the gray sea meets the horizon.

But perhaps the positive ugliness of the town is something redeemed by the vague air of romance and old-world mystery which pervades it. It is an exceptional place, and somewhat interesting thereby. The great Norman church upon the swampy waste, the scattered tombstones, bordered by the low and moss-grown walls, make a picture which is apt to dwell in the minds of those who look upon it, although it is by no means a pretty picture. The Rectory lies close to the church-yard; and a wicket-gate opens from Mr. Arundel's garden into a narrow pathway, leading across a patch of tangled grass and through a lane of sunken and lop-sided tombstones, to the low vestry door. The Rectory itself is a long, irregular building, to which one incumbent after another has built the additional chamber, or chimney, or porch, or bow-window, necessary for his accommodation. There is very little garden in front of the house, but a patch of lawn and shrubbery and a clump of old trees at the back.

"It's not a pretty house, is it, Miss Marchmont?" asked Edward, as he lifted his companion out of the carriage.

"No, not very pretty," Mary answered; "but I don't think any thing is pretty in Lincolnshire. Oh, there's the sea!" she cried, looking suddenly across the marshes to the low gray line in the distance. "How I wish we were as near the sea at Marchmont Towers!"

The young lady had something of a romantic passion for the wide-spreading ocean. It was an unknown region, that stretched far away, and that was wonderful and beautiful by reason of its solemn mystery. All her Corsair stories were allied to that far, fathomless deep. The white sail in the distance was Conrad's, perhaps; and he was speeding homeward to find Medora dead in her lonely watch-tower, with fading flowers upon her breast. The black hull yonder was the bark of some terrible pirate bound on rapine and ravage. (She was a coal-barge, I have no doubt, sailing Londonward with her black burden.) Nymphs and Lurleis, Mermaids and Mermen, and tiny water-babies with silvery tails, forever splashing in the sunshine, were all more or less associated with the long gray line toward which Mary Marchmont looked with solemn, yearning eyes.

"We'll drive down to the sea-shore some morning, Polly," said Mr. Arundel. He was beginning to call her Polly, now and then, in the easy familiarity of their intercourse. "We'll spend a long day on the sands, and I'll smoke cheroots while you pick up shells and sea-weed."

Miss Marchmont clasped her hands in silent rapture. Her face was irradiated by the new light of happiness. How good he was to her, this brave soldier, who must undoubtedly be made Commander-in-chief of the Army of the Indus in a year or so!

Edward Arundel led his companion across the flagged way between the iron gate of the Rectory garden and a half-glass door leading into the hall. Out of this simple hall, only furnished with a couple of chairs, a barometer, and an umbrella-stand, they went, without announcement, into a low old-fashioned room, half study, half parlor, where a young lady was sitting at a table writing.

She rose as Edward opened the door, and came to meet him.

"At last!" she said; "I thought your rich friends engrossed all your attention."

She paused, seeing Mary.

"This is Miss Marchmont, Olivia," said Edward; "the only daughter of my old friend. You must be very fond of her, please; for she is a dear little girl, and I know she means to love you."

Mary lifted her soft brown eyes to the face of the young lady, and then dropped her eyelids suddenly, as if half frightened by what she had seen there.

What was it? What was it in Olivia Arundel's handsome face from which those who looked at her so often shrank, repelled and disappointed? Every line in those perfectly-modeled features was beautiful to look at; but as a whole the face was not beautiful. Perhaps it was too much like a marble mask, exquisitely chiseled, but wanting in variety of expression. The handsome mouth was rigid; the dark gray eyes had a cold light in them. The thick bands of raven-black hair were drawn tightly off a square forehead, which was the brow of an intellectual and determined man rather than of a woman. . Yes, womanhood was the something wanted in Olivia Arundel's face. Intellect, resolution, courage, are rare gifts; but they are not the gifts whose tokens we look for most anxiously in a woman's face. If Miss Arundel had been a queen, her diadem would have become her nobly, and she might have been a very great queen; but Heav-

en help the wretched creature who had appealed from minor tribunals to *her* mercy! Heaven help delinquents of every kind whose last lingering hope had been in her compassion!

Perhaps Mary Marchmont vaguely felt something of all this, At any rate, the enthusiasm with which she had been ready to regard Edward Arundel cooled suddenly beneath the winter in that pale, quiet face.

Miss Arundel said a few words to her guest, kindly enough, but rather too much as if she had been addressing a child of six. Mary, who was accustomed to be treated as a woman, was wounded by her manner.

"How different she is to Edward!" thought Miss Marchmont. "I shall never like her as I like him."

"So this is the pale-faced child who is to have Marchmont Towers by-and-by," thought Miss Arundel; "and these rich friends are the people for whom Edward stays away from us."

The lines about the rigid mouth grew harder, the cold light in the gray eyes grew colder, as the young lady thought this.

It was thus that these two women met; while one was but a child in years; while the other was yet in the early bloom of womanhood: these two, who were predestined to hate each other, and inflict suffering upon each other in the days that were to come. It was thus that they thought of one another; each with an unreasoning dread, an undefined aversion gathering in her breast.

Six weeks passed, and Edward Arundel kept his promise of shooting the partridges on the Marchmont preserves. The wood behind the Towers and the stubbled corn-fields on the home-farm bristled with game. The young soldier heartily enjoyed himself through that delicious first week in September; and came home every afternoon, with a heavy game-bag and a light heart, to boast of his prowess before Mary and her father.

The young man was by this time familiar with every nook and corner of Marchmont Towers; and the builders were already at work at the tennis-court which John had promised to erect for his friend's pleasure. The site ultimately chosen was a bleak corner of the eastern front, looking to the wood; but as Edward declared the spot in every way eligible, John had no inclination to find fault with his friend's choice. There was other work for the builders; for Mr. Arundel had taken a wonderful fancy to a ruined boat-house upon the brink of the river; and this boat-house was to be rebuilt and restored, and made into a delightful pavilion, in the upper chambers of which Mary might sit with her father in the hot summer weather, while Mr. Arundel kept a couple of trim wherries in the recesses below.

So you see the young man made himself very much at home, in his own innocent, boyish fashion, at Marchmont Towers. But as he had brought life and light to the old Lincolnshire mansion nobody was inclined to quarrel with him for any liberties which he might choose to take; and every one looked forward sorrowfully to the dark days before Christmas, at which time he was under a promise to return to Dangerfield Park, there to spend the remainder of his leave of absence.

## CHAPTER VII.

### OLIVIA.

WHILE busy workmen were employed at Marchmont Towers, hammering at the fragile wooden walls of the tennis-court—while Mary Marchmont and Edward Arundel wandered, with the dogs at their heels, among the rustle of the fallen leaves in the wood behind the great gaunt Lincolnshire mansion—Olivia, the Rector's daughter, sat in her father's quiet study, or walked to and fro in the gloomy streets of Swampington, doing her duty day by day.

Yes, the life of this woman is told in these few words: she did her duty. From the earliest age at which responsibility can begin she had done her duty, uncomplainingly, unswervingly, as it seemed to those who watched her.

She was a good woman. The bishop of the diocese had specially complimented her for her active devotion to the holy work which falls somewhat heavily upon the only daughter of a widowed rector. All the stately dowagers about Swampington were loud in the praises of Olivia Arundel. Such devotion, such untiring zeal in a young person of three-and-twenty years of age were really most laudable, these solemn elders said, in tones of supreme patronage; for the young saint of whom they spoke wore shabby gowns, and was the portionless daughter of a poor man who had let the world slip by him, and who sat now amidst the dreary ruins of a wasted life, looking yearningly backward with hollow, regretful eyes, and bewailing the chances he had lost. Hubert Arundel loved his daughter; loved her with that passionate, sorrowful affection we feel for those who suffer for our sins, whose lives have been blighted by our follies. Every shabby garment which Olivia wore was a separate reproach to her father; every deprivation she endured stung him as cruelly as if she had turned upon him and loudly upbraided him for his wasted life and his squandered patrimony. He loved her; and he watched her day after day, doing her duty to him as to all others; doing her duty forever and forever; but when he most yearned to take her to his heart, her own cold perfections arose and separated him from the child he loved. What was he but a poor, vacillating, erring creature: weak, supine, idle, epicurean; unworthy to approach this girl, who never seemed to sicken of the hardness of her life—who never grew weary of well-doing?

But how was it that, for all her goodness, Olivia Arundel won so small a share of earthly reward? I do not speak of the gold and jewels and other worldly benefits with which the fairies in our children's story-books reward the benevolent mortals who take compassion upon them in the guise of old women; but rather of the love and gratitude, the tenderness and blessings which usually wait upon the footsteps of those who do good deeds. Olivia Arundel's charities were never-ceasing; her life was one perpetual sacrifice to her father's parishioners. There was no natural womanly vanity, no simple girlish fancy, which this woman had not trodden underfoot, and trampled out in the hard pathway she had chosen for herself.

The poor people knew this. Rheumatic men and women, crippled and bedridden, knew that the blankets which covered them had been bought out of money that would have purchased silk dresses for the Rector's handsome daughter, or luxuries for the frugal table at the Rectory. They knew this. They knew that, through frost and snow, through storm and rain, Olivia Arundel would come to sit beside their dreary hearths, their desolate sick-beds, and read holy books to them; sublimely indifferent to the foul weather without, to the stifling atmosphere within, to dirt, discomfort, poverty, inconvenience; heedless of all except the performance of the task she had set herself.

People knew this, and they were grateful to Miss Arundel, and submissive and attentive in her presence; they gave her such return as they were able to give for the benefits, spiritual and temporal, which she bestowed upon them; but they did not love her.

They spoke of her in reverential accents, and praised her whenever her name was mentioned; but they spoke with tearless eyes and unfaltering voices. Her virtues were beautiful, of course, as virtue in the abstract must always be; but I think there was a want of individuality in her goodness, a lack of personal tenderness in her kindness, which separated her from the people she benefited.

Perhaps there was something almost chilling in the dull monotony of Miss Arundel's benevolence. There was no blemish of moral weakness upon the good deeds she performed; and the recipients of her bounties, seeing her so far off, grew afraid of her, even by reason of her goodness, and *could* not love her.

She made no favorites among her father's parishioners. Of all the school-children she had taught she had never chosen one curly-headed urchin for a pet. She had no good days and bad days; she was never foolishly indulgent or extravagantly cordial. She was always the same —Church-of-England charity personified; meting out all mercies by line and rule; doing good with a note-book and a pencil in her hand; looking on every side with calm, scrutinizing eyes; rigidly just, terribly perfect.

It was a fearfully monotonous, narrow, and uneventful life which Olivia Arundel led at Swampington Rectory. At three-and-twenty years of age she could have written her history upon a few pages. The world outside that dull Lincolnshire town was shaken by convulsions, and made irrecognizable by repeated change; but all these outer changes and revolutions made themselves but little felt in the quiet grass-grown streets, and the flat surrounding swamps, within whose narrow boundary Olivia Arundel had lived from infancy to womanhood; performing and repeating the same duties from day to day, with no other progress to mark the lapse of her existence than the slow alternation of the seasons, and the dark hollow circles which had lately deepened beneath her gray eyes, and the depressed lines about the corners of her firm lower lip.

These outward tokens, beyond her own control, alone betrayed this woman's secret. She was weary of her life. She sickened under the dull burden which she had borne so long, and carried so patiently. The slow round of duty was loathsome to her. The horrible, narrow, unchanging existence, shut in by huge walls, which bounded her on every side and kept her prisoner to herself, was odious to her. The powerful intellect revolted against the fetters that bound and galled it. The proud heart beat with murderous violence against the bonds that kept it captive.

"Is my life always to be this—always, always, always?" The passionate nature burst forth sometimes, and the voice that had so long been stifled cried aloud in the black stillness of the night, "Is it to go on forever and forever; like the slow river that creeps under the broken wall? O my God! is the lot of other women never to be mine? Am I never to be loved and admired; never to be sought and chosen? Is my life to be all of one dull, gray, colorless monotony; without one sudden gleam of sunshine, without one burst of rainbow-light?"

How shall I anatomize this woman, who, gifted with no womanly tenderness of nature, unendowed with that pitiful and unreasoning affection which makes womanhood beautiful, yet tried, and tried unceasingly, to do her duty and to be good; clinging, in the very blindness of her soul, to the rigid formulas of her faith, but unable to seize upon its spirit? Some latent comprehension of the want in her nature made her only the more scrupulous in the performance of those duties which she had meted out for herself. The holy sentences she had heard, Sunday after Sunday, feebly read by her father, haunted her perpetually, and would not be put away from her. The tenderness in every word of those familiar gospels was a reproach to the want of tenderness in her own heart. She could be good to her father's parishioners, and she could make sacrifices for them; but she could not love them any more than they could love her.

That divine and universal pity, that spontaneous and boundless affection, which is the chief loveliness of womanhood and Christianity, had no part in her nature. She could understand Judith with the Assyrian general's gory head held aloft in her uplifted hand; but she could not comprehend that diviner mystery of sinful Magdalene sitting at her Master's feet with the shame and love in her face half-hidden by a veil of drooping hair.

No; Olivia Arundel was not a good woman in the commoner sense we attach to the phrase. It was not natural to her to be gentle and tender, to be beneficent, compassionate, and kind, as it is to the women we are accustomed to call "good." She was a woman who was forever fighting against her nature; who was forever striving to do right; forever walking painfully upon the difficult road mapped out for her; forever measuring herself by the standard she had set up for her self-abasement. And who shall say that such a woman as this, if she persevere unto the end, shall not wear a brighter crown than her more gentle sisters—the starry circlet of a martyr?

If she persevere unto the end! But was Olivia Arundel the woman to do this? The deepening circles about her eyes, the hollowing cheeks, and the feverish restlessness of manner which she could not always control, told how terrible the long struggle had become to her. If she could have died then—if she had fallen beneath the weight of her burden—what a record of sin and anguish might have remained unwritten in the history of woman's life! But this woman was one of those who can suffer, and yet not die. She bore her burden a little longer; only to fling it down by-and-by, and to abandon herself to the eager devils who had been watching for her so untiringly.

Hubert Arundel was afraid of his daughter. The knowledge that he had wronged her—wronged her even before her birth by the foolish waste of his patrimony, and wronged her through life by his lack of energy in seeking such advancement as a more ambitious man might have won—the knowledge of this, and of his daughter's superior virtues, combined to render the father ashamed and humiliated by the presence of his only child. The struggle between this fear and his passionate love of her was a very painful one; but fear had the mastery, and the Rector of Swampington was content to stand aloof, mutely watchful of his daughter, wondering feebly whether she was happy, striving vainly to discover that one secret, that keystone of the soul, which must exist in every nature, however outwardly commonplace.

Mr. Arundel had hoped that his daughter would marry, and marry well, even at Swampington; for there were rich young land-owners who visited at the Rectory. But Olivia's handsome face won her no admirers, and at three-and-twenty Miss Arundel had received no offer of marriage. The father reproached himself for this. It was he who had blighted the life of his penniless girl; it was his fault that no suitors came to woo his motherless child. Yet many dowerless maidens have been sought and loved; and I do not think it was Olivia's lack of fortune which kept admirers at bay. I believe it was rather that inherent want of tenderness which chilled and dispirited the timid young Lincolnshire squires.

Had Olivia ever been in love? Hubert Arundel constantly asked himself this question. He did so because he saw that some blighting influence, even beyond the poverty and dullness of her home, had fallen upon the life of his only child. What was it? What was it? Was it some hopeless attachment, some secret tenderness, which had never won the sweet return of love for love?

He would no more have ventured to question his daughter upon this subject than he would have dared to ask his fair young Queen, newly married in those days, whether she was happy with her handsome husband.

Miss Arundel stood by the Rectory gate in the early September evening, watching the western sunlight on the low sea-line beyond the marshes. She was wearied and worn out by a long day devoted to visiting among her parishioners; and she stood with her elbow leaning on the gate, and her head resting on her hand, in an attitude peculiarly expressive of fatigue. She had thrown off her bonnet, and her black hair was pushed carelessly from her forehead. Those masses of hair had not that purple lustre, nor yet that wandering glimmer of red gold, which gives peculiar beauty to some raven tresses. Olivia's hair was long and luxuriant; but it was of that dead, inky blackness, which is all shadow. It was dark, fathomless, inscrutable, like herself. The cold gray eyes looked thoughtfully seaward. Another day's duty had been done. Long chapters of Holy Writ had been read to troublesome old women afflicted with perpetual coughs; stifling, airless cottages had been visited: the dull, unvarying track had been beaten by the patient feet, and the yellow sun was going down upon another joyless day. But did the still evening hour bring peace to that restless spirit? No; by the rigid compression of the lips, by the feverish lustre in the eyes, by the faint hectic flush in the oval cheeks, by every outward sign of inward unrest, Olivia Arundel was not at peace. The listlessness of her attitude was merely the listlessness of physical fatigue. The mental struggle was not finished with the close of the day's work.

The young lady looked up suddenly as the tramp of a horse's hoofs, slow and lazy-sounding on the smooth road, met her ear. Her eyes dilated, and her breath went and came more rapidly; but she did not stir from her weary attitude.

The horse was from the stables at Marchmont Towers, and the rider was Mr. Arundel. He came smiling to the Rectory gate, with the low sunshine glittering in his yellow hair, and the light of careless, indifferent happiness irradiating his handsome face.

"You must have thought I'd forgotten you and my uncle, my dear Livy," he said, as he sprang lightly from his horse. "We've been so busy with the tennis-court, and the boat-house, and the partridges, and goodness knows what besides at the Towers, that I couldn't get the time to ride over till this evening. But to-day we dined early, on purpose that I might have the chance of getting here. I come upon an important mission, Livy, I assure you."

"What do you mean?"

There was no change in Miss Arundel's voice when she spoke to her cousin; but there was a change, not easily to be defined, in her face when she looked at him. It seemed as if that weary hopelessness of expression which had settled on her countenance grew ever more weary, more hopeless, as she turned toward this bright young soldier, glorious in the beauty of his own light-heartedness. It may have been merely the sharpness of contrast which produced this effect. It may have been an actual change arising out of some secret hidden in Olivia's breast.

"What do you mean by an important mission, Edward?" she said.

She had need to repeat the question; for the young man's attention had wandered from her, and he was watching his horse as the animal cropped the tangled herbage about the Rectory gate.

"Why, I've come with an invitation to a dinner at Marchmont Towers. There's to be a dinner-party; and, in point of fact, it's to be given on purpose for you and my uncle. John and Polly are full of it. You'll come, won't you, Livy?"

Miss Arundel shrugged her shoulders, with an impatient sigh.

"I hate dinner-parties," she said; "but, of course, if papa accepts Mr. Marchmont's invitation I can not refuse to go. Papa must choose for himself."

There had been some interchange of civilities between Marchmont Towers and Swampington Rectory during the six weeks which had passed since Mary's introduction to Olivia Arundel;

and this dinner-party was the result of John's simple desire to do honor to his friend's kindred.

"Oh, you must come, Livy," Mr. Arundel exclaimed. "The tennis-court is going on capitally. I want you to give us your opinion again. Shall I take my horse round to the stable? I am going to stop an hour or two, and ride back by moonlight."

Edward Arundel took the bridal in his hand, and the cousins walked slowly round by the low garden-wall to a dismal and rather dilapidated stable at the back of the Rectory, where Hubert Arundel kept a wall-eyed white horse, long-legged, shallow-chested, and large-headed, and a fearfully and wonderfully made phaeton, with high wheels and a mouldy leathern hood.

Olivia walked by the young soldier's side with that air of weary indifference that had so grown upon her very lately. Her eyelids drooped with a look of sullen disdain; but the gray eyes glanced furtively now and again at her companion's handsome face. He was very handsome. The glitter of golden hair and of bright fearless blue eyes; the careless grace which was the kind of man we call "a swell;" the gay insouciance of an easy, candid, generous nature—all combined to make Edward Arundel singularly attractive. These spoiled children of nature demand our admiration, in very spite of ourselves. These beautiful useless creatures call upon us to rejoice in their valueless beauty, like the flaunting poppies in the corn-field, and the gaudy wild-flowers in the grass.

The darkness of Olivia's face deepened after each furtive glance she cast at her cousin. Could it be that this girl, to whom nature had given strength but denied grace, envied the superficial attractions of the young man at her side? She did envy him; she envied him that sunny temperament which was so unlike her own; she envied him that wondrous power of taking life lightly. Why should existence be so bright and careless to him, while to her it was a terrible fever-dream, a long sickness, a never-ceasing battle?

"Is my uncle in the house?" Mr. Arundel asked, as he strolled from the stable into the garden with his cousin by his side.

"No; he has been out since dinner," Olivia answered; "but I expect him back every minute. I came out into the garden—the house seemed so hot and stifling to-night, and I have been sitting in close cottages all day."

"Sitting in close cottages!" repeated Edward. "Ah, to be sure; visiting your rheumatic old pensioners, I suppose. How good you are, Olivia!"

"Good!"

She echoed the word in the very bitterness of a scorn that could not be repressed.

"Yes; every body says so. The Millwards were at Marchmont Towers the other day, and they were talking of you, and praising your goodness, and speaking of your schools, and your blanket associations, and your invalid societies, and your relief clubs, and all your plans for the parish. Why, you must work as hard as a prime minister, Livy, by their account; you, who are only a few years older than me."

Only a few years! She started at the phrase, and bit her lip.

"I was three-and-twenty last month," she said.

"Ah, yes; to be sure. And I'm one-and-twenty. Then you're only two years older than me, Livy. But, then, you see, you're so clever, that you seem much older than you are. You make a fellow feel rather afraid of you, you know. Upon my word you do, Livy."

Miss Arundel did not reply to this speech of her cousin's. She was walking by his side up and down a narrow graveled pathway, bordered by a hazel-hedge; she had gathered one of the slender twigs, and was idly stripping away the fluffy ends.

"What do you think, Livy?" cried Edward, suddenly, bursting out laughing at the end of the question. "What do you think? It's my belief you've made a conquest."

"What do you mean?"

"There you go; turning upon a fellow as if you could eat him. Yes, Livy; it's no use your looking savage. You've made a conquest; and of one of the best fellows in the world, too. John Marchmont's in love with you."

Olivia Arundel's face flushed a vivid crimson to the roots of her black hair.

"How dare you come here to insult me, Edward Arundel?" she cried, passionately.

"Insult you? Now, Livy dear, that's too bad, upon my word," remonstrated the young man. "I come and tell you that as good a man as ever breathed is over head and ears in love with you, and that you may be mistress of one of the finest estates in Lincolnshire if you please, and you turn round upon me like no end of furies."

"Because I hate to hear you talk nonsense," answered Olivia, her bosom still heaving with that first outburst of emotion, but her voice suppressed and cold. "Am I so beautiful, or so admired or beloved, that a man who has not seen me half a dozen times should fall in love with me? Do those who know me estimate me so much, or prize me so highly, that a stranger should think of me? You *do* insult me, Edward Arundel, when you talk as you have talked to-night."

She looked out toward the low yellow light in the sky with a black gloom upon her face, which no reflected glimmer of the sinking sun could illumine; a settled darkness, near akin to the utter blackness of despair.

"But, good Heavens, Olivia, what do you mean?" cried the young man. "I tell you something that I think a good joke, and you go and make a tragedy out of it. If I'd told Letitia that a rich widower had fallen in love with her, she'd think it the finest fun in the world."

"I'm not your sister Letitia."

"No; but I wish you'd half as good a temper as she has, Livy. However, never mind; I'll say no more. If poor old Marchmont has fallen in love with you, that's his look-out. Poor dear old boy, he's let out the secret of his weakness half a dozen ways within these last few days. It's Miss Arundel this, and Miss Arundel the other; so handsome, so dignified, so ladylike, so good! That's the way he goes on, poor simple old dear, without having the remotest notion that he's making a confounded fool of himself."

Olivia tossed the rumpled hair from her forehead with an impatient gesture of her hand.

"Why should this Mr. Marchmont think all

this of me?" she said, "when—" She stopped abruptly.

"When—what, Livy?"

"When other people don't think it."

"How do you know what other people think? You haven't asked them, I suppose?"

The young soldier treated his cousin in very much the same free-and-easy manner which he displayed toward his sister Letitia. It would have been almost difficult for him to recognize any degree in his relationship to the two girls. He loved Letitia better than Olivia; but his affection for both was of exactly the same character.

Hubert Arundel came into the garden, wearied out, like his daughter, while the two cousins were walking under the shadow of the neglected hazels. He declared his willingness to accept the invitation to Marchmont Towers, and promised to answer John's ceremonious note the next day.

"Cookson, from Kemberling, will be there, I suppose," he said, alluding to a brother parson, "and the usual set? Well, I'll come, Ned, if you wish it. You'd like to go, Olivia?"

"If you like, papa."

There was a duty to be performed now—the duty of placid obedience to her father; and Miss Arundel's manner changed from angry impatience to a grave respect. She owed no special duty, be it remembered, to her cousin. She had no line or rule by which to measure her conduct to him.

She stood at the gate nearly an hour later, and watched the young man ride away in the dim moonlight. If every separate tramp of his horse's hoofs had struck upon her heart, it could scarcely have given her more pain than she felt as the sound of those slow footfalls died away in the distance.

"Oh my God!" she cried, "is this madness to undo all·that I have done? Is this folly to be the climax of my dismal life? Am I to die for the love of a frivolous, fair-haired boy, who laughs in my face when he tells me that his friend has pleased to 'take a fancy to me?'"

She walked away toward the house; then stopping, with a sudden shiver, she turned, and went back to the hazel-alley she had paced with Edward Arundel.

"Oh, my narrow life!" she muttered between her set teeth; "my narrow life! It is that which has made me the slave of this madness. I love him because he is the brightest and fairest thing I have ever seen. I love him because he brings me all I have ever known of a more beautiful world than that I live in. Bah! why do I reason with myself?" she cried, with a sudden change of manner. "I love him because I am mad."

She paced up and down the hazel-shaded pathway till the moonlight grew broad and full, and every ivy-grown gable of the Rectory stood sharply out against the vivid purple of the sky. She paced up and down, trying to trample the folly within her under her feet as she went; a fierce, passionate, impulsive woman, fighting against her mad love for a bright-faced boy.

"Two years older—only two years!" she said; "but he spoke of the difference between us as if it had been half a century. And then I am so clever, that I seem older than I am; and he is afraid of me! Is it for this that I have sat night after night in my father's study, poring over the books that were too difficult for him? What have I made of myself in my pride of intellect? What reward have I won for my patience?"

Olivia Arundel looked back at her long life of duty—a dull, dead level, unbroken by one of those monuments which mark the desert of the past; a desolate flat, unlovely as the marshes between the low Rectory wall and the shimmering gray sea.

---

## CHAPTER VIII.

### TEMPTATION.

MR. RICHARD PAULETTE, of that eminent legal firm, Paulette, Paulette, and Mathewson, coming to Marchmont Towers on business, was surprised to behold the quiet ease with which the sometime copying-clerk received the punctilious country gentry who came to sit at his board and do him honor.

Of all the legal fairy-tales, of all the parchment-recorded romances, of all the poetry run into affidavits, in which the solicitor had ever been concerned, this story seemed the strangest. Not so very strange in itself, for such romances are not uncommon in the history of a lawyer's experience; but strange by reason of the tranquil manner in which John Marchmont accepted his new position, and did the honors of his house to his late employer.

"Ah, Paulette," Edward Arundel said, clapping the solicitor on the back, "I don't suppose you believed me when I told you that my friend here was heir-presumptive to a handsome fortune."

The dinner-party at the Towers was conducted with that stately grandeur peculiar to such solemnities. There was the usual round of country-talk and parish-talk; the hunting squires leading the former section of the discourse, the rectors and rectors' wives supporting the latter part of the conversation. You heard on one side that Martha Harris's husband had left off drinking, and attended church morning and evening; and on the other, that the old gray fox that had been hunted nine seasons between Crackbin Bottom and Hollowcraft Gorse had perished ignobly in the poultry-yard of a recusant farmer. While your left ear became conscious of the fact that little Billy Smithers had fallen into a copper of scalding water, your right received the dismal tidings that all the young partridges had been drowned by the rains after St. Swithin, and that there were hardly any of this year's birds, Sir.

Mary Marchmont had listened to gayer talk in Oakley Street than any that was to be heard that night in her father's drawing-rooms, except indeed when Edward Arundel left off flirting with some pretty girls in blue, and hovered near her side for a little while, quizzing the company. Heaven knows the young soldier's jokes were commonplace enough; but Mary admired him as the most brilliant and accomplished of wits.

"How do you like my cousin, Polly?" he asked at last.

"Your cousin, Miss Arundel?"

"Yes."

"She is very handsome."

"Yes, I suppose so," the young man answered, carelessly. "Every body says that Livy's handsome; but it's rather a cold style of beauty, isn't it? A little too much of the Pallas Athenë about it for my taste. I like those girls in blue, with the crinkly auburn hair—there's a touch of red in it in the light—and the dimples. You've a dimple, Polly, when you smile."

Miss Marchmont blushed as she received this information, and her soft brown eyes wandered away, looking very earnestly at the pretty girls in blue. She looked at them with a strange interest, eager to discover what it was that Edward admired.

"But you haven't answered my question, Polly," said Mr. Arundel. "I am afraid you have been drinking too much wine, Miss Marchmont, and muddling that sober little head of yours with the fumes of your papa's tawny port. I asked you how you liked Olivia."

Mary blushed again.

"I don't know Miss Arundel well enough to like her—yet," she answered, timidly.

"But shall you like her when you've known her longer? Don't be jesuitical, Polly. Likings and dislikings are instantaneous and instinctive. I liked you before I'd eaten half a dozen mouthfuls of the roll you buttered for me at that breakfast in Oakley Street, Polly. You don't like my cousin Olivia, miss; I can see that very plainly. You're jealous of her."

"Jealous of her!"

The bright color faded out of Mary Marchmont's face and left it ashy pale.

"Do you like her, then?" she asked.

But Mr. Arundel was not such a coxcomb as to catch at the secret so naïvely betrayed in that breathless question.

"No, Polly," he said, laughing; "she's my cousin, you know, and I've known her all my life; and cousins are like sisters. One likes to tease and aggravate them, and all that; but one doesn't fall in love with them. But I think I could mention somebody who thinks a great deal of Olivia."

"Who?"

"Your papa."

Mary looked at the young soldier in utter bewilderment.

"Papa!" she echoed.

"Yes, Polly. How would you like a stepmamma? How would you like your papa to marry again?"

Mary Marchmont started to her feet as if she would have gone to her father in the midst of all those spectators. John was standing near Olivia and her father, talking to them, and playing nervously with his slender watch-chain when he addressed the young lady.

"My papa—marry again!" gasped Mary. "How dare you say such a thing, Mr. Arundel?"

Her childish devotion to her father arose in all its force; a flood of passionate emotion that overwhelmed her sensitive nature. Marry again! marry a woman who would separate him from his only child! Could he ever dream for one brief moment of such a horrible cruelty?

She looked at Olivia's sternly handsome face and trembled. She could almost picture that very woman standing between her and her father, and putting her away from him. Her indignation quickly melted into grief. Indignation, however intense, was always short-lived in that gentle nature.

"Oh, Mr. Arundel!" she said, piteously, appealing to the young man; "papa would never, never, never marry again—would he?"

"Not if it was to grieve you, Polly, I dare say," Edward answered, soothingly.

He had been dumbfounded by Mary's passionate sorrow. He had expected that she would have been rather pleased than otherwise at the idea of a young step-mother—a companion in those vast lonely rooms, an instructress and a friend as she grew to womanhood.

"I was only talking nonsense, Polly darling," he said. "You mustn't make yourself unhappy about any absurd fancies of mine. I think your papa admires my cousin Olivia; and I thought, perhaps, you'd be glad to have a step-mother."

"Glad to have any one who'd take papa's love away from me?" Mary said, plaintively. "Oh, Mr. Arundel, how could you think so?"

In all their familiarity the little girl had never learned to call her father's friend by his Christian name, though he had often told her to do so. She trembled to pronounce that simple Saxon name, which was so beautiful and wonderful because it was his; but when she read a very stupid novel, in which the hero was a namesake of Mr. Arundel's, the vapid pages seemed to be phosphorescent with light wherever the name appeared upon them.

I scarcely know why John Marchmont lingered by Miss Arundel's chair. He had heard her praises from every one. She was a paragon of goodness, an uncanonized saint, ever sacrificing herself for the benefit of others. Perhaps he was thinking that such a woman as this would be the best friend he could win for his little girl. He turned from the county matrons, the tender, kindly, motherly creatures, who would have been ready to take little Mary to the loving shelter of their arms, and looked to Olivia Arundel—this cold, perfect benefactress of the poor—for help in his difficulty.

"She who is so good to all her father's parishioners could not refuse to be kind to my poor Mary?" he thought.

But how was he to win this woman's friendship for his darling? He asked himself this question even in the midst of the frivolous people about him, and with the buzz of their conversation in his ears. He was perpetually tormenting himself about the future of his darling, which seemed more dimly perplexing now than it had ever appeared in Oakley Street, when the Lincolnshire property was a far-away dream, never to be realized. He felt that his brief lease of life was running out; he felt as if he and Mary had been standing upon a narrow tract of yellow sand, very bright, very pleasant under the sunshine, but with the slow-coming tide rising like a wall about them, and creeping stealthily onward to overwhelm them.

Mary might gather bright-colored shells and wet sea-weed in her childish ignorance; but he, who knew that the flood was coming, could but grow sick at heart with the dull horror of that hastening doom. If the black waters had been doomed to close over them both, the father might have been content to go down under the sullen waves, with his daughter clasped to his breast. But it was not to be so. He was to sink in that unknown stream, while she was left upon the tempest-tossed surface, to be beaten hither and thither, feebly battling with the stormy billows.

Could John Marchmont be a Christian, and yet feel this horrible dread of the death which must separate him from his daughter? I fear this frail, consumptive widower loved his child with an intensity of affection that is scarcely reconcilable with Christianity. Such great passions as these must be put away before the cross can be taken up and the troublesome path followed. In all love and kindness toward his fellow-creatures, in all patient endurance of the pains and troubles that befell himself, it would have been difficult to find a more single-hearted follower of Gospel teaching than John Marchmont; but in his affection for his motherless child he was a very pagan. He set up an idol for himself, and bowed himself before it. Doubtful and fearful of the future, he looked hopelessly forward. He could not trust his orphan child into the hands of God, and drop away himself into the fathomless-darkness, serene in the belief that she would be cared for and protected. No; he could not trust. He could be faithful for himself; simple and confiding as a child; but not for her. He saw the gloomy rocks lowering black in the distance; the pitiless waves beating far away yonder, impatient to devour the frail boat that was so soon to be left alone upon the waters. In the thick darkness of the future he could see no ray of light, except one—a new hope that had lately risen in his mind; the hope of winning some noble and perfect woman to be the future friend of his daughter.

The days were past in which, in his simplicity, he had looked to Edward Arundel as the future shelter of his child. The generous boy had grown into a stylish young man, a soldier, whose duty lay far away from Marchmont Towers. No; it was to a good woman's guardianship the father must leave his child.

Thus the very intensity of his love was the one motive which led John Marchmont to contemplate the step that Mary thought such a cruel and bitter wrong to her.

It was not till long after the dinner-party at Marchmont Towers that these ideas resolved themselves into any positive form, and that John began to think that for his daughter's sake he might be led to contemplate a second marriage. Edward Arundel had spoken the truth when he told his cousin that John Marchmont had repeatedly mentioned her name; but the careless and impulsive young man had been utterly unable to fathom the feeling lurking in his friend's mind. It was not Olivia Arundel's handsome face which had won John's admiration: it was the constant reiteration of her praises upon every side which had led him to believe that this woman, of all others, was the one whom he should win to be his child's friend and guardian in the dark days that were to come.

The knowledge that Olivia's intellect was of no common order, together with the somewhat imperious •dignity of her manner, strengthened this belief in John Marchmont's mind. It was not a good woman only whom he must seek in the friend he needed for his child; it was a woman powerful enough to shield her in the lonely path she would have to tread; a woman strong enough to help her, perhaps, by-and-by, to do battle with Paul Marchmont.

So, in the blind paganism of his love, John refused to trust his child into the hands of Providence, and chose for himself a friend and guardian who should shelter his darling. He made his choice with so much deliberation, and after such long nights and days of earnest thought, that he may be forgiven if he believed he had chosen wisely.

Thus it was that in the dark November days, while Edward and Mary played chess by the wide fire-place in the western drawing-room, or ball in the newly-erected tennis-court, John Marchmont sat in his study examining his papers, and calculating the amount of money at his own disposal, in serious contemplation of a second marriage.

Did he love Olivia Arundel? No. He admired her and respected her, and he firmly believed her to be the most perfect of women. No impulse had prompted the step he contemplated taking. He had loved his first wife truly and tenderly; but he had never suffered very acutely from any of those torturing emotions which form the several stages of the great tragedy called Love.

But had he ever thought of the likelihood of his deliberate offer being rejected by the young lady who had been the object of such careful consideration? Yes; he had thought of this, and was prepared to abide the issue. He should, at least, have tried his uttermost to secure a friend for his darling.

With such unloverlike feelings as these the owner of Marchmont Towers drove into Swampington one morning, deliberately bent upon offering Olivia Arundel his hand. He had consulted with his land-steward, and with Messrs. Paulette, and had ascertained how far he could endow his bride with the goods of this world. It was not much that he could give her, for the estate was strictly entailed; but there would be his own savings for the brief term of his life, and if he lived only a few years these savings might accumulate to a considerable amount, so limited were the expenses of the quiet Lincolnshire household; and there was a sum of money, something over nine thousand pounds, left him by Philip Marchmont, senior. He had something, then, to offer to the woman he sought to make his wife; and, above all, he had a supreme belief in Olivia Arundel's utter disinterestedness. He had seen her frequently since the dinner-party, and had always seen her the same —grave, reserved, dignified; patiently employed in the strict performance of her duty.

He found Miss Arundel sitting in her father's study, busily cutting out coarse garments for the poor. A newly-written sermon lay open on the table. Had Mr. Marchmont looked closely at the manuscript, he would have seen that the ink was wet and that the writing was Olivia's. It was a relief to this strange woman to write sermons sometimes—fierce denunciatory protests against the inherent wickedness of the human heart. Can you imagine a woman with a wicked heart steadfastly trying to do good, and to be good? It is a dark and horrible picture, but it is the only true picture of the woman whom John Marchmont sought to win for his wife.

The interview between Mary's father and Olivia Arundel was not a very sentimental one, but it was certainly the very reverse of commonplace. John was too simple-hearted to disguise the purpose of his wooing. He pleaded not for a wife for himself, but a mother for his orphan child. He talked of Mary's helplessness in the future, not of his own love in the present. Carried away by the egotism of his one affection, he let his motives appear in all their nakedness. He spoke long and earnestly; he spoke until the blinding tears in his eyes made the face of her he looked at seem blotted and dim.

Miss Arundel watched him as he pleaded; sternly, unflinchingly. But she uttered no word until he had finished; and then, rising suddenly, with a dusky flush upon her face, she began to pace up and down the narrow room. She had forgotten John Marchmont. In the strength and vigor of her intellect this weak-minded widower, whose one passion was a pitiful love for his child, appeared so utterly insignificant that for a few moments she had forgotten his presence in that room—his very existence, perhaps. She turned to him presently, and looked him full in the face.

"You do not love me, Mr. Marchmont?" she said.

"Pardon me," John stammered; "believe me, Miss Arundel, I respect, I esteem you so much, that—"

"That you choose me as a fitting friend for your child. I understand. I am not the sort of woman to be loved. I have long comprehended that. My cousin Edward Arundel has often taken the trouble to tell me as much. And you wish me to be your wife in order that you may have a guardian for your child? It is very much the same thing as engaging a governess; only the engagement is to be more binding."

"Miss Arundel," exclaimed John Marchmont, "forgive me! You misunderstand me; indeed you do. Had I thought that I could have offended you—"

"I am not offended. You have spoken the truth where another man would have told a lie. I ought to be flattered by your confidence in me. It pleases me that people should think me good, and worthy of their trust."

She broke into a weary sigh as she finished speaking.

"And you will not reject my appeal?"

"I scarcely know what to do," answered Olivia, pressing her hand to her forehead.

She leaned against the angle of the deep casement window, looking out at the bleak garden, desolate and neglected in the black winter weather. She was silent for some minutes. John Marchmont did not interrupt her; he was content to wait patiently until she should choose to speak.

"Mr. Marchmont," she said at last, turning upon poor John with an abrupt vehemence that almost startled him, "I am three-and-twenty; and in the long, dull memory of the three-and-twenty years that have made my life I can not look back upon one joy—no, so help me 'Heaven, not one!" she cried passionately, lifting her hand toward the low ceiling as she spoke. "No prisoner in the Bastile, shut in a cell below the level of the Seine, and making companions of rats and spiders in his misery, ever led a life

more hopelessly narrow, more pitifully circum-
scribed, than mine has been. These grass-grown
streets have made the boundary of my existence.
The flat fenny country round me is not flatter
or more dismal than my life. You will say that
I should take an interest in the duties which I
do; and that they should be enough for me.
Heaven knows I have tried to do so; but my life
is hard. Do you think there has been nothing
in all this to warp my nature? Do you think,
after hearing this, that I am the woman to be a
second mother to your child?"

She sat down as she finished speaking, and
her hands dropped listlessly in her lap. The
unquiet spirit raging in her breast had been
stronger than herself, and had spoken. She had
lifted the dull veil through which the outer world
beheld her, and had shown John Marchmont her
natural face.

"I think you are a good woman, Miss Arundel," he said, earnestly. "If I had thought
otherwise I should not have come here to-day.
I want a good woman to be kind to my child;
kind to her when I am dead and gone," he added, in a lower voice.

Olivia Arundel sat silent and motionless, looking straight before her out into the black dullness of the garden. She was trying to think out
the dark problem of her life.

Strange as it may seem, there was a certain
fascination for her in John Marchmont's offer.
He offered her something, no matter what; it
would be a change. She had compared herself
to a prisoner in the Bastile; and I think she
felt very much as a prisoner might have felt
upon his jailer's offering to remove him to Vin-
cennes. The new prison might be worse than
the old one, perhaps; but it would be different.
Life at Marchmont Towers might be more monotonous, more desolate that at Swampington;
but it would be a new monotony, another desolation. Have you never felt, when suffering the
hideous throes of toothache, that it would be a
relief to have the earache or the rheumatism—
that variety even in torture would be agreeable?

Then again, Olivia Arundel, though unblessed
with many of the charms of womanhood, was
not entirely without its weaknesses. To marry
John Marchmont would be to avenge herself
upon Edward Arundel. Alas! she forgot how
impossible it is to inflict a dagger-thrust upon
him who is guarded by the impenetrable armor
of indifference. She saw herself the mistress
of Marchmont Towers, waited upon by liveried
servants, courted, not patronized, by the country
gentry, avenged upon the mercenary aunt who
had slighted her, who had bade her go out and
get her living as a nursery-governess. She saw
this; and all that was ignoble in her nature
arose, and urged her to snatch the chance offered her—the one chance of lifting herself out of
the horrible obscurity of her life. The ambition
which might have made her an empress lowered
its crest, and cried, "Take this; at least it is
something." But through all the better voices
which she had enlisted to do battle with the
natural voice of her soul cried, "This is a temptation of the devil; put it away from thee!"

But this temptation came to her at the very
moment when her life had become most intolerable; too intolerable to be borne, she thought.
She knew now, fatally, certainly, that Edward

Arundel did not love her; that the one only
day-dream she had ever made for herself had
been a snare and a delusion. That one dream
had been the single light of her life. That tak-
en away from her, the darkness was blacker
than the blackness of death; more horrible than
the obscurity of the grave.

In all the future she had not one hope; no,
not one. She had loved Edward Arundel with
all the strength of her soul; she had wasted a
world of intellect and passion upon this bright-
haired boy. This foolish, groveling madness
had been the blight of her life. But for this she
might have grown out of her natural self by force
of her conscientious desire to do right, and might
have become, indeed, a good and perfect woman.
If her life had been a wider one, this wasted love
would perhaps have shrunk into its proper insignificance; she would have loved, and suffered,
and recovered, as so many of us recover from
this foolish epidemic. But all the volcanic forces
of an impetuous nature, concentrated into one
narrow focus, wasted themselves upon this one
feeling, until what should have been a sentiment
became a madness.

To think that in some far-away future time
she might cease to love Edward Arundel, and
learn to love somebody else, would have seemed
about as reasonable to Olivia as to hope that she
could have new legs and arms in that distant
time. She could cut away this fatal passion with
a desperate stroke, it may be, just as she could
cut off her arm; but to believe that a new love
would grow in its place was quite as absurd as
to believe in the growing of a new arm. Some
cork monstrosity might replace the amputated
limb; some sham and simulated affection might
succeed the old love.

Olivia Arundel thought of all these things, in
about ten minutes by the little skeleton clock
upon the mantle-piece, and while John Marchmont waited very patiently for some definite answer to his appeal. Her mind came back at
last, after all its passionate wanderings, to the
rigid channel she had so laboriously worn for it
—the narrow groove of duty. Her first words
testified this.

"If I accept this responsibility I will perform
it faithfully," she said, rather to herself than to
Mr. Marchmont.

"I am sure you will, Miss Arundel," John
answered, eagerly; "I am sure you will. You
mean to undertake it, then? you mean to consider my offer? May I speak to your father?
may I tell him that I have spoken to you? may
I say that you have given me a hope of your
ultimate consent?"

"Yes, yes," Olivia said, rather impatiently;
"speak to my father; tell him any thing you
please. Let him decide for me; it is my duty
to obey him."

There was a terrible cowardice in this. Olivia
Arundel shrank from marrying a man she did
not love, prompted by no better desire than the
mad wish to wrench herself away from her hateful life. She wanted to fling the burden of responsibility in this matter away from her. Let another urge her to do this wrong and let another
er decide; let another urge her to do this wrong
and let the wrong be called a sacrifice.

So for the first time she set to work deliberately to cheat her own conscience. For the first
time she put a false mark upon the standard sh

had made for the measurement of her moral progress.

She sank into a crouching attitude on a low stool by the fire-place, in utter prostration of body and mind, when John Marchmont had left her. She let her weary head fall heavily against the carved oaken shaft that supported the old-fashioned mantle-piece, heedless that her brow struck sharply against the corner of the wood-work.

If she could have died then, with no more sinful secret than a woman's natural weakness hidden in her breast—if she could have died then, while yet the first step upon the dark pathway of her life was untrodden—how happy for herself! how happy for others! How miserable a record of sin and suffering might have remained unwritten in the history of woman's life!

She sat long in the same attitude. Once, and once only, two solitary tears arose in her eyes, and rolled slowly down her pale cheeks.

"Will you be sorry when I am married, Edward Arundel?" she murmured; "will you be sorry?"

---

## CHAPTER IX.

"WHEN SHALL I CEASE TO BE ALL ALONE?"

HUBERT ARUNDEL was not so much surprised as might have been anticipated at the proposal made him by his wealthy neighbor. Edward Arundel had prepared his uncle for the possibility of such a proposal by sundry jocose allusions and arch hints upon the subject of John Marchmont's admiration for Olivia. The frank and rather frivolous young man thought it was his cousin's handsome face that had captivated the master of Marchmont Towers, and was quite unable to fathom the hidden motive underlying all John's talk about Miss Arundel.

The Rector of Swampington, being a simple-hearted and not very far-seeing man, thanked God heartily for the chance that had befallen his daughter. She would be well off and well cared for, then, by the mercy of Providence, in spite of his own shortcomings, which had left her with no better provision for the future than a pitiful policy upon her father's life. She would be well provided for henceforward, and would live in a handsome house; and all those noble qualities which had been dwarfed and crippled in a narrow sphere would now expand, and display themselves in unlooked-for grandeur.

"People have called her a good girl," he thought; "but how could they ever know her goodness, unless they had seen, as I have, the horrible deprivations she has borne so uncomplainingly?"

John Marchmont, being newly instructed by his lawyer, was able to give Mr. Arundel a very clear statement of the provision he could make for his wife's future. He could settle upon her the nine thousand pounds left him by Philip Marchmont. He would allow her five hundred a year pin-money during his lifetime; he would leave her his savings at his death; and he would effect an insurance upon his life for her benefit. The amount of these savings would, of course, depend upon the length of John's life; but the money would accumulate very quickly, as his income was eleven thousand a year, and his expenditure was not likely to exceed three.

The Swampington living was worth little more than three hundred and fifty pounds a year; and out of that sum Hubert Arundel and his daughter had done treble as much good for the numerous poor of the parish as ever had been achieved by any previous rector or his family. Hubert and his daughter had patiently endured the most griuding poverty, the burden ever falling heavier on Olivia, who had the heroic faculty of endurance as regards all physical discomfort. Can it be wondered, then, that the Rector of Swampington thought the prospect offered to his child a very brilliant one? Can it be wondered that he urged his daughter to accept this altered lot?

He did urge her, pleading John Marchmont's cause a great deal more warmly than the widower had himself pleaded.

"My darling," he said, "my darling girl! if I can live to see you mistress of Marchmont Towers, I shall go to my grave contented and happy. Think, my dear, of the misery this marriage will save you from. Oh, my dear girl, I can tell you now what I never dared tell you before; I can tell you of the long, sleepless nights I have passed thinking of you, and of the wicked wrongs I have done you. Not willful wrongs, my love," the Rector added, with tears gathering in his eyes; "for you know how dearly I have always loved you. But a father's responsibility toward his children is a very heavy burden. I've only looked at it in this light lately, my dear—now that I've let the time slip by, and it is too late to redeem the past. I've suffered very much, Olivia; and all this has seemed to separate us, somehow. But that's past now, isn't it, my dear? and you'll marry this Mr. Marchmont. He seems to be a very good, conscientious man, and I think he'll make you happy."

The father and daughter were sitting together after dinner in the dusky November twilight, the room only lighted by the fire, which was low and dim. Hubert Arundel could not see his daughter's face as he talked to her; he could only see the black outline of her figure sharply defined against the gray window behind her, as she sat opposite to him. He could see by her attitude that she was listening to him, with her head drooping and her hands lying idle in her lap.

She was silent for some little time after he had finished speaking; so silent that he feared his words might have touched her too painfully, and that she was crying.

Heaven help this simple-hearted father! She had scarcely heard three consecutive words that he had spoken, but had only gathered dimly from his speech that he wanted her to accept John Marchmont's offer.

Every great passion is a supreme egotism. It is not the object which we hug so determinedly; it is not the object which coils itself about our weak hearts: it is our own madness we worship and cleave to, our own pitiable folly which we refuse to put away from us. What is Bill Sykes's broken nose or bull-dog visage to Nancy? The creature she loves and will not part with is not Bill, but her own love for Bill—the one delusion of a barren life; the one grand selfishness of a feeble nature.

C

Olivia Arundel's thoughts had wandered far away while her father had spoken so piteously to her. She had been thinking of her cousin Edward, and had been asking herself the same question over and over again. Would he be sorry? would he be sorry if she married John Marchmont?

But she understood presently that her father was waiting for her to speak; and, rising from her chair, she went toward him, and laid her hand upon his shoulder.

"I am afraid I have not done my duty to you, papa," she said.

Latterly she had been forever harping upon this one theme—her duty! That word was the key-note of her life; and her existence had latterly seemed to her so inharmonious that it was scarcely strange she should repeatedly strike that leading note in the scale.

"My darling," cried Mr. Arundel, "you have been all that is good."

"No, no, papa; I have been cold, reserved, silent."

"A little silent, my dear," the Rector answered, meekly; "but you have not been happy. I have watched you, my love, and I know you have not been happy. But that is not strange. This place is so dull, and your life has been so fatiguing. How different that would all be at Marchmont Towers!"

"You wish me to marry Mr. Marchmont, then, papa?"

"I do indeed, my love. For your own sake, of course," the Rector added, deprecatingly.

"You really wish it?"

"Very, very much, my dear."

"Then I will marry him, papa."

She took her hand from the Rector's shoulder, and walked away from him to the uncurtained window, against which she stood with her back to her father, looking out into the gray obscurity.

I have said that Hubert Arundel was not a very clever or far-seeing person; but he vaguely felt that this was not exactly the way in which a brilliant offer of marriage should be accepted by a young lady who was entirely fancy-free, and he had an uncomfortable apprehension that there was something hidden under his daughter's quiet manner.

"But, my dear Olivia," he said, nervously, "you must not for a moment suppose that I would force you into this marriage if it is in any way repugnant to yourself. You—you may have formed some prior attachment, or there may be somebody who loves you, and has loved you longer than Mr. Marchmont, who—"

His daughter turned upon him sharply as he rambled on.

"Somebody who loves me!" she echoed. "What have you ever seen that should make you think any one loved me?"

The harshness of her tone jarred upon Mr. Arundel, and made him still more nervous.

"My love, I beg your pardon. I have seen nothing. I—"

"Nobody loves me, or has ever loved me—but you," resumed Olivia, taking no heed of her father's feeble interruption. "I am not the sort of woman to be loved; I feel and know that. I have an aquiline nose, and a clear skin, and dark eyes, and people call me handsome;

but nobody loves me, or ever will, so long as I live."

"But Mr. Marchmont, my dear—surely he loves and admires you?" remonstrated the Rector.

"Mr. Marchmont wants a governess and *chaperon* for his daughter, and thinks me a suitable person to fill such a post; that is all the *love* Mr. Marchmont has for me. No, papa; there is no reason I should shrink from this marriage. There is no one who will be sorry for it; no one. I am asked to perform a duty toward this little girl, and I am prepared to perform it faithfully. That is my part of the bargain. Do I commit a sin in marrying John Marchmont in this spirit, papa?"

She asked the question eagerly, almost breathlessly, as if her decision depended upon her father's answer.

"A sin, my dear! How can you ask such a question?"

"Very well, then; if I commit no sin in accepting this offer I will accept it."

It was thus Olivia paltered with her conscience, holding back half the truth. The question she should have asked was this: "Do I commit a sin in marrying one man while my heart is filled with a mad and foolish love for another?"

Miss Arundel could not visit her poor upon the day after this interview with her father. Her monotonous round of duty seemed more than ever abhorrent to her. She wandered across the dreary marshes, down by the lonely sea-shore, in the gray November fog.

She stood for a long time, shivering with the cold dampness of the atmosphere, but not even conscious that she was cold, looking at a dilapidated boat that lay upon the rugged beach. The waters before her and the land behind her were hidden by a dense veil of mist. It seemed as if she stood alone in the world—utterly isolated, utterly forgotten.

"O my God!" she murmured; "if this boat at my feet could drift me away to some desert island, I could never be more desolate than I am among the people who do not love me."

Dim lights in distant windows were gleaming across the flats when she returned to Swampington, to find her father sitting alone and dispirited at his frugal dinner. Miss Arundel took her place quietly at the bottom of the table, with no trace of emotion upon her face.

"I am sorry I staid out so long, papa," she said; "I had no idea it was so late."

"Never mind, my dear. I know you have always enough to occupy you. Mr. Marchmont called while you were out. He seemed very anxious to hear your decision, and was delighted when he found that it was favorable to himself."

Olivia dropped her knife and fork, and rose from her chair suddenly, with a strange look, which was almost terror, in her face.

"It is quite decided, then?" she said.

"Yes, my love. But you are not sorry, are you?"

"Sorry! No; I am glad."

She sank back into her chair with a sigh of relief. She *was* glad. The prospect of this strange marriage offered a relief from the horrible oppression of her life.

"Henceforward to think of Edward Arundel

will be a sin," she thought. "I have not won another man's love, but I shall be another man's wife."

## CHAPTER X.

### MARY'S STEP-MOTHER.

PERHAPS there was never a quieter courtship than that which followed Olivia's acceptance of John Marchmont's offer. There had been no pretense of sentiment on either side; yet I doubt if John had been much more sentimental during his early love-making days, though he had very tenderly and truly loved his first wife. There were few sparks of the romantic or emotional fire in his placid nature. His love for his daughter, though it absorbed his whole being, was a silent and undemonstrative affection; a thoughtful and almost fearful devotion, which took the form of intense but hidden anxiety for his child's future rather than any outward show of tenderness.

Had his love been of a more impulsive and demonstrative character, he would scarcely have thought of taking such a step as that he now contemplated, without first ascertaining whether it was agreeable to his daughter.

But he never for a moment dreamed of consulting Mary's will upon this important matter. He looked with fearful glances toward the dim future, and saw his darling, a lonely figure upon a barren landscape, beset with enemies eager to devour her; and he snatched at this one chance of securing her a protectress, who would be bound to her by a legal as well as a moral tie; for John Marchmont meant to appoint his second wife the guardian of his child. He thought only of this; and he hurried on his suit at the Rectory, fearful lest death should come between him and his loveless bride, and thus deprive his darling of a second mother.

This was the history of John Marchmont's second marriage. It was not till a week before the day appointed for the wedding that he told his daughter what he was about to do. Edward Arundel knew the secret, but he had been warned not to reveal it to Mary.

The father and daughter sat together late one evening in the first week of December, in the great western drawing-room. Edward had gone to a party at Swampington, and was to sleep at the Rectory; so Mary and her father were alone.

It was nearly eleven o'clock; but Miss Marchmont had insisted upon sitting up until her father should retire to rest. She had always sat up in Oakley Street, she had remonstrated, though she was much younger then. She sat on a velvet-covered hassock at her father's feet, with her fair hair falling over his knee, as her head lay there in loving abandonment. She was not talking to him; for neither John nor Mary were great talkers; but she was with him—that was quite enough.

Mr. Marchmont's thin fingers twined themselves listlessly in and out of the fair curls upon his knee. Mary was thinking of Edward and the party at Swampington. Would he enjoy himself very, very much? Would he be sorry that she was not there? It was a grown-up party, and she wasn't old enough for grown-up parties yet. Would the pretty girls in blue be there? and would he dance with them?

Her father's face was clouded by a troubled expression, as he looked absently at the red embers in the low fire-place. He spoke presently, but his observation was a very commonplace one. The opening speeches of a tragedy are seldom remarkable for any ominous or solemn meaning. Two gentlemen meet each other in a street very near the footlights, and converse rather flippantly about the aspect of affairs in general; there is no hint of bloodshed and agony till we get deeper into the play.

So Mr. Marchmont, bent upon making rather an important communication to his daughter, and for the first time feeling very fearful as to how she would take it, began thus:

"You really ought to go to bed earlier, Polly dear; you are looking very pale lately, and I know such hours as these must be bad for you."

"Oh no, papa dear," cried the young lady; "I'm always pale; that's natural to me. Sitting up late doesn't hurt me, papa. It never did in Oakley Street, you know."

John Marchmont shook his head sadly.

"I don't know that," he said. "My darling had to suffer many evils through her father's poverty. If you had some one who loved you, dear, a lady, you know—for a man does not understand these sort of things—your health would be looked after more carefully, and—and—your education—and—in short, you would be altogether happier; wouldn't you, Polly darling?"

He asked the question in an almost piteously appealing tone. A terrible fear was beginning to take possession of him. His daughter might be grieved at this second marriage. The very step which he had taken for her happiness might cause her loving nature pain and sorrow. In the utter cowardice of his affection he trembled at the thought of causing his darling any distress in the present, even for her future welfare, even for her future good; and he knew that the step he was about to take would secure that. Mary started from her reclining position, and looked up into her father's face.

"You're not going to engage a governess for me, papa?" she cried, eagerly. "Oh, please don't. We are so much better as it is. A governess would keep me away from you, papa; I know she would. The Miss Landells, at Impley Grange, have a governess: and they only come down to dessert for half an hour, or go out for a drive sometimes, so that they very seldom see their papa. Lucy told me so; and they said they'd give the world to be always with their papa, as I am with you. Oh pray, pray, papa darling, don't let me have a governess."

The tears were in her eyes as she pleaded to him. The sight of those tears made him terribly nervous.

"My own dear Polly," he said, "I'm not going to engage a governess. I—Polly, Polly dear, you must be reasonable. You mustn't grieve your poor father. You are old enough to understand these things now, dear. You know what the doctors have said. I may die, Polly, and leave you alone in the world."

She clung closely to her father, and looked up, pale and trembling, as she answered him.

"When you die, papa, I shall die too. I could never, never live without you."

"Yes, yes, my darling, you would. You will live to lead a happy life, please God, and a safe one: but if I die, and leave you very young, very inexperienced, and innocent, as I may do, my dear, you must not be without a friend to watch over you, to advise, to protect you. I have thought of this long and earnestly, Polly; and I believe that what I am going to do is right."

"What you are going to do!" Mary cried, repeating her father's words, and looking at him in sudden terror. "What do you mean, papa? What are you going to do? Nothing that will part us! Oh papa, papa, you will never do any thing to part us?"

"No, Polly darling," answered Mr. Marchmont. "Whatever I do I do for your sake, and for that alone. I'm going to be married, my dear."

Mary burst into a low wail, more pitiful than any ordinary weeping.

"Oh papa, papa," she cried, "you never will, you never will!"

The sound of that piteous voice for a few moments quite unmanned John Marchmont; but he armed himself with a desperate courage. He determined not to be influenced by this child, to relinquish the purpose which he believed was to achieve her future welfare.

"Mary, Mary dear," he said, reproachfully, "this is very cruel of you. Do you think I haven't consulted your happiness before my own? Do you think I shall love you less because I take this step for your sake? You are very cruel to me, Mary."

The little girl rose from her kneeling attitude, and stood before her father, with the tears streaming down her white cheeks, but with a certain air of resolution about her. She had been a child for a few moments; a child, with no power to look beyond the sudden pang of that new sorrow which had come to her. She was a woman now, able to rise superior to her sorrow in the strength of her womanhood.

"I won't be cruel, papa," she said; "I was selfish and wicked to talk like that. If it will make you happy to have another wife, papa, I'll not be sorry. No, I won't be sorry, even if your new wife separates us—a little."

"But, my darling," John remonstrated, "I don't mean that she should separate us at all. I wish you to have a second friend, Polly; some one who can understand you better than I do, who may love you perhaps almost as well."

Mary Marchmont shook her head; she could not realize this possibility. "Do you understand me, my dear?" her father continued, earnestly. "I want you to have some one who will be a mother to you; and I hope—I am sure that Olivia—"

Mary interrupted him by a sudden exclamation, that was almost like a cry of pain.

"Not Miss Arundel!" she said. "Oh papa, it is not Miss Arundel you are going to marry!"

Her father bent his head in assent.

"What is the matter with you, Mary?" he said, almost fretfully, as he saw the look of mingled grief and terror in his daughter's face. "You are really quite unreasonable to-night. If I am to marry at all, who should I choose for

a wife? Who could be better than Olivia Arundel? Every body knows how good she is. Every body talks of her goodness."

In these two sentences Mr. Marchmont made confession of a fact he had never himself considered. It was not his own impulse, it was no instinctive belief in her goodness, that had led him to choose Olivia Arundel for his wife. He had been influenced solely by the reiterated opinions of other people.

"I know she is very good, papa," Mary cried; "but oh, why, why do you marry her? Do you love her so very, very much?"

"Love her!" exclaimed Mr. Marchmont, naïvely; "no, Polly dear; you know I never loved any one but you."

"Why do you marry her, then?"

"For your sake, Polly; for your sake."

"But don't, then, papa; oh pray, pray don't. I don't want her. I don't like her. I could never be happy with her."

"Mary! Mary!"

"Yes, I know it's very wicked to say so, but it's true, papa; I never, never, never could be happy with her. I know she is good, but I don't like her. If I did any thing wrong, I should never expect her to forgive me for it; I should never expect her to have mercy upon me. Don't marry her, papa; pray, pray don't marry her."

"Mary," said Mr. Marchmont, resolutely, "this is very wrong of you. I have given my word, my dear, and I can not recall it. I believe that I am acting for the best. You must not be childish now, Mary. You have been my comfort ever since you were a baby; you mustn't make me unhappy now."

Her father's appeal went straight to her heart. Yes, she had been his help and comfort since her earliest infancy, and she was not unused to self-sacrifice; why should she fail him now? She had read of martyrs, patient and holy creatures, to whom suffering was glory; she would be a martyr, if need were, for his sake. She would stand steadfast amidst the blazing fagots, or walk unflinchingly across the white-hot plowshare; for his sake, for his sake.

"Papa, papa," she cried, flinging herself upon her father's neck, "I will not make you sorry. I will be good and obedient to Miss Arundel, if you wish it."

Mr. Marchmont carried his little girl up to her comfortable bedchamber close at hand to his own. She was very calm when she bade him good-night, and she kissed him with a smile upon her face; but all through the long hours before the late winter morning Mary Marchmont lay awake, weeping silently and incessantly in her new sorrow; and all through the same weary hours the master of that noble Lincolnshire mansion slept a fitful and troubled slumber, rendered hideous by confused and horrible dreams, in which the black shadow that came between him and his child, and the cruel hand that thrust him forever from his darling, were Olivia Arundel's.

But the morning light brought relief to John Marchmont and his child. Mary arose with the determination to submit patiently to her father's choice, and to conceal from him all traces of her foolish and unreasoning sorrow. John awoke from troubled dreams to believe in the wisdom of the step he had taken, and to take comfort from the thought that in the far-away future his daughter would have reason to thank and bless him for the choice he had made.

So the few days before the marriage passed away—miserably short days, that flitted by with terrible speed; and the last day of all was made still more dismal by the departure of Edward Arundel, who left Marchmont Towers to go to Dangerfield Park, whence he was most likely to start once more for India.

Mary felt that her narrow world of love was indeed crumbling away from her. Edward was lost, and to-morrow her father would belong to another. Mr. Marchmont dined at the Rectory upon that last evening; for there were settlements to be signed and other matters to be arranged; and Mary was alone—quite alone—weeping over her lost happiness.

"This would never have happened," she thought, "if we hadn't come to Marchmont Towers. I wish papa had never had the fortune; we were so happy in Oakley Street—so very happy. I wouldn't mind a bit being poor again if I could be always with papa."

Mr. Marchmont had not been able to make himself quite comfortable in his mind, after that unpleasant interview with his daughter in which he had broken to her the news of his approaching marriage. Argue with himself as he might upon the advisability of the step he was about to take, he could not argue away the fact that he had grieved the child he loved so intensely. He could not blot away from his memory the pitiful aspect of her terror-stricken face as she had turned it toward him when he uttered the name of Olivia Arundel.

No; he had grieved and distressed her. The future might reconcile her to that grief, perhaps, as a by-gone sorrow which she had been allowed to suffer for her own ultimate advantage. But the future was a long way off; and in the mean time there was Mary's altered face, calm and resigned, but bearing upon it a settled look of sorrow, very close at hand; and John Marchmont could not be otherwise than unhappy in the knowledge of his darling's grief.

I do not believe that any man or woman is ever suffered to take any fatal step upon the roadway of life without receiving ample warning by the way. The stumbling-blocks are placed in the fatal path by a merciful hand; but we insist upon groping over them, and surmounting them in our blind obstinacy, to reach that shadowy something beyond, which we have in our ignorance appointed to be our goal. A thousand ominous whispers in his own breast warned John Marchmont that the step he considered so wise was not a wise one: and yet, in spite of all these subtle warnings, in spite of the ever-present reproach of his daughter's altered face, this man, who was too weak to trust blindly in his God, went on persistently upon his way, trusting, with a thousand times more fatal blindness, in his own wisdom.

He could not be content to confide his darling and her altered fortunes to the Providence which had watched over her in her poverty, and sheltered her from every harm. He could not trust his child to the mercy of God, but he cast her upon the love of Olivia Arundel.

A new life began for Mary Marchmont after the quiet wedding at Swampington Church. The bride and bridegroom went upon a brief honey-moon excursion far away among snow-clad Scottish mountains and frozen streams, upon whose bloomless margins poor John shivered dismally. I fear that Mr. Marchmont, having been, by the hard pressure of poverty, compelled to lead a Cockney life for the better half of his existence, had but slight relish for the grand and sublime in nature. I do not think he looked at the ruined walls which had once sheltered Macbeth and his strong-minded partner with all the enthusiasm which might have been expected of him. He had but one idea about Macbeth, and was rather glad to get out of the neighborhood associated with the war-like Thane; for his memories of the past presented King Duncan's murderer as a very stern and uncompromising gentleman, who was utterly intolerant of banners held awry, or turned with the blank and ignoble side toward the audience, and who objected vehemently to a violent fit of coughing on the part of any one of his guests during the blank Barmecide feast of pasteboard and Dutch metal with which he was wont to entertain them. No; John Marchmont had had quite enough of Macbeth, and rather wondered at the hot enthusiasm of other red-nosed tourists, apparently indifferent to the frosty weather.

I fear that the master of Marchmont Towers would have preferred Oakley Street, Lambeth, to Princes Street, Edinburgh; for the nipping and eager airs of the Modern Athens nearly blew him across the gulf between the new town and the old. A visit to the Calton Hill produced an attack of that chronic cough which had so severely tormented the weak-kneed supernumerary in the draughty corridors of Drury Lane. Melrose and Abbotsford fatigued this poor feeble tourist; he tried to be interested in the stereotyped round of associations beloved by other travelers, but he had a weary craving for rest, which was stronger than any hero-worship; and he discovered, before long, that he had done a very foolish thing in coming to Scotland in December and January, without having consulted his physician as to the propriety of such a step.

But above all personal inconvenience, above all personal suffering, there was one feeling ever present in his heart—a sick yearning for the little girl he had left behind him; a mournful longing to be back with his child. Already Mary's sad forebodings had been in some way realized; already his new wife had separated him, unintentionally of course, from his daughter. The aches and pains he endured in the bleak Scottish atmosphere reminded him only too forcibly of the warnings he had received from his physicians. He was seized with a panic almost when he remembered his own imprudence. What if he had needlessly curtailed the short span of his life! What if he were to die soon; before Olivia had learned to love her step-daughter; before Mary had grown affectionately familiar with her new guardian? Again and again he appealed to his wife, imploring her to be tender to the orphan child, if he should be snatched away suddenly.

"I know you will love her by-and-by, Olivia," he said; "as much as I do, perhaps; for you will discover how good she is, how patient and unselfish. But just at first, and before you know her very well, you will be kind to her, won't you, Olivia? She has been used to great indulgence; she has been spoiled, perhaps; but you'll remember all that, and be very kind to her."

"I will try and do my duty," Mrs. Marchmont answered. "I pray that I never may do less."

There was no tender yearning in Olivia Marchmont's heart toward the motherless girl. She herself felt that such a feeling was wanting, and comprehended that it should have been there. She would have loved her step-daughter in those early days if she could have done so; but *she could not*—she could not. All that was tender or womanly in her nature had been wasted upon her hopeless love for Edward Arundel. The utter wreck of that small freight of affection had left her nature warped and stunted, soured, disappointed, unwomanly.

How was she to love this child, this fair-haired, dove-eyed girl, before whom woman's life, with all its natural wealth of affection, stretched far away, a bright and fairy vista? How was she to love her—she, whose black future was uncheckered by one ray of light; who stood dissevered from the past, alone in the dismal, dreamless monotony of the present?

"No," she thought; "beggars and princes can never love each other. When this girl and I are equals—when she, like me, stands alone upon a barren rock, far out amidst the waste of waters, with not one memory to hold her to the past, with not one hope to lure her onward to the future, with nothing but the black sky above and the black waters around—*then* we may grow fond of each other."

But always more or less steadfast to the standard she had set up for herself, Olivia Marchmont intended to do her duty to her step-daughter. She had not failed in other duties, though no glimmer of love had brightened them, no natural affection had made them pleasant. Why should she fail in this?

If this belief in her own power should appear to be somewhat arrogant, let it be remembered that she had set herself hard tasks before now, and had performed them. Would the new furnace through which she was to pass be more terrible than the old fires? She had gone to God's altar with a man for whom she had no more love than she felt for the lowest or most insignificant of the miserable sinners in her father's flock. She had sworn to honor and obey him, meaning at least faithfully to perform that portion of her vow; and on the night before her loveless bridal she had groveled—white, writhing, mad, and desperate—upon the ground, and had plucked out of her lacerated heart her hopeless love for another man.

Yes; she had done this. Another woman might have spent that bridal eve in vain tears and lamentations, in feeble prayers, and such weak struggles as might have been evidenced by the destruction of a few letters, a tress of hair, some fragile foolish tokens of a wasted love. She would have burned five out of six letters, perhaps—that helpless, ordinary sinner—and would have kept the sixth, to hoard away hidden among her matrimonial trousseau; she would have thrown away fifteen-sixteenths of that tress of hair, and would have kept the sixteenth portion—one delicate curl of gold, slender as the thread by which her shattered hopes had hung

—to be wept over and kissed in the days that were to come. An ordinary woman would have played fast and loose with love and duty; and so would have been true to neither.

But Olivia Arundel did none of these things. She battled with her weakness as St. George battled with the fiery dragon. She plucked the rooted serpent from her heart, reckless as to how much of that desperate heart was to be wrenched away with its roots. A cowardly woman would have killed herself, perhaps, rather than endure this mortal agony. Olivia Arundel killed more than herself; she killed the passion that had become stronger than herself.

"Alone she did it;" unaided by any human sympathy, or compassion, unsupported by any human counsel, not upheld by her God; for the religion she had made for herself was a hard creed, and the many words of tender comfort which must have been familiar to her were unremembered in that long night of anguish.

It was the Roman's stern endurance, rather than the meek faithfulness of the Christian, which upheld this unhappy girl under her torture. She did not do this thing because it pleased her to be obedient to her God. She did not do it because she believed in the mercy of Him who inflicted the suffering, and looked forward hopefully, even amidst her passionate grief, to the day when she should better comprehend that which she now saw so darkly. No; she fought the terrible fight, and she came forth out of it a conqueror, by reason of her own indomitable power of suffering, by reason of her own extraordinary strength of will.

But she did conquer. If her weapon was the classic sword and not the Christian cross, she was nevertheless a conqueror. When she stood before the altar and gave her hand to John Marchmont, Edward Arundel was dead to her. The fatal habit of looking at him as the one centre of her narrow life was cured. In all her Scottish wanderings her thoughts never once went back to him; though a hundred chance words and associations tempted her, though a thousand memories assailed her, though some trick of his face in the faces of other people, though some tone of his voice in the voices of others perpetually offered to entrap her. No; she was steadfast.

Dutiful as a wife as she had been dutiful as a daughter, she bore with her husband when his feeble health made him a wearisome companion. She waited upon him when pain made him fretful, and her duties became little less arduous than those of a hospital-nurse. When, at the bidding of the Scotch physician who had been called in at Edinburgh, John Marchmont turned homeward, traveling slowly and resting often on the way, his wife was more devoted to him than his experienced servant, more watchful than the best trained sick-nurse. She recoiled from nothing, she neglected nothing; she gave him full measure of the honor and obedience which she had promised upon her wedding-day. And when she reached Marchmont Towers upon a dreary evening in January, she passed beneath the solemn portal of the western front, carrying in her heart the full determination to hold as steadfastly to the other half of her bargain, and to do her duty to her step-child.

Mary ran out of the western drawing-room to welcome her father and his wife. She had cast off her black dresses in honor of Mr. Marchmont's marriage, and she wore some soft, silken fabric, of a pale shimmering blue, which contrasted exquisitely with her soft flaxen hair and her fair tender face. She uttered a cry of mingled alarm and sorrow when she saw her father, and perceived the change that had been made in his looks by the northern journey; but she checked herself at a warning glance from her step-mother, and bade that dear father welcome, clinging about him with an almost desperate fondness. She greeted Olivia gently and respectfully.

"I will try to be very good, mamma," she said, as she took the passive hand of the lady who had come to rule at Marchmont Towers.

"I believe you will, my dear," Olivia answered, kindly.

She had been startled a little as Mary addressed her by that endearing corruption of the holy word mother. The child had been so long motherless, that she felt little of that acute anguish which some orphans suffer when they have to look up in a strange face and say "mamma." She had taught herself the lesson of resignation, and she was prepared to accept this stranger as her new mother, and to look up to her and obey her henceforward. No thought of her future position as sole owner of Marchmont Towers ever crossed her mind, womanly as that mind had become in the sharp experiences of poverty. If her father had told her that he had cut off the entail, and settled Marchmont Towers upon his new wife, I think she would have submitted meekly to his will, and would have seen no injustice in the act. She loved him blindly and confidingly. Indeed, she could only love after one fashion. The organ of veneration must have been abnormally developed in Mary Marchmont's head. To believe that any one she loved was otherwise than perfect, would have been, in her creed, an infidelity against love. Had any one told her that Edward Arundel was not eminently qualified for the post of General-in-Chief of the Army of the Indus; or that her father could by any possible chance be guilty of a fault or folly, she would have recoiled in horror from the treasonous slanderer.

A dangerous quality, perhaps, this quality of guilelessness which thinketh no evil, which can not be induced to see the evil under its very nose. But surely, of all the beautiful and pure things upon this earth, such blind confidence is the purest and most beautiful. I knew a lady, dead and gone—alas for this world, which could ill afford to lose so good a Christian!—who carried this trustfulness of spirit, this utter incapacity to believe in wrong, through all the strife and turmoil of a troubled life, unsullied and unlessened, to her grave. She was cheated and imposed upon, robbed and lied to, by people who loved her, perhaps, while they wronged her—for to know her was to love her. She was robbed systematically by a confidential servant for years, and for years refused to believe those who told her of his delinquencies. She *could* not believe that people were wicked. To the

day of her death she had faith in the scoundrels and scamps who had profited by her sweet compassion and untiring benevolence; and indignantly defended them against those who dared to say that they were any thing more than unfortunate. To go to her was to go to a never-failing fountain of love and tenderness. To know her goodness was to understand the goodness of God; for her love approached the Infinite, and might have taught a skeptic the possibility of Divinity. Threescore years and ten of worldly experience left her an accomplished lady, a delightful companion, but in guilelessness a child.

So Mary Marchmont, trusting implicitly in those she loved, submitted to her father's will, and prepared to obey her step-mother. The new life at the Towers began very peacefully; a perfect harmony reigned in the quiet household. Olivia took the reins of management with so little parade that the old housekeeper who had long been paramount in the Lincolnshire mansion, found herself superseded before she knew where she was. It was Olivia's nature to govern. Her strength of will asserted itself almost unconsciously. She took possession of Mary Marchmont as she had taken possession of her school-children at Swampington, making her own laws for the government of their narrow intellects. She planned a routine of study that was actually terrible to the little girl, whose education had hitherto been conducted in a somewhat slipslop manner by a weakly-indulgent father. She came between Mary and her one amusement—the reading of novels. The half-bound romances were snatched ruthlessly from this young devourer of light literature, and sent back to the shabby circulating library at Swampington. Even the gloomy old oak book-cases in the library at the Towers, and the Abbotsford edition of the Waverley novels, were forbidden to poor Mary; for though Sir Walter Scott's morality is irreproachable, it will not do for a young lady to be weeping over Lucy Ashton or Amy Robsart when she should be consulting her terrestrial globe, and informing herself as to the latitude and longitude of the Fiji islands.

So a round of dry and dreary lessons began for poor Miss Marchmont, and her brain grew almost dazed under that continuous and pelting shower of hard facts which many worthy people consider the one sovereign method of education. I have said that her mind was far in advance of her years; Olivia perceived this, and set her tasks in advance of her mind, in order that the perfection attained by a sort of steeple-chase of instruction might not be lost to her. If Mary learned difficult lessons with surprising rapidity, Mrs. Marchmont plied her with even yet more difficult lessons, thus keeping the spur perpetually in the side of this heavily-weighted racer on the road to learning. But it must not be thought that Olivia willfully tormented or oppressed her step-daughter. It was not so. In all this, John Marchmont's second wife implicitly believed that she was doing her duty to the child committed to her care. She fully believed that this dreary routine of education was wise and right, and would be for Mary's ultimate advantage. If she caused Miss Marchmont to get up at abnormal hours on bleak wintry mornings, for the purpose of wrestling with a difficult variation by Hertz or Schubert, she herself rose also and sat shivering by the piano, counting the time of the music which her step-daughter played.

Whatever pains and trouble she inflicted on Mary she most unshrinkingly endured herself. She waded through the dismal slough of learning side by side with the younger sufferer: Roman emperors, medieval schisms, early British manufactures, Philippa of Hainault, Flemish woolen stuffs, Magna Charta, the sidereal heavens, Luther, Newton, Huss, Galileo, Calvin, Loyola, Sir Robert Walpole, Cardinal Wolsey, conchology, Arianism in the Early Church, trial by jury, Habeas Corpus, zoology, Mr. Pitt, the American war, Copernicus, Confucius, Mohammed, Harvey, Jenner, Lycurgus, and Catherine of Aragon; through a very diabolical dance of history, science, theology, philosophy, and instruction of all kinds, did this devoted priestess lead her hapless victim, struggling onward toward that distant altar at which Pallas Athené waited, pale and inscrutable, to receive a new disciple.

But Olivia Marchmont did not mean to be unmerciful; she meant to be good to her step-daughter. She did not love her; but, on the other hand, she did not dislike her. Her feelings were simply negative. Mary understood this, and the submissive obedience she rendered to her step-mother was untempered by affection. So, for nearly two years these two people led a monotonous life, unbroken by any more important event than a dinner-party at Marchmont Towers, or a brief visit to Harrowgate or Scarborough.

This monotonous existence was not to go on forever. The fatal day, so horribly feared by John Marchmont, was creeping closer and closer. The sorrow which had been shadowed in every childish dream, in every childish prayer, came at last; and Mary Marchmont was left an orphan.

Poor John had never quite recovered the effects of his winter excursion to Scotland; neither his wife's devoted nursing, nor his physician's care, could avail forever; and late in the autumn of the second year of his marriage he sank slowly and peacefully enough as regards physical suffering, but not without bitter grief of mind. In vain Hubert Arundel talked to him: in vain did he himself pray for faith and comfort in this dark hour of trial. He could not bear to leave his child alone in the world. In the foolishness of his love he would have trusted in the strength of his own arm to shield her in the battle; he could not trust her hopefully to the arm of God. He prayed for her night and day, during the last week of his illness; while she was praying passionately, almost madly, that he might be spared to her, or that she might die with him. Better for her, according to all mortal reasoning, if she had. Happier for her, a thousand times, if she could have died as she wished to die, clinging to her father's breast.

The blow fell at last upon those two loving hearts. These were the awful shadows of death that shut his child's face from John Marchmont's fading sight. His feeble arms groped here and there for her in that dim and awful obscurity.

Yes, this was death. The narrow tract of yellow sand had little by little grown narrower and narrower. The dark and cruel waters were closing in; the feeble boat went down into the darkness; and Mary stood alone, with her dead father's hand clasped in hers—the last feeble link which bound her to the Past—looking blankly forward to an unknown Future.

---

## CHAPTER XI.

### THE DAY OF DESOLATION.

Yes; the terrible day had come. Mary Marchmont roamed hither and thither in the big gaunt rooms, up and down the long dreary corridors, white and ghostlike in her mute anguish, while the undertaker's men were busy in her father's chamber, and while John's widow sat in the study below, writing business letters, and making all necessary arrangements for the funeral.

In those early days no one attempted to comfort the orphan. There was something more terrible than the loudest grief in the awful quiet of the girl's anguish. The wan eyes, looking wearily out of a white haggard face, that seemed drawn and contracted as if by some hideous physical torture, were tearless. Except the one long wail of despair which had burst from her lips in the awful moment of her father's death-agony, no cry of sorrow, no utterance of pain, had given relief to Mary Marchmont's suffering.

She suffered, and was still. She shrank away from all human companionship; she seemed specially to avoid the society of her step-mother. She locked the door of her room upon all who would have intruded on her, and flung herself upon the bed, to lie there in a dull stupor for hour after hour. But when the twilight was gray in the desolate corridors, the wretched girl wandered out into the gallery on which her father's room opened, and hovered near that solemn death-chamber—fearful to go in, fearful to encounter the watchers of the dead, lest they should torture her by their hackneyed expressions of sympathy, lest they should agonize her by their commonplace talk of the lost.

Once during that brief interval, while the coffin still held terrible tenancy of the death-chamber, the girl wandered in the dead of the night, when all but the hired watchers were asleep, to the broad landing of the oaken staircase, and into a deep recess formed by an embayed window that opened over the great stone porch which sheltered the principal western entrance to Marchmont Towers.

The window had been left open; for even in the bleak autumn weather the atmosphere of the great house seemed hot and oppressive to its living inmates, whose spirits were weighed down by a vague sense of something akin to terror of the Awful Presence in that Lincolnshire mansion. Mary had wandered to this open window, scarcely knowing whither she went, after remaining for a long time on her knees by the threshold of her father's room, with her head resting against the oaken panel of the door—not praying; why should she pray now, unless her prayers could have restored the dead? She had come out upon the wide staircase, and past the ghostly pictured faces that looked grimly down upon her from the oaken wainscot against which they hung; she had wandered here in the dim gray light: there was light somewhere in the sky, but only a shadowy and uncertain glimmer of fading starlight or coming dawn. And she stood now with her head resting against one of the angles of the massive stone-work, looking out of the open window.

The morning which was already glimmering dimly in the eastern sky behind Marchmont Towers was to witness poor John's funeral. For nearly six days Mary Marchmont had avoided all human companionship; for nearly six days she had shunned all human sympathy and comfort. During all that time she had never eaten, except when forced to do so by her step-mother, who had visited her from time to time, and had insisted upon sitting by her bedside while she took the food that had been brought to her. Heaven knows how often the girl had slept during those six dreary days; but her feverish slumbers had brought her very little rest or refreshment. They had brought her nothing but cruel dreams, in which her father was still alive; in which she felt his thin arms clasped round her neck, his faint and fitful breath warm upon her cheek.

A great clock in the stables struck five while Mary Marchmont stood looking out of the Tudor window. The broad gray flat before the house stretched far away, melting into the shadowy sky. The pale stars grew paler as Mary looked at them; the black water pools began to glimmer faintly under the widening patch of light in the eastern sky. The girl's senses were bewildered by her suffering—her head was light and dizzy.

Her father's death had made so sudden and terrible a break in her existence, that she could scarcely believe the world had not come to an end, with all the joys and sorrows of its inhabitants. Would there be any thing more after to-morrow? she thought; would the blank days and nights go monotonously on when the story that had given them a meaning and a purpose had come to its dismal end? Surely not; surely, after those gaunt iron gates, far away across the swampy waste that was called a park, had closed upon her father's funeral train, the world would come to an end, and there would be no more time or space. I think she really believed this in the semi-delirium into which she had fallen within the last hour. She believed that all would be over, and that she and her despair would melt away into the emptiness that was to engulf the universe after her father's funeral.

Then suddenly the full reality of her grief flashed upon her with horrible force. She clasped her hands upon her forehead, and a low faint cry broke from her white lips.

It was not all over. Time and space would not be annihilated. The weary, monotonous, workaday world would still go on upon its course. *Nothing* would be changed. The great gaunt stone mansion would still stand, and the dull machinery of its interior would still go on: the same hours; the same customs; the same inflexible routine. John Marchmont would be carried out of the house that had owned him master, to lie in the dismal vault under Kemberling Church; and the world in which he had made so little stir would go on without him. The easy-chair in which he had been wont to sit

would be wheeled away from its corner by the fireplace in the western drawing-room. The papers in his study would be sorted and put away, or taken possession of by strange hands. Cromwells and Napoleons die, and the earth reels for a moment, only to be "alive and bold" again in the next instant, to the astonishment of poets, and the calm satisfaction of philosophers; and ordinary people eat their breakfasts while the telegram lies beside them upon the table, and the ink in which Mr. Reuter's message is recorded is still wet from the machine in Printing-House Square.

Anguish and despair more terrible than any of the tortures she had felt yet took possession of Mary Marchmont's breast. For the first time she looked out at her own future. Until now she had thought only of her father's death. She had despaired because he was gone; but she had never contemplated the horror of her future life —a life in which she was to exist without him. A sudden agony, that was near akin to madness, seized upon this girl, in whose sensitive nature affection had always had a morbid intensity. She shuddered with a wild dread at the blank prospect of that horrible future; and as she looked out at the wide stone steps below the window from which she was leaning, for the first time in her young life the idea of self-destruction flashed across her mind.

She uttered a cry, a shrill, almost unearthly cry, that was, notwithstanding, low and feeble, and clambered suddenly upon the broad stone sill of the Tudor casement. She wanted to fling herself down and dash her brains out upon the stone steps below; but in the utter prostration of her state she was too feeble to do this, and she fell backward and dropped in a heap upon the polished oaken flooring of the recess, striking her forehead as she fell. She lay there unconscious until nearly seven o'clock, when one of the women-servants found her, and carried her off to her own room, where she suffered herself to be undressed and put to bed.

Mary Marchmont did not speak until the good-hearted Lincolnshire house-maid had laid her in her bed, and was going away to tell Olivia of the state in which she had found the orphan girl.

"Don't tell my step-mother any thing about me, Susan," she said; "I think I was mad last night."

This speech frightened the house-maid, and she went straight to the widow's room. Mrs. Marchmont, always an early riser, had been up and dressed for some time, and went at once to look at her step-daughter.

She found Mary very calm and reasonable. There was no trace of bewilderment or delirium now in her manner; and when the principal doctor of Swampington came, a couple of hours afterward, to look at the young heiress, he declared that there was no cause for any alarm. The young lady was sensitive, morbidly sensitive, he said, and must be kept very quiet for a few days, and watched by some one whose presence would not annoy her. If there was any girl of her own age whom she had ever shown a predilection for, that girl would be the fittest companion for her just now. After a few days it would be advisable that she should have change of air and change of scene. She must not be allowed to brood continuously on her father's death. The doctor repeated this last injunction more than once. It was most important that she should not give way too perpetually to her grief.

So Mary Marchmont lay in her darkened room while her father's funeral train was moving slowly away from the western entrance. It happened that Mary's apartments looked out into the quadrangle, and she heard none of the subdued sounds which attended the departure of that solemn procession. In her weakness she had grown submissive to the will of others. She thought this feebleness and exhaustion gave warning of her approaching death. Her prayers would be granted after all. This anguish and despair would be but of brief duration, and she would ere long be carried to the vault under Kemberling Church, to lie beside her father in the black stillness of that dreadful place.

Mrs. Marchmont strictly obeyed the doctor's injunctions. A girl of seventeen, the daughter of a small tenant farmer near the Towers, had been a special favorite with Mary, who was not apt to make friends among strangers. This girl, Hester Pollard, was sent for, and, came, willingly and gladly, to watch her young patroness. She brought her needle-work with her, and sat near the window, busily employed, while Mary lay shrouded by the pure white curtains of the bed. All active services necessary for the comfort of the invalid were performed by Olivia or her own special attendant—an old servant who had lived with the Rector ever since his daughter's birth, and had only left him to follow that daughter to Marchmont Towers after her marriage. So Hester Pollard had nothing to do but to keep very quiet, and patiently await the time when Mary might be disposed to talk to her. The farmer's daughter was a gentle, unobtrusive creature, very well fitted for the duty imposed upon her.

----

## CHAPTER XII.

### PAUL.

OLIVIA MARCHMONT sat in her late husband's study while John's funeral train was moving slowly along under the misty October sky. A long stream of carriages followed the stately hearse, with its four black horses, and its voluminous draperies of rich velvet, and nodding plumes that were damp and heavy with the autumn atmosphere. The unassuming master of Marchmont Towers had won for himself a quiet popularity among the simple country gentry, and the best families in Lincolnshire had sent their chiefs to do honor to his burial, or at the least their empty carriages to represent them at that mournful ceremonial. Olivia sat in her dead husband's favorite chamber. Her head lay back upon the cushion of the roomy morocco-covered arm-chair in which he had so often sat. She had been working hard that morning, and indeed every morning since John Marchmont's death, sorting and arranging papers, with the aid of Richard Paulette, the Lincoln's Inn solicitor, and James Gormby, the landsteward. She knew that she had been left sole guardian of her step-daughter, and executrix to her husband's will; and she had lost no time in

making herself acquainted with the business details of the estate, and the full nature of the responsibilities intrusted to her.

She was resting now. She had done all that could be done until after the reading of the will. She had attended to her step-daughter. She had stood in one of the windows of the western drawing-room, watching the departure of the funeral cortège; and now she abandoned herself for a brief space to that idleness which was so unusual to her.

A fire burned in the low grate at her feet, and a rough cur—half shepherd's dog, half Scotch deer-hound, who had been fond of John but was not fond of Olivia—lay at the further extremity of the hearth-rug, watching her suspiciously.

Mrs. Marchmont's personal appearance had not altered during the two years of her married life. Her face was thin and haggard, but it had been thin and haggard before her marriage. And yet no one could deny that the face was handsome, and the features beautifully chiseled. But the gray eyes were hard and cold, the line of the faultless eyebrows gave a stern expression to the countenance; the thin lips were rigid and compressed. The face wanted both light and color. A sculptor copying it line by line would have produced a beautiful head. A painter must have lent his own glowing tints if he wished to represent Olivia Marchmont as a lovely woman.

Her pale face looked paler, and her dead black hair blacker, against the blank whiteness of her widow's cap. Her mourning dress clung closely to her tall, slender figure. She was little more than twenty-five, but she looked a woman of thirty. It had been her misfortune to look older than she was from a very early period in her life.

She had not loved her husband when she married him, nor had she ever felt for him that love which in most womanly natures grows out of custom and duty. It was not in her nature to love. Her passionate idolatry of her boyish cousin had been the one solitary affection that had ever held a place in her cold heart. All the fire of her nature had been concentrated in this one folly, this one passion, against which only heroic self-tortures had been able to prevail.

Mrs. Marchmont felt no grief, therefore, at her husband's loss. She had felt the shock of his death, and the painful oppression of his dead presence in the house. She had faithfully nursed him through many illnesses; she had patiently tended him until the very last; she had done her duty. And now, for the first time, she had leisure to contemplate the past, and look forward to the future.

So far this woman had fulfilled the task which she had taken upon herself; she had been true and loyal to the vow she had made before God's altar, in the church of Swampington. And now she was free. No, not quite free; for she had a heavy burden yet upon her hands—the solemn charge of her step-daughter during the girl's minority. But as regarded marriage-vows and marriage-ties she was free.

She was free to love Edward Arundel again.

The thought came upon her with a rush and an impetus wild and strong as the sudden uprising of a whirlwind, or the loosing of a mountain-torrent that had long been bound. She was a wife no longer. It was no longer a sin to think of the bright-haired soldier, fighting far away. She was free. When Edward returned to England by-and-by he would find her free once more; a young widow—young, handsome, and rich enough to be no bad prize for a younger son. He would come back and find her thus; and then—and then—

She flung one of her clenched hands up into the air, and struck it on her forehead in a sudden paroxysm of rage. What then? Would he love her any better than he had loved her two years ago? No; he would treat her with the same cruel indifference, the same commonplace cousinly friendliness with which he had mocked and tortured her before. Oh, shame! Oh, misery! Was there no pride in women, that there could be one among them fallen so low as her; ready to grovel at the feet of a fair-haired boy, and to cry aloud, "Love me, love me! or be pitiful, and strike me dead!"

Better that John Marchmont had lived forever, better that Edward Arundel should die far away upon some Eastern battle-field, before some Afghan fortress, than that he should return to inflict upon her the same tortures she had writhed under two years before.

"God grant that he may never come back!" she thought. "God grant that he may marry out yonder, and live and die there. God keep him from me forever and forever in this weary world!"

And yet in the next moment, with the inconsistency which is the chief attribute of that madness we call love, her thoughts wandered away dreamily into visions of the future; and she pictured Edward Arundel back again at Swampington, at Marchmont Towers. Her soul burst its bonds and expanded, and drank in the sunlight of gladness, and she dared to think that it *might* be so—there *might* be happiness yet for her. He had been a boy when he went back to India—careless, indifferent. He would return a man—graver, wiser, altogether changed; changed so much as to love her, perhaps.

She knew that, at least, no rival had shut her cousin's heart against her, when she and he had been together two years before. He had been indifferent to her; but he had been indifferent to others also. There was comfort in that recollection. She had questioned him very sharply as to his life in India and at Dangerfield, and she had discovered no trace of any tender memory of the past, no hint of a cherished dream of the future. His heart had been empty: a boyish, unawakened heart; a temple in which the niches were, untenanted, the shrine unhallowed by the goddess.

Olivia Marchmont thought of these things. For a few moments, if only for a few moments, she abandoned herself to such thoughts as these. She let herself go. She released the stern hold which it was her habit to keep upon her own mind; and in those bright moments of delicious abandonment the glorious sunshine streamed in upon her narrow life, and visions of a possible future expanded before her like a fairy panorama, stretching away into realms of vague light and splendor. It was *possible;* it was at least possible.

But, again, in the next moment the magical panorama collapsed and shriveled away, like a burning scroll; the fairy picture, whose gorgeous coloring she had looked upon with dazzled eyes, almost blinded with overpowering glory, shrank into a handful of black ashes, and was gone. The woman's strong nature reasserted itself; the iron will rose up, ready to do battle with the foolish heart.

"I *will* not be fooled a second time," she cried. "Did I suffer so little when I blotted that image out of my heart? Did the destruction of my cruel Juggernaut cost me so small an agony that I must needs be ready to elevate the false god again, and crush out my heart once more under the brazen wheels? *He will never love me!*"

She writhed; this self-sustained and resolute woman writhed in her anguish as she uttered those five words, "He will never love me!" She knew that they were true, that of all the changes that Time could bring to pass, it would never bring such a change as that. There was not one element of sympathy between herself and the young soldier; they had not one thought in common. Nay, more; there was an absolute antagonism between them, which, in spite of her love, Olivia fully recognized. Over the gulf that separated them no coincidence of thought or fancy, no sympathetic emotion, ever stretched its electric chain to draw them together in mysterious union. They stood aloof, divided by the width of an intellectual universe. The woman knew this, and hated herself for her folly, scorning alike her love and its object; but her love was not the less because of her scorn. It was a madness, an isolated madness, which stood alone in her soul, and fought for mastery over her better aspirations, her wiser thoughts. We are all familiar with strange stories of wise and great minds which have been ridden by some hobgoblin fancy, some one horrible monomania.

Had Olivia Marchmont lived a couple of centuries before, she would have gone straight to the nearest old crone, and would have boldly accused the wretched woman of being the author of her misery.

"You harbor a black cat and other noisome vermin, and you prowl about muttering to yourself o' nights," she might have said. "You have been seen to gather herbs, and you make strange and uncanny signs with your palsied old fingers. The black cat is the devil, your colleague; and the rats under your tumble-down roof are his imps, your associates. It is *you* who have instilled this horrible madness into my soul; for it *could* not come of itself."

And Olivia Marchmont, being resolute and strong-minded, would not have rested until her tormentor had paid the penalty of her foul work at a stake in the nearest market-place.

And, indeed, some of our madnesses are so mad, some of our follies are so foolish, that we might almost be forgiven if we believed that there was a company of horrible crones meeting somewhere on an invisible Brocken, and making incantations for our destruction. Take up a newspaper and read its hideous revelations of crime and folly, and it will be scarcely strange if you involuntarily wonder whether witchcraft is a dark fable of the Middle Ages, or a dreadful truth of the nineteenth century. Must not

some of these miserable creatures whose stories
we read be *possessed;* possessed by eager, relentless demons, who lash and goad them onward, until no black abyss of vice, no hideous
gulf of crime, is black or hideous enough to content them?

Olivia Marchmont might have been a good
and great woman. She had all the elements of
greatness. She had genius, resolution, an indomitable courage, an iron will, perseverance,
self-denial, temperance, chastity. But against
all these qualities was set a fatal and foolish love
for a boy's handsome face and frank and genial
manner. If Edward Arundel had never crossed
her path, her unfettered soul might have taken
the highest and grandest flight; but, chained
down, bound, trammeled by her love for him,
she groveled on the earth like some maimed and
wounded eagle, who sees his fellows afar off,
high in the purple empyrean, and loathes himself for his impotence.

"What do I love him for?" she thought. "Is
it because he has blue eyes and chestnut hair,
with wandering gleams of golden light in it? Is it
because he has gentlemanly manners, and is easy
and pleasant, genial and light-hearted? Is it
because he has a dashing walk, and the air of a
man of fashion? It must be for some of these
attributes, surely; for I know nothing more in
him Of all the things he has ever said, I can
remember nothing—and I remember his smallest words, Heaven help me!—that any sensible
person could think worth repeating. He is
brave, I dare say, and generous; but neither
braver nor more generous than other men of his
rank and position."

She sat lost in such a reverie as this while her
dead husband was being carried to the roomy
vault set apart for the owners of Marchmont
Towers and their kindred; she was absorbed in
some such thoughts as these, when one of the
grave, gray-headed old servants brought her a
card upon a heavy salver emblazoned with the
Marchmont arms.

Olivia took the card almost mechanically.
There are some thoughts which carry us a long
way from the ordinary occupations of everyday
life, and it is not easy to return to the dull jog-
trot routine. The widow passed her left hand
across her brow before she looked at the name
inscribed upon the card in her right.

"Mr. Paul Marchmont."

She started as she read the name. Paul
Marchmont! She remembered what her husband had told her of this man. It was not much;
for John's feelings on the subject of his cousin
had been of so vague a nature that he had
shrunk from expounding them to his stern, practical wife. He had told her, therefore, that he
did not very much care for Paul, and that he
wished no intimacy ever to arise between the
artist and Mary; but he had said nothing more
than this.

"The gentleman is waiting to see me, I suppose?" Mrs. Marchmont said.

"Yes, ma'am. The gentleman came to Kemberling by the 11.5 train from London, and has
driven over here in one of Harris's flys."

"Tell him I will come to him immediately.
Is he in the drawing-room?"

"Yes, ma'am."

The man bowed and left the room. Olivia

lingered by the fire-place with her foot on th
fender, her elbow resting on the carved-oa
chimney-piece.

"Paul Marchmont! He has come to the fu
neral, I suppose. And he expects to find him
self mentioned in the will, I dare say. I think,
from what my husband told me, he will be dis.
appointed in that. Paul Marchmont! If Mary
were to die unmarried, this man or his sisters
would inherit Marchmont Towers."

There was a looking-glass over the mantle-
piece; a narrow, oblong glass, in an old-fashioned carved-ebony frame, which was inclined
forward. Olivia looked musingly in this glass,
and smoothed the heavy bands of dead-black hair
under her cap.

"There are people who would call me handsome," she thought, as she looked with a moody
frown at her image in the glass; "and yet I
have seen Edward Arundel's eyes wander away
from my face to watch the swallows skimming
by in the sun, or the ivy-leaves flapping against
the wall."

She turned from the glass with a sigh, and went
out into a dusky corridor. The shutters of all
the principal rooms and the windows upon the
grand staircase were still closed; the wide hall
was dark and gloomy, and drops of rain spattered
every now and then upon the logs that smouldered on the wide old-fashioned hearth. The
misty October morning had heralded a wet day.

Paul Marchmont was sitting in a low easy-
chair before a blazing fire in the western drawing-
room, the red light full upon his face. It was a
handsome face, or perhaps, to speak more exactly, it was one of those faces that are generally
called "interesting;" the features were very delicate and refined, the pale grayish-blue eyes were
shaded by long brown lashes, and the small and
rather feminine mouth was overshadowed by a
slender auburn mustache, under which the rosy
tint of the lips was very visible. But it was Paul
Marchmont's hair which gave a peculiarity to a
personal appearance that might otherwise have
been in no way out of the common. This hair,
fine, silky, and luxuriant, was *white,* although
its owner could not have been more than thirty-
seven years of age.

The uninvited guest rose as Olivia Marchmont
entered the room.

"I have the honor of speaking to my cousin's
widow," he said, with a courteous smile.

"Yes; I am Mrs. Marchmont."

Olivia seated herself near the fire. The wet
day was cold and cheerless, the dark house dismal and chilly. Mrs. Marchmont shivered as
she extended her long thin hand to the blaze.

"And you are doubtless surprised to see me
here, Mrs. Marchmont," the artist said, leaning
upon the back of his chair in the easy attitude
of a man who means to make himself at home;
"but believe me, that although I never took advantage of a very friendly letter written to me
by poor John—"

Paul Marchmont paused for a moment, keeping sharp watch upon the widow's face; but no
sorrowful expression, no evidence of emotion,
was visible in that inflexible countenance.

"Although, I repeat, I never availed myself
of a sort of general invitation to come and shoot
his partridges, or borrow money of him, or take
advantage of any of those other little privileges

generally claimed by a man's poor relations, it is not to be supposed, my dear Mrs. Marchmont, that I was altogether forgetful of either Marchmont Towers or its owner, my cousin. I did not come here, because I am a hard-working man, and the idleness of a country house would have been ruin to me. But I heard sometimes of my cousin from neighbors of his."

"Neighbors!" repeated Olivia, in a tone of surprise.

"Yes; people near enough to be called neighbors in the country. My sister lives at Stanfield. She is married to a surgeon who practices in that delightful town. You know Stanfield, of course?"

"No, I have never been there. It is five-and-twenty miles from here."

"Indeed! too far for a drive, then. Yes, my sister lives at Stanfield. John never knew much of her in his adversity, and therefore may be forgiven if he forgot her in his prosperity. But she did not forget him. We poor relations have excellent memories. The Stanfield people have so little to talk about, that it is scarcely any wonder if they are inquisitive about the affairs of the grand country gentry round about them. I heard of John through my sister; I heard of his marriage through her"—he bowed to Olivia as he said this—"and I wrote immediately to congratulate him upon that happy event," he bowed again here; "and it was through Lavinia Weston, my sister, that I heard of poor John's death, one day before the announcement appeared in the columns of the *Times*. I am sorry to find that I am too late for the funeral. I could have wished to have paid my cousin the last tribute of esteem that one man can pay another."

"You would wish to hear the reading of the will?" Olivia said, interrogatively.

Paul Marchmont shrugged his shoulders, with a low, careless laugh; not an indecorous laugh —nothing that this man did or said ever appeared ill advised or out of place. The people who disliked him were compelled to acknowledge that they disliked him unreasonably, and very much on the Doctor-Fell principle; for it was impossible to take objection to either his manners or his actions.

"That important legal document can have very little interest for me, my dear Mrs. Marchmont," he said, gayly. "John can have had nothing to leave me. I am too well acquainted with the terms of my grandfather's will to have any mercenary hopes in coming to Marchmont Towers."

He stopped, and looked at Olivia's impassible face.

"What on earth could have induced this woman to marry my cousin?" he thought. "John could have had very little to leave his widow."

He played with the jingling ornaments at his watch-chain, looking reflectively at the fire for some moments.

"Miss Marchmont—my cousin, Mary Marchmont, I should say—bears her loss pretty well, I hope?"

Olivia shrugged her shoulders.

"I am sorry to say that my step-daughter displays very little Christian resignation," she said. And then a spirit within her arose and whispered, with a mocking voice, "What resignation do *you* show—you, who should be so good a

Christian? How have *you* learned to school your rebellious heart?"

"My cousin is very young," Paul Marchmont said, presently.

"She was fifteen last July."

"Fifteen! Very young to be the owner of Marchmont Towers and an income of eleven thousand a year," returned the artist. He walked to one of the long windows, and drawing aside the edge of the blind, looked out upon the stone terrace and the wide flats before the mansion. The rain dripped and splashed upon the stone steps; the rain-drops hung upon the grim adornments of the carved balustrade, soaking into moss-grown escutcheons and half-obliterated coats-of-arms. The weird willows by the pools far away, and a solitary poplar near the house, looked gaunt and black against the dismal gray sky.

Paul Marchmont dropped the blind, and turned away from the gloomy landscape with a half-contemptuous gesture. "I don't know that I envy my cousin after all," he said; "the place is as dreary as Tennyson's Moated Grange."

There was the sound of wheels on the carriage-drive before the terrace, and presently a subdued murmur of hushed voices in the hall. Mr. Richard Paulette, and the two medical men who had attended John Marchmont, had returned to the Towers for the reading of the will. Hubert Arundel had returned with them; but the other followers in the funeral train had departed to their several homes. The undertaker and his men had made their way back to Marchmont by the side-entrance, and were making themselves very comfortable after the fulfillment of their mournful duties.

The will was to be read in the dining-room; and Mr. Paulette and the clerk who had accompanied him to Marchmont Towers were already seated at one end of the long carved-oak table, busy with their papers and pens and ink, assuming an importance the occasion did not require. Olivia went out into the hall to speak to her father.

"You will find Mr. Marchmont's solicitor in the dining-room," she said to Paul, who was looking at some of the old pictures on the drawing-room walls.

A large fire was blazing in the wide grate at the end of the dining-room. The blinds had been drawn up. There was no longer need that the house should be wrapped in darkness. The Awful Presence had departed; and such light as there was in the gloomy October sky was free to enter the rooms which the death of one quiet, unobtrusive creature had made for a time desolate.

There was no sound in the room but the low voices of the two doctors talking of their late patient in under tones near the fire-place, and the occasional fluttering of the papers under the lawyer's hand. The clerk, who sat respectfully a little way behind his master, and upon the very edge of his ponderous morocco-covered chair, had been wont to give John Marchmont his orders, and to lecture him for being tardy with his work a few years before, in the Lincoln's Inn office. He was wondering now whether he should find himself remembered in the dead man's will, to the extent of a mourning-ring or an old-fashioned silver snuff-box.

Richard Paulette looked up as Olivia and her father entered the room, followed at a little distance by Paul Marchmont, who walked at a leisurely pace, looking at the carved doorways and the pictures against the wainscot, and appearing, as he had declared himself, very little concerned in the important business about to be transacted.

"We shall want Miss Marchmont here, if you please," Mr. Paulette said, as he looked up from his papers.

"Is it necessary that she should be present?" Olivia asked.

"Very necessary."

"But she is ill; she is in bed."

"It is most important that she should be here when the will is read. Perhaps Mr. Bolton"—the lawyer looked toward one of the medical men—"will see. He will be able to tell us whether Miss Marchmont can safely come down stairs "

Mr. Bolton, the Swampington surgeon who had attended Mary that morning, left the room with Olivia. The lawyer rose and warmed his hands at the blaze, talking to Hubert Arundel and the London physician as he did so. Paul Marchmont, who had not been introduced to any one, occupied himself entirely with the pictures for a little time; and then, strolling over to the fire-place, fell into conversation with the three gentlemen, contriving, adroitly enough, to let them know who he was. The lawyer looked at him with some interest—a professional interest, no doubt; for Mr. Paulette had a copy of old Philip Marchmont's will in one of the japanned deed-boxes, inscribed with poor John's name. He knew that this easy-going, pleasant-mannered, white-haired young gentleman was the Paul Marchmont named in that document, and stood next in succession to Mary. Mary might die unmarried, and it was as well to be friendly and civil to a man who was at least a possible client.

The four gentlemen stood upon the broad Turkey hearth-rug for some time talking of the dead man, the wet weather, the cold autumn, the dearth of partridges, and other very safe topics of conversation. Olivia and the Swampington doctor were a long time absent, and Richard Paulette, who stood with his back to the fire, glanced every now and then toward the door.

It opened at last, and Mary Marchmont came into the room, followed by her step-mother.

Paul Marchmont turned at the sound of the opening of that ponderous mansion-door, and for the first time saw his second cousin, the young mistress of Marchmont Towers. He started as he looked at her, though with a scarcely perceptible movement, and a change came over his face. The feminine pinky hue in his cheeks faded suddenly and left them white. It had been a peculiarity of Paul Marchmont's, from his boyhood, always to turn pale with every acute emotion.

What was the emotion which had now blanched his cheeks? Was he thinking, "Is this fragile creature the mistress of Marchmont Towers? Is this frail life all that stands between me and eleven thousand a year?"

The life which shone out of that feeble earthly tabernacle did indeed seem a frail and fitful flame, likely to be extinguished by any rude breath from the coarse outer world. Mary Marchmont was deadly pale; black shadows encircled her wistful hazel eyes. Her stiff new mourning-dress, with its heavy trimmings of lustreless crape, seemed to hang loose upon her slender figure; her soft brown hair, damp with the water with which her burning forehead had been bathed, fell in straight disordered tresses about her shoulders. Her eyes were tearless, her small mouth terribly compressed. The rigidity of her face betokened the struggle by which her sorrow was repressed. She sat down in an easy-chair which Olivia indicated to her, and with her hands lying on the white handkerchief in her lap, and her swollen eyelids drooping over her eyes, waited for the reading of her father's will. It would be the last, the very last, she would ever hear of that dear father's words. She remembered this, and was ready to listen attentively; but she remembered nothing else. What was it to her that she was sole heiress of all that great mansion, and of eleven thousand a year? She had never in her life thought of the Lincolnshire fortune with any reference to herself or her own pleasures, and she thought of it less than ever now.

The will was dated February 4, 1844, exactly two months after John's marriage. It had been made by the master of Marchmont Tower without the aid of a lawyer, and was only witnessed by John's housekeeper and by Corson the old valet, a confidential servant, who had attended upon Mr. Marchmont's predecessor.

Richard Paulette began to read; and Mary, for the first time since she had taken her seat near the fire, lifted her eyes, and listened breathlessly, with faintly tremulous lips. Olivia sat near her step-daughter; and Paul Marchmont stood in a careless attitude at one corner of the fire-place, with his shoulders resting against the massive oaken chimney-piece. The dead man's will ran thus:

"I John Marchmont of Marchmont Towe declare this to be my last will and testamen Being persuaded that my end is approaching feel my dear little daughter Mary will be lef unprotected by any natural guardian M young friend Edward Arundel I had hoped whe in my poverty would have been a friend and ad viser to her if not a protector but her tende years and his position in life must place this now out of the question and I may die before fond hope which I have long cherished can be realized and which may now never be realize I now desire to make my will more particularl to provide as well as I am permitted for th guardianship and care of my dear little Mar during her minority Now I will and desir that my wife Olivia shall act as guardian advise and mother to my dear little Mary and that she place herself under the charge and guardian ship of my wife And as she will be an heires of very considerable property I would wish he to be guided by the advice of my said wife i the management of her property and particular ly in the choice of a husband As my dear littl Mary will be amply provided for on my death make no provision for her by this my will but direct my executrix to present to her a diamon ring which I wish her to wear in memory of he loving father so that she may always have m in her thoughts and particularly of these my wishes as to her future life until she shall be of age and capable of acting on her own judgment I also request my executrix to present my young friend Edward Arundel also with a diamond ring of the value of at least one hundred guineas as a slight tribute of the regard and esteem which I have ever entertained for him . . . . As to all the property as well real as personal over which I may at the time of my death have any control and capable of claiming or bequeathing I give devise and bequeath to my wife Olivia absolutely And I appoint my said wife sole executrix of this my will and guardian of my dear little Mary"

There were a few very small legacies, a mourning-ring to the expectant clerk; and this was all. Paul Marchmont had been quite right. Nobody could be less interested than himself in this will.

But he was apparently very much interested in John's widow and daughter. He tried to enter into conversation with Mary; but the girl's piteous manner seemed to implore him to leave her unmolested; and Mr. Bolton approached his patient almost immediately after the reading of the will, and in a manner took possession of her. Mary was very glad to leave the room once more, and to go back into the dim chamber where Hester Pollard sat at needle-work. Olivia left her step-daughter to the care of this humble companion, and went back to the long dining-room, where the gentlemen still hung listlessly over the fire, not knowing very well what to do with themselves.

Mrs. Marchmont could not do less than invite Paul to stay a few days at the Towers. She was virtually mistress of the house during Mary's minority, and on her devolved all the troubles, duties, and responsibilities attendant on such a position. Her father was going to stay with her till the end of the week: and he therefore would be able to entertain Mr. Marchmont. Paul unhesitatingly accepted the widow's hospitality. The old place was picturesque and interesting, he said; there were some genuine Holbeins in the hall and dining-room, and one good Lely in the drawing-room. He would give himself a couple of days' holiday, and go to Stanfield by an early train on Saturday.

"I have not seen my sister for a long time," he said; "her life is dull enough and hard enough, Heaven knows, and she will be glad to see me upon my way back to London."

Olivia bowed. She did not persuade Mr. Marchmont to extend his visit. The common courtesy she offered him was kept within the narrowest limits. She spent the best part of the time in the dead man's study during Paul's two days' stay, and left the artist almost entirely to her father's companionship.

But she was compelled to appear at dinner, when she took her accustomed place at the head of the table; and Paul therefore had some opportunity of sounding the depths of the strangest nature he had ever tried to fathom. He talked to her very much, listening with unvarying attention to every word she uttered. He watched her—but with no obtrusive gaze—almost incessantly; and when he went away from Marchmont Towers, without having seen Mary since the reading of the will, it was of Olivia he

thought; it was the recollection of Olivia which interested as much as it perplexed him.

The few people waiting for the London train looked at the artist as he strolled up and down the quiet platform at Kemberling Station, with his head bent and his eyebrows slightly contracted. He had a certain easy, careless grace of dress and carriage, which harmonized well with his delicate face, his silken silvery hair, his carefully-trained auburn mustache, and rosy, womanish mouth. He was a romantic-looking man. He was the beau-ideal of the hero in a young lady's novel. He was a man whom schoolgirls would have called "a dear." But it had been better, I think, for any helpless wretch to be in the bull-dog hold of the sturdiest Bill Sykes ever loosed upon society by right of his ticket-of-leave than in the power of Paul Marchmont, artist and teacher of drawing at Charlotte Street, Fitzroy Square.

He was thinking of Olivia as he walked slowly up and down the bare platform, only separated by a rough wooden paling from the flat open fields on the outskirts of Kemberling.

"The little girl is as feeble as a pale February butterfly," he thought; "a puff of frosty wind might wither her away. But that woman, that woman—how handsome she is, with her accurate profile and iron mouth; but what a raging fire there is hidden somewhere in her breast, and devouring her beauty by day and night! If I wanted to paint the sleeping scene in *Macbeth*, I'd ask her to sit for the Thane's wicked wife. Perhaps she has some bloody secret as deadly as the murder of a gray-headed Duncan upon her conscience, and leaves her bedchamber in the stillness of the night to walk up and down those long oaken corridors at the Towers, and wring her hands and wail aloud in her sleep. Why did she marry John Marchmont? His life gave her little more than a fine house to live in. His death leaves her with nothing but ten or twelve thousand pounds in the Three per Cents. What is her mystery? what is her secret, I wonder? for she must surely have one."

Such thoughts as these filled his mind as the train carried him away from the lonely little station, and away from the neighborhood of Marchmont Towers, within whose stony walls Mary lay in her quiet chamber, weeping for her dead father, and wishing—God knows in what utter singleness of heart—that she had been buried in the vault by his side.

---

## CHAPTER XIII.

### OLIVIA'S DESPAIR.

THE life which Mary and her step-daughter led at Marchmont Towers after poor John's death was one of those tranquil and monotonous existences that leave very little to be recorded, except the slow progress of the weeks and months, the gradual changes of the seasons. Mary bore her sorrows quietly, as it was her nature to bear all things. The doctor's advice was taken, and Olivia removed her step-daughter to Scarborough soon after the funeral. But the change of scene was slow to effect any change in the state of dull despairing sorrow into which the girl had fallen. The sea-breezes brought no color into her pale cheeks. She obeyed her step-mother's behests unmurmuringly, and wandered wearily by the dreary sea-shore in the dismal November weather in search of health and strength. But wherever she went, she carried with her the awful burden of her grief; and in every changing cadence of the low winter winds, in every varying murmur of the moaning waves, she seemed to hear her dead father's funeral dirge.

I think that, young as Mary Marchmont was, this mournful period was the great crisis of her life. The past, with its one great affection, had been swept away from her, and as yet there was no friendly figure to fill the dismal blank of the future. Had any kindly matron, any gentle Christian creature, been ready to stretch out her arms to the desolate orphan, Mary's heart would have melted, and she would have crept to the shelter of that womanly embrace, to nestle there forever. But there was no one. Olivia Marchmont obeyed the letter of her husband's solemn appeal, as she had obeyed the letter of those Gospel sentences that had been familiar to her from her childhood, but was utterly unable to comprehend its spirit. She accepted the charge intrusted to her. She was unflinching in the performance of her duty; but no one glimmer of the holy light of motherly love and tenderness, the semi-divine compassion of womanhood, ever illumined the dark chambers of her heart. Every night she questioned herself upon her knees as to her rigid performance of the level round of duty she had allotted to herself; every night—scrupulous and self-relentless as the hardest judge who ever pronounced sentence upon a criminal—she took note of her own shortcomings, and acknowledged her deficiencies.

But, unhappily, this self-devotion of Olivia's pressed no less heavily upon Mary than on the widow herself. The more rigidly Mrs. Marchmont performed the duties which she understood to be laid upon her by her dead husband's last will and testament, the harder became the orphan's life. The weary tread-mill of education worked on, when the young student was wellnigh fainting upon every step on that hopeless ladder of knowledge. If Olivia, on communing with herself at night, found that the day just done had been too easy a one for both mistress and pupil, the morrow's allowance of Roman emperors and French grammar was made to do penance for yesterday's shortcomings.

"This girl has been intrusted to my care, and one of my first duties is to give her a good education," Olivia Marchmont thought. "She is inclined to be idle; but I must fight against her inclination, whatever trouble the struggle entails upon myself. The harder the battle, the better for me, if I am conqueror."

It was only thus that Olivia Marchmont could hope to be a good woman. It was only by the rigid performance of hard duties, the patient practice of tedious rites, that she could hope to attain that eternal crown which simpler Christians seem to win so easily.

Morning and night the widow and her step-daughter read the Bible together; morning and night they knelt side by side to join in the same familiar prayers: yet all these readings, and all these prayers, failed to bring them any nearer together. No tender sentence of inspiration, not the words of Christ Himself, ever struck the same chord in these two women's hearts, bringing both into sudden unison. They went to church three times upon each dreary Sunday—dreary from the terrible uniformity which made one day a mechanical repetition of another, and sat together in the same pew; and there were times when some solemn word, some sublime injunction, seemed to fall with a new meaning upon the orphan girl's heart; but if she looked at her step-mother's face, thinking to see some ray of that sudden light which had newly shone into her own mind reflected there, the blank gloom of Olivia's countenance seemed like a dead wall, across which no glimmer of radiance ever shone.

They went back to Marchmont Towers in the early spring. People imagined that the young widow would cultivate the society of her husband's old friends, and that morning callers would be welcome at the Towers, and the stately dinner-parties would begin again, when Mrs. Marchmont's year of mourning was over. But it was not so; Olivia closed her doors upon almost all society, and devoted herself entirely to the education of her step-daughter. The gossips of Swampington and Kemberling; the county gentry who had talked of her piety and patience; her unflinching devotion to the poor of her father's parish, talked now of her self-abnegation; the sacrifices she made for her step-daughter's sake; the noble manner in which she justified John Marchmont's confidence in her goodness. Other women would have intrusted the heiress's education to some hired governess, people said; other women would have been upon the look-out for a second husband; other women would have grown weary of the dullness of that lonely Lincolnshire mansion, the monotonous society of a girl of sixteen. They were never tired of lauding Mrs. Marchmont as a model for all step-mothers in time to come.

Did she sacrifice much this woman, whose spirit was a raging fire, who had the ambition of a Semiramis, the courage of a Boadicea, the resolution of a Lady Macbeth? Did she sacrifice much in resigning such provincial gayeties as might have adorned her life—a few dinner-parties, an occasional county ball, a flirtation with some ponderous landed gentleman or hunting squire?

No; these things would very soon have grown odious to her; more odious than the monotony of her empty life, more wearisome even than the perpetual weariness of her own spirit. I said that, when she accepted a new life by becoming the wife of John Marchmont, she acted in the spirit of a prisoner who is glad to exchange his old dungeon for a new one. But, alas, the novelty of the prison-house had very speedily worn off, and that which Olivia Arundel had been at Swampington Rectory, Olivia Marchmont was now in the gaunt country mansion—a wretched woman, weary of herself and all the world, devoured by a slow-consuming and perpetual fire.

This woman was for two long melancholy years Mary Marchmont's sole companion and instructress. I say sole companion advisedly; for the girl was not allowed to become intimate with the younger members of such few county families as still called occasionally at the Towers, lest she should become empty-headed and frivolous by such companionship, Olivia said. Alas! there was little fear of Mary's becoming empty-headed. As she grew taller and more slender, she seemed to get weaker and paler, and her heavy head drooped wearily under the load of knowledge which it had been made to carry, like some poor sickly flower oppressed by the weight of the dew-drops which would have revivified a hardier blossom.

Heaven knows to what end Mrs. Marchmont educated her step-daughter. Poor Mary could have told the precise date of any event in universal history, ancient or modern; she could have named the exact latitude and longitude of the remotest island in the least navigable ocean, and might have given an accurate account of the manners and customs of its inhabitants had she been called upon to do so. She was alarmingly learned upon the subject of tertiary and old red sandstone, and could have told you almost as much as Mr. Charles Kingsley himself about the history of a gravel-pit—though I doubt if she could have conveyed her information in quite such a pleasant manner; she could have pointed out every star in the broad heavens above Lincolnshire, and could have told the history of its discovery; she knew the hardest names that science had given to the familiar field-flowers she met in her daily walks; yet I can not say that her conversation was any the more brilliant because of this, or that her spirits grew any the lighter under the influence of this general mental illumination.

But Mrs. Marchmont did most earnestly believe that this laborious educationary process was one of the duties she owed her step-daughter; and when, at seventeen years of age, Mary emerged from the struggle, laden with such intellectual spoils as I have described above, the widow felt a quiet satisfaction as she contemplated her work, and said to herself, "In this, at least, I have done my duty."

Among all the dreary mass of instruction beneath which her health had nearly succumbed, the girl had learned one thing that was a source of pleasure to herself. She had learned to become a very brilliant musician. She was not a musical genius, remember; for no such vivid flame as the fire of genius had ever burned in her gentle breast; but all the tenderness of her nature, all the poetry of a hyper-poetical mind, centred in this one accomplishment, and, condemned to perpetual silence in every other tongue, found a new and glorious language here. The girl had been forbidden to read Byron and Scott, but she was not forbidden to sit at her piano when the day's toils were over, and the twilight was dusky in her quiet room, playing dreamy melodies by Beethoven and Mozart, or making her own poetry to Mendelssohn's wordless songs. I think her soul must have shrunk and withered away had it not been for this one resource, this one refuge, in which her mind regained its elasticity, springing up, like a trampled flower, into new life and beauty.

Olivia was well pleased to see the girl sit hour after hour at her piano. She had learned to play well and brilliantly herself, mastering all difficulties with the proud determination which was a part of her strong nature; but she had no special love for music. All things that compose the poetry and beauty of life had been denied to this

D

woman, in common with the tenderness which makes the chief loveliness of womankind. She sat by and listened while Mary's slight hands wandered over the instrument, carrying the player's soul away into trackless regions of dreamland and beauty; but she heard nothing in the music except so many chords, so many tones and semi-tones, played in such or such a time.

It would have been scarcely natural for Mary Marchmont, reserved and self-contained though she had been ever since her father's death, to have had no yearning for more genial companionship than that of her step-mother. The girl who had kept watch in her room by the doctor's suggestion was the one friend and confidante whom the young mistress of Marchmont Towers fain would have chosen. But here Olivia interposed, sternly forbidding any intimacy between the two girls. Hester Pollard was the daughter of a small tenant farmer, and no fit associate for Mrs. Marchmont's step-daughter. Olivia thought that this taste for obscure company was the fruit of Mary's early training; the taint left by those bitter, debasing days of poverty, in which John Marchmont and his daughter had lived in some wretched Lambeth lodging.

"But Hester Pollard is fond of me, mamma," the girl pleaded; "and I feel so happy at the old farm-house. They are all so kind to me when I go there—Hester's father, and mother, and little brothers and sisters, you know; and the poultry-yard, and the pigs and horses, and the green-pond, with the geese cackling round it, remind me of my aunt's farm in Berkshire. I went there once with poor papa for a day or two; it was such a change after Oakley Street."

But Mrs. Marchmont was inflexible upon this point. She would allow her step-daughter to pay a ceremonial visit now and then to Farmer Pollard's, and to be entertained with cowslip-wine and pound-cake in the low old-fashioned parlor, where all the polished mahogany chairs were so shining and slippery that it was a marvel how any body ever contrived to sit down upon them. Olivia allowed such solemn visits as these now and then, and she permitted Mary to renew the farmer's lease upon sufficiently advantageous terms, and to make occasional presents to her favorite, Hester. But all stolen visits to the farm-yard, all evening rambles with the farmer's daughter in the apple-orchard at the back of the low white farm-house, were strictly interdicted; and though Mary and Hester were friends still, they were fain to be content with a chance of meeting once in the course of a dreary interval of months, and a silent pressure of the hand.

"You mustn't think that I am proud of my money, Hester," Mary said to her friend, "or that I forget you now that we see each other so seldom. Papa used to let me come to the farm whenever I liked; but papa had seen a great deal of poverty. Mamma keeps me almost always at home at my studies; but she is very good to me, and of course I am bound to obey her; papa wished me to obey her."

The orphan girl never for a moment forgot the terms of her father's will. He had wished her to obey; what should she do then but be obedient? Her submission to Olivia's lightest wish was only a part of the homage which she paid to that beloved father's memory.

It was thus she grew to early womanhood: a child in gentle obedience and docility; a woman by reason of that grave and thoughtful character which had been peculiar to her from her very infancy. It was in a life such as this, narrow, monotonous, joyless, that her seventeenth birthday came and went, scarcely noticed, scarcely remembered, in the dull uniformity of the days which left no track behind them; and Mary Marchmont was a woman—a woman with all the tragedy of life before her; infantine in her innocence and inexperience of the world outside Marchmont Towers.

The passage of time had been so long unmarked by any break in its tranquil course, the dull routine of life had been so long undisturbed by change, that I believe the two women thought their lives would go on for ever and ever. Mary, at least, had never looked beyond the dull horizon of the present. Her habit of castle-building had died out with her father's death. What need had she to. build castles now that he could no longer inhabit them? Edward Arundel, the bright boy she remembered in Oakley Street, the dashing young officer who had come to Marchmont Towers, had dropped back into the chaos of the past. Her father had been the keystone in the arch of Mary's existence: he was gone, and a mass of chaotic ruins alone remained of the familiar visions which had once beguiled her. The world had ended with John Marchmont's death, and his daughter's life since that great sorrow had been at best only a passive endurance of existence. They had heard very little of the young soldier at Marchmont Towers. Now and then a letter from some member of the family at Dangerfield had come to the Rector of Swampington. The warfare was still raging far away in the East, cruel and desperate battles were being fought, and brave Englishmen were winning loot and laurels, or perishing under the cimeters of Sikhs and Afghans, as the case may be. Squire Arundel's youngest son was not doing less than his duty, the letters said. He had gained his captaincy, and was well spoken of by great soldiers, whose very names were like the sound of the war-trumpet to English ears. ·

Olivia heard all this. She sat by her father, sometimes looking over his shoulder at the crumpled letter, as he read aloud to her of her cousin's exploits. The familiar name seemed to be all ablaze with lurid light as the widow's greedy eyes devoured it. How commonplace the letters were! What frivolous nonsense Letitia Arundel intermingled with the news of her brother! "You'll be glad to hear that my gray pony has got the better of his lameness. Papa gave a hunting-breakfast on Tuesday week. Lord Mountlitchcombe was present; but the hunting-men are very much aggravated about the frost, and I fear we shall have no crocuses. Edward has got his captaincy, papa told me to tell you; Sir Charles Napier and Major Outram have spoken very highly of him; but he—Edward, I mean—got a sabre-cut on his left arm, besides a wound on his forehead, and was laid up for nearly a month. I dare say you remember old Colonel Tollesley, at Halburton Lodge? He died last November, and has left all his money to—" And the young lady ran on thus with such gossip as she thought might be pleasing to her uncle; and there were no more tidings of the young soldier, whose life-blood had so nearly been spilt for his country's glory.

Olivia thought of him as she rode back to Marchmont Towers. She thought of the sabrecut upon his arm, and pictured him wounded and bleeding, lying beneath the canvas shelter of a tent, comfortless, lonely, forsaken.

"Better for me if he had died," she thought; "better for me if I were to hear of his death tomorrow."

And with the idea the picture of such a calamity arose before her so vividly and hideously distinct that she thought for one brief moment of agony, "This is not a fancy, it is a presentiment; it is second sight; the thing will occur."

She imagined herself going to see her father as she had gone that morning. All would be the same: the low gray garden-wall of the Rectory; the ceaseless surging of the sea; the prim servant-maid; the familiar study, with its litter of books and papers; the smell of old cigarsmoke; the chintz curtains flapping in the open window; the dry leaves fluttering in the garden without. There would be nothing changed except her father's face, which would be a little graver than usual. And then, after a little hesitation, after a brief preamble about the uncertainty of life, the necessity for looking always beyond this world, the horrors of war—the dreadful words would be upon his lips, when she would read all the hideous truth in his face, and fall prone to the ground before he could say, "Edward Arundel is dead."

Yes; she felt all the anguish. It would be this—this sudden paralysis of black despair. She tested the strength of her endurance by this imaginary torture—scarcely imaginary, surely, when it seemed so real—and asked herself a strange question: "Am I strong enough to bear this, or would it be less terrible to go on, suffering forever—forever abased and humiliated by the degradation of my love for a man who does not care for me?"

So long as John Marchmont had lived this woman would have been true to the terrible victory she had won upon the eve of her bridal. She would have been true to herself and to her marriage vow; but her husband's death, in setting her free, had cast her back upon the madness of her youth. It was no longer a sin to think of Edward Arundel. Having once suffered this idea to arise in her mind, her idol grew too strong for her, and she thought of him by night and day.

Yes; she thought of him for ever and ever. The narrow life to which she doomed herself, the self-immolation which she called duty, left her a prey to this one thought. Her work was not enough for her. Her powerful mind wasted and shriveled for want of worthy employment. It was like one vast roll of parchment whereon half the wisdom of the world might have been inscribed, but on which was only written over and over again, in maddening iteration, the name of Edward Arundel. If Olivia Marchmont could have gone to America, and entered herself among the feminine professors of law and medicine—if she could have set up a printing-press in Bloomsbury, or even written a novel— I think she might have been saved. The superabundant energy of her mind would have found a new object. As it was, she did none of these things. She had only dreamed one dream, and by force of perpetual repetition the dream had become a madness.

But the monotonous life was not to go on forever. The dull, gray, leaden sky was to be illumined by sudden bursts of sunshine, and swept by black thunder-clouds, whose stormy violence was to shake the very universe for these two solitary women.

John Marchmont had been dead nearly three years. Mary's humble friend, the farmer's daughter, had married a young tradesman in the village of Kemberling, a mile and a half from the Towers. Mary was a woman now, and had seen the last of the Roman Emperors and all the dry-as-dust studies of her early girlhood. She had nothing to do but accompany her step-mother hither and thither among the poor cottagers about Kemberling and two or three other small parishes within a drive of the Towers, doing good, after Olivia's fashion, by line and rule. At home the young lady did what she pleased, sitting for hours together at her piano, or wading through gigantic achievements in the way of embroidery-work. She was even allowed to read novels now, but only such novels as were especially recommended to Olivia, who was one of the patronesses of a book-club at Swampington.

The two women went to Kemberling Church together three times every Sunday. It was rather monotonous; the same church, the same rector and curate, the same clerk, the same congregation, the same old organ-tunes and droning voices of Lincolnshire charity-children, the same sermons very often. But Mary had grown accustomed to monotony. She had ceased to hope or care for any thing since her father's death, and was very well contented to be let alone, and allowed to dawdle through a dreary life which was utterly without aim or purpose. She sat opposite her step-mother on one particular afternoon in the state pew at Kemberling, which was lined with faded red baize, and raised a little above the pews of meaner worshipers; she was sitting with her listless hands lying in her lap, looking thoughtfully at her step-mother's stony face, and listening to the dull droning of the rector's voice above her head. It was a sunny afternoon in early June, and the church was bright with a warm yellow radiance; one of the old diamond-paned windows was open, and the tinkling of a sheep-bell far away in the distance, and the hum of bees in the church-yard, sounded pleasantly in the quiet of the hot atmosphere.

The young mistress of Marchmont Towers felt the drowsy influence of that tranquil summer weather creeping stealthily upon her. The heavy eyelids drooped over her soft brown eyes, those wistful eyes which had looked so long wearily out upon a world in which there seemed so little joy. The rector's sermon was a very long one this warm afternoon, and there was a low sound of snoring somewhere in one of the shadowy and sheltered pews beneath the galleries. Mary tried very hard to keep herself awake. Mrs. Marchmont had frowned darkly at her once or twice already, for to fall asleep in church was a dire iniquity in Olivia's rigid creed;

but the drowsiness was not easily to be conquered, and the girl was sinking into a peaceful slumber in the face of her step-mother's menacing frowns, when the sound of a sharp footfall on one of the gravel pathways in the church-yard aroused her attention.

Heaven knows why she should have been awoke out of her sleep by the sound of that step. It was different perhaps to the footsteps of the Kemberling congregation. The brisk, sharp sound of the tread, striking lightly but firmly on the gravel, was not compatible with the shuffling gait of the tradespeople and farmers' men who formed the greater part of the worshipers at that quiet Lincolnshire church. Again, it would have been a monstrous sin in that tranquil place for any one member of the congregation to disturb the rest by entering at such a time as this. It was a stranger, then, evidently. What did it matter? Miss Marchmont scarcely cared to lift her eyelids to see who or what the stranger was; but the intruder let in such a flood of June sunshine when he pushed open the ponderous oaken door under the church porch that she was dazzled by that sudden burst of light, and involuntarily opened her eyes.

The stranger let the door swing softly to behind him, and stood beneath the shadow of the porch, not caring to advance any farther, or to disturb the congregation by his presence.

Mary could not see him very plainly at first. She could only dimly define the outline of his tall figure, the waving masses of chestnut hair tinged with gleams of gold; but, little by little, his face seemed to grow out of the shadow, until she saw it all—the handsome patrician features, the luminous blue eyes, the amber mustache—the face which in Oakley Street, eight years ago, she had elected as her type of all manly perfection, her ideal of heroic grace.

Yes; it was Edward Arundel. Her eyes lighted up with an unwonted rapture as she looked at him; her lips parted, and her breath came in faint gasps. All the monotonous years, the terrible agonies of sorrow, dropped away into the past; and there was nothing but the present, the all-glorious present.

The one friend of her childhood had come back. The one link, the almost forgotten link, that bound her to every day-dream of those foolish early days, was united once more by the presence of the young soldier. All that happy time, nearly five years ago—that happy time in which the tennis-court had been built, and the boat-house by the river restored—those sunny autumn days before her father's second marriage—returned to her. There was pleasure and joy in the world, after all; and then the memory of her father came back to her mind, and her eyes filled with tears. How sorry Edward would be to see his old friend's empty place in the western drawing-room; how sorry for her and for her loss! Olivia Marchmont saw the change in her step-daughter's face, and looked at her with stern amazement. But, after the first shock of that delicious surprise, Mary's training asserted itself. She folded her hands —they trembled a little, but Olivia did not see that—and waited patiently, with her eyes cast down and a faint flush lighting up her cheeks, until the sermon was finished and the congregation began to disperse. She was not impatient. She felt as if she could have waited thus peacefully and contentedly forever, knowing that the only friend she had on earth was near her.

Olivia was slow to leave her pew; but at last she opened the door and went out into the quiet aisle, followed by Mary, out under the shadowy porch and into the gravel-walk in the churchyard, where Edward Arundel was waiting for the two ladies.

John Marchmont's widow uttered no cry of surprise when she saw her cousin standing a little way apart from the slowly-dispersing Kemberling congregation. Her dark face faded a little, and her heart seemed to stop its pulsation suddenly, as if she had been turned into stone; but this was only for a moment. She held out her hand to Mr. Arundel in the next instant, and bade him welcome to Lincolnshire.

"I did not know you were in England," she said.

"Scarcely any one knows it yet," the young man answered; "and I have not even been home. I came to Marchmont Towers at once."

He turned from his cousin to Mary, who was standing a little behind her step-mother.

"Dear Polly," he said, taking both her hands in his, "I was so sorry for you when I heard—"

He stopped, for he saw the tears welling up to her eyes. It was not his allusion to her father's death that had distressed her. He had called her Polly, the old familiar name, which she had never heard since that dead father's lips had last spoken it.

The carriage was waiting at the gate of the church-yard, and Edward Arundel went back to Marchmont Towers with the two ladies. He had reached the house a quarter of an hour after they had left it for afternoon church, and had walked over to Kemberling.

"I was so anxious to see you, Polly," he said, "after all this long time, that I had no patience to wait until you and Livy came back from church."

Olivia started as the young man said this. It was Mary Marchmont whom he had come to see, then; not her. Was she never to be any thing? Was she to be forever insulted by this humiliating indifference? A dark flush came over her face, as she drew her head up with the air of an offended empress, and looked angrily at her cousin. Alas! he did not even see that indignant glance. He was bending over Mary, telling her in a low, tender voice, of the grief he had felt at learning the news of her father's death.

Olivia Marchmont looked with an eager, scrutinizing gaze at her step-daughter. Could it be possible that Edward Arundel might ever come to love this girl? Could such a thing be possible? A hideous depth of horror and confusion seemed to open before her with the thought. In all the past, among all things she had imagined, among all the calamities she had pictured to herself, she had never thought of any thing like this. Would such a thing ever come to pass? Would she ever grow to hate this girl—this girl, who had been intrusted to her by her dead husband—with the most terrible hatred that one woman could feel toward another?

In the next moment she was angry with herself for the abject folly of this new terror. She had never yet learned to think of Mary as a woman. She had never thought of her otherwise than as the pale childlike girl who had come to her meekly, day after day, to recite difficult lessons, standing in a submissive attitude before her, and rendering obedience to her in all things. Was it likely, was it possible, that this pale-faced girl would enter into the lists against her in the great battle of her life? Was it likely that she was to find her adversary and her conqueror here, in the meek child who had been committed to her charge?

She watched her step-daughter's face with a jealous, hungry gaze. Was it beautiful? No! The features were delicate; the brown eyes soft and dovelike, almost lovely, now that they were irradiated by a new light, as they looked shyly up at Edward Arundel. But the girl's face was wan and colorless. It lacked the splendor of beauty. It was only after you had looked at her for a very long time that you began to think the face rather pretty.

The five years during which Edward Arundel had been away had made little alteration in him. He was rather stouter, perhaps; his amber mustache thicker; his manner more dashing than of old. The mark of a sabre-cut under the clustering chestnut curls upon the temple gave him a certain soldierly dignity. He seemed a man of the world now, and Mary Marchmont was rather afraid of him. He was so different to the Lincolnshire squires, the bashful younger sons who were to be educated for the Church. He was so dashing, so elegant, so splendid! From the waving grace of his hair to the tip of the polished boot peeping out of his well-cut trowsers (there were no peg-tops in 1847, and it was le genre to show very little of the boot), he was a creature to be wondered at, to be almost reverenced, Mary thought. She could not help admiring the cut of his coat, the easy nonchalance of his manner, the waxed ends of his curved mustache, the dangling toys of gold and enamel that jingled at his watch-chain, the waves of perfume that floated away from his cambric handkerchief. She was childish enough to worship all these external attributes in her hero.

"Shall I invite him to Marchmont Towers?" Olivia thought; and while she was deliberating upon this question, Mary Marchmont cried out, "You will stop at the Towers, won't you, Mr. Arundel, as you did when poor papa was alive?"

"Most decidedly, Miss Marchmont," the young man answered. "I mean to throw myself upon your hospitality as confidingly as I did a long time ago in Oakley Street, when you gave me hot rolls for my breakfast."

Mary laughed aloud; perhaps for the first time since her father's death. Olivia bit her lip. She was of so little account, then, she thought, that they did not care to consult her. A gloomy shadow spread itself over her face. Already, already she began to hate this pale-faced, childish orphan girl, who seemed to be transformed into a new being under the spell of Edward Arundel's presence.

But she made no attempt to prevent his stopping at the Towers, though a word from her would have effectually hindered his coming. A dull torpor of despair took possession of her; a black apprehension paralyzed her mind. She felt that a pit of horror was opening before her ignorant feet. All that she had suffered was as nothing to what she was about to suffer. Let it be, then. What could she do to keep this torture away from her? Let it come, since it seemed that it must come in some shape or other.

She thought all this while she sat back in a corner of the carriage watching the two faces opposite to her, as Edward and Mary, seated with their backs to the horses, talked together in low, confidential tones, which scarcely reached her ear. She thought all this during the short drive between Kemberling and Marchmont Towers; and when the carriage drew up before the low Tudor portico, the dark shadow had settled on her face. Her mind was made up. Let Edward Arundel come; let the worst come. She had struggled; she had tried to do her duty; she had striven to be good. But her destiny was stronger than herself, and had brought this young soldier over land and sea, safe out of every danger, rescued from every peril, to be her destruction. I think that in this crisis of her life the last faint ray of Christian light faded out of this lost woman's soul, leaving utter darkness and desolation. The old landmarks, dimly descried in the weary desert, sank forever down into the quicksands, and she was left alone— alone with her despair. Her jealous soul prophesied the evil which she dreaded. This man, whose indifference to her was almost an insult, would fall in love with Mary Marchmont—with Mary Marchmont, whose eyes lit up into new beauty under the glances of his, whose pale face blushed into faint bloom as he talked to her. The girl's undisguised admiration would flatter the young man's vanity, and he would fall in love with her out of very frivolity and weakness of purpose.

"He is weak and vain, and foolish and frivolous, I dare say," Olivia thought: "and if I were to fling myself upon my knees at his feet, and tell him that I loved him, he would be flattered and grateful, and would be ready to return my affection. If I could tell him what this girl tells him in every look and word, he would be as pleased with me as he is with her."

Her lip curled with unutterable scorn as she thought this. She was so despicable to herself by the deep humiliation of her wasted love, that the object of that foolish passion seemed despicable also. She was forever weighing Edward Arundel against all the tortures she had endured for his sake, and forever finding him wanting. He must have been a demi-god if his perfections could have outweighed so much misery; and for this reason she was unjust to her cousin, and could not accept him for that which he really was—a generous - hearted, candid, honorable young man—not a great man or a wonderful man—a brave and honest-minded soldier, very well worthy of a good woman's love.

Mr. Arundel staid at the Towers, occupying the room which had been his in John Marchmont's lifetime; and a new existence began for Mary. The young man was delighted with his old friend's daughter. Amidst all the Calcutta belles whom he had danced with at Government-House balls and flirted with upon the Indian race-course, he could remember no one as fascinating as this girl, who seemed as childlike now, in her early womanhood, as she had been womanly while she was a child. Her naïve tenderness for himself bewitched and enraptured him. Who could have avoided being charmed by that pure and innocent affection, which was as freely given by the girl of eighteen as it had been by the child, and was unchanged in character by the lapse of years? The young officer had been so much admired and caressed in Calcutta that perhaps, by reason of his successes, he had returned to England heart-whole; and he abandoned himself, without any arrière-pensée, to the quiet happiness which he felt in Mary Marchmont's society. I do not say that he was intoxicated by her beauty, which was by no means of the intoxicating order, or that he was madly in love with her. The gentle fascination of her society crept upon him before he was aware of its influence. He had never taken the trouble to examine his own feelings; they were disengaged—as free as butterflies to settle upon which flower might seem the fairest; and he had therefore no need to put himself under a course of rigorous self-examination. As yet he believed that the pleasure he now felt in Mary's society was the same order of enjoyment he had experienced five years before, when he had taught her chess, and promised her long rambles by the sea-shore.

They had no long rambles now in solitary lanes and under flowering hedgerows beside the waving green corn. Olivia watched them with untiring eyes. The tortures to which a jealous woman may condemn herself are not much greater than those she can inflict upon others. Mrs. Marchmont took good care that her ward and her cousin were not too happy. Wherever they went she went also; whenever they spoke she listened; whatever arrangement was most likely to please them was opposed by her. Edward was not coxcomb enough to have any suspicion of the reason of this conduct on his cousin's part. He only smiled and shrugged his shoulders, and attributed her watchfulness to an overstrained sense of her responsibility and the necessity of surveillance.

"Does she think me such a villain and a traitor," he thought, "that she fears to leave me alone with my dead friend's orphan daughter, lest I should whisper corruption into her innocent ear? How little these good women know of us, after all! What vulgar suspicions and narrow-minded fears influence them against us! Are they honorable and honest toward each other, I wonder, that they can entertain such pitiful doubts of our honor and honesty?"

So hour after hour and day after day Olivia Marchmont kept watch and ward over Edward and Mary. It was strange that love could blossom in such an atmosphere; it seems strange that the cruel gaze of those hard gray eyes did not chill the two innocent hearts, and prevent their free expansion. But it was not so. The egotism of love was all omnipotent. Neither Edward nor Mary was conscious of the evil light in the glance that so often rested upon them. The universe narrowed itself to the one spot of earth upon which these two stood side by side.

Edward Arundel had been more than a month

at Marchmont Towers when Olivia went, upon a hot July evening, to Swampington, on a brief visit to the Rector—a visit of duty. She would doubtless have taken Mary Marchmont with her, but the girl had been suffering from a violent headache throughout the burning summer day, and had kept her room. Edward Arundel had gone out early in the morning upon a fishing excursion to a famous trout-stream seven or eight miles from the Towers, and was not likely to return until after nightfall. There was no chance, therefore, of a meeting between Mary and the young officer, Olivia thought; no chance of any confidential talk which she would not be by to hear.

Did Edward Arundel love the pale-faced girl who revealed her devotion to him with such child-like unconsciousness? Olivia Marchmont had not been able to answer that question. She had sounded the young man several times upon his feelings toward her step-daughter; but he had met her hints and insinuations with perfect frankness, declaring that Mary seemed as much a child to him now as she had appeared nearly nine years before in Oakley Street, and that the pleasure he took in her society was only such as he might have felt in that of any innocent and confiding child.

"Her simplicity is so bewitching, you know, Livy," he said; "she looks up in my face, and trusts me with all her little secrets, and tells me her dreams about her dead father, and all her foolish, innocent fancies, as confidingly as if I were some play-fellow of her own age and sex. She's so refreshing after the artificial belles of a Calcutta ball-room, with their stereotyped fascinations and their complete manual of flirtation, the same for ever and ever. She is such a pretty little spontaneous darling, with her soft, shy, brown eyes, and her low voice, which always sounds to me like the cooing of the doves in the poultry-yard."

I think that Olivia, in the depth of her gloomy despair, took some comfort from such speeches as these. Was this frank expression of regard for Mary Marchmont a token of love? No; not as the widow understood the stormy madness. Love to her had been a dark and terrible passion, a thing to be concealed, as monomaniacs have sometimes contrived to keep the secret of their mania, until its burst forth at last, fatal and irrepressible, in some direful work of wreck and ruin.

So Olivia Marchmont took an early dinner alone, and drove away from the Towers at four o'clock on a blazing summer afternoon, more at peace perhaps than she had been since Edward Arundel's coming. She paid her dutiful visit to her father, sat with him for some time, talked to the two old servants who waited upon him, walked two or three times up and down the neglected garden, and then drove back to the Towers.

The first object upon which her eyes fell as she entered the hall was Edward Arundel's fishing-tackle lying in disorder upon an oaken bench near the broad arched door that opened out into the quadrangle. An angry flush mounted to her face as she turned upon the servant near her.

"Mr. Arundel has come home?" she said.

"Yes, ma'am, he came in half an hour ago;

but he went out again almost directly with Miss Marchmont."

"Indeed! I thought Miss Marchmont was in her room?"

"No, ma'am; she came down to the drawing-room about an hour after you left. Her head was better, ma'am, she said."

"And she went out with Mr. Arundel? Do you know which way they went?"

"Yes, ma'am; I heard Mr. Arundel say he wanted to look at the old boat-house by the river."

"And they have gone there?"

"I think so, ma'am."

"Very good; I will go down to them. Miss Marchmont must not stop out in the night-air. The dew is falling already."

The door leading into the quadrangle was open, and Olivia swept across the broad threshold, haughty and self-possessed, very stately-looking in her long black garments. She still wore mourning for her dead husband. What inducement had she ever had to cast off that sombre attire? What need to trick herself out in gay colors? What loving eyes would be charmed by her splendor? She went out of the door, across the quadrangle, under a stone archway, and into the low stunted wood, which was gloomy even in the summer-time. The setting sun was shining upon the western front of the Towers; but here all seemed cold and desolate. The damp mists were rising from the sodden ground beneath the trees. The frogs were croaking down by the river-side. With her small white teeth set, and her breath coming in fitful gasps, Olivia Marchmont hurried to the water's edge, winding in and out between the trees, tearing her black dress among the brambles, scorning all beaten paths, heedless where she trod, so long as she made her way speedily to the spot she wanted to reach.

At last the black sluggish river and the old boat-house came in sight, between a long vista of ugly distorted trunks and gnarled branches of pollard oak and willow. The building was dreary and dilapidated looking, for the improvements commenced by Edward Arundel five years ago had never been fully carried out; but it was sufficiently substantial, and bore no traces of positive decay. Down by the water's edge there was a great cavernous recess for the shelter of the boats, and above this there was a pavilion, built of brick and stone, containing two decent-sized chambers, with latticed windows overlooking the river. A flight of stone steps with an iron balustrade led up to the door of this pavilion, which was supported upon the solid side-walls of the boat-house below.

In the stillness of the summer twilight Olivia heard the voices of those whom she came to seek. They were standing down by the edge of the water, upon a narrow pathway that ran along by the sedgy brink of the river, and only a few paces from the pavilion. The door of the boat-house was open; a long-disused wherry lay rotting upon the damp and mossy flags. Olivia crept into the shadowy recess. The door that faced the river had fallen from its rusty hinges, and the slimy wood-work lay in ruins upon the threshold of the dark recess. Sheltered by the stone archway that had once been closed by this door, Olivia listened to the voices beside the still water.

Mary Marchmont was standing close to the river's edge; Edward stood beside her, leaning against the trunk of a willow that grew close to the water.

"My childish darling," the young man murmured, as if in reply to something his companion had said, "and so you think, because you are simple-minded and innocent, I am not to love you. It is your innocence I love, Polly dear—let me call you Polly, as I used five years ago—and I wouldn't have you otherwise for all the world. Do you know that sometimes I am almost sorry I ever came back to Marchmont Towers?"

"Sorry you came back?" cried Mary, in a tone of alarm. "Oh, why do you say that, Mr. Arundel?"

"Because you are heiress to eleven thousand a year, Mary, and the Moated Grange behind us; and this dreary wood, and the river—the river is yours, I dare say, Miss Marchmont; and I wish you joy of the possession of so much sluggish water and so many square miles of swamp and fen."·

"But what then?" Mary asked, wonderingly.

"What then? Do you know, Polly darling, that if I ask you to marry me people will call me a fortune-hunter, and declare that I came to Marchmont Towers bent upon stealing its heiress's innocent heart before she had learned the value of the estate that must go along with it? God knows they'd wrong me, Polly, as cruelly as ever an honest man was wronged; for, so long as I have money to pay my tailor and tobacconist—and I've more than enough for both of them—I want nothing further of the world's wealth. What should I do with all this swamp and fen, Miss Marchmont—with all that horrible complication of expired leases to be renewed, and income-taxes to be appealed against, that rich people have to endure? If you were not rich, Polly, I—"

He stopped and laughed, striking the toe of his boot among the weeds, and knocking the pebbles into the water. The woman crouching in the shadow of the archway listened with whitened cheeks and glaring eyes; listened as she might have listened to the sentence of her death, drinking in every syllable, in her ravenous desire to lose no breath that told her of her anguish.

"If I were not rich!" murmured Mary; "what if I were not rich?"

"I should tell you how dearly I love you, Polly, and ask you to be my wife by-and-by."

The girl looked up at him for a few moments in silence, shyly at first, and then more boldly, with a beautiful light kindling in her eyes.

"I love you dearly too, Mr. Arundel," she said, at last; "and I would rather you had my money than any one else in the world; and there was something in papa's will that made me think—"

"He would wish this, Polly," cried the young man, clasping the trembling little figure to his breast. "Mr. Paulette sent me a copy of the will, Polly, when he sent my diamond ring; and I think there were some words in it that hinted at such a wish. Your father said he left me this legacy, darling—I have his letter still—the legacy of a helpless girl. God knows I will try to be worthy of such a trust, Mary dearest; God

knows I will be faithful to my promise, made nine years ago."

The woman listening in the dark archway sank down upon the damp flags at her feet, among the slimy rotten wood and rusty iron nails and hinges. She sat there for a long time, not unconscious, but quite motionless, her white face leaning against the moss-grown arch, staring blankly out of the black shadows. She sat there and listened, while the lovers talked in low tender murmurs of the sorrowful past and of the unknown future; the beautiful untrodden region, in which they were to go hand in hand through all the long years of quiet happiness between that moment and the grave. She sat and listened till the moonlight faintly shimmered upon the water, and the footsteps of the lovers died away upon the narrow pathway by which they went back to the house.

Olivia Marchmont did not move until an hour after they had gone. Then she raised herself with an effort, and walked with stiffened limbs slowly and painfully to the house, and to her own room, where she locked her door and flung herself upon the ground in the darkness.

Mary came to her to ask why she did not come to the drawing-room, and Mrs. Marchmont answered, with a hoarse voice, that she was ill, and wished to be alone. Neither Mary nor the old woman-servant who had nursed Olivia, and had some little influence over her, could get any other answer than this.

<hr/>

## CHAPTER XIV.

### DRIVEN AWAY.

MARY MARCHMONT and Edward Arundel were happy. They were happy; and how should they guess at the tortures of that desperate woman, whose benighted soul was plunged in a black gulf of horror by reason of their innocent love? How should these two—very children in their ignorance of all stormy passions, all direful emotions—know, that in the darkened chamber where Olivia Marchmont lay; suffering under some vague illness, for which the Swampington doctor was fain to prescribe quinine, in utter unconsciousness as to the real nature of the disease which he was called upon to cure—how should they know that in that gloomy chamber a wicked heart was abandoning itself to all the devils that had so long held patient watch for this day?

Yes, the struggle was over. Olivia Marchmont flung aside the cross she had borne in dull, mechanical obedience, rather than in Christian love and truth. Better to have been sorrowful Magdalene, forgiven for her love and tears, than this cold, haughty, stainless woman, who had never been able to learn the sublime lessons which so many sinners have taken meekly to heart. The religion which was wanting in the vital principle of Christianity, the faith which showed itself only in dogged obedience, failed this woman in the hour of her agony. Her pride arose; the defiant spirit of the fallen angel asserted its gloomy grandeur.

"What have I done that I should suffer like this?" she thought. "What am I that an empty-headed soldier should despise me, and that I should go mad because of his indifference? Is this the recompense for my long years of obedience? Is this the reward Heaven bestows upon me for my life of duty?"

She remembered the histories of other women —women who had gone their own way and had been happy; and a darker question arose in her mind, almost the question which Job asked in his agony.

"Is there neither truth nor justice in the dealings of God?" she thought. "Is it useless to be obedient and submissive, patient and untiring? Has all my life been a great mistake, which is to end in confusion and despair?"

And then she pictured to herself the life that might have been hers if Edward Arundel had loved her. How good she would have been! The hardness of her iron nature would have been melted and subdued in the depth of her love and tenderness for him. She would have learned to be loving and tender to others. Her wealth of affection for him would have overflowed in gentleness and consideration for every creature in the universe. The lurking bitterness which had lain hidden in her heart ever since she had first loved Edward Arundel, and first discovered his indifference to her; and the poisonous envy of happier women, who had loved and were beloved—would have been blotted away. Her whole nature would have undergone a wondrous transfiguration, purified and exalted by the strength of her affection. All this might have come to pass if he had loved her—if he had only loved her. But a pale-faced child had come between her and this redemption, and there was nothing left for her but despair.

Nothing but despair? Yes; perhaps something further—revenge.

But this last idea took no tangible shape. She only knew that in the black darkness of the gulf into which her soul had gone down there was, far away somewhere, one ray of lurid light. She only knew this as yet, and that she hated Mary Marchmont with a mad and wicked hatred. If she could have thought meanly of Edward Arundel—if she could have believed him to be actuated by mercenary motives in his choice of the orphan girl—she might have taken some comfort from the thought of his unworthiness, and of Mary's probable sorrow in the days to come. But she could not think this. Little as the young soldier had said in the summer twilight beside the river, there had been that in his tones and looks that had convinced the wretched watcher of his truth. Mary might have been deceived by the shallowest pretender; but Olivia's eyes devoured every glance; Olivia's greedy ears drank in every tone; and she knew that Edward Arundel loved her step-daughter.

She knew this, and she hated Mary Marchmont. What had she done, this girl who had never known what it was to fight a battle with her own rebellious heart—what had she done, that all this wealth of love and happiness should drop into her lap unsought—comparatively unvalued, perhaps?

John Marchmont's widow lay in her darkened chamber, thinking over these things; no longer fighting the battle with her own heart, but utterly abandoning herself to her desperation—reckless, hardened, impenitent.

Edward Arundel could not very well remain at the Towers while the reputed illness of his hostess kept her to her room. He went over to Swampington, therefore, upon a dutiful visit to his uncle; but rode to the Towers every day to inquire very particularly after his cousin's progress, and to dawdle on the sunny western terrace with Mary Marchmont.

Their innocent happiness needs little description. Edward Arundel retained a good deal of that boyish chivalry which had made him so eager to become the little girl's champion in the days gone by. Contact with the world had not much sullied the freshness of the young man's spirit. He loved his innocent childish companion with the purest and truest devotion; and he was proud of the recollection that in the day of his poverty John Marchmont had chosen him as the future shelterer of this tender blossom.

"You must never grow any older or more womanly, Polly," he said sometimes to the young mistress of Marchmont Towers. "Remember that I always love you best when I think of you as the little girl in the shabby pinafore, who poured out my tea for me one bleak December morning in Oakley Street."

They talked a great deal of John Marchmont. It was such a happiness to Mary to be able to talk unreservedly of her father to some one who had loved and comprehended him.

"My step-mamma was very good to poor papa, you know, Edward," she said; "and of course he was very grateful to her; but I don't think he ever loved her quite as he loved you. You were the friend of his poverty, Edward; he never forgot that."

Once, as they strolled side by side together upon the terrace in the warm summer noontide, Mary Marchmont put her little hand through her lover's arm, and looked up shyly in his face.

"Did papa say that, Edward?" she whispered; "did he really say that?"

"Did he really say what, darling?"

"That he left me to you as a legacy?"

"He did indeed, Polly," answered the young man; "I'll bring you the letter to-morrow."

And the next day he showed Mary Marchmont the yellow sheet of letter-paper and the faded writing, which had once been black and wet under her dead father's hand. Mary looked through her tears at the old familiar Oakley Street address, and the date of the very day upon which Edward Arundel had breakfasted in the shabby lodging. Yes; there were the words: "The legacy of a child's helplessness is the only bequest I can leave to the only friend I have."

"And you shall never know what it is to be helpless while I am near you, Polly darling," the soldier said, as he refolded his dead friend's epistle. "You may defy your enemies henceforward, Mary; if you have any enemies. Oh, by-the-by, you have never heard any thing of that Paul Marchmont, I suppose?"

"Papa's cousin, Mr. Marchmont the artist?"

"Yes."

"He came to the reading of papa's will."

"Indeed! and did you see much of him?"

"Oh no, very little. I was ill, you know," the girl added, the tears rising to her eyes at the recollection of that bitter time, "I was ill, and I didn't notice any thing. I know that Mr. Marchmont talked to me a little; but I can't remember what he said."

"And he has never been here since?"

"Never."

Edward Arundel shrugged his shoulders. This Paul Marchmont could not be such a designing villain, after all, or surely he would have tried to push his acquaintance with his rich cousin. "I dare say John's suspicion of him was only one of the poor fellow's morbid fancies," he thought. "He was always full of morbid fancies."

Mrs. Marchmont's rooms were in the western front of the house; and through her open windows she heard the fresh young voices of the lovers, as they strolled up and down the terrace. The cavalry officer was content to carry a watering-pot of water for the refreshment of his young mistress's geraniums in the stone vases on the balustrade, and to do other under-gardener's work for her pleasure. He talked to her of the Indian campaign; and she asked a hundred questions about midnight marches and solitary encampments, fainting camels, lurking tigers in the darkness of the jungle, intercepted supplies of provision, stolen ammunition, and all the other details of the war.

Olivia arose at last, before the Swampington surgeon's saline draughts and quinine mixtures had subdued the fiery light in her eyes, or cooled the raging fever that devoured her. She arose because she could no longer lie still in her desolation, knowing that for two hours in each long summer's day Edward Arundel and Mary Marchmont could be happy together in spite of her. She came down stairs, therefore, and renewed her watch, chaining her step-daughter to her side, and interposing herself forever between the lovers.

The widow arose from her sick-bed an altered woman, as it appeared to all who knew her. A mad excitement seemed to have taken sudden possession of her. She flung off her mourning-garments, and ordered silks and laces, velvets and satins, from a London milliner; she complained of the absence of society, the monotonous dullness of her Lincolnshire life; and, to the surprise of every one, sent out cards of invitation for a ball at the Towers in honor of Edward Arundel's return to England. She seemed to be seized with a desire to do something, she scarcely cared what, to disturb the even current of her days.

During the brief interval between Mrs. Marchmont's leaving her room and the evening appointed for the ball, Edward Arundel found no very convenient opportunity of informing his cousin of the engagement entered into between himself and Mary. He had no wish to hurry this disclosure; for there was something in the orphan girl's childishness and innocence that kept all definite ideas of an early marriage very far away from her lover's mind. He wanted to go back to India and win more laurels, to lay at the feet of the mistress of Marchmont Towers. He wanted to make a name for himself, which should cause the world to forget that he was a younger son—a name that the vilest tongue would never dare to blacken with the epithet of fortune-hunter.

The young man was silent, therefore, waiting for a fitting opportunity in which to speak to Mary's step-mother. Perhaps he rather dreaded the idea of discussing his attachment with Olivia; for she had looked at him with cold angry eyes, and a brow as black as thunder, upon those occasions on which she had sounded him as to his feelings for Mary.

"She wants poor Polly to marry some grandee, I dare say," he thought; "and will do all she can to oppose my suit. But her trust will cease with Mary's majority; and I don't want my confiding little darling to marry me until she is old enough to choose for herself, and to choose wisely. She will be one-and-twenty in three years; and what are three years? I would wait as long as Jacob for my pet, and serve my fourteen years' apprenticeship under Sir Charles Napier, and be true to her all the time."

Olivia Marchmont hated her step-daughter. Mary was not slow to perceive the change in the widow's manner toward her. It had always been cold, and sometimes severe; but it was now almost abhorrent. The girl shrank appalled from the sinister light in her step-mother's gray eyes, as they followed her unceasingly, dogging her footsteps with a hungry and evil gaze. The gentle girl wondered what she had done to offend her guardian, and then, being unable to think of any possible delinquency by which she might have incurred Mrs. Marchmont's displeasure, was fain to attribute the change in Olivia's manner to the irritation consequent upon her illness, and was thus more gentle and more submissive than of old; enduring cruel looks, returning no answer to bitter speeches, but striving to conciliate her supposed invalid by her sweetness and obedience.

But the girl's amiability only irritated the despairing woman. Her jealousy fed upon every charm of the rival who had supplanted her. That fatal passion fed upon Edward Arundel's every look and tone, upon the quiet smile which rested on Mary's face as the girl sat over her embroidery, in meek silence thinking of her lover. The self-tortures which Olivia Marchmont inflicted upon herself were so horrible to bear that she turned, with a mad desire for relief, upon those she had the power to torture. Day by day and hour by hour she contrived to distress the gentle girl, who had so long obeyed her, now by a word, now by a look, but always with that subtle power of aggravation which women possess in such an eminent degree; until Mary Marchmont's life became a burden to her—or would have so become, but for that inexpressible happiness, of which her tormentor could not deprive her—the joy she felt in her knowledge of Edward Arundel's love.

She was very careful to keep the secret of her step-mother's altered manner from the young soldier. Olivia was his cousin, and he had said long ago that she was to love her. Heaven knows she had tried to do so, and had failed most miserably; but her belief in Olivia's goodness was still unshaken. If Mrs. Marchmont was now irritable, capricious, and even cruel, there was doubtless some good reason for the alteration in her conduct, and it was Mary's duty to be patient. The orphan girl had learned to suffer quietly when the great affliction of her father's death had fallen upon her; and she suffered so quietly now, that even her lover failed to perceive any symptoms of her distress. How could she grieve him by telling him of her sorrows, when his very presence brought such unutterable joy to her?

So, on the morning of the ball at Marchmont Towers—the first entertainment of the kind that had been given in that grim Lincolnshire mansion since young Arthur Marchmont's untimely death—Mary sat in her room, with her old friend Farmer Pollard's daughter—who was now Mrs. Mapleson, the wife of the most prosperous carpenter in Kemberling. Hester had come up to the Towers to pay a dutiful visit to her young patroness; and upon this particular occasion Olivia had not cared to prevent Mary and her humble friend spending half an hour together. Mrs. Marchmont roamed from room to room upon this day, with a perpetual restlessness. Edward Arundel was to dine at the Towers, and was to sleep there after the ball. He was to drive his uncle over from Swampington, as the Rector had promised to show himself for an hour or two at his daughter's entertainment. Mary had met her step-mother several times that morning in the corridors and on the staircase; but the widow had passed her in silence, with a dark face, and a shivering, almost abhorrent gesture.

The bright July day dragged itself out at last, with hideous slowness for the desperate woman, who could not find peace or rest in all those splendid rooms, on all that grassy flat, dry and burning under the blazing summer sun. She had wandered out upon the waste of barren turf, with her head bared to the hot sky, and had loitered here and there by the still pools, looking gloomily at the black tideless water, and wondering what the agony of drowning was like. Not that she had any thought of killing herself. No; the idea of death was horrible to her; for after her death Edward and Mary would be happy. Could she ever find rest in the grave knowing this? Could there be any possible extinction that would blot out her jealous fury? Surely the fire of her hate—it was no longer love, but hate, that raged in her heart—would defy annihilation, eternal by reason of its intensity. When the dinner-hour came, and Edward and his uncle arrived at the Towers, Olivia Marchmont's pale face was lit up with eyes that flamed like fire; but she took her accustomed place very quietly, with her father opposite to her, and Mary and Edward upon either side.

"I'm sure you're ill, Livy," the young man said; "you're as pale as death, and your hand is dry and burning. I'm afraid you've not been obedient to the Swampington doctor."

Mrs. Marchmont shrugged her shoulders with a short contemptuous laugh.

"I am well enough," she said. "Who cares whether I am well or ill?"

Her father looked up at her in mute surprise. The bitterness of her tone startled and alarmed him; but Mary never lifted her eyes. It was in such a tone as this that her step-mother had spoken constantly of late.

But two or three hours afterward, when the flats before the house were silvered by the moonlight, and the long ranges of windows glittered with the lamps within, Mrs. Marchmont emerged from her dressing-room another creature, as it seemed.

Edward and his uncle were walking up and down the great oaken banqueting-hall, which had been decorated and fitted up as a ball-room for the occasion, when Olivia crossed the wide threshold of the chamber. The young officer looked up with an involuntary expression of surprise. In all his acquaintance with his cousin he had never seen her look thus. The gloomy, black-robed woman was transformed into a Semiramis. She wore a voluminous dress of a deep claret-colored velvet, that glowed with the warm hues of rich wine in the lamplight. Her massive hair was coiled in a knot at the back of her head, and diamonds glittered amidst the thick bands that framed her broad white brow. Her stern classical beauty was lit up by the unwonted splendor of her dress, and asserted itself as obviously as if she had said, "Am I a woman to be despised for the love of a pale-faced child?"

Mary Marchmont came into the room a few minutes after her step-mother. Her lover ran to welcome her, and looked fondly at her simple dress of shadowy white crape, and the pearl circlet that crowned her soft brown hair. The pearls she wore upon this night had been given to her by her father on her fourteenth birthday.

Olivia watched the young man as he bent over Mary Marchmont.

He wore his uniform to-night for the special gratification of his young mistress, and he was looking down with a tender smile at her childish admiration of the bullion ornaments upon his coat, and the decoration he had won in India.

The widow looked from the two lovers to an antique glass upon an ebony bureau in a niche opposite to her, which reflected her own face—her own face, more beautiful than she had ever seen it before, with a feverish glow of vivid crimson lighting up her hollow cheeks.

"I might have been beautiful if he had loved me," she thought; and then she turned to her father, and began to talk to him of his parishioners, the old pensioners upon her bounty, whose little histories were so hatefully familiar to her. Once more she made a feeble effort to tread the old hackneyed pathway, which she had toiled upon with such weary feet; but she could not—she could not. After a few minutes she turned away abruptly from her father, and seated herself in a recess of the window, from which she could see Edward and Mary.

But Mrs. Marchmont's duties as hostess soon demanded her attention. The county families began to arrive, the sound of carriage-wheels seemed perpetual upon the crisp gravel-drive before the western front, the names of half the great people in Lincolnshire were shouted by the old servants in the hall. The band in the music-gallery struck up a quadrille, and Edward Arundel led the youthful mistress of the mansion to her place in the dance.

To Olivia that long night seemed all glare and noise and confusion. She did the honors of the ball-room, she received her guests, she meted out due attention to all; for she had been accustomed from her earliest girlhood to the stereotyped round of country society. She neglected no duty; but she did all mechanically, scarcely knowing what she said or did in the feverish tumult of her soul.

Yet, amidst all the bewilderment of her senses, in all the confusion of her thoughts, two figures were always before her. Wherever Edward

Arundel and Mary Marchmont went her eyes followed them, her fevered imagination pursued them. Once, and once only, in the course of that long night, she spoke to her step-daughter. "How often do you mean to dance with Captain Arundel, Miss Marchmont?" she said.

But before Mary could answer her step-mother had moved away upon the arm of a portly country squire, and the girl was left in sorrowful wonderment as to the reason of Mrs. Marchmont's angry tone.

Edward and Mary were standing in one of the deep embayed windows of the banqueting-hall when the dancers began to disperse, long after supper. The girl had been very happy that evening, in spite of her step-mother's bitter words and disdainful glances. For almost the first time in her life the young mistress of Marchmont Towers had felt the contagious influence of other people's happiness. The brilliantly-lighted ball-room, the splendid dresses of the dancers, the joyous music, the low sound of suppressed laughter, the bright faces which smiled at each other upon every side, were as new as any thing in fairy-land to this girl, whose narrow life had been overshadowed by the gloomy figure of her step-mother forever interposed between her and the outer world. The young spirit arose and shook off its fetters, fresh and radiant as the butterfly that escapes from its chrysalis-shell. The new light of happiness illumined the orphan's delicate face, until Edward Arundel began to wonder at her loveliness, as he had wondered once before that night at the fiery splendor of his cousin Olivia.

"I had no idea that Olivia was so handsome, or you so pretty, my darling," he said, as he stood with Mary in the embrasure of the window. "You look like Titania, the queen of the fairies, Polly, with your cloudy draperies and crown of pearls."

The window was open, and Captain Arundel looked wistfully at the broad flagged quadrangle, beautified by the light of the full summer moon. He glanced back into the room; it was nearly empty now; and Mrs. Marchmont was standing near the principal doorway, bidding the last of her guests good-night.

"Come into the quadrangle, Polly," he said, "and take a turn with me under the colonnade. It was a cloister once, I dare say, in the good old days, before Harry the Eighth was king; and cowled monks have paced up and down under its shadow, muttering mechanical prayers, as the beads of their rosaries dropped slowly through their shriveled old fingers. Come out into the quadrangle, Polly; all the people we know or care about are gone; and we'll go out and walk in the moonlight, as true lovers ought."

The soldier led his young companion across the threshold of the window, and out into a cloister-like colonnade that ran along one side of the house. The shadows of the Gothic pillars were black upon the moonlit flags of the quadrangle, which was as light now as in the day; but a pleasant obscurity reigned in the sheltered colonnade.

"I think this little bit of pre-Lutheran masonry is the best of all your possessions, Polly," the young man said, laughing. "By-and-by, when I come home from India a general, as I mean to do, Miss Marchmont, before I ask you to become Mrs. Arundel, I shall stroll up and down here in the still summer evenings smoking my cheroots. You will let me smoke out of doors, won't you, Polly? But suppose I should leave some of my limbs on the banks of the Sutlej, and come limping home to you with a wooden leg, would you have me then, Mary; or would you dismiss me with ignominy from your sweet presence, and shut the doors of your stony mansion upon myself and my calamities? I'm afraid, from your admiration of my gold epaulets and silk sash, that glory in the abstract would have very little attraction for you."

Mary Marchmont looked up at her lover with widely-opened and wondering eyes, and the clasp of her hand tightened a little upon his arm.

"There is nothing that could ever happen to you that would make me love you less *now*," she said, naïvely. "I dare say at first I liked you a little because you were handsome, and different to every one else I had ever seen. You were so very handsome, you know," she added, apologetically; "but it was not because of that *only* that I loved you; I loved you because papa told me you were good and generous, and his true friend when he was in cruel need of a friend. Yes, you were his friend at school, when your cousin, Martin Mostyn, and the other pupils sneered at him and ridiculed him. How can I ever forget that, Edward? How can I ever love you enough to repay you for that?" In the enthusiasm of her innocent devotion she lifted her pure young brow, and the soldier bent down and kissed that white throne of all virginal thoughts, as the lovers stood side by side, half in the moonlight, half in the shadow.

Olivia Marchmont came into the embrasure of the open window, and took her place there to watch them.

She came again to the torture. From the remotest end of the long banqueting-room she had seen the two figures glide out into the moonlight. She had seen them, and had gone on with her courteous speeches, and had repeated her formula of hospitality, with the fire in her heart devouring and consuming her. She came again, to watch and to listen, and to endure her self-imposed agonies; as mad and foolish in her fatal passion as some besotted wretch who should come willingly to the wheel upon which his limbs had been well-nigh broken, and supplicate for a renewal of the torture. She stood rigid and motionless in the shadow of the arched window, hiding herself, as she had hidden in the dark cavernous recess by the river; she stood and listened to all the childish babble of the lovers as they loitered up and down the vaulted cloister. How she despised them in the haughty superiority of an intellect which might have planned a revolution or saved a sinking state! What bitter scorn curled her lip as their foolish talk fell upon her ear! They talked like Florizel and Perdita, like Romeo and Juliet, like Paul and Virginia, and they talked a great deal of nonsense, no doubt; soft, harmonious foolishness, with little more meaning in it than there is in the cooing of doves, but tender and musical, and more than beautiful, to each other's ears. A tigress, famished and desolate, and but lately robbed of her whelps, would not be likely to listen very patiently to the communing of a pair of prosperous ring-doves. Olivia Marchmont listened with her brain on fire, and the spirit of a murderess raging in her breast. What was she that she should be patient? All the world was lost to her. She was thirty years of age, and she had never yet won the love of any human being. She was thirty years of age, and all the sublime world of affection was a dismal blank for her. From the outer darkness in which she stood she looked with wild and ignorant yearning into that bright region which her accursed foot had never trodden, and saw Mary Marchmont wandering hand in hand with the only man she could have loved, the only creature who had ever had the power to awake the instinct of womanhood in her soul.

She stood and waited until the clock in the quadrangle struck the first quarter after three: the moon was fading out, and the colder light of early morning glimmered in the eastern sky.

"I mustn't keep you out here any longer, Polly," Captain Arundel said, pausing near the window. "It's getting cold, my dear, and it's high time the mistress of Marchmont should retire to her stony bower. Good-night, and God bless you, my darling! I'll stop in the quadrangle and smoke a cheroot before I go to my room. Your step-mamma will be wondering what has become of you, Mary, and we shall have a lecture upon the proprieties to-morrow; so, once more, good-night."

He kissed the fair young brow under the coronal of pearls, stopped to watch Mary while she crossed the threshold of the open window, and then strolled away into the flagged court with his cigar-case in his hand.

Olivia Marchmont stood a few paces from the window when her step-daughter entered the room, and Mary paused involuntarily, terrified by the cruel aspect of the face that frowned upon her: terrified by something that she had never seen before—the horrible darkness that overshadows the souls of the lost.

"Mamma!" the girl cried, clasping her hands in sudden affright, "mamma! why do you look at me like that? Why have you been so changed to me lately? I can not tell you how unhappy I have been. Mamma, mamma, what have I done to offend you?"

Olivia Marchmont grasped the trembling hands uplifted entreatingly to her and held them in her own—held them as if in a vice. She stood thus, with her step-daughter pinioned in her grasp, and her eyes fixed upon the girl's face. Two streams of lurid light seemed to emanate from those dilated gray eyes; two spots of crimson blazed in the widow's hollow cheeks.

"*What* have you done?" she cried. "Do you think I have toiled for nothing to do the duty which I promised my dead husband to perform for your sake? Has all my care of you been so little, that I am to stand by now and be silent, when I see what you are? Do you think that I am blind, or deaf, or besotted, that you defy me and outrage me, day by day, and hour by hour, by your conduct?"

"Mamma, mamma, what do you mean?"

"Heaven knows how rigidly you have been educated; how carefully you have been secluded from all society, and sheltered from every influence, lest harm or danger should come to you. I have done my duty, and I wash my hands of you. The debasing taint of your mother's low breeding reveals itself in your every action. You run after my cousin Edward Arundel, and advertise your admiration of him to himself, and every creature who knows you. You fling yourself into his arms, and offer him yourself and your fortune; and in your low cunning try to keep the secret from me, your protectress and guardian, appointed by the dead father whom you pretend to have loved so dearly."

Olivia Marchmont still held her step-daughter's wrists in her iron grasp. The girl stared wildly at her with her eyes distended, her trembling lips apart. She began to think that the widow had gone mad.

"I blush for you, I am ashamed of you," cried Olivia. It seemed as if the torrent of her words burst forth almost in spite of herself. "There is not a village-girl in Kemberling, there is not a scullery-maid in this house, who would have behaved as you have done. I have watched you, Mary Marchmont, remember, and I know all. I know your wanderings down by the river-side. I heard you. Yes, by the Heaven above me, I heard you offer yourself to my cousin."

Mary drew herself up with an indignant gesture, and over the whiteness of her face there swept a sudden glow of vivid crimson that faded as quickly as it came. Her submissive nature revolted against her step-mother's horrible tyranny. The dignity of innocence arose and asserted itself against Olivia's shameful upbraiding.

"If I offered myself to Edward Arundel, mamma," she said, "it was because we love each other very truly, and because I think and believe papa wished me to marry his old friend."

"Because *we* love each other very truly!" Olivia echoed, in a tone of unmitigated scorn. "You can answer for Captain Arundel's heart, I suppose, then, as well as for your own? You must have a tolerably good opinion of yourself, Miss Marchmont, to be able to venture so much. Bah!" she cried, suddenly, with a disdainful gesture of her head; "do you think your pitiful face has won Edward Arundel? Do you think he has not had women fifty times your superior, in every quality of mind and body, at his feet out yonder in India? Are you idiotic and besotted enough to believe that it is any thing but your fortune this man cares for? Do you know the vile things people will do, the lies they will tell, the base comedies of guilt and falsehood they will act, for the love of eleven thousand a year? And you think that he loves you! Child, dupe, fool, are you weak enough to be deluded by a fortune-hunter's pretty pastoral flatteries? Are you weak enough to be duped by a man of the world, worn out and jaded, no doubt, as to the world's pleasures; in debt, perhaps, and in pressing need of money; who comes here to try and redeem his fortunes by a marriage with a semi-imbecile heiress?"

Olivia Marchmont released her hold of the shrinking girl, who seemed to have become transfixed to the spot upon which she stood, a pale statue of horror and despair.

The iron will of the strong and resolute woman rode rough-shod over the simple confidence of the ignorant girl. Until this moment Mary Marchmont had believed in Edward Arundel as implicitly as she had trusted in her dead father. But now, for the first time, a dreadful region of doubt opened before her; the foundations of her world reeled beneath her feet. Edward Arundel a fortune-hunter! This woman, whom she had obeyed for five weary years, and who had acquired that ascendency over her which a determined and vigorous nature must always exercise over a morbidly sensitive disposition, told her that she had been deluded. This woman laughed aloud in bitter scorn of her credulity. This woman, who could have no possible motive for torturing her, and who was known to be scrupulously conscientious in all her dealings, told her, as plainly as the most cruel words could tell a cruel truth, that her own charms could not have won Edward Arundel's affection.

All the beautiful day-dreams of her life melted away from her. She had never questioned herself as to her worthiness of her lover's devotion. She had accepted it as she accepted the sunshine and the starlight, as something beautiful and incomprehensible, that came to her by the beneficence of God, and not through any merits of her own. But as the fabric of her happiness dwindled away, the fatal spell exercised over the girl's weak nature by Olivia's violent words evoked a hundred doubts. How should he love her? why should he love her in preference to every other woman in the world? Set any woman to ask herself this question, and you fill her mind with a thousand suspicions, a thousand jealous doubts of her lover, though he were the truest and noblest in the universe.

Olivia Marchmont stood a few paces from her step-daughter, watching her while the black shadow of doubt blotted every joy from her heart, and utter despair crept slowly into her innocent breast. The widow expected that the girl's self-esteem would assert itself; that she would contradict and defy the traducer of her lover's truth; but it was not so. When Mary spoke again her voice was low and subdued, her manner as submissive as it had been two or three years before, when she had stood before her step-mother, waiting to repeat some difficult lesson.

"I dare say you are right, mamma," she said, in a low dreamy tone, looking, not at her step-mother, but straight before her into vacancy, as if her tearless eyes were transfixed by the vision of all her shattered hopes, filling with wreck and ruin the desolate fore-ground of a blank future. "I dare say you are right, mamma; it was very foolish of me to think that Edward—that Captain Arundel could care for me, for—for—my own sake; but if—if he wants my fortune, I should wish him to have it. The money will never be any good to me, you know, mamma; and he was so kind to papa in his poverty—so kind. I will never, never believe any thing against him; but I couldn't expect him to love me. I shouldn't have offered to be his wife. I ought only to have offered him my fortune."

She heard her lover's footstep in the quadrangle without, in the stillness of the summer morning, and shivered at the sound. It was less than a quarter of an hour since she had been walking with him up and down the cloistered way, in which his footsteps were echoing with a hollow sound; and now— Even in the confusion of her anguish Mary Marchmont could not help wondering, as she thought in how short a time the happiness of a future might be swept away into chaos.

"Good-night, mamma," she said, presently, with an accent of weariness. She did not look at her step-mother, who had turned away from her now, and had walked toward the open window, but stole quietly from the room, crossed the hall, and went up the broad staircase to her own lonely chamber. Heiress though she was, she had no special attendant of her own; she had the privilege of summoning Olivia's maid whenever she had need of assistance; but she retained the simple habits of her early life, and very rarely troubled Mrs. Marchmont's grim and elderly Abigail.

Olivia stood looking out into the stony quadrangle. It was broad daylight now; the cocks were crowing in the distance, and a sky-lark singing somewhere in the blue heaven, high up above Marchmont Towers. The faded garlands in the banqueting-room looked wan in the morning sunshine; the lamps were burning still, for the servants waited until Mrs. Marchmont should have retired before they entered the room. Edward Arundel was walking up and down the cloister, smoking his second cigar.

He stopped presently, seeing his cousin at the window.

"What, Livy," he cried, "not gone to bed yet?"

"No; I am going directly."

"Mary has gone, I hope?"

"Yes; she has gone. Good-night."

"Good-morning, my dear Mrs. Marchmont," the young man answered, laughing. "If the partridges were in I should be going out shooting this lovely morning, instead of going ignominiously to bed, like a worn-out reveler who has drunk too much sparkling hock. I like the still best, by-the-by—the Johannisberger, that poor John's predecessor imported from the Rhine. But I suppose there is no help for it, and I must go to bed in the face of all that eastern glory. I should be mounting for a gallop on the race-course if I were in Calcutta. But I'll go to bed, Mrs. Marchmont, and humbly await your breakfast-hour. They're stacking the new hay in the meadows beyond the park. Don't you smell it?"

Olivia shrugged her shoulders with an impatient frown. Good Heavens! how frivolous and senseless this man's talk seemed to her! She was plunging her soul into an abyss of sin and ruin for his sake; and she hated him, and rebelled against him, because he was so little worthy of the sacrifice.

"Good-morning," she said, abruptly. "I'm tired to death."

She moved away and left him.

Five minutes afterward he went up the great oak staircase after her, whistling a serenade from *Fra Diavolo* as he went. He was one of those people to whom life seems all holiday. Younger son though he was, he had never known any of the pitfalls of debt and difficulty into which the junior members of rich families are so apt to plunge headlong in early youth, and from which they emerge, enfeebled and crippled, to endure an after-life embittered by all the shabby miseries which wait upon aristocratic pauperism. Brave, honorable, and simple-minded, Edward Arundel had fought the battle of life like a good soldier, and had carried a stainless shield where the fight was thickest, and victory hard to win. His sunshiny nature won him friends, and his better qualities kept them. Young men trusted and respected him, and old men, gray in the service of their country, spoke well of him. His handsome face was a pleasant decoration at any festival; his kindly voice and hearty laugh at a dinner-table were as good as the music in the gallery at the end of a banqueting-chamber.

He had that freshness of spirit which is the peculiar gift of some natures; and he had as yet never known sorrow, except, indeed, such tender and compassionate sympathy as he had often felt for the calamities of others.

Olivia Marchmont heard her cousin's cheery tenor voice as he passed her chamber. "How happy he is!" she thought. "His very happiness is one insult the more to me."

The widow paced up and down her room in the morning sunshine, thinking of the things she had said in the banqueting-hall below, and of her step-daughter's white despairing face. What had she done? What was the extent of the sin she had committed? Olivia Marchmont asked herself these two questions. The old habit of self-examination was not quite abandoned yet. She sinned, and then set herself to work to try and justify her sin. "How should he love her!" she thought. "What is there in her pale, unmeaning face that should win the love of a man who despises me?"

She stopped before a cheval-glass, and surveyed herself from head to foot, frowning angrily at her handsome image, hating herself for her despised beauty. Her white shoulders looked like stainless marble against the rich ruby darkness of her velvet dress. She had snatched the diamond ornaments from her head, and her long black hair fell about her bosom in thick waveless tresses.

"I am handsomer than she is, and cleverer; and I love him better, ten thousand times, than she loves him," Olivia Marchmont thought, as she turned contemptuously from the glass. "Is it likely, then, that he cares for any thing but her fortune? Any other woman in the world would have argued as I argued to-night. Any woman would have believed that she did her duty in warning this besotted girl against her folly. What do I know of Edward Arundel that should lead me to think him better or nobler than other men? and how many men sell themselves for the love of a woman's wealth! Perhaps good may come of my mad folly, after all; and I may have saved this girl from a life of misery by the words I have spoken to-night."

The devils—forever lying in wait for this woman, whose gloomy pride rendered her in some manner akin to themselves—may have laughed at her as she argued thus with herself.

She lay down at last to sleep, worn out by the excitement of the long night, and to dream horrible dreams. The servants, with the exception of one who rose betimes to open the great house, slept long after the unwonted festival. Edward Arundel slumbered as heavily as any member of that wearied household; and thus it was that there was no one in the way to see a shrinking, trembling figure creep down the sunlit staircase, and steal across the threshold of the wide hall-door.

There was no one to see Mary Marchmont's silent flight from the gaunt Lincolnshire mansion, in which she had known so little real happiness. There was no one to comfort the sorrow-stricken girl in her despair and desolation of spirit. She crept away, like some escaped prisoner, in the early morning, from the house which the law called her own.

And the hand of the woman whom John Marchmont had chosen to be his daughter's friend and counselor was the hand which drove that daughter from the shelter of her home. The voice of her whom the weak father had trusted in, fearful to confide his child into the hands of God, but blindly confident in his own judgment, was the voice which had uttered the lying words, whose every syllable had been as a separate dagger thrust in the orphan girl's lacerated heart. It was her father—her father who had placed this woman over her, and had entailed upon her the awful agony that drove her out into an unknown world, careless whither she went in her despair.

———◆———

## CHAPTER XV.

### MARY'S LETTER.

It was past twelve o'clock when Edward Arundel strolled into the dining-room. The windows were open, and the scent of the mignonette upon the terrace was blown in upon the warm summer breeze.

Mrs. Marchmont was sitting at one end of the long table, reading a newspaper. She looked up as Edward entered the room. She was pale, but not much paler than usual. The feverish light had faded out of her eyes, and they looked dim and heavy.

"Good-morning, Livy," the young man said. "Mary is not up yet, I suppose?"

"I believe not."

"Poor little girl! A long rest will do her good after her first ball. How pretty and fairy-like she looked in her white gauze dress, and with that circlet of pearls round her soft brown hair! Your taste, I suppose, Olivia? She looked like a snow-drop among all the other gaudy flowers—the roses and tiger-lilies, and peonies and dahlias. That eldest Miss Hickman is handsome, but she's so terribly conscious of her attractions. That little girl from Swampington with the black ringlets is rather pretty, and Laura Filmer is a jolly, dashing girl; she looks you full in the face, and talks to you about hunting with as much gusto as an old whipper-in. I don't think much of Major Hawley's three tall, sandy-haired daughters; but Fred Hawley's a capital fellow; it's a pity he's a civilian. In short, my dear Olivia, take it altogether, I think your ball was a success, and I hope you'll give us another in the hunting-season."

Mrs. Marchmont did not condescend to reply to her cousin's meaningless rattle. She sighed wearily, and began to fill the tea-pot from the old-fashioned silver urn. Edward loitered in one of the windows, whistling to a peacock that was stalking solemnly backward and forward upon the stone balustrade.

"I should like to drive you and Mary down to the sea-shore, Livy, after breakfast. Will you go?"

Mrs. Marchmont shook her head.

"I am a great deal too tired to think of going out to-day," she said, ungraciously.

"And I never felt fresher in my life," the young man responded, laughing; "last night's festivities seem to have revivified me.. I wish Mary would come down," he added, with a yawn; "I could give her another lesson in billiards, at any rate. Poor little girl, I am afraid she'll never make a cannon."

Captain Arundel sat down to his breakfast, and drank the cup of tea poured out for him by Olivia. Had she been a sinful woman of another type, she would have put arsenic into the cup perhaps, and so have made an end of the young officer and of her own folly. As it was, she only sat by, with her own untasted breakfast before her, and watched him while he ate a plateful of raised pie, and drank his cup of tea, with the healthy appetite which generally accompanies youth and a good conscience. He sprang up from the table directly he had finished his meal, and cried out, impatiently,

"What can make Mary so lazy this morning? she is usually such an early riser."

Mrs. Marchmont rose as her cousin said this, and a vague feeling of uneasiness took possession of her mind. She remembered the white face which had blanched beneath the angry glare of her eyes, the blank look of despair that had come over Mary's countenance a few hours before.

"I will go and call her myself," she said. "N—no; I'll send Barbara." She did not wait to ring the bell, but went into the hall and called sharply, "Barbara! Barbara!"

A woman came out of a passage leading to the housekeeper's room, in answer to Mrs. Marchmont's call; a woman of about fifty years of age, dressed in gray stuff, and with a grave inscrutable face, a wooden countenance that gave no token of its owner's character. Barbara Simmons might have been the best or the worst of women, a Mrs. Fry or a Mrs. Brownrigg, for any evidence her face afforded against either hypothesis.

"I want you to go up stairs, Barbara, and call Miss Marchmont," Olivia said. "Captain Arundel and I have finished breakfast."

The woman obeyed, and Mrs. Marchmont returned to the dining-room, where Edward was trying to amuse himself with the Times of the previous day.

Ten minutes afterward Barbara Simmons came into the room carrying a letter on a silver waiter. Had the document been a death-warrant, or a telegraphic announcement of the landing of the French at Dover, the well-trained servant would have placed it upon a salver before presenting it to her mistress.

"Miss Marchmont is not in her room, ma'am," she said; "the bed has not been slept on; and I found this letter, addressed to Captain Arundel, upon the table."

Olivia's face grew livid; a horrible dread rushed into her mind. Edward snatched the letter which the servant held toward him.

"Mary not in her room! What, in Heaven's name, can it mean?" he cried.

He tore open the letter. The writing was not easily decipherable for the tears which the orphan girl had shed over it:

"MY OWN DEAR EDWARD,—I have loved you so dearly and so foolishly, and you have been so kind to me, that I have quite forgotten how unworthy I am of your affection. But I am forgetful no longer. Something has happened which has opened my eyes to my own folly—I know now that you did not love me; that I had no claim to your love; no charms or attractions such as so many other women possess, and for which you might have loved me. I know this now, dear Edward, and that all my happiness has been a foolish dream; but do not think that I blame any but myself for what has happened. Take my fortune: long ago, when I was a little girl, I asked my father to let me share it with you. I ask you now to take it all, dear friend; and I go away forever from a house in which I have learnt how little happiness riches can give. Do not be unhappy about me. I shall pray for you always—always remembering your goodness to my dead father; always looking back to the day upon which you came to see us in our poor lodging. I am very ignorant of all worldly business, but I hope the law will let me give you Marchmont Towers and all my fortune, whatever it may be. Let Mr. Paulette see this latter part of my letter, and let him fully understand that I abandon all my rights to you from this day. Good-by, dear friend; think of me sometimes, but never think of me sorrowfully.

"MARY MARCHMONT."

This was all. This was the letter which the heart-broken girl had written to her lover. It was in no manner different from the letter she might have written to him nine years before in Oakley Street. It was as childish in its ignorance and inexperience; as womanly in its tender self-abnegation.

Edward Arundel stared at the simple lines like a man in a dream, doubtful of his own identity, doubtful of the reality of the world about him, in his hopeless wonderment. He read the letter line by line again and again, first in dull stupefaction and muttering the words mechanically as he read them, with the full light of their meaning dawning gradually upon him.

Her fortune! He had never loved her! She had discovered her own folly! What did it all mean? What was the clew to the mystery of this letter, which had stunned and bewildered him, until the very power of reflection seemed lost? The dawning of that day had seen their parting, and the innocent face had been lifted to his, beaming with love and trust. And now—? The letter dropped from his hand, and fluttered slowly to the ground. Olivia Marchmont stooped to pick it up. Her movement aroused the young man from his stupor, and in that moment he caught the sight of his cousin's livid face.

He started as if a thunder-bolt had burst at his feet. An idea, sudden as some inspired revelation, rushed into his mind.

"Read that letter, Olivia Marchmont!" he said.

The woman obeyed. Slowly and deliberately she read the childish epistle which Mary had written to her lover. In every line, in every word, the widow saw the effect of her own deadly work; she saw how deeply the poison, dropped from her own envenomed tongue, had sunk into the innocent heart of the girl.

Edward Arundel watched her with flaming eyes. His tall soldierly frame trembled in the intensity of his passion. He followed his cousin's eyes along the lines in Mary Marchmont's letter, waiting till she should come to the end. Then the tumultuous storm of indignation burst forth, until Olivia cowered beneath the lightning of her cousin's glance.

Was this the man she had called frivolous? Was this the boyish, red-coated dandy she had despised? Was this the curled and perfumed representative of swelldom, whose talk never soared to higher flights than the description of a day's snipe-shooting, or a run with the Burleigh fox-hounds? The wicked woman's eyelids drooped over her averted eyes; she turned away, shrinking from this fearless accuser.

"This mischief is some of *your* work, Olivia Marchmont!" Edward Arundel cried. "It is you who have slandered and traduced me to my dead friend's daughter! Who else would dare accuse a Dangerfield Arundel of baseness? who else would be vile enough to call my father's son a liar and a traitor? It is you who have whispered shameful insinuations into this poor child's innocent ear! I scarcely need the confirmation of your ghastly face to tell me this. It is you who have driven Mary Marchmont from the home in which you should have sheltered and protected her! You envied her, I suppose—envied her the thousands which might have ministered to your wicked pride and ambition; the pride which has always held you aloof from those who might have loved you; the ambition that has made you a soured and discontented woman, whose gloomy face repels all natural affection. You envied the gentle girl whom your dead husband committed to your care, and who should have been most sacred to you. You envied her, and seized the first occasion upon which you might stab her to the very core of her tender heart. What other motive could you have had for doing this deadly wrong? None, so help me Heaven!"

No other motive! Olivia Marchmont dropped down in a heap on the ground near her cousin's feet; not kneeling, but groveling upon the carpeted floor, with her hands twisted one in the other, and writhing convulsively, and with her head falling forward on her breast. She uttered no syllable of self-justification or denial. The pitiless words rained down upon her provoked no reply. But in the depths of her heart sounded the echo of Edward Arundel's words: "The pride which has always held you aloof from those who might have loved you; . . . a discontented woman, whose gloomy face repels all natural affection."

"O God!" she thought, "he *might* have loved me, then! He might have loved me, if I could have locked my anguish in my own heart, and smiled at him and flattered him!"

And then an icy indifference took possession of her. What did it matter that Edward Arundel repudiated and hated her? He had never loved her. His careless friendliness had made as wide a gulf between them as his bitterest hate could ever make. Perhaps, indeed, his new-born hate would be nearer to love than

his indifference had been, for at least he would think of her now, if he thought ever. so bitterly.

"Listen to me, Olivia Marchmont, the young man said, while the woman still crouched upon the ground near his feet, self-confessed in the abandonment of her despair. "Wherever this girl may have gone, driven hence by your wickedness, I will follow her. My answer to the lie you have insinuated against me shall be my immediate marriage with my old friend's orphan child. *He* knew me well enough to know how far I was above the baseness of a fortune-hunter, and he wished that I should be his daughter's husband. I should be a coward and a fool were I to be for one moment influenced by such a slander as that which you have whispered in Mary Marchmont's ear. It is not the individual only whom you traduce. You slander the cloth I wear, the family to which I belong; and my best justification will be the contempt in which I hold your infamous insinuations. When you hear that I have squandered Mary Marchmont's fortune, or cheated the children I pray God she may live to bear me, it will be time enough for you to tell the world that your kinsman, Edward Dangerfield Arundel, is a swindler and a traitor."

He strode out into the hall, leaving his cousin on the ground; and she heard his voice outside the dining-room door making inquiries of the servants.

They could tell him nothing of Mary's flight. Her bed had not been slept in; nobody had seen her leave the house; it was most likely, therefore, that she had stolen away very early, before the servants were astir.

Where had she gone? Edward Arundel's heart beat wildly as he asked himself that question. He remembered how often he had heard of women, as young and innocent as Mary Marchmont, who had rushed to destroy themselves in a tumult of agony and despair. How easily this poor child, who believed that the dream of happiness was forever broken, might have crept down through the gloomy wood to the edge of the sluggish river to drop into the weedy stream and hide her sorrow under the quiet water! He could fancy her, a new Ophelia, pale and pure as the Danish prince's slighted love, floating past the weird branches of the willows, borne up for a while by the current, to sink in silence among the shadows farther down the stream.

He thought of these things in one moment, and in the next dismissed the thought. Mary's letter breathed the spirit of gentle resignation rather than of wild despair. "I shall always pray for you; I shall always remember you," she had written. Her lover remembered how much sorrow the orphan girl had endured in her brief life. He looked back to her childish days of poverty and self-denial; her early loss of her mother; her grief at her father's second marriage; the shock of that beloved father's death. Her sorrows had followed each other in gloomy succession, with only narrow intervals of peace between each new agony. She was accustomed, therefore, to grief. It is the soul untutored by affliction, the rebellious heart that has never known calamity, which becomes mad and desperate, and breaks under the first blow. Mary

Marchmont had learned the habit of endurance in the hard school of sorrow. *

Edward Arundel walked out upon the terrace, and re-read the missing girl's letter. He was calmer now, and able to face the situation with all its difficulties and perplexities. He was losing time, perhaps, in stopping to deliberate; but it was no use to rush off in reckless haste, undetermined in which direction he should seek for the lost mistress of Marchmont Towers. One of the grooms was busy in the stables saddling Captain Arundel's horse, and in the mean time the young man went out alone upon the sunny terrace to deliberate upon Mary's letter.

Complete resignation was expressed in every line of that childish epistle. The heiress spoke most decisively as to her abandonment of her fortune and her home. It was clear, then, that she meant to leave Lincolnshire; for she would know that immediate steps would be taken to discover her hiding-place, and bring her back to Marchmont Towers.

Where was she likely to go in her inexperience of the outer world? where but to those humble relations of her dead mother's, of whom her father had spoken in his letter to Edward Arundel, and with whom the young man knew she had kept up an occasional correspondence, sending them many little gifts out of her pocket-money. These people were small tenant-farmers at a place called Marlingford, in Berkshire. Edward knew their name and the name of the farm.

"I'll make inquiries at the Kemberling station to begin with," he thought. "There's a through train from the north that stops at Kemberling at a little before six. My poor darling may have easily caught that, if she left the house at five."

Captain Arundel went back into the hall and summoned Barbara Simmons. The woman replied with rather a sulky air to his numerous questions; but she told him that Miss Marchmont had left her ball dress upon the bed, and had put on a gray cashmere dress trimmed with black ribbon, which she had worn as half-mourning for her father; a black straw bonnet, with a crape veil, and a silk mantle trimmed with crape. She had taken with her a small carpet-bag, some linen—for the linen drawer of her wardrobe was open, and the things scattered confusedly about—and the little morocco case in which she kept her pearl ornaments, and the diamond ring left her by her father.

"Had she any money?" Edward asked.

"Yes, Sir; she was never without money. She spent a good deal among the poor people she visited with my mistress; but I dare say she may have had between ten and twenty pounds in her purse."

"She will go to Berkshire," Edward Arundel thought: "the idea of going to her humble friends would be the first to present itself to her mind. She will go to her dead mother's sister, and give her all her jewels, and ask for shelter in the quiet farm-house. She will act like one of the heroines in the old-fashioned novels she used to read in Oakley Street, the simple-minded damsels of those innocent story-books, who think nothing of resigning a castle and a coronet, and going out into the world to work for their daily bread in a white satin gown, and

E

with a string of pearls to bind their disheveled locks."

Captain Arundel's horse was brought round to the terrace-steps, as he stood with Mary's letter in his hand, waiting to rush away to the rescue of his sorrowful love.

"Tell Mrs. Marchmont that I shall not return to the Towers till I bring her step-daughter with me," he said to the groom; and then, without stopping to utter another word, he shook the rein on his horse's neck, and galloped away along the graveled drive leading to the great iron gates of Marchmont Towers.

Olivia heard his message, which had been spoken in a clear loud voice, like some knightly defiance, sounding trumpet-like at a castle-gate. She stood in one of the windows of the dining-room, hidden by the faded velvet curtain, and watched her cousin ride away, brave and handsome as any knight-errant of the chivalrous past, and as true as Bayard himself.

———◆———

## CHAPTER XVI.

### A NEW PROTECTOR.

CAPTAIN ARUNDEL's inquiries at the Kemberling station resulted in an immediate success. A young lady—a young woman the railway official called her—dressed in black, wearing a crape veil over her face, and carrying a small carpet-bag in her hand, had taken a second-class ticket for London by the 5.50, a parliamentary train, which stopped at almost every station on the line, and reached Euston Square at half past twelve.

Edward looked at his watch. It was ten minutes to two o'clock. The express did not stop at Kemberling; but he would be able to catch it at Swampington at a quarter past three. Even then, however, he could scarcely hope to get to Berkshire that night.

"My darling girl will not discover how foolish her doubts have been until to-morrow," he thought. "Silly child! has my love so little the aspect of truth that she can doubt me?"

He sprang on his horse again, flung a shilling to the railway porter who had held the bridle, and rode away along the Swampington road. The clocks in the gray old Norman turrets were striking three as the young man crossed the bridge, and paid his toll at the little toll-house by the stone archway.

The streets were as lonely as usual in the hot July afternoon; and the long line of sea beyond the dreary marshes was blue in the sunshine. Captain Arundel passed the two churches, and the low-roofed rectory, and rode away to the outskirts of the town, where the station glared in all the brilliancy of new red bricks, and dazzling stuccoed chimneys, athwart a desert of waste ground.

The express train came tearing up to the quiet platform two minutes after Edward had taken his ticket; and in another minute the clanging bell pealed out its discordant signal, and the young man was borne, with a shriek and a whistle, away upon the first stage of his search for Mary Marchmont.

It was nearly seven o'clock when he reached Euston Square; and he only got to the Paddington station in time to hear that the last train for Marlingford had just started. There was no possibility of his reaching the little Berkshire village that night. No mail train stopped within a reasonable distance of the obscure station. There was no help for it therefore. Captain Arundel had nothing to do but to wait for the next morning.

He walked slowly away from the station, very much disheartened by this discovery.

"I'd better sleep at some hotel up this way," he thought, as he strolled listlessly in the direction of Oxford Street, "so as to be on the spot to catch the first train to-morrow morning. What am I to do with myself all this night, racked with uncertainty about Mary?"

He remembered that one of his brother officers was staying at the hotel in Covent Garden where Edward himself stopped, when business detained him in London for a day or two.

"Shall I go and see Lucas?" Captain Arundel thought. "He's a good fellow, and won't bore me with a lot of questions, if he sees I've something on my mind. There may be some letters for me at E——'s. Poor little Polly!"

He could never think of her without something of that pitiful tenderness which he might have felt for a young and helpless child, whom it was his duty and privilege to protect and succor. It may be that there was little of the lover's fiery enthusiasm mingled with the purer and more tender feelings with which Edward Arundel regarded his dead friend's orphan daughter; but in place of this there was a chivalrous devotion, such as woman rarely wins in these degenerate modern days.

The young soldier walked through the lamp-lit western streets thinking of the missing girl, now assuring himself that his instinct had not deceived him, and that Mary must have gone straight to the Berkshire farmer's house, and in the next moment seized with a sudden terror that it might be otherwise: the helpless girl might have gone out into a world of which she was as ignorant as a child, determined to hide herself from all who had ever known her. If it should be thus: if, on going down to Marlingford, he obtained no tidings of his friend's daughter; what was he to do; where was he to look for her next?

He would put advertisements in the papers, calling upon his betrothed to trust him and return to him. Perhaps Mary Marchmont was of all people in this world the least likely to look into a newspaper; but at least it would be doing something to do this, and Edward Arundel determined upon going straight off to Printing-House Square to draw up an appeal to the missing girl.

It was past ten o'clock when Captain Arundel came to this determination, and he had reached the neighborhood of Covent Garden and of the theatres. The staring play-bills adorned almost every threshold, and fluttered against every door-post; and the young soldier, going into a tobacconist's to fill his cigar-case, stared abstractedly at a gaudy blue-and-red announcement of the last dramatic attraction to be seen at Drury Lane. It was scarcely strange that the Captain's thoughts wandered back to his boyhood, that shadowy time, far away behind his later days of Indian warfare and glory, and

that he remembered the December night upon which he had sat with his cousin in a box at the great patent theatre, watching the consumptive supernumerary struggling under the weight of his banner. From the box at Drury Lane to the next morning's breakfast in Oakley Street was but a natural transition of thought; but with that recollection of the humble Lambeth lodging, with the picture of a little girl in a pinafore sitting demurely at her father's table, and meekly waiting on his guest, an idea flashed across Edward Arundel's mind, and brought the hot blood into his face.

What if Mary had gone to Oakley Street? Was not this even more likely than that she should seek refuge with her kinsfolk in Berkshire? She had lived in the Lambeth lodging for years, and had only left that plebeian shelter for the grandeur of Marchmont Towers. What more natural than that she should go back to the familiar habitation, dear to her by reason of a thousand associations with her dead father? What more likely than that she should turn instinctively, in the hour of her desolation, to the humble friends whom she had known in her childhood?

Edward Arundel was almost too impatient to wait while the smart young damsel behind the tobacconist's counter handed him change for the half sovereign which he had just tendered her. He darted out into the street, and shouted violently to the driver of a passing hansom—there are always loitering hansoms in the neighborhood of Covent Garden—who was, after the manner of his kind, looking on any side rather than that upon which Providence had sent him a fare.

"Oakley Street, Lambeth," the young man cried. "Double fare if you get there in ten minutes."

The tall, raw-boned horse rattled off at that peculiar pace common to his species, making as much noise upon the pavement as if he had been winning a metropolitan Derby, and at about twenty minutes past nine drew up, smoking and panting, before the dimly-lighted window of the Ladies' Wardrobe, where a couple of flaring tallow-candles illuminated the splendor of a fore-ground of dirty artificial flowers, frayed satin shoes, and tarnished gilt combs; a middle distance of blue gauzy tissue, embroidered with beetles' wings; and a back-ground of greasy black satin. Edward Arundel flung back the doors of the hansom with a bang, and leaped out upon the pavement. The proprietress of the Ladies' Wardrobe was lolling against the door-post, refreshing herself with the soft evening breezes from the roads of Westminster and Waterloo, and talking to a neighbor.

"Bless her pore innercent 'art!" the woman was saying; "she's cried herself to sleep at last. But you never heard any think so pitiful as she talked to me at fust, sweet love! and the very picture of my own poor Eliza Jane, as she looked. You might have said it was Eliza Jane come back to life, only paler and more sickly like, and not that beautiful fresh color, and ringlets curled all round in a crop, as Eliza Ja—"

Edward Arundel burst in upon the good woman's talk, which rambled on in an unintermitting stream, unbroken by much punctuation.

"Miss Marchmont is here," he said; "I know

she is. Thank God, thank God! Let me see her, please, directly. I am Captain Arundel, her father's friend, and her affianced husband. You remember me, perhaps? I came here nine years ago to breakfast, one December morning. I can recollect you perfectly, and I know that you were always good to my poor friend's daughter. To think that I should find her here! You shall be well rewarded for your kindness to her. But take me to her; pray take me to her at once!"

The proprietress of the wardrobe snatched up one of the candles that guttered in a brass flat-candlestick upon the counter, and led the way up the narrow staircase. She was a good lazy creature, and she was so completely borne down by Edward's excitement, that she could only mutter disjointed sentences, to the effect that the gentleman had brought her heart into her mouth, and that her legs felt all of a jelly, and that her poor knees was a'most giving way under her, and other incoherent statements concerning the physical effect of the mental shocks she had that day received.

She opened the door of that shabby sitting-room upon the first-floor, in which the crippled eagle brooded over the convex mirror, and stood aside upon the threshold while Captain Arundel entered the room. A tallow-candle was burning dimly upon the table, and a girlish form lay upon the narrow horse-hair sofa, shrouded by a woolen shawl.

"She went to sleep about half an hour ago, Sir," the woman said; "and she cried herself to sleep, pore lamb, I think. I made her some tea, and got her a few creases and a French roll, with a bit of best fresh; but she wouldn't touch nothin', or only a few spoonfuls of the tea, just to please me. What is it that's drove her away from her 'ome, Sir, and such a good 'ome, too? She showed me a diamond ring as her pore par give her in his will. He left me twenty pound, pore gentleman—which he always acted like a gentleman bred and born; and Mr. Pollit, the lawyer, sent his clerk along with it and his compliments—though I'm sure I never looked for nothink, havin' always had my rent faithful to the very minute; and Miss Mary used to bring it down to me so pretty, and—"

But the whispering had grown louder by this time, and Mary Marchmont awoke from her feverish sleep, and lifted her weary head from the hard horse-hair pillow and looked about her, half forgetful of where she was, and of what had happened within the last eighteen hours of her life. The soft brown eyes wandered here and there, doubtful as to the reality of what they looked upon, until the girl saw her lover's figure, tall and splendid in the humble apartment, a tender half-reproachful smile upon his face, and his handsome blue eyes beaming with love and truth. She saw him, and a faint shriek broke from her tremulous lips as she tottered a few paces forward and fell upon his breast.

"You love me, then, Edward," she cried; "you do love me!"

"Yes, my darling, as truly and tenderly as ever woman was loved upon this earth."

And then the soldier sat down upon the hard bristly sofa, and with Mary's head still resting upon his breast, and his strong hand straying among her disordered hair, he reproached her for her foolishness, and comforted and soothed her; while the proprietress of the apartment stood, with the brass candlestick in her hand, watching the young lovers and weeping over their sorrows, as if she had been witnessing a scene in a play. Their innocent affection was unrestrained by the good woman's presence; and when Mary had smiled upon her lover, and assured him that she would never, never, never doubt him again, Captain Arundel was fain to kiss the soft-hearted landlady in his enthusiasm, and to promise her the handsomest silk dress that had ever been seen in Oakley Street, among all the faded splendors of silk and satin that ladies'-maids brought for her consideration.

"And now, my darling, my foolish runaway Polly, what is to be done with you?" asked the young soldier. "Will you go back to the Towers to-morrow morning?"

Mary Marchmont clasped her hands before her face, and began to tremble violently.

"Oh no, no, no!" she cried; "don't ask me to go back, Edward. I can never go back to that house again, while—"

She stopped suddenly, looking piteously at her lover.

"While my cousin Olivia Marchmont lives there," Captain Arundel said, with an angry frown. "God knows it's a bitter thing for me to think that your troubles should come from any of my kith and kin, Polly. She has used you very badly, then, this woman? She has been very unkind to you?"

"No, no! never before last night. It seems so long ago; but it was only last night, was it? Until then she was always kind to me. I didn't love her, you know, though I tried to do so for papa's sake, and out of gratitude to her for taking such trouble with my education; but one can be grateful to people without loving them, and I never grew to love her. But last night—last night she said such cruel things to me—such cruel things. O Edward, Edward!" the girl cried, suddenly, clasping her hands and looking imploringly at Captain Arundel, "were the cruel things she said true? Did I do wrong when I offered to be your wife?"

How could the young man answer this question except by clasping his betrothed to his heart? So there was another little love-scene, over which Mrs. Pimpernel—the proprietress's name was Pimpernel—wept fresh tears, murmuring that the Capting was the sweetest young man, sweeter than Mr. Macready in Claude Melnock; and that the scene altogether reminded her of that "cutting" episode where the proud mother went on against the pore young man, and Miss Faucit came out so beautiful. They are a play-going population in Oakley Street, and compassionate and sentimental like all true play-goers.

"What shall I do with you, Miss Marchmont?" Edward Arundel asked, gayly, when the little love-scene was concluded. "My mother and sister are away, at a German watering-place, trying some unpronounceable Spa for the benefit of poor Letty's health. Reginald is with them, and my father's alone at Dangerfield. So I can't take you down there, as I might have done if my mother had been at home; I don't much care for the Mostyns, or you might have stopped in Montague Square.

There are no friendly friars nowadays who will marry Romeo and Juliet at half-an-hour's notice. You must live a fortnight somewhere, Polly: where shall it be?"

"Oh, let me stay here, please," Miss Marchmont pleaded; "I was always so happy here!"

"Lord love her precious heart!" exclaimed Mrs. Pimpernel, lifting up her hands in a rapture of admiration. "To think as she shouldn't have a bit of pride, after all the money her pore par come into!. To think as she should wish to stay in her old lodgin's, where every think shall be done to make her comfortable; and the air back and front is very 'ealthy though you might not believe it, and the Blind School and Bedlam hard by, and Kennington Common only a pleasant walk, and beautiful and open this warm summer weather."

"Yes, I should like to stop here, please," Mary murmured. Even in the midst of her agitation, overwhelmed as she was by the emotions of the present, her thoughts went back to the past, and she remembered how delightful it would be to go and see the accommodating butcher, and the green-grocer's daughter, the kind butterman who had called her "little lady," and the disreputable gray parrot. How delightful it would be to see these humble friends, now that she was grown up, and had money wherewith to make them presents in token of her gratitude!

"Very well, then, Polly," Captain Arundel said, "you'll stay here. And Mrs.—"

"Pimpernel," the landlady suggested.

"Mrs. Pimpernel will take as good care of you as if you were Queen of England, and the welfare of the nation depended upon your safety. And I'll stop at my hotel in Covent Garden; and I'll see Richard Paulette—he's my lawyer as well as yours, you know, Polly—and tell him something of what has happened, and make arrangements for our immediate marriage."

"Our marriage!"

Mary Marchmont echoed her lover's last words, and looked up at him almost with a bewildered air. She had never thought of an early marriage with Edward Arundel as the result of her flight from Lincolnshire. She had a vague notion that she would live in Oakley Street for years, and that in some remote time the soldier would come to claim her.

"Yes, Polly darling; Olivia Marchmont's conduct has made me decide upon a very bold step. It is evident to me that my cousin hates you; for what reason, Heaven only knows, since you can have done nothing to provoke her hate. When your father was a poor man, it was to me he would have confided you. He changed his mind afterward, very naturally, and chose another guardian for his orphan child. If my cousin had fulfilled this trust, Mary, I would have deferred to her authority, and would have held myself aloof until your minority was passed, rather than ask you to marry me without your step-mother's consent. But Olivia Marchmont has forfeited her right to be consulted in this matter. She has tortured you and traduced me by her poisonous slander. If you believe in me, Mary, you will consent to be my wife. My justification lies in the future. You will not find that I shall sponge upon your fortune, my dear, or lead an idle life because my wife is a rich woman."

Mary Marchmont looked up with shy tenderness at her lover.

"I would rather the fortune were yours than mine, Edward," she said. "I will do whatever you wish; I will be guided by you in every thing."

It was thus that John Marchmont's daughter consented to become the wife of the man she loved, the man whose image she had associated since her childhood with all that was good and beautiful in mankind. She knew none of those pretty stereotyped phrases by means of which well-bred young ladies can go through a graceful fencing-match of hesitation and equivocation to the anguish of a doubtful and adoring suitor. She had no notion of that delusive negative, that bewitching feminine "no," which is proverbially understood to mean "yes." Weary courses of Roman Emperors, South Sea Islands, Sidereal Heavens, Tertiary and Old Red Sandstone, had very ill-prepared this poor little girl for the stern realities of life.

"I will be guided by you, dear Edward," she said; "my father wished me to be your wife, and if I did not love you, it would please me to obey him."

It was eleven o'clock when Captain Arundel left Oakley Street. The hansom had been waiting all the time, and the driver, seeing that his fare was young, handsome, dashing, and what he called "milingtary-like," demanded an enormous sum when he landed the young soldier before the portico of the hotel in Covent Garden.

Edward took a hasty breakfast the next morning, and then hurried off to Lincoln's-Inn Fields. But here a disappointment awaited him. Richard Paulette had started for Scotland upon a piscatorial excursion. The elder Paulette lived in the south of France, and kept his name in the business as a fiction, by means of which elderly and obstinate country clients were deluded into the belief that the solicitor who conducted their affairs was the same legal practitioner who had done business for their fathers and grandfathers before them. Mathewson, a grim man, was away among the Yorkshire wolds, superintending the foreclosure of certain mortgages upon a bankrupt baronet's estate. It was not likely that Captain Arundel could sit down and pour his secrets into the bosom of a clerk, however trust-worthy and confidential a personage that employé might be.

The young man's desire had been that his marriage with Mary Marchmont should take place at least with the knowledge and approbation of her dead father's lawyer; but he was impatient to assume the only title by which he might have a right to be the orphan girl's champion and protector; and he had therefore no inclination to wait until the long vacation was over, and Messrs. Paulette and Mathewson returned from their northern wanderings. Again, Mary Marchmont suffered from a continual dread that her step-mother would discover the secret of her humble retreat, and would follow her and reassume authority over her.

"Let me be your wife before I see her again, Edward," the girl pleaded, innocently, when this terror was uppermost in her mind. "She could not say cruel things to me if I were your wife. I know it is wicked to be so frightened of her, because she was always good to me until that night; but I can not tell you how I tremble at the thought of being alone with her at Marchmont Towers. I dream sometimes that I am with her in the gloomy old house, and that we two are all alone there, even the servants all gone, and you far away in India, Edward—at the other end of the world."

It was as much as her lover could do to soothe and reassure the trembling girl when these thoughts took possession of her. Had he been less sanguine and impetuous, less careless in the buoyancy of his spirits, Captain Arundel might have seen that Mary's nerves had been terribly shaken by the scene between her and Olivia, and all the anguish which had given rise to her flight from Marchmont Towers. The girl trembled at every sound—the shutting of a door, the noise of a cab stopping in the street below, the falling of a book from the table to the floor, startled her almost as much as if a gunpowder-magazine had exploded in the neighborhood. The tears rose to her eyes at the slightest emotion. Her mind was tortured by vague fears, which she tried in vain to explain to her lover. Her sleep was broken by dismal dreams, foreboding visions of shadowy evil.

For a little more than a fortnight Edward Arundel visited his betrothed daily in the shabby first-floor in Oakley Street, and sat by her side while she worked at some fragile scrap of embroidery, and talked gayly to her of the happy future, to the intense admiration of Mrs. Pimpernel, who had no greater delight than to assist in the pretty little sentimental drama being enacted on her first floor.

Thus it was that, on a cloudy and autumnal August morning, Edward Arundel and Mary Marchmont were married in a great empty-looking church in the parish of Lambeth, by an indifferent curate, who shuffled through the service at railroad speed, and with far less reverence for the solemn rite than he would have displayed had he known that the pale-faced girl kneeling before the altar-rails was undisputed mistress of eleven thousand a year. Mrs. Pimpernel, the pew-opener, and the registrar, who was in waiting in the vestry, and who beguiled thence to give away the bride, were the only witnesses to this strange wedding. It seemed a dreary ceremonial to Mrs. Pimpernel, who had been married at the same church five-and-twenty years before, in a cinnamon satin spencer, and a coal-scuttle bonnet, and with a young person in the dress-making line in attendance upon her as bridemaid.

It was rather a dreary wedding, no doubt. The drizzling rain dripped ceaselessly in the street without, and there was a smell of damp plaster in the great empty church. The melancholy street-cries sounded dismally from the outer world, while the curate was hurrying through those portentous words which were to unite Edward Arundel and Mary Marchmont until the final day of earthly separation. The girl clung shivering to her lover, her husband now, as they went into the vestry to sign their names in the marriage-register. Throughout the service she had expected to hear a footstep in the aisle behind her, and Olivia Marchmont's cruel voice crying out to forbid the marriage.

"I am your wife now, Edward, am I not?" she said, when she had signed her name in the register.

"Yes, my darling, forever and forever.".

"And nothing can part us now?"

"Nothing but death, my dear."

In the exuberance of his spirits, Edward Arundel spoke of the King of Terrors as if he had been a mere nobody, whose power to change or mar the fortunes of mankind was so trifling as to be scarcely worth mentioning.

The vehicle in waiting to carry the mistress of Marchmont Towers upon the first stage of her bridal tour was nothing better than a hack cab. The driver's garments exhaled stale tobacco-smoke in the moist atmosphere, and in lieu of the flowers which are wont to bestrew the bridal pathway of an heiress, Miss Marchmont trod upon damp and mouldy straw. But she was happy—happy, with a fearful apprehension that her happiness could not be real—a vague terror of Olivia's power to torture and oppress her, which even the presence of her lover-husband could not altogether drive away. She kissed Mrs. Pimpernel, who stood upon the edge of the pavement, crying bitterly, with the slippery white lining of the new silk dress which Edward Arundel had given her for the wedding gathered tightly round her.

"God bless you, my dear!" cried the honest dealer in frayed satins and tumbled gauzes; "I couldn't take this more to heart if you was my own Eliza Jane going away with the young man as she was to have married, and as is now a widower with five children, two in arms, and the youngest brought up by hand. God bless your pretty face, my dear; and oh, pray take care of her, Captain Arundel, for she's a tender flower, Sir, and truly needs your care. And it's but a trifle, my own sweet young missy, for the acceptance of such as you, but it's given from a full heart, and given humbly."

The latter part of Mrs. Pimpernel's speech bore relation to a hard newspaper parcel, which she dropped into Mary's lap. Mrs. Arundel opened the parcel presently, when she had kissed her humble friend for the last time and the cab was driving toward Nine Elms, and found that Mrs. Pimpernel's wedding-gift was a Scotch shepherdess in china, with a great deal of gilding about her tartan garments, very red legs, a hat and feathers, and a curly sheep. Edward put this article of *virtù* very carefully away in his carpet-bag; for his bride would not have the present treated with any show of disrespect.

"How good of her to give it me!" Mary said; "it used to stand upon the back-parlor chimney-piece when I was a little girl; and I was too fond of it. Of course I am not fond of Scotch shepherdesses now, you know, dear; but how should Mrs. Pimpernel know that? She thought it would please me to have this one."

"And you'll put it in the western drawing-room at the Towers, won't you, Polly?" Captain Arundel asked, laughing.

"I won't put it any where to be made fun of, Sir," the young bride answered, with some touch of wifely dignity; "but I'll take care of it, and never have it broken or destroyed; and Mrs. Pimpernel shall see it, when she comes to the Towers—if I ever go back there," she added, with a sudden change of manner.

"*If* you ever go back there!" cried Edward. "Why, Polly, my dear, Marchmont Towers is your own house. My cousin Olivia is only there upon sufferance, and her own good sense will tell her she has no right to remain there when she ceases to be your friend and protectress. She is a proud woman, and her pride will surely never suffer her to remain where she must feel she can be no longer welcome."

The young wife's face turned white with terror at her husband's words.

"But I could never ask her to go, Edward," she said. "I wouldn't turn her out for the world. She may stay there forever if she likes. I never have cared for the place since papa's death; and I couldn't go back while she is there, I'm so frightened of her, Edward, I'm so frightened of her."

The vague apprehension burst forth in this childish cry. Edward Arundel clasped his wife to his breast, and bent over her, kissing her pale forehead, and murmuring soothing words, as he might have done to a child.

"My dear, my dear," he said, "my darling Mary, this will never do; my own love, this is so very foolish."

"I know, I know, Edward; but I can't help it, I can't, indeed; I was frightened of her long ago; frightened of her even the first day I saw her, the day you took me to the Rectory; I was frightened of her when papa first told me he meant to marry her; and I am frightened of her now; even now that I'm your wife, Edward, I'm frightened of her still."

Captain Arundel kissed away the tears that trembled on his wife's eyelids; but she had scarcely grown quite composed even when the cab stopped at the Nine-Elms railway station. It was only when she was seated in the carriage with her husband, and the rain cleared away as they advanced farther into the heart of the pretty pastoral country, that the bride's sense of happiness and safety in her husband's protection returned to her. But by that time she was able to smile in his face, and to look forward with delight to a brief sojourn in that pretty Hampshire village which Edward had chosen for the scene of his honey-moon.

"Only a few days of quiet happiness, Polly," he said; "a few days of utter forgetfulness of all the world except you, and then I must be a man of business again, and write to your step-mother, and my father and mother, and Messrs. Paulette and Mathewson, and all the people who ought to know of our marriage."

---

## CHAPTER XVII.

### PAUL'S SISTER.

OLIVIA MARCHMONT shut herself once more in her desolate chamber, making no effort to find the runaway mistress of the Towers; indifferent as to what the slanderous tongues of her neighbors might say of her; hardened, callous, desperate.

To her father, and to any one else who questioned her about Mary's absence—for the story of the girl's flight was soon whispered abroad, the servants at the Towers having received no injunctions to keep the matter secret — Mrs. Marchmont replied with such an air of cold and determined reserve as kept the questioners at bay ever afterward.

So the Kemberling people, and the Swampington people, and all the country gentry within reach of Marchmont Towers, had a mystery and a scandal provided for them, which afforded ample scope for repeated discussion, and considerably relieved the dull monotony of their lives. But there were some questioners whom Mrs. Marchmont found it rather difficult to keep at a distance; there were some intruders who dared to force themselves upon the gloomy woman's solitude, and who would not understand that their presence was hateful, and their society abhorrent to her.

These people were a surgeon and his wife, who had newly settled at Kemberling; the best practice in the village falling into the market by reason of the death of a steady-going, gray-headed old practitioner, who for many years had shared with one opponent the responsibility of watching over the health of the Lincolnshire village.

It was only a week after Mary Marchmont's flight when these unwelcome guests first came to the Towers.

Olivia sat alone in her dead husband's study —the same room in which she had sat upon the morning of John Marchmont's funeral—a dark and gloomy chamber, wainscoted with blackened oak, and lighted only by a massive stone-framed Tudor window looking out into the quadrangle, and overshadowed by that cloistered colonnade beneath whose shelter Edward and Mary had walked upon the morning of the girl's flight. This wainscoted study was an apartment which most women, having all the rooms in Marchmont Towers at their disposal, would have been likely to avoid; but the gloom of the chamber harmonized with that horrible gloom which had taken possession of Olivia's soul, and the widow turned from the sunny western front, as she turned from all the sunlight and gladness in the universe, to come here, where the summer radiance rarely crept through the diamond-panes of the window, where the shadow of the cloister shut out the glory of the blue sky.

She was sitting in this room—sitting near the open window in a high-backed chair of carved and polished oak, with her head resting against the angle of the embayed window, and her handsome profile thrown into sharp relief by the dark green cloth curtain, hanging in straight folds from the low ceiling to the ground, and making a sombre back-ground to the widow's figure. Mrs. Marchmont had put away all the miserable gewgaws and vanities which she had ordered from London in a sudden excess of folly or caprice, and had reassumed her mourning-robes of lustreless black. She had a book in her hand —some new and popular fiction, which all Lincolnshire was eager to read; but although her eyes were fixed upon the pages before her, and her hand mechanically turned over leaf after leaf at regular intervals of time, the fashionable romance was only a weary repetition of phrases, a dull current of words, always intermingled with the images of Edward Arundel and Mary Marchmont, which arose out of every page to mock the hopeless reader.

Olivia flung the book away from her, at last, with a smothered cry of rage.

"Is there no cure for this disease?" she muttered. "Is there no relief except madness or death?"

But in the infidelity which had arisen out of her despair this woman had grown to doubt if either death or madness could bring her oblivion of her anguish. She doubted the quiet of the grave, and half believed that the torture of jealous rage and slighted love might mingle even with that silent rest, haunting her in her coffin, shutting her out of heaven, and following her into a darker world, there to be her torment everlastingly. There were times when she thought madness must mean forgetfulness; but there were other moments when she shuddered, horror-stricken, at the thought that, in the wandering brain of a mad woman, the image of that grief which had caused the shipwreck of her senses might still hold its place, distorted and exaggerated—a gigantic unreality, ten thousand times more terrible than the truth. Remembering the dreams which disturbed her broken sleep —those dreams which, in their feverish horror, were little better than intervals of delirium—it is scarcely strange if Olivia Marchmont thought thus.

She had not succumbed without many struggles to her sin and despair. Again and again she had abandoned herself to the devils at watch to destroy her, and again and again she had tried to extricate her soul from their dreadful power; but her most passionate endeavors were in vain. Perhaps it was that she did not strive aright; it was for this reason, surely, that she failed so utterly to arise superior to her despair; for otherwise that terrible belief attributed to the Calvinists, that some souls are foredoomed to damnation, would be exemplified by this woman's experience. She could not forget. She could not put away the vengeful hatred that raged like an all-devouring fire in her breast, and she cried, in her agony, "There is no cure for this disease!"

I think her mistake was in this, that she did not go to the right physician. She practiced quackery with her soul as some people do with their bodies; trying her own remedies rather than the simple prescriptions of the Divine Healer of all woes. Self-reliant, and scornful of the weakness against which her pride revolted, she trusted to her intellect and her will to lift her out of the moral slough into which her soul had gone down. She said:

"I am not a woman to go mad for the love of a boyish face; I am not a woman to die for a foolish fancy that the veriest school-girl might be ashamed to confess to her companion. I am not a woman to do this, and I *will* cure myself of my folly."

Mrs. Marchmont made an effort to take up her old life, with its dull round of ceaseless duty, its perpetual self-denial. If she had been a Roman Catholic she would have gone to the nearest convent, and prayed to be permitted to take such vows as might soonest set a barrier between herself and the world; she would have spent the long, weary days in perpetual and secret prayer; she would have worn deeper indentations upon the stones already hollowed by faithful knees. As it was, she made a routine of penance for herself, after her own fashion: going long distances on foot to visit her poor, when she might have ridden in her carriage; courting exposure to rain and foul weather; wearing herself out with unnecessary fatigue, and returning foot-sore to her desolate home, to fall fainting into the strong arms of her grim attendant Barbara.

But this self-appointed penance could not shut Edward Arundel and Mary Marchmont from the widow's mind. Walking through a fiery furnace their images would have haunted her still, vivid and palpable even in the agony of death. The fatigue of the long, weary walks made Mrs. Marchmont wan and pale; the exposure to storm and rain brought on a tiresome hacking cough, which worried her by day and disturbed her fitful slumbers by night. No good whatever seemed to come of her endeavors; and the devils who rejoiced at her weakness and her failure claimed her as their own. They claimed her as their own; and they were not without terrestrial agents, working patiently in their service, and ready to help in securing their bargain.

The great clock in the quadrangle had struck the half hour after three; the atmosphere of the August afternoon was sultry and oppressive. Mrs. Marchmont had closed her eyes after flinging aside her book, and had fallen into a doze: her nights were broken and wakeful, and the hot stillness of the day had made her drowsy.

She was aroused from this half-slumber by Barbara Simmons, who came into the room carrying two cards upon a salver—the same old-fashioned and emblazoned salver upon which Paul Marchmont's card had been brought to the widow nearly three years before. The Abigail stood half-way between the door and the window by which the widow sat, looking at her mistress's face with a glance of sharp scrutiny.

"She's changed since he came back, and changed again since he went away," the woman thought; "just as she always changed at the Rectory at his coming and going. Why didn't he take to her, I wonder? He might have known her fancy for him, if he'd had eyes to watch her face, or ears to listen to her voice. She's handsomer than the other one, and cleverer in book-learning; but she keeps 'em off—she seems allers to keep 'em off."

I think Olivia Marchmont would have torn the very heart out of this waiting-woman's breast had she known the thoughts that held a place in it; had she known that the servant who attended upon her, and took wages from her, dared to pluck out her secret, and to speculate upon her suffering.

The widow awoke suddenly, and looked up with an impatient frown. She had not been awakened by the opening of the door, but by that unpleasant sensation which almost always reveals the presence of a stranger to a sleeper of nervous temperament.

"What is it, Barbara?" she asked; and then, as her eyes rested on the cards, she added, angrily, "Haven't I told you that I would not see any callers to-day? I am worn out with my cough, and feel too ill to see any one."

"Yes, Miss Livy," the woman answered— she called her mistress by this name still, now and then, so familiar had it grown to her during the childhood and youth of the Rector's daughter—"I didn't forget that, Miss Livy. I told Richardson you was not to be disturbed. But the lady and gentleman said if you saw what was wrote upon the back of one of the cards you'd be sure to make an exception in their favor. I think that was what the lady said. She's a middle-aged lady, very talkative and pleasant-mannered," added the grim Barbara, in nowise relaxing the stolid gravity of her own manner as she spoke.

Olivia snatched the cards from the salver.

"Why do people worry me so?" she cried, impatiently. "Am I not to be allowed even five minutes' sleep without being broken in upon by some intruder or other?"

Barbara Simmons looked at her mistress's face. Anxiety and sadness dimly showed themselves in the stolid countenance of the lady's-maid. A close observer, penetrating below that aspect of wooden solemnity which was Barbara's normal expression, might have discovered a secret: the quiet waiting-woman loved her mistress with a jealous and watchful affection, that took heed of every change in its object.

Mrs. Marchmont examined the two cards, which bore the names of Mr. and Mrs. Weston, Kemberling. On the back of the lady's card these words were written in pencil:

"Will Mrs. Marchmont be so good as to see Lavinia Weston, Paul Marchmont's younger sister, and a connection of Mrs. M.'s?"

Olivia shrugged her shoulders as she threw down the card.

"Paul Marchmont! Lavinia Weston!" she muttered; "yes, I remember he said something about a sister married to a surgeon at Stanfield. Let these people come to me, Barbara."

The waiting-woman looked doubtfully at her mistress.

"You'll maybe smooth your hair and freshen yourself up a bit, before you see the folks, Miss Livy," she said, in a tone of mingled suggestion and entreaty. "Ye've had a deal of worry lately, and it's made ye look a little fagged and hag-gard-like. I'd not like the Kemberling folks to say as you was ill."

Mrs. Marchmont turned fiercely upon the Abigail.

"Let me alone!" she cried. "What is it to you, or to any one, how I look? What good have my looks done me that I should worry my-self about them?" she added, under her breath. "Show these people in here, if they want to see me."

"They've been shown into the western draw-ing-room, ma'am — Richardson took 'em in there."

Barbara Simmons fought hard for the preser-vation of appearances. She wanted the Rector's daughter to receive these strange people, who had dared to intrude upon her, in a manner befit-ting the dignity of John Marchmont's widow. She glanced furtively at the disorder of the gloomy chamber. Books and papers were scat-tered here and there; the hearth and low fender were littered with heaps of torn letters—for Olivia Marchmont had no tenderness for the memorials of the past, and indeed took a fierce delight in sweeping away the unsanctified records of her joyless, loveless life. The high-backed oaken chairs had been pushed out of their places; the green-cloth cover had been drawn half off the massive table, and hung in trailing folds upon the ground. A book flung here, a shawl there, a handkerchief in another place; an open secre-taire, with scattered documents and uncovered ink-stand, littered the room, and bore mute wit-

ness of the restlessness of its occupant. It need-ed no very subtle psychologist to read aright those separate tokens of a disordered mind; of a weary spirit, which had sought distraction in a dozen occupations, and had found relief in none. It was some vague sense of this that caused Bar-bara Simmons's anxiety. She wished to keep strangers out of this room, in which her mistress —wan, haggard, and weary-looking—revealed her secret by so many signs and tokens. But before Olivia could make any answer to her servant's suggestion, the door, which Barbara had left ajar, was pushed open by a very gentle hand, and a sweet voice said, in cheery, chirp-ing accents,

"I am sure I may come in; may I not, Mrs. Marchmont? The impression my brother Paul's description gave me of you is such a very pleas-ant one that I venture to intrude uninvited, al-most forbidden, perhaps."

The voice and manner of the speaker was so airy and self-possessed, there was such a world of cheerfulness and amiability in every tone, that, as Olivia Marchmont rose from her chair, she put her hand to her head, dazed and confounded, as if by the too boisterous caroling of some caged bird. What did they mean, these accents of gladness, these clear and untroubled tones, which sounded shrill and almost discordant in the de-spairing woman's weary ears? She stood, pale and worn, the very picture of all gloom and mis-ery, staring hopelessly at her visitor; too much abandoned to her grief to remember, in that first moment, the stern demands of pride. She stood still; revealing, by her look, her attitude, her silence, her abstraction, a whole history to the watchful eyes that were looking at her.

Mrs. Weston lingered on the threshold of the chamber in a pretty, half-fluttering manner; which was charmingly expressive of a struggle between a modest poor-relation-like diffidence and an earnest desire to rush into Olivia's arms. The surgeon's wife was a delicate-looking little woman, with features that seemed a miniature and feminine reproduction of her brother Paul's, and with very light hair so light and pale that, had it turned as white as the artist's in a single night, very few people would have been likely to take heed of the change. Lavinia Weston was eminently what is generally called a *lady-like* woman. She always conducted her-self in that especial and particular manner which was exactly fitted to the occasion. She adjusted her behavior by the nicest shades of color and hair-breadth scale of measurement. She had, as it were, made for herself a homeopathic sys-tem of good manners, and could mete out polite-ness and courtesy in the veriest globules, never administering either too much or too little. To her husband she was a treasure beyond all price; and if the Lincolnshire surgeon—who was a fat, solemn-faced man, with a character as level and monotonous as the flats and fens of his native county—was hen-pecked, the feminine autocrat held the reins of government so lightly that her obedient subject was scarcely aware how very irresponsible his wife's authority had become.

As Olivia Marchmont stood confronting the timid, hesitating figure of the intruder, with the width of the chamber between them, Lavinia Weston, in her crisp muslin-dress and scarf, her neat bonnet and bright ribbons and primly-adjusted gloves, looked something like an adventurous canary who had a mind to intrude upon the den of a hungry lioness. The difference, physical and moral, between the timid bird and the savage forest-queen could be scarcely wider than that between the two women.

But Olivia did not stand forever embarrassed and silent in her visitor's presence. Her pride came to her rescue. She turned sternly upon the polite intruder.

"Walk in, if you please, Mrs. Weston," she said, "and sit down. I was denied to you just now because I have been ill, and have ordered my servants to deny me to every one."

"But, my dear Mrs. Marchmont," murmured Lavinia Weston in soft, almost dove-like accents, "if you have been ill, is not your illness another reason for seeing us, rather than for keeping us away from you? I would not, of course, say a word which could in any way be calculated to give offense to your regular medical attendant—you have a regular medical attendant, no doubt; from Swampington, I dare say—but a doctor's wife may often be useful when a doctor is himself out of place. There are little nervous ailments—depression of spirits, mental uneasiness—from which women, and sensitive women, suffer acutely, and which perhaps a woman's more refined nature alone can thoroughly comprehend. You are not looking well, my dear Mrs. Marchmont. I left my husband in the drawing-room, for I was so anxious that our first meeting should take place without witnesses. Men think women sentimental when they are only impulsive. Weston is a good, simple-hearted creature; but he knows as much about a woman's mind as he does of an Æolian harp. When the strings vibrate he hears the low plaintive notes, but he has no idea whence the music comes. It is thus with us, Mrs. Marchmont. These medical men watch us in the agonies of hysteria; they hear our sighs, they see our tears, and in their awkwardness and ignorance they prescribe commonplace remedies out of the pharmacopœia. No, dear Mrs. Marchmont, you do not look well. I fear it is the mind, the mind, which has been overstrained. Is it not so?"

Mrs. Weston put her head on one side as she asked this question, and smiled at Olivia with an air of gentle insinuation. If the doctor's wife wished to plumb the depths of the widow's gloomy soul she had an advantage here; for Mrs. Marchmont was thrown off her guard by the question, which had been perhaps asked hap-hazard, or, it may be, with a deeply-considered design. Olivia turned fiercely upon the polite questioner.

"I have been suffering from nothing but a cold which I caught the other day," she said; "I am not subject to any fine-ladylike hysteria, I can assure you, Mrs. Weston."

The doctor's wife pursed up her lips into a sympathetic smile, not at all abashed by this rebuff. She had seated herself in one of the high-backed chairs, with her muslin skirt spread out about her. She looked a living exemplification of all that is neat and prim and commonplace, in contrast with the pale, stern-faced woman, standing rigid and defiant in her long black robes.

"How very chy-arming!" exclaimed Mrs.

Weston. "You are really not nervous. Dee-ar me; and from what my brother Paul said, I should have imagined that any one so highly organized must be rather nervous. But I really fear I am impertinent, and that I presume upon our very slight relationship. It is a relationship, is it not, although such a very slight one?"

"I have never thought of the subject," Mrs. Marchmont replied, coldly. "I suppose, however, that my marriage with your brother's cousin—"

"And my cousin—"

"Made a kind of connection between us. But Mr. Marchmont gave me to understand that you lived at Stanfield, Mrs. Weston."

"Until last week, positively until last week," answered the surgeon's wife. "I see you take very little interest in village gossip, Mrs. Marchmont, or you would have heard of the change at Kemberling."

"What change?"

"My husband's purchase of poor old Mr. Dawnfield's practice. The dear old man died a month ago—you heard of his death, of course—and Mr. Weston negotiated the purchase with Mrs. Dawnfield in less than a fortnight. We came here early last week, and already we are making friends in the neighborhood. How strange that you should not have heard of our coming!"

"I do not see much society," Olivia answered, indifferently, "and I hear nothing of the Kemberling people."

"Indeed!" cried Mrs. Weston; "and we hear so much of Marchmont Towers at Kemberling."

She looked full in the widow's face as she spoke, her stereotyped smile subsiding into a look of greedy curiosity; a look whose intense eagerness could not be concealed.

That look, and the tone in which her last sentence had been spoken, said as plainly as the plainest words could have done, "I have heard of Mary Marchmont's flight."

Olivia understood this; but in the passionate depth of her own madness she had no power to fathom the meanings or the motives of other people. She revolted against this Mrs. Weston, and disliked her because the woman intruded upon her in her desolation; but she never once thought of Lavinia Weston's interest in Mary's movements; she never once remembered that the frail life of that orphan girl only stood between this woman's brother and the rich heritage of Marchmont Towers.

Blind and forgetful of every thing in the hideous egotism of her despair, what was Olivia Marchmont but a fitting tool, a plastic and easily-moulded instrument, in the hands of unscrupulous people, whose hard intellects had never been beaten into confused shapelessness in the fiery furnace of passion?

Mrs. Weston had heard of Mary Marchmont's flight; but she had heard half a dozen different reports of that event, as widely diversified in their details as if half a dozen heiresses had fled from Marchmont Towers. Every gossip in the place had a separate story as to the circumstances which had led to the girl's running away from her home. The accounts vied with each other in graphic force and minute elaboration; the conversations that had taken place between

Mary and her step-mother, between Edward Arundel and Mrs. Marchmont, between the Rector of Swampington and nobody in particular, would have filled a volume, as related by the gossips of Kemberling; but as every body assigned a different cause for the terrible misunderstanding at the Towers, and a different direction for Mary's flight—and as the railway official at the station, who could have thrown some light on the subject, was a stern and moody man, who had little sympathy with his kind, and held his tongue persistently—it was not easy to get very near the truth. Under these circumstances, then, Mrs. Weston determined upon seeking information at the fountain-head, and approaching the cruel step-mother, who, according to some of the reports, had starved and beaten her dead husband's child.

"Yes, dear Mrs. Marchmont," said Lavinia Weston, seeing that it was necessary to come direct to the point if she wished to wring the truth from Olivia; "yes, we hear of every thing at Kemberling; and I need scarcely tell you that we heard of the sad trouble which you have had to endure since your ball—the ball that is spoken of as the most chy-arming entertainment remembered in the neighborhood for a long time. We heard of this sad girl's flight."

Mrs. Marchmont looked up with a dark frown, but made no answer.

"Was she—it really is such a very painful question, that I almost shrink from—but was Miss Marchmont at all—eccentric—a little mentally deficient? Pray pardon me, if I have given you pain by such a question; but—"

Olivia started, and looked sharply at her visitor. "Mentally deficient? No!" she said. But as she spoke her eyes dilated, her pale cheeks grew paler, her upper lip quivered with a faint convulsive movement. It seemed as if some idea presented itself to her with a sudden force that almost took away her breath.

"Not mentally deficient!" repeated Lavinia Weston; "dee-ar me! It's a great comfort to hear that. Of course Paul saw very little of his cousin, and he was not, therefore, in a position to judge—though his opinions, however rapidly arrived at, are generally so very accurate—but he gave me to understand that he thought Miss Marchmont appeared a little—just a little—weak in her intellect. I am very glad to find he was mistaken."

Olivia made no reply to this speech. She had seated herself in her chair by the window; she looked straight before her into the flagged quadrangle, with her hands lying idle in her lap. It seemed as if she were actually unconscious of her visitor's presence, or as if, in her scornful indifference, she did not even care to affect any interest in that visitor's conversation.

Lavinia Weston returned again to the attack.

"Pray, Mrs. Marchmont, do not think me intrusive or impertinent," she said, pleadingly, "if I ask you to favor me with the true particulars of this sad event. I am sure you will be good enough to remember that my brother Paul, my sister, and myself are Mary Marchmont's nearest relatives on her father's side, and that we have, therefore, some right to feel interested in her."

By this very polite speech Lavinia Weston plainly reminded the widow of the insignificance of her own position at Marchmont Towers. In her ordinary frame of mind Olivia would have resented the lady-like slight; but to-day she neither heard nor heeded it; she was brooding with a stupid, unreasonable persistency over the words "mental deficiency," "weak intellect." She only roused herself by a great effort to answer Mrs. Weston's question when that lady had repeated it in very plain words.

"I can tell you nothing about Miss Marchmont's flight," she said, coldly, "except that she chose to run away from her home. I found reason to object to her conduct upon the night of the ball; and the next morning she left the house, assigning no reason—to me, at any rate —for her absurd and improper behavior."

"She assigned no reason to you, my dear Mrs. Marchmont; but she assigned a reason to somebody, I infer, from what you say?"

"Yes; she wrote a letter to my cousin, Captain Arundel."

"Telling him the reason of her departure?"

"I don't know—I forget. The letter told nothing clearly; it was wild and incoherent."

Mrs. Weston sighed; a long-drawn, desponding sigh.

"Wild and incoherent!" she murmured, in a pensive tone. "How grieved Paul will be to hear of this! He took such an interest in his cousin—a delicate and fragile-looking young creature, he told me. Yes, he took a very great interest in her, Mrs. Marchmont, though you may perhaps scarcely believe me when I say so. He kept himself purposely aloof from this place; his sensitive nature led him to abstain from even revealing his interest in Miss Marchmont. His position, you must remember, with regard to this poor dear girl, is a very delicate—I may say a very painful—one."

Olivia remembered nothing. The value of the Marchmont estates; the sordid worth of those wide-stretching farms, spreading far away into Yorkshire; the pitiful, closely-calculated revenue, which made Mary a wealthy heiress, were so far from the dark thoughts of this woman's desperate heart, that she no more suspected Mrs. Weston of any mercenary design in coming to the Towers than of burglarious intentions with regard to the silver spoons in the plate-room. She only thought that the surgeon's wife was a tiresome woman, against whose pertinacious civility her angry spirit chafed and rebelled, until she was almost driven to order her from the room.

In this cruel weariness of spirit Mrs. Marchmont gave a short impatient sigh, which afforded a sufficient hint to such an accomplished tactician as her visitor.

"I know I have tired you, my dear Mrs. Marchmont," the doctor's wife said, rising and arranging her muslin scarf as she spoke, in token of her immediate departure; "I am so sorry to find you a sufferer from that nasty hacking cough; but of course you have the best advice, Mr. Poolton from Swampington, I think you said?"—Olivia had said nothing of the kind—"and I trust the warm weather will prevent the cough taking any hold of your chest. If I might venture to suggest flannels—so many young women quite ridicule the idea of flannels—but, as the wife of a humble provincial practitioner, I have learned their value. Good-by, dear Mrs.

Marchmont. I may come again, may I not, now that the ice is broken, and we are so well acquainted with each other? Good-by."

Olivia could not refuse to take at least *one* of the two plump and tightly-gloved hands which were held out to her with an air of frank cordiality; but the widow's grasp was loose and nerveless, and inasmuch as two consentient parties are required to the shaking of hands, as well as to the getting up of a quarrel, the salutation was not a very hearty one.

The surgeon's pony must have been weary of standing before the flight of shallow steps leading to the western portico, when Mrs. Weston took her seat by her husband's side in the gig, which had been newly painted and varnished since the worthy couple's *Hegira* from Stanfield. The surgeon was not an ambitious man, nor a designing man; he was simply stupid and lazy; lazy, although, in spite of himself, he led an active and hard-working life; but there are many square men whose sides are cruelly tortured by the pressure of the round holes into which they are ill-advisedly thrust, and if our destinies were meted out to us in strict accordance with our temperaments, Mr. Weston should have been a lotus-eater. As it was, he was content to drudge on, mildly complying with every desire of his wife; doing what she told him, because it was less trouble to do the hardest work at her bidding than to oppose her. It would have been surely less painful to Macbeth to have finished that ugly business of the murder than to have endured my lady's black contemptuous scowl, and the bitter scorn and contumely concentrated in those four words, "Give *me* the daggers!"

Mr. Weston asked one or two commonplace questions about his wife's interview with John Marchmont's widow; but slowly apprehending that Lavinia did not care to discuss the matter, he relapsed into meek silence, and devoted all his intellectual powers to the task of keeping the pony out of the deeper ruts in the rugged road between Marchmont Towers and Kemberling High Street.

"What is the secret of that woman's life?" thought Lavinia Weston during that homeward drive; "has she ill-treated the girl, or is she plotting in some way or other to get hold of the Marchmont fortune? Pshaw! that's impossible. And yet she may be making a purse, somehow or other, out of the estate. Any how, there is bad blood between the two women."

---

## CHAPTER XVIII.

### A STOLEN HONEY-MOON.

THE village to which Edward Arundel took his bride was within a few miles of Winchester. The young soldier had become familiar with the place in his early boyhood, when he had gone to spend a part of one bright mid-summer holiday at the house of a school-fellow; and had ever since cherished a friendly remembrance of the winding trout-streams, the rich verdure of the valleys, and the sheltering hills that shut in the pleasant little cluster of thatched cottages, the pretty white-walled villas, and the gray old church.

But to Mary, whose experiences of town and country were limited to the dingy purlieus of Oakley Street and the fenny flats of Lincolnshire, this Hampshire village seemed a rustic paradise, which neither trouble nor sorrow could ever approach. She had trembled at the thought of Olivia's coming in Oakley Street; but here she seemed to lose all terror of her stern step-mother —here, sheltered and protected by her young husband's love, she fancied that she might live her life out happy and secure.

She told Edward this one sunny morning, as they sat by the young man's favorite trout-stream. Captain Arundel's fishing-tackle lay idle on the turf at his side, for he had been beguiled into forgetfulness of a ponderous trout he had been watching and finessing with for upward of an hour, and had flung himself at full length upon the mossy margin of the water, with his uncovered head lying in Mary's lap.

The childish bride would have been content to sit forever thus in that rural solitude, with her fingers twisted in her husband's chestnut curls, and her soft eyes keeping timid watch upon his handsome face—so candid and unclouded in its careless repose. The undulating meadow-land lay half-hidden in a golden haze, only broken here and there by the glitter of the brighter sunlight that lit up the rippling waters of the wandering streams that intersected the low pastures. The massive towers of the cathedral, the gray walls of St. Cross, loomed dimly in the distance; the bubbling plash of a mill-stream sounded like some monotonous lullaby in the drowsy summer atmosphere. Mary looked from the face she loved to the fair landscape about her, and a tender solemnity crept into her mind, a reverent love and admiration for this beautiful earth, which was almost akin to awe.

"How pretty this place is, Edward!" she said. "I had no idea there were such places in all the wide world. Do you know, I think I would rather be a cottage-girl here than an heiress in Lincolnshire. Edward, if I ask you a favor, will you grant it?"

She spoke very earnestly, looking down at her husband's upturned face; but Captain Arundel only laughed at her question, without even caring to lift the drowsy eyelids that drooped over his blue eyes.

"Well, my pet, if you want any thing short of the moon, I suppose your devoted husband is scarcely likely to refuse it. Our honey-moon is not a fortnight old yet, Polly dear; you wouldn't have me turn tyrant quite as soon as this. Speak out, Mrs. Arundel, and assert your dignity as a British matron. What is the favor I am to grant?"

"I want you to live here always, Edward darling," pleaded the girlish voice. "Not for a fortnight or a month, but for ever and ever. I have never been happy at Marchmont Towers. Papa died there, you know, and I can not forget that. Perhaps that ought to have made the place sacred to me; and so it has; but it is sacred like papa's tomb in Kemberling Church, and it seems like profanation to be happy in it, or to forget my dead father even for a moment. Don't let us go back there, Edward. Let my step-mother live there all her life. It would seem selfish and cruel to turn her out of the house she has so long been mistress of. Mr. Gormby will go on collecting the rents, you know, and can send me the.......... You never, never, never ............ would be so ......... to leave me. I know how ....... and ....... are, and I am proud to think ...... your ....... courage, and all the brave deeds ....... in India. But you *have* fought for your country, Edward; you ....... done your duty. Nobody can expect ...... of you; nobody shall take you from me. Oh, my darling, my husband, you promised to ....... and defend me while our lives last! You won't leave me—you won't leave me, will you?"

Captain Arundel opened his eyes, and lifted himself out of his reclining position before he answered his wife.

"My own precious Polly," he said, smiling fondly at the gentle childish face turned in such earnestness toward his own; "my runaway little wife, rich people have their duties to perform as well as poor people; and I am afraid it would never do for you to hide in this out-of-the-way Hampshire village, and play absentee from stately Marchmont and all its dependencies. I love that pretty, infantine, unworldly spirit of yours, my darling; and I sometimes wish we were two grown-up babes in the wood, and could wander about gathering wild flowers, and eating blackberries and hazel-nuts, until the shades of evening closed in, and the friendly robins came to bury us. Don't fancy I'm tired of our honeymoon, Polly, or that I care for Marchmont Towers any more than you do; but I fear the nonresidence plan would never answer. The world would call my little wife eccentric, if she ran away from her grandeur; and Paul Marchmont, the artist—of whom your poor father had rather a bad opinion, by-the-way—would be taking out a statute of lunacy against you."

"Paul Marchmont!" repeated Mary. "Did papa dislike Mr. Paul Marchmont?"

"Well, poor John had a sort of a prejudice against the man, I believe; but it was only a prejudice, for he freely confessed that he could assign no reason for it. But, whatever Mr. Paul Marchmont may be, you must live at the Towers, Mary, and be Lady Bountiful-in-chief in your neighborhood, and look after your property, and have long interviews with Mr. Gormby, and become altogether a woman of business; so that when I go back to India—"

Mary interrupted him with a little cry:

"Go back to India!" she exclaimed. "What do you mean, Edward?"

"I mean, my darling, that my business in life is to fight for my Queen and country, and not to sponge upon my wife's fortune. You don't suppose I'm going to lay down my sword at seven-and-twenty years of age, and retire upon my pension? No, Polly; you remember what Lord Nelson said on the deck of the Trafalgar. That saying can never be so hackneyed as to lose its force. I must do my duty, Polly; I must do my duty; even if duty and love pull different ways, and I have to leave my darling, in the service of my country."

Mary clasped her hands in despair, and looked piteously at her lover-husband, with the tears streaming down her pale cheeks.

"Oh, Edward," she cried, "how cruel you are; how very, very cruel you are to me! What is the use of my fortune if you won't share it with me—if you won't take it all; for it is yours, my dearest; it is all yours. I remember the words in the Marriage Service, 'with all my goods I thee endow.' I have given you Marchmont Towers, Edward; nobody in the world can take

Edward Arundel kissed the tears away from his wife's pale face, and drew her head upon his bosom.

"My love," he said, tenderly, "you can not tell how much pain it gives me to hear you talk like this. What can I do? To give up my profession would be to make myself next ...... to a pauper. What would the world say of me, Mary? Think of that. This runaway marriage would be a dreadful dishonor to me if it were followed by a life of lazy dependence on my wife's fortune. Nobody can dare to slander the soldier who spends the brightest years of his life in the service of his country. You would not surely have me be less than true to myself, Mary darling? For my honor's sake I must leave you."

"Oh no, no, no!" cried the girl, in a low wailing voice. Unselfish and devoted as she had been in every other crisis of her young life, she could not be reasonable or self-denying here; she was seized with despair at the thought of parting with her husband. No, not even for his honor's sake could she let him go. Better that they should both die now, in this early ...... of their happiness.

"Edward, Edward," she sobbed, clinging convulsively about the young man's neck, "don't leave me; don't leave me!"

"Will you go with me to India, then, Mary?"

She lifted her head suddenly, and looked him full in the face, with the gladness in her eyes shining through her tears, like an April sun through a watery sky.

"I would go to the end of the world with you, my own darling," she said; "the burning sands and the dreadful jungles would have no terrors for me if I were with you, Edward."

Captain Arundel smiled at her earnestness.

"I won't take you into the jungle, my love," he answered, playfully; "or, if I do, your palki shall be well guarded, and all ravenous beasts kept at a respectful distance from my little wife. A great many ladies go to India with their husbands, Polly, and come back very little the worse for the climate or the voyage; and except your money, there is no reason you should not go with me."

"Oh, never mind my money, let anybody have that."

"Polly," cried the soldier, very seriously, "we must consult ...... as to the future. I don't think I ...... in marrying you during ...... have delayed writing to him too long. These letters must be written this ......"

"The letter to ...... Paulette and to your father?"

"Yes, and the letter to my cousin Olivia."

...... face grew sorrowful again, as Captain
...... said then.

"...... you tell my step-mother of our mar......?" she said.

"...... naturally, my dear. Why should we
keep her in ignorance of it? Your father's will
gives her the privilege of advising you, but not
the power to interfere with your choice, whatever that choice might be. You were your own
mistress, Mary, when you married me. What
reason have you to fear my cousin Olivia?"

"No reason, perhaps," the girl answered,
sadly; "but I do fear her. I know I am very
foolish, Edward, and you have reason to despise
me—you, who are so brave. But I could never
tell you how I tremble at the thought of being
once more in my step-mother's power. She
said cruel things to me, Edward. Every word
she spoke seemed to stab me to the heart; but it
isn't that only. There's something more than
that; something that I can't describe, that I
can't understand; something which tells me
that she hates me."

"Hates you, darling?"

"Yes, Edward, yes; she hates me. It wasn't
always so, you know. She used to be only
cold and reserved; but lately her manner has
changed. I thought that she was ill, perhaps,
and that my presence worried her. People often
wish to be alone, I know, when they are ill. O
Edward, I have seen her shrink from me, and
shudder if her dress brushed against mine, as
if I had been some horrible creature. What
have I done, Edward, that she should hate
me?"

Captain Arundel knitted his brows, and set
himself to work out this womanly problem; but
he could make nothing of it. Yes, what Mary
had said was perfectly true: Olivia hated her.
The young man had seen that upon the morning of the girl's flight from Marchmont Towers.
He had seen vengeful fury and vindictive passion
raging in the dark face of John Marchmont's
widow. But what reason could the woman have
for her hatred of this innocent girl? Again
and again Olivia's cousin asked himself this
question; and he was so far away from the
truth at last that he could only answer it by
imagining the lowest motive for the widow's
bad feeling. "She envies my poor little girl
her fortune and position," he thought.

"But you won't have me alone with my step-
mother, will you, Edward?" Mary said, recurring to her old prayer. "I am not afraid of
her, nor of any body or any thing in the world,
while you are with me—how should I be?—but
I think, if I were to be alone with her again, I
should die. She would speak to me again as
she spoke upon the night of the ball, and her
bitter taunts would kill me. I could not bear to
be in her power again, Edward."

"And you shall not, my darling," answered
the young man, enfolding the slender, trembling
figure in his strong arms. "My own childish
pet, you shall never be exposed to any woman's
insolence or tyranny. You shall be sheltered
and protected, and hedged in on every side by
your husband's love. And when I go to India
you shall sail with me, my pearl. Mary, look
up and smile at me, and let's have no more talk
of cruel step-mothers. How strange it seems to
me, Polly dear, that you should have been so

womanly when you were a child, and yet are so
childlike now you are a woman!"

The mistress of Marchmont Towers looked
doubtfully at her husband, as if she feared her
childishness might be displeasing to him.

"You don't love me any the less because of
that, do you, Edward?" she asked, timidly.

"Because of what, my treasure?"

"Because I am so—childish?"

"Polly," cried the young man, "do you
think Jupiter liked Hebe any the less because
she was as fresh and innocent as the nectar she
served out to him? If he had, my dear, he'd
have sent for Clotho, or Atropos, or some one
or other of the elderly maiden ladies of Hades,
to wait upon him as cup-bearer. I wouldn't
have you otherwise than you are, Polly, by so
much as one thought."

The girl looked up at her husband in a rapture
of innocent affection.

"I am too happy, Edward," she said, in a
low, awe-stricken whisper. "I am too happy.
So much happiness can never last."

Alas! the orphan girl's experience of this life
had early taught her the lesson which some people learn so late. She had learned to distrust
the equal blue of a summer sky, the glorious
splendor of the blazing sunlight. She was accustomed to sorrow; but these brief glimpses of
perfect happiness filled her with a dim sense of
terror. She felt like some earthly wanderer
who had strayed across the threshold of Paradise. In the midst of her delight and admiration she trembled for the moment in which the
ruthless angels, bearing flaming swords, should
drive her from the celestial gates.

"It can't last, Edward," she murmured.

"Can't last, Polly!" cried the young man;
"why, my dove is transformed all at once into
a raven. We have outlived our troubles, Polly,
like the hero and heroine in one of your novels;
and what is to prevent our living happy ever
afterward, like them? If you remember, my
dear, no sorrows or trials ever fall to the lot of
people *after* marriage. The persecutions, the
separations, the estrangements, are all antenup-
tial. When once your true novelist gets his hero
and heroine up to the altar rails in real earnest—
he gets them into the church sometimes, and
then forbids the bans, or brings a former wife,
or a rightful husband, pale and denouncing,
from behind a pillar, and drives the wretched
pair out again, to persecute them through three
hundred pages more before he lets them get back
again—but when once the important words are
spoken and the knot tied the story's done, and
the happy couple get forty or fifty years' wedded bliss as a set-off against the miseries they
have endured in the troubled course of a twelvemonth's courtship. That's the sort of thing,
isn't it, Polly?"

The clock of St. Cross, sounding faintly
athwart the meadows, struck three as the
young man finished speaking.

"Three o'clock, Polly!" he cried; "we must
go home, my pet. I mean to be business-like
to-day."

Upon each day in that happy honey-moon holiday Captain Arundel had made some such declaration with regard to his intention of being
business-like; that is to say, setting himself deliberately to the task of writing those letters

which should announce and explain his marriage to the people who had a right to hear of it. But the soldier had a dislike to all letter-writing, and a special horror of any epistolary communication which could come under the denomination of a business-letter; so the easy summer-days slipped by—the delicious drowsy noontides, the soft and dreamy twilight, the tender moonlit nights—and the Captain put off the task for which he had no fancy, from after breakfast until after dinner, and from after dinner until after breakfast; always beguiled away from his open traveling-desk by a word from Mary, who called him to the window to look at a pretty child on the village green before the inn, or at the blacksmith's dog, or the tinker's donkey, or a tired Italian organ-boy who had strayed into that out-of-the-way nook, or at the smart butcher from Winchester, who rattled over in a pony-cart twice a week to take orders from the gentry round about, and to insult and defy the local purveyor, whose stock generally seemed to consist of one leg of mutton and a dish of pig's fry.

The young couple walked slowly through the meadows, crossing rustic wooden bridges that spanned the winding stream, loitering to look down into the clear water at the fish which Captain Arundel pointed out, but which Mary could never see, that young lady always fixing her eyes upon some long trailing weed afloat in the transparent water, while the silvery trout indicated by her husband glided quietly away to the sedgy bottom of the stream. They lingered by the water-mill, beneath whose shadow some children were fishing; they seized upon every pretext for lengthening that sunny homeward walk, and only reached the inn as the village-clocks were striking four, at which hour Captain Arundel had ordered dinner.

But—after the simple little repast, mild and artless in its nature as the fair young spirit of the bride herself; after the landlord, sympathetic yet respectful, had in his own person attended upon his two guests; after the pretty rustic chamber had been cleared of all evidence of the meal that had been eaten—Edward Arundel began to seriously consider the business in hand.

"The letters must be written, Polly," he said, seating himself at a table near the open window. Trailing branches of jasmine and honey-suckle made a frame-work round the diamond-paned casement; the scented blossoms blew into the room with every breath of the warm August breeze, and hung trembling in the folds of the chintz curtains. Mr. Arundel's gaze wandered dreamily away through this open window to the primitive picture without—the scattered cottages upon the other side of the green, the cattle standing in the pond, the cackling geese hurrying homeward across the purple ridge of common, the village gossips loitering beneath the faded sign that hung before the low white tavern at the angle of the road. He looked at all these things as he flung his leathern desk upon the table, and made a great parade of unlocking and opening it.

"The letters must be written," he repeated, with a smothered sigh. "Did you ever notice a peculiar property in stationery, Polly?"

Mrs. Edward Arundel only opened her brown eyes to their widest extent, and stared at her husband.

"No; I see you haven't," said the young man. "How should you, my fortunate Polly? you've never had to write any business-letters yet, though you are an heiress. The peculiarity of all stationery, my dear, is, that it is possessed of an intuitive knowledge of the object for which it is to be used. If one has to write an unpleasant letter, Polly, it might go a little smoother, you know; one might round one's paragraphs, and spell the difficult words—the 'believes' and 'receives,' the 'tills' and 'untils,' and all that sort of thing—better with a pleasant pen, an easy-going, jolly, soft-nibbed quill, that would seem to say, 'Cheer up, old fellow, I'll carry you through it; we'll get to "your very obedient servant" before you know where you are,' and so on. But, bless your heart, Polly, let a poor, unbusiness-like fellow try to write a business-letter, and every thing goes against him. The pen knows what he's at, and jibs and stumbles and shies about the paper like a broken-down screw; the ink turns thick and lumpy, the paper gets as greasy as a London pavement after a fall of snow, till a poor fellow gives up, and knocks under to the force of circumstances. You see if my pen doesn't splutter, Polly, the moment I address Richard Paulette."

Captain Arundel was very careful in the adjustment of his sheet of paper, and began his letter with an air of resolution:

"WHITE HART INN, MILLDALE, NEAR WINCHESTER,
    August 14.

"MY DEAR SIR"—

He wrote as much as this with great promptitude, and then, with his elbow on the table, fell to staring at his pretty young wife and drumming his fingers on his chin. Mary was sitting opposite her husband at the open window, working, or making a pretense of being occupied with some impossible fragment of Berlin wool-work, while she watched her husband.

"How pretty you look in that white frock, Polly!" said the soldier; "you call those things frocks, don't you? And that blue sash, too—you ought always to wear white, Mary, like your namesakes abroad who are vouée au blanc by their faithful mothers, and who are a blessing to the laundresses for the first seven or fourteen years of their lives. What shall I say to Paulette? He's such a jolly fellow, there oughtn't to be much difficulty about the matter. 'My dear Sir,' seems absurdly stiff; 'My dear Paulette'—that's better—'I write this to inform you that your client, Miss Mary March—' What's that, Polly?"

It was the postman, a youth upon a pony, with the afternoon letters from London. Captain Arundel flung down his pen and went to the window. He had some interest in this young man's arrival, as he had left orders that such letters as were addressed to him at the hotel in Covent Garden should be forwarded to him at Milldale.

"I dare say there's a letter from Germany, Polly," he said, eagerly. "My mother and Letitia are capital correspondents; I'll wager any thing there's a letter, and I can answer it in the one I'm going to write this evening, and that'll be killing two birds with one stone. I'll run down to the postman, Polly."

Captain Arundel had good reason to go after his letters, for there seemed little chance of those missives being brought to him. The youthful postman was standing in the porch drinking ale out of a ponderous earthen-ware mug, and talking to the landlord, when Edward went down. "Any letters for me, Dick?" the Captain asked. He knew the Christian name of almost every visitor or hanger-on at the little inn, though he had not staid there an entire fortnight, and was as popular and admired as if he had been some free-spoken young squire to whom all the land round about belonged.

"'Ees, Sir," the young man answered, shuffling off his cap; "there be two letters for ye."

He handed the two packets to Captain Arundel, who looked doubtfully at the address of the uppermost, which, like the other, had been redirected by the people at the London hotel. The original address of this letter was in a handwriting that was strange to him; but it bore the post-mark of the village from which the Dangerfield letters were sent.

The back of the inn looked into an orchard, and through an open door opposite to the porch Edward Arundel saw the low branches of the trees, and the ripening fruit red and golden in the afternoon sunlight. He went out into this orchard to read his letters, his mind a little disturbed by the strange handwriting upon the Dangerfield epistle.

The letter was from his father's housekeeper, imploring him most earnestly to go down to the Park without delay. Squire Arundel had been seized with an attack of paralysis, and was declared to be in imminent danger. Mrs. and Miss Arundel and Mr Reginald were away in Germany. The faithful old servant implored the younger son to lose no time in hurrying home, if he wished to see his father alive.

The soldier stood leaning against the gnarled gray trunk of an old apple-tree, staring at this letter with a white awe-stricken face.

What was he to do? He must go to his father, of course. He must go without a moment's delay. He must catch the first train that would carry him westward from Southampton. There could be no question as to his duty. He must go; he must leave his young wife.

His heart sank with a sharp thrill of pain, and with perhaps some faint shuddering sense of an unknown terror, as he thought of this.

"It was lucky I didn't write the letters," he reflected; "no one will guess the secret of my darling's retreat. She can stay here till I come back to her. God knows I shall hurry back the moment my duty sets me free. These people will take care of her. No one will know where to look for her. I'm very glad I didn't write to Olivia. We were so happy this morning! Who could think that sorrow would come between us so soon?"

Captain Arundel looked at his watch. It was a quarter to six o'clock, and he knew that an express left Southampton for the west at eight. There would be time for him to catch that train with the help of a sturdy pony belonging to the landlord of the White Hart, which would rattle him over to the station in an hour and a half. There would be time for him to catch the train;

but, oh, how little time to comfort his darling; how little time to reconcile his young wife to the temporary separation!

He hurried back to the porch, briefly explained to the landlord what had happened, ordered the pony and gig to be got ready immediately, and then went very, very slowly up stairs, to the room in which his young wife sat by the open window waiting for his return.

Mary looked up at his face as he entered the room, and that one glance told her of some new sorrow.

"Edward," she cried, starting up from her chair with a look of terror, "my step-mother has come!"

Even in his trouble the young man smiled at his foolish wife's all-absorbing fear of Olivia Marchmont.

"No, my darling," he said; "I wish to Heaven our worst trouble were the chance of your father's widow breaking in upon us. Something has happened, Mary; something very sorrowful, very serious for me. My father is ill, Polly dear, dangerously ill, and I must go to him."

Mary Arundel drew a long breath. Her face had grown very white, and the hands that were linked tightly together upon her husband's shoulder trembled a little.

"I will try to bear it," she said; "I will try to bear it."

"God bless you, my darling!" the soldier answered, fervently, clasping his young wife to his breast. "I know you will. It will be a very short parting, Mary dearest. I will come back to you directly I have seen my father. If he is worse, there will be little need for me to stop at Dangerfield; if he is better, I can take you back there with me. My own darling love, it is very bitter for us to be parted thus; but I know that you will bear it like a heroine. Won't you, Polly?"

"I will try to bear it, dear."

She said very little more than this, but clung about her husband, not with any desperate force, not with any clamorous and tumultuous grief, but with a half-despondent resignation; as a drowning man, whose strength is well-nigh exhausted, may cling, in his hopelessness, to a spar which he knows he must presently abandon.

Mary Arundel followed her husband hither and thither while he made his brief and hurried preparations for the sudden journey; but although she was powerless to assist him—for her trembling hands let fall every thing she tried to hold, and there was a mist before her eyes which distorted and blotted the outline of each object she looked at—she hindered him by no noisy lamentations, she distressed him by no tears. She suffered, as it was her habit to suffer, quietly and uncomplainingly.

The sun was sinking when she went with Edward down stairs to the porch, before which the landlord's pony and gig were in waiting, in custody of a smart lad who was to drive Mr. Arundel to Southampton. There was no time for any protracted farewell. It was better so, perhaps, Edward thought. He would be back so soon that the grief he felt in this parting —and it may be that his suffering was scarcely less than Mary's—seemed wasted anguish, to which it would have been sheer cowardice to give way. But for all this the soldier very nearly broke down when he saw his childish wife's piteous face, white in the evening sunlight, turned to him in mute appeal, as if the quivering lips would fain have entreated him to abandon all and to remain. He lifted the fragile figure in his arms—alas! it had never seemed so fragile as now—and covered the pale face with passionate kisses and fast-dropping tears. "God bless and defend you, Mary! God keep—"

He was ashamed of the huskiness of his voice, and putting his wife suddenly away from him, he sprang into the gig, snatched the reins from the boy's hand, and drove away at the pony's best speed. The old-fashioned vehicle disappeared in a cloud of dust; and Mary, looking after her husband with eyes that were as yet tearless, saw nothing but glaring light and confusion, and a pastoral landscape that reeled and heaved like a stormy sea.

It seemed to her, as she went slowly back to her room, and sat down amidst the disorder of open portmanteaus and overturned hat-boxes, which the young man had thrown here and there in his hurried selection of the few things necessary for him to take on his hasty journey—it seemed as if the greatest calamity of her life had now befallen her. As hopelessly as she had thought of her father's death, she now thought of Edward Arundel's departure. She could not see beyond the acute anguish of this separation. She could not realize to herself that there was no cause for all this terrible sorrow; that the parting was only a temporary one; and that her husband would return to her in a few days at the furthest. Now that she was alone, that the necessity for heroism was past, she abandoned herself utterly to the despair that had held possession of her soul from the moment in which Captain Arundel had told her of his father's illness.

The sun went down behind the purple hills that sheltered the western side of the little village. The tree-tops in the orchard below the open window of Mrs. Arundel's bedroom grew dim in the gray twilight. Little by little the sound of voices in the rooms below died away into stillness. The fresh rosy-cheeked country girl who had waited upon the young husband and wife came into the sitting-room with a pair of wax candles in old-fashioned silver candlesticks, and lingered in the room for a little time, expecting to receive some order from the lonely watcher. But Mary had locked the door of her bedchamber, and sat with her head upon the sill of the open window, looking wearily out into the dim orchard. It was only when the stars glimmered in the tranquil sky that the girl's blank despair gave way before a sudden burst of tears, and she flung herself down beside the white-curtained bed to pray for her young husband. She prayed for him in an ecstatic fervor of love and faith, carried away by the new hopefulness that arose out of her ardent supplications, and picturing him going triumphant on his course to find his father out of danger—restored to health, perhaps—and to return to her before the stars glimmered through the darkness of another summer's night. She prayed for him, hoping and believing every thing; though at the hour in which she knelt,

with the faint starlight shimmering upon her upturned face and clasped hands, Edward Arundel was lying, maimed and senseless, in the wretched waiting-room of a little railway-station in Dorsetshire, watched over by an obscure country surgeon, while the frightened officials scudded here and there in search of some vehicle in which the young man might be conveyed to the nearest town.

There had been one of those accidents which seem terribly common on every line of railway, however well managed. A signal-man had mistaken one train for another; a flag had been dropped too soon; and the down express had run into a heavy luggage-train blundering up from Exeter with farm produce for the London markets. Two men had been killed, and a great many passengers hurt; some very seriously. Edward Arundel's case was perhaps one of the most serious among these.

---

## CHAPTER XIX.

### SOUNDING THE DEPTHS.

Lavinia Weston spent the evening after her visit to Marchmont Towers at her writing-desk, which, like every thing else appertaining to her, was a model of neatness and propriety; perfect in its way, although it was no marvelous specimen of walnut-wood and burnished gold, no elegant structure of papier-maché and mother-of-pearl, but simply a school-girl's rosewood velvet-lined desk, bought for fifteen shillings or a guinea.

Mrs. Weston had administered the evening refreshment of weak tea, stale bread, and strong butter to her meek husband, and had dismissed him to the surgery, a sunken and rather cellar-like apartment opening out of the prim second-best parlor, and approached from the village street by a side-door. The surgeon was very well content to employ himself with the preparation of such draughts and boluses as were required by the ailing inhabitants of Kemberling, while his wife sat at her desk in the room above him. He left his gallipots and pestle and mortar once or twice in the course of the evening to clamber ponderously up the three or four stairs leading to the sitting-room, and stare through the keyhole of the door at Mrs. Weston's thoughtful face, and busy hand gliding softly over the smooth note-paper. He did this in no prying or suspicious spirit, but out of sheer admiration for his wife.

"What a mind she has!" he murmured, rapturously, as he went back to his work; "what a mind!"

The letter which Lavinia Weston wrote that evening was a very long one. She was one of those women who write long letters upon every convenient occasion. To-night she covered two sheets of note-paper with her small neat handwriting. Those two sheets contained a detailed account of the interview that had taken place that day between the surgeon's wife and Olivia; and the letter was addressed to the artist, Paul Marchmont.

Perhaps it was in consequence of the receipt of this letter that Paul Marchmont arrived at his sister's house at Kemberling two days after

Mrs. Weston's visit to Marchmont Towers. He told the surgeon that he came to Lincolnshire for a few days' change of air, after a long spell of very hard work; and George Weston, who looked upon his brother-in-law as an intellectual demi-god, was very well content to accept any explanation of Mr. Marchmont's visit.

"Kemberling isn't a very lively place for you, Mr. Paul," he said, apologetically—he always called his wife's brother Mr. Paul—"but I dare say Lavinia will contrive to make you comfortable. She persuaded me to come here when old Dawnfield died; but I can't say she acted with her usual tact, for the business ain't as good as my Stanfield practice; but I don't tell Lavinia so."

Paul Marchmont smiled.

"The business will pick up by-and-by, I dare say," he said. "You'll have the Marchmont Towers' family to attend to in good time, I suppose."

"That's what Lavinia said," answered the surgeon. "'Mrs. John Marchmont can't refuse to employ a relation,' she says; 'and as first cousin to Mary Marchmont's father, I ought'—meaning herself, you know—'to have some influence in that quarter.' But then, you see, the very week we come here the gal goes and runs away; which rather, as one may say, puts a spoke in our wheel, you know."

Mr. George Weston rubbed his chin reflectively as he concluded thus. He was a man given to spending his leisure hours—when he had any leisure, which was not very often—in tavern parlors, where the affairs of the nation were settled and unsettled every evening over sixpenny glasses of Hollands and water; and he regretted his removal from Stanfield, which had been as the uprooting of all his dearest associations. He was a solemn man, who never hazarded an opinion lightly—perhaps because he never had an opinion to hazard—and his stolidity won him a good deal of respect from strangers; but in the hands of his wife he was meeker than the doves that cooed in the pigeon-house behind his dwelling, and more plastic than the knob of white wax upon which industrious Mrs. Weston was wont to rub her thread when engaged in the mysteries of that elaborate and terrible science which women paradoxically call *plain* needle-work.

Paul Marchmont presented himself at the Towers upon the day after his arrival at Kemberling. His interview with the widow was a very long one. He had studied every line of his sister's letter; he had weighed every word that had fallen from Olivia's lips and had been recorded by Lavinia Weston; and taking the knowledge thus obtained as his starting-point, he took his dissecting-knife and went to work at an intellectual autopsy. He anatomized the wretched woman's soul. He made her tell her secret, and bare her tortured breast before him; now wringing some hasty word from her impatience, now entrapping her into some admission—if only as much as a defiant look, a sudden lowering of the dark brows, an involuntary compression of the lips. He *made* her reveal herself to him. Poor Rosencrantz and Guildenstern were sorry blunderers in that art which is vulgarly called pumping, and were easily put out by a few quips and quaint retorts from the

F

mad Danish prince; but Paul Marchmont *would* have played upon Hamlet more deftly than ever mortal musician played upon pipe or recorder, and would have fathomed the remotest depths of that sorrowful and erratic soul. Olivia writhed under the torture of that polite inquisition, for she knew that her secrets were being extorted from her; that her pitiful folly—that folly which she would have denied even to herself, if possible—was being laid bare in all its weak foolishness. She knew this; but she was compelled to smile in the face of her bland inquisitor, to respond to his commonplace expressions of concern about the protracted absence of the missing girl, and meekly to receive his suggestions respecting the course it was her duty to take. He had the air of responding to *her* suggestions, rather than of himself dictating any particular line of conduct. He affected to believe that he was only agreeing with some understood ideas of hers, while he urged his own views upon her.

"Then we are quite of one mind in this, my dear Mrs. Marchmont," he said, at last; "this unfortunate girl must not be suffered to remain away from her legitimate home any longer than we can help. It is our duty to find and bring her back. I need scarcely say that you, being bound to her by every tie of affection, and having, beyond this, the strongest claim upon her gratitude for your devoted fulfillment of the trust confided in you—one hears of these things, Mrs. Marchmont, in a country village like Kemberling—I need scarcely say that you are the most fitting person to win the poor child back to a sense of her duty—if she *can* be won to such a sense." Paul Marchmont added, after a sudden pause and a thoughtful sigh, "I sometimes fear—"

He stopped abruptly, waiting until Olivia should question him.

"You sometimes fear—?"

"That—that the error into which Miss Marchmont has fallen is the result of a mental rather than of a moral deficiency."

"What do you mean?"

"I mean this, my dear Mrs. Marchmont," answered the artist, gravely; "one of the most powerful evidences of the soundness of a man's brain is his capability of assigning a reasonable motive for every action of his life. No matter how unreasonable the action in itself may seem, if the motive for that action can be demonstrated. But the moment a man acts *without* motive, we begin to take alarm and to watch him. He is eccentric; his conduct is no longer amenable to ordinary rule; and we begin to trace his eccentricities to some weakness or deficiency in his judgment or intellect. Now, I ask you what motive Mary Marchmont can have had for running away from this house?"

Olivia quailed under the piercing scrutiny of the artist's cold gray eyes, but she did not attempt to reply to his question.

"The answer is very simple," he continued, after that long scrutiny; "the girl could have had no cause for flight; while, on the other hand, every reasonable motive that can be supposed to actuate a woman's conduct was arrayed against her. She had a happy home, a kind step-mother. She was within a few years of becoming undisputed mistress of a very large estate. *And yet, immediately after having assisted at a festive entertainment, to all appearance as gay and happy as the gayest and happiest there, this girl runs away in the dead of the night, abandoning the mansion which is her own property, and assigning no reason whatever for what she does. Can you wonder, then, if I feel confirmed in an opinion that I formed upon the day on which I heard the reading of my cousin's will?"

"What opinion?"

"That Mary Marchmont is as feeble in mind as she is fragile in body."

He launched this sentence boldly, and waited for Olivia's reply. He had discovered the widow's secret. He had fathomed the cause of her jealous hatred of Mary Marchmont; but even *he* did not yet understand the nature of the conflict in the desperate woman's breast. She could not be wicked all at once. Against every fresh sin she made a fresh struggle, and she would not accept the lie which the artist tried to force upon her.

"I do not think that there is any deficiency in my step-daughter's intellect," she said, resolutely.

She was beginning to understand that Paul Marchmont wanted to ally himself with her against the orphan heiress, but as yet she did not understand why he should do so. She was slow to comprehend feelings that were utterly foreign to her own nature. There was so little of mercenary baseness in this strange woman's soul, that had the flame of a candle alone stood between her and the possession of Marchmont Towers, I doubt if she would have cared to waste a breath upon its extinction. She had lived away from the world, and out of the world; and it was difficult for her to comprehend the mean and paltry wickednesses which arise out of the worship of Baal.

Paul Marchmont recoiled a little before the straight answer which the widow had given him.

"You think Miss Marchmont strong-minded, then, perhaps?" he said.

"No, not strong-minded."

"My dear Mrs. Marchmont, you deal in paradoxes," exclaimed the artist. "You say that your step-daughter is neither weak-minded nor strong-minded?"

"Weak enough, perhaps, to be easily influenced by other people; weak enough to believe any thing my cousin Edward Arundel might choose to tell her; but not what is generally called deficient in intellect."

"You think her perfectly able to take care of herself?"

"Yes; I think so."

"And yet this running away looks almost as if—but I have no wish to force any unpleasant belief upon you, my dear madam. I think—as you yourself appear to suggest—that the best thing we can do is to get this poor girl home again as quickly as possible. It will never do for the mistress of Marchmont Towers to be wandering about the world with Mr. Edward Arundel. Pray pardon me, Mrs. Marchmont, if I speak rather disrespectfully of your cousin; but I really can not think that the gentleman has acted very honorably in this business."

Olivia was silent. She remembered the pas-

sionate indignation of the young soldier, the angry defiance hurled at her, as Edward Arundel galloped away from the gaunt western façade. She remembered these things, and involuntarily contrasted them with the smooth blandness of. Paul Marchmont's talk, and the deadly purpose lurking beneath it—of which deadly purpose some faint suspicion was beginning to dawn upon her.

If she could have thought Mary Marchmont mad—if she could have thought Edward Arundel base—she would have been glad; for then there would have been some excuse for her own wickedness. But she could not think so. She slipped little by little down into the black gulf, dragged now by her own mad passion, now lured yet further downward by Paul Marchmont.

Between this man and eleven thousand a year the life of a fragile girl was the solitary obstacle. For three years it had been so, and for three years Paul Marchmont had waited—patiently, as it was his habit to wait—the hour and the opportunity for action. The hour and opportunity had come, and this woman, Olivia Marchmont, only stood in his way. She must become either his enemy or his tool, to be baffled or to be made useful. He had now sounded the depths of her nature, and he determined to make her his tool.

"It shall be my business to discover this poor child's hiding-place," he said; "when that is found, I will communicate with you, and I know you will not refuse to fulfill the trust confided to you by your late husband. You will bring your step-daughter back to this house, and henceforward protect her from the dangerous influence of Edward Arundel."

Olivia looked at the speaker with an expression which seemed like terror. It was as if she said,

"Are you the devil that you hold out this temptation to me, and twist my own passions to serve your purpose?"

And then she paltered with her conscience.

"Do you consider that it is my duty to do this?" she asked.

"My dear Mrs. Marchmont, most decidedly."

"I will do it then. I—I—wish to do my duty."

"And you can perform no greater act of charity than by bringing this unhappy girl back to a sense of *her* duty. Remember that her reputation, her future happiness, may fall a sacrifice to this foolish conduct, which, I regret to say, is very generally known in the neighborhood. Forgive me if I express my opinion too freely; but I can not help thinking that if Mr. Arundel's intentions had been strictly honorable, he would have written to you before this, to tell you that his search for the missing girl had failed; or, in the event of his finding her, he would have taken the earliest opportunity of bringing her back to her own home. My poor cousin's somewhat unprotected position, her wealth, and her inexperience of the world, place her at the mercy of a fortune-hunter; and Mr. Arundel has himself to thank if his conduct gives rise to the belief that he wishes to compromise this girl in the eyes of the scandalous, and thus make sure of your consent to a marriage which would give him command of my cousin's fortune."

Olivia Marchmont's bosom heaved with the stormy beating of her heart. Was she to sit calmly by and hold her peace while this man slandered the brave young soldier, the bold, reckless, generous-hearted lad, who had shone upon her out of the darkness of her life, as the very incarnation of all that is noble and admirable in mankind? Was she to sit quietly by and hear a stranger lie away her kinsman's honor, and truth, and manhood?

Yes, she must do so. This man had offered her a price for her truth and her soul. He was ready to help her to the revenge she longed for. He was ready to give her his aid in separating the innocent young lovers, whose pure affection had poisoned her life, whose happiness was worse than the worst death to her. She kept silent, therefore, and waited for Paul to speak again.

"I will go up to Town to-morrow, and set to work about this business," the artist said, as he rose to take leave of Mrs. Marchmont; "I do not believe that I shall have much difficulty in finding the young lady's hiding-place. My first task shall be to look for Mr. Arundel. You can perhaps give me the address of some place in London where your cousin is in the habit of staying?"

"I can."

"Thank you; that will very much simplify matters. I shall write you immediate word of any discovery I make, and will then leave all the rest to you. My influence over Mary Marchmont as an entire stranger could be nothing. Yours, on the contrary, must be unbounded. It will be for you to act upon my letter."

Olivia Marchmont waited for two days and nights for the promised letter. Upon the third morning it came. The artist's epistle was very brief:

"MY DEAR MRS. MARCHMONT,—I have made the necessary discovery. Miss Marchmont is to be found at the White Hart Inn, Milldale, near Winchester. May I venture to urge your proceeding there in search of her without delay?

"Yours very faithfully,
"PAUL MARCHMONT.
"CHARLOTTE STREET, FITZROY SQUARE, Aug. 15."

---

## CHAPTER XX.

### RISEN FROM THE GRAVE.

THE rain dripped ceaselessly upon the dreary earth under a gray November sky—a dull and lowering sky, that seemed to brood over this lower world with some menace of coming down to blot out and destroy it. The express train rushing headlong across the wet flats of Lincolnshire glared like a meteor in the gray fog; the dismal shriek of the engine was like the cry of a bird of prey. The few passengers who had chosen that dreary winter's day for their travels looked despondently out at the monotonous prospect, seeking in vain to descry some spot of hope in the joyless prospect; or made futile attempts to read their newspapers by the dim light of the lamp in the roof of the carriage. Sulky passengers shuddered savagely as they wrapped themselves in huge woolen rugs or ponderous coverings made from the skins of wild beasts. Melancholy passengers drew grotesque and hideous traveling-caps over their brows, and, coiling themselves in the corner of their seats, essayed to sleep away the weary hours. Every thing upon this earth seemed dismal and damp, cold and desolate, incongruous and uncomfortable.

But there was one first-class passenger in that Lincolnshire express who made himself especially obnoxious to his fellows by the display of an amount of restlessness and superabundant energy quite out of keeping with the lazy despondency of those about him.

This was a young man with a long tawny beard and a white face—a very handsome face, though wan and attenuated, as if with some terrible sickness, and somewhat disfigured by certain strappings of plaster, which were bound about a patch of his skull a little above the left temple. This young man had the side of one carriage to himself, and a sort of bed had been made up for him with extra cushions, upon which he lay at full length, when he was still, which was never for very long together. He was enveloped almost to the chin in voluminous railway-rugs, but, in spite of these coverings, shuddered every now and then as if with cold. He had a pocket-pistol among his traveling paraphernalia, which he applied occasionally to his dry lips. Sometimes drops of perspiration broke suddenly out upon his forehead, and were brushed away by a tremulous hand, that was scarcely strong enough to hold a cambric handkerchief. In short, it was sufficiently obvious to every one that this young man with the tawny beard had only lately risen from a sick-bed, and had risen therefrom considerably before the time at which any prudent medical practitioner would have given him license to do so.

It was evident that he was very, very ill, but that he was, if any thing, more ill at ease in mind than in body, and that some terrible gnawing anxiety, some restless care, some horrible uncertainty or perpetual foreboding of trouble, would not allow him to be at peace. It was as much as the three fellow-passengers who sat opposite to him could do to bear with his impatience, his restlessness, his short half-stifled moans, his long weary sighs; the horror of his fidgety feet shuffled incessantly upon the cushions; the suddenly convulsive jerks with which he would lift himself upon his elbow to stare fiercely into the dismal fog outside the carriage window; the groans that were wrung from him as he flung himself into new and painful positions; the frightful aspect of physical agony which came over his face, as he looked at his watch—and he drew out and consulted that ill-used chronometer, upon an average, once in a quarter of an hour; his impatient crumpling of the crisp leaves of a new "Bradshaw," which he turned over ever and anon, as if, by perpetual reference to that mysterious time-table, he might hasten the advent of the hour at which he was to reach his destination. He was, altogether, a most aggravating and exasperating traveling companion; and it was only out of Christian forbearance with the weakness of his physical state that his irritated fellow-passengers refrained from uniting themselves against him, and casting him bodily out of the window of the carriage; as a clown sometimes flings a venerable but tiresome pantaloon through a square trap or pitfall, lurking, undreamed of, in the façade of an honest tradesman's dwelling.

The three passengers had, in divers manners, expressed their sympathy with the invalid traveler; but their courtesies had not been responded to with any evidence of gratitude or heartiness. The young man had answered them in an absent fashion, scarcely deigning to look at them as he spoke, speaking altogether with the air of some sleep-walker, who roams hither and thither absorbed in a dreadful dream, making a world for himself, and peopling it with horrible images unknown to those about him.

Had he been ill? Yes, very ill. He had had a railway accident, and then brain-fever. He had been ill for a long time.

Somebody asked him how long?

He shuffled about upon the cushions, and groaned aloud at this question, to the alarm of the man who had asked it.

"How long?" he cried, in a fierce agony of mental or bodily uneasiness; "how long? Two months—three months—ever since the 14th of August."

Then another passenger, looking at the young man's very evident sufferings from a commercial point of view, asked him whether he had had any compensation.

"Compensation!" cried the invalid. "What compensation?"

"Compensation from the Railway Company. I hope you've a strong case against them, for you've evidently been a terrible sufferer."

It was dreadful to see the way in which the sick man writhed under this question.

"Compensation!" he cried. "What compensation can they give me for an accident that shut me in a living grave for three months, that separated me from—— You don't know what you're talking about, Sir," he added, suddenly; "I can't think of this business patiently; I can't be reasonable. If they'd hacked me to pieces, I shouldn't have cared. I've been under a red-hot Indian sun when we fellows couldn't see the sky above us for the smoke of the cannons and the flashing of the sabres about our heads, and I'm not afraid of a little cutting and smashing more or less; but when I think what others may have suffered through—— I'm almost mad, and——"

He couldn't say any more, for the intensity of his passion had shaken him as a leaf is shaken by a whirlwind; and he fell back upon the cushions, trembling in every limb, and groaning aloud. His fellow-passengers looked at each other rather nervously, and two out of the three entertained serious thoughts of changing carriages when the express stopped midway between London and Lincoln.

But they were reassured by-and-by; for the invalid, who was Captain Edward Arundel, or that pale shadow of the dashing young cavalry officer which had risen from a sick-bed, relapsed into silence, and displayed no more alarming symptoms than that perpetual restlessness and disquietude which is cruelly wearying even to the strongest nerves. He only spoke once more, and that was when the short day, in which there had been no actual daylight, was closing in, and

the journey nearly finished, when he startled his companions by crying out, suddenly,

"O my God, will this journey never come to an end? Shall I never be put out of this horrible suspense?"

The journey, or at any rate Captain Arundel's share of it, came to an end almost immediately afterward, for the train stopped at Swampington; and while the invalid was staggering feebly to his feet, eager to scramble out of the carriage, his servant came to the door to assist and support him.

"You seem to have borne the journey wonderfully, Sir," the man said, respectfully, as he tried to rearrange his master's wrappings, and to do as much as circumstances, and the young man's restless impatience, would allow of being done for his comfort.

"I have suffered the tortures of the infernal regions, Morrison," Captain Arundel ejaculated, in answer to his attendant's congratulatory address. "Get me a fly directly. I must go to the Towers at once."

"Not to-night, Sir, surely?" the servant remonstrated, in a tone of alarm. "Your Mar and the doctors said you must rest at Swampington for a night."

"I'll rest nowhere till I've been to Marchmont Towers," answered the young soldier, passionately. "If I must walk there—if I'm to drop down dead on the road—I'll go. If the corn-fields between this and the Towers were a blazing prairie or a raging sea, I'd go. Get me a fly, man; and don't talk to me of my mother or the doctors. I'm going to look for my wife. Get me a fly."

This demand for a commonplace hackney vehicle sounded rather like an anti-climax, after the young man's talk of blazing prairies and raging seas; but passionate reality has no ridiculous side, and Edward Arundel's most foolish words were sublime by reason of their earnestness.

"Get me a fly, Morrison," he said, grinding his heel upon the platform in the intensity of his impatience. "Or, stay, we should gain more in the end if you were to go to the George—it's not ten minutes' walk from here; one of the porters will take you—the people there know me, and they'll let you have some vehicle, with a pair of horses and a clever driver. Tell them it's for an errand of life and death, and that Captain Arundel will pay them three times their usual price, or six times, if they wish. Tell them any thing, so long as you get what we want."

The valet, an old servant of Edward Arundel's father, was carried away by the young man's mad impetuosity. The vitality of this broken-down invalid, whose physical weakness contrasted strangely with his mental energy, bore down upon the grave man-servant like an avalanche, and carried him whither it would. He was fain to abandon all hope of being true to the promises which he had given to Mrs. Arundel and the medical men, and to yield himself to the will of the fiery young soldier.

He left Edward Arundel sitting upon a chair in the solitary waiting-room, and hurried after the porter who had volunteered to show him the way to the George Inn, the most prosperous hotel in Swampington.

The valet had good reason to be astonished by

his young master's energy and determination; for Mary Marchmont's husband was as one rescued from the very jaws of death. For twelve weeks after that terrible concussion upon the Southwestern Railway, Edward Arundel had lain in a state of coma--helpless, mindless; all the story of his life blotted away, and his brain transformed into as blank a page as if he had been an infant lying on his mother's knees. A fractured skull had been the young Captain's chief share in those injuries which were dealt out pretty freely to the travelers in the Exeter mail on the 14th of August; and the young man had been conveyed to Dangerfield Park, while his father's corpse lay in stately solemnity in one of the chief rooms, almost as much a corpse as that dead father.

Mrs. Arundel's troubles had come, as the troubles of rich and prosperous people often do come, in a sudden avalanche, that threatened to overwhelm the tender-hearted matron. She had been summoned from Germany to attend her husband's death-bed; and she was called away from her faithful watch beside that death-bed, to hear tidings of the terrible accident that had befallen her younger son.

Neither the Dorsetshire doctor who attended the stricken traveler upon his homeward journey, and brought the strong man, helpless as a child, to claim the same tender devotion that had watched over his infancy, nor the Devonshire doctors who were summoned to Dangerfield, gave any hope of their patient's recovery. The sufferer might linger for years, they said; but his existence would be only a living death, a horrible blank, which it was a cruelty to wish prolonged. But when a great London surgeon appeared upon the scene, a new light, a wonderful gleam of hope, shone in upon the blackness of the mother's despair.

This great London surgeon, who was a very unassuming and matter-of-fact little man, and who seemed in a great hurry to earn his fee and run back to Saville Row by the next express, made a brief examination of the patient, asked a very few sharp and trenchant questions of the reverential provincial medical practitioners, and then declared that the chief cause of Edward Arundel's state lay in the fact that a portion of the skull was depressed—a splinter pressed upon the brain.

The provincial practitioners opened their eyes very wide; and one of them ventured to mutter something to the effect that he had thought as much for a long time. The London surgeon further stated, that until the pressure was removed from the patient's brain, Captain Edward Arundel would remain in precisely the same state as that into which he had fallen immediately upon the accident. The splinter could only be removed by a very critical operation, and this operation must be deferred until the patient's bodily strength was in some measure restored.

The surgeon gave brief but decisive directions to the provincial medical men as to the treatment of their patient during this interregnum, and then departed, after promising to return as soon as Captain Arundel was in a fit state for the operation. This period did not arrive till the first week in November, when the Devonshire doctors ventured to declare their patient's shattered frame in a great measure renovated by their devoted attention, and the tender care of the best of mothers.

The great surgeon came. The critical operation was performed, with such eminent success as to merit a very long description which afterward appeared in the *Lancet*; and slowly, like the gradual lifting of a curtain, the black shadows passed away from Edward Arundel's mind, and the memory of the past returned to him.

It was then that he raved madly about his young wife, perpetually demanding that she might be summoned to him; continually declaring that some great misfortune would befall her if she were not brought to his side, that, even in his feebleness, he might defend and protect her. His mother mistook his vehemence for the raving of delirium. The doctors fell into the same error, and treated him for brain-fever. It was only when the young soldier demonstrated to them that he could, by making an effort over himself, be as reasonable as they were, that he convinced them of their mistake. Then he begged to be left alone with his mother; and, with his feverish hands clasped in hers, asked her the meaning of her black dress, and the reason why his young wife had not come to him. He learned that his mother's mourning garments were worn in memory of his dead father. He learned also, after much bewilderment and passionate questioning, that no tidings of Mary Marchmont had ever come to Dangerfield.

It was then that the young man told his mother the story of his marriage: how that marriage had been contracted in haste, but with no real desire for secrecy; how he had, out of mere idleness, put off writing to his friends until that last fatal night; and how, at the very moment when the pen was in his hand and the paper spread out before him, the different claims of a double duty had torn him asunder, and he had been summoned from the companionship of his bride to the death-bed of his father.

Mrs. Arundel tried in vain to set her son's mind at rest upon the subject of his wife's silence.

"No, mother!" he cried; "it is useless talking to me. You don't know my poor darling. She has the courage of a heroine as well as the simplicity of a child. There has been some foul play at the bottom of this; it is treachery that has kept my wife from me. She would have come here on foot had she been free to come. I know whose hand is in this business. Olivia Marchmont has kept my poor girl a prisoner; Olivia Marchmont has set herself between me and my darling!"

"But you don't know this, Edward. I'll write to Mr. Paulette; he will be able to tell us what has happened."

The young man writhed in a paroxysm of mental agony.

"Write to Mr. Paulette!" he exclaimed. "No, mother; there shall be no delay, no waiting for return posts. That sort of torture would kill me in a few hours. No, mother; I will go to my wife by the first train that will take me on my way to Lincolnshire."

"You will go! You, Edward! in your state!"

There was a terrible outburst of remonstrance

and entreaty on the part of the poor mother. Mrs. Arundel went down upon her knees before her son, imploring him not to leave Dangerfield till his strength was recovered; imploring him to let her telegraph a summons to Richard Paulette; to let her go herself to Marchmont Towers in search of Mary; to do any thing rather than carry out that one mad purpose that he was bent on—the purpose of going himself to look for his wife.

The mother's tears and prayers were vain; no adamant was ever firmer than the young soldier. "She is my wife, mother," he said; "I have sworn to protect and cherish her; and I have reason to think she has fallen into merciless hands. If I die upon the road, I must go to her. It is not a case in which I can do my duty by proxy. Every moment I delay is a wrong to that poor helpless girl. Be reasonable, dear mother, I implore you; I should suffer fifty times more by the torture of suspense if I staid here, than I can possibly suffer in a railroad journey from here to Lincolnshire."

The soldier's strong will triumphed over every opposition. The provincial doctors held up their hands, and protested against the madness of their patient; but without avail. All that either Mrs. Arundel or the doctors could do was to make such preparations and arrangements as would render the weary journey easier; and it was under the mother's superintendence that the air-cushions, the brandy-flasks, the hartshorn, sal volatile, and railway-rugs had been provided for the Captain's comfort.

It was thus that, after a blank interval of three months, Edward Arundel, like some creature newly risen from the grave, returned to Swampington, upon his way to Marchmont Towers.

The delay seemed endless to this restless passenger, sitting in the empty waiting-room of the quiet Lincolnshire station, though the hostler and stable-boys at the George were bestirring themselves with good-will, urged on by Mr. Morrison's promise of liberal reward for their trouble, and though the man who was to drive the carriage lost no time in arraying himself for the journey. Captain Arundel looked at his watch three times while he sat in that dreary Swampington waiting-room. There was a clock over the mantle-piece, but he would not trust to that.

"Eight o'clock!" he muttered. "It will be ten before I get to the Towers, if the carriage doesn't come directly."

He got up, and walked from the waiting-room to the platform, and from the platform to the door of the station. He was so weak as to be obliged to support himself with his stick; and even with that help he tottered and reeled sometimes like a drunken man. But, in his eager impatience, he was almost unconscious of his own weakness, unconscious of nearly every thing except the intolerable slowness of the progress of time.

"Will it never come?" he muttered. "Will it never come?"

But even this almost unendurable delay was not quite interminable. The carriage-and-pair from the George Inn rattled up to the door of the station, with Mr. Morrison upon the box, and a postillion loosely balanced upon one of the long-legged, long-backed, bony gray horses.

Edward Arundel got into the vehicle before his valet could alight to assist him.

"Marchmont Towers!" he cried to the postillion; "and a five-pound note if you get there in less than an hour!"

He flung some money to the officials who had gathered about the door to witness his departure, and who had eagerly pressed forward to render him that assistance which, even in his weakness, he disdained.

These men looked gravely at each other as the carriage dashed off into the fog, blundering and reeling as it went along the narrow half-made road, that led from the desert patch of waste ground upon which the station was built into the high street of Swampington.

"Marchmont Towers!" said one of the men, in a tone that seemed to imply that there was something ominous even in the name of the Lincolnshire mansion. "What does he want at Marchmont Towers, I wonder?"

"Why, don't you know who he is, mate?" responded the other man, contemptuously.

"No."

"He's Parson Arundel's nevy—the young officer that some folks said ran away with the poor young miss oop at the Towers."

"My word! is he, now? Why, I shouldn't ha' known him."

"No; he's a'most like the ghost of what he was, poor young chap! I've heerd as he was in that accident as happened last August on the Sou'western."

The railway official shrugged his shoulders. "It's all a queer story," he said. "I can't make out naught about it; but I know I shouldn't care to go up to the Towers after dark."

Marchmont Towers had evidently fallen into rather evil repute among these simple Lincolnshire people.

The carriage in which Edward Arundel rode was a superannuated old chariot, whose uneasy springs rattled and shook the sick man to pieces. He groaned aloud every now and then from sheer physical agony; and yet I almost doubt if he knew that he suffered, so superior in its intensity was the pain of his mind to every bodily torture. Whatever consciousness he had of his racked and aching limbs was as nothing in comparison to the racking anguish of suspense, the intolerable agony of anxiety, which seemed multiplied by every moment. He sat with his face turned toward the open window of the carriage, looking out steadily into the night. There was nothing before him but a blank darkness and thick fog, and a flat country blotted out by the falling rain; but he strained his eyes until the pupils dilated painfully, in his desire to recognize some landmark in the hidden prospect.

"*When* shall I get there?" he cried aloud, in a paroxysm of rage and grief. "My own one, my pretty one, my wife, when shall I get to you?"

He clenched his thin hands until the nails cut into his flesh. He stamped upon the floor of the carriage. He cursed the rusty, creaking springs, the slow-footed horses, the pools of water through which the wretched animals floundered pastern-deep. He cursed the darkness of the night, the stupidity of the postillion, the length of the way—every thing and any thing that kept him back from the end which he wanted to reach.

At last the end came. The carriage drew up before the tall iron gates, behind which stretched, dreary and desolate as some patch of common-land, that melancholy waste which was called a park.

A light burned dimly in the lower window of the lodge—a little spot that twinkled faintly red and luminous through the darkness and the rain; but the iron gates were as closely shut as if Marchmont Towers had been a prison-house. Edward Arundel was in no humor to linger long for the opening of those gates. He sprang from the carriage, reckless of the weakness of his cramped limbs, before the valet could descend from the rickety box-seat, or the postillion could get off his horse, and shook the wet and rusty iron bars with his wasted hands. The gates rattled, but resisted the concussion. They had evidently been locked for the night. The young man seized an iron ring, dangling at the end of a chain, which hung beside one of the stone pillars, and.rang a peal that resounded like an alarm-signal through the darkness. A fierce watch-dog far away in the distance howled dismally at the summons, and the dissonant shriek of a peacock echoed across the flat.

The door of the lodge was opened about five minutes after the bell had rung, and an old man peered out into the night, holding a candle shaded by his feeble hand, and looking suspiciously toward the gate.

"Who is it?" he said.

"It is I—Captain Arundel. Open the gate, please."

The man, who was very old, and whose intellect seemed to have grown as dim and foggy as the night itself, reflected for a few moments, and then mumbled,

"Cap'en Arundel! ay, to be sure, to be sure. Parson Arundel's nevy; ay, ay."

He went back into the lodge, to the disgust and aggravation of the young soldier, who rattled fiercely at the gate once more in his impatience. But the old man emerged presently, as tranquil as if the black November night had been some sunshiny noontide in July, carrying a lantern and a bunch of keys, one of which he proceeded in a leisurely manner to apply to the great lock of the gate.

"Let me in," cried Edward Arundel; "man alive, do you think I came down here to stand all night staring through these iron bars? Is Marchmont Towers a prison, that you shut your gates as if they were never to be opened until the Day of Judgment?"

The old man responded with a feeble, chirpy laugh, an audible grin, senile and conciliatory.

"We've no need to keep t' geates open arter dark," he said; "folk don't coome to the Toowers arter dark."

He had succeeded by this time in turning the key in the lock; one of the gates rolled slowly back upon its rusty hinges, creaking and groaning as if in hoarse protest against all visitors to the Towers; and Edward Arundel entered the dreary domain which John Marchmont had inherited from his kinsman.

The postillion turned his horses from the high road without the gates into the broad drive leading up to the mansion. Far away, across the wet flats, the broad western front of that gaunt stone dwelling-place frowned upon the travelers, its black grimness only relieved by two or three dim red patches, that told of lighted windows and human habitation. It was rather difficult to associate friendly flesh and blood with Marchmont Towers on this dark November night. The nervous traveler would have ráther expected to find diabolical denizens lurking within those black and stony walls; hideous enchantments beneath that rain-bespattered roof; weird and incarnate horrors brooding by deserted hearths; and fearful shrieks of souls in perpetual pain breaking upon the stillness of the night.

Edward Arundel had no thought of these things. He knew that the place was darksome and gloomy, and that, in very spite of himself, he had always been unpleasantly impressed by it; but he knew nothing more. He only wanted to reach the house without delay, and to ask for the young wife whom he had parted with upon a balmy August evening three months before. He wanted this passionately, almost madly; and every moment made his impatience wilder, his anxiety more intense. It seemed as if all the journey from Dangerfield Park to Lincolnshire was as nothing compared to the space that still lay between him and Marchmont Towers.

"We've done it in double-quick time, Sir," the postillion said, complacently pointing to the steaming sides of his horses. "Master 'll gie it me for driving the beasts like this."

Edward Arundel looked at the panting animals. They had brought him quickly, then, though the way had seemed so long.

"You shall have a five-pound note, my lad," he said, "if you get me up to yonder house in five minutes."

He had his hand upon the door of the carriage, and was leaning against it for support, while he tried to recover enough strength with which to clamber into the vehicle, when his eye was caught by some white object flapping in the rain against the stone pillar of the gate, and made dimly visible in a flickering patch of light from the lodge-keeper's lantern.

"What's that!" he cried, pointing to this white spot upon the moss-grown stone.

The old man slowly raised his eyes to the spot toward which the soldier's finger pointed.

"That?" he mumbled. "Ay, to be sure, to be sure. Poor young lady! That's the printed bill as they stook oop. It's the printed bill, to be sure, to be sure. I'd a'most forgot it. It ain't been much good, any how; and I'd a'most forgot it."

"The printed bill! the young lady!" gasped Edward Arundel, in a hoarse, choking voice.

He snatched the lantern from the lodge-keeper's hand with a force that sent the old man reeling and tottering several paces backward; and, rushing to the stone pillar, held the light up above his head, on a level with the white placard which had attracted his notice. It was damp and dilapidated at the edges; but· that which was printed upon it was as visible to the soldier as though each commonplace character had been a fiery sign inscribed upon a blazing scroll.

This was the announcement which Edward Arundel read upon the gate-post of Marchmont Towers:

"ONE HUNDRED POUNDS REWARD.—Whereas, Miss Mary Marchmont left her home on Wednesday last, October 17th, and has not since been heard of, this is to give notice that the above reward will be given to any one who shall afford such information as will lead to her recovery if she be alive, or to the discovery of her body, if she be dead. The missing young lady is eighteen years of age, rather below the middle height, of fair complexion, light-brown hair, and hazel eyes. When she left her home she had on a gray silk dress, gray shawl, and straw bonnet. She was last seen near the riverside upon the afternoon of Wednesday, the 17th instant.
"MARCHMONT TOWERS, *Oct.* 20, 1848."

---

## CHAPTER XXI.

### FACE TO FACE.

IT is not easy to imagine a lion-hearted young cavalry-officer, whose soldiership in the Punjaub had won the praises of a Napier and an Outram, fainting away like a heroine of romance at the coming of evil tidings; but Edward Arundel, who had risen from a sick-bed to take a long and fatiguing journey in utter defiance of the doctors, was not strong enough to bear the dreadful welcome that greeted him upon the gate-post at Marchmont Towers.

He staggered, and would have fallen, had not the extended arms of his father's confidential servant been luckily opened to receive and support him. But he did not lose his senses.

"Get me into the carriage, Morrison," he cried. "Get me up to that house. They've tortured and tormented my wife while I've been lying like a log on my bed at Dangerfield. For God's sake, get me up there as quick as you can."

Mr. Morrison had read the placard on the gate across his young master's shoulder. He lifted the Captain into the carriage, shouted to the postillion to drive on, and took his seat by the young man's side.

"Begging your pardon, Mr. Edward," he said, gently; "but the young lady may be found by this time. That bill's been sticking there for upward of a month, you see, Sir, and it isn't likely but what Miss Marchmont has been found between that time and this."

The invalid passed his hand across his forehead, down which the cold sweat rolled in great beads.

"Give me some brandy," he whispered; "pour some brandy down my throat, Morrison, if you've any compassion upon me; I must get strength somehow for the struggle that lies before me."

The valet took a wicker-covered flask from his pocket, and put the neck of it to Edward Arundel's lips.

"She may be found, Morrison," muttered the young man, after drinking a long draught of the fiery spirit; he would willingly have drunk living fire itself, in his desire to obtain unnatural strength in this crisis. "Yes; you're right there. She may be found. But to think that she should have been driven away! To think that my poor, helpless, tender girl should have

been driven a second time from the home that is her own! Yes; her own by every law and every right. Oh, the relentless devil, the pitiless devil!—what can be the motive of her conduct? Is it madness, or the infernal cruelty of a fiend incarnate?"

Mr. Morrison thought that his young master's brain had been disordered by the shock he had just undergone, and that this wild talk was mere delirium.

"Keep your heart up, Mr. Edward," he murmured, soothingly; "you may rely upon it the young lady has been found."

But Edward was in no mind to listen to any mild consolatory remarks from his valet. He had thrust his head out of the carriage-window, and his eyes were fixed upon the dimly-lighted casements of the western drawing-room.

"The room in which John and Polly and I used to sit together when first I came from India," he murmured. "How happy we were! how happy we were!"

The carriage stopped before the stone portico, and the young man got out once more, assisted by his servant. His breath came short and quick now that he stood upon the threshold. He pushed aside the servant who opened the familiar door at the summons of the clanging bell, and strode into the hall. A fire burned on the wide hearth; but the atmosphere of the great stone-paved chamber was damp and chilly.

Captain Arundel walked straight to the door of the western drawing-room. It was there that he had seen lights in the windows; it was there that he expected to find Olivia Marchmont.

He was not mistaken. A shaded lamp burned dimly on a table near the fire. There was a low invalid-chair beside this table, an open book upon the floor, and an Indian shawl, one he had sent to his cousin, flung carelessly upon the pillows. The neglected fire burned low in the old-fashioned grate, and above the dull red blaze stood the figure of a woman, tall, dark, and gloomy of aspect.

It was Olivia Marchmont, in the mourning robes that she had worn, with but one brief intermission, ever since her husband's death. Her profile was turned toward the door by which Edward Arundel entered the room; her eyes were bent steadily upon the low heap of burning ashes in the grate. Even in that doubtful light the young man could see that her features were sharpened, and that a settled frown had contracted her straight black brows.

In her fixed attitude, in her air of death-like tranquillity, this woman resembled some sinful vestal sister, set, against her will, to watch a sacred fire, and brooding moodily over her crimes.

She did not hear the opening of the door; she had not even heard the trampling of the horses' hoofs, or the crashing of the wheels upon the gravel before the house. There were times when her sense of external things was, as it were, suspended and absorbed in the intensity of her obstinate despair.

"Olivia!" said the soldier.

Mrs. Marchmont looked up at the sound of that accusing voice, for there was something in Edward Arundel's simple enunciation of her name which seemed like an accusation or a menace. She looked up, with a great terror in her face, and stared aghast at her unexpected visitor. Her white cheeks, her trembling lips, and dilated eyes could not have more palpably expressed a great and absorbing horror had the young man standing quietly before her been a corpse newly risen from its grave.

"Olivia Marchmont," said Captain Arundel, after a brief pause, "I have come here to look for my wife."

The woman pushed her trembling hands across her forehead, brushing the dead black hair from either temple, and still staring with the same unutterable horror at the face of her cousin. Several times she tried to speak; but the broken syllables died away in her throat in hoarse, inarticulate mutterings. At last, with a great effort, the words came.

"I—I—never expected to see you," she said; "I heard that you were very ill; I heard that you—"

"You heard that I was dying," interrupted Edward Arundel; "or that if I lived I should drag out the rest of my existence in hopeless idiocy. The doctors thought as much a week ago, when one of them, cleverer than the rest, I suppose, had the courage to perform an operation that restored me to consciousness. Sense and memory came back to me by degrees. The thick veil that had shrouded the past was rent asunder; and the first image that came to me was the image of my young wife, as I had seen her upon the night of our parting. For more than three months I had been dead. I was suddenly restored to life. I asked those about me to give me tidings of my wife. Had she sought me out? had she followed me to Dangerfield? No! They could tell me nothing. They thought that I was delirious, and tried to soothe me with compassionate speeches, merciful falsehoods, promising me that I should see my darling. But I soon read the secret of their scared looks. I saw pity and wonder mingled in my mother's face, and I entreated her to be merciful to me, and to tell me the truth. She had compassion upon me, and told me all she knew, which was very little. She had never heard from my wife. She had never heard of any marriage between Mary Marchmont and me. The only communication which she had received from any of her Lincolnshire relations had been an occasional letter from my Uncle Hubert, in reply to one of hers telling him of my hopeless state.

"This was the shock that fell upon me when life and memory came back. I could not bear the imprisonment of a sick-bed. I felt that for the second time I must go out into the world to look for my darling; and in defiance of the doctors, in defiance of my poor mother, who thought that my departure from Dangerfield was a suicide, I am here. It is here that I come first to seek for my wife. I might have stopped in London to see Richard Paulette. I might sooner have gained tidings of my darling. But I came here; I came here without stopping by the way, because an uncontrollable instinct and an unreasoning impulse tells me that it is here I ought to seek her. I am here, her husband, her only true and legitimate defender; and woe be to those who stand between me and my wife!"

He had spoken rapidly in his passion; and he

stopped, exhausted by his own vehemence, and sank heavily into a chair near the lamplit table, and only a few paces from the widow.

Then for the first time that night Olivia Marchmont plainly saw her cousin's face, and saw the terrible change that had transformed the handsome young soldier since the bright August morning on which he had gone forth from Marchmont Towers. She saw the traces of a long and wearisome illness sadly visible in his waxen complexion, his hollow cheeks, the faded lustre of his eyes, his dry and pallid lips. She saw all this, the woman whose one great sin had been to love this man wickedly and madly, in spite of her better self, in spite of her womanly pride; she saw the change in him that had altered him from a young Apollo to a shattered and broken invalid. And did any revulsion of feeling arise in her breast? did any corresponding transformation in her own heart bear witness to the baseness of her love?

No; a thousand times, no! There was no thrill of disgust, how transient soever; not so much as one passing shudder of painful surprise, one pang of womanly regret. No! In place of these, a passionate yearning arose in this woman's haughty soul; a flood of sudden tenderness rushed across the black darkness of her mind. She would have flung herself upon her knees, in loving self-abasement, at the sick man's feet. She would have cried aloud amidst a tempest of passionate sobs,

"Oh my love, my love! you are dearer to me a hundred times by this cruel change. It was *not* your bright blue eyes and waving chestnut hair—it was not your handsome face, your brave, soldier-like bearing—that I loved. My love was not so base as that. I inflicted a cruel outrage upon myself when I thought that I was the weak fool of a handsome face. Whatever *I* have been, my love, at least, has been pure. My love is pure, though I am base. I will never slander that again, for I know now that it is immortal."

In the sudden rush of that flood-tide of love and tenderness, all these thoughts welled into Olivia Marchmont's mind. In all her sin and desperation she had never been so true a woman as now. She had never, perhaps, been so near being a good woman. But the tender emotion was swept out of her breast the next moment by the first words of Edward Arundel.

"Why do you not answer my question?" he said.

She drew herself up in the erect and rigid attitude that had become almost habitual to her. Every trace of womanly feeling faded out of her face as the sunlight disappears behind the sudden darkness of a thunder-cloud.

"What question?" she asked, with icy indifference.

"The question I have come to Lincolnshire to ask; the question I have periled my life, perhaps, to ask," cried the young man. "Where is my wife?"

The widow turned upon him with a horrible smile.

"I never heard that you were married," she said. "Who is your wife?"

"Mary Marchmont, the mistress of this house."

Olivia opened her eyes and looked at him in half-sardonic surprise.

"Then it was not a fable?" she said.

"What was not a fable?"

"The unhappy girl spoke the truth when she said that you had married her at some out-of-the-way church in Lambeth."

"The truth! Yes!" cried Edward Arundel. "Who should dare to say that she spoke other than the truth? Who should dare to disbelieve her?"

Olivia Marchmont smiled again—the same horrible smile that was almost too horrible for humanity, and yet had a certain dark and gloomy grandeur of its own. Satan, the star of the morning, may have so smiled despairing defiance upon the Archangel Michael.

"Unfortunately," she said, "no one believed the poor child. Her story was such a very absurd one, and she could bring forward no shred of evidence in support of it."

"O my God!" ejaculated Edward Arundel, clasping his hands above his head in a paroxysm of rage and despair. "I see it all; I see it all. My darling has been tortured to death. Woman!" he cried, "are you possessed by a thousand fiends? Is there no one sentiment of womanly compassion left in your breast? If there is one spark of womanhood in your nature, I appeal to that. I ask you what has happened to my wife?"

"My wife! my wife!" The reiteration of that familiar phrase was to Olivia Marchmont like the perpetual thrust of a dagger aimed at an open wound. It struck every time upon the same tortured spot, and inflicted the same agony.

"The placard upon the gates of this place can tell you as much as I can," she said.

The ghastly whiteness of the soldier's face told her that he had seen the placard of which she spoke.

"She has not been found then?" he said, hoarsely.

"No."

"How did she disappear?"

"As she disappeared upon the morning on which you followed her. She wandered out of the house, this time leaving no letter, nor message, nor explanation of any kind whatever. It was in the middle of the day that she went out; and for some time her absence caused no alarm, as she had been in the habit of going out alone into the grounds whenever she chose. But, after some hours, she was waited for and watched for very anxiously. Then a search was made."

"Where?"

"Wherever she had been in the habit of walking—in the park; in the wood; along the narrow path by the water; at Pollard's farm; at Hester's house at Kemberling—in every place where it might be reasonably imagined there was the slightest chance of finding her."

"And all this was without result?"

"It was."

"Why did she leave this place? God help you, Olivia Marchmont, if it was your cruelty that drove her away."

The widow took no notice of the threat implied in these words. Was there any thing upon earth that she feared now? No; nothing. Had she not endured the worst, long ago, in Edward Arundel's contempt? She had no fear of a battle with this man; or with any other creature in the world; or with the whole world arrayed and banded together against her, if need were. Among all the torments of those black depths to which her soul had gone down there was no such thing as fear. That cowardly baseness is for the happy and prosperous, who have something to lose. This woman was by nature dauntless and resolute as the hero of some classic story; but in her despair she had the desperate and reckless courage of a starving wolf. The hand of death was upon her; what could it matter how she died?

"I am very grateful to you, Edward Arundel," she said, bitterly, "for the good opinion you have always had of me. The blood of the Dangerfield Arundels must have had some drop of poison intermingled with it, I should think, before it could produce such a vile creature as me; and yet I have heard people say my mother was a good woman."

The young man writhed impatiently beneath the torture of his cousin's deliberate speech. Was there to be no end to this unendurable delay? Even now—now that he was in this house, face to face with the woman he had come to question, it seemed as if he could not get tidings of his wife.

So, often in his dreams, he had headed a besieging party against the Afghans, with the scaling-ladders reared against the wall, and his men behind urging him on to the encounter, and had felt himself paralyzed and helpless, with his sabre weak as a withered reed in his nerveless hand.

"For God's sake, let there be no quarreling with phrases between you and me, Olivia!" he cried. "If you or any other living being have injured my wife, the reckoning between us shall be no light one. But there will be time enough to talk of that by-and-by. I stand before you newly risen from a grave in which I have lain for more than three months; as dead to the world, and to every creature I have ever loved or hated, as if the Funeral Service had been read over my coffin. I come to demand from you an account of what has happened during that interval. If you palter or prevaricate with me, I shall know that it is because you fear to tell me the truth."

"Fear!"

"Yes; you have good reason to fear, if you have wronged Mary Arundel. Why did she leave this house?"

"Because she was not happy in it, I suppose. She chose to shut herself up in her own room, and to refuse to be governed, or advised, or consoled. I tried to do my duty to her; yes," cried Olivia Marchmont, suddenly raising her voice, as if she had been vehemently contradicted—"yes, I did try to do my duty to her. I urged her to listen to reason; I begged her to abandon her foolish falsehood about a marriage with you in London."

"You disbelieved in that marriage?"

"I did," answered Olivia.

"You lie," cried Edward Arundel. "You knew the poor child had spoken the truth. You knew her—you knew me—well enough to know that I should not have detained her away from her home an hour, except to make her my wife, except to give myself the strongest right to love and defend her."

"'I knew nothing of the kind, Captain Arundel; you and Mary Marchmont had taken good care to keep your secrets from me. I knew nothing of your plots, your intentions. *I* should have considered that one of the Dangerfield Arundels would have thought his honor sullied by such an act as a stolen marriage with an heiress, considerably under age, and nominally in the guardianship of her step-mother. I did, therefore, disbelieve the story Mary Marchmont told me. Another person, much more experienced than me, also disbelieved the unhappy girl's account of her absence."

"Another person? What other person?"

"Mr. Marchmont."

"Mr. Marchmont?"

"Yes; Paul Marchmont—my husband's first-cousin."

A sudden cry of rage and grief broke from Edward Arundel's lips.

"O my God!" he exclaimed, "there was some foundation for the warning in John Marchmont's letter, after all. And I laughed at him; I laughed at my poor friend's fears."

The widow looked at her kinsman in mute wonder.

"Has Paul Marchmont been in this house?" he asked.

"Yes."

"When was he here?"

"He has been here often. He comes here constantly. He has been living at Kemberling for the last three months."

"Why?"

"For his own pleasure, I suppose," Olivia answered, haughtily. "'It is no business of mine to pry into Mr. Marchmont's motives."

Edward Arundel ground his teeth in an access of ungovernable passion. It was not against Olivia but against himself this time that he was enraged. He hated himself for the arrogant folly, the obstinate presumption, with which he had ridiculed and slighted John Marchmont's vague fears of his kinsman Paul.

"So this man has been here—is here constantly," he muttered. "Of course; it is only natural that he should hang about the place. And you and he are stanch allies, I suppose?" he added, turning upon Olivia.

"Stanch allies! Why?"

"Because you both hate my wife."

"What do you mean?"

"You both hate her. You, out of a base envy of her wealth; because of her superior rights, which made you a secondary person in this house, perhaps—there is nothing else for which you *could* hate her. Paul Marchmont, because she stands between him and a fortune. Heaven help her! Heaven help my poor, gentle, guileless darling! Surely Heaven must have had some pity upon her when her husband was not by."

The young man dashed the blinding tears from his eyes. They were the first that he had shed since he had risen from that which many people had thought his dying bed to search for his wife.

But this was no time for tears or lamentations. Stern determination took the place of tender pity and sorrowful love. It was a time for resolution and promptitude.

"Olivia Marchmont," he said, "there has

been some foul play in this business. My wife has been missing a month; yet, when I asked my mother what had happened at this house during my illness, she could tell me nothing. Why did you not write to tell her of Mary's flight?"

"Because Mrs. Arundel has never done me the honor to cultivate any intimacy between us. My father writes to his sister-in-law sometimes. I scarcely ever write to my aunt. On the other hand, your mother had never seen Mary Marchmont, and could not be expected to take any great interest in her proceedings. There was, therefore, no reason for my writing a special letter to announce the trouble that had befallen me."

"You might have written to my mother about my marriage. You might have applied to her for confirmation of the story which you disbelieved."

Olivia Marchmont smiled.

"Should I have received that confirmation?" she said. "No. I saw your mother's letters to my father. There was no mention in those letters of any marriage; no mention whatever of Mary Marchmont. This in itself was enough to confirm my disbelief. Was it reasonable to imagine that you would have married, and yet have left your mother in total ignorance of the fact?"

"O God, help me!" cried Edward Arundel, wringing his hands. "It seems as if my own folly, my own vile procrastination, have brought this trouble upon my wife. Olivia Marchmont, have pity upon me! If you hate this girl, your malice must surely have been satisfied by this time. She has suffered enough. Pity me, and help me, if you have any human feeling in your breast. She left this house because her life here had grown unendurable; because she saw herself doubted, disbelieved, widowed in the first month of her marriage, utterly desolate and friendless. Another woman might have borne up against all this misery. Another woman would have known how to assert herself, and to defend herself, even in the midst of her sorrow and desolation. But my poor darling is a child; a baby in ignorance of the world. How should *she* protect herself against her enemies? Her only instinct was to run away from her persecutors—to hide herself from those whose pretended doubts flung the horror of dishonor upon her. I can understand all now; I can understand. Olivia Marchmont, this man Paul has a strong reason for being a villain. The motives that have induced you to do wrong must be very small in comparison to his. He plays an infamous game, I believe, but he plays for a high stake."

A high stake! Had not she periled her soul upon the casting of this die? Had she not flung down her eternal happiness in that fatal game of hazard?

"Help me, then, Olivia," said Edward, imploringly; "help me to find my wife; and atone for all that you have ever done amiss in the past. It is not too late."

His voice softened as he spoke. He turned to her, with his hands clasped, waiting anxiously for her answer. Perhaps this appeal was the last cry of her good angel, pleading against the devils for her redemption. But the devils had too long held possession of this woman's breast. They arose, arrogant and unpitying, and hardened her heart against that pleading voice.

"How much he loves her!" thought Olivia Marchmont; "how dearly he loves her; for her sake he humiliates himself to me."

Then, with no show of relenting in her voice or manner, she said, deliberately,

"I can only tell you again what I told you before. The placard you saw at the park gates can tell you as much as I can. Mary Marchmont ran away. She was sought for in every direction, but without success. Mr. Marchmont, who is a man of the world, and better able to suggest what is right in such a case as this, suggested that Mr. Paulette should be sent for. He was accordingly communicated with. He came and instituted a fresh search. He also caused a bill to be printed and distributed through the country. Advertisements were inserted in the *Times* and other papers. For some reason—I forget what reason—Mary Marchmont's name did not appear in these advertisements. They were so worded as to render the publication of the name unnecessary."

Edward Arundel pushed his hand across his forehead.

"Richard Paulette has been here!" he murmured, in a low voice.

He had every confidence in the lawyer; and a deadly chill came over him at the thought that the cool, hard-headed solicitor had failed to find the missing girl.

"Yes; he was here two or three days."

"And he could do nothing?"

"Nothing, except what I have told you."

The young man thrust his hand into his breast to still the cruel beating of his heart. A sudden terror had taken possession of him—a horrible dread that he should never look upon his young wife's face again. For some minutes there was a dead silence in the room, only broken once or twice by the falling of some ashes on the hearth. Captain Arundel sat with his face hidden behind his hand. Olivia still stood as she stood when her cousin entered the room, erect and gloomy, by the old-fashioned chimney-piece.

"There was something in that placard," the soldier said at last, in a hoarse, altered voice—"there was something about my wife having been seen last by the water-side. Who saw her there?"

"Mr. Weston, a surgeon of Kemberling—Paul Marchmont's brother-in-law."

"Was she seen by no one else?"

"Yes; she was seen at about the same time—a little sooner or later, we don't know which—by one of Farmer Pollard's men."

"And she has never been seen since?"

"Never; that is to say, we can hear of no one who has seen her."

"At what time in the day was she seen by this Mr. Weston?"

"At dusk; between five and six o'clock."

Edward Arundel put his hand suddenly to his throat, as if to check some choking sensation that prevented his speaking.

"Olivia," he said, "my wife was last seen by the river-side. Does any one think that, by any unhappy accident, by any terrible fatality, she lost her way after dark, and fell into the water?

or that—O God, that would be too horrible!—does any one suspect that she drowned herself?"

"Many things have been said since her disappearance," Olivia Marchmont answered. "Some people say one thing, some another."

"And it has been said that she—that she was drowned?"

"Yes, many people have said so. The river was dragged while Mr. Paulette was here, and after he went away. The men were at work with the drags for more than a week."

"And they found nothing?"

"Nothing."

"Was there any other reason for supposing that—that my wife fell into the river?"

"Only one reason."

"What was that?"

"I will show you," Olivia Marchmont answered.

She took a bunch of keys from her pocket, and went to an old-fashioned bureau or cabinet upon the other side of the room. She unlocked the upper part of this bureau, opened one of the drawers, and took from it something which she brought to Edward Arundel.

This something was a little shoe; a little shoe of soft bronzed leather, stained and discolored with damp and moss, and trodden down upon one side, as if the wearer had walked a weary way in it, and had been unaccustomed to so much walking.

Edward Arundel remembered, in that brief, childishly-happy honey-moon at the little village near Winchester, how often he had laughed at his young wife's propensity for walking about damp meadows in such delicate little slippers as were better adapted to the requirements of a ball-room. He remembered the slender foot, so small that he could take it in his hand; the feeble little foot that had grown tired in long wanderings by the Hampshire trout-streams, but which had toiled on in heroic self-abnegation so long as it was the will of the sultan to pedestrianize.

"Was this found by the river-side?" he asked, looking piteously at the slipper which Mrs. Marchmont had put into his hand.

"Yes; it was found among the rushes on the shore, a mile below the spot at which Mr. Weston saw my step-daughter."

Edward Arundel put the little shoe into his bosom.

"I'll not believe it," he cried, suddenly; "I'll not believe that my darling is lost to me. She was too good, far too good, to think of suicide; and Providence would never suffer my poor lonely child to be led away to a dreary death upon that dismal river-shore. No, no; she fled away from this place because she was too wretched here. She went away to hide herself among those whom she could trust, until her husband came to claim her. I will believe any thing in the world except that she is lost to me. And I will not believe that, I will never believe that, until I look down at her corpse; until I lay my hand on her cold breast, and feel that her true heart has ceased beating. As I went out of this place four months ago to look for her, I will go again now. My darling, my darling, my innocent pet, my childish bride; I will go to the very end of the world in search of you."

The widow ground her teeth as she listened

to her kinsman's passionate words. Why did he forever goad her to blacker wickedness by this parade of his love for Mary? Why did he force her to remember every moment how much cause she had to hate this pale-faced girl?

Captain Arundel rose, and walked a few paces, leaning on his stick as he went.

"You will sleep here to-night, of course?" Olivia Marchmont said.

"Sleep here!"

His tone expressed plainly enough that the place was utterly abhorrent to him.

"Yes; where else should you stay?"

"I meant to have stopped at the nearest inn."

"The nearest inn is at Kemberling."

"That would suit me well enough," the young man answered, indifferently; "I must be in Kemberling early to-morrow, for I must see Paul Marchmont. I am no nearer the comprehension of my wife's flight by anything that you have told me. It is to Paul Marchmont that I must look next. Heaven help him if he tries to keep the truth from me."

"You will see Mr. Marchmont here as easily as at Kemberling," Olivia answered. "He comes here every day."

"What for?"

"He has built a sort of painting-room down by the river-side, and he paints there whenever there is light."

"Indeed!" cried Edward Arundel; "he makes himself at home at Marchmont Towers, then?"

"He has a right to do so, I suppose," answered the widow, indifferently. "If Mary Marchmont is dead, this place and all belonging to it is his. As it is, I am only here on sufferance."

"He has taken possession, then?"

"On the contrary, he shrinks from doing so."

"And, by the Heaven above us, he does wisely," cried Edward Arundel. "No man shall seize upon that which belongs to my darling. No foul plot of this artist-traitor shall rob her of her own. God knows how little value I set upon her wealth; but I will stand between her and those who try to rob her, until my last gasp. No, Olivia, I'll not stay here; I'll accept no hospitality from Mr. Marchmont. I suspect him too much."

He walked to the door; but before he reached it the widow went to one of the windows, and pushed aside the blind.

"Look at the rain," she said; "hark at it; don't you hear it drip, drip, drip upon the stone? I wouldn't turn a dog out of doors upon such a night as this; and you—you are so ill—so weak. Edward Arundel, do you hate me so much that you refuse to share the same shelter with me, even for a night?"

There is nothing so difficult of belief to a man who is not a coxcomb as the simple fact that he is beloved by a woman whom he does not love, and has never wooed by word or deed. But for this surely Edward Arundel must, in that sudden burst of tenderness, that one piteous appeal, have discovered a clew to his cousin's secret.

He discovered nothing; he guessed nothing. But he was touched by her tone, even in spite of his utter ignorance of its meaning, and he replied, in an altered manner,

"Certainly, Olivia, if you really wish it, I will stay. Heaven knows I have no desire that you and I should be ill friends. I want your help; your pity, perhaps. I am quite willing to believe that any cruel things you said to Mary arose from an outbreak of temper. I can not think that you could be base at heart. I will even attribute your disbelief of the statement made by my poor girl as to our marriage to the narrow prejudices learned in a dismal country town. Let us be friends, Olivia."

He held out his hand. His cousin laid her cold fingers in his open palm, and he shuddered as if he had come in contact with a corpse. There was nothing very cordial in the salutation. The two hands seemed to drop asunder, lifeless and inert; as if to bear mute witness that between these two people there was no possibility of sympathy or union.

But Captain Arundel accepted his cousin's hospitality. Indeed, he had need to do so; for he found that his valet had relied upon his master's stopping at the Towers, and had sent the carriage back to Swampington. A tray with cold meat and wine was brought into the drawing-room for the young soldier's refreshment. He drank a glass of Madeira, and made some pretense of eating a few mouthfuls, out of courtesy to Olivia; but he did this almost mechanically. He sat silent and gloomy, brooding over the terrible shock that he had so newly received; brooding over the hidden things that had happened in that dreary interval, during which he had been as powerless to defend his wife from trouble as a dead man.

Again and again the cruel thought returned to him, each time with a fresh agony—that if he had written to his mother, if he had told her the story of his marriage, the things which had happened could never have come to pass. Mary would have been sheltered and protected by a good and loving woman. This thought, this horrible self-reproach, was the bitterest thing the young man had to bear.

"It is too great a punishment," he thought; "I am too cruelly punished for having forgotten every thing in my happiness with my darling."

The widow sat in her low easy-chair near the fire, with her eyes fixed upon the burning coals; the grate had been replenished, and the light of the red blaze shone full upon Olivia Marchmont's haggard face. Edward Arundel, aroused for a few moments out of his gloomy abstraction, was surprised at the change which an interval of a few months had made in his cousin. The gloomy shadow which he had often seen on her face had become a fixed expression; every line had deepened, as if by the wear and tear of ten years, rather than by the progress of a few months. Olivia Marchmont had grown old before her time. Nor was this the only change. There was a look, undefined and undefinable, in the large luminous gray eyes, unnaturally luminous now, which filled Edward Arundel with a vague sense of terror; a terror which he would not—which he dared not—attempt to analyze. He remembered Mary's unreasoning fear of her step-mother, and he now scarcely wondered at that fear. There was something almost weird and unearthly in the aspect of the woman sitting opposite to him by the broad hearth; no vestige of color in her gloomy face, a strange light burning in her eyes, and her black draperies falling round her in straight lustreless folds.

"I fear you havé been ill, Olivia," the young man said, presently.

Another sentiment had arisen in his breast side by side with that vague terror—a fancy that perhaps there was some reason why his cousin should be pitied.

"Yes," she answered, indifferently; as if no subject of which Captain Arundel could have spoken would have been of less concern to her —"yes, I have been very ill."

"I am sorry to hear it."

Olivia looked up at him and smiled. Her smile was the strangest he had ever seen upon a woman's face.

"I am very sorry to hear it. What has been the matter with you?"

"Slow fever, Mr. Weston said."

"Mr. Weston?"

"Yes; Mr. Marchmont's brother-in-law. He has succeeded to Mr. Dawnfield's practice at Kemberling. He attended me, and he attended my step-daughter."

"My wife was ill, then?"

"Yes; she had brain-fever; she' recovered from that, but she did not recover strength. Her low spirits alarmed me, and I considered it only right—Mr. Marchmont suggested also— that a medical man should be consulted."

"And what did this man, this Mr. Weston, say?"

"Very little; there' was nothing the matter with Mary, he said. He gave her a little medicine, but only in the desire of strengthening her nervous system. He could give her no medicine that would have any very good effect upon her spirits while she chose to keep herself obstinately apart from every one."

The young man's head sank upon his breast. The image of his desolate young wife arose before him; the image of a pale, sorrowful girl, holding herself apart from her persecutors, abandoned, lonely, despairing. Why had she remained at Marchmont Towers? Why had she, ever consented to go there, when she had again and again expressed such terror of her step-mother? Why had she not rather followed her husband down to Devonshire, and thrown herself upon his relatives for protection? Was it like this loving girl to remain quietly here in Lincolnshire, when the man she loved with such innocent devotion was lying between life and death away in the west?

"She is such a child," he thought—"such a child in her ignorance of the world. I must not reason about her as I would about another woman."

And then a sudden flush of passionate emotion rose to his face, as a new thought flashed into his mind. What if this helpless girl had been detained by force at Marchmont Towers?

"Olivia," he cried, "whatever baseness this man Paul Marchmont may be capable of, you at least must be superior to any deliberate sin. I have all my life believed in you, and respected you as a good woman. Tell me the truth, then, for pity's sake. Nothing that you can tell me

will fill up the dead blank that the horrible interval since my accident has made in my life. But you can give me some help. A few words from you may clear away much of this ,dark ness. How did you find my wife? How did you induce her to come back to this place? I know that she had an unreasonable dread of returning here."

"I found her through the agency of Mr. Marchmont," Olivia answered, quietly. "I had some difficulty in inducing her to return here; but after hearing of your accident—"

"How was the news of that broken to her?"

"Unfortunately she saw a paper that had happened to be left in her way."

"By whom?"

"By Mr. Marchmont."

"Where was this?"

"In Hampshire."

"Indeed! then Paul Marchmont went with you to Hampshire?"

"He did. He was of great service to me in this crisis. After seeing the paper my step-daughter was seized with brain-fever. She was unconscious when we brought her back to the Towers. She was nursed by my old servant Barbara, and had the highest medical care. I do not think that any thing more could have been done for her."

"No," answered Edward Arundel, bitterly; "unless you could have loved her."

"We can not force our affections," the widow said, in a hard voice.

Another voice in her breast seemed to whisper, "Why do you reproach me for not having loved this girl? If you had loved me, the whole world would have been different."

"Olivia Marchmont," said Captain Arundel, "by your own avowal there has never been any affection for this orphan girl in your heart. It is not my business to dwell upon the fact, as something almost unnatural under the peculiar circumstances through which that helpless child was cast upon your protection. It is needless to try to understand why you have hardened your heart against my poor wife. Enough that it is so. But I may still believe that, whatever your feelings may be toward your dead husband's daughter, you would not be guilty of any deliberate act of treachery against her. I can afford to believe this of you; but I can not believe it of Paul Marchmont. That man is my wife's natural enemy. If he has been here during my illness, he has been here to plot against her. When he came here, he came to attempt her destruction. She stands between him and this estate. Long ago, when I was a careless school-boy, my poor friend John Marchmont told me that, if ever the day came upon which Mary's interests should be opposed to the interests of her cousin, that man would be a dire and bitter enemy; so much the more terrible because in all appearance her friend. The day came; and I, to whom the orphan girl had been left as a sacred legacy, was not by to defend her. But I have risen from the bed that many have thought a bed of death; and I come to this' place with one indomitable resolution paramount in my breast—the determination to find my wife, and to bring condign punishment upon the man who has done her wrong."

Captain Arundel spoke in a low voice; but

his passion was not the more terrible because of the suppression of those common outward evidences by which fury ordinarily betrays itself. He relapsed into thoughtful silence.

Olivia made no answer to any thing that he had said. She sat looking at him steadily, with an admiring awe in her face. How splendid he was, this young hero, even in his sickness and feebleness! How splendid, by reason of the grand courage, the chivalrous devotion, that shone out of his blue eyes!

The clock struck eleven while the cousins sat opposite to each other—only divided, physically, by the width of the tapestried hearth-rug; but, oh, how many weary miles asunder in spirit!— and Edward Arundel rose, startled from his sorrowful reverie.

"If I were a strong man," he said, "I would see Paul Marchmont to-night. But I must wait till to-morrow morning. At what time does he come to his painting-room?"

"At eight o'clock when the mornings are bright; but later when the weather is dull."

"At eight o'clock! I pray Heaven the sun may shine early to-morrow. I pray Heaven I may not have to wait long before I find myself face to face with that man! Good-night, Olivia!"

He took a candle from a table near the door, and lit it almost mechanically. He found Mr. Morrison waiting for him, very sleepy and despondent, in a large bedchamber in which Captain Arundel had never slept before—a dreary apartment, decked out with the faded splendors of the past; a chamber in which the restless sleeper might expect to see a phantom lady in a ghostly sack, cowering over the embers, and spreading her transparent hands above the red light.

"It isn't particular comfortable, after Dangerfield," the valet muttered, in a melancholy voice; "and all I 'ope, Mr. Edward, is, that the sheets are not damp. I've been a stirrin' of the fire and puttin' on fresh coals for the last hour. There's a bed for me in the dressin'-room, within call."

Captain Arundel scarcely heard what his servant said to him. He was standing at the door of the spacious chamber, looking out into a long, low-roofed corridor, in which he had just encountered Barbara, Mrs. Marchmont's confidential attendant—the wooden-faced, inscrutable-looking woman who, according to Olivia, had watched and ministered to his wife.

"Was that the tenderest face that looked down upon my darling as she lay on her sickbed?" he thought. "I had almost as soon have had a ghoul to watch by my poor dear's pillow."

---

## CHAPTER XXII.

### THE PAINTING-ROOM BY THE RIVER.

EDWARD ARUNDEL lay awake through the best part of that November night, listening to the ceaseless dripping of the rain upon the terrace, and thinking of Paul Marchmont. It was of this man that he must demand an account of his wife. Nothing that Olivia had told him had in any way lessened this determination. The little slipper found by the water's edge; the

placard flapping on the moss-grown pillar at the entrance to the park; the story of a possible suicide, or a more probable accident—all these things were as nothing beside the young man's suspicion of Paul Marchmont. He had poohpoohed John's dread of his kinsman as weak and unreasonable; and now, with the same unreason, he was ready to condemn this man, whom he had never seen, as a traitor and a plotter against his young wife.

He lay tossing from side to side all that night, weak and feverish, with great drops of cold perspiration rolling down his pale face, sometimes falling into a fitful sleep, in whose distorted dreams Paul Marchmont was forever present, now, one man, now another. There was no sense of fitness in these dreams; for sometimes Edward Arundel and the artist were wrestling together with newly-sharpened daggers in their eager hands, each thirsting for the other's blood; and in the next moment they were friends, and had been friendly—as it seemed—for years.

The young man woke from one of these last dreams, with words of good-fellowship upon his lips, to find the morning light gleaming through the narrow openings in the damask window-curtains, and Mr. Morrison laying out his master's dressing apparatus upon the carved oak toilet-table.

Captain Arundel dressed himself as fast as he could, with the assistance of the valet, and then made his way down the broad staircase, with the help of his cane, upon which he had need to lean pretty heavily, for he was as weak as a child.

"You had better give me the brandy-flask, Morrison," he said. "I am going out before breakfast. You may as well come with me, by-the-by; for I doubt if I could walk as far as I want to go, without the help of your arm."

In the hall Captain Arundel found one of the servants. The western door was open, and the man was standing on the threshold looking out at the morning. The rain had ceased; but the day did not yet promise to be very bright, for the sun gleamed like a ball of burnished copper through a pale November mist.

"Do you know if Mr. Paul Marchmont has gone down to the boat-house?" Edward asked.

"Yes, Sir," the man answered; "I met him just now in the quadrangle. He'd been having a cup of coffee with my mistress."

Edward started. They were friends, then, Paul Marchmont and Olivia!—friends, but surely not allies! Whatever villainy this man might be capable of committing, Olivia must at least be guiltless of any deliberate treachery.

Captain Arundel took his servant's arm and walked out into the quadrangle, and from the quadrangle to the low-lying woody swamp, where the stunted trees looked grim and weird-like in their leafless ugliness. Weak as the young man was, he walked rapidly across the sloppy ground, which had been almost flooded by the continual rains. He was borne up by his fierce desire to be face to face with Paul Marchmont. The savage energy of his mind was stronger than any physical debility. He dismissed Mr. Morrison as soon as he was within sight of the boat-house, and went on alone, leaning on his stick, and pausing now and then to draw breath, angry with himself for his weakness.

The boat-house, and the pavilion above it, had been patched up by some country workmen. A handful of plaster here and there, a little new brickwork, and a mended window-frame, bore witness of this. The ponderous old-fashioned wooden-shutters had been repaired, and a good deal of the work which had been begun in John Marchmont's lifetime had now, in a certain rough manner, been completed. The place which had hitherto appeared likely to fall into utter decay had been rendered weather-tight and habitable; the black smoke creeping slowly upward from the ivy-covered chimney, gave evidence of occupation. Beyond this, a large wooden shed, with a wide window fronting the north, had been erected close against the boat-house. This rough shed Edward Arundel at once understood to be the painting-room which the artist had built for himself.

He paused a moment outside the door of this shed. A man's voice—a tenor voice, rather thin and metallic in quality—was singing a scrap of Rossini upon the other side of the frail wood-work.

Edward Arundel knocked with the handle of his stick upon the door. The voice left off singing to say " Come in."

The soldier opened the door, crossed the threshold, and stood face to face with Paul Marchmont in the bare wooden shed. The painter had dressed himself for his work. His coat and waistcoat lay upon a chair near the door. He had put on a canvas jacket, and had drawn a loose pair of linen trowsers over those which belonged to his usual costume. So far as this paint-besmeared coat and trowsers went, nothing could have been more slovenly than Paul Marchmont's appearance; but some tinge of foppery exhibited itself in the black velvet smoking-cap, which contrasted with and set off the silvery whiteness of his hair, as well as in the delicate curve of his amber mustache. A mustache was not a very common adornment in the year 1848. It was rather an eccentricity affected by artists, and permitted as the wild caprice of irresponsible beings, not amenable to the laws that govern rational and respectable people.

Edward Arundel sharply scrutinized the face and figure of the artist. He cast a rapid glance round the bare whitewashed walls of the shed, trying to read even in those bare walls some chance clew to the painter's character. But there was not much to be gleaned from the details of that almost empty chamber. A dismal, black-looking iron stove, with a crooked chimney, stood in one corner. A great easel occupied the centre of the room. A sheet of tin, nailed upon a wooden shutter, swung backward and forward against the northern window, blown to and fro by the damp wind that crept in through the crevices in the frame-work of the roughly-fashioned casement. A heap of canvases were piled against the walls, and here and there a half-finished picture—a lurid Turneresque landscape; a black stormy sky; a rocky mountain-pass, dyed blood-red by the setting sun—was propped up against the whitewashed back-ground. Scattered scraps of water-color, crayon, old engravings, sketches torn and tumbled, bits of rock-work and foliage, lay littered about the floor; and on a paint-stained deal-table of the roughest and plainest fashion were gathered the color-tubes

and pallets, the brushes and sponges and dirty cloths, the greasy and sticky tin cans, which form the paraphernalia of an artist. Opposite the northern window was the moss-grown stone staircase leading up to the pavilion over the boat-house. Mr. Marchmont had built his painting-room against the side of the pavilion, in such a manner as to shut in the staircase and doorway which formed the only entrance to it. His excuse for the awkwardness of this piece of architecture was the impossibility of otherwise getting the all-desirable northern light for the illumination of his rough studio.

This was the chamber in which Edward Arundel found the man from whom he came to demand an account of his wife's disappearance. The artist was evidently quite prepared to receive his visitor. He made no pretense of being taken off his guard, as a meaner pretender might have done. One of Paul Marchmont's theories was, that as it is only a fool who would use brass where he could as easily employ gold, so it is only a fool that tells a lie when he can conveniently tell the truth.

" Captain Arundel, I believe ?" he said, pushing a chair forward for his visitor. " I am sorry to say I recognize you by your appearance of ill health. Mrs. Marchmont told me you wanted to see me. Does my meerschaum annoy you? I'll put it out if it does. No? Then, if you'll allow me, I'll go on smoking. Some people say tobacco-smoke gives a tone to one's pictures. If so, mine ought to be Rembrandts in depth of color."

Edward Arundel dropped into the chair that had been offered to him. If he could by any possibility have rejected even this amount of hospitality from Paul Marchmont he would have done so; but he was a great deal too weak to stand, and he knew that his interview with the artist must be a long one.

" Mr. Marchmont," he said, " if my cousin Olivia told you that you might expect to see me here to-day, she most likely told you a great deal more. Did she tell you that I look to you to account to me for the disappearance of my wife ?"

Paul Marchmont shrugged his shoulders, as who should say, " This young man is an invalid. I must not suffer myself to be aggravated by his absurdity." Then taking his meerschaum from his lips, he set it down, and seated himself at a few paces from Edward Arundel, on the lowest of the moss-grown steps leading up to the pavilion.

" My dear Captain Arundel," he said, very gravely, " your cousin did repeat to me a great deal of last night's conversation. She told me that you had spoken of me with a degree of violence, natural enough, perhaps, to a hot-tempered young soldier, but in no manner justified by our relations. When you call upon me to account for the disappearance of Mary Marchmont, you act about as rationally as if you declared me answerable for the pulmonary complaint that carried away her father. If, on the other hand, you call upon me to assist you in the endeavor to fathom the mystery of her disappearance, you will find me ready and willing to aid you to the very uttermost. It is to my interest as much as to yours that this mystery should be cleared up."

"And in the mean time you take possession of this estate?"

"No, Captain Arundel. The law would allow me to do so; but I decline to touch one farthing of the revenue which this estate yields, or to commit one act of ownership, until the mystery of Mary Marchmont's disappearance, or of her death, is cleared up."

"The mystery of her death!" said Edward Arundel; "you believe, then, that she is dead?"

"I anticipate nothing; I think nothing," answered the artist; "I only wait. The mysteries of life are so many and so incomprehensible—the stories, which are every day to be read by any man who takes the trouble to look through a newspaper, are so strange, and savor so much of the improbabilities of a novel-writer's first wild fiction—that I am ready to believe every thing and any thing. Mary Marchmont struck me, from the first moment in which I saw her, as sadly deficient in mental power. Nothing she could do would astonish me. She may be hiding herself away from us, prompted only by some eccentric fancy of her own. She may have fallen into the power of designing people. She may have purposely placed her slipper by the water-side in order to give the idea of an accident or a suicide, or she may have dropped it there by chance and walked barefoot to the nearest railway station. She acted unreasonably before when she ran away from Marchmont Towers; she may have acted unreasonably again."

"You do not think, then, that she is dead?"

"I hesitate to form any opinion; I positively decline to express one."

Edward Arundel gnawed savagely at the ends of his mustache. This man's cool imperturbability, which had none of the studied smoothness of hypocrisy, but which seemed rather the plain candor of a thorough man of the world, who had no wish to pretend to any sentiment he did not feel, baffled and infuriated the passionate young soldier. Was it possible that this man, who met him with such cool self-assertion, who in no manner avoided any discussion of Mary Marchmont's disappearance—was it possible that he could have had any treacherous and guilty part in that calamity? Olivia's manner looked like guilt; but Paul Marchmont's seemed the personification of innocence. Not angry innocence, indignant that its purity should have been suspected; but the matter-of-fact, commonplace innocence of a man of the world, who is a great deal too clever to play any hazardous and villainous game.

"You can perhaps answer me this question, Mr. Marchmont," said Edward Arundel. "Why was my wife doubted when she told the story of her marriage?"

The artist smiled, and rising from his seat upon the stone step, took a pocket-book from one of the pockets of the coat that he had been wearing.

"I can answer that question," he said, selecting a paper from among others in the pocket-book. "This will answer it."

He handed Edward Arundel the paper, which was a letter folded lengthways, and indorsed, "From Mrs. Arundel, August 31st." Within this letter was another paper, indorsed, "Copy of letter to Mrs. Arundel, August 28th."

G

"You had better read the copy first," Mr. Marchmont said, as Edward looked doubtfully at the inner paper.

The copy was very brief, and ran thus:

"MARCHMONT TOWERS, *August* 28, 1848.

"MADAM,—I have been given to understand that your son, Captain Arundel, within a fortnight of his sad accident, contracted a secret marriage with a young lady whose name I, for several reasons, prefer to withhold.' If you can oblige me by informing me whether there is any foundation for this statement you will confer a very great favor upon

"Your obedient servant,
"PAUL MARCHMONT."

The answer to this letter, in the hand of Edward Arundel's mother, was equally brief:

"DANGERFIELD PARK, *August* 31, 1848.

"SIR,—In reply to your inquiry, I beg to state that there can be no foundation whatever for the report to which you allude. My son is too honorable to contract a secret marriage; and although his present unhappy state renders it impossible for me to receive the assurance from his own lips, my confidence in his high principles justifies me in contradicting any such report as that which forms the subject of your letter. I am, Sir, yours obediently,

"LETITIA ARUNDEL."

The soldier stood, mute and confounded, with his mother's letter in his hand. It seemed as if every creature had been against the helpless girl whom he had made his wife. Every hand had been lifted to drive her from the house that was her own; to drive her out upon the world, of which she was ignorant, a wanderer and an outcast; perhaps to drive her to a cruel death.

"You can scarcely wonder if the receipt of that letter confirmed me in my previous belief that Mary Marchmont's story of a marriage arose out of the weakness of a brain never too strong, and at that time very much enfeebled by the effect of a fever."

Edward Arundel was silent. He crushed his mother's letter in his hand. Even his mother—even his mother—that tender and compassionate woman, whose protection he had so freely promised, ten years before, in the lobby of Drury Lane, to John Marchmont's motherless child—even she, by some hideous fatality, had helped to bring grief and shame upon the lonely girl. All this story of his young wife's disappearance seemed enveloped in a wretched obscurity, through whose thick darkness he could not penetrate. He felt himself encompassed by a web of mystery athwart which it was impossible for him to cut his way to the truth. He asked question after question, and received answers which seemed freely given; but the story remained as dark as ever. What did it all mean? What was the clew to the mystery? Was this man, Paul Marchmont—busy among his unfinished pictures, and bearing in his every action, in his every word, the stamp of an easy-going, free-spoken soldier of fortune—likely to have been guilty of any dark and subtle villainy against the missing girl? He had disbelieved in the marriage; but he had had some reason for his doubt of a fact that could not very well be welcome to him.

The young man rose from his chair, and stood irresolute, brooding over these things.

"Come, Captain Arundel," cried Paul Marchmont, heartily, "believe me, though I have not much superfluous sentimentality left in my composition after a pretty long encounter with the world, still I can truly sympathize with your regret for this poor silly child. I hope, for your sake, that she still lives, and is hiding herself out of some persistent folly. Perhaps, now you are able to act in the business, there may be a better chance of finding her. I am old enough to be your father, and am ready to give you the help of any knowledge of the world which I may have gathered in the experience of a lifetime. Will you accept my help?"

Edward Arundel paused for a moment, with his head still bent, and his eyes fixed upon the ground. Then suddenly lifting his head, he looked full in the artist's face as he answered him.

"No!" he cried. "Your offer may be made in all good faith, and if so, I thank you for it; but no one loves this missing girl as I love her; no one has so good a right as I have to protect and shelter her. I will look for my wife, alone, unaided; except by such help as I pray that God may give me."

---

## CHAPTER XXIII.

### IN THE DARK.

EDWARD ARUNDEL walked slowly back to the Towers, shaken in body, perplexed in mind, baffled, disappointed, and most miserable; the young husband, whose married life had been shut within the compass of a brief honey-moon, went back to that dark and gloomy mansion within whose encircling walls Mary had pined and despaired.

"Why did she stop here?" he thought; "why didn't she come to me? I thought her first impulse would have brought her to me. I thought my poor childish love would have set out on foot to seek her husband, if need were."

He groped his way feebly and wearily amidst the leafless wood, and through the rotting vegetation decaying in oozy slime beneath the black shelter of the naked trees. He groped his way toward the dismal eastern front of the great stone dwelling-house, his face always turned toward the blank windows that stared down at him from the discolored walls.

"Oh, if they could speak!" he exclaimed, almost beside himself in his perplexity and desperation; "if they could speak! If those cruel walls could speak, and tell me what my darling suffered within their shadow! If they could tell me why she despaired, and ran away to hide herself from her husband and protector! If they could speak!"

He ground his teeth in a passion of sorrowful rage.

"I should gain as much by questioning yonder stone-wall as by talking to my cousin, Olivia Marchmont," he thought, presently. "Why is that woman so venomous a creature in her hatred of my innocent wife? Why is it that, whether I threaten or whether I appeal, I can gain nothing from her—nothing? She baffles me as completely by her measured answers, which seem to reply to my questions, and which yet tell me nothing, as if she were a brazen image set up by the dark ignorance of a heathen people, and dumb in the absence of an impostor-priest. She baffles me, question her how I will. And Paul Marchmont, again—what have I learned from him? Am I a fool, that people can prevaricate and lie to me like this? Has my brain no sense, and my arm no strength, that I can not wring the truth from the false throats of these wretches?"

The young man gnashed his teeth again in the violence of his rage.

Yes, it was like a dream; it was like nothing but a dream. In dreams he had often felt this terrible sense of impotence wrestling with a mad desire to achieve something or other. But never before in his waking hours had the young soldier experienced such a sensation.

He stopped, irresolute, almost bewildered, looking back at the boat-house, a black spot far away down by the sedgy brink of the slow river, and then again turning his face toward the monotonous lines of windows in the eastern frontage of Marchmont Towers.

"I let that man play with me to-day," he thought; "but our reckoning is to come. We have not done with each other yet."

He walked on to the low archway leading into the quadrangle.

The room which had been John Marchmont's study, and which his widow had been wont to occupy since his death, looked into this quadrangle. Edward Arundel saw his cousin's dark head bending over a book, or a desk perhaps, behind the window.

"Let her beware of me, if she has done any wrong to my wife!" he thought. "To which of these people am I to look for an account of my poor lost girl? To which of these two am I to look? Heaven guide me to find the guilty one; and Heaven have mercy upon that wretched creature when the hour of reckoning comes, for I will have none."

Olivia Marchmont, looking through the window, saw her kinsman's face while this thought was in his mind. The expression, which she saw there was so terrible, so merciless, so sublime in its grand and vengeful beauty, that her own face blanched even to a paler hue than that which had lately become habitual to it.

"Am I afraid of him?" she thought, as she pressed her forehead against the cold glass, and by a physical effort restrained the convulsive trembling that had suddenly shaken her frame. "Am I afraid of him? No! what injury can he inflict upon me worse than that which he has done me from the very first? If he could drag me to a scaffold, and deliver me with his own hands into the grasp of the hangman, he would do me no deeper wrong than he has done me from the hour of my earliest remembrance of him. He could inflict no new pangs, no sharper torture, than I have been accustomed to suffer at his hands. He does not love me. He has never loved me. He never will love me. That is my wrong; and it is for that I take my revenge!"

She lifted her head, which had rested in a sullen attitude against the glass, and looked at the soldier's figure slowly advancing toward the western side of the house.

Then, with a smile—the same horrible smile which Edward Arundel had seen light up her face on the previous night—she muttered between her set teeth,

"Shall I be sorry because this vengeance has fallen across my pathway? Shall I repent, and try to undo what I have done? Shall I thrust myself between others and Mr. Edward Arundel? Shall *I* make myself the ally and champion of this gallant soldier, who seldom speaks to me except to insult and upbraid me? Shall *I* take justice into my hands, and interfere for my kinsman's benefit? No; he has chosen to threaten me; he has chosen to believe vile things of me. From the first his indifference has been next kin to insolence. Let him take care of himself."

Edward Arundel took no heed of the gray eyes that watched him with such a vengeful light in their fixed gaze. He was still thinking of his missing wife, still feeling, to a degree that was intolerably painful, that miserable dream-like sense of utter helplessness and prostration. "What am I to do?" he thought. "Shall I be forever going backward and forward between my Cousin Olivia and Paul Marchmont? forever questioning them, first one and then the other, and never getting any nearer to the truth?"

He asked himself this question, because the extreme anguish, the intense anxiety, which he had endured seemed to have magnified the smallest events, and to have multiplied a hundredfold the lapse of time. It seemed as if he had already spent half a lifetime in his search after John Marchmont's lost daughter.

"Oh my friend, my friend!" he thought, as some faint link of association, some memory thrust upon him by the aspect of the place in which he was, brought back the simple-minded tutor who had taught him mathematics eighteen years before—"my poor friend, if this girl had not been my love and my wife, surely the memory of your trust in me would be enough to make me a desperate and merciless avenger of her wrongs."

He went into the hall, and from the hall to the tenantless western drawing-room—a dreary chamber, with its grim and faded splendor, its stiff, old-fashioned furniture; a chamber which, unadorned by the presence of youth and innocence, had the aspect of belonging to a day that was gone and people that were dead. So might have looked one of those sealed-up chambers in the buried cities of Italy, when the doors were opened, and eager living eyes first looked in upon the habitations of the dead.

Edward Arundel walked up and down the empty drawing-room. There were the ivory chessmen that he had brought from India, under a glass shade on an inlaid table in a window. How often he and Mary had played together in that very window! and how she had always lost her pawns, and left her bishops and knights undefended, while trying to achieve impossible conquests with her queen! The young man paced slowly backward and forward across the old-fashioned bordered carpet, trying to think what he should do. He must form some plan of action in his own mind, he thought. There was foul work somewhere, he most implicitly believed; and it was for him to discover the motive of the treachery and the person of the traitor.

Paul Marchmont! Paul Marchmont! His mind always traveled back to this point. Paul Marchmont was Mary's natural enemy. Paul Marchmont was therefore surely the man to be suspected, the man to be found out and defeated.

And yet, if there was any truth in appearances, it was Olivia who was most inimical to the missing girl; it was Olivia whom Mary had feared; it was Olivia who had driven John Marchmont's orphan child from her home once, and who might, by the same power to tyrannize and torture a weak and yielding nature, have so banished her again.

Or these two, Paul and Olivia, might both hate the defenseless girl, and might have between them plotted a wrong against her.

"Who will tell me the truth about my lost darling?" cried Edward Arundel. "Who will help me to look for my missing love?"

His lost darling; his missing love. It was thus that the young man spoke of his wife. That dark thought which had been suggested to him by the words of Olivia, by the mute evidence of the little bronze slipper picked up near the river-brink, had never taken root, or held even a temporary place in his breast. He would not—nay, more, he could not—think that his wife was dead. In all his confused and miserable dreams that dreary November night, no dream had ever shown him *that*. No image of death had mingled itself with the distorted shadows that had tormented his sleep. No still white face had looked up at him through a veil of murky waters. No moaning sob of a rushing stream had mixed its dismal sound with the many voices of his slumbers. No; he feared all manner of unknown sorrows: he looked vaguely forward to a sea of difficulty, to be waded across in blindness and bewilderment before he could clasp his rescued wife in his arms; but he never thought that she was dead.

Presently the idea came to him that it was outside Marchmont Towers—away beyond the walls of this grim, enchanted castle, where evil spirits seemed to hold possession—that he should seek for the clew to his wife's hiding-place.

"There is Hester, that girl who was fond of Mary," he thought. "She may be able to tell me something, perhaps. I will go to her."

He went out into the hall to look for his servant, the faithful Morrison, who had been eating a very substantial breakfast with the domestics of the Towers—"the sauce to meat" being a prolonged discussion of the facts connected with Mary Marchmont's disappearance and her relations with Edward Arundel—and who came, radiant and greasy from the enjoyment of hot buttered cakes, and Lincolnshire bacon, at the sound of his master's voice.

"I want you to get me some vehicle, and a lad who will drive me a few miles, Morrison," the young soldier said; "or you can drive me yourself, perhaps?"

"Certainly, Master Edward; I have driven your Pa often, when we was travelin' together. I'll go and see if there's a phee-aton or a chay that will suit you, Sir; something that goes easy on its springs."

"Get any thing," muttered Captain Arundel, "so long as you can get it without loss of time."

All fuss and anxiety upon the subject of his health worried the young man. He felt his head dizzied with weakness and excitement; his arm —that muscular right arm which had done him good service two years before in án encounter with a tigress—as weak as the jewel-bound wrist of a delicate woman. But he chafed against any thing like consideration of his weakness; he rebelled against any thing that seemed likely to ·hinder him in that one object upon which all the powers of his mind were bent.

Mr. Morrison went away with some show of briskness, but dropped into a very leisurely pace as soon as he was fairly out of his master's sight. He went straight to the stables, where he had a pleasant gossip with the grooms and hangers-on, and amused himself further by inspecting every bit of horse-flesh in the Marchmont stables, prior to selecting a quiet gray cob which he felt himself capable of driving, and an old-fashioned gig, with a yellow body and black-and-yellow wheels, bearing a strong resemblance to a monstrous wooden wasp.

While the faithful attendant to whom Mrs. Arundel had delegated the care of her son was thus employed, the soldier stood in the stone hall, looking out at the dreary wintry landscape, and pining to hurry away across the dismal swamps to the village in which he hoped to hear tidings of her he sought. He was lounging in a deep oaken window-seat, looking hopelessly at that barren prospect, that monotonous expanse of flat morass and leaden sky, when he heard a footstep behind him, and, turning round, saw Olivia's confidential servant, Barbara Simmons; the woman who had watched by his wife's sick-bed—the woman whom he had compared to a ghoul.

She was walking slowly across the hall toward Olivia's room, whither a bell had just summoned her. Mrs. Marchmont had lately grown fretful and capricious, and did not care to be waited upon by any one except this woman, who had known her from her childhood, and was no stranger to her darkest moods.

Edward Arundel had determined to appeal to every living creature who was likely to know any thing of his wife's disappearance, and he snatched the first opportunity of questioning this woman.

"Stop, Mrs. Simmons," he said, moving away from the window;" I want to speak to you; I want to talk to you about my wife."

The woman turned to him with a blank face, whose expressionless stare might mean either genuine surprise, or an obstinate determination not to understand any thing that might be said to her.

"Your wife, Captain Arundel," she said, in cold measured tones, but with an accent of astonishment.

"Yes, my wife. Mary Marchmont, my lawfully-wedded wife. Look here, woman," cried Edward Arundel; "if you can not accept the word of a soldier, and an honorable man, you can perhaps believe the evidence of your eyes."

He took a morocco memorandum-book from his breast-pocket. It was full of letters, cards, bank-notes, and miscellaneous scraps of paper, carelessly stuffed into it, and among them Captain Arundel found the certificate of his marriage, which he had put away at random upon

his wedding morning, and which had lain unheeded in his pocket-book ever since.

"Look here!" he cried, spreading the document before the waiting-woman's eyes, and pointing, with a shaking hand, to the lines. "You believe that, I suppose?"

"Oh yes, Sir," Barbara Simmons answered, after deliberately reading the certificate. "I have no reason to disbelieve it; no wish to disbelieve it."

"No, I suppose not," muttered Edward Arundel, "unless you too are leagued with Paul Marchmont."

The woman did not flinch at this hinted accusation, but answered the young man in that slow and emotionless manner which no change of circumstance seemed to have power to alter.

"I am leagued with no one, Sir," she said, coldly. "I serve no one except my mistress, Miss Olivia—I mean Mrs. Marchmont."

The study-bell rang for the second time while she was speaking.

"I must go to my mistress, now, Sir," she said. "You heard her ringing for me."

"Go, then, and let me see you as you come back. I tell you I must and will see you and speak to you. Every body in this house tries to avoid me. It seems as if I was not to get a straight answer from any one of you. But I will know all that is to be known about my lost wife. Do you hear, woman? I will know!"

"I will come back to you directly, Sir," Barbara Simmons answered, quietly.

The leaden calmness of this woman's manner irritated Edward Arundel beyond all power of expression. Before his Cousin Olivia's gloomy coldness he had been flung back upon himself as before an iceberg; but every now and then some sudden glow of fiery emotion had shot up amidst the frigid mass, lurid and blazing, and that iceberg had for a moment at least been transformed into an angry and passionate woman, who might in that moment of fierce emotion betray the dark secrets of her soul. But this woman's manner presented a passive barrier, athwart which the young soldier was as powerless to penetrate as he would have been to walk through a block of solid stone.

Olivia was like some black and stony castle, whose barred windows bade defiance to the besieger, but behind whose narrow casements transient flashes of light gleamed fitfully upon the watchers without, hinting at the mysteries that were hidden within the citadel.

Barbara Simmons resembled a black stone-wall, grimly confronting the eager traveler, and giving no indication of the unknown country on the other side.

She came back almost immediately, after being only a few moments in Olivia's room—certainly not long enough to consult with her mistress as to what she was to say or to leave unsaid—and presented herself before Captain Arundel.

"If you have any questions to ask, Sir, about Miss Marchmont, about your wife, I shall be happy to answer them," she said.

"I have a hundred questions to ask," exclaimed the young man; "but first answer me this one plainly and truthfully, Where do you think my wife has gone? What do you think has become of her?"

` The woman was silent for a few moments, and then answered very gravely,

"I would rather not say what I think, Sir."

"Why not?"

"Because I might say that which would make you unhappy."

"Can any thing be more miserable to me than the prevarication which I meet with on every side?" cried Edward Arundel. "If you or any one else will be straightforward with me—remembering that I come to this place like a man who has risen from the grave, depending wholly on the word of others for the knowledge of that which is more vital to me than any thing upon this earth—that person will be the best friend I have found since I rose from my sick-bed to come hither. You can have no motive—if you are not in Paul Marchmont's pay—for being cruel to my poor girl. Tell me the truth, then; speak, and speak fearlessly."

"I have no reason to fear, Sir," answered Barbara Simmons, lifting her faded eyes to the young man's eager face, with a gaze that seemed to say, "I have done no wrong, and I do not shrink from justifying myself." "I have no reason to fear, Sir; I was piously brought up, and have done my best always to do my duty in the state of life in which Providence has been pleased to place me. I have not had a particularly happy life, Sir; for thirty years ago I lost all that made me happy, in them that loved me, and had a claim to love me. I have attached myself to my mistress; but it isn't for me to expect a lady like her would stoop to make me more to her or nearer to her than I have a right to be as a servant."

There was no accent of hypocrisy or cant in any one of these deliberately spoken words. It seemed as if in this speech the woman had told the history of her life; a brief, unvarnished history of a barren life, out of which all love and sunlight had been early swept away, leaving behind a desolate blank that was not destined to be filled up by any affection from the young mistress so long and patiently served.

"I am faithful to my mistress, Sir," Barbara Simmons added, presently, "and I try my best to do my duty to her. I owe no duty to any one else."

"You owe a duty to humanity," answered Edward Arundel. "Woman, do you think duty is a thing to be measured by line and rule? Christ came to save the lost sheep of the children of Israel; but was He less pitiful to the Canaanitish woman when she carried her sorrows to His feet? You and your mistress have made hard precepts for yourselves, and have tried to live by them. You try to circumscribe the area of your Christian charity, and to do good within given limits. The traveler who fell among thieves would have died of his wounds for any help he might have had from you if he had lain beyond your radius. Have you yet to learn that Christianity is cosmopolitan, illimitable, inexhaustible, subject to no laws of time or space? The duty you owe to your mistress is a duty that she buys and pays for—a matter of sordid barter, to be settled when you take your wages; the duty you owe to every miserable creature in your pathway is a sacred debt, to be accounted for to God."

As the young soldier spoke thus, carried away by his passionate agitation, suddenly eloquent by

reason of the intensity of his feeling, a change came over Barbara's face. There was no very palpable evidence of emotion in that stolid countenance; but across the wooden blankness of the woman's face flitted a transient shadow, which was like the shadow of fear.

"I tried to do my duty to Miss Marchmont as well as to my mistress," she said. "I waited on her faithfully while she was ill. I sat up with her six nights running. I didn't take my clothes off for a week. There are folks in the house who can tell you as much."

"God knows I am grateful to you, and will reward you for any pity you may have shown my poor darling," the young man answered, in a more subdued tone; "only, if you pity me, and wish to help me, speak out, and speak plainly. What do you think has become of my lost girl?"

"I can not tell you, Sir. As God looks down upon me and judges me, I declare to you that I know no more than you know. But I think—"

"You think what?"

"That you will never see Miss Marchmont again."

Edward Arundel started as violently as if of all sentences this was the last he had expected to hear pronounced. His sanguine temperament, fresh in its vigorous and untainted youth, could not grasp the thought of despair. He could be mad with passionate anger against the obstacles that separated him from his wife, but he could not believe those obstacles to be insurmountable. He could not doubt the power of his own devotion and courage to bring him back his lost love.

"Never—see her—again!"

He repeated these words as if they had belonged to a strange language, and he were trying to make out their meaning.

"You think," he gasped hoarsely, after a long pause—"you think—that—she is—dead?"

"I think that she went out of this house in a desperate state of mind. She was seen—not by me, for I should have thought it my duty to stop her if I had seen her so—she was seen by one of the servants crying and sobbing awfully as she went away upon that last afternoon."

"And she was never seen again?"

"Never by me."

"And—you—you think she went out of this house with the intention of—of—destroying herself?"

The words died away in a hoarse whisper, and it was by the motion of his white lips that Barbara Simmons perceived what the young man meant.

"I do, Sir."

"Have you any—particular reason for thinking so?"

"No reason beyond what I have told you, Sir."

Edward Arundel bent his head, and walked away to hide his blanched face. He tried instinctively to conceal his mental suffering, as he had sometimes hidden physical torture in an Indian hospital, prompted by the involuntary impulse of a brave man. But though the woman's words had come upon him like a thunder-bolt, he had no belief in the opinion they expressed. No; his young spirit wrestled against and rejected the awful conclusion. Other people might think what they chose ; but he knew better than they. His wife was *not* dead. His life had been so smooth, so happy, so prosperous, so unclouded and successful, that it was scarcely strange he should be skeptical of calamity—that his mind should be incapable of grasping the idea of a catastrophe so terrible as Mary's suicide.

" She was intrusted to me by her father," he thought. " She gave her faith to me before God's altar. She *can not* have perished body and soul ; she *can not* have gone down to destruction for want of my arm outstretched to save her. God is too good to permit such misery."

The young soldier's piety was of the simplest and most unquestioning order, and involved an implicit belief that a right cause must always be ultimately victorious. With the same blind faith in which he had often muttered a hurried prayer before plunging in amidst the mad havoc of an Indian battle-field, confident that the justice of Heaven would never permit heathenish Afghans to triumph over Christian British gentlemen, he now believed that, in the darkest hour of Mary Marchmont's life, God's arm had held her back from the dread horror—the unatonable offense —of self-destruction.

" I thank you for having spoken frankly to me," he said to Barbara Simmons ; " I believe that you have spoken in good faith. But I do not think my darling is forever lost to me. I anticipate trouble and anxiety, disappointment, defeat, for a time—for a long time, perhaps ; but I *know* that I shall find her in the end. The business of my life henceforth is to look for her."

Barbara's dull eyes held earnest watch upon the young man's countenance as he spoke. Anxiety, and even fear, were in that gaze, palpable to those who knew how to read the faint indications of the woman's stolid face.

---

CHAPTER XXIV.

THE PARAGRAPH IN THE NEWSPAPER.

MR. MORRISON brought the gig and pony to the western porch while Captain Arundel was talking to his cousin's servant, and presently the invalid was being driven across the flat between the Towers and the high road to Kemberling.

Mary's old favorite, Farmer Pollard's daughter, came out of a low rustic shop as the gig drew up before her husband's door. This good-natured, tender-hearted Hester, advanced to matronly dignity under the name of Mrs. Jobson, carried a baby in her arms, and wore a white dimity hood, that made a pent-house over her simple rosy face. But at the sight of Captain Arundel nearly all the rosy color disappeared from the country-woman's plump cheeks, and she stared aghast at the unlooked-for visitor, almost ready to believe that, if any thing so substantial as a pony and gig could belong to the spiritual world, it was the phantom only of the soldier that she looked upon.

" Oh, Sir !" she said : " oh, Captain Arundel, is it really you ?"

. Edward alighted before Hester could recover from the surprise occasioned by his appearance.

" Yes, Mrs. Jobson," he said. " May I come into your house ? I wish to speak to you."

Hester courtesied, and stood aside to allow her visitor to pass her. Her manner was col respectful, and she looked at the young offi with a grave, reproachful face, which was strar to him. She ushered her guest into a parlor the back of the shop—a prim apartment, sple did with varnished mahogany, shell-work bo? —bought during Hester's honey-moon trip t Lincolnshire watering-place—and voluminc achievements in the way of crochet-work ; gorgeous and Sabbath - day chamber, looki across a stand of geraniums into a garden tl was orderly and trimly kept even in this d November weather.

Mrs. Jobson drew forward an uneasy eas chair, covered with horse-hair, and veiled by crochet-work representation of a peacock e bowered among roses. She offered this luxu ous seat to Captain Arundel, who, in his wea ness, was well content to sink down upon t slippery cushions.

" I have come here to ask you to help me my search for my wife, Hester," Edward Aru del said, in a scarcely audible voice.

It is not given to the bravest mind to be utte ly independent and defiant of the body ; and t soldier was beginning to feel that he had ve nearly run the length of his tether, and mi soon submit himself to be prostrated by she physical weakness.

" Your wife !" cried Hester, eagerly. " O Sir, is that true ?"

" Is what true ?"

" That poor Miss Mary was your lawful we ded wife ?"

" She was," replied Edward Arundel, sternl " my true and lawful wife. What else shou she have been, Mrs. Jobson ?"

The farmer's daughter burst into tears.

" Oh, Sir," she said, sobbing violently as s spoke—" Oh, Sir, the things that was said agai that poor dear in this place and all about t Towers ! The things that was said ! It mak my heart bleed to think of them ; it makes r heart ready to break when I think what my po sweet young-lady must have suffered. And set me against you, Sir ; and I thought you w a bad and cruel-hearted man !"

" What did they say ?" cried Edward ; " wh did they dare to say against her or agai me ?"

" They said that you had enticed her aw from her home, Sir, and that—that—there h been no marriage ; and that you'd deserted h afterward, and the railway accident had co upon you as a punishment like ; and that M? Marchmont had found poor Miss Mary all alo at a country inn, and had brought her back the Towers."

" But what if people did say this ?" exclaim Captain Arundel. " You could have contradi ed their foul slanders. You could have spok in defense of my poor helpless girl."

" Me, Sir !"

" Yes. You must have heard the truth fro my wife's own lips."

Hester Jobson burst into a new flood of tea as Edward Arundel said this.

" Oh no, Sir," she sobbed ; " that was the m cruel thing of all. I never could get to see M Mary ; they wouldn't let me see her."

" Who wouldn't let you ?"

" Mrs. Marchmont and Mr. Paul Marchmo

I was laid up, Sir, when the report first spread about that Miss Mary had come home. Things was kept very secret, and it was said that Mrs. Marchmont was dreadfully cut up by the disgrace that had come upon her step-daughter. My baby was born about that time, Sir; but as soon as ever I could get about I went up to the Towers, in the hope of seeing my poor dear miss. But Mrs. Simmon's, Mrs. Marchmont's own maid, told me that Miss Mary was ill, very ill, and that no one was allowed to see her except those that waited upon her and that she was used to. And I begged and prayed that I might be allowed to see her, Sir, with the tears in my eyes; for my heart bled for her, poor darling dear, when I thought of the cruel things that were said against her, and thought that, with all her riches and her learning, folks could dare to talk of her as they wouldn't dare to talk of a poor man's wife like me. And I went again and again, Sir; but it was no good; and, the last time I went, Mrs. Marchmont came out into the hall to me, and told me that I was intrusive and impertinent, and that it was me, and such as me, as had set all manner of scandal afloat about her step-daughter. But I went again, Sir, even after that, and I saw Mr. Paul Marchmont, and he was very kind to me, and frank and free-spoken—almost like you, Sir; and he told me that Mrs. Marchmont was rather stern and unforgiving toward the poor young lady—he spoke very kind and pitiful of poor Miss Mary—and that he would stand my friend, and he'd contrive that I should see my poor dear as soon as ever she picked up her spirits a bit, and was more fit to see me; and I was to come again in a week's time, he said."

"Well, and when you went"—

"When I went, Sir," sobbed the carpenter's wife, "it was the 18th of October, and Miss Mary had run away upon the day before, and every body at the Towers was being sent right and left to look for her. I saw Mrs. Marchmont for a minute that afternoon; and she was as white as a sheet, and all of a tremble from head to foot, and she walked about the place as if she was out of her mind like."

"Guilt," thought the young soldier; "guilt of some sort. God only knows what that guilt has been."

He covered his face with his hands, and waited to hear what more Hester Jobson had to tell him. There was no need of questioning here; no reservation or prevarication. With almost as tender regret as he himself could have felt, the carpenter's wife told him all that she knew of the sad story of Mary's disappearance.

"Nobody took much notice of me, Sir, in the confusion of the place," Mrs. Jobson continued; "and there is a parlor-maid at the Towers called Susan Rose, that had been a school-fellow with me ten years before, and I got her to tell me all about it. And she said that poor dear Miss Mary had been weak and ailing ever since she had recovered from the brain-fever, and that she had shut herself up in her room, and had seen no one except Mrs. Marchmont and Barbara Simmons; but on the seventeenth Mrs. Marchmont sent for her, asking her to come to the study. And the poor young lady went; and then Susan Rose thinks that there was high words between Mrs. Marchmont and her step-

daughter, for as Susan was crossing the hall, poor miss came out of the study, and her face was all smothered in tears, and she cried out, as she came into the hall, 'I can't bear it any longer. My life is too miserable; my fate is too wretched!' And then she ran up stairs, and Susan Rose followed up to her room and listened outside the door; and she heard the poor dear sobbing and crying out again and again, 'Oh papa, papa! If you knew what I suffer! Oh papa, papa, papa!'—so pitiful, that if Susan Rose had dared she would have gone in to try and comfort her; but Miss Mary had always been very reserved to all the servants, and Susan didn't dare intrude upon her. It was late that evening when my poor young lady was missed, and the servants sent out to look for her."

"And you, Hester—you knew my wife better than any of these people—where do you think she went?"

Hester Jobson looked piteously at the questioner.

"Oh, Sir," she cried; "Oh, Captain Arundel, don't ask me; pray, pray don't ask me!"

"You think like these other people—you think that she went away to destroy herself?"

"Oh, Sir, what can I think, what can I think except that? She was last seen down by the water-side, and one of her shoes was picked up among the rushes; and for all there's been such a search made after her, and a reward offered, and advertisements in the papers, and every thing done that mortal could do to find her, and no news of her, Sir—not a trace to tell of her being living; not a creature to come forward and speak to her being seen by them after that day. What can I think, Sir, what can I think, except—"

"Except that she threw herself into the river at the back of Marchmont Towers."

"I've tried to think different, Sir; I've tried to hope I should see that poor sweet lamb again; but I can't, I can't. I've worn mourning for these three last Sundays, Sir; for I seemed to feel as if it was a sin and a disrespectfulness toward her to wear colors, and sit in the church where I have seen her so often, looking so meek and beautiful, Sunday after Sunday."

Edward Arundel bowed his head upon his hands and wept silently. This woman's belief in Mary's death afflicted him more than he dared confess to himself. He had defied Olivia and Paul Marchmont, as enemies, who tried to force a false conviction upon him; but he could neither doubt nor defy this honest, warm hearted creature, who wept aloud over the memory of his wife's sorrows. He could not doubt her sincerity; but he still refused to accept the belief which on every side was pressed upon him. He still refused to think that his wife was dead.

"The river was dragged for more than a week," he said, presently, "and my wife's body was never found."

Hester Jobson shook her head mournfully.

"That's a poor sign, Sir," she answered; "the river's full of holes, I've heard say. My husband had a fellow-'prentice who drowned himself in that river seven year ago, and his body was never found."

Edward Arundel rose and walked toward the door.

"I do not believe that my wife is dead," he cried. He held out his hand to the carpenter's wife. "God bless you," he said. "I thank you from my heart for your tender feeling toward my lost girl."

He went out to the gig, in which Mr. Morrison waited for him, rather tired of his morning's work.

"There is an inn a little way further along the street, Morrison," Captain Arundel said. "I shall stop there."

The man stared at his master.

"And not go back to Marchmont Towers, Mr. Edward?"

"No."

Edward Arundel had held nature in abeyance for more than four-and-twenty hours, and this outraged nature now took her revenge by flinging the young man prostrate and powerless upon his bed at the simple Kemberling hostelry, and holding him prisoner there for three dreary days; three miserable days, with long, dark, interminable evenings, during which the invalid had no better employment than to lie brooding over his sorrows, while Mr. Morrison read the *Times* newspaper in a monotonous and droning voice for his sick master's entertainment.

How that helpless and prostrate prisoner, bound hand and foot in the stern grasp of retaliative Nature, loathed the leading articles, the foreign correspondence, in the leviathan journal! How he sickened at the fiery English of Printing-House Square, as expounded by Mr. Morrison! The sound of the valet's voice was like the unbroken flow of a dull river. The great names that surged up every now and then upon that sullen tide of oratory made no impression upon the sick man's mind. What was it to him if the glory of England were in danger, the freedom of a mighty people wavering in the balance? What was it to him if famine-stricken Ireland were perishing, and the far-away Indian possessions menaced by contumacious and treacherous Sikhs? What was it to him if the heavens were shriveled like a blazing scroll, and the earth reeling on its shaken foundations? What had he to do with any catastrophe except that which had fallen upon his innocent young wife?

"Oh my broken trust!" he muttered sometimes, to the alarm of the confidential servant; "Oh my broken trust!"

But during the three days in which Captain Arundel lay in the best chamber at the Black Bull—the chief inn of Kemberling, and a very splendid place of public entertainment long ago, when all the northward-bound coaches had passed through that quiet Lincolnshire village—he was not without a medical attendant to give him some feeble help in the way of drugs and doctor's stuff, in the battle which he was fighting with offended Nature. I don't know but what the help, however well intended, may have gone rather to strengthen the hand of the enemy; for in those days—the year '48 is very long ago when we take the measure of time by science—country practitioners were apt to place themselves upon the side of the disease rather than of the patient, and to assist grim Death in his siege, by lending the professional aid of purgatives and phlebotomy.

On this principle Mr. George Weston, the surgeon of Kemberling, and the submissive and well-tutored husband of Paul Marchmont's sister, would fain have set to work with the prostrate soldier, on the plea that the patient's skin was hot and dry, and his white lips parched with fever.

But Captain Arundel protested vehemently against any such treatment.

"You shall not take an ounce of blood out of my veins," he said, or give me one drop of medicine that will weaken me. What I want is strength; strength to get up and leave this intolerable room, and go about the business that I have to do. As to fever," he added, scornfully, "as long as I have to lie here and am hindered from going about the business of my life, every drop of my blood will boil with a fever that all the drugs in Apothecaries' Hall would have no power to subdue. Give me something to strengthen me. Patch me up somehow or other, Mr. Weston, if you can. But I warn you that, if you keep me long here, I shall leave this place either a corpse or a madman."

The surgeon, drinking tea with his wife and brother-in-law half an hour afterward, related the conversation that had taken place between himself and his patient, breaking up his narrative with a great many "I saids" and "said he's," and with a good deal of rambling commentary upon the text.

Lavinia Weston looked at her brother while the surgeon told his story.

"He is very desperate about his wife, then, this dashing young captain?" Mr. Marchmont said, presently.

"Awful," answered the surgeon; "regular awful. I never saw any thing like it. Really it was enough to cut a man up to hear him go on so. He asked me all sorts of questions about the time when she was ill and I attended upon her, and what did she say to me, and did she seem very unhappy, and all that sort of thing. Upon my word, you know, Mr. Paul—of course I'm very glad to think of your coming into the fortune, and I'm very much obliged to you for the kind promises you've made to me and Lavinia; but I almost felt as if I could have wished the poor young lady hadn't drowned herself."

Mrs. Weston shrugged her shoulders, and looked at her brother.

"*Imbecile!*" she muttered.

She was accustomed to talk to her brother very freely, in rather school-girl French before her husband, to whom that language was as the most recondite of tongues, and who heartily admired her for superior knowledge.

He sat staring at her now, and eating bread-and-butter with a simple relish, which in itself was enough to mark him out as a man to be trampled upon.

On the fourth day after his interview with Hester, Edward Arundel was strong enough to leave his chamber at the Black Bull.

"I shall go to London by to-night's mail, Morrison," he said to his servant; "but before I leave Lincolnshire, I must pay another visit to Marchmont Towers. You can stop here, and pack my portmanteau while I go."

A rumbling old fly—looked upon as a splendid equipage by the inhabitants of Kemberling —was furnished for Captain Arundel's accommodation by the proprietor of the Black Bull; and once more the soldier approached that ill-omened dwelling-place which had been the home of his wife.

He was ushered without any delay to the study in which Olivia spent the greater part of her time.

The dusky afternoon was already closing in. A low fire burned in the old-fashioned grate, and one lighted wax-candle stood upon an open davenport, at which the widow sat amidst a confusion of torn papers, cast upon the ground about her.

The open drawers of the davenport, the littered scraps of paper and loosely-tied documents, thrust, without any show of order, into the different compartments of the desk, bore testimony to that state of mental distraction which had been common to Olivia Marchmont for some time past. She herself, the gloomy tenant of the Towers, sat with her elbow resting on her desk, looking hopelessly and absently at the confusion before her.

"I am very tired," she said, with a sigh, as she motioned her cousin to a chair. "I have been trying to sort my papers, and to look for bills that have to be paid, and receipts. They come to me about every thing. I am very tired."

Her manner was changed from that stern defiance with which she had last confronted her kinsman to an air of almost piteous feebleness. She rested her head on her hand, repeating, in a low voice,

"Yes, I am very tired."

Edward Arundel looked earnestly at her faded face, so faded from that which he remembered it in its proud young beauty, that, in spite of his doubt of this woman, he could scarcely refrain from some touch of pity for her.

"You are ill, Olivia," he said.

"Yes, I am ill; I am worn out; I am tired of my life. Why does not God have pity upon me, and take the bitter burden away? I have carried it too long."

She said this not so much to her cousin as to herself. She was like Job in his despair, and cried aloud to the Supreme Himself in a gloomy protest against her anguish.

"Olivia," said Edward Arundel very earnestly, "what is it that makes you unhappy? Is the burden that you carry a burden on your conscience? Is the black shadow upon your life a guilty secret? Is the cause of your unhappiness that which I suspect it to be? Is it that, in some hour of passion, you consented to league yourself with Paul Marchmont against my poor innocent girl? For pity's sake, speak, and undo what you have done. You can not have been guilty of a crime. There has been some foul play, some conspiracy, some suppression; and my darling has been lured away by the machinations of this man. But he could not have got her into his power without your help. You hated her—Heaven alone knows for what reason—and in an evil hour you helped him, and now you are sorry for what you have done. But it is not too late, Olivia; Olivia, it is surely not too late. Speak, speak, woman, and undo what you have done. As you hope for mercy and forgiveness from God, undo what you have done. I will exact no atonement from you. Paul

Marchmont, this smooth traitor, this frank man of the world, who defied me with a smile—he only shall be called upon to answer for the sin done against my darling. Speak, Olivia, for pity's sake," cried the young man, casting himself upon his knees at his cousin's feet. "You are of my own blood; you must have some spark of regard for me; have compassion upon me, then, or have compassion upon your own guilty soul, which must perish everlastingly if you withhold the truth. Have pity, Olivia, and speak!"

The widow had risen to her feet, recoiling from the soldier as he knelt before her, and looking at him with an awful light in the eyes that alone gave light to her corpse-like face.

Suddenly she flung her arms up above her head, stretching her wasted hands toward the ceiling.

"By the God who has renounced and abandoned me," she cried, "I have no more knowledge than you have of Mary Marchmont's fate. From the hour in which she left this house, upon the 17th of October, until this present moment, I have neither seen her nor heard of her. If I have lied to you, Edward Arundel," she added, dropping her extended arms, and turning quietly to her cousin—"if I have lied to you in saying this, may the tortures which I suffer be doubled to me—if in the infinite of suffering there is any anguish worse than that I now endure."

Edward Arundel paused for a little while, brooding over this strange reply to his appeal. Could he disbelieve his cousin?

It is common to some people to make forcible and impious asseverations of an untruth shamelessly, in the very face of an insulted Heaven. But Olivia Marchmont was a woman who, in the very darkest hour of her despair, knew no wavering from her faith in the God she had offended.

"I can not refuse to believe you, Olivia," Captain Arundel said, presently. "I do believe in your solemn protestations, and I no longer look for help from you in my search for my lost love. I absolve you from all suspicion of being aware of her fate after she left this house. But so long as she remained beneath this roof she was in your care, and I hold you responsible for the ills that may have then befallen her. You, Olivia, must have had some hand in driving that unhappy girl away from her home."

The widow had resumed her seat by the open davenport. She sat with her head bent, her brows contracted, her mouth fixed and rigid, her left hand trifling absently with the scattered papers before her.

"You accused me of this once before, when Mary Marchmont left this house," she said, sullenly.

"And you were guilty then," answered Edward.

"I can not hold myself answerable for the actions of others. Mary Marchmont left this time as she left before, of her own free-will."

"Driven away by your cruel words."

"She must have been very weak," answered Olivia, with a sneer, "if a few harsh words were enough to drive her away from her own house."

"You deny, then, that you were guilty of

causing this poor deluded child's flight from this house?"

Olivia Marchmont sat for some moments in moody silence; then suddenly raising her head, she looked her cousin full in the face.

"I do," she exclaimed; "if any one except herself is guilty of an act which was her own, I am not that person."

"I understand," said Edward Arundel; "it was Paul Marchmont's hand that drove her out upon the dreary world. It was Paul Marchmont's brain that plotted against her. You were only a minor instrument, a willing tool, in the hands of a subtle villain. But he shall answer; he shall answer!"

The soldier spoke the last words between his clenched teeth. Then, with his chin upon his breast, he sat thinking over what he had just heard.

"How was it?" he muttered; "how was it? He is too consummate a villain to use violence. His manner the other morning told me that the law was on his side. He had done nothing to put himself into my power, and he defied me. How was it, then? By what means did he drive my darling to her despairing flight?"

As Captain Arundel sat thinking of these things his cousin's idle fingers still trifled with the papers on the desk; while, with her chin resting on her other hand, and her eyes fixed upon the wall before her, she stared blankly at the reflection of the flame of the candle on the polished oaken panel. Her idle fingers, following no design, strayed here and there among the scattered papers, until a few that lay nearest the edge of the desk slid off the smooth morocco, and fluttered to the ground.

Edward Arundel, as absent-minded as his cousin, stooped involuntarily to pick up the papers. The uppermost of those that had fallen was a slip cut from a country newspaper, to which was pinned an open letter, a few lines only. The paragraph in the newspaper-slip was marked by double ink-lines, drawn round it by a neat penman. Again, almost involuntarily, Edward Arundel looked at this marked paragraph. It was very brief:

"We regret to be called upon to state that another of the sufferers in the accident which occurred last August on the Southwestern Railway has expired from injuries received upon that occasion. Captain Arundel, of the H. E. I. C. S., died on Friday night at Dangerfield Park, Devon, the seat of his elder brother."

The letter was almost as brief as the paragraph:

"KEMBERLING, October 17.
"MY DEAR MRS. MARCHMONT,—The inclosed has just come to hand. Let us hope it is not true. But, in case of the worst, it should be shown to Miss Marchmont *immediately*. Better that she should hear the news from you than from a stranger.

"Yours sincerely,
"PAUL MARCHMONT."

"I understand every thing now," said Edward Arundel, laying these two papers before his cousin; "it was with this printed lie that you and

Paul Marchmont drove my wife to despair—perhaps to death. My darling, my darling," cried the young man, in a burst of uncontrollable agony, "I refused to believe that you were dead; I refused to believe that you were lost to me. I can believe it now; I can believe it now!"

———◆———

## CHAPTER XXV.

### EDWARD ARUNDEL'S DESPAIR.

YES; Edward Arundel could believe the worst now. He could believe now that his young wife, on hearing tidings of his death, had rushed madly to her own destruction; too desolate, too utterly unfriended and miserable, to live under the burden of her sorrows.

Mary had talked to her husband in the happy, loving confidence of her bright honey-moon; she had talked to him of her father's death, and the horrible grief she had felt; the heart-sickness, the eager yearning to be carried to the same grave, to rest in the same silent sleep.

"I think I tried to throw myself from the window upon the night before papa's funeral," she had said; "but I fainted away. I know it was very wicked of me. But I was mad. My wretchedness had driven me mad."

He remembered this. Might not this girl, this helpless child, in the first desperation of her grief, have hurried down to that dismal river, to hide her sorrows forever under its slow and murky tide?

Henceforward it was with a new feeling that Edward Arundel looked for his missing wife. The young and hopeful spirit which had wrestled against conviction, which had stubbornly preserved its own sanguine fancies against the gloomy forebodings of others, had broken down before the evidence of that false paragraph in the country newspaper. That paragraph was the key to the sad mystery of Mary Arundel's disappearance. Her husband could understand now why she ran away, why she despaired; and how, in that desperation and despair, she might have hastily ended her short life.

It was with altered feelings, therefore, that he went forth to look for her. He was no longer passionate and impatient, for he no longer believed that his young wife lived to yearn for his coming, and to suffer for the want of his protection; he no longer thought of her as a lonely and helpless wanderer driven from her rightful home, and in her childish ignorance straying farther and farther away from him who had the right to succor and to comfort her. No; he thought of her now with sullen despair at his heart; he thought of her now in utter hopelessness; he thought of her with a bitter and agonizing regret, that was almost too terrible for endurance.

But this grief was not the only feeling that held possession of the young soldier's breast. Stronger even than his sorrow was his eager yearning for vengeance, his savage desire for retaliation.

"I look upon Paul Marchmont as the murderer of my wife," he said to Olivia, on that November evening on which he saw the paragraph in the newspaper; "I look upon that man as the deliberate destroyer of a helpless girl; and he shall answer to me for her life. He shall answer to me for every pang she suffered, for every tear she shed. God have mercy upon her poor erring soul, and help me to my vengeance upon her destroyer."

He lifted his eyes to heaven as he spoke, and a solemn shadow overspread his pale face, like a dark cloud upon a winter landscape.

I have said that Edward Arundel no longer felt a frantic impatience to discover his wife's fate. The sorrowful conviction which at last had forced itself upon him left no room for impatience. The pale face he had loved was lying hidden somewhere beneath those dismal waters. He had no doubt of that. There was no need of any other solution to the mystery of his wife's disappearance. That which he had to seek for was the evidence of Paul Marchmont's guilt.

The outspoken young soldier, whose nature was as transparent as the stainless soul of a child, had to enter into the lists with a man who was so different to himself, that it was almost difficult to believe that the two individuals belonged to the same species.

Captain Arundel went back to London, and betook himself forthwith to the office of Messrs. Paulette, Paulette, and Matthewson. He had the idea, common to many of his class, that all lawyers, whatever claims they might have to respectability, were in a manner past-masters in every villainous art, and, as such, the proper people to deal with a villain.

"Richard Paulette will be able to help me," thought the young man; "Richard Paulette saw through Paul Marchmont, I dare say."

But Richard Paulette had very little to say about the matter. He had known Edward Arundel's father, and he had known the young soldier from his early boyhood, and he seemed deeply grieved to witness his client's distress; but he had nothing to say against Paul Marchmont.

"I can not see what right you have to suspect Mr. Marchmont of any guilty share in your wife's disappearance," he said. "Do not think I defend him because he is our client. You know that we are rich enough and honorable enough to refuse the business of any man whom we thought a villain. When I was in Lincolnshire, Mr. Marchmont did every thing that a man could do to testify his anxiety to find his cousin."

"Oh yes," Edward Arundel answered, bitterly; "that is only consistent with the man's diabolical artifice; that was a part of his scheme. He wished to testify that anxiety, and he wanted you as a witness to his conscientious search after my—poor—lost girl." His voice and manner changed for a moment as he spoke of Mary.

Richard Paulette shook his head.

"Prejudice, prejudice, my dear Arundel," he said; "this is all prejudice upon your part, I assure you. Mr. Marchmont behaved with perfect honesty and candor. 'I won't tell you that I'm sorry to inherit this fortune,' he said, 'because if I did you wouldn't believe me—what man in his senses could believe that a poor devil of a landscape-painter would regret coming into eleven thousand a year?—but I am very sorry for this poor little girl's unhappy fate.'

And I believe," added Mr. Paulette, decisively, "that the man was heartily sorry."

Edward Arundel groaned aloud.

"O God! this is too terrible," he muttered. "Every body will believe in this man rather than in me. How am I to be avenged upon the wretch who caused my darling's death?"

He talked for a long time to the lawyer, but with no result. Richard Paulette set down the young man's hatred of Paul Marchmont as a natural consequence of his grief for Mary's death.

"I can't wonder that you are prejudiced against Mr. Marchmont," he said; "it's natural, it's only natural; but, believe me, you are wrong. Nothing could be more straightforward, and even delicate, than his conduct. He refuses to take possession of the estate, or to touch a farthing of the rents. 'No,' he said, when I suggested to him that he had a right to enter in possession—'no; we will not shut the door against hope. My cousin may be hiding herself somewhere; she may return by-and-by. Let us wait a twelvemonth. If, at the end of that time she does not return, and if in the interim we receive no tidings from her, no evidence of her existence, we may reasonably conclude that she is dead; and I may fairly consider myself the rightful owner of Marchmont Towers. In the mean time, you will act as if you were acting as Mary Marchmont's agent, holding all moneys as in trust for her, but to be delivered up to me at the expiration of a year from the day on which she disappeared.' I do not think any thing could be more straightforward than that," added Richard Paulette, in conclusion.

"No," Edward answered, with a sigh; "it seems very straightforward. But the man who could strike at a helpless girl by means of a lying paragraph in a newspaper—"

"Mr. Marchmont may have believed in that paragraph."

Edward Arundel arose with a gesture of impatience.

"I came to you for help, Mr. Paulette," he said; "but I see you don't mean to help me. Good-day."

He left the office before the lawyer could remonstrate with him. He walked away, with passionate anger against all the world raging in his breast.

"Why, what a smooth-spoken, false-tongued world it is!" he thought. "Let a man succeed in the vilest scheme, and no living creature will care to ask by what foul means he may have won his success. What weapons can I use against this Paul Marchmont, who twists truth and honesty to his own ends, and masks his basest treachery under an appearance of candor?"

From Lincoln's Inn Fields Captain Arundel drove over Waterloo Bridge to Oakley Street. He went to Mrs. Pimpernel's establishment, without any hope of the glad surprise that had met him there a few months before. He believed implicitly that his wife was dead, and wherever he went in search of her he went in utter hopelessness, only prompted by the desire to leave no part of his duty undone.

The honest-hearted dealer in cast-off apparel wept bitterly when she heard how sadly the Captain's honey-moon had ended. She would have been content to detain the young soldier all day while she bemoaned the misfortunes that had come upon him; and now for the first time Edward heard of dismal forebodings, and horrible dreams, and unaccountable presentiments of evil, with which this honest woman had been afflicted on and before his wedding-day, and of which she had made special mention at the time to divers friends and acquaintance.

"I never shall forget how shivery-like I felt as the cab drove off, with that poor dear alook-in' and smilin' at me out of the window. I says to Mrs. Polson, as her husband is in the shoe-makin' line two doors further down—I says, 'I do hope Capting Harungdell's lady will get safe to the end of her jouney.' I felt the cold-shivers a-creepin' up my back just exjackly like I did a fortnight before my pore Jane died, and I couldn't but think as somethink sarious was goin' to happen."

From London Captain Arundel went to Winchester, much to the disgust of his valet, who was accustomed to a luxuriously idle life at Dangerfield Park, and who did not by any means relish this desultory wandering from place to place. Perhaps there was some faint ray of hope in the young man's mind as he drew near to that little village-inn beneath whose shelter he had been so happy with his childish bride. If she had *not* committed suicide; if she had indeed wandered away, to try and bear her sorrows in gentle Christian resignation; if she had sought some retreat where she might be safe from her tormentors—would not every instinct of her loving heart have led her here?—here, amidst these low meadows and winding streams, guarded and surrounded by the pleasant shelter of grassy hill-tops, crowned by waving trees?—here, where she had been so happy with the husband of her choice?

But, alas, that newly-born hope, which had made the soldier's heart beat and his cheek flush, was as delusive as many other hopes that lure men and women onward in their weary wanderings upon this earth. The landlord of the White Hart Inn answered Edward Arundel's question with stolid indifference.

No; the young lady had gone away with her Ma, and a gentleman who came with her Ma. She had cried a deal, poor thing, and had seemed very much cut up. (It was from the chamber-maid Edward heard this.) But her Ma and the gentleman had seemed in a great hurry to take her away. The gentleman said that a village-inn wasn't the place for her, and he said he was very much shocked to find her there; and he had a fly got, and took the two ladies away in it to the George, at Winchester, and they were to go from there to London; and the young lady was crying when she went away, and was as pale as death, poor dear.

This was all that Captain Arundel gained by his journey to Milldale. He went across country to the farming people near Reading, his wife's poor relatives. But they had heard nothing of her. They had wondered, indeed, at having no letters from her; for she had been very kind to them. They were terribly distressed when they heard of her disappearance.

This was the forlorn hope. It was all over now. Edward Arundel could no longer struggle against the cruel truth. He could do nothing now but avenge his wife's sorrows. He went down to Devonshire, saw his mother, and told her the sad story of Mary's flight. But he could not rest at Dangerfield, though Mrs. Arundel implored him to stay long enough to recruit his shattered health. He hurried back to London, made arrangements with his agent for the purchase of his captaincy among his brother officers, and then, turning his back upon the career that had been far dearer to him than his life, he went down to Lincolnshire once more in the dreary winter weather, to watch and wait patiently, if need were, for the day of retribution.

There was a detached cottage, a lonely place enough, between Kemberling and Marchmont Towers, that had been to let for a long time, being very much out of repair, and by no means inviting in appearance. Edward Arundel took this cottage. All necessary repairs and alterations were executed under the direction of Mr. Morrison, who was to remain permanently in the young man's service. Captain Arundel had a couple of horses brought down to his new stable, and hired a country lad, who was to act as groom under the eye of the factotum. Mr. Morrison and this lad, with one female servant, formed Edward's establishment.

Paul Marchmont lifted his auburn eyebrows when he heard of the new tenant of Kemberling Retreat. The lonely cottage had been christened Kemberling Retreat by a sentimental tenant, who had ultimately levanted with his rent three quarters in arrear. The artist exhibited a gentlemanly surprise at this new vagary of Edward Arundel's, and publicly expressed his pity for the foolish young man.

"I am so sorry that the poor fellow should sacrifice himself to a romantic grief for my unfortunate cousin," Mr. Marchmont said, in the parlor of the Black Bull, where he condescended to drop in now and then with his brother-in-law, and to make himself popular among the magnates of Kemberling and the tenant farmers, who looked to him as their future, if not their actual landlord. "I am really sorry for the poor lad. He's a handsome, high-spirited fellow, and I'm sorry he's been so weak as to ruin his prospects in the Company's service. Yes; I am heartily sorry for him."

Mr. Marchmont discussed the matter very lightly in the parlor of the Black Bull; but he kept silence as he walked home with the surgeon; and Mr. George Weston, looking askance at his brother-in-law's face, saw that something was wrong, and thought it advisable to hold his peace.

Paul Marchmont sat up late that night talking to his sister after the surgeon had gone to bed. The brother and sister conversed in subdued murmurs as they stood close together before the expiring fire, and the faces of both were very grave, almost apprehensive.

"He must be terribly in earnest," Paul Marchmont said, "or he would never have sacrificed his position. He has planted himself here, close upon us, with a determination of watching us. We shall have to be very careful."

It was early in the new year that Edward Arundel completed all his arrangements and took possession of Kemberling Retreat. He knew that, in retiring from the East India Company's service, he had sacrificed the prospect of a brilliant and glorious career, under some of the finest soldiers who ever fought for their country. But he had made this sacrifice willingly—as an offering to the memory of his lost love ; as an atonement for his broken trust. For it was one of his most bitter miseries to remember that his own want of prudence had been the first cause of all Mary's sorrows. Had he confided in his mother—had he induced her to return from Germany to be present at his marriage, and to accept the orphan girl as a daughter—Mary need never again have fallen into the power of Olivia Marchmont. His own imprudence, his own rashness, had flung his poor child, helpless and friendless, into the hands of the very man against whom John Marchmont had written a solemn warning—a warning that it would have been Edward's duty to remember. But who could have calculated on the railway accident; and who could have foreseen a separation in the first blush of the honey-moon? Edward Arundel had trusted in his own power to protect his bride from every ill that might assail her. In the pride of his youth and strength he forgot that he was not immortal, and the last idea that could have entered his mind was the thought that he should be stricken down by a sudden calamity, and rendered even more helpless than the girl he had sworn to shield and shelter.

The bleak winter crept slowly past, and the shrill March winds were loud amidst the leafless trees in the wood behind Marchmont Towers. This wood was open to any foot-passenger who might choose to wander that way ; and Edward Arundel often walked upon the bank of the slow river, and past the boat-house, beneath whose shadow he had wooed his young wife in the bright summer that was gone. The place had a mournful attraction for the young man, by reason of the memory of the past, and a different and far keener fascination in the fact of Paul Marchmont's frequent occupation of his roughly-built painting-room.

In a purposeless and unsettled frame of mind Edward Arundel kept watch upon the man he hated, scarcely knowing why he watched, or for what he hoped, but with a vague belief that something would be discovered ; that some accident might come to pass which would enable him to say to Paul Marchmont,

"It was by your treachery my wife perished ; and it is you who must answer to me for her death."

Edward Arundel had seen nothing of his Cousin Olivia during that dismal winter. He had held himself aloof from the Towers—that is to say, he had never presented himself there as a guest, though he had been often on horseback and on foot in the wood by the river. He had not seen Olivia, but he had heard of her through his valet, Mr. Morrison, who insisted on repeating the gossip of Kemberling for the benefit of his listless and indifferent master.

"They do say as Mr. Paul Marchmont is going to marry Mrs. John Marchmont, Sir," Mr. Morrison said, delighted at the importance of his information. "They say as Mr. Paul is always up at the Towers visitin' Mrs. John, and that she takes his advice about every thing as she

does, and that she's quite wrapped up in him like."

Edward Arundel looked at his attendant with unmitigated surprise.

"My Cousin Olivia marry Paul Marchmont!" he exclaimed. "You should be wiser than to listen to such foolish gossip, Morrison. You know what country people are, and you know they can't keep their tongues quiet."

Mr. Morrison took this reproach as a compliment to his superior intelligence.

"It ain't oftentimes I listen to their talk, Sir," he said ; "but if I've heard this said once I've heard it twenty times; and I've heard it at the Black Bull, too, Mr. Edward, where Mr. Marchmont frequents sometimes with his sister's husband ; and the landlord told me as it had been spoken of once before his face, and he didn't deny it."

Edward Arundel pondered gravely over this gossip of the Kemberling people. It was not so very improbable, perhaps, after all. Olivia only held Marchmont Towers on sufferance. It might be that, rather than be turned out of her stately home, she would accept the hand of its rightful owner. She would marry Paul Marchmont, perhaps, as she had married his brother—for the sake of a fortune and a position. She had grudged Mary her wealth, and now she sought to become a sharer in that wealth.

"Oh, the villainy, the villainy!" cried the soldier. "It is all one base fabric of treachery and wrong. A marriage between these two will be only a part of the scheme. Between them they have driven my darling to her death, and they will now divide the profits of their guilty work."

The young man determined to discover whether there had been any foundation for the Kemberling gossip. He had not seen his cousin since the day of his discovery of the paragraph in the newspaper, and he went forthwith to the Towers, bent on asking Olivia the straight question as to the truth of the reports that had reached his ears.

He walked over to the dreary mansion. He had regained his strength by this time, and he had recovered his good looks; but something of the brightness of his youth was gone ; something of the golden glory of his beauty had faded, He was no longer the young Apollo, fresh and radiant with the divinity of the skies. He had suffered ; and suffering had left its traces on his countenance. That virgin hopefulness, that supreme confidence in a bright future, which is the virginity of beauty, had perished beneath the withering influence of affliction.

Mrs. Marchmont was not to be seen at the Towers. She had gone down to the boat-house with Mr. Paul Marchmont and Mrs. Weston, the servant said.

"I will see them together," Edward Arundel thought. "I will see if my cousin dares to tell me that she means to marry this man."

He walked through the wood to the dilapidated building by the river. The March winds were blowing among the leafless trees, swirling the black pools of water that the rain had left in every hollow; the smoke from the chimney of Paul Marchmont's painting-room struggled hopelessly against the wind, and was beaten back upon the roof from which it tried to rise. Every thing succumbed before that pitiless northeaster.

Edward Arundel knocked at the door of the wooden edifice erected by his foe. He scarcely waited for the answer to his summons, but lifted the latch, and walked across the threshold, uninvited, unwelcome.

There were four people in the painting-room. Two or three seemed to have been talking together when Edward knocked at the door; but the speakers had stopped simultaneously and abruptly, and there was a dead silence when he entered.

Olivia Marchmont was standing under the broad northern window; the artist was sitting upon one of the steps leading up to the pavilion; and a few paces from him, in an old cane-chair near the easel, sat George Weston, the surgeon, with his wife leaning over the back of his chair. It was at this man that Edward Arundel looked longest, riveted by the strange expression of his face. The traces of intense agitation have a peculiar force when seen in a usually stolid countenance. Your mobile faces are apt to give an exaggerated record of emotion. We grow accustomed to their changeful expression, their vivid betrayal of every passing sensation. But this man's was one of those faces which are only changed from their apathetic stillness by some moral earthquake, whose shock arouses the dullest man from his stupid imperturbability. Such a shock had lately affected George Weston, the quiet surgeon of Kemberling, the submissive husband of Paul Marchmont's sister. His face was as white as death; a slow trembling shook his ponderous frame; with one of his big fat hands he pulled a cotton handkerchief from his pocket, and tremulously wiped the perspiration from his bald forehead. His wife bent over him, and whispered a few words in his ear; but he shook his head with a piteous gesture, as if to testify his inability to comprehend her. It was impossible for a man to betray more obvious signs of violent agitation than this man betrayed.

"It's no use, Lavinia," he murmured, hopelessly, as his wife whispered to him for the second time; "it's no use, my dear; I can't get over it."

Mrs. Weston cast one rapid, half-despairing half-appealing glance at her brother, and in the next moment recovered herself, by an effort only such as great women, or wicked women, are capable of.

"Oh, you men!" she cried, in her liveliest voice; "oh, you men! What big silly babies, what nervous creatures you are! Come, George, I won't have you giving way to this foolish nonsense, just because an extra glass or so of Mrs. Marchmont's very fine old port has happened to disagree with you. You must not think that we are a drunkard, Mr. Arundel," added the lady, turning playfully to Edward, and patting her husband's clumsy shoulder as she spoke; "we are only a poor village surgeon with a very weak head, and quite unaccustomed to pale old port. Come, Mr. George Weston, march out into the open air, Sir, and let us see if the March wind will bring you back your senses."

And without another word Lavinia Weston hustled her husband, who walked like a man in

a dream, out of the painting-room, and closed the door behind her.

Paul Marchmont laughed as the door shut upon his brother-in-law.

"Poor George!" he said, carelessly; "I thought he helped himself to the port a little too liberally. He never could stand a glass of wine; and he's the most stupid creature when he is drunk."

Excellent as all this by-play was, Edward Arundel was not deceived by it.

"The man was not drunk," he thought; "he was frightened. What could have happened to throw him into that state? What mystery are these people hiding among themselves, and what should he have to do with it?"

"Good - evening, Captain Arundel," Paul Marchmont said. "I congratulate you on the change in your appearance since you were last in this place. You seem to have quite recovered the effects of that terrible railway accident."

Edward Arundel drew himself up stiffly as the artist spoke to him.

"We can not meet except as enemies, Mr. Marchmont," he said. "My cousin has no doubt told you what I said of you when I discovered the lying paragraph which you caused to be shown to my wife."

"I only did what any one else would have done under the circumstances," Paul Marchmont answered, quietly. "I was deceived by some penny-a-liner's false report. How should I know the effect that report would have upon my unhappy cousin?"

"I can not discuss this matter with you," cried Edward Arundel, his voice tremulous with passion; "I am almost mad when I think of it. I am not safe; I dare not trust myself. I look upon you as the deliberate assassin of a helpless girl; but so skillful an assassin that nothing less than the vengeance of God can touch you. I cry aloud to Him night and day, in the hope that He will hear me and avenge my wife's death. I can not look to any earthly law for help; but I trust in God, I trust in God."

There are very few positive and consistent atheists in this world. Mr. Paul Marchmont was a philosopher of the infidel school, a student of Voltaire and the brotherhood of the Encyclopedia, and a believer in those liberal days before the Reign of Terror, when Frenchmen, in coffeehouses, discussed the Supreme under the sobriquet of Mons. l'Etre; but he grew a little paler as Edward Arundel, with kindling eyes and uplifted hand, declared his faith in a Divine Avenger.

The skeptical artist may have thought, "What if there should be some reality in the creed so many weak fools confide in? What if there is a God who can not abide iniquity?"

"I came here to look for you, Olivia," Edward Arundel said, presently. "I want to ask you a question. Will you come into the wood with me?"

"Yes, if you wish it," Mrs. Marchmont answered, quietly.

The cousins went out of the painting-room together, leaving Paul Marchmont alone. They walked on for a few yards in silence.

"What is the question you came here to ask me?" Olivia asked, abruptly.

"The Kemberling people have raised a report

about you which I should fancy would be scarcely agreeable to yourself. You would hardly wish to benefit by Mary Marchmont's death, would you, Olivia?"

He looked at her searchingly as he spoke. Her face was at all times so expressive of hidden cares, of cruel mental tortures, that there was little room in her countenance for any new emotion. Her cousin looked in vain for any change in it now.

"Benefit by her death!" she exclaimed. "How should I benefit by her death?"

"By marrying the man who inherits this estate. They say you are going to marry Paul Marchmont."

Olivia looked at him with an expression of surprise.

"Do they say that of me?" she asked. "Do people say that?"

"They do. Is it true, Olivia?"

The widow turned upon him almost fiercely.

"What does it matter to you whether it is true or not? What do you care whom I marry, or what becomes of me?"

"I care this much," Edward Arundel answered, "that I would not have your reputation lied away by the gossips of Kemberling. I should despise you if you married this man. But if you do not mean to marry him, you have no right to encourage his visits; you are trifling with your own good name. You should leave this place, and by that means give the lie to any false reports that have arisen about you."

"Leave this place!" cried Olivia Marchmont, with a bitter laugh. "Leave this place! Oh my God, if I could; if I could go away and bury myself somewhere at the other end of the world, and forget—and forget!" She said this as if to herself; as if it was a cry of despair wrung from her in despite of herself; then, turning to Edward Arundel, she said, in a quieter voice, "I can never leave this place till I leave it in my coffin. I am a prisoner here 'for life."

She turned from him, and walked slowly away, with her face toward the dying sunlight in the low western sky.

--------

CHAPTER XXVI.

EDWARD'S VISITORS.

PERHAPS no greater sacrifice had ever been made by an English gentleman than that which Edward Arundel willingly offered up as an atonement for his broken trust, as a tribute to his lost wife. Brave, ardent, generous, and sanguine, this young soldier saw before him a brilliant career in the profession which he loved. He saw glory and distinction beckoning to him from afar, and turned his back upon those shining Sirens. He gave up all; in the vague hope of, sooner or later, avenging Mary's wrongs upon Paul Marchmont.

He made no boast, even to himself, of that which he had done. Again and again memory brought back to him the day upon which he breakfasted in Oakley Street and walked across Waterloo Bridge with the Drury Lane supernumerary. Every word that John Marchmont had spoken; every look of the meek and trust-

ing eyes, the pale and thoughtful face; every pressure of the thin hand which had grasped his in grateful affection, in friendly confidence—came back to Edward Arundel after an interval of nearly ten years, and brought with them a bitter sense of self-reproach.

"He trusted his daughter to me," the young man thought. "Those last words in the poor fellow's letter are always in my mind: 'The only bequest which I can leave to the. only friend I have is the legacy of a child's helplessness.' And I have slighted his solemn warning : and I have been false to my trust."

In his scrupulous sense of honor, the soldier reproached himself as bitterly for that imprudence, out of which so much evil had arisen, as another man might have done after a willful betrayal of his trust. He could not forgive himself. He was for ever and ever repeating in his own mind that one brief phrase which is the universal chorus of erring men's regret : "If I had acted differently, if I had done otherwise, this or that would not have come to pass." We are perpetually wandering amidst the hopeless deviations of a maze, finding pitfalls and precipices, quicksands and morasses, at every turn in the painful way; and we look back at the end of our journey to discover a straight and pleasant roadway by which, had we been wise enough to choose it, we might have traveled safely and comfortably to our destination.

But Wisdom waits for us at the goal instead of accompanying us upon our journey. She is a divinity whom we only meet very late in life; when we are too near the end of our troublesome march to derive much profit from her counsels. We can only retail them to our juniors, who, not getting them from the fountain-head, have very small appreciation of their value.

The young captain of East Indian cavalry suffered very cruelly from the sacrifice which he had made. Day after day, day after day, the slow, dreary, changeless, eventless, and unbroken life dragged itself out; and nothing happened to bring him any nearer to the purpose of this monotonous existence; no promise of ultimate success rewarded his heroic self-devotion. Afar he heard of the rush and clamor of war, of dangers and terror, of conquest and glory. His own regiment was in the thick of the strife, his brothers in arms were doing wonders. Every mail brought some new record of triumph and glory.

The soldier's heart sickened as he read the story of each new encounter; his heart sickened with that terrible yearning—that yearning which seems physically palpable in its perpetual pain; the yearning with which a child at a hard school, lying broad awake in the long, gloomy, rush-lit bedchamber in the dead of the silent night, remembers the soft resting-place of his mother's bosom; the yearning with which a faithful husband far away from home sighs for the presence of the wife he loves. Even with such a heartsickness as this Edward Arundel pined to be among the familiar faces yonder in the East—to hear the triumphant yell of his men as they swarmed after him through the breach in an Afghan wall—to see the dark heathens blanch under the terror of Christian swords.

He read every record of the war again and again, again and again, till each scene arose before him—a picture, flaming and lurid, grandly beautiful, horribly sublime. The very words of those newspaper reports seemed to blaze upon the paper on which they were written, so palpable were the images which they evoked in the soldier's mind. He was frantic in his eager impatience for the arrival of every mail, for the coming of each new record of that Indian warfare. He was like a devourer of romances, who reads a thrilling story link by link, and who is impatient for every new chapter of the fiction. His dreams were of nothing but battle and victory, danger, triumph, and death; and he often woke in the morning exhausted by the excitement of those visionary struggles, those phantom terrors.

His sabre hung over the chimney-piece in his simple bedchamber. He took it down sometimes, and drew it from the sheath. He could have almost wept aloud over that idle sword. He raised his arm, and the weapon vibrated with a whizzing noise as he swept the glittering steel in a wide circle through the empty air. An infidel's head should have been swept from his vile carcass in that rapid circle of the keen-edged blade. The soldier's arm was as strong as ever, his wrist as supple, his muscular force unwasted by mental suffering. Thank Heaven for that. But after that brief thanksgiving his arm dropped inertly, and the idle sword fell out of his relaxing grasp.

"I seem a craven to myself," he cried; "I have no right to be here—I have no right to be here while those other fellows are fighting for their lives out yonder. O God, have mercy upon me! My brain gets dazed sometimes; and I begin to wonder whether I am most bound to remain here and watch Paul Marchmont, or to go yonder and fight for my country and my Queen."

There were many phases in this mental fever. At one time the young man was seized with a savage jealousy of the officer who had succeeded to his captaincy. He watched this man's name, and every record of his movements, and was constantly taking objection to his conduct. He was grudgingly envious of this particular officer's triumphs, however small. He could not feel generously toward this happy successor, in the bitterness of his own enforced idleness.

"What opportunities this man has!" he thought; "*I* never had such chances."

It is almost impossible for me to faithfully describe the tortures which this monotonous existence inflicted upon the impetuous young man. It is the specialty of a soldier's career that it unfits most men for any other life. They can not throw off the old habitudes. They can not turn from the noisy stir of war to the tame quiet of everyday life; and even when they fancy themselves wearied and worn-out, and willingly retire from service, their souls are stirred by every sound of the distant contest, as the war-steed is aroused by the blast of a trumpet. But Edward Arundel's career had been cut suddenly short at the very hour in which it was brightest with the promise of future glory. It was as if a torrent rushing madly down a mountain-side had been dammed up, and its waters bidden to stagnate upon a level plain. The rebellious waters boiled and foamed in a sullen fury. The soldier could not submit him-

self contentedly to his fate. He might strip off his uniform, and accept sordid coin as the price of the epaulets he had won so dearly; but he was at heart a soldier still. When he received the bank bills which were the price of his captaincy, it seemed to him almost as if he had sold his brother's blood.

It was summer-time now. Ten months had elapsed since his marriage with Mary Marchmont, and no new light had been thrown upon the disappearance of his young wife. No one could feel a moment's doubt as to her fate. She had perished in that lonely river which flowed behind Marchmont Towers, and far away down to the sea.

The artist had kept his word, and had as yet taken no step toward entering into possession of the estate which he inherited by his cousin's death. But Mr. Paul Marchmont spent a great deal of time at the Towers, and a great deal more time in the painting-room by the river-side, sometimes accompanied by his sister, sometimes alone.

The Kemberling gossips had grown by no means less talkative upon the subject of Olivia, and the new owner of Marchmont Towers. On the contrary, the voices that discussed Mrs. Marchmont's conduct were a great deal more numerous than heretofore; in other words, John Marchmont's widow was "talked about." Every thing is said in this phrase. It was scarcely that people said bad things of her; it was rather that they talked more about her than any woman can suffer to be talked of with safety to her fair fame. They began by saying that she was going to marry Paul Marchmont; they went on to wonder *whether* she was going to marry him; then they wondered *why* she didn't marry him. From this they changed the venue, and began to wonder whether Paul Marchmont meant to marry her—there was an essential difference in this new wonderment—and next, why Paul Marchmont didn't marry her. And by this time Olivia's reputation was overshadowed by a terrible cloud, which had arisen, no bigger than a man's hand, in the first conjecturings of a few ignorant villagers.

People made it their business first to wonder about Mrs. Marchmont, and then to set up their own theories about her; to which theories they clung with a stupid persistence, forgetting, as people generally do forget, that there might be some hidden clew, some secret key, to the widow's conduct, for want of which the cleverest reasoning respecting her was only so much groping in the dark.

Edward Arundel heard of the cloud which shadowed his cousin's name. Her father heard of it, and went to remonstrate with her, imploring her to come to him at Swampington, and to leave Marchmont Towers to the new lord of the mansion. But she only answered him with gloomy, obstinate reiteration, and almost in the same terms as she had answered Edward Arundel; declaring that she would stay at the Towers till her death; that she would never leave the place till she was carried thence in her coffin.

Hubert Arundel, always afraid of his daughter, was more than ever afraid of her now; and he was as powerless to contend against her sullen determination, as he would have been to float up the stream of a rushing river.

So Olivia was talked about. She had scared away all visitors after the ball at the Towers by the strangeness of her manner and the settled gloom in her face; and she lived unvisited and alone in the gaunt stony mansion; and people said that Paul Marchmont was almost perpetually with her, and that she went to meet him in the painting-room by the river.

Edward Arundel sickened of his wearisome life, and no one helped him to endure his sufferings. His mother wrote to him, imploring him to resign himself to the loss of his young wife, to return to Dangerfield, to begin a new existence, and to blot out the memory of the past.

"You have done all that the most devoted affection could prompt you to do," Mrs. Arundel wrote. "Come back to me, my dearest boy. I gave you up to the service of your country because it was my duty to resign you then. But I can not afford to lose you now; I can not bear to see you sacrificing yourself to a chimera. Return to me; and let me see you make a new and happier choice. Let me see my son the father of little children who will gather round my knees when I grow old and feeble."

"A new and happier choice!" Edward Arundel repeated the words with a melancholy bitterness. "No, my poor lost girl; no, my blighted wife, I will not be false to you. The smiles of happy women can have no sunlight for me while I cherish the memory of the sad eyes that watched me when I drove away from Milldale, the sweet sorrowful face that I was never to look upon again."

The dull empty days succeeded each other, and *did* resemble each other, with a wearisome similitude that well-nigh exhausted the patience of the impetuous young man. His fiery nature chafed against this miserable delay. It was so hard to have to wait for his vengeance. Sometimes he could scarcely refrain from planting himself somewhere in Paul Marchmont's way, with the idea of a hand-to-hand struggle in which either he or his enemy must perish.

Once he wrote the artist a desperate letter, denouncing him as an arch-plotter and villain; calling upon him, if his evil nature was redeemed by one spark of manliness, to fight him as men had been in the habit of fighting only a few years before, with a hundred times less reason than these two men had for their quarrel.

"I have called you a villain and traitor; in India we fellows would kill each other for smaller words than those," wrote the soldier. "But I have no wish to take any advantage of her military experience. I may be a better shot than you. Let us have only one pistol, and draw lots for it. Let us fire at each other across a dinner-table. Let us do any thing, so that we bring this miserable business to an end."

Mr. Marchmont read this letter slowly and thoughtfully, more than once; smiling as he read.

"He's getting tired," thought the artist. "Poor young man, I thought he would be the first to grow tired of this sort of work."

He wrote Edward Arundel a long letter; a friendly but rather facetious letter; such as he might have written to a child who had asked him to jump over the moon. He ridiculed the idea of a duel, as something utterly Quixotic and absurd.

"I am fifteen years older than you, my dear Mr. Arundel," he wrote, "and a great deal too old to have any inclination to fight with wind-mills; or to represent the wind-mill which a high-spirited young Quixote may choose to mistake for a villainous knight, and run his hot head against in that delusion. I am not offended with you for calling me bad names, and I take your anger merely as a kind of romantic manner you have of showing your love for my poor cousin. We are not enemies, and we never shall be enemies; for I will never suffer myself to be so foolish as to get into a passion with a brave and generous-hearted young soldier, whose only error is an unfortunate hallucination with regard to

"Your very humble servant,
"PAUL MARCHMONT."

Edward ground his teeth with savage fury as he read this letter.

"Is there no making this man answer for his infamy?" he muttered. "Is there no way of making him suffer?"

June was nearly over, and the year was wearing round to the anniversary of Edward's wedding-day, the anniversaries of those bright days which the young bride and bridegroom had loitered away by the trout-streams in the Hampshire meadows, when some most unlooked-for visitors made their appearance at Kemberling Retreat.

The cottage lay back behind a pleasant garden, and was hidden from the dusty high road by a hedge of lilacs and laburnums which grew within the wooden fence. It was Edward's habit, in this hot summer-time, to spend a great deal of his time in the garden; walking up and down the neglected paths with a cigar in his mouth; or lolling in an easy-chair on the lawn reading the papers. Perhaps the garden was almost prettier, by reason of the long neglect which it had suffered, than it would have been if kept in the trimmest order by the industrious hands of a skillful gardener. Every thing grew in a wild and wanton luxuriance, that was very beautiful in this summer-time, when the earth was gorgeous with all manner of blossoms. Trailing branches from the espaliered apple-trees hung across the pathways, intermingled with roses that had run wild; and made bits that a landscape-painter might have delighted to copy. Even the weeds, which a gardener would have looked upon in horror, were beautiful. The wild convolvulus flung its tendrils into fantastic wreaths and wild festoons about the bushes of sweet-brier; the honey-suckle, untutored by the pruning-knife, mixed its tall branches with seringa and clematis; the jasmine that crept about the house had mounted to the very chimney-pots, and strayed in through the open windows; even the stable-roof was half-hidden by hardy monthly roses that had clambered up to the thatch. But the young soldier took very little interest in this disorderly garden. He pined to be far away in the thick jungle, or on the burning plain. He hated the quiet and repose of an existence which seemed little better than the living death of a cloister.

The sun was low in the west at the close of a long mid-summer day when Mr. Arundel strolled

H

up and down the neglected pathways, backward and forward amidst the long tangled grass of the lawn, smoking a cigar, and brooding over his sorrows.

He was beginning to despair. He had defied Paul Marchmont, and no good had come of his defiance. He had watched him, and there had been no result of his watching. Day after day he had wandered down to the lonely pathway by the river-side; again and again he had reconnoitred the boat-house, only to hear Paul Marchmont's treble voice singing scraps out of modern operas as he worked at his easel; or on one or two occasions to see Mr. George Weston, the surgeon, or Lavinia his wife, emerge from the artist's painting-room.

Upon one of these occasions Edward Arundel had accosted the surgeon of Kemberling, and had tried to enter into conversation with him. But Mr. Weston had exhibited such utterly hopeless stupidity, mingled with a very evident terror of his brother-in-law's foe, that Edward had been fain to abandon all hope of any assistance from this quarter.

"I'm sure I'm very sorry for you, Mr. Arundel," the surgeon said, looking, not at Edward, but about and around him, in a hopeless, wandering manner, like some hunted animal that looks far and near for a means of escape from his pursuer—"I'm very sorry for you—and for all your trouble—and I was when I attended you at the Black Bull—and you were the first patient I ever had there—and it led to my having many more—as I may say—though that's neither here nor there. And I'm very sorry for you, and for the poor young woman too—particularly for the poor young woman—and I always tell Paul so—and—and Paul—"

And at this juncture Mr. Weston stopped abruptly, as if appalled by the hopeless entanglement of his own ideas, and with a brief "Good-evening, Mr. Arundel," shot off in the direction of the towers, leaving Edward at a loss to understand his manner.

So, on this mid-summer evening, the soldier walked up and down the neglected grass-plot, thinking of the men who had been his comrades, and of the career which he had abandoned for the love of his lost wife.

He was aroused from his gloomy reverie by the sound of a fresh girlish voice calling to him by his name.

"Edward! Edward!"

Who could there be in Lincolnshire, in the name of all that is miraculous, with the right to call to him thus by his Christian name? He was not long left in doubt. While he was asking himself the question the same feminine voice cried out again:

"Edward! Edward! Will you come and open the gate for me, please? Or do you mean to keep me out here forever?"

This time Mr. Arundel had no difficulty in recognizing the familiar tones of his sister Letitia, whom he had believed, until that moment, to be safe under the maternal wing at Dangerfield. And lo! here she was, on horseback at his own gate, with a cavalier hat and feathers overshadowing her girlish face, and with another young Amazon on a thorough-bred chestnut, and a groom on a thorough-bred bay in the back-ground.

Edward Arundel, utterly confounded by the advent of such visitors, flung away his cigar, and went to the low wooden gate beyond which his sister's steed was pawing the dusty road, impatient of this stupid delay, and eager to be cantering stableward through the scented summer air.

"Why, Letitia!" cried the young man, "what, in mercy's name, has brought you here?"

Miss Arundel laughed aloud at her brother's look of surprise.

"You didn't know I was in Lincolnshire, did you?" she asked; and then answered her own question in the same breath: "Of course you didn't, because I wouldn't let mamma tell you I was coming; for I wanted to surprise you, you know. And I think I have surprised you, haven't I? I never saw such a scared-looking creature in all my life. If I were a ghost coming here in the gloaming, you couldn't look more frightened than you did just now. I only came the day before yesterday, and I'm staying at Major Lawford's, twelve miles away from here; and this is Miss Lawford, who was at school with me at Bath. You've heard me talk of Belinda Lawford, my dearest, dearest friend? Miss Lawford, my brother; my brother, Miss Lawford. Are you going to open the gate and let us in, or do you mean to keep your citadel closed upon us altogether, Mr. Edward Arundel?"

At this juncture the young lady in the background drew a little nearer to her friend, and murmured a remonstrance to the effect that it was very late, and that they were expected home before dark; but Miss Arundel refused to hear the voice of wisdom.

"Why, we've only an hour's ride back," she cried; "and if it should be dark, which I don't think it will be, for it's scarcely dark all night through at this time of year, we've got Hoskins with us, and Hoskins will take care of us. Won't you, Hoskins?" demanded the young lady, turning to the groom with a most insinuating smile.

Of course Hoskins declared that he was ready to achieve all that man could do or dare in the defense of his liege ladies, or something pretty nearly to that effect, but delivered in a vile Lincolnshire patois not easily rendered in printer's ink.

Miss Arundel waited for no further discussion, but gave her hand to her brother, and vaulted lightly from her saddle.

Then, of course, Edward Arundel offered his services to his sister's companion, and for the first time he looked in Belinda Lawford's face, and even in that one first glance saw that she was a good and beautiful creature, and that her hair, of which she had a great quantity, was of the color of her horse's chestnut coat; that her eyes were the bluest he had ever seen, and that her cheeks were like the neglected roses in his garden. He held out his hand to her. She took it with a frank smile, and dismounted, and came in among the grass-grown pathways, amidst the confusion of trailing branches and bright garden-flowers growing wild.

In that moment began the second volume of Edward Arundel's life. The first volume had begun upon the Christmas night on which the boy of seventeen went to see the pantomime at Drury Lane Theatre. The old story had been a long, sad story, full of tenderness and pathos, but with a cruel and dismal ending. The new story began to-night, in this fading western sunshine, in this atmosphere of balmy perfume, amidst these dew-laden garden-flowers growing wild.

But, as I think I observed before at the outset of this story, we are rarely ourselves aware of the commencement of any new section in our lives. We look back afterward, and wonder to see upon what an insignificant incident the fate of after-years depended.

"If I had gone down Piccadilly instead of taking a short cut across the Green Park the day I walked from Brompton to Charing Cross, I should not have met the woman I adore, and who has hen-pecked me so cruelly for the last fifteen years," says Brown.

"If I had not invited Lord Claude FitzTudor to dinner, with a view to mortifying Robinson of the War-Office by the exhibition of an aristocratic acquaintance, that wretched story of domestic shame and horror might never have gone the round of the papers; Sir Cresswell Cresswell might never have been called on to decide upon a case in which I was the petitioner; and a miserable woman, now dragging out a blighted life in a tawdry lodging at Dieppe, might still be a pure English matron, a proud and happy mother!" says Jones, whose wife ran away from him with the younger son of a duke.

It is only after the fact that we recognize the awful importance which actions, in themselves most trivial, assume by reason of their consequences; and when the action, in itself so unimportant, in its consequences so fatal, has been in any way a deviation from the right, how bitterly we reproach ourselves for that false step!

"I am so *glad* to see you, Edward!" Miss Arundel exclaimed, as she looked about her, criticising her brother's domain; "but you don't seem a bit glad to see me, you poor gloomy old dear. And how much better you look than 'you did when you left Dangerfield! only a little careworn, you know,. still. And to think of your coming and burying yourself here, away from all the people who love you, you silly old darling! And Belinda knows the story, and she's so sorry for you. Ain't you, Linda? I call her Linda for short, and because it's prettier than *Be*-linda," added the young lady aside to her brother, and with a contemptuous emphasis upon the first syllable of her friend's name.

Miss Lawford, thus abruptly appealed to, blushed, and said nothing.

If Edward Arundel had been told that any other young lady was acquainted with the sad story of his married life, I think he would have been inclined to revolt against the very idea of her pity. But although he had only looked once at Belinda Lawford, that one look seemed to have told him a great deal. He felt instinctively that she was as good as she was beautiful, and that her pity must be a most genuine and tender emotion, not to be despised by the proudest man upon earth.

The two ladies seated themselves upon a dilapidated rustic seat amidst the long grass, and Mr. Arundel sat in the low basket-chair in which he was wont to lounge a great deal of his time away.

"Why don't you have a gardener, Ned?" Letitia Arundel asked, after looking rather contemptuously at the flowery luxuriance around her.

Her brother shrugged his shoulders with a despondent gesture.

"Why should I take any care of the place?" he said. "I only took it because it was near the spot where—where my poor girl—where I wanted to be. I have no object in beautifying it. I wish to Heaven I could leave it and go back to India."

He turned his face eastward as he spoke, and the two girls saw that half-eager, half-despairing yearning that was always visible in his face when he looked to the east. It was over yonder, the scene of strife, the red field of glory, only separated from him by a patch of purple ocean, and a strip of yellow sand. It was yonder. He could almost feel the hot blast of the burning air. He could almost hear the shouts of victory. And he was a prisoner here, bound by a sacred duty—by a duty which he owed to the dead.

"Major Lawford—Major Lawford is Belinda's papa; 33d Foot—Major Lawford knew that we were coming here, and he begged me to ask you to dinner; but I said you wouldn't come, for I knew you had shut yourself out of all society—though the Major's the dearest creature, and the Grange is a most delightful place to stay at. I was down here in the mid-summer holidays once, you know, while you were in India. But I give the message as the Major gave it to me; and you're to come to dinner whenever you like."

Edward Arundel murmured a few polite words of refusal. No; he saw no society; he was in Lincolnshire to achieve a certain object; he should remain there no longer than was necessary in order for him to do so.

"And you don't even say that you're glad to see me," exclaimed Miss Arundel, with an offended air, "though it's six months since you were last at Dangerfield! Upon my word you're a nice brother for an unfortunate girl to waste her affections upon!"

Edward smiled faintly at his sister's complaint.

"I am very glad to see you, Letitia," he said; "very, very glad."

And indeed the young hermit could not but confess to himself that those two innocent young faces seemed to bring light and brightness with them, and to shed a certain transitory glimmer of sunshine upon the horrible gloom of his life. Mr. Morrison had come out to offer his duty to the young lady—whom he had been intimate with from a very early period of her existence, and had carried upon his shoulder some fifteen years before—under the pretense of bringing wine for the visitors; and the stable-lad had been sent to a distant corner of the garden to search for strawberries for their refreshment. Even the solitary maid-servant had crept into the parlor fronting the lawn, and had shrouded herself behind the window-curtains, whence she could peep out at the two Amazons, and gladden her eyes with the sight of something that was young and beautiful.

But the young ladies would not stop to drink any wine, though Mr. Morrison informed Letitia that the sherry was from the Dangerfield cellar, and had been sent to Master Edward by his Ma; nor to eat any strawberries, though the stable-boy, who made the air odorous with the scent of hay and oats, brought a little heap of freshly-gathered fruit piled upon a cabbage-leaf, and surmounted by a rampant caterpillar of the woolly species. They could not stay any longer, they both declared, lest there should be terror at Lawford Grange because of their absence. So they went back to the gate, escorted by Edward and his confidential servant; and after Letitia had given her brother a kiss, which resounded almost like the report of a pistol through the still evening air, the two ladies mounted their horses, and cantered away in the twilight.

"I shall come and see you again, Ned," Miss Arundel cried, as she shook the reins upon her horse's neck; "and so will Belinda—won't you, Belinda?"

Miss Lawford's reply, if she spoke at all, was quite inaudible amidst the clattering of the horses' hoofs upon the hard high-road.

---

## CHAPTER XXVII.

### ONE MORE SACRIFICE.

LETITIA ARUNDEL kept her word and came very often to Kemberling Retreat; sometimes on horseback, sometimes in a little pony-carriage; sometimes accompanied by Belinda Lawford, sometimes accompanied by a younger sister of Belinda's as chestnut-haired and blue-eyed as Belinda herself, but at the school-room and bread-and-butter period of life, and not particularly interesting. Major Lawford came one day with his daughter and her friend, and Edward and the half-pay officer walked together up and down the grass-plot, smoking and talking of the Indian war, while the two girls roamed about the garden among the roses and butterflies, tearing the skirts of their riding-habits every now and then among the briers and gooseberry bushes. It was scarcely strange after this visit that Edward Arundel should consent to accept Major Lawford's invitation to name a day for dining at the Grange; he could not with a very good grace have refused. And yet—and yet—it seemed to him almost a treason against his lost love, his poor pensive Mary—whose face, with the very look it had worn upon that last day, was ever present with him—to mix with happy people who had never known sorrow. But he went to the Grange, nevertheless, and grew more and more friendly with the Major, and walked in the gardens—which were very large and old-fashioned, but most beautifully kept—with his sister and Belinda Lawford; with Belinda Lawford, who knew his story and was sorry for him. He always remembered *that* as he looked at her bright face, whose varying expression gave perpetual evidence of a compassionate and sympathetic nature.

"If my poor darling had had this girl for a friend," he thought, sometimes, "how much happier she might have been!"

I dare say there have been many lovelier women in this world than Belinda Lawford; many women whose faces, considered artistically, came nearer perfection; many noses more exquisitely chiseled, and scores of mouths bearing a closer affinity to Cupid's bow; but I doubt if any face was ever more pleasant to look upon than the face of this blooming English maiden. She had a beauty that is sometimes wanting in perfect faces, and lacking which the most splendid loveliness will pall at last upon eyes that have grown weary of admiring; she had a charm for want of which the most rigidly classical profiles, the most exquisitely statuesque faces, have seemed colder and harder than the marble it was their highest merit to resemble. She had the beauty of goodness, and to admire her was to do homage to the purest and highest attributes of womanhood. It was not only that her pretty little nose was straight and well-shaped, that her lips were rosy red, that her eyes were bluer than the summer heavens, her chestnut hair tinged with the golden light of a setting sun; above and beyond such commonplace beauties as these, the beauties of tenderness, truth, faith, earnestness, hope, and charity, were enthroned upon her broad white brow, and crowned her queen by right divine of womanly perfection. A loving and devoted daughter, an affectionate sister, a true and faithful friend, an untiring benefactress to the poor, a gentle mistress, a well-bred Christian lady; in every duty and in every position she bore out and sustained the impression which her beauty made on the minds of those who looked upon her. She was only nineteen years of age, and no sorrow had ever altered the brightness of her nature. She lived a happy life with a father who was proud of her, and with a mother who resembled her in almost every attribute. She led a happy but a busy life, and did her duty to the poor about her as scrupulously as even Olivia had done in the old days at Swampington Rectory; but in such a genial and cheerful spirit as to win, not cold thankfulness, but heart-felt love and devotion from all who partook of her benefits.

Upon the Egyptian darkness of Edward Arundel's life this girl arose as a star, and by-and-by all the horizon brightened under her influence. The soldier had been very little in the society of women. His mother, his sister Letitia, his cousin Olivia, and John Marchmont's gentle daughter, were the only women whom he had ever known in the familiar freedom of domestic intercourse; and he trusted himself in the presence of this beautiful and noble-minded girl in utter ignorance of any danger to his own peace of mind. He suffered himself to be happy at Lawford Grange; and in those quiet hours which he spent there he put away his old life, and forgot the stern purpose that alone held him a prisoner in England.

But when he went back to his lonely dwelling-place he reproached himself bitterly for that which he considered a treason against his love.

"What right have I to be happy among these people?" he thought; "what right have I to take life easily, even for an hour, while my darling lies in her unhallowed grave, and the man who drove her to her death remains unpunished? I will never go to Lawford Grange again."

It seemed, however, as if every body, except Belinda, was in a plot against this idle soldier;

for sometimes Letitia coaxed him to ride back with her after one of her visits to Kemberling Retreat, and very often the Major himself insisted, in a hearty military fashion, upon the young man's taking the empty seat in his dog-cart, to be driven over to the Grange. Edward Arundel had never once mentioned Mary's name to any member of this hospitable and friendly family. They were very good to him, and were prepared, he knew, to sympathize with him; but he could not•bring himself to talk of his lost wife.. The thought of that rash and desperate act which had ended her short life was too cruel to him. He would not speak of her, because he would have had to plead excuses for that one guilty act; and her image to him was so stainless and pure that he could not bear to plead for her as for a sinner who had need of men's pity rather than a claim to their reverence.

"Her life had been so sinless," he cried, sometimes; "and to think that it should have ended in sin! If I could forgive Paul Marchmont for all the rest, if I could forgive him for my loss of her, I would never forgive him for that."

The young widower kept silence, therefore, upon the subject which occupied so large a share of his thoughts, which was every day and every night the theme of his most earnest prayers; and Mary's name was never spoken in his presence at Lawford Grange.

But in Edward Arundel's absence the two girls sometimes talked of this sad story.

"Do you really think, Letitia, that your brother's wife committed suicide?" Belinda asked her friend.

"Oh, as for that, there can't be any doubt about it, dear," answered Miss Arundel, who was of a lively, not to say a flippant disposition, and had no very great reverence for solemn things; "the poor dear creature drowned herself. I think she must have been a little wrong in her head. I don't say so to Edward, you know; at least, I did say so once when he was at Dangerfield, and he flew into an awful passion, and called me hard-hearted and cruel, and all sorts of shocking things; so of course I've never said so since. But really, the poor dear thing's goings-on were so eccentric: first she ran away from her step-mother, and went and hid herself in a horrid lodging; and then she married Edward at a nasty church in Lambeth, without so much as a wedding-dress, or a creature to give her away, or a cake, or cards, or any thing Christian-like; and then she ran away again; and as her father had been a super—what's it's name? a man who carries banners in pantomimes, and all that—I dare say she'd seen Mr. Macready as Hamlet, and had Ophelia's death in her head when she ran down to the river-side and drowned herself. I'm sure it's a very sad story; and of course I'm awfully sorry for Edward."

The young lady said no more than this; but Belinda brooded over the story of that early marriage—the stolen honey-moon, the sudden parting. How dearly they must have loved each other, the young bride and bridegroom, absorbed in their own happiness, and forgetful of all the outer world! She pictured Edward Arundel's face as it must have been before care and sorrow had blotted out the brightest attribute of his

beauty. She thought of him, and pitied him, with such tender sympathy, that by-and-by the thought of this young man's sorrow seemed to shut almost every idea completely out of her mind. She went about all her duties still, cheerfully and pleasantly, as it was her nature to do every thing; but the zest with which she had performed each loving office, each act of sweet benevolence, seemed lost to her now.

Remember that she was a simple country damsel leading a quiet life, whose peaceful course was almost as calm and uneventless as the existence of a cloister; a life so quiet that a decently-written romance from the Swampington book-club was a thing to be looked forward to with impatience, to read with breathless excitement, and to brood upon afterward for months. Was it strange, then, that this romance in real life, this sweet story of love and devotion, with its sad climax—this story, the scene of which lay within a few miles of her home, the hero of which was her father's constant guest—was it strange that this story, whose saddest charm was its truth, should make a strong impression upon the mind of an innocent and unworldly woman, and that day by day and hour by hour she should, all unconsciously to herself, feel a stronger interest in the hero of the tale?

She was interested in him. Alas! the truth must be set down, even if it has to be in the plain old commonplace words. *She fell in love with him.* But love in this innocent and womanly nature was so different a sentiment to that which had raged in Olivia's stormy breast that even she who felt it was unconscious of its gradual birth. It was not "an Adam at its birth," by-the-by.· It did not leap, Minerva-like, from the brain; for I believe that love is born of the brain oftener than of the heart, being a. strange compound of fancy and folly, ideality, veneration, and delusion. It came rather like the gradual dawning of a summer's morning—first a little patch of light, far away in the east, very faint and feeble; then a slow widening of the rosy brightness; and at last a great blaze of splendor over all the width of the vast heavens. And then Miss Lawford grew·more reserved in her intercourse with her friend's brother. Her frank good nature gave place to a timid, shrinking bashfulness that made her ten times more fascinating than she had been before. She was so very young, and had mixed so little with the world, that she had yet to learn the comedy of life. She had yet to learn to smile when she was sorry, or to look sorrowful when she was pleased, as prudence might dictate; to blush at will, or to grow pale when it was politic to sport the lily tint. She was a natural, artless, spontaneous creature; and she was utterly powerless to conceal her emotions, or to pretend a sentiment she did not feel. She blushed rosy red when Edward Arundel spoke to her suddenly. She betrayed herself by a hundred signs; mutely confessed her love almost as artlessly as Mary had revealed her affection a twelvemonth before. But if Edward saw this he gave no sign of having made the discovery. His voice, perhaps, grew a little lower and softer in its tone when he spoke to Belinda; but there was a sad cadence in that low voice which was too mournful for the accent of a lover. Sometimes, when his eyes rested for a moment on the girl's blushing face, a shadow would darken his own, and a faint quiver of emotion stir his lower lip; but it is impossible to say what this emotion may have been. Belinda hoped nothing, expected nothing. I repeat that she was unconscious of the nature of her own feeling; and she had never for a moment thought of Edward otherwise than as a man who would go to his grave faithful to that sad love-story which had blighted the promise of his youth. She never thought of him otherwise than as Mary's constant mourner; she never hoped that time would alter his feelings or wear out his constancy; yet she loved him, notwithstanding.

All through July and August the young man visited at the Grange, and at the beginning of September Letitia Arundel went back to Dangerfield. But even then Edward was still a frequent guest at Major Lawford's, for his enthusiasm upon all military matters had made him a very great favorite with the old officer. But toward the end of September Mr. Arundel's visits suddenly were restricted to an occasional call upon the Major; he left off dining at the Grange; his evening rambles in the garden with Mrs. Lawford and her blooming daughters—Belinda had no less than four blue-eyed sisters, all more or less resembling herself—ceased altogether, to the wonderment of every one in the old-fashioned country-house.

Edward Arundel shut out the new light which had dawned upon his life and withdrew into the darkness. He went back to the stagnant monotony, the hopeless despondency, the bitter regret, of his old existence.

"While my sister was at the Grange I had an excuse for going there," he said to himself, sternly. "I have no excuse now."

But the old monotonous life was somehow or other a great deal more difficult to bear than it had been before. Nothing seemed to interest the young man now. Even the records of Indian victories were "flat, stale, and unprofitable." He wondered at the remembrance with what eager impatience he had once pined for the coming of the newspapers, with what frantic haste he had devoured every syllable of the Indian news. All his old feelings seemed to have gone away, leaving nothing in his mind but a blank waste, a weary sickness of life and all belonging to it. Leaving nothing else—positively nothing? "No!" he answered, in reply to these mute questionings of his own spirit—"no," he repeated doggedly, "nothing."

It was strange to find what a blank was left in his life by reason of his abandonment of the Grange. It seemed as if he had suddenly retired from an existence full of pleasure and delight into the gloomy solitude of La Trappe. And yet what was it that he had lost, after all? A quiet dinner at a country-house, and an evening spent half in the leafy silence of an old-fashioned garden, half in a pleasant drawing-room, among a group of well-bred girls, and only enlivened by simple English ballads or pensive melodies by Mendelssohn. It was not much to forego, surely. And yet Edward Arundel felt, in sacrificing these new acquaintance at the Grange to the stern purpose of his life, almost as if he had resigned a second captaincy for Mary's sake.

## CHAPTER XXVIII.

### THE CHILD'S VOICE IN THE PAVILION BY THE WATER.

THE year wore slowly on. Letitia Arundel wrote very long letters to her friend and confidante, Belinda Lawford, and in each letter demanded particular intelligence of her brother's doings. Had he been to the Grange? how had he looked? what had he talked about? etc. etc. But to these questions Miss Lawford could only return one monotonous reply: Mr. Arundel had not been to the Grange; or Mr. Arundel had called on papa one morning, but had only staid a quarter of an hour, and had not been seen by any female member of the family.

The year wore slowly on. Edward endured his self-appointed solitude, and waited, waited, with a vengeful hatred forever brooding in his breast, for the day of retribution. The year wore on, and the anniversary of the day upon which Mary ran away from the Towers, the 17th of October, came at last.

Paul Marchmont had declared his intention of taking possession of the Towers upon the day following this. The twelvemonth's probation which he had imposed upon himself had expired; every voice was loud in praise of his conscientious and honorable conduct. He had grown very popular during his residence at Kemberling. Tenant farmers looked forward to halcyon days under his dominion; to leases renewed on favorable terms; to repairs liberally executed; to every thing that is delightful between landlord and tenant. Edward Arundel heard all this through his faithful servitor, Mr. Morrison, and chafed bitterly at the news. This traitor was to be happy and prosperous, and to have the good word of honest men; while Mary lay in her unhallowed grave, and people shrugged their shoulders, half compassionately, half contemptuously, as they spoke of the mad heiress who had committed suicide.

Mr. Morrison brought his master tidings of all Paul Marchmont's doings about this time. He was to take possession of the Towers on the 19th. He had already made several alterations in the arrangement of the different rooms. He had ordered new furniture from Swampington — another man would have ordered it from London; but Mr. Marchmont was bent upon being popular, and did not despise even the good opinion of a local tradesman—and by several other acts, insignificant enough in themselves, had asserted his ownership of the mansion which had been the airy castle of Mary Marchmont's day-dreams ten years before.

The coming in of the new master of Marchmont Towers was to be, take it altogether, a very grand affair. The Chorley Castle foxhounds were to meet, at eleven o'clock, upon the great grass-plot, or lawn, as it was popularly called, before the western front. The country gentry from far and near had been invited to a hunting-breakfast. Open house was to be kept all day for rich and poor. Every male inhabitant of the district who could muster any thing in the way of a mount was likely to join the friendly gathering. Poor Reynard is decidedly England's most powerful leveler. All differences of rank and station, all distinctions which Mammon raises in every other quarter, melt away before the friendly contact of the hunting-field. The man who rides best is the best man; and the young butcher who makes light of sunk fences, and skims, bird-like, over bullfinches and timber, may hold his own with the dandy heir to half the country-side. The cook at Marchmont Towers had enough to do to prepare for this great day. It was the first meet of the season, and in itself a solemn festival. Paul Marchmont knew this; and though the Cockney artist of Fitzroy Square knew about as much of fox-hunting as he did of the source of the Nile, he seized upon the opportunity of making himself popular, and determined to give such a hunting-breakfast as had never been given within the walls of Marchmont Towers since the time of a certain rackety Hugh Marchmont, who had drunk himself to death early in the reign of George III. He spent the morning of the 17th in the steward's room, looking through the cellar-book with the old butler, selecting the wines that were to be drunk the following day, and planning the arrangements for the mass of visitors, who were to be entertained in the great stone entrance-hall, in the kitchens, in the housekeeper's room, in the servants' hall, in almost every chamber that afforded accommodation for a guest.

"You will take care that people get placed according to their rank," Paul said to the gray-haired servant. "You know every body about here, I dare say, and will be able to manage so that we may give no offense."

The gentry were to breakfast in the long dining-room and in the western drawing-room. Sparkling hocks and Burgundies, fragrant Moselles, Champagnes of choicest brand and·rarest bouquet, were to flow like water for the benefit of the country gentlemen who should come to do honor to Paul Marchmont's installation. Great cases of comestibles had been sent by rail from Fortnum and Mason's; and the science of the cook at the Towers had been taxed to the utmost, in the struggles which she made to prove herself equal to the occasion. Twenty-one great casks of ale, each cask containing twenty-one gallons, had been brewed long ago, at the birth of Arthur Marchmont, and had been laid in the cellar ever since, waiting for the majority of the young heir who was never to come of age. This very ale, with a certain sense of triumph, Paul Marchmont ordered to be brought forth for the refreshment of the. commoners.

"Poor young Arthur!" he thought, after he had given this order. "I saw him once when he was a pretty boy with fair ringlets, dressed in a suit of black velvet. His father brought him to my studio one day, when he came to patronize me and buy a picture of me —out of sheer charity, of course, for he cared as much for pictures as I do for fox-hounds. *I* was a poor relation then, and never thought to see the inside of Marchmont Towers. It was a lucky September morning that swept that bright-faced boy out of my pathway, and left only sickly John Marchmont and his daughter between me and fortune."

Yes; Mr. Paul Marchmont's year of probation was past. He had asserted himself to Messrs. Paulette, Paulette, and Mathewson, and before the face of all Lincolnshire, in the character of an honorable and high-minded man; slow to seize upon the fortune that had fallen to him, conscientious, punctilious, generous, and unselfish. He had done all this; and now the trial was over, and the day of triumph had come.

There has been a race of villains of late years very popular with the novel-writer and the dramatist, but not, I think, quite indigenous to this honest British soil; a race of pale-faced, dark-eyed, and all-accomplished scoundrels, whose chiefest attribute is imperturbability. The imperturbable villain has been guilty of every iniquity in the black catalogue of crimes; but he has never been guilty of an emotion. He wins a million of money at *trente et quarante*, to the terror and astonishment of all Homburg; and by not so much as one twinkle of his eye or one quiver of his lip does that imperturbable creature betray a sentiment of satisfaction. Ruin or glory, shame or triumph, defeat, disgrace, or death—all are alike to the callous ruffian of the Anglo-Gallic novel. He smiles, and murders while he smiles, and smiles while he murders. He kills his adversary, unfairly, in a duel, and wipes his sword on a cambric handkerchief; and withal he is so elegant, so fascinating, and so handsome, that the young hero of the novel has a very poor chance against him; and the reader can scarcely help being sorry when retribution comes with the last chapter, and some crushing catastrophe annihilates the well-bred scoundrel.

'Paul Marchmont was not this sort of man. He was a hypocrite when it was essential to his own safety to practice hypocrisy; but he did not accept life as a drama, in which he was forever to be acting a part. Life would scarcely be worth the having to any man upon such terms. It is all very well to wear heavy plate-armor, and a casque that weighs fourteen pounds or so, when we go into the thick of the fight. But to wear the armor always, to live in it, to sleep in it, to carry the ponderous protection about us forever and ever! Safety would be too dear if purchased by such a sacrifice of all personal ease. Paul Marchmont, therefore, being a selfish and self-indulgent man, only wore his armor of hypocrisy occasionally, and when it was vitally necessary for his preservation. ·He had imposed upon himself a penance, and acted a part in holding back for a year from the enjoyment of a splendid fortune; and he had made this one great sacrifice in order to give the lie to Edward Arundel's vague accusations, which might have had an awkward effect upon the minds of other people, had the artist grasped too eagerly at his missing cousin's wealth. Paul Marchmont had made this sacrifice; but he did not intend to act a part all his life. He meant to enjoy himself, and to get the fullest possible benefit out of his good fortune. He meant to do this; and upon the 17th of October he made no effort to restrain his spirits, but laughed and talked joyously with whoever came in his way, winning golden opinions from all sorts of men; for happiness is contagious, and every body likes happy people.

Forty years of poverty is a long apprenticeship to the very hardest of masters—an apprenticeship calculated to give the keenest possible zest to newly-acquired wealth. Paul Marchmont rejoiced in his wealth with an almost delirious sense of delight. It was his at last. At last! He had waited, and waited patiently; and at last, while his powers of enjoyment were still in their zenith, it had come. How often he had dreamed of this; how often he had dreamed of that which was to take place to-morrow! How often in his dreams he had seen the stone-built mansion, and heard the voices of the crowd doing him honor. He had felt all the pride and delight of possession, to awake suddenly in the midst of his triumph, and gnash his teeth at the remembrance of his poverty. And now the poverty was a thing to be dreamed about, and the wealth was his. He had always been a good son and a kind brother; and his mother and sister were to arrive upon the eve of his installation, and were to witness his triumph. The rooms that had been altered were those chosen by Paul for his mother and maiden sister, and the new furniture had been ordered for their comfort. It was one of his many pleasures upon this day to inspect the apartments, to see that all his directions had been faithfully carried out, and to speculate upon the effect which these spacious and luxurious chambers would have upon the minds of Mrs. Paul Marchmont and her daughter, newly come from shabby lodgings in Charlotte Street.

"My poor mother!" thought the artist, as he looked round the pretty sitting-room. This sitting-room opened into a noble bedchamber, beyond which there was a dressing-room. "My poor mother!" he thought; "she has suffered a long time, and she has been patient. She has never ceased to believe in me; and she will see now that there was some reason for that belief. I told her long ago, when our fortunes were at the lowest ebb, when I was painting landscapes for the furniture-brokers at a pound apiece—I told her I was meant for something better than a tradesman's hack; and I have proved it—I have proved it."

He walked about the room, arranging the furniture with his own hands; walking a few paces backward now and then to contemplate such and such an effect from an artistic point of view; flinging the rich stuff of the curtains into graceful folds; admiring and examining every thing, always with a smile on his face. He seemed thoroughly happy. If he had done any wrong, if by any act of treachery he had hastened Mary Arundel's death, no recollection of that foul work arose in his breast to disturb the pleasant current of his thoughts. Selfish and self-indulgent, only attached to those who were necessary to his own happiness, his thoughts rarely wandered beyond the narrow circle of his own cares or his own pleasures. He was thoroughly selfish. He could have sat at a Lord Mayor's feast with a famine-stricken population clamoring at the door of the banquet-chamber. He believed in himself as his mother and sister had believed; and he considered that he had a right to be happy and prosperous, whoever suffered sorrow or adversity.

Upon this 17th of October Olivia Marchmont sat in the little study looking out upon the quadrangle, while the household was busied with the preparations for the festival of the following day. She was to remain at Marchmont Towers as a guest of the new master of the mansion. She would be protected from all scandal, Paul had said, by the presence of his mother and sister. She could retain the apartments she had been accustomed to occupy; she could pursue her old mode of life. He himself was not likely to be very much at the Towers. He was going to travel and to enjoy life now that he was a rich man.

These were the arguments which Mr. Marchmont used when openly discussing the widow's residence in his house. But in a private conversation between Olivia and himself he had only said a very few words upon the subject.

"You must remain," he said; and Olivia submitted, obeying him with a sullen indifference that was almost like the mechanical submission of an irresponsible being.

John Marchmont's widow seemed entirely under the dominion of the new master of the Towers. It was as if the stormy passions which had arisen out of a slighted love had worn out this woman's mind, and had left her helpless to stand against the force of Paul Marchmont's keen and vigorous intellect. A remarkable change had come over Olivia's character. A dull apathy had succeeded that fiery energy of soul which had enfeebled and well-nigh worn out her body. There were no outbursts of passion now. She bore the miserable monotony of her life uncomplainingly. Day after day, week after week, month after month, idle and apathetic, she sat in her lonely room, or wandered slowly in the grounds about the Towers. She very rarely went beyond those grounds. She was seldom seen now in her old pew at Kemberling Church; and when her father went to her and remonstrated with her for her non-attendance, she told him sullenly that she was too ill to go. She was ill. George Weston attended her constantly; but he found it very difficult to administer to such a sickness as hers, and he could only shake his head despondently when he felt her feeble pulse, or listened to the slow beating of her heart. Sometimes she would shut herself up in her room for a month at a time, and see no one but Mr. Weston—whom, in her utter indifference, she seemed to regard as a kind of domestic animal, whose going or coming were alike unimportant—and her faithful servant Barbara. This stolid, silent Barbara waited upon her mistress with untiring patience. She bore with every change of Olivia's gloomy temper; she was a perpetual shield and protection to her. Even upon this day of preparation and disorder Mrs. Simmons kept guard over the passage leading to the study, and took care that no one intruded upon her mistress. At about four o'clock all Paul Marchmont's orders had been given, and the new master of the house dined for the first time by himself at the head of the long carved-oak dining-table, waited upon in solemn state by the old butler. His mother and sister were to arrive by a train that would reach Swampington at ten o'clock, and one of the carriages from the Towers was to meet them at the station. The artist had leisure in the mean time for any other business he might have to transact.

He ate his dinner slowly, thinking deeply all the time. He did not stop to drink any wine after dinner, but as soon as the cloth was removed rose from the table, and went straight to Olivia's room.

"I am going down to the painting-room," he said. "Will you come there presently? I want very much to say a few words to you."

Olivia was sitting near the window, with her hands lying idle in her lap. She rarely opened a book now, rarely wrote a letter, or occupied herself in any manner. She scarcely raised her eyes as she answered him.

"Yes," she said; "I will come."

"Don't be long, then. It will be dark very soon. I am not going down there to paint; I am going to fetch a landscape that I want to hang in my mother's room, and to say a few words about—"

He closed the door without stopping to finish the sentence, and went out into the quadrangle.

Ten minutes afterward Olivia Marchmont rose, and, taking a heavy woolen shawl from a chair near her, wrapped it loosely about her head and shoulders.

"I am his slave and his prisoner," she muttered to herself. "I must do as he bids me."

A cold wind was blowing in the quadrangle, and the stone pavement was wet with a drizzling rain. The sun had just gone down, and the dull autumn sky was darkening. The fallen leaves in the wood were sodden with damp, and rotted slowly on the swampy ground.

Olivia took her way mechanically along the narrow pathway leading to the river. Half-way between Marchmont Towers and the boat-house she came suddenly upon the figure of a man walking toward her through the dusk. This man was Edward Arundel.

The two cousins had not met since the March evening upon which Edward had gone to seek the widow in Paul Marchmont's painting-room. Olivia's pale face grew whiter as she recognized the soldier.

"I was coming to the house to speak to you, Mrs. Marchmont," Edward said, sternly. "I am lucky in meeting you here, for I don't want any one to overhear what I've got to say."

He had turned in the direction in which Olivia had been walking; but she made a dead stop, and stood looking at him.

"You were going to the boat-house," he said. "I will go there with you."

She looked at him for a moment, as if doubtful what to do, and then said,

"Very well. You can say what you have to say to me, and then leave me. There is no sympathy between us; there is no regard between us; we are only antagonists."

"I hope not, Olivia. I hope there is some spark of regard still, in spite of all. I separate you in my own mind from Paul Marchmont. I pity you, for I believe you to be his tool."

"Is this what you have to say to me?"

"No; I came here as your kinsman, to ask you what you mean to do now that Paul Marchmont has taken possession of the Towers?"

"I mean to stay there."

"In spite of the gossip that your remaining will give rise to among these country people!"

"In spite of every thing. Mr. Marchmont wishes me to stay. It suits me to stay. What does it matter what people say of me? What do I care for any one's opinion—now?"

"Olivia," cried the young man, "are you mad?"

"Perhaps I am," she answered, coldly. "Why is it that you shut yourself from the sympathy of those who have a right to care for you? What is the mystery of your life?"

His cousin laughed bitterly.

"Would you like to know, Edward Arundel?" she said. "You shall know, perhaps, some day. You have despised me all my life; you will despise me more and more then."

They had reached Paul Marchmont's painting-room by this time. Olivia opened the door and walked in, followed by Edward. Paul was not there. There was a picture covered with a green baize upon the easel, and the artist's hat stood upon the table amidst the litter of brushes and pallets; but the room was empty. The door at the top of the stone steps leading to the pavilion was ajar.

"Have you any thing more to say to me?" Olivia asked, turning upon her cousin as if she would have demanded why he had followed her.

"Only this: I want to know your determination; whether you will be advised by me—and by your father—I saw my uncle Hubert this morning, and his opinion exactly coincides with mine —or whether you mean obstinately to take your own course in defiance of every body?"

"I do," Olivia answered. "I shall take my own course. I defy every body. I have not been gifted with the power of winning people's affection. Other women possess that power, and trifle with it, and turn it to bad account. I have prayed, Edward Arundel — yes, I have prayed upon my knees to the God who made me, that He would give me some poor measure of that gift which Nature has lavished upon other women; but He would not hear me, He would not hear me. I was not made to be loved. Why, then, should I make myself a slave for the sake of winning people's esteem? If they have despised me, I can despise them."

"Who has despised you, Olivia?" Edward asked, perplexed by his cousin's manner.

"YOU HAVE!" she cried, with flashing eyes; "you have! From first to last—from first to last!" She turned away from him impatiently. "Go," she said; "why should we keep up a mockery of friendship and cousinship? We are nothing to each other."

Edward walked toward the door; but he paused upon the threshold, with his hat in his hand, undecided as to what he ought to do.

As he stood thus, perplexed and irresolute, a cry, the feeble cry of a child, sounded within the pavilion.

The young man started and looked at his cousin. Even in the dusk he could see that her face had suddenly grown livid.

"There is a child in that place," he said, pointing to the door at the top of the steps.

The cry was repeated as he spoke—the low, complaining wail of a child. There was no other voice to be heard—no mother's voice soothing a helpless little one. The cry of the child was followed by a dead silence.

"There is a child in that pavilion," Edward Arundel repeated.

"There is," Olivia answered.

"Whose child?"

"What does it matter to you?"

"Whose child?"

"I can not tell you, Edward Arundel."
The soldier strode toward the steps, but before he could reach them Olivia flung herself across his pathway.

"I will see whose child is hidden in that place," he said. "Scandalous things have been said of you, Olivia. I will know the reason of your visits to this place."

She clung about his knees and hindered him from moving; half-kneeling, half-crouching on the lowest of the stone-steps, she blocked his pathway and prevented him from reaching the door of the pavilion. It had been ajar a few minutes ago; it was shut now. But Edward had not noticed this.

"No, no, no!" shrieked Olivia; "you shall trample me to death before you enter that place. You shall walk over my corpse before you pass over that threshold." .

The young man struggled with her for a few moments; then he suddenly flung her from him —not violently, but with a contemptuous gesture.

"You are a wicked woman, Olivia Marchmont," he said; "and it matters very little to me what you do or what becomes of you. I know now the secret of the mystery between you and Paul Marchmont. I can guess your motive for perpetually haunting this place."

He left the solitary building by the river and walked slowly back through the wood.

His mind—predisposed to think ill of Olivia by the dark rumors he·had heard through his servant, and which had had a certain amount of influence upon him, as all scandals have, however baseless—could imagine only one solution to the mystery of a child's presence in the lonely building by the river. Outraged and indignant at the discovery he had made, he turned his back upon Marchmont Towers.

"I will stay in 'this hateful place no longer," he thought, as he went back to his solitary home; "but before I leave Lincolnshire the whole county shall know what I think of Paul Marchmont."

---

## CHAPTER XXIX.

### CAPTAIN ARUNDEL'S REVENGE.

EDWARD ARUNDEL went back to his lonely home with a settled purpose in his mind. He would leave Lincolnshire — and immediately. He had no motive for remaining. It may be, indeed, that he had a strong motive for going away from the neighborhood of Lawford Grange. There was a lurking danger in the close vicinage of that pleasant, old-fashioned country mansion, and the bright band of blue-eyed damsels who inhabited there.

"I will turn my back upon Lincolnshire forever," Edward Arundel said to himself once more, upon his way homeward through the October twilight; "but before I go, the whole country shall know what I think of Paul Marchmont."

He clenched his fists and ground his teeth involuntarily as he thought this.

It was quite dark when he let himself in at the old-fashioned half-glass door that led into his humble sitting-room at Kemberling Retreat. He looked round the little chamber, which had been furnished forty years before by the pro-

prietor of the cottage, and had served for one tenant after another, until it seemed as if the spindle-legged chairs and tables had grown attenuated and shadowy by much service. He looked at the simple room, lighted by a bright fire and a pair of wax-candles in antique silver candlesticks. The red fire-light flickered and trembled upon the painted roses on the walls, on the obsolete engravings in clumsy frames of imitation-ebony and tarnished gilt; the silver tea-service and Sèvres china cup and saucer, which Mrs. Arundel had sent to the cottage for her son's use, stood upon the small oval table; and a brown setter, a favorite of the young man's, lay upon the hearth-rug, with his chin upon his outstretched paws, blinking at the blaze.

As Mr. Arundel lingered in the doorway, looking at these things, an image arose before him, as vivid and distinct as any apparition of Professor Pepper's manufacture; and he thought of what that commonplace cottage - chamber· might have been if his young wife had lived. He could fancy her bending over the low silver tea-pot—the sprawling, inartistic tea-pot, that stood upon quaint knobs, like gouty feet, and had ·been long ago banished from the Dangerfield breakfast-table as utterly rococo and ridiculous. He conjured up the dear dead face, with faint blushes flickering amidst its lily pallor, and soft hazel eyes looking up at him through the misty steam of the tea-table, innocent and virginal as the eyes of that mythic nymph who was wont to appear to the old Roman king. How happy she would have been! How willing to give up fortune and station, and to have lived for ever and ever in that queer old cottage, ministering to him and loving him!

Presently the face changed. The hazel-brown hair was suddenly lit up with a glitter of barbaric gold; the hazel eyes grew blue and bright; and the cheeks blushed rosy red. The young man frowned at this new and brighter vision; but he contemplated it gravely for some moments, and then breathed a long sigh, which was somehow or other expressive of relief.

"No," he said to himself, "I am not false to my poor lost girl; I do not forget her. Her image is dearer to me than any living creature. The mournful shadow of her face is more precious to me than the brightest reality."

He sat down in one of the spindle-legged arm-chairs, and poured out a cup of tea. He drank it slowly, brooding over the fire as he sipped the innocuous beverage, and did not deign to notice the caresses of the brown setter, who laid his cold wet nose in his master's hand by way of a delicate attention.

After tea the young man rang the bell, which was answered by Mr. Morrison.

"Have I any clothes that I can hunt in, Morrison?" Mr. Arundel asked.

His factotum stared aghast at this question.

"You ain't a-goin' to 'unt, are you, Mr. Edward?" he inquired, anxiously.

"Never mind that. I asked you a question about my clothes, and I want a straightforward answer."

"But, Mr. Edward," remonstrated the old servant, "I don't mean no offense; and the 'orses is very tidy animals in their way; but if you're thinkin' of going across country—and a pretty stiffish country too, as I've heard, in the way of bull-finches and timber—neither of them horses has any more of a hunter in him than I have."

"I know that as well as you do," Edward Arundel answered, coolly; "but I am going to the meet at Marchmont Towers to-morrow morning, and I want you to look me out a decent suit of clothes; that's all. You can have Desperado saddled ready for me a little after eleven o'clock."

Mr. Morrison looked even more astonished than before. He knew his master's savage enmity toward Paul Marchmont; and yet that very master now deliberately talked of joining in an assembly which was to gather together for the special purpose of doing the same Paul Marchmont honor. However, as he afterward remarked to the two fellow-servants with whom he sometimes condescended to be familiar, it wasn't his place to interfere or to ask any questions, and he had held his tongue accordingly. Perhaps this respectful reticence was rather the result of prudence than of inclination; for there was a dangerous light in Edward Arundel's eyes upon this particular evening which Mr. Morrison never had observed before.

The factotum said something about this later in the evening.

"I do really think," he remarked, "that, what with that young 'ooman's death, and the solitood of this most dismal place, and the rainy weather—which those as says it always rains in Lincolnshire ain't far out—my pore young master is not the man he were."

He tapped his forehead ominously to give significance to his words, and sighed heavily over his supper-beer.

The sun shone upon Paul Marchmont on the morning of the 18th of October. The glorious autumn sunshine streamed into his gorgeous bedchamber—which had been luxuriously fitted for him under his own superintendence—and awoke the new master of Marchmont Towers. He opened his eyes, and looked about him. He raised himself among the down pillows, and contemplated the figures upon the tapestry in a drowsy reverie. He had been dreaming of his poverty, and had been disputing a poor-rate summons with an impertinent tax-collector in the dingy passage of the house in Charlotte Street, Fitzroy Square. Ah! that horrible house had so long been the only scene of his life that it had grown almost a part of his mind, and haunted him perpetually in his sleep, like a nightmare of brick and mortar, now that he was rich, and had done with it forever.

Mr. Marchmont gave a faint shudder, and shook off the influence of the bad dream. Then, propped up by the pillows, he amused himself by admiring his new bedchamber.

It was a handsome room, certainly; the very room for an artist and a sybarite. Mr. Marchmont had not chosen it without due consideration. It was situated in an angle of the house; and though its chief windows looked westward, being immediately above those of the western drawing-room, there was another casement, a great oriel window, facing the east, and admitting all the grandeur of the morning sun through painted glass, on which the Marchmont escutcheon was represented in gorgeous hues of sapphire and ruby, emerald and topaz, amethyst

and aqua marina. Bright splashes of these colors flashed and sparkled on the polished oaken floor, and mixed themselves with the Oriental gaudiness of a Persian carpet, stretched beneath the low Arabian bed, which was hung with ruby-colored draperies that trailed upon the ground. Paul Marchmont was fond of splendor, and meant to have as much of it as money could buy. There was a voluptuous pleasure in all this finery, which only a parvenu could feel; it was the sharpness of the contrast between the magnificence of the present and the shabby miseries of the past that gave a poignancy to the artist's enjoyment of his new habitation.

All the furniture and draperies of the chamber had been made by Paul Marchmont's direction; but its chief beauty was the tapestry that covered the walls, which had been worked three hundred years before, by a patient chatelaine of the house of Marchmont. This tapestry lined the room on every side. The low door had been cut in it; so that a stranger going into that apartment at night, a little under the influence of the Marchmont cellars, and unable to register the topography of the chamber upon the tablet of his memory, might have been sorely puzzled to find an exit the next morning. Most tapestried chambers have a certain dismal grimness about them, which is more pleasant to the sightseer than to the constant inhabitant; but in this tapestry the colors were almost as bright and glowing to-day as when the fingers that had handled the variegated worsteds were still warm and flexible. The subjects, too, were of a more pleasant order than usual. No mailed ruffians or drapery-clad barbarians menaced the unoffending sleeper with uplifted clubs, or horrible bolts, in the very act of being launched from ponderous cross-bows; no wicked-looking Saracens, with ferocious eyes and copper-colored visages, brandished murderous cimeters above their turbaned heads. No; here all was pastoral gayety and peaceful delight. Maidens, with flowing kirtles and crisped yellow hair, danced before great wagons loaded with golden wheat. Youths, in red and purple jerkins, frisked as they played the pipe and tabor. The Flemish horses dragging the heavy wain were hung with bells and garlands, as for a rustic festival, and tossed their untrimmed manes into the air, and frisked and gamboled with their awkward legs, in ponderous imitation of the youths and maidens. Afar off, in the distance, wonderful villages, very queer as to perspective, but all a-bloom with gaudy flowers and quaint roofs of bright red tiles, stood boldly out against a bluer sky than the most enthusiastic pre-Raphaelite of to-day would care to send to the Academy in Trafalgar Square.

Paul Marchmont smiled at the youths and maidens, the laden wagons, the revelers, and the impossible village. He was in a humor to be pleased with every thing to-day. He looked at his dressing-table, which stood opposite to him, in the deep oriel window. His valet—he had a valet now—had opened the great inlaid dressing-case, and the silver-gilt fittings reflected the crimson hues of the velvet lining, as if the gold had been flecked with blood. Glittering bottles of diamond-cut glass, that presented a thousand facets to the morning light, stood like crystal obelisks amidst the litter of carved ivory brushes, and Sèvres boxes of pomatums; and one rare hot-house flower, white and fragile, peeped out of a slender crystal vase, against a back-ground of dark shining leaves.

"It's better than Charlotte Street, Fitzroy Square," said Mr. Marchmont, throwing himself back among the pillows until such time as his valet should bring him a cup of strong tea to refresh and invigorate his nerves withal. "I remember the paper in·my room: drab hexagons and yellow spots upon a brown ground. So pretty! And then the dressing-table: deal, gracefully designed; with a shallow drawer that very rarely would consent to come out, and which, when out, had an insurmountable objection to going in again; a most delicious table, exquisitely painted in stripes, olive green upon stone color, picked out with the favorite brown. Oh, it was a most delightful life; but it's over, thank Providence; it's over!"

Mr. Paul Marchmont thanked Providence as devoutly as if he had been the most patient attendant upon the divine pleasure, and had never for one moment dreamed of intruding his own impious handiwork amidst the mysterious designs of Omnipotence.

The sun shone upon the new master of Marchmont Towers. This bright October morning was not the very best for hunting purposes; for there was a fresh breeze blowing from the north, and a blue unclouded sky. But it was most delightful weather for the breakfast, and the assembling on the lawn, and all the pleasant preliminaries of the day's sport. Mr. Paul Marchmont, who was a thorough-bred Cockney, troubled himself very little about the hunt as he basked in that morning light. He only thought that the sun was shining upon him, and that he had come at last—no matter by what crooked ways—to the realization of his great day-dream; and that he was to be happy and prosperous for the rest of his life.

He drank his tea, and then got up and dressed himself. He wore the conventional "pink," the whitest buckskins, the most approved boots and tops; and he admired himself very much in the cheval glass when this toilet was complete. He had put on the dress for the gratification of his vanity, rather than from any serious intention of doing what he was about as incapable of doing as he was of becoming a modern Rubens or a new Raphael. He would receive his friends in this costume, and ride to cover, and follow the hounds, perhaps—a little way. At any rate, it was very delightful to him to play the country gentleman; and he had never felt so much a country gentleman as at this moment, when he contemplated himself from head to heel in his hunting costume.

At ten o'clock the guests began to assemble; the meet was not to take place until twelve, so that there might be plenty of time for the breakfast.

·I don't think Paul Marchmont ever really knew what took place at that long table at which he sat for the first time in the place of host and master. He was intoxicated from the first with the sense of triumph and delight in his new position; and he drank a great deal, for he drank unconsciously, emptying his glass every time it was filled, and never knowing who filled it, or what was put into it. By this means he took a very considerable quantity of various sparkling and effervescing wines; sometimes hock, sometimes Moselle, very often Champagne, to say nothing of a steady undercurrent of unpronounceable German hocks and crusted Burgundies. But he was not drunk after the common fashion of mortals; he could not be upon this particular day. He was not stupid, or drowsy, or unsteady upon his legs; he was only preternaturally excited, looking at every thing through a haze of dazzling light, as if all the gold of his newly-acquired fortune had been melted into the atmosphere.

He knew that the breakfast was a great success; that the long table was spread with every delicious comestible that the science of a first-rate cook, to say nothing of Fortnum and Mason, could devise; that the profusion of splendid silver, the costly china, the hot-house flowers, and the sunshine, made a confused mass of restless glitter and glowing color that dazzled his eyes as he looked at it. He knew that every body courted and flattered him, and that he was almost stifled by the overpowering sense of his own grandeur. Perhaps he felt this most when a certain county magnate, a baronet, member of Parliament, and great landowner, rose—primed with Champagne, and rather thicker of utterance than a man should be who means to be in at the death, by-and-by—and took the opportunity of—hum—expressing, in a few words—haw—the very great pleasure which he—aw, yes—and he thought he might venture to remark—aw—every body about him—ha—felt on this most—arrah, arrah—interesting—er—occasion; and said a great deal more, which took a very long time to say, but the gist of which was, that all these country gentlemen were so enraptured by the new addition to their circle, and so altogether delighted with Mr. Paul Marchmont, that they really were at a loss to understand how it was they had ever managed to endure existence without him.

And then there was a good deal of rather unnecessary but very·enthusiastic thumping of the table, whereat the costly glass shivered, and the hot-house blossoms trembled, amidst the musical chinking of silver forks, while the fox-hunters declared in chorus that the new owner of Marchmont Towers was a jolly good fellow, which—viz., the fact of his jollity—nobody could deny.

It was not a very refined demonstration, but it was a very hearty one. Moreover, these noisy fox-hunters were all men of some standing in the county; and it is a proof of the artist's inherent snobbery that to him the husky voices of these half-drunken men were more delicious than the sweet soprano tones of an equal number of Pattis—penniless and obscure Pattis, that is to say—sounding his praises. He was lifted at last out of that poor artist-life, in which he had always been a groveler—not for lack of talent, but by reason of the smallness of his own soul—into a new sphere, where every body was rich and grand and prosperous; and where the pleasant pathways were upon the necks of prostrate slaves, in the shape of grooms and hirelings, respectful servants, and reverential trades-people!

Yes; Paul Marchmont was more drunken than any of his guests; but his drunkenness was of a different kind to theirs. It was not the wine, but his own grandeur that intoxicated and besotted him.

These fox-hunters might get the better of their drunkenness in half an hour or so; but his intoxication was likely to last for a very long time, unless he should receive some sudden shock, powerful enough to sober him. The hounds were yelping and baying upon the lawn, and the huntsmen and whippers-in were running backward and forward from the lawn to the servants' hall, devouring snacks of beef and ham—a pound and a quarter or so at one sitting; or crunching the bones of a frivolous young chicken—there were not half a dozen mouthfuls on such insignificant, half-grown fowls; or excavating under the roof of a great game-pie; or drinking a quart or so of strong ale, or half a tumbler of raw brandy, *en passant;* and doing a great deal more in the same way, merely to beguile the time until the gentlefolks should appear upon the broad stone terrace.

It was half past twelve o'clock, and Mr. Marchmont's guests were still drinking and speechifying. They had been on the point of making a move ever so many times; but it had happened that each time some gentleman, who had been very quiet until that moment, suddenly got upon his legs, and began to cling convulsively to the neck of a half empty Champagne-bottle, and to make swallowing and gasping noises, and to wipe his lips with a napkin; whereby it was understood that he was going to propose somebody's health. This had considerably lengthened the entertainment, and it seemed rather likely that the ostensible business of the day would be forgotten altogether. One gentleman, indeed, huskier than his neighbors, had been heard to mutter something about billiards and soda-water; and another, who was thick of speech, but not husky, and who had shed tears in proposing an unintelligible toast—which was supposed to be the health of her gracious Majesty—suggested a stretch on a sofa, and the removal of his boots. At last, at half past twelve, the county magnate, who had bidden Paul Marchmont a stately welcome to Lincolnshire, remembered that there were twenty couple of impatient hounds scratching up the turf in front of the long windows of the banquet-chamber, while as many eager young tenant farmers, stalwart yeomen, well-to-do butchers, and a herd of tag-rag and bobtail, were pining for the sport to begin—at last, I say, Sir Lionel Boport remembered this, and led the way to the terrace, leaving the renegades to repose on the comfortable sofas lurking here and there in the spacious rooms. Then the grim stone front of the house was suddenly lighted up into splendor. The long terrace was one blaze of pink, relieved here and there by patches of sober black and forester's green. Among all these stalwart, florid-visaged country gentlemen, Paul Marchmont, very elegant, very picturesque, but extremely unsportsman-like, the hero of the hour, walked slowly down the broad stone steps amidst the vociferous cheering of the crowd, the snapping and yelping of impatient hounds, and the distant braying of a horn.

It was the crowning moment of his life; the moment he had dreamed of again and again in the wretched days of poverty and obscurity. The scene was scarcely new to him—he had acted it so often in his imagination; he had heard the shouts and seen the respectful crowd. There was a little difference in detail—that was all. There was no disappointment, no shortcoming in the realization, as there so often is when our brightest dreams are fulfilled, and the one great good, the all-desired, is granted to us. No; the prize was his, and it was worth all that he had sacrificed to win it.

He looked up and saw his mother and his sisters in the great window over the porch. He could see the exultant pride in his mother's pale face; and the one redeeming sentiment of his nature, his love for the womankind who depended upon him, stirred faintly in his breast, amidst the tumult of gratified ambition and selfish joy. This one drop of unselfish pleasure filled the cup to the brim. He took off his hat and waved it high up above his head in answer to the shouting of the crowd. He had stopped half-way down the flight of steps to bow his acknowledgment of the cheering. He waved his hat, and the huzzas grew still louder; and a band upon the other side of the lawn played that familiar and triumphant march which is supposed to apply to every living hero, from a Wellington just come home from Waterloo to the winner of a boat-race, or a patent-starch proprietor newly elected by an admiring constituency.

There was nothing wanting. I think that in that supreme moment Paul Marchmont quite forgot the tortuous and perilous ways by which he had reached this all-glorious goal. I don't suppose the young princes, smothered in the Tower, were ever more palpably present in tyrant Richard's memory than when the murderous usurper groveled in Bosworth's miry clay, and knew that the great game of life was lost. It was only when Henry the Eighth took away the great seal that Wolsey was able to see the foolishness of man's ambition. In that moment memory and conscience, never very wakeful in the breast of Paul Marchmont, were dead asleep, and only triumph and delight reigned in their stead. No; there was nothing wanting. This glory and grandeur paid him a thousand-fold for his patience and self-abnegation during the past year. He turned half round to look up at those eager watchers at the window.

Good God! It was his sister Lavinia's face he saw; no longer full of triumph and pleasure, but ghastly pale, and staring at some one or something horrible in the crowd. Paul Marchmont turned to look for this horrible something, the sight of which had power to change his sister's face; and found himself confronted by a young man—a young man whose eyes flamed like coals of fire; whose cheeks were as white as a sheet of paper; and whose firm lips were locked as tightly as if they had been chiseled out of a block of granite.

This man was Edward Arundel—the young widower, the handsome soldier—whom every body remembered as the husband of poor lost Mary Marchmont.

He had sprung out from amidst the crowd only one moment before, and had dashed up the steps of the terrace before any one had time to think of hindering him or interfering with him. It seemed to Paul Marchmont as if he must have leaped out of the solid earth, so sudden and so unlooked-for was his coming. He stood upon the step immediately below the artist; but as the terrace steps were shallow, and as he was taller by half a foot than Paul, the faces of the men were level, and they confronted each other.

The soldier held a heavy hunting-whip in his hand, no foppish toy with a golden trinket for its head, but a stout handle of stag-horn, and a formidable leathern thong. He held this whip in his strong right hand, with the thong twisted round the handle; and throwing out his left arm, nervous and muscular as the limb of a young gladiator, he seized Paul Marchmont by the collar of that fashionably-cut scarlet coat which the artist had so much admired in the cheval glass that morning.

There was a shout of surprise and consternation from the gentlemen on the terrace and the crowd upon the lawn, a shrill scream from the women, and in the next moment Paul Marchmont was writhing under a shower of blows from the hunting-whip in Edward Arundel's hand. The artist was not physically brave, yet he was not such a cur as to submit unresistingly to this hideous disgrace; but the attack was so sudden and unexpected as to paralyze him; so rapid in its execution as to leave him no time for resistance. Before he had recovered his presence of mind; before he knew the meaning of Edward Arundel's appearance in that place; even before he could fully realize the mere fact of his being there—the thing was done; he was disgraced forever. He had sunk in that one moment from the very height of his new grandeur to the lowest depth of social degradation.

"Gentlemen!" Edward Arundel cried, in a loud voice, which was distinctly heard by every member of the gaping crowd, "when the law of the land suffers a scoundrel to prosper, honest men must take the law into their own hands. I wished you to know my opinion of the new master of Marchmont Towers; and I think I've expressed it pretty clearly. I know him to be a most consummate villain; and I give you fair warning that he is no fit associate for honorable men. Good-morning."

Edward Arundel lifted his hat, bowed to the assembly, and then ran down the steps. Paul Marchmont, livid, and foaming at the mouth, rushed after him, brandishing his clenched fists, and gesticulating in impotent rage; but the young man's horse was waiting for him at a few paces from the terrace, in the care of a butcher's apprentice, and he was in the saddle before the artist could overtake him.

"I shall not leave Kemberling for a week, Mr. Marchmont," he called out; and then he walked his horse away, holding himself erect as a dart, and staring defiance at the crowd.

I am sorry to have to testify to the fickle nature of the British populace; but I am bound to own that a great many of the stalwart yeomen who had eaten game-pies and drunk strong liquors at Paul Marchmont's expense not half an hour before, were base enough to feel an involuntary admiration for Edward Arundel, as he rode slowly away, with his head up and his eyes flaming. There is seldom very much genuine sympathy for a man who has been horsewhipped; and there is a pretty universal inclination to believe that the man who inflicts chastisement upon him must be right in the main. It is true that the tenant farmers, especially those whose leases were nearly run out, were very loud in their indignation against Mr. Arundel, and one adventurous spirit made a dash at the young man's bridle as he went by; but the general feeling was in favor of the conqueror, and there was a lack of heartiness even in the loudest expressions of sympathy.

The crowd made a lane for Paul Marchmont as he went back to the house, white and helpless, and sick with shame.

Several of the gentlemen upon the terrace came forward to shake hands with him, and to express their indignation, and to offer any friendly service that he might require of them by-and-by—such as standing by to see him shot, if he should choose an old-fashioned mode of retaliation; or bearing witness against Edward Arundel in a law-court, if Mr. Marchmont preferred to take legal measures. But even these men recoiled when they felt the cold dampness of the artist's hands, and saw that *he had been frightened.* These sturdy uproarious fox-hunters, who braved the peril of sudden death every time they took a day's sport, entertained a sovereign contempt for a man who *could* be frightened of any body or any thing. They made no allowance for Paul Marchmont's Cockney education; they were not in the dark secrets of his life, and knew nothing of his guilty conscience; and it was *that* which had made him more helpless than a child in the fierce grasp of Edward Arundel.

So, one by one, after this polite show of sympathy, the rich man's guests fell away from him; and the yelping hounds and the cantering horses left the lawn before Marchmont Towers; the sound of the brass band and the voices of the people died away in the distance; and the glory of the day was done.

Paul Marchmont crawled slowly back to that luxurious bedchamber which he had left only a few hours before, and, throwing himself at full length upon the bed, sobbed like a frightened child.

He was panic-stricken; not because of the horsewhipping, but because of a sentence that Edward Arundel had whispered close to his ear in the midst of the struggle.

"I know *every thing*," the young man had said. "I know the secrets you hide in the pavilion by the river!"

---

## CHAPTER XXX.

### THE DESERTED CHAMBERS.

EDWARD ARUNDEL kept his word. He waited for a week and upward, but Paul Marchmont made no sign; and after having given him three days' grace over and above the promised time the young man abandoned Kemberling Retreat, forever, as he thought, and went away from Lincolnshire.

He had waited, hoping that Paul Marchmont would try to retaliate, and that some desperate struggle, physical or legal—he scarcely cared which—would occur between them. He would have courted any hazard which might have given him some chance of revenge. But nothing happened. He sent out Mr. Morrison to beat up information about the master of Marchmont Towers; and the factotum came back with the intelligence that Mr. Marchmont was ill, and would see no one—"leastways" excepting his mother and Mr. George Weston.

Edward Arundel shrugged his shoulders when he heard these tidings.

"What a contemptible cur the man is!" he thought. "There was a time when I could have suspected him of any foul play against my lost girl. I know him better now, and know that he is not even capable of a great crime. He was only strong enough to stab his victim in the dark, with lying paragraphs in newspapers, and dastardly hints and innuendoes for his weapons."

It would have been only perhaps an act of ordinary politeness had Edward Arundel paid a farewell visit to his friends at the Grange. But he did not go near the hospitable old house. He contented himself with writing a cordial letter to Major Lawford, thanking him for his hospitality and kindness; and referring, vaguely enough, to the hope of a future meeting.

He dispatched this letter by Mr. Morrison, who was in very high spirits at the prospect of leaving Kemberling, and who went about his work with almost boyish activity in the exuberance of his delight. He worked so briskly as to complete all necessary arrangements in a couple of days; and on the 29th of October, late in the afternoon, all was ready, and Mr. Morrison had nothing to do but to superintend the departure of the two horses from the Kemberling railway-station, under the guardianship of the lad who had served as Edward's groom.

Throughout that last day Mr. Arundel wandered here and there about the house and garden that so soon were to be deserted. He was dreadfully at a loss what to do with himself, and, alas! it was not to-day only that he felt the burden of his hopeless idleness. He felt it always; a horrible load, not to be cast away from him. His life had been broken off short, as it were, by the catastrophe which had left him a widower before his honey-moon was well over. The story of his existence was abruptly broken asunder; all the better part of his life was taken away from him, and he did not know what to do with the blank and useless remnant. The raveled threads of a once harmonious web, suddenly wrenched in twain, presented a mass of inextricable confusion; and the young man's brain grew dizzy when he tried to draw them out, or to consider them separately.

His life was most miserable, most hopeless, by reason of its emptiness. He had no duty to perform, no task to achieve. That nature must be utterly selfish, entirely given over to sybarite rest and self-indulgence, which does not feel a lack of something, wanting these—a duty or a purpose. Better to be Sisyphus toiling up the mountain-side, than Sisyphus with the stone taken away from him, and no hope of ever reaching the top. I heard a man once—a bill-sticker, and not by any means a sentimental or philosophical person—declare that he had never known real prosperity until he had thirteen orphan grandchildren to support; and surely there was a universal moral in that bill-sticker's confession. He had been a drunkard before, perhaps—he didn't say any thing about that—and a reprobate, it may be; but those thirteen small mouths clamoring for food made him sober and earnest, brave and true. He had a duty to do,

and was happy in its performance. He was wanted in the world, and he was somebody. From Napoleon III., seated in that Spartan chamber at Vichy, holding the destinies of civilized Europe in his hands, and debating whether he shall recreate Poland,'or build a new boulevard, to Paterfamilias in a Government office, working for the little ones at home—and from Paterfamilias to the crossing-sweeper, who craves his diurnal half-penny from busy citizens, tramping to their daily toil—every man has his separate labor and his different responsibility. Forever and forever the busy wheel of life turns round; but duty and ambition are the motive powers that keep it going.

Edward Arundel felt the barrenness of his life now that he had taken the only revenge which was possible for him upon the man who had persecuted his wife. That had been a rapturous but brief enjoyment. It was over. He could do no more to the man, since there was no lower depth of humiliation—in these later days, when pillories, and whipping-posts, and stocks are exploded from our market-places—to which a degraded creature could descend. No; there was no more to be done. It was useless to stop in Lincolnshire. The sad suggestion of the little slipper found by the water-side was but too true. Paul Marchmont had not murdered his helpless cousin; he had only tortured her to death. He was quite safe from the law of the land, which, being of a positive and arbitrary nature, takes no cognizance of indefinable offenses. This most infamous man was safe, and was free to enjoy his ill-gotten grandeur—if he could take much pleasure in it, after the scene upon the stone terrace.

The only joy that had been left for Edward Arundel after his retirement from the East India Company's service was this fierce delight of vengeance. He had drained the intoxicating cup to the dregs, and had been drunken at first in the sense of his triumph. But he was sober now; and he paced up and down the neglected garden beneath a chill October sky, crunching the fallen leaves under his feet, with his arms folded and his head bent, thinking of the barren future. It was all bare—a blank stretch of desert land, with no city in the distance; no purple domes or airy minarets on the horizon. It was in the very nature of this young man to be a soldier; and he was nothing if not a soldier. He could never remember having had any other aspiration than that eager thirst for military glory. Before he knew the meaning of the word "war," in his very infancy, the sound of a trumpet or the sight of a waving banner, a glittering weapon, a sentinel's scarlet coat, had moved him to a kind of rapture. The unvarnished school-room records of Greek and Roman warfare had been as delightful to him as the finest passages of a Macaulay or a Froude, a Thiers or Lamartine. He was a soldier by the inspiration of Heaven, as all great soldiers are. He had never known any other ambition, or dreamed any other dream. Other lads had talked of the bar, and the senate, and their glories. Bah! how cold and tame they seemed! What was the glory of a parliamentary triumph, in which words were the only weapons wielded by the combatants, compared with a hand-to-hand struggle, ankle deep in the bloody mire of a crowded trench, or a cavalry charge, before which a phalanx of fierce Afghans fled like frightened sheep upon a moor. Edward Arundel was a soldier, like the Duke of Wellington or Sir Colin Campbell—one writes the old name involuntarily, because one loves it best—or Othello. The Moor's first lamentation when he believes that Desdemona is false, and his life is broken, is that sublime farewell to all the glories of the battle-field. It was almost the same with Edward Arundel. The loss of his wife and of his captaincy were blent and mingled in his mind, and he could only bewail the one great loss which left life most desolate.

He had never felt the full extent of his desolation until now, for heretofore he had been buoyed up by the hope of vengeance upon Paul Marchmont; and now that his solitary hope had been realized to the fullest possible extent, there was nothing left—nothing but to revoke the sacrifice he had made, and to regain his place in the Indian army at any cost.

He tried not to think of the possibility of this. It seemed to him almost an infidelity toward his dead wife to dream of winning honors and distinction, now that she, who would have been so proud of any triumph won by him, was forever lost.

So, under the gray October sky he passed up and down upon the grass-grown pathways, amidst the weeds and briers, the brambles and broken branches that crackled as he trod upon them; and late in the afternoon, when the day, which had been sunless and cold, was melting into dusky twilight, he opened the low wooden gateway and went out into the road. An impulse which he could not resist took him toward the river-bank, and the wood behind Marchmont' Towers. Once more, for the last time in his life, perhaps, he went down to that lonely shore. He went to look at the bleak, unlovely place which had been the scene of his betrothal.

It was not that he had any thought of meeting Olivia Marchmont; he had dismissed her from his mind ever since his last visit to the lonely boat-house. Whatever the mystery of her life might be, her secret lay at the bottom of a black depth which the impetuous soldier did not care to fathom. He did not want to discover that hideous secret. Tarnished honor, shame, falsehood, disgrace, lurked in the obscurity in which John Marchmont's widow had chosen to enshroud her life. Let them rest. It was not for him to drag away the curtain that sheltered his kinswoman from the world.

He had no thought, therefore, of prying into any secrets that might be hidden in the pavilion by the water. The fascination that lured him to the spot was the memory of the past. He could not go to Mary's grave; but he went, in as reverent a spirit as he would have gone thither, to the scene of his betrothal, to pay his farewell visit to the spot which had been forever hallowed by the confession of her innocent love.

It was nearly dark when he got to the river-side. He went by a path which quite avoided the grounds about Marchmont Towers—a narrow foot-path, which served as a towing-path sometimes when some black barge crawled by on its way out to the open sea. To-night the river was hidden by a mist—a white fog—that obscured land and water; and it was only by the sound of the horses' hoofs that Edward

Arundel had warning to step aside as a string of them went by, dragging a chain that grated on the pebbles by the river-side.

"Why should they say my darling committed suicide?" thought Edward Arundel, as he groped his way along the narrow pathway; "it was on such an evening as this that she ran away from home. What more likely than that she lost the track and wandered into the river? Oh, my own poor lost one, God grant it was so! God grant it was by His will, and not your own desperate act, that you were lost to me!"

Sorrowful as the thought of his wife's death was to him, it soothed him to believe that that death might have been accidental. There was all the difference between sorrow and despair in the alternative.

Wandering ignorantly and helplessly through this autumnal fog, Edward Arundel found himself at the boat-house before he was aware of its vicinity.

There was a light gleaming from the broad north window of the painting-room, and a slanting line of light streamed out of the half-open door. In this lighted doorway Edward saw the figure of a girl—an unkempt, red-headed girl, with a flat freckled face—a girl who wore a lavender-cotton pinafore and hobnailed boots, with a good deal of brass about the leather fronts, and a redundancy of rusty leather boot-lace twisted round the ankles.

The young man remembered having seen this girl once in the village of Kemberling. She had been in Mrs. Weston's service as a drudge, and was supposed to have received her education in the Swampington union.

This young lady was supporting herself against the half-open door, with her arms a-kimbo, and her hands planted upon her hips, in humble imitation of the matrons whom she had been wont to see lounging at their cottage-doors in the high street of Kemberling, when the labors of the day were done.

Edward Arundel started at the sudden apparition of this damsel.

"Who are you, girl?" he asked; "and what brings you to this place?"

He trembled as he spoke. A sudden agitation had seized upon him, which he had no power to account for. It seemed as if Providence had brought him to this spot to-night, and had placed this ignorant country girl in his way for some special purpose. Whatever the secrets of this place might be, he was to know them, it appeared, since he had been led here, not by the promptings of curiosity, but only by a reverent love for a scene that was associated with his dead wife.

"Who are you, girl?" he asked again.

"Oi be Bessy Murrel, Sir," the damsel answered; "some on 'em calls me 'Wuk-us Bet;' and I be coom here to cle-an oop a bit."

"To clean up what?"

"The paa-intin' room. There's a de-al o' moock about, and aw'm to fettle oop, and make all toidy agen t' squire gets well."

"Are you all alone here?"

"All alo-an? Oh yes, Sir."

"Have you been here long?"

The girl looked at Mr. Arundel with a cunning leer, which was one of her "wuk-us" acquirements.

"Aw've bin here off an' on ever since t' squire ke-ame," she said. "There's a deal o' cleanin' down 'ere."

Edward Arundel looked at her sternly; but there was nothing to be gathered from her stolid countenance after its agreeable leer had melted away. The young man might have scrutinized the figure-head of the black barge creeping slowly past upon the hidden river with quite as much chance of getting any information out of its play of feature.

He walked past the girl into Paul Marchmont's painting-room. Miss Bessy Murrel made no attempt to hinder him. She had spoken the truth as to the cleaning of the place, for the room smelled of soap-suds, and a pail and scrubbing-brush stood in the middle of the floor. The young man looked at the door behind which he had heard the crying of the child. It was ajar, and the stone steps leading up to it were wet, bearing testimony to Bessy Murrel's industry.

Edward Arundel took the flaming tallow-candle from the table in the painting-room and went up the steps into the pavilion. The girl followed, but she did not try to restrain him, or to interfere with him. She followed him with her mouth open, staring at him after the manner of her kind, and she looked the very image of rustic stupidity.

With the flaring candle shaded by his left hand, Edward Arundel examined the two chambers in the pavilion. There was very little to reward his scrutiny. The two small rooms were bare and cheerless. The repairs that had been executed had only gone so far as to make them tolerably inhabitable, and secure from wind and weather. The furniture was the same that Edward remembered having seen on his last visit to the Towers; for Mary had been fond of sitting in one of the little rooms, looking out at the slow river and the trembling rushes on the shore. There was no trace of recent occupation in the empty rooms, no ashes in the grates. The girl grinned maliciously as Mr. Arundel raised the light above his head, and looked about him. He walked in and out of the two rooms. He stared at the obsolete chairs, the rickety tables, the dilapidated damask curtains, flapping every now and then in the wind that rushed in through the crannies of the doors and windows. He looked here and there, like a man bewildered; much to the amusement of Miss Bessy Murrel, who, with her arms crossed, and her elbows in the palms of her moist hands, followed him backward and forward between the two small chambers.

"There was some one living here a week ago," he said; "some one who had the care of a—"

He stopped suddenly. If he had guessed rightly at the dark secret, it was better that it should remain forever hidden. This girl was perhaps more ignorant than himself. It was not for him to enlighten her.

"Do you know if any body has lived here lately?" he asked.

Bessy Murrel shook her head.

"Nobody has lived here—not that oi knows of," she replied; "not to take their victuals, and such loike. Missus brings her work down some-,times, and sits in one of these here rooms, while Muster Poll does his pictur' paa-intin'; that's all oi knows of."

Edward went back to the painting-room, and

set down his candle. The mystery of those empty chambers was no business of his. He began to think that his cousin Olivia was mad, and that her outbursts of terror and agitation had been only the raving of a mad woman after all. There had been a great deal in her manner during the last year that had seemed like insanity. The presence of the child might have been purely accidental; and his cousin's wild vehemence only a paroxysm of insanity. He sighed as he left Miss Murrel to her scouring. The world seemed out of joint; and he, whose energetic nature fitted him for the straightening of crooked things, had no knowledge of the means by which it might be set right.

"Good-by, lonely place," he said; "good-by to the spot where my young wife first told me of her love!"

He walked back to the cottage, where the bustle of packing and preparation was all over, and where Mr. Morrison was entertaining a select party of friends in the kitchen. Early the next morning Mr. Arundel and his servant left Lincolnshire; the key of Kemberling Retreat was given up to the landlord; and a wooden board, flapping above the dilapidated trellis-work of the porch, gave notice that the habitation was to be let.

---

<h2 style="text-align:center">CHAPTER XXXI.</h2>

TAKING IT QUIETLY.

ALL the county, or at least all that part of the county within a certain radius of Marchmont Towers, waited very anxiously for Mr. Paul Marchmont to make some move. The horse-whipping business had given quite a pleasant zest, a flavor of excitement, a dash of what it is the fashion nowadays to call "sensation," to the wind-up of the hunting breakfast. Poor Paul's thrashing had been more racy and appetizing than the finest olives that ever grew; and his late guests looked forward to a great deal more excitement and "sensation" before the business was done with. Of course Paul Marchmont would do something. He *must* make a stir; and the sooner he made it the better. Matters would have to be explained. People expected to know the *cause* of Edward Arundel's enmity; and of course the new master of the Towers would see the propriety of setting himself right in the eyes of his influential acquaintance, his tenantry, and retainers, especially if he contemplated standing for Swampington at the next general election.

This was what people said to each other. The scene at the hunting breakfast was a most fertile topic of conversation. It was almost as good as a popular murder, and furnished scandalous paragraphs *ad infinitum* for the provincial papers, most of them beginning, "It is understood—" or "It has been whispered in our hearing that—" or "Rochefoucault has observed that—" Every body expected that Paul Marchmont would write to the papers, and that Edward Arundel would answer him in the papers; and that a brisk and stirring warfare would be carried on in printer's ink—at least. But no line written by either of the gentlemen appeared in any one of the county journals; and by slow degrees it dawned upon people that there was no further

I

amusement to be got out of Paul's chastisement, and that the master of the Towers meant to take the thing quietly, and to swallow the horrible outrage, taking care to hide any wry faces he made during that operation.

Yes; Paul Marchmont let the matter drop. The report was circulated that he was very ill, and had suffered from a touch of brain-fever, which kept him a victim to incessant delirium until after Mr. Arundel had left the county. This rumor was set afloat by Mr. Weston, the surgeon; and as he was the only person admitted to his brother-in-law's apartment, it was impossible for any one to contradict his assertion.

The fox-hunting squires shrugged their shoulders, and I am sorry to say that the epithets "hound," "cur," "sneak," and "mongrel," were more often applied to Mr. Marchmont than was consistent with Christian feeling on the part of the gentlemen who uttered them. But a man who can swallow a sound thrashing, administered upon his own door-step, has to contend with the prejudices of society, and must take the consequences of being in advance of his age.

So, while his new neighbors talked about him, Paul Marchmont lay in his splendid chamber, with the frisking youths and maidens staring at him all day long, and simpering at him with their unchanging faces, until he grew sick at heart, and began to loathe all this new grandeur, which had so delighted him a little time ago. He no longer laughed at the recollection of shabby Charlotte Street. He dreamed one night that he was back again in the old bedroom, with the painted deal furniture, and the hideous paper on the walls, and that the Marchmont-Towers magnificence had been only a feverish vision; and he was glad to be back in that familiar place, and was sorry on awaking to find that Marchmont Towers was a splendid reality.

There was only one faint red streak upon his shoulders; for the thrashing had not been a brutal one. It was *disgrace* Edward Arundel had wanted to inflict, not physical pain, the commonplace punishment with which a man corrects his refractory horse. The lash of the hunting-whip had done very little damage to the artist's flesh; but it had slashed away his manhood, as the sickle sweeps the flowers amidst the corn.

He could never look up again. The thought of going out of this house for the first time, and the horror of confronting the altered faces of his neighbors, was as dreadful to him as the anticipation of that awful exit from the Debtor's Door, which is the last step but one into eternity, must be to the condemned criminal.

"I shall go abroad," he said to his mother, when he made his appearance in the western drawing-room, a week after Edward's departure. "I shall go on the Continent, mother; I have taken a dislike to this place since that savage attacked me the other day."

Mrs. Marchmont sighed.

"It will seem hard to lose you, Paul, now that you are rich. You were so constant to us through all our poverty; and we might be so happy together now."

The artist was walking up and down the room, with his hands in the pockets of his braided velvet coat. He knew that in the conventional costume of a well-bred gentleman he showed to a disadvantage among other men; and he affected a picturesque and artistic style of dress, whose brighter hues and looser outlines lighted up his pale face, and gave a grace to his spare figure.

"You think it worth something, then, mother?" he said, presently, half-kneeling, half-lounging in a deep cushioned easy-chair near the table at which his mother sat. "You think our money is worth something to us? All these chairs and tables, this great rambling house, these servants who wait upon us, and the carriages we ride in, are worth something, are they not? they make us happier, I suppose. I know I always thought such things made up the sum of happiness when I was poor. I have seen a hearse going away from a rich man's door, carrying his cherished wife, or his only son perhaps; and I've thought, 'Ah! but he has forty thousand a year!' You are happier here than you were in Charlotte Street—eh, mother?"

Mrs. Marchmont was a Frenchwoman by birth, though she had lived so long in London as to become Anglicized. She only retained a slight accent of her native tongue, and a good deal more vivacity of look and gesture than is common to Englishwomen. Her eldest daughter was sitting on the other side of the broad fire-place. She was only a quieter and older likeness of Lavinia Weston.

"*Am* I happier?" exclaimed Mrs. Marchmont. "Need you ask me the question, Paul? But it is not so much for myself as for your sake that I value all this grandeur."

She held out her long thin hand, which was covered with rings, some old-fashioned and comparatively valueless, others lately purchased by her devoted son, and very precious. The artist took the shrunken fingers in his own and raised them to his lips.

"I'm very glad that I've made you happy, mother," he said; "that's something gained, at any rate."

He left the fire-place, and walked slowly up and down the room, stopping now and then to look out at the wintry sky, or the flat expanse of turf below it; but he was quite a different creature to that which he had been before his encounter with Edward Arundel. The chairs and tables palled upon him. The mossy velvet pile of the new carpets seemed to him like the swampy ground of a morass. The dark-green draperies of Genoa velvet deepened into black with the growing twilight, and seemed as if they had been fashioned out of palls.

What was it worth, this fine house, with the broad flat before it? Nothing, if he had lost the respect and consideration of his neighbors. He wanted to be a great man as well as a rich one. He wanted admiration and flattery, reverence and esteem; not from poor people, whose esteem and admiration were scarcely worth having, but from wealthy squires, his equals or his superiors by birth and fortune. He ground his teeth at the thought of his disgrace. He had drunk of the cup of triumph, and had tasted the very wine of life; and at the moment when that cup was fullest it had been snatched away from him by the ruthless hand of his enemy.

Christmas came, and gave Paul Marchmont a good opportunity of playing the country gentleman of the olden time. What was the cost of a couple of bullocks, a few hogsheads of ale, and a wagon-load of coals, if by such a sacrifice the master of the Towers could secure for himself the admiration due to a public benefactor? Paul gave *carte blanche* to the old servants; and tents were erected on the lawn, and monstrous bonfires blazed briskly in the frosty air; while the populace, who would have accepted the bounties of a new Nero fresh from the burning of a modern Rome, drank to the health of their benefactor, and warmed themselves by the unlimited consumption of strong beer.

Mrs. Marchmont and her invalid daughter assisted Paul in his attempt to regain the popularity he had lost upon the steps of the western terrace. The two women distributed square miles of flannel and blanketing among greedy claimants; they gave scarlet cloaks and poke-bonnets to old women; they gave an insipid feast upon temperance principles to the children of the National Schools. And they had their reward; for people began to say that this Paul Marchmont was a very noble fellow after all, by Jove, Sir! and that fellow Arundel must have been in the wrong, Sir; and no doubt Marchmont had his own reasons for not resenting the outrage, Sir; and a great deal more to the like effect.

After this roasting of the two bullocks the wind changed altogether. Mr. Marchmont gave a great dinner-party upon New-Year's Day. He sent out thirty invitations, and had only two refusals. So the long dining-room was filled with all the notabilities of the district, and Paul held his head up once more, and rejoiced in his own grandeur. After all, one horsewhipping can not annihilate a man with a fine estate and eleven thousand a year, if he knows how to make a splash with his money. Olivia Marchmont shared in none of the festivals that were held. Her father was very ill this winter; and she spent a good deal of her time at Swampington Rectory, sitting in Hubert Arundel's room, and reading to him. But her presence brought very little comfort to the sick man; for there was something in his daughter's manner that filled him with inexpressible terror; and he would lie for hours together watching her blank face, and wondering at its horrible rigidity. What was it? What was the dreadful secret which had transformed this woman? He tormented himself perpetually with this question, but he could imagine no answer to it. He did not know the power which a master-passion has upon these strong-minded women, whose minds are strong because of their narrowness, and who are the bonden slaves of one idea. He did not know that in a breast which holds no pure affection the master-fiend Passion rages like an all-devouring flame, perpetually consuming its victim. He did not know that in these violent and concentrative natures the line that separates reason from madness is so feeble a demarkation that very few can perceive the hour in which it is passed.

Olivia Marchmont had never been the most lively or delightful of companions. The tenderness which is the common attribute of a woman's nature had not been given to her. She ought to have been a great man. Nature makes these mistakes now and then, and the victim expiates the error. Hence come such imperfect histories as that of English Elizabeth and Swedish Christina. The fetters that had bound Olivia's nar-

row life had eaten into her very soul, and cankered there. If she could have been Edward Arundel's wife, she would have been the noblest and truest wife that ever merged her identity into that of another, and lived upon the refracted glory of her husband's triumphs. She would have been a Rachel Russell, a Mrs. Hutchinson, a Lady Nithisdale, a Madame de Lavalette. She would have been great by reason of her power of self-abnegation: and there would have been a strange charm in the aspect of this fierce nature attuned to harmonize with its master's soul, all the barbaric discords melting into melody, all the harsh combinations softening into perfect music; just as in Mr. Buckstone's most poetic drama we are bewitched by the wild huntress sitting at the feet of her lord, and admire her chiefly because we know that only that one man upon all the earth could have had power to tame her. To any one who had known Olivia's secret there could have been no sadder spectacle than this of her decay. The mind and body decayed together, bound by a mysterious sympathy. All womanly roundness disappeared from the spare figure, and Mrs. Marchmont's black dresses hung about her in loose folds. Her long, dead, black hair was pushed away from her thin face, and twisted into a heavy knot at the back of her head. Every charm that she had ever possessed was gone. The oldest women generally retain some traits of their lost beauty, some faint reflection of the sun that has gone down to light up the soft twilight of age, and even glimmer through the gloom of death. But this woman's face retained no token of the past. No empty hull, with shattered bulwarks crumbled by the fury of fierce seas, cast on a desert shore to rot and perish there, was ever more complete a wreck than she was. Upon her face and figure, in every look and gesture, in the tone of every word she spoke, there was an awful something, worse than the seal of death. Little by little the miserable truth dawned upon Hubert Arundel. His daughter was mad! He knew this; but he kept the dreadful knowledge hidden in his own breast; a hideous secret, whose weight oppressed him like an actual burden. He kept the secret; for it would have seemed to him the most cruel treason against his daughter to have confessed this discovery to any living creature, unless it should be absolutely necessary to do so. Meanwhile he set himself to watch Olivia, detaining her at the Rectory for a week together, in order that he might see her in all moods, under all phases.

He found that there were no violent or outrageous evidences of this mental decay. The mind had given way under the perpetual pressure of one set of thoughts. Hubert Arundel, in his ignorance of his daughter's secrets, could not discover the cause of her decadence; but that cause was very simple. If the body is a wonderful and complex machine which must not be tampered with—surely if this is so, that still more complex machine the mind must need careful treatment. If such and such a course of diet is fatal to the body's health, may not some thoughts be equally fatal to the health of the brain? may not a monotonous recurrence of the same ideas be above all injurious? If by reason of the peculiar nature of a man's labor he uses one limb or one muscle more than the rest;

'strange bosses rise up to testify to that ill-usage, the idle limbs wither, and the harmonious perfection of Nature gives place to deformity. So the brain, perpetually pressed ;upon, forever strained to its utmost tension by the wearisome succession of thoughts, becomes crooked and one-sided, always leaning one way, continually tripping up the wretched thinker.

John Marchmont's widow had only one set of ideas. On every subject but that one which involved Edward Arundel and his fortunes her memory had decayed. She asked her father the same questions—commonplace questions relating to his own comfort, or to simple household matters—twenty times a day, always forgetting that he had answered her. She had that impatience as to the passage of time which is one of the most painful signs of madness. She looked at her watch ten times an hour, and would wander out into the cheerless garden, indifferent to the bitter weather, in order to look at the clock in the church-steeple, under the impression that her own watch, and her father's, and all the time-keepers in the house, were slow.

She was sometimes restless, taking up one occupation after another, to throw all aside with equal impatience, and sometimes immobile for hours together. But as she was never violent, never in any way unreasonable, Hubert Arundel had not the heart to call science to his aid, and to betray her secret. The thought that his daughter's malady might be cured never entered his mind as within the range of possibility. There was nothing to cure; no delusions to be exorcised by medical treatment; no violent vagaries to be held in check by drugs and nostrums. The powerful intellect had decayed; its force and clearness were gone. No drugs that ever grew upon this earth could restore that which was lost. This was the conviction which kept the rector silent. It would have given him unutterable anguish to have told his daughter's secret to any living being; but he would have endured that misery if she could have been benefited thereby. He most firmly believed that she could not, and that her state was irremediable.

"My poor girl!" he thought to himself; "how proud I was of her ten years ago! I can do nothing for her; nothing except to love and cherish her, and hide her humiliation from the world."

But Hubert Arundel was not allowed to do even this much for the daughter he loved; for when Olivia had been with him a little more than a week, Paul Marchmont and his mother drove over to Swampington Rectory one morning and carried her away with them. The rector then saw for the first time that his once strong-minded daughter was completely under the dominion of these two people, and that they knew the nature of her malady quite as well as he did. He resisted her return to the Towers; but his resistance was useless. She submitted herself willingly to her new friends, declaring that she was better in their house than anywhere else. So she went back to her old suit of apartments, and her old servant Barbara waited upon her; and she sat alone in dead John Marchmont's study, listening to the January winds shrieking in the quadrangle, the distant rooks calling to each other among the bare branches of the poplars, the banging of the doors in the corridor, and occasional gusts of laughter from

the open door of the dining-room, while Paul Marchmont and his guests gave a jovial welcome to the new year.

While the master of the Towers reasserted his grandeur, and made stupendous efforts to regain the ground he had lost, Edward Arundel wandered far away in the depths of Brittany, traveling on foot, and making himself familiar with the simple peasants, who were ignorant of his troubles. He had sent Mr. Morrison down to Dangerfield with the greater part of his luggage; but he had not the heart to go back himself—yet a while. He was afraid of his mother's sympathy, and he went away into the lonely Breton villages to try and cure himself of his great grief before he began life again as a soldier. It was useless for him to strive against his vocation. Nature had made him a soldier, and nothing else; and wherever there was a good cause to be fought for his place was on the battle-field.

---

## CHAPTER XXXII.

### MISS LAWFORD SPEAKS HER MIND.

MAJOR LAWFORD and his blue-eyed daughters were not among those guests who accepted Paul Marchmont's princely hospitalities. Belinda Lawford had never heard the story of Edward's lost bride as he himself could have told it; but she had heard an imperfect version of the sorrowful history from Letitia, and that young lady had informed her friend of Edward's animus against the new master of the Towers.

"The poor dear foolish boy will insist upon thinking that Mr. Marchmont was at the bottom of it all," she had said, in a confidential chat with Belinda, "somehow or other; but whether he was, or whether he wasn't, I'm sure I can't say. But if one attempts to take Mr. Marchmont's part with Edward, he does get so violent and go on so, that one's obliged to say all sorts of dreadful things about Mary's cousin for the sake of peace. But, really, when I saw him one day in Kemberling, with a black velvet shooting-coat, and his beautiful smooth white hair and auburn mustache, I thought him most interesting. And so would you, Belinda, if you weren't so wrapped up in that doleful brother of mine."

Whereupon, of course, Miss Lawford had been compelled to declare that she was not "wrapped up" in Edward, whatever state of feeling that obscure phrase might signify; and to express, by the vehemence of her denial, that, if any thing, she rather detested Miss Arundel's brother. By-the-by, did you ever know a young lady who could understand the admiration aroused in the breast of other young ladies for that most uninteresting object, a *brother*? Or a gentleman who could enter with any warmth of sympathy into his friend's feelings respecting the auburn tresses or the Grecian nose of "a sister?" Belinda Lawford, I say, knew something of the story of Mary Arundel's death, and she implored her father to reject all hospitalities offered by Paul Marchmont.

"You won't go to the Towers, papa dear?" she said, with her hands clasped upon her father's arm, her cheeks kindling, and her eyes filling with tears as she spoke to him; "you won't go and sit at Paul Marchmont's table, and drink his wine, and shake hands with him? I know that he had something to do with Mary Arundel's death. He had, indeed, papa. I don't mean any thing that the world calls crime; I don't mean any act of open violence. But he was cruel to her, papa; he was cruel to her. He tortured her and tormented her until she—" The girl paused for a moment, and her voice faltered a little. "Oh, how I wish that I had known her, papa," she cried, presently, "that I might have stood by her and comforted her all through that sad time!"

The major looked down at his daughter with a tender smile—a smile that was a little significant perhaps, but full of love and admiration. "You would have stood by Arundel's poor little wife, my dear?" he said. "You would stand by her now, if she were alive, and needed your friendship?"

"I would indeed, papa," Miss Lawford answered, resolutely.

"I believe it, my dear; I believe it with all my heart. You are a good girl, my Linda; you are a noble girl. You are as good as a son to me, my dear."

Major Lawford was silent for a few minutes, holding his daughter in his arms and pressing his lips upon her broad forehead.

"You are fit to be a soldier's daughter, my darling," he said, "or—or a soldier's wife." He kissed her once more, and then left her, sighing thoughtfully as he went away.

This is how it was that neither Major Lawford nor any of his family were present at those splendid entertainments which Paul Marchmont gave to his new friends. Mr. Marchmont knew almost as well as the Lawfords themselves why they did not come, and the absence of them at his glittering board made his bread bitter to him and his wine tasteless. He wanted these people as much as the others—more than the others perhaps; for they had been Edward Arundel's friends; and he wanted them to turn their backs upon the young man, and join in the general outcry against his violence and brutality. The absence of Major Lawford at the lighted banquet-table tormented this modern rich man as the presence of Mordecai at the gate tormented Haman. It was not enough that all the others should come if these staid away, and by their absence tacitly testified to their contempt for the master of the Towers.

He met Belinda sometimes on horseback with the old gray-headed groom behind her, a fearless young Amazon, breasting the January winds, with her blue eyes sparkling, and her auburn hair blowing away from her candid face; he met her, and looked out at her from the luxurious barouche in which it was his pleasure to loll by his mother's side, half buried among soft furry rugs and sleek leopard-skins, making the chilly atmosphere through which he rode odorous with the scent of perfumed hair, and smiling over cruelly delicious criticisms in newly-cut reviews. He looked out at this fearless girl, whose friends so obstinately stood by Edward Arundel; and the cold contempt upon Miss Lawford's face cut him more keenly than the sharpest wind of that bitter January.

Then he took counsel with his womankind, not telling them his thoughts, fears, doubts, or wishes—it was not his habit to do that—but

taking their ideas, and only telling them so much as it was necessary for them to know in order that they might be useful to him. Paul Marchmont's life was regulated by a few rules, so simple that a child might have learned them; indeed I regret to say that some children are very apt pupils in that school of philosophy to which the master of Marchmont Towers belonged, and cause astonishment to their elders by the precocity of their intelligence. Mr. Marchmont might have inscribed upon a very small scrap of parchment the moral maxims by which he regulated his dealings with mankind.

"Always conciliate," said this philosopher. "Never tell an unnecessary lie. Be agreeable and generous to those who serve you. N.B. No good carpenter would allow his tools to get rusty. Make yourself master of the opinions of others, but hold your own tongue. Seek to obtain the maximum of enjoyment with the minimum of risk."

Such golden saws as these did Mr. Marchmont make for his own especial guidance; and he hoped to pass smoothly onward upon the railway of life, riding in a first-class carriage, on the greased wheels of a very easy conscience. As for any unfortunate fellow-travelers pitched out of the carriage-window in the course of the journey, or left lonely and helpless at desolate stations on the way, Providence, and not Mr. Marchmont, was responsible for their welfare. Paul had a high appreciation of Providence, and was fond of talking—very piously, as some people said; very impiously, as others secretly thought—about the inestimable Wisdom which governed all the affairs of this lower world. Nowhere, according to the artist, had the hand of Providence been more clearly visible than in this matter about Paul's poor little cousin Mary. If Providence had intended John Marchmont's daughter to be a happy bride, a happy wife, prosperous mistress of that stately habitation, why all that sad business of old Mr. Arundel's sudden illness, Edward's hurried journey, the railway accident, and all the complications that had thereupon arisen? Nothing would have been easier than for Providence to have prevented all this; and then he, Paul, would have been still in Charlotte Street, Fitzroy Square, patiently waiting for a friendly lift upon the high road of life. Nobody could say that he had ever been otherwise than patient. Nobody could say that he had ever intruded himself upon his rich cousins at the Towers, or had been heard to speculate upon his possible inheritance of the estate; or that he had, in short, done any thing but that which the best, truest, most conscientious and disinterested of mankind should do.

In the course of that bleak, frosty January, Mr. Marchmont sent his mother and his sister Lavinia to make a call at the Grange. The Grange people had never called upon Mrs. Marchmont; but Paul did not allow any flimsy ceremonial law to stand in his way when he had a purpose to achieve. So the ladies went to the Grange and were politely received; for Miss Lawford and her mother were a great deal too innocent and noble-minded to imagine that these pale-faced, delicate-looking women could have had any part, either directly or indirectly, in that cruel treatment which had driven Edward's young wife from her home. Mrs. Marchmont and Mrs. Weston were kindly received, therefore; and in a little conversation with Belinda about birds, and dahlias, and worsted-work, and the most innocent subjects imaginable, the wily Lavinia contrived to lead up to Miss Letitia Arundel, and thence, by the easiest conversational short cut, to Edward and his lost wife. Mrs. Weston was obliged to bring her cambric handkerchief out of her muff when she talked, about her cousin Mary; but she was a clever woman, and she had taken to heart Paul's pet maxim about the folly of *unnecessary* lies; and she was so candid as to entirely disarm Miss Lawford, who had a school-girlish notion that every kind of hypocrisy and falsehood was outwardly visible in a servile and slavish manner. She was not upon her guard against those practiced adepts in the art of deception, who have learned to make that subtle admixture of truth and falsehood which defy detection, like some fabrics in whose woof silk and cotton are so cunningly blended that only a practiced eye can discover the inferior material.

So when Lavinia dried her eyes and put her handkerchief back in her muff, and said, betwixt laughing and crying,

"Now you know, my dear Miss Lawford, you mustn't think that I would for a moment pretend to be sorry that my brother has come into this fortune. Of course any such pretense as that would be ridiculous, and quite useless into the bargain, as it isn't likely any body would believe me. Paul is a dear, kind creature, the best of brothers, the most affectionate of sons, and deserves any good fortune that could fall to his lot; but I am truly sorry for that poor little girl. I am truly sorry, believe me, Miss Lawford; and I only regret that Mr. Weston and I did not come to Kemberling sooner, so that I might have been a friend to the poor little thing; for then, you know, I might have prevented that foolish runaway match, out of which almost all the poor child's troubles arose. Yes, Miss Lawford; I wish I had been able to befriend that unhappy child, although by my so doing Paul would have been kept out of the fortune he now enjoys—for some time, at any rate. I say for some time, because I do not believe that Mary Marchmont would have lived to be old under the happiest circumstances. Her mother died very young; and her father, and her father's father, were consumptive."

Then Mrs. Weston took occasion, incidentally of course, to allude to her brother's goodness; but even then she was on her guard, and took care not to say too much.

"The worst actors are those who overact their parts." That was another of Paul Marchmont's golden maxims.

"I don't know what my brother may be to the rest of the world," Lavinia said, "but I know how good he is to those who belong to him. I should be ashamed to tell you all he has done for Mr. Weston and me. He gave me this cashmere shawl at the beginning of the winter, and a set of sables fit for a duchess; though I told him they were not at all the thing for a village surgeon's wife,· who keeps only one servant and dusts her own best parlor."

And Mrs. Marchmont talked of her son, with no loud enthusiasm, but with a tone of quiet conviction that was worth any money to Paul.

To have an innocent person, some one not in the secret, to play a small part in the comedy of his life was a desideratum with the artist. His mother had always been this person, this unconscious actor, instinctively falling into the action of the play, and shedding real tears, and smiling actual smiles—the most useful assistant to a great schemer.

But during the whole of the visit nothing was said as to Paul's conduct toward his unhappy cousin; nothing was said either to praise or to exculpate; and when Mrs. Marchmont and her daughter drove away in one of the new equipages which Paul had selected for his mother they left only a vague impression in Belinda's breast. She didn't quite know what to think. These people were so frank and candid, they had spoken of Paul with such real affection, that it was almost impossible to doubt them. Paul Marchmont might be a bad man, but his mother and sister loved him, and surely they were ignorant of his wickedness.

Mrs. Lawford troubled herself very little about this unexpected morning call. She was an excellent, warm-hearted, domestic creature, and thought a great deal more about the grand question as to whether she should have new damask curtains for the drawing-room, or send the old ones to be dyed; or whether she should withdraw her custom from the Kemberling grocer, whose "best black" at four and sixpence was really now so very inferior; or whether Belinda's summer silk-dress could be cut down into a frock for Isabella to wear in the winter evenings—than about the rights or wrongs of that story of the horsewhipping which had been administered to Mr. Marchmont.

"I'm sure those Marchmont Towers people seem very nice, my dear," the lady said to Belinda, "and I really wish your papa would go and dine there. You know I like him to dine out a good deal in the winter, Linda; not that I want to save the housekeeping money, only it is so difficult to vary the dinners for a man who has been in the army, and has had mess-dinners and a French cook."

But Belinda stuck fast to her colors. She was a soldier's daughter, as her father said, and she was almost as good as a son. The major meant this latter remark for very high praise; for the great grief of his·life had been the want of a boy's brave face at his fireside. She was as good as a son; that is to say, she was braver and more outspoken than most women, although she was feminine and gentle withal, and by no means strong-minded. She would have fainted, perhaps, at the first sight of blood upon a battle-field; but she would have bled to death with the calm heroism of a martyr rather than have been false to a noble cause.

"I think papa is quite right not to go to Marchmont Towers, mamma," she said; the artful minx omitted to state that it was by reason of her entreaties her father had staid away. "I think he is quite right. Mrs. Marchmont and Mrs. Weston may be very nice, and of course it isn't likely *they* would be cruel to poor young Mrs. Arundel; but I *know* that Mr. Marchmont must have been unkind to that poor girl, or Mr. Arundel would never have done what he did."

It is in the nature of good and brave men to lay down their masculine rights when they leave their hats in the hall, and to submit themselves meekly to feminine government. It is only the whippersnapper, the sneak, the coward out of doors, who is a tyrant at home. See how meekly the Conqueror of Italy went home to his charming Creole wife! See how pleasantly the Liberator of Italy lolls in the carriage of his golden-haired Empress, when the young trees in that fair wood beyond the triumphal arch are green in the bright spring weather, and all the hired vehicles in Paris are making toward the cascade! Major Lawford's wife was too gentle, and too busy with her store-room and her domestic cares, to tyrannize over her lord and master; but the major was duly hen-pecked by his blue-eyed daughters, and went here and there as they dictated.

So he staid away from Marchmont Towers to please Belinda, and only said, "Haw," "Yes," "'Pon my honor, now!" "Bless my soul!" when his friends told him of the magnificence of Paul's dinners.

But although the major and his eldest daughter did not encounter Mr. Marchmont in his own house, they met him sometimes on the neutral ground of other people's dining-rooms, and upon one especial evening at a pleasant little dinner-party given by the rector of the parish in which the Grange was situated.

Paul made himself particularly agreeable upon this occasion; but in the brief interval before dinner he was absorbed in a conversation with Mr. Davenant, the rector, upon the subject of ecclesiastical architecture—he knew every thing, and could talk about every thing, this dear Paul—and made no attempt to approach Miss Lawford. He only looked at her now and then, with a furtive, oblique glance out of his almond-shaped, pale-gray eyes; a glance that was wisely hidden by their auburn lashes, for it had an unpleasant resemblance to the leer of an evil-natured sprite. Mr. Marchmont contented himself with keeping this furtive watch upon Belinda, while she talked gayly with the rector's two daughters in a pleasant corner near the piano; and as the artist took Mrs. Davenant down to the dining-room, and sat next her at dinner, he had no opportunity of fraternizing with Belinda during that meal; for the young lady was divided from him by the whole length of the table, and, moreover, very much occupied by the exclusive attentions of two callow-looking officers from the nearest garrison-town, who were afflicted with extreme youth, and were painfully conscious of their degraded state, but tried notwithstanding to carry it off with a high hand, and affected the opinions of used-up fifty.

Mr. Marchmont had none of his womankind with him at this dinner; for his mother and invalid sister had neither of them felt strong enough to come, and Mr. and Mrs. Weston had not been invited. The artist's special object in coming to this dinner was the conquest of Miss Belinda Lawford. She sided with Edward Arundel against him. She must be made to believe Edward wrong, and himself right; or she might go about spreading her opinions, and doing him mischief. Beyond that, he had another idea about this auburn-haired, blue-eyed Belinda; and he looked to this dinner as likely to afford him an opportunity of laying the foundation of a very diplomatic scheme, in which Miss Lawford should

unconsciously become his tool. He was vexed at being placed apart from her at the dinner-table, but he concealed his vexation; and he was aggravated by the rector's old-fashioned hospitality, which detained the gentlemen over their wine for some time after the ladies left the dining-room. But the opportunity that he wanted came nevertheless, and in a manner that he had not anticipated.

The two callow defenders of their country had sneaked out of the dining-room, and rejoined the ladies in the cozy countrified drawing-rooms. They had stolen away, these two young men; for they were oppressed by the weight of a fearful secret. *They couldn't drink claret!* No; they had tried to like it; they had smacked their lips and winked their eyes—both at once, for even winking with *one* eye is an accomplishment scarcely compatible with extreme youth — over vintages that had seemed to them like a happy admixture of red ink and green-gooseberry juice. They had perjured their boyish souls with hideous falsehoods as to their appreciation of pale tawny port, light dry wines, 42 ports, 45 ports; when in the secret recesses of their minds they affected sweet and "slab" compounds sold by publicans, and facetiously called "our prime old port, at four and sixpence." They were very young, these beardless soldiers. They liked strawberry ices, and were on the verge of insolvency from a predilection for clammy-bath-buns, jam-tarts, and cherry-brandy. They liked gorgeous waistcoats; and patent-leather boots in a state of virgin brilliancy; and little bouquets in their button-holes; and a deluge of *millefleurs* upon their flimsy handkerchiefs. They were very young; the men they met at dinner-parties to-day had tipped them at Eton or Woolwich only yesterday, as it seemed, and remembered it and despised them. It was only a few months since they had been snubbed for calling the Douro a mountain in Switzerland, and the Himalayas a cluster of islands in the Pacific, at horrible *viva voce* examinations, in which the cold perspiration had bedewed their pallid young cheeks. They were delighted to get away from those elderly creatures in the rector's dining-room to the snug little back drawing-room, where Belinda Lawford and the two Miss Davenants were murmuring softly in the fire-light, like young turtles in a sheltered dove-cot; while the matrons in the larger apartment sipped their coffee, and conversed in low, awful voices about the iniquities of house-maids and the insubordination of gardeners and grooms.

Belinda and her two companions were very polite to the helpless young wanderers from the dining-room; and they talked pleasantly enough of all manner of things, until somehow or other the conversation came round to the Marchmont Towers scandal, and Edward's treatment of his lost wife's kinsman.

One of the young men had been present at the hunting-breakfast on that bright October morning, and he was not a little proud of his superior acquaintance with the whole business.

"I was the-aw, Miss Lawford," he said. "I was on the tew-wace after bweakfast—and a vewy excellent bweakfast it was, I ass-haw you; the still Moselle was weally admiwable, and Marchmont has some Madewa that immeasurably surpasses any thing I can induce my wine-merchant to send me—I was on the tew-wace, and I saw Awundel comin' up the steps, awful pale, and gwaspin' his whip; and I was a witness of all the west that occurred; and if I'd been Marchmont I should have shot Awundel before he left the pawk, if I'd had to swing fow it, Miss Lawford; for I should have felt, b' Jove, that my own sense of honaw demanded the sacwifice. Howevaw, Marchmont seems a vewy good fella; so I suppose it's all wight as far as he goes; but it was a bwutal business altogethaw, and that fella Awundel must be a scoundwel."

Belinda could not bear this. She had borne a great deal already. She had been obliged to sit by very often, and hear Edward Arundel's conduct discussed by Thomas, Richard, and Henry, or any body else who chose to talk about it; and she had been patient, and had held her peace, with her heart'bumping indignantly in her breast, and passionate crimson blushes burning her cheeks. But she could not submit to hear a beardless, pale-faced, and rather weak-eyed young ensign—who had never done any greater service for his Queen and country than to cry "Shudd ruph!" to a detachment of raw recruits in a barrack-yard, in the early bleakness of a winter's morning—take upon himself to blame Edward Arundel, the brave soldier, the noble Indian hero, the devoted lover and husband, the valiant avenger of his dead wife's wrongs.

"I don't think you know any thing of the real story, Mr. Pallisser," Belinda said, boldly, to the half-fledged ensign. "If you did, I'm sure you would admire Mr. Arundel's conduct instead of blaming it. Mr. Marchmont fully deserved the disgrace which Edward—which Mr. Arundel inflicted upon him."

The words were still upon her lips when Paul Marchmont himself came softly through the flickering fire-light to the low chair upon which Belinda sat. He came behind her, and laying his hand lightly upon the scroll-work at the back of her chair, bent over her, and said, in a low, confidential voice:

"You are a noble girl, Miss Lawford; I am sorry that you should think ill of me; but I like you for having spoken so frankly. You are a most noble girl. You are worthy to be your father's daughter."

This was said with a tone of suppressed emotion; but it was quite a random shot. Paul didn't know any thing about the major, except that he had a comfortable income, drove a neat dog-cart, and was often seen riding on the flat Lincolnshire roads with his eldest daughter. For all Paul knew to the contrary, Major Lawford might have been the veriest bully and coward who ever made those about him miserable; but Mr. Marchmont's tone as good as expressed that he was intimately acquainted with the old soldier's career, and had long admired and loved him. It was one of Paul's happy inspirations, this allusion to Belinda's father; one of those bright touches of color laid on with a skillful recklessness, and giving sudden brightness to the whole picture; a little spot of vermilion dabbed upon the canvas with the point of the pallet-knife, and lighting up all the landscape with sunshine.

"You know my father?" said Belinda, surprised.

"Who does not know him?" cried the artist.

"Do you think, Miss Lawford, that it is necessary to sit at a man's dinner-table before you know what he is?. I know your father to be a good man and a brave soldier, as well as I know that the Duke of Wellington is a great general, though I never dined at Apsley House. I respect your father, Miss Lawford; and I have been very much distressed by his evident avoidance of me and mine."

This was coming to the point at once. Mr. Marchmont's manner was candor itself. Belinda looked at him with widely-opened, wondering eyes. She was looking for the evidence of his wickedness in his face. I think she half expected that Mr. Marchmont would have corked eyebrows, and a slouched hat like a stage ruffian. She was so innocent, this simple young Belinda, that she imagined wicked people must necessarily look wicked.

Paul Marchmont saw the wavering of her mind in that half-puzzled expression, and he went on boldly.

"I like your father, Miss Lawford," he said; "I like him, and I respect him; and I want to know him. Other people may misunderstand me, if they please. I can't help their opinions. The truth is generally strongest in the end; and I can afford to wait. But I can not afford to forfeit the friendship of a man I esteem; I can not afford to be misunderstood by your father, Miss Lawford; and I have been very much pained—yes, very much pained—by the manner in which the major has repelled my little attempts at friendliness."

Belinda's heart smote her. She knew that it was her influence that had kept her father away from Marchmont Towers. This young lady was very conscientious. She was a Christian, too; and a certain sentence touching wrongful judgments rose up against her while Mr. Marchmont was speaking. If she had wronged this man; if Edward Arundel had been misled by his passionate grief for Mary; if she had been deluded by Edward's error—how very badly Mr. Marchmont had been treated between them! She didn't say any thing, but sat looking thoughtfully at the fire; and Paul saw that she was more and more perplexed. This was just what the artist wanted. To talk his antagonist into a state of intellectual fog was almost always his manner of commencing an argument.

Belinda was silent, and Paul seated himself in a chair close to hers. The callow ensigns had gone into the lamp-lit front drawing-room, and were busy turning over the leaves—and never turning them over at the right moment—of a thundering duet which the Misses Davenant were performing for the edification of their papa's visitors. Miss Lawford and Mr. Marchmont were alone, therefore, in that cozy inner chamber, and a very pretty picture they made: the auburn-haired girl, and the pale, sentimental-looking artist sitting side by side in the glow of the low fire, with a back-ground of crimson curtains and gleaming picture-frames; winter flowers piled in grim Indian jars; the fitful light flickering now and then upon one sharp angle of the high carved mantle-piece, with all its litter of antique china; and the rest of the room in sombre shadow. Paul had the field all to himself, and felt that victory would be easy. He began to talk about Edward Arundel.

If he had said one word against the young soldier, I think this impetuous girl, who had not yet learned to count the cost of what she did, would have been passionately eloquent in defense of her friend's brother—for no other reason than that he was the brother of her friend, of course; what other reason should she have for defending Mr. Arundel?

But Paul Marchmont did not give her any occasion for indignation. On the contrary, he spoke in praise of the hot-headed young soldier who had assaulted him, making all manner of excuses for the young man's violence, and using that tone of calm superiority with which a man of the world might naturally talk about a foolish boy.

"He has been very unreasonable, Miss Lawford," Paul said, by-and-by; "he has been very unreasonable, and has most grossly insulted me. But, in spite of all, I believe him to be a very noble young fellow, and I can not find it in my heart to be really angry with him. What his particular grievance against me may be I really do not know."

The furtive glance from the long, narrow gray eyes kept close watch upon Belinda's face as Paul said this. Mr. Marchmont wanted to ascertain exactly how much Belinda knew of that grievance of Edward's; but he could see perplexity only in her face. She knew nothing definite, therefore; she had only heard Edward talk vaguely of his wrongs. Paul Marchmont was convinced of this, and he went on boldly now, for he felt that the ground was all clear before him.

"This foolish young soldier chooses to be angry with me because of a calamity which I was as powerless to avert as to prevent that accident upon the Southwestern Railway by which Mr. Arundel so nearly lost his life. I can not tell you how sincerely I regret the misconception that has arisen in his mind. Because I have profited by the death of John Marchmont's daughter this impetuous young husband imagines—what? I can not answer that question; nor can he himself, it seems, since he has made no definite statement of his wrongs to any living being."

The artist looked more sharply than ever at Belinda's listening face. There was no change in its expression. The same wondering look, the same perplexity—that was all.

"When I say that I regret the young man's folly, Miss Lawford," Paul continued, "believe me it is chiefly on his account rather than my own. Any insult which he can inflict upon me can only rebound upon himself, since every body in Lincolnshire knows that I am in the right, and he in the wrong."

Mr. Marchmont was going on very smoothly; but at this point Miss Lawford, who had by no means deserted her colors, interrupted his easy progress.

"It remains to be proved who is right and who wrong, Mr. Marchmont," she said. "Mr. Arundel is the brother of my friend. I can not easily believe him to have done wrong."

Paul looked at her with a smile—a smile that brought hot blushes to her face; but she returned his look without flinching. The brave blue eyes looked full at the narrow gray eyes sheltered under pale auburn lashes, and their steadfast gaze did not waver.

"Ah, Miss Lawford," said the artist, still smiling, "when a young man is handsome, brave, chivalrous, and generous-hearted, it is very difficult to convince a woman that he can do wrong. Edward Arundel has done wrong. His ultra-Quixotism has made him blind to the folly of his own acts. I can afford to forgive him. But I repeat that I regret his infatuation about this poor lost girl far more upon his account than on my own; for I know—at least, I venture to think—that a way lies open to him of a happier and a better life than he could ever have known with my poor childish cousin Mary Marchmont. I have reason to know that he has formed another attachment, and that it is only a chivalrous delusion about that poor girl—whom he was never really in love with, and whom he only married because of some romantic notion inspired by my cousin John—that withholds him from that other and brighter prospect."

He was silent for a few moments, and then he said, hastily,

"Pardon me, Miss Lawford; I have been betrayed into saying much that I had better have left unsaid, more especially to you. I—"

He hesitated a little, as if embarrassed, and then rose and looked into the next room, where the duet had been followed by a solo.

One of the rector's daughters came toward the inner drawing-room, followed by a callow ensign.

"We want Belinda to sing," exclaimed Miss Davenant. "We want you to sing, you tiresome Belinda, instead of hiding yourself in that dark room all the evening."

Belinda came out of the darkness with her cheeks flushed and her eyelids drooping. Her heart was beating so fast as to make it quite impossible to speak just yet, or to sing either. But she sat down before the piano, and, with hands that trembled in spite of herself, began to play one of her pet sonatas.

Unhappily Beethoven requires precision of touch in the pianist who is bold enough to seek to interpret him; and upon this occasion I am compelled to admit that Miss Lawford's fingering was eccentric, not to say ridiculous—in common parlance, she made a mess of it; and just as she was going to break down, friendly Clara Davenant cried out,

"That won't do, Belinda! We want you to sing, not to play. You are trying to cheat us. We would rather have one of Moore's melodies than all Beethoven's sonatas."

So Miss Lawford, still blushing, with her eyelids still drooping, played Sir John Stevenson's simple symphony, and, in a fresh swelling voice that filled the room with melody, began:

"Oh, the days are gone when beauty bright
My heart's chain wove;
When my dream of life, from morn till night,
Was love, still love!"

And Paul Marchmont, sitting at the other end of the room turning over Miss Davenant's scrap-book, looked up through his auburn lashes, and smiled at the beaming face of the singer.

He felt that he had improved the occasion.

"I am not afraid of Miss Lawford now," he thought to himself.

This candid, fervent girl was only another piece in the schemer's game of chess, and he saw a way of making her useful in the attainment of that great end which, in the strange simplicity of cunning, he believed to be the one purpose of *every* man's life—Self-Aggrandizement.

It never for a moment entered into his mind that Edward Arundel was any more *real* than he was himself. There can be no perfect comprehension where there is no sympathy. Paul believed that Edward had tried to become master of Mary Marchmont's heritage, and had failed, and was angry because of his failure. He believed this passionate young man to be a schemer like himself, only a little' more impetuous and blundering in his manner of going to work.

---

## CHAPTER XXXIII.

### THE RETURN OF THE WANDERER.

THE March winds were blowing among the oaks in Dangerfield Park, when Edward Arundel went back to the house which had never been his home since his boyhood. He went back because he had grown weary of lonely wanderings in that strange Breton country. He had grown weary of himself, and of his own thoughts. He was worn out by the eager desire that devoured him by day and by night—the passionate yearning to be far away beyond that low Eastern horizon line; away amidst the carnage and riot of an Indian battle-field.

So he went back at last to his mother, who had written to him again and again, imploring him to return to her, and to rest, and to be happy in the familiar household where he was beloved. He left his luggage at the little inn where the coach that had brought him from Exeter stopped, and then he walked quietly homeward in the' gloaming. The' early spring evening was bleak and chill. The blacksmith's fire roared at him as he went by the smithy. All the lights in the queer latticed windows twinkled and blinked at him, as if in friendly welcome to the wanderer. He remembered them all: the quaint, misshapen, lop-sided roofs; the tumble-down chimneys; the low doorways, that had sunk down below the level of the village street, until all the front parlors became cellars, and strange pedestrians butted their heads against the flower-pots in the bedroom windows; the withered iron frame and pitiful oil-lamp hung out at the corner of the street, and making a faint spot of feeble light upon the rugged pavement; mysterious little shops in diamond-paned parlor windows, where Dutch dolls and stationery, stale gingerbread and pickled-cabbage, were mixed up with wooden peg-tops, rickety paper-kites, green apples, and string—they were all familiar to him.

It had been a fine thing once to come into this village with Letitia, and buy stale gingerbread and rickety kites of a snuffy old pensioner of his mother's. The kites had always stuck in the upper branches of the oaks, and the gingerbread had invariably choked him; but with the memory of the kites and gingerbread came back all the freshness of his youth, and he looked with a pensive tenderness at the homely little shops, the merchandise flickering in the red fire-light, that filled each quaint interior with a genial glow of warmth and color.

He passed unquestioned by a wicket at the side of the great gates. The fire-light was rosy in the windows of the lodge, and he heard a woman's voice singing a monotonous song to a sleepy child. Every where in this pleasant England there seemed to be the glow of cottage-fires, and friendliness, and love, and home. The young man sighed as he remembered that great stone mansion far away in dismal Lincolnshire, and thought how happy he might have been in this bleak spring twilight, if he could have sat by Mary Marchmont's side in the western drawing-room, watching the fire-light and the shadows trembling on her fair young face.

It never had been, and it never was to be. The happiness of a home; the sweet sense of ownership; the delight of dispensing pleasure to others ; all the simple domestic joys which make life beautiful—had never been known to John Marchmont's daughter since that early time in which she shared her father's lodging in Oakley Street, and went out in the cold December morning to buy rolls for Edward Arundel's breakfast. From the bay-window of his mother's favorite sitting-room the same red light that he had seen in every lattice in the village streamed out upon the growing darkness of the lawn. There was a half-glass door leading into a little lobby near this sitting-room. Edward Arundel opened it and went in, very quietly. He expected to find his mother and his sister in the room with the bay-window.

The door of this familiar apartment was ajar; he pushed it open and went in. It was a very pretty room, and all the womanly litter of open books and music, needle-work and drawing materials, made it homelike. The fire-light flickered upon every thing—on the pictures and picture-frames, the black oak paneling, the open piano, a cluster of snow-drops in a tall glass on the table, the scattered worsteds by the embroidery-frame, the sleepy dogs upon the hearth-rug. A young lady stood in the bay-window with her back to the fire. Edward Arundel crept softly up to her, and put his arm round her waist.

" Letty."

It was not Letitia, but a young lady with very blue eyes, who blushed scarlet, and turned upon the young man rather fiercely ; and then recognizing him, dropped into the nearest chair, and began to tremble and grow pale.

" I am sorry I startled you, Miss Lawford," Edward said, gently; "I really thought you were my sister. · I did not even know that you were here."

"No, of course not. I—you didn't startle me much, Mr. Arundel, only you were not exepected home. I thought you were far away in Brittany. I had no idea that there was any chance of your returning. I thought you meant to be away all the summer; Mrs. Arundel told me so."

Belinda Lawford said all this in that fresh girlish voice which was familiar to Mr. Arundel; but she was still very pale, and she still trembled a little, and there was something almost apologetic in the way in which she assured Edward that she had believed he would be abroad throughout the summer. It seemed almost as if she had said : "I did not come here because I thought I should see you. I had no thought or hope of meeting you."

But Edward Arundel was not a coxcomb, and he was very slow to understand any such signs as these. He saw that he had startled the young lady, and that she had turned pale and trembled as she recognized him; and he looked at her with a half-wondering, half-pensive expression in his face.

She blushed as he looked at her. She went to the table and began to gather together the silks and worsteds, as if the arrangement of her work-basket were a matter of vital importance, to be achieved at any sacrifice of politeness. Then suddenly remembering that she ought to say something to Mr. Arundel, she gave evidence of the originality of her intellect by the following remark:

"How surprised Mrs. Arundel and Letitia will be to see you!"

Even as she said this her eyes were still bent upon the skeins of worsted in her hand.

"Yes; I think they will be surprised. I did not mean to come home until the autumn. But I got so tired of wandering about a strange country alone. Where are they—my mother and Letitia?"

"They have gone down the village to the school. They will be back to tea. Your brother is away; and we dine at three o'clock, and drink tea at eight. It is so much pleasanter than dining late."

This was quite an effort of genius; and Miss Lawford went on sorting the skeins of worsted in the fire-light. Edward Arundel had been standing all this time with his hat in his hand, almost as if he had been a visitor making a late morning call upon Belinda; but he put his hat down now, and seated himself near the table by which the young lady stood busy with the arrangement of her work-basket.

Her heart was beating very fast, and she was straining her arithmetical powers to the uttermost, in the endeavor to make a very abstruse calculation as to the time in which Mrs. Arundel and Letitia could walk to the village school-house and back to Dangerfield, and the delay that might arise by reason of sundry interruptions from obsequious gaffers and respectful goodys, eager for a word of friendly salutation from their patroness.

The arrangement of the work-basket could not last forever. It had become the most pitiful pretense by the time Miss Lawford shut down the wicker lid, and seated herself primly in a low chair by the fire-place. She sat looking down at the fire, and twisting a slender gold chain in and out between her smooth white fingers. She looked very pretty in that fitful fire-light, with her waving brown hair pushed off her forehead, and her white eyelids hiding the tender blue eyes. She sat twisting the chain in her fingers, and dared not lift her eyes to Mr. Arundel's face; and if there had been a whole flock of geese in the room she could not have said " Bo!" to one of them.

And yet she was not a stupid girl. Her father could have indignantly refuted any such slander as that against the azure-eyed Hebe who made his home pleasant to him. To the major's mind Belinda was all that man could desire in the woman of his choice, whether as daughter or wife. She was the bright genius of the old man's home, and he loved her with

that chivalrous devotion which is common to brave soldiers, who are the simplest and gentlest of men when you chain them to their firesides, and keep them away from the din of the camp and the confusion of the transport-ship.

Belinda Lawford was clever, but only just clever enough to be charming. I don't think she could have got through "Paradise Lost," or Gibbon's "Decline and Fall," or a volume by Adam Smith or M'Culloch, though you had promised her a diamond necklace when she came conscientiously to "Finis." But she could read Shakspeare for the hour together, and did read him aloud to her father in a fresh, clear voice, that was like music on the water. And she read Macaulay's "History of England," with eyes that kindled when the historian's pages flamed out with burning words that were like the characters upon a blazing scroll. She could play Mendelssohn and Beethoven—plaintive sonatas, tender songs, that had no need of words to expound the mystic meaning of the music. She could sing old ballads and Irish melodies, that thrilled the souls of those who heard her, and made hard men pitiful to brazen Hibernian beggars in the London streets for the memory of that pensive music. She could read the leaders in the Times, with no false quantities in the Latin quotations, and knew what she was reading about; and had her favorites at St. Stephen's, and adored Lord Palmerston, and was Liberal to the core of her tender young heart. She was as brave as a true Englishwoman should be, and would have gone to the wars with her old father, and served him as his page; or would have followed him into captivity, and tended him in prison, if she had lived in the days when there was such work for a high-spirited girl to do.

But she sat opposite Mr. Edward Arundel, and twisted her chain round her fingers, and listened for the footsteps of the returning mistress of the house. She was like a bashful school-girl who has danced with an officer at her first ball. And yet amidst her shy confusion, her fears that she should seem agitated and embarrassed, her struggles to appear at her ease, there was a sort of pleasure in being seated here by the low fire with Edward Arundel opposite to her. There was a strange pleasure, an almost painful pleasure, mingled with her feelings in those quiet moments. She was acutely conscious of every sound that broke the stillness—the sighing of the wind in the wide chimney; the falling of the cinders on the hearth; the occasional snort of one of the sleeping dogs; and the beating of her own restless heart. And though she dared not lift her eyelids to the young soldier's face, that handsome, earnest countenance, with the chestnut hair lit up with gleams of gold, the firm lips shaded by a brown mustache, the pensive smile, the broad white forehead, the dark blue handkerchief tied loosely under a white collar, the careless gray traveling-dress, even the attitude of the hand and arm, the bent head drooping a little over the fire, were as present to her inner sight, as if her eyes had kept watch all this time, and had never wavered in their steady gaze.

There is a second sight that is not recognized by grave professors of magic; a second sight which common people call Love.

But by-and-by Edward began to talk, and then

Miss Lawford found courage, and took heart to question him about his wanderings in Brittany. She had only been a few weeks in Devonshire, she said. Her thoughts went back to the dreary autumn in Lincolnshire as she spoke; and she remembered the dull October day upon which her father had come into the girls' morning-room at the Grange with Edward's farewell letter in his hand. She remembered this, and all the talk that there had been about the horsewhipping of Mr. Paul Marchmont upon his own threshold. She remembered all the warm discussions, the speculations, the ignorant conjectures, the praise, the blame; and how it had been her business to sit by, and listen, and hold her peace, except upon that one never-to-be-forgotten night at the rectory, when Paul Marchmont had hinted at something whose perfect meaning she had never dared to imagine, but which had, somehow or other, mingled vaguely with all her day-dreams ever since.

Was there any truth in that which Paul Marchmont had said to her? Was it true that Edward Arundel had never really loved his young bride?

Letitia had said as much, not once, but twenty times.

"It's quite ridiculous to suppose that he could have ever been in love with the poor, dear, sickly thing," Miss Arundel had exclaimed; "it was only the absurd romance of the business that captivated him; for Edward is really ridiculously romantic; and her father having been a supernumer—it's no use; I don't think any body ever did know how many syllables there are in that word—and having lived in Oakley Street, and having written a pitiful letter to Edward about this motherless daughter, and all that sort of thing; just like one of those tiresome old novels with a baby left at a cottage-door, and all the *s*'s looking like *f*'s, and the last word of the page repeated at the top of the next page, you know. *That* was why my brother married Miss Marchmont, you may depend upon it, Linda; and all I hope is, that he'll be sensible enough to marry again soon, and to have a Christian-like wedding, with carriages, and a breakfast, and two clergymen; and *I* should wear white glacé silk, with tulle puffings, and a tulle bonnet (I suppose I must wear a bonnet, being only a bridemaid?), all showered over with clematis, as if I'd stood under a clematis-bush when the wind was blowing, you know, Linda."

With such discourse as this Miss Arundel had frequently entertained her friend; and she had indulged in numerous innuendoes of an embarrassing nature as to the propriety of old friends and school-fellows being united by the endearing tie of sister-in-law-hood, and other observations to the like effect.

Belinda knew that if Edward ever came to love her—whenever she did venture to speculate upon such a chance, she never dared to come at all near it, but thought of it as a thing that might come to pass in half a century or so—if he should choose her for his second wife, she knew that she would be gladly and tenderly welcomed at Dangerfield. Mrs. Arundel had hinted as much as this. Belinda knew how anxiously that loving mother hoped that her son might, by-and-by, form new ties, and cease to lead a purposeless life, wasting his brightest years in lam-

entations for his lost bride. She knew all this; and sitting opposite to the young man in the fire-light, there was a dull pain at her heart, for there was something in the soldier's sombre face that told her he had not yet ceased to lament that irrevocable past.

But Mrs. Arundel and Letitia came in presently, and gave utterance to loud rejoicings; and preparations were made for the physical comfort of the wanderer—bells were rung, lighted wax-candles and a glittering tea-service were brought in, a cloth was laid, and cold meats and other comestibles spread forth, with that profusion that has made the west country as proverbial as the north for its hospitality. I think Miss Lawford would have sat opposite the traveler for a week without asking any such commonplace question as to whether Mr. Arundel required refreshment. She had read in her Hort's *Pantheon* that the gods sometimes ate and drank like ordinary mortals; yet it had never entered into her mind that Edward could be hungry. But she now had the satisfaction of seeing Mr. Arundel eat a very good dinner, while she herself poured out the tea to oblige Letitia, who was in the middle of the third volume of a new novel, and went on reading it as coolly as if there had been no such person as that handsome young soldier in the world.

"The books must go back to the club tomorrow morning, you know, mamma dear, or I wouldn't read at tea-time," the young lady remarked, apologetically. "I want to know whether he'll marry Theodora or that nasty Miss St. Leger. Linda thinks he'll marry Miss St. Leger, and be miserable, and Theodora will die. I believe Linda likes love-stories to end unhappily. I don't. I hope if he *does* marry Miss St. Leger—and he'll be a wicked wretch if he does, after the things he has said to Theodora—I hope, if he does, she'll die—catch cold at a *déjeuner* at Twickenham, or something of that kind, you know; and then he'll marry Theodora afterward, and all will end happily. Do you know, Linda, I always fancy that you're like Theodora, and that Edward's like *him*."

After which speech Miss Arundel went back to her book, and Edward helped himself to a slice of tongue rather awkwardly; and Belinda Lawford, who had her hand upon the urn, suffered the tea-pot to overflow among the cups and saucers.

---

## CHAPTER XXXIV.

### A WIDOWER'S PROPOSAL.

For some time after his return Edward Arundel was very restless and gloomy, roaming about the country by himself, under the influence of a pretended passion for pedestrianism, reading hard for the first time in his life, shutting himself in his dead father's library, and sitting hour after hour in a great easy-chair, reading the histories of all the wars that have ever ravaged this earth, from the days in which the elephants of a Carthaginian ruler trampled upon the soldiery of Rome, to the era of that Corsican barrister's wonderful son, who came out of his simple island home to conquer the civilized half of a world.

Edward Arundel showed himself a very indifferent brother; for, do what she would, Letitia
could not induce him to join in any of her pursuits. She caused a butt to be set up upon the
lawn; but all she could say about Belinda's best
gold could not bring the young man out upon
the grass to watch the two girls shooting. He
looked at them by stealth sometimes through
the window of the library, and sighed as he
thought of the blight upon his manhood, and of
all the things that might have been.
Might not those things even yet come to pass?
Had he not done his duty to the dead; and was
he not free now to begin a fresh life? His mother was perpetually hinting at some bright prospect that lay smiling before him, if he chose to
take the blossom-bestrewn path that led to that
fair country. His sister told him still more plainly of a prize that was within his reach, if he were
but brave enough to stretch out his hand and
claim the precious treasure for his own. But
when he thought of all this—when he pondered
whether it would not be wise to drop the dense
curtain of forgetfulness over that sad picture of
the past—whether it would not be well to let the
dead bury their dead, and to accept that other
blessing which the same Providence that had
blighted his first hope seemed to offer to him
now—the shadowy phantom of John Marchmont
arose out of the mystic realms of the dead, and
a ghostly voice cried to him,
"I charged you with my daughter's safe-
keeping; I trusted you with her innocent love;
I gave you the custody of her helplessness.
What have you done to show yourself worthy
of my faith in you?"
These thoughts tormented the young widower
perpetually, and deprived him of all pleasure in
the congenial society of his sister and Belinda
Lawford; or infused so sharp a flavor of remorse
into his cup of enjoyment that pleasure was akin
to pain.
So I don't know how it was that, in the dusky
twilight of a bright day in early May, nearly
two months after his return to Dangerfield, Edward Arundel, coming by chance upon Miss
Lawford as she sat alone in the deep bay-window
where he had found her on his first coming, confessed to her the terrible struggle of feeling that
made the great trouble of his life, and asked her
if she was willing to accept a love which, in its
warmest fervor, was not quite unclouded by the
shadows of the sorrowful past.
"I love you dearly, Linda," he said; "I love,
I esteem, I admire you; and I know that it is
in your power to give me the happiest future
that ever a man imagined in his youngest, brightest dreams. But if you do accept my love, dear,
you must take my memory with it. I can not
forget, Linda. I have tried to forget. I have
prayed that God, in His mercy, might give me
forgetfulness of that irrevocable past. But the
prayer has never been granted; the boon has
never been bestowed. I think that love for
the living and remorse for the dead must forever reign side by side in my heart. It is no
falsehood to you that makes me remember her;
it is no forgetfulness of her that makes me love
you. I offer my brighter and happier self to
you, Belinda; I consecrate my sorrow and my
tears to her. I love you with all my heart, Belinda; but even for the sake of your love I will

not pretend that I can forget her. If John
Marchmont's daughter had died with her head
upon my breast and a prayer on her lips, I might
have regretted her as other men regret their
wives, and I might have learned by-and-by to look
back upon my grief with only a tender and natural regret, that would have left my future life
unclouded. But it can never be so. The poison
of remorse is blended with that sorrowful memory. If I had done otherwise—if I had been
wiser and more thoughtful—my darling need
never have suffered; my darling need never
have sinned. It is the thought that her death
may have been a sinful one that is most cruel
to me, Belinda. I have seen her pray, with her
pale, earnest face uplifted, and the light of faith
shining in her gentle eyes; I have seen the inspiration of God upon her face; and I can not
bear to think that, in the darkness that came
down upon her young life, that holy light was
quenched; I can not bear to think that Heaven
was ever deaf to the pitiful cry of my innocent
lamb."
And here Mr. Arundel paused, and sat silently looking out at the long shadows of the trees
upon the darkening lawn; and I fear that, for
the time being, he forgot that he had just made
Miss Lawford an offer of his hand and so much
of his heart as a widower may be supposed to
have at his disposal.
Ah me! we can only live and die once. There
are some things, and those the most beautiful
of all things, that can never be renewed: the
bloom on a butterfly's wing; the morning dew
upon a newly-blown rose; our first view of the
ocean; our first pantomime, when all the fairies
were fairies forever, and when the imprudent
consumption of the contents of a pewter quart-
measure in sight of the stage-box could not dis-
enchant us with that elfin creature Harlequin,
the graceful, faithful betrothed of Columbine the
fair. The firstlings of life are most precious.
When the black wing of the angel of death swept
over agonized Egypt, and the children were smitten, offended Heaven, eager for a sacrifice, took
the first-born. The young mothers would have
other children, perhaps; but between those others and the mother's love there would be the pale
shadow of that lost darling whose tiny hands first
drew undreamed-of melodies from the sleeping
chords, first evoked the slumbering spirit of maternal love. Among the latter lines—the most
passionate, the most sorrowful—that George
Gordon Noel Byron wrote, are some brief verses
that breathed a lament for the lost freshness, the
never-to-be-recovered youth:

"Oh, could I feel as I have felt; or be what I have been;
Or weep as I could once have wept!"

cried the poet when he complained of that "mortal coldness of the soul," which is "like death
itself."
Edward Arundel had grown to love Belinda
Lawford unconsciously, and in spite of himself;
but the first love of his heart, the first fruit of
his youth, had perished. He could not feel quite
the same devotion, the same boyish chivalry,
that he had felt for the innocent bride who had
wandered beside him in the sheltered meadows
near Winchester. He might begin a new life,
but he could not live the old life over again. He
must wear his rue with a difference this time.
But he loved Belinda very dearly, nevertheless;

and he told her so, and by-and-by·won from her ·a tearful avowal of affection.

Alas! she had no power to question the manner of his wooing. He loved her—he had said as much; and all the good she had desired in this universe became hers from the moment of Edward Arundel's utterance of those words. He loved her; that was enough. That he should cherish a remorseful sorrow for that lost wife made him only the truer, nobler, and dearer in Belinda's sight. She was not vain, or exacting, or selfish. It was not in her nature to begrudge poor dead Mary the tender thoughts of her husband. She was generous, impulsive, believing; and she had no more inclination to doubt Edward's love for her, after he had once avowed such a sentiment, than to disbelieve in the light of heaven when she saw the sun shining. Unquestioning, and unutterably happy, she received her lover's betrothal kiss, and went with him to his mother, blushing and trembling, to receive that lady's blessing.

"Ah, if you knew how I have prayed for this, Linda!" Mrs. Arundel exclaimed, as she folded the girl's slight figure in her arms.

"And I shall wear white glacé with pinked flounces, instead of tulle puffings, you sly Linda," cried Letitia.

"And I'll give Ted the home farm, and the white house to live in, if he likes to try his hand at the new system of farming," said Reginald Arundel, who had come home from the Continent, and had amused himself for the last week by strolling about his estate, and staring at his timber, and almost wishing that there was a necessity for cutting down all the oaks in the avenue, so that he might have something to occupy him until the 12th of August.

Never was promised bride more welcome to a household than bright Belinda Lawford; and as for the young lady herself, I must confess that she was almost childishly happy, and that it was all that she could do to prevent her light step from falling into a dance as she floated hither and thither through the house at Dangerfield— a fresh young Hebe in crisp muslin robes; a gentle goddess, with smiles upon her face and happiness in her heart.

"I loved you from the first, Edward," she whispered one day to her lover. "I knew that you were good, and brave, and noble; and I loved you because of that."

And a little for the golden glimmer in his clustering auburn curls; and a little for his handsome profile, his dark-blue eyes, and that distinguished air peculiar to the defenders of their country, more especially peculiar, perhaps, to those who ride on horseback when they sally forth to defend her. Once a soldier forever a soldier, I think. You may rob the noble warrior of his uniform, if you will; but the *je ne sais quoi*, the nameless air of the "long-sword, saddle, bridle," will hang round him still.

Mrs. Arundel and Letitia took matters quite out of the hands of the two lovers. The elder lady fixed the wedding-day, by agreement with Major Lawford, and sketched out the route for the wedding-tour. The younger lady chose the fabrics for the dresses of the bride and her attendants; and all was done before Edward and Belinda well knew what their friends were about. I think that Mrs. Arundel feared her son might change his mind if matters were not brought swiftly to a climax, and that she hurried on the irrevocable day in order that he might have no breathing-time until the vows had been spoken and Belinda Lawford was his wedded wife. It had been arranged that Edward should escort Belinda back to Lincolnshire, and that his mother and Letitia, who was to be chief bridemaid, should go with them. The marriage was to be solemnized at Hillingsworth Church, which was within a mile and a half of the Grange.

The 1st of July was the day appointed by agreement between Major and Mrs. Lawford and Mrs. Arundel, and on the 18th of June Edward was to accompany his mother, Letitia, and Belinda to Lincolnshire. They were to break the journey by stopping in town for a few days, in order to make a great many purchases necessary for Miss Lawford's wedding paraphernalia, for which the major had sent a bouncing check to his favorite daughter.

And all this time the only person at all unsettled, the only person whose mind was ill at ease, was Edward Arundel; the young widower who was about to take to himself a second wife. His mother, who watched him with a maternal comprehension of every change in his face, saw this, and trembled for her son's happiness.

"And yet he can not be otherwise than happy with Belinda Lawford," Mrs. Arundel thought to herself.

But upon the eve of that journey to London Edward sat alone with his mother in the drawing-room at Dangerfield, after the two younger ladies had retired for the night. They slept in adjoining apartments, these two young ladies; and I regret to say that a great deal of their conversation was about Valenciennes lace, and flounces cut upon the cross, moire antique, mull muslin, glacé silk, and the last "sweet thing" in bonnets. It was only when loquacious Letitia was shut out that Miss Lawford knelt alone in the still moonlight, and prayed that she might be a good wife to the man who had chosen her. I don't think she ever prayed that she might be faithful, and true, and pure; for it never entered into her mind that any creature bearing the sacred name of wife could be otherwise. She only prayed for the mysterious power to preserve her husband's affection, and make his life happy.

Mrs. Arundel, sitting *tête-à-tête* with her younger son in the lamp-lit drawing-room, was startled by hearing the young man breathe a deep sigh. She looked up from her work to see a sadder expression in his face than perhaps ever clouded the countenance of an expectant bridegroom.

"Edward!" she exclaimed.

"What, mother?"

"How heavily you sighed just now!"

"Did I?" said Mr. Arundel, abstractedly. Then, after a brief pause, he said, in a different tone, "It is no use trying to hide these things from you, mother. The truth is, I am not happy."

"Not happy, Edward!" cried Mrs. Arundel; "but surely you—"

"I know what you are going to say, mother. Yes, mother; I love this dear girl, Linda, with all my heart; I love her most sincerely; and I could look forward to a life of unalloyed happiness with her, if—if there was not some inexplicable dread, some vague and most miserable feeling always coming between me and my hopes. I have tried to look forward to the future, mother; I have tried to think of what my life may be with Belinda; but I can not, I can not. I can not look forward; all is dark to me. I try to build up a bright palace, and an unknown hand shatters it. I try to turn away from the memory of my old sorrows; but the same hand plucks me back, and chains me to the past. If I could retract what I have done; if I could, with any show of honor, draw back, even now, and not go upon this journey to Lincolnshire; if I *could* break my faith to this poor girl who loves me, and whom I love, as God knows, with all truth and earnestness—I would do so; I would do so."

"Edward!"

"Yes, mother; I would do it. It is not in me to forget. My dead wife haunts me by night and day. I hear her voice crying to me, 'False, false, false; cruel and false; heartless and forgetful!' There is never a night that I do not dream of that dark sluggish river down in Lincolnshire. There is never a dream that I have, however ridiculous, however inconsistent in all its other details, in which I do not see her dead face looking up at me through the murky waters. Even when I am talking to Linda, when words of love for her are on my lips, my mind wanders away back—always back—to the sunset by the boat-house, when my little wife gave me her hand, to the trout-stream in the meadow, where we sat side by side and talked about the future."

For a few minutes Mrs. Arundel was quite silent. She abandoned herself for that brief interval to complete despair. It was all over. The bridegroom would cry off; insulted Major Lawford would come post-haste to Dangerfield, to annihilate this dismal widower, who did not know his own mind. All the shimmering fabrics —the gauzes, and laces, and silks, and velvets— that were in course of preparation in the upper chambers would become so much useless finery, to be hidden in out-of-the-way cupboards, and devoured by misanthropical moths—insect iconoclasts, who take a delight in destroying the decorations of the human temple.

Poor Mrs. Arundel took a mental photograph of all the complicated horrors of the situation. An offended father; a gentle, loving girl crushed like some broken lily; gossip, slander, misery of all kinds. And then the lady plucked up courage, and gave her recreant son a sound lecture, to the effect that his conduct was atrociously wicked; and that if this trusting young bride, this fair young second wife, were to be taken away from him as the first had been, such a calamity would only be a fitting judgment upon him for his folly.

But Edward told his mother very quietly that he had no intention of being false to his newly-plighted troth.

"I love Belinda," he said; "and I will be true to her, mother. But I can not forget the past. It hangs about me like a bad dream."

———

## CHAPTER XXXV.

### HOW THE TIDINGS WERE RECEIVED IN LINCOLN-SHIRE.

THE young widower made no further lamentation, but did his duty to his betrothed bride with a cheerful visage. Ah, what a pleasant journey it was to Belinda, that progress through London on the way to Lincolnshire! It was like that triumphant journey of last March, when the royal bridegroom led his Northern bride through a surging sea of eager, smiling faces, to the musical jangling of a thousand bells. If there were neither populace nor joy-bells on this occasion, I scarcely think Miss Lawford knew that those elements of a triumphal progress were missing. To her ears all the universe was musical with the sounds of mystic joy-bells; all the earth was glad with the brightness of happy faces. The railway-carriage, the commonplace vehicle, frouzy with the odor of wool and morocco, was like a fairy chariot, more wonderful than Queen Mab's; the white chalk-cutting in the hill was a shining cleft in a mountain of silver; the wandering streams were melted diamonds; the stations were enchanted castles. The pale sherry, carried in a pocket-flask, and sipped out of a little silver tumbler—there is apt to be a warm flatness about sherry taken out of pocket-flasks that is scarcely agreeable to the connoisseur—was like nectar newly brewed for the gods; even the anchovies in the sandwiches were like the enchanted fish in the Arabian story. A magical philter had been infused into the atmosphere: the flavor of first love was in every sight and sound.

Was ever bridegroom more indulgent, more devoted, than Edward Arundel? He sat at the counters of silk-mercers for the hour together, while Mrs. Arundel and the two girls deliberated over crisp fabrics unfolded for their inspection. He was always ready to be consulted, and gave his opinion upon the conflicting merits of peach color and pink, apple-green and maize, with unwearying attention. But sometimes, even while Belinda was smiling at him, with the rippling silken stuff held up in her white hands, and making a lustrous cascade upon the counter, the mystic hand plucked him back, and his mind wandered away to that childish bride who had chosen no splendid garments for her wedding, but had gone with him to the altar as trustfully as a baby goes in its mother's arms to the cradle. If he had been left alone with Belinda, with tender, sympathetic Belinda—who loved him well enough to understand him, and was always ready to take her cue from his face, and to be joyous or thoughtful according to his mood—it might have been better for him. But his mother and Letitia reigned paramount during this ante-nuptial week, and Mr. Arundel was scarcely suffered to take breath. He was hustled hither and thither in the hot summer noontide. He was taken to Howell and James's to choose a dressing-case for his bride; and he was made to look at glittering objects until his eyes ached, and he could see nothing but a bewildering dazzle of ormolu and silver-gilt. He was taken to a great emporium in Bond Street to select perfumery, and made to sniff at divers essences until his nostrils were unnaturally distended, and his olfactory nerves afflicted with temporary paralysis. There was jewelry of his mother's and of Belinda's mother's to be re-set; and the hymeneal victim was compelled to sit for an hour or so, blinking at fiery-crested serpents that were destined to coil up his wife's arms, and emerald padlocks that were to lie upon her breast. And then, when his soul was weary of glaring splendors and glittering confusions, they took him round the Park, in a whirlpool of diaphanous bonnets, and smiling faces, and brazen harness, and emblazoned hammer-cloths, on the margin of a river whose waters were like molten gold under the blazing sun. And then they gave him a seat in an opera-box, and the crash of a monster orchestra, blended with the hum of a thousand voices, to soothe his nerves withal.

But the more wearied this young man became with glitter, and dazzle, and sunshine, and silk-mercer's ware, the more surely his mind wandered back to the still meadows, and the limpid trout-stream, the sheltering hills, the solemn shadows of the cathedral, the distant voices of the rooks high up in the waving elms.

The bustle of preparation was over at last, and the bridal party went down to Lincolnshire. Pleasant chambers had been prepared at the Grange for Mr. Arundel and his mother and sister; and the bridegroom was received with enthusiasm by Belinda's blue-eyed younger sisters, who were enchanted to find that there was going to be a wedding, and that they were to have new frocks.

So Edward would have been a churl indeed had he seemed otherwise than happy, had he been any thing but devoted to the bright girl who loved him.

Tidings of the coming wedding flew like wildfire through Lincolnshire. Edward Arundel's romantic story had elevated him into a hero; all manner of reports had been circulated about his devotion to his lost young wife. He had sworn never to mingle in society again, people said. He had sworn never to have a new suit of clothes, or to have his hair cut, or to shave, or to eat a hot dinner. And Lincolnshire by no means approved of the defection implied by his approaching union with Belinda. He was only a commonplace widower after all, it seemed; ready to be consoled as soon as the ceremonious interval of decent grief was over. People had expected something better of him. They had expected to see him in a year or two with long gray hair, shabby clothes, and his beard upon his breast, prowling about the village of Kemberling, baited by little children. Lincolnshire was very much disappointed by the turn that affairs had taken. Shaksperian aphorisms were current among the gossips at comfortable tea-tables; and people talked about funeral baked meats, and the propriety of building churches if you have any ambitious desire that your memory should outlast your life, and other bitter observations, familiar to all admirers of the great dramatist.

But there were some people in Lincolnshire to whom the news of Edward Arundel's intended marriage was more welcome than the early Mayflowers to rustic children eager for a festival. Paul Marchmont heard the report, and rubbed his hands stealthily, and smiled to himself as he sat reading in the sunny western drawing-room. The good seed that he had sown that night at the Rectory had borne this welcome fruit. Edward Arundel with a young wife would not be very much less formidable than Edward Arundel single and discontented, prowling about the neighborhood of Marchmont Towers, and perpetually threatening vengeance upon Mary's cousin.

It was busy little Lavinia Weston who first brought her brother the tidings. He took both her hands in his, and kissed them in his enthusiasm.

"My best of sisters," he said, "you shall have a pair of diamond ear-rings for this."

"For only bringing you the news, Paul?"

"For only bringing me the news. When a messenger carries the tidings of a great victory to his king, the king makes him a knight upon the spot. This marriage is a victory to me, Lavinia. From to-day I shall breathe freely."

"But they are not married yet. Something may happen, perhaps, to prevent—"

"What should happen?" asked Paul, rather sharply. "By-the-by, it will be as well to keep this from Mrs. John," he added, thoughtfully; "though really now I fancy it matters very little what she hears."

He tapped his forehead lightly with his two slim fingers, and there was a horrible significance in the action.

"She is not likely to hear any thing," Mrs. Weston said; "she sees no one but Barbara Simmons."

"Then I should be glad if you would give Simmons a hint to hold her tongue. This news about the wedding would disturb her mistress."

"Yes, I'll tell her so. Barbara is a very excellent person. I can always manage Barbara. But, oh, Paul, I don't know what I'm to do with that poor weak-witted husband of mine."

"How do you mean?"

"Oh, Paul, I have had such a scene with him to-day. Such a scene! You remember the way he went on that day down in the boat-house when Edward Arundel came in upon us unexpectedly? Well, he's been going on as badly as that to-day, Paul—or worse, I really think."

Mr. Marchmont frowned, and flung aside his newspaper, with a gesture expressive of considerable vexation.

"Now, really, Lavinia, this is too bad," he said; "if your husband is a fool, I am not going to be bored about his folly. You have managed him for fifteen years: surely you can go on managing him now without annoying me about him? If Mr. George Weston doesn't know when he's well off, he's an ungrateful cur, and you may tell him so, with my compliments."

He picked up his newspaper again, and began to read. But Lavinia Weston, looking anxiously at her brother's face, saw that his pale auburn brows were contracted in a thoughtful frown; and that, if he read at all, the words upon which his eyes rested could convey very little meaning to his brain.

She was right; for presently he spoke to her, still looking at the page before him, and with an attempt at carelessness.

"Do you think that fellow would go to Australia, Lavinia?"

"Alone?" asked his sister.

"Yes, alone, of course," said Mr. Marchmont, putting down his paper, and looking at Mrs. Weston rather dubiously; "I don't want you to go to the antipodes; but if—if the fellow refused to go without you, I'd make it well worth your while to go out there, Lavinia. You shouldn't have any reason to regret obliging me, my dear girl."

The dear girl looked rather sharply at her affectionate brother.

"It's like your selfishness, Paul, to propose such a thing," she said, "after all I've done—"

"I have not been illiberal to you, Lavinia."

"No, you've been generous enough to me, I know, in the matter of gifts; but you're rich, Paul, and you can afford to give. I don't like the idea that you're so willing to pack me out of the way now that I can be no longer useful to you."

Mr. Marchmont shrugged his shoulders.

"For Heaven's sake, Lavinia, don't be sentimental. If there's one thing I despise more than another, it is this kind of mawkish sentimentality. You've been a very good sister to me, and I've been a very decent brother to you. If you have served me, I have made it answer your purpose to do so. I don't want you to go away. You may bring all your goods and chattels to this house to-morrow, if you like, and live at free quarters here for the rest of your existence. But if George Weston is a pig-headed brute, who can't understand upon which side his bread is buttered, he must be got out of the way somehow. I don't care what it costs me; but he must be got out of the way. I'm not going to live the life of a modern Damocles, with a blundering sword always dangling over my head, in the person of Mr. George Weston. And if the man objects to leave the country without you, why, I think your going with him would be only a sisterly act toward me. I hate selfishness, Lavinia, almost as much as I detest sentimentality."

Mrs. Weston was silent for some minutes, absorbed in reflection. Paul got up, kicked aside a foot-stool, and walked up and down the room with his hands in his pockets.

"Perhaps I might get George to leave England, if I promised to join him as soon as he was comfortably settled in the colonies," Mrs. Weston said, at last.

"Yes," cried Paul; "nothing could be more easy. I'll act very liberally toward him, Lavinia; I'll treat him well; but he shall not stay in England. No, Lavinia; after what you have told me to-day, I feel that he must be got out of the country."

Mr. Marchmont went to the door and looked out, to see if by chance any one had been listening to him. The coast was quite clear. The stone-paved hall looked as some undiscovered chamber in an Egyptian temple. The artist went back to Lavinia, and seated himself by her side. For some time the brother and sister talked together earnestly.

They settled every thing for poor hen-pecked George Weston. He was to sail for Sydney immediately. Nothing could be more easy than for Lavinia to declare that her brother had accidentally heard of some grand opening for a medical practitioner in the metropolis of the antipodes. The surgeon was to have a very handsome sum given him, and Lavinia would, *of course*, join him as soon as he was settled. Paul Marchmont even looked through the *Shipping*

*Gazette* in search of an Australian vessel which should speedily convey his brother-in-law to a distant shore.

Lavinia Weston went home armed with all necessary credentials. She was to promise almost any thing to her husband, provided that he gave his consent to an early departure.

———◆———

## CHAPTER XXXVI.

### MR. WESTON REFUSES TO BE PUT UPON.

UPON the 31st of June, the eve of Edward Arundel's wedding-day, Olivia Marchmont sat in her own room—the room that she had chiefly occupied ever since her husband's death—the study looking out into the quadrangle. She sat alone in that dismal chamber, dimly lighted by a pair of wax-candles, in tall, tarnished, silver candlesticks. There could be no greater contrast than that between this desolate woman and the master of the house. All about him was bright, and fresh, and glittering, and splendid; around her there was only ruin and decay, thickening dust, and gathering cobwebs—outward evidences of an inner wreck. John Marchmont's widow was of no importance in that household. The servants did not care to trouble themselves about her whims or wishes, nor to put her rooms in order. They no longer courtesied to her when they met her, wandering—with a purposeless step and listless feet that dragged along the ground—up and down the corridor, or out in the dreary quadrangles. *They knew that she was mad.* What was to be gained by any show of respect to her, whose brain was too weak to hold the memory of their conduct for five minutes together? Of all the cruel calamities that can befall humanity, surely this living death called madness is the worst.

Barbara Simmons only was faithful to her mistress with an unvarying fidelity. She made no boast of her devotion; she expected neither fee nor reward for her self-abnegation. That rigid religion of discipline which had not been strong enough to preserve Olivia's stormy soul from danger and ruin was at least all-sufficient for this lower type of woman. Barbara Simmons had been taught to do her duty, and she did it without question or complaint. As she went through rain, snow, hail, or sunshine twice every Sunday to Kemberling Church—as she sat upon a hard seat in an uncomfortable angle of the servants' pew, with the sharp edges of the wood-work cutting her thin shoulders, to listen patiently to dull rambling sermons upon the hardest texts of St. Paul—so she attended upon her mistress, submitting to every caprice, putting up with every hardship; because it was her duty to do so. The only relief she allowed herself was an hour's gossip now and then in the housekeeper's room; but she never alluded to her mistress's infirmities, nor would it have been safe for any other servant to have spoken lightly of Mrs. John Marchmont in stern Barbara's presence.

Upon this summer evening, when happy people were still lingering among the wild flowers in shady lanes, or in the dusky pathways by the quiet river, Olivia sat alone, staring at the candles.

K

Was there any thing in her mind, or was she only a human automaton slowly decaying into dust? There was no speculation in those large lustreless eyes fixed upon the dim light of the candles. But for all that the mind was not a blank. The pictures of the past, forever changing, like the scenes in some magic panorama, revolved before her. She had no memory· of that which had happened a quarter of an hour ago; but she could remember every word that Edward Arundel had said to her in the Rectory garden at Swampington—every intonation of the voice in which those words were spoken.

There was a tea-service on the table: an attenuated little silver tea-pot; a lopsided cream-jug, with thin worn edges and one dumpy little foot missing; and an antique dragon china cup and saucer with the gilding washed off. That meal, which is generally called social, has but a dismal aspect when it is only prepared for one. The solitary tea-cup, half filled with cold, stagnant tea, with a leaf or two floating upon the top, like weeds on the surface of a tideless pond; the tea-spoon thrown askew across a little pool of spilled milk in the tea-tray—looked as dreary as the ruins of a deserted city.

In the western drawing-room Paul was strolling backward and forward, talking to his mother and sisters, and admiring his pictures. He had spent a great deal of money upon art since taking possession of the Towers, and the western drawing-room was quite a different place to what it had been in John Marchmont's lifetime. Etty's divinities smiled through hazy draperies, more transparent than the summer vapors that float before the moon. Pearly-complexioned nymphs, with faces archly peeping round the corner of soft rosy shoulders, frolicked amidst the silver spray of classic fountains. Turner's Grecian temples glimmered through sultry summer mists; while glimpses of ocean sparkled here and there, and were as beautiful as if the artist's brush had been dipped in melted opals. Stanfield's breezy beaches made cool spots of freshness on the wall. Panting deer upon dizzy crags, amidst the misty Highlands, testified to the hand of Landseer. Low down, in the corners of the room, there lurked quaint cottage-scenes by Faed. Ward's patched and powdered beaux and beauties—a Rochester, in a light periwig; a Nell Gwynne, showing her white teeth across a basket of oranges—made a blaze of color upon the walls; and among all these glories of to-day there were prim Madonnas and stiff-necked angels by Raphael and Tintoretto; a brown-faced grinning boy by Murillo (no collection ever was complete without that inevitable brown-faced boy); an obese Venus, by the great Peter Paul; and a pale Charles the First, with martyrdom foreshadowed in his pensive face, by Vandyke.

Paul Marchmont contemplated his treasures complacently as he strolled about the room, with his coffee-cup in his hand; while his mother watched him admiringly from her comfortable cushioned nest at one end of a luxurious sofa.

"Well, mother," Mr. Marchmont said, presently, "let people say what they may of me, they can never say that I have used my money badly. When I am dead and gone these pictures will remain to speak for me; posterity will say, 'At any rate, the fellow was a man of taste.' Now

what, in Heaven's name, could that miserable little Mary have done with eleven thousand a year, if—if she had lived to enjoy it?"

The minute-hand of the little clock in Mrs. John Marchmont's study was creeping slowly toward the quarter before eleven, when Olivia was aroused suddenly from that long reverie, in which the images of the past had shone upon her across the dull stagnation of the present, like the domes and minarets in a Phantasm City gleaming athwart the barren desert sands.

She was aroused by a cautious tap upon the outside of her window. She got up, opened the window, and looked out. The night was dark and starless, and there was a faint whisper of wind among the trees, that sounded like the presage of a storm.

"Don't be frightened," whispered a timid voice; "it's only me, George Weston. I want to talk to you, Mrs. John. I've got something particular to tell you—awful particular; but they mustn't hear it; they mustn't know I'm here. I came round this way on purpose. You can let me in at the little door in the lobby, can't you, Mrs. John? I tell you I must tell you what I've got to tell you," cried Mr. Weston, indifferent to tautology in his excitement. "Do let me in, there's a dear good soul. The little door in the lobby, you know; it's locked, you know, but the key ain't taken away, I dessay."

"The door in the lobby?" repeated Olivia, in a dreamy voice.

"Yes, you know. Do let me in now, that's a good creature. It's awful particular, I tell you. It's about Edward Arundel."

Edward Arundel! The sound of that name seemed to act upon the woman's shattered nerves like a stroke of electricity. The drooping head reared itself erect. The eyes, so lustreless before, flashed fire from their sombre depths. Comprehension, animation, energy returned, as suddenly as if the wand of an enchanter had summoned the dead back to life.

"Edward Arundel!" she cried, in a clear voice, that was utterly unlike the dull deadness of her usual tones.

"Hush!" whispered Mr. Weston; "don't speak loud, for goodness gracious sake. I dessay there's all manner of spies about. Let me in, and I'll tell you every thing."

"Yes, yes; I'll let you in. The door by the lobby—I understand; come, come."

Olivia disappeared from the window. The lobby of which the surgeon had spoken was close to her own apartment. She found the key in the lock of the door. The place was dark; she opened the door almost noiselessly, and Mr. Weston crept in on tip-toe. He followed Olivia into the study, closed the door behind him, and drew a long breath.

"I've got in," he said; "and now I am in, wild horses shouldn't hold me from speaking my mind, much less Paul Marchmont."

He turned the key in the door as he spoke, and, even as he did so, glanced rather suspiciously toward the window. To his mind the very atmosphere of that house was pervaded by the presence of his brother-in-law.

"Oh, Mrs. John!" exclaimed the surgeon, in piteous accents, "the way that I've been put upon! You've been put upon, Mrs. John, but you don't seem to mind it; and perhaps it's better to bring one's self to that, if one can; but I can't. I've tried to bring myself to it; I've even taken to drinking, Mrs. John, much as it goes against me; and I've tried to drown my feelings as a man in rum-and-water. But the more spirits I consume, Mrs. John, the more of a man I feel."

Mr. Weston struck the top of his hat with his clenched fist, and stared fiercely at Olivia, breathing very hard, and breathing rum-and-water with a faint odor of lemon-peel.

"Edward Arundel!—what about Edward Arundel?" said Olivia, in a low, eager voice.

"I'm coming to that, Mrs. John, in due c'ourse," returned Mr. Weston, with an air of dignity that was superior even to hiccough. "What I say, Mrs. John," he added, in a confidential and argumentative tone, "is this: I won't be put upon!" Here his voice sank to an awful whisper, "Of course it's pleasant enough to have one's rent provided for, and not to be kept awake by poor's rates, Mrs. John; but, good gracious me! I'd rather have the Queen's taxes and the poor-rates following me up day and night, and a man in possession to provide for at every meal—and you don't know how contemptuous a man in possession can look at you if you offer him salt butter, or your table in a general way don't meet his views—than the conscience I've had since Paul Marchmont came into Lincolnshire. I feel, Mrs. John, as if I'd committed oceans of murders. It's a miracle to me that my hair hasn't turned white before this; and it would have done it, Mrs. J., if it wasn't of that stubborn nature which is too wiry to give expression to a man's sufferings. Oh, Mrs. John, when I think how my pangs of conscience have been made game of—when I remember the insulting names I have been called, because my heart didn't happen to be made of adamant, my blood boils; it boils, Mrs. John, to that degree that I feel the time has come for action. I have been put upon until the spirit of manliness within me blazes up like a fiery furnace. I've been trodden upon, Mrs. John; but I'm not the worm they took me for. To-day they've put the finisher upon it." The surgeon paused to take breath. His mild and sheep-like countenance was flushed; his fluffy eyebrows twitched convulsively in his endeavors to give expression to the violence of his feelings. "To-day they've put the finisher upon it," he repeated. "I'm to go to Australia, am I? Ha! ha! we'll see about that. There's a nice opening in the medical line, is there? and dear Paul will provide the funds to start me! Ha! ha! two can play at that game. It's all brotherly kindness, of course, and friendly interest in my welfare— that's what it's called, Mrs. J. Shall I tell you what it is? I'm to be got rid of, at any price, for fear my conscience should get the better of me, and I should speak. I've been made a tool of. and I've been put upon; but they've been obliged to trust me. I've got a conscience, and I don't suit their views. If I hadn't got a conscience, I might stop here and have my rent and taxes provided for, and riot in rum-and-water to the end of my days. But I've a conscience that all the pine-apple rum in Jamaica wouldn't drown, and they're frightened of me."

Olivia had listened to all this with an impa-

tient frown upon her face. I doubt if she knew the meaning of Mr. Weston's complaints. She had been listening only for the one name that had power to transform her from a breathing automaton into a living, thinking, reasoning woman. She grasped the surgeon's wrist fiercely.

"You told me· you came here to speak about Edward Arundel," she said. "Have you been only trying to make a fool of me?"

"No, Mrs. John; I have come to speak about him, and I come to you, because I think you're not so bad as Paul Marchmont. I think that you've been a tool, like myself; and they've led you on, step by step, from bad to worse, pretty much as they have led me. You're·Edward Arundel's blood-relation, and it's your business to look to any wrong that's done him more than it is mine. But if you don't speak, Mrs. John, Edward Arundel is going to be married."

"Going to be married!" The words burst from Olivia's lips in a kind of shriek, and she stood glaring hideously at the surgeon, with her lips apart and her eyes dilated. Mr. Weston was fascinated by the horror of that gaze, and stared at her in silence for some moments. "You are a madman!" she exclaimed, after a pause; "you are a madman! Why do you come here with your idiotic fancies? Surely my life is miserable enough without this!"

"I ain't mad, Mrs. John, any more than—" Mr. Weston was going to say, "than you are;" but it struck him that, under existing circumstances, the comparison might be ill-advised— "I ain't any madder than other people," he said, presently. "Edward Arundel is going to be married. I have seen the young lady in Kemberling with her Pa; and she's a very sweet young woman to look at; and her name's Belinda Lawford; and the wedding is to be at eleven o'clock to-morrow morning at Hillingsworth Church."

Olivia slowly lifted her hands to her head, and swept the loose hair away from· her brow. All the mists that had obscured her brain melted slowly away, and showed her the past as it had really been in all its naked horror. Yes; step by step the cruel hand had urged her on from bad to worse; from bad to worse; until it had driven her here. ¹

It was for this that she had sold her soul to the powers of hell. It was for this that she had helped to torture that innocent girl whom a dying father had given into her pitiless hand. For this! For this! To find at last that all her iniquity had been wasted, and that Edward Arundel had chosen another bride—fairer, perhaps, than the first. The mad, unholy jealousy of her nature awoke from the obscurity of mental decay, a fierce ungovernable spirit. But another spirit arose in the next moment. Conscience, which so long had slumbered, awoke, and cried to her, in an awful voice, "Sinner, whose sin has been wasted, repent! restore! It is not yet too late."

The stern precepts of her religion came back to her. She had rebelled against those rigid laws, she had cast off those iron fetters, only to fall into a worse bondage; only to submit to a stronger tyranny. She had been a servant of the God of Sacrifice, and had rebelled when an offering was demanded of her. She had cast off the yoke of her Master, and had yielded herself up the slave of sin. And now, when she discovered whither her chains had dragged her, she was seized with a sudden panic, and wanted to go back to her old Master.

She stood for some minutes with her open palms pressed upon her forehead, and her chest heaving as if a stormy sea had raged in her bosom.

"This marriage must not take place," she cried, at last.

"Of course it mustn't," answered Mr. Weston; "didn't I say so just now? And if you don't speak to Paul and prevent it, I will. I'd rather you spoke to him, though," added the surgeon, thoughtfully; "because, you see, it would come better from you, wouldn't it now?"

Olivia Marchmont did not answer. Her hands had dropped from her head, and she was standing looking at the floor.

"There shall be no marriage," she muttered, with a wild laugh. "There's another heart to be broken—that's all. Stand aside, man," she cried; "stand aside, and let me go to him; let me go to him."

She pushed the terrified surgeon out of her pathway, unlocked the door, hurried along the passage and across the hall. She opened the door of the western drawing-room and went in.

Mr. Weston stood in the corridor looking after her. He waited for a few minutes, listening for any sound that might come from the western drawing-room. But the wide stone hall was between him and that apartment; and however loudly the voices might have been uplifted no breath of them could have reached the surgeon's ear. He waited for about five minutes, and then crept into the lobby and let himself out into the quadrangle.

"At any rate, nobody can say that I'm a coward," he thought complacently, as he went under a stone archway that led into the park. "But what a whirlwind that woman is! O my gracious, what a perfect whirlwind she is!"

---

## CHAPTER XXXVII.

### "GOING TO BE MARRIED!"

PAUL MARCHMONT was still strolling hither and thither about the room, admiring his pictures, and smiling to himself at the recollection of the easy manner in which he had obtained George Weston's consent to the Australian arrangement. For in his sober moments the surgeon was ready to submit to any thing his wife and brother-in-law imposed upon him. It was only under the influence of pine-apple rum that his manhood asserted itself. Paul was still contemplating his pictures when Olivia burst into the room; but Mrs. Marchmont and her invalid daughter had retired for the night, and the artist was alone — alone with his own thoughts, which were rather of a triumphal and agreeable character just now; for Edward's marriage and Mr. Weston's departure were equally pleasant to him.

He was startled a little by Olivia's abrupt entrance, for it was not her habit to intrude upon him or any member of that household; on the contrary, she had shown an obstinate determination to shut herself up in her own room, and to avoid every living creature except her servant Barbara Simmons.

Paul turned and confronted her very deliberately, and with the smile that was almost habitual to him upon his thin, pale lips. Her sudden appearance had blanched his face a little; but beyond this he betrayed no sign of agitation.

"My dear Mrs. Marchmont, you quite startle me. It is so very unusual to see you here, and at this hour especially."

It did not seem as if she had heard his voice. She went sternly up to him, with her thin listless arms hanging at her side, and her haggard eyes fixed upon his face.

"Is this true?" she asked.

He started a little, in spite of himself; for he understood in a moment what she meant. Some one, it scarcely mattered who, had told her of the coming marriage.

"Is what true, my dear Mrs. John?" he said, carelessly.

"Is this true that George Weston tells me?" she cried, laying her thin hand upon his shoulder. Her wasted fingers closed involuntarily upon the collar of his coat, her thin lips contracted into a ghastly smile, and a sudden fire kindled in her eyes. A strange sensation awoke in the tips of those tightening fingers, and thrilled through every vein of the woman's body—such a horrible thrill as vibrates along the nerves of a monomaniac, when the sight of a dreadful terror in his victim's face first arouses the murderous impulse in his breast.

Paul's face whitened as he felt the thin finger-points tightening upon his neck. He was afraid of Olivia.

"My dear Mrs. John, what is it you want of me?" he said, hastily. "Pray do not be violent."

"I am not violent."

She dropped her hand from his breast. It was true, she was not violent. Her voice was low; her hand fell loosely by her side. But Paul was frightened of her, nevertheless; for he saw that if she was not violent, she was something worse—she was dangerous.

"Did George Weston tell me truth just now?" she said.

Paul bit his nether lip savagely. George Weston had tricked him, then, after all, and had communicated with this woman. But what of that? She would scarcely be likely to trouble herself about this business of Edward Arundel's marriage. She must be past any such folly as that. She would not dare to interfere in the matter. She could not.

"Is it true?" she said; "is it? Is it true that Edward Arundel is going to be married to-morrow?"

She waited, looking with fixed, widely-opened eyes at Paul's face.

"My dear Mrs. John, you take me so completely by surprise that I—"

"That you have not got a lying answer ready for me," said Olivia, interrupting him. "You need not trouble yourself to invent one. I see that George Weston told me the truth. There was reality in his words. There is nothing but falsehood in yours."

Paul stood looking at her, but not listening to her. Let her abuse and upbraid him to her heart's content; it gave him leisure to reflect, and plan his course of action; and perhaps these bitter words might exhaust the fire within her, and leave her malleable to his skillful hands once more. He had time to think this, and to settle his own line of conduct while Olivia was speaking to him. It was useless to deny the marriage. She had heard of it from George Weston, and she might hear of it from any one else whom she chose to interrogate. It was useless to try to stifle this fact.

"Yes, Mrs. John," he said, "it is quite true. Your cousin, Mr. Arundel, is going to marry Belinda Lawford; a very lucky thing for us, believe me, as it will put an end to all questioning and watching and suspicion, and place us beyond all danger."

Olivia looked at him, with her bosom heaving, her breath growing shorter and louder with every word he spoke.

"You mean to let this be, then?" she said, when he had finished speaking.

"To let what be?"

"This marriage. You will let it take place?"

"Most certainly. Why should I prevent it?"

"Why should you prevent it?" she cried, fiercely; and then, in an altered voice, in tones of anguish, that were like a wail of despair, she exclaimed, "O my God! my God! what a dupe I have been; what a miserable tool in this man's hands! O my offended God! why didst Thou so abandon me, when I turned away from Thee, and made Edward Arundel the idol of my wicked heart?"

Paul sank into the nearest chair, with a faint sigh of relief.

"She will wear herself out," he thought, "and then I shall be able to do what I like with her."

But Olivia turned to him again while he was thinking this.

"Do you imagine that I will let this marriage take place?" she asked.

"I do not think you will be so mad as to prevent it. That little mystery which you and I have arranged between us is not exactly child's play, Mrs. John. We can neither of us afford to betray the other. Let Edward Arundel marry, and work for his wife, and be happy; nothing could be better for us than his marriage. Indeed, we have every reason to be thankful to Providence for the turn that affairs have taken," Mr. Marchmont concluded, piously.

"Indeed!" said Olivia; "and Edward Arundel is to have another bride. He is to be happy with another wife; and I am to hear of their happiness, to see him some day, perhaps, sitting by her side and smiling at her, as I have seen him smile at Mary Marchmont. He is to be happy, and I am to know of his happiness. Another baby-faced girl is to glory in the knowledge of his love; and I am to be quiet—I am to be quiet. Is it for this that I have sold my soul to you, Paul Marchmont? Is it for this I have shared your guilty secrets? Is it for this I have heard her feeble wailing sounding in my wretched feverish slumbers, as I have heard it every night since the day she left this house? Do you remember what you said to me? Do you remember how it was you tempted me? Do you remember how you played upon my misery, and traded on the tortures of my jealous heart? 'He

has despised your love,' you said: 'will you consent to see him happy with another woman?' That was your argument, Paul Marchmont. You allied yourself with the devil that held possession of my breast, and together you were too strong for me. I was set apart to be damned, and you were the chosen instrument of my damnation. You bought my soul, Paul Marchmont. You shall not cheat me of the price for which I sold it. You shall hinder this marriage."

"You are a mad woman, Mrs. John Marchmont, or you would not propose any such thing."

"Go," she said, pointing to the door; "go to Edward Arundel, and do something, no matter what, to prevent this marriage."

"I shall do nothing of the kind."

He had heard that a monomaniac was always to be subdued by indomitable resolution, and he looked at Olivia, thinking to tame her by his unfaltering glance. He might about as well have tried to look the raging sea into calmness.

"I am not a fool, Mrs. John Marchmont," he said, "and I shall do nothing of the kind."

He had risen, and stood by the lamp-lit table, trifling rather nervously with its elegant litter of delicately-bound books, jeweled-handled paper-knives, newly-cut periodicals, and pretty womanly toys collected by the women of the household.

The faces of the two were nearly upon a level as they stood opposite to each other, with only the table between them.

"Then I will prevent it!" Olivia cried, turning toward the door.

Paul Marchmont saw the resolution stamped upon her face. She would do what she threatened. He ran to the door and had his hand upon the lock before she could reach it.

"No, Mrs. John," he said, standing at the door, with his back turned to Olivia, and his fingers busy with the bolts and key. In spite of himself, this woman had made him a little nervous, and it was as much as he could do to find the handle of the key. "No, no, my dear Mrs. John; you shall not leave this house, nor this room, in your present state of mind. If you choose to be violent and unmanageable, we will give you the full benefit of your violence, and we will give you a better sphere of action. A padded room will be more suitable to your present temper, my dear madam. If you favor us with this sort of conduct, we will find people more fitted to restrain you."

He said all this in a sneering tone, that had a trifling tremulousness in it, while he locked the door, and assured himself that it was safely secured. Then he turned, prepared to fight the battle out somehow or other.

At the very moment of his turning there was a sudden crash, a shiver of broken glass, and the cold night wind blew into the room. One of the long French windows was wide open, and Olivia Marchmont was gone.

He was out upon the terrace in the next moment; but even then he was too late, for he could not see her right or left of him upon the long stone platform. There were three separate flights of steps, three different paths, widely diverging across the broad grassy flat before Marchmont Towers. She might have gone either way. There was the great porch, and all manner of stone abutments along the grim façade of the house. She might have concealed herself behind any one of them. The night was hopelessly dark. A pair of handsome bronze lamps, which Paul had placed before the principal doorway, only made two spots of light in the gloom. He ran along the terrace, looking into every nook and corner which might have served as a hiding-place; but he did not find Olivia.

She had left the house with the avowed intention of doing something to prevent the marriage. What would she do? What course would this desperate woman take in her jealous rage? Would she go straight to Edward Arundel and tell him—

Yes; this was most likely; for how else could she hope to prevent the marriage?

Paul stood quite still upon the terrace for a few minutes, thinking. There was only one course for him. To try and find Olivia would be next to hopeless. There were half a dozen outlets from the park. There were ever so many different pathways through the woody labyrinth at the back of the Towers. This woman might have taken any one of them. To waste the night in searching for her would be worse than useless.

There was only one thing to be done. He must counter-check this desperate creature's movements.

He went back to the drawing-room, shut the window, and then rang the bell.

There were not many of the old servants who had waited upon John Marchmont at the Towers now. The man who answered the bell was a person whom Paul had brought down from London.

"Get the chestnut saddled for me, Peterson," said Mr. Marchmont. "My poor cousin's widow has left the house, and I am going after her. She has given me very great alarm to-night by her conduct. I tell you this in confidence; but you can say as much to Mrs. Simmons, who knows more about her mistress than I do. See that there's no time lost in saddling the chestnut. I want to overtake this unhappy woman if I can. Go and give the order, and then bring me my hat."

The man went away to obey his master. Paul walked to the chimney-piece and looked at the clock.

"They'll be gone to bed at the Grange," he thought to himself. "Will she go there and knock them up, I wonder? Does she know that Edward's there? I doubt that; but yet Weston may have told her. At any rate, I can be there before her. It would take her a long time to get there on foot. I think I did the right thing in saying what I said to Peterson. I must have the report of her madness spread every where. I must face it out. But how—but how? So long as she was quiet I could manage every thing. But with her against me, and George Weston—oh, the cur, the white-hearted villain, after all that I've done for him and Lavinia! But what can a man expect when he's obliged to put his trust in a fool?"

He went to the window, and stood there looking out until he saw the groom coming along the gravel roadway below the terrace, leading a horse by the bridle. Then he put on the hat that the servant had brought him, ran down the steps, and got into the saddle.

"All right, Jeffreys," he said; "tell them

not to expect me back till to-morrow morning. Let Mrs. Simmons sit up for her mistress. Mrs. John may return at any hour in the night."

He galloped away along the smooth carriage-drive. At the lodge he stopped to inquire if any one had been through that way. No, the woman said; she had opened the gates for no one. Paul had expected no other answer. There was a footpath that led to a little wicket-gate opening on the high-road; and of course Olivia had chosen that way, which was a good deal shorter than the carriage-drive.

---

## CHAPTER XXXVIII.

### THE TURNING OF THE TIDE.

It was past two o'clock in the morning of the day which had been appointed for Edward Arundel's wedding, when Paul Marchmont drew rein before the white gate that divided Major Lawford's garden from the high-road. There was no lodge, no pretense of grandeur here. An old-fashioned garden surrounded an old-fashioned red-brick house. There was an apple-orchard upon one side of the low white gate, and a flower-garden, with a lawn and fish-pond, upon the other. The carriage-drive wound sharply round to a shallow flight of steps, and a broad door with a narrow window upon each side of it.

Paul got off his horse at the gate, and went in, leading the animal by the bridle. He was a cockney heart and soul, and had no sense of any enjoyments that were not of a cockney nature. So the horse he had selected for himself was any thing but a fiery creature. He liked plenty of bone and very little blood in the steed he rode, and was contented to go at a comfortable jog-trot, seven-miles-an-hour pace, along the wretched country roads.

There was a row of old-fashioned wooden posts, with iron chains swinging between them, upon both sides of the doorway. Paul fastened the horse's bridle to one of these, and went up the steps. He rang a bell that went clanging and jangling through the house in the stillness of the summer night. All the way along the road he had looked right and left, expecting to pass Olivia; but he had seen no sign of her. This was nothing, however; for there were by-ways by which she might come from Marchmont Towers to Lawford Grange.

"I must be before her, at any rate," Paul thought to himself, as he waited patiently for an answer to his summons.

The time seemed very long to him, of course; but at last he saw a light glimmering through the mansion windows, and heard a shuffling foot in the hall. Then the door was opened very cautiously, and a woman's scared face peered out at Mr. Marchmont through the opening.

"What is it?" the woman asked, in a frightened voice.

"It is I, Mr. Marchmont, of Marchmont Towers. Your master knows me. Mr. Arundel is here, is he not?"

"Yes, and Mrs. Arundel too; but they're all abed."

"Never mind that. I must see Major Lawford immediately."

"But they're all abed.'♦
"Never mind that, my good woman; I tell you I must see him."
"But won't to-morrow mornin' do? It's near three o'clock, and to-morrow's our eldest miss's weddin'-day; and they're all abed."
"I *must* see your master. For mercy's sake, my good woman, do what I tell you. Go and call up Major Lawford—you can do it quietly—and tell him I must speak to him at once."

The woman, with the chain of the door still between her and Mr. Marchmont, took a timid survey of Paul's face. She had heard of him often enough, but had never seen him before, and she was rather doubtful as to his identity. She knew that thieves and robbers resorted to all sorts of tricks in the course of their evil vocation. Mightn't this application for admittance in the dead of the night be only a part of some burglarious plot against the spoons and forks, and that hereditary silver urn with lions' heads holding rings in their mouths for handles, the fame of which had no doubt circulated throughout all Lincolnshire? Mr. Marchmont had neither a black mask nor a dark-lantern, and to Martha Philpot's mind these were essential attributes of the legitimate burglar; but he might be burglariously disposed, nevertheless, and it would be well to be on the safe side.

"I'll go and tell 'em," the discreet Martha said, civilly; "but perhaps you won't mind my leaving the chain oop. It ain't like as if it was winter," she added, apologetically.

"You may shut the door if you like," answered Paul; "only be quick and wake your master. You can tell him that I want to see him upon a matter of life and death."

Martha hurried away, and Paul stood upon the broad stone steps waiting for her return. Every moment was precious to him, for he wanted to be beforehand with Olivia. He had no thought except that she would come straight to the Grange to see Edward Arundel; unless, indeed, she was by any chance ignorant of his whereabouts.

Presently the light appeared again in the narrow windows, and this time a man's foot sounded upon the stone-flagged hall. This time, too, Martha let down the chain, and opened the door wide enough for Mr. Marchmont to enter. She had no fear of burglarious marauders now that the valiant Major was at her elbow.

"Mr. Marchmont," exclaimed the old soldier, opening a door leading into a little study, "you'll excuse me if I seem rather bewildered by your visit. When an old fellow like me is called up in the middle of the night he can't be expected to have his wits about him just at first. Martha, bring us a light. Sit down, Mr. Marchmont. There's a chair at your elbow there. And now may I ask the reason—"

"The reason I've disturbed you in this abrupt manner. The occasion that brings me here is a very painful one; but I believe that my coming may save you and yours from much annoyance."

"Save us from annoyance! Really, my dear Sir, you—"

"I mystify you for the moment, no doubt," Paul interposed, blandly; "but if you will have a little patience with me, Major Lawford, I think I can make every thing very clear—

only too painfully clear. You have heard of my relative, Mrs. John Marchmont—my cousin's widow?"

"I have," answered the Major, gravely.

The dark scandals that had been current about wretched Olivia Marchmont came into his mind with the mention of her name, and the memory of those miserable slanders overshadowed his frank face.

Paul waited while Martha brought in a smoky lamp, with the half-lighted wick sputtering and struggling in its oily socket. Then he went on, in a calm, dispassionate voice, which seemed the voice of a benevolent Christian, sublimely remote from other people's sorrows, but tenderly pitiful of suffering humanity, nevertheless.

"You have heard of my unhappy cousin. You have no doubt heard that she is—mad?"

He dropped his voice into so low a whisper that he only seemed to shape this last word with his thin, flexible lips.

"I have heard some rumor to that effect," the Major answered; "that is to say, I have heard that Mrs. John Marchmont has lately become eccentric in her habits."

"It has been my dismal task to watch the slow decay of a very powerful intellect," continued Paul. "When I first came to Marchmont Towers, about the time of my cousin Mary's unfortunate elopement with Mr. Arundel, that mental decay had already set in. Already the compass of Olivia Marchmont's mind had become reduced to a monotone, and the one dominant thought was doing its ruinous work. It was my fate to find the clew to that sad decay; it was my fate very speedily to discover the nature of that all-absorbing thought which, little by little, had grown into monomania."

Major Lawford stared at his visitor's face. He was a plain-spoken man, and could scarcely see his way clearly through all this obscurity of fine words.

"You mean to say you found out what had driven your cousin's widow mad?" he said, bluntly.

"You put the question very plainly, Major Lawford. Yes; I discovered the secret of my unhappy relative's morbid state of mind. That secret lies in the fact, that for the last ten years Olivia Marchmont has cherished a hopeless affection for her cousin, Mr. Edward Arundel."

The Major almost bounded off his chair in horrified surprise.

"Good gracious!" he exclaimed; "you surprise me, Mr. Marchmont, and—and—rather ∙ unpleasantly."

"I should never have revealed this secret to you or to any other living creature, Major Lawford, had not circumstances compelled me to do so. As far as Mr. Arundel is concerned, I can set your mind quite at ease. He has chosen to insult me very grossly; but let that pass. I must do him the justice to state that I believe him to have been from first to last utterly ignorant of the state of his cousin's mind."

"I hope so, Sir; egad, I hope so!" exclaimed the Major, rather fiercely. "If I thought that this young man had trifled with the lady's affection; if I thought—"

"You need think nothing to the detriment of Mr. Arundel," answered Paul, with placid politeness, "except that he is hot-headed, obstinate, and foolish. He is a young man of excellent principles, and has never fathomed the secret of his cousin's conduct toward him. I am rather a close observer—something of a student of human nature—and I have watched this unhappy woman. She loves, and has loved, her cousin Edward Arundel; and hers is one of those concentrative natures in which a great passion is near akin to a monomania. It was this hopeless, unreturned affection that embittered her character, and made her a harsh step-mother to my poor cousin Mary. For a long time this wretched woman has been very quiet; but her tranquillity has been only a deceitful calm. To-night the storm broke. Olivia Marchmont heard of the marriage that is to take place to-morrow; and, for the first time, a state of melancholy mania developed into absolute violence. She came to me, and attacked me upon the subject of this intended marriage. She accused me of having plotted to give Edward Arundel another bride; and then, after exhausting herself by a torrent of passionate invective against me, against her cousin Edward, your daughter—every one concerned in to-morrow's event—this wretched woman rushed out of the house in a jealous fury, declaring that she would do something—no matter what—to hinder the celebration of Edward Arundel's second marriage."

"Good Heavens!" gasped the Major. "And you mean to say—"

"I mean to say, that there is no knowing what may be attempted by a mad woman, driven mad by a jealousy in itself almost as terrible as madness. Olivia Marchmont has sworn to hinder your daughter's marriage. What has not been done by unhappy creatures in this woman's state of mind? Every day we read of such things in the newspapers—deeds of horror at which the blood grows cold in our veins; and we wonder that Heaven can permit such misery. It is not any frivolous motive that brings me here in the dead of the night, Major Lawford. I come to tell you that a desperate woman has sworn to hinder to-morrow's marriage. Heaven knows what she may do in her jealous frenzy. She may attack your daughter."

The father's face grew pale. His Linda, his darling, exposed to the fury of a mad woman! He could conjure up the scene: the fair girl clinging to her lover's breast, and desperate Olivia Marchmont swooping down upon her like an angry tigress.

"For mercy's sake, tell me what I am to do, Mr. Marchmont!" cried the Major. "God bless you, Sir, for bringing me this warning. But what am I to do? What do you advise? Shall we postpone the wedding?"

"On no account. All you have to do is to keep this wretched woman at bay. Shut your doors upon her. Do not let her be admitted to this house upon any pretense whatever. Get the wedding over an hour earlier than has been intended, if it is possible for you to do so, and hurry the bride and bridegroom away upon the first stages of their wedding-tour. If you wish to escape all the wretchedness of a public scandal, avoid seeing this woman."

"I will, I will," answered the bewildered Major. "It's a most awful situation. My poor Belinda! Her wedding-day! And a mad woman to attempt— Upon my word, Mr. March-

mont, I don't know how to thank you for the trouble you have taken."

"Don't speak of that. This woman is my cousin's widow: any shame of hers is disgrace to me. Avoid seeing her. If by any chance she does contrive to force herself upon you, turn a deaf ear to all she may say. She horrified me to-night by her mad assertions. Be prepared for any thing she may declare. She is possessed by all manner of delusions, remember, and may make the most ridiculous assertions. There is no limit to her hallucinations. She may offer to bring Edward Arundel's dead wife from the grave, perhaps. But you will not, on any account, allow her to obtain access to your daughter."

"No, no; on no account. My poor Belinda! I am very grateful to you, Mr. Marchmont, for this warning. You'll stop here for the rest of the night? Martha's beds are always aired. You'll accept the shelter of our spare room until to-morrow morning!"

"You are very good, Major Lawford; but I must hurry away directly. Remember that I am quite ignorant as to where my unhappy relative may be wandering at this hour of the night. She may have returned to the Towers. Her jealous fury may have exhausted itself; and in that case I have exaggerated the danger. But, at any rate, I thought it best to give you this warning."

"Most decidedly, my dear Sir; I thank you from the bottom of my heart. But you'll take something—wine, tea, brandy-and-water—eh?"

Paul had put on his hat and made his way into the hall by this time. There was no affectation in his eagerness to be away. He glanced uneasily toward the door every now and then while the Major was offering hospitable hindrance to his departure. He was very pale, with a haggard, ashen pallor that betrayed his anxiety, in spite of his bland calmness of manner.

"You are very kind. No; I will get away at once. I have done my duty here; I must now try and do what I can for this wretched woman. Good-night. Remember; shut your doors upon her."

He unfastened the bridle of his horse, mounted, and rode away slowly, so long as there was any chance of the horse's tread being heard at the Grange. But when he was a quarter of a mile away from Major Lawford's house, he urged the horse into a gallop. He had no spurs; but he used his whip with a ruthless hand, and went off at a tearing pace along a narrow lane, where the ruts were deep.

He rode for fifteen miles; and it was gray morning when he drew rein at a dilapidated five-barred gate leading into the great, tenantless yard of an uninhabited farm-house. The place had been unlet for some years; and the farm was in the charge of a hind in Mr. Marchmont's service. The hind lived in a cottage at the other extremity of the farm; and Paul had erected new buildings, with engine-houses and complicated machinery for pumping the water off the low-lying lands. Thus it was that the old farm-house and the old farm-yard were suffered to fall into decay. The empty sties, the ruined barns and outhouses, the rotting straw, and pools of rank corruption, made this tenantless farm-yard the very abomination of desolation. Paul Marchmont opened the gate and went in. He picked his way very cautiously through the mud and filth, leading his horse by the bridle till he came to an outhouse, where he secured the animal. Then he picked his way across the yard, lifted the rusty latch of a narrow wooden door set in a plastered wall, and went into a dismal stone court, where one lonely hen was moulting in miserable solitude.

Long rank grass grew in the interstices of the flags. The lonely hen set up a roopy cackle, and fluttered into a corner at sight of Paul Marchmont. There were some rabbit-hutches, tenantless; a dove-cote, empty; a dog-kennel, and a broken chain rusting slowly in a pool of water, but no dog. The court-yard was at the back of the house, looked down upon by a range of latticed windows, some with closed shutters, others with shutters swinging in the wind, as if they had been fain to beat themselves to death in very desolation of spirit.

Mr. Marchmont opened a door and went into the house. There were empty cellars and pantries, dairies and sculleries, right and left of him. The rats and mice scuttled away at sound of the intruder's footfall. The spiders ran upon the damp-stained walls, and the disturbed cobwebs floated slowly down from the cracked ceilings and tickled Mr. Marchmont's face.

Further on in the interior of the gloomy habitation Paul found a great stone-paved kitchen, at the darkest end of which there was a rusty grate, in which a minimum of flame struggled feebly with a maximum of smoke. An open oven-door revealed a dreary black cavern; and the very manner of the rusty door, and loose, half-broken handle, was an advertisement of incapacity for any homely hospitable use. Pale, sickly fungi had sprung up in clusters at the corners of the damp hearth-stone. Spiders and rats, damp and cobwebs, every sign by which Decay writes its name upon the dwelling man has deserted, had set its separate mark upon this ruined place.

Paul Marchmont looked round him with a contemptuous shudder. He called "Mrs. Brown! Mrs. Brown!" two or three times, each time waiting for an answer; but none came, and Mr. Marchmont passed on into another room.

Here at least there was some poor pretense of comfort. The room was in the front of the house, and the low latticed window looked out upon a neglected garden, where some tall fox-gloves reared their gaudy heads among the weeds. Across the garden there was a stout brick wall, with pear-trees trained against it, and dragon's-mouth and wall-flower waving in the morning breeze.

There was a bed in this room, empty; an easy-chair near the window; near that a little table, and a *set of Indian chessmen.* Upon the bed there were some garments scattered, as if but lately flung there; and upon the floor, near the fire-place, there were the fragments of a child's first toys—a tiny trumpet, bought at some village fair, a baby's rattle, and a broken horse.

Paul Marchmont looked about him; a little puzzled first, then with a vague dread in his haggard face.

"Mrs. Brown!" he cried, in a loud voice, hurrying across the room toward an inner door as he spoke.

The inner door was opened before Paul could reach it, and a woman appeared; a tall, gaunt-looking woman, with a hard face and bare, brawny arms.

"Where, in Heaven's name, have you been hiding yourself, woman?" Paul cried, impatiently. "And where's your patient?"

"Gone, Sir."

"Gone! Where?"

"With her step-mamma, Mrs. Marchmont—not half an hour ago. As it was your wish I should stop behind to clear up, I've done so, Sir; but I did think it would have been better for me to have gone with—"

Paul clutched the woman by the arm, and dragged her toward him.

"Are you mad?" he cried, with an oath. "Are you mad or drunk? Who gave you leave to let that woman go? Who—?"

He couldn't finish the sentence. His throat grew dry, and he gasped for breath, while all the blood in his body seemed to rush into his swollen forehead.

"You sent Mrs. Marchmont to fetch my patient away, Sir," exclaimed the woman, looking frightened. "You did, didn't you? She said so!"

"She is a liar; and you are a fool or a cheat. She paid you, I dare say! Can't you speak, woman? Has the person I left in your care, whom you were paid, and paid well, to take care of—have you let her go? Answer me that."

"I have, Sir," the woman faltered—she was big and brawny, but there was that in Paul Marchmont's face that frightened her, notwithstanding—"seeing as it was your orders."

"That will do," cried Paul Marchmont, holding up his hand, and looking at the woman with a ghastly smile; "that will do. You have ruined me; do you hear? You have undone a work, that has cost me— Oh, my God! why do I waste my breath in talking to such a creature as this? All my plots, my difficulties, my struggles and victories, my long sleepless nights, my bad dreams—has it all come to this? Ruin, unutterable ruin, brought upon me by a mad woman!"

He sat down in the chair by the window, and leaned upon the table, scattering the Indian chessmen with his elbow. He did not weep. That relief—terrible relief though it is for a man's breast—was denied him. He sat there with his face covered, moaning aloud. That helpless moan was scarcely like the complaint of a man; it was rather like the hopeless, dreary utterance of a brute's anguish; it sounded like the miserable howling of a beaten cur.

---

## CHAPTER XXXIX.

### BELINDA'S WEDDING-DAY.

THE sun shone upon Belinda Lawford's wedding-day. The birds were singing in the garden under her window as she opened the lattice and looked out. The word lattice is not a poetical license in this case; for Miss Lawford's chamber was a roomy, old-fashioned apartment at the back of the house, with deep window-seats and diamond-paned casements.

The sun shone, and the roses bloomed in all their summer glory. "'Twas in the time of

roses," as gentle-minded Thomas Hood so sweetly sang: surely the time of all others for a bridal
morning. The girl looked out into the sunshine,
with her loose auburn hair falling about her
shoulders, and lingered a little, looking at the
familiar garden, with a half-pensive smile.

"Oh, how often, how often," she said, "I
have walked up and down by those laburnums,
Letty!" There were two pretty white-curtained bedsteads in the old-fashioned room, and Miss
Arundel had shared her friend's apartment for
the last week. "How often mamma and I have
sat under the dear old cedar, making our poor
children's frocks! People say monotonous lives
are not happy: mine has been the same thing,
over and over again; and yet how happy I have
been! And to think that we"—she paused a
moment, and the rosy color in her cheeks deepened by just one shade; it was so sweet to 'use
that simple monosyllable "we" when Edward
Arundel was the other half of the pronoun—" to
think that we shall be in Paris to-morrow!"

"Driving in the Bois," exclaimed Miss Arundel, "dining at the Maison Dorée, or the Café
de Paris. Don't dine at Meurice's, Linda; it's
dreadfully slow dining at one's hotel. And
you'll be a young married woman, and can do
any thing, you know. If I were a young married woman I'd ask my husband to take me to
the Mabille, just for half an hour, with an old
bonnet and a thick veil. I knew a girl whose
first cousin married a cornet in the Guards, and
they went to the Mabille one night. Come, Belinda, if you mean to have your back hair done
at all, you'd better sit down at once and let me
commence operations."

Miss Arundel had stipulated that, upon this
particular morning, she was to dress her friend's
hair; and she turned up the frilled sleeves of
her white dressing-gown, and set to work in
the orthodox manner, spreading a net-work of
shining auburn tresses about Miss Lawford's
shoulders, prior to the weaving of elaborate
plaits that were to make a crown for the fair
young bride. Letitia's tongue went as fast as
her fingers; but Belinda was very silent.

She was thinking of the bounteous Providence
that had given her the man she loved for her
husband. She had been on her knees in the
early morning, long before Letitia's awakening,
breathing out innocent thanksgiving for the happiness that overflowed her fresh young heart.
A woman had need to be country-bred, and to
have been reared in the narrow circle of a happy home, to feel as Belinda Lawford felt. Such
love as hers is only given to bright and innocent spirits, untarnished even by the knowledge
of sin.

Down stairs Edward Arundel was making a
wretched pretense of breakfasting tête-à-tête with
his future father-in-law.

The Major had held his peace as to the unlooked-for visitant of the past night. He had
given particular orders that no stranger should
be admitted to the house, and that was all. But,
being of a naturally frank, not to say loquacious
disposition, the weight of this secret was a very
terrible burden to the honest half-pay soldier.
·He ate his dry toast uneasily, looking at the
door every now and then, in the perpetual expectation of beholding that barrier burst open by
mad Olivia Marchmont.

The breakfast was not a very cheerful meal,
therefore. I don't suppose any ante-nuptial
breakfast ever is very jovial. There was the
state banquet — the wedding breakfast — to be
eaten by-and-by; and Mrs. Lawford, attended
by all the females of the establishment, was engaged in putting the last touches to the groups
of fruit and confectionery, the pyramid of flowers, and that crowning glory, the wedding-cake.
"Remember, the still Hock and Madeira are
to go round first, and then the sparkling; and
tell Gogram to be particular about the corks,
Martha," Mrs. Lawford said to her confidential
maid, as she gave a nervous last look at the table. "I was at a breakfast once where a Cham-
pagne-cork hit the bridegroom on the bridge of
his nose at the very moment he rose to return
thanks; and being a nervous man, poor fellow!
—in point of fact, he was a curate, and the bride
was the rector's daughter, with two hundred a
year of her own—it quite overcame him, and he
didn't get over it all through the breakfast. And
now I must run and put on my bonnet."

There was nothing but putting on bonnets,
and pinning lace shawls, and wild outcries for
hair-pins, and interchanging of little feminine
services, upon the bedroom floor for the next
half-hour.

Major Lawford walked up and down the hall,
putting on his white gloves, which were too
large for him—elderly men's white gloves always are too large for them—and watching the
door of the citadel. Olivia must pass over a
father's body, the old soldier thought, before she
should annoy Belinda on her bridal morning.

By-and-by the carriages came round to the
door. The girl bridemaids came crowding down
the stairs, hustling each other's crisped garments,
and disputing a little in a sisterly fashion; then
Letitia Arundel, with nine rustling flounces of
white silk ebbing and flowing and·surging about
her, and with a pleased simper upon her face;
and then followed Mrs. Arundel, stately in sil-
ver-gray moire, and Mrs. Lawford, in violet silk
—until the hall was a show of bonnets and bouquets and muslin.

And last of all, Belinda Lawford, robed in
cloud-like garments of spotless lace, with bridal
flowers trembling round her hair, came slowly
down the broad old-fashioned staircase, to see
her lover loitering in the hall below.

He looked very grave; but he greeted his
bride with a tender smile. He loved her, but
he could not forget. Even upon this his wedding-day the haunting shadow of the past was
with him: not to be shaken off.

He did not wait till Belinda reached the bottom of the staircase. There was a sort of ceremonial law to be observed, and he was not to
speak to Miss Lawford upon this special morning until he met her in the vestry at Hillingsworth Church; so Letitia and Mrs. Arundel
hustled the young man into one of the carriages,
while Major Lawford ran to receive his daughter at the foot of the stairs.

The Arundel carriage drove off about five
minutes before the vehicle that was to convey
Major Lawford, Belinda, and as many of the
girl bridemaids as could be squeezed into it without detriment to lace· and muslin. The rest
went with Mrs. Lawford in the third and last
carriage. Hillingsworth Church was about three-

quarters of a mile from the Grange. It was a pretty, irregular old place, lying in a little nook under the shadow of a great yew-tree. Behind the square Norman tower there was a row of poplars, black against the blue summer sky; and between the low gate of the church-yard and the gray, moss-grown porch there was an avenue of good old elms. The rooks were calling to each other in the topmost branches of the trees as Major Lawford's carriage drew up at the church-yard gate.

Belinda was a great favorite among the poor of Hillingsworth parish, and the place had put on a gala-day aspect in honor of her wedding. Garlands of honey-suckle and wild clematis were twined about the stout oaken gate-posts. The school-children were gathered in clusters in the church-yard, with their pinafores full of fresh flowers from shadowy lanes and from prim cottage gardens—bright, homely blossoms, with the morning dew still upon them.

The rector and his curate were standing in the porch waiting for the coming of the bride; and there were groups of well-dressed people dotted about here and there in the drowsy sheltered pews near the altar. There were humbler spectators clustered under the low ceiling of the gallery—tradesmen's wives and daughters, radiant with new ribbons, and whispering to one another in delighted anticipation of the show.

Every body round about the Grange loved pretty, genial Belinda Lawford, and there was universal rejoicing because of her happiness.

The wedding party came out of the vestry presently in appointed order; the bride with her head drooping, and her face hidden by her veil; the bridemaids' garments making a fluttering noise as they came up the aisle, like the sound of a summer breeze faintly stirring a field of corn.

Then the grave voice of the rector began the service with the brief preliminary exordium; and then, in a tone that grew more solemn with the increasing solemnity of the words, he went on to that awful charge which is addressed especially to the bridegroom and the bride:

"I require and charge you both, as ye will answer at the dreadful Day of Judgment, when the secrets of all hearts shall be disclosed, that if either of you know any impediment why ye may not be lawfully joined together in matrimony, ye do now confess it. For be ye well assured—"

The rector read no further; for a woman's voice from out the dusky shadows at the further end of the church cried "Stop!"

There was a sudden silence; people stared at each other with pale, scared faces, and then turned in the direction whence the voice had come. The bride lifted her head for the first time since leaving the vestry, and looked round about her, ashy pale and trembling.

"Oh Edward, Edward!" she cried, "what is it?"

The rector waited, with his hand still upon the open book. He waited, looking toward the other end of the chancel. He had no need to wait long: a woman, with a black veil thrown back from a white, haggard face, and with dusty garments dragging upon the church-floor, came slowly up the aisle.

Her two hands were clasped upon her breast,

and her breath came in gasps, as if she had been running.

"Olivia!" cried Edward Arundel, "what, in Heaven's name—"

But Major Lawford stepped forward, and spoke to the rector.

"Pray let her be got out of the way," he said, in a low voice. "I was warned of this. I was quite prepared for some such disturbance." He sank his voice to a whisper. "She is mad!" he said, close in the rector's ear.

The whisper was like whispering in general —more distinctly audible than the rest of the speech. Olivia Marchmont heard it.

"Mad until to-day," she cried; "but not mad to-day. Oh, Edward Arundel! a hideous wrong has been done by me and through me. Your wife—your wife—"

"My wife! what of her? She—"

"She is alive!" gasped Olivia; "an hour's walk from here. I came on foot. I was tired, and I came slowly. I thought that I should be in time to stop you before you got to the church; but I am very weak. I ran the last part of the way—"

She dropped her hands upon the altar-rails, and seemed as if she would have fallen. The rector put his arm about her to support her, and she went on:

"I thought I should have spared her this," she said, pointing to Belinda; "but I can't help it. She must bear her misery as well as others. It can't be worse for her than it has been for others. She must bear—"

"My wife!" said Edward Arundel; "Mary, my poor sorrowful darling—alive?"

Belinda turned away, and buried her face upon her mother's shoulder. She could have borne any thing better than this.

His heart—that supreme treasure, for which she had rendered up thanks to her God—had never been hers, after all. A word, a breath, and she was forgotten; his thoughts went back to that other one. There was unutterable joy, there was unspeakable tenderness in his tone, as he spoke of Mary Marchmont, though she stood by his side, in all her foolish bridal finery, with her heart newly broken.

"Oh, mother," she cried, "take me away! take me away, before I die!"

Olivia flung herself upon her knees by the altar-rails, where the pure young bride was to have knelt by her lover's side; this wretched sinner cast herself down, sunk far below all common thoughts in the black depth of her despair.

"Oh, my sin, my sin!" she cried, with clasped hands lifted up above her head. "Will God ever forgive my sin? will God ever have pity upon me? Can He pity, can He forgive, such guilt as mine? Even this work of to-day is no atonement to be reckoned against my wickedness. I was jealous of her; I was jealous! Earthly passion was still predominant in this miserable breast."

She rose suddenly, as if this outburst had never been, and laid her hand upon Edward Arundel's arm.

"Come!" she said; "come!"

"To her—to Mary—my wife?"

They had taken Belinda away by this time; but Major Lawford stood looking on. He tried to draw Edward aside; but Olivia's hand upon the young man's arm held him like a vice. "She is mad," whispered the Major. "Mr. Marchmont came to me last night, and warned me of all this. He told me to be prepared for any thing; she has all sorts of delusions. Get her away, if you can, while I go and explain matters to Belinda. Edward, if you have a spark of manly feeling, get this woman away."

But Olivia held the bridegroom's arm with a tightening grasp.

"Come!" she said; "come! Are you turned to stone, Edward Arundel? Is your love worth no more than this? I tell you, your wife, Mary Marchmont, is alive. Let those who doubt me come and see for themselves."

The eager spectators, standing up in the pews or crowding in the narrow aisle, were only too ready to respond to this invitation.

Olivia led her cousin out into the church-yard; she led him to the gate where the carriages were waiting. The crowd flocked after them; and the people outside began to cheer as they came out. That cheer was the signal for which the school-children had waited; and they set to work scattering flowers upon the narrow pathway, before they looked up to see who was coming to tread upon the rosebuds and jasmine, the woodbine and seringa. But they drew back, scared and wondering, as Olivia came along the pathway, sweeping those tender blossoms after her with her trailing black garments, and leading the pale bridegroom by his arm.

She led him to the door of the carriage beside which Major Lawford's gray-haired groom was waiting, with a big white-satin favor pinned upon his breast, and a bunch of roses in his button-hole. There were favors in the horses' ears, and favors upon the breasts of the Hillingsworth trades-people who supplied bread and butcher's meat and grocery to the family at the Grange. The bell-ringers up in the church-tower saw the crowd flock out of the porch, and thought the marriage ceremony was over. The jangling bells pealed out upon the hot summer air as Edward stood by the church-yard gate, with Olivia Marchmont by his side.

"Lend me your carriage," he said to Major Lawford, "and come with me. I must see the end of this. It may be all a delusion; but I must see the end of it. If there is any truth in instinct, I believe that I shall see my wife—alive."

He got into the carriage without further ceremony, and Olivia and Major Lawford followed him.

"Where is my wife?" the young man asked, letting down the front window as he spoke.

"At Kemberling, at Hester Jobson's."

"Drive to Kemberling," Edward said to the coachman—"to Kemberling High Street, as fast as you can go."

The man drove away from the church-yard gate. The humbler spectators, who were restrained by no niceties of social etiquette, hurried after the vehicle, raising white clouds of dust upon the high-road with their eager feet. The higher classes lingered about the church-yard, talking to each other and wondering.

Very few people stopped to think of Belinda Lawford. "Let the stricken deer go weep." A stricken deer is a very uninteresting object when

there are hounds in full chase hard by, and another deer to be hunted.

"Since when has my wife been at Kemberling?" Edward Arundel asked Olivia, as the carriage drove along the high-road between the two villages.

"Since daybreak this morning."

"Where was she before then?"

"At Stony-Stringford Farm."

"And before then?"

"In the pavilion over the boat-house at Marchmont."

"My God! And—"

The young man did not finish his sentence. He put his head out of the window looking toward Kemberling, and straining his eyes to catch the earliest sight of the straggling village street.

"Faster!" he cried every now and then to the coachman; "faster!"

In little more than half an hour from the time at which it had left the church-yard gate the carriage stopped before the little carpenter's-shop. Mr. Jobson's doorway was adorned by a painted representation of two very doleful-looking mutes standing at a door; for Hester's husband combined the more aristocratic avocation of undertaker with the homely trade of carpenter and joiner.

Olivia Marchmont got out of the carriage before either of the two men could alight to assist her. Power was the supreme attribute of this woman's mind. Her purpose never faltered; from the moment she had left Marchmont Towers until now she had known neither rest of body nor wavering of intention.

"Come," she said to Edward Arundel, looking back as she stood upon the threshold of Mr. Jobson's door; "and you too," she added, turning to Major Lawford— "follow us, and see whether I am MAD."

She passed through the shop, and into that prim, smart parlor in which Edward Arundel had lamented his lost wife.

The latticed windows were wide open, and the warm summer sunshine filled the room.

A girl, with loose traces of hazel-brown hair falling about her face, was sitting on the floor, looking down at a beautiful fair-haired nursling of a twelvemonth old.

The girl was John Marchmont's daughter; the child was Edward Arundel's son. It was his childish cry that the young man had heard upon that October night in the pavilion by the water.

"Mary Arundel," said Olivia, in a hard voice, "I give you back your husband!"

The young mother got up from the ground and fell into her husband's arms. Edward carried her to a sofa and laid her down, white and senseless, and then knelt down beside her, crying over her, and sobbing out inarticulate thanksgiving to the God who had given his lost wife back to him.

"Poor, sweet lamb!" murmured Hester Jobson; "she's as weak as a baby; and she's gone through so much a'ready this morning."

It was some time before Edward Arundel raised his head from the pillow upon which his wife's pale face lay, half-hidden amidst the tangled hair. But when he did look up, he turned to Major Lawford and stretched out his hand.

"Have pity upon me," he said. "I have been the dupe of a villain. Tell your poor child how much I esteem her, how much I regret that—that—we should have loved each other as we have. The instinct of my heart would have kept me true to the past; but it was impossible to know your daughter and not love her. The villain who has brought this sorrow upon us shall pay dearly for his infamy. Go back to your daughter; tell her every thing. Tell her what you have seen here. I know her heart, and I know that she will open her arms to this poor ill-used child."

The Major went away. Hester Jobson bustled about bringing restoratives and pillows, stopping every now and then in an outburst of affection by the slippery horse-hair couch on which Mary lay.

Mrs. Jobson had prepared her best bedroom for her beloved visitor, and Edward carried his young wife up to the clean, airy chamber. He went back to the parlor to fetch the child. He carried the fair-haired little one up stairs in his own arms; but I regret to say that the infant showed an inclination to whimper in his newly-found father's embrace. It is only in the British Drama that newly-discovered fathers are greeted with an outburst of ready-made affection. Edward Arundel went back to the sitting-room presently, and sat down, waiting till Hester should bring him fresh tidings of his wife. Olivia Marchmont stood by the window, with her eyes fixed upon Edward.

"Why don't you speak to me?" she said, presently. "Can you find no words that are vile enough to express your hatred of me? Is that why you are silent?"

"No, Olivia," answered the young man, calmly. "I am silent, because I have nothing to say to you. Why you have acted as you have acted —why you have chosen to be the tool of a black-hearted villain—is an unfathomable mystery to me. I thank God that your conscience was aroused this day, and that you have at least hindered the misery of an innocent girl. But why you have kept my wife hidden from me—why you have been the accomplice of Paul Marchmont's crime—is more than I can even attempt to guess."

"Not yet?" said Olivia, looking at him with a strange smile. "Even yet I am a mystery to you?"

"You are, indeed, Olivia."

She turned away from him with a laugh.

"Then I had better remain so till the end," she said, looking out into the garden. But after a moment's silence she turned her head once more toward the young man. "I will speak," she said; "I *will* speak, Edward Arundel. I hope and believe that I have not long to live, and that all my shame and misery, my obstinate wickedness, my guilty passion, will come to an end, like a long feverish dream. O God, have mercy on my waking, and make it brighter than this dreadful sleep! I loved you, Edward Arundel. You don't know what that word 'love' means, do you? You think you love that childish girl yonder, don't you? but I can tell you that you don't know what love is. *I* know what it is. I have loved. For ten years—for ten long, dreary, desolate, miserable years, fifty-two weeks in every year, fifty-two Sundays, with long idle hours between the two church services —I have loved you, Edward. Shall I tell you

what it is to love? It is to suffer, to hate. Yes, to hate even the object of your love, when that love is hopeless;—we hate him for the very attributes that have made you love him; to grudge the gifts and graces that have made him dear. It is to hate every creature upon whom his eyes look with greater tenderness than they look on you; to watch one face until its familiar lines become a perpetual torment to you, and you can not sleep because of its eternal presence staring at you in all your dreams. Love! How many people upon this great earth know the real meaning of that hideous word. I have learned it until my soul loathes the lesson. They will tell you that I am mad, Edward, and they will tell you something near the truth; but not quite the truth. My madness has been my love. From long ago, Edward, when you were little more than a boy—you remember, don't you, the long days at the Rectory?—*I* remember every word you ever spoke to me, every sentiment you ever expressed, every look of your changing face— you were the first bright thing that came across my barren life; and I loved you. I married John Marchmont—why, do you think?—because I wanted to make a barrier between you and me. I wanted to make my love for you impossible by making it a sin. I did not think it was in my nature to sin. But since then—oh, I hope I have been mad since then; I hope that God may forgive my sins because I have been mad!"

Her thoughts wandered away to that awful question which had been so lately revived in her mind—Could she be forgiven? Was it within the compass of Heavenly mercy to forgive such a sin as hers?

---

## CHAPTER XL.

### MARY'S STORY.

One of the minor effects of any great shock, any revolution, natural or political, social or domestic, is a singular unconsciousness or an exaggerated estimate of the passage of time. Sometimes we fancy that the common functions of the universe have come to a dead stop during the tempest which has shaken our being to its remotest depths. Sometimes, on the other hand, it seems to us that, because we have endured an age of suffering, or half a lifetime of bewildered joy, the terrestrial globe has spun round in time to the quickened throbbing of our passionate hearts, and that all the clocks upon earth have been standing still.

When the sun sank upon the summer's day that was to have been the day of Belinda's bridal Edward Arundel thought that it was still early in the morning. He wondered at the rosy light all over the western sky, and that great ball of molten gold dropping down below the horizon. He was fain to look at his watch, in order to convince himself that the low light was really the familiar sun, and not some unnatural appearance in the heavens.

And yet, although he wondered at the closing of the day, with a strange inconsistency his mind could scarcely grapple with the idea that only last night he had sat by Belinda Lawford's side, her betrothed husband, and had pondered, Heaven only knows with what sorrowful regret, upon the unknown grave in which his dead wife lay. "I only knew it this morning," he thought; "I only knew this morning that my young wife still lives, and that I have a son."

He.was sitting by the open window in Hester Jobson's best bedroom. He was sitting in an old-fashioned easy-chair, placed between the head of the bed and the open window—a pure cottage window, with diamond panes of thin greenish glass, and a broad painted ledge, with a great jug of homely garden-flowers standing on it. The young man was sitting by the side of the bed upon which his newly-found wife and son lay asleep; the child's head nestled on his mother's breast, one flushed cheek peeping out of a tangled confusion of hazel-brown and baby-ish flaxen hair.

The white dimity curtains overshadowed the loving sleepers. The pretty fluffy knotted fringe —neat Hester's handiwork — made fantastical tracery upon the sunlit counterpane. Mary slept with one arm folded round her child, and with her face turned to her husband. She had fallen asleep, with her hand clasped in his, after a succession of fainting-fits that had left her terribly prostrate.

Edward Arundel watched that tender picture with a smile of ineffable affection.

"I can understand now why Roman Catholics worship the Virgin Mary," he thought. "I can comprehend the inspiration that guided Raphael's hand when he painted the Madonna de la Chaise. In all the world there is no picture so beautiful. From all the universe he could have chosen no subject more sublime. Oh, my darling wife, given back to me out of the grave, restored to me, and not alone restored! My little son! my baby-son! whose feeble voice I heard that dark October night. To think that I was so wretched a dupe! to think that my dull ears could hear that sound, and no instinct rise up in my heart to reveal the presence of my child! I was so near them, not once, but several times —so near, and I never knew—I never guessed!"

He clenched his fists involuntarily at the remembrance of those purposeless visits to the lonely boat-house. His young wife was restored to him. But nothing could wipe away the long interval of agony in which he and she had been the dupe of a villainous trickster and a jealous woman. Nothing could give back the first year of that baby's life—that year which should have been one long holiday of love and rejoicing. Upon what a dreary world those innocent eyes had opened, when they should have looked only upon sunshine and flowers, and the tender light of a loving father's smile!

"Oh, my darling, my darling!" the young husband thought, as he looked at his wife's wan face, upon which the evidence of all that past agony was only too painfully visible—"how bitterly we two have suffered! But how much more terrible must have been your suffering than mine, my poor gentle darling, my broken lily!"

In his rapture at finding the wife he had mourned as dead, the young man had for a time almost forgotten the villainous plotter who had kept her hidden from him. But now, as he sat quietly by the bed upon which Mary and her baby lay, he had leisure to think of Paul Marchmont.

What was he to do with that man? What vengeance could he wreak upon the head of that wretch who, for nearly two years, had condemned an innocent girl to cruel suffering and shame? To shame; for Edward knew now that one of the most bitter tortures which Paul Marchmont had inflicted upon his cousin had been his pretended disbelief in her marriage.

"What can I do to him?" the young man asked himself. "What can I do to him? There is no personal chastisement worse than that which he has endured already at my hands. The scoundrel! the heartless villain! the false, cold-blooded cur! What can I do to him? I can only repeat that shameful degradation, and I will repeat it. This time he shall howl under the lash like some beaten hound. This time I will drag him through the village street, and let every idle gossip in Kemberling see how a scoundrel writhes under an honest man's whip. I will—"

Edward Arundel's wife woke while he was thinking what chastisement he should inflict upon her deadly foe; and the baby opened his round innocent blue eyes in the next moment, and sat up, staring at his new parent.

Mr. Arundel took the child in his arms, and held him very tenderly, though perhaps rather awkwardly. The baby's round eyes opened wider at sight of the golden absurdities dangling at his father's watch chain, and the little pudgy hands began to play with the big man's lockets and seals.

"He comes to me, you see, Mary!" Edward said, with naïve wonder.

And then he turned the baby's face toward him, and tenderly contemplated the bright, surprised blue eyes, the tiny dimples, the soft moulded chin. I don't know whether fatherly vanity prompted the fancy, but Edward Arundel certainly did fancy that he saw some faint reflection of his own features in that pink and white baby-face; a shadowy resemblance, like a tremulous image looking up out of a river. But while Edward was half-thinking this, half-wondering whether there could be any likeness to him in that infant countenance, Mary settled the question with womanly decision.

"Isn't he like you, Edward?" she whispered.

"It was only for his sake that I bore my life all through that miserable time; and I don't think I could have lived even for him, if he hadn't been so like you. I used to look at his face sometimes for hours and hours together, crying over him, and thinking of you. I don't think I ever cried except when he was in my arms. Then something seemed to soften my heart, and the tears came to my eyes. I was very, very, very ill, for a long time before my baby was born; and I didn't know how the time went, or where I was. I used to fancy sometimes I was back in Oakley Street, and that papa was alive again, and that we were quite happy together, except for some heavy hammer that was always beating, beating, beating upon both our heads, and the dreadful sound of the river rushing down the street under our windows. I heard Mr. Weston tell his wife that it was a miracle I lived through that time."

Hester Jobson came in presently with a tea-tray, that made itself heard, by a jingling of tea-spoons and rattling of cups and saucers, all th way up the narrow staircase.

The friendly carpenter's wife had produced her best china and her silver tea-pot—an heir-loom inherited from a wealthy maiden aunt of her husband's. She had been busy all the afternoon, preparing that elegant little collation of cake and fruit which accompanied the tea-tray; and she spread the lavender-scented table-cloth, and arranged the cups and saucers, the plates and dishes, with mingled pride and delight.

But she had to endure a terrible disappointment by-and-by; for neither of her guests was in a condition to do justice to her hospitality. Mary got up and sat in the roomy easy-chair, propped up with pillows. Her pensive eyes kept a loving watch upon the face of her husband, turned toward her own, and slightly crimsoned by that rosy flush fading out in the western sky. She sat up and sipped a cup of tea; and in that lovely summer twilight, with the scent of the flowers blowing in through the open window, and a stupid moth doing his best to beat out his brains against one of the diamond panes in the lattice, the tortured heart, for the first time since the ruthless close of that brief honey-moon, felt the heavenly delight of repose.

"Oh, Edward!" murmured the young wife, "how strange it seems to be happy!"

He was at her feet, half-kneeling, half-sitting on a hassock of Hester's handiwork, with both his wife's hands clasped in his, and his head leaning upon the arm of her chair. Hester Jobson had carried off the baby, and these two were quite alone, all in all to each other, with a cruel gap of two years to be bridged over by sorrowful memories, by tender words of consolation. They were alone, and they could talk quite freely now, without fear of interruption; for although in purity and beauty an infant is first cousin to the angels, and although I most heartily concur in all that Mr. Bennett and Mr. Buchanan can say or sing about the species, still it must be owned that a baby is rather a hindrance to conversation, and that a man's eloquence does not flow quite so smoothly when he has to stop every now and then to rescue his infant son from the imminent peril of strangulation, caused by a futile attempt at swallowing one of his own fists.

Mary and Edward were alone; they were together once more, as they had been by the trout-stream in the Winchester meadows. A curtain had fallen upon all the wreck and ruin of the past, and they could hear the soft, mysterious music that was to be the prelude of a new act in life's drama.

"I shall try to forget all that time," Mary said, presently; "I shall try to forget it, Edward. I think the very memory of it would kill me, if it was to come back perpetually in the midst of my joy, as it does now, even now, when I am so happy—so happy that I dare not speak of my happiness."

She stopped, and her face drooped upon her husband's clustering hair.

"You are crying, Mary!"

"Yes, dear. There is something painful in happiness when it comes after such suffering."

The young man lifted his head, and looked in his wife's face. How deathly pale it was, even in that shadowy twilight; how worn and haggard and wasted since it had smiled at him in his brief honey-moon! Yes, joy is painful when it comes after a long continuance of suffering;

it is painful because we have become skeptical by reason of the endurance of such anguish. We have lost the power to believe in happiness. It comes, the bright stranger; but we shrink appalled from its beauty, lest, after all, it should be nothing but a phantom.

Heaven knows how anxiously Edward Arundel looked at his wife's altered face. Her eyes shone upon him with the holy light of love. She smiled at him with a tender, reassuring smile; but it seemed to him that there was something almost supernal in the brightness of that white, wasted face; something that reminded him of the countenance of a martyr who has ceased to suffer the anguish of death in a foretaste of the joys of heaven.

"Mary," he said, presently, "tell me every cruelty that Paul Marchmont or his tools inflicted upon you; tell me every thing, and I will never speak of our miserable separation again. I will only punish the cause of it," he added, in an undertone. "Tell me, dear. It will be painful for you to speak of it; but it will be only once. There are some things I must know. Remember, darling, that you are in my arms now, and that nothing but death can ever again part us."

The young man had his arms round his wife. He felt, rather than heard, a low, plaintive sigh as he spoke those last words.

"Nothing but death, Edward; nothing but death," Mary said, in a solemn whisper. "Death would not come to me when I was very miserable. I used to pray that I might die, and the baby too; for I could not have borne to leave him behind. I thought that we might both be buried with you, Edward. I have dreamed sometimes that I was lying by your side in a tomb, and I have stretched out my dead hand to clasp yours. I used to beg and entreat them to let me be buried with you when I died; for I believed that you were dead, Edward. I believed it most firmly. I had not even one lingering hope that you were alive. If I had felt such a hope, no power upon earth would have kept me prisoner."

"The wretches!" muttered Edward between his set teeth; "the dastardly wretches! the foul liars!"

"Don't, Edward; don't, darling. There is a pain in my heart when I hear you speak like that. I know how wicked they have been; how cruel—how cruel. I look back at all my suffering as if it were some one else who suffered; for, now that you are with me, I can not believe that miserable, lonely, despairing creature was really me—the same creature whose head now rests upon your shoulder, whose breath is mixed with yours. I look back and see all my past misery, and I can not forgive them, Edward; I am very wicked, for I can not forgive my cousin Paul and his sister—yet. But I don't want you to speak of them; I only want you to love me; I only want you to smile at me, and tell me again and again and again that nothing can part us now—but death."

She paused for a few moments, exhausted by having spoken so long. Her head lay upon her husband's shoulder, and she clung a little closer to him, with a slight shiver.

"What is the matter, darling?"

"I feel as if it couldn't be real."

"What, dear?"

"The present—all this joy. Oh, Edward, is it real? Is it—is it? Or am I only dreaming? Shall I wake presently and feel the cold air blowing in at the window, and see the moonlight on the wainscot at Stony Stringford? Is it all real?"

"It is, my precious one. As real as the mercy of God, who will give you compensation for all you have suffered; as real as God's vengeance, which will fall most heavily upon your persecutors. And now, darling, tell me—tell me all. I must know the story of these two miserable years during which I have mourned for my lost love."

' Mr. Arundel forgot to mention that during those two miserable years he had engaged himself to become the husband of another woman. But perhaps, even when he is best and truest, a man is always just a shade behind a woman in the matter of constancy.

"When you left me in Hampshire, Edward, I was very, very miserable," Mary began, in a low voice; "but I knew that it was selfish and wicked of me to think only of myself. I tried to think of your poor father, who was ill and suffering; and I prayed for him, and hoped that he would recover, and that you would come back to me very soon. The people at the inn were very kind to me. I sat at the window from morning till night upon the day after you left me, and upon the day after that; for I was so foolish as to fancy, every time I heard the sound of horses' hoofs or carriage-wheels upon the high-road, that you were coming back to me, and that all my grief was over. I sat at the window and watched the road till I knew the shape of every tree and housetop, every ragged branch of the hawthorn-bushes in the hedge. At last—it was the third day after you went away—I heard carriage-wheels, that slackened as they came to the inn. A fly stopped at the door, and oh, Edward, I did not wait to see who was in it; I never imagined the possibility of its bringing any body but you. I ran down stairs, with my heart beating so that I could hardly breathe, and I scarcely felt the stairs under my feet. But when I got to the door—oh my love, my love!—I can not bear to think of it; I can not endure the recollection of it—"

She stopped, gasping for breath, and clinging to her husband; and then, with an effort, went on again:

"Yes, I will tell you, dear; I must tell you. My cousin Paul and my step-mother were standing in the little hall at the foot of the stairs. I think I fainted in my step-mother's arms; and when my consciousness came back, I was in our sitting-room—the pretty rustic room, Edward, in which you and I had been so happy together.

"I must not stop to tell you every thing. It would take me so long to speak of all that happened in that miserable time. I knew that something must be wrong, from my cousin Paul's manner; but neither he nor my step-mother would tell me what it was. I asked them if you were dead; but they said, 'No, you were not dead.' Still I could see that something dreadful had happened. But by-and-by, by accident, I saw your name in a newspaper that was lying on the table with Paul's hat and gloves. I saw the description of an accident on the railway by which I knew you had traveled. My heart sank at once, and I think I guessed all that had happened. I read your name among those of the people who had been dangerously hurt. Paul shook his head when I asked him if there was any hope.

"They brought me back here. I scarcely know how I came, how I endured all that misery. I implored them to let me come to you again and again, on my knees at their feet. But neither of them would listen to me. It was impossible, Paul said. He always seemed very, very kind to me; always spoke softly; always told me that he pitied me, and was sorry for me. But though my step-mother looked sternly at me, and spoke, as she always used to speak, in a harsh, cold voice, I sometimes think she might have given way at last and let me come to you, but for him—but for my cousin Paul. He could look at me with a smile upon his face when I was almost mad with my misery; and he never wavered; he never hesitated.

"So they took me back to the Towers. I let them take me; for I scarcely felt my sorrow any longer. I only felt tired·; oh, so dreadfully tired; and I wanted to lie down upon the ground in some quiet place, where no one could come near me. I thought that I was dying. I believe I was very ill when we got back to the Towers. My step-mother and Barbara Simmons watched by my bedside day after day, night after night. Sometimes I knew them;. sometimes I had all sorts of fancies. And often—ah, how often, darling!—I thought that you were with me. My cousin Paul came every day and stood by my bedside. I can't tell you how hateful it was to me to have him there. He used to come into the room as silently as if he had been walking upon snow; but however noiselessly he came, however fast asleep I was when he entered the room, I always knew that he was there, standing by my bedside, smiling at me. I always woke with a shuddering horror thrilling through my veins, as if a rat had run across my face.

"By-and-by, when the delirium was quite gone, I felt ashamed of myself for this. It seemed so wicked to feel this unreasonable antipathy to my dear father's cousin; but he had brought me bad news of you, Edward, and it was scarcely strange that I should hate him. One day he sat down by my bedside, when I was getting better, and was strong enough to talk. There was no one besides ourselves in the room, except my step-mother, and she was standing at the window, with her head turned away from us, looking out. My cousin Paul sat down by the bedside, and began to talk to me in that gentle, compassionate way that used to torture me and irritate me in spite of myself.

"He asked me what had happened to me after my leaving the Towers on the day after the ball.

"I told him every thing, Edward—about your coming to me in Oakley Street—about our marriage. But oh! my darling, my husband, he wouldn't.believe me—he wouldn't. believe. Nothing that I could say would make him believe me. Though I swore to him again and again—by my dead father in heaven, as I hoped for the mercy of my God—that I had spoken the truth, and the truth only, he wouldn't believe me—he wouldn't believe. He shook his head, and said he scarcely wondered I should try to deceive him; that it was a very sad story, a very miserable and shameful story, and my attempted falsehood was little more than natural.

"And then he spoke against you, Edward—against you. He talked of my childish ignorance, my confiding love, and your villainy. Oh, Edward, he said such shameful things—such shameful, horrible things! You had plotted to become master of my fortune; to get me into your power, because of my money; and you had not married me. You had *not* married me; he persisted in saying that.

"I was delirious again after this—almost mad, I think. All through the delirium I kept telling my cousin Paul of our marriage. Though he was very seldom in the room, I constantly thought that he was there, and told him the same thing—the same thing—till my brain was on fire. I don't know how long it lasted. I know that, once in the middle of the night, I saw my step-mother lying upon the ground, sobbing aloud and crying out about her wickedness; crying out that God would never forgive her sin.

"I got better at last, and then I went down stairs; and I used to sit sometimes in poor papa's study. The blind was always down, and none of the servants, except Barbara Simmons, ever came into the room. My cousin Paul did not live at the Towers; but he came there every day, and often staid there all day. He seemed the master of the house. My step-mother obeyed him in every thing, and consulted him about every thing.

"Sometimes Mrs. Weston came. She was like her brother. She always smiled at me with a grave, compassionate smile, just like his; and she always seemed to pity me. But she wouldn't believe in my marriage. She spoke cruelly about you, Edward—cruelly, but in soft words, that seemed only spoken out of compassion for me. No one would believe in my marriage.

"No stranger was allowed to see me. I was never suffered to go out. They treated me as if I was some shameful creature, who must be hidden away from the sight of the world.

"One day I entreated my cousin Paul to go to London and see Mrs. Pimpernel. She would be able to tell him of our marriage. I had forgotten the name of the clergyman who married us, and the church at which we were married. And I could not tell Paul those; but I gave him Mrs. Pimpernel's address. And I wrote to her, begging her to tell my cousin all about my marriage; and I gave him the note unsealed.

"He went to London about a week afterward; and when he came back he brought me my note. He had been to Oakley Street, he said; but Mrs. Pimpernel had left the neighborhood, and no one knew where she was gone."

"A lie! a villainous lie!" muttered Edward Arundel. "Oh, the scoundrel! the infernal scoundrel!"

"No words would ever tell the misery of that time; the bitter anguish; the unendurable suspense. When I asked them about you they would tell me nothing. Sometimes I thought that you had forgotten me; that you had only married me out of pity for my loneliness; and

that you were glad to be freed from me. Oh, forgive me, Edward, for that wicked thought; but I was so very miserable, so utterly desolate. At other times I fancied that you were very ill, helpless, and unable to come to me. I dared not think that you were dead. I put away that thought from me with all my might; but it haunted me day and night. It was with me always like a ghost. I tried to shut it away from my sight; but I knew that it was there.

"The days were all alike—long, dreary, and desolate; so I scarcely know how the time went. My step-mother brought me religious books, and told me to read them; but they were hard, difficult books, and I couldn't find one word of comfort in them. They must have been written to frighten very obstinate and wicked people, I think. The only book that ever gave me any comfort was that dear Book I used to read to papa on a Sunday evening in Oakley Street. I read that, Edward, in those miserable days; I read the story of the widow's only son who was raised up from the dead because his mother was so wretched without him. I read that sweet, tender story again and again, until I used to see the funeral train, the pale, still face upon the bier, the white, uplifted hand, and that sublime and lovely countenance, whose image always comes to us when we are most miserable, the tremulous light upon the golden hair, and in the distance the glimmering columns of white temples, the palm-trees standing out against the purple Eastern sky. I thought that He who raised up a miserable woman's son chiefly because he was her only son, and she was desolate without him, would have more pity upon me than the God in Olivia's books; and I prayed to Him, Edward, night and day, imploring Him to bring you back to me.

"I don't know what day it was, except that it was autumn, and the dead leaves were blowing about in the quadrangle, when my step-mother sent for me one afternoon to my room, where I was sitting, not reading, not even thinking—only sitting with my head upon my hands, staring stupidly out at the drifting leaves and the gray, cold sky. My step-mother was in papa's study, and I was to go to her there. I went, and found her standing there, with a letter crumpled up in her clenched hand, and a slip of newspaper lying on the table before her. She was as white as death, and she was trembling violently from head to foot.

"'See,' she said, pointing to the paper; 'your lover is dead. But for you he would have received the letter that told him of his father's illness upon an earlier day; he would have gone to Devonshire by a different train. It was by your doing that he traveled when he did. If this is true, and he is dead, his blood be upon your head; his blood be upon your head!'

"I think her cruel words were almost exactly those. I did not hope for a minute that those horrible lines in the newspaper were false. I thought they must be true, and I was mad, Edward—I was mad; for utter despair came to me with the knowledge of your death. I went to my own room, and put on my bonnet and shawl; and then I went out of the house, down into that dreary wood, and along the narrow pathway by the river-side. I wanted to drown

L

myself; but the sight of the black water filled me with a shuddering horror. I was frightened, Edward; and I went on by the river, scarcely knowing where I was going, until it was quite dark; and I was tired, and sat down upon the damp ground by the brink of the river, all among the broad green flags and the wet rushes. I sat there for hours, and I saw the stars shining feebly in a dark sky. I think I was delirious; for sometimes I knew that I was there by the waterside, and then the next minute I thought that I was in my bedroom at the Towers; sometimes I fancied that I was with you in the meadows near Winchester, and the sun was shining, and you were sitting by my side, and I could see your float dancing up and down in the sunlit water. At last, after I had been there a very, very long time, two people came with a lantern, a man and woman; and I heard a startled voice say, 'Here she is; here, lying on the ground!' And then another voice, a woman's voice, very low and frightened, said, 'Alive!' And then two people lifted me up; the man carried me in his arms, and the woman took the lantern. I couldn't speak to them; but I knew that they were my cousin Paul and his sister Mrs. Weston. I remember being carried some distance in Paul's arms; and then I think I must have fainted away; for I can recollect nothing more until I woke up one day and found myself lying in a bed in the pavilion over the boat-house, with Mr. Weston watching by my bedside.

"I don't know how the time passed; I only know that it seemed endless. I think my illness was rheumatic fever, caught by lying on the damp ground nearly all that night when I ran away from the Towers. A long time went by: there was frost and snow. I saw the river once out of the window when I was lifted out of bed for an hour or two, and it was frozen; and once at midnight I heard the Kemberling Church bells ringing in the New Year. I was very ill, but I had ño doctor; and all that time I saw no one but my cousin Paul, and Lavinia Weston, and a servant called Betsy, a rough country-girl, who took care of me when my cousins were away. They were kind to me, and took great care of me."

"You did not see Olivia, then, all this time?" Edward asked, eagerly.

"No; I did not see my step-mother till some time after the New Year began. She came in suddenly one evening when Mrs. Weston was with me, and at first she seemed frightened at seeing me. She spoke to me kindly afterward, but in a strange, terror-stricken voice; and she laid her head down upon the counterpane of the bed, and sobbed aloud; and then Paul took her away, and spoke to her cruelly, very cruelly—taunting her with her love for you. I never understood till then why she hated me: but I pitied her after that; yes, Edward, miserable as I was, I pitied her, because you had never loved her. In all my wretchedness I was happier than her; for you had loved me, Edward—you had loved me!"

Mary lifted her face to her husband's lips, and those dear lips were pressed tenderly upon her pale forehead.

"Oh my love, my love!" the young man murmured; "my poor suffering angel! Can God ever forgive these people for their cruelty to you?

But, my darling, why did you make no effort to escape?"

"I was too ill to move; I believed that I was dying."

"But afterward, darling, when you were better, stronger, did you make no effort then to escape from your persecutors?"

Mary shook her head mournfully.

"Why should I try to escape from them?" she said. "What was there for me beyond that place? It was as well for me to be there as any where else. I thought you were dead, Edward; I thought you were dead, and life held nothing more for me. I could do nothing but wait till He who raised the widow's son should have pity upon me, and take me to the heaven where I thought you and papa had gone before me. I didn't want to go away from those dreary rooms over the boat-house. What did it matter to me whether I was there or at Marchmont Towers? I thought you were dead, and all the glories and grandeurs of the world were nothing to me. Nobody ill-treated me; I was let alone. Mrs. Weston told me that it was for my own sake they kept me hidden from every body about the Towers. I was a poor disgraced girl, she told me; and it was best for me to stop quietly in the pavilion till people had got tired of talking of me, and then my cousin Paul would take me away to the Continent, where no one would know who I was. She told me that the honor of my father's name, and of my family altogether, would be saved by this means. I replied that I had brought no dishonor on my dear father's name; but she only shook her head mournfully, and I was too weak to dispute with her. What did it matter? I thought you were dead, and that the world was finished for me. I sat day after day by the window; not looking out, for there was a Venetian blind that my cousin Paul had nailed down to the window-sill, and I could only see glimpses of the water through the long, narrow openings between the laths. I used to sit there listening to the moaning of the wind among the trees, or the sounds of horses' feet upon the towing-path, or the rain dripping into the river upon wet days. I think that even in my deepest misery God was good to me, for my mind sank into a dull apathy, and I seemed to lose even the capacity of suffering.

"One day—one day in March, when the wind was howling, and the smoke blew down the narrow chimney and filled the room—Mrs. Weston brought her husband, and he talked to me a little, and then talked to his wife in whispers. He seemed terribly frightened, and he trembled all the time, and kept saying, 'Poor thing; poor young woman!' but,his wife was cross to him, and wouldn't let him stop long in the room. After that Mr. Weston came very often, always with Lavinia, who seemed cleverer than he was, even as a doctor; for she dictated to him, and ordered him about in every thing. Then, by-and-by, when the birds were singing and the warm sunshine came into the room, my baby was born, Edward — my baby was born. I thought that God, who raised the widow's son, had heard my prayer, and had raised you up from the dead; for the baby's eyes were like yours, and I used to think sometimes that your soul was looking out of them and comforting me.

"Do you remember that poor foolish German

woman who believed that the spirit of a dead king came to her in the shape of a raven? She was not a good woman, I know, dear; but she must have loved the king very truly, or she never could have believed any thing so foolish. I don't believe in people's love when they love 'wisely,' Edward: the truest love is that which loves 'too well.'

"From the time of my baby's birth every thing was changed. I was more miserable, perhaps, because that dull, dead apathy cleared away, and my memory came back, and I thought of you, dear, and cried over my little angel's face as he slept. But I wasn't alone any longer. The world seemed narrowed into the little circle round my darling's cradle. I don't think he is like other babies, Edward. I think he has known of my sorrow from the very first, and has tried in his mute way to comfort me. The God who worked so many miracles, all separate tokens of His love and tenderness and pity for the sorrows of mankind, could easily make my baby different from other children, for a wretched mother's consolation.

"In the autumn after my darling's birth, Paul and his sister came for me one night, and took me away from the pavilion by the water to a deserted farm-house, where there was a woman to wait upon me and take care of me. She was not unkind to me, but she was rather neglectful of me. I did not mind that, for I wanted nothing except to be alone with my precious boy—your son, Edward; your son. The woman let me walk in the garden sometimes. It was a neglected garden, but there were bright flowers growing wild, and when the spring came again my pet used to lie on the grass and play with the butter-cups and daisies that I threw into his lap; and I think we were both of us happier and better than we had been in those two close rooms over the boat-house.

"I have told you all now, Edward—all except what happened this morning, when my step-mother and Hester Jobson came into my room in the early daybreak, and told me that I had been deceived, and that you were alive. My step-mother threw herself upon my knees at my feet, and asked me to forgive her, for she was a miserable sinner, who had been abandoned by God; and I forgave her, Edward, and kissed her; and you must forgive her too, dear, for I know that she has been very, very wretched. And she took the baby in her arms, and kissed him—oh, so passionately!—and cried over him. And then they brought me here in Mr. Jobson's cart, for Mr. Jobson was with them, and Hester held me in her arms all the time. And then, darling, then, after a long time, you came to me."

Edward put his arms round his wife, and kissed her once more. "We will never speak of this again, darling," he said. "I know all now; I understand it all. I will never again distress you by speaking of your cruel wrongs."

"And you will forgive Olivia, dear?"

"Yes, my pet, I will forgive—Olivia."

He said no more, for there was a footstep on the stair, and a glimmer of light shone through the crevices of the door. Hester Jobson came into the room with a pair of lighted wax-candles in white crockery candlesticks. But Hester was not alone; close behind her came a lady in a rustling silk gown, a tall matronly lady, who cried out,

"Where is she, Edward? Where is she? Let me see this poor ill-used child!"

It was Mrs. Arundel, who had come to Kemberling to see her newly-found daughter-in-law.

"Oh, my dear mother," cried the young man, "how good of you to come! Now, Mary, you need never again know what it is to want a protector, a tender womanly protector, who will shelter you from every harm."

Mary got up and went to Mrs. Arundel, who opened her arms to receive her son's young wife. But before she folded Mary to her friendly breast she took the girl's two hands in hers, and looked earnestly at her pale, wasted face.

She gave a long sigh as she contemplated those wan features, the shining light in the eyes, that looked unnaturally large by reason of the girl's hollow cheeks.

"Oh, my dear," cried Mrs. Arundel, "my poor, long-suffering child, how cruelly they have treated you!"

Edward looked at his mother, frightened by the earnestness of her manner; but she smiled at him with a bright, reassuring look.

"I shall take you home to Dangerfield with me, my poor love," she said to Mary; "and I shall nurse you, and make you as plump as a partridge, my poor wasted pet. And I'll be a mother to you, my motherless child. Oh, to think that there should be any wretch vile enough to—— But I won't agitate you, my dear. I'll take you away from this bleak horrid county by the first train to-morrow morning, and you shall sleep to-morrow night in the blue bedroom at Dangerfield, with the roses and myrtles waving against your window; and Edward shall go with us, and you sha'n't come back here till you're well and strong; and you'll try and love me, won't you, dear? And oh, Edward, I've seen the boy! and he's a *superb* creature, the very *image* of what you were at a twelvemonth old—and he came to me, and smiled at me, almost as if he knew I was his grandmother; and he has got FIVE teeth, but I'm *sorry* to tell you he's cutting them cross-wise, the top first instead of the bottom, Hester says."

"And Belinda, mother dear?" Edward said, presently, in a grave undertone.

"Belinda is an angel," Mrs. Arundel answered, quite as gravely. "She has been in her own room all day, and no one has seen her but her mother; but she came down to the hall as I was leaving the house this evening, and said to me, 'Dear Mrs. Arundel, tell him that he must not think I am so selfish as to be sorry for what has happened. Tell him that I am very glad to think his young wife has been saved.' She put her hand up to my lips to stop my speaking, and then went back again to her room; and if that isn't acting like an angel, I don't know what is."

--------

CHAPTER XLI.

"ALL WITHIN IS DARK AS NIGHT."

PAUL MARCHMONT did not leave Stony-Stringford Farm-house till dusk upon that bright summer's day; and the friendly twilight is slow to come in the early days of July, however a man may loathe the sunshine. Paul Marchmont stopped at the deserted farm-house, wandering in and out of the empty rooms, strolling listlessly about the neglected garden, or coming to a dead stop sometimes, and standing stock-still for ten minutes at a time, staring at the wall before him, and counting the slimy traces of the snails upon the branches of a plum-tree, or the flies in a spider's web. Paul Marchmont was afraid to leave that lonely farm-house. He was afraid as yet. He scarcely knew what he feared, for a kind of stupor had succeeded the violent emotions of the past few hours; and the time slipped by him, and his brain grew bewildered when he tried to realize his position.

It was very difficult for him to do this. The calamity that had come upon him was a calamity that he had never anticipated. He was a clever man, and he had put his trust in his own cleverness. He had never expected to be *found out.*

Until this hour every thing had been in his favor. His dupes and victims had played into his hands. Mary's grief, which had rendered her a passive creature, utterly indifferent to her own fate — her peculiar education, which had taught her every thing except knowledge of the world in which she was to live — had enabled Paul Marchmont to carry out a scheme so infamous and daring that it was beyond the suspicion of honest men, almost too base for the comprehension of ordinary villains.

He had never expected to be found out. All his plans had been deliberately and carefully prepared. Immediately after Edward's marriage and safe departure for the Continent, Paul had intended to convey Mary and the child, with the grim attendant whom he had engaged for them, far away, to one of the remotest villages in Wales.

Alone he would have done this; traveling by night, and trusting no one; for the hired attendant knew nothing of Mary's real position. She had been told that the girl was a poor relation of Paul's, and that her story was a very sorrowful one. If the poor creature had strange fancies and delusions, it was no more than might be expected; for she had suffered enough to turn a stronger brain than her own. Every thing had been arranged, and so cleverly arranged, that Mary and the child would disappear after dusk one summer's evening, and not even Lavinia Weston would be told whither they had gone.

Paul had never expected to be found out. But he had least of all expected betrayal from the quarter whence it had come. He had made Olivia his tool; but he had acted cautiously even with her. He had confided nothing to her; and although she had suspected some foul play in the matter of Mary's disappearance, she had been certain of nothing. She had uttered no falsehood when she swore to Edward Arundel that she did not know where his wife was. But for her accidental discovery of the secret of the pavilion, she would never have known of Mary's existence after that October afternoon on which the girl left Marchmont Towers.

But here Paul had been betrayed by the carelessness of the hired girl who acted as Mary Arundel's jailer and attendant. It was Olivia's habit to wander often in that dreary wood by the

water during the winter in which Mary was kept prisoner in the pavilion over the boat-house. Lavinia Weston and Paul Marchmont spent each of them a great deal of their time in the pavilion; but they could not be always on guard there. There was the world to be hoodwinked; and the surgeon's wife had to perform all her duties as a matron before the face of Kemberling, and had to give some plausible account of her frequent visits to the boat-house. Paul liked the place for his painting, Mrs. Weston informed her friends; and he was so enthusiastic in his love of art, that it was really a pleasure to participate in his enthusiasm; so she liked to sit with him, and talk to him or read to him while he painted. This explanation was quite enough for Kemberling, and Mrs. Weston went to the pavilion at Marchmont Towers three or four times a week without causing any scandal thereby.

But however well you may manage things yourself, it is not always easy to secure the careful co-operation of the people you employ. Betsy Murrel was a stupid, narrow-minded young person, who was very safe so far as regarded the possibility of any sympathy with, or compassion for, Mary Arundel arising in her stolid nature; but the stupid stolidity which made her safe in one way rendered her dangerous in another. One day, while Mrs. Weston was with the hapless young prisoner, Miss Murrel went out upon the water-side to converse with a good-looking young bargeman, who was a connection of her family, and perhaps an admirer of the young lady herself; and the door of the painting-room being left wide open, Olivia Marchmont wandered listlessly into the pavilion—there was a dismal fascination for her in that spot, on which she had heard Edward Arundel declare his love for John Marchmont's daughter — and heard Mary's voice in the chamber at the top of the stone steps.

This was how Olivia had surprised Paul's secret; and from that hour it had been the artist's business to rule this woman by the only weapon which he possessed against her—her own secret, her own weak folly, her mad love of Edward Arundel and jealous hatred of the woman whom he had loved. This weapon was a very powerful one, and Paul used it unsparingly.

When the woman who for seven-and-twenty years of her life had lived without sin, who from the hour in which she had been old enough to know right from wrong until Edward Arundel's second return from India had sternly done her duty—when this woman, who little by little had slipped away from her high standing-point and sunk down into a morass of sin—when this woman remonstrated with Mr. Marchmont he turned upon her and lashed her with the scourge of her own folly.

"You come and upbraid me," he said, "and you call me villain and arch-traitor, and say that you can not abide this your sin; and that your guilt, in keeping our secret, cries to you in the dead hours of the night; and you call upon me to undo what I have done, and to restore Mary Marchmont to her rights. Do you remember what her highest right is? Do you remember that which I must restore to her when I give her back this house and the income that goes along with it? If I restore Marchmont Towers I must restore to her *Edward Arundel's love.* You have forgotten that, perhaps. If she ever re-enters this house she will come back to it leaning on his arm. You will see them together. You will hear of their happiness ; and do you think that *he* will ever forgive you for your part of the conspiracy ? Yes, it *is* a conspiracy, if you like. If you are not afraid to call it by a hard name, why should I fear to do so ? Will he ever forgive you, do you think, when he knows that his young wife has been the victim of a senseless, vicious love ? Yes, Olivia Marchmont, any love is vicious which is given unsought, and is so strong a passion, so blind and unreasoning a folly, that honor, mercy, truth, and Christianity are trampled down before it. How will you endure Edward Arundel's contempt for you ? How will you tolerate his love for Mary, multiplied twentyfold by all this romantic business of separation and persecution ?

"You talk to me of my sin. Who was it who first sinned ? Who was it who drove Mary Marchmont from this house—not once only, but twice—by her cruelty ? Who was it who persecuted her and tortured her day by day and hour by hour, not openly, not with an uplifted hand or blows that could be warded off, but by cruel hints and innuendoes, by unwomanly sneers and hellish taunts. Look into your heart, Olivia Marchmont; and when you make atonement for your sin I will make restitution for mine. In the mean time, if this business is painful to you, the way lies open before you ; go and take Edward Arundel to the pavilion yonder, and give him back his wife ; give the lie to all your past life, and restore these devoted young lovers to each other's arms."

This weapon never failed in its effect ; Olivia Marchmont might loathe herself, and her sin, and her life, which was made hideous to her because of her sin ; but she *could* not bring herself to restore Mary to her lover-husband ; she could not tolerate the idea of their happiness. Every night she groveled on her knees, and swore to her offended God that she would do this thing, she would render this sacrifice of atonement ; but every morning, when her weary eyes opened on the hateful sunlight, she cried, "Not to-day ; not to-day."

Again and again, during Edward Arundel's residence at Kemberling Retreat, she had set out from Marchmont Towers with the intention of revealing to him the place where his young wife was hidden ; but, again and again, she had turned back and left her work undone. She *could* not ; she could not. In the dead of the night, under pouring rain, with the bleak winds of winter blowing in her face, she had set out upon that unfinished journey, only to stop midway, and cry out, "No, no, no ; not to-night ; I can not endure it yet !"

It was only when another and a fiercer jealousy was awakened in this woman's breast that she arose all at once, strong, resolute, and undaunted, to do the work she had so miserably deferred. As one poison is said to neutralize the evil power of another, so Olivia Marchmont's jealousy of Belinda seemed to blot out and extinguish her hatred of Mary. Better any thing than that Edward Arundel should have a new and perhaps a fairer bride. The jealous woman had always looked upon Mary Marchmont as a despicable rival. Better that Edward should be

tied to this girl than that he should rejoice in the smiles of a lovelier woman, worthier of his affection. *This* was the feeling paramount in Olivia's breast, although she was herself half unconscious how entirely this was the motive power which had given her new strength and resolution. She tried to think that it was the awakening of her conscience that had made her strong enough to do this one good work ; but, in the semi-darkness of her own mind, there was still a feeble glimmer of the light of truth ; and it was this that had prompted her to cry out on her knees before the altar in Hillingsworth Church, and declare the sinfulness of her nature.

Paul Marchmont stopped several times before the ragged, untrimmed fruit-trees in his purposeless wanderings in the neglected garden at Stony Stringford, before the vaporous confusion cleared away from his brain, and he was able to understand what had happened to him.

His first reasonable action was to take out his watch ; but even then he stood for some moments staring at the dial before he remembered why he had taken the watch from his pocket, or what it was that he wanted to know. By Mr. Marchmont's chronometer it was ten minutes past seven o'clock ; but the watch had been unwound upon the previous night, and had run down. Paul put it back in his waistcoat-pocket, and then walked slowly along the weedy pathway to that low latticed window in which he had often seen Mary Arundel standing with her child in her arms. He went to this window and looked in, with his face against the glass. The room was neat and orderly now, for the woman whom Mr. Marchmont had hired had gone about her work as usual, and was in the act of filling a little brown earthen-ware tea-pot from a kettle on the hob when Paul stared in at her.

She looked up as Mr. Marchmont's figure came between her and the light, and nearly dropped the little brown tea-pot in her terror of her offended employer.

But Paul pulled open the window, and spoke to her very quietly : "Stop where you are," he said ; "I want to speak to you ; I'll come in."

He went into the house by a door that had once been the front and principal entrance, which opened into a low wainscoted hall. From this room he went into the parlor, which had been Mary Arundel's apartment, and in which the hired nurse was now preparing her breakfast. "I thought I might as well get a cup of tea, Sir, while I waited for your orders," the woman murmured, apologetically ; "for bein' knocked up so early this morning, you see, Sir, has made my head *that* bad, I could scarcely bear myself ; and—"

Paul lifted his hand to stop the woman's talk, as he had done before. He had no consciousness of what she was saying, but the sound of her voice pained him. His eyebrows contracted with a spasmodic action, as if something had hurt his head.

There was a Dutch clock in the corner of the room, with a long pendulum swinging against the wall. By this clock it was half past eight. "Is your clock right ?" Paul asked.

"Yes, Sir. Leastways it may be five minutes too slow ; but not more."

Mr. Marchmont took out his watch, wound it up, and regulated it by the Dutch clock. "Now," he said, "perhaps you can tell me clearly what happened. I want no excuses, remember; I only want to know what occurred, and what was said, word for word, remember!"

He sat down, but got up again directly and walked to the window; then he paced up and down the room two or three times, and then went back to the fire-place and sat down again. He was like a man who, in the racking torture of some physical pain, finds a miserable relief in his own restlessness.

"Come," he said; "I am waiting."

"Yes, Sir; which, begging your parding, if you wouldn't mind sitting still like, while I'm a-telling of you, which it do remind me of the wild beastes in the Zoological, Sir, to that degree, that the boil, to which I am subjeck, Sir, and have been from a child, might prevent me bein' as truthful as I should wish. Mrs. Marchmount, Sir, she come before it was light, in a cart, Sir, which it was a shaycart, and made comfortable with cushions and straw, and such like, or I should not have let the young lady go away in it; and she bring with her a respectable homely-looking young person, which she call Hester Jobling or Gobson, or somethink of that sound like, which my memory is treechrous, and I don't wish to tell a story on no account; and Mrs. Marchmount she go straight up to my young lady, and she shakes her by the shoulder; and then the young woman called Hester, she wakes up my young lady quite gentle like, and kisses her and cries over her; and a man as drove the cart, which looked a small tradesman well-to-do, brings his trap round to the front door—you may see the trax of the wheels upon the gravel now, Sir, if you disbelieve me. And Mrs. Marchmount and the young woman called Hester, between 'em they gets my young lady up, and dresses her, and dresses the child; and does it all so quick, and overrides me to such a degree, that I hadn't no power to prevent 'em; but I say to Mrs. Marchmount, I say: 'Is it Mr. Marchmount's orders as his cousin should be took away this morning?' and she stare at me hard, and say, 'Yes;' and she have allus an abrumpt way, but was abrumpter than ordinary this morning. And oh, Sir, bein' a pore lone woman, what was I to do?"

"Have you nothing more to tell me?"

"Nothing, Sir; leastways except as they lifted my young lady into the cart, and the man got in after 'em, and drove away as fast as his horse would go; and they had been gone two minutes when I began to feel all in a tremble like, for fear as I might have done wrong in lettin' of 'em go."

"You did do wrong," Paul answered, sternly; "but no matter. If these officious friends of my poor weak-witted cousin choose to take her away, so much the better for me, who have been burdened with her long enough. Since your charge has gone, your services are no longer wanted. I sha'n't act illiberally to you, though I am very much annoyed by your folly and stupidity. Is there any thing due to you?"

Mrs. Brown hesitated for a moment, and then replied, in a very insinuating tone,

"Not wages, Sir; there ain't no wages doo to me—which you paid me a quarter in advance last Saturday was a week, and took a receipt, Sir, for the amount. But I have done my dooty, Sir, for my 'ealth ain't what it was when I answered your advertisement requirin' a respectable motherly person, to take charge of a invalid lady, not objectin' to the country—which I freely tell you, Sir, if I'd known that the country was a rheumatic old place like this, with rats enough to scare away a regyment of soldiers, I would not have undertook the situation; so any present as you might think sootable, considerin' all things, and—"

"That will do," said Paul Marchmont, taking a handful of loose money from his waistcoat-pocket; "I suppose a ten-pound note would satisfy you?"

"Indeed it would, Sir, and very liberal of you too."

"Very well. I've got a five-pound note here and five sovereigns. The best thing you can do is to get back to London at once; there's a train leaves Milsome Station at eleven o'clock—Milsome's not more than a mile and a half from here. You can get your things together; there's a boy about the place who will carry them for you, I suppose."

"Yes, Sir; there's a boy by the name of William."

"He can go with you, then; and if you look sharp, you can catch the eleven o'clock train."

"Yes, Sir; and thank you kindly, Sir."

"I don't want any thanks. See that you don't miss the train; that's all you have to take care of."

Mr. Marchmont went out into the garden again. He had done something, at any rate; he had arranged for getting this woman out of the way.

If—if by any remote chance there might be yet a possibility of keeping the secret of Mary's existence, here was one witness already got rid of.

But was there any chance? Mr. Marchmont sat down on a rickety old garden-seat, and tried to think—tried to take a deliberate survey of his position.

No; there was no hope for him. Look which way he could, there was not one ray of light. With George Weston and Olivia, Betsy Murrel, the servant-girl, and Hester Jobson, to bear witness against him, what could he hope?

The surgeon would be able to declare that the child was Mary's son, her legitimate son, sole heir to that estate of which Paul had taken possession.

There was no hope. There was no possibility that Olivia should waver in her purpose; for had she not brought with her two witnesses—Hester Jobson and her husband?

From that moment the case was taken out of her hands. The honest carpenter and his wife would see that Mary had her rights.

"It will be a glorious speculation for them," thought Paul Marchmont, who naturally measured other people's characters by a standard derived from an accurate knowledge of his own.

Yes, his ruin was complete. Destruction had come upon him, swift and sudden as the caprice of a madwoman—or—the thunder-bolt of an offended Providence. What should he do? Run away, sneak away by back-lanes and narrow foot-paths to the nearest railway-station, hide himself in a third-class carriage going London-wards, and from London get away to Liverpool, to creep on board some emigrant vessel bound for New York.

He could not even do this; for he was without the means of getting so much as the railway-ticket that should carry him on the first stage of his flight. After having given ten pounds to Mrs. Brown, he had only a few shillings in his waistcoat-pocket. He had only one article of any value about him, and that was his watch, which had cost fifty pounds. But the March-mont arms were emblazoned on the outside of the case; and Paul's name in full, and the address of Marchmont Towers, were ostentatiously engraved inside, so that any attempt to dispose of the watch must inevitably lead to the identification of the owner.

Paul Marchmont had made no provision for this evil day. Supreme in the consciousness of his own talents, he had never imagined discovery and destruction. His plans had been so well arranged. On the very day after Edward's second marriage Mary and her child would have been conveyed away to the remotest district in Wales; and the artist would have laughed at the idea of danger. The shallow schemer might have been able to manage this poor broken-hearted girl, whose many sorrows had brought her to look upon life as a thing which was never meant to be joyful, and which was only to be endured patiently, like some slow disease that would be surely cured in the grave. It had been so easy to deal with this ignorant and gentle victim that Paul had grown bold and confident, and had ignored the possibility of such ruin as had now come down upon him.

What was he to do? What was the nature of his crime, and what penalty had he incurred? He tried to answer these questions; but, as his offense was of no common kind, he knew of no common law which could apply to it. Was it a felony, this appropriation of another person's property, this concealment of another person's existence? or was it only a conspiracy amenable to no criminal law, and would he be called upon merely to make restitution of that which he had spent and wasted? What did it matter? Either way there was nothing for him but ruin, irretrievable ruin.

There are some men who can survive discovery and defeat, and begin a new life in a new world, and succeed in a new career. But Paul Marchmont was not one of these. He could not stick a hunting-knife and a brace of revolvers in his leathern belt, sling a game-bag across his shoulders, take up his breech-loading rifle, and go out into the back-woods of an uncivilized country, to turn sheep-breeder, and hold his own against a race of agricultural savages. He was a Cockney, and for him there was only one world—a world in which men wore varnished boots, and enameled shirt-studs with portraits of La Montespan or La Dubarry, and lived in chambers in the Albany, and treated each other to little dinners at Greenwich and Richmond, and cut a grand figure at a country house, and collected a gallery of art and a museum of *bric a brac*. This was the world upon the outer edge of which Paul Marchmont had lived so long, looking in at the brilliant inhabitants with hun-

gry, yearning eyes, through all the days of his poverty and obscurity. This was the world into which he had pushed himself at last by means of a crime.

He was forty years of age; and in all his life he had never had but one ambition—and that was to be master of Marchmont Towers. The remote chance of that inheritance had hung before him ever since his boyhood, a glittering prize, far away in the distance, but so brilliant as to blind him to the brightness of all nearer chances. Why should he slave at his easel, and toil to become a great painter? When would art earn him eleven thousand a year? The greatest painter of Mr. Marchmont's time lived in a miserable lodging at Chelsea. It was before the days of the "Railway Station" and the "Derby Day;" or perhaps Paul might have made an effort to become that which Heaven never meant him to be—a great painter. No; art was only a means of living with this man. He painted, and sold his pictures to his few patrons, who beat him down unmercifully, giving him a small profit upon his canvas and colors, for the encouragement of native art; but he only painted to live.

He was waiting. From the time when he could scarcely speak plain Marchmont Towers had been a familiar word in his ears and on his lips. He knew the number of lives that stood between his father and the estate, and had learned to say, naïvely enough then,

"Oh, pa, don't you wish that Uncle Philip, and Uncle Marmaduke, and Cousin John would die soon?"

He was two-and-twenty years of age when his father died; and he felt a faint thrill of satisfaction, even in the midst of his sorrow, at the thought that there was one life the less between him and the end of his hopes. But other lives had sprung up in the interim. There was young Arthur and little Mary; and Marchmont Towers was like a caravanserai at which seems to be further and further away as the weary traveler strives to reach it.

Still Paul hoped, and watched, and waited. He had all the instincts of a sybarite, and he fancied, therefore, that he was destined to be a rich man. He watched, and waited, and hoped, and cheered his mother and sister when they were downcast with the hope of better days. When the chance came he seized upon it, and plotted, and succeeded, and reveled in his brief success.

But now ruin had come to him what was he to do? He tried to make some plan for his own conduct, but he could not. His brain reeled with the effort which he made to realize his own position.

He walked up and down one of the path-ways in the garden until a quarter to ten o'clock; then he went into the house, and waited till Mrs. Brown had departed from Stony-Stringford Farm, attended by the boy, who carried two bundles, a band-box, and a carpet-bag.

"Come back here when you have taken those things to the station," Paul said: "I shall want you."

He watched the dilapidated five-barred gate swing to after the departure of Mrs. Brown and her attendant, and then went to look at his horse. The patient animal had been standing in a shed all this time, and had had neither food nor water. Paul searched among the empty barns and outhouses, and found a few handfuls of fodder. He took this to the animal, and then went back to the garden—to that quiet garden, where the bees were buzzing about in the sunshine with a drowsy, booming sound, and where a great tabby cat was sleeping, stretched flat upon its side, on one of the flower-beds.

Paul Marchmont waited here very impatiently till the boy came back.

"I must see Lavinia," he thought. "I dare not leave this place till I have seen Lavinia. I don't know what may be happening at Hillingsworth or Kemberling. These things are taken up sometimes by the populace. They may make a party against me; they may—"

He stood still, gnawing the edges of his nails, and staring down at the gravel-walk.

He was thinking of things that he had read in the newspapers—cases in which some cruel mother who had ill-used her child, or some suspected assassin who, in all human probability, had poisoned his wife, had been well-nigh torn piecemeal by an infuriated mob, and had been glad to cling for protection to the officers of justice, or to beg leave to stay in prison after acquittal, for safe shelter from honest men and women's indignation.

He remembered one special case in which the populace, unable to get at a man's person, tore down his house, and vented their fury upon unsentient bricks and mortar.

Mr. Marchmont took out a little memorandum-book, and scrawled a few lines in pencil:

"I am here, at Stony-Stringford Farm-house," he wrote. "For God's sake, come to me, Lavinia, and at once; you can drive here yourself. I want to know what has happened at Kemberling and at Hillingsworth. Find out every thing for me, and come.    P. M."

It was nearly twelve o'clock when the boy returned. Paul gave him this letter, and told the lad to get on his own horse, and ride to Kemberling as fast as he could go. He was to leave the horse at Kemberling, in Mr. Weston's stable, and was to come back to Stony Stringford with Mrs. Weston. This order Paul particularly impressed upon the boy, lest he should stop in Kemberling, and reveal the secret of Paul's hiding-place.

Mr. Paul Marchmont was afraid. A terrible sickening dread had taken possession of him, and what little manliness there had ever been in his nature seemed to have deserted him to-day.

Oh, the long, dreary hours of that miserable day! the hideous sunshine that scorched Mr. Marchmont's bare head as he loitered about the garden!—he had left his hat in the house; but he did not even know that he was bareheaded. Oh, the misery of that long day of suspense and anguish! The sick consciousness of utter defeat, the thought of the things that he might have done, the purse that he might have made with the money that he had lavished on pictures, and decorations, and improvements, and the profligate extravagance of splendid entertainments! This is what he thought of, and these were the thoughts that tortured him. But in all that miserable day he never felt one pang of remorse for the agonies that he had inflicted

upon his innocent victim; on the contrary, he hated her because of this discovery, and gnashed his teeth as he thought how she and her young husband would enjoy all the grandeur of Marchmont Towers—all that noble revenue which he had hoped to hold till his dying day.

It was growing dusk when Mr. Marchmont heard the sound of wheels in the dusty lane outside the garden-wall. He went through the house, and into the farm-yard, in time to receive his sister Lavinia at the gate. It was the wheels of her pony-carriage he had heard. She drove a pair of ponies which Paul had given her. He gnashed his teeth as he remembered that this was another piece of extravagance—another sum of money recklessly squandered, when it might have gone toward the making of a rich provision for this evil day.

Mrs. Weston was very pale, and her brother could see by her face that she brought him no good news. She left her ponies to the care of the boy, and went into the garden with her brother.

"Well, Lavinia?"

"Well, Paul, it is a dreadful business," Mrs. Weston said, in a low voice.

"It's all George's doing! It's all the work of that infernal scoundrel!" cried Paul, passionately. "But he shall pay bitterly for—"

"Don't let us talk of him, Paul; no good can come of that. What are you going to do?"

"I don't know. I sent for you because I wanted your help and advice. What's the good of your coming if you bring me no help?"

"Don't be cruel, Paul. Heaven knows I'll do my best. But I can't see what's to be done—except for you to get away, Paul. Every thing's known. Olivia stopped the marriage publicly in Hillingsworth Church; and all the Hillingsworth people followed Edward Arundel's carriage to Kemberling. The report spread like wild-fire; and oh, Paul! the Kemberling people have taken it up, and our windows have been broken, and there's been a crowd all day upon the terrace at the Towers, and they've tried to get into the house, declaring that they know you're hiding somewhere. Paul, Paul, what are we to do? The people hooted after me as I drove away from the High Street, and the boys threw stones at the ponies. Almost all the servants have left the Towers. The constables have been up there trying to get the crowd off the terrace. But what are we to do, Paul? what are we to do?"

"Kill ourselves," answered the artist, savagely. "What else should we do? What have we to live for? You have a little money, I suppose; I have none. Do you think I can go back to the old life? Do you think I can go back, and live in that shabby house in Charlotte Street, and paint the same rocks and boulders, the same long stretch of sea, the same low lurid streaks of light—all the old subjects over again—for the same starvation prices? Do you think I can ever tolerate shabby clothes again, or miserable makeshift dinners—bashed mutton, with ill-cut hunks of lukewarm meat floating about in greasy slop called gravy, and washed down with flat porter fetched half an hour too soon from a public house—do you think I can go back to that? No; I have tasted the cream of life: I have lived; and I'll never go back to the living death called poverty. Do you think I can stand in that passage in Charlotte' Street again, Lavinia, to be bullied by an illiterate tax-gatherer, or insulted by an infuriated baker? No, Lavinia; I have made my venture, and I have failed."

"But what will you do, Paul?"

"I don't know," he answered, moodily. This was a lie. He knew well enough what he meant to do: he would kill himself. That resolution inspired him with a desperate kind of courage. He would escape from the mob; he would get away somewhere or other quietly, and there kill himself. He didn't know how as yet; but he would deliberate upon that point at his leisure, and choose the death that was supposed to be least painful.

"Where are my mother and Clarissa?" he asked, presently.

"They are at our house; they came to me directly they heard the rumor of what had happened. I don't know how they heard it; but every one heard of it simultaneously as it seemed. My mother is in a dreadful state. I dared not tell her that I had known it all along."

"Oh, of course not," answered Paul, with a sneer; "let me bear the burden of my guilt alone. What did my mother say?"

"She kept saying again and again, 'I can't believe it. I can't believe that he could do any thing cruel; he has been such a good son.'"

"I was not cruel," Paul Marchmont cried, vehemently; "the girl had every comfort. I never grudged money for her comfort. She was a miserable, apathetic creature, to whom fortune was almost a burden rather than an advantage. If I separated her from her husband—bah!—was that such a cruelty? She was no worse off than if Edward Arundel had been killed in that railway accident; and it might have been so."

He didn't waste much time by reasoning on this point. He thought of his mother and sisters. From first to last he had been a good son and a good brother.

"What money have you, Lavinia?"

"A good deal; you have been very generous to me, Paul; and you shall have it all back again if you want it. I have got upward of two thousand pounds altogether; for I have been very careful of the money you have given me."

"You have been wise. Now listen to me, Lavinia. I have been a good son, and I have borne my burdens uncomplainingly. It is your turn now to bear yours. I must get back to Marchmont Towers, if I can, and gather together whatever personal property I have there. It isn't much—only a few trinkets, and such like. You must send me some one you can trust to fetch those to-night; for I shall not stay an hour in the place. I may not even be admitted into it; for Edward Arundel may have already taken possession in his wife's name. Then you will have to decide where you are to go. You can't stay in this part of the country. Weston must be liable to some penalty or other for his share in the business, unless he's bought over as a witness to testify to the identity of Mary's child. I haven't time to think of all this. I want you to promise me that you will take care of your mother and your invalid sister."

"I will, Paul; I will indeed. But tell me

what you are going to do yourself, and where you are going."

"I don't know," Paul Marchmont answered, in the same tone as before; "but whatever I do I want you to give me your solemn promise that you will be good to my mother and sister."

"I will, Paul; I promise you to do as you have done."

"You had better leave Kemberling by the first train to-morrow morning; take my mother and Clarissa with you; take every thing that is worth taking, and leave Weston behind you to bear the brunt of this business. You can get a lodging in the old neighborhood, and no one will molest you when you once get away from this place. But remember one thing, Lavinia: if Mary Arundel's child should die, and Mary herself should die childless, Clarissa will inherit Marchmont Towers. Don't forget that. There's a chance far away, and unlikely enough; but it is a chance."

"But you are more likely to outlive Mary and her child than Clarissa is," Mrs. Weston answered, with a feeble attempt at hopefulness; "try and think of that, Paul, and let the hope cheer you."

"Hope!" cried Mr. Marchmont, with a discordant laugh. "Yes; I'm forty years old, and for five-and-thirty of those years I've hoped and waited for Marchmont Towers. I can't hope any longer, or wait any longer. I give it up; I've fought hard, but I'm beaten."

It was nearly dark by this time, the shadowy darkness of a mid-summer's evening; and there were stars shining faintly out of the sky.

"You can drive me back to the Towers," Paul Marchmont said. "I don't want to lose any time in getting there; I may be locked out by Mr. Edward Arundel if I don't take care."

Mrs. Weston and her brother went back to the farm-yard. It was sixteen miles from Kemberling to Stony Stringford; and the ponies were steaming, for Lavinia had come at a good rate. But it was no time for the consideration of horse-flesh. Paul took a rug from the empty seat and wrapped himself in it. He would not be likely to be recognized in the darkness, sitting back in the low seat, and made bulky by the ponderous covering in which he had enveloped himself. Mrs. Weston took the whip from the boy, gathered up the reins, and drove off. Paul had left no orders about the custody of the old farm-house. The boy went home to his master, at the other end of the farm; and the night-winds wandered wherever they listed through the deserted habitation.

## CHAPTER XLII.

"THERE IS CONFUSION WORSE THAN DEATH."

THE brother and sister exchanged very few words during the drive between Stony-Stringford and Marchmont Towers. It was arranged between them that Mrs. Weston should drive by a back way leading to a lane that skirted the edge of the river: and that Paul should get out at a gate opening into the wood, and by that means make his way unobserved, to the house which had so lately been to all intents and purposes his own.

He dared not attempt to enter the Towers by any other way; for the indignant populace might still be lurking about the front of the house, eager to inflict summary vengeance upon the persecutor of a helpless girl.

It was between nine and ten o'clock when Mr. Marchmont got out at the little gate. All here was as still as death ; and Paul heard the croaking of the frogs upon the margin of a little pool in the wood, and the sound of horses' hoofs a mile away upon the loose gravel by the water-side.

"Good-night, Lavinia," he said. "Send for the things as soon as you go back; and be sure you send a safe person for them."

"Oh yes, dear ; but hadn't you better take any thing of value yourself?" Mrs. Weston asked, anxiously. "You say you have no money. Perhaps it would be best for you to send me the jewelry, though, and I can send you what money you want by my messenger."

"I sha'n't want any money—at least I have enough for what I want. What have you done with your savings?"

"They are in a London bank. But I have plenty of ready money in the house. You must want money, Paul?"

"I tell you, no. I have as much as I want."

"But tell me your plans, Paul ; I must know your plans before I leave Lincolnshire myself. Are *you* going away?"

"Yes."

"Immediately?"

"Immediately."

"Shall you go to London?"

"Perhaps. I don't know yet."

"But when shall we see you again, Paul? or how shall we hear of you?"

"I'll write to you."

"Where?"

"At the post-office in Rathbone Place. Don't bother me with a lot of questions to-night, Lavinia ; I'm not in the humor to answer them."

Paul Marchmont turned away from his sister impatiently, and opened the gate; but before she had driven off he went back to her:

"Shake hands, Lavinia," he said ; "shake hands, my dear; it may be a long time before you and I meet again."

He bent down and kissed his sister.

"Drive home as fast as you can, and send the messenger directly. He had better come to the door of the lobby, near Olivia's room. Where is Olivia, by-the-by? Is she still with the step-daughter she loves so dearly?"

"No; she went to Swampington early in the afternoon. A fly was ordered from the Black Bull, and she went away in it."

"So much the better," answered Mr. March-mont. "Good-night, Lavinia. Don't let my mother think ill of me. I tried to do the best I could to make her happy. Good-by."

"Good-by, dear Paul; God bless you!"

The blessing was invoked with as much sincerity as if Lavinia Weston had been a good woman, and her brother a good man. Perhaps neither of those two was able to realize the extent of the crime which they had assisted each other to commit.

Mrs. Weston drove away; and Paul went up to the back of the Towers, and under an arch-way leading into the quadrangle. All about the house was as quiet as if the Sleeping Beauty and her court had been its only occupants.

The inhabitants of Kemberling and the neigh-borhood were an orderly people, who burnt few candles between May and September; and how-ever much they might have desired to avenge Mary Arundel's wrongs by tearing Paul March-mont to pieces, their patience had been exhaust-ed by nightfall, and they had been glad to re-turn to their respective abodes to discuss Paul's iniquities comfortably over the nine o'clock beer.

Paul stood still in the quadrangle for a few moments, and listened. He could hear no hu-man breath or whisper; he only heard the sound of the corn-crake in the fields to the right of the Towers, and the distant rumbling of wagon-wheels on the high-road. There was a glimmer of light in one of the windows belonging to the servants' offices—only one dim glimmer, where there had usually been a row of brilliantly-light-ed casements. Lavinia was right, then ; almost all the servants had left the Towers. Paul tried to open the half-glass door leading into the lob-by ; but it was locked. He rang a bell; and after about three minutes' delay a buxom coun-try-girl appeared in the lobby carrying a candle. She was some kitchen-maid, or dairy-maid, or scullery-maid, whom Paul could not remember to have ever seen until now. She opened the door and admitted him, dropping a courtesy as he passed her. There was some relief even in this. Mr. Marchmont had scarcely expected to get into the house at all; still less to be received with common civility by any of the servants, who had so lately obeyed him and fawned upon him.

"Where are all the rest of the servants?" he asked.

"They're all gone, Sir; except him as you brought down from London—Mr. Peterson—and me and mother. Mother's in the laundry, Sir; and I'm scullery-maid."

"Why did the other servants leave the place?"

"Mostly because they was afraid of the mob upon the terrace, I think, Sir; for there's been people all the afternoon throwin' stones and breakin' the windows; and I don't think as there's a whole pane of glass in the front of the house, Sir ; and Mr. Gormby, Sir, he come about four o'clock, and he got the people to go away, Sir, by tellin' 'em as it warn't your property, Sir, but the young lady's, Miss Mary Marchmont—least-ways, Mrs. Airendale—as they was destroyin' of; but most of the servants had gone before that,· Sir, except Mr. Peterson; and Mr. Gorm-by give orders as me and mother was to lock all the doors, and let no one in ·upon no account whatever; and he's coming to-morrow mornin' to take possession, he says; and please, Sir, you can't come in; for his special orders to me and mother was, no one, and you in particklar."

"Nonsense, girl!" exclaimed Mr. Marchmont, decisively ; "who is Mr. Gormby, that he should give orders as to who comes in or stops out? I'm only coming in for half an hour, to pack my port-manteau. Where's Peterson?"

"In the dinin'-room, Sir; but please, Sir, you mustn't—"

The girl made a feeble effort to intercept Mr. Marchmont, in accordance with the steward's special orders: which were that Paul should, upon no pretense whatever, be suffered to enter that house. But the artist snatched the candlestick from her hand, and went away toward the dining-room, leaving her to stare after him in stupid amazement.

Paul found his valet Peterson, taking what he called a snack, in the dining-room. A cloth was spread upon the corner of the table; and there was a fore-quarter of cold roast lamb, a bottle of French brandy, and a decanter half full of Madeira before the valet.

He started as his master entered the room, and looked up, not very respectfully, but with no unfriendly glance.

"Give me half a tumbler of that brandy, Peterson," said Mr. Marchmont.

The man obeyed; and Paul drained the fiery spirit as if it had been so much water. It was four-and-twenty hours since meat or drink had crossed his dry white lips.

"Why didn't you go away with the rest?" he asked, as he set down the empty glass.

"It's only rats, Sir, that run away from a falling house. I stopped, thinkin' you'd be goin' away somewhere, and that you'd want me."

The solid and unvarnished truth of the matter was that Peterson had taken for granted that his master had made an excellent purse against this evil day, and would be ready to start for the Continent or America, there to lead a pleasant life upon the proceeds of his iniquity. The valet never imagined his master guilty of such besotted folly as to leave himself unprepared for this catastrophe.

"I thought you might still want me, Sir," he said; "and wherever you're going, I'm quite ready to go to. You've been a good master to me, Sir; and I don't want to leave a good master because things go against him."

Paul Marchmont shook his head, and held out the empty tumbler for his servant to pour more brandy into it.

"I am going away," he said; "but I want no servant where I'm going; but I'm grateful to you for your offer, Peterson. Will you come up stairs with me? I want to pack a few things."

"They're all packed, Sir. I knew you'd be leaving, and I've packed every thing."

"My dressing-case?"

"Yes, Sir. You've got the key of that."

"Yes; I know, I know."

Paul Marchmont was silent for a few minutes, thinking. Every thing that he had in the way of personal property of any value was in the dressing-case of which he had spoken. There was five or six hundred pounds' worth of jewelry in Mr. Marchmont's dressing-case; for the first instinct of the *nouveau riche* exhibits itself in diamond shirt-studs; cameo rings; malachite death's-heads with emerald eyes; grotesque and pleasing charms in the form of coffins, coal-scuttles, and hob-nailed boots; fantastical lockets of ruby and enamel; wonderful bands of massive yellow gold, studded with diamonds wherein to insert the two ends of flimsy lace cravats. Mr. Marchmont reflected upon the amount of his possessions, and their security in the jewel-drawer of his dressing-case. The dressing-case was furnished with a Chubb's lock, the key of which he carried in his waistcoat pocket. Yes, it was all safe.

"Look here, Peterson," said Paul Marchmont; "I think I shall sleep at Mrs. Weston's to-night. I should like you to take my dressing-case down there at once."

"And how about the other luggage, Sir—the portmanteaus and hat-boxes?"

"Never mind those. I want you to put the dressing-case safe in my sister's hands. I can send here for the rest to-morrow morning. You needn't wait for me now. I'll follow you in half an hour."

"Yes, Sir. You want the dressing-case carried to Mrs. Weston's house, and I'm to wait for you there?"

"Yes; you can wait for me."

"But is there nothing else I can do, Sir?"

"Nothing whatever. I've only got to collect a few papers, and then I shall follow you."

"Yes, Sir."

The discreet Peterson bowed, and retired to fetch the dressing-case. He put his own construction upon Mr. Marchmont's evident desire to get rid of him, and to be left alone at the Towers. Paul had, of course, made a purse, and had doubtless put his money away in some very artful hiding-place, whence he now wanted to take it at his leisure. He had stuffed one of his pillows with bank-notes, perhaps; or had hidden a cash-box behind the tapestry in his bedchamber; or had buried a bag of gold in the flower-garden below the terrace. Mr. Peterson went up stairs to Paul's dressing-room, put his hand through the strap of the dressing-case, which was very heavy, went down stairs again, met his master in the hall, and went out at the lobby-door.

Paul locked the door upon his valet, and then went back into the lonely house, where the ticking of the clocks in the tenantless rooms sounded unnaturally loud in the stillness. All the windows had been broken; and though the shutters were shut, the cold night-air blew in at many a crack and cranny, and well-nigh extinguished Mr. Marchmont's candle as he went from room to room looking about him.

He went into the western drawing-room, and lighted some of the lamps in the principal chandelier. The shutters were shut, for the windows here, as well as elsewhere, had been broken; fragments of shivered glass, great, jagged stones, and handfuls of gravel, lay about upon the rich carpet—the velvet-pile which he had chosen with such artistic taste, such careful deliberation. He lit the lamps and walked about the room, looking for the last time at his treasures. Yes, *his* treasures. It was he who had transformed this chamber from a prim, old-fashioned sitting-room, with quaint, japanned cabinets, and shabby, chintz-cushioned cane-chairs, cracked Indian vases, and a faded carpet, into a saloon that would have been no discredit to Buckingham Palace or Alton Towers.

It was he who had made the place what it was. He had squandered the savings of Mary's minority upon pictures that the richest collector in England might have been proud to own; upon porcelain that would have been worthy of a place in the Vienna Museum or the Bernal Collection. He had done this, and these things were to pass into the possession of the man he hated—the fiery young soldier who had horsewhipped him before the face of wondering Lincolnshire. He walked about the room, thinking of his life since he had come into possession of this place, and of what it had been before that time, and what it must be again, unless he summoned up a desperate courage—and killed him-self.

His heart beat fast and loud, and he felt an icy chill creeping slowly through his every vein as he thought of this. How was he to kill himself? He had no poison in his possession—no deadly drug that would reduce the agony of death to the space of a lightning's flash. There were pistols, rare gems of choicest workmanship, in one of the buhl-cabinets in that very room; there was a fowling-piece and ammunition in Mr. Marchmont's dressing-room; but the artist was not expert with the use of fire-arms, and he might fail in the attempt to blow out his brains, and only maim or disfigure himself hideously. There was the river—the slow, black river: but then, drowning is a slow death, and Heaven only knows how long the agony may seem to the wretch who endures it! Alas! the ghastly truth of the matter is, that Mr. Marchmont was afraid of death. Look at the King of Terrors how he would he could not discover any pleasing aspect under which he could meet the grim monarch without flinching.

He looked at life; but if life was less terrible than death, it was not less dreary. He looked forward with a shudder to see—what? Humiliation, disgrace, perhaps punishment—life-long transportation, it may be; for this base conspiracy might be a criminal offense,·amenable to criminal law. Or, escaping all this, what was there for him? What was there for this man even then? For forty years he had been steeped to the lips in poverty, and had endured his life. He looked back now, and wondered how it was that he had been patient; he wondered why he had not made an end of himself and his obscure trouble twenty years before this night. But after looking back a little longer, he saw the star which had illumined the darkness of that miserable and sordid existence, and he understood the reason of his endurance. He had hoped. Day after day he had got up to go through the same troubles, to endure the same humiliations; but every day, when his life had been hardest to him, he had said, "To-morrow I may be master of Marchmont Towers." But he could never hope this any more; he could not go back to watch and wait again, beguiled by the faint hope that Mary Arundel's son might die, and to hear by-and-by that other children were born to her to widen the great gulf betwixt him and fortune.

He looked back, and he saw that he had lived from day to day, from year to year, lured on by this one hope. He looked forward, and he saw that he could not live without it.

There had never been but this one road to good fortune open to him. He was a clever man, but his was not the cleverness which can transmute itself into solid cash. He could only paint indifferent pictures; and he had existed long enough by picture-painting to realize the utter hopelessness of success in that career.

He had borne his life while he was in it, but he could not bear to go back to it. He had been out of it, and had tasted another phase of existence; and he could see it all now plainly, as if he had been a spectator sitting in the boxes and watching a dreary play performed upon a stage before him. The performers in the remotest provincial theatre believe in the play they are acting. The omnipotence of passion creates dewy groves and moonlit atmospheres, ducal robes and beautiful women. But the metropolitan spectator, in whose mind the memory of better things is still fresh, sees that moonlit trees are poor distemper daubs, pushed on by dirty carpenters, and the moon a green bottle borrowed from a druggist's shop; the ducal robes, cotton velvet and tarnished tinsel; and the heroine of the drama old and ugly.

So Paul looked at the life he had endured, and wondered as he saw how horrible it was.

He could see the shabby lodging, the faded furniture, the miserable handful of fire struggling with the smoke in a shallow grate, that had been half blocked up with bricks by some former tenant as badly off as himself. He could look back at that dismal room, with the ugly paper on the walls, the scanty curtains flapping in the wind that they pretended to shut out; the figure of his mother sitting near the fireplace, with that pale,·anxious face, which was a perpetual complaint against hardship and discomfort. He could see his sister standing at the window in the dusky twilight, patching up some worn-out garment, and straining her eyes for the sake of economizing in the matter of half an inch of candle. And the street below the window—the shabby-genteel street, with a dingy shop breaking out here and there, and children playing on the door-steps, and a muffin-bell jingling through the evening fog, and a melancholy Italian grinding "Home, sweet Home!" in the patch of lighted road opposite the pawnbroker's. He saw it all; and it was all alike sordid, miserable, hopeless.

Paul Marchmont had never sunk so low as his cousin John. He had never descended so far in the social scale as to carry a banner at Drury Lane, or to live in one room in Oakley Street, Lambeth. But there had been times when to pay the rent of three rooms had been next kin to an impossibility to the artist, and when the honorarium of a shilling a night would have been very acceptable to him. He had drained the cup of poverty to the dregs; and now the cup was filled again, and the bitter draught was offered to him.

He must drink that, or another potion—a sleeping-draught, which is commonly called Death. He must die! But how? His coward heart sank as the horrible alternative pressed closer upon him. He must die—to-night—at once—in that house; so that when they came in the morning to eject him they would have little trouble; they would only have to carry out a corpse.

He walked up and down the room, biting his finger-nails to the quick, but coming to no resolution, until he was interrupted by the ringing of the bell at the lobby-door. It was the messenger from his sister, no doubt. Paul drew his watch from his waistcoat-pocket, unfastened his chain, took a set of gold studs from the breast of his shirt, and a signet-ring from his finger; then he sat down at a writing-table, and packed the watch and chain, the studs and signet-ring, and a bunch of keys, in a large envelope. He sealed this packet, and addressed it to his sister; then he took a candle and went to the lobby. Mrs. Weston had sent a young man who was an assistant and pupil of her husband's—a good-tempered young fellow, who willingly served her in her hour of trouble. Paul gave this young man the key of his dressing-case and packet. "You will be sure and put that in my sister's hands," he said.

"Oh yes, Sir. Mrs. Weston gave me this letter for you, Sir. Am I to wait for an answer?"

"No; there will be no answer. Good-night." "Good-night, Sir."

The young man went away, and Paul Marchmont heard him whistle a popular melody as he walked along the cloistered way and out of the quadrangle by a low archway commonly used by the trades-people who came to the Towers.

The artist stood and listened to the young man's departing footsteps. Then, with a horrible thrill of anguish, he remembered that he had seen his last of human kind; he had heard his last of human voices: for he was to kill himself that night. He stood in the dark lobby, looking out into the quadrangle. He was quite alone in the house; for the girl who had let him in was in the laundry with her mother. He could see the figures of the two women moving about in a great gas-lit chamber upon the other side of the quadrangle—a building which had no communication with the rest of the house. He was to die that night; and he had not yet even determined how he was to die.

He mechanically opened Mrs. Weston's letter. It was only a few lines, telling him that Peterson had arrived with the portmanteau and dressing-case, and that there would be a comfortable room prepared for Mr. Marchmont. "I am so glad you have changed your mind, and are coming to me, Paul," Mrs. Weston concluded. "Your manner when we parted to-night almost alarmed me."

Paul groaned aloud as he crushed the letter in his hand. Then he went back to the western drawing-room. He heard strange noises in the empty rooms as he passed by their open doors, weird, creaking sounds and melancholy moanings in the wide chimneys. It seemed as if all the ghosts of Marchmont Towers were astir to-night, moved by an awful prescience of some coming horror.

Paul Marchmont was an atheist; but atheism, although a very pleasing theme for a critical and argumentative discussion after a lobster supper and unlimited Champagne, is but a poor staff to lean upon when the worn-out traveler approaches the mysterious portals of the unknown land.

The artist had boasted of his belief in annihilation, and had declared himself perfectly satisfied with a materialistic or pantheistic arrangement of the universe, and very indifferent as to whether he cropped up in future years as a summer-cabbage or a new Raphael, so long as the ten stone or so of matter of which he was composed was made use of somehow or other, and did its duty in the great scheme of a scientific universe. But oh! how that empty, soulless creed slipped away from him now, when he stood alone in this tenantless house, shuddering at strange spirit noises, and horrified by a host of mystic fears—gigantic, shapeless terrors—that crowded in his empty, godless mind, and filled it with their hideous presence!

He had refused to believe in a personal God. He had laughed at the idea that there was any deity to whom the individual can appeal in his hour of grief or trouble, with the hope of any separate mercy, any special grace. He had rejected the Christian's simple creed, and now—now that he had floated away from the shores of life, and felt himself borne upon an irresistible current to that mysterious other side, what did he not believe in?

Every superstition that has ever disturbed the soul of ignorant man lent some one awful feature to that crowd of hideous images uprising in this man's mind. Awful Chaldean gods and Carthaginian goddesses, thirsting for the hot blood of human sacrifices, greedy for hecatombs of children flung shrieking into fiery furnaces, or torn limb from limb by savage beasts; Babylonian abominations; Egyptian Isis and Osiris; classical divinities, with flaming swords and pale impassible faces, rigid as the Destiny whose type they were; ghastly Germanic demons and witches—all the dread avengers that man, in the knowledge of his own wickedness, has ever shadowed for himself out of the darkness of his ignorant mind, swelled that ghastly crowd, until the artist's brain reeled, and he was fain to sit with his head in his hands, trying, by a great effort of the will, to exorcise these loathsome phantoms.

"I must be going mad," he muttered to himself. "I am going mad."

But still the great question was unanswered, How was he to kill himself?

"I must settle that," he thought. "I dare not think of any thing that may come afterward. Besides, what *should* come? I *know* that there is nothing. Haven't I heard it demonstrated by cleverer men than I am? Haven't I looked at it in every light, and weighed it in every scale—always with the same result? Yes; I know that there is nothing *after* the one short pang, any more than there is pain in the nerve of a tooth when the tooth is gone. The nerve was the soul of the tooth, I suppose; but wrench away the body, and the soul is dead. Why should I be afraid? One short pain—it will seem long, I dare say—and then I shall lie still for ever and ever, and melt slowly back into the elements out of which I was created. Yes; I shall lie still—and be *nothing*."

Paul Marchmont sat thinking of this for a long time. Was it such a great advantage, after all, this annihilation, the sovereign good of the atheist's barren creed? It seemed to-night to this man as if it would be better to be any thing, to suffer any anguish, any penalty for his sins, than to be blotted out for ever and ever from any conscious part in the grand harmony of the universe. If he could have believed in that Roman Catholic doctrine of purgatory, and that after cycles of years of suffering he might rise at last, purified from his sins, worthy to dwell among the angels, how differently would death have appeared to him! He might have gone away to hide himself in some foreign city, to perform patient daily sacrifices, humble acts of self-abnegation, every one of which should be a new figure, however small a one, to be set against the great sum of his sin.

But he could not believe. There is a vulgar proverb which says, "You can not have your loaf and eat it;" or, if proverbs would only be grammatical, it might be better worded, "You can not eat your loaf, and have it to eat on some future occasion." Neither can you indulge in rationalistic discussions or epigrammatic pleasantry about the great Creator who made you, and then turn to Him in the dreadful hour of your despair: "O my God, whom I have insulted and offended, help the miserable wretch who for twenty years has obstinately shut his heart against Thee!" It may be that God would forgive and hear even at that last supreme moment, as He heard the penitent thief upon the cross; but the penitent thief had been a sinner, not an unbeliever, and he *could* pray. The hard heart of the atheist freezes in his breast when he would repent and put away his iniquities. When he would fain turn to his offended Maker, the words that he tries to speak die away upon his lips; for the habit of blasphemy is too strong upon him; he can *blague* upon all the mighty mysteries of heaven and hell, but he *can not* pray.

Paul Marchmont could not fashion a prayer. Horrible witticisms arose up between him and the words he would have spoken—ghastly *bon mots*, that had seemed so brilliant at a lamp-lit dinner-table, spoken to a joyous accompaniment of Champagne-corks and laughter. Ah me! the world was behind this man now, with all its pleasures; and he looked back upon it, and thought that, even when it seemed gayest and brightest, it was only like a great roaring fair, with flaring lights, and noisy showmen clamoring forever to a struggling crowd.

How should he die! Should he go up stairs and cut his throat?

He stood before one of his pictures—a pet picture, a girl's face by Millais, looking through the moonlight, fantastically beautiful. He stood before this picture and he felt one small separate pang amidst all his misery as he remembered that Edward and Mary Arundel were now possessors of this particular gem.

"They sha'n't have it," he muttered to himself; "they sha'n't have *this*, at any rate."

He took a penknife from his pocket, and ripped the canvas across and across savagely, till it hung in ribbons from the deep-gilded frame.

Then he smiled to himself, for the first time since he had entered that house, and his eyes flashed with a sudden light.

"I have lived like Sardanapalus for the last year," he cried aloud, "and I will die like Sardanapalus!"

There was a fragile piece of furniture near him —an *étagère* of marqueterie work, loaded with costly *bric a brac*, Oriental porcelain, Sèvres and Dresden, old Chelsea and crown Derby cups and saucers, and quaint tea-pots, crawling vermin in Pallissy ware, Indian monstrosities, and all manner of expensive absurdities, heaped together in artistic confusion. Paul Marchmont struck the slim leg of the *étagère* with his foot, and laughed aloud as the fragile toys fell into a ruined heap upon the carpet. He stamped upon the broken china; and the frail cups and saucers crackled like egg-shells under his savage feet.

"I will die like Sardanapalus!" he cried; "the King Arbaces shall never rest in the palace I have beautified.

"'Now order here
Fagots, pine-nuts, and wither'd leaves, and such
Things as catch fire with one sole spark;
Bring cedar, too, and precious drugs, and spices,
And mighty planks, to nourish a tall pile;
Bring frankincense and myrrh, too; for it is
For a great sacrifice I build the pyre.'

I don't think much of your blank verse, George Gordon Noel Byron. Your lines end on lame syllables; your ten-syllable blank verse lacks the fiery ring of your rhymes. I wonder whether Marchmont Towers is insured? Yes, I remember paying a premium last Christmas. They may have a sharp tussle with the insurance companics though. Yes, I will die like Sardanapalus—no, not like him, for I have no Myrrha to mount the pile and cling about me to the last. Pshaw! a modern Myrrha would leave Sardanapalus to perish alone, and be off to make herself safe with the new king."

Paul snatched up the candle, and went out into the hall. His gray eyes had a strange light in them. His manner had that feverish excitement which the French call exaltation. He ran up the broad stairs leading to the long corridor, out of which his own rooms, and his mother's and sister's rooms opened.

Ah, how pretty they were! How elegant he had made them in his reckless disregard of expense, his artistic delight in the task of beautification! There were no shutters here, and the summer breeze blew in through the broken windows, and stirred the gauzy muslin curtains, the gay chintz draperies, the cloud-like festoons of silk and lace. Paul Marchmont went from room to room with the flaring candle in his hand, and wherever there were curtains or draperies about the windows, the beds, the dressing-tables, the low lounging-chairs, and cozy little sofas, he set a light to them. He did this with wonderful rapidity, leaving flames behind him as he traversed the long corridor, and coming back thus to the stairs. He went down stairs again, and returned to the western drawing-room. Then he blew out his candle, turned out the gas, and waited.

"How soon will it come?" he thought.

The shutters were shut, and the room was quite dark.

"Shall I ever have courage to stop till it comes?" Paul Marchmont thought.

He groped his way to the door, double-locked it, and then took the key from the lock.

He went to one of the windows, clambered upon a chair, opened the top shutter, and flung the key out through the broken window. He heard it strike jingling upon the stone terrace, and then bound away Heaven knows where.

"I sha'n't be able to go out by the door, at any rate," he thought.

It was quite dark in the room, but outside it was as light as day. Mr. Marchmont went away from the window, feeling his way among the chairs and tables. He could see the red light through the crevices of the shutters, and a lurid patch of sky through that one window, the upper half of which he had left open. He sat down, somewhere near the centre of the room, and waited.

"The smoke will kill me," he thought. "I shall know nothing of the fire."

He sat quite still. He had trembled violently while he had gone from room to room doing his horrible work; but his nerves seemed steadier now. Steadier! why, he was transformed to stone! His heart seemed to have stopped beating; and he only knew by a sick anguish, a dull aching pain, that it was still in his breast.

He sat waiting and thinking. In that time all the long story of the past was acted before him, and he saw what a wretch he had been. I do not know whether this was penitence; but looking at that enacted story, Paul Marchmont thought that his own part in the play was a mistake, and that it was a foolish thing to be a villain.

When a great flock of frightened people, with a fire-engine out of order, and drawn by whooping men and boys, came hurrying up to the Towers, they found a blazing edifice, which looked like an enchanted castle—great stone-framed windows vomiting flame; tall chimneys toppling down upon a fiery roof; molten lead, like water turned to fire, streaming in flaming cataracts upon the terrace; and all the sky lit up by that vast pile of blazing ruin. Only salamanders, or poor Mr. Braidwood's own chosen band, could have approached Marchmont Towers that night. The Kemberling firemen and the Swampington firemen, who came by-and-by, were neither salamanders nor Braidwoods. They stood aloof and squirted water at the flames, and recoiled aghast by-and-by when the roof came down like an avalanche of blazing timber, leaving only a gaunt gigantic skeleton of red-hot stone where Marchmont Towers once had been.

When it was safe to venture in among the ruins—and this was not for many hours after the fire had burnt itself out—people looked for Paul Marchmont; but amidst all that vast chaos of smouldering ashes there was nothing found that could be identified as the remains of a human being. No one knew where the artist had been at the time of the fire, or indeed whether he had been in the house at all; and the popular opinion was, that Paul had set fire to the mansion, and had fled away before the flames began to spread.

But Lavinia Weston knew better than this. She knew now why her brother had sent her every scrap of valuable property belonging to him. She understood now why he had come back to her to bid her good-night for the second time, and press his cold lips to hers.

---

CHAPTER THE LAST.

"DEAR IS THE MEMORY OF OUR WEDDED LIVES."

MARY and Edward Arundel saw the awful light in the sky, and heard the voices of the people shouting in the street below, and calling to one another that Marchmont Towers was on fire.

The young mistress of the burning pile had very little concern for her property. She only kept saying, again and again, "Oh, Edward! I hope there is no one in the house. God grant there may be no one in the house!"

And when the flames were highest, and it seemed by the light in the sky as if all Lincolnshire had been blazing, Edward Arundel's wife flung herself upon her knees, and prayed aloud for any unhappy creature that might be in peril.

Oh, if we could dare to think that this innocent girl's prayer was heard before the throne of an awful Judge, pleading for the soul of a wicked man!

Early the next morning Mrs. Arundel came from Lawford Grange with her confidential maid, and carried off her daughter-in-law and the baby on the first stage of the journey into Devonshire. Before she left Kemberling Mary was told that no dead body had been found among the ruins of the Towers; and this assertion deluded her into the belief that no unhappy creature had perished. So she went to Dangerfield happier than she had ever been since the sunny days of her honey-moon, to wait there for the coming of Edward Arundel, who was to stay behind to see Richard Paulette and Mr. Gormby, and to secure the testimony of Mr. Weston and Betsy Murrel with a view to the identification of Mary's little son, who had been neither registered nor christened.

I have no need to dwell upon this process of identification, registration, and christening through which Master Edward Arundel had to pass in the course of the next month. I had rather skip this dry-as-dust business, and go on to that happy time which Edward and his young wife spent together under the oaks at Dangerfield; that bright second honey-moon season, while they were as yet houseless; for a pretty villa-like mansion was being built on the Marchmont property, far away from the dank wood and the dismal river, in a pretty pastoral little nook, which was a fair oasis amidst the general dreariness of Lincolnshire.

I need scarcely say that the grand feature of this happy time was THE BABY. It will be of course easily understood that this child stood alone among babies. There never had been another such infant; it was more than probable there would never again be such a one. In every attribute of babyhood he was a twelvemonth in advance of the rest of his race. Prospective greatness was stamped upon his brow. He would be a Clive or a Wellington, unless indeed he should have a fancy for the Bar and the Woolsack, in which case he would be a little more erudite than Lyndhurst, a trifle more eloquent than Brougham. All this was palpable to the meanest capacity in the very manner in which this child crowed in his nurse's arms, or choked himself with farinaceous food, or smiled recognition at his young father, or performed the simplest act common to infancy.

I think Mr. Sant would have been pleased to paint one of those summer scenes at Dangerfield. The proud soldier-father; the pale young wife; the handsome, matronly grandmother; and, as the mystic centre of that magic circle, the toddling, flaxen-haired baby, held up by his father's hands, and taking caricature strides in imitation of papa's big steps.

To my mind, it is a great pity that children are not children forever—that the pretty baby-boy by Sant, all rosy, and flaxen, and blue-eyed, should ever grow into a great, angular, pre-Raphaelite hobadahoy, horribly big and out of drawing. But neither Edward, nor Mary, nor, above all, Mrs. Arundel, were of this opinion. They were as eager for the child to grow up and enter for the great races of this life, as some speculative turf magnate who has given a fancy price for a yearling, and is pining to see the animal a far-famed three-year-old, and winner of the double event.

Before the child had cut a double-tooth Mrs. Arundel, senior, had decided in favor of Eton as opposed to Harrow, and was balancing the conflicting advantages of classical Oxford and mathematical Cambridge; while Edward could not see the baby-boy rolling on the grass, with blue ribbons and sashes fluttering in the breeze, without thinking of his son's future appearance in the uniform of his own regiment, gorgeous in the splendid crash of a levee at St. James's.

How many airy castles were erected in that happy time, with the baby for the foundation-stone of all of them! *The* BABY! Why, that definite article alone expresses an infinity of foolish love and admiration. Nobody says *the* father, the husband, the mother. It is "my" father, my husband, as the case may be. But every baby, from St. Giles's to Belgravia, from Tyburnia to St. Luke's, is "the" baby. The infant's reign is short, but his royalty is supreme, and no one presumes to question his despotic rule.

Edward Arundel almost worshiped the little child whose feeble cry he had heard in the October twilight, and had *not* recognized. He was never tired of reproaching himself for this omission. That baby-voice *ought* to have awakened a strange thrill in the young father's breast.

That time at Dangerfield was the happiest period of Mary's life. All her sorrows had melted away. They did not tell her of Paul Marchmont's suspected fate; they only told her that her enemy had disappeared, and that no one knew whither he had gone. Mary asked once, and once only, about her step-mother, and she was told that Olivia was at Swampington Rectory, living with her father; and that people said she was mad. George Weston had emigrated to Australia with his wife, and his wife's mother and sister. There had been no prosecution for conspiracy; the disappearance of the principal criminal had rendered that unnecessary.

This was all that Mary ever heard of her persecutors. She did not wish to hear of them. She had forgiven them long ago. I think that, in the inner depths of her innocent heart, she had forgiven them from the moment she had fallen on her husband's breast in Hester's parlor at Kemberling, and had felt his strong arms clasped about her, sheltering her from all harm for evermore.

She was very happy; and her nature, always gentle, seemed sublimated by the sufferings she had endured, and already akin to that of the angels. Alas, this was Edward Arundel's chief sorrow! This young wife, so precious to him in her fading loveliness, was slipping away from him, even in the hour when they were happiest together, was separated from him even when they were most united. She was separated from him by that unconquerable sadness in his heart which was prophetic of a great sorrow to come.

Sometimes, when Mary saw her husband looking at her with a mournful tenderness, an almost despairing love in his eyes, she would throw herself into his arms, and say to him:

"You must remember how happy I have been, Edward. Oh my darling! promise me always to remember how happy I have been."

When the first chill breezes of autumn blew among the Dangerfield oaks Edward Arundel took his wife southward, with his mother and the inevitable baby in her train. They went to Nice, and they were very quiet, very happy, in the pretty southern town, with snow-clad mountains behind them, and the purple Mediterranean before.

The villa was building all this time in Lincolnshire. Edward's agent sent him plans and sketches for Mrs. Arundel's approval; and every evening there was some fresh talk about the arrangement of the rooms, and the laying out of gardens. Mary was always pleased to see the plans and drawings, and to discuss the progress of the work with her husband. She would talk of the billiard-room, and the cozy little smoking-room, and the nurseries for the baby, which were to have a southern aspect, and every advantage calculated to assist the development of that rare and marvelous blossom; and she would plan the comfortable apartments that were to be specially kept for dear grandmamma, who would of course spend a great deal of her time at the Sycamores—the new place was to be called the Sycamores. But Edward could never get his wife to talk of a certain boudoir opening into a tiny conservatory, which he himself had added on to the original architect's plan. He could never get Mary to speak of this particular chamber; and once, when he asked her some question about the color of the draperies, she said to him, very gently,

"I would rather you would not think of that room, darling."

"Why, my pet?"

"Because it will make you sorry afterward."

"Mary, my darling—"

"Oh, Edward! you know—you must know, dearest—that I shall never see that place?"

But her husband took her in his arms, and declared that this was only a morbid fancy, and that she was getting better and stronger every day, and would live to see her grandchildren playing under the maples that sheltered the northern side of the new villa. Edward told his wife this, and he believed in the truth of what he said. He could not believe that he was to lose this young wife, restored to him after so many trials. Mary did not contradict him just then; but that night, when she was sitting in her room reading by the light of a shaded lamp after she had gone to bed—Mary went to bed very early, by order of the doctors, and indeed lived altogether according to medical régime—she called her husband to her.

"I want to speak to you, dear," she said; "there is something that I must say to you."

The young man knelt down by his wife's bed.

"What is it, darling?" he asked.

"You know what we said to-day, Edward?"

"What, darling? We say so many things every day—we are so happy together, and have so much to talk about."

"But you remember, Edward—you remember what I said about never seeing the Sycamores? Ah, don't stop me, dear love," Mary said reproachfully, for Edward put his lips to hers to stay the current of mournful words; "don't stop me, dear, for I must speak to you. I want you to know that *it must be*, Edward, darling. I want you to remember how happy

I have been, and how willing I am to part with you, dear, since it is God's will that we should be parted. And there is something else that I want to say, Edward. Grandmamma told me something—all about Belinda. I want you to promise me that Belinda shall be happy by-and-by; for she has suffered so much, poor girl! And you will love her, and she will love the baby. But you won't love her quite the same way that you loved me, will you, dear? because you never knew her when she was a little child, and very poor. She has never been an orphan, and quite lonely, as I have been. You have never been *all the world* to her."

The Sycamores was finished by the following mid-summer, but no one took possession of the newly-built house; no brisk upholsterer's men came with three-foot rules and pencils and memorandum-books to take measurements of windows and floors: no wagons of splendid furniture made havoc of the gravel-drive before the principal entrance. The only person who came to the new house was a snuff-taking crone from Stanfield, who brought a turn-up bedstead, a Dutch clock, and a few minor articles of furniture, and encamped in a corner of the best bedroom.

Edward Arundel, senior, was away in India, fighting under Napier and Outram; and Edward Arundel, junior, was at Dangerfield, under the charge of his grandmother.

Perhaps the most beautiful monument in one of the English cemeteries at Nice is that tall white marble cross and kneeling figure, before which strangers pause to read an inscription to the memory of Mary, the beloved wife of Edward Dangerfield Arundel.

---

## EPILOGUE.

FOUR years after the completion of that pretty stuccoed villa, which seemed destined never to be inhabited, Belinda Lawford walked alone up and down the sheltered shrubbery-walk in the Grange garden in the fading September daylight.

Miss Lawford was taller and more womanly-looking than she had been on the day of her interrupted wedding. The vivid bloom had left her cheeks; but I think she was all the prettier because of that delicate pallor, which gave a pensive cast to her countenance. She was very grave, and gentle, and good; but she had never forgotten the shock of that broken bridal ceremonial in Hillingsworth Church.

The Major had taken his eldest daughter abroad almost immediately after that July day; and Belinda and her father had traveled together very peaceful, exploring quiet Belgian cities, looking at celebrated altar-pieces in dusky cathedrals, and wandering round battle-fields, which the intermingled blood of rival nations had once made one crimson swamp. They had been nearly a twelvemonth absent, and then Belinda returned to assist at the marriage of a younger sister, and to hear that Edward Arundel's wife had died of a lingering pulmonary complaint at Nice.

She was told this, and she was told how Olivia

Marchmont still lived with her father at Swampington, and how day by day she went the same round from cottage to cottage, visiting the sick; teaching little children, or sometimes rough-bearded men, to read and write and cipher; reading to old decrepit pensioners; listening to long histories of sickness and trial; and exhibiting an unwearying patience that was akin to sublimity. Passion had burned itself out in this woman's breast, and there was nothing in her mind now but remorse, and the desire to perform a long penance by reason of which she might in the end be forgiven.

But Mrs. Marchmont never visited any one alone. Wherever she went Barbara Simmons accompanied her, constant as her shadow. The Swampington people said this was because the rector's daughter was not quite right in her mind; and there were times when she forgot where she was, and would have wandered away in a purposeless manner, Heaven knows where, had she not been accompanied by her faithful servant. Clever as the Swampington people and the Kemberling people might be in finding out the business of their neighbors, they never knew that Olivia Marchmont had been consentient to the hiding away of her step-daughter. They looked upon her, indeed, with considerable respect, as a heroine by whose exertions Paul Marchmont's villainy had been discovered. In the hurry and confusion of the scene at Hillingsworth Church, nobody had taken heed of Olivia's incoherent self-accusations. Hubert Arundel was therefore spared the misery of knowing the extent of his daughter's sin.

Belinda Lawford came home in order to be present at her sister's wedding; and the old life began again for her, with all the old duties that had once been so pleasant. She went about them very cheerfully now. She worked for her poor pensioners, and took the chief burden of the housekeeping off her mother's hands. But though she jingled her keys with a cheery music as she went about the house, and though she often sang to herself over her work, the old happy smile rarely lit up her face. She went about her duties rather like some widowed matron who has lived her life, than a girl before whom the future lies, mysterious and unknown.

It has been said that happiness comes to the sleeper—the meaning of which proverb I take to be, that Joy generally comes to us when we least look for her lovely face. And it was on this September afternoon, when Belinda loitered in the garden after her round of small duties was finished, and she was free to think or dream at her leisure, that happiness came to her—unexpected, unhoped-for, supreme; for turning at one end of the sheltered alley, she saw Edward Arundel standing at the other end, with his hat in his hand, and the summer wind blowing among his hair.

Miss Lawford stopped quite still. The old-fashioned garden reeled before her eyes, and the hard graveled path seemed to become a quaking bog. She could not move; she stood still and waited while Edward came toward her.

"Letitia has told me about you, Linda," he said; "she has told me how true and noble you have been; and she sent me here to look for a wife, to make new sunshine in my empty home

M

—a young mother to smile upon my motherless boy."

Edward and Belinda walked up and down the sheltered alley for a long time, talking a great deal of the sad past, a little of the fair-seeming future; and it was growing dusk before they went in at the old-fashioned half-glass door leading into the drawing-room, where Mrs. Lawford and her younger daughters were sitting, and where Lydia, who was next to Belinda, and had been three years married to the Curate of Hillingsworth, was nursing her second baby.

"Has she said yes?" this young matron cried directly; for she had been told of Edward's errand to the Grange; "but of course she has. What else should she say, after refusing all manner of people, and giving herself the airs of an old maid.- Yes, um pressus Pops, um Aunty Lindy's going be marriedy-parriedy," concluded the curate's wife, addressing her three-months' old baby in that peculiar patois which is supposed to be intelligible to infants by reason of being unintelligible to every body else.

"I suppose you are not aware that my future brother-in-law is a major?" said Belinda's third sister, who had been struggling with a variation by Thalberg, all octaves and accidentals, and who twisted herself round upon her music-stool to address her sister. "I suppose you are not aware that you have been talking to Major Arundel, who has done all manner of splendid things in the Punjaub? Papa told us all about it five minutes ago."

It was as much as Belinda could do to support the clamorous felicitations of her sisters, especially the unmarried damsels, who were eager to exhibit themselves in the capacity of bridemaids; but by-and-by, after dinner, the curate's wife drew her sisters away from that shadowy window in which Edward Arundel and Belinda were sitting, and the lovers were left to themselves.

That evening was very peaceful, very happy, and there were many other evenings like it before Edward and Belinda completed that ceremonial which they had left unfinished more than five years before.

The Sycamores was very prettily furnished under Belinda's superintendence; and as Reginald Arundel had lately married, Edward's mother came to live with her younger son, and brought with her the idolized grandchild, who was now a tall, yellow-haired boy of six years old.

There was only one room in the Sycamores which was never tenanted by any one of that little household except Edward himself, who kept the key of the little chamber in his writing-desk, and only allowed the servants to go in at stated intervals to keep every thing bright and orderly in the apartment.

This·shut-up chamber was the boudoir which Edward Arundel had planned for his first wife. He had ordered it to be furnished with the very furniture which he had intended for Mary. The rosebuds and butterflies on the walls, the guipure curtains lined with pale blush-rose silk, the few chosen books in the little cabinet near the fire-place, the Dresden breakfast-service, the statuettes and pictures, were things he had fixed upon long ago in his own mind as the decorations for his wife's apartment. He went into the room now and then, and looked at his first wife's picture—a crayon sketch taken in London before Mary and her husband started for the south of France. He looked a little wistfully at this picture, even when he was happiest in the new ties that bound him to life, and all that is brightest in life.

Major Arundel took his eldest son into this room one day, when young Edward was eight or nine years old, and showed the boy his mother's portrait.

"When you are a man this place will be yours, Edward," the father said. "You can give your wife this room, although I have never given it to mine. You will tell her that it was built for your mother, and that it was built for her by a husband who, even when most grateful to God for every new blessing he enjoyed, never ceased to be sorry for the loss of his first love."

And so I leave my soldier-hero to repose upon laurels that have been hardly won, and secure in that modified happiness which is chastened by the memory of sorrow. I leave him with bright children crowding round his knees, a loving wife smiling at him across those fair childish heads. I leave him happy, and good, and useful, filling his place in the world, and bringing up his children to be wise and virtuous men and women in the days that are to come. I leave him, above all, with the serene lamp of faith forever burning in his soul, lighting the image of that other world in which there is neither marrying nor giving in marriage, and where his dead wife will smile upon him from amidst the vast throng of angel faces—a child for ever and ever before the throne of God.

THE END.

# HYACINTHE;

OR,

# THE CONTRAST.

## BY MRS. GREY.

AUTHOR OF "LENA CAMERON; OR, THE FOUR SISTERS,"
"THE BELLE OF THE FAMILY," "SYBIL LENNARD, A
RECORD OF WOMAN'S LIFE," "THE DUKE AND THE
COUSIN," "THE LITTLE WIFE," "THE MANŒU-
VRING MOTHER," "BARONET'S DAUGHTERS,"
"YOUNG PRIMA DONNA," "HARRY
MONK," "THE OLD DOWER HOUSE,"
"ALICE SEYMOUR," ETC., ETC.

"What is our duty here? to tend
From good to better—thence to best;
Grateful to drink life's cup,—then bend
Unmurmuring to our bed of rest."

Philadelphia: •
T. B. PETERSON, No. 102 CHESTNUT STREET.
ABOVE THIRD, GIRARD STORES.

# HYACINTHE;

## OR,

# THE CONTRAST.

---

### CHAPTER I.

"O friendly to the best pursuits of man,
Friendly to thought, to virtue, and to peace,
Domestic life in rural pleasures pass'd."

In a retired village in Monmouthshire lived Farmer Wilmot and
his wife. They were industrious, worthy people, and resided on a
neat little farm, which was at once their means of subsistence, and a
constant source of occupation and pleasure.

Although their resources were very limited, their wants were proportionally small, for children were not among the blessings which
had been bestowed upon them; and this was a drawback to their
happiness; as although, had they been possessed of offspring, their
labours must have been much heavier, and many a hard struggle
would they have had to support a family; still, regrets would mingle
themselves with those feelings of gratitude with which they viewed
their peaceful situation, and all the tranquil happiness it afforded
them. Placed in a sphere of life, where the world, and what is
falsely named the world's pleasures, fail to fix and captivate the mind,
the heart looks with more ardent longing for those objects of natural
affection on which to lavish that tenderness and love inherent in
every virtuous bosom; and it was with many a sigh that Jane Wilmot contemplated the blooming children of her neighbours; at times
inwardly exclaiming, "Oh! if it had pleased God to have blessed
me with a child, what happiness it would have been to me, to have

worked—to have toiled unceasingly for it; no exertion, no labour could have been irksome, with so dear an inducement!"

However, notwithstanding these occasional murmurs, Jane Wilmot was too right-minded and pious to give way to a spirit of repining at the divine will of Him who appoints all things; she felt that every event was arranged by an Almighty hand, and therefore submitted to her fate with cheerful meekness, recalling to her thoughts, with gratitude, the many blessings she already enjoyed. Indeed, she was a happy woman; happy in the possession of an excellent husband, with good health and strength to assist them in their labours; and, although they were poor, hitherto they had never been in need.

Jane Wilmot had formerly been in the service of a lady of high consideration, on whom it was her peculiar duty to attend; besides being employed in offices, which evinced the confidence her integrity merited. Her good qualities had quickly gained for her the esteem of her mistress, who manifested the interest she had excited by zealously seeking to improve the natural intelligence of her mind, and by inculcating those precepts of religion and piety without which she well knew her mental acquirements would be unprofitable. This excellent lady died very suddenly, and Jane was thus deprived of a sincere and valuable friend. James Wilmot had been many years her fellow-servant, and an attachment had long subsisted between them.

A legacy to each from their late mistress, and some savings of their own, enabled them to marry; and, having stocked a small farm, though in a very limited manner, by unceasing industry and good behaviour this worthy couple contrived to live on with tolerable comfort and success. Jane and her husband were always neat and respectable in their appearance, while their house, by its order and cleanliness, equally betokened the propriety of their ideas. The little garden surrounding their dwelling, arranged with the taste they had not failed to acquire in the service of their refined and lamented mistress, was a perfect paradise of sweets; and it was their dearest recreation to work in it, or with honest pride to display their garden treasures to their kind friend and frequent visiter, Mr. Neville, the clergyman of the parish.

The village of Fairbrook was particularly favoured in having for its pastor such a man as Mr. Neville, to whom his parishioners were his dearest objects of interest—their welfare, his heart's most fervent desire; and, while he sought by the earnestness of his precepts so to enlighten their minds and sanctify their feelings, that they might taste of that happiness which the world can neither give nor take away, he was not unmindful of their temporal concerns; and, with the advice his superior intelligence enabled him to afford, and the pecuniary assistance a well-economized income left at his disposal, he rescued many a grateful villager from the embarrassments incidental to an agricultural life.

Farmer Wilmot and his wife were perhaps the two persons of his humble flock for whom he felt the liveliest interest; for it rejoiced his kind heart to witness such real worth—such true and simple piety; and after he had visited them in their quiet and pleasant dwelling, he would return home with that pleasurable feeling in his bosom, which a good man feels in witnessing conduct so praiseworthy, and hearts so pure.

Jane Wilmot was loved throughout the village; and even the envy which at times finds a shelter in the breast of the rustic as of the courtier, was hushed and tongue-tied by her unfailing kindness and unassuming manners. Her love for children led her most frequently to those houses of her neighbours that were inhabited by those endearing beings, which her own heart told her every virtuous mother must regard as blessings. Attached by her tenderness, every child loved her; and if sickness attacked any of them, Jane was always to be found by the sufferer's bed, assisting the mother, and acting as the nurse. Farmer Wilmot used sometimes almost to chide her for thus spending so much of her time; and would good-naturedly reproach her for employments which he fancied must take her from necessary occupations at home: but she would always stop his chidings by saying, "Oh! James, you must only scold me when you find that I have neglected one single duty;" and so scrupulous was she in fulfilling them all, that he was immediately silenced; and only stifled a feeling of regret that the child upon whom she lavished her caresses was not her own.

---

## CHAPTER II.

"I see a column of slow rising smoke
O'ertop the lofty wood that skirts the wild.
A vagabond and useless tribe there eat
Their miserable meal."　＊　＊

Close to the farm which Farmer Wilmot rented was a long and retired lane. It was, unfortunately for him, the resort of gangs of gipsies, and many were the petty depredations which they committed

on his property.  However, so generally kind and humane was the
farmer known to be, that perhaps he escaped better than his neighbours; for even these lawless people in a manner respected him;
and farther than trifling misdemeanors he had not much to complain
of.  He thought that as a Christian, it was his duty to be very kind
to every fellow-creature, however weak and erring; it was not for
him to turn his back upon the frail; and, pitying the condition of
these miserable people, he never wantonly persecuted them, and even
occasionally assisted them by allowing them to mend his kitchen
utensils, buying from them baskets or mats, and showing much benevolent consideration should sickness have overtaken any of the gang.

One day as Jane Wilmot was returning home from taking a basket
of fresh-laid eggs to a gentleman's house, whose park-gates were
situated not far from the extremity of the lane, her attention was
attracted by a spectacle which greatly shocked her kind heart.  A
troop of gipsies had lately encamped in the lane; and the rough covering to a wretched hovel which had been hastily erected, was drawn
aside, with the view, it appeared, of giving air to an apparently dying
female, to whom the extreme sultriness of the day seemed to give
additional cause of suffering.

Mrs. Wilmot drew near, and asked some questions of an old crone,
who was bending over the afflicted creature, and learnt that the sick
woman was in the last stage of a decline, which was the reason of the
sudden halt of the gang, as it was supposed not many hours could
elapse before she breathed her last.

Jane beheld with much emotion a little child apparently about
three years old, who was crouching close to the dying woman.  The
infant was pale and thin, but its beauty was still most striking, as it
turned its large black eyes with shrinking fear upon the admiring
Mrs. Wilmot.  Clusters of dark curling hair hung over, and formed
almost her only covering; while her delicately formed mouth, with a
rosy under lip as yet unfaded by famine, completed the singular loveliness of infantile attraction.

"What a beautiful creature!" exclaimed Mrs. Wilmot, most
intently observing the child, "will her father take care of her when
her mother is dead?"

"As for that matter," answered the old woman, "I don't much
know.  I wish the useless little baggage might die with the woman,
for the good it will be to us:—get along, you nasty cross brat," pursued the hag, giving the poor babe a kick; for it had begun to cry,
probably suffering from hunger—"I wish our eyes had never lighted
upon you, for you have never been much profit or pleasure."

"Poor miserable little creature!" exclaimed Jane, taking the little girl into her arms, and tenderly looking at her; "how I pity you!—what would I give to take you home with me, and be henceforth a mother to you!"

The child, attracted by her gentleness and mild countenance, laid its head upon her shoulder; and when Jane wished to put her down, in order that she might return home, clung to her and wept bitterly.

Jane mingled tears with hers, and could not repress them during her walk home. The image of the poor ill-treated child was before her eyes; and when she met her husband, she told her story in most pathetic terms, adding—"The idea of the treatment this poor baby will receive when her mother is dead really distracts me. Oh! James, if you could but see what an interesting lovely creature she is!"

Farmer Wilmot, who always sympathized in his wife's feelings, promised to accompany her to the lane, and endeavour to ascertain whether the father of the child was equally devoid of humanity or tenderness as the old gipsy, which there was too much reason to apprehend; and in the evening they sallied forth, taking with them some gruel and other comforts for the sick woman.

When they drew near, several of the gang were sitting round their evening repast, consisting of poultry,—it was not unreasonable to consider as the spoil stolen the previous night from some neighbouring hen-roost. They were ferocious-looking beings, and Jane shuddered as she approached them. She inquired respecting the sick woman, and was told that "she was as bad as she could be." They drew near the wretched pallet, which had been formed for her with straw, covered with a few dirty rags. Death was visible upon the countenance of the sufferer. The little girl was fast asleep, her head resting upon the lap of her mother. A heated flush animated her pale cheeks; her beautiful ringlets nature had arranged with the truest grace about her forehead; her long dark eyelashes were fringed with tears; and as she lay, one little bare shoulder bore the marks of rude violence, being bruised, as if a heavy hand had roughly used it.

Jane pointed to the child, and the farmer was almost as much affected as his weeping wife.

The dying woman lay apart from the rest of the gipsy group, and Jane and her husband found themselves alone with her.

She looked at them, and motioned with her hand for Jane to stoop down, that she might speak to her. Jane knelt by her side—death is always awful to the beholder, and she felt that now she saw it surrounded by all its worst horrors—a soul about to take its departure from this earth under such circumstances! Where was the hope that supports the Christian?—alas! not here. In darkness the unfortunate woman had lived—in darkness she must die!

The dying gipsy whispered in low broken phrases, "That poor child—what will become of it when I am dead?—they will want to get rid of it—perhaps murder it—she has no father here—Brian hates it. He says the child may get him hanged—he stole it—." Here her words were interrupted by a dreadful spasm suddenly seizing her. Jane called for help, and in one minute the gipsies surrounded the woman; but she was dead! They suddenly grasped the child, and threw it at a distance: Jane could contain herself no longer.

"Give me the child," she cried in agony; and turning to her husband, with streaming eyes and supplicating action, she sobbed, "Oh! my dear husband, let me take her home, and be a mother to her. We may be certain the Almighty will bless our undertaking. Consider the happiness of saving perhaps a soul from everlasting destruction. What will be the fate of the poor infant if she is left with these dreadful people? If her life be spared, how will she be brought up? Poor innocent babe, she will be taught to be wicked; and, I am sure, from her sweet countenance she is not so by nature. Do, dear James, grant my request. We shall never miss the little she will cost us. Oh! no; God will assist us, and this act of humanity will increase, rather than diminish our means. Do not hesitate—shall we offer to take her?"

James looked grave and irresolute; he longed to grant his wife's request, and yet he felt that they were about to take upon themselves a heavy responsibility.

"I wish," he said, "we could first consult Mr. Neville."

"Well, go, dear husband, and ask his advice," Jane replied, quickly, sanguine as to the results; "I will remain by the child until you return—but pray do not be long, for I tremble at the looks of these terrible people." She then seated herself apart from the gipsies, and, taking the poor little girl in her arms, lulled it again to rest.

The gipsies were busying themselves about the corpse of the dead woman; and seeing that Mrs. Wilmot, far from watching them, was heedless of their proceedings, while centering all her attention in the child she held, they allowed her to remain in tranquillity until her husband returned, accompanied by Mr. Neville.

## CHAPTER III.

"There are these angels sent by heaven to guide '
Our earthly barks through time's deceitful tide;
Faith, Hope, and Charity—benignant three!
Charity fairest—follow Charity!"

JAMES WILMOT found Mr. Neville disengaged, and, in much haste and agitation, told him the purport of his visit. This excellent man was much interested by the account he gave of the destitute situation of the child, and willingly accompanied him to the lane, where they found Jane, with the poor baby asleep upon her knee.

Mr. Neville was struck with the beauty of the little girl, and equally shocked by her emaciated and neglected appearance. Jane renewed her entreaties that she might be allowed to take charge of her; and so earnest were her solicitations, that Mr. Neville joined with her in hoping that James would yield to her wishes. It was no difficult matter to obtain his hearty concurrence in the benevolent plan ; for from the first his heart inclined to it, although a fear that the step might not be a prudent one had for a moment made him hesitate. They had now only to speak to the gipsies.

Mr. Neville requested the father of the child to approach them : a man of a most ferocious appearance came reluctantly forward.

"You are the father of the child ?" inquired Mr. Neville.—"May be I am," gruffly replied the man ; "bad luck to me !" "Will you object to part with her, and allow this good woman to take charge of her, and bring her up as her own child ?" continued Mr. Neville, while Jane waited in dreadful suspense for the reply of the brutal gipsy.—"Ay, and thank her too; but—" hesitated the ruffian, "I must have my price for her: the little good-for-nought should bring me some price for the trouble she's been to my dead missis there."

Mr. Neville, thoroughly disgusted, and more than ever anxious to take the child out of such hands, offered him a sovereign ; and telling the man that he did not intend to give him any more, desired Mrs. Wilmot to go home with her charge—an order she with the most heartfelt joy obeyed ; and pressing the sleeping treasure to her bosom, she with rapid steps had nearly reached the farm, when she was joined by a young gipsy girl, who, out of breath, begged her for an instant to stop.

"Oh ! ma'am, I have run so fast, just to ask you to let me have
2

one more look at poor little May.  I heard you were taking her away; and, poor heart, I am the only one in the world who ever was kind to her."

Mrs. Wilmot willingly paused, and the good-natured looking gipsy girl affectionately kissed the sleeping child.  "Ah! poor May," she said, "a hard life you have had; and I am glad you have found a kind friend.  Good bye—good bye"—and, again kissing her, she wiped a tear, which the parting seemed to call to her bright black eyes, and ran back to join her companions,

Mr. Neville remained still with the gipsy group to give further orders.  He desired them peremptorily to leave the neighbourhood by the morning, promising to defray all expenses of the funeral if they would decamp without delay.

The carpenter of the village speedily constructed a shell for the body of the deceased woman, which was conveyed to the poor-house, and by the next morning the gipsy tribe had finally departed.

On Jane Wilmot reaching her home, the little girl, whom we shall now call "May," awaking from her deep sleep, opened her large dark eyes, and gazed fearfully around her.  Her first impulse was to cry; but the mild, kind looks which met her timid glances, almost immediately checked her grief; and a nice basin of bread and milk, which her new protectress had prepared for her, was devoured by the poor famished babe with the utmost eagerness.

Jane then hastened to take off the filthy rags with which poor May's emaciated body was scantily clothed, with some little reluctance cut off the thick and matted curls which covered her head, and then washed her completely with warm water; and so gently and kindly did she perform this office, that the child, though evidently unaccustomed to such a process, submitted to it without murmuring.

Many tears did Jane shed when she saw the pitiable state of the poor child's body, as, added to filth and neglect, evident marks of savage treatment were to be discovered.  She was almost crippled from ill usage, while her little form, thin and wretched in the extreme, was covered with innumerable scars, which, though slight, bore sad evidence of the cruelty she had undergone: however, one scar on her forehead seemed to attest greater barbarity than all the rest, and had been apparently inflicted by some sharp instrument; for although it was easily perceptible that the wound had been made some length of time back, still it was so indelible as to promise to accompany her down to the grave—a grave Jane almost feared her fragile charge could scarcely be long preserved from.

"Poor, darling child! what have you suffered!—Did they beat you very hard?" she inquired of the child; who replied, looking round as if she almost anticipated the repetition of their savage treatment, "Oh, yes; beat me, and kicked me; nobody loved me but mammy a little, and brown Bet."

After the child was made thoroughly clean and comfortable, Jane placed her in a little bed, which she had made close to her own. It was quite a matter of surprise to see how immediately the little girl conformed herself as it were to her new position. She seemed as if renewing old habits, instead of acquiring new. A sweet happy smile was on her countenance when Jane kissed her, and laid her down; and the beauty of the expression of her features when she fell asleep, lighted up by that bright flush which generally accompanies the slumber of children, can only be imagined by those who have gazed on that most touching sight; the heavenly tranquil sleep of a lovely child.

Jane hung over her in silent rapture, and on her knees implored that a blessing might be vouchsafed on her by that gracious God, whose property is ever to have mercy. She prayed also that her undertaking might be sanctified by His almighty protection, and that the little destitute girl might grow up to be an honour to the holy name of Christian, and thus form the pride and happiness of her adopted parents.

After this pious duty was performed, Mrs. Wilmot's thoughts again turned to the temporal necessity of her charge, and she began to reflect how she should clothe her new-found daughter. As for the rags which had partially covered her, they had been immediately consigned to the fire. Whilst she was considering which of her own garments she should cut up to furnish clothing for little May, she heard a gentle tap at the door, and soon beheld the welcome form of Mr. Neville, accompanied by his sister, Mrs. Villars.

They came laden with two complete suits for the little stranger, of which they always kept a store for the village children. Jane conducted her visiters to the bedside of the child, and felt happy in perceiving they were equally moved and interested, as herself by the appearance of the sleeping babe.

Her brother had told Mrs. Villars of the wretched plight in which the infant had been found; and on seeing its present peaceful and improved state, she could not resist taking the hand of the excellent Jane and offering commendations for that active charity, which, under the blessing of her God, had taught her thus to rescue a suffering fellow-creature from a condition of hopeless misery.

'CHAPTER IV.

"Though I could read the books of prophecy,  &c.,
· Withdraw the veil of heavenly mystery;
Though Science led me through her various way,
And I had power, power from above to say,
'Remove thou mountain:'—this were nought, and I
An useless nothing, without Charity."

As the whole transactions related in the foregoing chapter, had taken place, in so short a time, and as no one, but the persons already mentioned, knew any thing of the circumstances attending the manner in which little May became domesticated in the family of Farmer Wilmot, Mr. Neville and his sister considered that it would be advisable to keep the details concerning it as quiet as possible.

The Wilmots lived very much to themselves; never entered into the gossip of the village, and had few intimate friends; therefore they hoped to escape without many questions; and it was agreed that they should merely say, with reference to May, that they had adopted her; determining to decline all other explanation, should farther inquiries be made.

Of course rumour and curiosity were busy for some little time, and many were the conjectures formed upon the mysterious arrival of our little heroine: however, it proved like all other novelties, a "nine days' wonder," and finding that no light was thrown upon the matter, surmise at length wore itself out, and the Wilmots were left in peaceful enjoyment of their newly-acquired child.

Every day inspired these good people with more love for this little foundling; the sweetness of her disposition developing itself, in proportion as confidence and happiness dawned upon her feelings.

. At first she was timid and shrinking to a fearful excess, and weakness and fever, brought on evidently by neglect, made her ill and low-spirited; but kindness and cleanliness soon brought the roses into her pale cheeks; her beautiful eyes began to beam with happiness, and her lovely hair growing again in clustering ringlets, rendered her beauty almost unearthly.

Jane watched her returning health with the anxiety of a mother; and indeed no mother could be more adored by her child than she was by little May: it appeared as if all the affection of her nature was brought forth by the warm beams of kindness which emanated from the benevolent countenance of Mrs. Wilmot, who, indulging in all the endearing tenderness to childhood, so natural to her bosom, and which was rendered still more active by the recollection of what she had rescued her from, felt a happiness of which she could have formed no previous conception.

What a beatified virtue is benevolence!—It is a precious tie existing between man and man as children of one common father,—a tie wholly unaffected by difference of age, station, kindred, or country, and over which the artificial distinctions of a vain world have little power. If we consider our blessed Lord simply in his human character, how bright—how lovely and engaging does this particular virtue appear! And when contemplating, with adoring veneration, the tenderness of His compassion—the activity of His benevolence, let it be remembered that these are *imitable* virtues. We cannot, like Him, recall the fleeting soul to its earthly tabernacle; we cannot say to the angry wave, "Peace, be still!" but we may all cheer, and soothe, and be kind one to another.

Jane had ever acted the part of the good Samaritan, and now she reaped the reward of her habitual charity, for every morning she rose with greater alacrity and happiness. She had indeed, now an incitement to exertion; and what a real interest she felt in possessing a child which in every respect seemed to her maternal bosom all her own! Kind as her husband was upon the occasion, she was sensible she ought to strive never to let him find that her precious May was ever an encumbrance to him; therefore with increased diligence and exactitude she laboured in the performance of every duty. She counted too with greater eagerness her eggs, watched with an anxious eye the well-doing of her poultry, beheld with gladness the rich milk yielded by her cows, and was more than ever desirous that her butter should be of the finest quality. She always found a ready sale for these articles at the Hall, as the housekeeper declared that Mrs. Wilmot was the cleanest and most honest dealer who ever approached the house.

It was from the Hall also that Jane had occasionally been supplied with needlework, and she now anxiously inquired for further employment of that nature.

"How is it," said Mrs. Smith, "that you are so very desirous for work?—I hope you are doing well at home?"

"O yes, thank you, ma'am," Jane replied, slightly blushing at the housekeeper's remark; "every thing goes on as well as our hearts could wish; but we have taken charge of a little girl, and I feel that I ought now to work more than I used to do, when we had no one to think of but ourselves."

The hint was sufficient for the good woman. She made interest with the ladies' maids, and work poured in upon Jane from many quarters, so that every Saturday night she, returned home from the Hall with a little treasure, which she with joyful pride counted out before her husband, whose kind and honest heart glowed with satisfaction and gratitude in the possession of so excellent a wife, while he rendered her equally happy by evincing as tender an interest in their pretty charge as occupied her own affectionate bosom.

---

## CHAPTER V.

" 'Tis sweet, in journeying tnrough this vale of tears,
  To gather its fair flowers; to pay and prove
  Blessings and sympathies, and acts of love,
  And so to sink into the lap of years."

MR. NEVILLE and his sister, whose feelings from the first had been greatly interested in Mrs. Wilmot's *protégée*, as time went on, still continued sensible to her irresistible, though infantine attractions; indeed, she was a child whose every act gave the fairest promise of excellence; and, as she grew in years, evinced, with a mind full of vigour and intelligence, the unusual accompaniment of a heart of rare and sweet simplicity.

Many were the conversations which took place between the brother and sister upon the subject of the child. It was evident from the dying words of the gipsy woman, and the unnatural behaviour of the reputed father, that there were the strongest reasons for believing she was in reality a stolen child. This at first had been a subject of great disquietude to the Wilmots, who, by the idea, felt their possession of the little May rendered an uncertain one: but by degrees it passed wholly from their minds, and they almost ceased to remember that she was other than their own dear offspring. But it was very different with Mr. Neville, though he kindly avoided alluding to his suspicions to the farmer, on whom they could only inflict a useless anxiety; and every day both the pastor and his sister became more and more convinced, that the little foundling came of no common parentage. At times they fancied that perhaps the romance of her story gave rise to these surmises; but when they beheld her every every action marked by innate elegance, and witnessed her high-bred, and, what some might have termed, aristocratic appearance, they felt inwardly persuaded these were the legible stamps of superior birth. Her delicate feet—her long and taper fingers—her beautifully turned head—her symmetric and swanlike neck—were, they well knew, traits almost peculiar to the patrician daughters of the land ; and how was it that all this exclusive cast of loveliness united itself in the form of the lowly-born May ? Her disposition, though truly tender and affectionate, was retiring, sensitive, and shy ; and it was not difficult to imagine that in a different sphere of life, with another system of education, some shades of haughtiness might have mingled themselves with the otherwise gentle qualities of her heart. Now such feelings were never called forth : to her village companions she was ever kind, though evincing no inclination to form or cherish with them any intimacy; but to her father and mother, and her kind friends Mr. Neville and his sister, her affection was ardent in the extreme, and seemed to centre in them alone.

For Jane Wilmot her attachment was so deep—so absorbing, that even at her young age, it approached almost to enthusiasm; towards her adopted father it took the character of an affection at once tender and relying ; while again, with the tact of a delicate mind, she early evinced for Mr. Neville and his sister a most touching sense of veneration, mingled with a grateful love.

With regard to Mr. Neville, it was impossible for him to be known without exciting the liveliest feelings of respect, admiration, and attachment. In the early part of his life he had travelled much, and had stored his mind with information and those acquirements, which now, in the calm and even tenor of a clerical life, afforded him a never-failing source of interest and pleasing recollection.

His sister, justly beloved by her brother, was in want of a home. Her husband had died suddenly, and left her with scarcely any resources. Devotedly attached to her husband, the heart of the widow appeared to be almost broken; and with youth offering the prospect of a long, though sorrowing life, her pilgrimage in this world promised to be a sad and weary one. She knew not where to go—in what part of the world to fix herself. Mr. Neville entreated his sister to become the mistress of his house ; and by thus convincing her that there were still duties remaining to her in this world, her dormant energies were awakened, and restored her to herself.

Mrs. Villars proved a real solace to her brother in his retirement; and contributing every day to his comfort, aiding him in all his benevolent pursuits, entering into his renfined and simple amusements, and receiving daily from his virtuous example fresh incitements to calmness and peace of mind, she became once more, what she had

heretofore been, an active friend, an intelligent companion, and the
most affectionate and devoted of sisters.

Mrs. Villars often urged her brother to allow her to give the little
May the advantage of a superior and enlightened education. Possessing herself every accomplishment necessary to render her a perfect
instructress, willingly would she have devoted her time in bestowing
them upon a child of so much promise; but Mr. Neville always opposed this measure. He would say—" Teach her to be a good Christian and a good daughter to the excellent people who have adopted
her. In her present obscurity she will probably pass her life; why
teach her what may raise her wishes beyond the humble home the
Almighty has provided for her? Indeed, my dear sister, it is one of
the errors of the times in which we live—the system of over-educa-
tion adopted in every family. I am speaking now without any reference to our simple-minded May; but it distresses me when I look
around, and see the manner in which parents are educating, or suffering others to educate, their children. *Show* is evidently the end
to which all their efforts tend; and it is only when a glittering list
of arts and accomplishments has been forced on the boy they have
rendered trifling and self-sufficient—on the girl they have made vain
and forward, that they consider their purposes have been answered;
forgetting to teach the awful truth; that all have an immortal soul—
or in what manner that soul is to be made acceptable for Heaven.
And is it not dreadful to see parents thus failing to reflect how suddenly their children may be called into a world, where all the acquirements, for which they now sacrifice every thing, will be as worth-
less as the painted dust which adorns the butterfly's wings? where
all that is not founded on religion, and on the reason and virtue which
religion teaches, shall have passed away with the other gaudy trappings of the world? You will think me very prosy, my dear sister,"
continued Mr. Neville, taking a book from the table before him; " but
here are some lines which express so well my opinion relative to the
education of females, that I must read them to you. Speaking of the
modern systems which are creeping in, the poet asks,—

> 'Are ye not apt
> To taint the infant mind; to point the way
> To fashionable folly, strew with flowers
> The path of vice, and teach the wayward child
> Extravagance and pride? Who learns in you
> To be the prudent wife, or pious mother?—
> To be her parent's staff, or husband's joy!
> —'Tis you dissolve the links that once held fast
> Domestic happiness—'Tis you untie

The matrimonial knot—'Tis you divide  
The parent and his child—Yes, 'tis to you  
We owe the ruin of our dearest bliss.  
The best instructress for the growing girl  
Is she that bare her. Let her first be taught,  
And we shall see the path of virtue smooth  
With often treading. She can best dispense  
That frequent medicine the soul requires,  
And make it grateful to the lip of youth,  
By mixture of affection. She can charm  
When others fail, and leave the work undone.  
She will not faint, for she instructs her own.  
She will not torture, for she feels herself.  
So education thrives, and the sweet maid  
Improves in beauty, like the shapeless rock  
Under the Sculptor's chisel; till at length  
She undertakes her progress through the world  
A woman fair and good, as child for parent,  
Parent for child, or man for wife, could wish.'

"And now," pursued Mr. Neville, after his sister had acknowledged the truth of the lines which he had read, "and now, but one word more regarding our little favourite. Let us cultivate in her every species of useful acquirement which will render her happy in her present station, giving her at the same time a perfect knowledge of religion, that she may walk blameless before her God. To this really blessed end, let all our endeavours be directed; and lovely and fascinating as she already promises to be, do not give her merely exterior embellishments, which may one day only lead her into the temptations and follies of the world, and possibly render her a victim to the snares to which the young, the beautiful, and the unprotected, are so often exposed. The obscurity and mystery of her birth is great, but why should we wish to withdraw the veil which hangs over it? She can scarcely be happier than she now is, or own a greater blessing than being a child of such excellent and virtuous parents as those who now so tenderly cherish her.

And indeed May was happy; her home, though humble, was comfortable and cheerful in the extreme, and the gladness of her youthful heart might be traced in the blithe and melodious song with which she greeted the morning's early hour, when, like the lark which carolled above her head, she left her slumbers for the sweet duties of the day. Gaily and with delight would she hasten to assist her dear mother in her various labours—labours which were only so in name, for to her every occupation was an active pleasure. But her dearest office was that of making herself useful to her father; and with playful

3

earnestness she would prevent all assistance, nor allow Mrs. Wilmot
to interfere with her in preparing his meals, or in arranging and keeping in the most perfect order his linen, and the few books and pamphlets which constituted the farmer's library. Indeed, there could
be scarcely a greater punishment inflicted upon her than to have
anticipated her in these kind duties; but, above all, that which she
would consider most exclusively her own, was the gay task of preparing breakfast—a meal her watchful affection soon told her was his
most favourite one. Her delight in spreading the snowy cloth, in
cutting the bread and butter, in placing before him a delicate jar or
honey—the produce of her own bees—and the plate of fresh water-
cresses which she had risen early to procure, was only equalled by
the pleasure these kind attentions taught her protectors' hearts to feel.

It was a touching and beautiful sight to behold this lovely child
thus occupied. Her graceful form and high-bred demeanour seemed
scacely belonging to a cottage; and yet the affection which beamed
from her countenance, whilst bestowing these tender cares, spoke of
the genuine feelings of rustic life, at the same time that it indicated
filial attachment in its most attractive form.

What happiness it is for those parents who thus witness the active
goodness of their child!—and be assured, my young readers, that
domestic duties are not less pleasing, nor less acceptable, in the sight
of your Heavenly Father. They must ever hold pre-eminently the
first place in the ordinary range of Christian services; and while you
are watching the sick bed of a suffering parent, soothing the sad hours
of disease by tender assiduities, or seeking to enliven the closing eve
of, life's little day of some aged relative, by your presence and considerate attentions, you may rejoice in the belief that you are acting
righteously in the sight of God; and by thus following the precepts
of your Saviour, may, after a life well spent, hear the joyful invitation,
" Come, ye blessed of my Father!".

James Wilmot fully appreciated the happiness of possessing so
excellent a daughter, in which light he ever considered the virtuous
little May; and in a measure reaped in this world the reward of the
benevolence which had led him to foster her. May rejoiced in his
affection, and in the tender words of compliment which he lavished
upon her; and if in a moment of pre-occupation the farmer failed to
utter the usual " Thank you, my own darling;" or, " What a happy
man I am to have so good a little daughter!" she would wait her
time with a delicate tact, and then, when she knew she might, without being troublesome, claim his attention, put both arms around his
neck, and say with mock gravity, " What a pity my father no longer

loves h s poor little May!" and then, smiling and chiding him by turns, delight and amuse the worthy Wilmot by her fascinating playfulness.

---

## CHAPTER VI.

"Within my infant breast parental care
The living seed of young devotion planted,
And watch'd and water'd it—and pray'd and panted
That it might spring, and bud, and blossom there."

For two hours every day, Mary went to the Rectory, where Mrs Villars instructed her in reading, writing, and needle-work of every kind; farther than that she did not go, with the exception of selecting for her books of a superior order, which expanded and improved her mind, affording her at the same time the most engrossing amusement.

May was a child of great natural abilities, with a memory so singularly good, that she could retain with the utmost accuracy any thing she had either read or heard. Mr. Neville's sermons, which were to her subjects of absorbing interest, she could repeat in a most extraordinary manner; and once during an illness of many weeks' duration, which confined Farmer Wilmot to his house, May regularly repeated to him the sermon, of which he was unfortunately deprived the benefit of hearing.

Brookside Farm was situated in a most retired spot, which afforded so few neighbours that May formed few acquaintances of her own age; indeed she was brought up so differently from the other children of the village, that Mrs. Wilmot, and her friends at the Rectory, were not anxious that she should associate much with them. However, although she was a child of most retiring manners, she was loved by all who knew her, for never was May found to be unkind; and there was something in her calm and even dignified manner, contrasting so strongly with that of others, and which imparted to her an air of such decided superiority, that there was a degree of respect shown towards her by every one. One little girl looked up to her with peculiar regard and admiration—Susan Ashfield, the daughter of a farmer in the neighbourhood. She was unhappy, poor girl, in having lost an excellent mother; and on the second marriage of her father with a woman of a harsh and unkind disposition, she learnt more deeply to regret the treasure she had been deprived of. Susan Ashfield was a girl of high spirit, and, perhaps, sometimes made matters worse, by giving way to the impulses of wounded feelings. She had not yet sufficiently studied that most important of lessons—to "bear and forbear;" she however possessed a good-heart and a grateful disposition, and kindness would always produce that impression, which no degree of harshness could create.

Susan passed many a wretched hour; and one day was discovered by the tender-hearted May, sitting on a bank near her father's house, weeping bitterly. She had that morning been beaten cruelly by her stepmother for some trifling misdemeanor.

May mingled her tears with those of the poor girl, and, thinking that she should suffer if her mother even looked unkindly upon her, she seated herself by the side of her afflicted young friend, and asked her kindly what was the exact cause of her present distress.

"Why, dear May," she said, "perhaps I am also to blame, but my stepmother is so unkind to me, that it may be I am sometimes a little pert. But now if any thing goes wrong, it is always thought my fault; if her baby cries, it is I who have hurt it.. I am obliged to nurse it from morning to night; and though I do not mind that, for I love the child, still I am blamed, and ordered about in such a manner, and so hard-worked, and so seldom know what it is to have a kind word said to me, that I believe my temper is becoming bad. But," continued the poor girl, sobbing violently, "I think of my dear mother who is dead, and remember how *she* loved me; and then I become indifferent to every thing in this world, and dislike—and, I fear I may almost say, hate—the unworthy woman who has taken her place."

"Oh! do not say so, my dear Susan," said May, "remember she is your father's wife: and have you so completely forgotten the precepts of our good friend, Mr. Neville, in his discourses to us every Sunday, what a point he makes of Christian forbearance towards each other? I know in your case it is a difficult task for you to bear with so much unkindness, and I heard Mr. Neville say, that the sweetest natural disposition may be soured by constant ill-treatment: but we must seek for that forbearance, that feeling for those with whom we live, that will lead us to give up our own interests for those of others. Dear Susan," May continued, still more earnestly, as she perceived that her words seemed to have weight, and pressing the poor weeping girl's hands within her own,—"Dear Susan, do you not recollect that a kind word often turneth away wrath? and if you were to strive and please your mother, you must in time make some impression upon her; at least she would have no excuse for ill-treating you; and, above all, you would have no cause for self-reproach. How much we hear, almost every Sunday, upon the subject of the regulation of our tempers! I particularly recollect a part of the last sermon, when Mr. Neville said we were not to think highly of the offences we may commit for want of due command over one's temper, or suppose ourselves responsible for them to our fellow creature only; but—and, O Susan, how solemn his voice sounded as he continued—'be assured you must give a strict account of them all to the Supreme Governor of the world, and who has made this a great part of your appointed trial upon earth. Well did our Lord declare, 'Blessed are the peacemakers, for they shall be called the children of God;' and yet how little of this spirit is there upon earth! When we look around us in the world, who would believe that relationship exists among its inhabitants? When we see the quarrels and the coldnesses, the lawsuits and the strifes between those who are not only bound by the common tie of Christian fraternity, but by the closest and most indissoluble bonds of blood, are we not tempted to inquire, can these indeed be 'brethren?' Can they be all trusting to the same hope of salvation, and expecting to dwell together in the same heaven? It is impossible; with such feelings the same eternal mansions could not contain them. If they were admitted there, heaven would be no heaven if it were a place where so many differing families were all to congregate together in one eternal abode.' "

"How forcible is this appeal, Susan!" May continued, after a short pause, only broken by the sighs of her attentive and interested hearer: "when I was listening to it, how thankful I felt that my lot was cast where I enjoy so sweetly the delights of peace and kindness. I know I am a most fortunate girl, and my happiness only makes me the more feel for your very different lot; but still I think you may amend it. Try to bear gently with your mother's unkindness, and you will be happier when you consider, that to cultivate such feelings is absolutely requisite to the attainment of higher felicity in the world to come."

"Yes, May, all this is very true, I know; but our tempers are not in our own power, and if mine is bad it is rather my unhappiness than my fault."

"I do not like to hear you speak thus, dear Susan; but do not think I venture to disapprove from imagining myself superior to you: indeed you would wrong me if you did. I know that I have never been tried; my life has been one of continual happiness; nor have I known what it was to have a harsh word said to me: therefore I ought only to be grateful and humble, and endeavour not to draw down the displeasure of the Almighty by arrogance or self-sufficiency; but again must I say, that I am sure it is at least worth the trial to endeavour to meet your mother's severity with gentleness and temper. It is true we are not all equally happy in our dispositions, but we must endeavour to check and subdue every propensity to do wrong. I have heard Mr. Neville repeat to those who sought his advice, ' Watch the symptoms of ill-temper as they rise with a firm resolution to conquer them, before they are even perceived by any other person. In every such inward conflict call upon your God to assist the feeble nature he has given you, and sacrifice to him every feeling that would tempt you to disobedience; so will you at length attain the true Christian meekness, which is blessed in the sight of God and man; which has the promise of this life as well as that which is to come. Then will you pity in others those infirmities which you have conquered in yourself, and you will think yourself as much bound to assist, by your patience and gentleness, those who are so unhappy as to be under the dominion of evil passions, as you are to impart charity to the poor and miserable.' "

Susan listened with the deepest attention to the advice of her young monitress; indeed it would have been difficult to avoid being impressed by the animated and almost inspired manner of our dear May, whose countenance while she repeated the words of her revered friend was lighted with an expression almost heavenly.

I have thus narrated the foregoing conversation, to impart to my young readers some idea of the character of this child, which was of no common stamp. Brought up as she was in obscurity, and only educated in the plainest manner, still did her mind evince a depth and strength rarely to be found in one so young. Beholding on all sides the exercise of religion in its purest form, and early taught to make it her first and dearest object, she was deeply impressed with a sense of its importance. In her home the day was begun and ended in prayer; her last words at night were praises to her Heavenly Father; and as she knelt down with her parents to pour forth an evening prayer of thanksgiving, it was heartfelt devotion, not mere lip service, which directed their aspirations to the Throne of Grace.

"How devoutly must it be desired, that a greater portion of the spirit of prayer was shed abroad upon us unprofitable servants, that there might be more of that secret communing with God—that habitual and strict intercourse with Him, the absence of which throws such coldness over the feelings of us his people, and such a formality and deadness over our best services! You cannot ask more than your

Redeemer is ready to grant. You cannot seek too near an access to him in whom you believe; and be assured if you are really sincere in your desire of 'drawing nigh unto God,' and earnest in prayer, the Spirit of Grace will not be wanting to encourage; the power of Christ will not be wanting to bring you unto him, though all the weakness of human nature should place itself between you."

## CHAPTER VII.

"What is our duty here ? ,to tend
From good to better—thence to best;
Grateful to drink life's cup—then bend,
Unmurmuring to our bed of rest;
To pluck the flowers that round us blow,
Scattering their fragrance as we go."

FARMER WILMOT had been very prosperous in all his concerns, and they were now able to afford the additional expense of keeping a female servant to assist in the household labours. By these means May had now considerable time to instruct and amuse herself; and though she had ever shared the occupations of Mrs. Wilmot with unvarying cheerfulness and industry, she was not unconscious of the advantage it was to be now freed from the obligation of so strict an attention to the duties of the house and farm.

May was now nearly fifteen; at least so they calculated by her appearance when they had first taken her from the misery in which she had been found, and her tall and improving figure now confirmed their surmises. She had now much leisure to pass a considerable portion of her time with her kind friends at the Rectory, where she always gained additional knowledge and intelligence; but it was not without some doubt and apprehension that Mr. Neville saw her young mind imbibing tastes and ideas which he feared might raise her wishes beyond her present prospects. However, May was thoroughly satisfied with her home; and never for a moment did she wish for any thing beyond the peace and contentment she at present enjoyed, cross her imagination : indeed, how could it, when she contrasted her happy life with that of the village children ?—and often, after having witnessed the discomfort or misconduct of some youthful neighbour, she would exclaim with emotions of fervent gratitude, "What have I done to receive such happiness ?"

May derived much satisfaction from seeing that her young friend

Susan Ashfield was much more comfortable than she used to be. May's admonitions had produced their proper effect upon her mind; and, determining to try the result of perfect forbearance on her part, not an impertinent word or look escaped her when her stepmother scolded her. So completely did she repress any ebullition of temper, that soon there was no excuse for ill-treatment; and in time, notwithstanding Mrs. Ashfield's natural violence of disposition, she was obliged to confess that Susan had really become a very good girl.

Happy indeed was the situation of May in every respect. Adored by her kind and indulgent parents, sincerely loved by the friends she so highly revered, surrounded by comfort on every side, there was nothing left for her heart to wish. Constantly occupied in performing her duty, and pleasing those whose slightest wish was her law; enjoying health and liberty, and the varied amusements which the country affords, she certainly partook of the felicity which is most congenial to our natures, and approaching more nearly to that state in which we were originally created, though luxury and refinement have done much to disturb such pure and simple sources of happiness.

May's amusements were never-ending; for nature supplied her most amply with pleasures, while the same kind Providence had endowed her with a heart capable of appreciating them. Her flowers, her poultry-yard, her dairy, her bees, were all delights, though necessitating, constant, and laborious occupation: but May was a busy little person, and her only regret was that she could not make her day twice as long.

How widely distinct, and how greatly superior in advantages is the life led by the happy child, whose parents are enabled to rear it among the healthful and improving pleasures afforded by the country, to that state of artificial existence which marks the young days of those whose natural protectors, by choice or necessity, confine their charges to the polluted atmosphere and corrupting influence of our large towns! Withheld from the enjoyment and the contemplation of the beauties of nature, which to the unsophisticated heart of childhood is known to offer the best and dearest joys, what are the amusements and pursuits of that poor prisoner, that victim to the tastes and situation of its parents, a town-bred child? Exchanging the invigorating influence of exercise in the pure air, amidst woods and verdant fields, for the splendid pageantry and the refinement of art it is unable to appreciate—what does the young mind gain by the exchange?—Alas! a worldliness of heart that always comes too early; and that disrelish for simple pleasures, the sad penalty of our advances in luxurious indulgence, and of years misspent. Ignorant of the garden's

treasures, scarcely distinguishing even by name those flowery adornments of earth, bestowed by the profuse hand of God. All they
know of the pure happiness, felt by the country-child, is from books,
or perhaps from the artless description of some happier little friend;
and when they see the faded, ill-odoured bouquet' (the prize from
some green-grocer's stall) with which, as a matter of taste, their
governess may decorate the school-room chimney-piece, well may
they doubt the accuracy of those histories which seek to describe the
treasures of Flora as sources of rejoicing and innocent delight.

Unacquainted with the wild bliss which it is to the healthful child
to exercise its limbs unrestrainedly in the green meadow, or on the
healthy down, whose activity learns to be more active, the fragile inhabitants of the town school-room, ignorant of country sports and
country joys, find its pleasures confined to the stiff, formal walk—the
new dress, of which the elegance is only valued as being superior to
that worn by some less *recherché* neighbour—or to the ball, which,
with its previous practisings and laboured exhibitions, ought rather to
be considered as a placard of the dancing-master's talents, and is
nothing like the merry fête we should expect to find in a youthful
ball-room.

Of the many artificial habits and recreations of a town-life, perhaps
none are more objectionable than these midnight revels, where the
child, the *real* child, soon loses all sense of enjoyment, and yawns
with music, in a position decidedly foreign to its impulses and to its
very nature. Nor is *ennui* the only evil genius conjured up at these
assemblies. Too often have we seen the love of admiration and display find birth in a young heart, which, but for these ill-judged pastimes, might never have known such dangerous inmates. Too often
have we seen the worldliness and the jealousies of maturer years dis-
torting at a juvenile ball the lovely faces of mere babes.

These public assemblies, as we have frequently witnessed them,
become snares for parent as well as child; for, once imperceptibly
drawn into the vortex of false ambition, it is greatly to be feared, that
parents will run many risks, and make many compromises, which at
other times they would shrink from, rather than forego for their children one of the fictitious advantages coveted for the lovely idols of
their hearts. But the beautiful child may not grow up to be the admired woman; beauty is evanescent at all times, and many a disappointed mother has learnt, with misplaced grief, how particularly it is
so in childhood. The parents, too, who are now able to gratify the
wishes and pamper to the utmost these worshipped images of their
vanity, may not live to continue their indulgence; and the heart must

4

ache with commiseration at the thought of the sufferings of that poor little being, who, bereft of the enervating though fostering care of a fond mother, finds itself with all the artificial wants engendered by over-indulgence, consigned to the cold, unfeeling care of uninterested hirelings. Oh that parents would bring up their children *as children*, in innocence and nature, with fond care, but with grave correction, and not suffer them to forestall those false and exciting joys which the ways of a degenerate world have rendered customary! Surely as Christians they ought to aim higher for their children, nor ambition for them that admiration which is shared by the opera-dancer and the professional performer. Let children dance to improve their strength, to give grace and vigour to their limbs, and as a recreation to themselves; and let them even occasionally meet together to enjoy this innocent amusement with their young playmates and companions. Dancing is peculiarly suited to childhood; and we should rejoice to see their young and happy faces beaming with the redoubled glow of animation and healthful exercise, every pleasure being heightened by the presence of their beloved parents and their dearest friends; but let them not be decked out as puppets for the amusement of a crowd, who probably return home to laugh at the credulous parents, who by thus feeding the natural inclination of the human heart for vanity, help to rivet a chain about their offspring, which, linking them too powerfully to the things of this world, may impede their progress even to the gates of heaven, open only to those who use this world without abusing it

---

## CHAPTER VIII.

"Still raise for good the supplicating voice,
But leave to Heaven the measure and the choice:
Safe in His power, whose eyes discern afar
The secret ambush of a specious prayer.
Implore his aid, in his decisions rest,
Secure whate'er He gives, He gives the best."

It was an evening in spring, fine and bright, but sufficiently cold to make the fire, which May was anxiously stirring into a blaze, likely to prove acceptable to the farmer, whom they were expecting to return home from the neighbouring town, where he had gone upon business early in the morning. He was unusually late; and poor May, after returning, for at least the twentieth time, from looking over

the garden gate, down the road which she knew he must 'take, exclaimed with undissembled anxiety, "Dear mother, what can have
become of my father? His supper will all be spoilt; and it is very
late for him to be out, for there is a very cold wind, and he was complaining of not feeling well this morning. Besides, he promised too
to bring me home a warm shawl for poor old Sarah, and I promised
to take it to her this evening; but if he does not make haste, I shall
not be able, for it is already getting dark."

"Indeed, I never knew your father so late, my dear," Mrs. Wilmot
replied, sharing May's inquietude; "but hark! do I not hear the
sound of a horse?"

"Yes, mother; here he is!"—and out flew May, full of glee; and
with plenty of questions ready to pour upon the farmer; but in an
instant her gaiety was checked. No smile greeted her animated
approach. The farmer looked grave and very sad; and, getting off
his horse, without saying a word or even looking at his eager child;
he led it into the stable; and so unlike himself did he appear, that
May felt alarmed, and did not venture to follow him, as she was accustomed to do; but waiting until he again appeared, she narrowly
observed him, and her heart sunk within her, for his eyes were evidently red, and she could not help fearing that he had been weeping.
She said not a word, but followed him into the house, pale and
trembling: there she found her mother, who, not at first perceiving
the symptoms which had struck such a damp over the feelings of
May, began questioning her husband upon the reason of the lateness
of his return.

"Do not ask me any questions just now, wife," he replied, "for I
am very tired, and do not feel well." 

"Sit down in your arm-chair, father, and let me give you something to revive you;—a glass of wine, dearest father, for I know you
are ill:"—and May threw her arms round his neck, and began to weep
bitterly. A foreboding of evil struck her forcibly: she was sure something had happened to vex him dreadfully, for never had she seen his
countenance so disturbed.

Farmer Wilmot sat down, and drawing his darling girl upon his
knee, and hiding his face upon her shoulder, was soon heard by his
alarmed wife to mingle sobs and tears with those of May; and convulsive was the emotion which appeared to shake the frame of the
worthy farmer.

"What is the matter?—for mercy's sake tell me!" repeated many
times poor Mrs. Wilmot; but no answer could she obtain. May was
becoming every moment more and more agitated by seeing the suf-

ferings of her father; and Mrs. Wilmot was amazed and distracted by witnessing a scene so distressing and so unaccountable.

At this moment a knock was heard at the door, and Mr. Neville entered the apartment: he too looked very grave, and, as he regarded the melancholy group before him, became evidently much agitated.

Both May and her mother rushed towards him, and entreated him to tell them what was the cause of the farmer's excessive grief.

Mr. Neville did not answer this question, but going up to Farmer Wilmot, he took him by the hand, and said, in a tone of commiseration and feeling, " My good friend, this utter despondency is wrong; you must and ought to struggle against it."

" But, sir, how will my poor wife bear this blow ?"

" Leave her to me, Wilmot ; I will break to her what has happened, and I shall rely upon her fortitude, and the sense of religion which I know she possesses, to carry her through the trial she has to encounter. Leave the room, my excellent friend, and calm yourself; and remember that submission to the will of God is a duty strictly required of us."

The farmer obeyed the wishes of his revered pastor, and Mr. Neville was left alone with the terror-struck wife and poor weeping May.

." Now, dear May, listen to what I have to say," said this kind friend, as he seated himself between her and her mother.: " and you, my good Mrs. Wilmot, summon up all your fortitude, and remember, ' that the Lord gave, and the Lord taketh away : blessed be the name of the Lord.' " Mr. Neville paused for a moment; then, taking the hand of May within his own, continued :—" You have never been told, my dear child, that you are not the daughter of these excellent people, who have indeed been parents to you in the excess of care and affection they have shown you; but who are in reality unallied to you. Nay, start not, nor give way to so much emotion; you must listen to me with patience. You were found by them in want and misery, brought on you by the wickedness of evil people; and they took you home and fostered you, and felt for you all the tenderness of the kindest of parents. Now I entreat you again to receive what I am now obliged to impart with as much calmness as you can command. Rouse all your energies, my beloved child, my worthy good girl, for I must now tell you that your real parents have discovered your existence, and are about to claim you as their own.".

A scream of terror from May stopped Mr. Neville abruptly in his communication, and he then perceived that Mrs. Wilmot had fainted away.

The scene which ensued may be imagined, but is far too painful to be described.

The utter wretchedness of all the inhabitants of the farm was profound and overwhelming. The love which these excellent people felt for the child of their adoption,—the manner in which she had become necessary to their happiness, was so great that the idea of losing her was to them almost as dreadful an affliction as if they had seen the grave close over her. Henceforth she was to live, to smile, to be a joy to those around her, but not for them were all her sweet and endearing qualities to be exercised! At this moment their grief was too absorbing, and for a short time threw a veil over those better feelings—those feelings of resignation, which a true and lively faith in the mercy and wisdom of God ought to suggest, to teach us never to doubt, never to despair, if we are visited by the severest trials, but to feel assured that they are as much the fruits of our heavenly Father's love as his more obvious blessings; and if we are called upon to give up our dearest possession, that same faith will teach us, even amidst nature's keenest sufferings, to kiss the rod while worshipping Him whose inscrutable will appoints our trials, and in the darkest hour of nature's woe, to remember with confidence that "God will provide."

There are, however, afflictions so deep and overwhelming, the sorrowing feelings they occasion must be indulged in; and it was thus with the family at the farm; but God in his mercy allows us tears for the relief of such bitter griefs. We *may* mourn, but not as "those that are not to be comforted; and after nature has found vent in the natural expression of our sorrow, we must look to the God of our salvation, who solaces all those who turn to him in heart and in spirit.

---

## CHAPTER IX.

"If bitterness drug our earthly cup,
If sorrow disturb our career;
Eternity's joys can well fill up
The chasms of suffering here."

My readers will no doubt be very anxious to hear every particular relating to the events of the last chapter, and I must lose no time in narrating to them the history of the disclosure, which will restore our heroine to her rightful parents.

A gang of gipsies, of the worst description, had been taken up, some of the party having been implicated in a most atrocious murder, of which they were found guilty. One of the wretched men before he was executed, made a full confession of his guilt, and also of the crimes of his past life. Amongst many dreadful deeds, he mentioned having been accessory to stealing a little girl from the park of the Earl of Avondale, near Bristol, and who he believed was their only child. She had been laid asleep upon a haycock, whilst the nurse was amusing herself by having her fortune told by one of the women belonging to the gang. They were instigated to this daring and outrageous act by the splendour of an ornament that attracted them, and which was hung round the neck of the sleeping child. Fearful of detection, they immediately embarked on board a vessel which was on the point of sailing for Cork, and they remained in Ireland until they imagined the pursuit after the child might be relaxed. The gipsy said, he believed she had been with the gang about two years, when they happened to be encamped in the neighbourhood of Brookside Farm, where the child was taken from them by a farmer of the name of Wilmot, who promised to bring her up as his own child; and they were very glad to get rid of her, for they were always afraid of detection. Once, indeed, the gipsy had thought of informing the Earl of Avondale of these particulars, first stipulating for a large reward, and the sacred promise that no punishment should be inflicted; but a long transportation for some theft had driven the matter from his mind, nor had it since occurred to him. He said the child had a peculiar mark upon her forehead, a scar, which appeared to have been inflicted by a sharp instrument. It was in the month of May that they found the child, and in consequence of that circumstance they had always called her May. The confession went on further to state, that the child was remarkable for the darkness of her eyes, and for her long curling dark hair.

This extraordinary confession soon met the notice of the Earl and Countess of Avondale, who had for many years sought in vain for their lost and only child;—a child so doubly valuable to them, for she was heiress at once to their title, and to the immense hereditary estates which accompanied it.

Lord Avondale, as may well be imagined, lost no time in making the further inquiries which were necessary; and the result was so far in corroboration of his hopes, that after travelling with the most incredible expedition, a few hours before the scene described in the foregoing chapter, he had arrived in the most painful state of agitation and suspense at the Parsonage.

He hastily demanded an interview with Mr. Neville, who, as the clergyman of the place, he considered the most likely person to satisfy his inquiries.

In a few words Mr. Neville was able to dispel his doubts, and convinced the enraptured father that his child was within a short distance of him.

At this moment the farmer happened to stop at the Parsonage gate, on his way home, to leave a letter which he had brought for Mr. Neville from the neighbouring town.   Mr. Neville desired him to be shown in; and, whilst the Earl was almost on his knees before the good man, expressing in the most fervent and enthusiastic terms his gratitude and joy for all his tender care of his child, the poor farmer scarcely knew how to restrain a burst of grief at the idea of so completely losing her in whom he centred all a parent's affection.

Would an Earl's daughter continue to love a simple farmer?— would she not look back with shame on the years passed in an humble cottage?   But even should his gentle May always love him, and think of him with affection, still she would be for ever lost to him; and he knew too well that the difference of their stations would place a gulf between them never to be surmounted.  He felt almost broken-hearted on the conclusion of Mr. Neville's communications, and was obliged hastily to leave Lord Avondale's presence to conceal the anguish which unmanned him.

Lord Avondale's impatience to see his child was of course excessive; and it was with much difficulty that he was persuaded by Mr. Neville and his sister to defer the interview until the morning.  They told his lordship the farmer and his wife were not common characters, and that they were full of deep and refined feeling; that their love for the child of their adoption was of the purest and most fervent nature, their existence appearing wrapt up in her; while her affection for those she considered her parents was equally lively and tender.  By these representations they at length convinced the Earl that one night's preparation was quite necessary to tutor their feelings into calmness to bear the shock, which the idea of her removal would cause the party; and, after at last having obtained his promise to wait with patience until the morning, Mr. Neville went to the farm to discuss these events with its inhabitants.  He was soon followed by his sister, who did indeed take a true part in their grief, and offered what consolation she could then suggest; but she found it a difficult task, as she was almost as unhappy as her poor friends, for dearly did she love their darling May, whose distress and agitation was most painful to behold. Her enthusiastic and affectionate heart had known no other attachment but that which she felt towards her supposed parents and her dear friends at the Rectory, and the idea of leaving them overwhelmed with agony her gentle heart.  Mrs. Villars passed much of the night alternately at the bedside of her poor friends; and at last succeeded in obtaining a promise of composure from May, in order that by some rest she might be able to meet her father the Earl the next day with propriety, and the semblance at least of calmness.

Lord Avondale could not enter into the feelings which so bitterly evinced themselves at the farm. He had always lived for the world, nor could he imagine happiness unconnected with it; and to him it appeared that the transition from obscurity to splendour must be happiness itself. Although possessed of excellent natural feelings, they had never been brought forth or matured, and lay dormant, if not totally extinct, within his bosom. His marriage had been one of *convenance*. Lady Avondale was a beautiful woman of high rank and large fortune; but I grieve to say, as she is the mother of our interesting May, that she was indeed a mere lady of fashion, without one quality, one feeling, which bespoke a heart possessed of those gentle virtues so endearing in a woman.

Such a wife was not likely to elicit from a husband's bosom those benign charities of our nature which bade us see in every man a brother, and teach us to seek him as our friend; and though Lord Avondale was really amiable, yet thrown amongst the society attracted to their circle by his worldly-minded wife, he degenerated like them into the mere ephemeral flutterer of the day, forgetting alike his higher destinies in this life and the life to come.

CHAPTER X.

" But thou art fled
Like some bright exhalation, which the dawn
Robes in its golden beams ;—ah ! thou hast fled!
The kind, the gentle, and the beautiful—
The child of grace and virtue."

MRS. VILLARS had, with as much caution as possible, broken to Lady Hyacinthe, (for we must now exchange the simple name of May for this more high-sounding appellation,) that her father intended taking her to London on the following day. This abrupt step appeared hasty and inconsiderate; but still much was to be said for the anxiety of the mother, who had so long been deprived of the society of her child : in short, Lord Avondale was peremptory, and no choice was left her but to obey. His lordship was profuse in his professions of gratitude, and to ev nce it there was no pecuniary recompense which he was not willing to make to the farmer and his wife. He talked of settling thousands upon them, and was with difficulty convinced by Mr. Neville that five hundred a year was perfectly equal, if not more than sufficient, to satisfy all their bounded wishes : but how great was the Earl's surprise, when, on questioning Farmer Wilmot as to the method by which it were better this sum should be placed at his disposal, he at once gently but firmly refused all emolument from the hands which were destined to wrest his beloved May from his bosom ! It was in vain they expostulated with him on this indifference to the benefits of fortune : he would shake his head with a mournful expression, saying, "The wealth of the Indies could not reconcile me to the loss of my child. It is only from the same Almighty hand which thus chastens us that I and my poor Jane can look to for peace and consolation."

Mr. Neville in some measure reconciled Lord Avondale to the unbending refusals of the farmer, by intimating that he would always have it in his power to watch over his welfare, and administer to his wants and wishes ; adding, that he was certain the most perfect satisfaction his lordship could impart to these most excellent people, would be the promise that they should occasionally see the beloved being upon whom they had lavished so much affection. To this no answer was returned ; but in the grave, confused expression of his countenance, Mr. Neville read, as plainly as though the Earl had spoken it, poor Hyacinthe's eternal separation from the friends of her youth.

Poor child ! dreary were her feelings when she left her bed the sad morning of her departure, and looking round her own dear little room, felt that it was for the last time.

The last time ! What a sound of wretchedness do these three words convey to the heart ! And for the last time was she soon to be clasped in the arms of her mother !—that mother who saved her from destruction—who had been so tender, so kind to her. And must she for the last time implore a blessing from that father, to whom she knew she was the solace and delight—the happiness of his declining years ? What would they do without her ? It was for them she mourned, for them she wept. "My father, my dearest mother, what is to be done for them ? They love me so very much, their hearts will break. I know well that I made them happy, that they depended upon me for many things ; and now that they are growing old, I am to be torn from them, when I am becoming every day more necessary to their comfort."

5

"My dear madam," said the sorrowing girl, addressing Mrs. Vil, lars in a broken and tremulous voice, "I have only one favour to request, which is, that you will send for Susan Ashford. You tell me that this lord who is my father will do any thing for my poor parents here that money will purchase; therefore I know that, by offering a sum of money, Mrs. Ashford will give up Susan, and I think she may be some little comfort here when I am gone. I need not ask you, kind friends, to console their affliction by your presence; your good- ness I know too well. To part from you is my third great misery, and never can I forget all you have done for me. My poor expres- sions in vain endeavour to convey to you all the gratitude I feel for your unremitting care and tenderness to the poor little foundling who was thrown upon your kindness. But you will write to me, dear, dear Mrs. Villars, and your letters will be my only happiness; and be assured that they will continue to be my guides, my monitors, through- out my life. All your precepts and counsels are engraven in my heart, and will, I trust, be my support in the new and dreaded existence which I shall have now to endure."

Mrs. Villars at this moment was as much affected as her dear young friend, and it was with the greatest effort that she conquered her emo- tion sufficiently to calm Hyacinthe, and bring her spirits to that state of firmness which would enable her to meet Lord Avondale without any distressing marks of agitation; but she did at last induce her to subdue her feelings to that degree which permitted her to receive her father with propriety; and, when he entered the room, she gracefully submitted to the tender embrace that he bestowed upon her.

Much was Lord Avondale agitated in beholding his long-lost child!—tears of gratitude and genuine feeling fell from his eyes as he looked at her, and pressed her again and again to his bosom, in delighted admiration at the beautiful girl, who, as she now stood be- fore him in glowing loveliness, he saw was in form and feature the very image of her high-born mother, but with all her own benevolent and intellectual qualities shining forth in her bright and expressive countenance.

Anxiously and eagerly did the happy father part the clustering ringlets on her forehead to look for the scar, which was one great proof of her identity; and joyfully did he discover it, although it had now dwindled into a little white mark, scarcely visible.

"You cannot think how much distress that scar caused your mother, my dear child," the Earl said, smiling as he observed it: "your nurse let you fall from her knee upon the edge of a sharp fender, and so dreadful was the wound, that it was feared it would destroy your beauty altogether. However, that has fortunately not been the case, he added, looking with pride upon the blushing and lovely face of his daughter, so unused to listen to eulogiums on personal endowments. . We must pass over the wretched parting which took place between Hyacinthe and her afflicted friends. Indeed every heart must feel for them, if we think for a moment of that being—that object which we love the dearest, the most devotedly upon earth—and then imagine it taken away from us for ever; with all our past happiness, every thing which engaged our thoughts, and influenced our affections, imbittered by this one sad bereavement!

Alas! there are few of us who could support such a visitation without murmurs—without tearful repinings—though still conscious the affliction comes direct from the hands of our Heavenly Father. Nature will rise up—that is, our earthly feelings—and the groan of anguish will burst from the over-charged heart. But it ought not to be thus—and let us all emulate the Christian resignation of the excellent Wilmot and his wife, who, bowing humbly to the dispensations of their God, though with spirits heavy with the bitterness of grief, were yet soon able to say with the voice of piety, and faith in the supreme and unerring wisdom of their Maker, "Thy will, O Lord, be done!"

But the recollection of that moment of trial never passed from their hearts; and often, with the retrospective eye of sad regret, did they again see their beloved May, as they still in their affections called her, borne fainting into the carriage, and placed in the arms of her newly-discovered father, conveyed rapidly away, far from the peaceful scenes of her contented childhood!—it was a painful image, but it would again and again recur, and was only to be banished by the hope that all this was ultimately to prove instrumental to the happiness of the dear child of their adoption.

---

## CHAPTER XI.

"From the recesses of a lowly spirit
Her humble prayer ascends. O Father! hear it!
Upsoaring on the wings of fear and meekness."

For many miles poor Hyacinthe was too much absorbed in grief to be any thing but a most sorrowful companion to her father; but by degrees the violence of her sufferings in some measure abated, and she began to recollect the parting admonition of Mrs. Villars, who bade her ever remember that she must now regard Lord Avondale as her rightful father, and evince towards him the requisite affection and respect; and that, moreover, it was her duty to bear always in mind, that giving way to inordinate grief savours too much of rebellion against the Divine will, who, we know, orders every event which happens to us his creatures. It had been an early lesson, that to question the wisdom of the Almighty's decrees was an impiety, which led to deeper crimes: she therefore sought, by praying meekly within herself for fortitude to bear the trials awarded by His chastening hand —rather to increase the spirit of righteousness in her bosom, than to shrink from the visitations which might be sent to prove it. Her pious aspirations were not without effect, and a sensation of hope and consolation evinced their holy power.

However, we cannot avoid feeling for our poor Hyacinthe, and sympathizing in that sickly sorrow, "which is felt when we are first transplanted from a happy home;"—a sorrow the most difficult of endurance among those which mark our path in this lower world, because generally the first. "There are after-griefs which wound more deeply, which leave behind the scars never to be effaced, that bruise the spirit, and sometimes break the heart; but never do we feel so keenly the sense of utter desolation as when first leaving the haven of our home." It is then, when, as it were, launched on the stream of life, 'an aching void pains our inmost soul; the want of love—the necessity of being loved—aggravates our feelings of loneliness and desertion: while images of past happiness rise up to heighten and complete the sum of bitterness. Alas! too early was poor Hyacinthe brought acquainted with such woe—too soon-was the home of her childhood, the kind friends of her infant years, but an image of regretful memory.

Nothing could exceed the attentions and tenderness of Lord Avondale; and, at the close of the three days which nearly brought them to the end of their journey, Hyacinthe began to feel real affection for her newly acquired parent. Her heart, however, sunk within her, when Lord Avondale informed her that they were entering London: she would now soon be in the presence of her mother! But would this mother love her?—should she receive from her the same endearing affection which the kind-hearted Mrs. Wilmot had ever evinced towards her? Her noble mother would, she feared, look with contempt upon her countrified child; and how could she ever accustom herself to the fastidious refinements of society after the humble life she had hitherto led?

"Can I ever feel happiness in this crowded city?" she mentally exclaimed, as the carriage rapidly-flew through the bustling streets, and a sensation of fear nearly overpowered her spirits. "O my peaceful happy home—my dear father and mother!—would that I had ever remained in ignorance of my real fate, and that I could have passed the remainder of my life in tranquillity with you!—what happiness I have lost!" She was interrupted in these reflections by Lord Avondale saying, "Now, Hyacinthe, we shall soon arrive—we are in Grosvenor Square," and in a moment the carriage stopped at the door, of a splendid mansion, which was instantly thrown open, and displayed the interior of a well lighted hall, filled with liveried and other servants.

Hyacinthe was almost lifted from the carriage by her father; for fear and emotion nearly deprived her of the use of her limbs. When she entered, her eyes were dazzled by the glare of light and bustle which appeared to surround her.

"Where is her ladyship?" hastily inquired Lord Avondale.

"My lady desired I would tell your lordship," answered the pompous-looking groom of the chambers, who poor Hyacinthe imagined must at least be another lord—"that she was obliged to dine at the Duke of C——'s, and that her ladyship will not be at home before twelve o'clock."

The Earl looked hurt and mortified, and Hyacinthe's heart heaved heavily. What a reception for a long-lost child!

Lord Avondale led his daughter into a splendidly lighted apartment, where refreshments were laid out. He soon perceived that Hyacinthe was both weary and ill at ease: he therefore proposed her retiring to rest, to which she gladly consented.

Lord Avondale rang the bell, and ordering Mademoiselle Victorine, the Countess's maid, to be summoned, kissed Hyacinthe affectionately, and placed her in charge of the fine lady who immediately made her appearance.

Poor Hyacinthe looked round with surprise and dismay upon her conductress. Her idea of a servant was extremely limited; and when she beheld a lady attired in a blue silk dress, her neck covered with gold chains, her fingers overwhelmed in rings, and her hair arranged in the last Parisian fashion, she thought there must be some mistake, and that some high-born friend of her mother's must have kindly taken upon herself to show these attentions.

The size and magnificence of the house, instead of giving her pleasure, filled her more and more with awe ; and she shrunk with fear and timidity at the view of the numerous domestics whom she passed, and who evidently appeared to scan her person with the utmost curiosity.

Lord Avondale had taken care to supply her at the first good town through which they passed, with a handsome pelisse and bonnet of a more fashionable construction than those with which she had quitted the farm; and her natural carriage was so good, so graceful and dis-; tinguished, that no remarks to her disadvantage could be made: on the contrary, on all sides was whispered, "The very image of my lady!—her own stately walk! Well, to be sure, she does not look as if she had lived all her life in a farm-house!"

At length our poor weary heroine reached the door of her apartment, the sanctuary in which she hoped to repose undisturbed; but Mademoiselle, after throwing open the door, followed her into it. Nothing could exceed the elegance with which the apartment was fitted up; and if the sorrowful Hyacinthe had been in a more composed state of mind, she must have been struck by its magnificence: subdued as her spirits now were, she scarcely saw what was before her.

Mademoiselle Victorine began immediately offering her services in assisting her to undress. In vain Hyacinthe assured her she would rather be without them. "Oh! miladi, her ladyship your mamma would be so displeased; she would think it so very shocking for a young lady to be able to undress herself: and besides which, she desired me to arrange your hair, and make you look as well as possible for her to see you to-morrow; *mais comme elle sera charmée, car vraiment vous êtes belle comme l'amour!* Yes, miladi," she continued, regarding her astonished auditor as she stepped back a few paces back the better to observe her, "you are very beautiful, and very like Madame la Comtesse: you will indeed be exquisite when dressed *comme il faut; mais il y a beaucoup à faire,—beaucoup, beaucoup.*"

Hyacinthe blushed deeply at this tirade. Flattery had never before reached her ears; and as she was by nature and education taught to condemn it, it grated upon her feelings and disgusted her. However, she submitted to her fate, and allowed herself to be pulled to pieces by the person whom she now discovered must be a servant.

Poor girl! she would have been abashed had she seen the super-cilious look of contempt with which Mademoiselle regarded every part of her dress as she disrobed her. She was soon apparelled in a lace dressing-gown; and when Mademoiselle proceeded to take down her luxuriant hair, there was no describing the extravagance of the French-woman's raptures: it all ended, however, in her exclaiming with un-affected satisfaction, "Oh, how happy miladi la Comtesse will be when she beholds this superb head of hair!—*vraiment c'est magnifique!*" And indeed it was beautiful; bright, and glossy to the touch, it fell in the most graceful ringlets, rendering superfluous all the art

of the experienced Victorine, who, seeing that it was unnecessary to
go through the ceremony of placing it *en papillotte*, after passing a
beautiful ornamented hairbrush gently through it, placed a pretty night-
cap upon the lovely head of the Lady Hyacinthe; and, seeing her
spring hastily into the bed, she lighted a little silver lamp, and politely wishing her good night, left the apartment, and hastened to the
steward's room, where she was assailed by a host of questions.  All
that was then learned was, that the newly-found heiress was certainly
very beautiful, but dressed in the lowest style possible; and, assuredly,
for a young lady who had always associated with farmers and farmers'
wives, she was wondrous cold and proud.

,Poor Hyacinthe! how falsely did these words describe her feelings
that night!—and who could have attributed cold-heartedness and
pride to her, had they seen the emotion and deep humility with which,
on the servant leaving the room, she threw herself from her bed, and,
falling on her knees, hastened to pay her evening devotions, and to
ask for protection and support to lead her through the difficulties of
her new station of life?  She foresaw many trials, and shrunk with
aversion from the change; but she prayed with fervour, and soon felt
soothed and comforted.  However, still some natural tears would flow
in bitter streams, when her mind reverted to the sorrowing friends she
had left behind.  " My poor darling mother!" she mentally exclaimed,
" she is still no doubt thinking of her child.  And my father, he is
perhaps trying to console her; but how?—with a breaking heart I
fear.  And here I am—oh, how can I believe it?—a high-born and
wealthy personage, surrounded by luxury and riches, heiress to estates
and titles!  But will all this ever make me happy?  Alas! at this
moment I feel, that once more to find myself under the dear roof
which has so long sheltered me, and safe in the arms of my kind
friends, would be bliss for which how delightedly would I give up
all my possessions and expectations: but, as far as I only am concerned, I will endeavour to submit meekly to the will of God; and
oh! may the Almighty vouchsafe his protection to my dearest friends!
Gracious Father! I implore thee to soothe their sorrow, and bring
their minds to bear with resignation thy dispensations."

Hyacinthe returned to her bed, but her mind was in too agitated a
state to permit her to sleep.  Thoughts would intrude themselves;
and it required all her fortitude and strength of mind to prevent her
murmuring at the idea, that such excellent and really religious people
as the Wilmots should be destined to meet with such a return for all
their goodness towards her. ."Did they not rescue me from destruction, and bring me up in the paths of virtue—and were not all their

best affections centred in me alone? And now I am torn from them
for ever; for much I dread from the words of Lord Avondale, 'that
my proud mother will allow of no communication between me and
persons whom she considers low-born. Oh! if she did but know
half their real worth—their goodness, piety, and honourable feelings!
Softened by these reflections, she wept again most bitterly. It was
long before she could compose herself: but at length fatigue and exhaustion overcame her, and she was just dropping asleep, when she
was aroused with a start by a thundering knock at the hall door. At
first her rustic ears, little accustomed to such sounds, made her doubt
from whence they proceeded; but she at last remembered what it
was, and was again endeavouring to go to sleep, when her attention
was attracted by voices whispering at her door, and presently it was
softly opened. Hyacinthe's heart beat violently within her bosom;—
it might be her mother! In this instance we cannot say much for the
force of nature, for so great was her dread of meeting her new parent,
that, although deceit had ever been foreign to her nature, it certainly
for the first time entered her mind; and the thought occurred to her
to feign sleep, and thus put off the dreaded moment. She accordingly closed her eyes, but not before she had caught a glimpse of a
radiant looking personage, followed by Mademoiselle, who advanced
with cautious steps towards the bed. She then heard the following
words:—" For Heaven's sake, Victorine, walk softly! I would not
wake her for the world." These expressions fell sweetly upon the
heart of her child, and they were uttered by a voice whose silvery
tones were like music to her ear; but the warm glow of satisfied feelings was immediately dispelled by those which followed,—" I dread
a scene, and fear that I shall faint with horror when I hear her countrified dialect. Look gently, and tell me if I may examine her in
safety."

Victorine approached on tiptoe, and, seeing Hyacinthe in what she
imagined a deep sleep, motioned to her lady that she might draw
near.

Perhaps at no time could Lady Avondale have seen her lovely child
to more advantage. The agitation she had undergone had more than
usually flushed her youthful countenance, while her long black eyelashes were shown to full perfection shading the roses on her cheek.
Her full red lips, compressed to conceal every internal emotion, enabled the beholder to judge accurately of the beautiful form of her
mouth; while her dark and silken ringlets, which clustered round a
forehead of marble purity, were only partially concealed by the little
lace night-cap that confined them. Lying as she did amidst the

white drapery of the bed-clothes, her appearance of beauty, innocence, and freshness, was indeed most striking.

The Countess gazed at her for some moments without uttering a word : we will give her credit for some natural feeling overpowering her heart when she looked for the first time on her long lost and only child. Indeed, Mademoiselle was thunder-struck, by perceiving that for a moment her ladyship's eyes were actually filled with tears. She was about to run for sal volatile, camphor, julap, *eau de fleur d'orange*, and all such restoratives which are usually resorted to by fine ladies on those occasions when nature struggles against the *sang froid* imposed by custom ; but her steps were arrested by an exclamation from Lady Avondale, which plainly evinced that she was rapidly descending from her temporary exaltation of feeling. "Thank Heaven!" she at length murmured, and then again she paused, apparently overwhelmed with gratitude—" Thank Heaven!" she again repeated with fervour—" she is at least pretty !"

At these words Hyacinthe turned quickly in her bed ; a feeling of mortification, anger, and even disgust, made her anxious to put an end to a scrutiny which brought forth such a result. Was it for the paltry advantage of those personal attractions she was supposed to possess, that her own mother uttered expressions of gratitude to Heaven?

Lady Avondale was now anxious to depart, fearing she had roused her daughter ; but Mademoiselle told her that she need not be alarmed, for that people who had been brought up in cottages slept as sound as rocks. The Countess therefore lingered some time longer by the side of the silken bed on which her child reclined. All she said farther did not tend to reassure poor Hyacinthe. "Victorine, she appears to be very tall ;—how old she will make me look !" " Oh no, miladi, she is so beautiful, she will appear like your twin-sister." " But, Victorine, before you bring her to me in the morning, mind that you dress her properly, for I have not nerves for vulgarity. How is her complexion—not *very* brown, I hope?—and her hands—good Heavens! are they very coarse? Victorine, you must really send to Delcroix for quantities of *pâte de miel*, unless he can recommend something of quicker operation—and her feet, with the dreadful shoes she must have worn all her life—poor unfortunate child, they must be entirely spoiled !"—and here tears actually returned to her ladyship's eyes.

Mademoiselle assured her lady that every thing was better than could be expected. " And indeed, miladi," said the consoling Abigail, " her ladyship has a high manner about her which rather surprised me ; and I could not help remarking to Monsieur Vol-au-vent, in the

6

steward's room; that the butler's English proverb, 'What is bred in
the bone, will come out in the flesh,' was very applicable to the Lady
Hyacinthe; for there was not a symptom of the farm-house to be perceived in her.   However, miladi, I ought to have excepted the dress
—such inventions!"—and here the lady's-maid made a grimace, expressing most eloquently her disgust; " but happily I was able to put
every thing aside before vulgar eyes had seen the frightful coarseness
of the linen of your ladyship's lovely daughter."

"'Thank Heaven! thank Heaven!" reiterated the mother, as she
quitted the chamber, after listening with the utmost patience to the
familiar remarks of the indulged Victorine.

Hyacinthe could not resist the inclination which tempted her to
take one look at the being who gave her birth; she therefore hastily
looked round as they were leaving the room, and the beautiful vision
that met her eyes caused her heart to palpitate with admiration and
astonishment.   Her fairy dreams seemed all realised in the person of
this lovely woman.   She appeared young in the extreme, and her
dress was so brilliant—so unlike any thing our rustic heroine had ever
before beheld, that her delighted surprise was quite overpowering.

At length she exclaimed, "Is it possible that any being so lovely
can possess a heart apparently so cold! so dead to natural feeling?"
and then she fondly thought that it could not be; that the world, the
situation in which she had lived, might have only partially perverted
the disposition and ideas of her beautiful mother.

"Perhaps if she had lived near dear Mr. Neville," continued the
anxious Hyacinthe, almost audibly communing with herself—" if she
had possessed the advantage of being instructed by him—of hearing
his excellent and righteous precepts, this beauteous creature might
have been equally an angel in mind as she is now in person.   A d
that sweet voice!—does it not seem in itself to show that she must be
naturally good?   Oh that I might be the happy means, the weak instrument in the hand of the Almighty, to endeavour to convey to her
the blessing I have received of religious instructions; then indeed I
should not have lived in vain!   My poor mother, cast among the
giddy pleasures of the world, has perhaps never heard the voice of
pious remonstrance, or affectionate counsel.   Her heart too has been
hitherto closed to the tender calls of maternal affection: who can say
that when it opens to the claims of her long-lost child, it will not gain
every other good and holy feeling?"

Hyacinthe again prayed fervently; and the spirit of prayer came
with healing on its wings, soothing her agitated mind; so that she
soon sank sweetly into a deep repose.

## CHAPTER XIII.

"Accomplishments have taken Virtue's place,
And Wisdom falls before exterior grace:
We slight the precious kernel of the stone,
And toil to polish its rough coat alone.
A just deportment, manners graced with ease,
Elegant phrase, and figure form'd to please,
Are qualities, that seem to comprehend
Whatever parents, guardians, schools, intend."

HYACINTHE's slumbers were profound; and it was not until a late hour that she was awakened by Mademoiselle Victorine, who entered the room, followed by another almost equally smart lady, carrying all the variety of paraphernalia composing the toilet and attire of an elegant female.

Hyacinthe soon found herself under the inevitable dominion of these two accomplished Abigails; and after various most tiresome trials of corsets, shoes, dresses, and an infinitude of minor, though not less important articles, she was at length equipped to their satisfaction.

They discovered that her height was exactly that of Lady Avondale; and with slight alterations made on the moment, one of her dresses answered remarkably well. A small pair of Melnotte's shoes soon decked her pretty feet, and some delicate French gloves concealed a trifling coarseness in her otherwise well-formed hands.

Mademoiselle then gave our heroine's hair a few more twitches, turned her two or three times round to see that all was right, and then with an air of satisfaction led the way.

Poor Hyacinthe trembled violently whilst she followed her conductress to the apartments of Lady Avondale. She was, at length, after a few minutes employed in descending the splendid staircase, and traversing a gallery heated by invisible means, ushered by a little page who was lounging on a *fauteuil* at the door, into the boudoir of her mother! What a crowd of tumultuous feelings pressed in the overcharged heart of the agitated Hyacinthe—feelings, which (she already knew sufficient of her mother to be aware) must be smothered, if not wholly subdued.

Lady Avondale was reclining listlessly on a couch, and her lovely person appeared no less attractive than on the preceding evening, though attired simply in a loose morning-gown, and a close lace cap; while Hyacinthe felt that she could approach her with more confi-

dence, gaze on her with less rear, tnan when she was glittering in all
the elegance of dress and diamonds.

Lady Avondale half-raised herself when her daughter entered ; and
on her drawing near to her, took her hand ,and affectionately kissed
her, and then held her from her that she might take an ample survey
of her person.

Our poor rustic May stood abashed. Her eyes were cast down and
full of tears, her colour was heightened, and her bosom heaved heavily.
She longed to throw herself into her mother's arms, to implore her to
bless her, and to love her as she had been accustomed to be loved—
loved for herself, not for her fragile and exterior beauty.  But every
word that her mother uttered proved to her too 'truly that she would
be appreciated merely according to outward circumstances, unless from
some happy chance her mother's mind should acquire some other tone.

All this pressed rapidly on her thoughts, while Lady Avondale was
almost lost in the contemplation of the young creature who stood before her; and so pensively beautiful was the cast of her countenance,
while the attitude which she had unconsciously taken was so perfectly
graceful, that the Countess was wrapt in the delight which such a contemplation afforded ; and if her heart was ever susceptible of tender
feelings, it was at this present moment.

. With her naturally sweet tone of voice, she said, at the same time
making Hyacinthe sit down beside her, " My dear girl, why do you
look so sad ?   The happiest period of your poor life is now arrived.
You must forget all your past privations—all the misery of, your
former years, for you are now perhaps the most favoured and enviable
being in the universe.  You have the whole world before you—
wealth, rank, youth, and indeed, I rejoice to add, great beauty.
What a sensation she will create !" said her ladyship, turning to
Mademoiselle.  " People may now be silent about the beauty of Lady
Greville's girls.  Has she one to compare with mine ?  My poor
sister-in-law must now indeed hide her diminished head !" ..

At this moment the little page in crimson and gold announced that
Lord Avondale's valet had come to inform the Lady Hyacinthe that
his lordship waited breakfast for her in the library : with her mother's
permission, she not unreluctantly obeyed the summons ; and thus
ended the first interview with her beauteous parent, and which had
filled her whole heart with trepidation and anxiety.

As days passed on, Hyacinthe soon found herself surrounded by
every description of instruction.

Two governesses were installed as her immediate preceptresses—a
French and Italian lady ; for it was soon discovered that her English

education had been carefully regulated, and her mind by these means at once refined and enlightened. But this was not sufficient for the ill-judging Lady Avondale. She required that in her daughter should be united all the brilliant acquirements which were alone of value in her worldly eyes; and poor Hyacinthe was speedily made to endure every species of torture, which, for the perfect development of her form, and her initiation into the artificial graces of the *ballet* master, it was considered necessary should be inflicted. Masters of every description attended her daily; and studies, which, if they had been separately taught, would have been a delight to her, were now too much confounded in the chaos of knowledge and the scientific means for display now forced upon the pupil, for her to benefit by the elaborate instructions lavished upon her.

She was any thing but happy, for she was conscious that she was doing very little good: while the difference of her present life with that she had passed was so very great, that the restrictions and the confinement of it preyed upon her health and spirits.

All day immured in a gloomy school room, with no other prospect than blackened leads and smoke-encircled chimneys, how often did Hyacinthe sigh for the lost joys and the liberty of her former life! How did she pant to breathe the fresh air, to have her eyes regaled by the sight of the flowers, and the green fields of her dear country home!

Her walks were now limited to the dismal square; where, accompanied by the two stiff, uninteresting women, who were styled her governesses, both discoursing in a language quite unfamiliar to her ear, she found little benefit, and less pleasure, in pacing to and fro the stunted and smoky shrubberies of the monotonous inclosure.

Of her mother she saw very little, and of her father not much more; for it was but seldom that she was permitted to escape from her prison room to join him in his library.

For Lord Avondale, Hyacinthe felt much affection. His mild, kind manners went directly to her heart, and she longed with the warmth of young and natural feelings to be able to contribute to his happiness and live in his society. But for her mother, with all her anxious endeavours to entertain for her the affection of a child, she could not tutor her heart to feel that glow of love and tender veneration which a mother ought to inspire.

This was scarcely to be wondered at; for the excellent though youthful judgment of poor Hyacinthe could not fail to detect a thousand errors and weaknesses, which a less interested or less unsophisticated observer might have passed unnoticed.

Lady Avondale was at once the most frivolous, and most completely
worldly-minded, of her sex. In her intercourse with her daughter,
her only aim appeared to make her instrumental to her own vanity;
and if the poor girl, when she appeared before her, looked pale and
languid, or less beautiful than usual, she was received with coldness,
and dismissed with undissembled disgust. However, of all the miseries she endured, her Sunday trials were by far the most bitter.

Hyacinthe had been brought up in the strictest observance of religion in her late home; and with the friends of her youth, it was made
no secondary consideration, but rather was the first, the dearest care
of their existence.

Sunday was ever anticipated by them as a day of pious rest—a day
which they willingly and joyfully dedicated to that service, which
was to them their hope, their solace, throughout their pilgrimage on
earth. How gladly did they prepare for this holy day! How busy
was May on Saturday, preparing every thing for the coming festival,
that every unnecessary labour should be abridged, or dispensed with
on that sacred day; and when she arose on Sunday morning, it was
with a heart filled with pious gratitude for the blessings she possessed
in the advantage of living beneath the spiritual care of such a pastor
as Mr. Neville. Neatly attired, how happily did she walk with her
supposed parents to the village church: and there her innocent heart
poured forth praises to her God, who looketh with peculiar pity upon
the young and helpless.

Hyacinthe was always permitted on that day to remain at the Parsonage until after the second service, as she actively assisted Mrs.
Villars in the duties of her Sunday-school, for which she felt much
interest.

What a contrast were her waking feelings, the first Sunday morning she passed in Grosvenor Square! After the almost stunning confusion of the week she had spent, she looked forward to Sunday as at
least a day of rest: but on awaking, Hyacinthe's ears were assailed
with sounds the same as usual; as much of the busy avocations of the
extensive household seemed renewed; as much business and activity
among the under servants; as much *exigeance* and idly performed
duties of the upper. Lady Avondale's page still lounged in his velvet
chair, listlessly reading the Court Journal. Monsieur Vol-au-vent still
gossipped in the hall with the porter, occasionally whistling a ma-
zourka; while the same elaborate meal was spread on the breakfast-
table, with all the splendid appointments which usually decorated it,
and not even the daily papers were omitted! Every thing passed the
same, and no one said, "It is Sunday!"

Her own (French maid could, give her no information as to the movements of the family; but Hyacinthe requested her to ask Mademoiselle Victorine at what hour her lady went to church. The answer to this question was a shrug of the shoulders, "Ah, ciel! miladi seldom go to church; she too delicate!"

Hyacinthe recollected with a sigh, that her mother had been at the opera the night before!

The distressed girl then descended to the breakfast-room, where she found Lord Avondale: and with a face which betrayed no small degree of anxiety, she asked whether he had the intention of going to church.

"To be sure, my little daughter, we will go together to-day," he answered, with a smile, as he rang the bell; and after he had ordered the carriage, added kindly, that he should soon swallow his coffee, when he would immediately complete his toilet, and be in readiness to accompany her.

"But do you not always go to church, dear papa?" said Hyacinthe, in a tone of inquietude.

"Do not be too inquisitive about my concerns, you grave little monitress," answered Lord Avondale, smiling at her earnestness, but inwardly satisfied with the good feeling it evinced: "I shall go much oftener, now I have you for my companion."

"How happy that will make me!" said Hyacinthe joyfully; "for, my dearest papa, I have been taught to make the exercise of religion so *very dear* an object—to consider it of *such vital* importance—that to see those I love neglect it, terrifies and afflicts me."

Lord Avondale sighed, and soon after left the room to prepare for church.

A fine-toned organ and good singing delighted and charmed Hyacinthe's very soul; and the sermon was delivered by a popular preacher of some merit, whose discourse impressed deeply on her heart; but how truly was she surprised and disgusted by the scene which took place immediately upon the congregation rising from their knees! Whispering, smiling, nodding, was then the order of the day. She heard one lady say to another, "What a beautiful colour your pelisse is!"—while her neighbour in a loud whisper remarked, "How exceedingly full the opera was last night!—how well Taglioni danced the new pas Russe!" Another old lady exclaimed, at the same time yawning terrifically, "How dreadfully long the sermon was! It is a great shame that any one should take the liberty of detaining a congregation more than twenty minutes."

Hyacinthe felt quite shocked, and turned pale with amaze-

ᵗment; almost beginning to fancy that she had entered the modern
Babylon.

Our heroine's life had been so retired, her education so strict, that
she could scarcely believe the evidence of her eyes and ears: and she
returned home grave and dejected.  Her heart was full of sorrow and
heaviness; for how could she hope to obtain that future happiness, to
which she had been taught to look forward with such joy, if she were
destined to live among those who, although they might know there
was a God, appeared neither to fear nor to love him?          ⁱⁱ

Hyacinthe was endeavouring to lose these anxious thoughts in the·
perusal of a book of devotion, the gift of her revered Mr. Neville,
when she received a summons from Lady 'Avondale to desire her to
be in readiness to accompany her in a drive.  She asked eagerly if it
would prevent her from attending the afternoon service ; and was still
more unhappy when she found that it certainly would, and that very
few people ever thought of doing such a thing as to go to church twice
in the same day in London.

Poor Hyacinthe feared to disobey her mother; and, after allowing
herself to be attired in a beautiful new dress and bonnet, accompanied
Lady Avondale to pay some visits.  They then went into the Park,
and finished the afternoon in Kensington Gardens.

Adulation and admiration were poured into her ears from every
side.  Her romantic history rendered her the topic of conversation and
curiosity to all ranks, and her great beauty of course heightened the
interest which was naturally felt for her.

Lady Avondale was provoked and angry with her lovely daughter,
and she could not comprehend why she looked so sad in the midst
of so much happiness.  At first she attributed it to timidity, and then
to ill-temper; and vented her spleen in ·invectives against the good
people who had educated her, who, she said, had infected her with such
grovelling ideas, that it took away all her pleasure in having recovered her.

Poor Hyacinthe's unhappiness was thus increased ; she grieved to
find herself unloved by her mother, who she found, with deep sorrow,
would never enter into her feelings upon the subject of the want of
enjoyment of her present life.

Her Sunday was ended in being again most elegantly attired, and
brought forward at a large evening party, given by Lady Avondale on purpose to display to the admiring world the beauty of her
daughter.

What a Sabbath for the pious May to spend! And when, at length,
she was allowed to retire for the night, which was not until a very

late hour, she was so tired, so subdued, that her evening devotions were not as they used to be, but poured forth in bitterness and sadness of spirit.

---

## CHAPTER XIV.

"Peace, murmuring spirit! bruised and writhing still,
Confess the living fount of life is near:
Take up thy cross, repine not at the will
Which bids thee meekly bow, and calmly bear the pain!"

WE shall now leave our heroine for a short period, and take a retrospective glance at the inhabitants of the village in which she had spent so many happy days—days of childhood and joy; such as never come after the quick pulse of youth is lowered by the cares and anxieties of approaching maturity,—after the sunny brow of childhood is clouded by the consciousness of the responsibilities of life, and we "look upon the dial's hand, and note that hours are passing."

Grief had laid its heavy hand upon the once cheerful occupants of Brookside Farm. The loss of the darling May was a bereavement felt most bitterly, not only by them, but also by the excellent rector and his sister; and, although they endeavoured to console the good farmer and his wife, tears, most bitter tears, mingled themselves with every soothing word they uttered.

Their little paradise had now lost its chief attraction—the gentle being who had formed so great an object of delight was removed far from them, and was now only as a dream of the past. She had vanished entirely from the eyes which had so loved to dwell upon her; and like a sweet perfume, or a sweeter melody, which passes away, leaving only the memory of the enjoyment, with the sad knowledge that it cannot be recalled. It is true that this treasure of their affections still lived for others; but for them they felt, with a deep regret, that she was gone for ever!

Lord Avondale had taken the earliest opportunity of informing Mr. Neville that the Countess' views and ideas were such, that she would never allow her daughter any personal communication with those who were not of her own rank in life. Mr. Neville could only acquiesce in the wishes his lordship's words were meant to convey, and instruct his sister of the barrier raised between her and her idolized May.

In the quiet and retired life they led, the lovely and virtuous girl

7

had been an unceasing object of interest and excitement; and sadly did Mrs. Villars now pursue her morning's employment, unbroken by the presence of this child of her adoption.  Habit and affection made her start, and her heart beat, whenever a footstep was heard about the time that she was accustomed to see her dear pupil, who never entered the Rectory but with a countenance beaming with delight; not only at the idea of spending some hours with her revered friends, but also from the real pleasure she took in the improving, and to her delightful studies, through which she was conducted by Mrs. Villars and her brother.

This excellent lady now felt a void—a blank which could not be filled up; and well did she enter into the feelings of the afflicted family at the farm, although she was aware she had less to deplore than them.  Though it would be an altered intercourse, she believed she might be allowed to see the Lady Hyacinthe again; but she felt that their lowly station was an insuperable objection to the renewal of the affectionate familiarity hearts like theirs could alone be contented with.

Mrs. Villars had made it her first care, immediately on Hyacinthe's departure, to send Susan Ashfield to the farm; and a small sum of money easily persuaded her mother to dispense with her services for a short period.

Susan was an excellent girl, and most anxious to be of use to the friends of her beloved and youthful monitress.  They were sensible of her well-meant endeavours; but what could compensate to them for what they had lost?

The farmer had long been in a delicate state of health, although his ailments had scarcely confined him to the house; he was, however, now threatened with a malady which too often proves fatal to those whom it attacks.

Mrs. Villars, on repairing to the farm a few mornings after the afflicting departure of Hyacinthe, witnessed a scene which contributed much to the depressed state of her spirits.

The agitation and grief caused by the separation from the young and idolized being who had twined so closely round his heart, had brought on a violent fit of spasms; and poor Farmer Wilmot, after a night of intense suffering, was now seated in his arm-chair, pale and languid,—and with such evident and touching marks of sorrow in his countenance, that Mrs. Villars was obliged to turn away to conceal the tears with which sympathy filled her eyes.

At this moment she felt that she was unable to address one word of comfort to the poor mourner; therefore Mrs. Villars inquired of

Susan, where she might find Mrs. Wilmot; and on being told that she was up stairs, she immediately went in search of her, and discovered the poor woman seated upon the bed in the little room formerly occupied by May, weeping most bitterly.

"My good friend," said Mrs. Villars, kindly and soothingly, "you must indeed endeavour to shake off this violent affliction, and rouse yourself to enable you to enter into your customary occupations. I have come to beg that you and your husband will come to the Rectory and pass the day; the change will do you good."

"No, madam," sobbed out poor Mrs. Wilmot; "I thank you most kindly, but at present I like no place but this. I love to look upon the seat on which my darling sat—at the bed on which she lay; nothing consoles me but what reminds me of her. It is a sorrow which soothes my mind."

"But for your husband, my dear Jane, for his sake you must endeavour to reconcile yourself to the loss you have met with," said Mrs. Villars, with gentleness and compassion in her voice.

"Ah! madam—and it is for him that my heart doubly bleeds," replied poor Mrs. Wilmot, with the most poignant distress expressed in her countenance. "No one can imagine how fondly—how distractedly he doted upon that child; and you do not know how much his health has been declining lately—so that I much fear now that he will no longer have a motive for exertion, he will sink into a state of listlessness and confirmed ill health. As long as we possessed our dear child, he never would give up: he used to say, if disinclined to go out, 'I must work, or how will our May's little fortune go on?'— and he never willingly thought of himself while she remained to us. We have now far too much for ourselves. Our interest in life is over for ever; and now all we have to do is to sit down and wish for the hour when it shall please the Almighty to take us from hence."

"This is very wrong, my good friend," replied Mrs. Villars; "you are still in the prime of life. You have probably many days still before you. Do you not think it would be a sin for you to spend them uselessness? Hitherto your life has been one of great and almost uninterrupted happiness; such as was never intended to be the lot of human beings; and we must ever be prepared for the dispensations of our God, and bend with submission to his decrees. He brings us sorrow to awaken us from our vain and foolish dreams of security and self-confidence, in order that we may become more deeply acquainted with the fulness of grace and mercy that dwelleth in Christ Jesus." Mrs. Villars paused for a few moments, and then continued, with a mournful intonation of voice, "This lesson, my good Jane, is often most effectually learned under the pressure of intense affliction. I speak most feelingly.' There was a time when I enjoyed happiness. the most pure and heavenly—happiness which I vainly thought might last for ever. But the cup of joy was dashed from my lips—I had to behold the destruction of my dearest hopes—my heart's fondest wishes; yet here I am, calm, and I trust fully resigned to the will of God." Again Mrs. Villars paused, her emotion being too deep for utterance. After a short silence, she again continued;—"When visited with acute personal affliction, or suffering under the removal of a beloved object, we are awakened to a touching conviction of our utter helplessness,—to a strong sense of the precarious tenure of our earthly blessings; and we begin to perceive that God is every thing, and man nothing. It is then that we look round for some 'city of refuge' in which we may take shelter. We cast an anxious and timid glance upon past months and years; and listen, perhaps for the first time, to the reproachful voice of conscience: it is then, that remembering the indifference with which we have received, and the ingratitude with which we have wasted, the rich gifts of Providence, we seek to approach God in penitence and prayer."

"Ah! madam, I feel every word that you utter, and I shall indeed endeavour to show you that they have not been spoken to an unmindful ear: let me convince you that your kindness has not been bestowed in vain—let me go to my husband, that my calmness and resignation may induce him to master his grief—though I fear, alas! that his failing health renders him less capable of struggling with his feelings."

Indeed, Mrs. Villars felt seriously uneasy when she again saw Farmer Wilmot. Mr. Neville was seated by his side, and had been administering to him all the comfort it was in his power to bestow: but he complained of pain and weariness, which arose from bodily as well as mental suffering.

A messenger had been despatched for a doctor, who, after seeing his patient, communicated to Mr. Neville his fear that he had certainly a complaint of the heart, of long standing, and which was a disease which generally baffled all medical aid. He, however, bled him; and, prescribing quiet and repose, begged that his mind might be left as tranquil as possible.

At this moment this was a hard task to perform; but every attention which an attached wife could bestow, and every kindness which friendship and sympathizing feelings could suggest, he received from the benevolent Rector and his sister.

He had the further comfort of welcoming the most tender and

affectionate letter from his dear child, which he still continued to call her.

Hyacinthe was permitted to correspond with her friends, at the Rectory; and also to write to the parents who had so tenderly nurtured the lovely child of her adoption. This was most soothing to them, while proving to her her only source of happiness.

In a short time there were no more lamentations to be heard at the farm, and tears were no longer seen streaming down the cheeks of the honest Wilmot and his wife; while to the casual observer every thing seemed to go on as heretofore.

They were now resigned to their loss, although their sad hearts were still oppressed and full of grief; but they remembered from whom their present trial was sent, and bowed their heads meekly to the will of God. Such is the power of faith and real religion!

---

## CHAPTER XV.

" Then let the sands of existence fall,
    The current of life flow fast;
    Our times are in God's hands, and all—
    All will be well at last."

WE must now return to the Lady Hyacinthe, and follow her through the privations and vexations connected with the new situation in which she was placed; at the same time that we describe the enjoyments with which Providence strews the path which is even the most distasteful to us.

It was a great relief to Hyacinthe, when her mother (having made an exhibition of her, until she was tired. of hearing eulogiums and flattering expressions which were not addressed immediately to herself,) resigned her wholly to her governesses; telling her that she must now work hard, and endeavour to make up for lost time, by acquiring what was really useful in the world, instead of cant phrases and antiquated ways only fit for a Methodist, and certainly not for a young lady of rank and fashion.

Thus poor Hyacinthe was consigned completely to the charge of her governesses, and to the masters who assisted them in imparting the numerous accomplishments conceived essential to her station in life: and unless it was that she occasionally breakfasted with Lord Avondale, and was permitted now and then to take a walk with him, her life was one of uniform dulness, and wearisome application to studies, whose endless variety were sources of considerable embarrassment.

Lord Avondale indeed was kindness itself; and had it only depended on him, his Hyacinthe would have been his dear and constant companion; but he had been so long accustomed to succumb to every wish and caprice of his imperious Countess, than even in this most interesting and important subject he weakly acquiesced, and that too against his better judgment. Yet he beheld with deep though unavailing regret, the thraldom his child endured—a thraldom the more vexatious, insomuch that it was injudicious, and could not possibly tend to any desirable result.

Lord Avondale kindly indulged and seconded Hyacinthe's wish of being tenderly mindful and attentive to her beloved friends in the country; and scarcely ever did she return home from a walk with him without having selected some present which should speak of her affectionate recollection of the kind protectors of her childhood. All the newest and choicest publications were regularly sent to the Rectory—an arrival most precious to Mr. Neville; and eagerly did she endeavour to suit each taste in her careful selection of gifts for the individuals so every way dear to her. Lord Avondale's wishes for gratifying her were boundless, while he was equally anxious with herself to testify his own gratitude to her valuable friends

We may say that it was Hyacinthe's only delight to be enabled to send package after package filled with treasures, sometimes directed to the farm, and sometimes to the Rectory; while the letters she was suffered to send with them were a gratification that for the moment made her forget all the irksomeness of her present life. Still a deep regret would mingle itself with the pleasure she experienced in this correspondence with the friends of her childish years; it was also perceptible in their letters, notwithstanding their mutual endeavours to conceal the feelings of sadness which still rested on their hearts.

One acute source of affliction to the anxious girl, was the hint, which, though obscurely given, conveyed too plainly to her mind, that her dear foster-father's health was certainly declining. What would she not have given to have flown to him, and to have rendered him that attendance which an affectionate child would know so well how to bestow! "He only wants me," she would often mentally exclaim; "if I were with him, he should soon be well—I know so well how to nurse him—he misses me, dear darling father—he longs to see his own little May, and that is the reason of his illness—I was sure he could not live without me."

But she knew how vain were all her ardent wishes upon the subject: happiness like that was not within her reach.

One morning Hyacinthe received a message from Lady Avondale, desiring her to be ready to accompany her in the carriage, as she intended to introduce her to her aunt, Lady Greville, and her cousins. Poor Hyacinthe was again in distress. She had often heard the Countess allude to this aunt; and it was always with a degree of sarcasm and dislike, which latter feeling was unconsciously imparted to her; and she had rather rejoiced at the delay which had as yet deferred her presentation to this unknown relative.

Hyacinthe expected she must be something very awful, very repulsive—that she should again have to undergo the unfeeling scrutiny she had suffered from her mother, and one or two of her high-born connections—in short, that she should find her aunt a fine lady!—and, as the carriage stopped at one of the most splendid houses in London, and they were ushered in with the usual pomp of servants and retinue, our heroine trembled with the expectation of finding renewed ostentation and worldly-mindedness.

They were told that her ladyship was in her morning-room, and into that apartment (using the privilege of near relations) they were introduced.

What a surprise and relief to Hyacinthe was the scene which the interior of that room offered! Lady Greville was working, and by her side sat one of her daughters reading aloud. Two other sweet-looking girls were busily employed with their drawing; whilst a pretty child of six years old, the youngest pet of the family, sat on an ottoman at her mother's feet, eagerly endeavouring to emulate her mamma's abilities in the working department, by constructing a little cotton petticoat for some infant pensioner.

Lady Greville, advancing, kindly received Lady Avondale, and most affectionately embraced the nervous Hyacinthe; and, taking her by the hand, introduced her to her cousins; who all came forward with countenances beaming with amiability and kindness of heart.

Hyacinthe was almost overcome with the feeling of comfort and happiness which this unlooked-for reception yielded her; and when she looked into the countenance of her aunt, which, though not possessing the dazzling beauty of her mother, owned the utmost degree of sweetness, intelligence, and benevolence,) she could scarcely refrain from throwing herself into her arms, and beseeching her to love and cherish her as she had been loved and cherished by those friends whose remembrance was forcibly called to her mind by thus finding the heart's affections, and tenderness of manner, not wholly confined to the village of Fairbrook.

Hyacinthe's ideas of what is technically termed "high life," were very much limited : and we fear, from what she had witnessed since her inauguration to the distinguished station to which she was born, .not very exalted. It is true that she could feel most strongly the wide distinction between the simple and rustic home she had left, with the splendid one she now inhabited; but the contrast was all in favour of the virtuous poverty and rational enjoyments of former days; while her well-regulated mind shrunk with intuitive dread from all around her; which certainly betrayed the condemned pomps and vanities of the world, without offering any of the intrinsic advantages and blessings which wealth and power may give, if properly appreciated and employed. Under the present influence of her feelings, it might indeed appear to her difficult for a "rich man to enter into the kingdom of heaven;" but she did not then reflect, that it is the misapplication, not the possession of worldly advantages, which will exclude the prosperous man from the mansions of everlasting bliss,— and that wealth and exalted rank, when *used* without being *abused*, only tend to make virtue shine more brilliantly, while the force of righteous example is rendered more beneficial from being more conspicuous and extended.

Thus it was in the Greville family. High in birth and fortune, they were models of worth and excellence. Warmly and devotedly attached to their children, truly devout and earnest in the exercise of their religion, they led a life of social and intellectual enjoyment; offering to the observation of others the gratifying spectacle of excessive refinement of taste with simplicity of heart, extensive liberality with strict economy of expenditure, and pre-eminent piety with cheerfulness and humility of demeanour. The station of Lord Greville brought him into public life, which rendered a residence in London therefore indispensable. In consequence, though with much regret, his family removed every year for some months to the metropolis, leaving their beautiful country residence with lively sorrow; for that was their sphere, the scene of their best enjoyments, and not the crowded, dissipated, and sin-sheltering town. However, Lady Greville felt, it was an imperious duty scrupulously to comply with all the exactions which her position in life demanded. While entering the brilliant scenes of ostentatious display, and sacrificing precious hours to the claims of the gay world,—both alike distasteful to her, but persisted in from the consideration that it was presumptuous and wrong to shrink from those duties which she could plainly see were

incumbent on her position in this life,—she hailed with heartfelt satisfaction the evident predilection evinced by her children for the pure
and domestic joys of their country home. It would have been incon
sistent with her sense of justice to have insisted on the necessity of
seclusion and retirement to young females, whose tastes led them into
the busy circles of pleasure, and whose future life might place them
amongst them: and had such been her daughters' choice, with the
armour of true religion, and the love of God deeply rooted in their
hearts, she would have trusted that the trials offered by the dissipation of the world should prove tests of faith and virtue, instead of the
fatal stumbling-blocks they so often become. But as it was, Lady
Greville was spared the anxiety the ordeal might have cost her; and
found, with a deep sense of thankfulness, that the young beings consigned by Providence to her charge, had already learnt, by her precepts and example, that true happiness is only to be found in the
exercise of Christian duties; and that, already discerning the emptiness of indiscriminate society and the appalling nature of the glare
and bustle of fashionable life, they returned to scenes of tranquillity
and retirement equally delighted with herself, there to partake of the
pure and precious joy arising from the best affections of the heart, the
enlightenment of the mind, and an uninterrupted worship of their
Almighty Father

---

## CHAPTER XVI.

> " 'Tis in the silence, in the shade,
> That light from Heaven illumes our road;
> And man, even mortal man, is made,
> If not a God—almost a God."

HYACINTHE had soon an opportunity of forming a judgment mucn
more favourable of the high-born inhabitants of the metropolis, than
that which had filled her ideas before her acquaintance with the
Greville family.

A fever of a very malignant nature attacked one of the servants of
Lord Avondale's establishment; and he, as well as Lady Avondale,
were too happy to avail themselves of Lady Greville's considerate
offer of taking Hyacinthe into her own house, whilst her brother and
sister-in-law paid some visits previous to their settling for the autumn
at Avondale Castle; by these means avoiding the hazard of infection,

8

Lady Greville and her family were to remain a fortnight longer in London, from whence they were to proceed to their own home in the country; and it was arranged that after remaining a short time there, Hyacinthe was to rejoin her parents and governesses at the seat of her ancestors.

With unfeigned joy did Hyacinthe prepare to accompany her aunt to Park Lane, although her pleasure suffered some alloy from the idea of leaving her indulgent and courtly father.

Lady Avondale coldly bade her adieu, requesting at the same time that she would take care of her complexion, and never forget to wear her gloves. "I have had a great deal of trouble," added this *anxious* parent, "to civilize your appearance, therefore pray be good enough to follow up my plans; and, if possible, spare me the disgrace of having a daughter with an odious freckled or tanned skin, with the plebeian accompaniment of coarse hands."

"Your aunt," her ladyship proceeded to say, "is a very improper person for you to be with, though this frightful typhus makes it a matter of necessity. She places very little importance in these matters, as little Eugenia's ruddy face may show.; and I must desire that you will take care not to add any of her strange notions to those you have unfortunately already acquired."

The announcement of Lady Greville's arrival interrupted this singular lecture; and Hyacinthe bounded joyfully into her aunt's carriage, with more elasticity of movement than she had displayed since her arrival in London.

How kindly she was received by her uncle and cousins! Her poor heart, which had been almost frozen by the coldness she had met with, since she had quitted the tender friends of her childhood, glowed again with its natural warmth under the influence of their affectionate manners.

These kind relations had soon discovered that Hyacinthe possessed no common character. They encouraged her to speak of her former life; and much were they interested and touched by her little history, entering most fully into all her feelings connected with the subject.

At Greville House, Hyacinthe beheld indeed a truly happy family; and it was here she found the realization of every blessing that can be desired in this life. However, the excess of earthly felicity had not engendered indifference, as in too many cases; or negligence in the observance of the duties from which no station exempts us. Lady Greville had taught her family to reflect that we have each an allotted part to sustain—appropriate engagements to fulfil—peculiar virtues to exercise—an immortal destiny to accomplish. She bade them consider that the flowery path and the rugged way were equally the appointments of God; but, as prosperity was their lot, they should partake of it with gratitude, ever remembering the hand from which it flowed. It was also impressed on their minds, that, as the gift of God, wealth is to be enjoyed gratefully and liberally, as one of the means of usefulness derived from the bounty of Heaven: but, like every other talént committed to our care, an exact account must be rendered unto Him, who, while He giveth liberally, requires the most minute fidelity in the trust. In that parable of our Saviour, of the ten pieces of money, the nobleman, who vests the charge in his servants, expressly declares, "Occupy until I come." By these memorable words, a day of account is strikingly referred to; and it was to that event Lady Greville most earnestly directed her children's minds, in order that their every action should be governed by a reference to that ordeal through which they must pass.

With these judicious counsels, and words of holy wisdom, Lady Greville had formed the hearts of her children to rejoice only in the exercise of virtue, and it is not to be wondered at that their domestic circle was one purely and eminently happy. Here was wealth and rank without one spark of ostentation: religion in the purest form, unmixed with gloom or narrow-mindedness; affection of the most devoted kind amongst all its members.

The education of the young ladies was conducted in the most delightful manner. Their governess was a sensible, excellent person, who went hand in hand with Lady Greville in her system with her pupils. The school-room opened into Lady Greville's morning-room, and the studies were superintended by her, and farther assisted by masters. She placed very little stress on mere accomplishments, her desire being that the understanding of her children should be cultivated and well directed; but, if they evinced any decided taste or wish to pursue any peculiar study, she was too happy to have the power of assisting their inclinations by the best instructions.

Hyacinthe was most charmed to be allowed to join the cheerful, joyful party at study in the morning; gnd so judiciously were those studies directed, that the hours passed delightfully, and much too swiftly. How different from the dull routine of ordinary schoolrooms! As a mother's eye—a mother's judgment was every thing, every lesson was appropriated to the capacity and taste of the pupil; and consequently each acquirement was achieved with facility and comfort. This was following nature and reason, instead of custom and fashion, and the result showed the good sense of the arrangements.

The morning after Hyacinthe's arrival, one of her cousins came to her before she had quitted her room, and begged to know whether she would like to join the family at prayers. Most willingly she followed her conductress to the apartment where all the household were assembled for the presenting a morning sacrifice of prayer and thanksgiving to their God!

Lord and Lady Greville considered it one of their most important duties to erect a "family altar" in their house, and with their assembled children and dependants, call upon the name of the Lord. They were not content with their own private devotions, leaving those whom God had brought beneath their roof to live and die in ignorance of Him who "truly to know is life eternal." They also felt that they did not possess one reasonable excuse for not being able to spare a single half hour for God; and no unholy shame of being thought too earnest in religion, or the fear of the "world's dread laugh," ever prompted them to neglect these pious duties. It is too often that the mockery of man is the cause of our neglect of God, but this is the weakest, the most unworthy plea that can be urged in extenuation of the omission of family prayer—an omission that occasions our losing the greatest and purest of comforts—that of acknowledging with one accord the mercies he has bestowed upon us, and petitioning together for a continuance of his blessings; while with one voice we confess our sins with open and acknowledged humility.

How happily did the fortnight glide on to Hyacinthe! She was now the joyous, cheerful being she had once been before she became rich and great. Her kind relatives were anxious to amuse as well as instruct her, and Hyacinthe, who had as yet seen nothing of London besides the parks and the streets at the west end of the town, was amazed and delighted by the sight of those objects of national splendour which it was their first care to enable her to inspect; and it was with surprise and pleasure she reviewed each monument of art, each stupendous specimen of the finest architecture, each museum teeming with the treasures of the old and new world, and which until now she had only known by those studies which had referred to them.

Much as she loved the country, Hyacinthe felt sorry when the time arrived for her to quit London. She dreaded any change from the happiness she was then enjoying. Besides, the time would be drawing near when she was to return home; for her imperious mother had only given permission for her to remain one fortnight at Beechwood; and, already her heart sunk within her at the idea of leaving her newly-acquired friends. They were all so good—so kind—father, mother, the son, and the daughters, were all alike estimable in their different characters.

The day fixed for the departure of the family for the country at length arrived; and great was the joy expressed by every branch of it. They were going home—to their own dear home, to all the pursuits and pleasures so delightful to them. London was their trial; it did not suit any of their tastes; but to be with their father reconciled them to any thing; and Lady Greville would have considered a paradise a desert without the presence of her dear and excellent husband.

If Hyacinthe considered this family happy in London, what did she think when she contemplated them at Beechwood? It was a beautiful place, situated in one of the loveliest counties in England. The house, the very palace of comfort; while the little village, scattered near the park g tes, was picturesque, and its thatched cottages were pictures of neatness.

It was a touching and gratifying sight to witness the reception which the family received. Every individual appeared to feel that they were welcoming their dearest friends. Each cottager flew to his door to wave his hat, and catch one glance from the eye of one of the members of this beloved family.

Then the joy of the young people to revisit all their possessions in the shape of flower-gardens, poultry-yards, aviary, ponies, dogs, and all the treasures which made their country pleasures so abundant.

They had been met at the hall door by the clergyman of the parish; and it brought tears down the cheeks of Hyacinthe to witness their meeting with this most excellent person. Each cousin embraced him most cordially and affectionately. He was to them a very dear friend; one who had been their spiritual guide and monitor; and who had ably assisted their parents in leading them into the paths of virtue and goodness: and, as Hyacinthe beheld the tenderness of his greeting to them, she thought of her own loved Mr. Neville, and felt that in Mr. Coventry she beheld the union of all those perfections which distinguished him. The vicarage was close to the park gates, as well as the simple village church; but they were both gothic structures of a very ancient date, and by their venerable and picturesque character, formed rather pleasing ornaments, than deteriorated by their vicinity from the imposing aspect of Beechwood.

Many were the questions poured into Mr. Coventry's ears by the young beings who crowded round him, relative to all their pensioners, and those inhabitants of the village, in whom they took most interest, their school, their clothing-club, and all the various institutions of usefulness and relief for the neighbouring poor, of which they were the chief supporters and managers.

The next day, when Hyacinthe accompanied her cousins to the village, it was a beautiful sight to witness the joy, which their presence inspired. They were greeted by young and old, in every house, with the most respectful delight, and looked upon as harbingers of comfort and relief.

Lady Greville had taught her daughters not to be merely satisfied by coldly relieving the temporal wants of their fellow-creatures; that is easily done when the means are abundant; but the charity she inculcated was that of soothing the afflicted, whether their sufferings proceeded from mental or bodily anguish; and, young as they were, she encouraged them to occupy their well-directed minds with the essential and ulterior improvement of the poor.

. This was done in great humility, and never in a manner likely to offend, but under the cognizance and guidance of Mr. Coventry; and these amiable girls had the heartfelt joy of beholding the success of their plan for the benefit of the distressed.

Youth is the season for kind and warm emotions; and in this sphere of probation, in which sickness, sorrow, and suffering so much abound, opportunities of exercising Christian love can neither be few nor rare; and Lady Greville was most anxious to impress upon the minds of her children that they are never *too young* to fulfil duties of this nature.

The heart is easily touched by distress, and melts at the sight of human misery; and let me admonish my young readers to cherish these emotions; but let them not mistake feelings for virtues, nor dwell with too much complacency upon casual acts of kindness which may have cost no personal sacrifice. Real emotions of charity must prompt you to exertion and self-denial, blended with the principle of Christian love; and these actions, by repetition, will be wrought into habits until they become permanent graces of the soul.

## CHAPTER XVII.

" Some measure of evil seems to be necessary in the present state of man, for his discipline and improvement, and to prepare him for higher enjoyment; nor have we any reason to think more is permitted than is necessary for these valuable purposes."

By her residence at Beechwood the mind of Hyacinthe became more deeply impressed with the opinion of the exquisite felicity enjoyed by its inhabitants; nor could she discover one drawback that any had to the perfect happiness of their lot; but she felt they highly merited it all; and her heart rejoiced at the prospect of its continuance. A short time after her arrival she was walking with her aunt quite alone, and she could not help expressing to her all she felt upon the subject.

" My dear aunt," she said, " I always thought that uninterrupted happiness was not to be the lot of human beings; yet in vain have I endeavoured to discover what is your trial; for nowhere can I perceive it."

Lady Greville smiled; but in that smile was mingled a grave and touching sadness. At last, after a pause, she said, " Follow me, Hyacinthe, and I will show you that the Almighty is too wise, too just, not to dispense afflictions upon all his servants; in mercy and infinite wisdom convincing us, that this world at best is not to be one of unmixed felicity."

Lady Greville led the way in silence until they came to the church. Having arrived there, she opened a small side-door, by a key which she carried about her; and, entering with Hyacinthe, she told her to follow. When she had reached the middle of the aisle she stopped, and desired her anxious companion to read the inscription upon a plain white marble tablet which was placed upon the wall of the church. Hyacinthe ran her eye hastily over it, and beheld these words: " Sacred to the memory of Henry and Percy Mansfield, twin sons of George Barton Greville, and Mary his wife.—Henry died, aged 10 years, January 5th, 18—, and Percy followed his brother on the 2d of the ensuing April.

' Early, bright, transient, pure as morning dew,
They sparkled, were exhaled, and went to heaven!' "

Hyacinthe felt inexpressibly shocked and distressed. She looked at her aunt in fear and trembling; but she was calm, though very pale.

"My dear girl," she at length said, in a low, but clear voice, seating herself upon a bench opposite the monument, and desiring Hyacinthe to do the same—"you have so lately entered your own family, that you are scarcely acquainted with the minutes of its history. I do not think you are even aware that Augustus is your uncle's son by a former marriage; indeed I sometimes almost forget the circumstance, so dearly do I love him. I never had a son besides those two beloved children whose death, you there see recorded. They were twins, and always evidenced much delicacy of constitution. Perhaps that circumstance made me regard them with peculiar tenderness; but certainly they were most interesting boys. The Almighty had adorned them with every degree of loveliness. I can see them now in my mind's eye, with their bright joyous countenances, their curling hair and beautiful complexions, sporting in happy play together, or seated with an arm round each other's neck, learning at the same time their task, or reading for their amusement out of the same book. Their attachment to each other was the strongest I ever beheld. They were never separate, and all their little possessions appeared considered by them as their joint property. Certainly they were the joy and happiness of my life—my sunshine, my dearest delight; and much, alas! I fear too much, was my heart engaged by these two treasures. And yet not only I, but every one loved them; they were so affectionate—so good! Well," continued Lady Greville, after a sad pause, which was interrupted by a torrent of tears, " I must finish my melancholy story. The scarlet fever, that scourge of families, attacked my children; all my girls had the complaint slightly and most favourably. Henry sickened, and, oh! wretched moment—never to be forgotten!—he died in torture in my arms. Percy, who was a stronger child, lived through the disease, but never got over the effects of it. He lingered some months; but one circumstance I am almost certain—that grief for the loss of his treasured brother really caused his death. He was a child possessing the strongest affections; and his mind and health previously weakened by all he had suffered, it was evident wanted strength to reconcile himself to the loss of his second self. It would be impossible for me to describe to you the happy frame of mind in which this adored child at last died. He was perfectly resigned to the idea of leaving this world; and so heaven-ward were his ideas directed, that the humble hope which he entertained of meeting his brother in a future life made him look forward to his release with joy. How constantly he endeavoured

to comfort and reconcile me and his father, whose grief was more
intense! For my part I was supported, as long as he lived, with
almost supernatural firmness. But when it was all over—when the
emaciated form of my boy was taken from these arms, which had so
long been his support, then I felt all the blankness of despair. Long
and dreary were the days of my grief. I mourned as one who was not
to be comforted. Thanks be to the God of comfort, I was roused from
this state of sinful despair by my good and sincere friend Mr. Coventry.
He brought me a letter which had been confided to his care by my
own sainted boy, and did not fear to make me read it. He knew me
well, and hoped my days of darkness would soon pass; and that,
through the grace of God, I should soon look for comfort, from whom
only it is to be derived. Here is the precious letter," continued
Lady Greville, as she took it from a small velvet case: "it never
leaves me, and its perusal always affords me a calm and holy pleasure." She then read as follows—

"Dearest Mother,—Do not grieve too much for me when I am
gone. Remember where I hope to be—in the presence of that Redeemer you have taught me to adore. And you know how much I
loved Henry, poor dear Henry! I think of him now as a bright angel
in the courts of God: may I not trust to be with him also? and soon
we may together join in praises to our God and king. Be comforted,
dear mother; think of your little boys, but not with sorrow, for remember that all our griefs are ended, and we rest in peace, where we
shall no longer be assailed by sickness or sorrow: and where, through
the mediation of our Saviour, we shall await with joy our re-union
with you, dearest papa, and our sweet sisters. Darling mother, farewell. When you will receive this, your Percy will be free from
pain."

Hyacinthe's sobs were no longer to be controlled. She threw
her arms round her aunt, and wept upon her bosom; and for some
moments they mingled their tears together: however, they were not
bitter tears. Lady Greville had long subdued every feeling like that
of murmuring against the Divine will; and, although her tenderly
maternal heart mourned silently over every memento of her boys, it
was a grief which we may hope even the Almighty would not
condemn.

"My dearest Hyacinthe," she said, as soon as she had regained
her calmness—"I brought you here, not to afflict you, but in order
to convey to you a useful lesson. Do not think that there exists, in
this life, undisturbed happiness; it is not intended that it should be
the case. In every cup there is a drop of bitterness; but the hand

9

which dispenses afflictions, at the same time offers relief; and those trials appointed by God, are never without intended benefit to us. If human nature at first shrinks from sorrow, faith and Christian hope soon come to its support. Indeed we ought to rejoice that it pleases the Almighty to visit us with trials and sufferings in this world, instead of permitting us to enter upon eternity with hearts too devoted to the fascinations and delusions of the life we are called upon to renounce. What are a few years of worldly sorrow, if we have the supporting hand of God with us, who sees fit thus to prepare us for his heavenly kingdom? But now let us leave this dear and sacred spot," said Lady Greville, rising; "and recollect, my dear niece, that although our Creator has showered blessings without number upon me and mine, he has in his mercy, and for my eternal welfare, made me acquainted with grief. Oh! may it have its due effect upon me, and fit me to hope with confidence to meet my angels again, where we shall be for ever united!"

---

## CHAPTER XVIII.

> "O Charity! our helpless nature's pride,
> Thou friend to him who knows no friend beside,
> Thine are the ample views that, unconfined,
> Stretch to the utmost walks of human kind;
> Thine is the spirit, that with widest plan
> Brother to brother binds, and man to man!"

How delightful was a Sabbath passed at Beechwood! So calm, so serene, so happy-minded did all its inhabitants appear, that well might it give one the idea of its being the Almighty's "favourite day."

Lady Greville ever made it a rule, that on Saturday every necessary duty should be performed; indeed it was universally considered by each member of the family as a day of preparation. All urgent letters were written. If any matters were in agitation, Lady Greville endeavoured that they should be definitely arranged during the week; particularly desiring that her children should disencumber their memories of trifles, such as orders, promises, or engagements, that they might not intrude themselves on the morrow. On Saturday evening every arrangement was completed. The house looked as if every thing was put in order for an entertainment. Fresh flowers were in the vases, fresh perfumes in the crystal essence-bottles which decorated the tables, while superb engravings from scriptural paintings, in ample portfolios, were placed on ornamental stands.

Hyacinthe inquired if company was expected. "Yes," replied her aunt, "we shall have company, "but not of the kind you imagine we are to see. We do nothing on Saturday evening but prepare for Sunday. We collect our poor neighbours to instruct them in religion, and prepare their hearts for the Sabbath occupations, and, as far as we can, remove any little anxieties they may have on their minds, or reconcile any differences which may have arisen between them. We then give them tea in a large room which we keep on purpose for this little parish business."

On Sunday morning, after breakfast, every one was occupied in the perusal of some lesson of piety till the church bell rang. Then all were expected to assemble, and proceed together to attend Divine worship in the temple dedicated to God, among their pious friends and neighbours.

On their return home, Lady Greville said to Hyacinthe, "It is our rule now to separate, and pass our time alone, but we shall meet again at the hour of afternoon church. My girls go to their rooms, or into the gardens. Our doors are closed to visitors; and charged as I am with the care of so large a family, the right to be alone with my God, and do nothing but communicate with Him, is a privilege that I cannot forego for any consideration. Do you not agree with me in thinking, my dear Hyacinthe, that it is an inexpressible comfort to be able one day in the week to give up ourselves entirely to thoughts and to pursuits, the fruits of which are love and holiness and joy; to have no other occupation, than to 'acquaint ourselves with God, and be at peace?' It always gives me an idea of the happiness we are to enjoy hereafter; for if there is such peace in an earthly Sabbath, interrupted as it is with our coldness, and carelessness, and worldliness, what will be the bliss of that eternal Sabbath for which we are preparing? A little while, and what is now but a brief foretaste, a passing semblance of celestial joy, will be an eternal and unchanging reality; a little while, and the smile of our Father will no more be averted: the world, renounced, will no more resume its power, and self-submitted will no more rebel. Now adieu, my dear niece, until three o'clock. I feel assured that the pupil of the excellent Mr. Neville must enjoy the method in which we spend our Sabbath."

After the afternoon service, the party assembled at dinner, cheerful and happy, talking or silent as they pleased; but no one seemed inclined to speak of yesterday's business or to-morrow's plans.

In the evening sacred music was the proposed amusement; and books were on the tables if any one liked to read; but, they were books of a strictly religious tendency. Prayers ended this day of holy peace; and Hyacinthe retired for the night with a heart over-flowing with admiration of the practical piety of her exemplary relatives, and with a holy love towards her God.

The happiness which Hyacinthe was now enjoying was soon to come to an end; and at length the dreaded day arrived when she was to leave Beechwood; and it was announced to her, that Lord Avondale had sent a carriage and a confidential servant to escort her home.

Poor Hyacinthe clung in sorrow to her aunt; who, much attached to her young and affectionate niece, felt real regret in losing her; particularly knowing how far from happy, or congenial to her taste or disposition, was the home to which she was about to return. She said every thing in her power to soothe her, and to strengthen her mind to bear her trials with fortitude; but it was with a saddened heart that she saw her depart.

Hyacinthe arrived at Avondale Castle with very different feelings to those with which she had entered Beechwood. The magnificence of the place, instead of imparting delight, gave her that impression of awe and dread which was connected with every thing belonging to the abode of Lady Avondale; and with sinking spirits she entered her splendid home, where she was soon met and most kindly greeted by her father.

Lord Avondale told her that the Countess was far from well, having caught a violent cold at the opera the night before she left London, which she had never been able to shake off; and when Hyacinthe was conducted into the presence of her mother, she was much shocked to observe a visible and distressing alteration in her appearance.

However, Lady Avondale was in no way softened or subdued by her illness. She raised herself upon the sofa for a few minutes, evidently scanning with a most scrutinizing glance her daughter's appearance. She must have been struck by its most visible improvement; for a month's undisturbed tranquillity and happiness had done more towards the embellishment of Hyacinthe, than all the labour which had been bestowed upon her external charms by dancing masters, calisthenic professors, milliners, hair-dressers, mantua-makers, and lady's maids; while the advantage of associating intimately with those whose manners were distinguished by the purest refinement and most graceful simplicity was perceptible in her improved address.

Perhaps it was not possible to see any thing more blooming or beautiful than the countenance of this lovely girl; and Lady Avondale could not help expressing the admiration which beauty always extorted from her. "How well you are looking, child!" she said, with animation; then added, in a changed, fretful, and impatient tone of voice—"But do you not think I am in very bad looks? Am I not grown very thin, and very sallow?"

Hyacinthe was at a loss how to answer; and she felt shocked and unhappy. Her mother, with more irritation, repeated, "Why don't you answer, Hyacinthe? I know by your silence that you think I am looking hideous; but I suppose you are so puffed up with the idea of your own beauty, that you do not care to see me faded and ill."

Hyacinthe was distressed beyond measure. With tears she at length found courage to say, that she certainly thought that Lady Avondale looked as if she had been suffering from recent illness; but that, doubtless, when the complaint was removed, her good looks would return, as her beauty was not gone, only a little less brilliant.

"Heaven knows," said Lady Avondale, "that if I am to look old and ugly, I cannot see much pleasure in living!"

Hyacinthe inwardly shuddered. Was it for the pleasure of admiration that she alone existed; and with such ideas was she in a state to die? How she longed to exhort her mother to remember that she had an immortal soul to save—to implore her to call her ways to remembrance—to humble herself before the throne of God, and, kneeling at the cross of Christ, to exclaim with deep humility, "There is indeed no health in me!"

Lady Avondale was evidently in a precarious state. A neglected cold had settled upon her lungs, and symptoms of consumption were but too perceptible. However, no one dared to utter the apprehensions which all felt were painfully well grounded; none dared to impart to the mind of the patient a sense of her own danger.

It was, indeed, melancholy to Hyacinthe to behold her mother, whom she had left so bright and beautiful, suddenly changed into a suffering and fast-sinking invalid. What love she could now have felt for her, if its evidence had been allowed! How she should have nursed her—have waited upon her, and prayed with her, as well as for her! But Lady Avondale was not yet softened by illness. Surrounded by people who fostered every feeling of vanity and worldly enjoyment, and who chased the very name of religion from the sick

room for fear of its inducing gloom or. melancholy, little did Lady
Avondale think upon the subject; or she would have learnt that it
brought "healing on its wings:" and blessed by its soothing influence, she would have been reassured by the conviction, that even
sighs of penitence breathed in secret, tears unseen by human eyes,
are precious in His sight who "willeth not the death of a sinner;"
put hails such symptoms as the harbinger of that repentance which
"leadeth unto salvation."

How different was the whole system of Avondale Castle, to the arrangements of Beechwood! Although Lady Avondale was so great
an invalid, from the intermittent nature of her malady, she was at
times able to see company; the house was therefore full of visitors, as
she could not endure the *ennui* of being in a country-house with only
a family party.

Hyacinthe was again consigned to the charge of her governesses;
and how woful was the change from the intellectual companions she
had quitted!

Lady Avondale had chosen her governesses as most ladies do; she
had selected those who asked the highest salary, and had lived with
people of the highest rank; but she had never inquired whether they
were fitting companions for a girl of fifteen. Hyacinthe could not
love her instructresses, for they were selfish and indifferent, and had
too little dignity to inspire respect.

Still loving the country with all the enthusiasm of the rustic May,
Hyacinthe hoped to enjoy the pleasures of nature in her loveliest
garb, in a home which offered every species of beauty, from the
smiling flower-garden and tranquil lake, to the dark wood of towering pines and foaming torrent. But her expectations were in vain.
If she asked to walk in the grounds, she was still to be accompanied
by one of the governesses; and they were usually followed by a smart
gentleman, who styled himself the head-gardener, armed with a slight
*spud* in the shape of a walking-stick, and who, if she attempted to
gather a flower, was ready in a moment to assist her with his scissors
to save her the trouble of stooping. How he would have been
startled and surprised could he have known that the high-born Lady
Hyacinthe longed to assist in labours to which he even could not condescend: and that the brilliant parterres failed to interest her as
much as her own humble ones had formerly done when she had superintended and laboured in their cultivation! Indeed, this ceremonious inspection of Flora's beauties was any thing but satisfactory to
poor Hyacinthe, who then would long to bound off to the wilder
beauties of the park, but was always checked by her French governess,

who, in her tight silk slippers, felt unequal to any rougher path than that offered by the velvet lawn. This was all very vexatious, but she tried to submit with resignation to the deprivation.

But what most distressed our gentle heroine, was the scorn, and almost anger, which her mother evinced when she begged to be allowed to visit the cottages by which they occasionally drove, and make acquaintance with the poor of the neighbouring village. "Would it be consistent," asked Lady Avondale, contemptuously, "with the refinement and dignity of the Lady Hyacinthe Tremaine, to be seen in the dirty abodes of the peasantry; to say nothing of the fevers and complaints she might imbibe by visiting their miserable habitations?"

Strict orders were henceforth given to the governesses not to allow her for a moment out of their sight; "for with her extraordinary low propensities," added her ladyship, "there is no saying in what filthy hovel she might be found."

Lady Avondale could not at all enter into her daughter's ideas of what true charity consisted in; and she really exerted herself to enter into the subject with Hyacinthe, saying, that she considered that they did every thing that was necessary in that way. "Perhaps," she said, "you are not aware of the expenses at which we are every year for the paupers who surround the castle. We pay an annual stipend to a schoolmaster to teach their dirty brats; and we subscribe to endless clubs and institutions for their benefit. Besides which," added her ladyship, with a most satisfied air, "I cannot tell you how many oxen and sheep, blankets, flannels, coals, and candles, we order to be distributed every Christmas—what would you do more?—and yet I believe they are a very ungrateful, dissatisfied set!"

All this was very true; but it still did not satisfy Hyacinthe. She had seen charity exercised in its purest form, from her earliest infancy; and at Beechwood, from the addition of wealth and power, it was exhibited in a still more extended manner. Often, on beholding her excellent aunt enduring fatigue and anxiety to ascertain the sincerity and claims of some pitiable sufferer, she had felt tempted to exclaim,—

"How few like thee inquire the wretched out,
And court the offices of soft humanity!
Like thee reserve their raiment for the naked,
Reach out their bread to feed the helpless orphan,
Or mix the pitying tear with those who weep!"

And on witnessing the blessed effects of such active benevolence, she was·reminded of thé days of her childhood, when she·was sometimes allowed to accompany the good Rector and his sister into the dwellings of the unfortunate, or into some mournful cottage, where poverty and sorrow dwelt together. There she beheld true charity— that charity so beautifully described by the Apostle, " which suffereth long, and is kind, which never faileth;" and which indeed gives lustre and grace to every thing performed by those whom it inspires, likening man to his Creator.

Experience might have taught Lady Avondale, that mistaken charity, or the giving alms indiscriminately, is more injurious than beneficial : for it·promotes idleness, by teaching poverty to rely on other aid than personal industry. Alms alone, however liberal, however extended, neither are, nor can be, the whole of the duty or nature of Christian charity; but that which Hyacinthe had witnessed at Brookside farm and Beechwood, she felt was that she ought to, imitate; for indeed with truth could her excellent models have said, " When the ear heard me, then it blessed me ; and when the eye saw me, it gave witness to me ; because I delivered the poor that cried, the fatherless and those who had none to help them. The blessing of him that was ready to perish came upon me, and I caused the widow's heart to sing for joy !"

---

## CHAPTER XIX.

"When life flow'd by, and, like an angel, Death
Came to release them to the world on high,
Praise trembled still on each expiring breath,
And holy triumph beamed from every eye."

WE will now for a brief space of time leave all the splendours of Avondale Castle, and return to the humble limits of Brookside farm ; but such of my young readers who feel an interest in the kind and amiable persons who inhabit that peaceful spot, will be grieved with the sorrowful details I have now to relate.

With Hyacinthe's departure, the cheerfulness and joy which had before reigned in that happy home had also fled, and were succeeded by a gloom and sadness, which even imparted itself to the inhabitants of the Rectory. Mr. Neville and his sister hardly knew, until they had lost her, how fondly they loved the young foundling; and each experienced a degree of dejection that required their best efforts to shake off. The garden did not look so blooming, and the Sunday school seemed much to miss the energetic young assistant; in short, May was wanted every where.

But at the farm, matters assumed a much more grievous aspect. The disease under which the good Wilmot suffered, though of long standing, was now, with its fatal effects, for the first time, most fearfully perceptible; and, from day to day, and week to week, was becoming rapidly worse. The best assistance afforded by the first medical advice was administered to him, and every comfort which friendship and affection could suggest; but the dread fiat had gone forth, and it was evident to every one that he soon must die. But how calm and heavenly was the composure of this excellent man! His hope had always been in a better world; and to that world he now looked forward with confidence tempered by humility. This life to him had been one of great happiness, although marked by privations and toil; and he thanked God for all the blessings he had enjoyed, and also for the comforting reflection that in quitting it he should leave none dear to him in want. He grieved at the idea of parting with the affectionate companion of his days of joy and of ease; but there again the Christian's hope supported him, and the expectation of a blessed reunion chastened his natural sorrow with pious resignation. He submitted to the will of the great Author of his being, happy in the calm which arises from a holy assurance of approaching felicity, and which is the inseparable attendant of a life of faith.

If however there was one worldly feeling in his heart, and which made the idea of death at times painful to this good man, and created the wish that he still might linger in this vale of tears; it was the remembrance of his darling child—his own precious May. The idea of never again beholding her in this life, of not again pressing her loved form to his paternal bosom, imbittered many moments, and brought frequent tears of sadness to his venerable cheeks. When depressed by the spasms, with which his malady almost constantly afflicted him, it wrung the hearts of all around him to hear his pathetic words concerning his dear lost child.

"My darling May!" he would exclaim, "why is she not here to soothe my dying spirit? These eyes would close in peace, could they once more rest upon my child. Once more to hold her to my

10

heart is now my only desire ; and, alas! this craving wish is the link
that still binds my thoughts to earth—still draws me from my God!"

Mr. Neville, when he saw the anxious state of the poor sufferer,
and considered the comfort which an interview with Lady Hyacinthe
would be to him, could hesitate no longer. He had felt a great reluctance to address the proud relatives of his dear young friend ; but
he now believed that it was an imperative duty to do so, and to venture every thing to bring comfort to the dying moments of so good a
man. He accordingly wrote to Lord Avondale, giving a most touching account of the state of Farmer Wilmot, and beseeching him
to allow his daughter to pass a week with him at the Rectory, in
order that she might take a final farewell of one who had been to her
for so many years the most tender of parents. Mr. Neville then
reminded the Earl how really urgent was this request, in consideration of all he owed Mr. and Mrs. Wilmot, for having been the means,
through the assistance of the Almighty, of saving his child from utter
destruction.

. This letter had the desired effect. Lord Avondale was naturally
kind-hearted ; but, possessing an indolent mind, had allowed himself
to be too much under the dominion of his Countess, with whose imperious character my readers are already acquainted.

Hyacinthe was sitting with Lord Avondale when the letters were
delivered to him ; and seeing the well-known handwriting of Mr.
Neville, watched with anxiety her father's countenance, whilst he
perused its contents. She soon perceived that he was agitated by
what he read ; and when he had finished the letter, she started up,
and approaching quickly towards him, entreated that she might be
allowed also to see it. Agonizing indeed were the poor girl's feelings on its perusal ; and casting herself on her knees before her father,
she besought him by every endearing expression, and every argument
that occurred to her distressed mind, to suffer her to lose no time in
setting out for Brookside.

. "But your mother, my dear child," said Lord Avondale, hesitat-
ingly,—" how are we to overrule her objections?—in her weak state
I dare not agitate her?"

This was indeed a most perplexing idea: however, the Earl promised to do his best to obtain her consent. I will not enter into the
particulars of all that Lord Avondale and Hyacinthe had to encounter
in their endeavours to gain her mother's permission to her departure ;
thus prejudicing my readers still more against the unhappy woman,
whose doom was as nearly sealed as that of the excellent farmer. I

ʃ will only add, that the urgent entreaties of Lord Avondale, joined to those of the poor distressed Hyacinthe, at last prevailed; and a reluctant consent was extorted from Lady Avondale, that she might spend one fortnight with her friends.

There are few minds so callous as to revisit the scenes of their childhood without experiencing some emotion, or receiving some salutary lesson. And whether these scenes be in the crowded city, amidst the coarse and ordinary scenes of vulgar life, or in the lovely valley, with its green hills and its gliding streams—the same searching feelings swell the heart, as the thoughts of the past rush over it, speaking to us with impressive truth of the careless days of our childhood—of the gay dreams of our youth—of the transient pleasures of our prime—of the faded joy of our old age. They speak to us of parents now sleeping in the dust—of playfellows in a far distant land —of companions altered or alienated. They speak to us, it may be, of time misspent, of talents misapplied, of warnings neglected, of blessings unappreciated, of peace departed. And oh! how dark and apathetic must that mind be, which can find itself once more in the home of childhood, without being inspired by such, or similarly wholesome reflections! Retrospect of every kind must be for our good, for by retrospect we are alone corrected and instructed; and there is something of a solemn reproof, when returning to a parent's house, (whether a father's arms are open to receive his long-absent child, or whether the eye that would have welcomed, or the tongue which would have blessed, are now mouldering in the grave,) which bids the erring mortal turn from his evil ways. Oh! many are the wild, tumultuous waves, that roll over the human mind, and obliterate many of its fairest characters—its fondest recollections; but still the indelible impressions of a parent's love remain stamped upon the heart. One little spot will still be found, consecrated to the purest, the holiest of earthly affections.

The feelings of Hyacinthe were most overpowering when she entered the pretty village of Fairbrook. It was to a father's arms she was returning—to the dear haunts of her happy childhood; and but for the sad, sad duty which brought her hither, how happy she would have felt! She had viewed fairer scenes than those her tearful eye now rested upon, and had gazed with enthusiasm on the inanimate objects of nature; but however they had charmed her senses, or filled her imagination, they wanted that deep and powerful interest which seemed to entwine with her very existence—the love of her early home.

The carriage that conveyed her stopped at the gate of the Rectory. She rushed from it, and was soon in the arms of her dear Mrs. Villars, which she only quitted to be clasped tenderly to the bosom of Mr. Neville. With what admiration they gazed upon the beautiful, high-born girl that stood before them; and who, with the most humble affection, besought them to bless her and love her, as they used to do in those happy days when she knew no other friends than those who called her their own little May.

For a few minutes, indeed, in the buoyancy of youthful excitement, Hyacinthe almost forgot her very grief; and with childish eagerness she passed quickly through every well-known room in the Rectory. She then made à rapid circuit of the dearly loved garden, and re-newed her acquaintance with the old respectable domestics, who at first shrunk back, not knowing how they might be received by the fine lady Hyacinthe Tremaine; but who, they soon found, had not lost one portion of the kindness and urbanity possessed by the humble May.

The excitement of the first few moments over, the recollection of *why* she was there, rushed to the mind of Hyacinthe with full force; and bitter tears started into her eyes, as she asked in a low trembling voice, "How is he?—when may I see him?"

Mr. Neville and his sister looked very sad. "My dear child," he then said, "you must prepare yourself for much agitation; our poor friend is very altered, and so weakened by his disease, that I fear he is near his last hour. Nay, my love," added he, seeing Hyacinthe give way to a paroxysm of grief, "you have come here to yield com-fort, not to add to affliction by giving way to your own sorrow. I know it is a justifiable sorrow; for one of the deepest wounds which our hearts can receive in this world, is caused by the death of those who are dear to us; and it admits of no other consolation than that which is found in absolute submission to the will of God—that gra-cious Being who never afflicts us but for our good, and who will repay with heavenly bliss our resignation to earthly sorrows. We may lament the approaching fate of our good friend, but the change him is exceeding gain: the mercy of God takes him from the evil to come, and he is well prepared to meet his Almighty Father."

"And my dear mother!—for so I will ever call her—how does she support her affliction?" sobbed poor Hyacinthe.

"She endures her trial in silence," replied Mr. Neville, "with an humble mind, yet with invincible courage—patient in hope, strong only in God, and deriving support and consolation from him alone·

she recalls to her mind the image of her dying Saviour, remembers his meek acceptance of that bitter cup, because it was sent to him by his Heavenly Father; and says with him, 'My God, not my will, but thine be done!' "

We can imagine the feelings of the tender-hearted Hyacinthe, when she accompanied Mr. Neville to the farm: her tears were all dried up, but her pale countenance and trembling steps plainly indicated her inward sufferings.

She arrived at length at the beautiful and picturesque farm, and entered the garden, once the pride of its possessors; but in the rapid glance which Hyacinthe cast over it, she read an accurate history of grief in the careless state of this once cherished spot. One part of it alone appeared never to have lost its interest with the inhabitants of the farm: it was an arbour formed from a large hawthorn-tree, and was surrounded by a tiny flower-garden. This spot they used to call "May's Bower;" and it had been fostered with the tenderest care, whilst every thing else had been neglected. A tear rose to her eye as she passed it; but she checked every contending emotion, and endeavoured to nerve herself for the approaching interview.

And indeed it required all her fortitude to suppress her sobs, when she felt herself in the arms of her kindest and fondest of friends. And when she read in her pale and worn countenance the inroads which grief had made in her heart, she again sunk upon Mrs. Wilmot's bosom, exclaiming—"My mother! your May has returned to you unchanged, and with all the fond affection of your own child;— she is come to mingle her tears with yours—to share your anxieties, and to endeavour to soothe you with her tenderest love. Oh! this dear, once happy home—would that I had never left it! But my father!—when may I see him?"

"My dear child," replied Mrs. Wilmot, much affected, "he is now sleeping, and we must not disturb him, for he has little rest from pain; but you shall go with me and look at him. His sleep, from the opium which has been administered, is profound; and I would rather you should get over the first sight of his altered appearance before he sees you. But promise me to be calm; you always obeyed your mother, darling, and I know I may rely upon you."

She then opened a door which led into a room on the same floor, to which Farmer Wilmot had been removed; for before his illness became so fatally severe, he had been able occasionally to walk in the garden, and sit for awhile in the hawthorn bower, which the spring had covered with the sweetest May blossoms.

Hyacinthe, with an effort over her feelings, followed Mrs. Wilmot into the room, and there she beheld the excellent being whom she still continued in the light of a father. He was lying in a deep sleep, supported by pillows. Could Hyacinthe, in this pale, spectral form, recognize the athletic person of the well-looking farmer? Disease had indeed done its worst; and yet the same kind benevolent expression was still there; no impatient frown clouded his brow, and a serene smile seemed to play upon his half-closed lips. A portrait of herself, which Hyacinthe had sent to him, was hung exactly opposite the bed, and in such a position that he could always see it; while close to it hung a little straw bonnet and a grey cloak, which she immediately recognized as her former possessions. The room was ornamented with presents which she at different times had despatched to the farm, every thing evincing how much his thoughts were fixed upon herself; while in his thin hand, which was lying on the coverlid, she perceived the last letter she had written to him.

Affected beyond measure, poor Hyacinthe sunk upon a chair by the bedside, and wept in silence. Mrs. Wilmot drew the curtain so as to shut out the sight of the afflicted Hyacinthe, should her husband suddenly awake; and then seated herself by her darling child, who, throwing an arm round her neck, wept gently upon her bosom.

In about a quarter of an hour Farmer Wilmot moved. His wife was immediately by his side. "Jane," he exclaimed, in a voice hollow and weak, "I have had such a delightful dream. I fancied that our child was here, and that I was holding her by the hand. But I suppose," he added, with a deep sigh of disappointment, "it was this dear letter which suggested the idea. However, she will soon be here—will she not?"

"Very, very soon, my dear husband," Mrs. Wilmot replied, endeavouring to speak calmly. "But you must promise me, that when you see her you will be perfectly still. You know how every exertion brings on a return of your complaint; therefore, when I tell you she is come, you must be as tranquil and as composed as possible, under such an agitating meeting."

"I promise every thing, dear Jane; but when do you think I shall see her? Recollect my life is ebbing fast; and I so pray for a few days' enjoyment of her society."

"May is already at the Rectory," said Mrs. Wilmot, wishing to prepare her husband by degrees. Then watching his countenance with anxiety to see how it affected him, she added with caution, "indeed she is now on her way to the farm, nor should I wonder should she arrive immediately: dear James,"'she at length said, taking his hand with tenderness, "if I tell you that you shall see her this moment, will you promise your poor wife not to agitate yourself —will you be calm?"

The farmer bowed his head in acquiescence; and his own May, who could no longer control her feelings, drawing back the curtain, sunk upon her knees, before the bed, and exclaimed, "Here, father, is your child."

We will pass over the first half hour of this happy meeting; for it is not for the pen to describe its sacred nature. But it will be pleasing to my readers to look again at our high-born heroine, once more assuming the character of the humble May; for in a very short space of time she had taken her place in the sick-room, and, as if she had never quitted him, was again her father's nurse—his tender and watchful servant. She seemed to fall back immediately into all her old habits of affection and usefulness; and the good man might well forget that he had ever been deprived of her society. Even Mrs. Wilmot became a secondary assistant in the dying man's chamber. No one smoothed his pillows so well as May; no food tasted so well as that which he saw her fingers prepare; no one read so sweetly to him; no one slept so lightly by his side, as his sweet May, who had insisted upon taking Mrs Wilmot's post upon a sofa at night, as the poor grieving wife was very nearly worn out by watching and care.

For a few days after Hyacinthe's arrival, Farmer Wilmot appeared better; so much did happiness and gratified affection excite and revive him: but the flame which for a moment flashed with re-newed life, sunk again; and the medical man pronounced that his death was fast approaching. This was no distressing hearing to this true Christian. The happiness he had enjoyed in again beholding his beloved foundling, the comfort which her presence afforded him, and the assurance that in her his poor widow would always find an affectionate and zealous friend, only inspired him with more lively gratitude towards the Author of this good.

With her hand clasped in his, and supported by his excellent wife, he felt he could die in peace. "Dearest child," he would say, "think of me when I am gone, and may my last moments be a source of comfort to you! for they will, I trust, show you the happi-ness with which he who trusteth in the atonement of a Saviour, and who claims the pardon gained for him by his all-sufficient sacrifice upon the cross, leaves a world which can only be a preparation for that which is to come. Oh! may it teach you, my beloved child, to cherish that faith—those holy affections and habits, which will enable you to rejoice in the bright prospect of a happy death! and surely it ought to confirm and strengthen your faith to behold a weak mortal just about to die, full of joy and peace; enabled by that same holy trust to contemplate with delight the approaching moment, when he may hope to be associated with kindred spirits in everlasting joy and love. May you, my sweet child, ever taste with a grateful heart the blessings which the unwearied hand of Providence has scattered in your path! But do not lose sight of the far greater delights—the transcendant glories of your eternal throne. Remember that you are a candidate for an inheritance among the saints in bliss—for the society of angels, and of God. May you, my child—may you, my beloved wife, be numbered among those active servants whom the Lord at his coming shall find ready!"

Thus, with his latest breath, did this excellent man discourse with those around him.

Ten days after Hyacinthe's arrival he died calmly and without pain. His last words were addressed to his God—his last look was riveted upon the child of his adoption. So heavenly tranquil was his departure, that how could his weeping survivors wish that he was still lingering in this world of trouble?

Such an end throws a soft and holy light over the dark valley of the shadow of death. It bids the mourner and the sufferer "to be of good cheer," and thus patiently and cheerfully to await the coming of the Lord. It often softens the pangs of separation from those who are dear to us; teaching us that by a holy and righteous life, a perfect submission to the will of God—a faith in his promises, death will be robbed of its sting, and the grave of its victory.

## CHAPTER XX.

" Look above thee—there, indeed,
May thy thoughts repose delighted ;
If thy wounded bosom bleed,
If thy fondest hopes are blighted,
There a stream of comfort flows."

Hyacinthe remained at Brookside farm until after she had witnessed the last sad offices performed for the mortal remains of her
much-loved friend. We will pass over the details of that melancholy
day, when all that was left of one so dearly prized was for ever removed from the home which had so long been his delight, to be
consigned to the dreary earth. We can all feel for the grief of those
who had loved the mild beauties of the character of the departed
Christian.

Hyacinthe was most affectionately anxious to arrange some plan
for the future comfort of the dear widow. She found that she still
wished to linger in the abode where she had spent the happiest, as
well as the saddest days of her life; therefore the farm and the offices
connected with agricultural pursuits were let off to a friendly neighbour, and Mrs. Wilmot was left in possession of the house and
garden.

Hyacinthe had received *carte blanche* from her father, that she
might spare no expense to satisfy any of the wishes of her foster-
mother ; but they were few in number, and it was a great comfort to
the considerate girl to find that she was able to make arrangements
for the continued residence of Susan Ashfield at the farm, whose kindness and activity had much endeared her to Mrs. Wilmot.

Bitter was the idea of the approaching parting to Hyacinthe and
her adopted mother. It was almost heart-breaking to our poor
heroine, who felt that she would now be leaving Mrs. Wilmot without that stay, that comfort which had hitherto softened every pain.
Henceforth she was to be alone in a place where every object, every
circumstance, must remind her of that dear husband whom she loved
next to God ; and whom she would never again behold in a mortal
state. But when the Almighty in His infinite wisdom imposes a
sacrifice upon us, and takes from us some beloved object, he does
not leave us to endure the stroke unsustained ; and if through th

11

veil of probationary sorrow which he spreads over us, we look up to
Him for aid, we shall receive it, and feel assured that by means of
such mortal trials we are to reap everlasting joy.

Jane Wilmot now shone forth as a true disciple of our Lord.
" My child," she said to Hyacinthe, who was weeping bitterly by her
side, " weep not for me, for God will not reject the prayer of the
poor and desolate, nor despise the broken and contrite heart.   What
comfort does he not·vouchsafe us, if in the hour of affliction we
rest on him?   Let us not then, my beloved girl, by the repining of
wounded hearts, forego this blessed assurance of consolation.   His
holy word teaches and enables us to endure whatever may be our lot
in this passing scene ; bidding us remember that it is *here* where we
must make good our claims to happiness *hereafter*.   And, after all,
how selfishly we mourn for the remaining days of a being whom indeed we fondly loved, but who must now be far happier with his
God, from whose sight sorrow and sighing flee away—in whose presence is fulness of joy, and at whose right hand are pleasures for evermore!   Such is the healing power of faith and true love towards
God, it sanctifies even the severest trials, and gives the mourner
power to say, ' Our light afflictions, which are but for a moment, are
not worthy to be compared with the glory that shall be revealed in
us,' if we pass through them in pious submission to the Divine
will."

Thus did this excellent woman combat with her own grief, to
impart consolation to her dear child.   Oh! blessed are they who even
in the anguish of their spirit can bring their fainting hearts before the
footstool of their God!   With such, " weeping may endure for a
night, but joy cometh in the morning."

Before Hyacinthe quitted her early home, she felt that it would be
a melancholy gratification to pay a parting visit to one spot, from peculiar circumstances most dear to her : it was her own May bower,
her former precious territory, and which had been so tenderly treasured by her dear departed friend.   There had they together planted
at its entrance a honeysuckle and a wild rose ; and daily were they
tended, and fondly were they watched by him, as long as his feeble
limbs had permitted him to reach the spot.   During her absence they
had grown and flourished ; but the sweetness of both were passed for
a season, and their long and slender branches now hung in mournful
desolation.

With sad and faltering steps, the last morning of Hyacinthe's stay
at Brookside, she approached the spot which brought such painful,

ıthough tender recollections to her mind—each bush, each ı stone, ıtold its noiseless tale ( of neglect and perished life ; ' while the very silence that surrounded her, spoke more eloquently than' words coula have done of the loss her heart had sustained.  She entered the mossy bower, so long her favourite retreat, and gave way to the feelings which oppressed her.  Here it was almost a luxury to weep ; it seemed as if these mute witnesses of her early pleasures were now become the sympathetic depositaries of her sacred and maturer sorrow.  Here she could almost fancy, in the excitement wrought by memory on her imagination, that the spirit of the tender friend for whom she grieved hovered near her.  "Dearest father," she cried, as if addressing him, "hear your child ! Your pure spirit will rejoice, when she promises never to forget you, or the precepts it was your constant care to inculcate in her mind.  Ever remembering them, I will endeavour to tread with watchfulness the path of duty which lies before me ; still imagining that I am cheered by your kind smile of approbation ; and, in adversity or prosperity, I trust I may prove myself worthy of the love and care which charity first, and then affection, bestowed on the destitute May."

Hyacinthe was roused from a melancholy reverie, which followed this apostrophe to the being who had so fondly sheltered and protected her childhood, by the arrival of Mr. Neville, who came to inform her that every thing was in readiness for her departure. She therefore prepared to bid a long, a last adieu to the home of her youth ; but I should vainly attempt to depict the feelings which that gave rise to :

> "Ye who have known what 'tis to dote upon
> A few dear objects, will in sadness feel
> Such partings break the heart."

It was a very different scene to which Hyacinthe was returning, although she was again to undergo the trials offered by the chamber of death.

Since her departure Lady Avondale had become considerably worse, and was now entirely confined to her room.

Lord Avondale met Hyacinthe on her arrival with a countenance grave and dejected.  He took her hand with mournful tenderness, as he said, "Your mother, my dear girl, has been dreadfully ill since you were here, and her spirits are now in a very irritable and depressed state.  She declares that she will not see you ; adding, she is sure you will be so dismal, and that you will tell such melancholy histories of the scenes you have lately witnessed. Therefore you must not attempt to see her, until of her own accord she sends for you. She is indeed, very, very ill, and in a wretched state of mind."

Lord Avondale was much agitated, and his daughter partook too much of his feelings to be able to speak.

"Hyacinthe," he again said, after a dismal pause, "how I wish that your poor mother had ever experienced the blessings of religious instruction! she might then have had some comfort in her present state; but now I fear she has no hope in this world, or in the next."

"Oh! say not so," exclaimed Hyacinthe, in an agony of terror; whilst there is life there is hope, both for her soul and body: Our gracious Lord freely offers his 'preserving grace' to enable a willing soul to come to him. He does not content himself with calling home his wandering sheep, but seeks those that are lost, and when he has found them rejoiceth. If my poor mamma would only fix her thoughts steadfastly upon her Redeemer, He has both the power and will to restore her soul, and to reconcile her to her Heavenly Father. Her wanderings cannot have been too wide to hinder the effect of his divine influence;—an influence which will not only *speak* to her heart, but *change* her heart, and bring her at once to her God. Let us send for the good Mr. Neville," she continued, with a quickness of utterance and gentle earnestness which spoke her interest in her words; "he has always been successful in his endeavours to soften the pangs of the sick or the dying. By the kindest manner, and the most soothing expressions, he will draw her mind by degrees from this world, and induce her to rely on our Saviour's mediation to secure her salvation. Is there any thing too weak for him to strengthen—too yielding for him to render firm? Oh! no: believe me, my dearest father, that his voice can call, cheer, and encourage her, and make her more than conqueror over the most fearful adversary of her soul."

"Hyacinthe," replied Lord Avondale, "we will endeavour to do the best to calm your afflicted mother; but I scarcely know how we shall ever be able to introduce the subject of religion. She would immediately think that we considered her in danger, and then the agonies of her mind would be beyond measure great. She has had a life of what she considers happiness. The world is her idol, and the idea of quitting it, for one with which she has so little acquaintance, would be anguish and bitterness beyond endurance."

"I do not despair, papa," Hyacinthe replied thoughtfully; "with great care and caution much may be done; and I have been brought up to consider it a most severe and bounden duty, that we all use our endeavours, however feeble they may be, to assist each other on our way to Heaven."

Whilst thus Hyacinthe was in the act of speaking to her father, one of Lady Avondale's female attendants hastily entered the room, to say that her ladyship had been suddenly seized with a fainting fit, and begged Lord Avondale to come to her immediately.

Hyacinthe followed her father up the noble staircase, adorned with vases and statues, with graceful lamps at every landing. And oh! the sumptuous, the splendid air of every thing within the chamber of sickness! contrasting so strangely with the rustic simplicity of that in which she had so lately administered the services of love and watchfulness. But the dispensations of Providence are fearful levelers of the factitious distinctions among men. "Little boots it to the course of Death, whether he plucks his prey from the downy couch curtained with satin, or the wretched pallet of a prison or workhouse. And what are all the dazzling splendours of rank and riches?—what have they of solace or mitigation to him bidden "to turn his face to the wall"—to look his last on life, "its toys and tinsel?" Resignation to the will of God yields a softer pillow to the dying one, than the utmost refinements of art; Christian faith beams more sweetly on the closing lid, than the "attempered light shed by perfumed oil from an agate lamp."

Lady Avondale, after a short time, recovered from the succession of fainting fits which had so alarmed her attendants; but she appeared suffering and much exhausted. Lord Avondale thought this would be a favourable opportunity of introducing Hyacinthe into the presence of her mother, and therefore motioned her to approach from the adjoining dressing-room, at the door of which she had stationed herself; her heart beating with anxiety to be of assistance, but withheld by the timidity of her gentle nature. She advanced, and, kneeling by the side of this still lovely woman, pressed to her lips one of her hands, which hung listlessly over the sofa. How Hyacinthe's affectionate bosom thrilled with joy, when she beheld her mother's eye to her with a kind expression! Oh! how she longed to impart to her all she felt! but she recollected that her only chance of gaining any influence over her, would be in the most cautious conduct and by the slowest degrees.

When Lady Avondale was more recovered, Hyacinthe said to her in a cheerful voice, "Mamma, you must not tell me to leave you; for do not imagine that I shall be a dismal companion. I trust if you will try me, that you will find that I shall amuse, rather than depress you."

"Well, pretty Hyacinthe, I will try you," replied Lady Avondale; adding, with a faint smile, "to tell you the truth, I am rather tired of all my present attendants. They were very attentive when I was first taken ill; but now that my illness has lasted so long, I evidently see that they are tired of the confinement it imposes on them. They are all an ungrateful set. Victorine is angry, because I do not give her almost every day some dress that I have scarcely worn; and all the others have some equally selfish cause of dissatisfaction."

"Oh! then, my dearest mamma, you must allow me to become your nurse," Hyacinthe exclaimed, rejoicing at the ground she had gained: "you know that I have not been brought up as a fine lady; and if you will but try me, you will find how useful I can make myself; and I hope you know that only one feeling will actuate me—that of pleasing, and being of service to you."

"Very well; I think I must adopt you as a nurse, my pretty Hyacinthe; but recollect, I am to have no dismalities—no religion forced upon me. I am sure," the Countess added, beginning to weep, "that I am miserable enough already, and want nothing to make me still more wretched and melancholy."

Hyacinthe was so glad to have gained an access to her mother's room on any terms, that she abstained from any premature anxiety to draw her mind to subjects which were really calculated to soothe it.

In a few days a circumstance occurred, which quite established Hyacinthe about the person of Lady Avondale. Mademoiselle Victorine having heard of an eligible situation, and knowing that there was little probability of her present lady ever entering again into that course of life, which alone offered a harvest and occupation pleasing to her peculiar talents, abruptly left her place; and Hyacinthe soon evinced such intelligence and promptness, added to the most winning softness and ability in attending to her mother, that soon she could not bear her to leave her sight.

With a degree of skill and tact, scarcely in accordance with the youth of our heroine, she at length introduced the dreaded subject of religion. But oh! how distressing was the state in which she found her poor parent's mind! No ray of light or hope appeared to illuminate it—all was darkness and confusion. . She had lived only for this world; and now that it was receding from her grasp, she knew not what to cling to—where to look for consolation.

How different was this bed of sickness and of death to the one Hyacinthe had so lately watched! There the poor sufferer's every pang was soothed by the Divine hand by which he was supported. The greater his pain and weakness the nearer he felt to his Redeemer. Here, racked with suffering, and with life drawing to its close, Lady Avondale's heart still fixed itself with frightful tenacity on the things of this world. Her impatience and fretfulness were dreadful to witness; and when these evidences of temper subsided, they were succeeded by despondence and wretchedness equally distressing to those around.

The decay of her beauty appeared to give her most disturbance; and the pleasures of dress, its study, and adornments to her invalid frame, were still the paramount occupations of Lady Avondale's mind. The knowledge of what was passing in the world was the next subject of interest; and for the gratification of both these tastes, she could not have had a more able assistant than in the accomplished Abigail who replaced Victorine. It was with no small degree of sorrow and unhappiness that Hyacinthe beheld from day to day the shrinking form baffle even the skill of the talented lady's maid, to give the newly invented wrapping-gown the intended fall; while the increasing hollow of the cheek, and the deepening yellow of the complexion, mocked equally all attempts for the partial concealment of the ravages of sickness, by the exquisite lace cap and the delicate tinted ribbon. Hyacinthe recoiled from the vain effort to make death look lovely, and with shrinking terror asked herself, whether it was thus an immortal spirit was to prepare to present itself at the judgment-seat of its God? But, after a short time, as the disease under which the Countess laboured increased in violence, it was the Almighty's gracious will to send his blessed assistance to subdue her worldly feelings.

In her hours of loneliness—in the dark monotony of a sick room, the obligation seemed almost peremptorily enforced on her "to commune with her heart, and be still." There, no festive sounds disturbed her melancholy, but wholesome musings; no voices of gay companions broke upon her solitude; no insidious flatterer recalled the dream of vanity to her sinking heart. Conscience awoke from its deep slumber. She called her ways to remembrance; she cast a backward glance at the life of forgetfulness which she had led, and a sense of wrong mingled with the recollections which crowded upon her mind. Talents perverted, duties slighted, time unredeemed, furnish but too many sources of terror and humiliation to an awakened conscience. She began, though late, to feel that there was no refuge from evil, no guard from sin, but in the knowledge of the Almighty God: and then a glimmering light broke over her benighted soul, telling her there could be no pardon for past unrighteousness but through the merits and mediation of a blessed Redeemer. The holy radiance shed by the Spirit stayed not here its blessed influence; brighter and brighter grew its light; and soon with holy fervour and heart-felt eagerness, the spontaneous prayer burst from her trembling lips—" God be merciful to me a sinner?"

At first this happy dawn was unperceived by Hyacinthe. She had been accustomed, when observing the sufferings of Lady Avondale more intense than usual, to kneel by her bedside, and pray in a low but earnest voice that her mother's agony might be softened, and her mind tranquillized. At first Lady Avondale appeared to take little notice of this action; but by degrees Hyacinthe saw that she sometimes listened, and soon found that it evidently gave her satisfaction; for her countenance became more tranquil, and once or twice she had whispered " go on."

One day, after Hyacinthe had been praying some time, in the words of a beautiful prayer, which had been written by Mr. Neville expressly for the chamber of death and sickness, Lady Avondale, who had listened with deep attention, at length said to her daughter in a voice of intense emotion,—.

" Oh! Hyacinthe, would that I could live some years longer to make my peace with God! that God whom I have never tried to love! Oh! if you could know what it was to feel as I do now, you would pity me. I am aware that I must die; and now, for the first time, have learnt to reflect on what is to follow death. What is to become of one who feels that she is, what your prayer has just taught her, ' a stranger in the courts of the Lord?' What a lesson am I to those who, like me, have only lived for the enjoyments of this world; who forget that there is an end to all things, and that there is an ever-enduring hereafter? what is to become of me, dear Hyacinthe? I feel I have no time left to reconcile me to the God whom I have so selfishly neglected. And for what? Alas! alas! how paltry and grovelling appear the joys for which I have hitherto alone lived! How loathsome the luxury for which I have bartered my salvation! But despair and sickness change most fearfully the aspect of every thing ; and I fancy now that I would gladly submit to the severest penury to get rid of the upbraidings of my feelings. Oh! my child, how different I must appear to you when compared to the good Farmer Wilmot, who led a life of duty and religious excel lence! to such a person, death and sickness must have been disarmed of all the horrors which now so appal me!"

Lady Avondale sunk exhausted on her· pillow, overcome by the painful violence of her remorseful feelings ; while sobs and sighs showed their continuance in her mind. But her words and dreadful agitation, however they pained the tender heart of her daughter, were not without comfort. She knew that it was that state of mind alone which would bring with it ultimate peace : and she inwardly thanked her God, that her poor mother was at length brought to the knowledge of her great and absolute want of the atoning power and assistance of our Saviour and the Holy Spirit.

Hyacinthe's whole time and conversation from this day past were devoted to pious subjects. Much was she enabled to say that soothed and consoled her dying parent. She assured her how precious in the sight of God were those sighs·of penitence breathed in secret—those tears unseen by human eyes ;—that our tender Father views with attentive and compassionate regards the first faint effort to return to Him ;—that he strengthens us by his grace ; he encourages us by his promises ; he guides us by his Spirit ; and receives us into the number of his children ; that—

> " His ear is open to the faintest cry,
> His grace descends to meet the lifted eye,
> He reads the language of a silent tear,
> And sighs are incense from a heart sincere."

Thus soothed and encouraged by her virtuous daughter, Lady Avondale passed the remaining months of her life. She learnt to look forward with hope to that kingdom, the only subject worthy the struggles and exertions of an immortal spirit. She looked back, with shame and contempt to the frivolous pleasures and paltry gratifications by which the stream of her life had been so polluted and disturbed. Objects once contemplated with delight, were seen in their real proportions ; and they appeared less than nothing—the nothingness of vanity! She felt the absurdity and evil of those high thoughts of her bosom which, engendering pride, had led to

12

bitterness and every unworthy passion, and deeply did she now con-
temn them.

She at length learnt with deep humility to hope that pardon would
be extended, notwithstanding the past unrighteousness of her days;
she learnt to believe that she had "an advocate with the Father—
even Jesus Christ the righteous;" that "Him hath God exalted to
be a Prince and Saviour, to give repentance to Israel, *and forgiveness of sins!*"

With this deep conviction Lady Avondale's last moments were
gilded. She sank into her eternal rest, from the arms of her daughter
and husband, who himself benefited by the rays of holiness shed on
the pillow of death; and we must hope that her humble and contrite
heart, with all its affections increased and purified, was received as a
peace-offering by a merciful God!

---

## CHAPTER XXI.

" Hope gladdens the world with its living ray,
    And smiles serenely on all;
It scatters a thousand charms in its way
    Over this earthly ball;
It has streams of peace, and joy, and love,
    To water this valley of death;
And brings the flowers of heaven from above
    For virtue's undying wreath."

HYACINTHE is now about to take her leave of her kind readers.
We have seen her sustain more than one character, and I trust it
has been in a manner likely to edify those of my young friends
who may chance to peruse this simple tale. But we will not
leave her in sorrow and affliction. The Almighty hand showered
much felicity upon her during the remainder of her life: not that
she escaped the pains and troubles which we must all expect to
meet with in the course of our pilgrimage through a world, the paths
of which are, for the wisest reasons, strewed alike with thorns and
roses. She had her share of human woe; but it was so chastened
and supported by the aid to which she always looked, that every
sorrow was softened. Rich is the reward, even on earth, in peace

of conscience, to those who only trust in God. He will hear the voice of our prayers—He will send his Holy Spirit to guard us from the pollutions, and guide us through the perplexities of the world; and he will ultimately welcome us to that eternal home, where the ransomed of the Lord shall meet to taste of everlasting joy.

After the sad scene which Lord Avondale and Hyacinthe had witnessed at the castle, Lord Avondale was anxious that by change of place the sorrowful impression left on their minds should be in a measure obviated: they therefore made a short tour on the continent. On their return Hyacinthe was delighted by her father proposing a visit to Beechwood; and too happy was she to find herself once more in the arms of her dear aunt and amiable cousins.

Lord Avondale, soon after their arrival, told her that business would take him from her for a few weeks, and that he would then return to accompany her back to Avondale Castle.

It was with much regret that Hyacinthe parted with her father; her young affectionate heart clung with the truest filial love to one who had endeared himself to her by such constant tenderness and indulgence; but he promised her soon to return, and added, that his leaving her was in order to insure her future happiness. He said this with a look so full of cheerful satisfaction, that it communicated pleasure to the heart of his daughter. Her thoughts instantly glanced towards her dear friends at Fairbrook; but Lord Avondale had been so invariably silent upon the subject, that, with the delicacy which was natural to her, she had scarcely ever ventured to express her feelings or wishes relative to the objects of her early affection, from the fear that it might be irksome to him.

At the expiration of six weeks Lord Avondale returned, improved in looks and spirits. He would not hear of extending their stay at Beechwood beyond the next day, and appeared all anxiety to be at home.

What joy—what happiness awaited our heroine, on her arrival at the castle!

"Hyacinthe," said Lord Avondale, when they had entered the hall, "I wish to show you an alteration I have made in your apartments."

She followed the Earl with eagerness, seeing by his countenance that some joyful surprise awaited her: and indeed most joyful were her feelings, when, on entering her sitting-room, she was clasped to the bosom of her foster mother.

"We are never again to part, my darling child," exclaimed this excellent woman; while Hyacinthe, who wept from excess of emotion, could only falter out, as she for a moment turned from her embrace, to throw herself into the arms of Lord Avondale, "Oh! this is indeed happiness!—how can I ever thank you sufficiently, my dear, kind father?"

After a few minutes given to the delight of this meeting, Mrs. Wilmot opened a door which communicated to apartments Lord Avondale had destined for her use; and there Hyacinthe found the good Susan Ashfield, who had a room appropriated to her, close to those of her mistress.

Mrs. Wilmot was to reside at the castle as long as she lived; where indeed her days might pass as quietly as at her cottage. She was put into possession of a bed-room and a small dressing-closet with a charming sitting-room, looking into a beautiful flower-garden, which she was also to consider her own. A private staircase communicated with these rooms, which led to a small vestibule, by which she could at once descend to her little territory, from whence a path led to the most secluded and beautiful parts of the park. Her dear child could be with her the greatest part of the day; for it is needless to state that the two governesses appointed to attend on the Lady Hyacinthe had long since been dismissed, her future education being more judiciously designed. And how felicitous it was to the high-born heiress of Avondale Castle, to feel that she could now watch over the declining years of one who had succoured the destitute little May; and by unwearied kindness and attention endeavour to repay her for all that had been done for her during her more than usually helpless childhood! And poor Mrs. Wilmot—how did her pious heart expand with gratitude to God, who thus rewarded her by a protected and happy old age for the deeds of charity done in earlier years!

"But, my dear Mrs. Villars, and dear good Mr. Neville, how you will miss them, my own darling mother!—and how distressed they must have been to have lost you!" said Hyacinthe, with a shaded countenance, after the first joyous excitement had subsided.

"Ask no questions, dearest, and wait with patience, and you will find they are almost as happy as I am."

With this delightful assurance of Mrs. Wilmot, Hyacinthe was obliged to be satisfied; for she could elicit nothing further either from her or Lord Avondale.

Much did it delight this affectionate girl to witness the attentive

kindness of the Earl's manner to Mrs. Wilmot, who with tears of
gratitude told the history of her being now domesticated at the castle.

Lord Avondale had come in person to the farm, to solicit her to
take up her abode under the same roof with her adopted daughter.
"I felt much, my dear child," she added, "in leaving the spot
where rested all that remained to me of my precious husband;
and at first I felt that it would be impossible for me to tear myself
away from my dear home: but at length I considered how he would
have wished me to have acted, and at once my mind was altered.
I knew that to give you happiness would have been his most fervent
wish; and believe me, my child, it is mine also. Life once more
will become interesting to me, for I can now again devote myself to
you; and in seeing your happiness I shall have fresh and daily
cause of adoring the Divine source from whence it flows.

The next day was Sunday. Hyacinthe, now mistress of her own
actions, and of her father's establishment, was anxious to introduce,
by degrees, into Avondale Castle, the habits of Beechwood. How
happy it would make her if she could induce those around her to
consider this holy day as one of rest and recollection, and of communion with God: in which the Lord's name was to be honoured
and praised, from the rising up of the sun to the going down
thereof!

With very varied feelings did this amiable girl pursue her path
towards the church, leaning on the arm of her father, who seemed,
by a tender pressure of the hand, whose trembling was perceptible
to him, to seek to calm the agitation of which he himself partook.

Hyacinthe certainly felt calmer and happier than she had ever
done before at Avondale Castle; but still tears of sorrow rose to
her eyes, when she remembered the young and lovely mother who
was now in her untimely and much dreaded grave. She was about
to visit the church, where in the cold, dark vault, rested all that
remained of one whose happiness had been in luxury: here was the
mouldering form of her whose pride had been perishable beauty,
and those riches, of which all that now availed to the short-lived
worldling was the escutcheoned coffin which held her inanimate
dust! It was an awful and afflicting lesson; but the agitated Hyacinthe then thought of the last scene of the existence of her mother
with a composing satisfaction, and prayed with inward but intense
fervour that she was received by God as a truly penitent sinner,
although indeed she came to Him for pardon but at the "eleventh
hour."

On entering the pew, to which they had access by a private door, Hyacinthe sunk on her knees in pious prayer. But what voice was it that startled her in her meditations?—what well-known accents met her ear, when, as if in accordance with the subject of her meditations, the clergyman commenced the service with the words, "The sacrifices of God are a broken spirit: a broken and a contrite heart, O God, thou wilt not despise!"

Hyacinthe hastily rose, and, going forward in the pew, looked anxiously towards the reading-desk, where she beheld her dear friend, the pious instructor of her early years, the venerated Mr. Neville! Softened and saddened by the reflections which had previously filled her mind, the unexpected sight filled her bosom wi h emotion, and she cast her eyes towards Lord Avondale to seek some explanation of the occurence. His were beaming with tenderness on herself; and inwardly he felt most happy that the surprise should in a measure disturb the mournful thoughts, which, from the peculiar character of her mind, he had felt sure would be created by her first visit to the holy edifice where rested the marble sepulchre of her mother. The eyes of Hyacinthe were again turned towards Mr. Neville, whose voice faltered in a slight degree as his regard met hers; but he instantly recovered, and he proceeded with the service in his usual impressive manner.

The sermon explained to our heroine the mystery of Mr. Neville's appearance at Avondale. He addressed his congregation for the first time, and presented himself as their future Rector. His discourse was most eloquent and touching; and tears were drawn from the eyes of many of the congregation. As for Hyacinthe, hers flowed in torrents; but they were tears of joy, of gratitude, and surprise.

At the conclusion of the service she was conducted by her father into the arms of Mrs. Villars, who was waiting for her in the porch; and in a moment she found herself in the Rectory, which was adjoining the church, pressed alternately to the bosom of her two kind friends.

The history of all this happiness was briefly thus. The living of Avondale became vacant a few months before; and it was Lord Avondale's earnest wish, both on his own account and Hyacinthe's, to present it to Mr. Neville. For this purpose he visited Fairbrook, and, in the kindest and most delicate way, besought his acceptance of it.

No expense or pains had been spared to make their new abode delightful, and indeed it was a lovely spot. What joy—what happiness did these arrangements insure to Hyacinthe! How·could she be sufficiently grateful to her considerate parent?—" Only," she exclaimed, with fervour, pressing his hand again·and again to her lips, " by devoting my life to you, and by making your pleasure my first and dearest care."

Hyacinthe is so happy now, that it is a favourable opportunity of allowing the curtain to fall on her and her delighted friends. However, trusting she has excited some little· interest in the minds of my young readers, for their gratification we will just take a little peep into her maturer years, and add, that our amiable heroine had a long life of happiness—that she was the joy and comfort of Lord Avondale's old age, the pride and delight of the good Rector and his sister, and the solace and blessing of her adopted mother.

Hyacinthe shone no less brightly in her character of wife and mother; and was rewarded by finding an excellent husband in the son of Lord Greville.

It was new life and existence to the good Mrs. Wilmot, when she held in her arms another little " May ;" for so was named our heroine's first child. " Mother" was the endearing name by which the excellent woman was called by the children of " her child," as she still fondly styled the'Lady Hyacinthe Mansfield ; and in superintending these dear charges she felt she had something to live for : and she was indeed loved by them and their gentle mother with an affection at once tender and enduring.

And now, my readers, farewell. I trust that my Hyacinthe may be as kindly received as her predecessor, "Alice Seymour;" and that her life may offer amusement as well as instruction to those who peruse these pages. I have essayed in this Tale, as in my first, to make it a practical lesson ; and to show that a deep sense of religion will alone gild the path of life with permanent brightness; and that the measure of happiness enjoyed by rational beings, even in this world, depends more upon their personal qualities—upon the principles, habits, and dispositions they cultivate, than upon external circumstances; and that no course of life can be safe or satisfactory which is pursued without reference to God. I seek not to prove that riches and prosperity are not good, or that sickness and suffering are not evils; but I would wish to show that both may be sanctified, and each state rendered subservient to the glory of Him who dispenses both good and evil. Only let us "watch and pray," and trust in Him ; let us earnestly implore the assistance of his Holy

Spirit, that we may be enabled temperately to enjoy, and meekly to suffer, all that is decreed by his will.; thus insuring to ourselves a strong, constant, and sustaining sense of his protecting goodness and unfailing wisdom. Then, whether our path lead amidst sunny pastures or through the barren wilderness, we shall perceive that a heavenly arm directs, and a heavenly smile invites us to press forward in well-doing, even through storms and darkness, to that pure region where all is cloudless and serene.

## THE END.

Lightning Source UK Ltd.
Milton Keynes UK
UKHW021935051118
331797UK00009B/469/P